OATHBRINGER

BOOKS BY
BRANDON SANDERSON

THE STORMLIGHT ARCHIVE
The Way of Kings
Words of Radiance
Oathbringer

THE MISTBORN SAGA
THE ORIGINAL TRILOGY
Mistborn
The Well of Ascension
The Hero of Ages
THE WAX AND WAYNE SERIES
The Alloy of Law
Shadows of Self
The Bands of Mourning

Elantris
Warbreaker
Arcanum Unbounded: The Cosmere Collection

The Rithmatist

ALCATRAZ VS. THE EVIL LIBRARIANS
Alcatraz vs. the Evil Librarians
The Scrivener's Bones
The Knights of Crystallia
The Shattered Lens
The Dark Talent

THE RECKONERS
Steelheart
Firefight
Calamity

BRANDON SANDERSON

OATHBRINGER

Book Three of
THE STORMLIGHT ARCHIVE

A TOM DOHERTY ASSOCIATES BOOK • NEW YORK

OATHBRINGER

Copyright © 2017 by Dragonsteel Entertainment, LLC

Brandon Sanderson® is a registered trademark of Dragonsteel Entertainment, LLC

All rights reserved.

Edited by Moshe Feder

Illustrations preceding chapters 39 and 58 by Dan dos Santos
Illustrations preceding chapters 8, 15, 25, 27, 33, 67, 99, 108, and 116 by Ben McSweeney
Illustrations preceding chapters 77 and 94 by Miranda Meeks
Illustrations preceding chapters 44 and 104 by Kelley Harris
Maps and illustrations preceding chapters 1, 5, 53, 61, 89, and 120 by Isaac Stewart
Viewpoint icons by Isaac Stewart, Ben McSweeney, and Howard Lyon
Map of the inside of the dust jacket by Isaac Stewart
Front endpapers by Dan dos Santos
Rear endpapers by Howard Lyon

Designed by Greg Collins

A Tor Book
Published by Tom Doherty Associates
175 Fifth Avenue
New York, NY 10010

www.tor-forge.com

Tor® is a registered trademark of Macmillan Publishing Group, LLC.

The Library of Congress Cataloging-in-Publication Data is available upon request.

ISBN 978-0-7653-2637-9 (hardcover)
ISBN 978-1-250-16949-5 (international, sold outside the U.S., subject to rights availability)
ISBN 978-1-250-16216-8 (signed)
ISBN 978-0-7653-9983-0 (ebook)

Our books may be purchased in bulk for promotional, educational, or business use. Please contact your local bookseller or the Macmillan Corporate and Premium Sales Department at 1-800-221-7945, extension 5442, or by email at MacmillanSpecialMarkets@macmillan.com.

First Edition: November 2017

Printed in the United States of America

10 9 8 7 6 5 4 3 2 1

For Alan Layton
    Who was cheering for Dalinar
        (And me)
    Before Stormlight even existed.

PREFACE AND ACKNOWLEDGMENTS

Welcome to *Oathbringer*! It's been a long road, creating this book. I thank you for your patience. Stormlight books are a huge undertaking—which you might be able to infer from the large list of people below.

If you haven't had the chance to read *Edgedancer*—a separate Stormlight novella taking place between books two and three—I'd recommend it to you now. Find it sold on its own, or in the story collection *Arcanum Unbounded*, which has novellas and novelettes from all across the Cosmere. (The universe in which this series, *Mistborn, Elantris, Warbreaker,* and others take place.)

That said, as always, every series is written so it can be read and enjoyed on its own, without knowledge of these other series or books. If you're intrigued, you can find a longer explanation I've written at brandonsanderson.com/cosmere.

Now, on to the parade of names! As I often say, though my name goes on the cover, there are tons of people involved in bringing you these books. They deserve my most hearty of thanks, and yours as well, for their tireless work across the three years it took to write this novel.

My main agent for these books (and everything else) is the wonderful Joshua Bilmes, of JABberwocky. Others at the agency who worked on them include Brady McReynolds, Krystyna Lopez, and Rebecca Eskildsen. Special thanks also go to John Berlyne, my UK agent, of Zeno—along with all of the sub-agents who work with us around the world.

My editor at Tor on this project was the ever-brilliant Moshe Feder. Special thanks to Tom Doherty, who has believed in the Stormlight project for years, and Devi Pillai, who provided essential publishing and editorial aid during the course of the novel's creation.

Others at Tor who provided help include Robert Davis, Melissa Singer, Rachel Bass, and Patty Garcia. Karl Gold was our Production Manager and Nathan Weaver the Managing Editor, with Meryl Gross and Rafal Gibek in trade production. Irene Gallo was our Art Director, Michael Whelan the cover designer, Greg Collins the interior designer, and Carly Sommerstein our proofreader.

At Gollancz/Orion (my UK publisher) thanks goes to Gillian Redfearn, Stevie Finegan, and Charlotte Clay.

Our copyeditor on this book was Terry McGarry, who has done excellent work on many of my novels. The ebook was prepared by Victoria Wallis and Caitlin Buckley at Macmillan.

Many people at my own company worked long hours to produce this book. A Stormlight novel is "crunch time" for us here at Dragonsteel, and so make sure to give the team a thumbs-up (or, in Peter's case, a block of cheese) next time you meet them. Our manager and Chief Operations Officer is my lovely wife, Emily Sanderson. Vice President and Editorial Director is the Insistent Peter Ahlstrom. Art Director is Isaac Stʒwart.

Our shipping manager (and the one who ships you all our signed books and T-shirts via the brandonsanderson.com store) is Kara Stewart. Continuity editor—and holy keeper of our internal continuity wiki—is Karen Ahlstrom. Adam Horne is my executive assistant and publicity/marketing director. Emily's assistant is Kathleen Dorsey Sanderson and our executive minion is Emily "Mem" Grange.

The audiobook was read by my personal favorite audiobook narrators, Michael Kramer and Kate Reading. Thanks again, guys, for making time in your schedule for this!

Oathbringer continues the tradition of filling The Stormlight Archive with beautiful art. We again have a fantastic cover illustration by Michael Whelan, whose attention to detail has given us an incredibly accurate rendition of Jasnah Kholin. I love that she gets a place to shine on the cover of this book, and I continue to feel honored and grateful that Michael takes time away from his gallery work to paint the world of Roshar.

It takes a variety of artists to recreate the styles found in the ephemera of another world, so this time around we've worked with even more artists than before. Dan dos Santos and Howard Lyon are responsible for the paintings of the Heralds on the front and back endpapers. I wanted these to have a style evoking classical paintings of the Renaissance and the later Romantic era, and both Dan and Howard exceeded expectations. These pieces are not only great art for a book, they are great art period, deserving of a place in any gallery.

I should note that Dan and Howard also contributed their talents to the interior art, for which I'm also grateful. Dan's fashion pieces are good enough to be cover art, and Howard's linework for some of the new chapter icons is something I hope to see more of in future volumes.

Ben McSweeney joins us again, providing nine pieces of art from Shallan's sketchbook. Between a cross-continent move, a demanding day job, and the needs of a growing family, Ben has been ever consistent in delivering top-notch illustrations. He is a great artist and a quality human being.

Also lending their talents to this volume with full-page illustrations are Miranda Meeks and Kelley Harris. Both have done fantastic work for us in the past, and I think you'll love their contributions this time around.

In addition, a variety of wonderful people helped behind the scenes as consultants or facilitated other aspects of the art in this book: The David Rumsey Map Collection, Brent at Woodsounds Flutes, Angie and Michelle at Two Tone Press, Emily Dunlay, David and Doris Stewart, Shari Lyon, Payden McRoberts, and Greg Davidson.

My writing group for *Oathbringer* (and they often read submissions each week at 5–8x the normal size) included Karen Ahlstrom, Peter Ahlstrom, Emily Sanderson, Eric James Stone, Darci Stone, Ben Olsen, Kaylynn Zo-Bell, Kathleen Dorsey Sanderson, Alan "Leyten from Bridge Four" Layton, Ethan "Skar from Bridge Four" Skarstedt, and Ben "Don't put me in Bridge Four" Olsen.

Special thanks go to Chris "Jon" King for feedback on some particularly tricky scenes involving Teft, Will Hoyum for some advice on paraplegics, and Mi'chelle Walker for some special advisement on passages involving specific mental health issues.

Beta readers included (take a deep breath) Aaron Biggs, Aaron Ford, Adam Hussey, Austin Hussey, Alice Arneson, Alyx Hoge, Aubree Pham, Bao Pham, Becca Horn Reppert, Bob Kluttz, Brandon Cole, Darci Cole, Brian T. Hill, Chris "Jon" King, Chris Kluwe, Cory Aitchison, David Behrens, Deana Covel Whitney, Eric Lake, Gary Singer, Ian McNatt, Jessica Ashcraft, Joel Phillips, Jory Phillips, Josh Walker, Mi'chelle Walker, Kalyani Poluri, Rahul Pantula, Kellyn Neumann, Kristina Kugler, Lyndsey "Lyn" Luther, Mark Lindberg, Marnie Peterson, Matt Wiens, Megan Kanne, Nathan "Natam" Goodrich, Nikki Ramsay, Paige Vest, Paul Christopher, Randy MacKay, Ravi Persaud, Richard Fife, Ross Newberry, Ryan "Drehy" Dreher Scott, Sarah "Saphy" Hansen, Sarah Fletcher, Shivam Bhatt, Steve Godecke, Ted Herman, Trae Cooper, and William Juan.

Our beta reader comment coordinators were Kristina Kugler and Kellyn Neumann.

Our gamma readers included many of the beta readers again, plus: Benjamin R. Black, Chris "Gunner" McGrath, Christi Jacobsen, Corbett Rubert, Richard Rubert, Dr. Daniel Stange, David Han-Ting Chow, Donald Mustard III, Eric Warrington, Jared Gerlach, Jareth Greeff,

Jesse Y. Horne, Joshua Combs, Justin Koford, Kendra Wilson, Kerry Morgan, Lindsey Andrus, Lingting Xu, Loggins Merrill, Marci Stringham, Matt Hatch, Scott Escujuri, Stephen Stinnett, and Tyson Thorpe.

As you can see, a book like this is a *huge* undertaking. Without the efforts of these many people, you'd be holding a far, far inferior book.

As always, some final thanks go to my family: Emily Sanderson, Joel Sanderson, Dallin Sanderson, and Oliver Sanderson. They put up with a husband/father who is often off in another world, thinking about highstorms and Knights Radiant.

Finally, thanks to you all, for your support of these books! They don't always come out as quickly as I'd like, but that is in part because I want them to be as perfect as they can get. You hold in your hands a volume I've been preparing and outlining for almost two decades. May you enjoy your time in Roshar.

Journey before destination.

CONTENTS

ILLUSTRATIONS

NOTE: *Many illustrations, titles included, contain spoilers for material that comes before them in the book. Look ahead at your own risk.*

BOOK
THREE

·⋄·

OATHBRINGER

Roshar
Endless Ocean
Rall Elorim
Quili
Abri
Resh
Kasitor
Iri
Rira
Kurth
Resh
Eila
The Misted Mountains
Babatharnam
Panatham
Marabeth
The Purela
Shinovar
Aimian Sea
Yulay
Fu Na
Desh
Azir
Aimia
Alm
Yezier
Urithiru
Azimir
The Val
Yeddaw
Emul
Liafor
Tashikk
Steen
Sesemalex Dar
Tukar
Mara
Icewater
N
Leeward
Stormward
S
Southern Depths

STEAMWATER OCEAN

ISLES

Sea

ALAY

SUMI

AKAK

Northgrip

HERDAZ

Mourn's
Vault

Varikev

Ru Parat

JAH KEVED

Elanar

Kholinar

Shulin

ALETHKAR

UNCLAIMED HILLS

Tu

Bayla

Valath

Horneater Peaks

BAVLAND

Rathalas

Dawn's
Shadow

Silnasen

TRIAX

Vedenar

Dumadari

Shattered
Plains

Tarat Sea

Karanak

New Natanan

Kharbranth

FROSTLANDS

Longbrow's

Thaylen City

Kina

The Shallow Crypts

THAYLENAH

OCEAN OF ORIGINS

FOR HIS ROYAL MAJESTY KING GAVILAR KHOLIN
BY HIS ROYAL HIGH CARTOGRAPHER
ISASIK SHULIN
1167

PROLOGUE

TO WEEP

SIX YEARS AGO

Eshonai had always told her sister that she was certain something wonderful lay over the next hill. Then one day, she'd crested a hill and found *humans*.

She'd always imagined humans—as sung of in the songs—as dark, formless monsters. Instead they were wonderful, bizarre creatures. They spoke with no discernible rhythm. They wore clothing more vibrant than carapace, but couldn't grow their own armor. They were so terrified of the storms that even when traveling they hid inside vehicles.

Most remarkably, they had only *one form*.

She first assumed the humans must have forgotten their forms, much as the listeners once had. That built an instant kinship between them.

Now, over a year later, Eshonai hummed to the Rhythm of Awe as she helped unload drums from the cart. They'd traveled a great distance to see the human homeland, and each step had overwhelmed her further. That experience culminated here, in this incredible city of Kholinar and its magnificent palace.

This cavernous unloading dock on the western side of the palace was so large, two hundred listeners had packed in here after their first arrival, and still hadn't filled the place. Indeed, most of the listeners couldn't attend the feast upstairs—where the treaty between their two peoples was being witnessed—but the Alethi had seen to their refreshment anyway, providing mountains of food and drink for the group down here.

She stepped out of the wagon, looking around the loading dock, humming to Excitement. When she'd told Venli she was determined to map the world, she'd imagined a place of natural discovery. Canyons and hills, forests and laits overgrown with life. Yet all along, *this* had been out here. Waiting just beyond their reach.

Along with more listeners.

When Eshonai had first met the humans, she'd seen the little listeners they had with them. A hapless tribe who were trapped in dullform. Eshonai had assumed the humans were taking care of the poor souls without songs.

Oh, how innocent those first meetings had been.

Those captive listeners had not been merely some small tribe, but instead representative of an enormous population. And the humans had not been caring for them.

The humans owned them.

A group of these parshmen, as they were called, clustered around the outside of Eshonai's ring of workers.

"They keep trying to help," Gitgeth said to Curiosity. He shook his head, his beard sparkling with ruby gemstones that matched the prominent red colors of his skin. "The little rhythmless ones want to be near us. They sense that something is wrong with their minds, I tell you."

Eshonai handed him a drum from the back of the cart, then hummed to Curiosity herself. She hopped down and approached the group of parshmen.

"You aren't needed," she said to Peace, spreading her hands. "We would prefer to handle our own drums."

The ones without songs looked at her with dull eyes.

"Go," she said to Pleading, waving toward the nearby festivities, where listeners and human servants laughed together, despite the language barrier. Humans clapped along to listeners singing the old songs. "Enjoy yourselves."

A few looked toward the singing and cocked their heads, but they didn't move.

"It won't work," Brianlia said to Skepticism, resting her arms across a drum nearby. "They simply can't *imagine* what it is to live. They're pieces of property, to be bought and sold."

What to make of this idea? Slaves? Klade, one of the Five, had gone to the slavers in Kholinar and purchased a person to see if it truly was possible. He hadn't even bought a parshman; there had been *Alethi* for sale. Apparently the parshmen were expensive, and considered high-quality slaves. The listeners had been told this, as if it were supposed to make them proud.

She hummed to Curiosity and nodded to the side, looking toward the others. Gitgeth smiled and hummed to Peace, waving for her to go. Everyone was used to Eshonai wandering off in the middle of jobs. It wasn't that she was unreliable. . . . Well, perhaps she was, but at least she was consistent.

Regardless, she'd be wanted at the king's celebration soon anyway; she was one of the best among the listeners at the dull human tongue, which she'd taken to naturally. It was an advantage that had earned her a place on this expedition, but it was also a problem. Speaking the human tongue made her important, and people who grew too important couldn't be allowed to go off chasing the horizon.

She left the unloading bay and walked up the steps into the palace proper, trying to take in the ornamentation, the artistry, the sheer overwhelming *wonder* of the building. Beautiful and terrible. People who were bought and sold maintained this place, but was that what freed the humans to create great works like the carvings on the pillars she passed, or the inlaid marble patterns on the floor?

She passed soldiers wearing their artificial carapace. Eshonai didn't have armor of her own at the moment; she wore workform instead of warform, as she liked its flexibility.

Humans didn't have a choice. They hadn't lost their forms as she'd first assumed; they *only had one.* Forever in mateform, workform, and warform all at once. And they wore their emotions on their faces far more than listeners. Oh, Eshonai's people would smile, laugh, cry. But not like these Alethi.

The lower level of the palace was marked by broad hallways and galleries, lit by carefully cut gemstones that made light sparkle. Chandeliers hung above her, broken suns spraying light everywhere. Perhaps the plain appearance of the human bodies—with their bland skin that was various shades of tan—was another reason they sought to ornament everything, from their clothing to these pillars.

Could we do this? she thought, humming to Appreciation. *If we knew the right form for creating art?*

The upper floors of the palace were more like tunnels. Narrow stone corridors, rooms like bunkers dug into a mountainside. She made her way toward the feast hall to check if she was needed, but stopped here and there to glance into rooms. She'd been told she could wander as she pleased, that the palace was open to her save for areas with guards at the doors.

She passed a room with paintings on all the walls, then one with a bed and furniture. Another door revealed an indoor privy with running water, a marvel that she still didn't understand.

She poked through a dozen rooms. As long as she reached the king's celebration in time for the music, Klade and the others of the Five wouldn't complain. They were as familiar with her ways as everyone else. She was always wandering off, poking into things, peeking into doors . . .

And finding the king?

Eshonai froze, the door cracked open, allowing her to see into a lush room with a thick red rug and bookshelves lining the walls. So much information just lying around, casually ignored. More surprisingly, King Gavilar himself stood pointing at something on a table, surrounded by five others: two officers, two women in long dresses, and one old man in robes.

Why wasn't Gavilar at the feast? Why weren't there guards at the door? Eshonai attuned Anxiety and pulled back, but not before one of the women prodded Gavilar and pointed toward Eshonai. Anxiety pounding in her head, she pulled the door closed.

A moment later a tall man in uniform stepped out. "The king would like to see you, Parshendi."

She feigned confusion. "Sir? Words?"

"Don't be coy," the soldier said. "You're one of the interpreters. Come in. You aren't in trouble."

Anxiety shaking her, she let him lead her into the den.

"Thank you, Meridas," Gavilar said. "Leave us for a moment, all of you."

They filed out, leaving Eshonai at the door attuning Consolation and humming it loudly—even though the humans wouldn't understand what it meant.

"Eshonai," the king said. "I have something to show you."

He knew her name? She stepped farther into the small, warm room, holding her arms tightly around her. She didn't understand this man. It was more than his alien, dead way of speaking. More than the fact that she couldn't anticipate what emotions might be swirling in there, as warform and mateform contested within him.

More than any human, this man baffled her. Why *had* he offered them such a favorable treaty? At first it had seemed an accommodation between tribes. That was before she'd come here, seen this city and the Alethi armies. Her people had once possessed cities of their own, and armies to envy. They knew that from the songs.

That had been long ago. They were a fragment of a lost people. Traitors who had abandoned their gods to be free. This man could have crushed the listeners. They'd once assumed that their Shards—weapons they had so far kept hidden from the humans—would be enough to protect them. But she'd now seen over a dozen Shardblades and suits of Shardplate among the Alethi.

Why did he smile at her like that? What was he hiding, by not singing to the rhythms to calm her?

"Sit, Eshonai," the king said. "Oh, don't be frightened, little scout. I've been wanting to speak to you. Your mastery of our language is unique!"

She settled on a chair while Gavilar reached down and removed something from a small satchel. It glowed with red Stormlight, a construction of gemstones and metal, crafted in a beautiful design.

"Do you know what this is?" he asked, gently pushing it toward her.

"No, Your Majesty."

"It's what we call a fabrial, a device powered by Stormlight. This one makes warmth. Just a smidge, unfortunately, but my wife is confident her scholars can create one that will heat a room. Wouldn't that be wonderful? No more smoky fires in hearths."

It seemed lifeless to Eshonai, but she didn't say so. She hummed to Praise so he'd feel happy telling her of this, and handed it back.

"Look closely," King Gavilar said. "Look deep into it. Can you see what's moving inside? It's a spren. That is how the device works."

Captive like in a gemheart, she thought, attuning Awe. *They've built devices that mimic how we apply the forms?* The humans did so much with their limitations!

"The chasmfiends aren't your gods, are they," he said.

"What?" she asked, attuning Skepticism. "Why ask that?" What a strange turn in the conversation.

"Oh, it's merely something I've been thinking about." He took the fabrial back. "My officers feel so superior, as they think they have you figured out. They think you're savages, but they are so wrong. You're not savages. You're an enclave of memories. A window into the past."

He leaned forward, the light from the ruby leaking between his fingers. "I need you to deliver a message to your leaders. The Five? You're close to them, and I'm being watched. I need their help to achieve something."

She hummed to Anxiety.

"Now, now," he said. "I'm going to help you, Eshonai. Did you know, I've discovered how to bring your gods back?"

No. She hummed to the Rhythm of the Terrors. *No . . .*

"My ancestors," he said, holding up the fabrial, "first learned how to hold a spren inside a gemstone. And with a very special gemstone, you can hold even a god."

"Your Majesty," she said, daring to take his hand in hers. He couldn't feel the rhythms. He didn't know. "Please. We no longer worship those gods. We left them, *abandoned* them."

"Ah, but this is for your good, and for ours." He stood up. "We live without honor, for your gods once brought ours. Without them, we have no *power.* This world is trapped, Eshonai! Stuck in a dull, lifeless state of transition." He looked toward the ceiling. "Unite them. I need a threat. Only danger will unite them."

"What . . ." she said to Anxiety. "What are you saying?"

"Our enslaved parshmen were once like you. Then we somehow robbed them of their ability to undergo the transformation. We did it by capturing a spren. An ancient, *crucial* spren." He looked at her, green eyes alight.

"I've seen how that can be reversed. A new storm that will bring the Heralds out of hiding. A new war."

"Insanity." She rose to her feet. "Our gods tried to destroy you."

"The old Words must be spoken again."

"You can't . . ." She trailed off, noticing for the first time that a map covered the table nearby. Expansive, it showed a land bounded by oceans—and the artistry of it put her own attempts to shame.

She rose and stepped to the table, gaping, the Rhythm of Awe playing in her mind. *This is gorgeous.* Even the grand chandeliers and carved walls were nothing by comparison. This was knowledge *and* beauty, fused into one.

"I thought you'd be pleased to hear that we are allies in seeking the return of your gods," Gavilar said. She could almost hear the Rhythm of Reprimand in his dead words. "You claim to fear them, but why fear that which made you live? My people need to be united, and I need an empire that won't simply turn to infighting once I am gone."

"So you seek for *war*?"

"I seek for an end to something that we never finished. My people were Radiant once, and your people—the parshmen—were vibrant. Who is served by this drab world where my people fight each other in endless squabbles, without light to guide them, and your people are as good as corpses?"

She looked back at the map. "Where . . . where is the Shattered Plains? This portion here?"

"That is all of Natanatan you gesture toward, Eshonai! This is the Shattered Plains." He pointed at a spot not much bigger than his thumbnail, when the entire map was as large as the table.

It gave her a sudden dizzying perspective. This was the world? She'd assumed that in traveling to Kholinar, they'd crossed almost as far as the land could go. Why hadn't they shown her this before!

Her legs weakened, and she attuned Mourning. She dropped back into her seat, unable to stand.

So vast.

Gavilar removed something from his pocket. A sphere? It was dark, yet somehow still glowed. As if it had . . . an aura of blackness, a phantom light that was not light. Faintly violet. It seemed to suck in the light around it.

He set it on the table before her. "Take that to the Five and explain what I told you. Tell them to remember what your people once were. *Wake up*, Eshonai."

He patted her on the shoulder, then left the room. She stared at that terrible light, and—from the songs—knew it for what it was. The forms of power had been associated with a dark light, a light from the king of gods.

She plucked the sphere off the table and went running.

⁘

When the drums were set up, Eshonai insisted on joining the drummers. An outlet for her anxiety. She beat to the rhythm in her head, banging as hard as she could, trying with each beat to banish the things the king had said.

And the things she'd just done.

The Five sat at the high table, the remnants of their final course uneaten.

He intends to bring back our gods, she'd told the Five.

Close your eyes. Focus on the rhythms.

He can do it. He knows so much.

Furious beats pulsing through her soul.

We have to do something.

Klade's slave was an assassin. Klade claimed that a *voice*—speaking to the rhythms—had led him to the man, who had confessed his skills when pressed. Venli had apparently been with Klade, though Eshonai hadn't seen her sister since earlier in the day.

After a frantic debate, the Five had agreed this was a sign of what they were to do. Long ago, the listeners had summoned the courage to adopt dullform in order to escape their gods. They'd sought freedom at any cost.

Today, the cost of maintaining that freedom would be high.

She played the drums. She felt the rhythms. She wept softly, and didn't look as the strange assassin—wearing flowing white clothing provided by Klade—left the room. She'd voted with the others for this course of action.

Feel the peace of the music. As her mother always said. *Seek the rhythms. Seek the songs.*

She resisted as the others pulled her away. She wept to leave the music behind. Wept for her people, who might be destroyed for tonight's action. Wept for the world, which might never know what the listeners had done for it.

Wept for the king, whom she had consigned to death.

The drums cut off around her, and dying music echoed through the halls.

PART

ONE

United

DALINAR • SHALLAN •
KALADIN • ADOLIN

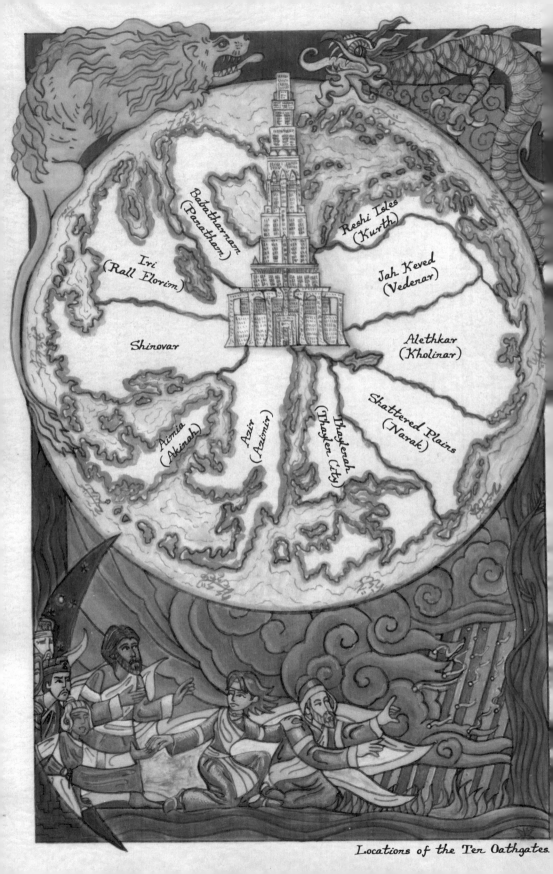

Iri
(Rall Elorim)

Babatharnam
(Panatham)

Reshi Isles
(Kurth)

Jah Keved
(Vedenar)

Shinovar

Alethkar
(Kholinar)

Aimia
(Akinah)

Azir
(Azimir)

Thaylenah
(Thaylen City)

Shattered Plains
(Narak)

Locations of the Ten Oathgates.

I

BROKEN
AND DIVIDED

I'm certain some will feel threatened by this record. Some few may feel liberated. Most will simply feel that it should not exist.

—From *Oathbringer*, preface

Dalinar Kholin appeared in the vision standing beside the memory of a dead god.

It had been six days since his forces had arrived at Urithiru, legendary holy tower city of the Knights Radiant. They had escaped the arrival of a new devastating storm, seeking refuge through an ancient portal. They were settling into their new home hidden in the mountains.

And yet, Dalinar felt as if he knew nothing. He didn't understand the force he fought, let alone how to defeat it. He barely understood the storm, and what it meant in returning the Voidbringers, ancient enemies of men.

So he came here, into his visions. Seeking to pull secrets from the god—named Honor, or the Almighty—who had left them. This particular vision was the first that Dalinar had ever experienced. It began with him standing next to an image of the god in human form, both perched atop a cliff overlooking Kholinar: Dalinar's home, seat of the government. In the vision, the city had been destroyed by some unknown force.

The Almighty started speaking, but Dalinar ignored him. Dalinar had become a Knight Radiant by bonding the Stormfather himself—soul of the highstorm, most powerful spren on Roshar—and Dalinar had discovered he could now have these visions replayed for him at will. He'd already heard this monologue three times, and had repeated it word for word to Navani for transcription.

This time, Dalinar instead walked to the edge of the cliff and knelt to look out upon the ruins of Kholinar. The air smelled dry here, dusty and warm. He squinted, trying to extract some meaningful detail from the chaos of broken buildings. Even the windblades—once magnificent, sleek rock formations exposing countless strata and variations—had been shattered.

The Almighty continued his speech. These visions were like a diary, a set of immersive messages the god had left behind. Dalinar appreciated the help, but right now he wanted details.

He searched the sky and discovered a ripple in the air, like heat rising from distant stone. A shimmer the size of a building.

"Stormfather," he said. "Can you take me down below, into the rubble?"

You are not supposed to go there. That is not part of the vision.

"Ignore what I'm supposed to do, for the moment," Dalinar said. "Can you do it? Can you transport me to those ruins?"

The Stormfather rumbled. He was a strange being, somehow connected to the dead god, but not exactly the same thing as the Almighty. At least today he wasn't using a voice that rattled Dalinar's bones.

In an eyeblink, Dalinar was transported. He no longer stood atop the cliff, but was on the plains down before the ruins of the city.

"Thank you," Dalinar said, striding the short remaining distance to the ruins.

Only six days had passed since their discovery of Urithiru. Six days since the awakening of the Parshendi, who had gained strange powers and glowing red eyes. Six days since the arrival of the new storm—the Everstorm, a tempest of dark thunderheads and red lightning.

Some in his armies thought that it was finished, the storm over as one catastrophic event. Dalinar knew otherwise. The Everstorm would return, and would soon hit Shinovar in the far west. Following that, it would course across the land.

Nobody believed his warnings. Monarchs in places like Azir and Thaylenah admitted that a strange storm had appeared in the east, but they didn't believe it would return.

They couldn't guess how destructive this storm's return would be. When it had first appeared, it had clashed with the highstorm, creating a unique cataclysm. Hopefully it would not be as bad on its own—but it would still be a storm blowing the wrong way. And it would awaken the world's parshman servants and make them into Voidbringers.

What do you expect to learn? the Stormfather said as Dalinar reached the rubble of the city. *This vision was constructed to draw you to the ridge to speak with Honor. The rest is backdrop, a painting.*

"Honor put this rubble here," Dalinar said, waving toward the broken walls heaped before him. "Backdrop or not, his knowledge of the world and our enemy couldn't help but affect the way he made this vision."

Dalinar hiked up the rubble of the outer walls. Kholinar had been . . . storm it, Kholinar *was* . . . a grand city, like few in the world. Instead of hiding in the shadow of a cliff or inside a sheltered chasm, Kholinar trusted in its enormous walls to buffer it from highstorm winds. It *defied* the winds, and did not bow to the storms.

In this vision, something had destroyed it anyway. Dalinar crested the detritus and surveyed the area, trying to imagine how it had felt to settle here so many millennia ago. Back when there had been no walls. It had been a hardy, stubborn lot who had grown this place.

He saw scrapes and gouges on the stones of the fallen walls, like those made by a predator in the flesh of its prey. The windblades had been smashed, and from up close he could see claw marks on one of those as well.

"I've seen creatures that could do this," he said, kneeling beside one of the stones, feeling the rough gash in the granite surface. "In my visions, I witnessed a stone monster that ripped itself free of the underlying rock.

"There are no corpses, but that's probably because the Almighty didn't populate the city in this vision. He just wanted a symbol of the coming destruction. He didn't think Kholinar would fall to the Everstorm, but to the Voidbringers."

Yes, the Stormfather said. *The storm will be a catastrophe, but not nearly on the scale of what follows. You can find refuge from storms, Son of Honor. Not so with our enemies.*

Now that the monarchs of Roshar had refused to listen to Dalinar's warning that the Everstorm would soon strike them, what else could Dalinar do? The real Kholinar was reportedly consumed by riots—and the queen had gone silent. Dalinar's armies had limped away from their first confrontation with the Voidbringers, and even many of his own highprinces hadn't joined him in that battle.

A war was coming. In awakening the Desolation, the enemy had rekindled a millennia-old conflict of ancient creatures with inscrutable motivations and unknown powers. Heralds were supposed to appear and lead the charge against the Voidbringers. The Knights Radiant should have already been in place, prepared and trained, ready to face the enemy. They were supposed to be able to trust in the guidance of the Almighty.

Instead, Dalinar had only a handful of new Radiants, and there was no sign of help from the Heralds. And beyond that, the Almighty—God himself—was dead.

Somehow, Dalinar was supposed to save the world anyway.

The ground started to tremble; the vision was ending with the land falling away. Atop the cliff, the Almighty would have just concluded his speech.

A final wave of destruction rolled across the land like a highstorm. A metaphor designed by the Almighty to represent the darkness and devastation that was coming upon humankind.

Your legends say that you won, he had said. *But the truth is that we lost. And we are losing. . . .*

The Stormfather rumbled. *It is time to go.*

"No," Dalinar said, standing atop the rubble. "Leave me."

But—

"Let me feel it!"

The wave of destruction struck, crashing against Dalinar, and he shouted defiance. He had not bowed before the highstorm; he would not bow before this! He faced it head-on, and in the blast of power that ripped apart the ground, he saw something.

A golden light, brilliant yet terrible. Standing before it, a dark figure in black Shardplate. The figure had nine shadows, each spreading out in a different direction, and its eyes glowed a brilliant red.

Dalinar stared deep into those eyes, and felt a chill wash through him. Though the destruction raged around him, vaporizing rocks, those *eyes* frightened him more. He saw something terribly familiar in them.

This was a danger far beyond even the storms.

This was the enemy's champion. And he was coming.

UNITE THEM. QUICKLY.

Dalinar gasped as the vision shattered. He found himself sitting beside Navani in a quiet stone room in the tower city of Urithiru. Dalinar didn't need to be bound for visions any longer; he had enough control over them that he had ceased acting them out while experiencing them.

He breathed deeply, sweat trickling down his face, his heart racing. Navani said something, but for the moment he couldn't hear her. She seemed distant compared to the rushing in his ears.

"What was that light I saw?" he whispered.

I saw no light, the Stormfather said.

"It was brilliant and golden, but terrible," Dalinar whispered. "It bathed everything in its heat."

Odium, the Stormfather rumbled. *The enemy.*

The god who had killed the Almighty. The force behind the Desolations.

"Nine shadows," Dalinar whispered, trembling.

Nine shadows? The Unmade. His minions, ancient spren.

Storms. Dalinar knew of them from legend only. Terrible spren who twisted the minds of men.

Still, those eyes haunted him. As frightening as it was to contemplate the Unmade, he feared that figure with the red eyes the most. Odium's champion.

Dalinar blinked, looking to Navani, the woman he loved, her face painfully concerned as she held his arm. In this strange place and stranger time, she was something real. Something to hold on to. A mature beauty—in some ways the picture of a perfect Vorin woman: lush lips, light violet eyes, silvering black hair in perfect braids, curves accentuated by the tight silk havah. No man would ever accuse Navani of being scrawny.

"Dalinar?" she asked. "Dalinar, what happened? Are you well?"

"I'm . . ." He drew in a deep breath. "I'm well, Navani. And I know what we must do."

Her frown deepened. "What?"

"I have to unite the world against the enemy faster than he can destroy it."

He had to find a way to make the other monarchs of the world listen to him. He had to prepare them for the new storm and the Voidbringers. And, barring that, he had to help them survive the effects.

But if he succeeded, he wouldn't have to face the Desolation alone. This was not a matter of one nation against the Voidbringers. He needed the kingdoms of the world to join him, and he needed to find the Knights Radiant who were being created among their populations.

Unite them.

"Dalinar," she said, "I think that's a worthy goal . . . but storms, what of ourselves? This mountainside is a wasteland—what are we going to feed our armies?"

"The Soulcasters—"

"Will run out of gemstones eventually," Navani said. "And they can create only the basic necessities. Dalinar, we're half frozen up here, broken and divided. Our command structure is in disarray, and it—"

"Peace, Navani," Dalinar said, rising. He pulled her to her feet. "I know. We have to fight anyway."

She embraced him. He held to her, feeling her warmth, smelling her perfume. She preferred a less floral scent than other women—a fragrance with spice to it, like the aroma of newly cut wood.

"We can do this," he told her. "My tenacity. Your brilliance. Together, we *will* convince the other kingdoms to join with us. They'll see when the storm returns that our warnings were right, and they'll unite against the enemy. We can use the Oathgates to move troops and to support each other."

The Oathgates. Ten portals, ancient fabrials, were gateways to Urithiru. When a Knight Radiant activated one of the devices, those people standing upon its surrounding platform were brought to Urithiru, appearing on a similar device here at the tower.

They only had one pair of Oathgates active now—the ones that moved people back and forth between Urithiru and the Shattered Plains. Nine more could theoretically be made to work—but unfortunately, their research determined that a mechanism inside each of them had to be unlocked from *both* sides before they'd work.

If he wanted to travel to Vedenar, Thaylen City, Azimir, or any of the other locations, they'd first need to get one of their Radiants to the city and unlock the device.

"All right," she said. "We'll do it. Somehow we'll make them listen—even if they've got their fingers planted firmly in their ears. Makes one wonder how they manage it, with their heads rammed up their own backsides."

He smiled, and suddenly thought himself foolish for idealizing her just earlier. Navani Kholin was not some timid, perfect ideal—she was a sour storm of a woman, set in her ways, stubborn as a boulder rolling down a mountain and increasingly impatient with things she considered foolish.

He loved her the most for that. For being open and genuine in a society that prided itself on secrets. She'd been breaking taboos, and hearts, since their youth. At times, the idea that she loved him back seemed as surreal as one of his visions.

A knock came at the door to his room, and Navani called for the person to enter. One of Dalinar's scouts poked her head in through the door. Dalinar turned, frowning, noting the woman's nervous posture and quick breathing.

"What?" he demanded.

"Sir," the woman said, saluting, face pale. "There's . . . been an incident. A corpse discovered in the corridors."

Dalinar felt something building, an energy in the air like the sensation of lightning about to strike. "Who?"

"Highprince Torol Sadeas, sir," the woman said. "He's been murdered."

2

ONE PROBLEM SOLVED

I needed to write it anyway.

—From *Oathbringer*, preface

"S top! What do you think you're doing?" Adolin Kholin strode over to a group of workers in crem-stained work outfits who were unloading boxes from the back of a wagon. Their chull twisted, trying to search out rockbuds to munch on. Fruitlessly. They were deep within the tower, for all the fact that this cavern was as large as a small town.

The workers had the decency to look chagrined, though they probably didn't know what for. A flock of scribes trailing Adolin checked the contents of the wagon. Oil lamps on the ground did little to push back the darkness of the enormous room, which had a ceiling that went up four stories.

"Brightlord?" one of the workers asked, scratching at his hair beneath his cap. "I was just unloadin'. That's what I think I was doin'."

"Manifest says beer," Rushu—a young ardent—told Adolin.

"Section two," Adolin said, rapping the knuckles of his left hand against the wagon. "Taverns are being set up along the central corridor with the lifts, six crossroads inward. My aunt *expressly* told your highlords this."

The men just stared at him blankly.

"I can have a scribe show you. Pick these boxes back up."

The men sighed, but started reloading their wagon. They knew better than to argue with the son of a highprince.

Adolin turned to survey the deep cavern, which had become a dumping ground for both supplies and people. Children ran past in groups. Workers set up tents. Women gathered water at the well in the center. Soldiers carried torches or lanterns. Even axehounds raced this way and that. Four entire warcamps full of people had frantically crossed the Shattered Plains to Urithiru, and Navani had struggled to find the right spot for them all.

For all the chaos, though, Adolin was glad to have these people. They were fresh; they hadn't suffered the battle with the Parshendi, the attack of the Assassin in White, and the terrible clash of two storms.

The Kholin soldiers were in terrible shape. Adolin's own sword hand was wrapped and still throbbing, his wrist broken during the fighting. His face had a nasty bruise, and he was one of the more lucky ones.

"Brightlord," Rushu said, pointing at another wagon. "That looks like wines."

"Delightful," Adolin said. Was *nobody* paying attention to Aunt Navani's directives?

He dealt with this wagon, then had to break up an argument among men who were angry they had been set to hauling water. They claimed that was parshman work, beneath their nahn. Unfortunately, there were no parshmen any longer.

Adolin soothed them and suggested they could start a water haulers' guild if forced to continue. Father would approve that for certain, though Adolin worried. Would they have the funds to pay all these people? Wages were based on a man's rank, and you couldn't just make slaves of men for no reason.

Adolin was glad for the assignment, to distract him. Though he didn't have to see to each wagon himself—he was here to supervise—he threw himself into the details of the work. He couldn't exactly spar, not with his wrist in this shape, but if he sat alone too long he started thinking about what had happened the day before.

Had he really done that?

Had he really *murdered* Torol Sadeas?

It was almost a relief when at long last a runner came for him, whispering that something had been discovered in the corridors of the third floor.

Adolin was certain he knew what it was.

· · ·

Dalinar heard the shouts long before he arrived. They echoed down the tunnels. He knew that tone. Conflict was near.

He left Navani and broke into a run, sweating as he burst into a wide intersection between tunnels. Men in blue, lit by the harsh light of lanterns, faced off against others in forest green. Angerspren grew from the floor like pools of blood.

A corpse with a green jacket draped over the face lay on the ground.

"Stand down!" Dalinar bellowed, charging into the space between the two groups of soldiers. He pulled back a bridgeman who had gotten right up in the face of one of Sadeas's soldiers. "Stand down, or I'll have you all in the stockade, every man!"

His voice hit the men like stormwinds, drawing eyes from both sides. He pushed the bridgeman toward his fellows, then shoved back one of Sadeas's soldiers, praying the man would have the presence of mind to resist attacking a highprince.

Navani and the scout stopped at the fringes of the conflict. The men from Bridge Four finally backed down one corridor, and Sadeas's soldiers retreated up the one opposite. Just far enough that they could still glare at one another.

"You'd better be ready for Damnation's own thunder," Sadeas's officer shouted at Dalinar. "Your men *murdered* a highprince!"

"We found him like this!" Teft of Bridge Four shouted back. "Probably tripped on his own knife. Serves him well, the storming bastard."

"Teft, *stand down!*" Dalinar shouted at him.

The bridgeman looked abashed, then saluted with a stiff gesture.

Dalinar knelt, pulling the jacket back from Sadeas's face. "That blood is dried. He's been lying here for some time."

"We've been looking for him," said the officer in green.

"Looking for him? You *lost* your highprince?"

"The tunnels are confusing!" the man said. "They don't go natural directions. We got turned about and . . ."

"Thought he might have returned to another part of the tower," a man said. "We spent last night searching for him there. Some people said they thought they'd seen him, but they were wrong, and . . ."

And a highprince was left lying here in his own gore for half a day, Dalinar thought. *Blood of my fathers.*

"We couldn't find him," the officer said, "because your men murdered him and moved the body—"

"That blood has been pooling there for hours. Nobody moved the body." Dalinar pointed. "Place the highprince in that side room there and send for Ialai, if you haven't. I want to have a better look."

⁂

Dalinar Kholin was a connoisseur of death.

Even since his youth, the sight of dead men had been a familiar thing to him. You stay on the battlefield long enough, and you become familiar with its master.

So Sadeas's bloodied, ruined face didn't shock him. The punctured eye, smashed up into the socket by a blade that had been rammed into the brain. Fluid and blood had leaked out, then dried.

A knife through the eye was the sort of wound that killed an armored man wearing a full helm. It was a maneuver you practiced to use on the battlefield. But Sadeas had not been wearing armor and had not been on a battlefield.

Dalinar leaned down, inspecting the body lit by flickering oil lanterns as it lay on the table.

"Assassin," Navani said, clicking her tongue and shaking her head. "Not good."

Behind him, Adolin and Renarin gathered with Shallan and a few of the bridgemen. Across from Dalinar stood Kalami; the thin, orange-eyed woman was one of his more senior scribes. They'd lost her husband, Teleb, in the battle against the Voidbringers. He hated to call upon her in her time of grief, but she insisted that she remain on duty.

Storms, he had so few high officers left. Cael had fallen in the clash between Everstorm and highstorm, almost making it to safety. He'd lost Ilamar and Perethom to Sadeas's betrayal at the Tower. The only highlord he had left was Khal, who was still recuperating from a wound he'd taken during the clash with the Voidbringers—one he'd kept to himself until everyone else was safe.

Even Elhokar, the king, had been wounded by assassins in his palace while the armies were fighting at Narak. He'd been recuperating ever since. Dalinar wasn't certain if he would come to see Sadeas's body or not.

Either way, Dalinar's lack of officers explained the room's other occupants: Highprince Sebarial and his mistress, Palona. Likable or not, Sebarial was one of the two living highprinces who had responded to Dalinar's call to march for Narak. Dalinar had to rely on someone, and he didn't trust most of the highprinces farther than the wind could blow them.

Sebarial, along with Aladar—who had been summoned but had not yet arrived—would have to form the foundation of a new Alethkar. Almighty help them all.

"Well!" said Palona, hands on hips as she regarded Sadeas's corpse. "I guess that's one problem solved!"

Everyone in the room turned toward her.

"What?" she said. "Don't tell me you weren't all thinking it."

"This is going to look bad, Brightlord," Kalami said. "Everyone is going to act like those soldiers outside and assume you had him assassinated."

"Any sign of the Shardblade?" Dalinar asked.

"No, sir," one of the bridgemen said. "Whoever killed him probably took it."

Navani rubbed Dalinar on the shoulder. "I wouldn't have put it as Palona did, but he *did* try to have you killed. Perhaps this is for the best."

"No," Dalinar said, voice hoarse. "We needed him."

"I know you're desperate, Dalinar," Sebarial said. "My presence here is sufficient proof of *that*. But surely we haven't sunk so far as to be better off with Sadeas among us. I agree with Palona. Good riddance."

Dalinar looked up, inspecting those in the room. Sebarial and Palona. Teft and Sigzil, the lieutenants from Bridge Four. A handful of other soldiers, including the young scout woman who had fetched him. His sons, steady Adolin and impenetrable Renarin. Navani, with her hand on his shoulder. Even the aging Kalami, hands clasped before her, meeting his eyes and nodding.

"You all agree, don't you?" Dalinar asked.

Nobody objected. Yes, this murder was inconvenient for Dalinar's reputation, and they certainly wouldn't have gone so far as to kill Sadeas themselves. But now that he was gone . . . well, why shed any tears?

Memories churned inside Dalinar's head. Days spent with Sadeas, listening to Gavilar's grand plans. The night before Dalinar's wedding, when he'd shared wine with Sadeas at a rowdy feast that Sadeas had organized in his name.

It was hard to reconcile that younger man, that *friend,* with the thicker, older face on the slab before him. The adult Sadeas had been a murderer whose treachery had caused the deaths of better men. For those men, abandoned during the battle at the Tower, Dalinar could feel only satisfaction at finally seeing Sadeas dead.

That troubled him. He knew *exactly* how the others were feeling. "Come with me."

He left the body and strode out of the room. He passed Sadeas's guards, who hurried back in. They would deal with the corpse; hopefully he'd defused the situation enough to prevent an impromptu clash between his forces and theirs. For now, the best thing to do was get Bridge Four away from here.

Dalinar's retinue followed him through the halls of the cavernous tower, bearing oil lamps. The walls were twisted with lines—natural strata of alternating earthy colors, like those made by crem drying in layers. He didn't blame the soldiers for losing track of Sadeas; it was strikingly easy to get lost in this place, with its endless passageways all leading into darkness.

Fortunately, he had an idea of where they were, and led his people to the outer rim of the tower. Here he strode through an empty chamber and stepped out onto a balcony, one of many similar ones that were like wide patios.

Above him rose the enormous tower city of Urithiru, a strikingly high structure built up against the mountains. Created from a sequence of ten ringlike tiers—each containing eighteen levels—the tower city was adorned with aqueducts, windows, and balconies like this one.

The bottom floor also had wide sections jutting out at the perimeter: large stone surfaces, each a plateau in its own right. They had stone railings at their edges, where the rock fell away into the depths of the chasms between mountain peaks. At first, these wide flat sections of stone had baffled them. But the furrows in the stone, and planter boxes on the inner edges, had revealed their purpose. Somehow, these were *fields.* Like the large spaces for gardens atop each tier of the tower, this area had been farmed, despite the cold. One of these fields extended below this balcony, two levels down.

Dalinar strode up to the edge of the balcony and rested his hands on the smooth stone retaining wall. The others gathered behind him. Along the way they'd picked up Highprince Aladar, a distinguished bald Alethi with dark tan skin. He was accompanied by May, his daughter: a short, pretty woman in her twenties with tan eyes and a round face, her jet-black Alethi hair worn short and curving around her face. Navani whispered to them the details of Sadeas's death.

Dalinar swept his hand outward in the chill air, pointing away from the balcony. "What do you see?"

The bridgemen gathered to look off the balcony. Their number included the Herdazian, who now had two arms after regrowing the one with Stormlight. Kaladin's men had begun manifesting powers as Windrunners—though apparently they were merely "squires." Navani said it was a type of apprentice Radiant that had once been common: men and women whose abilities were tied to their master, a full Radiant.

The men of Bridge Four had not bonded their own spren, and—though they had started manifesting powers—had lost their abilities when Kaladin had flown to Alethkar to warn his family of the Everstorm.

"What do I see?" the Herdazian said. "I see clouds."

"*Lots* of clouds," another bridgeman added.

"Some mountains too," another said. "They look like teeth."

"Nah, horns," the Herdazian argued.

"We," Dalinar interrupted, "are above the storms. It's going to be easy to forget the tempest the rest of the world is facing. The Everstorm will return, bringing the Voidbringers. We have to assume that this city—our armies—will soon be the only bastion of order left in the world. It is our calling, our *duty,* to take the lead."

"Order?" Aladar said. "Dalinar, have you *seen* our armies? They fought an impossible battle only six days ago, and despite being rescued, we technically *lost*. Roion's son is woefully underprepared for dealing with the remnants of his princedom. Some of the strongest forces—those of Thanadal and Vamah—*stayed behind* in the warcamps!"

"The ones who did come are already squabbling," Palona added. "Old Torol's death back there will only give them something else to dissent about."

Dalinar turned around, gripping the top of the stone wall with both hands, fingers cold. A chill wind blew against him, and a few windspren passed like little translucent people riding on the breeze.

"Brightness Kalami," Dalinar said. "What do you know of the Desolations?"

"Brightlord?" she asked, hesitant.

"The Desolations. You've done scholarly work on Vorin theory, yes? Can you tell us of the Desolations?"

Kalami cleared her throat. "They were destruction made manifest, Brightlord. Each one was so profoundly devastating that humankind was left broken. Populations ruined, society crippled, scholars dead. Humankind was forced to spend generations rebuilding after each one. Songs tell of how the losses compounded upon one another, causing us to slide farther each time, until the Heralds left a people with swords and fabrials and returned to find them wielding sticks and stone axes."

"And the Voidbringers?" Dalinar asked.

"They came to annihilate," Kalami said. "Their goal was to wipe humankind from Roshar. They were specters, formless—some say they are spirits of the dead, others spren from Damnation."

"We will have to find a way to stop this from happening again," Dalinar said softly, turning back to the group. "We are the ones this world must be able to look to. We must provide stability, a rallying point.

"This is why I cannot rejoice to find Sadeas dead. He was a thorn in my side, but he was a capable general and a brilliant mind. We needed him. Before this is through, we'll need everyone who can fight."

"Dalinar," Aladar said. "I used to bicker. I used to be like the other highprinces. But what I saw on that battlefield . . . those red eyes . . . Sir, I'm with you. I will follow you to the ends of the storms themselves. What do you want me to do?"

"Our time is short. Aladar, I name you our new Highprince of Information, in command of the judgment and law of this city. Establish order in Urithiru and make sure that the highprinces have clearly delineated realms of control within it. Build a policing force, and patrol these hallways. Keep the peace, and prevent clashes between soldiers like the one we avoided earlier.

"Sebarial, I name you Highprince of Commerce. Account our supplies and establish marketplaces in Urithiru. I want this tower to become a functioning city, not just a temporary waystop.

"Adolin, see that the armies are put into a training regimen. Count the troops we have, from all the highprinces, and convey to them that their spears will be required for the defense of Roshar. So long as they remain here, they are under my authority as Highprince of War. We'll crush their squabbling beneath a weight of training. We control the Soulcasters, and we control the food. If they want rations, they'll have to listen."

"And us?" the scruffy lieutenant of Bridge Four asked.

"Continue to explore Urithiru with my scouts and scribes," Dalinar said. "And let me know the moment your captain returns. Hopefully he will bring good news from Alethkar."

He took a deep breath. A voice echoed in the back of his mind, as if distant. *Unite them.*

Be ready for when the enemy's champion arrives.

"Our ultimate goal is the preservation of all Roshar," Dalinar said softly. "We've seen the cost of division in our ranks. Because of it, we failed to stop the Everstorm. But that was just the trial run, the sparring before the real fight. To face the Desolation, I will find a way to do what my ancestor the Sunmaker failed to do through conquest. I *will* unify Roshar."

Kalami gasped softly. No man had ever united the entire continent— not during the Shin invasions, not during the height of the Hierocracy, not during the Sunmaker's conquest. This was his task, he was increasingly certain. The enemy would unleash his worst terrors: the Unmade and the Voidbringers. That phantom champion in the dark armor.

Dalinar would resist them with a unified Roshar. Such a shame he hadn't found a way to somehow convince Sadeas to join in his cause.

Ah, Torol, he thought. *What we could have done together, if we hadn't been so divided. . . .*

"Father?" A soft voice drew his attention. Renarin, who stood beside Shallan and Adolin. "You didn't mention us. Me and Brightness Shallan. What is our task?"

"To practice," Dalinar said. "Other Radiants will be coming to us, and you two will need to lead them. The knights were once our greatest weapon against the Voidbringers. They will need to be so again."

"Father, I . . ." Renarin stumbled over the words. "It's just . . . Me? I can't. I don't know how to . . . let alone . . ."

"Son," Dalinar said, stepping over. He took Renarin by the shoulder. "I trust you. The Almighty and the spren have granted you powers to defend and protect this people. Use them. *Master* them, then report back to me what you can do. I think we're all curious to find out."

Renarin exhaled softly, then nodded.

3

MOMENTUM

THIRTY-FOUR YEARS AGO

Rockbuds crunched like skulls beneath Dalinar's boots as he charged across the burning field. His elites pounded after him, a handpicked force of soldiers both lighteyed and dark. They weren't an honor guard. Dalinar didn't need *guards*. These were simply the men he considered competent enough not to embarrass him.

Around him, rockbuds smoldered. Moss—dried from the summer heat and long days between storms this time of year—flared up in waves, setting the rockbud shells alight. Flamespren danced among them. And, like a spren himself, Dalinar charged through the smoke, trusting in his padded armor and thick boots to protect him.

The enemy—pressed on the north by his armies—had pulled back into this town just ahead. With some difficulty Dalinar had waited, so he could bring his elites in as a flanking force.

He hadn't expected the enemy to fire this plain, desperately burning their own crops to block the southern approach. Well, the fires could go to Damnation. Though some of his men were overwhelmed by the smoke or heat, most stayed with him. They'd crash into the enemy, pressing them back against the main army.

Hammer and anvil. His favorite kind of tactic: the type that didn't allow his enemies to get away from him.

As Dalinar burst from the smoky air, he found a few lines of spearmen hastily forming ranks on the southern edge of the town. Anticipationspren—like red streamers growing from the ground and whipping in the wind—clustered around them. The low town wall had been torn down in a contest a few years back, so the soldiers had only rubble as a fortification—though a large ridge to the east made a natural windbreak against the storms, which had allowed this place to sprawl almost like a real city.

Dalinar bellowed at the enemy soldiers, beating his sword—just an ordinary longsword—against his shield. He wore a sturdy breastplate, an open-fronted helm, and iron-reinforced boots. The spearmen ahead of him wavered as his elites roared from amid the smoke and flame, shouting a bloodthirsty cacophony.

A few of the spearmen dropped their weapons and ran. Dalinar grinned. He didn't need Shards to intimidate.

He hit the spearmen like a boulder rolling through a grove of saplings, his sword tossing blood into the air. A good fight was about *momentum*. Don't stop. Don't think. Drive forward and convince your enemies that they're as good as dead already. That way, they'll fight you less as you send them to their pyres.

The spearmen thrust their spears frantically—less to try to kill, more to try to push away this madman. Their ranks collapsed as too many of them turned their attention toward him.

Dalinar laughed, slamming aside a pair of spears with his shield, then disemboweling one man with a blade deep in the gut. The man dropped his spear in agony, and his neighbors backed away at the horrific sight. Dalinar came in with a roar, killing them with a sword that bore their friend's blood.

Dalinar's elites struck the now-broken line, and the real slaughter began. He pushed forward, keeping momentum, shearing through the ranks until he reached the back, then breathed deeply and wiped ashen sweat from his face. A young spearman wept on the ground nearby, screaming for his mother as he crawled across the stone, trailing blood. Fearspren mixed with orange, sinewy painspren all around. Dalinar shook his head and rammed his sword down into the boy's back as he passed.

Men often cried for their parents as they died. Didn't matter how old they were. He'd seen greybeards do it, same as kids like this one. *He's not much younger than me,* Dalinar thought. Maybe seventeen. But then, Dalinar had never felt young, regardless of his age.

His elites carved the enemy line in two. Dalinar danced, shaking off his bloodied blade, feeling alert, excited, but not yet *alive*. Where was it?

Come on. . . .

A larger group of enemy soldiers was jogging down the street toward him, led by several officers in white and red. From the way they suddenly pulled up, he guessed they were alarmed to find their spearmen falling so quickly.

Dalinar charged. His elites knew to watch, so he was rapidly joined by fifty men—the rest had to finish off the unfortunate spearmen. Fifty would do. The crowded confines of the town would mean Dalinar shouldn't need more.

He focused his attention on the one man riding a horse. The fellow wore plate armor obviously meant to resemble Shardplate, though it was only of common steel. It lacked the beauty, the power, of true Plate. He still looked like he was the most important person around. Hopefully that would mean he was the best.

The man's honor guard rushed to engage, and Dalinar felt something stir inside him. Like a thirst, a physical need.

Challenge. He needed a *challenge*!

He engaged the first member of the guard, attacking with a swift brutality. Fighting on a battlefield wasn't like dueling in an arena; Dalinar didn't dance around the fellow, testing his abilities. Out here, that sort of thing got you stabbed in the back by someone else. Instead, Dalinar slammed his sword down against the enemy, who raised his shield to block. Dalinar struck a series of quick, powerful blows, like a drummer pounding out a furious beat. *Bam, bam, bam, bam!*

The enemy soldier clutched his shield over his head, leaving Dalinar squarely in control. Dalinar raised his own shield before him and shoved it against the man, forcing him back until he stumbled, giving Dalinar an opening.

This man didn't get a chance to cry for his mother.

The body dropped before him. Dalinar let his elites handle the others; the way was open to the brightlord. Who was he? The highprince fought to the north. Was this some other important lighteyes? Or . . . didn't Dalinar remember hearing something about a son during Gavilar's endless planning meetings?

Well, this man certainly looked grand on that white mare, watching the battle from within his helm's visor, cape streaming around him. The foe raised his sword to his helm toward Dalinar in a sign of challenge accepted.

Idiot.

Dalinar raised his shield arm and pointed, counting on at least one of his strikers to have stayed with him. Indeed, Jenin stepped up, unhooked the shortbow from his back, and—as the brightlord shouted his surprise— shot the horse in the chest.

"Hate shooting horses," Jenin grumbled as the beast reared in pain. "Like throwing a thousand broams into the storming ocean, Brightlord."

"I'll buy you two when we finish this," Dalinar said as the brightlord tumbled off his horse. Dalinar dodged around flashing hooves and squeals of pain, seeking out the fallen man. He was pleased to find the enemy rising.

They engaged, sweeping at one another, frantic. Life was about *momentum*. Pick a direction and don't let anything—man or storm—turn you aside. Dalinar battered at the brightlord, driving him backward, furious and persistent.

He felt like he was winning the contest, controlling it, right up until he slammed his shield at the enemy and—in the moment of stress—felt something *snap*. One of the straps that held the shield to his arm had broken.

The enemy reacted immediately. He shoved the shield, twisting it around Dalinar's arm, snapping the other strap. The shield tumbled free.

Dalinar staggered, sweeping with his sword, trying to parry a blow that didn't come. The brightlord instead lunged in close and rammed Dalinar with his shield.

Dalinar ducked the blow that followed, but the backhand hit him solidly on the side of the head, sending him stumbling. His helm twisted, bent metal biting into his scalp, drawing blood. He saw double, his vision swimming.

He's coming in for the kill.

Dalinar roared, swinging his blade up in a lurching, wild parry that connected with the brightlord's weapon and swept it completely out of his hands.

The man instead punched Dalinar in the face with a gauntlet. His nose crunched.

Dalinar fell to his knees, sword slipping from his fingers. His foe was breathing deeply, cursing between breaths, winded by the short, frantic contest. He reached to his belt for a knife.

An emotion stirred inside Dalinar.

It was a fire that filled the pit within. It washed through him and awakened him, bringing clarity. The sounds of his elites fighting the brightlord's honor guard faded, metal on metal becoming clinks, grunts becoming merely a distant humming.

Dalinar smiled. Then the smile became a toothy grin. His vision returned as the brightlord—knife in hand—looked up and started, stumbling back. He seemed horrified.

Dalinar roared, spitting blood and throwing himself at the enemy. The swing that came at him seemed pitiful and Dalinar ducked it, ramming his shoulder against his foe's lower body. Something thrummed inside Dalinar, the pulse of the battle, the rhythm of killing and dying.

The Thrill.

He knocked his opponent off balance, then went searching for his sword. Dym, however, hollered Dalinar's name and tossed him a poleaxe, with a hook on one side and a broad, thin axe blade on the other. Dalinar seized it from the air and spun, hooking the brightlord around the ankle with the axehead, then yanked.

The brightlord fell in a clatter of steel. Before Dalinar could capitalize on this, two men of the honor guard managed to extricate themselves from Dalinar's men and come to the defense of their brightlord.

Dalinar swung and buried the axehead into one guard's side. He ripped it free and spun again—smashing the weapon down on the rising brightlord's helm and sending him to his knees—before coming back and barely catching the remaining guard's sword on the haft of the poleaxe.

Dalinar pushed upward, holding the poleaxe in two hands, sweeping the guard's blade into the air over his head. Dalinar stepped forward until he was face-to-face with the fellow. He could feel the man's breath.

He spat blood draining from his nose into the guard's eyes, then kicked him in the stomach. He turned toward the brightlord, who was trying to flee. Dalinar growled, full of the Thrill. He swung the poleaxe with one hand, hooking the spike into the brightlord's side, and yanked, dropping him yet again.

The brightlord rolled over. He was greeted by the sight of Dalinar slamming his poleaxe down with both hands, driving the spike right through the breastplate and into his chest. It made a satisfying crunch, and Dalinar pulled it out bloodied.

As if that blow had been a signal, the honor guard finally broke before his elites. Dalinar grinned as he watched them go, gloryspren popping up around him as glowing golden spheres. His men unhooked shortbows and shot a good dozen of the fleeing enemy in the back. Damnation, it felt good to best a force larger than your own.

Nearby, the fallen brightlord groaned softly. "Why . . ." the man said from within his helm. "Why us?"

"Don't know," Dalinar said, tossing the poleaxe back to Dym.

"You . . . you *don't know*?" the dying man said.

"My brother chooses," Dalinar said. "I just go where he points me." He gestured toward the dying man, and Dym rammed a sword into the armored man's armpit, finishing the job. The fellow had fought reasonably well; no need to extend his suffering.

Another soldier approached, handing Dalinar his sword. It had a chip the size of a thumb right in the blade. Looked like it had bent as well. "You're supposed to stick it into the squishy parts, Brightlord," Dym said, "not pound it against the hard parts."

"I'll keep that in mind," Dalinar said, tossing the sword aside as one of his men selected a replacement from among the fallen.

"You . . . all right, Brightlord?" Dym asked.

"Never been better," Dalinar said, voice faintly distorted by the clogged nose. Hurt like Damnation itself, and he drew a small flock of painspren—like little sinewy hands—up from the ground.

His men formed up around him, and Dalinar led the way farther down the street. Before too long, he could make out the bulk of the enemy still fighting ahead, harried by his army. He halted his men, considering his options.

Thakka, captain of the elites, turned to him. "Orders, sir?"

"Raid those buildings," Dalinar said, pointing at a line of homes. "Let's see how well they fight while they watch us rounding up their families."

"The men will want to loot," Thakka said.

"What is there to loot in hovels like these? Soggy hogshide and old rockbud bowls?" He pulled off his helm to wipe the blood from his face. "They can loot afterward. Right now I need hostages. There are civilians somewhere in this storming town. Find them."

Thakka nodded, shouting the orders. Dalinar reached for some water. He'd need to meet up with Sadeas, and—

Something slammed into Dalinar's shoulder. He caught only a brief sight of it, a black blur that hit with the force of a roundhouse kick. It threw him down, and pain flared up from his side.

He blinked as he found himself lying on the ground. A storming *arrow* sprouted from his right shoulder, with a long, thick shaft. It had gone straight through the chain mail, just to the side of where his cuirass met his arm.

"Brightlord!" Thakka said, kneeling, shielding Dalinar with his body. "Kelek! Brightlord, are you—"

"Who in Damnation shot that?" Dalinar demanded.

"Up there," one of his men said, pointing at the ridge above the town.

"That's got to be over *three hundred yards*," Dalinar said, shoving Thakka aside and standing. "That can't—"

He was watching, so he was able to jump out of the way of the next arrow, which dropped a mere foot from him, cracking against the stone ground. Dalinar stared at it, then started shouting. "Horses! Where are the storming horses!"

A small group of soldiers came trotting forward, bringing all eleven horses, which they'd guided carefully across the field. Dalinar had to dodge *another* arrow as he seized the reins of Fullnight, his black gelding, and heaved himself into the saddle. The arrow in his arm was a cutting pain, but he felt something more pressing drawing him forward. Helping him focus.

He galloped back the way they'd come in, getting out of the archer's sight, trailed by ten of his best men. There had to be a way up that slope. . . . There! A rocky set of switchbacks, shallow enough that he didn't mind running Fullnight up them.

Dalinar worried that by the time he reached the top, his quarry would have escaped. However, when he eventually burst onto the top of the ridge, an arrow slammed into his *left* breast, going straight through the breastplate near the shoulder, nearly throwing him from the saddle.

Damnation! Dalinar hung on somehow, clenching the reins in one hand, and leaned low, peering ahead as the archer—still a distant figure—stood upon a rocky knob and launched another arrow. And another. Storms, the fellow was quick!

He jerked Fullnight to one side, then the other, feeling the thrumming sense of the Thrill surge within him. It drove away the pain, let him focus.

Ahead, the archer finally seemed to grow alarmed, and leaped from his perch to flee.

Dalinar charged Fullnight over that knob a moment later. The archer turned out to be a man in his twenties wearing rugged clothing, with arms and shoulders that looked like they could have lifted a chull. Dalinar had the option of running him down, but instead galloped Fullnight past and kicked the man in the back, sending him sprawling.

As Dalinar pulled up his horse, the motion sent a spike of pain through his arm. He forced it down, eyes watering, and turned toward the archer, who lay in a heap amid spilled black arrows.

Dalinar lurched from the saddle, an arrow sprouting from each shoulder, as his men caught up. He seized the archer and hauled the fellow to his feet, noting the blue tattoo on his cheek. The archer gasped and stared at Dalinar. He expected he was quite a sight, covered in soot from the fires, his face a mask of blood from the nose and the cut scalp, stuck with not one but *two* arrows.

"You waited until my helm was off," Dalinar demanded. "You are an assassin. You were set here *specifically* to kill me."

The man winced, then nodded.

"Amazing!" Dalinar said, letting go of the fellow. "Show me that shot again. How far *is* that, Thakka? I'm right, aren't I? Over three hundred yards?"

"Almost four," Thakka said, pulling over his horse. "But with a height advantage."

"Still," Dalinar said, stepping up to the lip of the ridge. He looked back at the befuddled archer. "Well? Grab your bow!"

"My . . . bow?" the archer said.

"Are you deaf, man?" Dalinar snapped. "Go get it!"

The archer regarded the ten elites on horseback, grim-faced and danger-ous, before wisely deciding to obey. He picked up an arrow, then his bow—which was made of a sleek black wood Dalinar didn't recognize.

"Went right through my storming armor," Dalinar muttered, feeling at the arrow that had hit him on the left. That one didn't seem too bad—it had punctured the steel, but had lost most of its momentum in doing so. The one on his right, though, had cut through the chain and was sending blood down his arm.

He shook his head, shading his eyes with his left hand, inspecting the battlefield. To his right, the armies clashed, and his main body of elites had come up to press at the flank. The rearguard had found some civilians and was shoving them into the street.

"Pick a corpse," Dalinar said, pointing toward an empty square where a skirmish had happened. "Stick an arrow in one down there, if you can."

The archer licked his lips, still seeming confused. Finally, he took a spyglass off his belt and studied the area. "The one in blue, near the over-turned cart."

Dalinar squinted, then nodded. Nearby, Thakka had climbed off his horse and had slid out his sword, resting it on his shoulder. A not-so-subtle warning. The archer drew his bow and launched a single black-fletched arrow. It flew true, sticking into the chosen corpse.

A single awespren burst around Dalinar, like a ring of blue smoke. "Stormfather! Thakka, before today, I'd have bet you half the princedom that such a shot wasn't possible." He turned to the archer. "What's your name, assassin?"

The man raised his chin, but didn't reply.

"Well, in any case, welcome to my elites," Dalinar said. "Someone get the fellow a horse."

"What?" the archer said. "I tried to *kill* you!"

"Yes, from a distance. Which shows remarkably good judgment. I can make use of someone with your skills."

"We're enemies!"

Dalinar nodded toward the town below, where the beleaguered enemy army was—at long last—surrendering. "Not anymore. Looks like we're all allies now!"

The archer spat to the side. "Slaves beneath your brother, the tyrant."

Dalinar let one of his men help him onto his horse. "If you'd rather be killed, I can respect that. Alternatively, you can join me and name your price."

"The life of my brightlord Yezriar," the archer said. "The heir."

"Is that the fellow . . . ?" Dalinar said, looking to Thakka.

". . . That you killed down below? Yes, sir."

"He's got a hole in his chest," Dalinar said, looking back to the assassin. "Tough break."

"You . . . you monster! Couldn't you have captured him?"

"Nah. The other princedoms are digging in their heels. Refuse to recognize my brother's crown. Games of catch-me with the high lighteyes just encourage people to fight back. If they know we're out for blood, they'll think twice." Dalinar shrugged. "How about this? Join with me, and we won't pillage the town. What's left of it, anyway."

The man looked down at the surrendering army.

"You in or not?" Dalinar said. "I promise not to make you shoot anyone you like."

"I . . ."

"Great!" Dalinar said, turning his horse and trotting off.

A short time later, when Dalinar's elites rode up to him, the sullen archer was on a horse with one of the other men. The pain surged in Dalinar's right arm as the Thrill faded, but it was manageable. He'd need surgeons to look at the arrow wound.

Once they reached the town again, he sent orders to stop the looting. His men would hate that, but this town wasn't worth much anyway. The riches would come once they started into the centers of the princedoms.

He let his horse carry him in a leisurely gait through the town, passing soldiers who had settled down to water themselves and rest from the protracted engagement. His nose still smarted, and he had to forcibly prevent himself from snorting up blood. If it was well and truly broken, that wouldn't turn out well for him.

Dalinar kept moving, fighting off the dull sense of . . . nothingness that often followed a battle. This was the worst time. He could still remember being alive, but now had to face a return to mundanity.

He'd missed the executions. Sadeas already had the local highprince's head—and those of his officers—up on spears. Such a showman, Sadeas was. Dalinar passed the grim line, shaking his head, and heard a muttered curse from his new archer. He'd have to talk to the man, reinforce that in striking at Dalinar earlier, he'd shot an arrow at an enemy. That was to be respected. If he tried something against Dalinar or Sadeas now, it would be different. Thakka would already be searching out the fellow's family.

"Dalinar?" a voice called.

He stilled his horse, turning toward the sound. Torol Sadeas—resplendent in golden yellow Shardplate that had already been washed clean—pushed through a cluster of officers. The red-faced young man looked far older than he had a year ago. When they'd started all this, he'd still been a gangly youth. No longer.

"Dalinar, are those *arrows*? Stormfather, man, you look like a thornbush! What happened to your face?"

"A fist," Dalinar said, then nodded toward the heads on spears. "Nice work."

"We lost the crown prince," Sadeas said. "He'll mount a resistance."

"That would be impressive," Dalinar said, "considering what I did to him."

Sadeas relaxed visibly. "Oh, Dalinar. What would we do without you?"

"Lose. Someone get me something to drink and a pair of surgeons. In that order. Also, Sadeas, I promised we wouldn't pillage the city. No looting, no slaves taken."

"You *what*?" Sadeas demanded. "Who did you promise?"

Dalinar thumbed over his shoulder at the archer.

"Another one?" Sadeas said with a groan.

"He's got amazing aim," Dalinar said. "Loyal, too." He glanced to the side, where Sadeas's soldiers had rounded up some weeping women for Sadeas to pick from.

"I was looking forward to tonight," Sadeas noted.

"And I was looking forward to breathing through my nose. We'll live. More than can be said for the kids we fought today."

"Fine, fine," Sadeas said, sighing. "I suppose we could spare one town. A symbol that we are not without mercy." He looked over Dalinar again. "We need to get you some Shards, my friend."

"To protect me?"

"Protect you? Storms, Dalinar, at this point I'm not certain a *rockslide* could kill you. No, it just makes the rest of us look bad when you accomplish what you do while practically unarmed!"

Dalinar shrugged. He didn't wait for the wine or the surgeons, but instead led his horse back to gather his elites and reinforce the orders to guard the city from looting. Once finished, he walked his horse across smoldering ground to his camp.

He was done living for the day. It would be weeks, maybe months, before he got another opportunity.

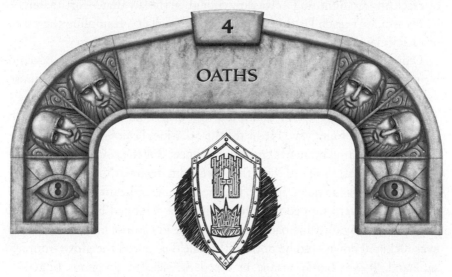

4

OATHS

I know that many women who read this will see it only as further proof that I am the godless heretic everyone claims.

—From *Oathbringer*, preface

Two days after Sadeas was found dead, the Everstorm came again. Dalinar walked through his chambers in Urithiru, pulled by the unnatural storm. Bare feet on cold rock. He passed Navani— who sat at the writing desk working on her memoirs again—and stepped onto his balcony, which hung straight out over the cliffs beneath Urithiru.

He could feel something, his ears popping, cold—even more cold than usual—blowing in from the west. And something else. An inner chill.

"Is that you, Stormfather?" Dalinar whispered. "This feeling of dread?"

This thing is not natural, the Stormfather said. *It is unknown.*

"It didn't come before, during the earlier Desolations?"

No. It is new.

As always, the Stormfather's voice was far off, like very distant thunder. The Stormfather didn't always reply to Dalinar, and didn't remain near him. That was to be expected; he was the soul of the storm. He could not—should not—be contained.

And yet, there was an almost childish petulance to the way he sometimes ignored Dalinar's questions. It seemed that sometimes he did so merely because he didn't want Dalinar to think that he would come whenever called.

The Everstorm appeared in the distance, its black clouds lit from within by crackling red lightning. It was low enough in the sky that—fortunately—its top wouldn't reach Urithiru. It surged like a cavalry, trampling the calm, ordinary clouds below.

Dalinar forced himself to watch that wave of darkness flow around Urithiru's plateau. Soon it seemed as if their lonely tower were a lighthouse looking over a dark, deadly sea.

It was hauntingly silent. Those red lightning bolts didn't rumble with thunder in the proper way. He heard the occasional *crack*, stark and shocking, like a hundred branches snapping at once. But the sounds didn't seem to match the flashes of red light that rose from deep within.

The storm was so quiet, in fact, that he was able to hear the telltale rustle of cloth as Navani slipped up behind him. She wrapped her arms around him, pressing against his back, resting her head against his shoulder. His eyes flickered down, and he noticed that she'd removed the glove from her safehand. It was barely visible in the dark: slender, gorgeous fingers—delicate, with the nails painted a blushing red. He saw it by the light of the first moon above, and by the intermittent flashes of the storm beneath.

"Any further word from the west?" Dalinar whispered. The Everstorm was slower than a highstorm, and had hit Shinovar many hours before. It did not recharge spheres, even if you left them out during the entire Everstorm.

"The spanreeds are abuzz. The monarchs are delaying a response, but I suspect that soon they'll realize they *have* to listen to us."

"I think you underestimate the stubbornness a crown can press into a man or woman's mind, Navani."

Dalinar had been out during his share of highstorms, particularly in his youth. He'd watched the chaos of the stormwall pushing rocks and refuse before it, the sky-splitting lightning, the claps of thunder. Highstorms were the ultimate expression of nature's power: wild, untamed, sent to remind man of his insignificance.

However, highstorms never seemed hateful. This storm was different. It felt *vengeful*.

Staring into that blackness below, Dalinar thought he could see what it had done. A series of impressions, thrown at him in anger. The storm's experiences as it had slowly crossed Roshar.

Houses ripped apart, screams of the occupants lost to the tempest.

People caught in their fields, running in a panic before the unpredicted storm.

Cities blasted with lightning. Towns cast into shadow. Fields swept barren.

And vast seas of glowing red eyes, coming awake like spheres suddenly renewed with Stormlight.

Dalinar hissed out a long, slow breath, the impressions fading. "Was that real?" he whispered.

Yes, the Stormfather said. *The enemy rides this storm. He's aware of you, Dalinar.*

Not a vision of the past. Not some possibility of the future. His kingdom, his people, his entire *world* was being attacked. He drew a deep breath. At the very least, this wasn't the singular tempest that they'd experienced when the Everstorm had clashed with the highstorm for the first time. This seemed less powerful. It wouldn't tear down cities, but it did rain destruction upon them—and the winds would attack in bursts, hostile, even *deliberate.*

The enemy seemed more interested in preying upon the small towns. The fields. The people caught unaware.

Though it was not as destructive as he'd feared, it would still leave thousands dead. It would leave cities broken, particularly those without shelter to the west. More importantly, it would steal the parshmen laborers and turn them into Voidbringers, loosed on the public.

All in all, this storm would exact a price in blood from Roshar that hadn't been seen since . . . well, since the Desolations.

He lifted his hand to grasp Navani's, as she in turn held to him. "You did what you could, Dalinar," she whispered after a time watching. "Don't insist on carrying this failure as a burden."

"I won't."

She released him and turned him around, away from the sight of the storm. She wore a dressing gown, not fit to go about in public, but also not precisely immodest.

Save for that hand, with which she caressed his chin. "I," she whispered, "don't believe you, Dalinar Kholin. I can read the truth in the tightness of your muscles, the set of your jaw. I know that you, while being crushed beneath a boulder, would insist that you've got it under control and ask to see field reports from your men."

The scent of her was intoxicating. And those entrancing, brilliant violet eyes.

"You need to relax, Dalinar," she said.

"Navani . . ." he said.

She looked at him, questioning, so beautiful. Far more gorgeous than when they'd been young. He'd swear it. For how could anyone be as beautiful as she was now?

He seized her by the back of the head and pulled her mouth to his own. Passion woke within him. She pressed her body to his, breasts pushing against him through the thin gown. He drank of her lips, her mouth, her scent. Passionspren fluttered around them like crystal flakes of snow.

Dalinar stopped himself and stepped back.

"Dalinar," she said as he pulled away. "Your stubborn refusal to get seduced is making me question my feminine wiles."

"Control is important to me, Navani," he said, his voice hoarse. He gripped the stone balcony wall, white knuckled. "You know how I was, what I became, when I was a man with no control. I will not surrender now."

She sighed and sidled up to him, pulling his arm free of the stone, then slipping under it. "I won't push you, but I need to know. Is this how it's going to continue? Teasing, dancing on the edge?"

"No," he said, staring out over the darkness of the storm. "That would be an exercise in futility. A general knows not to set himself up for battles he cannot win."

"Then what?"

"I'll find a way to do it right. With oaths."

The oaths were vital. The promise, the act of being bound together.

"How?" she said, then poked him in the chest. "I'm as religious as the next woman—more than most, actually. But Kadash turned us down, as did Ladent, even Rushu. She squeaked when I mentioned it and *literally* ran away."

"Chanada," Dalinar said, speaking of the senior ardent of the warcamps. "She spoke to Kadash, and had him go to each of the ardents. She probably did it the moment she heard we were courting."

"So no ardent will marry us," Navani said. "They consider us siblings. You're stretching to find an impossible accommodation; continue with this, and it's going to leave a lady wondering if you actually care."

"Have you ever thought that?" Dalinar said. "Sincerely."

"Well . . . no."

"You are the woman I love," Dalinar said, pulling her tight. "A woman I have always loved."

"Then who cares?" she said. "Let the ardents hie to Damnation, with ribbons around their ankles."

"Blasphemous."

"I'm not the one telling everyone that God is dead."

"Not *everyone*," Dalinar said. He sighed, letting go of her—with reluctance—and walked back into his rooms, where a brazier of coal radiated welcome warmth, as well as the room's only light. They had recovered his fabrial heating device from the warcamps, but didn't yet have the Stormlight to run it. The scholars had discovered long chains and cages, apparently used for lowering spheres down into the storms, so they'd be able to renew their spheres—if the highstorms ever returned. In other parts of the world, the Weeping had restarted, then fitfully stopped. It might start again. Or the proper storms might start up. Nobody knew, and the Stormfather refused to enlighten him.

Navani entered and pulled the thick drapings closed over the doorway, tying them tightly in place. This room was heaped with furniture, chairs lining the walls, rolled rugs stacked atop them. There was even a standing mirror. The images of twisting windspren along its sides bore the distinctly rounded look of something that had been carved first from weevilwax, then Soulcast into hardwood.

They had deposited all this here for him, as if worried about their highprince living in simple stone quarters. "Let's have someone clear this out for me tomorrow," Dalinar said. "There's room enough for it in the chamber next door, which we can turn into a sitting room or a common room."

Navani nodded as she settled onto one of the sofas—he saw her reflected in the mirror—her hand still casually uncovered, gown dropping to the side, exposing neck, collarbone, and some of what was beneath. She wasn't trying to be seductive right now; she was merely comfortable around him. Intimately familiar, past the point where she felt embarrassed for him to see her uncovered.

It was good that one of them was willing to take the initiative in the relationship. For all his impatience to advance on the battlefield, this was one area in which he'd always needed encouragement. Same as it had been all those years ago . . .

"When I married last," Dalinar said softly, "I did many things wrong. I *started* wrong."

"I wouldn't say that. You married *Shshshsh* for her Shardplate, but many marriages are for political reasons. That doesn't mean you were wrong. If you'll recall, we all encouraged you to do it."

As always, when he heard his dead wife's name, the word was replaced to his hearing with a breezy sound of rushing air—the name couldn't gain purchase in his mind, any more than a man could hold to a gust of wind.

"I'm not trying to replace her, Dalinar," Navani said, suddenly sounding concerned. "I know you still have affection for *Shshshsh*. It's all right. I can share you with her memory."

Oh, how little they all understood. He turned toward Navani, set his jaw against the pain, and said it.

"I don't remember her, Navani."

She looked to him with a frown, as if she thought she hadn't heard him correctly.

"I can't remember my wife at all," he said. "I don't know her face. Portraits of her are a fuzzy smudge to my eyes. Her name is taken from me whenever spoken, like someone has plucked it away. I don't remember what she and I said when we first met; I can't even remember seeing her at the feast that night when she first arrived. It's all a blur. I can remember some events surrounding my wife, but nothing of the actual details. It's all just . . . gone."

Navani raised her safehand fingers to her mouth, and from the way her brow knit with concern, he figured he must look like he was in agony.

He slumped down in a chair across from her.

"The alcohol?" she asked softly.

"Something more."

She breathed out. "The Old Magic. You said you knew both your boon and your curse."

He nodded.

"Oh, Dalinar."

"People glance at me when her name comes up," Dalinar continued, "and they give me these looks of pity. They see me keeping a stiff expression, and they assume I'm being stoic. They infer hidden pain, when really I'm just trying to keep up. It's hard to follow a conversation where half of it keeps slipping away from your brain.

"Navani, maybe I did grow to love her. I can't remember. Not one moment of intimacy, not one fight, not a *single word* she ever said to me. She's gone, leaving debris that mars my memory. I can't remember how she died. That one gets to me, because there are parts of that day I *know* I should remember. Something about a city in rebellion against my brother, and my wife being taken hostage?"

That . . . and a long march alone, accompanied only by hatred and the Thrill. He remembered those emotions vividly. He'd brought vengeance to those who had taken his wife from him.

Navani settled down on the seat beside Dalinar, resting her head on his shoulder. "Would that I could create a fabrial," she whispered, "to take away this kind of pain."

"I think . . . I think losing her must have hurt me terribly," Dalinar whispered, "because of what it drove me to do. I am left with only the scars. Regardless, Navani, I want it to be *right* with us. No mistakes. Done properly, with oaths, spoken to you before someone."

"Mere words."

"Words are the most important things in my life right now."

She parted her lips, thoughtful. "Elhokar?"

"I wouldn't want to put him in that position."

"A foreign priest? From the Azish, maybe? They're *almost* Vorin."

"That would be tantamount to declaring myself a heretic. It goes too far. I will not defy the Vorin church." He paused. "I might be willing to side-step it though. . . ."

"What?" she asked.

He looked upward, toward the ceiling. "Maybe we go to someone with authority greater than theirs."

"You want a *spren* to marry us?" she said, sounding amused. "Using a foreign priest would be heretical, but not a spren?"

"The Stormfather is the largest remnant of Honor," Dalinar said. "He's a sliver of the Almighty himself—and is the closest thing to a god we have left."

"Oh, I'm not objecting," Navani said. "I'd let a confused dishwasher marry us. I just think it's a little unusual."

"It's the best we're going to get, assuming he is willing." He looked to Navani, then raised his eyebrows and shrugged.

"Is that a proposal?"

". . . Yes?"

"Dalinar Kholin," she said. "Surely you can do better."

He rested his hand on the back of her head, touching her black hair, which she had left loose. "Better than you, Navani? No, I don't think that I could. I don't think that any man has ever had a chance better than this."

She smiled, and her only reply was a kiss.

◆◆

Dalinar was surprisingly nervous as, several hours later, he rode one of Urithiru's strange fabrial lifts toward the roof of the tower. The lift resembled a balcony, one of many that lined a vast open shaft in the middle of Urithiru—a columnar space as wide as a ballroom, which stretched up from the first floor to the last one.

The tiers of the city, despite looking circular from the front, were actually more half-circles, with the flat sides facing east. The edges of the lower levels melded into the mountains to either side, but the very center was open to the east. The rooms up against that flat side had windows there, providing a view toward the Origin.

And here, in this central shaft, those windows made up one wall. A pure, single unbroken pane of glass hundreds of feet tall. In the day, that lit the shaft with brilliant sunlight. Now, it was dark with the gloom of night.

The balcony crawled steadily along a vertical trench in the wall; Adolin and Renarin rode with him, along with a few guards and Shallan Davar. Navani was already up above. The group stood on the other side of the balcony, giving him space to think. And to be nervous.

Why should he be nervous? He could hardly keep his hands from shaking. Storms. You'd think he was some silk-covered virgin, not a general well into his middle years.

He felt a rumbling deep within him. The Stormfather was being responsive at the moment, for which he was grateful.

"I'm surprised," Dalinar whispered to the spren, "you agreed to this so willingly. Grateful, but still surprised."

I respect all oaths, the Stormfather responded.

"What about foolish oaths? Made in haste, or in ignorance?"

There are no foolish oaths. All are the mark of men and true spren over beasts and subspren. The mark of intelligence, free will, and choice.

Dalinar chewed on that, and found he was not surprised by the extreme opinion. Spren *should* be extreme; they were forces of nature. But was this how Honor himself, the Almighty, had thought?

The balcony ground its inexorable way toward the top of the tower. Only a handful of the dozens of lifts worked; back when Urithiru flourished, they all would have been going at once. They passed level after level of unexplored space, which bothered Dalinar. Making this his fortress was like camping in an unknown land.

The lift finally reached the top floor, and his guards scrambled to open the gates. Those were from Bridge Thirteen these days—he'd assigned Bridge Four to other responsibilities, considering them too important for simple guard duty, now that they were close to becoming Radiants.

Increasingly anxious, Dalinar led the way past several pillars designed with representations of the orders of Radiants. A set of steps took him up through a trapdoor onto the very roof of the tower.

Although each tier was smaller than the one below it, this roof was still over a hundred yards wide. It was cold up here, but someone had set up braziers for warmth and torches for light. The night was strikingly clear, and high above, starspren swirled and made distant patterns.

Dalinar wasn't sure what to make of the fact that no one—not even his sons—had questioned him when he'd announced his intent to marry in the middle of the night, on the roof of the tower. He searched out Navani, and was shocked to see that she'd found a traditional bridal crown. The intricate headdress of jade and turquoise complemented her wedding gown. Red for luck, it was embroidered with gold and shaped in a much looser style than the havah, with wide sleeves and a graceful drape.

Should Dalinar have found something more traditional to wear himself? He suddenly felt like a dusty, empty frame hung beside the gorgeous painting that was Navani in her wedding regalia.

Elhokar stiffly stood at her side wearing a formal golden coat and loose takama underskirt. He was paler than normal, following the failed assassination attempt during the Weeping, where he'd nearly bled to death. He'd been resting a great deal lately.

Though they'd decided to forgo the extravagance of a traditional Alethi wedding, they had invited some others. Brightlord Aladar and his daughter, Sebarial and his mistress. Kalami and Teshav to act as witnesses. He felt relieved to see them there—he'd feared Navani would be unable to find women willing to notarize the wedding.

A smattering of Dalinar's officers and scribes filled out the small procession. At the very back of the crowd gathered between the braziers, he spotted a surprising face. Kadash, the ardent, had come as requested. His scarred, bearded face didn't look pleased, but he *had* come. A good sign. Perhaps with everything else happening in the world, a highprince marrying his widowed sister-in-law wouldn't cause too much of a stir.

Dalinar stepped up to Navani and took her hands, one shrouded in a sleeve, the other warm to his touch. "You look amazing," he said. "How did you find that?"

"A lady must be prepared."

Dalinar looked to Elhokar, who bowed his head to Dalinar. *This will further muddy the relationship between us,* Dalinar thought, reading the same sentiment on his nephew's features.

Gavilar would not appreciate how his son had been handled. Despite his best intentions, Dalinar had trodden down the boy and seized power. Elhokar's time recuperating had worsened the situation, as Dalinar had grown accustomed to making decisions on his own.

However, Dalinar would be lying to himself if he said that was where it had begun. His actions had been done for the good of Alethkar, for the good of Roshar itself, but that didn't deny the fact that—step by step— he'd usurped the throne, despite claiming all along he had no intention of doing so.

Dalinar let go of Navani with one hand and rested it on his nephew's shoulder. "I'm sorry, son," he said.

"You always are, Uncle," Elhokar said. "It doesn't stop you, but I don't suppose that it should. Your life is defined by deciding what you want, then seizing it. The rest of us could learn from that, if only we could figure out how to keep up."

Dalinar winced. "I have things to discuss with you. Plans that you might appreciate. But for tonight, I simply ask your blessing, if you can find it to give."

"This will make my mother happy," Elhokar said. "So, fine." Elhokar kissed his mother on the forehead, then left them, striding across the rooftop. At first Dalinar worried the king would stalk down below, but he stopped beside one of the more distant braziers, warming his hands.

"Well," Navani said. "The only one missing is your spren, Dalinar. If he's going to—"

A strong breeze struck the top of the tower, carrying with it the scent of recent rainfall, of wet stone and broken branches. Navani gasped, pulling against Dalinar.

A presence emerged in the sky. The Stormfather encompassed everything, a face that stretched to both horizons, regarding the men imperiously. The air became strangely still, and everything but the tower's top seemed to fade. It was as if they had slipped into a place outside of time itself.

Lighteyes and guards alike murmured or cried out. Even Dalinar, who had been expecting this, found himself taking a step backward—and he had to fight the urge to cringe down before the spren.

OATHS, the Stormfather rumbled, ARE THE SOUL OF RIGHTEOUSNESS. IF YOU ARE TO SURVIVE THE COMING TEMPEST, OATHS MUST GUIDE YOU.

"I am comfortable with oaths, Stormfather," Dalinar called up to him. "As you know."

YES. THE FIRST IN MILLENNIA TO BIND ME. Somehow, Dalinar felt the spren's attention shifting to Navani. AND YOU. DO OATHS HOLD MEANING TO YOU?

"The right oaths," Navani said.

AND YOUR OATH TO THIS MAN?

"I swear it to him, and to you, and any who care to listen. Dalinar Kholin is mine, and I am his."

YOU HAVE BROKEN OATHS BEFORE.

"All people have," Navani said, unbowed. "We're frail and foolish. This one I will not break. I vow it."

The Stormfather seemed content with this, though it was far from a traditional Alethi wedding oath. BONDSMITH? he asked.

"I swear it likewise," Dalinar said, holding to her. "Navani Kholin is mine, and I am hers. I love her."

SO BE IT.

Dalinar had anticipated thunder, lightning, some kind of celestial trump of victory. Instead, the timelessness ended. The breeze passed. The Stormfather vanished. All through the gathered guests, smoky blue awespren rings burst out above heads. But not Navani's. Instead she was ringed by gloryspren, the golden lights rotating above her head. Nearby, Sebarial rubbed his temple—as if trying to understand what he'd seen. Dalinar's new guards sagged, looking suddenly exhausted.

Adolin, being Adolin, let out a whoop. He ran over, trailing joyspren in the shape of blue leaves that hurried to keep up with him. He gave Dalinar—then Navani—enormous hugs. Renarin followed, more reserved but—judging from the wide grin on his face—equally pleased.

The next part became a blur, shaking hands, speaking words of thanks.

Insisting that no gifts were needed, as they'd skipped that part of the traditional ceremony. It seemed that the Stormfather's pronouncement had been dramatic enough that everyone accepted it. Even Elhokar, despite his earlier pique, gave his mother a hug and Dalinar a clasp on the shoulder before going below.

That left only Kadash. The ardent waited to the end. He stood with hands clasped before him as the rooftop emptied.

To Dalinar, Kadash had always looked wrong in those robes. Though he wore the traditional squared beard, it was not an ardent that Dalinar saw. It was a soldier, with a lean build, dangerous posture, and keen light violet eyes. He had a twisting old scar running up to and around the top of his shaved head. Kadash's life might now be one of peace and service, but his youth had been spent at war.

Dalinar whispered a few words of promise to Navani, and she left him to go to the level below, where she'd ordered food and wine to be set up. Dalinar stepped over to Kadash, confident. The pleasure of having finally done what he'd postponed for so long surged through him. He was *married* to Navani. This was a joy that he'd assumed lost to him since his youth, an outcome he hadn't even allowed himself to *dream* would be his.

He would not apologize for it, or for her.

"Brightlord," Kadash said quietly.

"Formality, old friend?"

"I wish I could only be here as an old friend," Kadash said softly. "I have to report this, Dalinar. The ardentia will not be pleased."

"Surely they cannot deny my marriage if the Stormfather himself blessed the union."

"A spren? You expect us to accept the authority of a *spren*?"

"A remnant of the Almighty."

"Dalinar, that's *blasphemy*," Kadash said, voice pained.

"Kadash. You know I'm no heretic. You've fought by my side."

"That's supposed to reassure me? Memories of what we did together, Dalinar? I appreciate the man you have become; you should avoid reminding me of the man you once were."

Dalinar paused, and a memory swirled up from the depths inside him— one he hadn't thought of in years. One that surprised him. Where had it come from?

He remembered Kadash, bloodied, kneeling on the ground having retched until his stomach was empty. A hardened soldier who had encountered something so vile that even he was shaken.

He'd left to become an ardent the next day.

"The Rift," Dalinar whispered. "Rathalas."

"Dark times need not be dredged up," Kadash said. "This isn't about . . . that day, Dalinar. It's about today, and what you've been spreading among the scribes. Talk of these things you've seen in visions."

"Holy messages," Dalinar said, feeling cold. "Sent by the Almighty."

"Holy messages claiming the Almighty is *dead*?" Kadash said. "Arriving on the eve of the return of the Voidbringers? Dalinar, can't you see how this looks? I'm your ardent, technically your *slave*. And yes, perhaps still your friend. I've tried to explain to the councils in Kharbranth and Jah Keved that you mean well. I tell the ardents of the Holy Enclave that you're looking back toward when the Knights Radiant were pure, rather than their eventual corruption. I tell them that you have no control over these visions.

"But Dalinar, that was before you started teaching that the Almighty was dead. They're angry enough over that, and now you've gone and defied convention, spitting in the eyes of the ardents! I personally don't think it matters if you marry Navani. That prohibition is outdated to be sure. But what you've done tonight . . ."

Dalinar reached to place a hand on Kadash's shoulder, but the man pulled away.

"Old friend," Dalinar said softly, "Honor might be dead, but I have felt . . . something else. Something beyond. A warmth and a light. It is not that God has died, it is that the Almighty was *never* God. He did his best to guide us, but he was an impostor. Or perhaps only an agent. A being not unlike a spren—he had the power of a god, but not the pedigree."

Kadash looked at him, eyes widening. "Please, Dalinar. Don't ever repeat what you just said. I think I can explain away what happened tonight. Maybe. But you don't seem to realize you're aboard a ship barely afloat in a storm, while you insist on doing a jig on the prow!"

"I will not hold back truth if I find it, Kadash," Dalinar said. "You just saw that I am *literally* bound to a spren of oaths. I don't dare lie."

"I don't think you would lie, Dalinar," Kadash said. "But I do think you can make mistakes. Do not forget that I was there. You are *not* infallible."

There? Dalinar thought as Kadash backed up, bowed, then turned and left. *What does he remember that I cannot?*

Dalinar watched him go. Finally, he shook his head, and went to join the midnight feast, intent on being done with it as soon as was seemly. He needed time with Navani.

His wife.

Map of Alethkar, oriented to the greatest diametrical length from the Sea North to the Sea South

Annotated for your convenience.

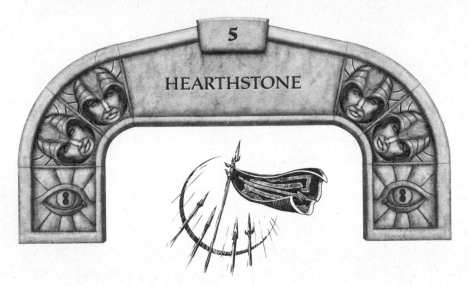

5

HEARTHSTONE

I can point to the moment when I decided for certain this record had to be written. I hung between realms, seeing into Shadesmar— the realm of the spren—and beyond.

—From *Oathbringer*, preface

Kaladin trudged through a field of quiet rockbuds, fully aware that he was too late to prevent a disaster. His failure pressed down on him with an almost physical sensation, like the weight of a bridge he was forced to carry all on his own.

After so long in the eastern part of the stormlands, he had nearly forgotten the sights of a fertile landscape. Rockbuds here grew almost as big as barrels, with vines as thick as his wrist spilling out and lapping water from the pools on the stone. Fields of vibrant green grass pulled back into burrows before him, easily three feet tall when standing at height. The field was dappled with glowing lifespren, like motes of green dust.

The grass back near the Shattered Plains had barely reached as high as his ankle, and had mostly grown in yellowish patches on the leeward side of hills. He was surprised to find that he distrusted this taller, fuller grass. An ambusher could hide in that, by crouching down and waiting for the grass to rise back up. How had Kaladin never noticed? He'd run through fields like this playing catch-me with his brother, trying to see who was quick enough to grab handfuls of grass before it hid.

Kaladin felt drained. Used up. Four days ago, he'd traveled by Oathgate to the Shattered Plains, then flown to the northwest at speed. Filled to bursting with Stormlight—and carrying a wealth more in gemstones—he'd been determined to reach his home, Hearthstone, before the Everstorm returned.

After just half a day, he'd run out of Stormlight somewhere in Aladar's princedom. He'd been walking ever since. Perhaps he could have flown all the way to Hearthstone if he'd been more practiced with his powers. As it was, he'd traveled over a thousand miles in half a day, but this last bit—ninety or so miles—had taken an excruciating *three days*.

He hadn't beaten the Everstorm. It had arrived earlier in the day, around noon.

Kaladin noticed a bit of debris peeking out of the grass, and he trudged toward it. The foliage obligingly pulled back before him, revealing a broken wooden churn, the kind used for turning sow's milk into butter. Kaladin crouched and rested fingers on the splintered wood, then glanced toward another chunk of wood peeking out over the tops of the grass.

Syl zipped down as a ribbon of light, passing his head and spinning around the length of wood.

"It's the edge of a roof," Kaladin said. "The lip that hangs down on the leeward side of a building." Probably from a storage shed, judging by the other debris.

Alethkar wasn't in the harshest of the stormlands, but neither was this some soft-skinned Western land. Buildings here were built low and squat, sturdy sides pointed eastward toward the Origin, like the shoulder of a man set and ready to take the force of an impact. Windows would only be on the leeward—the westward—side. Like the grass and the trees, human-kind had learned to weather the storms.

That depended on storms always blowing in the same direction. Kaladin had done what he could to prepare the villages and towns he passed for the coming Everstorm, which would blow in the wrong direction and trans-form parshmen into destructive Voidbringers. Nobody in those towns had possessed working spanreeds, however, and he'd been unable to contact his home.

He hadn't been fast enough. Earlier today, he'd spent the Everstorm within a tomb he'd hollowed out of rock using his Shardblade—Syl her-self, who could manifest as any weapon he desired. In truth, the storm hadn't been nearly as bad as the one where he'd fought the Assassin in White. But the debris he found here proved that this one had been bad enough.

The mere memory of that red storm outside his hollow made panic rise inside him. The Everstorm was so *wrong*, so unnatural—like a baby born with no face. Some things just should not be.

He stood up and continued on his way. He had changed uniforms be-fore leaving—his old uniform had been bloodied and tattered. He now wore a spare generic Kholin uniform. It felt wrong not to bear the symbol of Bridge Four.

He crested a hill and spotted a river to his right. Trees sprouted along its banks, hungry for the extra water. That would be Hobble's Brook. So if he looked directly west . . .

Hand shading his eyes, he could see hills that had been stripped of grass and rockbuds. They'd soon be slathered with seed-crem, and lavis polyps would start to bud. That hadn't started yet; this was *supposed* to be the Weeping. Rain should be falling right now in a constant, gentle shower.

Syl zipped up in front of him, a ribbon of light. "Your eyes are brown again," she noted.

It took a few hours without summoning his Shardblade. Once he did that, his eyes would bleed to a glassy light blue, almost glowing. Syl found the variation fascinating; Kaladin still hadn't decided how he felt about it.

"We're close," Kaladin said, pointing. "Those fields belong to Hobbleken. We're maybe two hours from Hearthstone."

"Then you'll be home!" Syl said, her ribbon of light spiraling and taking the shape of a young woman in a flowing havah, tight and buttoning above the waist, with safehand covered.

Kaladin grunted, walking down the slope, longing for Stormlight. Being without it now, after holding so much, was an echoing hollowness within him. Was this what it would be like every time he ran dry?

The Everstorm hadn't recharged his spheres, of course. Neither with Stormlight nor some other energy, which he'd feared might happen.

"Do you like the new dress?" Syl asked, wagging her covered safehand as she stood in the air.

"Looks strange on you."

"I'll have you know I put a *ton* of thought into it. I spent positively hours thinking of just how— Oh! What's that?"

She turned into a little stormcloud that shot toward a lurg clinging to a stone. She inspected the fist-size amphibian on one side, then the other, before squealing in joy and turning into a perfect imitation of the thing—except pale white-blue. This startled the creature away, and she giggled, zipping back toward Kaladin as a ribbon of light.

"What were we saying?" she asked, forming into a young woman and resting on his shoulder.

"Nothing important."

"I'm *sure* I was scolding you. Oh, yes, you're home! Yay! Aren't you *excited*?"

She didn't see it—didn't realize. Sometimes, for all her curiosity, she could be oblivious.

"But . . . it's your home . . ." Syl said. She huddled down. "What's wrong?"

"The Everstorm, Syl," Kaladin said. "We were supposed to beat it here."
He'd *needed* to beat it here.

Surely someone would have survived, right? The fury of the storm, and then the worse fury after? The murderous rampage of servants turned into monsters?

Oh, Stormfather. Why hadn't he been *faster?*

He forced himself into a double march again, pack slung over his shoulder. The weight was still heavy, dreadfully so, but he found that he had to know. Had to see.

Someone had to witness what had happened to his home.

.·.

The rain resumed about an hour out of Hearthstone, so at least the weather patterns hadn't been *completely* ruined. Unfortunately, this meant he had to hike the rest of the way wet. He splashed through puddles where rainspren grew, blue candles with eyes on the very tip.

"It will be all right, Kaladin," Syl promised from his shoulder. She'd created an umbrella for herself, and still wore the traditional Vorin dress instead of her usual girlish skirt. "You'll see."

The sky had darkened by the time he finally crested the last lavis hill and looked down on Hearthstone. He braced himself for the destruction, but it shocked him nonetheless. Some of the buildings he remembered were simply . . . gone. Others stood without roofs. He couldn't see the entire town from his vantage, not in the gloom of the Weeping, but many of the structures he could make out were hollow and ruined.

He stood for a long time as night fell. He didn't spot a glimmer of light in the town. It was empty.

Dead.

A part of him scrunched up inside, huddling into a corner, tired of being whipped so often. He'd embraced his power; he'd taken the path of a Radiant. Why hadn't it been enough?

His eyes immediately sought out his own home on the outskirts of town. But no. Even if he'd been able to see it in the rainy evening gloom, he didn't want to go there. Not yet. He couldn't face the death he might find.

Instead, he rounded Hearthstone on the northwestern side, where a hill led up to the citylord's manor. The larger rural towns like this served as a kind of hub for the small farming communities around them. Because of that, Hearthstone was cursed with the presence of a lighteyed ruler of some status. Brightlord Roshone, a man whose greedy ways had ruined far more than one life.

Moash . . . Kaladin thought as he trudged up the hill toward the manor, shivering in the chill and the darkness. He'd have to face his friend's betrayal—and near assassination of Elhokar—at some point. For now, he had more pressing wounds that needed tending.

The manor was where the town's parshmen had been kept; they'd have begun their rampage here. He was pretty sure that if he ran across Roshone's broken corpse, he wouldn't be too heartbroken.

"Wow," Syl said. "*Gloomspren.*"

Kaladin looked up and noted an unusual spren whipping about. Long, grey, like a tattered streamer of cloth in the wind. It wound around him, fluttering. He'd seen its like only once or twice before.

"Why are they so rare?" Kaladin asked. "People feel gloomy all the time."

"Who knows?" Syl said. "Some spren are common. Some are uncommon." She tapped his shoulder. "I'm pretty sure one of my aunts liked to hunt these things."

"*Hunt* them?" Kaladin asked. "Like, try to spot them?"

"No. Like you hunt greatshells. Can't remember her name . . ." Syl cocked her head, oblivious to the fact that rain was falling through her form. "She wasn't really my aunt. Just an honorspren I referred to that way. What an odd memory."

"More seems to be coming back to you."

"The longer I'm with you, the more it happens. Assuming you don't try to kill me again." She gave him a sideways look. Though it was dark, she glowed enough for him to make out the expression.

"How often are you going to make me apologize for that?"

"How many times have I done it so far?"

"At least fifty."

"Liar," Syl said. "Can't be more than twenty."

"I'm sorry."

Wait. Was that light up ahead?

Kaladin stopped on the path. It *was* light, coming from the manor house. It flickered unevenly. Fire? Was the manor burning? No, it seemed to be candles or lanterns inside. Someone, it appeared, had survived. Humans or Voidbringers?

He needed to be careful, though as he approached, he found that he didn't want to be. He wanted to be reckless, angry, destructive. If he found the creatures that had taken his home from him . . .

"Be ready," he mumbled to Syl.

He stepped off the pathway, which was kept free of rockbuds and other plants, and crept carefully toward the manor. Light shone between boards that had been pounded across the building's windows, replacing glass that the Everstorm undoubtedly broke. He was surprised the manor had survived as well as it had. The porch had been ripped free, but the roof remained.

The rain masked other sounds and made it difficult to see much beyond that, but someone, or something, *was* inside. Shadows moved in front of the lights.

Heart pounding, Kaladin rounded toward the northern side of the building. The servants' entrance would be here, along with the quarters for the parshmen. An unusual amount of noise came from inside the manor house. Thumping. Motion. Like a nest full of rats.

He had to feel his way through the gardens. The parshmen had been housed in a small structure built in the manor's shadow, with a single open chamber and benches for sleeping. Kaladin reached it by touch and felt at a large hole ripped in the side.

Scraping came from behind him.

Kaladin spun as the back door of the manor opened, its warped frame grinding against stone. He dove for cover behind a shalebark mound, but light bathed him, cutting through the rain. A lantern.

Kaladin stretched his hand to the side, prepared to summon Syl, yet the person who stepped from the manor was no Voidbringer, but instead a human guardsman in an old helm spotted by rust.

The man held up his lantern. "Here now," he shouted at Kaladin, fumbling at the mace on his belt. "Here now! You there!" He pulled free the weapon and held it out in a quivering hand. "What are you? Deserter? Come here into the light and let me see you."

Kaladin stood up warily. He didn't recognize the soldier—but either someone had survived the Voidbringer assault, or this man was part of an expedition investigating the aftermath. Either way, it was the first hopeful sign Kaladin had seen since arriving.

He held his hands up—he was unarmed save for Syl—and let the guard bully him into the building.

6

FOUR LIFETIMES

I thought that I was surely dead. Certainly, some who saw farther than I did thought I had fallen.

—From *Oathbringer*, preface

Kaladin stepped into Roshone's manor, and his apocalyptic visions of death and loss started to fade as he recognized people. He passed Toravi, one of the town's many farmers, in the hallway. Kaladin remembered the man as being enormous, with thick shoulders. In actuality, he was shorter than Kaladin by half a hand, and most of Bridge Four could have outmatched him for muscles.

Toravi didn't seem to recognize Kaladin. The man stepped into a side chamber, which was packed with darkeyes sitting on the floor.

The soldier walked Kaladin along the candlelit hallway. They passed through the kitchens, and Kaladin noted dozens of other familiar faces. The townspeople filled the manor, packing every room. Most sat on the floor in family groups, and while they looked tired and disheveled, they were alive. Had they rebuffed the Voidbringer assault, then?

My parents, Kaladin thought, pushing through a small group of townspeople and moving more quickly. Where were his parents?

"Whoa, there!" said the soldier behind, grabbing Kaladin by the shoulder. He shoved his mace into the small of Kaladin's back. "Don't make me down you, son."

Kaladin turned on the guardsman, a clean-shaven fellow with brown eyes that seemed set a little too close together. That rusted cap was a disgrace.

"Now," the soldier said, "we're just going to go find Brightlord Roshone, and you're going to explain why you were skulking round the place. Act real nice, and maybe he won't hang you. Understand?"

The townspeople in the kitchens noticed Kaladin finally, and pulled away. Many whispered to one another, eyes wide, fearful. He heard the words "deserter," "slave brands," "dangerous."

Nobody said his name.

"They don't recognize you?" Syl asked as she walked across a kitchen countertop.

Why would they recognize this man he had become? Kaladin saw himself reflected in a pan hanging beside the brick oven. Long hair with a curl to it, the tips resting against his shoulders. A rough uniform that was a shade too small for him, face bearing a scruffy beard from several weeks without shaving. Soaked and exhausted, he looked like a vagabond.

This wasn't the homecoming he'd imagined during his first months at war. A glorious reunion where he returned as a hero wearing the knots of a sergeant, his brother delivered safe to his family. In his fancies, people had praised him, slapped him on the back and accepted him.

Idiocy. These people had never treated him or his family with any measure of kindness.

"Let's go," the soldier said, shoving him on the shoulder.

Kaladin didn't move. When the man shoved harder, Kaladin rolled his body with the push, and the shift of weight sent the guard stumbling past him. The man turned, angry. Kaladin met his gaze. The guard hesitated, then took a step back and gripped his mace more firmly.

"Wow," Syl said, zipping up to Kaladin's shoulder. "That is *quite* the glare you gave."

"Old sergeant's trick," Kaladin whispered, turning and leaving the kitchens. The guard followed behind, barking an order that Kaladin ignored.

Each step through this manor was like walking through a memory. There was the dining nook where he'd confronted Rillir and Laral on the night he'd discovered his father was a thief. This hallway beyond, hung with portraits of people he didn't know, had been where he'd played as a child. Roshone hadn't changed the portraits.

He'd have to talk to his parents about Tien. It was why he hadn't tried to contact them after being freed from slavery. Could he face them? Storms, he hoped they lived. But could he *face them*?

He heard a moan. Soft, underneath the sounds of people talking, still he picked it out.

"There were wounded?" he asked, turning on his guard.

"Yeah," the man said. "But—"

Kaladin ignored him and strode down the hallway, Syl flying along beside his head. Kaladin shoved past people, following the sounds of the tormented, and eventually stumbled into the doorway of the parlor. It had been transformed into a surgeon's triage room, with mats laid out on the floor bearing wounded.

A figure knelt by one of the pallets carefully splinting a broken arm. Kaladin had known as soon as he'd heard those moans of pain where he'd find his father.

Lirin glanced at him. Storms. Kaladin's father looked weathered, bags underneath his dark brown eyes. The hair was greyer than Kaladin remembered, the face gaunter. But he was the same. Balding, diminutive, thin, bespectacled . . . and amazing.

"What's this?" Lirin asked, turning back to his work. "Did the high-prince's house send soldiers already? That was faster than expected. How many did you bring? We can certainly use . . ." Lirin hesitated, then looked back at Kaladin.

Then his eyes opened wide.

"Hello, Father," Kaladin said.

The guardsman finally caught up, shouldering past gawking towns-people and waving his mace toward Kaladin like a baton. Kaladin sidestepped absently, then pushed the man so he stumbled farther down the hallway.

"It *is* you," Lirin said. Then he scrambled over and caught Kaladin in an embrace. "Oh, Kal. My boy. My little boy. Hesina! *HESINA!*"

Kaladin's mother appeared in the doorway a moment later, bearing a tray of freshly boiled bandages. She probably thought that Lirin needed her help with a patient. Taller than her husband by a few fingers, she wore her hair tied back with a kerchief just as Kaladin remembered.

She raised her gloved safehand to her lips, gaping, and the tray slipped down in her other hand, tumbling bandages to the floor. Shockspren, like pale yellow triangles breaking and re-forming, appeared behind her. She dropped the tray and reached to the side of Kaladin's face with a soft touch. Syl zipped around in a ribbon of light, laughing.

Kaladin couldn't laugh. Not until it had been said. He took a deep breath, choked on it the first time, then finally forced it out.

"I'm sorry, Father, Mother," he whispered. "I joined the army to protect him, but I could barely protect myself." He found himself shaking, and he put his back to the wall, letting himself sink down until he was seated. "I let Tien die. I'm sorry. It's my fault. . . ."

"Oh, Kaladin," Hesina said, kneeling down beside him and pulling him into an embrace. "We got your letter, but over a year ago they told us you had died as well."

"I should have saved him," Kaladin whispered.

"You shouldn't have gone in the first place," Lirin said. "But now . . . Almighty, now you're back." Lirin stood up, tears leaking down his cheeks. "My son! My son is *alive*!"

⁙

A short time later, Kaladin sat among the wounded, holding a cup of warm soup in his hands. He hadn't had a hot meal since . . . when?

"That's *obviously* a slave's brand, Lirin," a soldier said, speaking with Kaladin's father near the doorway into the room. "*Sas* glyph, so it happened here in the princedom. They probably told you he'd died to save you the shame of the truth. And then the *shash* brand—you don't get that for mere insubordination."

Kaladin sipped his soup. His mother knelt beside him, one hand on his shoulder, protective. The soup tasted of home. Boiled vegetable broth with steamed lavis stirred in, spiced as his mother always made it.

He hadn't spoken much in the half hour since he'd arrived. For now, he just wanted to be here with them.

Strangely, his memories had turned fond. He remembered Tien laughing, brightening the dreariest of days. He remembered hours spent studying medicine with his father, or cleaning with his mother.

Syl hovered before his mother, still wearing her little havah, invisible to everyone but Kaladin. The spren had a perplexed look on her face.

"The wrong-way highstorm did break many of the town's buildings," Hesina explained to him softly. "But our home still stands. We had to dedicate your spot to something else, Kal, but we can make space for you."

Kaladin glanced at the soldier. Captain of Roshone's guard; Kaladin thought he remembered the man. He almost seemed too pretty to be a soldier, but then, he *was* lighteyed.

"Don't worry about that," Hesina said. "We'll deal with it, whatever the . . . trouble is. With all these wounded pouring in from the villages around, Roshone will need your father's skill. Roshone won't go making a storm and risk Lirin's discontent—and you *won't* be taken from us again."

She talked to him as if he were a child.

What a surreal sensation, being back here, being treated like he was still the boy who had left for war five years ago. Three men bearing their son's name had lived and died in that time. The soldier who had been forged in Amaram's army. The slave, so bitter and angry. His parents had never met Captain Kaladin, bodyguard to the most powerful man in Roshar.

And then . . . there was the next man, the man he was becoming. A man who owned the skies and spoke ancient oaths. Five years had passed. And four lifetimes.

"He's a runaway slave," the guard captain hissed. "We can't just *ignore* that, surgeon. He probably stole the uniform. And even if for some reason he was allowed to hold a spear despite his brands, he's a deserter. Look at those haunted eyes and tell me you don't see a man who has done terrible things."

"He's my *son*," Lirin said. "I'll buy his writ of slavery. You're *not* taking him. Tell Roshone he can either let this slide, or he can go without a surgeon. Unless he assumes Mara can take over after just a few years of apprenticeship."

Did they think they were speaking softly enough that he couldn't hear?

Look at the wounded people in this room, Kaladin. You're missing something.

The wounded . . . they displayed fractures. Concussions. Very few lacerations. This was not the aftermath of a battle, but of a natural disaster. So what had happened to the Voidbringers? Who had fought them off?

"Things have gotten better since you left," Hesina promised Kaladin, squeezing his shoulder. "Roshone isn't as bad as he once was. I think he feels guilty. We can rebuild, be a family again. And there's something else you need to know about. We—"

"Hesina," Lirin said, throwing his hands into the air.

"Yes?"

"Write a letter to the highprince's administrators," Lirin said. "Explain the situation; see if we can get a forbearance, or at least an explanation." He looked to the soldier. "Will *that* satisfy your master? We can wait upon a higher authority, and in the meantime I can have my son back."

"We'll see," the soldier said, folding his arms. "I'm not sure how much I like the idea of a *shash*-branded man running around my town."

Hesina rose to join Lirin. The two had a hushed exchange as the guard settled back against the doorway, pointedly keeping an eye on Kaladin. Did he know how little like a soldier he looked? He didn't walk like a man acquainted with battle. He stepped too hard, and stood with his knees too straight. There were no dents in his breastplate, and his sword's scabbard knocked against things as he turned.

Kaladin sipped his soup. Was it any wonder that his parents still thought of him as a child? He'd come in looking ragged and abandoned, then had started sobbing about Tien's death. Being home brought out the child in him, it seemed.

Perhaps it was time, for once, to stop letting the rain dictate his mood. He couldn't banish the seed of darkness inside him, but Stormfather, he didn't need to let it rule him either.

Syl walked up to him in the air. "They're like I remember them."

"Remember them?" Kaladin whispered. "Syl, you never knew me when I lived here."

"That's true," she said.

"So how can you remember them?" Kaladin said, frowning.

"Because I do," Syl said, flitting around him. "Everyone is connected, Kaladin. Every*thing* is connected. I didn't know you then, but the winds did, and I am of the winds."

"You're honorspren."

"The winds are of Honor," she said, laughing as if he'd said something ridiculous. "We are kindred blood."

"You don't have blood."

"And you don't have an imagination, it appears." She landed in the air before him and became a young woman. "Besides, there was . . . another voice. Pure, with a song like tapped crystal, distant yet demanding . . ." She smiled, and zipped away.

Well, the world might have been upended, but Syl was as impenetrable as ever. Kaladin set aside his soup and climbed to his feet. He stretched to one side, then the other, feeling satisfying *pop*s from his joints. He walked toward his parents. Storms, but everyone in this town seemed smaller than he remembered. He hadn't been *that* much shorter when he'd left Hearthstone, had he?

A figure stood right outside the room, speaking with the guard with the rusty helmet. Roshone wore a lighteyes' coat that was several seasons out of fashion—Adolin would have shaken his head at that. The citylord wore a wooden foot on his right leg, and had lost weight since Kaladin had last seen him. His skin drooped on his figure like melted wax, bunching up at his neck.

That said, Roshone had the same imperious bearing, the same angry expression—his light yellow eyes seemed to blame everyone and everything in this insignificant town for his banishment. He'd once lived in Kholinar, but had been involved in the deaths of some citizens—Moash's grandparents—and had been shipped out here as punishment.

He turned toward Kaladin, lit by candles on the walls. "So, *you're* alive. They didn't teach you to keep yourself in the army, I see. Let me have a look at those brands of yours." He reached over and held up the hair in front of Kaladin's forehead. "Storms, boy. What did you do? Hit a lighteyes?"

"Yes," Kaladin said.

Then punched him.

He bashed Roshone right in the face. A solid hit, exactly like Hav had taught him. Thumb outside of his fist, he connected with the first two knuckles of his hand across Roshone's cheekbone, then followed through to slide across the front of the face. Rarely had he delivered such a perfect punch. It barely even hurt his fist.

Roshone dropped like a felled tree.

"That," Kaladin said, "was for my friend Moash."

7

A WATCHER AT THE RIM

I did not die.

I experienced something worse.

—From *Oathbringer*, preface

Kaladin!" Lirin exclaimed, grabbing him by the shoulder. "What are you *doing*, son?"

Roshone sputtered on the ground, his nose bleeding. "Guards, take him! You hear me!"

Syl landed on Kaladin's shoulder, hands on her hips. She tapped her foot. "He probably deserved that."

The darkeyed guard scrambled to help Roshone to his feet while the captain leveled his sword at Kaladin. A third joined them, running in from another room.

Kaladin stepped one foot back, falling into a guard position.

"Well?" Roshone demanded, holding his handkerchief to his nose. "Strike him down!" Angerspren boiled up from the ground in pools.

"Please, no," Kaladin's mother cried, clinging to Lirin. "He's just distraught. He—"

Kaladin held out a hand toward her, palm forward, in a quieting motion. "It's all right, Mother. That was only payment for a little unsettled debt between Roshone and me."

He met the eyes of the guards, each in turn, and they shuffled uncertainly. Roshone blustered. Unexpectedly, Kaladin felt in complete control of the situation—and . . . well, more than a little embarrassed.

Suddenly, the perspective of it crashed down on him. Since leaving

Hearthstone, Kaladin had met true evil, and Roshone hardly compared. Hadn't he sworn to protect even those he didn't like? Wasn't the whole *point* of what he had learned to keep him from doing things like this? He glanced at Syl, and she nodded to him.

Do better.

For a short time, it had been nice to just be Kal again. Fortunately, he wasn't that youth any longer. He was a new person—and for the first time in a long, *long* while, he was happy with that person.

"Stand down, men," Kaladin said to the soldiers. "I promise not to hit your brightlord again. I apologize for that; I was momentarily distracted by our previous history. Something he and I both need to forget. Tell me, what happened to the parshmen? Did they not attack the town?"

The soldiers shifted, glancing toward Roshone.

"I said *stand down*," Kaladin snapped. "For storm's sake, man. You're holding that sword like you're going to chop a stumpweight. And you? *Rust* on your cap? I know Amaram recruited most of the able-bodied men in the region, but I've seen messenger boys with more battle poise than you."

The soldiers looked to one another. Then, red-faced, the lighteyed one slid his sword back into its sheath.

"What are you doing?" Roshone demanded. "Attack him!"

"Brightlord, sir," the man said, eyes down. "I may not be the best soldier around, but . . . well, sir, trust me on this. We should just pretend that punch never happened." The other two soldiers nodded their heads in agreement.

Roshone sized Kaladin up, dabbing at his nose, which wasn't bleeding badly. "So, they *did* make something out of you in the army, did they?"

"You have no idea. We need to talk. Is there a room here that isn't clogged full of people?"

"Kal," Lirin said. "You're speaking foolishness. Don't give orders to Brightlord Roshone!"

Kaladin pushed past the soldiers and Roshone, walking farther down the hallway. "Well?" he barked. "Empty room?"

"Up the stairs, sir," one of the soldiers said. "Library is empty."

"Excellent." Kaladin smiled to himself, noting the "sir." "Join me up there, men."

Kaladin started toward the stairs. Unfortunately, an authoritative bearing could only take a man so far. Nobody followed, not even his parents.

"I gave you people an order," Kaladin said. "I'm not fond of repeating myself."

"And what," Roshone said, "makes you think you can order anyone around, boy?"

Kaladin turned back and swept his arm before him, summoning Syl. A
bright, dew-covered Shardblade formed from mist into his hand. He spun

the Blade and rammed her down into the floor in one smooth motion. He held the grip, feeling his eyes bleed to blue.

Everything grew still. Townspeople froze, gaping. Roshone's eyes bulged. Curiously, Kaladin's father just lowered his head and closed his eyes.

"Any other questions?" Kaladin asked.

⁂

"They were gone when we went back to check on them, um, Brightlord," said Aric, the short guard with the rusty helm. "We'd locked the door, but the side was ripped clean open."

"They didn't attack a soul?" Kaladin asked.

"No, Brightlord."

Kaladin paced through the library. The room was small, but neatly organized with rows of shelves and a fine reading stand. Each book was exactly flush with the others; either the maids were extremely meticulous, or the books were not often moved. Syl perched on one shelf, her back to a book, swinging her legs girlishly over the edge.

Roshone sat on one side of the room, periodically pushing both hands along his flushed cheeks toward the back of his head in an odd nervous gesture. His nose had stopped bleeding, though he'd have a nice bruise. That was a fraction of the punishment the man deserved, but Kaladin found he had no passion for abusing Roshone. He had to be better than that.

"What did the parshmen look like?" Kaladin asked of the guardsmen. "They changed, following the unusual storm?"

"Sure did," Aric said. "I peeked when I heard them break out, after the storm passed. They looked like Voidbringers, I tell you, with big bony bits jutting from their skin."

"They were taller," the guard captain added. "Taller than me, easily as tall as you are, Brightlord. With legs thick as stumpweights and hands that could have strangled a whitespine, I tell you."

"Then why didn't they attack?" Kaladin asked. They could have easily taken the manor; instead, they'd run off into the night. It spoke of a more disturbing goal. Perhaps Hearthstone was too small to be bothered with.

"I don't suppose you tracked their direction?" Kaladin said, looking toward the guards, then Roshone.

"Um, no, Brightlord," the captain said. "Honestly, we were just worried about surviving."

"Will you tell the king?" Aric asked. "That storm ripped away *four* of our silos. We'll be starving afore too long, with all these refugees and no food. When the highstorms start coming again, we won't have half as many homes as we need."

"I'll tell Elhokar." But Stormfather, the rest of the kingdom would be just as bad.

He needed to focus on the Voidbringers. He couldn't report back to Dalinar until he had the Stormlight to fly home, so for now it seemed his most useful task would be to find out where the enemy was gathering, if he could. What were the Voidbringers planning? Kaladin hadn't experienced their strange powers himself, though he'd heard reports of the Battle of Narak. Parshendi with glowing eyes and lightning at their command, ruthless and terrible.

"I'll need maps," he said. "Maps of Alethkar, as detailed as you have, and some way to carry them through the rain without ruining them." He grimaced. "And a horse. Several of them, the finest you have."

"So you're robbing me now?" Roshone asked softly, staring at the floor.

"Robbing?" Kaladin said. "We'll call it renting instead." He pulled a handful of spheres from his pocket and dropped them on the table. He glanced toward the soldiers. "Well? Maps? Surely Roshone keeps survey maps of the nearby areas."

Roshone was not important enough to have stewardship over any of the highprince's lands—a distinction Kaladin had never realized while he lived in Hearthstone. Those lands would be watched over by much more important lighteyes; Roshone would only be a first point of contact with surrounding villages.

"We'll want to wait for the lady's permission," the guard captain said. "Sir."

Kaladin raised an eyebrow. They'd disobey Roshone for him, but not the manor's lady? "Go to the house ardents and tell them to prepare the things I request. Permission will be forthcoming. And locate a spanreed connected to Tashikk, if any of the ardents have one. Once I have the Stormlight to use it, I'll want to send word to Dalinar."

The guards saluted and left.

Kaladin folded his arms. "Roshone, I'm going to need to chase those parshmen and see if I can figure out what they're up to. I don't suppose any of your guards have tracking experience? Following the creatures would be hard enough without the rain swamping everything."

"Why do they matter so much?" Roshone asked, still staring at the floor.

"Surely you've guessed," Kaladin said, nodding to Syl as her ribbon of light flitted over to his shoulder. "Weather in turmoil and terrors transformed from common servants? That storm with the red lightning, blowing the wrong direction? The Desolation is here, Roshone. The Voidbringers have returned."

Roshone groaned, leaning forward, arms wrapped around himself as if he were going to be sick.

"Syl?" Kaladin whispered. "I might need you again."

"You sound apologetic," she replied, cocking her head.

"I am. I don't like the idea of swinging you about, smashing you into things."

She sniffed. "Firstly, I *don't* smash into things. I am an *elegant* and *graceful* weapon, stupid. Secondly, why would you be bothered?"

"It doesn't feel right," Kaladin replied, still whispering. "You're a woman, not a weapon."

"Wait . . . so this is about me being a girl?"

"No," Kaladin said immediately, then hesitated. "Maybe. It just feels strange."

She sniffed. "You don't ask your other weapons how they feel about being swung about."

"My other weapons aren't people." He hesitated. "Are they?"

She looked at him with head cocked and eyebrows raised, as if he'd said something very stupid.

Everything has a spren. His mother had taught him that from an early age.

"So . . . some of my spears have been women, then?" he asked.

"Female, at least," Syl said. "Roughly half, as these things tend to go." She flitted up into the air in front of him. "It's your fault for personifying us, so no complaining. Of course, some of the old spren have four genders instead of two."

"What? Why?"

She poked him in the nose. "Because humans didn't imagine those ones, silly." She zipped out in front of him, changing into a field of mist. When he raised his hand, the Shardblade appeared.

He strode to where Roshone sat, then stooped down and held the Shardblade before the man, point toward the floor.

Roshone looked up, transfixed by the weapon's blade, as Kaladin had anticipated. You couldn't be near one of these things and *not* be drawn by it. They had a magnetism.

"How did you get it?" Roshone asked.

"Does it matter?"

He didn't reply, but they both knew the truth. Owning a Shardblade was enough—if you could claim it, and not have it taken from you, it was yours. With one in his possession, the brands on his head were meaningless. No man, not even Roshone, would imply otherwise.

"You," Kaladin said, "are a cheat, a rat, and a murderer. But as much as I hate it, we don't have time to oust Alethkar's ruling class and set up something better. We are under attack by an enemy we do not understand, and which we could not have anticipated. So you're going to have to stand up and lead these people."

Roshone stared at the blade, looking at his reflection.

"We're not powerless," Kaladin said. "We can and will fight back—but first we need to survive. The Everstorm will return. Regularly, though I don't know the interval yet. I need you to prepare."

"How?" Roshone whispered.

"Build homes with slopes in both directions. If there's not time for that, find a sheltered location and hunker down. I can't stay. This crisis is bigger than one town, one people, even if it's *my* town and *my* people. I have to rely on you. Almighty preserve us, you're all we have."

Roshone slumped down farther in his seat. Great. Kaladin stood and dismissed Syl.

"We'll do it," a voice said from behind him.

Kaladin froze. Laral's voice sent a shiver down his spine. He turned slowly, and found a woman who did not at all match the image in his head. When he'd last seen her, she'd been wearing a perfect lighteyed dress, beautiful and young, yet her pale green eyes had seemed hollow. She'd lost her betrothed, Roshone's son, and had instead become engaged to the father—a man more than twice her age.

The woman he confronted was no longer a youth. Her face was firm, lean, and her hair was pulled back in a no-nonsense tail of black peppered with blonde. She wore boots and a utilitarian havah, damp from the rain.

She looked him up and down, then sniffed. "Looks like you went and grew up, Kal. I was sorry to hear the news of your brother. Come now. You need a spanreed? I've got one to the queen regent in Kholinar, but that one hasn't been responsive lately. Fortunately, we do have one to Tashikk, as you asked about. If you think that the king will respond to you, we can go through an intermediary."

She walked back out the doorway.

"Laral . . ." he said, following.

"I hear you stabbed my floor," she noted. "That's good hardwood, I'll have you know. Honestly. Men and their weapons."

"I dreamed of coming back," Kaladin said, stopping in the hallway outside the library. "I imagined returning here a war hero and challenging Roshone. I wanted to save you, Laral."

"Oh?" She turned back to him. "And what made you think I needed

saving?"

"You can't tell me," Kaladin said softly, waving backward toward the library, "that you've been happy with *that*."

"Becoming a lighteyes does not grant a man any measure of decorum, it appears," Laral said. "You will stop insulting my husband, Kaladin. Shardbearer or not, another word like that, and I'll have you thrown from my home."

"Laral—"

"I *am* quite happy here. Or I was, until the winds started blowing the wrong direction." She shook her head. "You take after your father. Always feeling like you need to save everyone, even those who would rather you mind your own business."

"Roshone brutalized my family. He sent my brother to his death and did everything he could to destroy my father!"

"And your father spoke against my husband," Laral said, "disparaging him in front of the other townspeople. How would you feel, as a new brightlord exiled far from home, only to find that the town's most important citizen is openly critical of you?"

Her perspective was skewed, of course. Lirin had tried to befriend Roshone at first, hadn't he? Still, Kaladin found little passion to continue the argument. What did he care? He intended to see his parents moved from this city anyway.

"I'll go set up the spanreed," she said. "It might take some time to get a reply. In the meantime, the ardents should be fetching your maps."

"Great," Kaladin said, pushing past her in the hallway. "I'm going to go speak with my parents."

Syl zipped over his shoulder as he started down the steps. "So, that's the girl you were going to marry."

"No," Kaladin whispered. "That's a girl I was never going to marry, no matter what happened."

"I like her."

"You would." He reached the bottom of the steps and looked back up. Roshone had joined Laral at the top of the stairs, carrying the gems Kaladin had left on the table. How much had that been?

Five or six ruby broams, he thought, and maybe a sapphire or two. He did the calculations in his head. Storms . . . That was a ridiculous sum— more money than the goblet full of spheres that Roshone and Kaladin's father had spent years fighting over back in the day. That was now mere pocket change to Kaladin.

He'd always thought of all lighteyes as rich, but a minor brightlord in an insignificant town . . . well, Roshone was actually poor, just a different kind of poor.

Kaladin searched back through the house, passing people he'd once known—people who now whispered "Shardbearer" and got out of his way with alacrity. So be it. He'd accepted his place the moment he'd seized Syl from the air and spoken the Words.

Lirin was back in the parlor, working on the wounded again. Kaladin stopped in the doorway, then sighed and knelt beside Lirin. As the man reached toward his tray of tools, Kaladin picked it up and held it at the ready. His old position as his father's surgery assistant. The new apprentice was helping with wounded in another room.

Lirin eyed Kaladin, then turned back to the patient, a young boy who had a bloodied bandage around his arm. "Scissors," Lirin said.

Kaladin proffered them, and Lirin took the tool without looking, then carefully cut the bandage free. A jagged length of wood had speared the boy's arm. He whimpered as Lirin palpated the flesh nearby, covered in dried blood. It didn't look good.

"Cut out the shaft," Kaladin said, "and the necrotic flesh. Cauterize."

"A little extreme, don't you think?" Lirin asked.

"Might want to remove it at the elbow anyway. That's going to get infected for sure—look how dirty that wood is. It will leave splinters."

The boy whimpered again. Lirin patted him. "You'll be fine. I don't see any rotspren yet, and so we're not going to take the arm off. Let me talk to your parents. For now, chew on this." He gave the boy some bark as a relaxant.

Together, Lirin and Kaladin moved on; the boy wasn't in immediate danger, and Lirin would want to operate after the anesthetic took effect.

"You've hardened," Lirin said to Kaladin as he inspected the next patient's foot. "I was worried you'd never grow calluses."

Kaladin didn't reply. In truth, his calluses weren't as deep as his father might have wanted.

"But you've also become one of them," Lirin said.

"My eye color doesn't change a thing."

"I wasn't speaking of your eye color, son. I don't give two chips whether a man is lighteyed or not." He waved a hand, and Kaladin passed him a rag to clean the toe, then started preparing a small splint.

"What you've become," Lirin continued, "is a killer. You solve problems with the fist and the sword. I had hoped that you would find a place among the army's surgeons."

"I wasn't given much choice," Kaladin said, handing over the splint, then preparing some bandages to wrap the toe. "It's a long story. I'll tell you sometime." *The less soul-crushing parts of it, at least.*

"I don't suppose you're going to stay."

"No. I need to follow those parshmen."

"More killing, then."

"And you honestly think we shouldn't fight the *Voidbringers*, Father?"

Lirin hesitated. "No," he whispered. "I know that war is inevitable. I just didn't want *you* to have to be a part of it. I've seen what it does to men. War flays their souls, and those are wounds I can't heal." He secured the splint, then turned to Kaladin. "We're surgeons. Let others rend and break; *we* must not harm others."

"No," Kaladin said. "You're a surgeon, Father, but I'm something else. A watcher at the rim." Words spoken to Dalinar Kholin in a vision. Kaladin stood up. "I will protect those who need it. Today, that means hunting down some Voidbringers."

Lirin looked away. "Very well. I am . . . glad you returned, son. I'm glad you're safe."

Kaladin rested his hand on his father's shoulder. "Life before death, Father."

"See your mother before you leave," Lirin said. "She has something to show you."

Kaladin frowned, but made his way out of the healing chamber to the kitchens. The entire place was lit only by candles, and not many of them. Everywhere he went, he saw shadows and uncertain light.

He filled his canteen with fresh water and found a small umbrella. He'd need that for reading maps in this rain. From there, he went hiking up to check on Laral in the library. Roshone had retreated to his room, but she was sitting at a writing table with a spanreed before her.

Wait. The spanreed was *working*. Its ruby glowed.

"Stormlight!" Kaladin said, pointing.

"Well, of course," she said, frowning at him. "Fabrials require it."

"How do you have *infused* spheres?"

"The highstorm," Laral said. "Just a few days back."

During the clash with the Voidbringers, the Stormfather had summoned an irregular highstorm to match the Everstorm. Kaladin had flown before its stormwall, fighting the Assassin in White.

"That storm was unexpected," Kaladin said. "How in the world did you know to leave your spheres out?"

"Kal," she said, "it's not so hard to hang some spheres out once a storm starts blowing!"

"How many do you have?"

"Some," Laral said. "The ardents have a few—I wasn't the only one to think of it. Look, I've got someone in Tashikk willing to relay a message to Navani Kholin, the king's mother. Wasn't that what you implied you wanted? You really think she'll respond to you?"

The answer, blessedly, came as the spanreed started writing. " 'Captain?' " Laral read. " 'This is Navani Kholin. Is it really you?' "

Laral blinked, then looked up at him.

"It is," Kaladin said. "The last thing I did before leaving was speak with Dalinar at the top of the tower." Hopefully that would be enough to authenticate him.

Laral jumped, then wrote it.

"'Kaladin, this is Dalinar,'" Laral read as the message came back. "'What is your status, soldier?'"

"Better than expected, sir," Kaladin said. He outlined what he'd discovered, in brief. He ended by noting, "I'm worried that they left because Hearthstone wasn't important enough to bother destroying. I've ordered horses and some maps. I figure I can do a little scouting and see what I can find about the enemy."

"'Careful,'" Dalinar responded. "'You don't have any Stormlight left?'"

"I might be able to find a little. I doubt it will be enough to get me home, but it will help."

It took a few minutes before Dalinar replied, and Laral took the opportunity to change the paper on the spanreed board.

"'Your instincts are good, Captain,'" Dalinar finally sent. "'I feel blind in this tower. Get close enough to discover what the enemy is doing, but don't take unnecessary risks. Take the spanreed. Send us a glyph each evening to know you are safe.'"

"Understood, sir. Life before death."

"'Life before death.'"

Laral looked to him, and he nodded that the conversation was over. She packed up the spanreed for him without a word, and he took it gratefully, then hurried out of the room and down the steps.

His activities had drawn quite a crowd of people, who had gathered in the small entry hall before the steps. He intended to ask if anyone had infused spheres, but was interrupted by the sight of his mother. She was speaking with several young girls, and held a toddler in her arms. What was she doing with . . .

Kaladin stopped at the foot of the steps. The little boy was perhaps a year old, chewing on his hand and babbling around his fingers.

"Kaladin, meet your brother," Hesina said, turning toward him. "Some of the girls were watching him while I helped with the triage."

"A brother," Kaladin whispered. It had never occurred to him. His mother would be forty-one this year, and . . .

A brother.

Kaladin reached out. His mother let him take the little boy, hold him in hands that seemed too rough to be touching such soft skin. Kaladin trembled, then pulled the child tight against him. Memories of this place had not broken him, and seeing his parents had not overwhelmed him, but this . . .

He could not stop the tears. He felt like a fool. It wasn't as if this changed anything—Bridge Four were his brothers now, as close to him as any blood relative.

And yet he wept.

"What's his name?"

"Oroden."

"Child of peace," Kaladin whispered. "A good name. A very good name."

Behind him, an ardent approached with a scroll case. Storms, was that Zeheb? Still alive, it seemed, though she'd always seemed older than the stones themselves. Kaladin handed little Oroden back to his mother, then wiped his eyes and took the scroll case.

People crowded at the edges of the room. He was quite the spectacle: the surgeon's son turned slave turned Shardbearer. Hearthstone wouldn't see this much excitement for another hundred years.

At least not if Kaladin had any say about it. He nodded to his father—who had stepped out of the parlor room—then turned to the crowd. "Does anyone here have infused spheres? I will trade you, two chips for one. Bring them forth."

Syl buzzed around him as a collection was made, and Kaladin's mother made the trades for him. What he ended up with was only a pouch's worth, but it seemed vast riches. At the very least, he wasn't going to need those horses any longer.

He tied the pouch closed, then looked over his shoulder as his father stepped up. Lirin took a small glowing diamond chip from his pocket, then handed it toward Kaladin.

Kaladin accepted it, then glanced at his mother and the little boy in her arms. His *brother*.

"I want to take you to safety," he said to Lirin. "I need to leave now, but I'll be back soon. To take you to—"

"No," Lirin said.

"Father, it's the *Desolation*," Kaladin said.

Nearby, people gasped softly, their eyes haunted. Storms; Kaladin should have done this in private. He leaned in toward Lirin. "I know of a place that is safe. For you, Mother. For little Oroden. Please don't be stubborn, for once in your life."

"You can take them, if they'll go," Lirin said. "But I'm staying here. Particularly if . . . what you just said is true. These people will need me."

"We'll see. I'll return as soon as I can." Kaladin set his jaw, then walked to the front door of the manor. He pulled it open, letting in the sounds of rain, the scents of a drowned land.

He paused, looked back at the room full of dirtied townspeople, homeless and frightened. They'd overheard him, but they'd known already. He'd heard them whispering. Voidbringers. The Desolation.

He couldn't leave them like this.

"You heard correctly," Kaladin said loudly to the hundred or so people gathered in the manor's large entry hall—including Roshone and Laral, who stood on the steps up to the second floor. "The Voidbringers have returned."

Murmurs. Fright.

Kaladin sucked in some of the Stormlight from his pouch. Pure, luminescent smoke began to rise from his skin, distinctly visible in the dim room. He Lashed himself upward so he rose into the air, then added a Lashing downward, leaving him to hover about two feet above the floor, glowing. Syl formed from mist as a Shardspear in his hand.

"Highprince Dalinar Kholin," Kaladin said, Stormlight puffing before his lips, "has refounded the Knights Radiant. And this time, we will *not* fail you."

The expressions in the room ranged from adoring to terrified. Kaladin found his father's face. Lirin's jaw had dropped. Hesina clutched her infant child in her arms, and her expression was one of pure delight, an awespren bursting around her head in a blue ring.

You I will protect, little one, Kaladin thought at the child. *I will protect them all.*

He nodded to his parents, then turned and Lashed himself outward, streaking away into the rain-soaked night. He'd stop at Stringken, about half a day's walk—or a short flight—to the south and see if he could trade spheres there.

Then he'd hunt some Voidbringers.

8

A POWERFUL LIE

That moment notwithstanding, I can honestly say this book has been brewing in me since my youth.

—From *Oathbringer*, preface

Shallan drew.

She scraped her drawing pad with agitated, bold streaks. She twisted the charcoal stick in her fingers every few lines, seeking the sharpest points to make the lines a deep black.

"Mmm . . ." Pattern said from near her calves, where he adorned her skirt like embroidery. "Shallan?"

She kept drawing, filling the page with black strokes.

"Shallan?" Pattern asked. "I understand why you hate me, Shallan. I did not mean to help you kill your mother, but it is what I did. It is what I did. . . ."

Shallan set her jaw and kept sketching. She sat outside at Urithiru, her back against a cold chunk of stone, her toes frigid, coldspren growing up like spikes around her. Her frazzled hair whipped past her face in a gust of air, and she had to pin the paper of her pad down with her thumbs, one trapped in her left sleeve.

"Shallan . . ." Pattern said.

"It's all right," Shallan said in a hushed voice as the wind died down. "Just . . . just let me draw."

"Mmm . . ." Pattern said. "A powerful lie . . ."

A simple landscape; she should be able to draw a simple, calming landscape. She sat on the edge of one of the ten Oathgate platforms, which rose ten feet higher than the main plateau. Earlier in the day, she'd activated this Oathgate, bringing forth a few hundred more of the thousands who were waiting at Narak. That would be it for a while: each use of the device used an incredible amount of Stormlight. Even with the gemstones that the newcomers had brought, there wasn't much to go around.

Plus, there wasn't much of *her* to go around. Only an active, full Knight Radiant could work the control buildings at the center of each platform, initiating the swap. For now, that meant only Shallan.

It meant she had to summon her Blade each time. The Blade she'd used to kill her mother. A truth she'd spoken as an Ideal of her order of Radiants.

A truth that she could no longer, therefore, stuff into the back of her mind and forget.

Just draw.

The city dominated her view. It stretched impossibly high, and she struggled to contain the enormous tower on the page. Jasnah had searched this place out in the hope of finding books and records here of ancient date; so far, they hadn't found anything like that. Instead, Shallan struggled to *understand* the tower.

If she locked it down into a sketch, would she finally be able to grasp its incredible size? She couldn't get an angle from which to view the entire tower, so she kept fixating on the little things. The balconies, the shapes of the fields, the cavernous openings—maws to engulf, consume, overwhelm.

She ended up with a sketch not of the tower itself, but instead a crisscrossing of lines on a field of softer charcoal. She stared at the sketch, a windspren passing and troubling the pages. She sighed, dropping her charcoal into her satchel and getting out a damp rag to wipe her freehand fingers.

Down on the plateau, soldiers ran drills. The thought of them all living in that place disturbed Shallan. Which was stupid. It was just a *building*.

But it was one she couldn't sketch.

"Shallan . . ." Pattern said.

"We'll work it out," she said, eyes forward. "It's not *your* fault my parents are dead. You didn't cause it."

"You can hate me," Pattern said. "I understand."

Shallan closed her eyes. She didn't *want* him to understand. She wanted him to convince her she was wrong. She needed to be *wrong*.

"I don't hate you, Pattern," Shallan said. "I hate the sword."

"But—"

"The sword isn't you. The sword is me, my father, the life we led, and the way it got twisted all about."

"I . . ." Pattern hummed softly. "I don't understand."

I'd be shocked if you did, Shallan thought. *Because I sure don't.* Fortunately, she had a distraction coming her way in the form of a scout climbing up the ramp to the platform where Shallan perched. The darkeyed woman wore white and blue, with trousers beneath a runner's skirt, and had long, dark Alethi hair.

"Um, Brightness Radiant?" the scout asked after bowing. "The highprince has requested your presence."

"Bother," Shallan said, while inwardly relieved to have something to do. She handed the scout her sketchbook to hold while she packed up her satchel.

Dun spheres, she noted.

While three of the highprinces had joined Dalinar on his expedition to the center of the Shattered Plains, the greater number had remained behind. When the unexpected highstorm had come, Hatham had received word via spanreed from scouts out along the plains.

His warcamp had been able to get out most of their spheres for recharging before the storm hit, giving him a huge amount of Stormlight compared to the rest of them. He was becoming a wealthy man as Dalinar traded for infused spheres to work the Oathgate and bring in supplies.

Compared to that, providing spheres to her to practice her Lightweaving wasn't a terrible expense—but she still felt guilty to see that she'd drained two of them by consuming Stormlight to help her with the chill air. She'd have to be careful about that.

She got everything packed, then reached back for the sketchbook and found the scout woman flipping through the pages with wide eyes. "Brightness . . ." she said. "These are amazing."

Several were sketches as if looking up from the base of the tower, catching a vague sense of Urithiru's stateliness, but more giving a sense of vertigo. With dissatisfaction, Shallan realized she'd enhanced the surreal nature of the sketches with impossible vanishing points and perspective.

"I've been trying to draw the tower," Shallan said, "but I can't get it from the right angle." Maybe when Brightlord Brooding-Eyes returned, he could fly her to another peak along the mountain chain.

"I've never seen anything like these," the scout said, flipping pages. "What do you call it?"

"Surrealism," Shallan said, taking the large sketchbook back and tucking it under her arm. "It was an old artistic movement. I guess I defaulted to it when I couldn't get the picture to look how I wanted. Hardly anyone bothers with it anymore except students."

"It made my eyes make my brain think it forgot to wake up."

Shallan gestured, and the scout led the way back down and across the plateau. Here, Shallan noticed that more than a few soldiers on the field had stopped their drills and were watching her. Bother. She would never again return to being just Shallan, the insignificant girl from a backwater town. She was now "Brightness Radiant," ostensibly from the Order of Elsecallers. She'd persuaded Dalinar to pretend—in public, at least—that Shallan was from an order that couldn't make illusions. She needed to keep that secret from spreading, or her effectiveness would be weakened.

The soldiers stared at her as if they expected her to grow Shardplate, shoot gouts of flame from her eyes, and fly off to tear down a mountain or two. *Probably should try to act more composed,* Shallan thought to herself. *More . . . knightly?*

She glanced at a soldier who wore the gold and red of Hatham's army. He immediately looked down and rubbed at the glyphward prayer tied around his upper right arm. Dalinar was determined to recover the reputation of the Radiants, but storms, you couldn't change an entire nation's perspective in a matter of a few months. The ancient Knights Radiant had betrayed humankind; while many Alethi seemed willing to give the orders a fresh start, others weren't so charitable.

Still, she tried to keep her head high, her back straight, and to walk more like her tutors had always instructed. Power was an illusion of perception, as Jasnah had said. The first step to being in control was to see yourself as capable of being in control.

The scout led her into the tower and up a flight of stairs, toward Dalinar's secure section. "Brightness?" the woman asked as they walked. "Can I ask you a question?"

"As that was a question, apparently you can."

"Oh, um. Huh."

"It's fine. What did you want to know?"

"You're . . . a Radiant."

"That one was actually a statement, and that's making me doubt my previous assertion."

"I'm sorry. I just . . . I'm curious, Brightness. How does it work? Being a Radiant? You have a Shardblade?"

So that was where this was going. "I assure you," Shallan said, "it is quite possible to remain properly feminine while fulfilling my duties as a knight."

"Oh," the scout said. Oddly, she seemed *disappointed* by that response. "Of course, Brightness."

Urithiru seemed to have been crafted straight from the rock of a mountain, like a sculpture. Indeed, there weren't seams at the corners of rooms, nor were there distinct bricks or blocks in the walls. Much of the stone exposed thin lines of strata. Beautiful lines of varied hue, like layers of cloth stacked in a merchant's shop.

The corridors often twisted about in strange curves, rarely running straight toward an intersection. Dalinar suggested that perhaps this was to fool invaders, like a castle fortification. The sweeping turns and lack of seams made the corridors feel like tunnels.

Shallan didn't need a guide—the strata that cut through the walls had distinctive patterns. Others seemed to have trouble telling those apart, and talked of painting the floors with guidelines. Couldn't they distinguish the pattern here of wide reddish strata alternating with smaller yellow ones? Just go in the direction where the lines were sloping slightly upward, and you'd head toward Dalinar's quarters.

They soon arrived, and the scout took up duty at the door in case her services were needed again. Shallan entered a room that only a day before had been empty, but was now arrayed with furniture, creating a large meeting place right outside Dalinar and Navani's private rooms.

Adolin, Renarin, and Navani sat before Dalinar, who stood with hands on hips, contemplating a map of Roshar on the wall. Though the place was stuffed with rugs and plush furniture, the finery fit this bleak chamber like a lady's havah fit a pig.

"I don't know how to approach the Azish, Father," Renarin was saying as she entered. "Their new emperor makes them unpredictable."

"They're *Azish*," Adolin said, giving Shallan a wave with his unwounded hand. "How can they *not* be predictable? Doesn't their government mandate how to peel your fruit?"

"That's a stereotype," Renarin said. He wore his Bridge Four uniform, but had a blanket over his shoulders and was holding a cup of steaming tea, though the room wasn't particularly cold. "Yes, they have a large bureaucracy. A change in government is still going to cause upheaval. In fact, it might be *easier* for this new Azish emperor to change policy, since policy is well defined enough to change."

"I wouldn't worry about the Azish," Navani said, tapping her notepad with a pen, then writing something in it. "They'll listen to reason; they always do. What about Tukar and Emul? I wouldn't be surprised if that war of theirs is enough to distract them even from the return of the Desolations."

Dalinar grunted, rubbing his chin with one hand. "There's that warlord in Tukar. What's his name?"

"Tezim," Navani said. "Claims he's an aspect of the Almighty."

Shallan sniffed as she slipped into the seat beside Adolin, setting her satchel and drawing pad on the floor. "Aspect of the Almighty? At least he's humble."

Dalinar turned toward her, then clasped his hands behind his back. Storms. He always seemed so . . . *large*. Bigger than any room he was in, brow perpetually furrowed by the deepest of thoughts. Dalinar Kholin could make choosing what to have for breakfast look like the most important decision in all of Roshar.

"Brightness Shallan," he said. "Tell me, how would you deal with the Makabaki kingdoms? Now that the storm has come as we warned, we have an opportunity to approach them from a position of strength. Azir is the most important, but just faced a succession crisis. Emul and Tukar are, of course, at war, as Navani noted. We could certainly use Tashikk's information networks, but they're so isolationist. That leaves Yezier and Liafor. Perhaps the weight of their involvement would persuade their neighbors?"

He turned toward her expectantly.

"Yes, yes . . ." Shallan said, thoughtful. "I *have* heard of several of those places."

Dalinar drew his lips to a line, and Pattern hummed in concern on her skirts. Dalinar did not seem the type of man you joked with.

"I'm sorry, Brightlord," Shallan continued, leaning back in her chair. "But I'm confused as to why you want *my* input. I know of those kingdoms, of course—but my knowledge is an academic thing. I could probably name their primary export for you, but as to foreign policy . . . well, I'd never even spoken to someone from *Alethkar* before leaving my homeland. And we're neighbors!"

"I see," Dalinar said softly. "Does your spren offer some counsel? Could you bring him out to speak to us?"

"Pattern? He's not particularly knowledgeable about our kind, which is sort of why he's here in the first place." She shifted in her seat. "And to be frank, Brightlord, I think he's scared of you."

"Well, he's obviously not a fool," Adolin noted.

Dalinar shot his son a glance.

"Don't be like that, Father," Adolin said. "If anyone would be able to go about intimidating forces of nature, it would be you."

Dalinar sighed, turning and resting his hand on the map. Curiously, it was Renarin who stood up, setting aside his blanket and cup, then walked over to put his hand on his father's shoulder. The youth looked even more spindly than normal when standing beside Dalinar, and though his hair wasn't as blond as Adolin's, it was still patched with yellow. He seemed such a strange contrast to Dalinar, cut from almost entirely different cloth.

"It's just so big, son," Dalinar said, looking at the map. "How can I unite all of Roshar when I've never even *visited* many of these kingdoms? Young Shallan spoke wisdom, though she might not have recognized it. We don't know these people. Now I'm expected to be responsible for them? I wish I could *see* it all. . . ."

Shallan shifted in her seat, feeling as if she'd been forgotten. Perhaps he'd sent for her because he'd wanted to seek the aid of his Radiants, but the Kholin dynamic had always been a family one. In that, she was an intruder.

Dalinar turned and walked to fetch a cup of wine from a warmed pitcher near the door. As he passed Shallan, she felt something unusual. A leaping within her, as if part of her were being *pulled* by him.

He walked past again, holding a cup, and Shallan slipped from her seat, following him toward the map on the wall. She breathed in as she walked, drawing Stormlight from her satchel in a shimmering stream. It infused her, glowing from her skin.

She rested her freehand against the map. Stormlight poured off her, illuminating the map in a swirling tempest of Light. She didn't exactly understand what she was doing, but she rarely did. Art wasn't about understanding, but about *knowing*.

The Stormlight streamed off the map, passing between her and Dalinar in a rush, causing Navani to scramble off her seat and back away. The Light swirled in the chamber and became another, larger map—floating at about table height—in the center of the room. Mountains grew up like furrows in a piece of cloth pressed together. Vast plains shone green from vines and fields of grass. Barren stormward hillsides grew splendid shadows of life on the leeward sides. Stormfather . . . as she watched, the topography of the landscape became *real*.

Shallan's breath caught. Had *she* done that? How? Her illusions usually required a previous drawing to imitate.

The map stretched to the sides of the room, shimmering at the edges. Adolin stood up from his seat, crashing through the middle of the illusion somewhere near Kharbranth. Wisps of Stormlight broke around him, but when he moved, the image swirled and neatly re-formed behind him.

"How . . ." Dalinar leaned down near their section, which detailed the Reshi Isles. "The detail is amazing. I can almost see the cities. What did you do?"

"I don't know if I did *anything*," Shallan said, stepping into the illusion, feeling the Stormlight swirl around her. Despite the detail, the perspective was still from very far away, and the mountains weren't even as tall as one of her fingernails. "I couldn't have created this, Brightlord. I don't have the knowledge."

"Well *I* didn't do it," Renarin said. "The Stormlight quite certainly came from you, Brightness."

"Yes, well, your father was tugging on me at the time."

"Tugging?" Adolin asked.

"The Stormfather," Dalinar said. "This is his influence—this is what he sees each time a storm blows across Roshar. It wasn't me or you, but *us*. Somehow."

"Well," Shallan noted, "you *were* complaining about not being able to take it all in."

"How much Stormlight did this take?" Navani asked, rounding the outside of the new, vibrant map.

Shallan checked her satchel. "Um . . . all of it."

"We'll get you more," Navani said with a sigh.

"I'm sorry for—"

"No," Dalinar said. "Having my Radiants practice with their powers is among the most valuable resources I could purchase right now. Even if Hatham makes us pay through the nose for spheres."

Dalinar strode through the image, disrupting it in a swirl around him. He stopped near the center, beside the location of Urithiru. He looked from one side of the room to the other in a long, slow survey.

"Ten cities," he whispered. "Ten kingdoms. Ten Oathgates connecting them from long ago. This is how we fight it. This is how we begin. We don't start by saving the world—we start with this simple step. We protect the cities with Oathgates.

"The Voidbringers are everywhere, but we can be more mobile. We can shore up capitals, deliver food or Soulcasters quickly between kingdoms. We can make those ten cities bastions of light and strength. But we must be quick. He's coming. The man with nine shadows . . ."

"What's this?" Shallan said, perking up.

"The enemy's champion," Dalinar said, eyes narrowing. "In the visions, Honor told me our best chance of survival involved forcing Odium to accept a contest of champions. I've seen the enemy's champion—a creature in black armor, with red eyes. A parshman perhaps. It had nine shadows."

Nearby, Renarin had turned toward his father, eyes wide, jaw dropping. Nobody else seemed to notice.

"Azimir, capital of Azir," Dalinar said, stepping from Urithiru to the center of Azir to the west, "is home to an Oathgate. We need to open it and gain the trust of the Azish. They will be important to our cause."

He stepped farther to the west. "There's an Oathgate hidden in Shinovar. Another in the capital of Babatharnam, and a fourth in far-off Rall Elorim, City of Shadows."

"Another in Rira," Navani said, joining him. "Jasnah thought it was in Kurth. A sixth was lost in Aimia, the island that was destroyed."

Dalinar grunted, then turned toward the map's eastern section. "Vedenar makes seven," he said, stepping into Shallan's homeland. "Thaylen City is eight. Then the Shattered Plains, which we hold."

"And the last one is in Kholinar," Adolin said softly. "Our home."

Shallan approached and touched him on the arm. Spanreed communication into the city had stopped working. Nobody knew the status of Kholinar; their best clue had come via Kaladin's spanreed message.

"We start small," Dalinar said, "with a few of the most important to holding the world. Azir. Jah Keved. Thaylenah. We'll contact other nations, but our focus is on these three powerhouses. Azir for its organization and political clout. Thaylenah for its shipping and naval prowess. Jah Keved for its manpower. Brightness Davar, any insight you could offer into your homeland—and its status following the civil war—would be appreciated."

"And Kholinar?" Adolin asked.

A knock at the door interrupted Dalinar's response. He called admittance, and the scout from before peeked in. "Brightlord," she said, looking concerned. "There's something you need to see."

"What is it, Lyn?"

"Brightlord, sir. There's . . . there's been another murder."

9

THE THREADS OF A SCREW

The sum of my experiences has pointed at this moment. This decision.

—From *Oathbringer*, preface

One benefit of having become "Brightness Radiant" was that for once, Shallan was *expected* to be a part of important events. Nobody questioned her presence during the rush through the corridors, lit by oil lanterns carried by guards. Nobody thought she was out of place; nobody even considered the propriety of leading a young woman to the scene of a brutal murder. What a welcome change.

From what she overheard the scout telling Dalinar, the corpse had been a lighteyed officer named Vedekar Perel. He was from Sebarial's army, but Shallan didn't know him. The body had been discovered by a scouting party in a remote part of the tower's second level.

As they drew nearer, Dalinar and his guards jogged the rest of the distance, outpacing Shallan. Storming Alethi long legs. She tried to suck in some Stormlight—but she'd used it all on that blasted map, which had disintegrated into a puff of Light as they'd left.

That left her exhausted and annoyed. Ahead of her, Adolin stopped and looked back. He danced a moment, as if impatient, then hurried to her instead of running ahead.

"Thanks," Shallan said as he fell into step beside her.

"It's not like he can get more dead, eh?" he said, then chuckled awkwardly. Something about this had him seriously disturbed.

He reached for her hand with his hurt one, which was still splinted, then winced. She took his arm instead, and he held up his oil lantern as they hurried on. The strata here spiraled, twisting around the floor, ceiling, and walls like the threads of a screw. It was striking enough that Shallan took a Memory of it for later sketching.

Shallan and Adolin finally caught up to the others, passing a group of guards maintaining a perimeter. Though Bridge Four had discovered the body, they'd sent for Kholin reinforcements to secure the area.

They protected a medium-sized chamber now lit by a multitude of oil lamps. Shallan paused in the doorway right before a ledge that surrounded a wide square depression, perhaps four feet deep, cut into the stone floor of the room. The wall strata here continued their curving, twisting medley of oranges, reds, and browns—ballooning out across the sides of this chamber in wide bands before coiling back into narrow stripes to continue down the hall that led out the other side.

The dead man lay at the bottom of the cavity. Shallan steeled herself, but even so found the sight nauseating. He lay on his back, and had been stabbed right through the eye. His face was a bloody mess, his clothing disheveled from what looked to have been an extended fight.

Dalinar and Navani stood on the ledge above the pit. His face was stiff, a stone. She stood with her safehand raised to her lips.

"We found him just like this, Brightlord," said Peet the bridgeman. "We sent for you immediately. Storm me if it doesn't look exactly the same as what happened to Highprince Sadeas."

"He's even lying in the same position," Navani said, grabbing her skirts and descending a set of steps into the lower area. It made up almost the entire room. In fact . . .

Shallan looked toward the upper reaches of the chamber, where several stone sculptures—like the heads of horses—extended from the walls with their mouths open. *Spouts,* she thought. *This was a bathing chamber.*

Navani knelt beside the body, away from the blood running toward a drain on the far side of the basin. "Remarkable . . . the positioning, the puncturing of the eye . . . It's *exactly* like what happened to Sadeas. This has to be the same killer."

Nobody tried to shelter Navani from the sight—as if it were completely proper for the king's mother to be poking at a corpse. Who knew? Maybe in Alethkar, ladies were expected to do this sort of thing. It was still odd to Shallan how temerarious the Alethi were about towing their women into battle to act as scribes, runners, and scouts.

She looked to Adolin to get his read on the situation, and found him staring, aghast, mouth open and eyes wide. "Adolin?" Shallan asked. "Did you know him?"

He didn't seem to hear her. "This is impossible," he muttered. "*Impossible.*"

"Adolin?"

"I . . . No, I didn't know him, Shallan. But I'd assumed . . . I mean, I figured the death of Sadeas was an isolated crime. You know how he was. Probably got himself into trouble. Any number of people could have wanted him dead, right?"

"Looks like it was something more than that," Shallan said, folding her arms as Dalinar walked down the steps to join Navani, trailed by Peet, Lopen, and—remarkably—Rlain of Bridge Four. That one drew attention from the other soldiers, several of whom positioned themselves subtly to protect Dalinar from the Parshendi. They considered him a danger, regardless of which uniform he wore.

"Colot?" Dalinar said, looking toward the lighteyed captain who led the soldiers here. "You're an archer, aren't you? Fifth Battalion?"

"Yes, sir!"

"We have you scouting the tower with Bridge Four?" Dalinar asked.

"The Windrunners needed extra feet, sir, and access to more scouts and scribes for maps. My archers are mobile. Figured it was better than doing parade drills in the cold, so I volunteered my company."

Dalinar grunted. "Fifth Battalion . . . who was your policing force?"

"Eighth Company," Colot said. "Captain Tallan. Good friend of mine. He . . . didn't make it, sir."

"I'm sorry, Captain," Dalinar said. "Would you and your men withdraw for a moment so I can consult with my son? Maintain that perimeter until I tell you otherwise, but do inform King Elhokar of this and send a messenger to Sebarial. I'll visit and tell him about this in person, but he'd best get a warning."

"Yes, sir," the lanky archer said, calling orders. The soldiers left, including the bridgemen. As they moved, Shallan felt something prickle at the back of her neck. She shivered, and couldn't help glancing over her shoulder, hating how this unfathomable building made her feel.

Renarin was standing right behind her. She jumped, letting out a pathetic squeak. Then she blushed furiously; she'd forgotten he was even with them. A few shamespren faded into view around her, floating white and red flower petals. She'd rarely attracted those, which was a wonder. She'd have thought they would take up permanent residence nearby.

"Sorry," Renarin mumbled. "Didn't mean to sneak up on you."

Adolin walked down into the room's basin, still looking distracted. Was he *that* upset by finding a murderer among them? People tried to kill him practically every day. Shallan grabbed the skirt of her havah and followed him down, staying clear of the blood.

"This is troubling," Dalinar said. "We face a terrible threat that would wipe our kind from Roshar like leaves before the stormwall. I don't have time to worry about a murderer slinking through these tunnels." He looked up at Adolin. "Most of the men I'd have assigned to an investigation like this are dead. Niter, Malan . . . the King's Guard is no better, and the bridgemen—for all their fine qualities—have no experience with this sort of thing. I'll need to leave it to you, son."

"*Me?*" Adolin said.

"You did well investigating the incident with the king's saddle, even if that turned out to be something of a wind chase. Aladar is Highprince of Information. Go to him, explain what happened, and set one of his policing teams to investigate. Then work with them as my liaison."

"You want me," Adolin said, "to investigate who killed Sadeas."

Dalinar nodded, squatting down beside the corpse, though Shallan had no idea what he expected to see. The fellow was very dead. "Perhaps if I put my son on the job, it will convince people I'm serious about finding the killer. Perhaps not—they might just think I've put someone in charge who can keep the secret. Storms, I miss Jasnah. She would have known how to spin this, to keep opinion from turning against us in court.

"Either way, son, stay on this. Make sure the remaining highprinces at least know that we consider these murders a priority, and that we are dedicated to finding the one who committed them."

Adolin swallowed. "I understand."

Shallan narrowed her eyes. What had gotten into him? She glanced toward Renarin, who still stood up above, on the walkway around the empty pool. He watched Adolin with unblinking sapphire eyes. He was *always* a little strange, but he seemed to know something she didn't.

On her skirt, Pattern hummed softly.

Dalinar and Navani eventually left to speak with Sebarial. Once they were gone, Shallan seized Adolin by the arm. "What's wrong?" she hissed. "You knew that dead man, didn't you? Do you know who killed him?"

He looked her in the eyes. "I have no idea who did this, Shallan. But I *am* going to find out."

She held his light blue eyes, weighing his gaze. Storms, what was she thinking? Adolin was a wonderful man, but he was about as deceitful as a newborn.

He stalked off, and Shallan hurried after him. Renarin remained in the room, looking down the hall after them until Shallan got far enough away that—over her shoulder—she could no longer see him.

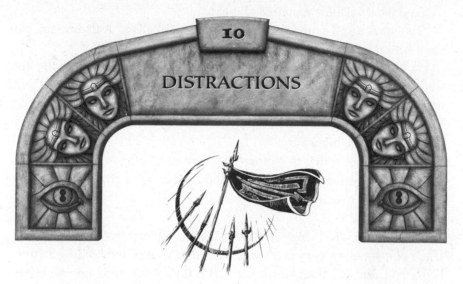

10

DISTRACTIONS

Perhaps my heresy stretches back to those days in my childhood, where these ideas began.

—From *Oathbringer*, preface

Kaladin leaped from a hilltop, preserving Stormlight by Lashing himself upward just enough to give him some lift.

He soared through the rain, angled toward another hilltop. Beneath him, the valley was clogged with vivim trees, which wound their spindly branches together to create an almost impenetrable wall of forestation.

He landed lightly, skidding across the wet stone past rainspren like blue candles. He dismissed his Lashing, and as the force of the ground reasserted itself, he stepped into a quick march. He'd learned to march before learning the spear or shield. Kaladin smiled. He could almost hear Hav's voice barking commands from the back of the line, where he helped stragglers. Hav had always said that once men could march together, learning to fight was easy.

"Smiling?" Syl said. She'd taken the shape of a large raindrop streaking through the air beside him, falling the wrong way. It was a natural shape, but also completely wrong. Plausible impossibility.

"You're right," Kaladin said, rain dribbling down his face. "I should be more solemn. We're chasing down Voidbringers." Storms, how odd it sounded to say that.

"I didn't intend it as a reprimand."

"Hard to tell with you sometimes."

"And what was *that* supposed to mean?"

"Two days ago, I found that my mother is still alive," Kaladin said, "so the position is not, in fact, vacant. You can stop trying to fill it."

He Lashed himself upward slightly, then let himself slide down the wet stone of the steep hill, standing sideways. He passed open rockbuds and wiggling vines, glutted and fat from the constant rainfall. Following the Weeping, they'd often find as many dead plants around the town as they did after a strong highstorm.

"Well, I'm not trying to mother you," Syl said, still a raindrop. Talking to her could be a surreal experience. "Though perhaps I chide you on occasion, when you're being sullen."

He grunted.

"Or when you're being uncommunicative." She transformed into the shape of a young woman in a havah, seated in the air and holding an umbrella as she moved along beside him. "It is my solemn and important duty to bring *happiness, light,* and *joy* into your world when you're being a dour idiot. Which is most of the time. So there."

Kaladin chuckled, holding a little Stormlight as he ran up the side of the next hill, then skidded down into the next valley. This was prime farmland; there was a reason why the Akanny region was prized by Sadeas. It might be a cultural backwater, but these rolling fields probably fed half the kingdom with their lavis and tallew crops. Other villages focused on raising large passels of hogs for leather and meat. Gumfrems, a kind of chull-like beast, were less common pasture animals harvested for their gemhearts, which—though small—allowed Soulcasting of meat.

Syl turned into a ribbon of light and zipped in front of him, making loops. It was difficult not to feel uplifted, even in the gloomy weather. He'd spent the entire sprint to Alethkar worrying—and then assuming—that he'd be too late to save Hearthstone. To find his parents alive . . . well, it was an unexpected blessing. The type his life had been severely lacking.

So he gave in to the urging of the Stormlight. Run. *Leap.* Though he'd spent two days chasing the Voidbringers, Kaladin's exhaustion had faded. There weren't many empty beds to be found in the broken villages he passed, but he had been able to find a roof to keep him dry and something warm to eat.

He'd started at Hearthstone and worked his way outward in a spiral—visiting villages, asking after the local parshmen, then warning people that the terrible storm would return. So far, he hadn't found a single town or village that had been attacked.

Kaladin reached the next hilltop and pulled to a stop. A weathered stone post marked a crossroads. During his youth, he'd never gotten this far from Hearthstone, though he wasn't more than a few days' walk away.

Syl zipped up to him as he shaded his eyes from the rain. The glyphs and simple map on the stone marker would indicate the distance to the next town—but he didn't need that. He could make it out as a smudge in the gloom. A fairly large town, by local standards.

"Come on," he said, starting down the hillside.

"I think," Syl said, landing on his shoulder and becoming a young woman, "I would make a *wonderful* mother."

"And what inspired this topic?"

"You're the one who brought it up."

In comparing Syl to his mother for nagging him? "Are you even capable of having children? Baby spren?"

"I have no idea," Syl proclaimed.

"You call the Stormfather . . . well, Father. Right? So he birthed you?"

"Maybe? I think so? Helped shape me, is more like it. Helped us find our voices." She cocked her head. "Yes. He made some of us. Made me."

"So maybe you could do that," Kaladin said. "Find little, uh, bits of the wind? Or of Honor? Shape them?"

He used a Lashing to leap over a snarl of rockbuds and vines, and startled a pack of cremlings as he landed, sending them scuttling away from a nearly clean mink skeleton. Probably the leavings of a larger predator.

"Hmmm," Syl said. "I *would* be an excellent mother. I'd teach the little spren to fly, to coast the winds, to harass you. . . ."

Kaladin smiled. "You'd get distracted by an interesting beetle and fly off, leaving them in a drawer somewhere."

"Nonsense! Why would I leave my babies in a drawer? Far too boring. A highprince's shoe though . . ."

He flew the remaining distance to the village, and the sight of broken buildings at the western edge dampened his mood. Though the destruction continued to be less than he'd feared, every town or village had lost people to the winds or the terrible lightning.

This village—Hornhollow, the map called it—was in what once would have been considered an ideal location. The land here dipped into a depression, and a hill to the east cut the brunt of the highstorms. It held about two dozen structures, including two large storm sanctuaries where travelers could stay—but there were also many outer buildings. This was the highprince's land, and an industrious darkeyes of high enough nahn could get a commission to work an unused hill out by itself, then keep a portion of the crop.

A few sphere lanterns gave light to the square, where people had gathered for a town meeting. That was convenient. Kaladin dropped toward the lights and held his hand to the side. Syl formed there by unspoken command, taking the shape of a Shardblade: a sleek, beautiful sword with the symbol of the Windrunners prominent on the center, with lines sweeping off it toward the hilt—grooves in the metal that looked like flowing tresses of hair. Though Kaladin preferred a spear, the Blade was a symbol.

Kaladin hit the ground in the center of the village, near its large central cistern, used to catch rainwater and filter away the crem. He rested the Sylblade on his shoulder and stretched out his other hand, preparing his speech. *People of Hornhollow. I am Kaladin, of the Knights Radiant. I have come—*

"Lord Radiant!" A portly lighteyed man stumbled out of the crowd, wearing a long raincloak and a wide-brimmed hat. He looked ridiculous, but it was the Weeping. Constant rain didn't exactly encourage heights of fashion.

The man clapped his hands in an energetic motion, and a pair of ardents stumbled up beside him, bearing goblets full of glowing spheres. Around the perimeter of the square, people hissed and whispered, anticipation-spren flapping in an unseen wind. Several men held up small children to get a better look.

"Great," Kaladin said softly. "I've become a menagerie act."

In his mind, he heard Syl giggle.

Well, best to put on a good show of it. He lifted the Sylblade high over-head, prompting a cheer from the crowd. He would have bet that most of the people in this square used to curse the name of the Radiants, but none of that was manifest now in the people's enthusiasm. It was hard to believe that centuries of mistrust and vilification would be forgotten so quickly. But with the sky breaking and the land in turmoil, people would look to a symbol.

Kaladin lowered his Blade. He knew all too well the danger of symbols. Amaram had been one to him, long ago.

"You knew of my coming," Kaladin said to the citylord and the ardents. "You've been in contact with your neighbors. Have they told you what I've been saying?"

"Yes, Brightlord," the lighteyed man said, gesturing eagerly for him to take the spheres. As he did so—replacing them with spent ones he'd traded for previously—the man's expression fell noticeably.

Expected me to pay two for one as I did at the first few towns, did you? Kaladin thought with amusement. Well, he dropped a few extra dun spheres in. He'd rather be known as generous, particularly if it helped word spread, but he couldn't halve his spheres each time he went through them.

"This is good," Kaladin said, fishing out a few small gemstones. "I can't visit every holding in the area. I need you to send messages to each nearby village, carrying words of comfort and command from the king. I will pay for the time of your runners."

He looked out at the sea of eager faces, and couldn't help but remember a similar day in Hearthstone where he and the rest of the townspeople had waited, eager to catch a glimpse of their new citylord.

"Of course, Brightlord," the lighteyed man said. "Would you wish to rest now, and take a meal? Or would you rather visit the location of the attack immediately?"

"*Attack?*" Kaladin said, feeling a spike of alarm.

"Yes, Brightlord," the portly lighteyes said. "Isn't that why you're here? To see where the rogue parshmen assaulted us?"

Finally! "Take me there. *Now.*"

⁘

They'd attacked a grain storage just outside town. Squashed between two hills and shaped like a dome, it had weathered the Everstorm without so much as a loosed stone. That made it a particular shame that the Voidbringers had ripped open the door and pillaged what was inside.

Kaladin knelt within, flipping over a broken hinge. The building smelled of dust and tallew, but was too wet. Townspeople who would suffer a dozen leaks in their bedroom would go to great expense to keep their grain dry.

It felt odd to not have the rain on his head, though he could still hear it pattering outside.

"May I continue, Brightlord?" the ardent asked him. She was young, pretty, and nervous. Obviously she didn't know where he fit into the scheme of her religion. The Knights Radiant had been founded by the Heralds, but they were also traitors. So . . . he was either a divine being of myth or a cretin one step above a Voidbringer.

"Yes, please," Kaladin said.

"Of the five eyewitnesses," the ardent said, "four, um, independently counted the number of attackers at . . . fifty or so? Anyway, it's safe to say that they've got large numbers, considering how many sacks of grain they were able to carry away in such a short time. They, um, didn't look exactly like parshmen. Too tall, and wearing armor. The sketch I made . . . Um . . ."

She tried showing him her sketch again. It wasn't much better than a child's drawing: a bunch of scribbles in vaguely humanoid shapes.

"Anyway," the young ardent continued, oblivious to the fact that Syl had landed on her shoulder and was inspecting her face. "They attacked right after first moonset. They had the grain out by middle of second moon, um, and we didn't hear anything until the change of guard happened. Sot raised the alarm, and that chased the creatures off. They only left four sacks, which we moved."

Kaladin took a crude wooden cudgel off the table next to the ardent. The ardent glanced at him, then quickly looked back to her paper, blushing. The room, lit by oil lamps, was depressingly hollow. This grain should have gotten the village to the next harvest.

To a man from a farming village, nothing was more distressing than an empty silo at planting time.

"The men who were attacked?" Kaladin said, inspecting the cudgel, which the Voidbringers had dropped while fleeing.

"They've both recovered, Brightlord," the ardent said. "Though Khem has a ringing in his ear he says won't go away."

Fifty parshmen in warform—which was what the descriptions sounded most like to him—could easily have overrun this town and its handful of militia guards. They could have slaughtered everyone and taken whatever they wished; instead, they'd made a surgical raid.

"The red lights," Kaladin said. "Describe them again."

The ardent started; she'd been looking at him. "Um, all five witnesses mentioned the lights, Brightlord. There were several small glowing red lights in the darkness."

"Their eyes."

"Maybe?" the ardent said. "If those were eyes, it was only a few. I went and asked, and none of the witnesses specifically saw eyes glowing—and Khem got a look right in one of the parshmen's faces as they struck him."

Kaladin dropped the cudgel and dusted off his palms. He took the sheet with the picture on it out of the young ardent's hands and inspected it, just for show, then nodded to her. "You did well. Thank you for the report."

She sighed, grinning stupidly.

"Oh!" Syl said, still on the ardent's shoulder. "She thinks you're pretty!"

Kaladin drew his lips to a line. He nodded to the woman and left her, striking back into the rain toward the center of town.

Syl zipped up to his shoulder. "Wow. She must be *desperate* living out here. I mean, look at you. Hair that hasn't been combed since you flew across the continent, uniform stained with crem, and that *beard*."

"Thank you for the boost of confidence."

"I guess when there's nobody about but farmers, your standards really drop."

"She's an ardent," Kaladin said. "She'd have to marry another ardent."

"I don't think she was thinking about marriage, Kaladin . . ." Syl said, turning and looking backward over her shoulder. "I know you've been busy lately fighting guys in white clothing and stuff, but *I've* been doing research. People lock their doors, but there's plenty of room to get in underneath. I figured, since you don't seem inclined to do any learning yourself, I should study. So if you have questions . . ."

"I'm well aware of what is involved."

"You sure?" Syl asked. "Maybe we could have that ardent draw you a picture. She seems like she'd be really eager."

"Syl . . ."

"I just want you to be happy, Kaladin," she said, zipping off his shoulder and running a few rings around him as a ribbon of light. "People in relationships are happier."

"That," Kaladin said, "is demonstrably false. Some might be. I know a lot who aren't."

"Come on," Syl said. "What about that Lightweaver? You seemed to like her."

The words struck uncomfortably close to the truth. "Shallan is engaged to Dalinar's son."

"So? You're better than him. I don't trust him one bit."

"You don't trust anyone who carries a Shardblade, Syl," Kaladin said with a sigh. "We've been over this. It's not a mark of bad character to have bonded one of the weapons."

"Yes, well, let's have someone swing around the corpse of *your* sisters by the feet, and we'll see whether you consider it a 'mark of bad character' or not. This is a distraction. Like that Lightweaver could be for you . . ."

"Shallan's a lighteyes," Kaladin said. "That's the end of the conversation."

"But—"

"End," he said, stepping into the home of the village lighteyes. Then he added under his breath, "And stop spying on people when they're being intimate. It's creepy."

The way she spoke, she expected to be *there* when Kaladin . . . Well, he'd never considered that before, though she went with him everywhere else. Could he convince her to wait outside? She'd still listen, if not sneak in to watch. Stormfather. His life just kept getting stranger. He tried—unsuccessfully—to banish the image of lying in bed with a woman, Syl sitting on the headboard and shouting out encouragement and advice. . . .

"Lord Radiant?" the citylord asked from inside the front room of the small home. "Are you well?"

"Painful memory," Kaladin said. "Your scouts are certain of the direction the parshmen went?"

The citylord looked over his shoulder at a scraggly man in leathers, bow on his back, standing by the boarded-up window. Trapper, with a writ from the local highlord to catch mink on his lands. "Followed them half a day out, Brightlord. They never deviated. Straight toward Kholinar, I'd swear to Kelek himself."

"Then that's where I'm going as well," Kaladin said.

"You want me to lead you, Brightlord Radiant?" the trapper asked.

Kaladin drew in Stormlight. "Afraid you'd just slow me down." He nodded to the men, then stepped out and Lashed himself upward. People clogged the road and cheered from rooftops as he left the town behind.

<hr />

The scents of horses reminded Adolin of his youth. Sweat, and manure, and hay. Good scents. *Real* scents.

He'd spent many of those days, before he was fully a man, on campaign with his father during border skirmishes with Jah Keved. Adolin had been afraid of horses back then, though he'd never have admitted it. So much faster, more intelligent, than chulls.

So alien. Creatures all covered in hair—which made him shiver to touch—with big glassy eyes. And those hadn't even been *real* horses. For all their pedigree breeding, the horses they'd rode on campaign had just been ordinary Shin Thoroughbreds. Expensive, yes. But by definition, therefore, not *priceless*.

Not like the creature before him now.

They were housing the Kholin livestock in the far northwest section of the tower, on the ground floor, near where winds from outside blew along the mountains. Some clever constructions in the hallways by the royal engineers had ventilated the scents away from the inner corridors, though that left the region quite chilly.

Gumfrems and hogs clogged some rooms, while conventional horses stabled in others. Several even contained Bashin's axehounds, animals who never got to go on hunts anymore.

Such accommodations weren't good enough for the Blackthorn's horse. No, the massive black Ryshadium stallion had been given his own field. Large enough to serve as a pasture, it was open to the sky and in an enviable spot, if you discounted the scents of the other animals.

As Adolin emerged from the tower, the black monster of a horse came galloping over. Big enough to carry a Shardbearer without looking small, Ryshadium were often called the "third Shard." Blade, Plate, and Mount.

That didn't do them justice. You couldn't earn a Ryshadium simply by defeating someone in combat. They chose their riders.

But, Adolin thought as Gallant nuzzled his hand, *I suppose that was how it used to be with Blades too. They were spren who chose their bearers.*

"Hey," Adolin said, scratching the Ryshadium's snout with his left hand. "A little lonely out here, isn't it? I'm sorry about that. Wish you weren't alone any—" He cut off as his voice caught in his throat.

Gallant stepped closer, towering over him, but somehow still gentle. The horse nuzzled Adolin's neck, then blew out sharply.

"Ugh," Adolin said, turning the horse's head. "*That's* a scent I could do without." He patted Gallant's neck, then reached with his right hand into his shoulder pack—before a sharp pain from his wrist reminded him yet again of his wound. He reached in with the other hand and took out some sugar lumps, which Gallant consumed eagerly.

"You're as bad as Aunt Navani," Adolin noted. "That's why you came running, isn't it? You smelled treats."

The horse turned his head, looking at Adolin with one watery blue eye, rectangular pupil at the center. He almost seemed . . . offended.

Adolin often had felt he could read his own Ryshadium's emotions. There had been a . . . bond between him and Sureblood. More delicate and indefinable than the bond between man and sword, but still there.

Of course, Adolin *was* the one who talked to his sword sometimes, so he had a habit of this sort of thing.

"I'm sorry," Adolin said. "I know the two of you liked to run together. And . . . I don't know if Father will be able to get down as much to see you. He'd already been withdrawing from battle before he got all these new responsibilities. I thought I'd stop by once in a while."

The horse snorted loudly.

"Not to *ride* you," Adolin said, reading indignation in the Ryshadium's motions. "I just thought it might be nice for both of us."

The horse poked his snout at Adolin's satchel until he dug out another sugar cube. It seemed like agreement to Adolin, who fed the horse, then leaned back against the wall and watched him gallop through the pasture.

Showing off, Adolin thought with amusement as Gallant pranced past him. Maybe Gallant would let him brush his coat. That would feel good, like the evenings he'd spent with Sureblood in the dark calm of the stables. At least, that was what he'd done before everything had gotten busy, with Shallan and the duels and everything else.

He'd ignored the horse right up until he'd needed Sureblood in battle. And then, in a flash of light, he was gone.

Adolin took a deep breath. Everything seemed insane these days. Not just Sureblood, but what he'd done to Sadeas, and now the investigation . . .

Watching Gallant seemed to help a little. Adolin was still there, leaning against the wall, when Renarin arrived. The younger Kholin poked his head through the doorway, looking around. He didn't shy away when Gallant galloped past, but he did regard the stallion with wariness.

"Hey," Adolin said from the side.

"Hey. Bashin said you were down here."

"Just checking on Gallant," Adolin said. "Because Father's been so busy lately."

Renarin approached. "You could ask Shallan to draw Sureblood," Renarin said. "I bet, um, she'd be able to do a good job. To remember."

It wasn't a bad suggestion, actually. "Were you looking for me, then?"

"I . . ." Renarin watched Gallant as the horse pranced by again. "He's excited."

"He likes an audience."

"They don't fit, you know."

"Don't fit?"

"Ryshadium have stone hooves," Renarin said, "stronger than ordinary horses'. Never need to be shod."

"And that makes them not fit? I'd say that makes them fit better. . . ." Adolin eyed Renarin. "You mean ordinary horses, don't you?"

Renarin blushed, then nodded. People had trouble following him sometimes, but that was merely because he tended to be so thoughtful. He'd be thinking about something deep, something brilliant, and then would only mention a part. It made him seem erratic, but once you got to know him, you realized he wasn't trying to be esoteric. His lips just sometimes failed to keep up with his brain.

"Adolin," he said softly. "I . . . um . . . I have to give you back the Shardblade you won for me."

"Why?" Adolin said.

"It hurts to hold," Renarin said. "It always has, to be honest. I thought it was just me, being strange. But it's all of us."

"Radiants, you mean."

He nodded. "We can't use the dead Blades. It's not right."

"Well, I suppose I could find someone else to use it," Adolin said, running through options. "Though you should really be the one to choose. By right of bestowal, the Blade is yours, and you should pick the successor."

"I'd rather you do it. I've given it to the ardents already, for safekeeping."

"Which means you'll be unarmed," Adolin said.

Renarin glanced away.

"Or not," Adolin said, then poked Renarin in the shoulder. "You've got a replacement already, don't you."

Renarin blushed again.

"You mink!" Adolin said. "You've managed to create a Radiant Blade? Why didn't you tell us?"

"It just happened. Glys wasn't certain he could do it . . . but we need more people to work the Oathgate . . . so . . ."

He took a deep breath, then stretched his hand to the side and summoned a long glowing Shardblade. Thin, with almost no crossguard, it had waving folds to the metal, like it had been forged.

"Gorgeous," Adolin said. "Renarin, it's fantastic!"

"Thanks."

"So why are you embarrassed?"

"I'm . . . not?"

Adolin gave him a flat stare.

Renarin dismissed the Blade. "I simply . . . Adolin, I was starting to *fit in*. With Bridge Four, with being a Shardbearer. Now, I'm in the darkness again. Father expects me to be a Radiant, so I can help him unite the world. But how am I supposed to learn?"

Adolin scratched his chin with his good hand. "Huh. I assumed that it just kind of came to you. It hasn't?"

"Some has. But it . . . frightens me, Adolin." He held up his hand, and it started to glow, wisps of Stormlight trailing off it, like smoke from a fire. "What if I hurt someone, or ruin things?"

"You're not going to," Adolin said. "Renarin, that's the power of the Almighty himself."

Renarin only stared at that glowing hand, and didn't seem convinced. So Adolin reached out with his good hand and took Renarin's, holding it.

"This is good," Adolin said to him. "You're not going to hurt anyone. You're here to save us."

Renarin looked to him, then smiled. A pulse of Radiance washed through Adolin, and for an instant he saw himself *perfected*. A version of himself that was somehow complete and whole, the man he could be.

It was gone in a moment, and Renarin pulled his hand free and murmured an apology. He mentioned again the Shardblade needing to be given away, then fled back into the tower.

Adolin stared after him. Gallant trotted up and nudged him for more sugar, so he reached absently into his satchel and fed the horse.

Only after Gallant trotted off did Adolin realize he'd used his right hand. He held it up, amazed, moving his fingers.

His wrist had been completely healed.

11

THE RIFT

THIRTY-THREE YEARS AGO

Dalinar danced from one foot to the other in the morning mist, feeling a new power, an *energy* in every step. Shardplate. His *own* Shardplate.

The world would never be the same place. They'd all expected he would someday have his own Plate or Blade, but he'd never been able to quiet the whisper of uncertainty from the back of his mind. What if it never happened?

But it had. Stormfather, it *had*. He'd won it himself, in combat. Yes, that combat had involved kicking a man off a cliff, but he'd defeated a Shardbearer regardless.

He couldn't help but bask in how grand it felt.

"Calm, Dalinar," Sadeas said from beside him in the mist. Sadeas wore his own golden Plate. "Patience."

"It won't do any good, Sadeas," Gavilar—clad in bright blue Plate— said from Dalinar's other side. All three of them wore their faceplates up for the moment. "The Kholin boys are chained axehounds, and we smell blood. We can't go into battle breathing calming breaths, centered and serene, as the ardents teach."

Dalinar shifted, feeling the cold morning fog on his face. He wanted to dance with the anticipationspren whipping in the air around him. Behind, the army waited in disciplined ranks, their footsteps, clinkings, coughs, and murmured banter rising through the fog.

He almost felt as if he didn't need that army. He wore a massive hammer on his back, so heavy an unaided man—even the strongest of them— wouldn't be able to lift it. He barely noticed the weight. Storms, this *power*. It felt remarkably like the Thrill.

"Have you given thought to my suggestion, Dalinar?" Sadeas asked.

"No."

Sadeas sighed.

"If Gavilar commands me," Dalinar said, "I'll marry."

"Don't bring me into this," Gavilar said. He summoned and dismissed his Shardblade repeatedly as they talked.

"Well," Dalinar said, "until you say something, I'm staying single." The only woman he'd ever wanted belonged to Gavilar. They'd married—storms, they had a child now. A little girl.

His brother must never know how Dalinar felt.

"But think of the *benefit*, Dalinar," Sadeas said. "Your wedding could bring us alliances, Shards. Perhaps you could win us a princedom—one we wouldn't have to storming drive to the brink of collapse before they join us!"

After two years of fighting, only four of the ten princedoms had accepted Gavilar's rule—and two of those, Kholin and Sadeas, had been easy. The result was a united Alethkar: *against* House Kholin.

Gavilar was convinced that he could play them off one another, that their natural selfishness would lead them to stab one another in the back. Sadeas, in turn, pushed Gavilar toward greater brutality. He claimed that the fiercer their reputation, the more cities would turn to them willingly rather than risk being pillaged.

"Well?" Sadeas asked. "Will you at least consider a union of political necessity?"

"Storms, you still on that?" Dalinar said. "Let me fight. You and my brother can worry about politics."

"You can't escape this forever, Dalinar. You realize that, right? We'll have to worry about feeding the darkeyes, about city infrastructure, about ties with other kingdoms. *Politics.*"

"You and Gavilar," Dalinar said.

"All of us," Sadeas said. "All three."

"Weren't you trying to get me to relax?" Dalinar snapped. Storms.

The rising sun finally started to disperse the fog, and that let him see their target: a wall about twelve feet high. Beyond that, nothing. A flat rocky expanse, or so it appeared. The chasm city was difficult to spot from this direction. Named Rathalas, it was also known as the Rift: an entire city that had been built inside a rip in the ground.

"Brightlord Tanalan is a Shardbearer, right?" Dalinar asked.

Sadeas sighed, lowering his faceplate. "We only went over this *four* times, Dalinar."

"I was drunk. Tanalan. Shardbearer?"

"Blade only, Brother," Gavilar said.

"He's mine," Dalinar whispered.

Gavilar laughed. "Only if you find him first! I've half a mind to give that Blade to Sadeas. At least *he* listens in our meetings."

"All right," Sadeas said. "Let's do this carefully. Remember the plan. Gavilar, you—"

Gavilar gave Dalinar a grin, slammed his faceplate down, then took off running to leave Sadeas midsentence. Dalinar whooped and joined him, Plated boots grinding against stone.

Sadeas cursed loudly, then followed. The army remained behind for the moment.

Rocks started falling; catapults from behind the wall hurled solitary boulders or sprays of smaller rocks. Chunks slammed down around Dalinar, shaking the ground, causing rockbud vines to curl up. A boulder struck just ahead, then bounced, spraying chips of stone. Dalinar skidded past it, the Plate lending a spring to his motion. He raised his arm before his eye slit as a hail of arrows darkened the sky.

"Watch the ballistas!" Gavilar shouted.

Atop the wall, soldiers aimed massive crossbowlike devices mounted to the stone. One sleek bolt—the size of a spear—launched directly at Dalinar, and it proved far more accurate than the catapults. He threw himself to the side, Plate grinding on stone as he slid out of the way. The bolt hit the ground with such force that the wood shattered.

Other shafts trailed netting and ropes, hoping to trip a Shardbearer and render him prone for a second shot. Dalinar grinned, feeling the Thrill awaken within him, and recovered his feet. He leaped over a bolt trailing netting.

Tanalan's men delivered a storm of wood and stone, but it wasn't nearly enough. Dalinar took a stone in the shoulder and lurched, but quickly regained his momentum. Arrows were useless against him, the boulders too random, and the ballistas too slow to reload.

This was how it should be. Dalinar, Gavilar, Sadeas. Together. Other responsibilities didn't matter. Life was about the *fight*. A good battle in the day—then at night, a warm hearth, tired muscles, and a good vintage of wine.

Dalinar reached the squat wall and *leaped*, propelling himself in a mighty jump. He gained just enough height to grab one of the crenels of the wall's top. Men raised hammers to pound his fingers, but he hurled himself over the lip and onto the wall walk, crashing down amid panicked defenders. He jerked the release rope on his hammer—dropping it on an enemy behind—then swung out with his fist, sending men broken and screaming.

This was almost too easy! He seized his hammer, then brought it up and swung it in a wide arc, tossing men from the wall like leaves before a gust of wind. Just beyond him, Sadeas kicked over a ballista, destroying the device with a casual blow. Gavilar attacked with his Blade, dropping corpses by the handful, their eyes burning. Up here, the fortification worked against the defenders, leaving them cramped and clumped up—perfect for Shard-bearers to destroy.

Dalinar surged through them, and in a few moments likely killed more men than he had in his entire life. At that, he felt a surprising yet profound dissatisfaction. This was not about his skill, his momentum, or even his reputation. You could have replaced him with a toothless gaffer and pro-duced practically the same result.

He gritted his teeth against that sudden useless emotion. He dug deeply within, and found the Thrill waiting. It filled him, driving away dissatis-faction. Within moments he was roaring his pleasure. Nothing these men did could touch him. He was a destroyer, a conqueror, a glorious maelstrom of death. A *god*.

Sadeas was saying something. The silly man gestured in his golden Shardplate. Dalinar blinked, looking out over the wall. He could see the Rift proper from this vantage, a deep chasm in the ground that hid an entire city, built up the sides of either cliff.

"Catapults, Dalinar!" Sadeas said. "Bring down those catapults!"

Right. Gavilar's armies had started to charge the walls. Those catapults—near the way down into the Rift proper—were still launching stones, and would drop hundreds of men.

Dalinar leaped for the edge of the wall and grabbed a rope ladder to swing down. The ropes, of course, immediately snapped, sending him top-pling to the ground. He struck with a crash of Plate on stone. It didn't hurt, but his pride took a serious blow. Above, Sadeas looked at him over the edge. Dalinar could practically hear his voice.

Always rushing into things. Take some time to think once in a while, won't you?

That had been a flat-out greenvine mistake. Dalinar growled and climbed to his feet, searching for his hammer. Storms! He'd bent the handle in his fall. How had he done *that*? It wasn't made of the same strange metal as Blades and Plate, but it was still good steel.

Soldiers guarding the catapults swarmed toward him while the shadows of boulders passed overhead. Dalinar set his jaw, the Thrill saturating him, and reached for a stout wooden door set into the wall nearby. He ripped it free, the hinges popping, and stumbled. It came off more easily than he'd expected.

There was more to this armor than he'd ever imagined. Maybe he wasn't any better with the Plate than some old gaffer, but he would change that. At that moment, he determined that he'd never be surprised again. He'd wear this Plate morning and night—he'd *sleep* in the storming stuff—until he was more comfortable in it than out.

He raised the wooden door and swung it like a bludgeon, sweeping soldiers away and opening a path to the catapults. Then he dashed forward and grabbed the side of one catapult. He ripped its wheel off, splintering wood and sending the machine teetering. He stepped onto it, grabbing the catapult's arm and breaking it free.

Only ten more to go. He stood atop the wrecked machine when he heard a distant voice call his name. "Dalinar!"

He looked toward the wall, where Sadeas reached back and heaved his Shardbearer's hammer. It spun in the air before slamming into the catapult next to Dalinar, wedging itself into the broken wood.

Sadeas raised a hand in salute, and Dalinar waved back in gratitude, then grabbed the hammer. The destruction went a lot faster after that. He pounded the machines, leaving behind shattered wood. Engineers—many of them women—scrambled away, screaming, "Blackthorn, Blackthorn!"

By the time he neared the last catapult, Gavilar had secured the gates and opened them to his soldiers. A flood of men entered, joining those who had scaled the walls. The last of the enemies near Dalinar fled down into the city, leaving him alone. He grunted and kicked the final broken catapult, sending it rolling backward across the stone toward the edge of the Rift.

It tipped, then fell over. Dalinar stepped forward, walking onto a kind of observation post, a section of rock with a railing to prevent people from slipping over the side. From this vantage, he got his first good look down at the city.

"The Rift" was a fitting name. To his right, the chasm narrowed, but here at the middle he'd have been hard-pressed to throw a stone across to the other side, even with Shardplate. And within it, there was life. Gardens bobbing with lifespren. Buildings built practically on top of one another down the V-shaped cliff sides. The place teemed with a network of stilts, bridges, and wooden walkways.

Dalinar turned and looked back at the wall that ran in a wide circle around the opening of the Rift on all sides except the west, where the canyon continued until it opened up below at the shores of the lake.

To survive in Alethkar, you had to find shelter from the storms. A wide cleft like this one was perfect for a city. But how did you protect it? Any attacking enemy would have the high ground. Many cities walked a risky line between security from storms and security from men.

Dalinar shouldered Sadeas's hammer as groups of Tanalan's soldiers flooded down from the walls, forming up to flank Gavilar's army on both right and left. They'd try to press against the Kholin troops from both sides, but with three Shardbearers to face, they were in trouble. Where was Highlord Tanalan himself?

Behind, Thakka approached with a small squad of elites, joining Dalinar on the stone viewing platform. Thakka put his hands on the railing, whistling softly.

"Something's going on with this city," Dalinar said.

"What?"

"I don't know. . . ." Dalinar might not pay attention to the grand plans Gavilar and Sadeas made, but he was a soldier. He knew battlefields like a woman knew her mother's recipes: he might not be able to give you measurements, but he could taste when something was off.

The fighting continued behind him, Kholin soldiers clashing with Tanalan's defenders. Tanalan's armies didn't fare well; demoralized by the advancing Kholin army, the enemy ranks quickly broke and scrambled into a retreat, clogging the ramps down into the city. Gavilar and Sadeas didn't give chase; they had the high ground now. No need to rush into a potential ambush.

Gavilar clomped across the stone, Sadeas beside him. They'd want to survey the city and rain arrows upon those below—maybe even use stolen catapults, if Dalinar had left any functional. They'd siege this place until it broke.

Three Shardbearers, Dalinar thought. *Tanalan has to be planning to deal with us somehow. . . .*

This viewing platform was the best vantage for looking into the city. And they'd situated the catapults right next to it—machines that the Shardbearers were certain to attack and disable. Dalinar glanced to the sides, and saw cracks in the stone floor of the viewing platform.

"No!" Dalinar shouted to Gavilar. "Stay back! It's a—"

The enemy must have been watching, for the moment he shouted, the ground fell out from beneath him. Dalinar caught a glimpse of Gavilar—held back by Sadeas—looking on in horror as Dalinar, Thakka, and a handful of other elites were toppled into the Rift.

Storms. The entire section of stone where they'd been standing—the lip hanging out over the Rift—had broken free! As the large section of rock tumbled down into the first buildings, Dalinar was flung into the air above the city. Everything spun around him.

A moment later, he crashed into a building with an awful *crunch.* Something hard hit his arm, an impact so powerful he heard his armor there shatter.

The building failed to stop him. He tore right through the wood and continued, helm grinding against stone as he somehow came in contact with the side of the Rift.

He hit another surface with a loud crunch, and blessedly here he finally stopped. He groaned, feeling a sharp pain from his left hand. He shook his head, and found himself staring upward some fifty feet through a shattered section of the near-vertical wooden city. The large section of falling rock had torn a swath through the city along the steep incline, smashing homes and walkways. Dalinar had been flung just to the north, and had eventually come to rest on the wooden roof of a building.

He didn't see signs of his men. Thakka, the other elites. But without Shardplate . . . He growled, angerspren boiling around him like pools of blood. He shifted on the rooftop, but the pain in his hand made him wince. His armor all down his left arm had shattered, and in falling he appeared to have broken a few fingers.

His Shardplate leaked glowing white smoke from a hundred fractures, but the only pieces he'd lost completely were from his left arm and hand.

He gingerly pried himself from the rooftop, but as he shifted, he broke through and fell into the home. He grunted as he hit, members of a family screaming and pulling back against the wall. Tanalan apparently hadn't told the people of his plan to crush a section of his own city in a desperate attempt to deal with the enemy Shardbearers.

Dalinar got to his feet, ignoring the cowering people, and shoved open the door—breaking it with the strength of his push—and stepped out onto a wooden walkway that ran before the homes on this tier of the city.

A hail of arrows immediately fell on him. He turned his right shoulder toward them, growling, shielding his eye slit as best he could while he inspected the source of the attack. Fifty archers were set up on a garden platform on the other storming side of the Rift from him. Wonderful.

He recognized the man leading the archers. Tall, with an imperious bearing and stark white plumes on his helm. Who put chicken feathers on their helms? Looked ridiculous. Well, Tanalan was a fine enough fellow. Dalinar had beat him once at pawns, and Tanalan had paid the bet with a hundred glowing bits of ruby, each dropped into a corked bottle of wine. Dalinar had always found that amusing.

Reveling in the Thrill, which rose in him and drove away pain, Dalinar charged along the walkway, ignoring arrows. Above, Sadeas was leading a force down one of the ramps outside the path of the rockfall, but it would be slow going. By the time they arrived, Dalinar intended to have a new Shardblade.

He charged onto one of the bridges that crossed the Rift. Unfortunately, he knew exactly what *he* would do if preparing this city for an assault. Sure enough, a pair of soldiers hurried down the other side of the Rift, then used axes to attack the support posts to Dalinar's bridge. It had Soulcast metal ropes holding it up, but if they could get those posts down—dropping the lines—his weight would surely cause the entire thing to fall.

The bottom wash of the Rift was easily another hundred feet below. Growling, Dalinar made the only choice he could. He threw himself over the side of his walkway, dropping a short distance to one below. It looked sturdy enough. Even so, one foot smashed through the wooden planks, nearly followed by his entire body.

He heaved himself up and continued running across. Two more soldiers reached the posts holding up this bridge, and they began frantically hacking away.

The walkway shook beneath Dalinar's feet. Stormfather. He didn't have much time, but there were no more walkways within jumping distance. Dalinar pushed himself to a run, roaring, his footfalls cracking boards.

A single black arrow fell from above, swooping like a skyeel. It dropped one of the soldiers. Another arrow followed, hitting the second soldier even as he gawked at his fallen ally. The walkway stopped shaking, and Dalinar grinned, pulling to a stop. He turned, spotting a man standing near the sheared-off section of stone above. He lifted a black bow toward Dalinar.

"Teleb, you storming miracle," Dalinar said.

He reached the other side and plucked an axe from the hands of a dead man. Then he charged up a ramp toward where he'd seen Highlord Tanalan.

He found the place easily, a wide wooden platform built on struts connected to parts of the wall below, and draped with vines and blooming rockbuds. Lifespren scattered as Dalinar reached it.

Centered in the garden, Tanalan waited with a force of some fifty soldiers. Puffing inside his helm, Dalinar stepped up to confront them. Tanalan was armored in simple steel, no Shardplate, though a brutal-looking Shardblade—wide, with a hooked tip—appeared in his grasp.

Tanalan barked for his soldiers to stand back and lower their bows. Then he strode toward Dalinar, holding the Shardblade with both hands.

Everyone always fixated upon Shardblades. Specific weapons had lore dedicated to them, and people traced which kings or brightlords had carried which sword. Well, Dalinar had used both Blade and Plate, and if given the choice of one, he'd pick Plate every time. All he needed to do was get in one solid hit on Tanalan, and the fight would be over. The highlord, however, had to contend with a foe who could resist his blows.

The Thrill thrummed inside Dalinar. Standing between two squat trees, he set his stance, keeping his exposed left arm pointed away from the highlord while gripping the axe in his gauntleted right hand. Though it was a war axe, it felt like a child's plaything.

"You should not have come here, Dalinar," Tanalan said. His voice bore a distinctively nasal accent common to this region. The Rifters always had considered themselves a people apart. "We had no quarrel with you or yours."

"You refused to submit to the king," Dalinar said, armor plates clinking as he rounded the highlord while trying to keep an eye on the soldiers. He wouldn't put it past them to attack him once he was distracted by the duel. It was what he himself would have done.

"The king?" Tanalan demanded, angerspren boiling up around him. "There hasn't been a throne in Alethkar for generations. Even if we *were* to have a king again, who is to say the Kholins deserve the mantle?"

"The way I see it," Dalinar said, "the people of Alethkar deserve a king who is the strongest and most capable of leading them in battle. If only there were a way to prove that." He grinned inside his helm.

Tanalan attacked, sweeping in with his Shardblade and trying to leverage his superior reach. Dalinar danced back, waiting for his moment. The Thrill was a heady rush, a lust to prove himself.

But he needed to be cautious. Ideally Dalinar would prolong this fight, relying on his Plate's superior strength and the stamina it provided. Unfortunately, that Plate was still leaking, and he had all these guards to deal with. Still, he tried to play it as Tanalan would expect, dodging attacks, acting as if he were going to drag out the fight.

Tanalan growled and came in again. Dalinar blocked the blow with his arm, then made a perfunctory swing with his axe. Tanalan dodged back easily. Stormfather, that Blade was long. Almost as tall as Dalinar was.

Dalinar maneuvered, brushing against the foliage of the garden. He couldn't even feel the pain of his broken fingers anymore. The Thrill called to him.

Wait. Act like you're drawing this out as long as possible. . . .

Tanalan advanced again, and Dalinar dodged backward, faster because of his Plate. And then when Tanalan tried his next strike, Dalinar ducked *toward him.*

He deflected the Shardblade with his arm again, but this blow hit hard, shattering the arm plate. Still, Dalinar's surprise rush let him lower his shoulder and slam it against Tanalan. The highlord's armor *clanged*, bending before the force of the Shardplate, and the highlord tripped.

Unfortunately, Dalinar was off balance just enough from his rush to fall alongside the highlord. The platform shook as they hit the ground, the wood cracking and groaning. Damnation! Dalinar had *not* wanted to go to the ground while surrounded by foes. Still, he had to stay inside the reach of that Blade.

Dalinar dropped off his right gauntlet—without the arm piece connecting it to the rest of the armor, it was dead weight—as the two of them twisted in a heap. He'd lost the axe, unfortunately. The highlord battered against Dalinar with the pommel of his sword, to no effect. But with one hand broken and the other lacking the power of Plate, Dalinar couldn't get a good hold on his foe.

Dalinar rolled, finally positioning himself above Tanalan, where the weight of the Shardplate would keep his foe pinned. At that moment though, the other soldiers attacked. Just as he'd expected. Honorable duels like this—on a battlefield at least—always lasted only until your lighteyes was losing.

Dalinar rolled free. The soldiers obviously weren't ready for how quickly he responded. He got to his feet and scooped up his axe, then lashed out. His right arm still had the pauldron and down to the elbow brace, so when he swung, he had *power*—a strange mix of Shard-enhanced strength and frailty from his exposed arms. He had to be careful not to snap his own wrist.

He dropped three men with a flurry of axe slices. The others backed away, blocking him with polearms as their fellows helped Tanalan to his feet.

"You speak of the people," Tanalan said hoarsely, gauntleted hand feeling at his chest where the cuirass had been bent significantly by Dalinar's rush. He seemed to be having trouble breathing. "As if this were about *them*. As if it were for their good that you loot, you pillage, you *murder*. You're an uncivilized brute."

"You can't civilize war," Dalinar said. "There's no painting it up and making it pretty."

"You don't have to pull sorrow behind you like a sledge on the stones, scraping and crushing those you pass. You're a *monster*."

"I'm a soldier," Dalinar said, eyeing Tanalan's men, many of whom were preparing their bows.

Tanalan coughed. "My city is lost. My plan has failed. But I can do Alethkar one last service. I can take you down, you bastard."

The archers started to loose.

Dalinar roared and threw himself to the ground, hitting the platform with the weight of Shardplate. The wood cracked around him, weakened by the fighting earlier, and he broke through it, shattering struts underneath.

The entire platform came crashing down around him, and together they fell toward the tier below. Dalinar heard screams, and he hit the next walkway hard enough to daze him, even with Shardplate.

Dalinar shook his head, groaning, and found his helm cracked right down the front, the uncommon vision granted by the armor spoiled. He pulled the helm free with one hand and gasped for breath. Storms, his good arm hurt too. He glanced at it and found splinters piercing his skin, including one chunk as long as a dagger.

He grimaced. Below, the few remaining soldiers who had been positioned to cut down bridges came charging up toward him.

Steady, Dalinar. Be ready!

He got to his feet, dazed, exhausted, but the two soldiers didn't come for him. They huddled around Tanalan's body where it had fallen from the platform above. The soldiers grabbed him, then fled.

Dalinar roared and awkwardly gave pursuit. His Plate moved slowly, and he stumbled through the wreckage of the fallen platform, trying to keep up with the soldiers.

The pain from his arms made him mad with rage. But the Thrill, the *Thrill* drove him forward. He would not be beaten. He would not stop! Tanalan's Shardblade had not appeared beside his body. That meant his foe still lived. Dalinar had *not yet won*.

Fortunately, most of the soldiers had been positioned to fight on the other side of the city. This side was practically empty, save for huddled townspeople—he caught glimpses of them hiding in their homes.

Dalinar limped up ramps along the side of the Rift, following the men dragging their brightlord. Near the top, the two soldiers set their burden down beside an exposed portion of the chasm's rock wall. They did something that caused a portion of that wall to open inward, revealing a hidden door. They towed their fallen brightlord into it, and two other soldiers—responding to their frantic calls—rushed out to meet Dalinar, who arrived moments later.

Helmless, Dalinar saw red as he engaged them. They bore weapons; he did not. They were fresh, and he had wounds nearly incapacitating both arms.

The fight still ended with the two soldiers on the ground, broken and bleeding. Dalinar kicked open the hidden door, Plated legs functioning enough to smash it down.

He lurched into a small tunnel with diamond spheres glowing on the walls. That door was covered in hardened crem on the outside, making it seem like a part of the wall. If he hadn't seen them enter, it would have taken days, maybe weeks to locate this place.

At the end of a short walk, he found the two soldiers he'd followed. Judging by the blood trail, they'd deposited their brightlord in the closed room behind them.

They rushed Dalinar with the fatalistic determination of men who knew they were probably dead. The pain in Dalinar's arms and head seemed nothing before the Thrill. He had rarely felt it so strong as he did now, a beautiful clarity, such a *wonderful* emotion.

He ducked forward, supernaturally quick, and used his shoulder to crush one soldier against the wall. The other fell to a well-placed kick, then Dalinar burst through the door beyond them.

Tanalan lay on the ground here, blood surrounding him. A beautiful woman was draped across him, weeping. Only one other person was in the small chamber: a young boy. Six, perhaps seven. Tears streaked the child's face, and he struggled to lift his father's Shardblade in two hands.

Dalinar loomed in the doorway.

"You can't have my daddy," the boy said, words distorted by his sorrow. Painspren crawled around the floor. "You *can't*. You . . . you . . ." His voice fell to a whisper. "Daddy said . . . we fight monsters. And with faith, we will win. . . ."

⁙

A few hours later, Dalinar sat on the edge of the Rift, his legs swinging over the broken city below. His new Shardblade rested across his lap, his Plate—deformed and broken—in a heap beside him. His arms were bandaged, but he'd chased away the surgeons.

He stared out at what seemed an empty plain, then flicked his eyes toward the signs of human life below. Dead bodies in heaps. Broken buildings. Splinters of civilization.

Gavilar eventually walked up, trailed by two bodyguards from Dalinar's elites, Kadash and Febin today. Gavilar waved them back, then groaned as he settled down beside Dalinar, removing his helm. Exhaustionspren spun overhead, though—despite his fatigue—Gavilar looked thoughtful. With those keen, pale green eyes, he'd always seemed to know so much. Growing up, Dalinar had simply assumed that his brother would always be right in whatever he said or did. Aging hadn't much changed his opinion of the man.

"Congratulations," Gavilar said, nodding toward the Blade. "Sadeas is irate it wasn't his."

"He'll find one of his own eventually," Dalinar said. "He's too ambitious for me to believe otherwise."

Gavilar grunted. "This attack nearly cost us too much. Sadeas is saying we need to be more careful, not risk ourselves and our Shards in solitary assaults."

"Sadeas is smart," Dalinar said. He reached gingerly with his right hand, the less mangled one, and raised a mug of wine to his lips. It was the only drug he cared about for the pain—and maybe it would help with the shame too. Both feelings seemed stark, now that the Thrill had receded and left him deflated.

"What do we do with them, Dalinar?" Gavilar asked, waving down toward the crowds of civilians the soldiers were rounding up. "Tens of thousands of people. They won't be cowed easily; they won't like that you killed their highlord *and* his heir. Those people will resist us for years. I can feel it."

Dalinar took a drink. "Make soldiers of them," he said. "Tell them we'll spare their families if they fight for us. You want to stop doing a Shardbearer rush at the start of battles? Sounds like we'll need some expendable troops."

Gavilar nodded, considering. "Sadeas is right about other things too, you know. About us. And what we're going to have to become."

"Don't talk to me about that."

"Dalinar . . ."

"I lost half my elites today, my captain included. I've got enough problems."

"Why are we here, fighting? Is it for honor? Is it for Alethkar?"

Dalinar shrugged.

"We can't just keep acting like a bunch of thugs," Gavilar said. "We can't rob every city we pass, feast every night. We need discipline; we need to hold the land we have. We need bureaucracy, order, laws, *politics.*"

Dalinar closed his eyes, distracted by the shame he felt. What if Gavilar found out?

"We're going to have to grow up," Gavilar said softly.

"And become soft? Like these highlords we kill? *That's* why we started, isn't it? Because they were all lazy, fat, corrupt?"

"I don't know anymore. I'm a father now, Dalinar. That makes me wonder about what we do once we have it all. How do we make a kingdom of this place?"

Storms. A kingdom. For the first time in his life, Dalinar found that idea horrifying.

Gavilar eventually stood up, responding to some messengers who were calling for him. "Could you," he said to Dalinar, "at least try to be a *little* less foolhardy in future battles?"

"This coming from you?"

"A thoughtful me," Gavilar said. "An . . . exhausted me. Enjoy Oathbringer. You earned it."

"Oathbringer?"

"Your sword," Gavilar said. "Storms, didn't you listen to *anything* last night? That's Sunmaker's old sword."

Sadees, the Sunmaker. He had been the last man to unite Alethkar, centuries ago. Dalinar shifted the Blade in his lap, letting the light play off the pristine metal.

"It's yours now," Gavilar said. "By the time we're done, I'll have it so that nobody even thinks of Sunmaker anymore. Just House Kholin and Alethkar."

He walked away. Dalinar rammed the Shardblade into the stone and leaned back, closing his eyes again and remembering the sound of a brave boy crying.

NEGOTIATIONS

I ask not that you forgive me. Nor that you even understand.

—From *Oathbringer*, preface

Dalinar stood beside the glass windows in an upper-floor room of Urithiru, hands clasped behind his back. He could see his reflection hinted in the window, and beyond it vast openness. The sky cloud-free, the sun burning white.

Windows as tall as he was—he'd never seen anything like them. Who would dare build something of glass, so brittle, and face it *toward* the storms? But of course, this city was above the storms. These windows seemed a mark of defiance, a symbol of what the Radiants had meant. They had stood above the pettiness of world politics. And because of that height, they could see so far. . . .

You idealize them, said a distant voice in his head, like rumbling thunder. *They were men like you. No better. No worse.*

"I find that encouraging," Dalinar whispered back. "If they were like us, then it means we can be like them."

They eventually betrayed us. Do not forget that.

"Why?" Dalinar asked. "What happened? What changed them?"

The Stormfather fell silent.

"Please," Dalinar said. "Tell me."

Some things are better left forgotten, the voice said to him. *You of all men should understand this, considering the hole in your mind and the person who once filled it.*

Dalinar drew in a sharp breath, stung by the words.

"Brightlord," Brightness Kalami said from behind. "The emperor is ready for you."

Dalinar turned. Urithiru's upper levels held several unique rooms, including this amphitheater. Shaped like a half-moon, the room had windows at the top—the straight side—then rows of seats leading down to a speaking floor below. Curiously, each seat had a small pedestal beside it. For the Radiant's spren, the Stormfather told him.

Dalinar started down the steps toward his team: Aladar and his daughter, May. Navani, wearing a bright green havah, sitting in the front row with feet stretched out before her, shoes off and ankles crossed. Elderly Kalami to write, and Teshav Khal—one of Alethkar's finest political minds—to advise. Her two senior wards sat beside her, ready to provide research or translation if needed.

A small group, prepared to change the world.

"Send my greetings to the emperor," Dalinar instructed.

Kalami nodded, writing. Then she cleared her throat, reading the response that the spanreed—writing as if on its own—relayed. "You are greeted by His Imperial Majesty Ch.V.D. Yanagawn the First, Emperor of Makabak, King of Azir, Lord of the Bronze Palace, Prime Aqasix, grand minister and emissary of Yaezir."

"An imposing title," Navani noted, "for a fifteen-year-old boy."

"He supposedly raised a child from the dead," Teshav said, "a miracle that gained him the support of the viziers. Local word is that they had trouble finding a new Prime after the last two were murdered by our old friend the Assassin in White. So the viziers picked a boy with questionable lineage and made up a story about him saving someone's life in order to demonstrate a divine mandate."

Dalinar grunted. "Making things up doesn't sound very Azish."

"They're fine with it," Navani said, "as long as you can find witnesses willing to fill out affidavits. Kalami, thank His Imperial Majesty for meeting with us, and his translators for their efforts."

Kalami wrote, and then she looked up at Dalinar, who began to pace the center of the room. Navani stood to join him, eschewing her shoes, walking in socks.

"Your Imperial Majesty," Dalinar said, "I speak to you from the top of Urithiru, city of legend. The sights are breathtaking. I invite you to visit me here and tour the city. You are welcome to bring any guards or retinue you see fit."

He looked to Navani, and she nodded. They'd discussed long how to approach the monarchs, and had settled on a soft invitation. Azir was first, the most powerful country in the west and home to what would be the most central and important of the Oathgates to secure.

The response took time. The Azish government was a kind of beautiful mess, though Gavilar had often admired it. Layers of clerics filled all levels—where both men and women wrote. Scions were kind of like ardents, though they weren't slaves, which Dalinar found odd. In Azir, being a priest-minister in the government was the highest honor to which one could aspire.

Traditionally, the Azish Prime claimed to be emperor of all Makabak—a region that included over a half-dozen kingdoms and princedoms. In reality, he was king over only Azir, but Azir did cast a long, long shadow.

As they waited, Dalinar stepped up beside Navani, resting his fingers on one of her shoulders, then drew them across her back, the nape of her neck, and let them linger on the other shoulder.

Who would have thought a man his age could feel so giddy?

"'Your Highness,'" the reply finally came, Kalami reading the words. "'We thank you for your warning about the storm that blew from the wrong direction. Your timely words have been noted and recorded in the official annals of the empire, recognizing you as a friend to Azir.'"

Kalami waited for more, but the spanreed stopped moving. Then the ruby flashed, indicating that they were done.

"That wasn't much of a response," Aladar said. "Why didn't he reply to your invitation, Dalinar?"

"Being noted in their official records is a great honor to the Azish," Teshav said, "so they've paid you a compliment."

"Yes," Navani said, "but they are trying to dodge the offer we made. Press them, Dalinar."

"Kalami, please send the following," Dalinar said. "I am honored, though I wish my inclusion in your annals could have been due to happier circumstances. Let us discuss the future of Roshar together, here. I am eager to make your personal acquaintance."

They waited as patiently as they could for a response. It finally came, in Alethi. "'We of the Azish crown are saddened to share mourning for the fallen with you. As your noble brother was killed by the Shin destroyer, so were beloved members of our court. This creates a bond between us.'"

That was all.

Navani clicked her tongue. "They're not going to be pushed into an answer."

"They could at least explain themselves!" Dalinar snapped. "It feels like we're having two different conversations!"

"The Azish," Teshav said, "do not like to give offense. They're almost as bad as the Emuli in that regard, particularly with foreigners."

It wasn't only an Azish attribute, in Dalinar's estimation. It was the way of politicians worldwide. Already this conversation was starting to feel like his efforts to bring the highprinces to his side, back in the warcamps. Half answer after half answer, mild promises with no bite to them, laughing eyes that mocked him even while they pretended to be perfectly sincere.

Storms. Here he was again. Trying to unite people who didn't want to listen to him. He couldn't afford to be bad at this, not any longer.

There was a time, he thought, *when I united in a different way.* He smelled smoke, heard men screaming in pain. Remembered bringing blood and ash to those who defied his brother.

Those memories had become particularly vivid lately.

"Another tactic maybe?" Navani suggested. "Instead of an invitation, try an offer of aid."

"Your Imperial Majesty," Dalinar said. "War is coming; surely you have seen the changes in the parshmen. The Voidbringers have returned. I would have you know that the Alethi are your allies in this conflict. We would share information regarding our successes and failures in resisting this enemy, with hope that you will report the same to us. Mankind must be unified in the face of the mounting threat."

The reply eventually came: "'We agree that aiding one another in this new age will be of the utmost importance. We are glad to exchange information. What do you know of these transformed parshmen?'"

"We engaged them on the Shattered Plains," Dalinar said, relieved to make some kind of headway. "Creatures with red eyes, and similar in many ways to the parshmen we found on the Shattered Plains—only more dangerous. I will have my scribes prepare reports for you detailing all we have learned in fighting the Parshendi over the years."

"'Excellent,'" the reply finally came. "'This information will be extremely welcome in our current conflict.'"

"What is the status of your cities?" Dalinar asked. "What have the parshmen been doing there? Do they seem to have a goal beyond wanton destruction?"

Tensely, they waited for word. So far they'd been able to discover blessed little about the parshmen the world over. Captain Kaladin sent reports using scribes from towns he visited, but knew next to nothing. Cities were in chaos, and reliable information scarce.

"'Fortunately,'" came the reply, "'our city stands, and the enemy is not actively attacking any longer. We are negotiating with the hostiles.'"

"Negotiating?" Dalinar said, shocked. He turned to Teshav, who shook her head in wonder.

"Please clarify, Your Majesty," Navani said. "The Voidbringers are willing to *negotiate* with you?"

"'Yes,'" came the reply. "'We are exchanging contracts. They have very detailed demands, with outrageous stipulations. We hope that we can forestall armed conflict in order to gather ourselves and fortify the city.'"

"They can write?" Navani pressed. "The Voidbringers themselves are sending you *contracts*?"

"'The average parshman cannot write, so far as we can tell,'" the reply came. "'But some are different—stronger, with strange powers. They do not speak like the others.'"

"Your Majesty," Dalinar said, stepping up to the spanreed writing table, speaking more urgently—as if the emperor and his ministers could hear his passion through the written word. "I need to talk to you directly. I can come myself, through the portal we wrote of earlier. We must get it working again."

Silence. It stretched so long that Dalinar found himself grinding his teeth, itching to summon a Shardblade and dismiss it, over and over, as had been his habit as a youth. He'd picked it up from his brother.

A response finally came. "'We regret to inform you that the device you mention,'" Kalami read, "'is not functional in our city. We have investigated it, and have found that it was destroyed long ago. We cannot come to you, nor you to us. Many apologies.'"

"He's telling us this now?" Dalinar said. "Storms! That's information we could have used as soon as he learned it!"

"It's a lie," Navani said. "The Oathgate on the Shattered Plains functioned after centuries of storms and crem buildup. The one in Azimir is a monument in the Grand Market, a large dome in the center of the city."

Or so she'd determined from maps. The one in Kholinar had been incorporated into the palace structure, while the one in Thaylen City was some kind of religious monument. A beautiful relic like this wouldn't simply be destroyed.

"I agree with Brightness Navani's assessment," Teshav said. "They are worried about the idea of you or your armies visiting. This is an excuse." She frowned, as if the emperor and his ministers were little more than spoiled children disobeying their tutors.

The spanreed started writing again.

"What does it say?" Dalinar said, anxious.

"It's an affidavit," Navani said, amused. "That the Oathgate is not functional, signed by imperial architects and stormwardens." She read further. "Oh, this is delightful. Only the Azish would assume you'd want *certification* that something is broken."

"Notably," Kalami added, "it only certifies that the device 'does not function as a portal.' But of course it would not, not unless a Radiant were to visit and work it. This affidavit basically says that when turned off, the device doesn't work."

"Write this, Kalami," Dalinar said. "Your Majesty. You ignored me once. Destruction caused by the Everstorm was the result. Please, this time listen.

You cannot negotiate with the Voidbringers. We *must* unify, share information, and protect Roshar. Together."

She wrote it and Dalinar waited, hands pressed against the table.

"'We misspoke when we mentioned negotiations,'" Kalami read. "'It was a mistake of translation. We agree to share information, but time is short right now. We will contact you again to further discuss. Farewell, Highprince Kholin.'"

"Bah!" Dalinar said, pushing himself back from the table. "Fools, idiots! Storming lighteyes and *Damnation's* own politics!" He stalked across the room, wishing he had something to kick, before forcing his temper under control.

"That's more of a stonewall than I expected," Navani said, folding her arms. "Brightness Khal?"

"In my experiences with the Azish," Teshav said, "they are extremely proficient at saying very little in as many words as possible. This is not an unusual example of communication with their upper ministers. Don't be put off; it will take time to accomplish anything with them."

"Time during which Roshar burns," Dalinar said. "Why did they pull back regarding their claim to have had negotiations with the Voidbringers? Are they thinking of allying themselves to the enemy?"

"I hesitate to guess," Teshav said. "But I would say that they simply decided they'd given away more information than intended."

"We *need* Azir," Dalinar said. "Nobody in Makabak will listen to us unless we have Azir's blessing, not to mention that Oathgate. . . ." He trailed off as a different spanreed on the table started blinking.

"It's the Thaylens," Kalami said. "They're early."

"You want to reschedule?" Navani asked.

Dalinar shook his head. "No, we can't afford to wait another few days before the queen can spare time again." He took a deep breath. Storms, talking to politicians was more exhausting than a hundred-mile march in full armor. "Proceed, Kalami. I'll contain my frustration."

Navani settled down on one of the seats, though Dalinar remained standing. Light poured in through the windows, pure and bright. It flowed down, bathing him. He breathed in, almost feeling as if he could taste the sunlight. He'd spent too many days inside the twisting stone corridors of Urithiru, lit by the frail light of candles and lamps.

"'Her Royal Highness,'" Kalami read, "'Brightness Fen Rnamdi, queen of Thaylenah, writes to you.'" Kalami paused. "Brightlord . . . pardon the interruption, but that indicates that the queen holds the spanreed herself rather than using a scribe."

To another woman, that would have been intimidating. To Kalami, it was merely one of many footnotes—which she added copiously to the bottom of the page before preparing the reed to relay Dalinar's words.

"Your Majesty," Dalinar said, clasping his hands behind his back and pacing the stage at the center of the seats. *Do better. Unite them.* "I send you greetings from Urithiru, holy city of the Knights Radiant, and extend to you our humblest invitation. This tower is truly a sight to behold, matched only by the glory of a sitting monarch. I would be honored to present it for you to experience."

The spanreed quickly scribbled a reply. Queen Fen was writing directly in Alethi. "'Kholin,'" Kalami read, "'you old brute. Quit spreading chull scat. What do you really want?'"

"I always *did* like her," Navani noted.

"I'm being sincere, Your Majesty," Dalinar said. "My only desire is for us to meet in person, and to talk to you and show you what we've discovered. The world is changing around us."

"'Oh,'" came the reply, "'the world is changing, is it? What led you to this incredible conclusion? Was it the fact that our slaves suddenly became Voidbringers, or was it perhaps the storm that blew the *wrong way*,'—She wrote that twice as large as the line around it, Brightlord—'ripping our cities apart?'"

Aladar cleared his throat. "Her Majesty seems to be having a bad day."

"She's insulting us," Navani said. "For Fen, that actually implies a good day."

"She's always been perfectly civil the few times I've met her," Dalinar said with a frown.

"She was being queenly then," Navani said. "You've got her talking to you directly. Trust me, it's a good sign."

"Your Majesty," Dalinar said, "please tell me of your parshmen. The transformation came upon them?"

"'Yes,'" she replied. "'Storming monsters stole our best ships—almost everything in the harbor from single-masted sloops on up—and escaped the city.'"

"They . . . sailed?" Dalinar said, again shocked. "Confirm. They didn't attack?"

"'There were some scuffles,'" Fen wrote, "'but most everyone was too busy dealing with the effects of the storm. By the time we got things somewhat sorted out, they were sailing away in a grand fleet of royal warships and private trading vessels alike.'"

Dalinar drew a breath. *We don't know half as much about the Voidbringers as we assumed.* "Your Majesty," he continued. "You might remember that we *warned* you about the imminent arrival of that storm."

"'I believed you,'" Fen said. "'If only because we got word from New Natanan confirming it. We tried to prepare, but a nation cannot upend four millennia worth of tradition at a snap of the fingers. Thaylen City is a shambles, Kholin. The storm broke our aqueducts and sewer systems, and ripped apart our docks—flattened the entire outer market! We have to fix all our cisterns, reinforce our buildings to withstand storms, and rebuild society—all without any parshman laborers and in the middle of the storming Weeping. I don't have *time* for sightseeing.'"

"It's hardly sightseeing, Your Majesty," Dalinar said. "I am aware of your problems, and dire though they are, we cannot ignore the Voidbringers. I intend to convene a grand conference of kings to fight this threat."

"'Led by you,'" Fen wrote in reply. "'Of course.'"

"Urithiru is the natural location for a meeting," Dalinar said. "Your Majesty, the Knights Radiant have returned—we speak again their ancient oaths, and bind the Surges of nature to us. If we can restore your Oathgate to functionality, you can be here in an afternoon, then return the same evening to direct the needs of your city."

Navani nodded at this tactic, though Aladar folded his arms, looking thoughtful.

"What?" Dalinar asked him as Kalami wrote.

"We need a Radiant to travel to the city to activate their Oathgate, right?" Aladar asked.

"Yes," Navani said. "A Radiant needs to unlock the gate on this side—which we can do at any moment—then one has to travel to the destination city and undo the lock there as well. That done, a Radiant can initiate a transfer from either location."

"Then the only one we have that can theoretically get to Thaylen City is the Windrunner," Aladar said. "But what if it takes him months to get back here? Or what if he's captured by the enemy? Can we even make good on our promises, Dalinar?"

A troubling problem, but one that Dalinar thought he might have an answer to. There was a weapon that he'd decided to keep hidden for now. It might work as well as a Radiant's Shardblade in opening the Oathgates—and might let someone reach Thaylen City by flight.

That was moot for the time being. First he needed a willing ear on the other side of the spanreed.

Fen's reply came. "'I will admit that my merchants are intrigued by these Oathgates. We have lore surrounding them here, that the one most Passionate could cause the portal of worlds to open again. I think every girl in Thaylenah dreams of being the one to invoke it.'"

"The Passions," Navani said with a downward turn of her lips. The Thaylens had a pagan pseudo-religion, and that had always been a curious aspect in dealing with them. They would praise the Heralds one moment, then speak of the Passions the next.

Well, Dalinar wasn't one to fault another for unconventional beliefs.

"'If you want to send me what you know about these Oathgates, well, that sounds great,'" Fen continued. "'But I'm not interested in some grand conference of kings. You let me know what you boys come up with, because I'm going to be here frantically trying to rebuild my city.'"

"Well," Aladar said, "at least we finally got an honest response."

"I'm not convinced this is honest," Dalinar said. He rubbed his chin, thinking. He'd only met this woman a few times, but something seemed *off* about her responses.

"I agree, Brightlord," Teshav said. "I think any Thaylen would jump at the chance to come pull strings at a meeting of monarchs, if only to see if she can find a way to get trade deals out of them. She is most certainly hiding something."

"Offer troops," Navani said, "to help her rebuild."

"Your Majesty," Dalinar said, "I am deeply grieved to hear of your losses. I have many soldiers here who are currently unoccupied. I would gladly send you a battalion to help repair your city."

The reply was slow in coming. "'I'm not sure what I think of having Alethi troops on my stone, well intentioned or not.'"

Aladar grunted. "She's worried about invasion? Everyone knows Alethi and ships don't mix."

"She's not worried about us arriving on ships," Dalinar said. "She's worried about an army of troops suddenly materializing in the center of her city."

A very rational worry. If Dalinar had the inclination, he could send a Windrunner to secretly open a city's Oathgate, and invade in an unprecedented assault that appeared right behind enemy lines.

He needed allies, not subjects, so he wouldn't do it—at least not to a potentially friendly city. Kholinar, however, was another story. They still didn't have reliable word of what was happening in the Alethi capital. But if the rioting was still going on, he'd been thinking that there might be a way to get armies in and restore order.

For now, he needed to focus on Queen Fen. "Your Majesty," he said, nodding for Kalami to write, "consider my offer of troops, please. And as you do, might I suggest that you begin searching among your people for budding Knights Radiant? They are the key to working Oathgates.

"We have had a number of Radiants manifest near the Shattered Plains. They are formed through an interaction with certain spren, who seem to be searching for worthy candidates. I can only assume this is happening worldwide. It is entirely likely that among the people of your city, someone has already spoken the oaths."

"You're giving up quite an advantage, Dalinar," Aladar noted.

"I'm planting a seed, Aladar," Dalinar said. "And I'll plant it on any hill I can find, regardless of who owns it. We must fight as a unified people."

"I don't dispute that," Aladar said, standing up and stretching. "But your knowledge of the Radiants is a bargaining point, one that can perhaps draw people to you—force them to work *with* you. Give up too much, and you might find a 'headquarters' for the Knights Radiant in every major city across Roshar. Rather than working together, you'll have them competing to recruit."

He was right, unfortunately. Dalinar hated turning knowledge into bargaining chips, but what if this was why he'd always failed in his negotiations with the highprinces? He wanted to be honest, straightforward, and let the pieces fall where they may. But it seemed that someone better at the game—and more willing to break the rules—always snatched the pieces from the air as he dropped them, then set them down the way they wanted.

"And," he said quickly for Kalami to add, "we would be happy to send our Radiants to train those you discover, then introduce them to the system and fraternity of Urithiru, to which each of them has a right by nature of their oaths."

Kalami added this, then twisted the spanreed to indicate they were done and waiting for a reply.

"'We will consider this,'" Kalami read as the spanreed scribbled across the page. "'The crown of Thaylenah thanks you for your interest in our people, and we will consider negotiations regarding your offer of troops. We have sent some of our few remaining cutters to track down the fleeing parshmen, and will inform you of what we discover. Until we speak again, Highprince.'"

"Storms," Navani said. "She reverted to queenspeak. We lost her somewhere in there."

Dalinar sat down in the seat next to her and let out a long sigh.

"Dalinar . . ." she said.

"I'm fine, Navani," he said. "I can't expect glowing commitments to cooperation on my first attempt. We'll just have to keep trying."

The words were more optimistic than he felt. He wished he could talk to these people in person, instead of over spanreed.

They talked to the princess of Yezier next, followed by the prince of Tashikk. They didn't have Oathgates, and were less essential to his plan, but he wanted to at least open lines of communication with them.

Neither gave him more than vague answers. Without the Azish emperor's blessing, he wouldn't be able to get any of the smaller Makabaki kingdoms to commit. Perhaps the Emuli or the Tukari would listen, but he'd only ever get one of those two, considering their long-standing feud.

At the end of the last conference, Aladar and his daughter excusing themselves, Dalinar stretched, feeling worn down. And this wasn't the end of it. He would have discussions with the monarchs of Iri—it had three, strangely. The Oathgate at Rall Elorim was in their lands, making them important—and they held sway over nearby Rira, which had another Oathgate.

Beyond that, of course, there were the Shin to deal with. They hated using spanreeds, so Navani had poked at them through a Thaylen merchant who had been willing to relay information.

Dalinar's shoulder protested as he stretched. He had found middle age to be like an assassin—quiet, creeping along behind him. Much of the time he would go about his life as he always had, until an unexpected ache or pain gave warning. He was not the youth he had once been.

And bless the Almighty for that, he thought idly, bidding farewell to Navani—who wanted to sift through information reports from various spanreed stations around the world. Aladar's daughter and scribes were gathering them in bulk for her.

Dalinar collected several of his guards, leaving others for Navani should she need some extra hands, and climbed up along the rows of seats to the room's exit at the top. Hovering just outside the doorway—like an axehound banished from the warmth of the fire—stood Elhokar.

"Your Majesty?" Dalinar said, starting. "I'm glad you could make the meeting. Are you feeling better?"

"Why do they refuse you, Uncle?" Elhokar asked, ignoring the question. "Do they think perhaps you will try to usurp their thrones?"

Dalinar drew in his breath sharply, and his guards looked embarrassed to be standing nearby. They backed up to give him and the king privacy.

"Elhokar . . ." Dalinar said.

"You likely think I say this in spite," the king said, poking his head into the room, noting his mother, then looking back at Dalinar. "I don't. You *are* better than I am. A better soldier, a better person, and certainly a better king."

"You do yourself a disservice, Elhokar. You must—"

"Oh, save your platitudes, Dalinar. For once in your life, just be *honest* with me."

"You think I haven't been?"

Elhokar raised his hand and lightly touched his own chest. "Perhaps you have been, at times. Perhaps the liar here is me—lying to tell myself I could do this, that I could be a fraction of the man my father was. No, don't interrupt me, Dalinar. Let me have my say. Voidbringers? Ancient cities full of wonder? The *Desolations*?" Elhokar shook his head. "Perhaps . . . perhaps I'm a fine king. Not extraordinary, but not an abject failure. But in the face of these events, the world needs better than fine."

There seemed a fatalism to his words, and that sent a worried shiver through Dalinar. "Elhokar, what are you saying?"

Elhokar strode into the chamber and called down to those at the bottom of the rows of seats. "Mother, Brightness Teshav, would you witness something for me?"

Storms, no, Dalinar thought, hurrying after Elhokar. "Don't do this, son."

"We all must accept the consequences of our actions, Uncle," Elhokar said. "I've been learning this very slowly, as I can be as dense as a stone."

"But—"

"Uncle, am I your king?" Elhokar demanded.

"Yes."

"Well, I shouldn't be." He knelt, shocking Navani and causing her to pull to a stop three-quarters of the way up the steps. "Dalinar Kholin," Elhokar said in a loud voice, "I swear to you now. There are princes and highprinces. Why not kings and highkings? I give an oath, immutable and witnessed, that I accept you as my monarch. As Alethkar is to me, I am to you."

Dalinar breathed out, looking to Navani's aghast face, then down to his nephew, kneeling as a vassal on the floor.

"You *did* ask for this, Uncle," Elhokar said. "Not specifically in words, but it is the only place we could have gone. You have slowly been taking command ever since you decided to trust those visions."

"I've tried to include you," Dalinar said. Silly, impotent words. He should be better than that. "You are right, Elhokar. I'm sorry."

"Are you?" Elhokar asked. "Are you really?"

"I'm sorry," Dalinar said, "for your pain. I'm sorry that I didn't handle this better. I'm sorry that this . . . this must be. Before you make this oath, tell me what you expect that it entails?"

"I've already said the words," Elhokar said, growing red faced. "Before witnesses. It is done. I've—"

"Oh, stand up," Dalinar said, grabbing him by the arm and hauling him to his feet. "Don't be dramatic. If you really want to swear this oath, I'll let you. But let's not pretend you can sweep into a room, shout a few words, and assume it's a legal contract."

Elhokar pulled his arm free and rubbed it. "Won't even let me abdicate with dignity."

"You're *not* abdicating," Navani said, joining them. She shot a glare at the guards, who stood watching with slack jaws, and they grew white at the glare. She pointed at them as if to say, *Not a word of this to anyone else.* "Elhokar, you intend to shove your uncle into a position above you. He's right to ask. What will this mean for Alethkar?"

"I . . ." Elhokar swallowed. "He should give up his lands to his heir. Dalinar is a king of somewhere else, after all. Dalinar, Highking of Urithiru, maybe the Shattered Plains." He stood straighter, speaking more certainly. "Dalinar must stay out of the direct management of my lands. He can give me commands, but *I* decide how to see them accomplished."

"It sounds reasonable," Navani said, glancing at Dalinar.

Reasonable, but gut-wrenching. The kingdom he'd fought for—the kingdom he'd forged in pain, exhaustion, and blood—now rejected him.

This is my land now, Dalinar thought. *This tower covered in coldspren.* "I can accept these terms, though at times I might need to give commands to your highprinces."

"As long as they're in your domain," Elhokar said, a hint of stubbornness to his voice, "I consider them under your authority. While they visit Urithiru or the Shattered Plains, command as you wish. When they return to my kingdom, you must go through me." He looked to Dalinar, and then glanced down, as if embarrassed to be making demands.

"Very well," Dalinar said. "Though we need to work this out with scribes before we make the change officially. And before we go too far, we should make certain there is still an Alethkar for you to rule."

"I've been thinking the same thing. Uncle, I want to lead our forces to Alethkar and recapture our homeland. Something is wrong in Kholinar. More than these riots or my wife's supposed behavior, more than the spanreeds going still. The enemy is doing something in the city. I'll take an army to stop it, and save the kingdom."

Elhokar? Leading troops? Dalinar had been imagining himself leading a force, cutting through the Voidbringer ranks, sweeping them from Alethkar and marching into Kholinar to restore order.

Truth was, though, it didn't make sense for either of them to lead such an assault. "Elhokar," Dalinar said, leaning in. "I've been considering something. The Oathgate is attached to the *palace itself.* We don't need to march an army all the way to Alethkar. All we need to do is restore that device! Once it works, we can transport our forces into the city to secure the palace, restore order, and fend off the Voidbringers."

"Get into the city," Elhokar said. "Uncle, to do that we might *need* an army in the first place!"

"No," Dalinar said. "A small team could reach Kholinar far faster than an army. As long as there was a Radiant with them, they could sneak in, restore the Oathgate, and open the way for the rest of us."

Elhokar perked up. "Yes! I'll do it, Uncle. I'll take a team and reclaim our home. Aesudan is there; if the rioting is still happening, she's fighting against it."

That wasn't what the reports—before they'd cut off—had suggested to Dalinar. If anything, the queen was the *cause* of the riots. And he certainly hadn't been intending Elhokar to go on this mission himself.

Consequences. The lad was earnest, as he'd always been. Besides, Elhokar seemed to have learned something from his near death at the hands of assassins. He was certainly humbler now than he'd been in years past.

"It is fitting," Dalinar said, "that their king should be the one who saves them. I will see that you have whatever resources you need, Elhokar."

Glowing gloryspren orbs burst around Elhokar. He grinned at them. "I only seem to see those when I'm around you, Uncle. Funny. For all that I should resent you, I don't. It's hard to resent a man who is doing his best. I'll do it. I'll save Alethkar. I need one of your Radiants. The hero, preferably."

"The hero?"

"The bridgeman," Elhokar said. "The soldier. He needs to go with me, so if I screw up and fail, someone will be there to save the city anyway."

Dalinar blinked. "That's very . . . um . . ."

"I've had ample chances to reflect lately, Uncle," Elhokar said. "The Almighty has preserved me, despite my stupidity. I'll bring the bridgeman with me, and I'll observe him. Figure out why he's so special. See if he'll teach me to be like him. And if I fail . . ." He shrugged. "Well, Alethkar is in safe hands regardless, right?"

Dalinar nodded, bemused.

"I need to make plans," Elhokar said. "I've only just recovered from my wounds. But I can't leave until the hero returns anyway. Could he fly me and my chosen team to the city? That would certainly be the fastest way. I will want every report we've had from Kholinar, and I need to study the Oathgate device in person. Yes, and have drawings done comparing it to the one in the city. And . . ." He beamed. "Thank you, Uncle. Thank you for believing in me, if only this small amount."

Dalinar nodded to him, and Elhokar retreated, a spring in his step. Dalinar sighed, feeling overwhelmed by the exchange. Navani hovered by his side as he settled down in one of the seats for the Radiants, beside a pedestal for a little spren.

On one side, he had a king swearing to him an oath he didn't want. On the other, he had an entire group of monarchs who wouldn't listen to his most rational of suggestions. Storms.

"Dalinar?" Kalami said. "Dalinar!"

He leaped to his feet, and Navani spun. Kalami was watching one of the spanreeds, which had started writing. What was it now? What terrible news awaited him?

"'Your Majesty,'" Kalami read from the page, "'I consider your offer generous, and your advice wise. We have located the device you call an Oathgate. One of my people has come forward, and—remarkably—claims to be Radiant. Her spren directed her to speak with me; we plan to use her Shardblade to test the device.

"'If it works, I will come to you in all haste. It is well that someone is attempting to organize a resistance to the evils that befall us. The nations of Roshar must put aside their squabbles, and the reemergence of the holy city of Urithiru is proof to me that the Almighty guides your hand. I look forward to counseling with you and adding my forces to yours in a joint operation to protect these lands.'" She looked up at him, amazed. "It was sent by Taravangian, king of Jah Keved and Kharbranth."

Taravangian? Dalinar hadn't expected him to reply so quickly. He was said to be a kindly, if somewhat simple man. Perfect for ruling a small city-state with the help of a governing council. His elevation to king of Jah Keved was widely seen as an act of spite from the former king, who hadn't wanted to give the throne to any of his rivals' houses.

The words still warmed Dalinar. Someone had listened. Someone was willing to join him. Bless that man, *bless him*.

If Dalinar failed everywhere else, at least he would have King Taravangian at his side.

13

CHAPERONE

I ask only that you read or listen to these words.

—From *Oathbringer*, preface

Shallan breathed out Stormlight and stepped through it, feeling it
envelop her, transform her.

She'd been moved, upon request, to Sebarial's section of Urithiru,
in part because he'd promised her a room with a balcony. Fresh air and a
view of the mountain peaks. If she couldn't be completely free of this
building's shadowed depths, then at least she could have a home on the
borders.

She pulled at her hair, pleased to see it had turned black. She had become
Veil, a disguise she'd been working on for some time.

Shallan held up hands that were callused and worked—even the safehand. Not that Veil was unfeminine. She kept her nails filed, and liked to
dress nicely, keep her hair brushed. She simply didn't have time for frivoli-
ties. A good sturdy coat and trousers suited Veil better than a flowing havah.
And she had *no* time for an extended sleeve covering her safehand. She'd
wear a glove, thank you very much.

At the moment she was dressed in her nightgown; she'd change later,
once she was ready to sneak out into Urithiru's halls. She needed some practice first. Though she felt bad about the use of Stormlight when everyone
else was scrimping, Dalinar *had* told her to train with her powers.

She strode through her chamber, adopting Veil's gait—confident and
sturdy, never prim. You couldn't balance a book on Veil's head as she walked,

but she'd happily balance one on your face after she knocked you unconscious.

She circled the room several times, crossing the patch of evening light from the window. Her room was ornamented by bright circular patterns of strata on the walls. The stone was smooth to the touch, and a knife couldn't scratch it.

There wasn't much furniture, though Shallan was hopeful that the latest scavenging expeditions to the warcamps would return with something she could appropriate from Sebarial. For now she did what she could with some blankets, a single stool, and—blessedly—a hand mirror. She'd hung it on the wall, tied to a stone knob that she assumed was for hanging pictures.

She checked her face in the mirror. She wanted to get to the point where she could become Veil at a moment's notice, without needing to review sketches. She prodded at her features, but of course as the more angular nose and pronounced forehead were a result of Lightweaving, she couldn't feel them.

When she frowned, Veil's face mimicked the motion perfectly. "Something to drink, please," she said. No, rougher. "Drink. Now." Too strong?

"Mmm," Pattern said. "The voice becomes a good lie."

"Thank you. I've been working on sounds." Veil's voice was deeper than Shallan's, rougher. She'd started to wonder, how far could she go in changing how things sounded?

For now, she wasn't sure she'd gotten the lips right in the illusion. She sauntered over to her art supplies and flipped open her sketchbook, looking for renditions of Veil she'd drawn instead of going to dinner with Sebarial and Palona.

The first page of the sketchbook was of the corridor with the twisting strata she'd passed through the other day: lines of madness curling toward darkness. She flipped to the next, a picture of one of the tower's budding markets. Thousands of merchants, washwomen, prostitutes, innkeepers, and craftsmen of all varieties were setting up in Urithiru. Shallan knew well how many—she'd been the one to bring them all through the Oathgate.

In her sketch, the black upper reaches of the large market cavern loomed over tiny figures scurrying between tents, holding fragile lights. The next was another tunnel into darkness. And the next. Then a room where the strata coiled about one another in a mesmerizing manner. She hadn't realized she'd done so many. She flipped twenty pages before she found her sketches of Veil.

Yes, the lips were right. The build was wrong, however. Veil had a lean strength, and that wasn't coming through in the nightgown. It looked too much like Shallan's figure beneath.

Someone knocked on the wooden plate hung outside her rooms. She had just a cloth draping the doorway right now. Many of the tower's doors had warped over the years; hers had been ripped out, and she was still waiting on a replacement.

The one knocking would be Palona, who had once again noticed that Shallan had skipped dinner. Shallan sucked in a breath, destroying the image of Veil, recovering some of the Stormlight from her Lightweaving. "Come," she said. Honestly, it didn't seem to matter to Palona that Shallan was a storming *Knight Radiant* now, she'd still mother her all the—

Adolin stepped in, carrying a large plate of food in one hand, some books under the other arm. He saw her and stumbled, nearly dropping it all.

Shallan froze, then yelped and tucked her bare safehand behind her back. Adolin didn't even have the decency to blush at finding her practically naked. He balanced the food in his hand, recovering from his stumble, and then grinned.

"Out!" Shallan said, waving her freehand at him. "Out, out, out!"

He backed away awkwardly, through the draped cloth over the doorway. Stormfather! Shallan's blush was probably so bright they could have used her as a signal to send the army to war. She pulled on a glove, then wrapped that in a safepouch, then threw on the blue dress she had draped over the back of her chair and did up the sleeve. She didn't have the presence of mind to pull on her bodice vest first, not that she really needed one anyway. She kicked it under a blanket instead.

"In my defense," Adolin said from outside, "you *did* invite me in."

"I thought you were Palona!" Shallan said, doing up the buttons on the side of her dress—which proved difficult, with three layers covering her safehand.

"You know, you could *check* to see who is at your door."

"Don't make this my fault," Shallan said. "You're the one slipping into young ladies' bedrooms practically unannounced."

"I knocked!"

"The knock was feminine."

"It was . . . Shallan!"

"Did you knock with one hand or two?"

"I'm carrying a storming platter of food—for *you*, by the way. Of course the knock was one-handed. And seriously, who knocks with *two*?"

"It was quite feminine, then. I'd have thought that imitating a woman to catch a glimpse of a young lady in her undergarments was beneath you, Adolin Kholin."

"Oh, for Damnation's sake, Shallan. Can I come in *now*? And just so we're clear, I'm a *man* and your betrothed, my name is Adolin Kholin, I was born under the sign of the nine, I have a birthmark on the back of my left thigh, and I had crab curry for breakfast. Anything else you need to know?"

She poked her head out, pulling the cloth tight around her neck. "Back of your left thigh, eh? What's a girl got to do to sneak a glimpse of *that*?"

"Knock like a man, apparently."

She gave him a grin. "Just a sec. This dress is being a pain." She ducked back into the room.

"Yes, yes. Take your time. I'm not standing out here holding a heavy platter of food, smelling it after having skipped dinner so I could dine with you."

"It's good for you," Shallan said. "Builds strength, or something. Isn't that the sort of thing you do? Strangle rocks, stand on your head, throw boulders around."

"Yes, I have quite my share of murdered rocks stuffed under my bed."

Shallan grabbed her dress with her teeth at the neck to pull it tight, helping with the buttons. Maybe.

"What *is* it with women and their undergarments anyway?" Adolin said, the platter clinking as some of the plates slid against one another. "I mean, that shift covers basically the same parts as a formal dress."

"It's the decency of it," Shallan said around a mouthful of fabric. "Besides, certain things have a tendency to poke out through a shift."

"Still seems arbitrary to me."

"Oh, and men aren't arbitrary about clothing? A uniform is basically the same as any other coat, right? Besides, aren't you the one who spends his afternoons searching through fashion folios?"

He chuckled and started a reply, but Shallan, finally dressed, swept back the sheet on her doorway. Adolin stood up from leaning against the wall of the corridor and took her in—frazzled hair, dress that she had missed two buttons on, cheeks flushed. Then he grinned a dopey grin.

Ash's eyes . . . he actually thought she was pretty. This wonderful, princely man actually *liked* being with her. She'd traveled to the ancient city of the Knights Radiant, but compared to Adolin's affection, all the sights of Urithiru were dun spheres.

He liked her. *And* he brought her food.

Do not *find a way to screw this up,* Shallan thought to herself as she took the books from under his arm. She stepped aside, letting him enter and set the platter on the floor. "Palona said you hadn't eaten," he said, "and then she found out I'd skipped dinner. So, uh . . ."

"So she sent you with a lot," Shallan said, inspecting the platter piled high with dishes, flatbreads, and shellfood.

"Yeah," Adolin said, standing and scratching at his head. "I think it's a Herdazian thing."

Shallan hadn't realized how hungry she was. She'd been intending to get something at one of the taverns later tonight while prowling about wearing Veil's face. Those taverns had set up in the main market, despite Navani's attempts to send them elsewhere, and Sebarial's merchants had quite the stock to sell.

Now that this was all before her . . . well, she didn't worry much about decorum as she settled down on the ground and started to spoon herself up a thin, watery curry with vegetables.

Adolin remained standing. He *did* look sharp in that blue uniform, though admittedly she'd never really seen him in anything else. *Birthmark on the thigh, eh . . .*

"You'll have to sit on the ground," Shallan said. "No chairs yet."

"I just realized," he said, "this is your bedroom."

"And my drawing room, and my sitting room, and my dining room, and my 'Adolin says obvious things' room. It's quite versatile, this room— singular—of mine. Why?"

"I'm just wondering if it's proper," he said, then actually blushed— which was adorable. "For us to be in here alone."

"*Now* you're worried about propriety?"

"Well, I did recently get lectured about it."

"That wasn't a lecture," Shallan said, taking a bite of food. The succulent tastes overwhelmed her mouth, bringing on that delightful sharp pain and mixing of flavor that you only got from the first bite of something sweet. She closed her eyes and smiled, savoring it.

"So . . . not a lecture?" Adolin said. "Was there to be more to that quip?"

"Sorry," she said, opening her eyes. "It wasn't a lecture, it was a creative application of my tongue to keep you distracted." Looking at his lips, she could think of some other creative applications for her tongue. . . .

Right. She took a deep breath.

"It *would* be inappropriate," Shallan said, "if we were alone. Fortunately, we are not."

"Your ego doesn't count as a separate individual, Shallan."

"Ha! Wait. You think I have an ego?"

"It just sounded good—I don't mean . . . Not that . . . Why are you grinning?"

"Sorry," Shallan said, making two fists before herself and shivering in glee. She'd spent so *long* feeling timid, it was so satisfying to hear a reference to her confidence. It was working! Jasnah's teaching about practicing and acting like she was in control. It was *working.*

Well, except for that whole part about having to admit to herself that she'd killed her mother. As soon as she thought of it, she instinctively tried to shove the memory away, but it wouldn't budge. She'd spoken it to Pattern as a truth—which were the odd Ideals of the Lightweavers.

It was stuck in her mind, and every time she thought about it, the gaping wound flared up with pain again. Shallan had killed her mother. Her father had covered it up, pretended he'd murdered his wife, and the event had destroyed his life—driving him to anger and destruction.

Until eventually Shallan had killed him too.

"Shallan?" Adolin asked. "Are you well?"

No.

"Sure. Fine. Anyway, we *aren't* alone. Pattern, come here please." She held out her hand, palm up.

He reluctantly moved down from the wall where he'd been watching. As always, he made a ripple in whatever he crossed, be it cloth or stone—like there was something under the surface. His complex, fluctuating pattern of lines was always changing, melding, vaguely circular but with surprising tangents.

He crossed up her dress and onto her hand, then split out from beneath her skin and rose into the air, expanding fully into three dimensions. He hovered there, a black, eye-bending network of shifting lines—some patterns shrinking while others expanded, rippling across his surface like a field of moving grass.

She would *not* hate him. She could hate the sword she'd used to kill her mother, but not him. She managed to push aside the pain for now—not forgetting it, but hopefully not letting it spoil her time with Adolin.

"Prince Adolin," Shallan said, "I believe you've heard my spren's voice before. Let me introduce you formally. This is Pattern."

Adolin knelt, reverent, and stared at the mesmerizing geometries. Shallan didn't blame him; she'd lost herself more than once in that network of lines and shapes that almost seemed to repeat, but never quite did.

"Your spren," Adolin said. "A Shallanspren."

Pattern sniffed in annoyance at that.

"He's called a Cryptic," she said. "Every order of Radiant bonds a different variety of spren, and that bond lets me do what I do."

"Craft illusions," Adolin said softly. "Like that one with the map the other day."

Shallan smiled and—realizing she had just a smidge of Stormlight left from her illusion earlier—was unable to resist showing off. She raised her sleeved safehand and breathed out, sending a shimmering patch of Stormlight above the blue cloth. It formed into a small image of Adolin from her sketches of him in his Shardplate. This one remained frozen, Shardblade on his shoulder, faceplate up—like a little doll.

"This is an incredible talent, Shallan," Adolin said, poking at the version of himself—which fuzzed, offering no resistance. He paused, then poked at Pattern, who shied back. "Why do you insist on hiding this, pretending that you're a different order than you are?"

"Well," she said, thinking fast and closing her hand, dismissing the image of Adolin. "I just think it might give us an edge. Sometimes secrets are important."

Adolin nodded slowly. "Yeah. Yeah, they are."

"Anyway," Shallan said. "Pattern, you're to be our chaperone tonight."

"What," Pattern said with a hum, "is a chaperone?"

"That is someone who watches two young people when they are together, to make certain they don't do anything inappropriate."

"Inappropriate?" Pattern said. "Such as . . . dividing by zero?"

"What?" Shallan asked, looking to Adolin, who shrugged. "Look, just keep an eye on us. It will be all right."

Pattern hummed, melting down into his two-dimensional form and taking up residence on the side of a bowl. He seemed content there, like a cremling snuggled into its crack.

Unable to wait any longer, Shallan dug into her meal. Adolin settled down across from her and attacked his own food. For a time, Shallan ignored her pain and savored the moment—good food, good company, the setting sun casting ruby and topaz light across the mountains and into the room. She felt like drawing this scene, but knew it was the type of moment she couldn't capture on a page. It wasn't about content or composition, but the pleasure of living.

The trick to happiness wasn't in freezing every momentary pleasure and clinging to each one, but in ensuring one's life would produce many future moments to anticipate.

Adolin—after finishing an entire plate of stranna haspers steamed in the shell—picked out a few chunks of pork from a creamy red curry, then put them on a plate and handed them in her direction. "Wanna try a bite?"

Shallan made a gagging noise.

"Come on," he said, wagging the plate. "It's delicious."

"It would burn my lips off, Adolin Kholin," Shallan said. "Don't think I didn't notice you picking the absolute *spiciest* concoction Palona sent. Men's food is dreadful. How can you taste anything beneath all that spice?"

"Keeps it from being bland," Adolin said, stabbing one of the chunks and popping it in his mouth. "There's nobody here but us. You can try it."

She eyed it, remembering the times as a child when she'd sneaked tastes of men's food—though not this specific dish.

Pattern buzzed. "Is this the inappropriate thing I'm supposed to stop you from doing?"

"No," Shallan said, and Pattern settled back down. *Perhaps a chaperone,* she thought, *who believes basically everything I tell him isn't going to be the most effective.*

Still, with a sigh, she grabbed a chunk of the pork in some flatbread. She *had* left Jah Keved hunting new experiences, after all.

She tried a bite, and was given immediate reason to regret her decisions in life.

Eyes brimming with tears, she scrambled for the cup of water Adolin, insufferably, had picked up to hand toward her. She gulped that down, though it didn't seem to do anything. She followed it by wiping her tongue with a napkin—in the most feminine way possible, of course.

"I hate you," she said, drinking *his* water next.

Adolin chuckled.

"Oh!" Pattern said suddenly, bursting up from the bowl to hover in the air. "You were talking about *mating*! I'm to make sure you don't accidentally mate, as mating is forbidden by human society until you have first performed appropriate rituals! Yes, yes. Mmmm. Dictates of custom require following certain patterns before you copulate. I've been studying this!"

"Oh, Stormfather," Shallan said, covering her eyes with her freehand. A few shamespren even peeked in for a glimpse before vanishing. Twice in one week.

"Very well, you two," Pattern said. "No mating. *NO MATING.*" He hummed to himself, as if pleased, then sank down onto a plate.

"Well, that was humiliating," Shallan said. "Can we maybe talk about those books you brought? Or ancient Vorin theology, or strategies for counting grains of sand? Anything other than what just happened? Please?"

Adolin chuckled, then reached for a slim notebook that was on top of the pile. "May Aladar sent teams to question Vedekar Perel's family and friends. They discovered where he was before he died, who last saw him, and wrote down anything suspicious. I thought we could read the report."

"And the rest of the books?"

"You seemed lost when Father asked you about Makabaki politics," Adolin said, pouring some wine, merely a soft yellow. "So I asked around, and it seems that some of the ardents hauled their entire libraries out here. I was able to get a servant to locate you a few books I'd enjoyed on the Makabaki."

"Books?" Shallan said. "You?"

"I don't spend *all* my time hitting people with swords, Shallan," Adolin said. "Jasnah and Aunt Navani made very certain that my youth was filled with interminable periods spent listening to ardents lecture me on politics and trade. Some of it stuck in my brain, against my natural inclinations.

Those three books are the best of the ones I remember having read to me, though the last one is an updated version. I thought it might help."

"That's thoughtful," she said. "Really, Adolin. Thank you."

"I figured, you know, if we're going to move forward with the betrothal . . ."

"Why wouldn't we?" Shallan said, suddenly panicked.

"I don't know. You're a *Radiant*, Shallan. Some kind of half-divine being from mythology. And all along I was thinking we were giving *you* a favorable match." He stood up and started pacing. "Damnation. I didn't mean to say it like that. I'm sorry. I just . . . I keep worrying that I'm going to screw this up somehow."

"You worry *you're* going to screw it up?" Shallan said, feeling a warmth inside that wasn't completely due to the wine.

"I'm not good with relationships, Shallan."

"Is there anyone who actually is? I mean, is there *really* someone out there who looks at relationships and thinks, 'You know what, I've got this'? Personally, I rather think we're all collectively idiots about it."

"It's worse for me."

"Adolin, dear, the last man *I* had a romantic interest in was not only an ardent—forbidden to court me in the first place—but also turned out to be an assassin who was merely trying to obtain my favor so he could get close to Jasnah. I think you overestimate everyone else's capability in this regard."

He stopped pacing. "An assassin."

"Seriously," Shallan said. "He almost killed me with a loaf of poisoned bread."

"Wow. I have to hear this story."

"Fortunately, I just told it to you. His name was Kabsal, and he was so incredibly sweet to me that I can almost forgive him for trying to kill me."

Adolin grinned. "Well, it's nice to hear that I don't have a high bar to jump—all I have to do is *not* poison you. Though you shouldn't be telling me about past lovers. You'll make me jealous."

"Please," Shallan said, dipping her bread in some leftover sweet curry. Her tongue *still* hadn't recovered. "You've courted, like, half the warcamps."

"It's not that bad."

"Isn't it? From what I hear, I'd have to go to Herdaz to find an eligible woman you haven't pursued." She held out her hand to him, to help her to her feet.

"Are you mocking my failings?"

"No, I'm *lauding* them," she said, standing up beside him. "You see, Adolin dear, if you hadn't wrecked all those other relationships, you wouldn't be here. With me." She pulled close. "And so, in reality, you're the *greatest* at relationships there ever was. You ruined only the wrong ones, you see."

He leaned down. His breath smelled of spices, his uniform of the crisp, clean starch Dalinar required. His lips touched hers, and her heart fluttered. So warm.

"No mating!"

She started, pulling out of the kiss to find Pattern hovering beside them, pulsing quickly through shapes.

Adolin bellowed a laugh, and Shallan couldn't help joining in at the ridiculousness of it. She stepped back from him, but kept hold on his hand. "Neither of us is going to mess this up," she said to him, squeezing his hand. "Despite what might at times seem like our best efforts otherwise."

"Promise?" he asked.

"I promise. Let's look at this notebook of yours and see what it says about our murderer."

14

SQUIRES CAN'T CAPTURE

In this record, I hold nothing back. I will try not to shy away from difficult topics, or paint myself in a dishonestly heroic light.

—From *Oathbringer*, preface

Kaladin crept through the rains, sidling in a wet uniform across the rocks until he was able to peek through the trees at the Voidbringers. Monstrous terrors from the mythological past, enemies of all that was right and good. Destroyers who had laid waste to civilization countless times.

They were playing cards.

What in Damnation's depths? Kaladin thought. The Voidbringers had posted a single guard, but the creature had simply been sitting on a tree stump, easy to avoid. A decoy, Kaladin had assumed, figuring he would find the true guard watching from the heights of the trees.

If there was a hidden guard though, Kaladin had missed spotting them—and they'd missed Kaladin in equal measure. The dim light served him well, as he was able to settle between some bushes right at the edge of the Voidbringer camp. Between trees they had stretched tarps, which leaked horribly. In one place they'd made a proper tent, fully enclosed with walls—and he couldn't see what was inside.

There wasn't enough shelter, so many sat out in the rain. Kaladin spent a torturous few minutes expecting to be spotted. All they had to do was notice that these bushes had drawn in their leaves at his touch.

Nobody looked, fortunately. The leaves timidly peeked back out, obscuring him. Syl landed on his arm, hands on her hips as she surveyed the

Voidbringers. One of them had a set of wooden Herdazian cards, and he sat at the edge of the camp—directly before Kaladin—using a flat surface of stone as a table. A female sat opposite him.

They looked different from what he expected. For one thing, their skin was a different shade—many parshmen here in Alethkar had marbled white and red skin, rather than the deep red on black like Rlain from Bridge Four. They didn't wear warform, though neither did they wear some terrible, powerful form. Though they were squat and bulky, their only carapace ran along the sides of their forearms and jutted out at their temples, leaving them with full heads of hair.

They still wore their simple slave smocks, tied at the waists with strings. No red eyes. Did that change, perhaps, like his own eyes?

The male—distinguished by a dark red beard, the hairs each unnaturally thick—finally placed a card on the rock next to several others.

"Can you *do* that?" the female asked.

"I think so."

"You said squires can't capture."

"Unless another card of mine is touching yours," the male said. He scratched at his beard. "I think?"

Kaladin felt cold, like the rainwater was seeping in through his skin, penetrating all the way to his blood and washing through him. They spoke like Alethi. Not a hint of an accent. With his eyes closed, he wouldn't have been able to tell these voices from those of common darkeyed villagers from Hearthstone, save for the fact that the female had a deeper voice than most human women.

"So . . ." the female said. "You're saying you don't know how to play the game after all."

The male began gathering up the cards. "I *should* know, Khen. How many times did I watch them play? Standing there with my tray of drinks. I should be an expert at this, shouldn't I?"

"Apparently not."

The female stood and walked over to another group, who were trying to build a fire under a tarp without much success. It took a special kind of luck to be able to get flames going outside during the Weeping. Kaladin, like most in the military, had learned to live with the constant dampness.

They had the stolen sacks of grain—Kaladin could see them piled underneath one of the tarps. The grain had swollen, splitting several of the sacks. Several were eating soggy handfuls, since they had no bowls.

Kaladin wished he didn't immediately taste the mushy, awful stuff in his own mouth. He'd been given unspiced, boiled tallew on many occasions. Often he'd considered it a blessing.

The male who'd been speaking continued to sit on his rock, holding up a wooden card. They were a lacquered set, durable. Kaladin had occasionally seen their like in the military. Men would save for months to get a set like this, that wouldn't warp in the rain.

The parshman looked so forlorn, staring down at his card, shoulders slumped.

"This is wrong," Kaladin whispered to Syl. "We've been so *wrong*. . . ." Where were the destroyers? What had happened to the beasts with the red eyes that had tried to crush Dalinar's army? The terrible, haunting figures that Bridge Four had described to him?

We thought we understood what was going to happen, Kaladin thought. *I was so sure. . . .*

"Alarm!" a sudden, shrill voice called. "Alarm! You fools!"

Something zipped through the air, a glowing yellow ribbon, a streak of light in the dim afternoon shade.

"He's there," the shrill voice said. "You're being watched! Beneath those shrubs!"

Kaladin burst up through the underbrush, ready to suck in Stormlight and be away. Though fewer towns had any now, as it was running out again, he had a little left.

The parshmen seized cudgels made from branches or the handles of brooms. They bunched together and held the sticks like frightened villagers, no stance, no control.

Kaladin hesitated. *I could take them all in a fight even without Stormlight.* He'd seen men hold weapons like that many times before. Most recently, he'd seen it inside the chasms, when training the bridgemen.

These were no warriors.

Syl flitted up to him, prepared to become a Blade. "No," Kaladin whispered to her. Then he held his hands to the sides, speaking more loudly. "I surrender."

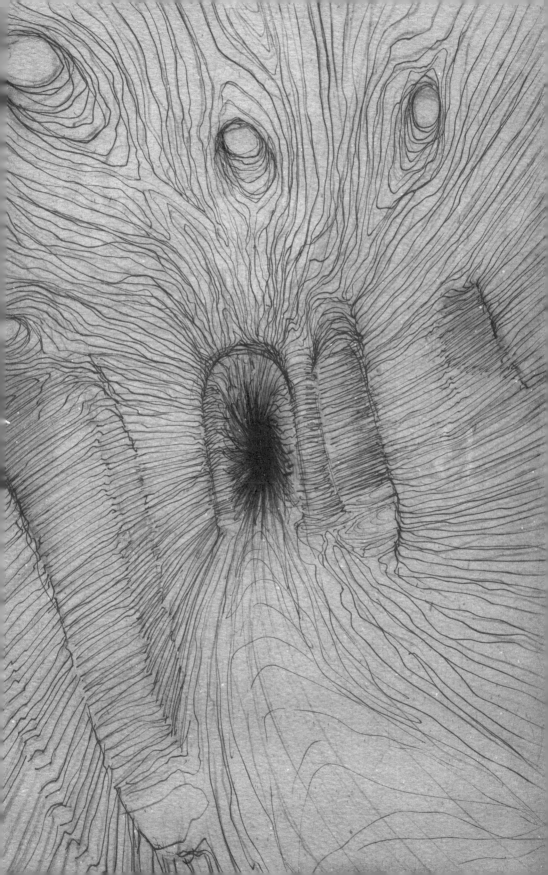

15

BRIGHTNESS RADIANT

I will express only direct, even brutal, truth. You must know what I have done, and what those actions cost me.

—From *Oathbringer*, preface

Brightlord Perel's body was found in the same area as Sadeas's," Shallan said, pacing back and forth in her room as she flipped through pages of the report. "That *can't* be a coincidence. This tower is far too big. So we know where the murderer is prowling."

"Yeah, I suppose," Adolin said. He lounged with his back against the wall, coat unbuttoned while tossing a small leather ball filled with dried grain into the air and catching it again. "I just think the murders could have been done by two different people."

"Same *exact* method of murder," Shallan said. "Body positioned the same way."

"Nothing else connecting them," Adolin said. "Sadeas was slime, widely hated, and usually accompanied by guards. Perel was quiet, well-liked, and known for his administrative prowess. He was less a soldier than a manager."

The sun had fully set by now, and they'd set out spheres on the floor for light. The remnants of their meal had been carted away by a servant, and Pattern hummed happily on the wall near Adolin's head. Adolin glanced at him occasionally, looking uncomfortable, which she fully understood. She'd grown used to Pattern, but his lines *were* strange.

Wait until Adolin sees a Cryptic in Shadesmar form, she thought, *with a full body but twisting shapes for his head.*

Adolin tossed the little stitched ball into the air and caught it with his right hand—the one that Renarin, amazingly, had healed. She wasn't the only one practicing with her powers. She was especially glad someone else had a Shardblade now. When the highstorms returned, and they began working the Oathgate in earnest, she'd have help.

"These reports," Shallan said, tapping the notebook against her hand, "are both informative and useless. Nothing connects Perel and Sadeas save their both being lighteyes—that and the part of the tower they were in. Perhaps mere *opportunity* drove the killer's choice of victims."

"You're saying someone happened to kill a highprince," Adolin said, "by accident? Like . . . a back-alley murder outside a pub?"

"Maybe. Brightness Aladar suggests in here that your father lay down some rules on people moving alone through empty parts of the tower."

"I still think there might be two murderers," Adolin said. "You know . . . like someone saw Sadeas dead, and figured they could get away with killing someone else, blaming it on the first fellow."

Oh, Adolin, Shallan thought. He'd arrived at a theory he liked, and now wouldn't let it go. It was a common mistake warned of in her scientific books.

Adolin did have one point—a highprince being murdered was unlikely to be random chance. There were no signs of Sadeas's Shardblade, Oathbringer, being used by anyone, not even a rumor of it.

Maybe the second death is a kind of decoy? Shallan thought, riffling through the report again. *An attempt to make it seem like random attacks?* No, that was too convoluted—and she had no more evidence for it than Adolin had for his theory.

That did leave her thinking. Maybe everyone was paying attention to these two deaths because they'd happened to important lighteyes. Could there be other deaths they hadn't noticed because they'd happened to less prominent individuals? If a beggar had been found in Adolin's proverbial back alley behind a pub, would anyone have remarked upon it—even if he'd been stabbed through the eye?

I need to get out there among them and see what I can find. She opened her mouth to tell him she should probably turn in, but he was already standing, stretching.

"I think we've done what we can with that," he said, nodding toward the report. "At least for tonight."

"Yeah," Shallan said, feigning a yawn. "Probably."

"So . . ." Adolin said, then took a deep breath. "There's . . . something else."

Shallan frowned. Something else? Why did he suddenly look like he was preparing to do something difficult?

He's going to break off our betrothal! a part of her mind thought, though she pounced on that emotion and shoved it back behind the curtains where it belonged.

"Okay, this isn't easy," Adolin said. "I don't want to offend, Shallan. But . . . you know how I had you eat that man's food?"

"Um, yes. If my tongue is particularly spicy in the coming days, I blame you."

"Shallan, there's something similar that we need to talk about. Something about you we can't just ignore."

"I . . ." *I killed my parents. I stabbed my mother through the chest and I strangled my father while singing to him.*

"You," Adolin said, "have a Shardblade."

I didn't want to kill her. I had to. I had *to.*

Adolin grabbed her by the shoulders and she started, focusing on him. He was . . . grinning?

"You have a *Shardblade*, Shallan! A *new* one. That's incredible. I dreamed for years of earning my Blade! So many men spend their lives with that very dream and never see it fulfilled. And here you have one!"

"And that's a good thing, right?" she said, held in his grip with arms pulled tight against her body.

"Of course it is!" Adolin said, letting go of her. "But, I mean, you're a woman."

"Was it the makeup that tipped you off, or the dress? Oh, it was the breasts, wasn't it? Always giving us away."

"Shallan, this is serious."

"I know," she said, calming her nerves. "Yes, Pattern can become a Shardblade, Adolin. I don't see what this has to do with anything. I can't give it away. . . . Stormfather. You want to teach me how to use it, don't you?"

He grinned. "You said that Jasnah was a Radiant too. Women, gaining Shardblades. It's weird, but it's not like we can *ignore* it. What about Plate? Do you have that hidden somewhere too?"

"Not that I know of," she said. Her heart was beating quickly, her skin growing cold, her muscles tense. She fought against the sensation. "I don't know where Plate comes from."

"I know it's not feminine, but who cares? You've got a sword; you should know how to use it, and custom can go to Damnation. There, I said it." He took a deep breath. "I mean, the bridgeboy can have one, and he's *darkeyed*. Well, he was. Anyway, it's not so different from that."

Thank you, Shallan thought, *for ranking all women as something equivalent to peasants.* But she held her tongue. This was obviously an important moment for Adolin, and he *was* trying to be broad-minded.

But . . . thinking of what she'd done pained her. Holding the weapon would be worse. So much worse.

She wanted to hide. But she couldn't. This truth refused to budge from her mind. Could she explain? "So, you're right, but—"

"Great!" Adolin said. "Great. I brought the Blade guards so we won't hurt each other. I stashed them back at the guard post. I'll go fetch them."

He was out the door a moment later. Shallan stood with her hand stretched toward him, objections dying on her lips. She curled her fingers up and brought her hand to her breast, her heart thundering within.

"Mmmm," Pattern said. "This is good. This needs to be done."

Shallan scrambled through the room to the small mirror she'd hung from the wall. She stared at herself, eyes wide, hair an utter mess. She'd started breathing in sharp, quick gasps. "I can't—" she said. "I can't be this person, Pattern. I can't just wield the sword. Some brilliant knight on a tower, pretending she should be followed."

Pattern hummed softly a tone she'd come to recognize as confusion. The bewilderment of one species trying to comprehend the mind of another.

Sweat trickled down Shallan's face, running beside her eye as she stared at herself. What did she expect to see? The thought of breaking down in front of Adolin heightened her tension. Her every muscle grew taut, and the corners of her vision started to darken. She could see only before herself, and she wanted to run, go somewhere. *Be away.*

No. No, just be someone else.

Hands shaking, she scrambled over and dug out her drawing pad. She ripped pages, flinging them out of the way to reach an empty one, then seized her charcoal pencil.

Pattern moved over to her, a floating ball of shifting lines, buzzing in concern. "Shallan? Please. What is wrong?"

I can hide, Shallan thought, drawing at a frenzied pace. *Shallan can flee and leave someone in her place.*

"It's because you hate me," Pattern said softly. "I can die, Shallan. I can go. They will send you another to bond."

A high-pitched whine started to rise in the room, one Shallan didn't immediately recognize as coming from the back of her own throat. Pattern's words were like knives to her side. *No, please. Just draw.*

Veil. Veil would be fine holding a sword. She didn't have Shallan's broken soul, and hadn't killed her parents. She'd be able to do this.

No. No, what would Adolin do if he returned and found a completely different woman in the room? He couldn't know of Veil. The lines she sketched, ragged and unrefined from the shaking pencil, quickly took the shape of her own face. But hair in a bun. A poised woman, not as flighty as Shallan, not as unintentionally silly.

A woman who hadn't been sheltered. A woman hard enough, strong enough, to wield this sword. A woman like . . . like Jasnah.

Yes, Jasnah's subtle smile, composure, and self-confidence. Shallan outlined her own face with these ideals, creating a harder version of it. Could . . . could she be this woman?

I have to be, Shallan thought, drawing in Stormlight from her satchel, then breathing it out in a puff around her. She stood up as the change took hold. Her heartbeat slowed, and she wiped the sweat from her brow, then calmly undid her safehand sleeve, tossed aside the foolish extra pouch she'd tied around her hand inside, then rolled the sleeve back to expose her still-gloved hand.

Good enough. Adolin couldn't possibly expect her to put on sparring clothing. She pulled her hair back into a bun and fixed it in place with hairspikes from her satchel.

When Adolin returned to the room a moment later, he found a poised, calm woman who wasn't *quite* Shallan Davar. *Brightness Radiant is her name,* she thought. *She will go only by title.*

Adolin carried two long, thin pieces of metal that somehow could meld to the front of Shardblades and make them less dangerous for use in sparring. Radiant inspected them with a critical eye, then held her hand to the side, summoning Pattern. The Blade formed—a long, thin weapon nearly as tall as she was.

"Pattern," she said, "can modulate his shape, and will dull his edge to safe levels. I shan't need such a clunky device." Indeed, Pattern's edge rippled, dulling.

"Storms, that's handy. I'll still need one though." Adolin summoned his own Blade, a process that took him ten heartbeats—during which he turned his head, looking at her.

Shallan glanced down, realizing that she'd enhanced her bust in this guise. Not for him, of course. She'd just been making herself look more like Jasnah.

Adolin's sword finally appeared, with a thicker blade than her own, sinuous along the sharp edge, with delicate crystalline ridges along the back. He put one of the guards on the sword's edge.

Radiant put one foot forward, Blade lifted high in two hands beside her head.

"Hey," Adolin said. "That's not bad."

"Shallan *did* spend quite a lot of time drawing you all."

Adolin nodded thoughtfully. He approached and reached toward her with a thumb and two fingers. She thought he was going to adjust her grip, but instead he pressed his fingers against her collarbone and shoved lightly.

Radiant stumbled backward, almost tripping.

"A stance," Adolin said, "is about more than just looking great on the battlefield. It's about footing, center of balance, and control of the fight."

"Noted. So how do I make it better?"

"I'm trying to decide. Everyone I've worked with before had been using a sword since their youth. I'm wondering how Zahel would have changed my training if I'd never even *picked up* a weapon."

"From what I've heard of him," Radiant said, "it will depend on where there are any convenient rooftops nearby to jump off."

"That's how he trained with Plate," Adolin said. "This is Blade. Should I teach you dueling? Or should I teach you how to fight in an army?"

"I shall settle," Radiant said, "for knowing how to avoid cutting off any of my own appendages, Brightlord Kholin."

"Brightlord Kholin?"

Too formal. Right. That was how Radiant would act, of course—but she could allow herself some familiarity. Jasnah had done that.

"I was merely," Radiant said, "attempting to show the respect due a master from his humble pupil."

Adolin chuckled. "Please. We don't need that. But here, let's see what we can do about that stance. . . ."

Over the next hour, Adolin positioned her hands, her feet, and her arms a dozen times over. He picked a basic stance for her that she could eventually adapt into several of the formal stances—the ones like Windstance, which Adolin said wouldn't rely on strength or reach as much as mobility and skill.

She wasn't certain why he'd bothered fetching the metal sparring sleeves, as the two of them didn't exchange any blows. Other than correcting her stance ten thousand times, he spoke about the art of the duel. How to treat your Shardblade, how to think of an opponent, how to show respect to the institutions and traditions of the duel itself.

Some of it was very practical. Shardblades were dangerous weapons, which explained the demonstrations on how to hold hers, how to walk with it, how to take care not to slice people or things while casually turning.

Other parts of his monologue were more . . . mystical.

"The Blade is part of you," Adolin said. "The Blade is more than your tool; it is your life. Respect it. It will not fail you—if you are bested, it is because you failed the sword."

Radiant stood in what felt like a very stiff pose, Blade held before herself in two hands. She'd only scraped Pattern on the ceiling two or three times; fortunately, most of the rooms in Urithiru had high ceilings.

Adolin gestured for her to perform a simple strike, as they'd been practicing. Radiant raised both arms, tilting the sword, then took a step forward while bringing it down. The entire angle of movement couldn't have been more than ninety degrees—barely a strike at all.

Adolin smiled. "You're catching it. A few thousand more of those, and it will start to feel natural. We'll have to work on your breathing though."

"My breathing?"

He nodded absently.

"Adolin," Radiant said, "I assure you, I have been breathing—without fail—my entire life."

"Yeah," he said. "That's why you're going to have to unlearn it."

"How I stand, how I think, how I breathe. I have trouble distinguishing what is actually relevant, and what is part of the subculture and superstition of swordsmen."

"It's all relevant," Adolin said.

"Eating chicken before a match?"

Adolin grinned. "Well, maybe some things are personal quirks. But the swords *are* part of us."

"I know mine is part of me," Radiant said, resting the Blade at her side and setting her gloved safehand on it. "I've bonded it. I suspect this is the origin of the tradition among Shardbearers."

"So academic," Adolin said, shaking his head. "You need to *feel* this, Shallan. *Live* it."

That would not have been a difficult task for Shallan. Radiant, however, preferred not to feel things she hadn't considered in depth beforehand.

"Have you considered," she said, "that your Shardblade was once a living spren, wielded by one of the Knights Radiant? Doesn't that change how you look at it?"

Adolin glanced toward his Blade, which he'd left summoned, strapped with the sheath and set across her blankets. "I've always *kind of* known. Not that it was alive. That's silly. Swords aren't alive. I mean . . . I've always known there was something special about them. It's part of being a duelist, I think. We all know it."

She let the matter drop. Swordsmen, from what she'd seen, were superstitious. As were sailors. As were . . . well, basically everyone but scholars like Radiant and Jasnah. It *was* curious to her how much of Adolin's rhetoric about Blades and dueling reminded her of religion.

How strange that these Alethi often treated their actual religion so flippantly. In Jah Keved, Shallan had spent hours painting lengthy passages from the Arguments. You'd speak the words out loud over and over, committing them to memory while kneeling or bowing, before finally burning the paper. The Alethi instead preferred to let the ardents deal with the Almighty, like he was some annoying parlor guest who could be safely distracted by servants offering a particularly tasty tea.

Adolin let her do some more strikes, perhaps sensing that she was growing tired of having her stance constantly adjusted. As she was swinging, he grabbed his own Blade and fell in beside her, modeling the stance and the strikes.

After a short time of that she dismissed her Blade, then picked up her sketchbook. She quickly flipped past the drawing of Radiant, and started to sketch Adolin in his stance. She was forced to let some of Radiant bleed away.

"No, stand there," Shallan said, pointing at Adolin with her charcoal. "Yes, like that."

She sketched out the stance, then nodded. "Now strike, and hold the last position."

He did so. By now he'd removed his jacket, standing in only shirt and trousers. She did like how that tight shirt fit him. Even Radiant would admire that. She wasn't *dead*, just pragmatic.

She looked over the two sketches, then resummoned Pattern and fell into position.

"Hey, *nice*," Adolin said as Radiant performed the next few strikes. "Yeah, you've got it."

He again fell in beside her. The simple attack he'd taught her was obviously a poor test of his skills, but he executed it with precision nonetheless, then grinned and started talking about the first few lessons he'd had with Zahel long ago.

His blue eyes were alight, and Shallan loved seeing that glow from him. Almost like Stormlight. She knew that passion—she'd felt what it was to be alive with interest, to be consumed by something so fully that you lost yourself in the wonder of it. For her it was art, but watching him, she thought that the two of them weren't so different.

Sharing these moments with him and drinking of his excitement felt special. Intimate. Even more so than their closeness had been earlier in the evening. She let herself be Shallan in some of the moments, but whenever the pain of holding the sword started to spike—whenever she really *thought* about what she was doing—she was able to become Radiant and avoid it.

She was genuinely reluctant to see the time end, so she let it stretch into the late evening, well past when she should have called a halt. At long last, Shallan bade a tired, sweaty farewell to Adolin and watched him trot down the strata-lined hallway outside, a spring to his step, a lamp in his hands, blade guards held on his shoulder.

Shallan would have to wait another night to visit taverns and hunt for answers. She trailed back into her room—strangely contented for all that the world might be in the middle of ending. That night she slept, for once, in peace.

16

WRAPPED
THREE TIMES

For in this comes the lesson.

—From *Oathbringer*, preface

A legend rested on the stone slab before Dalinar. A weapon pulled from the ancient mists of time, and said to have been forged during the shadowdays by the hand of God himself. The Blade of the Assassin in White, claimed by Kaladin Stormblessed during their clash above the storm.

Upon cursory inspection, it was indistinguishable from an ordinary Shardblade. Elegant, relatively small—in that it was barely five feet long— it was thin and curved like a tusk. It had patterns only at the base of the blade near the hilt.

He'd lit it with four diamond broams, placed at the corners of the altarlike stone slab. This small room had no strata or paintings on the walls, so the Stormlight lit only him and that alien Blade. It did have one oddity.

There was no gemstone.

Gemstones were what allowed men to bond to Shardblades. Often affixed at the pommel, though occasionally at the spot where hilt met blade, the gem would flash when you first touched it, initiating the process. Keep the Blade with you for a week, and the Blade became yours—dismissible and returnable in time with your heartbeat.

This Blade didn't have one. Dalinar hesitantly reached out and rested his fingers on its silvery length. It was warm to the touch, like something alive.

"It doesn't scream when I touch it," he noted.

The knights, the Stormfather said in his head, *broke their oaths. They aban-doned everything they'd sworn, and in so doing killed their spren. Other Blades are the corpses of those spren, which is why they scream at your touch. This weapon, instead, was made directly from Honor's soul, then given to the Heralds. It is also the mark of an oath, but a different type—and does not have the mind to scream on its own.*

"And Shardplate?" Dalinar asked.

Related, but different, the Stormfather rumbled. *You haven't spoken the oaths required to know more.*

"You cannot break oaths," Dalinar said, fingers still resting on the Honor-blade. "Right?"

I cannot.

"What of the thing we fight? Odium, the origin of the Voidbringers and their spren. Can he break oaths?"

No, the Stormfather said. *He is far greater than I, but the power of ancient Adonalsium permeates him. And controls him. Odium is a force like pressure, gravitation, or the movement of time. These things cannot break their own rules. Nor can he.*

Dalinar tapped the Honorblade. A fragment of Honor's own soul, crystallized into metallic form. In a way, the death of their god gave him hope—for if Honor had fallen, surely Odium could as well.

In visions, Honor had left Dalinar with a task. *Vex Odium, convince him that he can lose, and appoint a champion. He will take that chance instead of risk-ing defeat again, as he has suffered so often. This is the best advice I can give you.*

"I've seen that the enemy is preparing a champion," Dalinar said. "A dark creature with red eyes and nine shadows. Will Honor's suggestion work? Can I make Odium agree to a decisive contest between me and that champion?"

Of course Honor's suggestion would work, the Stormfather said. *He spoke it.*

"I mean," Dalinar said, "*why* would it work? Why would this Odium ever agree to a contest of champions? It seems too momentous a matter to risk on something so small and inferior as the prowess and will of men."

Your enemy is not a man like you, the Stormfather replied, voice rum-bling, thoughtful. Even . . . frightened. *He does not age. He feels. He is angry. But this does not change, and his rage does not cool. Epochs can pass, and he will remain the same.*

To fight directly might coax out forces that could hurt him, as he has been hurt before. Those scars do not heal. To pick a champion, then lose, will only cost him time. He has that in plenitude. He still will not agree easily, but it is possible he will agree. If presented with the option in the right moment, the right way. Then he will be bound.

"And we win . . ."

Time, the Stormfather said. *Which, though dross to him, is the most valuable thing a man can have.*

Dalinar slipped the Honorblade off the slab. At the side of the room, a shaft cut into the ground. Two feet wide, it was one of many strange holes, corridors, and hidden corners they'd found in the tower city. This one was probably part of a sewage system; judging by the rust on the edges of the hole, there had once been a metal pipe here connecting the stone hole in the floor to one in the ceiling.

One of Navani's primary concerns was figuring out how all this worked. For now, they'd gotten by using wooden frames to turn certain large, communal rooms with ancient baths into privies. Once they had more Stormlight, their Soulcasters could deal with the waste, as they'd done in the warcamps.

Navani found the system inelegant. Communal privies with sometimes long lines made for an inefficient city, and she claimed that these tubes indicated a widespread piping and sanitation system. It was exactly the sort of large-scale civic project that engaged her—he'd never known anyone to get as excited by sewage as Navani Kholin.

For now, this tube was empty. Dalinar knelt and lowered the sword into the hole, sliding it into a stone sheath he'd cut in the side. The upper lip of the hole shielded the protruding hilt from sight; you'd have to reach down and feel in the hole to find the Honorblade.

He stood up, then gathered his spheres and made his way out. He hated leaving it there, but he could think of nothing safer. His rooms didn't feel secure enough yet—he had no vault, and a crowd of guards would only draw attention. Beyond Kaladin, Navani, and the Stormfather himself, nobody even knew that Dalinar had this. If he masked his movements, there was virtually no chance of the Blade being discovered in this vacant portion of the tower.

What will you do with it? the Stormfather asked as Dalinar entered the empty corridors. *It is a weapon beyond parallel. The gift of a god. With it, you would be a Windrunner unoathed. And more. More that men do not understand, and cannot. Like a Herald, nearly.*

"All the more reason," Dalinar said, "to think very carefully before using it. Though I wouldn't mind if you kept an eye on it for me."

The Stormfather actually laughed. *You think I can see all things?*

"I kind of assumed . . . The map we made . . ."

I see what is left out in the storms, and that darkly. I am no god, Dalinar Kholin. No more than your shadow on the wall is you.

Dalinar reached the steps downward, then wound around and around, holding a broam for light. If Captain Kaladin didn't return soon, the Honorblade would provide another means of Windrunning—a way to get to

Thaylen City or Azir at speed. Or to get Elhokar's team to Kholinar. The Stormfather had also confirmed it could work Oathgates, which might prove handy.

Dalinar reached more inhabited sections of the tower, which bustled with movement. A chef's assistants hauling supplies from the storage dump right inside the tower gates, a couple of men painting lines on the floor to guide, families of soldiers in a particularly wide hallway, sitting on boxes along the wall and watching children roll wooden spheres down a slope into a room that had probably been another bath.

Life. Such an odd place to make a home, yet they'd transformed the barren Shattered Plains into one. This tower wouldn't be so different, assuming they could keep farming operations going on the Shattered Plains. And assuming they had enough Stormlight to keep those Oathgates working.

He was the odd man out, holding a sphere. Guards patrolled with lanterns. The cooks worked by lamp oil, but their stores were starting to run low. The women watching children and darning socks used only the light of a few windows along the wall here.

Dalinar passed near his rooms. Today's guards, spearmen from Bridge Thirteen, waited outside. He waved for them to follow him.

"Is all well, Brightlord?" one asked, catching up quickly. He spoke with a slow drawl—a Koron accent, from near the Sunmaker Mountains in central Alethkar.

"Fine," Dalinar said tersely, trying to determine the time. How long had he spent speaking with the Stormfather?

"Good, good," the guard said, spear held lightly to his shoulder. "Wouldn't want anything ta have happened ta you. While you were out. Alone. In the corridors. When you said nobody should be going about alone."

Dalinar eyed the man. Clean-shaven, he was a little pale for an Alethi and had dark brown hair. Dalinar vaguely thought the man had shown up among his guards several times during the last week or so. He liked to roll a sphere across his knuckles in what Dalinar found to be a distracting way.

"Your name?" Dalinar asked as they walked.

"Rial," the man said. "Bridge Thirteen." The soldier raised a hand and gave a precise salute, so careful it could have been given by one of Dalinar's finest officers, except he maintained the same lazy expression.

"Well, Sergeant Rial, I was *not* alone," Dalinar said. "Where did you get this habit of questioning officers?"

"It isn't a habit if you only do it once, Brightlord."

"And you've only ever done it once?"

"Ta you?"

"To anyone."

"Well," Rial said, "those don't count, Brightlord. I'm a new man. Reborn in the bridge crews."

Lovely. "Well, Rial, do you know what time it is? I have trouble telling in these storming corridors."

"You could use the clock device Brightness Navani sent you, sir," Rial said. "I think that's what they're for, you know."

Dalinar affixed him with another glare.

"Wasn't questioning you, sir," Rial said. "It wasn't a question, see. . . ."

Dalinar finally turned and stalked back down the corridor to his rooms. Where was that package Navani had given him? He found it on an end table, and from inside it removed a leather bracer somewhat like what an archer would wear. It had two clock faces set into the top. One showed the time with three hands—even seconds, as if that mattered. The other was a stormclock, which could be set to wind down to the next projected high-storm.

How did they get it all so small? he wondered, shaking the device. Set into the leather, it also had a painrial—a gemstone fabrial that would take pain from him if he pressed his hand on it. Navani had been working on various forms of pain-related fabrials for use by surgeons, and had mentioned using him as a test subject.

He strapped the device to his forearm, right above the wrist. It felt conspicuous there, wrapping around the outside of his uniform sleeve, but it *had* been a gift. In any case, he had an hour until his next scheduled meeting. Time to work out some of his restless energy. He collected his two guards, then made his way down a level to one of the larger chambers near where he housed his soldiers.

The room had black and grey strata on the walls, and was filled with men training. They all wore Kholin blue, even if just an armband. For now both lighteyes and dark practiced in the same chamber, sparring in rings with padded cloth mats.

As always, the sounds and smells of sparring warmed Dalinar. Sweeter than the scent of flatbread baking was that of oiled leather. More welcoming than the sound of flutes was that of practice swords rapping against one another. Wherever he was, and whatever station he obtained, a place like this would always be home.

He found the swordmasters assembled at the back wall, seated on cushions and supervising their students. Save for one notable exception, they all had squared beards, shaved heads, and simple, open-fronted robes that tied at the waist. Dalinar owned ardents who were experts in all manner of specialties, and per tradition any man or woman could come to them and be apprenticed in a new skill or trade. The swordmasters, however, were

his pride.

Five of the six men rose and bowed to him. Dalinar turned to survey the room again. The smell of sweat, the clang of weapons. They were the signs of preparation. The world might be in chaos, but Alethkar prepared.

Not Alethkar, he thought. *Urithiru. My kingdom.* Storms, it was going to be difficult to accustom himself to that. He would always be Alethi, but once Elhokar's proclamation came out, Alethkar would no longer be his. He still hadn't figured out how to present that fact to his armies. He wanted to give Navani and her scribes time to work out the exact legalities.

"You've done well here," Dalinar said to Kelerand, one of the sword-masters. "Ask Ivis if she'd look at expanding the training quarters into adjacent chambers. I want you to keep the troops busy. I'm worried about them getting restless and starting more fights."

"It will be done, Brightlord," Kelerand said, bowing.

"I'd like a spar myself," Dalinar said.

"I shall find someone suitable, Brightlord."

"What about you, Kelerand?" Dalinar said. The swordmaster bested Dalinar two out of three times, and though Dalinar had given up delusions of someday becoming the better swordsman—he was a soldier, not a duelist—he liked the challenge.

"I will," Kelerand said stiffly, "of course do as my highprince commands, though if given a choice, I shall pass. With all due respect, I don't feel that I would make a suitable match for you today."

Dalinar glanced toward the other standing swordmasters, who lowered their eyes. Swordmaster ardents weren't generally like their more religious counterparts. They could be formal at times, but you could laugh with them. Usually.

They were still ardents though.

"Very well," Dalinar said. "Find me someone to fight."

Though he'd intended it only as a dismissal of Kelerand, the other four joined him, leaving Dalinar. He sighed, leaning back against the wall, and glanced to the side. One man still lounged on his cushion. He wore a scruffy beard and clothing that seemed an afterthought—not dirty, but ragged, belted with rope.

"Not offended by my presence, Zahel?" Dalinar asked.

"I'm offended by everyone's presence. You're no more revolting than the rest, Mister Highprince."

Dalinar settled down on a stool to wait.

"You didn't expect this?" Zahel said, sounding amused.

"No. I thought . . . well, they're *fighting* ardents. Swordsmen. Soldiers, at heart."

"You're dangerously close to threatening them with a decision, Brightlord:

choose between God and their highprince. The fact that they like you doesn't make the decision easier, but more difficult."

"Their discomfort will pass," Dalinar said. "My marriage, though it seems dramatic now, will eventually be a mere trivial note in history."

"Perhaps."

"You disagree?"

"Every moment in our lives seems trivial," Zahel said. "Most are forgotten while some, equally humble, become the points upon which history pivots. Like white on black."

"White . . . on black?" Dalinar asked.

"Figure of speech. I don't really care what you did, Highprince. Lighteyed self-indulgence or serious sacrilege, either way it doesn't affect me. But there *are* those who are asking how far you're going to end up straying."

Dalinar grunted. Honestly, had he expected *Zahel* of all people to be helpful? He stood up and began to pace, annoyed at his own nervous energy. Before the ardents could return with someone for him to duel, he stalked back into the middle of the room, looking for soldiers he recognized. Men who wouldn't feel inhibited sparring with a highprince.

He eventually located one of General Khal's sons. Not the Shardbearer, Captain Halam Khal, but the next oldest son—a beefy man with a head that had always seemed a little too small for his body. He was stretching after some wrestling matches.

"Aratin," Dalinar said. "You ever sparred with a highprince?"

The younger man turned, then immediately snapped to attention. "Sir?"

"No need for formality. I'm just looking for a match."

"I'm not equipped for a proper duel, Brightlord," he said. "Give me some time."

"No need," Dalinar said. "I'm fine for a wrestling match. It's been too long."

Some men would rather not spar with a man as important as Dalinar, for fear of hurting him. Khal had trained his sons better than that. The young man grinned, displaying a prominent gap in his teeth. "Fine with me, Brightlord. But I'll have you know, I've not lost a match in months."

"Good," Dalinar said. "I need a challenge."

The swordmasters finally returned as Dalinar, stripped to the waist, was pulling on a pair of sparring leggings over his undershorts. The tight leggings came down only to his knees. He nodded to the swordmasters—ignoring the gentlemanly lighteyes they'd sought out for him to spar—and stepped into the wrestling ring with Aratin Khal.

His guards gave the swordmasters a kind of apologetic shrug, then Rial counted off a start to the wrestling match. Dalinar immediately lunged forward and slammed into Khal, grabbing him under the arms, struggling to hold his feet back and force his opponent off balance. The wrestling match would eventually go to the ground, but you wanted to be the one who controlled when and how that happened.

There was no grabbing the leggings in a traditional vehah match, and of course no grabbing hair, so Dalinar twisted, trying to get his opponent into a sturdy hold while preventing the man from shoving Dalinar over. Dalinar scrambled, his muscles taut, his fingers slipping on his opponent's skin.

For those frantic moments, he could focus only on the match. His strength against that of his opponent. Sliding his feet, twisting his weight, straining for purchase. There was a purity to the contest, a simplicity that he hadn't experienced in what seemed like ages.

Aratin pulled Dalinar tight, then managed to twist, tripping Dalinar over his hip. They went to the mat, and Dalinar grunted, raising his arm to his neck to prevent a chokehold, turning his head. Old training prompted him to twist and writhe before the opponent could get a good grip on him.

Too slow. It had been years since he'd done this regularly. The other man moved with Dalinar's twist, forgoing the attempt at a chokehold, instead getting Dalinar under the arms from behind and pressing him down, face against the mat, his weight on top of Dalinar.

Dalinar growled, and by instinct reached out for that extra reserve he'd always had. The pulse of the fight, the edge.

The Thrill. Soldiers spoke of it in the quiet of the night, over campfires. That battle rage unique to the Alethi. Some called it the power of their ancestors, others the true mindset of the soldier. It had driven the Sunmaker to glory. It was the open secret of Alethi success.

No. Dalinar stopped himself from reaching for it, but he needn't have worried. He couldn't remember feeling the Thrill in months—and the longer he'd been apart from it, the more he'd begun to recognize that there was something profoundly *wrong* about the Thrill.

So he gritted his teeth and struggled—cleanly and fairly—with his opponent.

And got pinned.

Aratin was younger, more practiced at this style of fight. Dalinar didn't make it easy, but he was on the bottom, lacked leverage, and simply wasn't as young as he'd once been. Aratin twisted him over, and before too long Dalinar found himself pressed to the mat, shoulders down, completely immobilized.

Dalinar knew he was beaten, but couldn't bring himself to tap out. Instead he strained against the hold, teeth gritted and sweat pouring down the sides of his face. He became aware of something. Not the Thrill . . . but Stormlight in the pocket of his uniform trousers, lying beside the ring.

Aratin grunted, arms like steel. Dalinar smelled his own sweat, the rough cloth of the mat. His muscles protested the treatment.

He knew he could seize the Stormlight power, but his sense of fairness protested at the mere thought. Instead he arched his back, holding his breath and heaving with everything he had, then twisted, trying to get back on his face for the leverage to escape.

His opponent shifted. Then groaned, and Dalinar felt the man's grip slipping . . . slowly. . . .

"Oh, for storm's sake," a feminine voice said. "Dalinar?"

Dalinar's opponent let go immediately, backing away. Dalinar twisted, puffing from exertion, to find Navani standing outside the ring with arms folded. He grinned at her, then stood up and accepted a light takama overshirt and towel from an aide. As Aratin Khal retreated, Dalinar raised a fist to him and bowed his head—a sign that Dalinar considered Aratin the victor. "Well played, son."

"An honor, sir!"

Dalinar threw on the takama, turning to Navani and wiping his brow with the towel. "Come to watch me spar?"

"Yes, what every wife loves," Navani said. "Seeing that in his spare time, her husband likes to roll around on the floor with half-naked, sweaty men." She glanced at Aratin. "Shouldn't you be sparring with men closer to your own age?"

"On the battlefield," Dalinar said, "I don't have the luxury of choosing the age of my opponent. Best to fight at a disadvantage here to prepare." He hesitated, then said more softly, "I think I almost had him anyway."

"Your definition of 'almost' is particularly ambitious, gemheart."

Dalinar accepted a waterskin from an aide. Though Navani and her aides weren't the only women in the room, the others were ardents. Navani in her bright yellow gown still stood out like a flower on a barren stone field.

As Dalinar scanned the chamber, he found that many of the ardents—not just the swordmasters—failed to meet his gaze. And there was Kadash, his former comrade-in-arms, speaking with the swordmasters.

Nearby, Aratin was receiving congratulations from his friends. Pinning the Blackthorn was considered quite the accomplishment. The young man accepted their praise with a grin, but he held his shoulder and winced when someone slapped him on the back.

I should have tapped out, Dalinar thought. Pushing the contest had endangered them both. He was annoyed at himself. He'd specifically chosen someone younger and stronger, then became a poor loser? Getting older was something he needed to accept, and he was kidding himself if he actually thought this would help him on the battlefield. He'd given away his armor, no longer carried a Shardblade. When exactly did he expect to be fighting in person again?

The man with nine shadows.

The water suddenly tasted stale in his mouth. He'd been expecting to fight the enemy's champion himself, assuming he could even make the contest happen to their advantage. But wouldn't assigning the duty to someone like Kaladin make far more sense?

"Well," Navani said, "you might want to throw on a uniform. The Iriali queen is ready."

"The meeting isn't for a few hours."

"She wants to do it now. Apparently, her court tidereader saw something in the waves that means an earlier meeting is better. She should be contacting us any minute."

Storming Iriali. Still, they had an Oathgate—two, if you counted the one in the kingdom of Rira, which Iri had sway over. Among Iri's three monarchs, currently two kings and a queen, the latter had authority over foreign policy, so she was the one they needed to talk to.

"I'm fine with moving up the time," Dalinar said.

"I'll await you in the writing chamber."

"Why?" Dalinar said, waving a hand. "It's not like she can see me. Set up here."

"Here," Navani said flatly.

"Here," Dalinar said, feeling stubborn. "I've had enough of cold chambers, silent save for the scratching of reeds."

Navani raised an eyebrow at him, but ordered her assistants to get out their writing materials. A worried ardent came over, perhaps to try to dissuade her—but after a few firm orders from Navani, he went running to get her a bench and table.

Dalinar smiled and went to select two training swords from a rack near the swordmasters. Common longswords of unsharpened steel. He tossed one to Kadash, who caught it smoothly, but then placed it in front of him with point down, resting his hands on the pommel.

"Brightlord," Kadash said, "I would prefer to give this task to another, as I don't particularly feel—"

"Tough," Dalinar said. "I need some practice, Kadash. As your master, I demand you give it to me."

Kadash stared at Dalinar for a protracted moment, then let out an annoyed huff and followed Dalinar to the ring. "I won't be much of a match for you, Brightlord. I have dedicated my years to scripture, not the sword. I was only here to—"

"—check up on me. I know. Well, maybe I'll be rusty too. I haven't fought with a common longsword in decades. I always had something better."

"Yes. I remember when you first got your Blade. The world itself trembled on that day, Dalinar Kholin."

"Don't be melodramatic," Dalinar said. "I was merely one in a long line of idiots given the ability to kill people too easily."

Rial hesitantly counted the start to the match, and Dalinar rushed in swinging. Kadash rebuffed him competently, then stepped to the side of the ring. "Pardon, Brightlord, but you *were* different from the others. You were much, much better at the killing part."

I always have been, Dalinar thought, rounding Kadash. It was odd to remember the ardent as one of his elites. They hadn't been close then; they'd only become so during Kadash's years as an ardent.

Navani cleared her throat. "Hate to interrupt this stick-wagging," she said, "but the queen is ready to speak with you, Dalinar."

"Great," he said, not taking his eyes off Kadash. "Read me what she says."

"While you're sparring?"

"Sure."

He could practically feel Navani roll her eyes. He grinned, coming in at Kadash again. She thought he was being silly. Perhaps he was.

He was also failing. One at a time, the world's monarchs were shutting him out. Only Taravangian of Kharbranth—known to be slow witted—had agreed to listen to him. Dalinar was doing something wrong. In an extended war campaign, he'd have forced himself to look at his problems from a new perspective. Bring in new officers to voice their ideas. Try to approach battles from different terrain.

Dalinar clashed blades with Kadash, smashing metal against metal.

"'Highprince,'" Navani read as he fought, "'it is with wondrous awe at the grandeur of the One that I approach you. The time for the world to undergo a glorious new experience has arrived.'"

"Glorious, Your Majesty?" Dalinar said, swiping at Kadash's leg. The man dodged back. "Surely you can't *welcome* these events?"

"'All experience is welcome,'" came the reply. "'We are the One experiencing itself—and this new storm is glorious even if it brings pain.'"

Dalinar grunted, blocking a backhand from Kadash. Swords rang loudly.

"I hadn't realized," Navani noted, "that she was so religious."

"Pagan superstition," Kadash said, sliding back across the mat from Dalinar. "At least the Azish have the decency to worship the Heralds, although they blasphemously place them above the Almighty. The Iriali are no better than Shin shamans."

"I remember, Kadash," Dalinar said, "when you weren't nearly so judgmental."

"I've been informed that my laxness might have served to encourage you."

"I always found your perspective to be refreshing." He stared right at Kadash, but spoke to Navani. "Tell her: Your Majesty, as much as I welcome a challenge, I fear the suffering these new . . . experiences will bring. We must be unified in the face of the coming dangers."

"Unity," Kadash said softly. "If that is your goal, Dalinar, then why do you seek to rip apart your own people?"

Navani started writing. Dalinar drew closer, passing his longsword from one hand to the other. "How do you know, Kadash? How do you *know* the Iriali are the pagans?"

Kadash frowned. Though he wore the square beard of an ardent, that scar on his head wasn't the only thing that set him apart from his fellows. They treated swordplay like just another art. Kadash had the haunted eyes of a soldier. When he dueled, he kept watch to the sides, in case someone tried to flank him. An impossibility in a solo duel, but all too likely on a battlefield.

"How can you ask that, Dalinar?"

"Because it should be asked," Dalinar said. "You claim the Almighty is God. Why?"

"Because he simply *is*."

"That isn't good enough for me," Dalinar said, realizing for the first time it was true. "Not anymore."

The ardent growled, then leaped in, attacking with real determination this time. Dalinar danced backward, fending him off, as Navani read—loudly.

"'Highprince, I will be frank. The Iriali Triumvirate is in agreement. Alethkar has not been relevant in the world since the Sunmaker's fall. The power of the ones who control the new storm, however, is undeniable. They offer gracious terms.'"

Dalinar stopped in place, dumbfounded. "You'd side with the *Voidbringers*?" he asked toward Navani, but then was forced to defend himself from Kadash, who hadn't let up.

"What?" Kadash said, clanging his blade against Dalinar's. "Surprised someone is willing to side with evil, Dalinar? That someone would pick darkness, superstition, and heresy instead of the Almighty's light?"

"I am *not* a heretic." Dalinar slapped Kadash's blade away—but not before the ardent scored a touch on Dalinar's arm. The hit was hard, and though the swords were blunted, that would bruise for certain.

"You just *told* me you doubted the Almighty," Kadash said. "What is left, after that?"

"I don't know," Dalinar said. He stepped closer. "I don't know, and that *terrifies* me, Kadash. But Honor spoke to me, confessed that he was beaten."

"The princes of the Voidbringers," Kadash said, "were said to be able to blind the eyes of men. To send them lies, Dalinar."

He rushed in, swinging, but Dalinar danced back, retreating around the rim of the dueling ring.

"'My people,'" Navani said, reading the reply from the queen of Iri, "'do not want war. Perhaps the way to prevent another Desolation is to let the Voidbringers take what they wish. From our histories, sparse though they are, it seems that this was the one option men never explored. An experience from the One we rejected.'"

Navani looked up, obviously as surprised to read the words as Dalinar was to hear them. The pen kept writing. "'Beyond that,'" she added, "'we have reasons to distrust the word of a thief, Highprince Kholin.'"

Dalinar groaned. So *that* was what this was all about—Adolin's Shardplate. Dalinar glanced at Navani. "Find out more, try to console them?"

She nodded, and started writing. Dalinar gritted his teeth and charged Kadash again. The ardent caught his sword, then grabbed his takama with his free hand, pulling him close, face to face.

"The Almighty is *not dead*," Kadash hissed.

"Once, you'd have counseled me. Now you glare at me. What happened to the ardent I knew? A man who had lived a real life, not just watched the world from high towers and monasteries?"

"He's frightened," Kadash said softly. "That he's somehow failed in his most solemn duty to a man he deeply admires."

They met eyes, their swords still locked, but neither one actually trying to push the other. For a moment, Dalinar saw in Kadash the man he'd always been. The gentle, understanding model of everything good about the Vorin church.

"Give me something to take back to the curates of the church," Kadash pled. "Recant your insistence that the Almighty is dead. If you do that, I can make them accept the marriage. Kings have done worse and retained Vorin support."

Dalinar set his jaw, then shook his head.

"Dalinar . . ."

"Falsehoods serve nobody, Kadash," Dalinar said, pulling back. "If the Almighty is dead, then pretending otherwise is pure stupidity. We need real hope, not faith in lies."

Around the room, more than a few men had stopped their bouts to watch or listen. The swordmasters had stepped up behind Navani, who was still exchanging some politic words with the Iriali queen.

"Don't throw out everything we've believed because of a few dreams, Dalinar," Kadash said. "What of our society, what of *tradition*?"

"Tradition?" Dalinar said. "Kadash, did I ever tell you about my first sword trainer?"

"No," Kadash said, frowning, glancing at the other ardents. "Was it Rembrinor?"

Dalinar shook his head. "Back when I was young, our branch of the Kholin family didn't have grand monasteries and beautiful practice grounds. My father found a teacher for me from two towns over. His name was Harth. Young fellow, not a true swordmaster—but good enough.

"He was very focused on proper procedure, and wouldn't let me train until I'd learned how to put on a takama the right way." Dalinar gestured at the takama shirt he was wearing. "He wouldn't have stood for me fighting like this. You put on the skirt, then the overshirt, then you wrap your cloth belt around yourself three times and tie it.

"I always found that annoying. The belt was too tight, wrapped three times—you had to pull it hard to get enough slack to tie the knot. The first time I went to duels at a neighboring town, I felt like an idiot. Everyone else had long drooping belt ends at the front of their takamas.

"I asked Harth why we did it differently. He said it was the right way, the *true* way. So, when my travels took me to Harth's hometown, I searched out his master, a man who had trained with the ardents in Kholinar. He insisted that this was the right way to tie a takama, as he'd learned from his master."

By now, they'd drawn an even larger crowd. Kadash frowned. "And the point?"

"I found my master's master's master in Kholinar after we captured it," Dalinar said. "The ancient, wizened ardent was eating curry and flatbread, completely uncaring of who ruled the city. I asked him. Why tie your belt three times, when everyone else thinks you should do it twice?

"The old man laughed and stood up. I was shocked to see that he was terribly short. 'If I only tie it twice,' he exclaimed, 'the ends hang down so low, I trip!'"

The chamber fell silent. Nearby, one soldier chuckled, but quickly cut himself off—none of the ardents seemed amused.

"I love tradition," Dalinar said to Kadash. "I've *fought* for tradition. I make my men follow the codes. I uphold Vorin virtues. But merely being tradition does not make something worthy, Kadash. We can't just assume that because something is *old* it is *right*."

He turned to Navani.

"She's not listening," Navani said. "She insists you are a thief, not to be trusted."

"Your Majesty," Dalinar said. "I am led to believe that you would let nations fall, and men be slaughtered, because of a petty grievance from the past. If my relations with the kingdom of Rira are prompting you to consider supporting the enemies of all humankind, then perhaps we could discuss a personal reconciliation first."

Navani nodded at that, though she glanced at the people watching and cocked an eyebrow. She thought all this should have been done in private. Well, perhaps she was right. At the same time, Dalinar felt he'd needed this. He couldn't explain why.

He raised his sword to Kadash in a sign of respect. "Are we done here?"

In response, Kadash came running at him, sword raised. Dalinar sighed, then let himself get touched on the left, but ended the exchange with his weapon leveled at Kadash's neck.

"That's not a valid dueling strike," the ardent said.

"I'm not much of a duelist these days."

The ardent grunted, then shoved away Dalinar's weapon and lunged at him. Dalinar, however, caught Kadash's arm, then spun the man with his own momentum. He slammed Kadash down to the ground and held him there.

"The world is ending, Kadash," Dalinar said. "I can't simply rely on tradition. I need to know *why*. Convince me. Offer me proof of what you say."

"You shouldn't *need* proof in the Almighty. You sound like your niece!"

"I'll take that as a compliment."

"What . . . what of the Heralds?" Kadash said. "Do you deny *them*, Dalinar? They were servants of the Almighty, and their existence proved his. They had *power*."

"Power?" Dalinar said. "Like this?"

He sucked in Stormlight. Murmuring rose from those watching as Dalinar began to glow, then did . . . something else. Commanded the Light. When he rose, he left Kadash stuck to the ground in a pool of Radiance that held him fast, binding him to the stone. The ardent wriggled, helpless.

"The Knights Radiant have returned," Dalinar said. "And yes, I accept the authority of the Heralds. I accept that there was a being, once, named Honor—the Almighty. He helped us, and I would welcome his help again. If you can prove to me that Vorinism as it currently stands is what the Heralds taught, we will speak again."

He tossed his sword aside and stepped up to Navani.

"Nice show," she said softly. "That was for the room, not just Kadash, I assume?"

"The soldiers need to know where I stand in relation to the church. What does our queen say?"

"Nothing good," she muttered. "She says you can contact her with arrangements for the return of the stolen goods, and she'll consider."

"Storming woman," Dalinar said. "She's after Adolin's Shardplate. How valid is her claim?"

"Not very," Navani said. "You got that through marriage, and to a light-eyes from Rira, not Iri. Yes, the Iriali claim their sister nation as a vassal, but even if the claim weren't disputed, the queen doesn't have any actual relation to Evi or her brother."

Dalinar grunted. "Rira was never strong enough to try to claim the Plate back. But if it will bring Iri to our side, then I'd consider it. Maybe I can agree to . . ." He trailed off. "Wait. What did you say?"

"Hum?" Navani said. "About . . . oh, right. You can't hear her name."

"Say it again," Dalinar whispered.

"What?" Navani said. "Evi?"

Memories blossomed in Dalinar's head. He staggered, then slumped against the writing table, feeling as if he'd been struck by a hammer to the head. Navani called for physicians, implying his dueling had overtaxed him.

That wasn't it. Instead, it was the burning in his mind, the sudden shock of a word spoken.

Evi. He could *hear his wife's name.*

And he suddenly remembered her face.

17

TRAPPED
IN SHADOWS

It is not a lesson I claim to be able to teach. Experience herself is the great teacher, and you must seek her directly.

—From *Oathbringer*, preface

I still think we should kill him," Khen—the parshwoman who had been playing cards—said to the others.

Kaladin sat tied and bound to a tree. He'd spent the night there. They'd let him up several times to use the latrine today, but otherwise kept him bound. Though their knots were good, they always posted guards, even though he'd turned himself in to them in the first place.

His muscles were stiff, and the posture was uncomfortable, but he had endured worse as a slave. Almost the entire afternoon had passed so far—and they were still arguing about him.

He didn't see that yellow-white spren again, the one that had been a ribbon of light. He almost thought he'd imagined it. At least the rain had finally stopped. Hopefully that meant the highstorms—and Stormlight—were close to returning.

"Kill him?" another of the parshmen said. "Why? What danger is he to us?"

"He'll tell others where we are."

"He found us easily enough on his own. I doubt others will have trouble, Khen."

The parshmen didn't seem to have a specific leader. Kaladin could hear them talking from where they stood, huddled together beneath a tarp. The air smelled wet, and the clump of trees shivered when a gust of wind blew through. A shower of water drops came down on top of him, somehow more cold than the Weeping itself.

Soon, blessedly, this would all dry up and he could finally see the sun again.

"So we let him go?" Khen asked. She had a gruff voice, angry.

"I don't know. Would you actually do it, Khen? Bash his head in yourself?"

The tent fell silent.

"If it means they can't take us again?" she said. "Yes, I'd kill him. I won't go back, Ton."

They had simple, darkeyed Alethi names—matched by their uncomfortably familiar accents. Kaladin didn't worry for his safety; though they'd taken his knife, spanreed, and spheres, he could summon Syl at a moment's notice. She flitted nearby on gusts of wind, dodging between the branches of trees.

The parshmen eventually left their conference, and Kaladin dozed. He was later roused by the noise of them gathering up their meager belongings: an axe or two, some waterskins, the nearly ruined bags of grain. As the sun set, long shadows stretched across Kaladin, plunging the camp into darkness again. It seemed that the group moved at night.

The tall male who had been playing cards the night before approached Kaladin, who recognized the pattern of his skin. He untied the ropes binding Kaladin to the tree, the ones around his ankles—but left the bonds on Kaladin's hands.

"You *could* capture that card," Kaladin noted.

The parshman stiffened.

"The card game," Kaladin said. "The squire can capture if supported by an allied card. So you were right."

The parshman grunted, yanking on the rope to tow Kaladin to his feet. He stretched, working stiff muscles and painful cramps, as the other parshmen broke down the last of the improvised tarp tents: the one that had been fully enclosed. Earlier in the day, though, Kaladin had gotten a look at what was inside.

Children.

There were a dozen of them, dressed in smocks, of various ages from toddler to young teenager. The females wore their hair loose, and the males wore theirs tied or braided. They hadn't been allowed to leave the tent except at a few carefully supervised moments, but he had heard them laughing. He'd first worried they were captured human children.

As the camp broke, they scattered about, excited to finally be released. One younger girl scampered across the wet stones and seized the empty hand of the man leading Kaladin. Each of the children bore the distinctive look of their elders—the not-quite-Parshendi appearance with the armored portions on the sides of their heads and forearms. For the children, the color of the carapace was a light orange-pink.

Kaladin couldn't define why this sight seemed so strange to him. Parshmen did breed, though people often spoke of them *being bred*, like animals. And, well, that wasn't far from the truth, was it? Everyone knew it.

What would Shen—Rlain—think if Kaladin had said those words out loud?

The procession moved out of the trees, Kaladin led by his ropes. They kept talk to a minimum, and as they crossed through a field in the darkness, Kaladin had a distinct impression of familiarity. Had he been here before, done this before?

"What about the king?" his captor said, speaking in a soft voice, but turning his head to direct the question at Kaladin.

Elhokar? What . . . *Oh, right. The cards.*

"The king is one of the most powerful cards you can place," Kaladin said, struggling to remember all the rules. "He can capture any other card except another king, and can't be captured himself unless touched by three enemy cards of knight or better. Um . . . and he is immune to the Soulcaster." *I think.*

"When I watched men play, they used this card rarely. If it is so powerful, why delay?"

"If your king gets captured, you lose," Kaladin said. "So you only play him if you're desperate or if you are certain you can defend him. Half the times I've played, I left him in my barrack all game."

The parshman grunted, then looked to the girl at his side, who tugged on his arm and pointed. He gave her a whispered response, and she ran on tiptoes toward a patch of flowering rockbuds, visible by the light of the first moon.

The vines pulled back, blossoms closing. The girl, however, knew to squat at the side and wait, hands poised, until the flowers reopened—then she snatched one in each hand, her giggles echoing across the plain. Joyspren followed her like blue leaves as she returned, giving Kaladin a wide berth.

Khen, walking with a cudgel in her hands, urged Kaladin's captor to keep moving. She watched the area with the nervousness of a scout on a dangerous mission.

That's it, Kaladin thought, remembering why this felt familiar. *Sneaking away from Tasinar.*

It had happened after he'd been condemned by Amaram, but before he'd been sent to the Shattered Plains. He avoided thinking of those months. His repeated failures, the systematic butchering of his last hints of idealism . . . well, he'd learned that dwelling on such things took him to dark places. He'd failed so many people during those months. Nalma had been one of those. He could remember the touch of her hand in his: a rough, callused hand.

That had been his most successful escape attempt. It had lasted five days.

"You're not monsters," Kaladin whispered. "You're not soldiers. You're not even the seeds of the void. You're just . . . runaway slaves."

His captor spun, yanking on Kaladin's rope. The parshman seized Kaladin by the front of his uniform, and his daughter hid behind his leg, dropping one of her flowers and whimpering.

"Do you *want* me to kill you?" the parshman asked, pulling Kaladin's face close to his own. "You insist on reminding me how your kind see us?"

Kaladin grunted. "Look at my forehead, parshman."

"And?"

"Slave brands."

"What?"

Storms . . . parshmen weren't branded, and they didn't mix with other slaves. Parshmen were actually too valuable for that. "When they make a human into a slave," Kaladin said, "they brand him. I've been here. Right where you are."

"And you think that makes you understand?"

"Of course it does. I'm one—"

"*I* have spent my entire *life* living in a fog," the parshman yelled at him. "Every day knowing I should say something, do *something* to stop this! Every night clutching my daughter, wondering why the world seems to move around us in the light—while we are trapped in shadows. They sold her mother. *Sold her.* Because she had birthed a healthy child, which made her good breeding stock.

"Do you understand *that,* human? Do you understand watching your family be torn apart, and knowing you should object—knowing deep in your soul that something is *profoundly* wrong? Can you know that feeling of being unable to say a *single storming word* to stop it?"

The parshman pulled him even closer. "They may have taken your freedom, but they took our *minds.*"

He dropped Kaladin and whirled, gathering up his daughter and holding her close as he jogged to catch up to the others, who had turned back at the outburst. Kaladin followed, yanked by his rope, stepping on the little girl's flower in his forced haste. Syl zipped past, and when Kaladin tried to catch her attention, she just laughed and flew higher on a burst of wind.

His captor suffered several quiet chastisements when they caught up;

this column couldn't afford to draw attention. Kaladin walked with them, and remembered. He did understand a little.

You were never free while you ran; you felt as if the open sky and the endless fields were a torment. You could feel the pursuit following, and each morning you awoke expecting to find yourself surrounded.

Until one day you were right.

But parshmen? He'd accepted Shen into Bridge Four, yes. But accepting that a sole parshman could be a bridgeman was starkly different from accepting the entire people as . . . well, human.

As the column stopped to distribute waterskins to the children, Kaladin felt at his forehead, tracing the scarred shape of the glyphs there.

They took our minds. . . .

They'd tried to take his mind too. They'd beaten him to the stones, stolen everything he loved, and murdered his brother. Left him unable to think straight. Life had become a blur until one day he'd found himself standing over a ledge, watching raindrops die and struggling to summon the motivation to end his life.

Syl soared past in the shape of a shimmering ribbon.

"Syl," Kaladin hissed. "I need to talk to you. This isn't the time for—"

"Hush," she said, then giggled and zipped around him before flitting over and doing the same to his captor.

Kaladin frowned. She was acting so carefree. Too carefree? Like she'd been back before they forged their bond?

No. It couldn't be.

"Syl?" he begged as she returned. "Is something wrong with the bond? Please, I didn't—"

"It's not that," she said, speaking in a furious whisper. "I think parshmen might be able to see me. Some, at least. And that other spren is still here too. A higher spren, like me."

"Where?" Kaladin asked, twisting.

"He's invisible to you," Syl said, becoming a group of leaves and blowing around him. "I think I've fooled him into thinking I'm just a windspren."

She zipped away, leaving a dozen unanswered questions on Kaladin's lips. *Storms . . . is that spren how they know where to go?*

The column started again, and Kaladin walked for a good hour in silence before Syl next decided to come back to him. She landed on his shoulder, becoming the image of a young woman in her whimsical skirt. "He's gone ahead for a little bit," she said. "And the parshmen aren't looking."

"The spren is guiding them," Kaladin said under his breath. "Syl, this spren must be . . ."

"From *him*," she whispered, wrapping her arms around herself and growing small—actively shrinking to about two-thirds her normal size. "Voidspren."

"There's more," Kaladin said. "These parshmen . . . how do they know how to talk, how to act? Yes, they've spent their lives around society—but to be this, well, normal after such a long time half asleep?"

"The Everstorm," Syl said. "Power has filled the holes in their souls, bridging the gaps. They didn't just wake, Kaladin. They've been healed, Connection refounded, Identity restored. There's more to this than we ever realized. Somehow when you conquered them, you stole their ability to change forms. You literally ripped off a piece of their souls and locked it away." She turned sharply. "He's coming back. I will stay nearby, in case you need a Blade."

She left, zipping straight into the air as a ribbon of light. Kaladin continued to shuffle behind the column, chewing on her words, before speeding up and stepping beside his captor.

"You're being smart, in some ways," Kaladin said. "It's good to travel at night. But you're following the riverbed over there. I know it makes for more trees, and more secure camping, but this is literally the first place someone would look for you."

Several of the other parshmen gave him glances from nearby. His captor didn't say anything.

"The big group is an issue too," Kaladin added. "You should break into smaller groups and meet up each morning, so if you get spotted you'll seem less threatening. You can say you were sent somewhere by a lighteyes, and travelers might let you go. If they run across all seventy of you together, there's no chance of that. This is all assuming, of course, you don't want to fight—which you don't. If you fight, they'll call out the highlords against you. For now they've got bigger problems."

His captor grunted.

"I can help you," Kaladin said. "I might not understand what you've been through, but I *do* know what it feels like to run."

"You think I'd trust you?" the parshman finally said. "You will *want* us to be caught."

"I'm not sure I do," Kaladin said, truthful.

His captor said nothing more and Kaladin sighed, dropping back into position behind. Why had the Everstorm not granted these parshmen powers like those on the Shattered Plains? What of the stories of scripture and lore? The Desolations?

They eventually stopped for another break, and Kaladin found himself a smooth rock to sit against, nestled into the stone. His captor tied the rope to a nearby lonely tree, then went to confer with the others. Kaladin leaned back, lost in thought until he heard a sound. He was surprised to find his captor's daughter approaching. She carried a waterskin in two hands, and stopped right beyond his reach.

She didn't have shoes, and the walk so far had not been kind to her feet, which—though tough with calluses—were still scored by scratches and scrapes. She timidly set the waterskin down, then backed away. She didn't flee, as Kaladin might have expected, when he reached for the water.

"Thank you," he said, then took a mouthful. It was pure and clear—apparently the parshmen knew how to settle and scoop their water. He ignored the rumbling of his stomach.

"Will they really chase us?" the girl asked.

By Mishim's pale green light, he decided this girl was not as timid as he had assumed. She was nervous, but she met his eyes with hers.

"Why can't they just let us go?" she asked. "Could you go back and tell them? We don't want trouble. We just want to go away."

"They'll come," Kaladin said. "I'm sorry. They have a lot of work to do in rebuilding, and they'll want the extra hands. You are a . . . resource they can't simply ignore."

The humans he'd visited hadn't known to expect some terrible Voidbringer force; many thought their parshmen had merely run off in the chaos.

"But why?" she said, sniffling. "What did we do to them?"

"You tried to destroy them."

"No. We're nice. We've always been nice. I never hit anyone, even when I was mad."

"I didn't mean you specifically," Kaladin said. "Your ancestors—the people like you from long ago. There was a war, and . . ."

Storms. How did you explain slavery to a seven-year-old? He tossed the waterskin to her, and she scampered back to her father—who had only just noticed her absence. He stood, a stark silhouette in the night, studying Kaladin.

"They're talking about making camp," Syl whispered from nearby. She had crawled into a crack in the rock. "The Voidspren wants them to march on through the day, but I don't think they're going to. They're worried about their grain spoiling."

"Is that spren watching me right now?" Kaladin asked.

"No."

"Then let's cut this rope."

He turned and hid what he was doing, then quickly summoned Syl as a knife to cut himself free. That would change his eye color, but in the darkness, he hoped the parshmen wouldn't notice.

Syl puffed back into a spren. "Sword now?" she said. "The spheres they took from you have all run out, but they'll scatter at seeing a Blade."

"No." Kaladin instead picked up a large stone. The parshmen hushed, noticing his escape. Kaladin carried his rock a few steps, then dropped it, crushing a rockbud. He was surrounded a few moments later by angry parshmen carrying cudgels.

Kaladin ignored them, picking through the wreckage of the rockbud. He held up a large section of shell.

"The inside of this," he said, turning it over for them, "will still be dry, despite the rainfall. The rockbud needs a barrier between itself and the water outside for some reason, though it always seems eager to drink after a storm. Who has my knife?"

Nobody moved to return it.

"If you scrape off this inner layer," Kaladin said, tapping at the rockbud shell, "you can get to the dry portion. Now that the rain has stopped, I should be able to get us a fire going, assuming nobody has lost my tinder bag. We need to boil that grain, then dry it into cakes. They won't be tasty, but they'll keep. If you don't do something soon, your supplies *will* rot."

He stood up and pointed. "Since we're already here, we should be near enough the river that we can gather more water. It won't flow much longer with the end of the rains.

"Rockbud shells don't burn particularly well, so we'll want to harvest some real wood and dry it at the fire during the day. We can keep that one small, then do the cooking tomorrow night. In the dark, the smoke is less likely to reveal us, and we can shield the light in the trees. I just have to figure out how we're going to cook without any pots to boil the water."

The parshmen stared at him. Then Khen finally pushed him away from the rockbud and took up the shard he'd been holding. Kaladin spotted his original captor standing near the rock where Kaladin had been sitting. The parshman held the rope Kaladin had cut, rubbing its sliced-through end with his thumb.

After a short conference, the parshmen dragged him to the trees he'd indicated, returned his knife—standing by with every cudgel they had—and demanded that he prove he could build a fire with wet wood.

He did just that.

DOUBLE VISION

You cannot have a spice described to you, but must taste it for yourself.

—From *Oathbringer*, preface

Shallan became Veil.

Stormlight made her face less youthful, more angular. Nose pointed, with a small scar on the chin. Her hair rippled from red to Alethi black. Making an illusion like this took a larger gem of Stormlight, but once it was going, she could maintain it for hours on just a smidgen.

Veil tossed aside the havah, instead pulling on trousers and a tight shirt, then boots and a long white coat. She finished with only a simple glove on the left hand. Veil, of course, wasn't in the least embarrassed at that.

There was a simple relief for Shallan's pain. There was an easy way to hide. Veil hadn't suffered as Shallan had—and she was tough enough to handle that sort of thing anyway. Becoming her was like setting down a terrible burden.

Veil threw a scarf around her neck, then slung a rugged satchel—acquired for Veil specifically—over her shoulder. Hopefully the conspicuous knife handle sticking out from the top would look natural, even intimidating.

The part at the back of her mind that was still Shallan worried about this. Would she look fake? She'd almost certainly missed some subtle clues encoded in her behavior, dress, or speech. These would indicate to the right people that Veil didn't have the hard-bitten experience she feigned.

Well, she would have to do her best and hope to recover from her inevitable mistakes. She tied another knife onto her belt, long, but not quite a sword, since Veil wasn't lighteyed. Fortunately. No lighteyed woman would be able to prance around so obviously armed. Some mores grew lax the farther you descended the social ladder.

"Well?" Veil asked, turning to the wall, where Pattern hung.

"Mmm . . ." he said. "Good lie."

"Thank you."

"Not like the other."

"Radiant?"

"You slip in and out of her," Pattern said, "like the sun behind clouds."

"I just need more practice," Veil said. Yes, that voice sounded excellent. Shallan *was* getting far better with sounds.

She picked Pattern up—which involved pressing her hand against the wall, letting him pass over to her skin and then her coat. With him humming happily, she crossed her room and stepped out onto the balcony. The first moon had risen, violet and proud Salas. She was the least bright of the moons, which meant it was mostly dark out.

Most rooms on the outside had these small balconies, but hers on the second level was particularly advantageous. It had steps down to the field below. Covered in furrows for water and ridges for planting rockbuds, the field also had boxes at the edges for growing tubers or ornamental plants. Each tier of the city had a similar one, with eighteen levels inside separating them.

She stepped down to the field in the darkness. How had anything ever grown up here? Her breath puffed out in front of her, and coldspren grew around her feet.

The field had a small access doorway back into Urithiru. Perhaps the subterfuge of not exiting through her room wasn't necessary, but Veil preferred to be careful. She wouldn't want guards or servants remarking on how Brightness Shallan went about during odd hours of the night.

Besides, who knew where Mraize and his Ghostbloods had operatives? They hadn't contacted her since that first day in Urithiru, but she knew they'd be watching. She still didn't know what to do about them. They had admitted to assassinating Jasnah, which should be grounds enough to hate them. They also seemed to know things, important things, about the world.

Veil strolled through the corridor, carrying a small hand lamp for light, as a sphere would make her stand out. She passed evening crowds that kept the corridors of Sebarial's quarter as busy as his warcamp had been. Things never seemed to slow down here as much as they did in Dalinar's quarter.

The strangely mesmerizing strata of the corridors guided her out of Sebarial's quarter. The number of people in the hallways slackened. Just Veil and those lonely, endless tunnels. She felt as if she could sense the weight of the other levels of the tower, empty and unexplored, bearing down on her. A mountain of unknown stone.

She hurried on her way, Pattern humming to himself from her coat.

"I like him," Pattern said.

"Who?" Veil said.

"The swordsman," Pattern said. "Mmm. The one you can't mate with yet."

"Can we please stop talking about him that way?"

"Very well," Pattern said. "But I like him."

"You hate his sword."

"I have come to understand," Pattern said, growing excited. "Humans . . . humans *don't care about the dead*. You build chairs and doors out of corpses! You *eat* corpses! You make clothing from the skins of corpses. Corpses are *things* to you."

"Well, I guess that's true." He seemed unnaturally excited by the revelation.

"It is grotesque," he continued, "but you all must *kill* and *destroy* to live. It is the way of the Physical Realm. So I should not hate Adolin Kholin for wielding a corpse!"

"You just like him," Veil said, "because he tells Radiant to respect the sword."

"Mmm. Yes, very, very nice man. Wonderfully smart too."

"Why don't you marry him, then?"

Pattern buzzed. "Is that—"

"No that's not an option."

"Oh." He settled down into a contented buzz on her coat, where he appeared as a strange kind of embroidery.

After a short time walking, Shallan found she needed to say something more. "Pattern. Do you remember what you said to me the other night, the first time . . . we became Radiant?"

"About dying?" Pattern asked. "It may be the only way, Shallan. Mmm . . . You must speak truths to progress, but you will hate me for making it happen. So I can die, and once done you can—"

"No. No, *please* don't leave me."

"But you hate me."

"I hate myself too," she whispered. "Just . . . *please*. Don't go. Don't die."

Pattern seemed pleased by this, as his humming increased—though his sounds of pleasure and his sounds of agitation could be similar. For the moment, Veil let herself be distracted by the night's quest. Adolin continued his efforts to find the murderer, but hadn't gotten far. Aladar was Highprince of Information, and his policing force and scribes were a resource—but Adolin wanted badly to do as his father asked.

Veil thought that perhaps both were looking in the wrong places. She finally saw lights ahead and quickened her pace, eventually stepping out onto a walkway around a large cavernous room that stretched up several stories. She had reached the Breakaway: a vast collection of tents lit by many flickering candles, torches, or lanterns.

The market had sprung up shockingly fast, in defiance of Navani's carefully outlined plans. Her idea had been for a grand thoroughfare with shops along the sides. No alleyways, no shanties or tents. Easily patrolled and carefully regulated.

The merchants had rebelled, complaining about lack of storage space, or the need to be closer to a well for fresh water. In reality, they wanted a larger market that was much harder to regulate. Sebarial, as Highprince of Commerce, had agreed. And despite having made a mess of his ledgers, he was sharp when it came to trade.

The chaos and variety of it excited Veil. Hundreds of people, despite the hour, attracting spren of a dozen varieties. Dozens upon dozens of tents of varied colors and designs. In fact, some weren't tents at all, but were better described as stands—roped-off sections of ground guarded by a few burly men with cudgels. Others were actual buildings. Small stone sheds that had been built inside this cavern, here since the days of the Radiants.

Merchants from all ten original warcamps mixed at the Breakaway. She passed three different cobblers in a row; Veil had never understood why merchants selling the same things congregated. Wouldn't it be better to set up where you wouldn't have competition literally next door?

She packed away her hand lamp, as there was plenty of light here from the merchant tents and shops, and sauntered along. Veil felt more comfortable than she had in those empty, twisted corridors; here, life had gained a foothold. The market grew like the snarl of wildlife and plants on the leeward side of a ridge.

She made her way to the cavern's central well: a large, round enigma that rippled with crem-free water. She'd never seen an actual well before—everyone normally used cisterns that refilled with the storms. The many wells in Urithiru, however, never ran out. The water level didn't even drop, despite people constantly drawing from them.

Scribes talked about the possibility of a hidden aquifer in the mountains, but where would the water come from? Snows at the tops of the peaks nearby didn't seem to melt, and rain fell very rarely.

Veil sat on the well's side, one leg up, watching the people who came and went. She listened to the women chatter about the Voidbringers, about family back in Alethkar, and about the strange new storm. She listened to the men worry about being pressed into the military, or about their dark-eyed nahn being lowered, now that there weren't parshmen to do common work. Some lighteyed workers complained about supplies trapped back in Narak, waiting for Stormlight before they could be transferred here.

Veil eventually ambled off toward a particular row of taverns. *I can't interrogate too hard to get my answers,* she thought. *If I ask the wrong kind of questions, everyone will figure me for some kind of spy for Aladar's policing force.*

Veil. Veil didn't hurt. She was comfortable, confident. She'd meet people's eyes. She'd lift her chin in challenge to anyone who seemed to be sizing her up. Power was an illusion of perception.

Veil had her own kind of power, that of a lifetime spent on the streets knowing she could take care of herself. She had the stubbornness of a chull, and while she was cocky, that confidence was a power of its own. She got what she wanted and wasn't embarrassed by success.

The first bar she chose was inside a large battle tent. It smelled of spilled lavis beer and sweaty bodies. Men and women laughed, using over-turned crates as tables and chairs. Most wore simple darkeyed clothing: laced shirts—no money or time for buttons—and trousers or skirts. A few men dressed after an older fashion, with a wrap and a loose filmy vest that left the chest exposed.

This was a low-end tavern, and likely wouldn't work for her needs. She'd need a place that was lower, yet somehow richer. More disreputable, but with access to the powerful members of the warcamp undergrounds.

Still, this seemed a good place to practice. The bar was made of stacked boxes and had some actual chairs beside it. Veil leaned against the "bar" in what she hoped was a smooth way, and nearly knocked the boxes over. She stumbled, catching them, then smiled sheepishly at the bartender—an old darkeyed woman with grey hair.

"What do you want?" the woman asked.

"Wine," Veil said. "Sapphire." The second most intoxicating. Let them see that Veil could handle the hard stuff.

"We got Vari, kimik, and a nice barrel of Veden. That one will cost you though."

"Uh . . ." Adolin would have known the differences. "Give me the Veden." Seemed appropriate.

The woman made her pay first, with dun spheres, but the cost didn't seem outrageous. Sebarial wanted the liquor flowing—his suggested way to make sure tensions didn't get too high in the tower—and had subsidized the prices with low taxes, for now.

While the woman worked behind her improvised bar, Veil suffered beneath the gaze of one of the bouncers. Those didn't stay near the entrance, but instead waited here, beside the liquor and the money. Despite what Aladar's policing force would like, this place was not completely safe. If unexplained murders *had* been glossed over or forgotten, they would have happened in the Breakaway, where the clutter, worry, and press of tens of thousands of camp followers balanced on the edge of lawlessness.

The barkeep plunked a cup in front of Veil—a *tiny* cup, with a clear liquid in it.

Veil scowled, holding it up. "You got mine wrong, barkeep; I ordered sapphire. What is this, water?"

The bouncer nearest Veil snickered, and the barkeep stopped in place, then looked her over. Apparently Shallan had already made one of those mistakes she'd been worried about.

"Kid," the barkeep said, somehow leaning on the boxes near her and not knocking any over. "That's the same stuff, just without the fancy infusions the lighteyes put in theirs."

Infusions?

"You some kind of house servant?" the woman asked softly. "Out for your first night on your own?"

"Of course not," Veil said. "I've done this a hundred times."

"Sure, sure," the woman replied, tucking a stray strand of hair behind her ear. It popped right back up. "You certain you want that? I might have some wines back here done with lighteyed colors, for you. In fact, I know I've got a nice orange." She reached to reclaim the cup.

Veil seized it and knocked the entire thing back in a single gulp. That proved to be one of the worst mistakes of her life. The liquid *burned*, like it was on fire! She felt her eyes go wide, and she started coughing and almost threw up right there on the bar.

That was wine? Tasted more like lye. What was wrong with these people? There was no sweetness to it at all, not even a hint of flavor. Just that burning sensation, like someone was scraping her throat with a scouring brush! Her face immediately grew warm. It hit her so fast!

The bouncer was holding his face, trying—and failing—not to laugh out loud. The barkeep patted Shallan on the back as she kept coughing. "Here," the woman said, "let me get you something to chase that—"

"No," Shallan croaked. "I'm just happy to be able to drink this . . . again after so long. Another. Please."

The barkeep seemed skeptical, though the bouncer was all for it—he'd settled down on the stool to watch Shallan, grinning. Shallan placed a sphere on the bar, defiant, and the barkeep reluctantly filled her cup again.

By now, three or four other people from nearby seats had turned to watch. Lovely. Shallan braced herself, then drank the wine in a long, extended gulp.

It wasn't any better the second time. She held for a moment, eyes watering, then let out an explosion of coughing. She ended up hunched over, shaking, eyes squeezed closed. She was pretty sure she let out a long squeak as well.

Several people in the tent clapped. Shallan looked back at the amused barkeep, her eyes watering. "That was awful," she said, then coughed. "You *really* drink this dreadful liquid?"

"Oh, hon," the woman said. "That's not *nearly* as bad as they get."

Shallan groaned. "Well, get me another."

"You sure—"

"Yes," Shallan said with a sigh. She probably wasn't going to be establishing a reputation for herself tonight—at least not the type she wanted. But she could try to accustom herself to drinking this cleaning fluid.

Storms. She was already feeling lighter. Her stomach did *not* like what she was doing to it, and she shoved down a bout of nausea.

Still chuckling, the bouncer moved a seat closer to her. He was a younger man, with hair cut so short it stood up on end. He was as Alethi as they came, with a deep tan skin and a dusting of black scrub on his chin.

"You should try sipping it," he said to her. "Goes down easier in sips."

"Great. That way I can savor the terrible flavor. So bitter! Wine is supposed to be sweet."

"Depends on how you make it," he said as the barkeep gave Shallan another cup. "Sapphire can sometimes be distilled tallew, no natural fruit in it—just some coloring for accent. But they don't serve the really hard stuff at lighteyed parties, except to people who know how to ask for it."

"You know your alcohol," Veil said. The room shook for a moment before settling. Then she tried another drink—a sip this time.

"It comes with the job," he said with a broad smile. "I work a lot of fancy events for the lighteyes, so I know my way around a place with tablecloths instead of boxes."

Veil grunted. "They need bouncers at fancy lighteyed events?"

"Sure," he said, cracking his knuckles. "You just have to know how to 'escort' someone out of the feast hall, instead of throwing them out. It's actually easier." He cocked his head. "But strangely, more dangerous at the same time." He laughed.

Kelek, Veil realized as he scooted closer. *He's flirting with me.*

She probably shouldn't have found it so surprising. She'd come in alone, and while Shallan would never have described Veil as "cute," she wasn't ugly. She was kind of normal, if rugged, but she dressed well and obviously had money. Her face and hands were clean, her clothing—while not rich silks—a generous step up from worker garb.

Initially she was offended by his attention. Here she'd gone to all this trouble to make herself capable and hard as rocks, and the first thing she did was attract some guy? One who cracked his knuckles and tried to tell her how to drink her alcohol?

Just to spite him, she downed the rest of her cup in a single shot.

She immediately felt guilty for her annoyance at the man. Shouldn't she be flattered? Granted, Adolin *could* have destroyed this man in any conceivable way. Adolin even cracked his knuckles louder.

"So . . ." the bouncer said. "Which warcamp you from?"

"Sebarial," Veil said.

The bouncer nodded, as if he'd expected that. Sebarial's camp had been the most eclectic. They chatted a little longer, mostly with Shallan making the odd comment while the bouncer—his name was Jor—went off on various stories with many tangents. Always smiling, often boasting.

He wasn't too bad, though he didn't seem to care what she actually said, so long as it prompted him to keep talking. She drank some more of the terrible liquid, but found her mind wandering.

These people . . . they each had lives, families, loves, dreams. Some slumped at their boxes, lonely, while others laughed with friends. Some kept their clothing, poor though it was, reasonably clean—others were stained with crem and lavis ale. Several of them reminded her of Tyn, the way they talked with confidence, the way their interactions were a subtle game of one-upping each other.

Jor paused, as if expecting something from her. What . . . what had he been saying? Following him was getting harder, as her mind drifted.

"Go on," she said.

He smiled, and launched into another story.

I'm not going to be able to imitate this, she thought, leaning against her box, *until I've lived it. No more than I could draw their lives without having walked among them.*

The barkeep came back with the bottle, and Shallan nodded. That last cup hadn't burned nearly as much as the others.

"You . . . sure you want more?" the bouncer asked.

Storms . . . she was starting to feel *really* sick. She'd had four cups, yes, but they were little cups. She blinked, and turned.

The room spun in a blur, and she groaned, resting her head on the table. Beside her, the bouncer sighed.

"I could have told you that you were wasting your time, Jor," the barkeep said. "This one will be out before the hour is done. Wonder what she's trying to forget . . ."

"She's just enjoying a little free time," Jor said.

"Sure, sure. With eyes like those? I'm sure that's it." The barkeep moved away.

"Hey," Jor said, nudging Shallan. "Where are you staying? I'll call you a palanquin to cart you home. You awake? You should get going before things go too late. I know some porters who can be trusted."

"It's . . . not even late yet . . ." Shallan mumbled.

"Late enough," Jor said. "This place can get dangerous."

"Yeaaah?" Shallan asked, a glimmer of memory waking inside of her. "People get stabbed?"

"Unfortunately," Jor said.

"You know of some . . . ?"

"Never happens here in this area, at least not yet."

"Where? So I . . . so I can stay away . . ." Shallan said.

"All's Alley," he said. "Keep away from there. Someone got stabbed behind one of the taverns just last night there. They found him dead."

"Real . . . real strange, eh?" Shallan asked.

"Yeah. You heard?" Jor shivered.

Shallan stood up to go, but the room upended about her, and she found herself slipping down beside her stool. Jor tried to catch her, but she hit the ground with a thump, knocking her elbow against the stone floor. She immediately sucked in a little Stormlight to help with the pain.

The cloud around her mind puffed away, and her vision stopped spinning. In a striking moment, her drunkenness simply vanished.

She blinked. *Wow.* She stood up without Jor's help, dusting off her coat and then pulling her hair back away from her face. "Thanks," she said, "but that's exactly the information I need. Barkeep, we settled?"

The woman turned, then froze, staring at Shallan, pouring liquid into a cup until it overflowed.

Shallan picked up her cup, then turned it and shook the last drop into her mouth. "That's good stuff," she noted. "Thanks for the conversation, Jor." She set a sphere on the boxes as a tip, pulled on her hat, then patted Jor fondly on the cheek before striding out of the tent.

"Stormfather!" Jor said from behind her. "Did I just get played for a fool?"

It was still busy out, reminding her of Kharbranth, with its midnight markets. That made sense. Neither sun nor moon could penetrate to these halls; it was easy to lose track of time. Beyond that, while most people had been put immediately to work, many of the soldiers had free time without plateau runs to do any longer.

Shallan asked around, and managed to get pointed toward All's Alley. "The Stormlight made me sober," she said to Pattern, who had crawled up her coat and now dimpled her collar, folded over the top.

"Healed you of poison."

"That will be useful."

"Mmmm. I thought you'd be angry. You drank the poison on purpose, didn't you?"

"Yes, but the point wasn't to get drunk."

He buzzed in confusion. "Then why drink it?"

"It's complicated," Shallan said. She sighed. "I didn't do a very good job in there."

"Of getting drunk? Mmm. You gave it a good effort."

"As soon as I got drunk, as soon as I lost control, Veil slipped away from me."

"Veil is just a face."

No. Veil was a woman who didn't giggle when she got drunk, or whine, fanning her mouth when the drink was too hard for her. She never acted like a silly teenager. Veil hadn't been sheltered, practically locked away, until she went crazy and murdered her own family.

Shallan stopped in place, suddenly frantic. "My brothers. Pattern, I didn't kill them, right?"

"What?" he said.

"I talked to Balat over spanreed," Shallan said, hand to her forehead. "But . . . I had Lightweaving then . . . even if I didn't fully know it. I could have fabricated that. Every message from him. My own memories . . ."

"Shallan," Pattern said, sounding concerned. "No. They live. Your brothers live. Mraize said he rescued them. They are on their way here. This isn't the lie." His voice grew smaller. "Can't you tell?"

She adopted Veil again, her pain fading. "Yes. Of course I can tell." She started forward again.

"Shallan," Pattern said. "This is . . . mmm . . . there is something wrong with these lies you place upon yourself. I don't understand it."

"I just need to go deeper," she whispered. "I can't be Veil only on the surface."

Pattern buzzed with a soft, anxious vibration—fast paced, high pitched. Veil hushed him as she reached All's Alley. A strange name for a tavern, but she had seen stranger. It wasn't an alley at all, but a big set of five tents sewn together, each a different color. It glowed dimly from within.

A bouncer stood out front, short and squat, with a scar running up his cheek, across his forehead, and onto his scalp. He gave Veil a critical looking-over, but didn't stop her as she sauntered—full of confidence—into the tent. It smelled worse than the other pub, with all these drunken people crammed together. The tents had been sewn to create partitioned-off areas, darkened nooks—and a few had tables and chairs instead of boxes. The people who sat at them didn't wear the simple clothing of workers, but instead leathers, rags, or unbuttoned military coats.

Both richer than the other tavern, Veil thought, *and lower at the same time.*

She rambled through the room, which—despite oil lamps on some tables—was quite dim. The "bar" was a plank set across some boxes, but they'd draped a cloth over the middle. A few people waited for drinks; Veil ignored them. "What's the strongest thing you've got?" she asked the barkeep, a fat man in a takama. She thought he might be lighteyed. It was too dim to tell for certain.

He looked her over. "Veden saph, single barrel."

"Right," Veil said dryly. "If I wanted water, I'd go to the well. Surely you've got something stronger."

The barkeep grunted, then reached behind himself and took out a jug of something clear, with no label. "Horneater white," he said, thumping it down on the table. "I have no idea what they ferment to make the stuff, but it takes paint off real nicely."

"Perfect," Veil said, clacking a few spheres onto the improvised counter. The others in line had been shooting her glares for ignoring the line, but at this their expressions turned to amusement.

The barkeep poured Veil a very small cup of the stuff and set it before her. She downed it in one gulp. Shallan trembled inside at the burning that followed—the immediate warmth to her cheeks and almost instant sense of nausea, accompanied by a tremor through her muscles as she tried to resist throwing up.

Veil was expecting all this. She held her breath to stifle the nausea, and *relished* the sensations. *No worse than the pains already inside,* she thought, warmth radiating through her.

"Great," she said. "Leave the jug."

Those idiots beside the bar continued to gawk as she poured another cup of the Horneater white and downed it, feeling its warmth. She turned to inspect the tent's occupants. Who to approach first? Aladar's scribes had checked watch records for anyone else killed the same way as Sadeas, and they'd come up empty—but a killing in an alleyway might not get reported. She hoped that the people here would know of it regardless.

She poured some more of that Horneater drink. Though it was even fouler-tasting than the Veden saph, she found something strangely appealing about it. She downed the third cup, but drew in a tiny bit of Stormlight from a sphere in her pouch—just a smidge that instantly burned away and didn't make her glow—to heal herself.

"What are you looking at?" she said, eyeing the people in line at the bar.

They turned away as the bartender moved to put a stopper on the jug. Veil put her hand on top of it. "I'm not done with that yet."

"You are," the bartender said, brushing her hand away. "One of two things is going to happen if you continue like that. You'll either puke all over my bar, or you'll drop dead. You're not a Horneater; this *will* kill you."

"That's my problem."

"The mess is *mine*," the barkeep said, yanking the jug back. "I've seen your type, with that haunted look. You'll get yourself drunk, then pick a fight. I don't care what it is you want to forget; go find some other place to do it."

Veil cocked an eyebrow. Getting kicked out of the most disreputable bar in the market? Well, at least her reputation wouldn't suffer here.

She caught the barkeep's arm as he pulled it back. "I'm not here to tear your bar down, friend," she said softly. "I'm here about a murder. Someone who was killed here a few days back."

The barkeep froze. "Who are you? You with the guard?"

"Damnation, no!" Veil said. *Story. I need a cover story.* "I'm hunting the man who killed my little sister."

"And that has to do with my bar how?"

"I've heard rumors of a body found near here."

"A grown woman," the barkeep said. "So not your sister."

"My sister didn't die here," Veil said. "She died back in the warcamps; I'm just hunting the one who did it." She hung on as the barkeep tried to pull away again. "Listen. I'm not going to make trouble. I just need information. I hear there were . . . unusual circumstances about this death. This *rumored* death. The man who killed my sister, he has something strange about him. He kills in the same way every time. Please."

The barkeep met her eyes. *Let him see,* Veil thought. *Let him see a woman with a hard edge, but wounds inside.* A story reflected in her eyes—a narrative she needed this man to believe.

"The one who did it," the barkeep said softly, "has already been dealt with."

"I need to know if your murderer is the same one I've been hunting," Veil said. "I need details of the killing, however gruesome they may be."

"I can't say anything," the barkeep whispered, but he nodded toward one of the alcoves made from the stitched-together tents, where shadows indicated some people were drinking. "They might."

"Who are they?"

"Just your everyday, ordinary thugs," the barkeep said. "But they're the ones I pay to keep my bar out of trouble. If someone *had* disturbed this establishment in a way that risked the authorities shutting the place down—as that Aladar is so fond of doing—those are the people who would have taken care of said problem. I won't say more."

Veil nodded in thanks, but didn't let go of his arm. She tapped her cup and cocked her head hopefully. The barkeep sighed and gave her one more hit of the Horneater white, which she paid for, then sipped as she walked away.

The alcove he'd indicated held a single table full of a variety of ruffians. The men wore the clothing of the Alethi upper crust: jackets and stiff uniform-style trousers, belts and buttoned shirts. Here, their jackets were undone, their shirts loose. Two of the women even wore the havah, though another was in trousers and a jacket, not too different from what Veil wore. The whole group reminded her of Tyn in the way they lounged in an almost *deliberate* way. It took effort to look so indifferent.

There was an unoccupied seat, so Veil strolled right in and took it. The lighteyed woman across from her hushed a jabbering man by touching his lips. She wore the havah, but without a safehand sleeve—instead, she wore a glove with the fingers brazenly cut off at the knuckles.

"That's Ur's seat," the woman said to Veil. "When he gets back from the pisser, you'd best have moved on."

"Then I'll be quick," Veil said, downing the rest of her drink, savoring the warmth. "A woman was found dead here. I think the murderer might have also killed someone dear to me. I've been told the murderer was 'dealt with,' but I need to know for myself."

"Hey," said a foppish man wearing a blue jacket, with slits in the outer layer to show yellow underneath. "You're the one that was drinking the Horneater white. Old Sullik only keeps that jug as a joke."

The woman in the havah laced her fingers before herself, inspecting Veil.

"Look," Veil said, "just tell me what the information will cost me."

"One can't buy," the woman said, "what isn't for sale."

"Everything is for sale," Veil said, "if you ask the right way."

"Which you're not doing."

"Look," Veil said, trying to catch the woman's eyes. "Listen. My kid sister, she—"

A hand fell on Shallan's shoulder, and she looked up to find an enormous Horneater man standing behind her. Storms, he had to be nearly seven feet tall.

"This," he said, drawing out the *i* sound to an *e* instead, "is my spot."

He pulled Veil off the chair, tossing her backward to roll on the ground, her cup tumbling away, her satchel twisting and getting wound up in her arms. She came to a rest, blinking as the large man sat on the chair. She felt she could hear its soul groaning in protest.

Veil growled, then stood up. She yanked off her satchel and dropped it, then removed a handkerchief and the knife from inside. This knife was narrow and pointed, long but thinner than the one on her belt.

She picked up her hat and dusted it off before replacing it and strolling back up to the table. Shallan disliked confrontation, but Veil loved it.

"Well, well," she said, resting her safehand on the top of the large Horneater's left hand, which was lying flat on the tabletop. She leaned down beside him. "You say it's your place, but I don't see it marked with your name."

The Horneater stared at her, confused by the strangely intimate gesture of putting her safehand on his hand.

"Let me show you," she said, removing her knife and placing the point onto the back of her hand, which was pressed against his.

"What is this?" he asked, sounding amused. "You put on an act, being tough? I have seen men pretend—"

Veil rammed the knife down through her hand, through his, and into the tabletop. The Horneater screamed, whipping his hand upward, making Veil pull the knife out of both hands. The man toppled out of his chair as he scrambled away from her.

Veil settled down in it again. She took the cloth from her pocket and wrapped it around her bleeding hand. That would obscure the cut when she healed it.

Which she didn't do at first. It would need to be seen bleeding. Instead—a part of her surprised at how calm she remained—she retrieved her knife, which had fallen beside the table.

"You're crazy!" the Horneater said, recovering his feet, holding his bleeding hand. "You're *ana'kai crazy*."

"Oh wait," Veil said, tapping the table with her knife. "Look, I see your mark here, in blood. Ur's seat. I was wrong." She frowned. "But mine's here too. Suppose you can sit in my lap, if you want."

"I'll throttle you!" Ur said, shooting a glare at the people in the main room of the tent, who had crowded around the entrance to this smaller room, whispering. "I'll—"

"Quiet, Ur," the woman in the havah said.

He sputtered. "But Betha!"

"You think," the woman said to Veil, "assaulting my friends is going to make me *more* likely to talk?"

"Honestly, I just wanted the seat back." Veil shrugged, scratching at the tabletop with her knife. "But if you want me to start hurting people, I suppose I could do that."

"You really are crazy," Betha said.

"No. I just don't consider your little group a threat." She continued scratching. "I've tried being nice, and my patience is running thin. It's time to tell me what I want to know before this turns ugly."

Betha frowned, then glanced at what Veil had scratched into the tabletop. Three interlocking diamonds.

The symbol of the Ghostbloods.

Veil gambled that the woman would know what it meant. They seemed the type who would—small-time thugs, yes, but ones with a presence in an important market. Veil wasn't certain how secretive Mraize and his people were with their symbol, but the fact that they got it tattooed on their bodies indicated to her that it wasn't supposed to be terribly secret. More a warning, like cremlings who displayed red claws to indicate they were poisonous.

Indeed, the moment Betha saw the symbol, she gasped softly. "We . . . we want nothing to do with your type," Betha said. One of the men at the table stood up, trembling, and looked from side to side, as if expecting assassins to tackle him right then.

Wow, Veil thought. Even cutting the hand of one of their members hadn't provoked this strong a reaction.

Curiously though, one of the other women at the table—a short, younger woman wearing a havah—leaned forward, interested.

"The murderer," Veil said. "What happened to him?"

"We had Ur drop him off the plateau outside," Betha said. "But . . . how could this be a man *you* would be interested in? It was just Ned."

"Ned?"

"Drunk, from Sadeas's camp," said one of the men. "Angry drunk; always got into trouble."

"Killed his wife," Betha said. "Pity too, after she followed him all the way out here. Guess none of us had much choice, with that crazy storm. But still . . ."

"And this Ned," Veil said, "murdered his wife with a knife through the eye?"

"What? No, he strangled her. Poor bastard."

Strangled? "That's it?" Veil said. "No knife wounds?"

Betha shook her head, seeming confused.

Stormfather, Veil thought. So it was a dead end? "But I heard that the murder was strange."

"No," the standing man said, then settled back down beside Betha, knife out. He set it on the table, in front of them. "We knew Ned would go too far at some point. Everyone did. I don't think any of us was surprised when, after she tried to drag him away from the tavern that night, he finally went over the edge."

Literally, Shallan thought. *At least once Ur got hold of him.*

"It appears," Veil said, standing up, "that I have wasted your time. I will leave spheres with the barkeep; your tab is my debt, tonight." She spared a glance for Ur, who hunched nearby and regarded her with a sullen expression. She waved her bloodied fingers at him, then made her way back toward the main tent room of the tavern.

She hovered just inside it, contemplating her next move. Her hand throbbed, but she ignored it. Dead end. Perhaps she'd been foolish to think she could solve in a few hours what Adolin had spent weeks trying to crack.

"Oh, don't look so sullen, Ur," Betha said from behind, voice drifting out of the tent alcove. "At least it was just your hand. Considering who that was, it could have been a *lot* worse."

"But why was she so interested in Ned?" Ur said. "Is she going to come back because I killed him?"

"She wasn't after him," one of the other women snapped. "Didn't you listen? Ain't nobody that cares Ned killed poor Rem." She paused. "Course, it could have been about the other woman he killed."

Veil felt a shock run through her. She spun, striding back into the alcove. Ur whimpered, hunching down and holding his wounded hand.

"There was *another* murder?" Veil demanded.

"I . . ." Betha licked her lips. "I was going to tell you, but you left so fast that—"

"Just talk."

"We'd have let the watch take care of Ned, but he couldn't leave it at killing just poor Rem."

"He killed another person?"

Betha nodded. "One of the barmaids here. *That* we couldn't let pass. We protect this place, you see. So Ur had to take a long walk with Ned."

The man with the knife rubbed his chin. "Strangest thing, that he'd come back and kill a barmaid the next night. Left her body right around the corner from where he killed poor Rem."

"He screamed the whole time we were taking him to his fall that he hadn't killed the second one," Ur muttered.

"He did," Betha said. "That barmaid was strangled the exact same way as Rem, body dropped in the same position. Even had the marks of his ring scraping her chin like Rem did." Her light brown eyes had a hollow cast to them, like she was staring at the body again, as it had been found. "Exact same marks. Uncanny."

Another double murder, Veil thought. *Storms. What does it mean?*

Veil felt dazed, though she didn't know if it was from drink or the unwelcome image of the strangled women. She went and gave the barkeep some spheres—probably too many—and hooked the jug of Horneater white with her thumb, then carted it out with her into the night.

19

THE SUBTLE ART
OF DIPLOMACY

THIRTY-ONE YEARS AGO

Acandle flickered on the table, and Dalinar lit the end of his napkin in it, sending a small braid of pungent smoke into the air. Stupid decorative candles. What was the point? Looking pretty? Didn't they use spheres because they were better than candles for light?

At a glare from Gavilar, Dalinar stopped burning his napkin and leaned back, nursing a mug of deep violet wine. The kind you could smell from across the room, potent and flavorful. A feast hall spread before him, dozens of tables set on the floor of the large stone room. The place was far too warm, and sweat prickled on his arms and forehead. Too many candles maybe.

Outside the feast hall, a storm raged like a madman who'd been locked away, impotent and ignored.

"But how do you deal with highstorms, Brightlord?" Toh said to Gavilar. The tall, blond-haired Westerner sat with them at the high table.

"Good planning keeps an army from needing to be out during a storm except in rare situations," Gavilar explained. "Holdings are common in Alethkar. If a campaign takes longer than anticipated, we can split the army and retreat back to a number of these towns for shelter."

"And if you're in the middle of a siege?" Toh asked.

"Sieges are rare out here, Brightlord Toh," Gavilar said, chuckling.

"Surely there are cities with fortifications," Toh said. "Your famed Kholinar has majestic walls, does it not?" The Westerner had a thick accent and spoke in a clipped, annoying way. Sounded silly.

"You're forgetting about Soulcasters," Gavilar said. "Yes, sieges happen now and then, but it's very hard to starve out a city's soldiers while there are Soulcasters and emeralds to make food. Instead we usually break down the walls quickly, or—more commonly—we seize the high ground and use that vantage to pound the city for a while."

Toh nodded, seeming fascinated. "Soulcasters. We have not these things in Rira or Iri. Fascinating, fascinating . . . And so many Shards here. Perhaps half the world's wealth of Blades and Plates, all contained in Vorin kingdoms. The Heralds themselves favor you."

Dalinar took a long pull on his wine. Outside, thunder shook the bunker. The highstorm was in full force now.

Inside, servants brought out slabs of pork and lanka claws for the men, cooked in a savory broth. The women dined elsewhere, including, he'd heard, Toh's sister. Dalinar hadn't met her yet. The two Western lighteyes had arrived barely an hour before the storm hit.

The hall soon echoed with the sounds of people chatting. Dalinar tore into his lanka claws, cracking them with the bottom of his mug and biting out the meat. This feast seemed too polite. Where was the music, the laughter? The women? Eating in separate rooms?

Life had been different these last few years of conquest. The final four highprinces stood firm in their unified front. The once-frantic fighting had stalled. More and more of Gavilar's time was required by the administration of his kingdom—which was half as big as they wanted it to be, but still demanding.

Politics. Gavilar and Sadeas didn't make Dalinar play at it too often, but he still had to sit at feasts like this one, rather than dining with his men. He sucked on a claw, watching Gavilar talk to the foreigner. Storms. Gavilar actually looked regal, with his beard combed like that, glowing gemstones on his fingers. He wore a uniform of the newer style. Formal, rigid. Dalinar instead wore his skirtlike takama and an open overshirt that went down to midthigh, his chest bare.

Sadeas held court with a group of lesser lighteyes at a table across the hall. Every one of that group had been carefully chosen: men with uncertain loyalties. He'd talk, persuade, convince. And if he was worried, he'd find ways to eliminate them. Not with assassins, of course. They all found that sort of thing distasteful; it wasn't the Alethi way. Instead, they'd maneuver the man into a duel with Dalinar, or would position him at the front of an assault. Ialai, Sadeas's wife, spent an impressive amount of time cooking up new schemes for getting rid of problematic allies.

Dalinar finished the claws, then turned toward his pork, a succulent slab of meat swimming in gravy. The food *was* better at this feast. He just wished that he didn't feel so useless here. Gavilar made alliances; Sadeas dealt with problems. Those two could treat a feast hall like a battlefield.

Dalinar reached to his side for his knife so he could cut the pork. Except the knife wasn't there.

Damnation. He'd lent it to Teleb, hadn't he? He stared down at the pork, smelling its peppery sauce, his mouth watering. He reached to eat with his fingers, then thought to look up. Everyone else was eating primly, with utensils. But the servers had forgotten to bring him a knife.

Damnation again. He sat back, wagging his mug for more wine. Nearby, Gavilar and that foreigner continued their chat.

"Your campaign here *has* been impressive, Brightlord Kholin," Toh said. "One sees a glint of your ancestor in you, the great Sunmaker."

"Hopefully," Gavilar noted, "my accomplishments won't be as ephemeral as his."

"Ephemeral! He reforged Alethkar, Brightlord! You shouldn't speak so of one like him. You're his descendant, correct?"

"We all are," Gavilar said. "House Kholin, House Sadeas . . . all ten princedoms. Their founders were his sons, you know. So yes, signs of his touch are here—yet his empire didn't last even a single generation past his death. Leaves me wondering what was wrong with his vision, his planning, that his great empire broke apart so quickly."

The storm rumbled. Dalinar tried to catch the attention of a servant to request a dinner knife, but they were too busy scuttling about, seeing to the needs of other demanding feastgoers.

He sighed, then stood—stretching—and walked to the door, holding his empty mug. Lost in thought, he threw aside the bar on the door, then shoved open the massive wooden construction and stepped outside.

A sheet of icy rain suddenly washed over his skin, and wind blasted him fiercely enough that he stumbled. The highstorm was at its raging height, lightning blasting down like vengeful attacks from the Heralds.

Dalinar struck out into the storm, his overshirt whipping about him. Gavilar talked more and more about things like legacy, the kingdom, responsibility. What had happened to the fun of the fight, to riding into battle laughing?

Thunder crashed, and the periodic strikes of lightning were barely enough to see by. Still, Dalinar knew his way around well enough. This was a highstorm waystop, a place built to house patrolling armies during storms. He and Gavilar had been positioned at this one for a good four months now, drawing tribute from the nearby farms and menacing House Evavakh from just inside its borders.

Dalinar found the particular bunker he was looking for and pounded on the door. No response. So he summoned his Shardblade, slid the tip between the double doors, and sliced the bar inside. He pushed open the door to find a group of wide-eyed armed men scrambling into defensive lines, surrounded by fearspren, weapons held in nervous grips.

"Teleb," Dalinar said, standing in the doorway. "Did I lend you my belt knife? My favorite one, with the whitespine ivory on the grip?"

The tall soldier, who stood in the second rank of terrified men, gaped at him. "Uh . . . your *knife*, Brightlord?"

"Lost the thing somewhere," Dalinar said. "I lent it to you, didn't I?"

"I gave it back, sir," Teleb said. "You used it to pry that splinter out of your saddle, remember?"

"Damnation. You're right. What *did* I do with that blasted thing?" Dalinar left the doorway and strode back out into the storm.

Perhaps Dalinar's worries had more to do with himself than they did Gavilar. The Kholin battles were so calculated these days—and these last months had been more about what happened off the battlefield than on it. It all seemed to leave Dalinar behind like the discarded shell of a cremling after it molted.

An explosive burst of wind drove him against the wall, and he stumbled, then stepped backward, driven by instincts he couldn't define. A large boulder slammed into the wall, then bounced away. Dalinar glanced and saw something luminous in the distance: a gargantuan figure that moved on spindly glowing legs.

Dalinar stepped back up to the feast hall, gave the whatever-it-was a rude gesture, then pushed open the door—throwing aside two servants who had been holding it closed—and strode back in. Streaming with water, he walked up to the high table, where he flopped into his chair and set down his mug. Wonderful. Now he was wet and he *still* couldn't eat his pork.

Everyone had gone silent. A sea of eyes stared at him.

"Brother?" Gavilar asked, the only sound in the room. "Is everything . . . all right?"

"Lost my storming knife," Dalinar said. "Thought I'd left it in the other bunker." He raised his mug and took a loud, lazy slurp of rainwater.

"Excuse me, Lord Gavilar," Toh stammered. "I . . . I find myself in need of refreshment." The blond-haired Westerner stood from his place, bowed, and retreated across the room to where a master-servant was administering drinks. His face seemed even paler than those folk normally were.

"What's wrong with him?" Dalinar asked, scooting his chair closer to his brother.

"I assume," Gavilar said, sounding amused, "that people he knows don't casually go for strolls in highstorms."

"Bah," Dalinar said. "This is a fortified waystop, with walls and bunkers. We needn't be scared of a little wind."

"Toh thinks differently, I assure you."

"You're grinning."

"You may have just proven in one moment, Dalinar, a point I've spent a half hour trying to make politically. Toh wonders if we're strong enough to protect him."

"Is that what the conversation was about?"

"Obliquely, yes."

"Huh. Glad I could help." Dalinar picked at a claw on Gavilar's plate. "What does it take to get one of these fancy servants to get me a storming knife?"

"They're master-servants, Dalinar," his brother said, making a sign by raising his hand in a particular way. "The sign of need, remember?"

"No."

"You really need to pay better attention," Gavilar said. "We aren't living in huts anymore."

They'd never lived in huts. They were Kholin, heirs to one of the world's great cities—even if Dalinar had never seen the place before his twelfth year. He didn't like that Gavilar was buying into the story the rest of the kingdom told, the one that claimed their branch of the house had until recently been ruffians from the backwaters of their own princedom.

A gaggle of servants in black and white flocked to Gavilar, and he requested a new dining knife for Dalinar. As they split to run the errand, the doors to the women's feast hall opened, and a figure slipped in.

Dalinar's breath caught. Navani's hair glowed with the tiny rubies she'd woven into it, a color matched by her pendant and bracelet. Her face a sultry tan, her hair Alethi jet black, her red-lipped smile so knowing and clever. And a figure . . . a figure to make a man weep for desire.

His brother's wife.

Dalinar steeled himself and raised his arm in a gesture like the one Gavilar had made. A serving man stepped up with a springy gait. "Brightlord," he said, "I will see to your desires of course, though you might wish to know that the sign is off. If you'll allow me to demonstrate—"

Dalinar made a rude gesture. "Is this better?"

"Uh . . ."

"Wine," Dalinar said, wagging his mug. "Violet. Enough to fill this three times at least."

"And what vintage would you like, Brightlord?"

He eyed Navani. "Whichever one is closest."

Navani slipped between tables, followed by the squatter form of Ialai Sadeas. Neither seemed to care that they were the only lighteyed women in the room.

"What happened to the emissary?" Navani said as she arrived. She slid between Dalinar and Gavilar as a servant brought her a chair.

"Dalinar scared him off," Gavilar said.

The scent of her perfume was heady. Dalinar scooted his chair to the side and set his face. Be firm, don't let her know how she warmed him, brought him to life like nothing else but battle.

Ialai pulled a chair over for herself, and a servant brought Dalinar's wine. He took a long, calming drink straight from the jug.

"We've been assessing the sister," Ialai said, leaning in from Gavilar's other side. "She's a touch vapid—"

"A *touch*?" Navani asked.

"—but I'm reasonably sure she's being honest."

"The brother seems the same," Gavilar said, rubbing his chin and inspecting Toh, who was nursing a drink near the bar. "Innocent, wide-eyed. I think he's genuine though."

"He's a sycophant," Dalinar said with a grunt.

"He's a man without a home, Dalinar," Ialai said. "No loyalty, at the mercy of those who take him in. And he has only one piece he can play to secure his future."

Shardplate.

Taken from his homeland of Rira and brought east, as far as Toh could get from his kinsmen—who were reportedly outraged to find such a precious heirloom stolen.

"He doesn't have the armor with him," Gavilar said. "He's at least smart enough not to carry it. He'll want assurances before giving it to us. Powerful assurances."

"Look how he stares at Dalinar," Navani said. "You impressed him." She cocked her head. "Are you wet?"

Dalinar ran his hand through his hair. Storms. He hadn't been embarrassed to stare down the crowd in the room, but before her he found himself blushing.

Gavilar laughed. "He went for a stroll."

"You're kidding," Ialai said, scooting over as Sadeas joined them at the high table. The bulbous-faced man settled down on her chair with her, the two of them sitting half on, half off. He dropped a plate on the table, piled with claws in a bright red sauce. Ialai attacked them immediately. She was one of the few women Dalinar knew who liked masculine food.

"What are we discussing?" Sadeas asked, waving away a master-servant with a chair, then draping his arm around his wife's shoulders.

"We're talking about getting Dalinar married," Ialai said.

"What?" Dalinar demanded, choking on a mouthful of wine.

"That *is* the point of this, right?" Ialai said. "They want someone who can protect them, someone their family will be too afraid to attack. But

Toh and his sister, they'll want more than just asylum. They'll want to be part of things. Inject their blood into the royal line, so to speak."

Dalinar took another long drink.

"You *could* try water sometime you know, Dalinar," Sadeas said.

"I had some rainwater earlier. Everyone stared at me funny."

Navani smiled at him. There wasn't enough wine in the world to prepare him for the gaze behind the smile, so piercing, so appraising.

"This could be what we need," Gavilar said. "It gives us not only the Shard, but the appearance of speaking for Alethkar. If people outside the kingdom start coming to me for refuge and treaties, we might be able to sway the remaining highprinces. We might be able to unite this country not through further war, but through sheer weight of *legitimacy*."

A servant, at long last, arrived with a knife for Dalinar. He took it eagerly, then frowned as the woman walked away.

"What?" Navani asked.

"This little thing?" Dalinar asked, pinching the dainty knife between two fingers and dangling it. "How am I supposed to eat a pork steak with *this*?"

"Attack it," Ialai said, making a stabbing motion. "Pretend it's some thick-necked man who has been insulting your biceps."

"If someone insulted my biceps, I wouldn't attack him," Dalinar said. "I'd refer him to a physician, because *obviously* something is wrong with his eyes."

Navani laughed, a musical sound.

"Oh, Dalinar," Sadeas said. "I don't think there's another person on Roshar who could have said that with a straight face."

Dalinar grunted, then tried to maneuver the little knife into cutting the steak. The meat was growing cold, but still smelled delicious. A single hungerspren started flitting about his head, like a tiny brown fly of the type you saw out in the west near the Purelake.

"What defeated Sunmaker?" Gavilar suddenly asked.

"Hmm?" Ialai said.

"Sunmaker," Gavilar said, looking from Navani, to Sadeas, to Dalinar. "He united Alethkar. Why did he fail to create a lasting empire?"

"His kids were too greedy," Dalinar said, sawing at his steak. "Or too weak maybe. There wasn't one of them that the others would agree to support."

"No, that's not it," Navani said. "They might have united, if the Sunmaker himself could have been bothered to *settle* on an heir. It's his fault."

"He was off in the west," Gavilar said. "Leading his army to 'further glory.' Alethkar and Herdaz weren't enough for him. He wanted the whole world."

"So it was his ambition," Sadeas said.

"No, his greed," Gavilar said quietly. "What's the point of conquering if you can never sit back and enjoy it? Shubreth-son-Mashalan, Sunmaker, even the Hierocracy . . . they all stretched farther and farther until they collapsed. In all the history of mankind, has any conqueror decided they had enough? Has any man just said, 'This is good. This is what I wanted,' and gone home?"

"Right now," Dalinar said, "what I want is to eat my storming steak." He held up the little knife, which was bent in the middle.

Navani blinked. "How in the Almighty's tenth name did you do that?"

"Dunno."

Gavilar stared with that distant, far-off look in his green eyes. A look that was becoming more and more common. "Why are we at war, Brother?"

"This again?" Dalinar said. "Look, it's not so complicated. Can't you remember how it was back when we started?"

"Remind me."

"Well," Dalinar said, wagging his bent knife. "We looked at this place here, this kingdom, and we realized, 'Hey, all these people have *stuff*.' And we figured . . . hey, maybe *we* should have that stuff. So we took it."

"Oh Dalinar," Sadeas said, chuckling. "You are a gem."

"Don't you ever think about what it meant though?" Gavilar asked. "A kingdom? Something grander than yourself?"

"That's foolishness, Gavilar. When people fight, it's about the stuff. That's it."

"Maybe," Gavilar said. "Maybe. There's something I want you to listen to. The Codes of War, from the old days. Back when Alethkar meant something."

Dalinar nodded absently as the serving staff entered with teas and fruit to close the meal; one tried to take his steak, and he growled at her. As she backed away, Dalinar caught sight of something. A woman peeking into the room from the other feast hall. She wore a delicate, filmy dress of pale yellow, matched by her blonde hair.

He leaned forward, curious. Toh's sister Evi was eighteen, maybe nineteen. She was tall, almost as tall as an Alethi, and small of chest. In fact, there was a certain sense of flimsiness to her, as if she were somehow less real than an Alethi. The same went for her brother, with his slender build.

But that *hair*. It made her stand out, like a candle's glow in a dark room.

She scampered across the feast hall to her brother, who handed her a drink. She tried to take it with her left hand, which was tied inside a small pouch of yellow cloth. The dress didn't have sleeves, strangely.

"She kept trying to eat with her safehand," Navani said, eyebrow cocked.

Ialai leaned down the table toward Dalinar, speaking conspiratorially. "They go about half-clothed out in the far west, you know. Rirans, Iriali, the Reshi. They aren't as inhibited as these prim Alethi women. I bet she's quite exotic in the bedroom. . . ."

Dalinar grunted. Then finally spotted a knife.

In the hand hidden behind the back of a server clearing Gavilar's plates.

Dalinar kicked at his brother's chair, breaking a leg off and sending Gavilar toppling to the ground. The assassin swung at the same moment, clipping Gavilar's ear, but otherwise missing. The wild swing struck the table, driving the knife into the wood.

Dalinar leaped to his feet, reaching over Gavilar and grabbing the assassin by the neck. He spun the would-be killer around and slammed him to the floor with a satisfying *crunch*. Still in motion, Dalinar grabbed the knife from the table and pounded it into the assassin's chest.

Puffing, Dalinar stepped back and wiped the rainwater from his eyes. Gavilar sprang to his feet, Shardblade appearing in his hand. He looked down at the assassin, then at Dalinar.

Dalinar kicked at the assassin to be sure he was dead. He nodded to himself, righted his chair, sat down, then leaned over and yanked the man's knife from his chest. A fine blade.

He washed it off in his wine, then cut off a piece of his steak and shoved it into his mouth. *Finally.*

"Good pork," Dalinar noted around the bite.

Across the room, Toh and his sister were staring at Dalinar with looks that mixed awe and terror. He caught a few shockspren around them, like triangles of yellow light, breaking and re-forming. Rare spren, those were.

"Thank you," Gavilar said, touching his ear and the blood that was dripping from it.

Dalinar shrugged. "Sorry about killing him. You probably wanted to question him, eh?"

"It's no stretch to guess who sent him," Gavilar said, settling down, waving away the guards who—belatedly—rushed to help. Navani clutched his arm, obviously shaken by the attack.

Sadeas cursed under his breath. "Our enemies grow desperate. Cowardly. An assassin during a storm? An Alethi should be ashamed of such action."

Again, everyone in the feast was gawking at the high table. Dalinar cut his steak again, shoving another piece into his mouth. What? He wasn't going to *drink* the wine he'd washed the blood into. He wasn't a barbarian.

"I know I said I wanted you free to make your own choice in regard to a bride," Gavilar said. "But . . ."

"I'll do it," Dalinar said, eyes forward. Navani was lost to him. He needed to just storming accept that.

"They're timid and careful," Navani noted, dabbing at Gavilar's ear with her napkin. "It might take more time to persuade them."

"Oh, I wouldn't worry about that," Gavilar said, looking back at the corpse. "Dalinar is nothing if not *persuasive*."

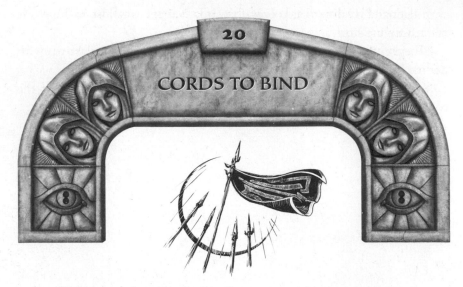

20

CORDS TO BIND

However, with a dangerous spice, you can be warned to taste lightly. I would that your lesson may not be as painful as my own.

—From *Oathbringer*, preface

Now this," Kaladin said, "isn't actually that serious a wound. I know it looks deep, but it's often better to be cut deep by a sharp knife than to be raggedly gouged by something dull."

He pressed the skin of Khen's arm together and applied the bandage to her cut. "Always use clean cloth you've boiled—rotspren love dirty cloth. Infection is the real danger here; you'll spot it as red along the outsides of the wound that grows and streaks. There will be pus too. Always wash out a cut before binding it."

He patted Khen's arm and took back his knife, which had caused the offending laceration when Khen had been using it to cut branches off a fallen tree for firewood. Around her, the other parshmen gathered the cakes they'd dried in the sun.

They had a surprising number of resources, all things considered. Several parshmen had thought to grab metal buckets during their raid—which had worked as pots for boiling—and the waterskins were going to be a lifesaver. He joined Sah, the parshman who had originally been his captor, among the trees of their improvised camp. The parshman was lashing a stone axehead to a branch.

Kaladin took it from him and tested it against a log, judging how well it split the wood. "You need to lash it tighter," Kaladin said. "Get the leather strips wet and really pull as you wrap it. If you aren't careful, it'll fall off on you midswing."

Sah grunted, taking back the hatchet and grumbling to himself as he undid the lashings. He eyed Kaladin. "You can go check on someone else, human."

"We should march tonight," Kaladin said. "We've been in one spot too long. And break into small groups, like I said."

"We'll see."

"Look, if there's something wrong with my advice . . ."

"Nothing is wrong."

"But—"

Sah sighed, looking up and meeting Kaladin's eyes. "Where did a slave learn to give orders and strut about like a lighteyes?"

"My entire life was not spent as a slave."

"I hate," Sah continued, "feeling like a child." He started rewrapping the axehead, tighter this time. "I hate being taught things that I should already know. Most of all, I hate needing your help. We ran. We escaped. Now what? You leap in, start telling us what to do? We're back to following Alethi orders again."

Kaladin stayed silent.

"That yellow spren isn't any better," Sah muttered. "Hurry up. Keep moving. She tells us we're free, then with the very next breath berates us for not obeying quickly enough."

They were surprised that Kaladin couldn't see the spren. They'd also mentioned to him the sounds they heard, distant rhythms, almost music.

"'Freedom' is a strange word, Sah," Kaladin said softly, settling down. "These last few months, I've probably been more 'free' than at any time since my childhood. You want to know what I did with it? I stayed in the same place, serving another highlord. I wonder if men who use cords to bind are fools, since tradition, society, and momentum are going to tie us all down anyway."

"I don't have traditions," Sah said. "Or society. But still, my 'freedom' is that of a leaf. Dropped from the tree, I just blow on the wind and pretend I'm in charge of my destiny."

"That was almost poetry, Sah."

"I have no idea what that is." He pulled the last lashing tight and held up the new hatchet.

Kaladin took it and buried it into the log next to him. "Better."

"Aren't you worried, human? Teaching us to make cakes is one thing. Giving us weapons is quite another."

"A hatchet is a tool, not a weapon."

"Perhaps," Sah said. "But with this same chipping and sharpening method you taught, I will eventually make a spear."

"You act as if a fight is inevitable."

Sah laughed. "You don't think it is?"

"You have a choice."

"Says the man with the brand on his forehead. If they're willing to do that to one of their *own*, what brutality awaits a bunch of thieving parshmen?"

"Sah, it *doesn't* have to come to war. You *don't* have to fight the humans."

"Perhaps. But let me ask you this." He set the axe across his lap. "Considering what they did to me, why *wouldn't* I?"

Kaladin couldn't force out an objection. He remembered his own time as a slave: the frustration, powerlessness, anger. They'd branded him with *shash* because he was dangerous. Because he'd fought back.

Dared he demand this man do otherwise?

"They'll want to enslave us again," Sah continued, taking the hatchet and hacking at the log next to him, starting to strip off the rough bark as Kaladin had instructed, so they could have tinder. "We're money lost, and a dangerous precedent. Your kind will expend a fortune figuring out what changed to give us back our minds, and they'll find a way to reverse it. They'll strip from me my sanity, and set me to carrying water again."

"Maybe . . . maybe we can convince them otherwise. I know good men among the Alethi lighteyes, Sah. If we talk to them, show them how you can talk and think—that you're like regular people—they'll listen. They'll agree to give you your freedom. That's how they treated your cousins on the Shattered Plains when they first met."

Sah slammed the hatchet down into the wood, sending a chip fluttering into the air. "And that's why we should be free now? Because we're acting like you? We deserved slavery before, when we were different? It's all right to dominate us when we won't fight back, but now it's not, because we can *talk*?"

"Well, I mean—"

"That's why I'm angry! Thank you for what you're showing us, but don't expect me to be happy that I need you for it. This just reinforces the belief within you, maybe even within myself, that your people should be the ones who decide upon our freedom *in the first place*."

Sah stalked off, and once he was gone, Syl appeared from the underbrush and settled on Kaladin's shoulder, alert—watching for the Voidspren—but not immediately alarmed.

"I think I can sense a highstorm coming," she whispered.

"What? Really?"

She nodded. "It's distant still. A day or three." She cocked her head.

"I suppose I could have done this earlier, but I didn't need to. Or know I wanted to. You always had the lists."

Kaladin took a deep breath. How to protect these people from the storm? He'd have to find shelter. He'd . . .

I'm doing it again.

"I can't do this, Syl," Kaladin whispered. "I can't spend time with these parshmen, see their side."

"Why?"

"Because Sah is right. This *is* going to come to war. The Voidspren will drive the parshmen into an army, and rightly so, after what was done to them. Our kind will have to fight back or be destroyed."

"Then find the middle ground."

"Middle ground only comes in war after lots of people have died—and only after the important people are worried they might actually lose. Storms, I shouldn't be here. I'm starting to want to defend these people! Teach them to fight. I don't dare—the only way I can fight the Voidbringers is to pretend there's a difference between the ones I have to protect and the ones I have to kill."

He trudged through the underbrush and started helping tear down one of the crude tarp tents for the night's march.

I am no storyteller, to entertain you with whimsical yarns.

—From *Oathbringer*, preface

Aclamorous, insistent knocking woke Shallan. She still didn't have a bed, so she slept in a heap of red hair and twisted blankets.

She pulled one of these over her head, but the knocking persisted, followed by Adolin's annoyingly charming voice. "Shallan? Look, this time I'm going to wait to come in until you're *really* sure I should."

She peeked out at the sunlight, which poured through her balcony window like spilled paint. Morning? The sun was in the wrong place.

Wait . . . Stormfather. She'd spent the night out as Veil, then slept to the afternoon. She groaned, tossing off sweaty blankets, and lay there in just her shift, head pounding. There was an empty jug of Horneater white in the corner.

"Shallan?" Adolin said. "Are you decent?"

"Depends," she said, voice croaking, "on the context. I'm decent at sleeping."

She put hands over her eyes, safehand still wrapped in an improvised bandage. What had gotten into her? Tossing around the symbol of the Ghostbloods? Drinking herself silly? *Stabbing a man* in front of a gang of armed thugs?

Her actions felt like they'd taken place in a dream.

"Shallan," Adolin said, sounding concerned. "I'm going to peek in. Palona says you've been in here all day."

She yelped, sitting up and grabbing the bedding. When he looked, he found her bundled there, a frizzy-haired head protruding from blankets—which she had pulled tight up to her chin. He looked perfect, of course. Adolin could look perfect after a storm, six hours of fighting, and a bath in cremwater. Annoying man. How *did* he make his hair so adorable? Messy in just the right way.

"Palona said you weren't feeling well," Adolin said, pushing aside the cloth door and leaning in the doorway.

"Blarg."

"Is it, um, girl stuff?"

"Girl stuff," she said flatly.

"You know. When you . . . uh . . ."

"I'm aware of the biology, Adolin, thank you. Why is it that every time a woman is feeling a little odd, men are so quick to blame her cycle? As if she's suddenly unable to control herself because she has some pains. Nobody thinks that for men. 'Oh, stay away from Venar today. He sparred too much yesterday, so his muscles are sore, and he's likely to *rip your head off.*'"

"So it's our fault."

"Yes. Like everything else. War. Famine. Bad hair."

"Wait. Bad hair?"

Shallan blew a lock of it out of her eyes. "Loud. Stubborn. Oblivious to our attempts to fix it. The Almighty gave us messy hair to prepare us for living with men."

Adolin brought in a small pot of warm washwater for her face and hands. Bless him. And Palona, who had probably sent it with him.

Damnation, her hand ached. And her head. She remembered occasionally burning off the alcohol last night, but hadn't ever held enough Stormlight to completely fix the hand. And never enough to make her completely sober.

Adolin set the water down, perky as a sunrise, grinning. "So what *is* wrong?"

She pulled the blanket up over her head and pulled it tight, like the hood of a cloak. "Girl stuff," she lied.

"See, I don't think men would blame your cycle nearly as much if you all didn't do the same. I've courted my share of women, and I once kept track. Deeli was once sick for womanly reasons four times in the same month."

"We're very mysterious creatures."

"I'll say." He lifted up the jug and gave it a sniff. "Is this *Horneater white?*" He looked to her, seeming shocked—but perhaps also a little impressed.

"Got a little carried away," Shallan grumbled. "Doing investigations about your murderer."

"In a place serving Horneater moonshine?"

"Back alley of the Breakaway. Nasty place. Good booze though."

"Shallan!" he said. "You went alone? That's not safe."

"Adolin, dear," she said, finally pulling the blanket back down to her shoulders, "I could *literally* survive being stabbed with a sword through the chest. I think I'll be fine with some ruffians in the market."

"Oh. Right. It's kind of easy to forget." He frowned. "So . . . wait. You could survive all kinds of nasty murder, but you still . . ."

"Get menstrual cramps?" Shallan said. "Yeah. Mother Cultivation can be hateful. I'm an all-powerful, Shardblade-wielding pseudo-immortal, but nature still sends a friendly reminder every now and then to tell me I should be getting around to having children."

"No mating," Pattern buzzed softly on the wall.

"But I shouldn't be blaming yesterday on that," Shallan added to Adolin. "My time isn't for another few weeks. Yesterday was more about psychology than it was about biology."

Adolin set the jug down. "Yeah, well, you might want to watch out for the Horneater wines."

"It's not so bad," Shallan said with a sigh. "I can burn away the intoxication with a little Stormlight. Speaking of which, you don't have any spheres with you, do you? I seem to have . . . um . . . eaten all of mine."

He chuckled. "I have *one*. A single sphere. Father lent it to me so I could stop carrying a lantern everywhere in these halls."

She tried to bat her eyelashes at him. She wasn't exactly sure how one did that, or why, but it seemed to work. At the very least, he rolled his eyes and handed over a single ruby mark.

She sucked in the Light hungrily. She held her breath so it wouldn't puff out when she breathed, and . . . suppressed the Light. She could do that, she'd found. To prevent herself from glowing or drawing attention. She'd done that as a child, hadn't she?

Her hand slowly reknit, and she let out a relieved sigh as the headache vanished as well.

Adolin was left with a dun sphere. "You know, when my father explained that good relationships required investment, I don't think this is what he meant."

"Mmm," Shallan said, closing her eyes and smiling.

"Also," Adolin added, "we have the *strangest* conversations."

"It feels natural to have them with you, though."

"I think that's the oddest part. Well, you'll want to start being more careful with your Stormlight. Father mentioned he was trying to get you more infused spheres for practice, but there just aren't any."

"What about Hatham's people?" she said. "They left out lots of spheres in the last highstorm." That had only been . . .

She did the math, and found herself stunned. It had been *weeks* since the unexpected highstorm where she'd first worked the Oathgate. She looked at the sphere between Adolin's fingers.

Those should all have gone dun by now, she thought. *Even the ones renewed most recently.* How did they have *any* Stormlight at all?

Suddenly, her actions the night before seemed even more irresponsible. When Dalinar had commanded her to practice with her powers, he probably hadn't meant practicing how to avoid getting too drunk.

She sighed, and—still keeping the blanket on—reached for the bowl of washing water. She had a lady's maid named Marri, but she kept sending her away. She didn't want the woman discovering that she was sneaking out or changing faces. If she kept on like that, Palona would probably assign the woman to other work.

The water didn't seem to have any scents or soaps applied to it, so Shallan raised the small basin and then took a long, slurping drink.

"I washed my feet in that," Adolin noted.

"No you didn't." Shallan smacked her lips. "Anyway, thanks for dragging me out of bed."

"Well," he said, "I have selfish reasons. I'm kind of hoping for some moral support."

"Don't hit the message too hard. If you want someone to believe what you're telling them, come to your point gradually, so they're with you the entire time."

He cocked his head.

"Oh, not *that* kind of moral," Shallan said.

"Talking to you can be weird sometimes."

"Sorry, sorry. I'll be good." She sat as primly and attentively as she could, wrapped in a blanket with her hair sticking out like the snarls of a thornbush.

Adolin took a deep breath. "My father finally persuaded Ialai Sadeas to speak with me. Father hopes she'll have some clues about her husband's death."

"You sound less optimistic."

"I don't like her, Shallan. She's strange."

Shallan opened her mouth, but he cut her off.

"Not strange like you," he said. "Strange . . . bad strange. She's always weighing everything and everyone she meets. She's never treated me as anything other than a child. Will you go with me?"

"Sure. How much time do I have?"

"How much do you need?"

Shallan looked down at herself, huddled in her blankets, frizzy hair tickling her chin. "A *lot*."

"Then we'll be late," Adolin said, standing up. "It's not like her opinion of me could get any worse. Meet me at Sebarial's sitting room. Father wants me to take some reports from him on commerce."

"Tell him the booze in the market is good."

"Sure." Adolin glanced again at the empty jug of Horneater white, then shook his head and left.

⁂

An hour later, Shallan presented herself—bathed, makeup done, hair somewhat under control—to Sebarial's sitting room. The chamber was larger than her room, but notably, the doorway out onto the balcony was enormous, taking up half the wall.

Everyone was out on the wide balcony, which overlooked the field below. Adolin stood by the railing, lost to some contemplation. Behind him, Sebarial and Palona lay on cots, their backs exposed to the sun, getting *massages*.

A flight of Horneater servants massaged, tended coal braziers, or stood dutifully with warmed wine and other conveniences. The air, particularly in the sun, wasn't as chilly as it had been most other days. It was almost pleasant.

Shallan found herself caught between embarrassment—this plump, bearded man wearing only a *towel* was the highprince—and outrage. She'd just taken a *cold* bath, pouring ladles of water on her own head while shivering. She'd considered that a luxury, as she hadn't been required to fetch the water herself.

"How is it," Shallan said, "that I am still sleeping on the floor, while you have cots *right here*."

"Are you highprince?" Sebarial mumbled, not even opening his eyes.

"No. I'm a Knight Radiant, which I should think is higher."

"I see," he said, then groaned in pleasure at the masseuse's touch, "and so you can pay to have a cot carried in from the warcamps? Or do you still rely on the stipend *I* give you? A stipend, I'll add, that was supposed to pay for your help as a scribe for my accounts—something I haven't seen in weeks."

"She did save the world, Turi," Palona noted from Shallan's other side. The middle-aged Herdazian woman also hadn't opened her eyes, and though she lay chest-down, her safehand was tucked only halfway under a towel.

"See, I don't think she saved it, so much as delayed its destruction. It's a *mess* out there, my dear."

Nearby, the head masseuse—a large Horneater woman with vibrant red hair and pale skin—ordered a round of heated stones for Sebarial. Most of the servants were probably her family. Horneaters did like to be in business together.

"I will note," Sebarial said, "that this Desolation of yours is going to undermine years of my business planning."

"You can't possibly blame me for that," Shallan said, folding her arms.

"You did chase me out of the warcamps," Sebarial said, "even though they survived quite well. The remnants of those domes shielded them from the west. The big problem was the parshmen, but those have all cleared out now, marching toward Alethkar. So I plan to go back and reclaim my land there before others seize it." He opened his eyes and glanced at Shallan. "Your young prince didn't want to hear that—he worries I will stretch our forces too thin. But those warcamps are going to be vital for trade; we can't leave them completely to Thanadal and Vamah."

Great. Another problem to think about. No wonder Adolin looked so distracted. He'd noted they'd be late to visiting Ialai, but didn't seem particularly eager to be on the move.

"You be a good Radiant," Sebarial told her, "and get those other Oathgates working. I've prepared quite the scheme for taxing passage through them."

"Callous."

"Necessary. The only way to survive in these mountains will be to tax the Oathgates, and Dalinar knows it. He put me in charge of commerce. Life doesn't stop for a war, child. Everyone will still need new shoes, baskets, clothing, wine."

"And we need massages," Palona added. "Lots of them, if we're going to have to live in this frozen wasteland."

"You two are hopeless," Shallan snapped, walking across the sunlit balcony to Adolin. "Hey. Ready?"

"Sure." She and Adolin struck out through the hallways. Each of the eight highprincedoms' armies in residence at the tower had been granted a quarter of the second or third level, with a few barracks on the first level, leaving most of that level reserved for markets and storage.

Of course, not even the first level had been completely explored. There were so many hallways and bizarre tangents—hidden sets of rooms tucked away behind everything else. Maybe eventually each highprince would rule his quarter in earnest. For now, they occupied little pockets of civilization within the dark frontier that was Urithiru.

Exploration on the upper levels had been completely halted, as they no longer had Stormlight to spare in working the lifts.

They left Sebarial's quarter, passing soldiers and an intersection with painted arrows on the floor leading to various places, such as the nearest privy. The guards' checkpoint didn't look like a barricade, but Adolin had pointed out the boxes of rations, the bags of grain, set in a specific way before the soldiers. Anyone rushing this corridor from the outside would get tangled in all of that, plus face pikemen beyond.

The soldiers nodded to Adolin, but didn't salute him, though one did bark an order to two men playing cards in a nearby room. The fellows stood up, and Shallan was startled to recognize them. Gaz and Vathah.

"Thought we'd take your guards today," Adolin said.

My guards. Right. Shallan had a group of soldiers made up of deserters and despicable murderers. She didn't mind that part, being a despicable murderer herself. But she also had no idea what to do with them.

They saluted her lazily. Vathah, tall and scruffy. Gaz, short with a single brown eye, the other socket covered by a patch. Adolin had obviously already briefed them, and Vathah sauntered out to guard them in the front, while Gaz lingered behind.

Hoping they were far enough away not to hear, Shallan took Adolin by the arm.

"Do we *need* guards?" she whispered.

"Of course we do."

"Why? You're a Shardbearer. I'm a Radiant. I think we'll be fine."

"Shallan, being guarded isn't always about safety. It's about prestige."

"I've got plenty. Prestige is practically leaking from my nose these days, Adolin."

"That's not what I meant." Adolin leaned down, whispering. "This is for them. You don't need guards, maybe, but you do need an honor guard. Men to be *honored* by their position. It's part of the rules we play by—you get to be someone important, and they get to share in it."

"By being useless."

"By being part of what you're doing," Adolin said. "Storms, I forget how new you are to all this. What have you been doing with these men?"

"Letting them be, mostly."

"What of when you need them?"

"I don't know if I will."

"You will," Adolin said. "Shallan, you're their commander. Maybe not their military commander, as they're a civil guard, but it amounts to the same thing. Leave them idle, make them assume they're inconsequential, and you'll ruin them. Give them something important to do instead, work they'll be proud of, and they'll serve you with honor. A failed soldier is often one that has *been* failed."

She smiled.

"What?"

"You sound like your father," she said.

He paused, then looked away. "Nothing wrong with that."

"I didn't say there was. I like it." She held his arm. "I'll find something to do with my guards, Adolin. Something useful. I promise."

Gaz and Vathah didn't seem to think the duty was all that important, from the way they yawned and slouched as they walked, holding out oil lamps, spears at their shoulders. They passed a large group of women carrying water, and then some men carrying lumber to set up a new privy. Most made way for Vathah; seeing a personal guard was a cue to step to the side.

Of course, if Shallan had really wanted to exude importance, she'd have taken a palanquin. She didn't mind the vehicles; she'd used them extensively in Kharbranth. Maybe it was the part of Veil inside of her, though, that made her resist Adolin whenever he suggested she order one. There was an independence to using her own feet.

They reached the stairwell up, and at the top, Adolin dug in his pocket for a map. The painted arrows weren't all finished up here. Shallan tugged his arm and pointed the way down a tunnel.

"How can you know that so easily?" he said.

"Don't you see how wide those strata are?" she asked, pointing to the wall of the corridor. "It's this way."

He tucked away his map and gestured for Vathah to lead the way. "Do you really think I'm like my father?" Adolin said softly as they walked. There was a worried sense to his voice.

"You are," she said, pulling his arm tight. "You're just like him, Adolin. Moral, just, and capable."

He frowned.

"What?"

"Nothing."

"You're a terrible liar. You're worried you can't live up to his expectations, aren't you?"

"Maybe."

"Well you have, Adolin. You have lived up to them in every way. I'm certain Dalinar Kholin couldn't hope for a better son, and . . . storms. That idea *bothers* you."

"What? No!"

Shallan poked Adolin in the shoulder with her freehand. "You're not telling me something."

"Maybe."

"Well, thank the Almighty for that."

"Not . . . going to ask what it is?"

"Ash's eyes, no. I'd rather figure it out. A relationship needs *some* measure of mystery."

Adolin fell silent, which was all well and good, because they were approaching the Sadeas section of Urithiru. Though Ialai had threatened to relocate back to the warcamps, she'd made no such move. Likely because there was no denying that this city was now the seat of Alethi politics and power.

They reached the first guard post, and Shallan's two guards pulled up close to her and Adolin. They exchanged hostile glares with the soldiers in forest-green-and-white uniforms as they were allowed past. Whatever Ialai Sadeas thought, her men had obviously made up their minds.

It was strange how much difference a few steps could make. In here, they passed far fewer workers or merchants, and far more soldiers. Men with dark expressions, unbuttoned coats, and unshaved faces of all varieties. Even the scribes were different—more makeup, but sloppier clothing.

It felt like they'd stepped from law into disorder. Loud voices echoed down hallways, laughing raucously. The stripes painted to guide the way were on the walls here rather than the floor, and the paint had been allowed to drip, spoiling the strata. They'd been smeared in places by men who had walked by, their coats brushing the still-wet paint.

The soldiers they passed all sneered at Adolin.

"They feel like gangs," Shallan said softly, looking over her shoulder at one group.

"Don't mistake them," Adolin said. "They march in step, their boots are sturdy, and their weapons well maintained. Sadeas trained good soldiers. It's just that where Father used discipline, Sadeas used competition. Besides, here, looking too clean will get you mocked. You can't be mistaken for a Kholin."

She'd hoped that maybe, now that the truth about the Desolation had been revealed, Dalinar would have an easier time of uniting the highprinces. Well, that obviously wasn't going to happen while these men blamed Dalinar for Sadeas's death.

They eventually reached the proper rooms and were ushered in to confront Sadeas's wife. Ialai was a short woman with thick lips and green eyes. She sat in a throne at the center of the room.

Standing beside her was Mraize, one of the leaders of the Ghostbloods.

22

THE DARKNESS WITHIN

I am no philosopher, to intrigue you with piercing questions.

—From *Oathbringer*, preface

Maize. His face was crisscrossed by scars, one of which deformed his upper lip. Instead of his usual fashionable clothing, today he wore a Sadeas uniform, with a breastplate and a simple skullcap helm. He looked exactly like the other soldiers they'd passed, save for that face.

And the chicken on his shoulder.

A *chicken*. It was one of the stranger varieties, pure green and sleek, with a wicked beak. It looked much more like a predator than the bumbling things she'd seen sold in cages at markets.

But seriously. Who walked around with a pet chicken? They were for eating, right?

Adolin noted the chicken and raised an eyebrow, but Mraize didn't give any sign that he knew Shallan. He slouched like the other soldiers, holding a halberd and glaring at Adolin.

Ialai hadn't set out chairs for them. She sat with her hands in her lap, sleeved safehand beneath her freehand, lit by lamps on pedestals at either side of the room. She looked particularly vengeful by that unnatural flickering light.

"Did you know," Ialai said, "that after whitespines make a kill, they will eat, then hide near the carcass?"

"It's one of the dangers in hunting them, Brightness," Adolin said. "You assume that you're on the beast's trail, but it might be lurking nearby."

"I used to wonder at this behavior until I realized the kill will attract scavengers, and the whitespine is not picky. The ones that come to feast on its leavings become another meal themselves."

The implication of the conversation seemed clear to Shallan. *Why have you returned to the scene of the kill, Kholin?*

"We want you to know, Brightness," Adolin said, "that we take the murder of a highprince *very* seriously. We are doing everything we can to prevent this from happening again."

Oh, Adolin . . .

"Of course you are," Ialai said. "The other highprinces are now too afraid to stand up to you."

Yes, he'd walked right into that one. But Shallan didn't take over; this was Adolin's task, and he'd invited her for support, not to speak for him. Honestly, she wouldn't be doing much better. She'd just be making different mistakes.

"Can you tell us of anyone who might have had the opportunity and motive for killing your husband?" Adolin said. "*Other* than my father, Brightness."

"So even you admit that—"

"It's strange," Adolin snapped. "My mother always said she thought you were clever. She admired you, and wished she had your wit. Yet here, *I* see no proof of that. Honestly, do you *really* think that my father would withstand Sadeas's insults for years—weather his betrayal on the Plains, suffer that dueling fiasco—only to *assassinate him* now? Once Sadeas was proven wrong about the Voidbringers, and my father's position is secure? We both know my father wasn't behind your husband's death. To claim otherwise is simple idiocy."

Shallan started. She hadn't expected *that* from Adolin's lips. Strikingly, it seemed to her to be the *precise* thing he'd needed to say. Cut away the courtly language. Deliver the straight and earnest truth.

Ialai leaned forward, inspecting Adolin and chewing on his words. If there was one thing Adolin could convey, it was authenticity.

"Fetch him a chair," Ialai said to Mraize.

"Yes, Brightness," he said, his voice thick with a rural accent that bordered on Herdazian.

Ialai then looked to Shallan. "And you. Make yourself useful. There are teas warming in the side room."

Shallan sniffed at the treatment. She was no longer some inconsequential ward, to be ordered about. However, Mraize lurched off in the same direction she'd been told to go, so Shallan bore the indignity and stalked after him.

The next room was much smaller, cut out of the same stone as the others, but with a muted pattern of strata. Oranges and reds that blended together so evenly you could almost pretend the wall was all one hue. Ialai's people had been using it for storage, as evidenced by the chairs in one corner. Shallan ignored the warm jugs of tea heating on fabrials on the counter and stepped close to Mraize.

"What are you doing here?" she hissed at him.

His chicken chirped softly, as if in agitation.

"I'm keeping an eye on that one," he said, nodding toward the other room. Here, his voice became refined, losing the rural edge. "We have interest in her."

"So she's not one of you?" Shallan asked. "She's not a . . . Ghostblood?"

"No," he said, eyes narrowing. "She and her husband were too wild a variable for us to invite. Their motives are their own; I don't think they align to those of anyone else, human or listener."

"The fact that they're crem didn't enter into it, I suppose."

"Morality is an axis that doesn't interest us," Mraize said calmly. "Only loyalty and power are relevant, for morality is as ephemeral as the changing weather. It depends upon the angle from which you view it. You will see, as you work with us, that I am right."

"I'm *not* one of you," Shallan hissed.

"For one so insistent," Mraize said, picking up a chair, "you were certainly free in using our symbol last night."

Shallan froze, then blushed furiously. So he knew about that? "I . . ."

"Your hunt is worthy," Mraize said. "And you are allowed to rely upon our authority to achieve your goals. That is a benefit of your membership, so long as you do not abuse it."

"And my brothers? Where are they? You promised to deliver them to me."

"Patience, little knife. It has been but a few weeks since we rescued them. You will see my word fulfilled in that matter. Regardless, I have a task for you."

"A task?" Shallan snapped, causing the chicken to chirp at her again. "Mraize, I'm not going to do some task for you people. You *killed* Jasnah."

"An enemy combatant," Mraize said. "Oh, don't look at me like that. You know full well what that woman was capable of, and what she got herself into by attacking us. Do you blame your wonderfully moral Blackthorn for what he did in war? The countless people *he* slaughtered?"

"Don't deflect your evils by pointing out the faults of others," Shallan said. "I'm not going to further your cause. I don't care how much you demand that I Soulcast for you, I'm not going to do it."

"So quick to insist, yet you acknowledge your debt. One Soulcaster lost, destroyed. But we forgive these things, for missions undertaken. And before you object again, know that the task we require of you is one you're *already* undertaking. Surely you have sensed the darkness in this place. The . . . wrongness."

Shallan looked about the small room, flickering with shadows from a few candles on the counter.

"Your task," Mraize said, "is to secure this location. Urithiru must remain strong if we are to properly use the advent of the Voidbringers."

"*Use* them?"

"Yes," Mraize said. "This is a power we will control, but we must not let either side gain dominance yet. Secure Urithiru. Hunt the source of the darkness you feel, and expunge it. This is your task. And for it I will give payment in information." He leaned closer to her and spoke a single word. "Helaran."

He lifted the chair and walked out, adopting a more bumbling gait, stumbling and almost dropping the chair. Shallan stood there, stunned. Helaran. Her eldest brother had died in Alethkar—where he'd been for mysterious reasons.

Storms, what did Mraize know? She glared after him, outraged. How dare he tease with that name!

Don't focus on Helaran right now. Those were dangerous thoughts, and she could not become Veil now. Shallan poured herself and Adolin cups of tea, then grabbed a chair under her arm and awkwardly navigated back out. She sat down beside Adolin, then handed him a cup. She took a sip and smiled at Ialai, who glared at her, then directed Mraize to fetch a cup.

"I think," Ialai said to Adolin, "that if you honestly wish to solve this crime, you won't be looking at my husband's former enemies. Nobody had the opportunity or motives that you would find in your warcamp."

Adolin sighed. "We established that—"

"I'm not saying Dalinar did this," Ialai said. She seemed calm, but she gripped the sides of her chair with white-knuckled hands. And her eyes . . . makeup could not hide the redness. She'd been crying. She was truly upset.

Unless it was an act. *I could fake crying,* Shallan thought, *if I knew that someone was coming to see me, and if I believed the act would strengthen my position.*

"Then what *are* you saying?" Adolin asked.

"History is rife with examples of soldiers assuming orders when there were none," Ialai said. "I agree that Dalinar would never knife an old friend in dark quarters. His soldiers may not be so inhibited. You want to know who did this, Adolin Kholin? Look among your own ranks. I would wager the princedom that somewhere in the Kholin army is a man who thought to do his highprince a service."

"And the other murders?" Shallan said.

"I do not know the mind of this person," Ialai said. "Maybe they have a taste for it now? In any case, I think we can agree this meeting serves no further purpose." She stood up. "Good day, Adolin Kholin. I hope you will share what you discover with me, so that my own investigator can be better informed."

"I suppose," Adolin said, standing. "Who is leading your investigation? I'll send him reports."

"His name is Meridas Amaram. I believe you know him."

Shallan gaped. "Amaram? *Highmarshal Amaram?*"

"Of course," Ialai said. "He is among my husband's most acclaimed generals."

Amaram. He'd killed her brother. She glanced at Mraize, who kept his expression neutral. Storms, what did he know? She still didn't understand where Helaran had gotten his Shardblade. What had led him to clash with Amaram in the first place?

"Amaram is *here?*" Adolin asked. "When?"

"He arrived with the last caravan and scavenging crew that you brought through the Oathgate. He didn't make himself known to the tower, but to me alone. We have been seeing to his needs, as he was caught out in a storm with his attendants. He assures me he will return to duty soon, and will make finding my husband's murderer a priority."

"I see," Adolin said.

He looked to Shallan, and she nodded, still stunned. Together they collected her soldiers from right inside the door, and left into the hallway beyond.

"Amaram," Adolin hissed. "Bridgeboy isn't going to be happy about this. They have a vendetta, those two."

Not just Kaladin.

"Father originally appointed Amaram to refound the Knights Radiant," Adolin continued. "If Ialai has taken him in after he was so soundly discredited . . . The mere act of it calls Father a liar, doesn't it? Shallan?"

She shook herself and took a deep breath. Helaran was long dead. She would worry about getting answers from Mraize later.

"It depends on how she spins things," she said softly, walking beside Adolin. "But yes, she implies that Dalinar is at the least overly judgmental in his treatment of Amaram. She's reinforcing her side as an alternative to your father's rule."

Adolin sighed. "I'd have thought that without Sadeas, maybe it would get easier."

"Politics is involved, Adolin—so by definition it can't be easy." She took his arm, wrapping hers around it as they passed another group of hostile guards.

"I'm terrible at this," Adolin said softly. "I got so annoyed in there, I almost punched her. You watch, Shallan. I'll ruin this."

"Will you? Because I think you're right about there being multiple killers."

"What? Really?"

She nodded. "I heard some things while I was out last night."

"When you weren't staggering around drunk, you mean."

"I'll have you know I'm a very graceful drunk, Adolin Kholin. Let's go . . ." She trailed off as a pair of scribes ran past in the hallway, heading toward Ialai's rooms at a shocking speed. Guards marched after them.

Adolin caught one by the arm, nearly provoking a fight as the man cursed at the blue uniform. The fellow, fortunately, recognized Adolin's face and held himself back, hand moving off the axe in a sling to his side.

"Brightlord," the man said, reluctant.

"What is this?" Adolin said. He nodded down the hall. "Why is everyone suddenly talking at that guard post farther along?"

"News from the coast," the guard finally said. "Stormwall spotted in New Natanan. The highstorms. They've returned."

I am no poet, to delight you with clever allusions.

—From *Oathbringer*, preface

I don't got any meat to sell," the old lighteyes said as he led Kaladin into the storm bunker. "But your brightlord and his men can weather in here, and for cheap." He waved his cane toward the large hollow building. It reminded Kaladin of the barracks on the Shattered Plains—long and narrow, with one small end pointed eastward.

"We'll need it to ourselves," Kaladin said. "My brightlord values his privacy."

The elderly man glanced at Kaladin, taking in the blue uniform. Now that the Weeping had passed, it looked better. He wouldn't wear it to an officer's review, but he'd spent some good time scrubbing out the stains and polishing the buttons.

Kholin uniform in Vamah lands. It could imply a host of things. Hopefully one of them was not "This Kholin officer has joined a bunch of runaway parshmen."

"I can give you the whole bunker," the merchant said. "Was supposed to be renting it to some caravans out of Revolar, but they didn't show."

"What happened?"

"Don't know," he said. "But it's storming strange, I'd say. Three caravans, with different masters and goods, all gone silent. Not even a runner to give me word. Glad I took ten percent up front."

Revolar. It was Vamah's seat, the largest city between here and Kholinar.

"We'll take the bunker," Kaladin said, handing over some dun spheres. "And whatever food you can spare."

"Not much, by an army's scale. Maybe a sack of longroots or two. Some lavis. Was expectin' one of those caravans to resupply me." He shook his head, expression distant. "Strange times, Corporal. That wrong-way storm. You reckon it will keep coming back?"

Kaladin nodded. The Everstorm had hit again the day before, its second occurrence—not counting the initial one that had only come in the far east. Kaladin and the parshmen had weathered this one, upon warning from the unseen spren, in an abandoned mine.

"Strange times," the old man said again. "Well, if you do need meat, there's been a nest of wild hogs rooting about in the ravine to the south of here. This is Highlord Cadilar's land though, so um. . . . Well, you just understand that." If Kaladin's fictional "brightlord" was traveling on the king's orders, they could hunt the lands. If not, killing another highlord's hogs would be poaching.

The old man spoke like a backwater farmer, light yellow eyes not-withstanding, but he'd obviously made something of himself running a waystop. A lonely life, but the money was probably quite good.

"Let's see what food I can find you here," the old man said. "Follow along. Now, you're *sure* a storm is coming?"

"I have charts promising it."

"Well, bless the Almighty and Heralds for that, I suppose. Will catch some people surprised, but it will be nice to be able to work my spanreed again."

Kaladin followed the man to a stone rootshed on the leeward edge of his home, and haggled—briefly—for three sacks of vegetables. "One other thing," Kaladin added. "You can't watch the army arrive."

"What? Corporal, it's my duty to see your people settled in—"

"My brightlord is a *very* private person. It's important nobody know of our passing. *Very important.*" He laid his hand on his belt knife.

The lighteyed man just sniffed. "I can be trusted to hold my tongue, *soldier.* And don't threaten me. I'm sixth dahn." He raised his chin, but when he hobbled back into his house, he shut the door tight and pulled closed the stormshutters.

Kaladin transferred the three sacks into the bunker, then hiked out to where he'd left the parshmen. He kept glancing about for Syl, but of course he saw nothing. The Voidspren was following him, hidden, likely to make sure he didn't do anything underhanded.

They made it back right before the storm.

Khen, Sah, and the others had wanted to wait until dark—unwilling to trust that the old lighteyes wouldn't spy on them. But the wind had started blowing, and they'd finally believed Kaladin that a storm was imminent.

Kaladin stood by the bunker's doorway, anxious as the parshmen piled in. They'd picked up other groups in the last few days, led by unseen Voidspren that he was told darted away once their charges were delivered. Their numbers were now verging on a hundred, including the children and elderly. Nobody would tell Kaladin their end goal, only that the spren had a destination in mind.

Khen was last through the door; the large, muscled parshwoman lingered, as if she wanted to watch the storm. Finally she took their spheres—most of which they'd stolen from him—and locked the sack into the iron-banded lantern on the wall outside. She waved Kaladin through the door, then followed, barring it closed.

"You did well, human," she said to Kaladin. "I'll speak for you when we reach the gathering."

"Thanks," Kaladin said. Outside, the stormwall hit the bunker, making the stones shake and the very ground rattle.

The parshmen settled down to wait. Hesh dug into the sacks and inspected the vegetables with a critical eye. She'd worked the kitchens of a manor.

Kaladin settled with his back to the wall, feeling the storm rage outside. Strange, how he could hate the mild Weeping so much, yet feel a thrill when he heard thunder beyond these stones. That storm had tried its best to kill him on several occasions. He felt a kinship to it—but still a wariness. It was a sergeant who was too brutal in training his recruits.

The storm would renew the gems outside, which included not only spheres, but the larger gemstones he'd been carrying. Once renewed, he—well, the parshmen—would have a wealth of Stormlight.

He needed to make a decision. How long could he delay flying back to the Shattered Plains? Even if he had to stop at a larger city to trade his dun spheres for infused ones, he could probably make it in under a day.

He couldn't dally forever. What were they doing at Urithiru? What was the word from the rest of the world? The questions hounded him. Once, he had been happy to worry only about his own squad. After that, he'd been willing to look after a battalion. Since when had the state of the entire world become his concern?

I need to steal back my spanreed at the very least, and send a message to Brightness Navani.

Something flickered at the edge of his vision. Syl had come back? He glanced toward her, a question on his lips, and barely stopped the words as he realized his error.

The spren beside him was glowing yellow, not blue-white. The tiny woman stood on a translucent pillar of golden stone that had risen from the ground to put her even with Kaladin's gaze. It, like the spren herself, was the yellow-white color of the center of a flame.

She wore a flowing dress that covered her legs entirely. Hands behind her back, she inspected him. Her face was shaped oddly—narrow, but with large, childlike eyes. Like someone from Shinovar.

Kaladin jumped, which caused the little spren to smile.

Pretend you don't know anything about spren like her, Kaladin thought. "Um. Uh . . . I can see you."

"Because I want you to," she said. "You *are* an odd one."

"Why . . . why do you want me to see you?"

"So we can talk." She started to stroll around him, and at each step, a spike of yellow stone shot up from the ground and met her bare foot. "Why are you still here, human?"

"Your parshmen took me captive."

"Your mother teach you to lie like that?" she asked, sounding amused. "They're less than a month old. Congratulations on fooling them." She stopped and smiled at him. "I'm a tad older than a month."

"The world is changing," Kaladin said. "The country is in upheaval. I guess I want to see where this goes."

She contemplated him. Fortunately, he had a good excuse for the bead of sweat that trickled down the side of his face. Facing a strangely intelligent, glowing yellow spren would unnerve anyone, not just a man with too many things to hide.

"Would you fight for us, deserter?" she asked.

"Would I be allowed?"

"My kind aren't *nearly* as inclined toward discrimination as yours. If you can carry a spear and take orders, then *I* certainly wouldn't turn you away." She folded her arms, smiling in a strangely knowing way. "The final decision won't be mine. I am but a messenger."

"Where can I find out for certain?"

"At our destination."

"Which is . . ."

"Close enough," the spren said. "Why? You have pressing appointments elsewhere? Off for a beard trim perhaps, or a lunch date with your grandmother?"

Kaladin rubbed at his face. He'd almost been able to forget about the hairs that prickled at the sides of his mouth.

"Tell me," the spren asked, "how did you know that there would be a highstorm tonight?"

"Felt it," Kaladin said, "in my bones."

"Humans can*not* feel storms, regardless of the body part in question."

He shrugged. "Seemed like the right time for one, with the Weeping having stopped and all."

She didn't nod or give any visible sign of what she thought of that comment. She merely held her knowing smile, then faded from his view.

24

MEN OF BLOOD
AND SORROW

I have no doubt that you are smarter than I am. I can only relate what happened, what I have done, and then let you draw conclusions.

—From *Oathbringer*, preface

Dalinar remembered.

Her name had been Evi. She'd been tall and willowy, with pale yellow hair—not true golden, like the hair of the Iriali, but striking in its own right.

She'd been quiet. Shy, both she and her brother, for all that they'd been willing to flee their homeland in an act of courage. They'd brought Shardplate, and . . .

That was all that had emerged over the last few days. The rest was still a blur. He could recall meeting Evi, courting her—awkwardly, since both knew it was an arrangement of political necessity—and eventually entering into a causal betrothal.

He didn't remember love, but he did remember attraction.

The memories brought questions, like cremlings emerging from their hollows after the rain. He ignored them, standing straight-backed with a line of guards on the field in front of Urithiru, suffering a bitter wind from the west. This wide plateau held some dumps of wood, as part of this space would probably end up becoming a lumberyard.

Behind him, the end of a rope blew in the wind, smacking a pile of wood again and again. A pair of windspren danced past, in the shapes of little people.

Why am I remembering Evi now? Dalinar wondered. *And why have I recovered only my first memories of our time together?*

He had always remembered the difficult years following Evi's death, which had culminated in his being drunk and useless on the night Szeth, the Assassin in White, had killed his brother. He assumed that he'd gone to the Nightwatcher to be rid of the pain at losing her, and the spren had taken his other memories as payment. He didn't know for certain, but that seemed right.

Bargains with the Nightwatcher were supposed to be permanent. Damning, even. So what was happening to him?

Dalinar glanced at his bracer clocks, strapped to his forearm. Five minutes late. Storms. He'd been wearing the thing barely a few days, and already he was counting minutes like a scribe.

The second of the two watch faces—which would count down to the next highstorm—still hadn't been engaged. A single highstorm had come, blessedly, carrying Stormlight to renew spheres. It seemed like so long since they'd had enough of that.

However, it would take until the next highstorm for the scribes to make guesses at the current pattern. Even then they could be wrong, as the Weeping had lasted far longer than it should have. Centuries—millennia—of careful records might now be obsolete.

Once, that alone would have been a catastrophe. It threatened to ruin planting seasons and cause famines, to upend travel and shipping, disrupting trade. Unfortunately, in the face of the Everstorm and the Voidbringers, it was barely third on the list of cataclysms.

The cold wind blew at him again. Before them, the grand plateau of Urithiru was ringed by ten large platforms, each raised about ten feet high, with steps up beside a ramp for carts. At the center of each one was a small building containing the device that—

With a bright flash, an expanding wave of Stormlight spread outward from the center of the second platform from the left. When the Light faded, Dalinar led his troop of honor guards up the wide steps to the top. They crossed to the building at the center, where a small group of people had stepped out and were now gawking at Urithiru, surrounded by awespren.

Dalinar smiled. The sight of a tower as wide as a city and as tall as a small mountain . . . well, there wasn't anything else like it in the world.

At the head of the newcomers was a man in burnt orange robes. Aged, with a kindly, clean-shaven face, he stood with his head tipped back and jaw lowered as he regarded the city. Near him stood a woman with silvery hair pulled up in a bun. Adrotagia, the head Kharbranthian scribe.

Some thought she was the true power behind the throne; others guessed it was that other scribe, the one they had left running Kharbranth in its king's absence. Whoever it was, they kept Taravangian as a figurehead—and Dalinar was happy to work through him to get to Jah Keved and Kharbranth. This man had been a friend to Gavilar; that was good enough for Dalinar. And he was more than glad to have at least one other monarch at Urithiru.

Taravangian smiled at Dalinar, then licked his lips. He seemed to have forgotten what he wanted to say, and had to glance at the woman beside him for support. She whispered, and he spoke loudly after the reminder.

"Blackthorn," Taravangian said. "It is an honor to meet you again. It has been too long."

"Your Majesty," Dalinar said. "Thank you so much for responding to my call." Dalinar had met Taravangian several times, years ago. He remembered a man of quiet, keen intelligence.

That was gone now. Taravangian had always been humble, and had kept to himself, so most didn't know he'd been intelligent once—before his strange illness five years ago, which Navani was fairly certain covered an apoplexy that had permanently wounded his mental capacities.

Adrotagia touched Taravangian's arm and nodded toward someone standing with the Kharbranthian guards: a middle-aged lighteyed woman wearing a skirt and blouse, after a Southern style, with the top buttons of the blouse undone. Her hair was short in a boyish cut, and she wore gloves on both hands.

The strange woman stretched her right hand over her head, and a Shardblade appeared in it. She rested it with the flat side against her shoulder.

"Ah yes," Taravangian said. "Introductions! Blackthorn, this is the newest Knight Radiant. Malata of Jah Keved."

⁙

King Taravangian gawked like a child as they rode the lift toward the top of the tower. He leaned over the side far enough that his large Thaylen bodyguard rested a careful hand on the king's shoulder, just in case.

"So many levels," Taravangian said. "And this balcony. Tell me, Brightlord. What makes it move?"

His sincerity was so unexpected. Dalinar had been around Alethi politicians so much that he found honesty an obscure thing, like a language he no longer spoke.

"My engineers are still studying the lifts," Dalinar said. "It has to do with conjoined fabrials, they believe, with gears to modulate speed."

Taravangian blinked. "Oh. I meant . . . is this Stormlight? Or is someone pulling somewhere? We had parshmen do ours, back in Kharbranth."

"Stormlight," Dalinar said. "We had to replace the gemstones with infused ones to make it work."

"Ah." He shook his head, grinning.

In Alethkar, this man would never have been able to hold a throne after the apoplexy struck him. An unscrupulous family would have removed him by assassination. In other families, someone would have challenged him for his throne. He'd have been forced to fight or abdicate.

Or . . . well, someone might have muscled him out of power, and acted like king in all but name. Dalinar sighed softly, but kept a firm grip on his guilt.

Taravangian wasn't Alethi. In Kharbranth—which didn't wage war—a mild, congenial figurehead made more sense. The city was *supposed* to be unassuming, unthreatening. It was a twist of luck that Taravangian had also been crowned king of Jah Keved, once one of the most powerful kingdoms on Roshar, following its civil war.

He would normally have had trouble keeping that throne, but perhaps Dalinar might lend him some support—or at least authority—through association. Dalinar certainly intended to do everything he could.

"Your Majesty," Dalinar said, stepping closer to Taravangian. "How well guarded is Vedenar? I have a great number of troops with too much idle time. I could easily spare a battalion or two to help secure the city. We can't afford to lose the Oathgate to the enemy."

Taravangian glanced at Adrotagia.

She answered for him. "The city is secure, Brightlord. You needn't fear. The parshmen made one push for the city, but there are still many Veden troops available. We fended the enemy off, and they withdrew eastward."

Toward Alethkar, Dalinar thought.

Taravangian again looked out into the wide central column, lit from the sheer glass window to the east. "Ah, how I wish this day hadn't come."

"You sound as if you anticipated it, Your Majesty," Dalinar said.

Taravangian laughed softly. "Don't you? Anticipate sorrow, I mean? Sadness . . . loss . . ."

"I try not to hasten my expectations in either direction," Dalinar said. "The soldier's way. Deal with today's problems, then sleep and deal with tomorrow's problems tomorrow."

Taravangian nodded. "I remember, as a child, listening to an ardent pray to the Almighty on my behalf as glyphwards burned nearby. I remember thinking . . . surely the sorrows can't be past us. Surely the evils didn't actually end. If they had, wouldn't we be back in the Tranquiline Halls even now?" He looked toward Dalinar, and surprisingly there were tears in his pale grey eyes. "I do not think you and I are destined for such a glorious place. Men of blood and sorrow don't get an ending like that, Dalinar Kholin."

Dalinar found himself without a reply. Adrotagia gripped Taravangian on the forearm with a comforting gesture, and the old king turned away, hiding his emotional outburst. What had happened in Vedenar must have troubled him deeply—the death of the previous king, the field of slaughter.

They rode the rest of the way in silence, and Dalinar took the chance to study Taravangian's Surgebinder. She'd been the one to unlock—then activate—the Veden Oathgate on the other side, which she'd managed after some careful instructions from Navani. Now the woman, Malata, leaned idly against the side of the balcony. She hadn't spoken much during their tour of the first three levels, and when she looked at Dalinar, she always seemed to have a hint of a smile on her lips.

She carried a wealth of spheres in her skirt pocket; the light shone through the fabric. Perhaps that was why she smiled. He himself felt relieved to have Light at his fingertips again—and not only because it meant the Alethi Soulcasters could get back to work, using their emeralds to transform rock to grain to feed the hungry people of the tower.

Navani met them at the top level, immaculate in an ornate silver and black havah, her hair in a bun and stabbed through with hairspikes meant to resemble Shardblades. She greeted Taravangian warmly, then clasped hands with Adrotagia. After a greeting, Navani stepped back and let Teshav guide Taravangian and his little retinue into what they were calling the Initiation Room.

Navani herself drew Dalinar to the side. "Well?" she whispered.

"He's as sincere as ever," Dalinar said softly. "But . . ."

"Dense?" she asked.

"Dear, *I'm* dense. This man has become an idiot."

"You're not dense, Dalinar," she said. "You're rugged. Practical."

"I've no illusions as to the thickness of my skull, gemheart. It's done right by me on more than one occasion—better a thick head than a broken one. But I don't know that Taravangian in his current state will be of much use."

"Bah," Navani said. "We've more than enough clever people around us, Dalinar. Taravangian was always a friend to Alethkar during your brother's reign, and a little illness shouldn't change our treatment of him."

"You're right, of course. . . ." He trailed off. "There's an earnestness to him, Navani. And a melancholy I hadn't remembered. Was that always there?"

"Yes, actually." She checked her own arm clock, like his own, though with a few more gemstones attached. Some kind of new fabrial she was tinkering with.

"Any news from Captain Kaladin?"

She shook her head. It had been days since his last check-in, but he'd likely run out of infused rubies. Now that the highstorms had returned, they'd expected something.

In the room, Teshav gestured to the various pillars, each representing an order of Knight Radiant. Dalinar and Navani waited in the doorway, separated from the rest.

"What of the Surgebinder?" Navani whispered.

"A Releaser. Dustbringer, though they don't like the term. She claims her spren told her that." He rubbed his chin. "I don't like how she smiles."

"If she's truly a Radiant," Navani said, "can she be anything but trustworthy? Would the spren pick someone who would act against the best interests of the orders?"

Another question he didn't know the answer to. He'd need to see if he could determine whether her Shardblade was only that, or if it might be another Honorblade in disguise.

The touring group moved down a set of steps toward the meeting chamber, which took up most of the penultimate level and sloped down to the level below. Dalinar and Navani trailed after them.

Navani, he thought. *On my arm.* It still gave him a heady, surreal feeling. Dreamlike, as if this were one of his visions. He could vividly remember desiring her. Thinking about her, captivated by the way she talked, the things she knew, the look of her hands as she sketched—or, storms, as she did something as simple as raising a spoon to her lips. He remembered staring at her.

He remembered a specific day on a battlefield, when he had almost let his jealousy of his brother lead him too far—and was surprised to feel Evi slipping into that memory. Her presence colored the old, crusty memory of those war days with his brother.

"My memories continue to return," he said softly as they paused at the door into the conference room. "I can only assume that eventually it will all come back."

"That shouldn't be happening."

"I thought the same. But really, who can say? The Old Magic is said to be inscrutable."

"No," Navani said, folding her arms, getting a stern expression on her face—as if angry with a stubborn child. "In each case I've looked into, the boon and curse both lasted until death."

"Each case?" Dalinar said. "How many did you find?"

"About three hundred at this point," Navani said. "It's been difficult to get any time from the researchers at the Palanaeum; everyone the world over is demanding research into the Voidbringers. Fortunately, His Majesty's impending visit here earned me special consideration, and I had some credit. They say it's best to patronize the place in person—at least Jasnah always said . . ."

She took a breath, steadying herself before continuing. "In any case, Dalinar, the research is definitive. We haven't been able to find a *single* case where the effects of the Old Magic wore off—and it's not like people haven't tried over the centuries. Lore about people dealing with their curses, and seeking any cure for them, is practically its own *genre*. As my researcher said, 'Old Magic curses aren't like a hangover, Brightness.'"

She looked up at Dalinar, and must have seen the emotion in his face, for she cocked her head. "What?" she asked.

"I've never had anyone to share this burden with," he said softly. "Thank you."

"I didn't find anything."

"It doesn't matter."

"Could you at least confirm with the Stormfather again that his bond with you is absolutely, for sure *not* what's causing the memories to come back?"

"I'll see."

The Stormfather rumbled. *Why would she want me to say more? I have spoken, and spren do not change like men. This is not my doing. It is not the bond.*

"He says it's not him," Dalinar said. "He's . . . annoyed at you for asking again."

She kept her arms crossed. This was something she shared with her daughter, a characteristic frustration with problems she couldn't solve. As if she were disappointed in the facts for not arranging themselves more helpfully.

"Maybe," she said, "something was different about the deal you made. If you can recount your visit to me sometime—with as much detail as you can remember—I'll compare it to other accounts."

He shook his head. "There wasn't much. The Valley had a lot of plants. And . . . I remember . . . I asked to have my pain taken away, and she took memories too. I think?" He shrugged, then noticed Navani pursing her lips, her stare sharpening. "I'm sorry. I—"

"It's not you," Navani said. "It's the Nightwatcher. Giving you a deal when you were probably too distraught to think straight, then erasing your memory of the details?"

"She's a spren. I don't think we can expect her to play by—or even understand—our rules." He wished he could give her more, but even if he could dredge up something, this wasn't the time. They should be paying attention to their guests.

Teshav had finished pointing out the strange glass panes on the inner walls that seemed like windows, only clouded. She moved on to the pairs of discs on the floor and ceiling that looked something like the top and bottom of a pillar that had been removed—a feature of a number of rooms they'd explored.

Once that was done, Taravangian and Adrotagia returned to the top of the room, near the windows. The new Radiant, Malata, lounged in a seat near the wall-mounted sigil of the Dustbringers, staring at it.

Dalinar and Navani climbed the steps to stand by Taravangian. "Breathtaking, isn't it?" Dalinar asked. "An even better view than from the lift."

"Overwhelming," Taravangian said. "So much space. We think . . . we think that we are the most important things on Roshar. Yet so much of Roshar is empty of us."

Dalinar cocked his head. Yes . . . perhaps some of the old Taravangian lingered in there somewhere.

"Is this where you'll have us meet?" Adrotagia asked, nodding toward the room. "When you've gathered all the monarchs, will this be our council chamber?"

"No," Dalinar said. "This seems too much like a lecture hall. I don't want the monarchs to feel as if they're being preached to."

"And . . . when will they come?" Taravangian asked, hopeful. "I am looking forward to meeting the others. The king of Azir . . . didn't you tell me there was a new one, Adrotagia? I know Queen Fen—she's very nice. Will we be inviting the Shin? So mysterious. Do they even have a king? Don't they live in tribes or something? Like Marati barbarians?"

Adrotagia tapped his arm fondly, but looked to Dalinar, obviously curious about the other monarchs.

Dalinar cleared his throat, but Navani spoke.

"So far, Your Majesty," she said, "you are the only one who has heeded our warning call."

Silence followed.

"Thaylenah?" Adrotagia asked hopefully.

"We've exchanged communications on five separate occasions," Navani said. "In each one, the queen has dodged our requests. Azir has been even more stubborn."

"Iri dismissed us almost outright," Dalinar said with a sigh. "Neither Marabethia nor Rira would respond to the initial request. There's no real government in the Reshi Isles or some of the middle states. Babatharnam's Most Ancient has been coy, and most of the Makabaki states imply that they're waiting for Azir to make a decision. The Shin sent only a quick reply to congratulate us, whatever that means."

"Hateful people," Taravangian said. "Murdering so many worthy monarchs!"

"Um, yes," Dalinar said, uncomfortable at the king's sudden change in attitude. "Our primary focus has been on places with Oathgates, for strategic reasons. Azir, Thaylen City, and Iri seem most essential. However, we've made overtures to everyone who will listen, Oathgate or no. New Natanan is being coy so far, and the Herdazians think I'm trying to trick them. The Tukari scribes keep claiming they will bring my words to their god-king."

Navani cleared her throat. "We actually got a reply from him, just a bit ago. Teshav's ward was monitoring the spanreeds. It's not exactly encouraging."

"I'd like to hear it anyway."

She nodded, and went to collect it from Teshav. Adrotagia gave him a questioning glance, but he didn't dismiss the two of them. He wanted them to feel they were part of an alliance, and perhaps they would have insights that would prove helpful.

Navani returned with a single sheet of paper. Dalinar couldn't read the script on it, but the lines seemed sweeping and grand—imperious.

"'A warning,'" Navani read, "'from Tezim the Great, last and first man, Herald of Heralds and bearer of the Oathpact. His grandness, immortality, and power be praised. Lift up your heads and hear, men of the east, of your God's proclamation.

"'None are Radiant but him. His fury is ignited by your pitiful claims, and your unlawful capture of his holy city is an act of rebellion, depravity, and wickedness. Open your gates, men of the east, to his righteous soldiers and deliver unto him your spoils.

"'Renounce your foolish claims and swear yourselves to him. The judgment of the final storm has come to destroy all men, and only his path will lead to deliverance. He deigns to send you this single mandate, and will not speak it again. Even this is far above what your carnal natures deserve.'"

She lowered the paper.

"Wow," Adrotagia said. "Well, at least it's clear."

Taravangian scratched at his head, brow furrowed, as if he didn't agree with that statement at all.

"I guess," Dalinar said, "we can cross the Tukari off our list of possible allies."

"I'd rather have the Emuli anyway," Navani said. "Their soldiers might be less capable, but they're also . . . well, *not crazy*."

"So . . . we are alone?" Taravangian said, looking from Dalinar to Adrotagia, uncertain.

"We are alone, Your Majesty," Dalinar said. "The end of the world has come, and still nobody will listen."

Taravangian nodded to himself. "Where do we attack first? Herdaz?

My aides say it is the traditional first step for an Alethi aggression, but they also point out that if you could somehow take Thaylenah, you'd completely control the Straits and even the Depths."

Dalinar listened to the words with dismay. It was the obvious assumption. So clear that even simpleminded Taravangian saw it. What else to make of Alethkar proposing a union? Alethkar, the great conquerors? Led by the Blackthorn, the man who had united his own kingdom by the sword?

It was the suspicion that had tainted every conversation with the other monarchs. *Storms,* he thought. *Taravangian didn't come because he believed in my grand alliance. He assumed that if he didn't, I wouldn't send my armies to Herdaz or Thaylenah—I'd send them to Jah Keved. To him.*

"We're not going to attack anyone," Dalinar said. "Our focus is on the Voidbringers, the true enemy. We will win the other kingdoms with diplomacy."

Taravangian frowned. "But—"

Adrotagia, however, touched him on the arm and quieted him. "Of course, Brightlord," she said to Dalinar. "We understand."

She thought he was lying.

And are you?

What would he do if nobody listened? How would he save Roshar without the Oathgates? Without resources?

If our plan to reclaim Kholinar works, he thought, *wouldn't it make sense to take the other gates the same way? Nobody would be able to fight both us and the Voidbringers. We could seize their capitals and force them—for their own good—to join our unified war effort.*

He'd been willing to conquer Alethkar for its own good. He'd been willing to seize the kingship in all but name, again for the good of his people.

How far would he go for the good of all Roshar? How far would he go to prepare them for the coming of that enemy? A champion with nine shadows.

I will unite instead of divide.

He found himself standing at that window beside Taravangian, staring out over the mountains, his memories of Evi carrying with them a fresh and dangerous perspective.

25

THE GIRL
WHO LOOKED UP

I will confess my murders before you. Most painfully, I have killed someone who loved me dearly.

—From *Oathbringer*, preface

The tower of Urithiru was a skeleton, and these strata beneath Shallan's fingers were veins that wrapped the bones, dividing and spreading across the entire body. But what did those veins carry? Not blood.

She slid through the corridors on the third level, in the bowels, away from civilization, passing through doorways without doors and rooms without occupants.

Men had locked themselves in with their light, telling themselves that they'd conquered this ancient behemoth. But all they had were outposts in the darkness. Eternal, waiting darkness. These hallways had *never* seen the sun. Storms that raged through Roshar never touched here. This was a place of eternal stillness, and men could no more conquer it than cremlings could claim to have conquered the boulder they hid beneath.

She defied Dalinar's orders that all were to travel in pairs. She didn't worry about that. Her satchel and safepouch were stuffed with new spheres recharged in the highstorm. She felt gluttonous carrying so many, breathing in the Light whenever she wished. She was as safe as a person could be, so long as she had that Light.

She wore Veil's clothing, but not yet her face. She wasn't truly exploring, though she did make a mental map. She just wanted to be in this place, sensing it. It could not be comprehended, but perhaps it could be *felt*.

Jasnah had spent years hunting for this mythical city and the information she'd assumed it would hold. Navani spoke of the ancient technology she was sure this place must contain. So far, she'd been disappointed. She'd cooed over the Oathgates, had been impressed by the system of lifts. That was it. No majestic fabrials from the past, no diagrams explaining lost technology. No books or writings at all. Just dust.

And darkness, Shallan thought, pausing in a circular chamber with corridors splitting out in seven different directions. She *had* felt the wrongness Mraize spoke of. She'd felt it the moment she'd tried to draw this place. Urithiru was like the impossible geometries of Pattern's shape. Invisible, yet grating, like a discordant sound.

She picked a direction at random and continued, finding herself in a corridor narrow enough that she could brush both walls with her fingers. The strata had an emerald cast here, an alien color for stone. A hundred shades of wrongness.

She passed several small rooms before entering a much larger chamber. She stepped into it, holding a diamond broam high for light, revealing that she was on a raised portion at the front of a large room with curving walls and rows of stone . . . benches?

It's a theater, she thought. *And I've walked out onto the stage.* Yes, she could make out a balcony above. Rooms like this struck her with their humanity. Everything else about this place was so empty and arid. Endless rooms, corridors, and caverns. Floors strewn with only the occasional bit of civilization's detritus, like rusted hinges or an old boot's buckle. Decayspren huddled like barnacles on ancient doors.

A theater was more *real.* More alive, despite the span of the epochs. She stepped into the center and twirled about, letting Veil's coat flare around her. "I always imagined being up on one of these. When I was a child, becoming a player seemed the grandest job. To get away from home, travel to new places." *To not have to be myself for at least a brief time each day.*

Pattern hummed, pushing out from her coat to hover above the stage in three dimensions. "What is it?"

"It's a stage for concerts or plays."

"Plays?"

"Oh, you'd like them," she said. "People in a group each pretend to be someone different, and tell a story together." She strode down the steps at the side, walking among the benches. "The audience out here watches."

Pattern hovered in the center of the stage, like a soloist. "Ah . . ." he said. "A group lie?"

"A wonderful, wonderful lie," Shallan said, settling onto a bench, Veil's satchel beside her. "A time when people all imagine together."

"I wish I could see one," Pattern said. "I could understand people . . . mmmm . . . through the lies they want to be told."

Shallan closed her eyes, smiling, remembering the last time she'd seen a play at her father's. A traveling children's troupe come to entertain her. She'd taken Memories for her collection—but of course, that was now lost at the bottom of the ocean.

"The Girl Who Looked Up," she whispered.

"What?" Pattern asked.

Shallan opened her eyes and breathed out Stormlight. She hadn't sketched this particular scene, so she used what she had handy: a drawing she'd done of a young child in the market. Bright and happy, too young to cover her safehand. The girl appeared from the Stormlight and scampered up the steps, then bowed to Pattern.

"There was a girl," Shallan said. "This was before storms, before memories, and before legends—but there was still a girl. She wore a long scarf to blow in the wind."

A vibrant red scarf grew around the girl's neck, twin tails extending far behind her and flapping in a phantom wind. The players had made the scarf hang behind the girl using strings from above. It had seemed so real.

"The girl in the scarf played and danced, as girls do today," Shallan said, making the child prance around Pattern. "In fact, most things were the same then as they are today. Except for one big difference. The wall."

Shallan drained an indulgent number of spheres from her satchel, then sprinkled the floor of the stage with grass and vines like from her homeland. Across the back of the stage, a wall grew as Shallan had imagined it. A high, terrible wall stretching toward the moons. Blocking the sky, throwing everything around the girl into shadow.

The girl stepped toward it, looking up, straining to see the top.

"You see, in those days, a wall kept out the storms," Shallan said. "It had existed for so long, nobody knew how it had been built. That did not bother them. Why wonder when the mountains began or why the sky was high? Like these things were, so the wall was."

The girl danced in its shadow, and other people sprang up from Shallan's Light. Each was a person from one of her sketches. Vathah, Gaz, Palona, Sebarial. They worked as farmers or washwomen, doing their duties with heads bowed. Only the girl looked up at that wall, her twin scarf tails streaming behind her.

She approached a man standing behind a small cart of fruit, wearing Kaladin Stormblessed's face.

"Why is there a wall?" she asked the man selling fruit, speaking with her own voice.

"To keep the bad things out," he replied.

"What bad things?"

"Very bad things. There is a wall. Do not go beyond it, or you shall die."

The fruit seller picked up his cart and moved away. And still, the girl looked up at the wall. Pattern hovered beside her and hummed happily to himself.

"Why is there a wall?" she asked the woman suckling her child. The woman had Palona's face.

"To protect us," the woman said.

"To protect us from what?"

"Very bad things. There is a wall. Do not go beyond it, or you shall die."

The woman took her child and left.

The girl climbed a tree, peeking out the top, her scarf streaming behind her. "Why is there a wall?" she called to the boy sleeping lazily in the nook of a branch.

"What wall?" the boy asked.

The girl thrust her finger pointedly toward the wall.

"That's not a wall," the boy said, drowsy. Shallan had given him the face of one of the bridgemen, a Herdazian. "That's just the way the sky is over there."

"It's a *wall*," the girl said. "A giant wall."

"It must be there for a purpose," the boy said. "Yes, it is a wall. Don't go beyond it, or you'll probably die."

"Well," Shallan continued, speaking from the audience, "these answers did not satisfy the girl who looked up. She reasoned to herself, if the wall kept evil things out, then the space on this side of it should be safe.

"So, one night while the others of the village slept, she sneaked from her home with a bundle of supplies. She walked toward the wall, and indeed the land *was* safe. But it was also dark. Always in the shadow of that wall. No sunlight, ever, directly reached the people."

Shallan made the illusion roll, like scenery on a scroll as the players had used. Only far, far more realistic. She had painted the ceiling with light, and looking up, you seemed to be looking only at an infinite sky—dominated by that wall.

This is . . . this is far more extensive than I've done before, she thought, surprised. Creationspren had started to appear around her on the benches, in the form of old latches or doorknobs, rolling about or moving end over end.

Well, Dalinar *had* told her to practice. . . .

"The girl traveled far," Shallan said, looking back toward the stage. "No predators hunted her, and no storms assaulted her. The only wind was the pleasant one that played with her scarf, and the only creatures she saw were the cremlings that clicked at her as she walked.

"At long last, the girl in the scarves stood before the wall. It was truly expansive, running as far as she could see in either direction. And its height! It reached almost to the Tranquiline Halls!"

Shallan stood and walked onto the stage, passing into a different land—an image of fertility, vines, trees, and grass, dominated by that terrible wall. It grew spikes from its front in bristling patches.

I didn't draw this scene out. At least . . . not recently.

She'd drawn it as a youth, in detail, putting her imagined fancies down on paper.

"What happened?" Pattern said. "Shallan? I must know what happened. Did she turn back?"

"Of course she didn't turn back," Shallan said. "She *climbed*. There were outcroppings in the wall, things like these spikes or hunched, ugly statues. She had climbed the highest trees all through her youth. She could do this."

The girl started climbing. Had her hair been white when she'd started? Shallan frowned.

Shallan made the base of the wall sink into the stage, so although the girl got higher, she remained chest-height to Shallan and Pattern.

"The climb took days," Shallan said, hand to her head. "At night, the girl who looked up would tie herself a hammock out of her scarf and sleep there. She picked out her village at one point, remarking on how small it seemed, now that she was high.

"As she neared the top, she finally began to fear what she would find on the other side. Unfortunately, this fear did not stop her. She was young, and questions bothered her more than fear. So it was that she finally struggled to the very top and stood to see the other side. The hidden side . . ."

Shallan choked up. She remembered sitting at the edge of her seat, listening to this story. As a child, when moments like watching the players had been the only bright spots in life.

Too many memories of her father, and of her mother, who had loved telling her stories. She tried to banish those memories, but they *wouldn't go*.

Shallan turned. Her Stormlight . . . she'd used up almost everything she'd pulled from her satchel. Out in the seats, a crowd of dark figures watched. Eyeless, just shadows, people from her memories. The outline of her father, her mother, her brothers and a dozen others. She couldn't create them, because she hadn't drawn them properly. Not since she'd lost her collection . . .

Next to Shallan, the girl stood triumphantly on the wall's top, her scarves and white hair streaming out behind her in a sudden wind. Pattern buzzed beside Shallan.

". . . and on that side of the wall," Shallan whispered, "the girl saw steps."

The back side of the wall was crisscrossed with enormous sets of steps leading down to the ground, so distant.

"What . . . what does it mean?" Pattern said.

"The girl stared at those steps," Shallan whispered, remembering, "and suddenly the gruesome statues on her side of the wall made sense. The spears. The way it cast everything into shadow. The wall did indeed hide something evil, something frightening. It was the people, like the girl and her village."

The illusion started to break down around her. This was too ambitious for her to hold, and it left her strained, exhausted, her head starting to pound. She let the wall fade, claiming its Stormlight. The landscape vanished, then finally the girl herself. Behind, the shadowed figures in the seats started to evaporate. Stormlight streamed back to Shallan, stoking the storm inside.

"That's how it ended?" Pattern asked.

"No," Shallan said, Stormlight puffing from her lips. "She goes down, sees a perfect society lit by Stormlight. She steals some and brings it back. The storms come as a punishment, tearing down the wall."

"Ah . . ." Pattern said, hovering beside her on the now-dull stage. "So that's how the storms first began?"

"Of course not," Shallan said, feeling tired. "It's a lie, Pattern. A story. It doesn't mean anything."

"Then why are you crying?"

She wiped her eyes and turned away from the empty stage. She needed to get back to the markets.

In the seats, the last of the shadowy audience members puffed away. All but one, who stood up and walked out the back doors of the theater. Startled, Shallan felt a sudden shock run through her.

That figure hadn't been one of her illusions.

She flung herself from the stage—landing hard, Veil's coat fluttering—and dashed after the figure. She held the rest of her Stormlight, a thrumming, violent tempest. She skidded into the hall outside, glad for sturdy boots and simple trousers.

Something shadowy moved down the corridor. Shallan gave chase, lips drawn to a sneer, letting Stormlight rise from her skin and illuminate her surroundings. As she ran, she pulled a string from her pocket and tied her hair back, becoming Radiant. Radiant would know what to do if she caught this person.

Can a person look that much like a shadow?

"Pattern," she shouted, thrusting her right hand forward. Luminescent fog formed there, becoming her Shardblade. Light escaped her lips, transforming her more fully into Radiant. Luminescent wisps trailed behind her, and she felt it chasing her. She charged into a small round chamber and skidded to a stop.

A dozen versions of herself, from drawings she'd done recently, split around her and dashed through the room. Shallan in her dress, Veil in her coat. Shallan as a child, Shallan as a youth. Shallan as a soldier, a happy wife, a mother. Leaner here, plumper there. Scarred. Bright with excitement. Bloodied and in pain. They vanished after passing her, collapsing one after another into Stormlight that curled and twisted about itself before vanishing away.

Radiant raised her Shardblade in the stance Adolin had been teaching her, sweat dripping down the sides of her face. The room would have been dark but for the Light curling off her skin and passing through her clothing to rise around her.

Empty. She'd either lost her quarry in the corridors, or it had been a spren and not a person at all.

Or there was nothing there in the first place, a part of her worried. *Your mind is not trustworthy these days.*

"What was that?" Radiant said. "Did you see it?"

No, Pattern thought to her. *I was thinking on the lie.*

She walked around the edge of the circular room. The wall was scored by a series of deep slots that ran from floor to ceiling. She could feel air moving through them. What was the purpose of a room like this? Had the people who had designed this place been mad?

Radiant noted faint light coming from several of the slots—and with it the sounds of people in a low, echoing clatter. The Breakaway market? Yes, she was in that region, and while she was on the third level, the market's cavern was a full four stories high.

She moved to the next slot and peered through it, trying to decide just where it let out. Was this—

Something moved in the slot.

A dark mass wriggled deep inside, squeezing between walls. Like goo, but with bits jutting out. Those were elbows, ribs, fingers splayed along one wall, each knuckle bending backward.

A spren, she thought, trembling. *It is some strange kind of spren.*

The thing twisted, head deforming in the tiny confines, and looked toward her. She saw eyes reflecting her light, twin spheres set in a mashed head, a distorted human visage.

Radiant pulled back with a sharp gasp, summoning her Shardblade again and holding it wardingly before herself. But what was she going to do? Hack her way through the stone to get to the thing? That would take forever.

Did she even want to reach it?

No. But she had to anyway.

The market, she thought, dismissing her Blade and darting back the way she'd come. *It's heading to the market.*

With Stormlight propelling her, Radiant dashed through corridors, barely noticing as she breathed out enough to transform her face into Veil's. She swerved through a network of twisted passages. This maze, these enigmatic tunnels, were not what she'd expected from the home of the Knights Radiant. Shouldn't this be a fortress, simple but grand—a beacon of light and strength in the dark times?

Instead it was a puzzle. Veil stumbled out of the back corridors into populated ones, then dashed past a group of children laughing and holding up chips for light and making shadows on the walls.

Another few turns took her out onto the balcony walk around the cavernous Breakaway market, with its bobbing lights and busy pathways. Veil turned left to see slots in the wall here. For ventilation?

The thing had come through one of these, but where had it gone after that? A scream rose, shrill and cold, from the floor of the market below. Cursing to herself, Veil took the steps at a reckless pace. Just like Veil. Running headlong into danger.

She sucked in her breath, and the Stormlight puffing around her pulled in, causing her to stop glowing. After a short dash, she found people gathering between two packed rows of tents. The stalls here sold various goods, many of which looked to be salvage from the more abandoned warcamps. More than a few enterprising merchants—with the tacit approval of their highprinces—had sent expeditions back to gather what they could. With Stormlight flowing and Renarin to help with the Oathgate, those had finally been allowed into Urithiru.

The highprinces had gotten first pick. The rest of their finds were heaped in the tents here, watched over by guards with long cudgels and short tempers.

Veil shoved her way to the front of the crowd, finding a large Horneater man cursing and holding his hand. *Rock,* she thought, recognizing the bridgeman though he wasn't in uniform.

His hand was bleeding. *Like it was stabbed right through the center,* Veil thought.

"What happened here?" she demanded, still holding her Light in to keep it from puffing out and revealing her.

Rock eyed her while his companion—a bridgeman she thought she'd seen before—wrapped his hand. "Who are you to ask me this thing?"

Storms. She was Veil right now, but she didn't dare expose the ruse, especially not in the open. "I'm on Aladar's policing force," she said, digging in her pocket. "I have my commission here . . ."

"Is fine," Rock said, sighing, his wariness seeming to evaporate. "I did nothing. Some person pulled knife. I did not see him well—long coat, and a hat. A woman in crowd screamed, drawing my attention. Then, this man, he attacked."

"Storms. Who is dead?"

"Dead?" The Horneater looked to his companion. "Nobody is dead. Attacker stabbed my hand, then ran. Was assassination attempt, maybe? Person got angry about rule of tower, so he attacked me, for being in Kholin guard?"

Veil felt a chill. *Horneater. Tall, burly.*

The attacker had chosen a man who looked very similar to the one she had stabbed the other day. In fact, they weren't far from All's Alley. Just a few "streets" over in the market.

The two bridgemen turned to leave, and Veil let them go. What more could she learn? The Horneater had been targeted not because of anything he'd done, but because of how he looked. And the attacker had been wearing a coat and hat. Like Veil usually did . . .

"I thought I'd find you here."

Veil started, then whirled around, hand going to her belt knife. The speaker was a woman in a brown havah. She had straight Alethi hair, dark brown eyes, bright red painted lips, and sharp black eyebrows almost certainly enhanced with makeup. Veil recognized this woman, who was shorter than she'd seemed while sitting down. She was one of the thieves that Veil had approached at All's Alley, the one whose eyes had lit up when Shallan had drawn the Ghostbloods' symbol.

"What did he do to you?" the woman asked, nodding toward Rock. "Or do you just have a thing for stabbing Horneaters?"

"This wasn't me," Veil said.

"I'm sure." The woman stepped closer. "I've been waiting for you to turn up again."

"You should stay away, if you value your life." Veil started off through the market.

The short woman scrambled after her. "My name is Ishnah. I'm an excellent writer. I can take dictations. I have experience moving in the market underground."

"You want to be my ward?"

"Ward?" The young woman laughed. "What are we, lighteyes? I want to join you."

The Ghostbloods, of course. "We're not recruiting."

"Please." She took Veil by the arm. "Please. The world is wrong now. Nothing makes sense. But you . . . your group . . . you know things. I don't want to be blind anymore."

Shallan hesitated. She could understand that desire to do something, rather than just feeling the world tremble and shake. But the Ghostbloods were despicable. This woman would not find what she desired among them. And if she did, then she was not the sort of person that Shallan would want to add to Mraize's quiver.

"No," Shallan said. "Do the smart thing and forget about me and my organization."

She pulled out of the woman's grip and hurried away through the bustling market.

TWENTY-NINE YEARS AGO

Incense burned in a brazier as large as a boulder. Dalinar sniffled as Evi threw a handful of tiny papers—each folded and inscribed with a very small glyph—into the brazier. Fragrant smoke washed over him, then whipped in the other direction as winds ripped through the warcamp, carrying windspren like lines of light.

Evi bowed her head before the brazier. She had strange beliefs, his betrothed. Among her people, simple glyphwards weren't enough for prayers; you needed to burn something more pungent. While she spoke of Jezrien and Kelek, she said their names strangely: Yaysi and Kellai. And she made no mention of the Almighty—instead she spoke of something called the One, a heretical tradition the ardents told him came from Iri.

Dalinar bowed his head for a prayer. *Let me be stronger than those who would kill me.* Simple and to the point, the kind he figured the Almighty would prefer. He didn't feel like having Evi write it out.

"The One watch you, near-husband," Evi murmured. "And soften your temper." Her accent, to which he was now accustomed, was thicker than her brother's.

"Soften it? Evi, that's not the point of battle."

"You needn't kill in anger, Dalinar. If you must fight, do it knowing that each death wounds the One. For we are all people in Yaysi's sight."

"Yeah, all right," Dalinar said.

The ardents didn't seem to mind that he was marrying someone half pagan. "It is wisdom to bring her to Vorin truth," Jevena—Gavilar's head ardent—had told him. Similar to how she'd spoken of his conquest. "Your sword will bring strength and glory to the Almighty."

Idly, he wondered what it would take to actually earn the ardents' displeasure.

"Be a man and not a beast, Dalinar," Evi said, then pulled close to him, setting her head on his shoulder and encouraging him to wrap his arms around her.

He did so with a limp gesture. Storms, he could hear the soldiers snicker as they passed by. The Blackthorn, being consoled before battle? Publicly hugging and acting lovey?

Evi turned her head toward him for a kiss, and he presented a chaste one, their lips barely touching. She accepted that, smiling. And she did have a beautiful smile. Life would have been a lot easier for him if Evi would have just been willing to move along with the marriage. But her traditions demanded a long engagement, and her brother kept trying to get new provisions into the contract.

Dalinar stomped away. In his pocket he held another glyphward: one provided by Navani, who obviously worried about the accuracy of Evi's foreign script. He felt at the smooth paper, and didn't burn the prayer.

The stone ground beneath his feet was pocked with tiny holes—the pinpricks of hiding grass. As he passed the tents he could see it properly, covering the plain outside, waving in the wind. Tall stuff, almost as high as his waist. He'd never seen grass that tall in Kholin lands.

Across the plain, an impressive force gathered: an army larger than any they'd faced. His heart jumped in anticipation. After two years of political maneuvering, here they were. A real battle with a real army.

Win or lose, *this* was the fight for the kingdom. The sun was on its way up, and the armies had arrayed themselves north and south, so neither would have it in their eyes.

Dalinar hastened to his armorers' tent, and emerged a short time later in his Plate. He climbed carefully into the saddle as one of the grooms brought his horse. The large black beast wasn't fast, but it *could* carry a man in Shardplate. Dalinar guided the horse past ranks of soldiers—spearmen, archers, lighteyed heavy infantry, even a nice group of fifty cavalrymen under Ilamar, with hooks and ropes for attacking Shardbearers. Anticipationspren waved like banners among them all.

Dalinar still smelled incense when he found his brother, geared up and mounted, patrolling the front lines. Dalinar trotted up beside Gavilar.

"Your young friend didn't show for the battle," Gavilar noted.

"Sebarial?" Dalinar said. "He's *not* my friend."

"There's a hole in the enemy line, still waiting for him," Gavilar said, pointing. "Reports say he had a problem with his supply lines."

"Lies. He's a coward. If he'd arrived, he'd have had to actually pick a side."

They rode past Tearim, Gavilar's captain of the guard, who wore Dalinar's extra Plate for this battle. Technically that still belonged to Evi. Not Toh, but Evi herself, which was strange. What would a woman do with Shardplate?

Give it to a husband, apparently. Tearim saluted. He was capable with Shards, having trained, as did many aspiring lighteyes, with borrowed sets.

"You've done well, Dalinar," Gavilar said as they rode past. "That Plate will serve us today."

Dalinar made no reply. Even though Evi and her brother had delayed such a painfully long time to even agree to the *betrothal*, Dalinar had done his duty. He just wished he felt more for the woman. Some passion, some true *emotion*. He couldn't laugh without her seeming confused by the conversation. He couldn't boast without her being disappointed in his bloodlust. She always wanted him to hold her, as if being alone for one *storming* minute would make her wither and blow away. And . . .

"Ho!" one of the scouts called from a wooden mobile tower. She pointed, her voice distant. "Ho, there!"

Dalinar turned, expecting an advance attack from the enemy. But no, Kalanor's army was still deploying. It wasn't men that had attracted the scout's attention, but *horses*. A small herd of them, eleven or twelve in number, galloping across the battlefield. Proud, majestic.

"Ryshadium," Gavilar whispered. "It's rare they roam this far east."

Dalinar swallowed an order to round up the beasts. Ryshadium? Yes . . . he could see the spren trailing after them in the air. Musicspren, for some reason. Made no storming sense. Well, no use trying to capture the beasts. They couldn't be held unless they chose a rider.

"I want you to do something for me today, Brother," Gavilar said. "Highprince Kalanor himself needs to fall. As long as he lives, there will be resistance. If he dies, his line goes with him. His cousin, Loradar Vamah, can seize power."

"Will Loradar swear to you?"

"I'm certain of it," Gavilar said.

"Then I'll find Kalanor," Dalinar said, "and end this."

"He won't join the battle easily, knowing him. But he's a Shardbearer. And so . . ."

"So we need to force him to engage."

Gavilar smiled.

"What?" Dalinar said.

"I'm simply pleased to see you talking of tactics."

"I'm not an idiot," Dalinar growled. He always paid attention to the tactics of a battle; he simply wasn't one for endless meetings and jaw wagging.

Though . . . even those seemed more tolerable these days. Perhaps it was familiarity. Or maybe it was Gavilar's talk of forging a dynasty. It was the increasingly obvious truth that this campaign—now stretching over many years—was no quick bash and grab.

"Bring me Kalanor, Brother," Gavilar said. "We need the Blackthorn today."

"All you need do is unleash him."

"Ha! As if anyone existed who could leash him in the first place."

Isn't that what you've been trying to do? Dalinar thought immediately. *Marrying me off, talking about how we have to be "civilized" now? Highlighting everything I do wrong as the things we must expunge?*

He bit his tongue, and they finished their ride down the lines. They parted with a nod, and Dalinar rode over to join his elites.

"Orders, sir?" asked Rien.

"Stay out of my way," Dalinar said, lowering his faceplate. The Shardplate helm sealed closed, and a hush fell over the elites. Dalinar summoned Oathbringer, the sword of a fallen king, and waited. The enemy had come to stop Gavilar's continued pillage of the countryside; they would have to make the first move.

These last few months spent attacking isolated, unprotected towns had made for unfulfilling battles—but had also put Kalanor in a terrible position. If he sat back in his strongholds, he allowed more of his vassals to be destroyed. Already those started to wonder why they paid Kalanor taxes. A handful had preemptively sent messengers to Gavilar saying they would not resist.

The region was on the brink of flipping to the Kholins. And so, Highprince Kalanor had been forced to leave his fortifications to engage here. Dalinar shifted on his horse, waiting, planning. The moment came soon enough; Kalanor's forces started across the plain in a cautious wave, shields raised toward the sky.

Gavilar's archers released flights of arrows. Kalanor's men were well trained; they maintained their formations beneath the deadly hail. Eventually they met Kholin heavy infantry: a block of men so armored that it might as well have been solid stone. At the same time, mobile archer units sprang out to the sides. Lightly armored, they were *fast*. If the Kholins won this battle—and Dalinar was confident of victory—it would be because of the newer battlefield tactics they'd been exploring.

The enemy army found itself flanked—arrows pounding the sides of their assault blocks. Their lines stretched, the infantry trying to reach the archers, but that weakened the central block, which suffered a beating from the heavy infantry. Standard spearman blocks engaged enemy units as much to position them as to do them harm.

This all happened on the scale of the battlefield. Dalinar had to climb off his horse and send for a groom to walk the animal as he waited. Inside, Dalinar fought back the Thrill, which urged him to ride in immediately.

Eventually, he picked a section of Kholin troops who were faring poorly against the enemy block. Good enough. He remounted and kicked his horse into a gallop. This was the right moment. He could *feel* it. He needed to strike now, when the battle was pivoting between victory and loss, to draw out his enemy.

Grass wriggled and pulled back in a wave before him. Like subjects bowing. This might be the end, his final battle in the conquest of Alethkar. What happened to him after this? Endless feasts with politicians? A brother who refused to look elsewhere for battle?

Dalinar opened himself to the Thrill and drove away such worries. He struck the line of enemy troops like a highstorm hitting a stack of papers. Soldiers scattered before him, shouting. Dalinar laid about with his Shardblade, killing dozens on one side, then the other.

Eyes burned, arms fell limp. Dalinar breathed in the joy of the conquest, the narcotic beauty of destruction. None could stand before him; all were tinder and he the flame. The soldier block should have been able to band together and rush him, but they were too frightened.

And why shouldn't they be? People spoke of common men bringing down a Shardbearer, but surely that was a fabrication. A conceit intended to make men fight back, to save Shardbearers from having to hunt them down.

He grinned as his horse stumbled trying to cross the bodies piling around it. Dalinar kicked the beast forward, and it leaped—but as it landed, something gave. The creature screamed and collapsed, dumping him.

He sighed, shoving aside the horse and standing. He'd broken its back; Shardplate was not meant for such common beasts.

One group of soldiers tried a counterattack. Brave, but stupid. Dalinar felled them with broad sweeps of his Shardblade. Next, a lighteyed officer organized his men to come press and try to trap Dalinar, if not with their skill, then their weight of bodies. He spun among them, Plate lending him energy, Blade granting him precision, and the Thrill . . . the Thrill giving him *purpose*.

In moments like this, he could see why he had been created. He was wasted listening to men blab. He was wasted doing anything but *this:* providing the ultimate test of men's abilities, proving them, demanding their lives at the edge of a sword. He sent them to the Tranquiline Halls primed and ready to fight.

He was not a man. He was *judgment.*

Enthralled, he cut down foe after foe, sensing a strange rhythm to the fighting, as if the blows of his sword needed to fall to the dictates of some unseen beat. A redness grew at the edges of his vision, eventually covering the landscape like a veil. It seemed to shift and move like the coils of an eel, trembling to the beats of his sword.

He was furious when a calling voice distracted him from the fight.

"Dalinar!"

He ignored it.

"Brightlord Dalinar! Blackthorn!"

That voice was like a screeching cremling, playing its song inside his helm. He felled a pair of swordsmen. They'd been lighteyed, but their eyes had burned away, and you could no longer tell.

"Blackthorn!"

Bah! Dalinar spun toward the sound.

A man stood nearby, wearing Kholin blue. Dalinar raised his Shardblade. The man backed away, raising hands with no weapon, still shouting Dalinar's name.

I know him. He's . . . Kadash? One of the captains among his elites. Dalinar lowered his sword and shook his head, trying to get the buzzing sound out of his ears. Only then did he see—really see—what surrounded him.

The dead. Hundreds upon hundreds of them, with shriveled coals for eyes, their armor and weapons sheared but their bodies eerily untouched. Almighty above . . . how many had he killed? He raised his hand to his helm, turning and looking about him. Timid blades of grass crept up among the bodies, pushing between arms, fingers, beside heads. He'd blanketed the plain so thoroughly with corpses that the grass had a difficult time finding places to rise.

Dalinar grinned in satisfaction, then grew chill. A few of those bodies with burned eyes—three men he could spot—wore blue. His own men, bearing the armband of the elites.

"Brightlord," Kadash said. "Blackthorn, your task is accomplished!" He pointed toward a troop of horsemen charging across the plain. They carried the silver-on-red flag bearing a glyphpair of two mountains. Left no choice, Highprince Kalanor had committed to the battle. Dalinar had destroyed several companies on his own; only another Shardbearer could stop him.

"Excellent," Dalinar said. He pulled off his helm and took a cloth from Kadash, using it to wipe his face. A waterskin followed. Dalinar drank the entire thing.

Dalinar tossed away the empty skin, his heart racing, the Thrill thrumming within. "Pull back the elites. Do not engage unless I fall." Dalinar pulled his helm back on, and felt the comforting tightness as the latches cinched it into place.

"Yes, Brightlord."

"Gather those of us who . . . fell," Dalinar said, waving toward the Kholin dead. "Make certain they, and theirs, are cared for."

"Of course, sir."

Dalinar dashed toward the oncoming force, his Shardplate crunching against stones. He felt sad to have to engage a Shardbearer, instead of continuing his fight against the ordinary men. No more laying waste; he now had only one man to kill.

He could vaguely remember a time when facing lesser challenges hadn't sated him as much as a good fight against someone capable. What had changed?

His run took him toward one of the rock formations on the eastern side of the field—a group of enormous spires, weathered and jagged, like a row of stone stakes. As he entered the shadows, he could hear fighting from the other side. Portions of the armies had broken off and tried to flank each other by rounding the formations.

At their base, Kalanor's honor guard split, revealing the highprince himself on horseback. His Plate was overlaid with a silver coloring, perhaps steel or silver leaf. Dalinar had ordered his Plate buffed back to its normal slate grey; he'd never understood why people would want to "augment" the natural majesty of Shardplate.

Kalanor's horse was a tall, majestic animal, brilliant white with a long mane. It carried the Shardbearer with ease. A Ryshadium. Yet Kalanor dismounted. He patted the animal fondly on the neck, then stepped forward to meet Dalinar, Shardblade appearing in his hand.

"Blackthorn," he called. "I hear you've been single-handedly destroying my army."

"They fight for the Tranquiline Halls now."

"Would that you had joined to lead them."

"Someday," Dalinar said. "When I am too old and weak to fight here, I'll welcome being sent."

"Curious, how quickly tyrants grow religious. It must be convenient to tell yourself that your murders belong to the Almighty instead."

"They'd better not belong to him!" Dalinar said. "I worked hard for those kills, Kalanor. The Almighty can't have them; he can merely credit them to me when weighing my soul!"

"Then let them weigh you down to Damnation itself." Kalanor waved back his honor guard, who seemed eager to throw themselves at Dalinar. Alas, the highprince was determined to fight on his own. He swiped with his sword, a long, thin Shardblade with a large crossguard and glyphs down its length. "If I kill you, Blackthorn, what then?"

"Then Sadeas gets a crack at you."

"No honor on this battlefield, I see."

"Oh, don't pretend you are any better," Dalinar said. "I know what you did to rise to your throne. You can't pretend to be a peacemaker now."

"Considering what you did to the peacemakers," Kalanor said, "I'll count myself lucky."

Dalinar leaped forward, falling into Bloodstance—a stance for someone who didn't care if he got hit. He was younger, more agile than his opponent. He counted on being able to swing faster, harder.

Strangely, Kalanor chose Bloodstance himself. The two clashed, bashing their swords against one another in a pattern that sent them twisting about in a quick shuffle of footings—each trying to hit the same section of Plate repeatedly, to open a hole to flesh.

Dalinar grunted, batting away his opponent's Shardblade. Kalanor was old, but skilled. He had an uncanny ability to pull back before Dalinar's strikes, deflecting some of the force of the impact, preventing the metal from breaking.

After furiously exchanging blows for several minutes, both men stepped back, a web of cracks on the left sides of their Plate leaking Stormlight into the air.

"It will happen to you too, Blackthorn," Kalanor growled. "If you do kill me, someone will rise up and take your kingdom from you. It will never last."

Dalinar came in for a power swing. One step forward, then a twist all the way about. Kalanor struck him on the right side—a solid hit, but insignificant, as it was on the wrong side. Dalinar, on the other hand, came in with a sweeping stroke that hummed in the air. Kalanor tried to move with the blow, but this one had too much momentum.

The Shardblade connected, destroying the section of Plate in an explosion of molten sparks. Kalanor grunted and stumbled to the side, nearly tripping. He lowered his hand to cover the hole in his armor, which continued to leak Stormlight at the edges. Half the breastplate had shattered.

"You fight like you lead, Kholin," he growled. "Reckless."

Dalinar ignored the taunt and charged instead.

Kalanor ran away, plowing through his honor guard in his haste, shoving some aside and sending them tumbling, bones breaking.

Dalinar almost caught him, but Kalanor reached the edge of the large rock formation. He dropped his Blade—it puffed away to mist—and sprang, grabbing hold of an outcropping. He started to climb.

He reached the base of the natural tower moments later. Boulders littered the ground nearby; in the mysterious way of the storms, this had probably been a hillside until recently. The highstorm had ripped most of it away, leaving this unlikely formation poking into the air. It would probably soon get blown down.

Dalinar dropped his Blade and leapt, snagging an outcropping, his fingers grinding on stone. He dangled before getting a footing, then proceeded to climb up the steep wall after Kalanor. The other Shardbearer tried to kick rocks down, but they bounced off Dalinar harmlessly.

By the time Dalinar caught up, they had climbed some fifty feet. Down below, soldiers gathered and stared, pointing.

Dalinar reached for his opponent's leg, but Kalanor yanked it out of the way and then—still hanging from the stones—summoned his Blade and began swiping down. After getting battered on the helm a few times, Dalinar growled and let himself slide down out of the way.

Kalanor gouged a few chunks from the wall to send them clattering at Dalinar, then dismissed his Blade and continued upward.

Dalinar followed more carefully, climbing along a parallel route to the side. He eventually reached the top and peeked over the edge. The summit of the formation was some flat-topped, broken peaks that didn't look terribly sturdy. Kalanor sat on one of them, Blade across one leg, his other foot dangling.

Dalinar climbed up a safe distance from his enemy, then summoned Oathbringer. Storms. There was barely enough room up here to stand. Wind buffeted him, a windspren zipping around to one side.

"Nice view," Kalanor said. Though the forces had started out with equal numbers, below them were far more fallen men in silver and red strewn across the grassland than there were men in blue. "I wonder how many kings get such prime seating to watch their own downfall."

"You were never a king," Dalinar said.

Kalanor stood and lifted his Blade, extending it in one hand, point toward Dalinar's chest. "That, Kholin, is all tied up in bearing and assumption. Shall we?"

Clever, bringing me up here, Dalinar thought. Dalinar had the obvious edge in a fair duel—and so Kalanor brought random chance into the fight. Winds, unsteady footing, a plunge that would kill even a Shardbearer.

At the very least, this would be a novel challenge. Dalinar stepped forward carefully. Kalanor changed to Windstance, a more flowing, sweeping style of fighting. Dalinar chose Stonestance for the solid footing and straightforward power.

They traded blows, shuffling back and forth along the line of small peaks. Each step scraped chips off the stones, sending them tumbling down. Kalanor obviously wanted to draw out this fight, to maximize the time for Dalinar to slip.

Dalinar tested back and forth, letting Kalanor fall into a rhythm, then broke it to strike with everything he had, battering down in overhand blows. Each fanned something burning inside of Dalinar, a thirst that his earlier rampage hadn't sated. The Thrill wanted more.

Dalinar scored a series of hits on Kalanor's helm, backing him up to the edge, one step away from a fall. The last blow destroyed the helm entirely, exposing an aged face, clean-shaven, mostly bald.

Kalanor growled, teeth clenched, and struck back at Dalinar with unexpected ferocity. Dalinar met it Blade with Blade, then stepped forward to turn it into a shoving match—their weapons locked, neither with room to maneuver.

Dalinar met his enemy's gaze. In those light grey eyes, he *saw* something. Excitement, energy. A familiar bloodlust.

Kalanor felt the Thrill too.

Dalinar had heard others speak of it, this euphoria of the contest. The secret Alethi edge. But seeing it right there, in the eyes of a man trying to kill him, made Dalinar furious. He should not have to share such an intimate feeling with this man.

He grunted and—in a surge of strength—tossed Kalanor back. The man stumbled, then slipped. He instantly dropped his Shardblade and, in a frantic motion, managed to grab the rock lip as he fell.

Helmless, Kalanor dangled. The sense of the Thrill in his eyes faded to panic. "Mercy," he whispered.

"This *is* a mercy," Dalinar said, then struck him straight through the face with his Shardblade.

Kalanor's eyes burned from grey to black as he dropped off the spire, trailing twin lines of black smoke. The corpse scraped rock before hitting far below, on the far side of the rock formation, away from the main army.

Dalinar breathed out, then sank down, wrung out. Shadows stretched long across the land as the sun met the horizon. It had been a fine fight. He'd accomplished what he'd wanted. He'd conquered all who stood before him.

And yet he felt empty. A voice within him kept saying, "That's it? Weren't we promised more?"

Down below, a group in Kalanor's colors made for the fallen body. The honor guard had seen where their brightlord had fallen? Dalinar felt a spike of outrage. That was *his* kill, *his* victory. He'd won those Shards!

He scrambled down in a reckless half-climb. The descent was a blur; he was seeing red by the time he hit the ground. One soldier had the Blade; others were arguing over the Plate, which was broken and mangled.

Dalinar attacked, killing six in moments, including the one with the Blade. Two others managed to run, but they were slower than he was. Dalinar caught one by the shoulder, whipping him around and smashing him down into the stones. He killed the last with a sweep of Oathbringer.

More. Where were more? Dalinar saw no men in red. Only some in blue—a beleaguered set of soldiers who flew no flag. In their center, however, walked a man in Shardplate. Gavilar rested here from the battle, in a place behind the lines, to take stock.

The hunger inside of Dalinar grew. The Thrill came upon him in a rush, overwhelming. Shouldn't the strongest rule? Why should he sit back so often, listening to men *chat* instead of *war*?

There. There was the man who held what he wanted. A throne . . . a throne and more. The woman Dalinar *should* have been able to claim. A love he'd been forced to abandon, for what reason?

No, his fighting today was *not* done. This was *not* all!

He started toward the group, his mind fuzzy, his insides feeling a deep ache. Passionspren—like tiny crystalline flakes—dropped around him.

Shouldn't he have passion?

Shouldn't he be rewarded for all he had accomplished?

Gavilar was weak. He intended to give up his momentum and rest upon what *Dalinar* had won for him. Well, there was one way to make certain the war continued. One way to keep the Thrill alive.

One way for Dalinar to get everything he deserved.

He was running. Some of the men in Gavilar's group raised hands in welcome. Weak. No weapons presented against him! He could slaughter them all before they knew what had happened. They *deserved* it! Dalinar deserved to—

Gavilar turned toward him, pulling free his helm and smiling an open, honest grin.

Dalinar pulled up, stopping with a lurch. He stared at Gavilar, his *brother*. *Oh, Stormfather,* Dalinar thought. *What am I doing?*

He let the Blade slip from his fingers and vanish. Gavilar strode up, unable to read Dalinar's horrified expression behind his helm. As a blessing, no shamespren appeared, though he should have earned a legion of them in that moment.

"Brother!" Gavilar said. "Have you seen? The day is won! Highprince Ruthar brought down Gallam, winning Shards for his son. Talanor took a Blade, and I hear you finally drew out Kalanor. Please tell me he didn't escape you."

"He . . ." Dalinar licked his lips, breathing in and out. "He is dead." Dalinar pointed toward the fallen form, visible only as a bit of silvery metal shining amid the shadows of the rubble.

"Dalinar, you wonderful, *terrible* man!" Gavilar turned toward his soldiers. "Hail the Blackthorn, men. Hail him!" Gloryspren burst around Gavilar, golden orbs that rotated around his head like a crown.

Dalinar blinked amid their cheering, and suddenly felt a shame so deep he wanted to crumple up. This time, a single spren—like a falling petal from a blossom—drifted down around him.

He had to do something. "Blade and Plate," Dalinar said to Gavilar urgently. "I won them both, but I give them to you. A gift. For your children."

"Ha!" Gavilar said. "Jasnah? What would she do with Shards? No, no. You—"

"Keep them," Dalinar pled, grabbing his brother by the arm. "Please."

"Very well, if you insist," Gavilar said. "I suppose you do already have Plate to give your heir."

"If I have one."

"You will!" Gavilar said, sending some men to recover Kalanor's Blade and Plate. "Ha! Toh will have to agree, finally, that we can protect his line. I suspect the wedding will happen within the month!"

As would, likely, the official re-coronation where—for the first time in centuries—all ten highprinces of Alethkar would bow before a single king.

Dalinar sat down on a stone, pulling free his helm and accepting water from a young messenger woman. *Never again*, he swore to himself. *I give way for Gavilar in all things. Let him have the throne, let him have love.*

I must never be king.

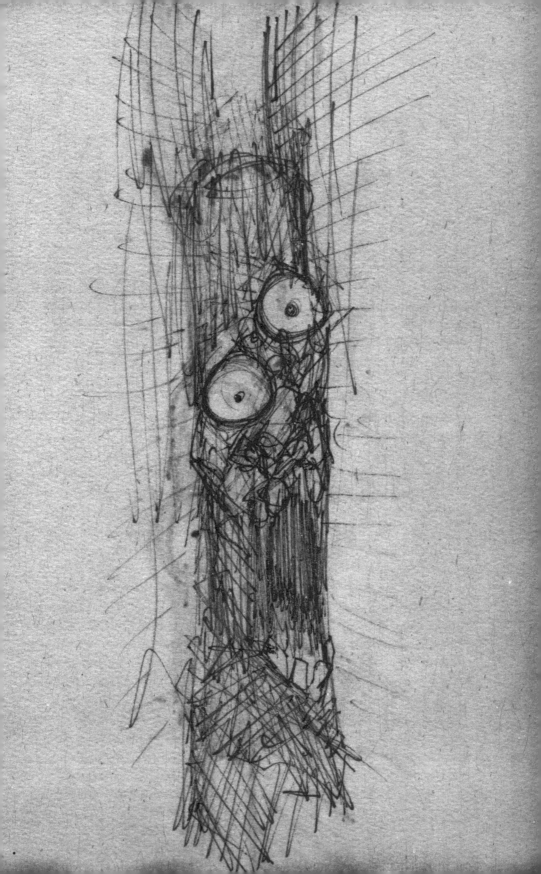

27

PLAYING PRETEND

I will confess my heresy. I do not back down from the things I have said, regardless of what the ardents demand.

—From *Oathbringer*, preface

The sounds of arguing politicians drifted to Shallan's ears as she sketched. She sat on a stone seat at the back of the large meeting room near the top of the tower. She'd brought a pillow to sit on, and Pattern buzzed happily on the little pedestal.

She sat with her feet up, thighs supporting her drawing pad, stockinged toes curling over the rim of the bench in front of her. Not the most dignified of positions; Radiant would be mortified. At the front of the auditorium, Dalinar stood before the glowing map that Shallan and he—somehow combining their powers—could create. He'd invited Taravangian, the highprinces, their wives, and their head scribes. Elhokar had come with Kalami, who was scribing for him lately.

Renarin stood beside his father in his Bridge Four uniform, looking uncomfortable—so basically, same as usual. Adolin lounged nearby, arms folded, occasionally whispering a joke toward one of the men of Bridge Four.

Radiant should be down there, engaging in this important discussion about the future of the world. Instead, Shallan drew. The light was just so *good* up here, with these broad glass windows. She was tired of feeling trapped in the dark hallways of the lower levels, always feeling that something was watching her.

She finished her sketch, then tipped it toward Pattern, holding the sketchbook with her sleeved safehand. He rippled up from his post to inspect her drawing: the slot obstructed by a mashed-up figure with bulging, inhuman eyes.

"Mmmm," Pattern said. "Yes, that is correct."

"It has to be some kind of spren, right?"

"I feel I should know," Pattern said. "This . . . this is a thing from long ago. Long, *long* ago . . ."

Shallan shivered. "Why is it here?"

"I cannot say," Pattern replied. "It is not a thing of us. It is of *him.*"

"An ancient spren of Odium. Delightful." Shallan flipped the page over the top of her sketchbook and started on another drawing.

The others spoke further of their coalition, Thaylenah and Azir recurring as the most important countries to convince, now that Iri had made it completely clear they had joined the enemy.

"Brightness Kalami," Dalinar was saying. "The last report. It listed a large gathering of the enemy in Marat, was it?"

"Yes, Brightlord," the scribe said from her position at the reading desk. "Southern Marat. You hypothesized it was the low population of the region that induced the Voidbringers to gather there."

"The Iriali have taken the chance to strike eastward, as they've always wanted to," Dalinar said. "They'll seize Rira and Babatharnam. Meanwhile, areas like Triax—around the southern half of central Roshar—continue to go dark."

Brightness Kalami nodded, and Shallan tapped her lips with her drawing pencil. The question raised an implication. How could cities go completely dark? These days major cities—particularly ports—would have hundreds of spanreeds in operation. Every lighteyes or merchant wanting to watch prices or keep in contact with distant estates would have one.

Those in Kholinar had started working as soon as the highstorms returned—and then they'd been cut off one by one. Their last reports claimed that armies were gathering near the city. Then . . . nothing. The enemy seemed to be able to locate spanreeds somehow.

At least they'd finally gotten word from Kaladin. A single glyph for time, implying they should be patient. He'd been unable to get to a town to find a woman to scribe for him, and just wanted them to know he was safe. Assuming someone else hadn't gotten the spanreed, and faked the glyph to put them off.

"The enemy is making a play for the Oathgates," Dalinar decided. "All of their motions, save for the gathering in Marat, indicate this. My instincts say that army is planning to strike back at Azir, or even to cross and try to assault Jah Keved."

"I trust Dalinar's assessment," Highprince Aladar added. "If he believes this course to be likely, we should listen."

"Bah," said Highprince Ruthar. The oily man leaned against the wall across from the others, barely paying attention. "Who cares what you say, Aladar? It's amazing you can even see, considering the place you've gone and stuck your head these days."

Aladar spun and thrust his hand to the side in a summoning posture. Dalinar stopped him, as Ruthar must have known that he would. Shallan shook her head, letting herself instead be drawn farther into her sketching. A few creationspren appeared at the top of her drawing pad, one a tiny shoe, the other a pencil like the one she used.

Her sketch was of Highprince Sadeas, drawn without a specific Memory. She'd never wanted to add *him* to her collection. She finished the quick sketch, then flipped to a sketch of Brightlord Perel, the other man they'd found dead in the hallways of Urithiru. She'd tried to re-create his face without wounds.

She flipped back and forth between the two. *They do look similar,* Shallan decided. *Same bulbous features. Similar build.* Her next two pages were pictures of the two Horneaters. Those two looked roughly similar as well. And the two murdered women? Why would the man who strangled his wife confess to that murder, but then *swear* he hadn't killed the second woman? One was already enough to get you executed.

That spren is mimicking the violence, she thought. *Killing or wounding in the same way as attacks from previous days. A kind of . . . impersonation?*

Pattern hummed softly, drawing her attention. Shallan looked up to see someone strolling in her direction: a middle-aged woman with short black hair cut almost to the scalp. She wore a long skirt and a buttoning shirt with a vest. Thaylen merchant clothing.

"What is that you're sketching, Brightness?" the woman asked in Veden.

Hearing her own language so suddenly was strange to Shallan, and her mind took a moment to sort through the words. "People," Shallan said, closing her drawing pad. "I enjoy figure drawing. You're the one who came with Taravangian. His Surgebinder."

"Malata," she said. "Though I am not his. I came to him for convenience, as Spark suggested we might look to Urithiru, now that it has been rediscovered." She surveyed the large auditorium. Shallan could see no sign of her spren. "Do you suppose we really filled this entire chamber?"

"Ten orders," Shallan said, "with hundreds of people in most. Yes, I'd assume we could fill it—in fact, I doubt everyone belonging to the orders could fit in here."

"And now there are four of us," she said idly, eyeing Renarin, who stood stiff beside his father, sweating beneath the scrutiny as people occasionally glanced at him.

"Five," Shallan said. "There's a flying bridgeman out there somewhere—and those are only the ones of us gathered here. There are bound to be others like you, who are still looking for a way to reach us."

"If they want to," Malata said. "Things don't have to be the way they were. Why should they? It didn't work out so well last time for the Radiants, did it?"

"Maybe," Shallan said. "But maybe this isn't the time to experiment either. The Desolation has started again. We could do worse than rely upon the past to survive this."

"Curious," the woman said, "that we have only the word of a few stuffy Alethi about this entire 'Desolation' business, eh sister?"

Shallan blinked at the casual way it was said, along with a wink. Malata smiled and sauntered back toward the front of the room.

"Well," Shallan whispered, "*she's* annoying."

"Mmm . . ." Pattern said. "It will be worse when she starts destroying things."

"Destroying?"

"Dustbringer," Pattern said. "Her spren . . . mmm . . . they like to break what is around them. They want to know what is inside."

"Pleasant," Shallan said, as she flipped back through her drawings. The thing in the crack. The dead men. This should be enough to present to Dalinar and Adolin, which she planned to do today, now that she had her sketches done.

And after that?

I need to catch it, she thought. *I watch the market. Eventually someone will be hurt. And a few days later, this thing will try to copy that attack.*

Perhaps she could patrol the unexplored parts of the tower? Look for it, instead of waiting for it to attack?

The dark corridors. Each tunnel like a drawing's impossible line . . .

The room had grown quiet. Shallan shook out of her reverie and looked up to see what was happening: Ialai Sadeas had arrived at the meeting, carried in a palanquin. She was accompanied by a familiar figure: Meridas Amaram was a tall man, tan eyed, with a square face and solid figure. He was also a murderer, a thief, and a traitor. He had been caught trying to steal a Shardblade—proof that what Captain Kaladin said about him was true.

Shallan gritted her teeth, but found her anger . . . cool. Not gone. No, she would not forgive this man for killing Helaran. But the uncomfortable truth was that she didn't know why, or how, her brother had fallen to Amaram. She could almost hear Jasnah whispering to her: *Don't judge without more details.*

Below, Adolin had risen and stepped toward Amaram, right into the center of the illusory map, breaking its surface, causing waves of glowing Stormlight to ripple across it. He stared murder at Amaram, though Dalinar rested his hand on his son's shoulder, holding him back.

"Brightness Sadeas," Dalinar said. "I am glad you have agreed to join the meeting. We could use your wisdom in our planning."

"I'm not here for your plans, Dalinar," Ialai said. "I'm here because it was a convenient place to find you all together. I've been in conference with my advisors back at our estates, and the consensus is that the heir, my nephew, is too young. This is no time for House Sadeas to be without leadership, so I've made a decision."

"Ialai," Dalinar said, stepping into the illusion beside his son. "Let's talk about this. Please. I have an idea that, though untraditional, might—"

"Tradition is our ally, Dalinar," Ialai said. "I don't think you've ever understood that as you should. Highmarshal Amaram is our house's most decorated and well-regarded general. He is beloved of our soldiers, and known the world over. I name him regent and heir to the house title. He is, for all intents, Highprince Sadeas now. I would ask the king to ratify this."

Shallan's breath caught. King Elhokar looked up from his seat, where he—seemingly—had been lost in thought. "Is this legal?"

"Yes," Navani said, arms folded.

"Dalinar," Amaram said, stepping down several of the steps toward the rest of them at the bottom of the auditorium. His voice gave Shallan chills. That refined diction, that perfect face, that crisp uniform . . . this man was what every soldier aspired to be.

I'm not the only one who is good at playing pretend, she thought.

"I hope," Amaram continued, "our recent . . . friction will not prevent us from working together for the needs of Alethkar. I have spoken to Brightness Ialai, and I think I have persuaded her that our differences are secondary to the greater good of Roshar."

"The greater good," Dalinar said. "You think you are one to speak about what is good?"

"Everything I've done is for the greater good, Dalinar," Amaram said, his voice strained. "*Everything.* Please. I know you intend to pursue legal action against me. I will stand at trial, but let us postpone that until *after* Roshar has been saved."

Dalinar regarded Amaram for an extended, tense moment. Then he finally looked to his nephew and nodded in a curt gesture.

"The throne acknowledges your act of regency, Brightness," Elhokar said to Ialai. "My mother will wish a formal writ, sealed and witnessed."

"Already done," Ialai said.

Dalinar met the eyes of Amaram across the floating map. "Highprince," Dalinar finally said.

"Highprince," Amaram said back, tipping his head.

"Bastard," Adolin said.

Dalinar winced visibly, then pointed toward the exit. "Perhaps, son, you should take a moment to yourself."

"Yeah. Sure." Adolin pulled out of his father's grip, stalking toward the exit.

Shallan thought only a moment, then grabbed her shoes and drawing pad and hurried after him. She caught up to Adolin in the hallway outside, near where the palanquins for the women were parked, and took his arm.

"Hey," she said softly.

He glanced at her, and his expression softened.

"You want to talk?" Shallan asked. "You seem angrier about him than you were before."

"No," Adolin muttered, "I'm just annoyed. We're finally rid of Sadeas, and now *that* takes his place?" He shook his head. "When I was young, I used to look up to him. I started getting suspicious when I was older, but I guess part of me still wanted him to be like they said. A man above all the pettiness and the politics. A true soldier."

Shallan wasn't certain what she thought of the idea of a "true soldier" being the type who didn't care about politics. Shouldn't the *why* of what a man was doing be important to him?

Soldiers didn't talk that way. There was some ideal she couldn't quite grasp, a kind of cult of obedience—of caring only about the battlefield and the challenge it presented.

They walked onto the lift, and Adolin fished out a free gemstone—a little diamond not surrounded by a sphere—and placed it into a slot along the railing. Stormlight began to drain from the stone, and the balcony shook, then slowly began to descend. Removing the gem would tell the lift to stop at the next floor. A simple lever, pushed one way or the other, would determine whether the lift crawled upward or downward.

They descended past the top tier, and Adolin took up position by the railing, looking out over the central shaft with the window all along one side. They were starting to call it the atrium—though it was an atrium that ran up dozens upon dozens of floors.

"Kaladin's not going to like this," Adolin said. "Amaram as a highprince? The two of us spent weeks in jail because of the things that man did."

"I think Amaram killed my brother."

Adolin wheeled around to stare at her. "*What?*"

"Amaram has a Shardblade," Shallan said. "I saw it previously in the hands of my brother, Helaran. He was older than I am, and left Jah Keved years ago. From what I can gather, he and Amaram fought at some point, and Amaram killed him—taking the Blade."

"Shallan . . . that Blade. You know where Amaram got that, right?"

"On the battlefield?"

"From *Kaladin*." Adolin raised his hand to his head. "The bridgeboy insisted that he'd saved Amaram's life by killing a Shardbearer. Amaram then killed Kaladin's squad and took the Shards for himself. That's basically the entire *reason* the two hate each other."

Shallan's throat grew tight. "Oh."

Tuck it away. Don't think about it.

"Shallan," Adolin said, stepping toward her. "Why would your brother try to kill Amaram? Did he maybe know the highlord was corrupt? Storms! Kaladin didn't know any of that. Poor bridgeboy. Everyone would have been better off if he'd just let Amaram die."

Don't confront it. Don't think about it.

"Yeah," she said. "Huh."

"But how did your brother know?" Adolin said, pacing across the balcony. "Did he say anything?"

"We didn't talk much," Shallan said, numb. "He left when I was young. I didn't know him well."

Anything to get off this topic. For this was something she could still tuck away in the back of her brain. She did *not* want to think about Kaladin and Helaran. . . .

It was a long, quiet ride to the bottom floors of the tower. Adolin wanted to go visit his father's horse again, but she wasn't interested in standing around smelling horse dung. She got off on the second level to make her way toward her rooms.

Secrets. *There are more important things in this world,* Helaran had said to her father. *More important even than you and your crimes.*

Mraize knew something about this. He was withholding the secrets from her like sweets to entice a child to obedience. But all he wanted her to do was investigate the oddities in Urithiru. That was a good thing, wasn't it? She'd have done it anyway.

Shallan meandered through the hallways, following a path where Sebarial's workers had affixed some sphere lanterns to hooks on the walls. Locked up and filled with only the cheapest diamond spheres, they shouldn't be worth the effort to break into, but the light they gave was also rather dim.

She should have stayed above; her absence must have destroyed the illusion of the map. She felt bad about that. Was there a way she could learn to leave her illusions behind her? They'd need Stormlight to keep going. . . .

In any case, Shallan had needed to leave the meeting. The secrets this
city hid were too engaging to ignore. She stopped in the hallway and dug

out her sketchbook, flipping through pages, looking at the faces of the dead men.

Absently turning a page, she came across a sketch she didn't recall making. A series of twisting, maddening lines, scribbled and unconnected.

She felt cold. "When did I draw this?"

Pattern moved up her dress, stopping under her neck. He hummed, an uncomfortable sound. "I do not remember."

She flipped to the next page. Here she'd drawn a rush of lines sweeping out from a central point, confused and chaotic, transforming to the heads of horses with the flesh ripping off, their eyes wide, equine mouths screaming. It was grotesque, nauseating.

Oh Stormfather . . .

Her fingers trembled as she turned to the next page. She'd scribbled it entirely black, using a circular motion, spiraling toward the center point. A deep void, an endless corridor, something terrible and unknowable at the end.

She snapped the sketchbook shut. "What is happening to me?"

Pattern hummed in confusion. "Do we . . . run?"

"Where."

"Away. Out of this place. Mmmmm."

"No."

She trembled, part of her terrified, but she couldn't abandon those secrets. She had to have them, hold them, make them hers. She turned sharply in the corridor, taking a path away from her room. A short time later, she strode into the barracks where Sebarial housed his soldiers. There were plentiful spaces like this in the tower: vast networks of rooms with built-in stone bunks in the walls. Urithiru *had* been a military base; that much was evident from its ability to efficiently house tens of thousands of soldiers on the lower levels alone.

In the common room of the barracks, men lounged with coats off, playing with cards or knives. Her passing caused a stir as men gaped, then leaped to their feet, debating between buttoning their coats and saluting. Whispers of "Radiant" chased her as she walked into a corridor lined with rooms, where the individual platoons bunked. She counted off doorways marked by archaic Alethi numbers etched into the stone, then entered a specific one.

She burst in on Vathah and his team, who sat inside playing cards by the light of a few spheres. Poor Gaz sat on the chamber pot in a corner privy, and he yelped, pulling closed the cloth on the doorway.

Guess I should have anticipated that, Shallan thought, covering her blush by sucking in a burst of Stormlight. She folded her arms and regarded the others as they—lazily—climbed to their feet and saluted. They were only twelve men now. Some had made their way to other jobs. A few others had died in the Battle of Narak.

She'd kind of been hoping that they would all drift away—if only so she wouldn't have to figure out what to do with them. She now realized that Adolin was right. That was a *terrible* attitude. These men were a resource and, all things considered, had been remarkably loyal.

"I," Shallan told them, "have been an awful employer."

"Don't know about that, Brightness," Red said—she still didn't know how the tall, bearded man had gotten his nickname. "The pay has come on time and you haven't gotten *too* many of us killed."

"Oi got killed," Shob said from his bunk, where he saluted—still lying down.

"Shut up, Shob," Vathah said. "You're not dead."

"Oi'm dyin' this time, Sarge. Oi'm sure of it."

"Then at least you'll be quiet," Vathah said. "Brightness, I agree with Red. You've done right by us."

"Yes, well, the free ride is over," Shallan said. "I have work for you."

Vathah shrugged, but some of the others looked disappointed. Maybe Adolin was right; maybe deep down, men like this did need something to do. They wouldn't have admitted that fact, though.

"I'm afraid it might be dangerous," Shallan said, then smiled. "And it will probably involve you getting a little drunk."

28

ANOTHER OPTION

Finally, I will confess my humanity. I have been named a monster, and do not deny those claims. I am the monster that I fear we all can become.

—From *Oathbringer*, preface

"The decision has been made,'" Teshav read, "'to seal off this Oathgate until we can destroy it. We realize this is not the path you wished for us to take, Dalinar Kholin. Know that the Prime of Azir considers you fondly, and looks forward to the mutual benefit of trade agreements and new treaties between our nations.

"'A magical portal into the very center of our city, however, presents too severe a danger. We will entertain no further pleas to open it, and suggest that you accept our sovereign will. Good day, Dalinar Kholin. May Yaezir bless and guide you.'"

Dalinar punched his fist into his palm as he stood in the small stone chamber. Teshav and her ward occupied the writing podium and seat beside it, while Navani had been pacing opposite Dalinar. King Taravangian sat in a chair by the wall, hunched forward with hands clasped, listening with a concerned expression.

That was it then. Azir was out.

Navani touched his arm. "I'm sorry."

"There's still Thaylenah," Dalinar said. "Teshav, see if Queen Fen will speak with me today."

"Yes, Brightlord."

He had Jah Keved and Kharbranth from Taravangian, and New

Natanan was responding positively. With Thaylenah, Dalinar could at least forge a unified Vorin coalition of all the Eastern states. That model might eventually persuade the nations of the west to join with them.

If anyone remained by then.

Dalinar started pacing again as Teshav contacted Thaylenah. He preferred little rooms like this one; the large chambers were a reminder of how enormous this place was. In a small room like this, you could pretend that you were in a cozy bunker somewhere.

Of course, even in a small chamber there were reminders that Urithiru wasn't normal. The strata on the walls, like the folds of a fan. Or the holes that commonly showed up at the tops of rooms, right where the walls met the ceiling. The one in this room couldn't help but remind him of Shallan's report. Was something in there, watching them? Could a *spren* really be murdering people in the tower?

It was nearly enough to make him pull out of the place. But where would they go? Abandon the Oathgates? For now, he'd quadrupled patrols and sent Navani's researchers searching for a possible explanation. At least until he could come up with a solution.

As Teshav wrote to Queen Fen, Dalinar stepped up to the wall, suddenly bothered by that hole. It was right by the ceiling, and too high for him to reach, even if he stood on a chair. Instead he breathed in Stormlight. The bridgemen had described using stones to climb walls, so Dalinar picked up a wooden chair and painted its back with shining light, using the palm of his left hand.

When he pressed the back of the chair against the wall, it stuck. Dalinar grunted, tentatively climbing up onto the seat of the chair, which hung in the air at about table height.

"Dalinar?" Navani asked.

"Might as well make use of the time," he said, carefully balancing on the chair. He jumped, grabbing the edge of the hole by the ceiling, and pulled himself up to look down it.

It was three feet wide, and about one foot tall. It seemed endless, and he could feel a faint breeze coming out of it. Was that . . . scraping he heard? A moment later, a mink slunk into the main tunnel from a shadowed crossroad, carrying a dead rat in its mouth. The tubular little animal twitched its snout toward him, then carried its prize away.

"Air *is* circulating through those," Navani said as he hopped down off the chair. "The method baffles us. Perhaps some fabrial we have yet to discover?"

Dalinar looked back up at the hole. Miles upon miles of even smaller tunnels threaded through the walls and ceilings of an already daunting system. And hiding in them somewhere, the thing that Shallan had drawn . . .

"She's replied, Brightlord!" Teshav said.

"Excellent," Dalinar said. "Your Majesty, our time is growing short. I'd like—"

"She's still writing," Teshav said. "Pardon, Brightlord. She says . . . um . . ."

"Just read it, Teshav," Dalinar said. "I'm used to Fen by now."

"'Damnation, man. Are you ever going to leave me alone? I haven't slept a full night in weeks. The Everstorm has hit us twice now; we're barely keeping this city from falling apart.'"

"I understand, Your Majesty," Dalinar said. "And am eager to send you the aid I promised. Please, let us make a pact. You've dodged my requests long enough."

Nearby, the chair finally dropped from the wall and clattered to the floor. He prepared himself for another round of verbal sparring, of half promises and veiled meanings. Fen had been growing increasingly formal during their exchanges.

The spanreed wrote, then halted almost immediately. Teshav looked at him, grave.

"'No,'" she read.

"*Your Majesty*," Dalinar said. "This is not a time to forge on alone! Please. I beg you. Listen to me!"

"'You have to know by now,'" came the reply, "'that this coalition is never going to happen. Kholin . . . I'm baffled, honestly. Your garnet-lit tongue and pleasant words make it seem like you really assume this will work.

"'Surely you see. A queen would have to be either stupid or desperate to let an Alethi army into the very center of her city. I've been the former at times, and I might be approaching the latter, but . . . storms, Kholin. No. I'm not going to be the one who finally lets Thaylenah fall to you people. And on the off chance that you're sincere, then I'm sorry.'"

It had an air of finality to it. Dalinar walked over to Teshav, looking at the inscrutable squiggles on the page that somehow made up the women's script. "Can you think of anything?" he asked Navani as she sighed and settled down into a chair next to Teshav.

"No. Fen is stubborn, Dalinar."

Dalinar glanced at Taravangian. Even he had assumed Dalinar's purpose was conquest. And who wouldn't, considering his history?

Maybe it would be different if I could speak to them in person, he thought. But without the Oathgates, that was virtually impossible.

"Thank her for her time," Dalinar said. "And tell her my offer remains on the table."

Teshav started writing, and Navani looked to him, noting what the scribe hadn't—the tension in his voice.

"I'm fine," he lied. "I just need time to think."

He strode from the room before she could object, and his guards outside fell into step behind him. He wanted some fresh air; an open sky always seemed so inviting. His feet didn't take him in that direction, however. He instead found himself roaming through the hallways.

What now?

Same as always, people ignored him unless he had a sword in his hand. Storms, it was like they *wanted* him to come in swinging.

He stalked the halls for a good hour, getting nowhere. Eventually, Lyn the messenger found him. Panting, she said that Bridge Four needed him, but hadn't explained why.

Dalinar followed her, Shallan's sketch a heavy weight in his mind. Had they found another murder victim? Indeed, Lyn led him to the section where Sadeas had been killed.

His sense of foreboding increased. Lyn led him to a balcony, where the bridgemen Leyten and Peet met him. "Who was it?" he asked as he met them.

"Who . . ." Leyten frowned. "Oh! It's not that, sir. It's something else. This way."

Leyten led him down some steps onto the wide field outside the first level of the tower, where three more bridgemen waited near some rows of stone planters, probably for growing tubers.

"We noticed this by accident," Leyten said as they walked among the planters. The hefty bridgeman had a jovial way about him, and talked to Dalinar—a highprince—as easily as he'd talk to friends at a tavern. "We've been running patrols on your orders, watching for anything strange. And . . . well, Peet noticed something strange." He pointed up at the wall. "See that line?"

Dalinar squinted, picking out a gouge cut into the rock wall. What could score stone like that? It almost looked like . . .

He looked down at the planter boxes nearest them. And there, hidden between two of them, was a hilt protruding from the stone floor.

A Shardblade.

It was easy to miss, as the blade had sunk all the way down into the rock. Dalinar knelt beside it, then took a handkerchief from his pocket and used it to grab the hilt.

Even though he didn't touch the Blade directly, he heard a very distant whine, like a scream in the back of someone's throat. He steeled himself, then yanked the Blade out and set it across the empty planter.

The silvery Blade curved at the end almost like a fishhook. The weapon was even wider than most Shardblades, and near the hilt it rippled in wave-like patterns. He knew this sword, knew it intimately. He'd carried it for decades, since winning it at the Rift all those years ago.

Oathbringer.

He glanced upward. "The killer must have dropped it out that window. It clipped the stone on its way down, then landed here."

"That's what we figured, Brightlord," Peet said.

Dalinar looked down at the sword. His sword.

No. Not mine at all.

He seized the sword, bracing himself for the screams. The cries of a dead spren. They weren't the shrill, painful shrieks he'd heard when touching other Blades, but more of a whimper. The sound of a man backed into a corner, thoroughly beaten and facing something terrible, but too tired to keep screaming.

Dalinar steeled himself and carried the Blade—a familiar weight—with the flat side against his shoulder. He walked toward a different entrance back into the tower city, followed by his guards, the scout, and the five bridgemen.

You promised to carry no dead Blade, the Stormfather thundered in his head.

"Calm yourself," Dalinar whispered. "I'm not going to bond it."

The Stormfather rumbled, low and dangerous.

"This one doesn't scream as loudly as others. Why?"

It remembers your oath, the Stormfather sent. *It remembers the day you won it, and better the day you gave it up. It hates you—but less than it hates others.*

Dalinar passed a group of Hatham's farmers who had been trying, without success, to get some lavis polyps started. He drew more than a few looks; even at a tower populated by soldiers, highprinces, and Radiants, someone carrying a Shardblade in the open was an unusual sight.

"Could it be rescued?" Dalinar whispered as they entered the tower and climbed a stairway. "Could we save the spren who made this Blade?"

I know of no way, the Stormfather said. *It is dead, as is the man who broke his oath to kill it.*

Back to the Lost Radiants and the Recreance—that fateful day when the knights had broken their oaths, abandoned their Shards, and walked away. Dalinar had witnessed that in a vision, though he still had no idea what had caused it.

Why? What had made them do something so drastic?

He eventually arrived at the Sadeas section of the tower, and though guards in forest green and white controlled access, they couldn't deny a highprince—particularly not Dalinar. Runners dashed before him to carry word. Dalinar followed them, using their path to judge if he was going in the right direction. He was; she was apparently in her rooms. He stopped at the nice wooden door, and gave Ialai the courtesy of knocking.

One of the runners he had chased here opened the door, still panting. Brightness Sadeas sat in a throne set in the center of the room. Amaram stood at her shoulder.

"Dalinar," Ialai said, nodding her head to him like a queen greeting a subject.

Dalinar heaved the Shardblade off his shoulder and set it carefully on the floor. Not as dramatic as spearing it through the stones, but now that he could hear the weapon's screams, he felt like treating it with reverence.

He turned to go.

"Brightlord?" Ialai said, standing up. "What is this in exchange for?"

"No exchange," Dalinar said, turning back. "That is rightfully yours. My guards found it today; the killer threw it out a window."

She narrowed her eyes at him.

"I didn't kill him, Ialai," Dalinar said wearily.

"I realize that. You don't have the bite left in you to do something like that."

He ignored the gibe, looking to Amaram. The tall, distinguished man met his gaze.

"I *will* see you in judgment someday, Amaram," Dalinar said. "Once this is done."

"As I said you could."

"I wish that I could trust your word."

"I stand by what I was forced to do, Brightlord," Amaram said, stepping forward. "The arrival of the Voidbringers only proves I was in the right. We need practiced Shardbearers. The stories of darkeyes gaining Blades are charming, but do you really think we have time for nursery tales now, instead of practical reality?"

"You murdered *defenseless men*," Dalinar said through gritted teeth. "Men who had saved your life."

Amaram stooped, lifting Oathbringer. "And what of the hundreds, even thousands, your wars killed?"

They locked gazes.

"I respect you greatly, Brightlord," Amaram said. "Your life has been one of grand accomplishment, and you have spent it seeking the good of Alethkar. But you—and take this with the respect I intend—are a *hypocrite*.

"You stand where you do because of a brutal determination to do what had to be done. It is because of that trail of corpses that you have the luxury to uphold some lofty, nebulous code. Well, it might make you feel better about your past, but morality is not a thing you can simply doff to put on the helm of battle, then put back on when you're done with the slaughter."

He nodded his head in esteem, as if he hadn't just rammed a sword through Dalinar's gut.

Dalinar spun and left Amaram holding Oathbringer. Dalinar's stride down the corridors was so quick that his entourage had to scramble to keep up.

He finally found his rooms. "Leave me," he said to his guards and the bridgemen.

They hesitated, storm them. He turned, ready to lash out, but calmed himself. "I don't intend to stray in the tower alone. I will obey my own laws. Go."

They reluctantly retreated, leaving his door unguarded. He passed into his outer common room, where he'd ordered most of the furniture to be placed. Navani's heating fabrial glowed in a corner, near a small rug and several chairs. They finally had enough Stormlight to power it.

Drawn by the warmth, Dalinar walked up to the fabrial. He was surprised to find Taravangian sitting in one of the chairs, staring into the depths of the shining ruby that radiated heat into the room. Well, Dalinar *had* invited the king to use this common room when he wished.

Dalinar wanted nothing but to be alone, and he toyed with leaving. He wasn't sure that Taravangian had noticed him. But that warmth was so welcoming. There were few fires in the tower, and even with the walls to block wind, you always felt chilled.

He settled into the other chair and let out a deep sigh. Taravangian didn't address him, bless the man. Together they sat by that not-fire, staring into the depths of the gem.

Storms, how he had failed today. There would be no coalition. He couldn't even keep the Alethi highprinces in line.

"Not quite like sitting by a hearth, is it?" Taravangian finally said, his voice soft.

"No," Dalinar agreed. "I miss the popping of the logs, the dancing of flamespren."

"It does have its own charm though. Subtle. You can see the Stormlight moving inside."

"Our own little storm," Dalinar said. "Captured, contained, and channeled."

Taravangian smiled, eyes lit by the ruby's Stormlight. "Dalinar Kholin . . . do you mind me asking you something? How do you know what is right?"

"A lofty question, Your Majesty."

"Please, just Taravangian."

Dalinar nodded.

"You have denied the Almighty," Taravangian said.

"I—"

"No, no. I am not decrying you as a heretic. I do not care, Dalinar. I've questioned the existence of deity myself."

"I feel there must be a God," Dalinar said softly. "My mind and soul rebel at the alternative."

"Is it not our duty, as kings, to ask questions that make the minds and souls of other men cringe?"

"Perhaps," Dalinar said. He studied Taravangian. The king seemed so contemplative.

Yes, there still is *some of the old Taravangian in there,* Dalinar thought. *We have misjudged him. He might be slow, but that doesn't mean he doesn't think.*

"I have felt warmth," Dalinar said, "coming from a place beyond. A light I can almost see. If there is a God, it was not the Almighty, the one who called himself Honor. He was a creature. Powerful, but still merely a creature."

"Then how do you know what is right? What guides you?"

Dalinar leaned forward. He thought he could see something larger within the ruby's light. Something that moved like a fish in a bowl.

Warmth continued to bathe him. Light.

"'On my sixtieth day,'" Dalinar whispered, "'I passed a town whose name shall remain unspoken. Though still in lands that named me king, I was far enough from my home to go unrecognized. Not even those men who handled my face daily—in the form of my seal imprinted upon their letters of authority—would have known this humble traveler as their king.'"

Taravangian looked to him, confused.

"It's a quote from a book," Dalinar said. "A king long ago took a journey. His destination was this very city. Urithiru."

"Ah . . ." Taravangian said. "*The Way of Kings,* is it? Adrotagia has mentioned that book."

"Yes," Dalinar said. "'In this town, I found men bedeviled. There had been a murder. A hogman, tasked in protecting the landlord's beasts, had been assaulted. He lived long enough, only, to whisper that three of the other hogmen had gathered together and done the crime.

"'I arrived as questions were being raised, and men interrogated. You see, there were *four* other hogmen in the landlord's employ. Three of them had been responsible for the assault, and likely would have escaped suspicion had they finished their grim job. Each of the four loudly proclaimed that he was the one who had not been part of the cabal. No amount of interrogation determined the truth.'"

Dalinar fell silent.

"What happened?" Taravangian asked.

"He doesn't say at first," Dalinar replied. "Throughout his book, he raises the question again and again. Three of those men were violent threats, guilty of premeditated murder. One was innocent. What do you do?"

"Hang all four," Taravangian whispered.

Dalinar—surprised to hear such bloodthirst from the other man—turned. Taravangian looked sorrowful, not bloodthirsty at all.

"The landlord's job," Taravangian said, "is to prevent further murders. I doubt that what the book records actually happened. It is too neat, too simple a parable. Our lives are far messier. But assuming the story did occur as claimed, and there was absolutely no way of determining who was guilty . . . you have to hang all four. Don't you?"

"What of the innocent man?"

"One innocent dead, but three murderers stopped. Is it not the best good that can be done, and the best way to protect your people?" Taravangian rubbed his forehead. "Stormfather. I sound like a madman, don't I? But is it not a particular madness to be charged with such decisions? It's difficult to address such questions without revealing our own hypocrisy."

Hypocrite, Amaram accused Dalinar in his mind.

He and Gavilar hadn't used pretty justifications when they'd gone to war. They'd done as men did: they'd conquered. Only later had Gavilar started to seek validation for their actions.

"Why not let them all go?" Dalinar said. "If you can't prove who is guilty—if you can't be *sure*—I think you should let them go."

"Yes . . . one innocent in four is too many for you. That makes sense too."

"No, *any* innocent is too many."

"You say that," Taravangian said. "Many people do, but our laws *will* claim innocent men—for all judges are flawed, as is our knowledge. Eventually, you *will* execute someone who does not deserve it. This is the burden society must carry in exchange for order."

"I hate that," Dalinar said softly.

"Yes . . . I do too. But it's not a matter of morality, is it? It's a matter of thresholds. How many guilty may be punished before you'd accept one innocent casualty? A thousand? Ten thousand? A hundred? When you consider, all calculations are meaningless except one. Has more good been done than evil? If so, then the law has done its job. And so . . . I must hang all four men." He paused. "And I would weep, every night, for having done it."

Damnation. Again, Dalinar reassessed his impression of Taravangian. The king was soft-spoken, but not slow. He was simply a man who liked to consider a great long time before committing.

"Nohadon eventually wrote," Dalinar said, "that the landlord took a modest approach. He imprisoned all four. Though the punishment should have been death, he mixed together the guilt and innocence, and determined that the *average* guilt of the four should deserve only prison."

"He was unwilling to commit," Taravangian said. "He wasn't seeking justice, but to assuage his own conscience."

"What he did was, nevertheless, another option."

"Does your king ever say what he would have done?" Taravangian asked. "The one who wrote the book?"

"He said the only course was to let the Almighty guide, and let each instance be judged differently, depending on circumstances."

"So he too was unwilling to commit," Taravangian said. "I would have expected more."

"His book was about his journey," Dalinar said. "And his questions. I think this was one he never fully answered for himself. I wish he had."

They sat by the not-fire for a time before Taravangian eventually stood and rested his hand on Dalinar's shoulder. "I understand," he said softly, then left.

He was a good man, the Stormfather said.

"Nohadon?" Dalinar said.

Yes.

Feeling stiff, Dalinar rose from his seat and made his way through his rooms. He didn't stop at the bedroom, though the hour was growing late, and instead made his way onto his balcony. To look out over the clouds.

Taravangian is wrong, the Stormfather said. *You are not a hypocrite, Son of Honor.*

"I am," Dalinar said softly. "But sometimes a hypocrite is nothing more than a person who is in the process of changing."

The Stormfather rumbled. He didn't like the idea of change.

Do I go to war with the other kingdoms, Dalinar thought, *and maybe save the world? Or do I sit here and pretend that I can do all this on my own?*

"Do you have any more visions of Nohadon?" Dalinar asked the Stormfather, hopeful.

I have shown you all that was created for you to see, the Stormfather said. *I can show no more.*

"Then I should like to rewatch the vision where I met Nohadon," Dalinar said. "Though let me go fetch Navani before you begin. I want her to record what I say."

Would you rather I show the vision to her as well? the Stormfather asked. *She could record it herself that way.*

Dalinar froze. "You can show the visions to *others?*"

I was given this leave: to choose those who would best be served by the visions. He paused, then grudgingly continued. *To choose a Bondsmith.*

No, he did not like the idea of being bonded, but it was part of what he'd been commanded to do.

Dalinar barely considered that thought.

The Stormfather could show the visions to *others.*

"Anyone?" Dalinar said. "You can show them to anyone?"

During a storm, I can approach anyone I choose, the Stormfather said. *But you do not have to be in a storm, so you can join a vision in which I have placed someone else, even if you are distant.*

Storms! Dalinar bellowed a laugh.

What have I done? the Stormfather asked.

"You've just solved my problem!"

The problem from The Way of Kings?

"No, the greater one. I've been wishing for a way to meet with the other monarchs in person." Dalinar grinned. "I think that in a coming highstorm, Queen Fen of Thaylenah is going to have a quite remarkable experience."

So sit back. Read, or listen, to someone who has passed between realms.

—From *Oathbringer,* preface

Veil prowled through the Breakaway market, hat pulled low, hands in her pockets. Nobody else seemed to be able to hear the beast that she did.

Regular shipments of supplies through Jah Keved via King Taravangian had set the market bustling. Fortunately, with a third Radiant capable of working the Oathgate now, less of Shallan's time was required.

Spheres that glowed again, and several highstorms as proof that that would persist, had encouraged everyone. Excitement was high, trading brisk. Drink flowed freely from casks emblazoned with the royal seal of Jah Keved.

Lurking within it all, somewhere, was a predator that only Veil could hear. She heard the thing in the silence between laughter. It was the sound of a tunnel extending into the darkness. The feel of breath on the back of your neck in a dark room.

How could they laugh while that void watched?

It had been a frustrating four days. Dalinar had increased patrols to almost ridiculous levels, but those soldiers weren't watching the right way. They were too easily seen, too disruptive. Veil had set her men to a more targeted surveillance in the market.

So far, they'd found nothing. Her team was tired, as was Shallan, who suffered from the long nights as Veil. Fortunately, Shallan wasn't doing anything particularly useful these days. Sword training with Adolin each day—

more frolicking and flirting than useful swordplay—and the occasional meeting with Dalinar where she had nothing to add but a pretty map.

Veil though . . . Veil hunted the hunter. Dalinar acted like a soldier: increased patrols, strict rules. He asked his scribes to find him evidence of spren attacking people in historical records.

He needed more than vague explanations and abstract ideas—but those were the very soul of art. If you could explain something perfectly, then you'd never *need* art. That was the difference between a table and a beautiful woodcutting. You could explain the table: its purpose, its shape, its nature. The woodcutting you simply had to experience.

She ducked into a tent tavern. Did it seem busier in here than on previous nights? Yes. Dalinar's patrols had people on edge. They were avoiding the darker, more sinister taverns in favor of ones with good crowds and bright lights.

Gaz and Red stood beside a pile of crates, nursing drinks and wearing plain trousers and shirts, not uniforms. She hoped they weren't too intoxicated yet. Veil pushed up to their position, crossing her arms on the boxes.

"Nothing yet," Gaz said with a grunt. "Same as the other nights."

"Not that we're complaining," Red added, grinning as he took a long pull on his drink. "This is the kind of soldiering I can really get behind."

"It's going to happen tonight," Veil said. "I can smell it in the air."

"You said that last night, Veil," Gaz said.

Three nights ago, a friendly game of cards had turned to violence, and one player had hit another over the head with a bottle. That often wouldn't have been lethal, but it had hit just right and killed the poor fellow. The perpetrator—one of Ruthar's soldiers—had been hanged the next day in the market's central square.

As unfortunate as the event had been, it was exactly what she'd been waiting for. A seed. An act of violence, one man striking the other. She'd mobilized her team and set them in the taverns near where the fight occurred. *Watch*, she'd said. *Someone will get attacked with a bottle, in exactly the same way. Pick someone who looks like the man who died, and watch.*

Shallan had done sketches of the murdered man, a short fellow with long drooping mustaches. Veil had distributed them; the men took her as no more than another employee.

Now . . . they waited.

"The attack *will* come," Veil said. "Who are your targets?"

Red pointed out two men in the tent who had mustaches and were of a similar height to the dead man. Veil nodded and dropped a few low-value spheres onto the table. "Get something in you other than booze."

"Sure, sure," Red said as Gaz grabbed the spheres. "But tell me, sweetness, don't you want to stay here with us a little longer?"

"Most men who have made a pass at me end up missing a finger or two, Red."

"I'd still have plenty left to satisfy you, I promise."

She looked back at him, then started snickering. "That was a decently good line."

"Thanks!" He raised his mug. "So . . ."

"Sorry, not interested."

He sighed, but raised his mug farther before taking a pull on it.

"Where did you come from, anyway?" Gaz said, inspecting her with his single eye.

"Shallan kind of sucked me up along the way, like a boat pulling flotsam into its wake."

"She does that," Red said. "You think you're done. Living out the last light of your sphere, you know? And then suddenly, you're an honor guard to a storming *Knight Radiant,* and everyone's looking up to you."

Gaz grunted. "Ain't that true. Ain't that true. . . ."

"Keep watch," Veil said. "You know what to do if something happens."

They nodded. They'd send one man to the meeting place, while the other tried to tail the attacker. They knew there might be something weird about the man they chased, but she hadn't told them everything.

Veil walked back to the meeting point, near a dais at the center of the market, close to the well. The dais looked like it had once held some kind of official building, but all that remained was the six-foot-high foundation with steps leading up to it on four sides. Here, Aladar's officers had set up central policing operations and disciplinary facilities.

She watched the crowds while idly spinning her knife in her fingers. Veil liked watching people. That she shared with Shallan. It was good to know how the two of them were different, but it was also good to know what they had in common.

Veil wasn't a true loner. She needed people. Yes, she scammed them on occasion, but she wasn't a thief. She was a lover of experience. She was at her best in a crowded market, watching, thinking, enjoying.

Now Radiant . . . Radiant could take people or leave them. They were a tool, but also a nuisance. How could they so often act *against* their own best interests? The world would be a better place if they'd all simply do what Radiant said. Barring that, they could at *least* leave her alone.

Veil flipped her knife up and caught it. Radiant and Veil shared efficiency. They liked seeing things done well, in the right way. They didn't suffer fools, though Veil could laugh at them, while Radiant simply ignored them.

Screams sounded in the market.

Finally, Veil thought, catching her knife and spinning. She came alert, eager, drawing in Stormlight. Where?

Vathah came barreling through the crowd, shoving aside a marketgoer. Veil ran to meet him.

"Details!" Veil snapped.

"It wasn't like you said," he said. "Follow me."

The two took off back the way he'd come.

"It wasn't a bottle to the head." Vathah said. "My tent is near one of the buildings. The stone ones that were here in the market, you know?"

"And?" she demanded.

Vathah pointed as they drew close. You couldn't miss the tall structure beside the tent he and Glurv had been watching. At the top, a corpse dangled from an outcropping, hanged by the neck.

Hanged. *Storm it. The thing didn't imitate the attack with the bottle . . . it imitated the execution that followed!*

Vathah pointed. "Killer dropped the person up there, leaving them to twitch. Then the killer *jumped* down. All that distance, Veil. How—"

"Where?" she demanded.

"Glurv is tailing," Vathah said, pointing.

The two charged in that direction, shoving their way through the crowds. They eventually spotted Glurv up ahead, standing on the edge of the well, waving. He was a squat man with a face that always looked swollen, as if it were trying to burst through its skin.

"Man wearing all black," he said. "Ran straight toward the eastern tunnels!" He pointed toward where troubled marketgoers were peering down a tunnel, as if someone had just passed them in a rush.

Veil dashed in that direction. Vathah stayed with her longer than Glurv— but with Stormlight, she maintained a sprint no ordinary person could match. She burst into the indicated hallway and demanded to know if anyone had seen a man pass this way. A pair of women pointed.

Veil followed, heart beating violently, Stormlight raging within her. If she failed the chase, she'd have to wait for two more people to be assaulted—if it even happened again. The creature might hide, now that it knew she was watching.

She sprinted down this hallway, leaving behind the more populated sections of the tower. A few last people pointed down a tunnel at her shouted question.

She was beginning to lose hope as she reached the end of the hallway at an intersection, and looked one way, then the other. She glowed brightly to light the corridors for a distance, but she saw nothing in either.

She let out a sigh, slumping against the wall.

"Mmmm . . ." Pattern said from her coat. "It's there."

"Where?" Shallan asked.

"To the right. The shadows are off. The wrong pattern."

She stepped forward, and something split out of the shadows, a figure that was jet black—though like a liquid or a polished stone, it reflected her light. It scrambled away, its shape *wrong*. Not fully human.

Veil ran, heedless of the danger. This thing might be able to hurt her—but the mystery was the greater threat. She *needed* to know these secrets.

Shallan skidded around a corner, then barreled down the next tunnel. She managed to follow the broken piece of shadow, but she couldn't quite catch it.

The chase led her deeper into the far reaches of the tower's ground floor, to areas barely explored, where the tunnels grew increasingly confusing. The air smelled of old things. Of dust and stone left alone for ages. The strata danced on the walls, the speed of her run making them seem to twist around her like threads in a loom.

The thing dropped to all fours, light from Shallan's glow reflecting off its coal skin. It ran, frantic, until it hit a turn in the tunnel ahead and *squeezed* into a hole in the wall, two feet wide, near the floor.

Radiant dropped to her knees, spotting the thing as it wriggled out the other side of the hole. *Not that thick,* she thought, standing. "Pattern!" she demanded, thrusting her hand to the side.

She attacked the wall with her Shardblade, slicing chunks free, dropping them to the floor with a clatter. The strata ran all the way through the stone, and the pieces she carved off had a forlorn, broken beauty to them.

Engorged with Light, she shoved up against the sliced wall, finally breaking through into a small room beyond.

Much of its floor was taken up by the mouth of a pit. Circled by stone steps with no railing, the hole bored down through the rock into darkness. Radiant lowered her Shardblade, letting it slice into the rock at her feet. A hole. Like her drawing of spiraling blackness, a pit that seemed to descend into the void itself.

She released her Shardblade, falling to her knees.

"Shallan?" Pattern asked, rising up from the ground near where the Blade had vanished.

"We'll need to descend."

"Now?"

She nodded. "But first . . . first, go and get Adolin. Tell him to bring soldiers."

Pattern hummed. "You won't go alone, will you?"

"No. I promise. Can you make your way back?"

Pattern buzzed affirmatively, then zipped off across the ground, dimpling the floor of the rock. Curiously, the wall near where she'd broken in showed the rust marks and remnants of ancient hinges. So there was a secret door to get into this place.

Shallan kept her word. She was drawn toward that blackness, but she wasn't stupid. Well, mostly not stupid. She waited, transfixed by the pit, until she heard voices from the hallway behind her. *He can't see me in Veil's clothing!* she thought, and started to reawaken. How long had she been kneeling there?

She took off Veil's hat and long white coat, then hid them behind the debris. Stormlight enfolded her, painting the image of a havah over her trousers, gloved hand, and tight buttoned shirt.

Shallan. She was Shallan again—innocent, lively Shallan. Quick with a quip, even when nobody wanted to hear it. Earnest, but sometimes over-eager. She could be that person.

That's you, a part of her cried as she adopted the persona. *That's the real you. Isn't it? Why do you have to paint that face over another?*

She turned as a short, wiry man in a blue uniform entered the room, grey dusting his temples. What was his name again? She'd spent some time around Bridge Four in the last few weeks, but still hadn't learned them all.

Adolin strode in next, wearing Kholin blue Shardplate, faceplate up, Blade resting on his shoulder. Judging from the sounds out in the hallway— and the Herdazian faces that peeked into the room—he had brought not only soldiers, but the *entirety* of Bridge Four.

That included Renarin, who clomped in after his brother, clad in slate-colored Shardplate. Renarin looked far less frail when fully armored, though his face didn't seem like a soldier's, even if he had stopped wearing his spectacles.

Pattern approached and tried to slide up her illusory dress, but then stopped, backing away and humming in pleasure at the lie. "I found him!" he proclaimed. "I found Adolin!"

"I see that," Shallan said.

"He came at me," Adolin said, "in the training rooms, screaming that you'd found the killer. Said that if I didn't come, you'd probably—and I quote—'go do something stupid without letting me watch.'"

Pattern hummed. "Stupidity. Very interesting."

"You should visit the Alethi court sometime," Adolin said, stepping over to the pit. "So . . ."

"We tracked the thing that has been assaulting people," Shallan said. "It killed someone in the market, then it came here."

"The . . . thing?" one of the bridgemen asked. "Not a person?"

"It's a spren," Shallan whispered. "But not like one I've ever seen. It's able to imitate a person for a time—but it eventually becomes something else. A broken face, a twisted shape . . ."

"Sounds like that girl you've been seeing, Skar," one of the bridgemen noted.

"Ha ha," Skar said dryly. "How about we toss you in that pit, Eth, and see how far down this thing goes?"

"So this spren," Lopen said, approaching the pit, "it, sure, killed Highprince Sadeas?"

Shallan hesitated. No. It had killed Perel in copying the Sadeas murder, but someone *else* had murdered the highprince. She glanced at Adolin, who must have been thinking the same thing, for how solemn his expression was.

The spren was the greater threat—it had performed multiple murders. Still, it made her uncomfortable to acknowledge that her investigation hadn't taken them a single step closer to finding who had killed the highprince.

"We must have passed by this point a dozen times," a soldier said from behind. Shallan started; that voice was *female*. Indeed, she'd mistaken one of Dalinar's scouts—the short woman with long hair—for another bridgeman, though her uniform was different. She was inspecting the cuts Shallan had made to get into this room. "Don't you remember scouting right past that curved hallway outside, Teft?"

Teft nodded, rubbing his bearded chin. "Yeah, you're right, Lyn. But why hide a room like this?"

"There's something down there," Renarin whispered, leaning out over the pit. "Something . . . ancient. You've felt it, haven't you?" He looked up at Shallan, then the others in the room. "This place is weird; this whole tower is weird. You've noticed it too, right?"

"Kid," Teft said, "you're the expert on what's weird. We'll trust your word."

Shallan looked with concern toward Renarin at the insult. He just grinned, as one of the other bridgemen slapped him on the back—Plate notwithstanding—while Lopen and Rock started arguing over who was truly the weirdest among them. In a moment of surprise, she realized that Bridge Four had actually assimilated Renarin. He might be the lighteyed son of a highprince, resplendent in Shardplate, but here he was just another bridgeman.

"So," one of the men said, a handsome, muscled fellow with arms that seemed too long for his body, "I assume we're heading down into this awful crypt of terror?"

"Yes," Shallan said. She thought his name was Drehy.

"Storming lovely," Drehy said. "Marching orders, Teft?"

"That's up to Brightlord Adolin."

"I brought the best men I could find," Adolin said to Shallan. "But I feel like I should bring an entire army instead. You sure you want to do this now?"

"Yes," Shallan said. "We have to, Adolin. And . . . I don't know that an army would make a difference."

"Very well. Teft, give us a hefty rearguard. I don't fancy having something sneak up on us. Lyn, I want accurate maps—stop us if we get too far ahead of your drawing. I want to know my *exact* line of retreat. We go slowly, men. Be ready to perform a controlled, careful retreat if I command it."

Some shuffling of personnel followed. Then the group finally started down the staircase, single file, Shallan and Adolin near the center of the pack. The steps jutted right from the wall, but were wide enough that people would be able to pass on their way up, so there was no danger of falling off. She tried to keep from brushing anyone, as it might disturb the illusion that she was wearing her dress.

The sound of their footsteps vanished into the void. Soon they were alone with the timeless, patient darkness. The light of the sphere lanterns the bridgemen carried didn't seem to stretch far in that pit. It reminded Shallan of the mausoleum carved into the hill near her manor, where ancient Davar family members had been Soulcast to statues.

Her father's body hadn't been placed there. They had lacked the funds to pay for a Soulcaster—and besides, they'd wanted to pretend he was alive. She and her brothers had burned the body, as the darkeyes did.

Pain . . .

"I have to remind you, Brightness," Teft said from in front of her, "you can't expect anything . . . extraordinary from my men. For a bit, some of us sucked up light and strutted about like we were Stormblessed. That stopped when Kaladin left."

"It'll come back, gancho!" Lopen said from behind her. "When Kaladin returns, we'll glow again good."

"Hush, Lopen," Teft said. "Keep your voice down. Anyway, Brightness, the lads will do their best, but you need to know what—and what not—to expect."

Shallan hadn't been expecting Radiant powers from them; she'd known about their limitation already. All she needed were soldiers. Eventually, Lopen tossed a diamond chip into the hole, earning him a glare from Adolin.

"It might be down there waiting for us," the prince hissed. "Don't give it warning."

The bridgeman wilted, but nodded. The sphere bounced as a visible pinprick below, and Shallan was glad to know that at least there was an end to this descent. She'd begun to imagine an infinite spiral, like with old Dilid, one of the ten fools. He ran up a hillside toward the Tranquiline Halls with sand sliding beneath his feet—running for eternity, but never making progress.

Several bridgemen let out audible sighs of relief as they finally reached the bottom of the shaft. Here, piles of splinters scattered at the edges of the round chamber, covered in decayspren. There had once been a banister for the steps, but it had fallen to the effects of time.

The bottom of the shaft had only one exit, a large archway more elaborate than others in the tower. Up above, almost everything was the same uniform stone—as if this whole tower had been carved in one go. Here, the archway was of separately placed stones, and the walls of the tunnel beyond were lined with bright mosaic tiles.

Once they entered the hall, Shallan gasped, holding up a diamond broam. Gorgeous, intricate pictures of the Heralds—made of thousands of tiles— adorned the ceiling, each in a circular panel.

The art on the walls was more enigmatic. A solitary figure hovering above the ground before a large blue disc, arms stretched to the side as if to embrace it. Depictions of the Almighty in his traditional form as a cloud bursting with energy and light. A woman in the shape of a tree, hands spreading toward the sky and becoming branches. Who would have thought to find pagan symbols in the home of the Knights Radiant?

Other murals depicted shapes that reminded her of Pattern, windspren . . . ten kinds of spren. One for each order?

Adolin sent a vanguard a short distance ahead, and soon they returned. "Metal doors ahead, Brightlord," Lyn said. "One on each side of the hall."

Shallan pried her eyes away from the murals, joining the main body of the force as they moved. They reached the large steel doors and stopped, though the corridor itself continued onward. At Shallan's prompting, the bridgemen tried them, but couldn't get them open.

"Locked," Drehy said, wiping his brow.

Adolin stepped forward, sword in hand. "I've got a key."

"Adolin . . ." Shallan said. "These are artifacts from another time. Valuable and precious."

"I won't break them too much," he promised.

"But—"

"Aren't we chasing a murderer?" he said. "Someone who is likely to, say, hide in a locked room?"

She sighed, then nodded as he waved everyone back. She tucked her safehand, which had brushed him, back under her arm. It was so strange to feel like she was wearing a glove, but to see her hand as sleeved. Would it really have been so bad to let Adolin know about Veil?

A part of her panicked at the idea, so she let go of it quickly.

Adolin rammed his Blade through the door just above where the lock or bar would be, then swept it down. Teft tried the door, and was able to shove it open, hinges grinding loudly.

The bridgemen ducked in first, spears in hand. For all Teft's insistence that she wasn't to expect anything exceptional of them, they took point without orders, even though there were two Shardbearers at the ready.

Adolin rushed in after the bridgemen to secure the room, though Renarin wasn't paying much attention. He'd walked a few steps farther down the main corridor, and now stood still, staring deeper into the depths, sphere held absently in one gauntleted hand, Shardblade in the other.

Shallan stepped up hesitantly beside him. A cool breeze blew from behind them, as if being sucked into that darkness. The mystery lurked in that direction, the captivating depths. She could sense it more distinctly now. Not an evil really, but a *wrongness*. Like the sight of a wrist hanging from an arm after the bone is broken.

"What is it?" Renarin whispered. "Glys is frightened, and won't speak."

"Pattern doesn't know," Shallan said. "He calls it ancient. Says it's of the enemy."

Renarin nodded.

"Your father doesn't seem to be able to feel it," Shallan said. "Why can we?"

"I . . . I don't know. Maybe—"

"Shallan?" Adolin said, looking out of the room, his faceplate up. "You should see this."

The wreckage inside the room was more decayed than most they'd found in the tower. Rusted clasps and screws clung to bits of wood. Decomposed heaps ran in rows, containing bits of fragile covers and spines.

A library. They'd finally found the books Jasnah had dreamed of discovering.

They were ruined.

With a sinking feeling, Shallan moved through the room, nudging at piles of dust and splinters with her toes, frightening off decayspren. She found some shapes of books, but they disintegrated at her touch. She knelt between two rows of fallen books, feeling lost. All that knowledge . . . dead and gone.

"Sorry," Adolin said, standing awkwardly nearby.

"Don't let the men disturb this. Maybe . . . maybe there's something Navani's scholars can do to recover it."

"Want us to search the other room?" Adolin asked.

She nodded, and he clanked off. A short time later, she heard hinges creak as Adolin forced open the door.

Shallan suddenly felt exhausted. If these books here were gone, then it was unlikely they'd find others better preserved.

Forward. She rose, brushing off her knees, which only reminded her that her dress wasn't real. *You aren't here for this secret anyway.*

She stepped out into the main hallway, the one with the murals. Adolin and the bridgemen were exploring the room on the other side, but a quick glance showed Shallan that it was a mirror of the one they'd left, furnished only with piles of debris.

"Um . . . guys?" Lyn, the scout, called. "Prince Adolin? Brightness Radiant?"

Shallan turned from the room. Renarin had walked farther down the corridor. The scout had followed him, but had frozen in the hallway. Renarin's sphere illuminated something in the distance. A large mass that reflected the light, like glistening tar.

"We shouldn't have come here," Renarin said. "We can't fight this. Stormfather." He stumbled backward. "Stormfather . . ."

The bridgemen hastened into the hallway in front of Shallan, between her and Renarin. At a barked order from Teft, they made a formation spanning from one side of the main hallway to the other: a line of men holding spears low, with a second line behind holding more spears higher in an overhand grip.

Adolin burst out of the second library room, then gaped at the undulating shape in the distance. A living darkness.

That darkness seeped down the hallway. It wasn't fast, but there was an inevitability about the way it coated everything, flowing up the sides of the walls, onto the ceiling. On the ground, shapes split from the main mass, becoming figures that stepped as if from the surf. Creatures that had two feet and soon grew faces, with clothing that rippled into existence.

"She's here," Renarin whispered. "One of the Unmade. Re-Shephir . . . the Midnight Mother."

"Run, Shallan!" Adolin shouted. "Men, start back up the hall."

Then—of course—he *charged* at the flood of things.

The figures . . . they look like us, Shallan thought, stepping back, farther from the line of bridgemen. There was one midnight creature that looked like Teft, and another that was a copy of Lopen. Two larger shapes seemed to be wearing Shardplate. Except they were made of shiny tar, their features blobby, imperfect.

The mouths opened, sprouting spiny teeth.

"Make a careful retreat, like the prince ordered!" Teft called. "Don't get boxed in, men! Hold the line! Renarin!"

Renarin still stood out in front, holding forth his Shardblade: long and thin, with a waving pattern to the metal. Adolin reached his brother, then grabbed his arm and tried to tow him back.

He resisted. He seemed mesmerized by that line of forming monsters.

"Renarin! Attention!" Teft shouted. "To the line!"

The boy's head snapped up at the command and he scrambled—as if he weren't the cousin of the king—to obey his sergeant's order. Adolin retreated with him, and the two fell into formation with the bridgemen. Together, they pulled backward through the main hall.

Shallan backed up, staying roughly twenty feet behind the formation. Suddenly, the enemy moved with a burst of speed. Shallan cried out, and the bridgemen cursed, turning spears as the main mass of darkness swept up along the sides of the corridor, covering the beautiful murals.

The midnight figures dashed forward, charging the line. An explosive, frantic clash followed, bridgemen holding formation and striking at creatures who suddenly began forming on the right and left, coming out of the blackness on the walls. The things bled vapor when struck, a darkness that hissed from them and dissipated into the air.

Like smoke, Shallan thought.

The tar swept down from the walls, surrounding the bridgemen, who circled to keep themselves from being attacked at the rear. Adolin and Renarin fought at the very front, hacking with Blades, leaving dark figures to hiss and gush smoke in pieces.

Shallan found herself separated from the soldiers, an inky blackness between them. There didn't seem to be a duplicate for her.

The midnight faces bristled with teeth. Though they thrust with spears, they did so awkwardly. They struck true now and then, wounding a bridgeman, who would pull back into the center of the formation to be hastily bandaged by Lyn or Lopen. Renarin fell into the center and started to glow with Stormlight, healing those who were hurt.

Shallan watched all this, feeling a numbing trance settle over her. "I . . . know you," she whispered to the blackness, realizing it was true. "I know what you're doing."

Men grunted and stabbed. Adolin swept before himself, Shardblade trailing black smoke from the creatures' wounds. He chopped apart dozens of the things, but new ones continued forming, wearing familiar shapes. Dalinar. Teshav. Highprinces and scouts, soldiers and scribes.

"You try to imitate us," Shallan said. "But you fail. You're a spren. You don't *quite* understand."

She stepped toward the surrounded bridgemen.

"Shallan!" Adolin called, grunting as he cleaved three figures before him. "Escape! Run!"

She ignored him, stepping up to the darkness. In front of her—at the closest point of the ring—Drehy stabbed a figure straight through the head, sending it stumbling back. Shallan seized its shoulders, spinning it toward her. It was Navani, a gaping hole in her face, black smoke escaping with a hiss. Even ignoring that, the features were off. The nose too big, one eye a little higher than the other.

It dropped to the floor, writhing as it deflated like a punctured wine-skin.

Shallan strode right up to the formation. The things fled her, shying to the sides. Shallan had the distinct and terrifying impression that these things could have swept the bridgemen away at will—overwhelming them in a terrible black tide. But the Midnight Mother wanted to learn; she wanted to fight with spears.

If that was so, however, she was growing impatient. The newer figures forming up were increasingly distorted, more bestial, spiny teeth spilling from their mouths.

"Your imitation is pathetic," Shallan whispered. "Here. Let me show you how it's done."

Shallan drew in her Stormlight, going alight like a beacon. Things screamed, pulling away from her. As she stepped around the formation of worried bridgemen—wading into the blackness at their left flank—figures extended from her, shapes growing from light. The people from her recently rebuilt collection.

Palona. Soldiers from the hallways. A group of Soulcasters she'd passed two days ago. Men and women from the markets. Highprinces and scribes. The man who had tried to pick up Veil at the tavern. The Horneater she'd stabbed in the hand. Soldiers. Cobblers. Scouts. Washwomen. Even a few kings.

A glowing, radiant force.

Her figures spread out to surround the beleaguered bridgemen like sentries. This new, glowing force drove the enemy monsters back, and the tar withdrew along the sides of the hall, until the path of retreat was open. The Midnight Mother dominated the darkness at the end of the hall, the direction they had not yet explored. It waited there, and did not recede farther.

The bridgemen relaxed, Renarin muttering as he healed the last few who had been hurt. Shallan's cohort of glowing figures moved forward and formed a line with her, between darkness and bridgemen.

The creatures formed again from the blackness ahead, growing more ferocious, like beasts. Featureless blobs with teeth sprouting from slit mouths.

"How are you doing this?" Adolin asked, voice ringing from within his helm. "Why are they afraid?"

"Has someone with a knife—not knowing who you were—ever tried to threaten you?"

"Yeah. I just summoned my Shardblade."

"It's a little like that." Shallan stepped forward, and Adolin joined her. Renarin summoned his Blade and took a few quick steps to reach them, his Plate clicking.

The darkness pulled back, revealing that the hallway opened up into a room ahead. As she approached, Shallan's Stormlight illuminated a bowl-like chamber. The center was dominated by a heaving black mass that undulated and pulsed, stretching from floor to ceiling some twenty feet above.

The midnight beasts tested forward against her light, no longer seeming as intimidated.

"We have to choose," Shallan said to Adolin and Renarin. "Retreat or attack?"

"What do you think?"

"I don't know. This creature . . . she's been watching me. She's changed how I see the tower. I feel like I *understand* her, a connection I cannot explain. That can't be a good thing, right? Can we even trust what I think?"

Adolin raised his faceplate and smiled at her. Storms, that smile. "Highmarshal Halad always said that to beat someone, you must first know them. It's become one of the rules we follow in warfare."

"And . . . what did he say about retreat?"

"'Plan every battle as if you will inevitably retreat, but fight every battle like there is no backing down.'"

The main mass in the chamber undulated, faces appearing from its tarry surface—pressing out as if trying to escape. There was something beneath the enormous spren. Yes, it was wrapped around a pillar that reached from the floor of the circular room to its ceiling.

The murals, the intricate art, the fallen troves of information . . . This place was important.

Shallan clasped her hands before herself, and the Patternblade formed in her palms. She twisted it in a sweaty grip, falling into the dueling stance Adolin had been teaching her.

Holding it immediately brought pain. Not the screaming of a dead spren. Pain inside. The pain of an Ideal sworn, but not yet overcome.

"Bridgemen," Adolin called. "You willing to give it another go?"

"We'll last longer than you will, gancho! Even with your fancy armor."

Adolin grinned and slammed his faceplate down. "At your word, Radiant."

She sent her illusions in, but the darkness didn't shy before them as it had previously. Black figures attacked her illusions, testing to find that they weren't real. Dozens of these midnight men clogged the way forward.

"Clear the way for me to the thing in the center," she said, trying to sound more certain than she felt. "I need to get close enough to touch her."

"Renarin, can you guard my back?" Adolin asked.

Renarin nodded.

Adolin took a deep breath, then charged into the room, bursting right through the middle of an illusion of his father. He struck at the first midnight man, chopping it down, then began sweeping around him in a frenzy.

Bridge Four shouted, rushing in behind him. Together, they began to form a path for Shallan, slaying the creatures between her and the pillar.

She walked through the bridgemen, a rank of them forming a spear line to either side of her. Ahead, Adolin pushed toward the pillar, Renarin at his back preventing him from being surrounded, bridgemen in turn pushing up along the sides to keep Renarin from being overwhelmed.

The monsters no longer bore even a semblance of humanity. They struck Adolin, too-real claws and teeth scraping his armor. Others clung to him, trying to weigh him down or find chinks in the Shardplate.

They know how to face men like him, Shallan thought, still holding her Shardblade in one hand. *Why then do they fear me?*

Shallan wove Light, and a version of Radiant appeared near Renarin. The creatures attacked it, leaving Renarin for a moment—unfortunately, most of her illusions had fallen, collapsing into Stormlight as they were disrupted again and again. She could have kept them going, she thought, with more practice.

Instead, she wove versions of herself. Young and old, confident and frightened. A dozen different Shallans. With a shock, she realized that several were pictures she'd lost, self-portraits she'd practiced with a mirror, as Dandos the Oilsworn had insisted was vital for an aspiring artist.

Some of her selves cowered; others fought. For a moment Shallan lost herself, and she even let Veil appear among them. She was those women, those girls, every one of them. And none of them were her. They were things she used, manipulated. Illusions.

"Shallan!" Adolin shouted, voice straining as Renarin grunted and ripped midnight men off him. "Whatever you're going to do, do it now!"

She'd stepped up to the front of the column the soldiers had won for her, right near Adolin. She tore her gaze away from a child Shallan dancing among the midnight men. Before her, the main mass—coating the pillar in the center of the room—bubbled with faces that stretched against the surface, mouths opening to scream, then submerged like men drowning in tar.

"Shallan!" Adolin said again.

That pulsing mass, so terrible, but so *captivating.*

The image of the pit. The twisting lines of the corridors. The tower that couldn't be completely seen. This was why she'd come.

Shallan strode forward, arm out, and let the illusory sleeve covering her hand vanish. She pulled off her glove, stepped right up to the mass of tar and voiceless screams.

Then pressed her safehand against it.

Listen to the words of a fool.

—From *Oathbringer*, preface

S hallan was open to this thing. Laid bare, her skin split, her soul gaping wide. It could get *in*.

It was also open to her.

She felt its confused fascination with humankind. It remembered men—an innate understanding, much as newborn mink kits innately knew to fear the skyeel. This spren was not completely aware, not completely cognizant. She was a creation of instinct and alien curiosity, drawn to violence and pain like scavengers to the scent of blood.

Shallan knew Re-Shephir at the same time as the thing came to know her. The spren tugged and prodded at Shallan's bond with Pattern, seeking to rip it free and insert herself instead. Pattern clung to Shallan, and she to him, holding on for dear life.

She fears us, Pattern's voice buzzed in her head. *Why does she fear us?*

In her mind's eye, Shallan envisioned herself holding tightly to Pattern in his humanoid form, the two of them huddled down before the spren's attack. That image was all she could see at the moment, for the room—and everything in it—had dissolved to black.

This thing was ancient. Created long ago as a splinter of the soul of something even more terrible, Re-Shephir had been ordered to sow chaos, spawning horrors to confuse and destroy men. Over time, slowly, she'd become increasingly intrigued by the things she murdered.

Her creations had come to imitate what she saw in the world, but **309** lacking love or affection. Like stones come alive, content to be killed or to kill with no attachment or enjoyment. No emotions beyond an over-powering curiosity, and that ephemeral attraction to violence.

Almighty above . . . it's like a creationspren. Only so, so wrong.

Pattern whimpered, huddled against Shallan in his shape of a man with a stiff robe and a moving pattern for a head. She tried to shield him from the onslaught.

Fight every battle . . . as if there is . . . no backing down.

Shallan looked into the depths of the swirling void, the dark spinning soul of Re-Shephir, the Midnight Mother. Then, growling, Shallan struck.

She didn't attack like the prim, excitable girl who had been trained by cautious Vorin society. She attacked like the frenzied child who had mur-dered her mother. The cornered woman who had stabbed Tyn through the chest. She drew upon the part of her that hated the way everyone assumed she was so nice, so sweet. The part of her that hated being described as *diverting* or *clever*.

She drew upon the Stormlight within, and pushed herself farther into Re-Shephir's essence. She couldn't tell if it was actually happening—if she was pushing her physical body farther into the creature's tar—or if this was all a representation of someplace else. A place beyond this room in the tower, beyond even Shadesmar.

The creature trembled, and Shallan finally saw the reason for its fear. It had been trapped. The event had happened recently in the spren's reckoning, though Shallan had the impression that in fact centuries upon centuries had passed.

Re-Shephir was terrified of it happening again. The imprisonment had been unexpected, presumed impossible. And it had been done by a Light-weaver like Shallan, who had *understood* this creature.

It feared her like an axehound might fear someone with a voice similar to that of its harsh master.

Shallan hung on, pressing herself against the enemy, but realization washed over her—the understanding that this thing was going to know her completely, discover each and every one of her secrets.

Her ferocity and determination wavered; her commitment began to seep away.

So she lied. She insisted that she wasn't afraid. She was *committed*. She'd always been that way. She would continue that way forever.

Power could be an illusion of perception. Even within yourself.

Re-Shephir broke. It screeched, a sound that vibrated through Shallan. A screech that remembered its imprisonment and feared something worse.

Shallan dropped backward in the room where they'd been fighting. Adolin caught her in a steel grip, going down on one knee with an audible crack of Plate against stone. She heard that echoing scream fading. Not dying. Fleeing, escaping, determined to get as far from Shallan as it could.

When she forced her eyes open, she found the room clean of the darkness. The corpses of the midnight creatures had dissolved. Renarin quickly knelt next to a bridgeman who had been hurt, removing his gauntlet and infusing the man with healing Stormlight.

Adolin helped Shallan sit up, and she tucked her exposed safehand under her other arm. Storms . . . she'd somehow kept up the illusion of the havah.

Even after all of that, she didn't want Adolin to know of Veil. She *couldn't*.

"Where?" she asked him, exhausted. "Where did it go?"

Adolin pointed toward the other side of the room, where a tunnel extended farther down into the depths of the mountain. "It fled in that direction, like moving smoke."

"So . . . should we chase it down?" Eth asked, making his way carefully toward the tunnel. His lantern revealed steps cut into the stone. "This goes down a long ways."

Shallan could feel a change in the air. The tower was . . . different. "Don't give chase," she said, remembering the terror of that conflict. She was more than happy to let the thing run. "We can post guards in this chamber, but I don't think she'll return."

"Yeah," Teft said, leaning on his spear and wiping sweat from his face. "Guards seem like a very, *very* good idea."

Shallan frowned at the tone of his voice, then followed his gaze, to look at the thing Re-Shephir had been hiding. The pillar in the exact center of the room.

It was set with thousands upon thousands of cut gemstones, most larger than Shallan's fist. Together, they were a treasure worth more than most kingdoms.

*If they cannot make you less foolish, at least let them give you
hope.*

—From *Oathbringer*, preface

Throughout his youth, Kaladin had dreamed of joining the military
and leaving quiet little Hearthstone. Everyone knew that soldiers
traveled extensively and saw the world.

And he had. He'd seen dozens upon dozens of empty hills, weed-covered
plains, and identical warcamps. Actual sights, though . . . well, that was
another story.

The city of Revolar was, as his hike with the parshmen had proven, only
a few weeks away from Hearthstone by foot. He'd never visited. Storms,
he'd never actually lived in a *city* before, unless you counted the warcamps.

He suspected most cities weren't surrounded by an army of parshmen as
this one was.

Revolar was built in a nice hollow on the leeward side of a series of hills,
the perfect spot for a little town. Except this was not a "little town." The
city had sprawled out, filling in the areas between the hills, going up the
leeward slopes—only leaving the tips completely bare.

He'd expected a city to look more organized. He'd imagined neat rows
of houses, like an efficient warcamp. This looked more like a snarl of plants
clumped in a chasm at the Shattered Plains. Streets running this way and
that. Markets that poked out haphazardly.

Kaladin joined his team of parshmen as they wound along a wide roadway kept level with smoothed crem. They passed through thousands upon

thousands of parshmen camped here, and more gathered by the hour, it seemed.

His, however, was the only group that carried stone-headed spears on their shoulders, packs of dried grain biscuits, and hogshide leather sandals. They tied their smocks with belts, and carried stone knives, hatchets, and tinder in waxed sleeves made from candles he'd traded for. He'd even begun teaching them to use a sling.

He probably shouldn't have shown them any of these things; that didn't stop him from feeling proud as he walked with them, entering the city.

Crowds thronged the streets. Where had all these parshmen come from? This was a force of at least forty or fifty thousand. He knew most people ignored parshmen . . . and, well, he'd done the same. But he'd always had tucked into the back of his mind this idea that there weren't *that* many out there. Each high-ranking lighteyes owned a handful. And a lot of the caravaneers. And, well, even the less wealthy families from cities or towns had them. And there were the dockworkers, the miners, the water haulers, the packmen they used when building large projects. . . .

"It's amazing," Sah said from where he walked beside Kaladin, carrying his daughter on his shoulder to give her a better view. She clutched some of his wooden cards, holding them close like another child might carry a favorite stuffed doll.

"Amazing?" Kaladin asked Sah.

"Our own city, Kal," he whispered. "During my time as a slave, barely able to think, I still dreamed. I tried to imagine what it would be like to have my own home, my own life. Here it is."

The parshmen had obviously moved into homes along the streets here. Were they running markets too? It raised a difficult, unsettling question. Where were all the humans? Khen's group walked deeper into the city, still led by the unseen spren. Kaladin spotted signs of trouble. Broken windows. Doors that no longer latched. Some of that would be from the Everstorm, but he passed a couple of doors that had obviously been hacked open with axes.

Looting. And ahead stood an inner wall. It was a nice fortification, right in the middle of the city sprawl. It probably marked the original city boundary, as decided upon by some optimistic architect.

Here, at long last, Kaladin found signs of the fight he'd expected during his initial trip to Alethkar. The gates to the inner city lay broken. The guardhouse had been burned, and arrowheads still stuck from some of the wood beams they passed. This was a conquered city.

But where had the humans been moved? Should he be looking for a prison camp, or a heaping pyre of burned bones? Considering the idea made him sick.

"Is this what it's about?" Kaladin said as they walked down a roadway in the inner city. "Is this what you want, Sah? To conquer the kingdom? Destroy humankind?"

"Storms, I don't know," he said. "But I can't be a slave again, Kal. I *won't* let them take Vai and imprison her. Would you defend them, after what they did to you?"

"They're my people."

"That's no excuse. If one of 'your people' murders another, don't you put them in prison? What is a just punishment for enslaving my entire race?"

Syl soared past, her face peeking from a shimmering haze of mist. She caught his eye, then zipped over to a windowsill and settled down, taking the shape of a small rock.

"I . . ." Kaladin said. "I don't know, Sah. But a war to exterminate one side or the other can't be the answer."

"You can fight alongside us, Kal. It doesn't have to be about humans against parshmen. It can be nobler than that. Oppressed against the oppressors."

As they passed the place where Syl was, Kaladin swept his hand along the wall. Syl, as they'd practiced, zipped up the sleeve of his coat. He could feel her, like a gust of wind, move up his sleeve then out his collar, into his hair. The long curls hid her, they'd determined, well enough.

"There are a *lot* of those yellow-white spren here, Kaladin," she whispered. "Zipping through the air, dancing through buildings."

"Any signs of humans?" Kaladin whispered.

"To the east," she said. "Crammed into some army barracks and old parshman quarters. Others are in big pens, watched under guard. Kaladin . . . there's another highstorm coming today."

"When?"

"Soon, maybe? I'm new to guessing this. I doubt anyone is expecting it. Everything has been thrown off; the charts will all be wrong until people can make new ones."

Kaladin hissed slowly through his teeth.

Ahead, his team approached a large group of parshmen. Judging by the way they'd been organized into large lines, this was some kind of processing station for new arrivals. Indeed, Khen's band of a hundred was shuffled into one of the lines to wait.

Ahead of them, a parshman in full carapace armor—like a Parshendi—strolled down the line, holding a writing board. Syl pulled farther into Kaladin's hair as the Parshendi man stepped up to Khen's group.

"What towns, work camps, or armies do you all come from?" His voice had a strange cadence, similar to the Parshendi Kaladin had heard on the Shattered Plains. Some of those in Khen's group had hints of it, but nothing this strong.

The scribe parshman wrote down the list of towns Khen gave him, then noted their spears. "You've been busy. I'll recommend you for special training. Send your captive to the pens; I'll write down a description here, and once you're settled, you can put him to work."

"He . . ." Khen said, looking at Kaladin. "He is not our captive." She seemed begrudging. "He was one of the humans' slaves, like us. He wishes to join and fight."

The parshman looked up in the air at nothing.

"Yixli is speaking for you," Sah whispered to Kaladin. "She sounds impressed."

"Well," the scribe said, "it's not unheard of, but you'll have to get permission from one of the Fused to label him free."

"One of the what?" Khen asked.

The parshman with the writing board pointed toward his left. Kaladin had to step out of the line, along with several of the others, to see a tall parshwoman with long hair. There was carapace covering her cheeks, running back along the cheekbones and into her hair. The skin on her arms prickled with ridges, as if there were carapace *under* the skin as well. Her eyes glowed red.

Kaladin's breath caught. Bridge Four had described these creatures to him, the strange Parshendi they'd fought during their push toward the center of the Shattered Plains. These were the beings who had summoned the Everstorm.

This one focused directly on Kaladin. There was something oppressive about her red gaze.

Kaladin heard a clap of thunder in the far distance. Around him, many of the parshmen turned toward it and began to mutter. Highstorm.

In that moment, Kaladin made his decision. He'd stayed with Sah and the others as long as he dared. He'd learned what he could. The storm presented a chance.

It's time to go.

The tall, dangerous creature with the red eyes—the Fused, they had called her—began walking toward Khen's group. Kaladin couldn't know if she recognized him as a Radiant, but he had no intention of waiting until she arrived. He'd been planning; the old slave's instincts had already decided upon the easiest way out.

It was on Khen's belt.

Kaladin sucked in the Stormlight, right from her pouch. He burst alight with its power, then grabbed the pouch—he'd need those gemstones—and yanked it free, the leather strap snapping.

"Get your people to shelter," Kaladin said to the surprised Khen. "A highstorm is close. Thank you for your kindness. No matter what you are told, know this: I do not wish to be your enemy."

The Fused began to scream with an angry voice. Kaladin met Sah's betrayed expression, then launched himself into the air.

Freedom.

Kaladin's skin shivered with joy. Storms, how he'd missed this. The wind, the openness above, even the lurch in his stomach as gravity let go. Syl spun around him as a ribbon of light, creating a spiral of glowing lines. Gloryspren burst up about Kaladin's head.

Syl took on the form of a person just so she could glower at the little bobbing balls of light. "Mine," she said, swatting one of them aside.

About five or six hundred feet up, Kaladin changed to a half Lashing, so he slowed and hovered in the sky. Beneath, that red-eyed parshwoman was gesturing and screaming, though Kaladin couldn't hear her. Storms. He hoped this wouldn't mean trouble for Sah and the others.

He had an excellent view of the city—the streets filled with figures, now making for shelter in buildings. Other groups rushed to the city from all directions. Even after spending so much time with them, his first reaction was one of discomfort. So many parshmen together in one place? It was unnatural.

This impression bothered him now as it never would have before.

He eyed the stormwall, which he could see approaching in the far distance. He still had time before it arrived.

He'd have to fly up above the storm to avoid being caught in its winds. But then what?

"Urithiru is out there somewhere, to the west," Kaladin said. "Can you guide us there?"

"How would I do that?"

"You've been there before."

"So have you."

"You're a force of nature, Syl," Kaladin said. "You can feel the storms. Don't you have some kind of . . . location sense?"

"*You're* the one from this realm," she said, batting away another gloryspren and hanging in the air beside him, folding her arms. "Besides, I'm less a force of nature and more one of the raw powers of creation transformed by collective human imagination into a personification of one of their ideals." She grinned at him.

"Where did you come up with *that*?"

"Dunno. Maybe I heard it somewhere once. Or maybe I'm just *smart*."

"We'll have to make for the Shattered Plains, then," Kaladin said. "We can strike out for one of the larger cities in southern Alethkar, swap gemstones there, and hopefully have enough to hop over to the war-camps."

That decided, he tied his gemstone pouch to his belt, then glanced down and tried to make a final estimate of troop numbers and parshman fortifications. It felt odd to not worry about the storm, but he'd just move up over it once it arrived.

From up here, Kaladin could see the great trenches cut into the stones to divert away floodwaters after a storm. Though most of the parshmen had fled for shelter, some remained below, craning necks and staring up at him. He read betrayal in their postures, though he couldn't even tell if these were members of Khen's group or not.

"What?" Syl asked, alighting on his shoulder.

"I can't help but feel a kinship to them, Syl."

"They conquered the city. They're *Voidbringers*."

"No, they're people. And they're *angry*, with good reason." A gust of wind blew across him, making him drift to the side. "I know that feeling. It burns in you, worms inside your brain until you forget everything but the injustice done to you. It's how I felt about Elhokar. Sometimes a world of rational explanations can become meaningless in the face of that all-consuming desire to *get what you deserve*."

"You changed your mind about Elhokar, Kaladin. You saw what was right."

"Did I? Did I find what was *right*, or did I just finally agree to see things the way you wanted?"

"Killing Elhokar *was* wrong."

"And the parshmen on the Shattered Plains that I killed? Murdering them wasn't wrong?"

"You were protecting Dalinar."

"Who was assaulting their homeland."

"Because they killed his brother."

"Which, for all we know, they did because they saw how King Gavilar and his people treated the parshmen." Kaladin turned toward Syl, who sat on his shoulder, one leg tucked beneath her. "So what's the difference, Syl? What is the difference between Dalinar attacking the parshmen, and these parshmen conquering that city?"

"I don't know," she said softly.

"And why was it worse for me to *let* Elhokar be killed for his injustices than it was for me to actively kill parshmen on the Shattered Plains?"

"One is wrong. I mean, it just feels wrong. Both do, I guess."

"Except one nearly broke my bond, while the other didn't. The bond isn't about what's right and wrong, is it, Syl. It's about what *you see* as right and wrong."

"What *we* see," she corrected. "And about oaths. You swore to protect Elhokar. Tell me that during your time planning to betray Elhokar, you didn't—deep down—think you were doing something wrong."

"Fine. But it's still about perception." Kaladin let the winds blow him, feeling a pit open in his belly. "Storms, I'd hoped . . . I'd hoped you could tell me, give me an absolute *right*. For once, I'd like my moral code not to come with a list of exceptions at the end."

She nodded thoughtfully.

"I'd have expected you to object," Kaladin said. "You're a . . . what, embodiment of human perceptions of honor? Shouldn't you at least *think* you have all the answers?"

"Probably," she said. "Or maybe if there are answers, I should be the one who wants to find them."

The stormwall was now fully visible: the great wall of water and refuse pushed by the oncoming winds of a highstorm. Kaladin had drifted along with the winds away from the city, so he Lashed himself eastward until they floated over the hills that made up the city's windbreak. Here, he spotted something he hadn't seen earlier: pens full of great masses of humans.

The winds blowing in from the east were growing stronger. However, the parshmen guarding the pens were just standing there, as if nobody had given them orders to move. The first rumblings of the highstorm had been distant, easy to miss. They'd notice it soon, but that might be too late.

"Oh!" Syl said. "Kaladin, those people!"

Kaladin cursed, then dropped the Lashing holding him upward, which made him fall in a rush. He crashed to the ground, sending out a puff of glowing Stormlight that expanded from him in a ring.

"Highstorm!" he shouted at the parshman guards. "Highstorm coming! Get these people to safety!"

They looked at him, dumbfounded. Not a surprising reaction. Kaladin summoned his Blade, shoving past the parshmen and leaping up onto the pen's low stone wall, for keeping hogs.

He held aloft the Sylblade. Townspeople swarmed to the wall. Cries of "Shardbearer" rose.

"A highstorm is coming!" he shouted, but his voice was quickly lost in the tumult of voices. Storms. He had little doubt that the Voidbringers could handle a group of rioting townsfolk.

He sucked in more Stormlight, raising himself into the air. That quieted them, even drove them backward.

"Where did you shelter," he demanded in a loud voice, "when the last storms came?"

A few people near the front pointed at the large bunkers nearby. For housing livestock, parshmen, and even travelers during storms. Could those hold an entire town's worth of people? Maybe if they crowded in.

"Get moving!" Kaladin said. "A storm will be here soon."

Kaladin, Syl's voice said in his mind. *Behind you.*

He turned and found parshman guards approaching his wall with spears. Kaladin hopped down as the townspeople finally reacted, climbing the walls, which were barely chest high and slathered with smooth, hardened crem.

Kaladin took one step toward the parshmen, then swiped his Blade, separating their spearheads from the hafts. The parshmen—who had barely more training than the ones he'd traveled with—stepped back in confusion.

"Do you want to fight me?" Kaladin asked them.

One shook her head.

"Then see that those people don't trample each other in their haste to get to safety," Kaladin said, pointing. "And keep the rest of the guards from attacking them. This isn't a revolt. Can't you hear the thunder, and feel the wind picking up?"

He launched himself onto the wall again, then waved for the people to move, shouting orders. The parshman guards eventually decided that instead of fighting a Shardbearer, they'd risk getting into trouble for doing what he said. Before too long, he had an entire team of them prodding the humans—often less gently than he'd have liked—toward the storm bunkers.

Kaladin dropped down beside one of the guards, a female whose spear he'd sliced in half. "How did this work the last time the storm hit?"

"We mostly left the humans to themselves," she admitted. "We were too busy running for safety."

So the Voidbringers hadn't anticipated that storm's arrival either. Kaladin winced, trying not to dwell on how many people had likely been lost to the impact of the stormwall.

"Do better," he said to her. "These people are your charge now. You've seized the city, taken what you want. If you wish to claim any kind of moral superiority, treat your captives better than they did you."

"Look," the parshwoman said. "Who *are* you? And why—"

Something large crashed into Kaladin, tossing him backward into the wall with a *crunch*. The thing had arms; a person who grasped for his throat, trying to strangle him. He kicked them off; their eyes trailed red.

A blackish-violet glow—like *dark Stormlight*—rose from the red-eyed parshman. Kaladin cursed and Lashed himself into the air.

The creature followed.

Another rose nearby, leaving a faint violet glow behind, flying as easily as he did. These two looked different from the one he'd seen earlier, leaner, with longer hair. Syl cried out in his mind, a sound like pain and surprise mixed. He could only assume that someone had run to fetch these, after he had taken to the sky.

A few windspren zipped past Kaladin, then began to dance playfully around him. The sky grew dark, the stormwall thundering across the land. Those red-eyed Parshendi chased him upward.

So Kaladin Lashed himself straight toward the storm.

It had worked against the Assassin in White. The highstorm was dangerous, but it was also something of an ally. The two creatures followed, though they overshot his elevation and had to Lash themselves back downward in a weird bobbing motion. They reminded him of his first experimentation with his powers.

Kaladin braced himself—holding to the Sylblade, joined by four or five windspren—and crashed through the stormwall. An unstable darkness swallowed him; a darkness that was often split by lightning and broken by phantom glows. Winds contorted and clashed like rival armies, so irregular that Kaladin was tossed by them one way, then the other. It took all his skill in Lashing to simply get going in the right direction.

He watched over his shoulder as the two red-eyed parshmen burst in. Their strange glow was more subdued than his own, and somehow gave off the impression of an *anti*-glow. A darkness that clung to them.

They were immediately disrupted, sent spinning in the wind. Kaladin smiled, then was nearly crushed by a boulder tumbling through the air. Sheer luck saved him; the boulder passed close enough that another few inches would have ripped off his arm.

Kaladin Lashed himself upward, soaring through the tempest toward its ceiling. "Stormfather!" he yelled. "Spren of storms!"

No response.

"Turn yourself aside!" Kaladin shouted into the churning winds. "There are people below! Stormfather. You *must* listen to me!"

All grew still.

Kaladin stood in that strange space where he'd seen the Stormfather before—a place that seemed outside of reality. The ground was far beneath him, dim, slicked with rain, but barren and empty. Kaladin hovered in the air. Not Lashed; the air was simply solid beneath him.

WHO ARE YOU TO MAKE DEMANDS OF THE STORM, SON OF HONOR?

The Stormfather was a face as wide as the sky, dominating like a sunrise.

Kaladin held his sword aloft. "I know you for what you are, Stormfather. A spren, like Syl."

I AM THE MEMORY OF A GOD, THE FRAGMENT THAT REMAINS. THE SOUL OF A STORM AND THE MIND OF ETERNITY.

"Then surely with that soul, mind, and memory," Kaladin said, "you can find mercy for the people below."

AND WHAT OF THE HUNDREDS OF THOUSANDS WHO HAVE DIED IN THESE WINDS BEFORE? SHOULD I HAVE HAD MERCY FOR THEM?

"Yes."

AND THE WAVES THAT SWALLOW, THE FIRES THAT CONSUME? YOU WOULD HAVE THEM STOP?

"I speak only of you, and only today. Please."

Thunder rumbled. And the Stormfather actually seemed to *consider* the request.

IT IS NOT SOMETHING I CAN DO, SON OF TANAVAST. IF THE WIND STOPS BLOWING, IT IS NOT A WIND. IT IS NOTHING.

"But—"

Kaladin dropped back into the tempest proper, and it seemed as if no time had passed. He ducked through the winds, gritting his teeth in frustration. Windspren accompanied him—he had two dozen now, a spinning and laughing group, each a ribbon of light.

He passed one of the glowing-eyed parshmen. The Fused? Did that term refer to all whose eyes glowed?

"The Stormfather really could be more helpful, Syl. Didn't he claim to be your father?"

It's complicated, she said in his mind. *He's stubborn though. I'm sorry.*

"He's callous," Kaladin said.

He's a storm, Kaladin. As people over millennia have imagined him.

"He could choose."

Perhaps. Perhaps not. I think what you're doing is like asking fire to please stop being so hot.

Kaladin zoomed down along the ground, quickly reaching the hills around Revolar. He had hoped to find that everyone was safe, but that was—of course—a frail hope. People were scattered across the pens and the ground near the bunkers. One of those bunkers still had the doors open, and a few men were trying—bless them—to gather the last people outside and carry them in.

Many were too far away. They huddled against the ground, holding to the wall or outcroppings of rock. Kaladin could barely make them out in flashes of lightning—terrified lumps alone in the tempest.

He had felt those winds. He'd been powerless before them, tied to the side of a building.

Kaladin . . . Syl said in his mind as he dropped.

The storm pulsed inside him. Within the highstorm, his Stormlight constantly renewed. It preserved him, had saved his life a dozen times over. That very power that had tried to kill him had been his salvation.

He hit the ground and dropped Syl, then seized the form of a young father clutching a son. He pulled them up, holding them secure, trying to run them toward the building. Nearby, another person—he couldn't see much of them—was torn away in a gust of wind and taken by the darkness.

Kaladin, you can't save them all.

He screamed as he grabbed another person, holding her tight and walking with them. They stumbled in the wind as they reached a cluster of people huddled together. Some two dozen or more, in the shadow of the wall around the pens.

Kaladin pulled the three he was helping—the father, the child, the woman—over to the others. "You can't stay out here!" he shouted at them all. "Together. You have to walk together, this way!"

With effort—winds howling, rain pelting like daggers—he got the group moving across the stony ground, arm in arm. They made good progress until a boulder crunched to the ground nearby, sending some of them huddling down in a panic. The wind rose, lifting some people up; only the clutching hands of the others kept them from blowing away.

Kaladin blinked away tears that mingled with the rain. He bellowed. Nearby, a flash of light illuminated a man being crushed as a portion of wall ripped away and towed his body off into the storm.

Kaladin, Syl said. *I'm sorry.*

"Being sorry isn't enough!" he yelled.

He clung with one arm to a child, his face toward the storm and its terrible winds. Why did it destroy? This tempest shaped them. Must it ruin them too? Consumed by his pain and feelings of betrayal, Kaladin surged with Stormlight and flung his hand forward as if to try to push back the wind itself.

A hundred windspren spun in as lines of light, twisting around his arm, wrapping it like ribbons. They surged with Light, then exploded outward in a blinding sheet, sweeping to Kaladin's sides and parting the winds around him.

Kaladin stood with his hand toward the tempest, and *deflected it.* Like a stone in a swift-moving river stopped the waters, he opened a pocket in the storm, creating a calm wake behind him.

The storm raged against him, but he held the point in a formation of windspren that spread from him like wings, diverting the storm. He managed to turn his head as the storm battered him. People huddled behind him, soaked, confused—surrounded by calm.

"Go!" he shouted. "*Go!*"

They found their feet, the young father taking his son back from Kaladin's leeward arm. Kaladin backed up with them, maintaining the windbreak. This group was only some of those trapped by the winds, yet it took everything Kaladin had to hold the tempest.

The winds seemed angry at him for his defiance. All it would take was one boulder.

A figure with glowing red eyes landed on the field before him. It advanced, but the people had finally reached the bunker. Kaladin sighed and released the winds, and the spren behind him scattered. Exhausted, he let the storm pick him up and fling him away. A quick Lashing gave him elevation, preventing him from being rammed into the buildings of the city.

Wow, Syl said in his mind. *What did you just do? With the storm?*

"Not enough," Kaladin whispered.

You'll never be able to do enough to satisfy yourself, Kaladin. That was still wonderful.

He was past Revolar in a heartbeat. He turned, becoming merely another piece of debris on the winds. The Fused gave chase, but lagged behind, then vanished. Kaladin and Syl pushed out of the stormwall, then rode it at the front of the storm. They passed over cities, plains, mountains—never running out of Stormlight, for there was a source renewing them from behind.

They flew for a good hour like that before a current in the winds nudged him toward the south.

"Go that way," Syl said, a ribbon of light.

"Why?"

"Just listen to the piece of nature incarnate, okay? I think Father wants to apologize, in his own way."

Kaladin growled, but allowed the winds to channel him in a specific direction. He flew this way for hours, lost in the sounds of the tempest, until finally he settled down—half of his own volition, half because of the pressing winds. The storm passed—leaving him in the middle of a large, open field of rock.

The plateau in front of the tower city of Urithiru.

32

COMPANY

For I, of all people, have changed.

—From *Oathbringer*, preface

Shallan settled in Sebarial's sitting room. It was a strangely shaped stone chamber with a loft above—he sometimes put musicians there—and a shallow cavity in the floor, which he kept saying he was going to fill with water and fish. She was fairly certain he made claims like that just to annoy Dalinar with his supposed extravagance.

For now, they'd covered the hole with some boards, and Sebarial would periodically warn people not to step on them. The rest of the room was decorated lavishly. She was pretty sure she'd seen those tapestries in a monastery in Dalinar's warcamp, and they were matched by luxurious furniture, golden lamps, and ceramics.

And a bunch of splintery boards covering a pit. She shook her head. Then—curled up on a sofa with blankets heaped over her—she gladly accepted a cup of steaming citrus tea from Palona. She still hadn't been able to rid herself of the lingering chill she'd felt since her encounter with Re-Shephir a few hours back.

"Is there anything else I can get you?" Palona asked.

Shallan shook her head, so the Herdazian woman settled herself on a sofa nearby, holding another cup of tea. Shallan sipped, glad for the company. Adolin had wanted her to sleep, but the last thing she wanted was to be alone. He'd handed her over to Palona's care, then stayed with Dalinar and Navani to answer their further questions.

"So . . ." Palona said. "What was it like?"

How to answer *that*? She'd touched the storming *Midnight Mother*. A name from ancient lore, one of the Unmade, princes of the Voidbringers. People sang about Re-Shephir in poetry and epics, describing her as a dark, beautiful figure. Paintings depicted her as a black-clad woman with red eyes and a sultry gaze.

That seemed to exemplify how little they really remembered about these things.

"It wasn't like the stories," Shallan whispered. "Re-Shephir is a spren. A vast, terrible spren who wants so *desperately* to understand us. So she kills us, imitating our violence."

There was a deeper mystery beyond that, a wisp of something she'd glimpsed while intertwined with Re-Shephir. It made Shallan wonder if this spren wasn't merely trying to understand humankind, but rather searching for something *it itself had lost*.

Had this creature—in distant, distant time beyond memory—once been human?

They didn't know. They didn't know *anything*. At Shallan's first report, Navani had set her scholars searching for information, but their access to books here was still limited. Even with access to the Palanaeum, Shallan wasn't optimistic. Jasnah had hunted for years to find Urithiru, and even then most of what she'd discovered had been unreliable. It had simply been too many years.

"To think it was here, all this time," Palona said. "Hiding down there."

"She was captive," Shallan whispered. "She eventually escaped, but that was centuries ago. She has been waiting here ever since."

"Well, we should find where the others are held, and make sure *they* don't get out."

"I don't know if the others were ever captured." She'd felt isolation and loneliness from Re-Shephir, a sense of being torn away while the others escaped.

"So . . ."

"They're out there, and always have been," Shallan said. She felt exhausted, and her eyes were drooping in direct defiance of her insistence to Adolin that she was not *that* kind of tired.

"Surely we'd have discovered them by now."

"I don't know," Shallan said. "They'll . . . they'll just be normal to us. The way things have always been."

She yawned, then nodded absently as Palona continued talking, her comments degenerating into praise of Shallan for acting as she had. Adolin had been the same way, which she hadn't minded, and Dalinar had been downright nice to her—instead of being his usual stern rock of a human being.

She didn't tell them how near she'd come to breaking, and how terrified she was that she might someday meet that creature again.

But . . . maybe she did deserve some acclaim. She'd been a child when she'd left her home, seeking salvation for her family. For the first time since that day on the ship, watching Jah Keved fade behind her, she felt like she actually might have a handle on all of this. Like she might have found some stability in her life, some control over herself and her surroundings.

Remarkably, she *kind of* felt like an adult.

She smiled and snuggled into her blankets, drinking her tea and—for the moment—putting out of her mind that basically an entire troop of soldiers had seen her with her glove off. She was *kind of* an adult. She could deal with a little embarrassment. In fact, she was increasingly certain that between Shallan, Veil, and Radiant, she could deal with anything life could throw at her.

A disturbance outside made her sit up, though it didn't sound dangerous. Some chatter, a few boisterous exclamations. She wasn't terribly surprised when Adolin stepped in, bowed to Palona—he did have nice manners—and jogged over to her, his uniform still rumpled from having worn Shardplate over it.

"Don't panic," he said. "It's a good thing."

"It?" she said, growing alarmed.

"Well, someone just arrived at the tower."

"Oh, that. Sebarial passed the news; the bridgeboy is back."

"Him? No, that's not what I'm talking about." Adolin searched for words as voices approached, and several other people stepped into the room.

At their head was Jasnah Kholin.

THE END OF

Part One

INTERLUDES

PUULI • ELLISTA • VENLI

PUULI

P uuli the lighthouse keeper tried not to let everyone know how excited he was for this new storm.

It was truly tragic. Truly tragic. He told Sakin this as she wept. She had thought herself quite high and blessed when she'd landed her new husband. She'd moved into the man's fine stone hut in a prime spot for growing a garden, behind the northern cliffs of the town.

Puuli gathered scraps of wood blown eastward by the strange storm, and piled them in his little cart. He pulled it with two hands, leaving Sakin to weep for her husband. Up to three now, she was, all lost at sea. Truly tragic.

Still, he was excited for the storm.

He pulled his cart past other broken homes here, where they should have been sheltered west of the cliffs. Puuli's grandfather had been able to remember when those cliffs hadn't been there. Kelek himself had broken apart the land in the middle of a storm, making a new prime spot for homes.

Where would the rich people put their houses now?

And they did have rich people here in town, never mind what the travelers on the ocean said. Those would stop at this little port, on the crumbling eastern edge of Roshar, and shelter from storms in their cove alongside the cliffs.

Puuli pulled his cart past the cove. Here, one of the foreigner captains— with long eyebrows and tan skin, rather than the proper blue skin—was trying to make sense of her ruined ship. It had been rocked in the cove, struck by lightning, then smashed back against the stones. Now only the mast was visible.

Truly tragic, Puuli said. He complimented the captain on the mast though. It was a very nice mast.

Puuli picked up a few planks from the broken ship that had washed onto the shore of the cove, then threw them into his cart. Even if it had destroyed many a ship, Puuli was happy for this new storm. Secretly happy.

Had the time finally come, that his grandfather had warned of? The time of changes, when the men from the hidden island of the Origin at last came to reclaim Natanatan?

Even if not, this new storm brought him so much *wood*. Scraps of rock-buds, branches from trees. He gathered it all eagerly, piling his cart high, then pulled it past fishers in huddles, trying to decide how they'd survive in a world with storms from both directions. Fishers didn't sleep away the Weeping, like lazy farmers. They worked it, for there were no winds. Lots of bailing, but no winds. Until now.

A tragedy, he told Au-lam while helping him clear the refuse of his barn. Many of the boards ended up in Puuli's cart.

A tragedy, he agreed with Hema-Dak as he watched her children so she could run a broth to her sister, who was sick with the fever.

A tragedy, he told the Drummer brothers as he helped them pull a tattered sail from the surf and stretch it out on the rocks.

At last, Puuli finished his rounds and pulled his little cart up the long, twisting road toward Defiance. That was his name for the lighthouse. Nobody else called it that, because to them it was just the lighthouse.

At the top, he left out an offering of fruit for Kelek, the Herald who lived in the storm. Then he pulled his wagon into the room on the bottom floor. Defiance wasn't a tall lighthouse. He'd seen paintings of the sleek, fashionable ones down along Longbrow's Straits. Lighthouses for rich folks who sailed ships that didn't catch fish. Defiance was only two stories tall, and built squat like a bunker. But she had good stonework, and a buffer of crem on the outside kept her from leaking.

She'd stood for over a hundred years, and Kelek hadn't decided to knock her down. The Stormfather knew how important she was. Puuli carried a load of wet stormwood and broken boards up to the top of the lighthouse, where he set them out beside the fire—which burned low during the day—to dry. He dusted off his hands, then stepped up to the rim of the lighthouse. At night, the mirrors would shine the light right out through this hole.

He looked over the cliffs, to the east. His family was a lot like the lighthouse themselves. Squat, short, but powerful. And enduring.

They'll come with Light in their pockets, Grandfather had said. *They'll come to destroy, but you should watch for them anyway. Because they'll come from the Origin. The sailors lost on an infinite sea. You keep that fire high at night, Puuli. You burn it bright until the day they come.*

They'll arrive when the night is darkest.

Surely that was now, with a new storm. Darkest nights. A tragedy.

And a sign.

ELLISTA

The Jokasha Monastery was ordinarily a very quiet place. Nestled in the forests on the western slopes of the Horneater Peaks, the monastery felt only rain at the passing of a highstorm. Furious rain, yes, but none of the terrible violence known in most parts of the world.

Ellista reminded herself every passing storm how lucky she was. Some ardents had fought half their lives to be transferred to Jokasha. Away from politics, storms, and other annoyances, at Jokasha you could simply *think.*

Usually.

"Are you *looking* at these numbers? Are your eyes *disconnected* from your brain?"

"We can't judge yet. Three instances are not enough!"

"Two data points to make a coincidence, three to make a sequence. The Everstorm travels at a consistent speed, unlike the highstorm."

"You can't possibly say that! One of your data points, so highly touted, is from the original passing of the storm, which happened as an uncommon event."

Ellista slammed her book closed and stuffed it into her satchel. She burst from her reading nook and gave a glare to the two ardents arguing in the hall outside, both wearing the caps of master scholars. They were so involved in their shouting match that they didn't even respond to the glare, though it had been one of her best.

She bustled from the library, entering a long hallway with sides open to the elements. Peaceful trees. A quiet brook. Humid air and mossy vines that popped and stretched as they lay out for the evening. Well, yes, a large swath of trees out there *had* been flattened by the new storm. But that was no reason for everyone to get upset! The rest of the world could worry.

Here, at the central home of the Devotary of the Mind, she was supposed to be able to just read.

She set her things out at a reading desk near an open window. The humidity wasn't good for books, but weak storms went hand-in-hand with fecundity. You simply had to accept that. Hopefully those new fabrials to draw water from the air would—

". . . Telling you, we're going to have to move!" a new voice echoed through the hallway. "Look, the storm is going to ravage those woods. Before long, this slope will be barren, and the storm will be hitting us full force."

"The new storm doesn't have that strong a wind factor, Bettam. It's *not* going to blow down the trees. Have you looked at my measurements?"

"I've disputed those measurements."

"But—"

Ellista rubbed her temples. She wore her head shaved, like the other ardents. Her parents still joked that she'd joined the ardentia simply because she hated bothering with her hair. She tried earplugs, but could hear the arguing through them, so she packed up her things again.

Maybe the low building? She took the long set of steps outside, traveling down the slope along a forested path. Before arriving at the monastery for the first time, she'd had illusions about what it would be like to live among scholars. No bickering. No politicking. She hadn't found that to be true—but generally people left her alone. And so she was lucky to be here. She told herself that again as she entered the lower building.

It was basically a zoo. Dozens of people gathering information from spanreeds, talking to one another, buzzing with talk of this or that highprince or king. She stopped in the doorway, took it all in for a moment, then turned on her heel and stalked back out.

Now what? She started back up the steps, but slowed. *It's probably the only route to peace* . . . she thought, looking out into the forest.

Trying not to think about the dirt, the cremlings, and the fact that something might drip on her head, she strode off into the forest. She didn't want to go too far, as who knew what might be out here? She chose a stump without *too* much moss on it and settled down among bobbing lifespren, book across her lap.

She could still hear ardents arguing, but they were distant. She opened her book, intent on finally getting something done today.

Wema spun away from Brightlord Sterling's forward advances, tucking her safehand to her breast and lowering her gaze from his comely locks. Such affection as to excite the unsavory mind could surely not satisfy her for an extended period, as though his attentions had at one time been fanciful delights to entertain her leisure hours, they now seemed to manifest his utmost impudence and greatest faults of character.

"What!" Ellista exclaimed, reading. "No, you silly girl! He's finally pronounced his affection for you. Don't you dare turn away now."

How could she accept this wanton justification of her once single-minded desires? Should she not, instead, select the more prudent choice, as advocated by the undeviating will of her uncle? Brightlord Vadam had an endowment of land upon the highprince's grace, and would have means to provide far beyond the satisfactions available to a simple officer, no matter how well regarded or what winds had graced his temperament, features, and gentle touch.

Ellista gasped. "Brightlord *Vadam*? You little whore! Have you forgotten how he locked away your father?"

"Wema," Brightlord Sterling intoned, "it seems I have gravely misjudged your attentions. In this, I find myself deposited deep within an embarrassment of folly. I shall be away, to the Shattered Plains, and you shall not again suffer the torment of my presence."

He bowed a true gentleman's bow, possessed of all proper refinement and deference. It was a supplication beyond what even a monarch could rightly demand, and in it Wema ascertained the true nature of Brightlord Sterling's regard. Simple, yet passionate. Respectful in deed. It lent great context to his earlier advance, which now appeared all at once to be a righteous division in otherwise sure armor, a window of vulnerability, rather than a model of avarice.

As he lifted the door's latch to forever make his exodus from her life, Wema surged with unrivaled shame and longing, twisted together not unlike two threads winding in a loom to construct a grand tapestry of desire.

"Wait!" Wema cried. "Dear Sterling, wait upon my words."

"Storms right you'd better wait, Sterling." Ellista leaned closer to the book, flipping the page.

Decorum seemed a vain thing to her now, lost upon the sea that was her need to feel Sterling's touch. She rushed to him, and upon his arm pressed her ensleeved hand, which then she lifted to caress his sturdy jaw.

It was so warm out here in the forest. Practically sweltering. Ellista put her hand to her lips, reading with wide eyes, trembling.

Would that the window through that statuesque armor could still be located, and that a similar wound within herself might be found, to press against his own and offer passage deep within her soul. If only—

"Ellista?" a voice asked.

"Yip!" she said, bolting upright, snapping the book closed, and spun toward the sound. "Um. Oh! Ardent Urv." The young Siln ardent was tall, gangly, and obnoxiously loud at times. Except, apparently, when sneaking up on colleagues in the forest.

"What was that you were studying?" he asked.

"Important works," Ellista said, then sat on the book. "Nothing to mind yourself with. What is it you want?"

"Um . . ." He looked down at her satchel. "You were the last one to check out the transcriptions from Bendthel's collected Dawnchant? The old versions? I just wanted to check on your progress."

Dawnchant. Right. They'd been working on that before this storm came, and everyone got distracted. Old Navani Kholin, in Alethkar, had somehow cracked the Dawnchant. Her story about visions was nonsense—the Kholin family was known for opaque politics—but her key was authentic, and had let them slowly work through the old texts.

Ellista started digging in her satchel. She came up with three musty codices and a sheaf of papers, the latter being the work she'd done so far.

Annoyingly, Urv settled on the ground beside her stump, taking the papers as she offered them. He laid his satchel across his lap and began reading.

"Incredible," he said a few moments later. "You've made more progress than I have."

"Everyone else is too busy worrying about that storm."

"Well, it *is* threatening to wipe out civilization."

"An overreaction. Everyone always overreacts to every little gust of wind."

He flipped through her pages. "What's this section? Why take such care for where each text was found? Fiksin concluded that these Dawnchant books had all spread from a central location, and so there's nothing to learn by where they ended up."

"Fiksin was a boot-licker, not a scholar," Ellista said. "Look, there's *easy* proof here that the same writing system was once used all across Roshar. I have references in Makabakam, Sela Tales, Alethela . . . Not a diaspora of texts, but real evidence they wrote naturally in the Dawnchant."

"Do you suppose they all spoke the same language?"

"Hardly."

"But Jasnah Kholin's *Relic and Monument*?"

"Doesn't claim everyone spoke the same language, only that they wrote it. It's foolish to assume that everyone used the same language across hundreds of years and dozens of nations. It makes more sense that there was a codified *written* language, the language of scholarship, just like you'll find many undertexts written in Alethi now."

"Ah . . ." he said. "And then a Desolation hit. . . ."

Ellista nodded, showing him a later page in her sheaf of notes. "This in-between, weird language is where people started using the Dawnchant script to *phonetically* transcribe their language. It didn't work so well." She flipped two more pages. "In this scrap we have one of the earliest emergences of the proto-Thaylo-Vorin glyphic radicals, and here is one showing a more intermediate Thaylen form.

"We've always wondered what happened to the Dawnchant. How could people forget how to read their own language? Well, it seems clear now. By the point this happened, the language had been moribund for millennia. They weren't speaking it, and hadn't been for generations."

"Brilliant," Urv said. He wasn't so bad, for a Siln. "I've been translating what I can, but got stuck on the Covad Fragment. If what you've been doing here is correct, it might be because Covad isn't true Dawnchant, but a phonetic transcription of another ancient language. . . ."

He glanced to the side, then cocked his head. Was he looking at her—

Oh, no. It was just the book, which she was still sitting on.

"An Accountability of Virtue." He grunted. "Good book."

"You've *read* it?"

"I have a fondness for Alethi epics," he said absently, flipping through her pages. "She really should have picked Vadam though. Sterling was a flatterer and a cadger."

"Sterling is a noble and upright officer!" She narrowed her eyes. "And *you* are just trying to get a rise out of me, Ardent Urv."

"Maybe." He flipped through her pages, studying a diagram she'd made of various Dawnchant grammars. "I have a copy of the sequel."

"There's a *sequel*?"

"About her sister."

"The mousy one?"

"She is elevated to courtly attention and has to choose between a strapping naval officer, a Thaylen banker, and the King's Wit."

"Wait. There are *three* different men this time?"

"Sequels always have to be bigger," he said, then offered her the stack of pages back. "I'll lend it to you."

"Oh you will, will you? And what is the cost for this magnanimous gesture, Brightlord Urv?"

"Your help translating a stubborn section of Dawnchant. A particular patron of mine has a strict deadline upon its delivery."

I-3

THE RHYTHM OF THE LOST

Venli attuned the Rhythm of Craving as she climbed down into the chasm. This wondrous new form, stormform, gave her hands a powerful grip, allowing her to hang hundreds of feet in the air, yet never fear that she would fall.

The chitin plating under her skin was far less bulky than that of the old warform, but at the same time nearly as effective. During the summoning of the Everstorm, a human soldier had struck her directly across the face. His spear had cut her cheek and across the bridge of her nose, but the mask of chitin armor underneath had deflected the weapon.

She continued to climb down the wall of stone, followed by Demid, her once-mate, and a group of her loyal friends. In her mind she attuned the Rhythm of Command—a similar, yet more powerful version of the Rhythm of Appreciation. Every one of her people could hear the rhythms—beats with some tones attached—yet she no longer heard the old, common ones. Only these new, superior rhythms.

Beneath her the chasm opened, where water from highstorms had carved a bulge. She eventually reached the bottom, and the others dropped around her, each landing with a thumping crunch. Ulim moved down the stone wall; the spren usually took the form of rolling lightning, moving across surfaces.

At the bottom, he formed from lightning into a human shape with odd eyes. Ulim settled on a patch of broken branches, arms folded, his long hair rippling in an unseen wind. She wasn't certain why a spren sent by Odium himself would look human.

"Around here somewhere," Ulim said, pointing. "Spread out and search."

Venli set her jaw, humming to the Rhythm of Fury. Lines of power rippled up her arms. "Why should I continue to obey your orders, spren? You should obey *me*."

The spren ignored her, which further stoked her anger. Demid, however, placed his hand on her shoulder and squeezed, humming to the Rhythm of Satisfaction. "Come, look with me this way."

She curtailed her humming and turned south, joining Demid, picking her way through debris. Crem buildup had smoothed the floor of the chasm, but the storm had left a great deal of refuse.

She attuned the Rhythm of Craving. A quick, violent rhythm. "I should be in charge, Demid. Not that spren."

"You are in charge."

"Then why haven't we been told anything? Our gods have returned, yet we've barely seen them. We sacrificed greatly for these forms, and to create the glorious true storm. We . . . we lost how many?"

Sometimes she thought about that, in strange moments when the new rhythms seemed to retreat. All of her work, meeting with Ulim in secret, guiding her people toward stormform. It had been about *saving* her people, hadn't it? Yet of the tens of thousands of listeners who had fought to summon the storm, only a fraction remained.

Demid and she had been scholars. Yet even scholars had gone to battle. She felt at the wound on her face.

"Our sacrifice was worthwhile," Demid told her to the Rhythm of Derision. "Yes, we have lost many, but humans sought our extinction. At least this way some of our people survived, and now we have great power!"

He was right. And, if she was being honest, a form of power was what she had always wanted. And she'd achieved one, capturing a spren in the storm within herself. That hadn't been one of Ulim's species, of course— lesser spren were used for changing forms. She could occasionally feel the pulsing, deep within, of the one she'd bonded.

In any case, this transformation had given her great power. The good of her people had always been secondary to Venli; now was a late time to be having a bout of conscience.

She resumed humming to Craving. Demid smiled and gripped her shoulder again. They'd shared something once, during their days in mateform. Those silly, distracting passions were not ones they currently felt, nor were they something that any sane listener would desire. But the memories of them did create a bond.

They picked through the refuse, passing several fresh human corpses, smashed into a cleft in the rock. Good to see those. Good to remember that her people had killed many, despite their losses.

"Venli!" Demid said. "Look!" He scrambled over a log from a large wooden bridge that was wedged in the center of the chasm. She followed, pleased by her strength. She would probably always remember Demid as the gangly scholar he had been before this change, but she doubted either of them would ever willingly return. Forms of power were simply too intoxicating.

Once across the log, she could see what Demid had spotted: a figure slumped by the wall of the chasm, helmeted head bowed. A Shardblade—shaped like frozen flames—rose from the ground beside her, rammed into the stone floor.

"Eshonai! Finally!" Venli leaped from the top of the log, landing near Demid.

Eshonai looked exhausted. In fact, she wasn't moving.

"Eshonai?" Venli said, kneeling beside her sister. "Are you well? Eshonai?" She gripped the Plated figure by the shoulders and lightly shook it.

The head rolled on its neck, limp.

Venli felt cold. Demid solemnly lifted Eshonai's faceplate, revealing dead eyes set in an ashen face.

Eshonai . . . no . . .

"Ah," Ulim's voice said. "Excellent." The spren approached across the stone wall, like crackling lightning moving through the stone. "Demid, your hand."

Demid obediently raised his hand, palm up, and Ulim shot across from the wall to the hand, then formed into his human shape, standing on the perch. "Hmmm. Plate looks completely drained. Broken along the back, I see. Well, it's said to regrow on its own, even now that it is separated from its master from so long ago."

"The . . . Plate," Venli said softly, numb. "You wanted the Plate."

"Well, the Blade too, of course. Why else would we be hunting a corpse? You . . . Oh, you thought she was *alive*?"

"When you said we needed to find my sister," Venli said, "I thought . . ."

"Yes, looks like she drowned in the storm's floodwaters," Ulim said, making a sound like a tongue clicking. "Rammed the sword into the stone, held on to it to stay in place, but couldn't breathe."

Venli attuned the Rhythm of the Lost.

It was one of the old, inferior rhythms. She hadn't been able to find those since transforming, and she had no idea how she happened upon this one. The mournful, solemn tone felt distant to her.

"Eshonai . . . ?" she whispered, and nudged the corpse again. Demid gasped. Touching the bodies of the fallen was taboo. The old songs spoke of days when humans had hacked apart listener corpses, searching for gemhearts. Leave the dead to peace instead; it was their way.

Venli stared into Eshonai's dead eyes. *You were the voice of reason*, Venli thought. *You were the one who argued with me. You . . . you were supposed to keep me grounded.*

What do I do without you?

"Well, let's get that Plate off, kids," Ulim said.

"Show respect!" Venli snapped.

"Respect for what? It's for the best that this one died."

"For the best?" Venli said. "For the *best*?" She stood, confronting the little spren on Demid's outstretched palm. "That is my sister. She is one of our greatest warriors. An inspiration, and a martyr."

Ulim rolled his head in an exaggerated way, as if perturbed—and bored—by the chastisement. How *dare* he! He was merely a spren. He was to be her *servant*.

"Your sister," Ulim said, "didn't undergo the transformation properly. She resisted, and we'd have eventually lost her. She was never dedicated to our cause."

Venli attuned the Rhythm of Fury, speaking in a loud, punctuating sequence. "You will not say such things. You are spren! You are to serve."

"And I do."

"Then you must obey me!"

"You?" Ulim laughed. "Child, how long have you been fighting your little war against the humans? Three, four years?"

"Six years, spren," Demid said. "Six long, bloody years."

"Well, do you want to guess how long *we've* been fighting this war?" Ulim asked. "Go ahead. Guess. I'm waiting."

Venli seethed. "It doesn't matter—"

"Oh, but it does," Ulim said, his red figure electrifying. "Do you know how to lead armies, Venli? *True* armies? Supply troops across a battlefront that spans hundreds of miles? Do you have memories and experiences that span eons?"

She glared at him.

"Our leaders," Ulim said, "know exactly what they're doing. Them I obey. But *I* am the one who escaped, the spren of redemption. I don't have to listen to you."

"I will be a queen," Venli said to Spite.

"If you survive? Maybe. But your sister? She and the others sent that assassin to kill the human king *specifically* to keep us from returning. Your people are traitors—though your personal efforts do you justice, Venli. You may be blessed further, if you are wise. Regardless, get that armor off your sister, shed your tears, and get ready to climb back up. These plateaus are crawling with men who stink of Honor. We must be away and see what your ancestors need us to do."

"Our ancestors?" Demid said. "What do the dead have to do with this?"

"Everything," Ulim replied, "seeing as they're the ones in charge. Armor. *Now.*" He zipped to the wall as a tiny streak of lightning, then moved off.

Venli attuned Derision at the way she'd been treated, then—defying taboos—helped Demid remove the Shardplate. Ulim returned with the others and ordered them to gather up the armor.

They hiked off, leaving Venli to bring the Blade. She lifted it from the stone, then lingered, regarding her sister's corpse—which lay there in only padded underclothing.

Venli felt something stir inside her. Again, distantly, she was able to hear the Rhythm of the Lost. Mournful, slow, with separated beats.

"I . . ." Venli said. "Finally, I don't have to listen to you call me a fool. I don't have to worry about you getting in the way. I can do what I want."

That terrified her.

She turned to go, but paused as she saw something. What was that small spren that had crept out from beneath Eshonai's corpse? It looked like a small ball of white fire; it gave off little rings of light and trailed a streak behind it. Like a comet.

"What are you?" Venli demanded to Spite. "Shoo."

She hiked off, leaving her sister's corpse there at the bottom of the chasm, stripped and alone. Food for either a chasmfiend or a storm.

PART
TWO

New Beginnings Sing

SHALLAN • JASNAH • DALINAR •
BRIDGE FOUR

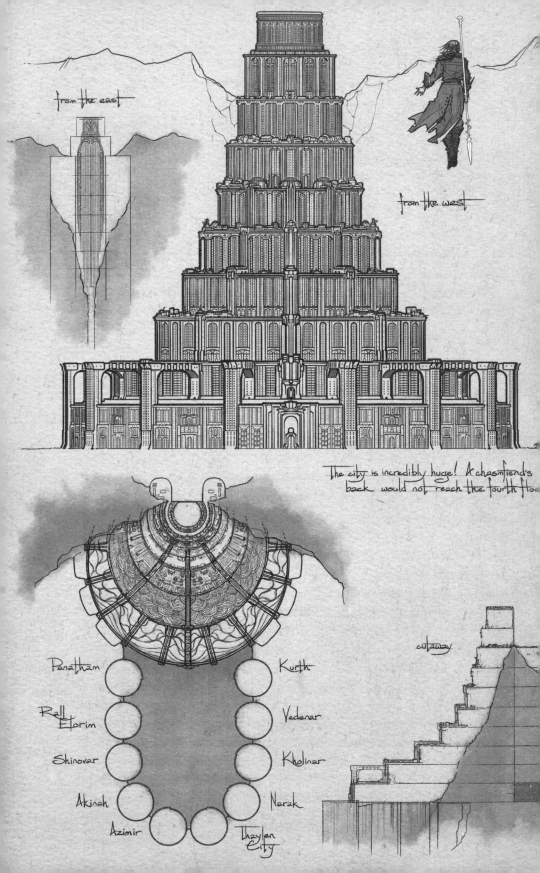

from the east

from the west

The city is incredibly huge! A chasmfiend's back would not reach the fourth floor

cutaway

Panatham

Rall Elorim

Shinovar

Akinah

Azimir

Kurth

Vedenar

Kholinar

Narak

Thaylen City

33

A LECTURE

Dearest Cephandrius,
I received your communication, of course.

Jasnah was alive.

Jasnah Kholin was *alive*.

Shallan was supposed to be recovering from her ordeal, never mind that the bridgemen had handled the fighting. All she'd done was grope an eldritch spren. Still, she spent the next day holed up in her room sketching and thinking.

Jasnah's return sparked something in her. Shallan had once been more analytical in her drawing, including notes and explanations with the sketches. Lately she'd only been doing pages and pages of twisted images.

Well, she'd been trained as a scholar, hadn't she? She shouldn't just draw; she should analyze, extrapolate, speculate. So, she addressed herself to fully recording her experiences with the Unmade.

Adolin and Palona visited her separately, and even Dalinar came to check on her while Navani clicked her tongue and asked after her health. Shallan endured their company, then eagerly returned to her drawing. There were so many questions. Why exactly had she been able to drive the thing away? What was the meaning of its creations?

Hanging over her research, however, was a single daunting fact. Jasnah was alive.

Storms . . . Jasnah was alive.

That changed *everything*.

Eventually, Shallan couldn't remain locked up any longer. Though Navani mentioned Jasnah was planning to visit her later in the evening,

Shallan washed and dressed, then threw her satchel over her shoulder and went searching for the woman. She had to know *how* Jasnah had survived.

In fact, as Shallan stalked the hallways of Urithiru, she found herself increasingly perturbed. Jasnah claimed to always look at things from a logical perspective, but she had a flair for the dramatic to rival any story-teller. Shallan well remembered that night in Kharbranth when Jasnah had lured thieves in, then dealt with them in stunning—and brutal—fashion.

Jasnah didn't want to merely prove her points. She wanted to drive them right into your skull, with a flourish and a pithy epigram. Why hadn't she written via spanreed to let everyone know she had survived? Storms, where had she *been* all this time?

A few inquiries led Shallan back to the pit with its spiraling stairs. Guards in sharp Kholin blue confirmed that Jasnah was below, so Shallan started trudging down those steps again, and was surprised to find that she felt no anxiety at the descent. In fact . . . the oppressive feelings she'd felt since they'd arrived at the tower seemed to have evaporated. No more fear, no more formless sense of wrongness. The thing she'd chased away had been its cause. Somehow, its aura had pervaded the entire tower.

At the base of the stairs, she found more soldiers. Dalinar obviously wanted this place well guarded; she certainly couldn't complain about that. These let her pass without incident, save a bow and a murmur of "Bright-ness Radiant."

She strode down the muraled hallway, the sphere lanterns set along the base of the walls making it pleasingly bright. Once she'd passed the empty library rooms to either side, she heard voices drifting toward her from ahead. She stepped up into the room where she'd faced the Midnight Mother, and got her first good look at the place when it *wasn't* covered in writhing darkness.

The crystal pillar at the center really was something incredible. It wasn't a single gemstone, but a myriad of them fused together: emerald, ruby, topaz, sapphire . . . All ten varieties seemed to have been melted into a single thick pillar, twenty feet tall. Storms . . . what would it look like if all those gems were somehow *infused*, rather than dun as they were at the moment?

A large group of guards stood at a barricade near the other side of the room, looking down into the tunnel where the Unmade had vanished. Jasnah rounded the giant pillar, freehand resting on the crystal. The princess wore red, lips painted to match, hair up and run through with swordlike hair-spikes with rubies on the pommels.

Storms. She was perfect. A curvaceous figure, tan Alethi skin, light vi-olet eyes, and not a hint of aberrant color to her jet-black hair. Making

Jasnah Kholin as beautiful as she was brilliant was one of the most unfair things the Almighty had ever done.

Shallan hesitated in the doorway, feeling much as she had upon seeing Jasnah for the first time in Kharbranth. Insecure, overwhelmed, and—if she was honest—incredibly envious. Whatever ordeals Jasnah had been through, she looked no worse for wear. That was remarkable, considering that the last time Shallan had seen Jasnah, the woman had been lying unconscious on the floor while a man rammed a knife through her chest.

"My mother," Jasnah said, hand still on the pillar, not looking toward Shallan, "thinks this must be some kind of incredibly intricate fabrial. A logical assumption; we've always believed that the ancients had access to great and wonderful technology. How else do you explain Shardblades and Shardplate?"

"Brightness?" Shallan said. "But . . . Shardblades aren't fabrials. They're spren, transformed by the bond."

"As are fabrials, after a manner of speaking," Jasnah said. "You do know how they're made, don't you?"

"Only vaguely," Shallan said. This was how their reunion went? A lecture? *Fitting.*

"You capture a spren," Jasnah said, "and imprison it inside a gemstone crafted for the purpose. Artifabrians have found that specific stimuli will provoke certain responses in the spren. For example, flamespren give off heat—and by pressing metal against a ruby with a flamespren trapped inside, you can increase or decrease that heat."

"That's . . ."

"Incredible?"

"*Horrible,*" Shallan said. She'd known some of this, but to contemplate it directly appalled her. "Brightness, we're *imprisoning* spren?"

"No worse than hitching a wagon to a chull."

"Sure, if in order to get a chull to pull a wagon, you first had to lock it in a box forever."

Pattern hummed softly from her skirts in agreement.

Jasnah just cocked an eyebrow. "There are spren and there are spren, child." She rested her fingers on the pillar again. "Do a sketch of this for me. Be certain to get the proportions and colors right, if you please."

The careless presumption of the command hit Shallan like a slap in the face. What was she, some servant to be given orders?

Yes, a part of her affirmed. *That's* exactly *what you are. You're Jasnah's ward.* The request wasn't at all unusual in that light, but compared to how she had grown accustomed to being treated, it was . . .

Well, it wasn't worth taking offense at, and she should accept that.

Storms, when had she grown so touchy? She took out her sketchpad and got to work.

"I was heartened to hear that you had made it here on your own," Jasnah said. "I . . . apologize for what happened on *Wind's Pleasure*. My lack of foresight caused the deaths of many, and doubtless hardship for you, Shallan. Please accept my regret."

Shallan shrugged, sketching.

"You've done *very* well," Jasnah continued. "Imagine my amazement when I reached the Shattered Plains, only to discover that the warcamp had already relocated to this tower. What you have accomplished is brilliant, child. We will need to speak further, however, about the group that again tried to assassinate me. The Ghostbloods will almost certainly start targeting you, now that you've begun progressing toward your final Ideals."

"You're sure it was the Ghostbloods that attacked the ship?"

"Of course I am." She glanced at Shallan, lips turning down. "Are you certain you are well enough to be about, child? You seem uncharacteristically reserved."

"I'm fine."

"You're displeased because of the secrets I kept."

"We all need secrets, Brightness. I know this more than anyone. But it would have been nice if you had let us know you were alive." *Here I was assuming I could handle things on my own—assuming I'd have to handle things on my own. But all that time, you were on your way back to toss everything into the air again.*

"I only had the opportunity upon reaching the warcamps," Jasnah said, "and there decided that I couldn't risk it. I was tired and unprotected. If the Ghostbloods wished to finish me off, they could have done so at their leisure. I determined that a few more days of everyone believing I was dead would not greatly increase their distress."

"But how did you even survive in the first place?"

"Child, I'm an Elsecaller."

"Of course. An Elsecaller, Brightness. A thing you never explained; a word which no one but the most dedicated scholar of the esoteric would recognize! That explains it perfectly."

Jasnah smiled for some reason.

"All Radiants have an attachment to Shadesmar," Jasnah said. "Our spren originate there, and our bond ties us to them. But my order has special control over moving between realms. I was able to shift to Shadesmar to escape my would-be assassins."

"And that helped with the knife in your storming chest?"

"No," Jasnah said. "But surely by now you've learned the value of a little Stormlight when it comes to bodily wounds?"

Of course she had, and she could probably have guessed all of this. But for some reason she didn't want to accept that. She wanted to remain annoyed at Jasnah.

"My true difficulty was not escaping, but *returning*," Jasnah said. "My powers make it easy to transfer to Shadesmar, but getting back to this realm is no small feat. I had to find a transfer point—a place where Shadesmar and our realm touch—which is far, far more difficult than one might assume. It's like . . . going downhill one way, but uphill to get back."

Well, perhaps her return would take some pressure off Shallan. Jasnah could be "Brightness Radiant" and Shallan could be . . . well, whatever she was.

"We will need to converse further," Jasnah said. "I would hear the exact story, from your perspective, of the discovery of Urithiru. And I assume you have sketches of the transformed parshmen? That will tell us much. I . . . believe I once disparaged the usefulness of your artistic skill. I now find reason to call myself foolish for that presumption."

"It's fine, Brightness," Shallan said with a sigh, still sketching the pillar. "I can get you those things, and there *is* a lot to talk about." But how much of it would she be able to say? How would Jasnah react, for instance, to finding that Shallan had been dealing with the Ghostbloods?

It's not like you're really a part of their organization, Shallan thought to herself. *If anything, you're using* them *for information.* Jasnah might find that admirable.

Shallan still wasn't eager to broach the topic.

"I feel lost . . ." Jasnah said.

Shallan looked up from her sketchbook to find the woman regarding the pillar again, speaking softly, as if to herself.

"For years I was at the very forefront of all this," Jasnah said. "One short stumble, and I find myself scrambling to stay afloat. These visions that my uncle is having . . . the refounding of the Radiants in my absence . . .

"That Windrunner. What do you think of him, Shallan? I find him much as I imagined his order, but I have only met him once. It has all come so quickly. After years of struggling in the shadows, everything coming to light—and despite my years of study—I understand so very little."

Shallan continued her sketch. It was nice to be reminded that, for all their differences, there were occasional things that she and Jasnah shared.

She just wished that ignorance weren't at the top of the list.

34

RESISTANCE

I noticed its arrival immediately, just as I noticed your many intrusions into my land.

I<small>T IS TIME</small>, the Stormfather said.

All went dark around Dalinar, and he entered a place between his world and the visions. A place with a black sky and an infinite floor of bone-white rock. Shapes made of smoke seeped through the stone ground, then rose around him, dissipating. Common things. A chair, a vase, a rockbud. Sometimes people.

I <small>HAVE HER</small>. The Stormfather's voice shook this place, eternal and vast. T<small>HE</small> T<small>HAYLEN</small> <small>QUEEN</small>. M<small>Y STORM HITS HER CITY NOW</small>.

"Good," Dalinar said. "Please give her the vision."

Fen was to see the vision with the Knights Radiant falling from the sky, come to deliver a small village from a strange and monstrous force. Dalinar wanted her to see the Knights Radiant firsthand, as they had once been. Righteous, protecting.

W<small>HERE SHALL</small> I <small>PUT HER</small>? the Stormfather asked.

"The same place you put me my first time," Dalinar said. "In the home. With the family."

A<small>ND YOU</small>?

"I'll observe, then talk to her after."

Y<small>OU MUST BE PART OF EVENTS</small>, the Stormfather said, sounding stubborn. Y<small>OU MUST TAKE THE ROLE OF SOMEONE</small>. T<small>HIS IS HOW IT WORKS</small>.

"Fine. Pick someone. But if possible, make Fen see me as myself, and let me see her." He felt at the side sword he wore at his belt. "And can you let me keep this? I'd rather not have to fight with a poker again."

The Stormfather rumbled in annoyance, but did not object. The place of endless white stone faded.

"What was that place?" Dalinar asked.

IT IS NO PLACE.

"But everything else in these visions is real," Dalinar said. "So why is it that—"

IT IS NO PLACE, the Stormfather insisted firmly.

Dalinar fell silent, letting himself be taken by the vision.

I IMAGINED IT, the Stormfather said more softly, as if he were admitting something embarrassing. ALL THINGS HAVE A SOUL. A VASE, A WALL, A CHAIR. AND WHEN A VASE IS BROKEN, IT MIGHT DIE IN THE PHYSICAL REALM, BUT FOR A TIME ITS SOUL REMEMBERS WHAT IT WAS. SO ALL THINGS DIE TWICE. ITS FINAL DEATH IS WHEN MEN FORGET IT WAS A VASE, AND THINK ONLY OF THE PIECES. I IMAGINE THE VASE FLOATING AWAY THEN, ITS FORM DISSOLVING INTO THE NOTHINGNESS.

Dalinar had never heard anything so philosophical from the Stormfather. He hadn't imagined it was possible that a spren—even a mighty one of the highstorms—could dream in such a way.

Dalinar found himself hurtling through the air.

Flailing his arms, he shouted in panic. First moon's violet light bathed the ground far below. His stomach lurched and his clothes flapped in the wind. He continued yelling until he realized that he wasn't actually getting closer to the ground.

He *wasn't* falling, he was *flying*. The air was rushing against the top of his head, not his face. Indeed, now he saw that his body was glowing, Stormlight streaming off him. He didn't feel like he was holding it though—no raging inside his veins, no urge to action.

He shielded his face from the wind and looked forward. A Radiant flew ahead, resplendent in blue armor that glowed, the light brightest at the edges and in the grooves. The man was looking back at Dalinar, doubtless because of his cries.

Dalinar saluted him to indicate he was all right. The armored man nodded, looking forward again.

He's a Windrunner, Dalinar thought, piecing it together. *I've taken the place of his companion, a female Radiant.* He'd seen these two in the vision before; they were flying to save the village. Dalinar wasn't moving under his own power—the Windrunner had Lashed the female Radiant into the sky, as Szeth had done to Dalinar during the Battle of Narak.

It was still difficult to accept that he wasn't falling, and a sinking feeling persisted in the pit of his stomach. He tried to focus on other things. He was wearing an unfamiliar brown uniform, though he was glad to note that he had his side sword as requested. But why didn't he have on Shardplate?

In the vision, the woman had worn a set that glowed amber. Was this the result of the Stormfather trying to make him look like himself to Fen?

Dalinar still didn't know why Radiant Plate glowed, while modern Shardplate did not. Was the ancient Plate "living" somehow, like Radiant Blades lived?

Perhaps he could find out from that Radiant ahead. He had to ask his questions carefully, however. Everyone would see Dalinar as the Radiant he had replaced, and if his questions were uncharacteristic, that tended only to confuse people, rather than get him answers.

"How far away are we?" Dalinar asked. The sound was lost in the wind, so he shouted it more loudly, drawing the attention of his companion.

"Not long now," the man shouted back, voice echoing inside his helm, which glowed blue—most strongly at the edges and across the eye slit.

"I think something might be wrong with my armor!" Dalinar shouted to him. "I can't make my helm retract!"

In response, the other Radiant made his vanish. Dalinar caught sight of a puff of Light or mist.

Beneath the helm, the man had dark skin and curly black hair. His eyes glowed blue. "Retract your helm?" he shouted. "You haven't summoned your armor yet; you had to dismiss it so I could Lash you."

Oh, Dalinar thought. "I mean earlier. It wouldn't vanish when I wanted it to."

"Talk to Harkaylain then, or to your spren." The Windrunner frowned. "Will this be a problem for our mission?"

"I don't know," Dalinar shouted. "But it distracted me. Tell me again how we know where to go, and what we know of the things we're going to fight?" He winced at how awkward that sounded.

"Just be ready to back me up against the Midnight Essence, and use Regrowth on any wounded."

"But—"

You will find difficulty getting useful answers, Son of Honor, the Stormfather rumbled. *These do not have souls or minds. They are re-creations forged by Honor's will, and do not have the memories of the real people.*

"Surely we can learn things," Dalinar said under his breath.

They were created to convey only certain ideas. Further pressing will merely reveal the thinness of the facade.

This brought up memories of the fake city Dalinar had visited in his first vision, the destroyed version of Kholinar that was more prop than reality. But there *had* to be things he could learn, things that Honor might not have intended, but had included by chance.

I need to get Navani and Jasnah in here, he thought. *Let them pick at these*

re-creations.

Last time in this vision, Dalinar had taken the place of a man named Heb: a husband and father who had defended his family with only a fireplace poker for a weapon. He remembered his frantic struggle with a beast of oily, midnight skin. He had fought, bled, agonized. He'd spent what seemed like an eternity trying—and eventually failing—to protect his wife and daughter.

Such a personal memory. False though it was, he had *lived* it. In fact, seeing the small town ahead—in the lait created by a large ridge of rock—made emotions well up inside Dalinar. It was a painful irony that he should have such vivid feelings about this place, these people, when his memories of Evi were still so shadowy and confused.

The Windrunner slowed Dalinar by grabbing his arm. They drew to a stop in midair, hovering above the rocky flats outside the village.

"There." The Windrunner pointed to the field around the town, where weird black creatures were swarming. About the size of an axehound, they had oily skin that reflected the moonlight. While they moved on all sixes, they were like no natural animal. They had spindly legs like a crab's, but a bulbous body and a sinuous head, featureless except for a slit of a mouth bristling with black teeth.

Shallan had faced the source of these things deep beneath Urithiru. Dalinar had slept a little less secure each night since, knowing that one of the Unmade had been hidden in the bowels of the tower. Were the other eight similarly lurking nearby?

"I'll go down first," the Windrunner said, "and draw their attention. You make for the town and help the people there." The man pressed his hand against Dalinar. "You'll drop in about thirty seconds."

The man's helm materialized, then he plunged toward the monsters. Dalinar remembered that descent from the vision—like a falling star come to rescue Dalinar and the family.

"How," Dalinar whispered to the Stormfather. "How do we get the armor?"

Speak the Words.

"Which words?"

You will know or you will not.

Great.

Dalinar saw no sign of Taffa or Seeli—the family he'd protected—below. In his version they'd been out here, but their flight had been his doing. He couldn't be sure how the vision had played out this time.

Storms. He hadn't planned this very well, had he? In his mind's eye, he'd anticipated getting to Queen Fen and helping her along, making sure she wasn't in too much danger. Instead, he'd wasted time flying here.

Stupid. He needed to learn to be more specific with the Stormfather.

Dalinar began to descend in a controlled float. He had some idea of how the Windrunner Surges worked together, but he was impressed none-theless. Just as he touched down, the feeling of lightness left him and the Stormlight rising from his skin puffed away. This left him as much less of a target in the darkness than the other Radiant, who glowed like a bril-liant blue beacon, sweeping about himself with a grand Shardblade as he fought the Midnight Essence.

Dalinar crept through the town, his common side sword feeling frail compared to a Shardblade—but at least it wasn't an iron poker. Some of the creatures scrambled by on the main thoroughfare, but Dalinar hid beside a boulder until they passed.

He easily identified the proper house, which had a small barn out back, nestled against the stone cliff that sheltered the town. He crept up, and found that the barn wall had been ripped open. He remembered hiding in there with Seeli, then fleeing as a monster attacked.

The barn was empty, so he headed for the house, which was much finer. Made of crem bricks, and larger, though it seemed only one family lived in it. For a house this big, that would be an oddity, wouldn't it? Space was at a premium in laits.

Some of his assumptions obviously didn't hold in this era. In Alethkar, a fine wooden mansion would be a symbol of wealth. Here, however, many of the other houses were of wood.

Dalinar slipped into the house, feeling increasingly worried. Fen's real body couldn't be harmed by what happened in the vision, but she could still feel pain. So while the injuries might not be real, her anger at Dalinar certainly would be. He could ruin any chance of her listening to him.

She's already given up on listening, he assured himself. Navani agreed—this vision couldn't make things worse.

He felt in his uniform's pocket, and was pleased to find some gem-stones. A Radiant would have Stormlight. He took out a small diamond the size of a pebble and used its white light to inspect the room. The table had been overturned, chairs scattered. The door hung open and creaked softly in a breeze.

There was no sign of Queen Fen, but Taffa's body lay facedown near the hearth. She wore a single-piece brown dress, now in tatters. Dalinar sighed, sheathing his sword and kneeling to gently touch her back in a spot un-raked by monster claws.

It's not real, he told himself, *not now. This woman lived and died thousands of years ago.*

It still hurt to see her. He walked to the swinging door and stepped outside into the night, where howls and cries rang out from the town.

He strode quickly down the roadway, feeling a sense of urgency. No . . . not just urgency, impatience. Seeing Taffa's corpse had changed something. He was not a confused man trapped in a nightmare, as he'd feared when first visiting this place. Why was he sneaking? These visions belonged to *him*. He should not fear their contents.

One of the creatures scuttled out of the shadows. Dalinar drew in Stormlight as it leaped and bit at his leg. Pain flared up his side, but he ignored it, and the wound reknit. He glanced down as the creature lunged again, with similar lack of results. It scurried backward a few paces, and he could sense *confusion* in its posture. This was not how its prey was supposed to act.

"You don't eat the corpses," Dalinar said to it. "You kill for pleasure, don't you? I often think of how spren and man are so different, but this we share. We can both murder."

The unholy thing came at him again, and Dalinar seized it in both hands. The body felt springy to the touch, like a wineskin filled to bursting. He painted the writhing monster with Stormlight and spun, hurling it toward a nearby building. The creature hit the wall back-first and stuck there several feet above the ground, legs scrambling.

Dalinar continued on his way. He simply cut through the next two creatures that came for him. Their disjointed bodies twitched, black smoke leaking from the carcasses.

What is that light? It danced in the night ahead, growing stronger. Harsh, orange, flooding the end of the street.

He didn't remember a fire from before. Were homes burning? Dalinar approached, and found a *bonfire*, flickering with flamespren, built of furniture. It was surrounded by dozens of people holding brooms and crude picks: men and women alike, armed with whatever they could find. Even an iron poker or two.

Judging by the fearspren gathered around them, the townspeople were terrified. They managed some semblance of ranks anyway—with children at the center, nearer the fires—as they frantically defended themselves from the midnight monsters. A figure near the fire commanded from the top of a box. Fen's voice had no accent; to Dalinar, her shouts seemed to be in perfect Alethi, though—in the strange way of these visions—everyone present was actually speaking and thinking in an ancient language.

How did she manage this so quickly? Dalinar wondered, mesmerized by the fighting townsfolk. Some of them fell in bloody, screaming heaps, but others pinned down the monsters and stabbed open their backs—sometimes with kitchen knives—to deflate them.

Dalinar remained on the outskirts of the battle until a dramatic figure in glowing blue swept down upon the scene. The Windrunner made short work of the remaining creatures.

At the end, he saved a glare for Dalinar. "What are you doing standing there? Why haven't you helped?"

"I—"

"We'll have words about this when we return!" he shouted, pointing toward one of the fallen. "Go, help the wounded!"

Dalinar followed the gesture, but walked toward Fen instead of the wounded. Some of the townspeople huddled and wept, though others exulted in survival, cheering and holding up their improvised weapons. He'd seen these aftereffects of a battle before. The welling up of emotions came in a variety of ways.

The bonfire's heat caused Dalinar's brow to sweat. Smoke churned in the air, reminding him of the place he'd been before he'd fully entered this vision. He'd always loved the warmth of an actual fire, dancing with flamespren, so eager to burn themselves out and die.

Fen was over a foot shorter than Dalinar, with an oval face, yellow eyes, and white Thaylen eyebrows she kept curled to hang down beside her cheeks. She did not braid her grey hair like an Alethi woman would have, but instead let it fall down to cover her shoulders. The vision had given her a simple shirt and trousers to wear—the costume of the man she'd replaced—though she'd found a glove for her safehand.

"Now the Blackthorn himself shows up?" she said. "Damnation, this is a strange dream."

"Not quite a dream, Fen," Dalinar said, looking back toward the Radiant, who had charged a small group of midnight monsters coming down the street. "I don't know if I have time to explain."

"I can slow it down," one of the villagers said in the Stormfather's voice.

"Yes, please," Dalinar said.

Everything stopped. Or . . . slowed greatly. The bonfire's flames shimmered lethargically, and the people slowed to a crawl.

Dalinar was unaffected, as was Fen. He sat down on a box beside the one Fen stood on, and she hesitantly settled down next to him. "A *very* strange dream."

"I assumed I was dreaming myself, when I saw the first vision," Dalinar said. "When they kept happening, I was forced to acknowledge that no dream is this crisp, this logical. In no dream could we be having this conversation."

"In every dream I've experienced, what happened felt natural at the time."

"Then you will know the difference when you wake. I can show many more of these visions to you, Fen. They were left for us by . . . a being with some interest in helping us survive the Desolations." Best not to get into his heresy at the moment. "If one isn't persuasive enough, I understand. I'm dense enough that I didn't trust them for months."

"Are they all this . . . invigorating?"

Dalinar smiled. "This was the most powerful of them, to me." He looked to her. "You did better than I did. I worried only about Taffa and her daughter, but just ended up getting them surrounded by monsters anyway."

"I let the woman die," Fen said softly. "I ran with the child, and let the thing kill her. Used her almost as bait." She looked to Dalinar, eyes haunted. "What was your purpose in this, Kholin? You imply you have power over these visions. Why did you trap me in this one?"

"Honestly, I just wanted to talk to you."

"Send me a storming letter."

"In person, Fen." He nodded toward the gathered townspeople. "You did *this*. You organized the town, pitted them against the enemy. It's remarkable! You expect me to accept that you will turn your back on the world in a similar moment of need?"

"Don't be dense. My kingdom is suffering. I'm seeing to my people's needs; I'm not turning my back on anyone."

Dalinar looked to her and pursed his lips, but said nothing.

"Fine," she snapped. "Fine, Kholin. You want to dig into it for real? Tell me this. You *really* expect me to believe that the storming *Knights Radiant* are back and that the Almighty chose *you*—a tyrant and a murderer—to lead them?"

In response, Dalinar stood up and drew in Stormlight. His skin began glowing with luminescent smoke, drifting from his body. "If you wish proof, I can persuade you. Incredible though it seems, the Radiants *have* returned."

"And of the second part? Yes, there is a new storm, and perhaps new manifestations of power. Fine. What I don't accept is that you, Dalinar Kholin, have been told by the Almighty to lead us."

"I have been commanded to unite."

"A mandate from God—the *very* same argument the Hierocracy used for seizing control of the government. What about Sadees, the Sunmaker? He claimed he had a calling from the Almighty too." She stood and walked among the people of the town—who stood as if frozen, barely moving. She turned and swept a hand back toward Dalinar. "Now here *you* are, saying the same things in the same way—not quite threats, but insistent. Let us join forces! If we don't, the world is doomed."

Dalinar felt his patience slipping. He clenched his jaw, forced himself to be calm, and rose. "Your Majesty, you're being irrational."

"Am I? Oh, let me storming reconsider, then. All I need to do is let the storming *Blackthorn himself* into my city, so he can take control of my armies!"

"What would you have me *do*?" Dalinar shouted. "Would you have me watch the world crumble?"

She cocked her head at his outburst.

"Maybe you're right, and I am a tyrant! Maybe letting my armies into your city is a terrible risk. But maybe you don't have good options! Maybe all the good men are dead, so all you have is me! Spitting into the storm isn't going to change that, Fen. You can risk *possibly* being conquered by the Alethi, or you can *definitely* fall to the Voidbringer assault alone!"

Curiously, Fen crossed her arms and raised her left hand to her chin, inspecting Dalinar. She didn't seem the least bit fazed by his shouting.

Dalinar stepped past a squat man who was slowly—as if through tar—turning toward where they'd once been seated. "Fen," Dalinar said. "You don't like me. Fine. You tell me *to my face* that trusting me is worse than a Desolation."

She studied him, aged eyes thoughtful. What was wrong? What had he said?

"Fen," he tried again. "I—"

"Where was this passion earlier?" she asked. "Why didn't you speak like this in your letters to me?"

"I . . . Fen, I was being *diplomatic*."

She sniffed. "That made it sound like I was talking to a committee. It's what one always assumes anyway, when communicating via spanreed."

"So?"

"So compared to that, it's good to hear some honest shouting." She eyed the people standing around them. "And this is *exceptionally* creepy. Can we get away from this?"

Dalinar found himself nodding, mostly to buy some time to think. Fen seemed to think his anger was . . . a good thing? He gestured at a path through the crowd and Fen joined him, walking away from the bonfire.

"Fen," he said, "you say you expected to talk to a committee through the spanreed. What's wrong with that? Why would you want me to *shout* at you instead?"

"I don't want you to shout at me, Kholin," she said. "But storms, man. Don't you know what has been said about you these last few months?"

"No."

"You've been the hottest topic on the spanreed informant networks! Dalinar Kholin, the Blackthorn, has gone mad! He claims to have killed the Almighty! One day he refuses to fight, then the next day he marches his armies off on an insane quest into the Shattered Plains. He says he's going to enslave the Voidbringers!"

"I didn't say—"

"Nobody expects every report to be true, Dalinar, but I had extremely good information claiming you'd lost your mind. Refounding the Knights Radiant? Raving about a Desolation? You seized the throne of Alethkar in all but title, but refused to fight the other highprinces, and instead ran your armies off into the Weeping. Then you told everyone a new storm was coming. That was enough to convince me that you really *were* mad."

"But then the storm came," Dalinar said.

"But then the storm came."

The two walked down the quiet street, light from behind flooding across them, making their shadows lengthen. To their right, a calm blue light shone between buildings—the Radiant, who fought monsters in slowed time.

Jasnah could probably learn something from these buildings, with their old architecture. These people wearing unfamiliar clothing. He'd have expected everything in the past to be crude, but it wasn't. The doors, the buildings, the clothing. It was well made, just . . . lacking something he couldn't define.

"The Everstorm proved I wasn't mad?" Dalinar asked.

"It proved that *something* was happening."

Dalinar suddenly stopped. "You think I'm working *with* them! You think that explains my behavior, my foreknowledge. You think I've been acting erratically because I've been in *contact* with the Voidbringers!"

"All I knew," Fen said, "was that the voice on the other end of the spanreed was *not* the Dalinar Kholin I'd expected. The words were too polite, too calm, to be trusted."

"And now?" Dalinar asked.

Fen turned. "Now . . . I'll consider. Can I see the rest of it? I want to know what happens to the little girl."

Dalinar followed her gaze and saw—for the first time—little Seeli sitting, huddled with some other children near the fire. She had a haunted cast to her eyes. He could imagine her horror as Fen ran away, Taffa—the child's mother—screaming as she was ripped apart.

Seeli suddenly lurched into motion, turning her head to stare with a hollow gaze at a woman who knelt beside her, offering something to drink. The Stormfather had restored the vision's normal speed.

Dalinar backed up, letting Fen rejoin the people and experience the end of the vision. As he folded his arms to watch, he noted a shimmering in the air beside him.

"We'll want to send her more of these," Dalinar said to the Stormfather. "We can only be served by more people knowing the truths the Almighty left behind. Can you bring in only one person per storm, or can we accelerate that somehow? And can you bring two people into two different visions at once?"

The Stormfather rumbled. *I do not like to be ordered about.*

"And you prefer the alternative? Letting Odium win? How far will your pride push you, Stormfather?"

It is not pride, the Stormfather said, sounding stubborn. *I am not a man. I do not bend or cower. I do what is in my nature, and to defy that is pain.*

The Radiant finished off the last of the midnight creatures and stepped up to the gathered people, then looked at Fen. "Your upbringing might be humble, but your talent for leadership is impressive. I have rarely seen a man—king or commander—organize people for defense as well as you did here today."

Fen cocked her head.

"No words for me, I see," the knight said. "Very well. But should you wish to learn true leadership, come to Urithiru."

Dalinar turned to the Stormfather. "That's almost exactly what the knight said to me last time."

By design, certain things always happen in the visions, the Stormfather replied. *I do not know Honor's every intention, but I know he wished you to interact with Radiants and know that men could join them.*

"All who resist are needed," the Radiant said to Fen. "Indeed, any who have a desire to fight should be compelled to come to Alethela. We can teach you, help you. If you have the soul of a warrior, that passion could destroy you, unless you are guided. Come to us."

The Radiant strode off, then Fen jumped as Seeli stood up and started talking to her. The girl's voice was too quiet for Dalinar to hear, but he could guess what was happening. At the end of each vision, the Almighty himself spoke through one of the people, passing along wisdom that—at first—Dalinar had assumed was interactive.

Fen seemed troubled by what she heard. As well she should be. Dalinar remembered the words.

This is important, the Almighty had said. *Do not let strife consume you. Be strong. Act with honor, and honor will aid you.*

Except Honor was dead.

At the end of it, Fen turned toward Dalinar, her eyes measuring.

She still does not trust you, the Stormfather said.

"She wonders if I created this vision with the power of the Voidbringers. She no longer thinks I'm mad, but she does continue to wonder if I've joined the enemy."

So you've failed again.

"No," Dalinar said. "Tonight she listened. And I think she'll end up taking the gamble of coming to Urithiru."

The Stormfather rumbled, sounding confused. *Why?*

"Because," Dalinar said, "I know how to talk to her now. She doesn't want polite words or diplomatic phrases. She wants me to be myself. I'm fairly certain that's something I can deliver."

35

FIRST INTO THE SKY

You think yourself so clever, but my eyes are not those of some petty noble, to be clouded by a false nose and some dirt on the cheeks.

Someone bumped Sigzil's cot, waking him from a dream. He yawned, and Rock's breakfast bell began ringing in the next room.

He'd been dreaming in Azish. He'd been back home, studying for the governmental service tests. Passing would have qualified him to enter a real school, with a shot at becoming a clerk to someone important. Only, in the dream, he'd been panicked to realize he'd forgotten how to read.

After so many years away, thinking of his mother tongue felt strange. He yawned again, settling on his cot, back to the stone wall. They had three small barracks and a common room in the center.

Out there, everyone pushed, ramble-scramble, up to the breakfast table. Rock had to shout at them—yet again—to organize themselves. Months in Bridge Four, now apprentice Knights Radiant, and the lot of them *still* couldn't figure out how to line up properly. They wouldn't last a day in Azir, where queuing in an orderly way wasn't only expected, it was practically a mark of *national pride.*

Sigzil rested his head against the wall, remembering. He'd been the first from his family in generations with a real shot at passing the exams. A silly dream. Everyone in Azir *talked* about how even the humblest man could become Prime, but the son of a laborer had so little time to study.

He shook his head, then washed with a basin of water he'd fetched the night before. He took a comb to his hair, and inspected himself in a polished length of steel. His hair was growing far too long; the tight black curls had a tendency to stick straight out.

He set out a sphere to use its light for a shave—he had acquired his own razor. Soon after he started, however, he nicked himself. He sucked in a breath at the pain, and his sphere winked out. What . . .

His skin started glowing, letting off a faint luminescent smoke. Oh, right. Kaladin was back.

Well, that was going to solve *so* many problems. He got out another sphere, and did his best not to eat this one as he finished shaving. Afterward, he pressed his hand against his forehead. Once, he'd had slave brands there. The Stormlight had healed those, though his Bridge Four tattoo remained.

He rose and put on his uniform. Kholin blue, sharp and neat. He slid his new hogshide notebook into his pocket, then stepped out into the common room—and stopped short as Lopen's face swung *down* right in front of him. Sigzil almost slammed into the Herdazian, who was stuck by the bottoms of his feet to the storming *ceiling*.

"Hey," Lopen said, bowl of morning porridge held upside down—or, well, right-side up, but upside down to Lopen—in front of him. The Herdazian tried to take a bite, but the porridge slipped off his spoon and splatted to the ground.

"Lopen, what are you *doing*?"

"Practicing. I've got to show them how good I am, hooch. It's like with women, only it involves sticking yourself to the ceiling and learning not to spill food on the heads of people you like."

"Move, Lopen."

"Ah, you have to ask the right way. I'm not one-armed anymore! I can't be shoved around. Say, do you know how to get *two armed* Herdazians to do what you want?"

"If I did, we wouldn't be having this conversation."

"Well, you take away both of their spears, obviously." He grinned. A few feet away, Rock laughed with a loud "Ha!"

Lopen wiggled his fingers at Sigzil, as if to taunt him, fingernails glistening. Like all Herdazians, he had fingernails that were dark brown and hard as crystal. A bit reminiscent of carapace.

He still had a tattoo on his head too. Though so far only a few of Bridge Four had learned to draw in Stormlight, each of those had kept their tattoos. Only Kaladin was different; his tattoo had melted off once he took in Stormlight, and his scars refused to heal.

"Remember that one for me, hooch," Lopen said. He never would explain what "hooch" meant, or why he used it only to refer to Sigzil. "I'll need, sure, lots and lots of new jokes. Also sleeves. Twice as many of those, except on vests. Then the same number."

"How did you even manage to get up there, so you could stick your feet . . . no, don't start. I don't actually want to know." Sigzil ducked under Lopen.

The men were still scrambling for food, laughing and shouting in complete disarray. Sigzil shouted to get their attention. "Don't forget! The captain wanted us up and ready for inspection by second bell!"

Sigzil could barely be heard. Where was Teft? They actually listened when he gave orders. Sigzil shook his head, weaving his way toward the door. Among his people, he was of average height—but he'd gone and moved among the *Alethi*, who were practically giants. So here, he was a few inches shorter than most.

He slipped out into the hallway. The bridge crews occupied a sequence of large barracks on the tower's first floor. Bridge Four were gaining Radiant powers, but there were hundreds more men in the battalion who were still ordinary infantry. Perhaps Teft had gone to inspect the other crews; he'd been given responsibility for training them. Hopefully it wasn't the other thing.

Kaladin bunked in his own small suite of rooms at the end of the hallway. Sigzil made his way there, going over his scribbles in the notebook. He used Alethi glyphs, as was acceptable for a man out here, and had never learned their actual writing system. Storms, he'd been away so long, the dream was probably right. He might have trouble writing in the Azish script.

What would life be like if he hadn't turned into a failure and a disappointment? If he'd passed the tests, instead of getting into trouble, needing to be rescued by the man who had become his master?

The list of problems first, he decided, reaching Kaladin's door and knocking.

"Come!" the captain's voice said from inside.

Sigzil found Kaladin doing morning push-ups on the stone floor. His blue jacket was draped over a chair.

"Sir," Sigzil said.

"Hey, Sig," Kaladin said, grunting as he continued his push-ups. "Are the men up and mustered?"

"Up, yes," Sigzil said. "When I left them, they seemed bordering on a food fight, and only half were in uniform."

"They'll be ready," Kaladin said. "Was there something you wanted, Sig?"

Sigzil settled down in the chair next to Kaladin's coat and opened his notebook. "A lot of things, sir. Not the least of which is the fact that you should have a real scribe, not . . . whatever I am."

"You're my clerk."

"A poor one. We've a full battalion of fighting men with only four lieutenants and no official scribes. Frankly, sir, the bridge crews are a mess. Our finances are in shambles, requisition orders are piling up faster than Leyten can deal with them, and there's an entire host of problems requiring an officer's attention."

Kaladin grunted. "The fun part of running an army."

"Exactly."

"That was sarcasm, Sig." Kaladin stood up and wiped his brow with a towel. "All right. Go ahead."

"We'll start with something easy," Sigzil said. "Peet is now officially betrothed to the woman he's been seeing."

"Ka? That's wonderful. Maybe she could help you with scribe duties."

"Perhaps. I believe that you were looking into requisitioning housing for men with families?"

"Yeah. That was before the whole mess with the Weeping, and the expedition onto the Shattered Plains, and . . . And I should go back to Dalinar's scribes about it, shouldn't I?"

"Unless you expect the married couples to share a bunk in the standard barracks, then I'd say that yes, you should." Sigzil looked to the next page in his book. "I believe that Bisig is close to being betrothed as well."

"Really? He's so quiet. I never know what's going on behind those eyes of his."

"Not to mention Punio, who I found out recently is *already* married. His wife drops off food for him."

"I thought that was his sister!"

"He wanted to fit in, I believe," Sigzil said. "His broken Alethi already makes that hard. And then there's the matter of Drehy . . ."

"What matter?"

"Well, he's been courting a man, you see . . ."

Kaladin threw on his coat, chuckling. "I *did* know about that one. You only now noticed?"

Sigzil nodded.

"It's Dru he's been seeing, still? From the district quartermaster's offices?"

"Yes, sir." Sigzil looked down. "Sir, I . . . Well, it's just that . . ."

"Yes?"

"Sir, Drehy hasn't filled out the proper forms," Sigzil said. "If he wants to court another man, he needs to apply for social reassignment, right?"

Kaladin rolled his eyes. So, there were no forms for that in Alethkar.

Sigzil couldn't say he was surprised, as the Alethi didn't have proper procedures for anything. "Then how do you apply for social reassignment?"

"We don't." Kaladin frowned. "Is this really that big a problem to you, Sig? Maybe—"

"Sir, it's not this specifically. Right now, there are four religions represented in Bridge Four."

"Four?"

"Hobber follows the Passions, sir. Four, even if you don't count Teft, who I can't figure out rightly. And now there's all this talk of Brightlord Dalinar claiming the Almighty is dead, and . . . Well, I feel responsible, sir."

"For Dalinar?" Kaladin frowned.

"No, no." He took a deep breath. There had to be a way to explain this. What would his master do?

"Now," Sigzil said, scrambling at an idea, "everybody knows that Mishim—the third moon—is the most clever and wily of the moons."

"All right . . . And this is relevant, why?"

"Because of a story," Sigzil said. "Hush. Uh, I mean, please listen, sir. You see, there are three moons, and the third moon is the cleverest. And she doesn't want to be in the sky, sir. She wants to escape.

"So one night, she tricked the queen of the Natan people—this was a long time ago, so they were still around. I mean, they're still around now, but they were more around then, sir. And the moon tricked her, and then they traded places until they stopped. And now the Natan people have blue skin. Does that make sense?"

Kaladin blinked. "I have no idea what you just said."

"Um, well," Sigzil said. "It's obviously fanciful. Not the real reason that the Natan people have blue skin. And, um . . ."

"It was supposed to explain something?"

"It's how my master always did things," Sigzil said, looking at his feet. "He'd tell a story anytime someone was confused, or when people were angry at him. And, well, it changed everything. Somehow." He looked to Kaladin.

"I suppose," Kaladin said slowly, "that maybe you feel . . . like a moon. . . ."

"No, not really." It was about responsibility, but he had really not explained it well. Storms. Master Hoid had named him a full Worldsinger, and here he couldn't even tell a story straight.

Kaladin clapped him on the shoulder. "It's all right, Sig."

"Sir," Sigzil said. "The other men don't have any *direction*. You've given them purpose, a reason to be good men. They *are* good men. But in some ways, it was easy when we were slaves. What do we do if not all the men manifest the ability to draw in Stormlight? What is our place in the army?

Brightlord Kholin released us from guard duty, as he said he wanted us practicing and training as Radiants instead. But what *is* a Knight Radiant?"

"We'll need to figure it out."

"And if the men need guidance? If they need a moral center? Someone has to talk to them when they're doing something wrong, but the ardents ignore us, since they associate us with the things Brightlord Dalinar is saying and doing."

"You think you can be the one to guide the men instead?" Kaladin asked.

"Someone should, sir."

Kaladin waved for Sigzil to follow him out into the corridor. Together they started walking toward the Bridge Four barracks, Sigzil holding out a sphere for light.

"I don't mind if you want to be something like our unit's ardent," Kaladin said. "The men like you, Sig, and they put a lot of stock in what you have to say. But you should try to understand what they want out of life, and respect that, rather than projecting onto them what you think they *should* want out of life."

"But sir, some things are just *wrong*. You know what Teft has gotten into, and Huio, he's been visiting the prostitutes."

"That's not forbidden. Storms, I've had some sergeants who suggested it as the key to a healthy mind in battle."

"It's wrong, sir. It's imitating an oath without the commitment. Every major religion agrees to this, except the Reshi, I suppose. But they're pagans even among *pagans*."

"Your master teach you to be this judgmental?"

Sigzil stopped short.

"I'm sorry, Sig," Kaladin said.

"No, he said the same thing about me. All the time, sir."

"I give you permission to sit down with Huio and explain your worries," Kaladin said. "I won't forbid you from expressing your morals—I'd encourage it. Just don't present your beliefs as our code. Present them as *yours*, and make a good argument. Maybe the men will listen."

Sigzil nodded, hurrying to catch up. To cover his embarrassment—more at completely failing to tell the right story than anything else—he dug into his notebook. "That does raise another issue, sir. Bridge Four is down to twenty-eight members, after our losses during the first Everstorm. Might be time for some recruitment."

"Recruitment?" Kaladin said. He cocked his head.

"Well, if we lose any more members—"

"We *won't*," Kaladin said. He always thought that.

"—or, even if we don't, we're down from the thirty-five or forty of a good bridge crew. Maybe we don't need to keep that number, but a good active unit should always be watching for people to recruit.

"What if someone else in the army has been displaying the right attitude to be a Windrunner? Or, more pointedly, what if our men start swearing oaths and bonding their own spren? Would we dissolve Bridge Four, and let each man be their own Radiant?"

The idea of dissolving Bridge Four seemed to pain Kaladin almost as much as the idea of losing men in battle. They walked in silence for a short time. They weren't going to the Bridge Four barracks after all; Kaladin had taken a turn deeper into the tower. They passed a water wagon, pulled by laborers to deliver water from the wells to the officers' quarters. Normally that would be parshman work.

"We should at least put out a call for recruitment," Kaladin finally said, "though honestly I can't think of how I'll cull hopefuls down to a manageable number."

"I'll try to come up with some strategies, sir," Sigzil said. "If I might ask, where are we . . ." He trailed off as he saw Lyn hurrying down the hallway toward them. She carried a diamond chip in her palm for light, and wore her Kholin uniform, her dark Alethi hair pulled back in a tail.

She drew up when she saw Kaladin, then saluted him smartly. "Just the man I was looking for. Quartermaster Vevidar sends word that 'your unusual request has been fulfilled,' sir."

"Excellent," Kaladin said, marching through the hallway past her. Sigzil shot her a look as she fell in with him, and she shrugged. She didn't know what the unusual request was, only that it had been fulfilled.

Kaladin eyed Lyn as they walked. "You're the one who has been helping my men, right? Lyn, was it?"

"Yes, sir!"

"In fact, it seems you've been making excuses to run messages to Bridge Four."

"Um, yes, sir."

"Not afraid of the 'Lost Radiants' then?"

"Frankly, sir, after what I saw on the battlefield, I'd rather be on your side than bet on the opposition."

Kaladin nodded, thoughtful as he walked. "Lyn," he finally said, "how would you like to join the Windrunners?"

The woman stopped in place, jaw dropping. "Sir?" She saluted. "Sir, I'd *love* that! Storms!"

"Excellent," Kaladin said. "Sig, can you get her our ledgers and accounts?"

Lyn's hand drooped from her brow. "Ledgers? Accounts?"

"The men will also need letters written to family members," Kaladin said. "And we should probably write a history of Bridge Four. People will be curious, and a written account will save me from having to explain it all the time."

"Oh," Lyn said. "A scribe."

"Of course," Kaladin said, turning back toward her in the hallway, frowning. "You're a woman, aren't you?"

"I thought you were asking . . . I mean, in the highprince's visions, there were women who were Knights Radiant, and with Brightness Shallan . . ." She blushed. "Sir, I didn't join the scouts because I liked sitting around staring at ledgers. If that's what you're offering, I'll have to pass."

Her shoulders fell, and she wouldn't meet Kaladin's eyes. Sigzil found, strangely, that he wanted to punch his captain. Not hard, mind you. Just a gentle "wake up" punch. He couldn't remember feeling that way with Kaladin since the time the captain had woken him up that first morning, back in Sadeas's warcamp.

"I see," Kaladin said. "Well . . . we're going to have tryouts to join the order proper. I suppose I could extend you an invitation. If you'd like."

"Tryouts?" she said. "For real positions? Not just doing accounts? Storms, I'm in."

"Speak with your superior, then," Kaladin said. "I haven't devised the proper test yet, and you'd need to pass it before you could be let in. Either way, you'd need clearance to change battalions."

"Yes, sir!" she said, and bounded off.

Kaladin watched her go, then grunted softly.

Sigzil—without even thinking about it—mumbled, "Did your master teach you to be that insensitive?"

Kaladin eyed him.

"I have a suggestion, sir," Sigzil continued. "Try to understand what people want out of life, and respect that, rather than projecting onto them what you think they *should*—"

"Shut it, Sig."

"Yes, sir. Sorry, sir."

They continued on their way, and Kaladin cleared his throat. "You don't have to be so formal with me, you know."

"I know, sir. But you're a lighteyes now, and a Shardbearer and . . . well, it feels right."

Kaladin stiffened, but didn't contradict him. In truth, Sigzil had always felt . . . awkward trying to treat Kaladin like any other bridgeman. Some of the others could do it—Teft and Rock, Lopen in his own strange way. But Sigzil felt more comfortable when the relationship was set out and clear. Captain and his clerk.

Moash had been the closest to Kaladin, but he wasn't in Bridge Four any longer. Kaladin hadn't said what Moash had done, only that he had "removed himself from our fellowship." Kaladin got stiff and unresponsive whenever Moash's name was mentioned.

"Anything else on that list of yours?" Kaladin asked as they passed a guard patrol in the hallway. He received crisp salutes.

Sigzil looked through his notebook. "Accounts and the need for scribes . . . Code of morals for the men . . . Recruitment . . . Oh, we're still going to need to define our place in the army, now that we're no longer bodyguards."

"We're still bodyguards," Kaladin said. "We just protect anyone who needs it. We have bigger problems, in that storm."

It had come again, a third time, this event proving that it was even more regular than the highstorms. Right around every nine days. Up high as they were, its passing was only a curiosity—but throughout the world, each new arrival strained already beleaguered cities.

"I realize that, sir," Sigzil said. "But we still have to worry about procedure. Here, let me ask this. Are we, as Knights Radiant, still an Alethi military organization?"

"No," Kaladin said. "This war is bigger than Alethkar. We're for all mankind."

"All right, then what's our chain of command? Do we obey King Elhokar? Are we still his subjects? And what dahn or nahn are we in society? You're a Shardbearer in Dalinar's court, aren't you?"

"Who pays the wages of Bridge Four? What about the other bridge crews? If there is a squabble over Dalinar's lands in Alethkar, can he call you—and Bridge Four—up to fight for him, like a normal liege-vassal relationship? If not, then can we still expect him to pay us?"

"Damnation," Kaladin breathed.

"I'm sorry, sir. It—"

"No, they're good questions, Sig. I'm lucky to have you to ask them." He clasped Sigzil on the shoulder, stopping in the hallway just outside the quartermaster's offices. "Sometimes I wonder if you're wasted in Bridge Four. You should've been a scholar."

"Well, that wind blew past me years ago, sir. I . . ." He took a deep breath. "I failed the exams for government training in Azir. I wasn't good enough."

"Then the exams were stupid," Kaladin said. "And Azir lost out, because they missed the chance to have you."

Sigzil smiled. "I'm glad they did." And . . . strangely, he felt it was true. A nameless weight he'd been carrying seemed to slide off his back. "Honestly, I feel like Lyn. I don't want to be huddled over a ledger when Bridge Four takes to the air. I want to be first into the sky."

"I think you'll have to fight Lopen for that distinction," Kaladin said with a chuckle. "Come on." He strode into the quartermaster's office, where a group of waiting guardsmen immediately made space for him. At the counter, a beefy soldier with rolled-up sleeves searched through boxes and crates, muttering to himself. A stout woman—presumably his wife—inspected requisition forms. She nudged the man and pointed at Kaladin.

"Finally!" the quartermaster said. "I'm tired of having these here, drawing everyone's eyes and making me sweat like a spy with too many spren."

He shuffled over to a pair of large black sacks in the corner that, best that Sigzil could tell, weren't drawing any eyes at all. The quartermaster hefted them and glanced at the scribe, who double-checked a few forms, then nodded, presenting them for Kaladin to stamp with his captain's seal. Paperwork done, the quartermaster handed a sack to Kaladin and another to Sigzil.

They clinked when moved, and were surprisingly heavy. Sigzil undid the ties and glanced into his.

A flood of green light, powerful as sunlight, shone out over him. Emeralds. The large type, not in spheres, probably cut from the gemhearts of chasmfiends hunted on the Shattered Plains. In a moment, Sigzil realized that the guards filling the room weren't here to get something from the quartermaster. They were here to protect this wealth.

"That's the royal emerald reserve," the quartermaster said. "Held for emergency grain, renewed with Light in the storm this morning. How you talked the highprince into letting you take it is beyond me."

"We're only borrowing them," Kaladin said. "We'll have them back before evening arrives. Though be warned, some will be dun. We'll need to check them out tomorrow again. And the day after that . . ."

"I could buy a *princedom* for that much," the quartermaster said with a grunt. "What in Kelek's name do you need them for?"

Sigzil, however, had already guessed. He grinned like a fool. "We're going to practice being Radiant."

HERO

TWENTY-FOUR YEARS AGO

Dalinar cursed as smoke billowed out of the fireplace. He shoved his weight against the lever and managed to budge it, reopening the chimney flue. He coughed, backing up and waving smoke away from his face.

"We are going to need to see that replaced," Evi said from the sofa where she was doing needlework.

"Yeah," Dalinar said, thumping down to the floor before the fire.

"At least you got to it quickly. Today we will not need to scrub the walls, and the life will be as white as a sun at night!"

Evi's native idioms didn't always translate well into Alethi.

The fire's heat was welcome, as Dalinar's clothing was still damp from the rains. He tried to ignore the ever-present sound of the Weeping's rain outside, instead watching a pair of flamespren dance along one of the logs. These seemed vaguely human, with ever-shifting figures. He followed one with his eyes as it leaped toward the other.

He heard Evi rise, and thought she might be off to seek the privy again. She instead settled down next to him and took his arm, then sighed in contentment.

"That can't be comfortable," Dalinar said.

"And yet you are doing it."

"I'm not the one who is . . ." He looked at her belly, which had begun to round.

Evi smiled. "My condition does not make me so frail that I risk *breaking* by sitting on the floor, beloved." She pulled his arm tighter. "Look at them. They play so eagerly!"

"It's like they're sparring," Dalinar said. "I can almost see the little blades in their hands."

"Must everything be fighting to you?"

He shrugged.

She leaned her head on his arm. "Can't you just enjoy it, Dalinar?"

"Enjoy what?"

"Your life. You went through so much to make this kingdom. Can't you be satisfied, now that you've won?"

He stood up, pulling his arm from her grip, and crossed the chamber to pour himself a drink.

"Don't think I haven't noticed the way you act," Evi said. "Perking up whenever the king speaks of the smallest conflict beyond our borders. Having the scribes read to you of great battles. Always talking about the next duel."

"I'm not to have that much longer," Dalinar grumbled, then took a sip of wine. "Gavilar says it's foolish to endanger myself, says someone is bound to try to use one of those duels as a ploy against him. I'll have to get a champion." He stared at his wine.

He'd never had a high opinion of dueling. It was too fake, too sanitized. But at least it was something.

"It's like you're dead," Evi said.

Dalinar looked over at her.

"It's like you only live when you can fight," she continued. "When you can kill. Like a blackness from old stories. You live only by taking lives from others."

With that pale hair and light golden skin, she was like a glowing gemstone. She was a sweet, loving woman who deserved better than the treatment he gave her. He forced himself to go back and sit down beside her.

"*I* still think the flamespren are playing," she said.

"I've always wondered," Dalinar said. "Are they *made* of fire themselves? It looks like they are, and yet what of emotion spren? Are angerspren then *made* of anger?"

Evi nodded absently.

"And what of gloryspren?" Dalinar said. "Made of glory? What *is* glory? Could gloryspren appear around someone who is delusional, or perhaps very drunk—who only *thinks* they've accomplished something great, while everyone else is standing around mocking them?"

"A mystery," she said, "sent by Shishi."

"But don't you ever wonder?"

"To what end?" Evi said. "We will know eventually, when we return to the One. No use troubling our minds now about things we cannot understand."

Dalinar narrowed his eyes at the flamespren. That one *did* have a sword. A miniature Shardblade.

"This is why you brood so often, husband," Evi said. "It isn't healthy to have a stone curdling in your stomach, still wet with moss."

"I . . . What?"

"You must not think such strange thoughts. Who put such things into your mind anyway?"

He shrugged, but thought of two nights before, staying up late and drinking wine beneath the rain canopy with Gavilar and Navani. She'd talked and talked about her research into spren, and Gavilar had simply grunted, while making notations in glyphs on a set of his maps. She'd spoken with such passion and excitement, and Gavilar had ignored her.

"Enjoy the moment," Evi told him. "Close your eyes and contemplate what the One has given you. Seek the peace of oblivion, and bask in the joy of your own sensation."

He closed his eyes as she suggested, and tried to simply enjoy being here with her. "Can a man actually change, Evi? Like those spren change?"

"We are all different aspects of the One."

"Then can you change from one aspect to another?"

"Of course," Evi said. "Is not your own doctrine about transformation? About a man being Soulcast from crass to glorious?"

"I don't know if it's working."

"Then petition the One," she said.

"In prayer? Through the ardents?"

"No, silly. Yourself."

"In *person*?" Dalinar asked. "Like, at a temple?"

"If you wish to meet the One in person, you must travel to the Valley," she said. "There you can speak with the One, or to his avatar, and be granted—"

"The Old Magic," Dalinar hissed, opening his eyes. "The Nightwatcher. Evi, don't say things like that." Storms, her pagan heritage popped up at the strangest times. She could be talking good Vorin doctrine, then out came something like *that*.

Fortunately, she spoke of it no more. She closed her eyes and hummed softly. Finally, a knock came at the outer door to his rooms.

Hathan, his room steward, would answer that. Indeed, Dalinar heard the man's voice outside, and that was followed by a light rap on the chamber door. "It is your brother, Brightlord," Hathan said through the door.

Dalinar leaped, opening the door and passing the short master-servant. Evi followed, trailing along with one hand touching the wall, a habit of hers. They passed open windows that looked down upon a sodden Kholinar, flickering lanterns marking where people moved through the streets.

Gavilar waited in the sitting room, dressed in one of those new suits with the stiff jacket and buttons up the sides of the chest. His dark hair curled to his shoulders, and was matched by a fine beard.

Dalinar hated beards; they got caught in your helm. He couldn't deny its effect on Gavilar though. Looking at Gavilar in his finery, one didn't see a backwater thug—a barely civilized warlord who had crushed and conquered his way to the throne. No, this man was a *king*.

Gavilar rapped a set of papers against the palm of his hand.

"What?" Dalinar asked.

"Rathalas," Gavilar said, shoving the papers toward Evi as she entered.

"Again!" Dalinar said. It had been years since he'd visited the Rift, that giant trench where he'd won his Shardblade.

"They're demanding your Blade back," Gavilar said. "They claim that Tanalan's heir has returned, and deserves the Shard, as you never won it in a true contest."

Dalinar felt cold.

"Now, I know this to be patently false," Gavilar said, "because when we fought at Rathalas all those years ago, you said you *dealt* with the heir. You *did* deal with the heir, did you not, Dalinar?"

He remembered that day. He remembered darkening that doorway, the Thrill pulsing inside him. He remembered a weeping child holding a Shardblade. The father, lying broken and dead behind. That soft voice, pleading.

The Thrill had vanished in a moment.

"He was a child, Gavilar," Dalinar said, his voice hoarse.

"Damnation!" Gavilar said. "He's a descendant of the old regime. That was . . . storms, that was a decade ago. He's old enough to be a threat! The whole city is going into rebellion, the entire *region*. If we don't act, the whole Crownlands could break off."

Dalinar smiled. The emotion shocked him, and he quickly stifled the grin. But surely . . . surely someone would need to go and rout the rebels.

He turned and caught sight of Evi. She was beaming at him, though he'd have expected her to be indignant at the idea of more wars. Instead, she stepped up to him and took his arm. "You spared the child."

"I . . . He could barely lift the Blade. I gave him to his mother, and told her to hide him."

"Oh, Dalinar." She pulled him close.

He felt a swelling of pride. Ridiculous, of course. He had endangered the kingdom—how would people react if they knew the Blackthorn himself had broken before a crisis of conscience? They'd laugh.

In that moment, he didn't care. So long as he could be a hero to this woman.

"Well, I suppose rebellion was to be expected," Gavilar said as he stared out the window. "It's been years since the formal unification; people are going to start asserting their independence." He raised his hand toward Dalinar, turning. "I know what you want, Brother, but you'll have to forbear. I'm not sending an army."

"But—"

"I can nip this thing with politics. We can't have a show of force be our *only* method of maintaining unity, or Elhokar will spend his entire life putting out fires after I'm gone. We need people to start thinking of Alethkar as a unified kingdom, not separate regions always looking for an advantage against one another."

"Sounds good," Dalinar said.

It wasn't going to happen, not without the sword to remind them. For once, however, he was fine not being the one to point that out.

*You mustn't worry yourself about Rayse. It is a pity about Aona
and Skai, but they were foolish—violating our pact from the very
beginning.*

Numuhukumakiaki'aialunamor had always been taught that the
first rule of warfare was to know your enemy. One might assume that such lessons weren't terribly relevant in his life
anymore. Fortunately, making a good stew was a lot like going to war.

Lunamor—called Rock by his friends, on account of their thick, lowlander tongues being incapable of proper speech—stirred his cauldron with
an enormous wooden spoon the size of a longsword. A fire burned rockbud
husks underneath, and a playful windspren whipped at the smoke, making
it blow across him no matter where he stood.

He had placed the cauldron on a plateau of the Shattered Plains, and—
beautiful lights and fallen stars—he was surprised to discover that he had
missed this place. Who would have thought he could become fond of this
barren, windswept flatland? His homeland was a place of extremes: bitter
ice, powdery snow, boiling heat, and blessed humidity.

Down here, everything was so . . . moderate, and the Shattered Plains
were the worst of all. In Jah Keved he'd found vine-covered valleys. In
Alethkar they had fields of grain, rockbuds spreading endlessly like the
bubbles of a boiling cauldron. Then the Shattered Plains. Endless empty
plateaus with barely anything growing on them. Strangely, he loved them.

Lunamor hummed softly as he stirred with two hands, churning the
stew and keeping the bottom from burning. When the smoke wasn't in his
face—this cursed, too-thick wind had too much air to behave properly—

he could smell the scent of the Shattered Plains. An . . . open scent. The scent of a high sky and baking stones, but spiced by the hint of life in the chasms. Like a pinch of salt. Humid, alive with the odors of plants and rot intermingling.

In those chasms, Lunamor had found himself again after a long time being lost. Renewed life, renewed purpose.

And stew.

Lunamor tasted his stew—using a fresh spoon of course, as he wasn't a barbarian like some of these lowlander cooks. The longroots still had further to cook before he could add the meat. Real meat, from finger crabs he'd spent all night shelling. Couldn't cook that too long, or it got rubbery.

The rest of Bridge Four stood arrayed on the plateau, listening to Kaladin. Lunamor had set up so that his back was toward Narak, the city at the center of the Shattered Plains. Nearby, one of the plateaus flashed as Renarin Kholin worked the Oathgate. Lunamor tried not to be distracted by that. He wanted to look out westward. Toward the old warcamps.

Not much longer now to wait, he thought. *But don't dwell on that. The stew needs more crushed limm.*

"I trained many of you in the chasms," Kaladin said. The men of Bridge Four had been augmented by some members of the other bridge crews, and even a couple of soldiers that Dalinar had suggested for training. The group of five scout women was surprising, but who was Lunamor to judge?

"I could train people in the spear," Kaladin continued, "because I myself had been trained in the spear. What we're attempting today is different. I barely understand how I learned to use Stormlight. We're going to have to stumble through this together."

"It's all good, gancho," Lopen called. "How hard can it be to learn how to fly? Skyeels do it all the time, and they are ugly and stupid. Most bridgemen are only one of those things."

Kaladin stopped in line near Lopen. The captain seemed in good spirits today, for which Lunamor took credit. He had, after all, made Kaladin's breakfast.

"The first step will be to speak the Ideal," Kaladin said. "I suspect a few of you have already said it. But for the rest, if you wish to be a squire to the Windrunners, you will need to swear it."

They began belting out the words. Everyone knew the right ones by now. Lunamor whispered the Ideal.

Life before death. Strength before weakness. Journey before destination.

Kaladin handed Lopen a pouch full of gemstones. "The real test, and proof of your squireship, will be learning to draw Stormlight into yourselves. A few of you have learned it already—"

Lopen started glowing immediately.

"—and they will help the rest learn. Lopen, take First, Second, and Third Squads. Sigzil, you've got Fourth, Fifth, and Sixth. Peet, don't think I haven't seen you glowing. You take the other bridgemen, and Teft, you take the scouts and . . ."

Kaladin looked around. "Where is Teft?"

He was only just noticing? Lunamor loved their captain, but he got distracted sometimes. Maybe airsickness.

"Teft didn't come back to the barracks last night, sir," Leyten called, looking uncomfortable.

"Fine. I'll help the scouts. Lopen, Sigzil, Peet, talk your squads through how to draw in Stormlight. Before the day is done, I want everyone on this plateau glowing like they swallowed a lantern."

They broke up, obviously eager. Translucent red streamers rose from the stone, whipping as if in the wind, one end connected to the ground. Anticipationspren. Lunamor gave them the sign of respect, hand to his shoulder, then his forehead. These were lesser gods, but still holy. He could see their true shapes beyond the streamers, a faint shadow of a larger creature at the bottom.

Lunamor handed off his stirring to Dabbid. The young bridgeman didn't talk, and hadn't since Lunamor had helped Kaladin pull him from the battlefield. He could stir though, and run waterskins. He had become something of an unofficial mascot for the team, as he'd been the first bridgeman that Kaladin had saved. When bridgemen passed Dabbid, they gave a subtle salute.

Huio was on kitchen duty with Lunamor today, as was becoming more common. Huio requested it, and the others avoided it. The squat, beefy Herdazian man was humming softly to himself as he stirred the shiki, a brownish Horneater drink that Lunamor had chilled overnight in metal bins on the plateau outside Urithiru.

Strangely, Huio took a handful of lazbo from a pot and sprinkled it into the liquid.

"What are you doing, crazy man!" Lunamor bellowed, stomping up. "Lazbo? In drink? That thing is spicy powder, airsick lowlander!"

Huio said something in Herdazian.

"Bah!" Lunamor said. "I do not speak this crazy language you use. Lopen! Come here and talk to this cousin you have! He is ruining our drinks!"

Lopen, however, was gesturing wildly at the sky and talking about how he'd stuck himself to the ceiling earlier.

Lunamor grunted and looked back at Huio, who proffered a spoon dripping with liquid.

"Airsick fool," Lunamor said, taking a sip. "You will ruin . . ."

Blessed gods of sea and stone. That was *good*. The spice added just the right *kick* to the chilled drink, combining flavors in a completely unexpected— yet somehow complementary—way.

Huio smiled. "Bridge Four!" he said in thickly accented Alethi.

"You are lucky man," Lunamor said, pointing. "I will not kill you today." He took another sip, then gestured with the spoon. "Go do this thing to other bins of shiki."

Now, where was Hobber? The lanky, gap-toothed man couldn't be *too* far away. That was one advantage of having an assistant chef who could not walk; he usually stayed where you put him.

"Watch me now, carefully!" Lopen said to his group, Stormlight puffing from his mouth as he spoke. "All right. Here it is. I, the Lopen, will now fly. You may applaud as you feel is appropriate."

He jumped up, then crashed back to the plateau.

"Lopen!" Kaladin called. "You're supposed to be helping the others, not showing off!"

"Sorry, gon!" Lopen said. He quivered on the ground, his face pressed to the stone, and didn't rise.

"Did you . . . did you stick yourself to the *ground*?" Kaladin asked.

"Just part of the plan, gon!" Lopen called back. "If I am to become a delicate cloud upon the sky, I must first convince the ground that I am not abandoning her. Like a worried lover, sure, she must be comforted and reassured that I will return following my dramatic and regal ascent to the sky."

"You're not a king, Lopen," Drehy said. "We've been over this."

"Of course I am not. I am a *former* king. You are obviously one of the stupid ones I mentioned earlier."

Lunamor grunted in amusement and rounded his little cooking station toward Hobber, who he now remembered was peeling tubers by the side of the plateau. Lunamor slowed. Why was Kaladin kneeling before Hobber's stool, holding out . . . a gemstone?

Ahhh . . . Lunamor thought.

"I had to *breathe* to draw it in," Kaladin explained softly. "I'd been doing it unconsciously for weeks, maybe months, before Teft explained the truth to me."

"Sir," Hobber said, "I don't know if . . . I mean, sir, I'm no Radiant. I was never that good with the spear. I'm barely a passable cook."

Passable was a stretch. But he was earnest and helpful, so Lunamor was happy to have him. Besides, he needed a job he could do sitting. A month back, the Assassin in White had swept through the king's palace at the warcamps, trying to kill Elhokar—and the attack had left Hobber with dead legs.

Kaladin folded the gemstone in Hobber's fingers. "Just try," the captain said softly. "Being a Radiant isn't so much about your strength or skill, but about your heart. And yours is the best of all of us."

The captain seemed intimidating to many outsiders. A perpetual storm for an expression, an intensity that made men wilt when it turned on them. But there was also an astonishing tenderness to this man. Kaladin gripped Hobber on the arm, and almost seemed to be tearing up.

Some days, it seemed you couldn't break Kaladin Stormblessed with all the stones on Roshar. Then one of his men would get wounded, and you'd see him crack.

Kaladin headed back toward the scouts he'd been helping, and Lunamor jogged to catch up. He bowed to the little god who rode on the bridge captain's shoulder, then asked, "You think Hobber can do this thing, Kaladin?"

"I'm sure he can. I'm sure *all* of Bridge Four can, and perhaps some of these others."

"Ha!" Lunamor said. "Finding a smile on your face, Kaladin Stormblessed, is like finding lost sphere in your soup. Surprising, yes, but very nice too. Come, I have drink you must try."

"I need to get back to—"

"Come! Drink you must try!" Lunamor guided him to the big pot of shiki and poured him a cup.

Kaladin slurped it down. "Hey, that's pretty good, Rock!"

"Is not my recipe," Lunamor said. "Huio has changed this thing. I now have to either promote him or push him off side of plateau."

"Promote him to what?" Kaladin asked, getting himself another cup.

"To airsick lowlander," Lunamor said, "second class."

"You might be too fond of that term, Rock."

Nearby, Lopen talked to the ground, against which he was still pressed. "Don't worry, dear one. The Lopen is vast enough to be possessed by many, many forces, both terrestrial and celestial! I *must* soar to the air, for if I were to remain only on the ground, surely my growing magnitude would cause the land to crack and break."

Lunamor looked to Kaladin. "I am fond of term, yes. But only because this thing has astounding number of applications among you."

Kaladin grinned, sipping his shiki and watching the men. Farther along the plateau, Drehy suddenly raised his long arms and called out, "Ha!" He was glowing with Stormlight. Bisig soon followed. That should fix his hand—he too had been injured by the Assassin in White.

"This *will* work, Rock," Kaladin said. "The men have been close to the power for months now. And once they have it, they'll be able to heal. I won't have to go into battle worrying which of you I'll lose."

"Kaladin," Lunamor said softly. "This thing we have begun, it is still war. Men will die."

"Bridge Four will be protected by their power."

"And the enemy? They will not have power?" He stepped closer. "Surely I do not wish to dampen Kaladin Stormblessed when he is optimistic, but nobody is ever perfectly safe. This is sad truth, my friend."

"Maybe," Kaladin admitted. He got a distant look on his face. "Your people only let younger sons go to war, right?"

"Only tuanalikina, fourth son and younger, can be wasted in war. First, second, and third sons are too valuable."

"Fourth son and younger. So hardly ever."

"Ha! You do not know the size of Horneater families."

"Still, it has to mean fewer men dying in battle."

"Peaks are different place," Lunamor said, smiling at Sylphrena as she rose off Kaladin's shoulder and started dancing on the nearby winds. "And not just because we have right amount of air for brains to work. To attack another peak is costly and difficult, requiring much preparation and time. We speak of this thing more than we do him."

"It sounds nice."

"You will visit with me someday!" Lunamor said. "You and all Bridge Four, as you are family now."

"Ground," Lopen insisted, "I *will* still love you. I'm not attracted to anyone the way I am to you. Whenever I leave, I'll come right back!"

Kaladin glanced at Lunamor.

"Perhaps," Lunamor noted, "when that one is away from too much toxic air, he will be less . . ."

"Lopen?"

"Though upon consideration, this thing would be sad."

Kaladin chuckled, handing Lunamor his cup. Then he leaned in. "What happened to your brother, Rock?"

"My two brothers are well, so far as I know."

"And the third brother?" Kaladin said. "The one who died, moving you from fourth to third, and making you a cook instead of a soldier? Don't deny it."

"Is sad story," Lunamor said. "And today is not day for sad stories. Today is day for laughter, stew, flight. These things."

And hopefully . . . hopefully something even grander.

Kaladin patted him on the shoulder. "If you ever need to talk, I'm here."

"That is good to know. Though today, I believe someone else wishes to talk." Lunamor nodded toward someone crossing a bridge onto their plateau. A figure in a stiff blue uniform, with a silver circlet on his head. "The king has been eager to speak with you. Ha! Asked us several times if we knew when you would return. As if we are appointment keepers for our glorious flying leader."

"Yes," Kaladin said. "He came to see me the other day." Kaladin braced himself visibly, setting his jaw, then walked to the king, who had just marched onto the plateau, trailed by a cluster of guards from Bridge Eleven.

Lunamor positioned himself working on the soup where he could listen, as he was curious.

"Windrunner," Elhokar said, nodding to Kaladin. "It seems you are right, your men have had their powers restored. How soon will they be ready?"

"They're in fighting shape already, Your Majesty. But to master their powers . . . well, I can't say, honestly."

Lunamor sipped his soup and didn't turn toward the king, but stirred and listened.

"Have you given thought to my request?" Elhokar said. "Will you fly me to Kholinar, so we can reclaim the city?"

"I'll do as my commander tells me."

"No," Elhokar said. "I'm asking you, personally. Will you come? Will you help me reclaim our homeland?"

"Yes," Kaladin said softly. "Give me some time, a few weeks at least, to train my men. I'd prefer to bring a few squire Windrunners with us—and if we're lucky, I might be able to leave a full Radiant behind to lead if something happens to me. But either way . . . yes, Elhokar. I'll go with you to Alethkar."

"Good. We have some time, as Uncle wishes to try contacting people in Kholinar using his visions. Perhaps twenty days? Can you train your squires in that time?"

"I'll have to, Your Majesty."

Lunamor glanced at the king, who folded his arms, watching the Windrunners, prospective and current. He seemed to have come not just to speak with Kaladin, but to watch the training. Kaladin walked back to the scouts—his god following in the air after him—so Lunamor brought the king something to drink. Then he hesitated beside the bridge that Elhokar had crossed to reach this plateau.

Their old bridge, from the bridge runs, had been repurposed for moving people around these plateaus closest to Narak. Permanent bridges were still being reconstructed. Lunamor patted the wood. They'd thought this lost, but a salvage party had discovered it wedged in a chasm a short distance away. Dalinar had agreed to have it hauled up, at Teft's request.

Considering what it had been through, the old bridge was in good shape. It was made of tough wood, Bridge Four was. He looked beyond it, and was unsettled by the sight of the next plateau over—or the rubble of it. A stump of a plateau, made of broken rock that extended only twenty feet or so from the chasm floor. Rlain said that had been an ordinary plateau, before the meeting of Everstorm and highstorm at the Battle of Narak.

During that terrible cataclysm when storms met, entire plateaus had been ripped up and shattered. Though the Everstorm had returned several times, the two storms had not again met over a populated area. Lunamor patted the old bridge, then shook his head, walking back toward his cooking station.

They could have trained at Urithiru, perhaps, but none of the bridgemen had complained at coming here. The Shattered Plains were far better than the lonesome plain before the tower. This place was just as barren, but it was also *theirs*.

They also hadn't questioned when Lunamor had decided to bring along his cauldrons and supplies to make lunch. It was inefficient, true, but a hot meal would make up for it—and beyond that, there was an unspoken rule. Though Lunamor, Dabbid, and Hobber didn't participate in the training or sparring, they were still Bridge Four. They went where the others went.

He had Huio add the meat—with a strict charge to *ask* before changing any spices. Dabbid continued to stir placidly. He seemed content, though it was hard to tell with that one. Lunamor washed his hands in a pot, then got to work on the bread.

Cooking *was* like warfare. You had to know your enemy—though his "enemies" in this contest were his friends. They came to each meal expecting greatness, and Lunamor fought to prove himself time and time again. He waged war with breads and soups, sating appetites and satisfying stomachs.

As he worked, hands deep within the dough, he could hear his mother's humming. Her careful instructions. Kaladin was wrong; Lunamor hadn't *become* a cook. He'd always been one, since he could toddle up the stepstool to the counter and stick his fingers in the sticky dough. Yes, he'd once trained with a bow. But soldiers needed to eat, and nuatoma guards each did several jobs, even guards with his particular heritage and blessings.

He closed his eyes, kneading and humming his mother's song to a beat he could almost, barely, just *faintly* hear.

A short time later, he heard soft footsteps crossing the bridge behind. Prince Renarin stopped beside the cauldron, his duty of transferring people through the Oathgate finished for now. On the plateau, more than a third of Bridge Four had figured out how to draw in Stormlight, but none of the newcomers had managed it, despite Kaladin's coaching.

Renarin watched with flushed cheeks. He'd obviously run to get here once released from his other duty, but now he was hesitant. Elhokar had set up to watch near some rocks, and Renarin stepped toward him, as if sitting at the side and watching was his place too.

"Hey!" Lunamor said. "Renarin!"

Renarin jumped. The boy wore his blue Bridge Four uniform, though his seemed somehow . . . neater than the others.

"I could use some help with this bread," Lunamor said.

Renarin smiled immediately. All the youth ever wanted was to be treated like the rest of them. Well, that attitude benefited a man. Lunamor would have the highprince himself kneading dough, if he could get away with it. Dalinar seemed like he could use a good session of making bread.

Renarin washed his hands, then sat on the ground across from Lunamor and followed his lead. Lunamor ripped off a piece of dough about as wide as his hand, flattened it, then slapped it against one of the large stones he'd put to warm by the fire. The dough stuck to the stone, where it would cook until one peeled it off.

Lunamor didn't push Renarin to talk. Some people you wanted to press, draw them out. Others you wanted to let move at their own pace. Like the difference between a stew you brought to a boil and one you kept at a simmer.

But where is his god? Lunamor could see all spren. Prince Renarin had bonded one, except Lunamor had never been able to spot it. He bowed when Renarin wasn't looking, just in case, and made a sign of reverence to the hidden god.

"Bridge Four is doing well," Renarin finally said. "He'll have them all drinking Stormlight soon."

"Likely so," Lunamor said. "Ha! But they have much time until they catch up to you. Truthwatcher! Is good name. More people should watch truth, instead of lies."

Renarin blushed. "I . . . I suppose it means I can't be in Bridge Four anymore, doesn't it?"

"Why not?"

"I'm a different order of Radiant," Renarin said, eyes down as he formed a perfectly round piece of dough, then carefully set it onto a stone.

"You have power to heal."

"The Surges of Progression and Illumination. I'm not sure how to make the second one work though. Shallan has explained it seven times, but I can't create even the smallest illusion. Something's wrong."

"Still, only healing for now? This thing will be very useful to Bridge Four!"

"I can't *be* Bridge Four anymore."

"That is nonsense. Bridge Four is not Windrunners."

"Then what is it?"

"It is us," Lunamor sad. "It is me, it is them, it is you." He nodded toward Dabbid. "That one, he will never hold spear again. He will not fly, but he is Bridge Four. I am forbidden to fight, but I am Bridge Four. And you, you might have fancy title and different powers." He leaned forward. "But I know Bridge Four. And you, Renarin Kholin, are Bridge Four."

Renarin smiled widely. "But Rock, don't you ever worry that you aren't the person everyone thinks you are?"

"Everyone thinks I am loud, insufferable lout!" Lunamor said. "So to be something else would not be bad thing."

Renarin chuckled.

"You think this about yourself?" Lunamor said.

"Maybe," Renarin said, making another perfectly round piece of dough. "I don't know *what* I am most days, Rock, but I seem to be the only one. Since I could walk, everyone was saying, 'Look how bright he is. He should be an ardent.'"

Lunamor grunted. Sometimes, even if you were loud and insufferable, you knew when not to say anything.

"Everyone thinks it's *so obvious*. I have a mind for figures, don't I? Yes, join the ardents. Of course, nobody *says* I'm much less of a man than my brother, and nobody points out that it *sure* would be nice for the succession if the sickly, strange younger brother were safely tucked away in a monastery."

"When you say these things, you are *almost* not bitter!" Lunamor said. "Ha! Much practice must have been required."

"A lifetime."

"Tell me," Lunamor said. "Why do you wish to be man who fights, Renarin Kholin?"

"Because it's what my father always wanted," Renarin said immediately. "He may not realize it, but it's there, Rock."

Lunamor grunted. "Perhaps this is stupid reason, but it is reason, and I can respect that. But tell me, why do you *not* want to become ardent or stormwarden?"

"Because everyone assumes I will be!" Renarin said, slapping bread down on the heated stones. "If I go and do it, I'm giving in to what they all say." He looked for something to fidget with, and Lunamor tossed him more dough.

"I think," Lunamor said, "your problem is different than you say. You claim you are not the person everyone thinks you are. Maybe you worry, instead, that you *are* that person."

"A sickly weakling."

"No," Lunamor said, leaning in. "You can be you without this being bad thing. You can admit you act and think differently from your brother, but can learn not to see this as flaw. It is just Renarin Kholin."

Renarin started kneading the dough furiously.

"Is good," Lunamor said, "that you learn to fight. Men do well learning many different skills. But men also do well using what the gods have given them. In the Peaks, a man may not have such choices. Is privilege!"

"I suppose. Glys says . . . Well, it's complicated. I could talk to the ardents, but I'm hesitant to do anything that would make me stand out from the other bridgemen, Rock. I'm already the oddest one in this bunch."

"Is that so?"

"Don't deny it, Rock. Lopen is . . . well, Lopen. And you're obviously . . . um . . . you. But *I'm* still the strange one. I've always been the strangest one."

Lunamor slapped dough onto a rock, then pointed toward where Rlain—the Parshendi bridgeman they used to call Shen—sat on a rock near his squad, watching quietly as the others laughed at Eth having accidentally stuck a stone to his hand. He wore warform, and so was taller and stronger than he had been before—but the humans seemed to have completely forgotten that he was there.

"Oh," Renarin said. "I don't know if he counts."

"This thing is what everyone always tells him," Lunamor said. "Over and over again."

Renarin stared for a long time while Lunamor continued to make bread. Finally, Renarin stood up and dusted off his uniform, walked across the stone plateau, and settled down beside Rlain. Renarin fidgeted and didn't say anything, but Rlain seemed to appreciate the company anyway.

Lunamor smiled, then finished the last of the bread. He rose and set up the shiki drink with a stack of wooden cups. He took another drink himself, then shook his head and glanced at Huio, who was harvesting the bread. The Herdazian man was glowing faintly—clearly, he'd already learned how to draw in Stormlight.

Airsick Herdazian. Lunamor raised a hand and Huio tossed him a flatbread, which Lunamor bit. He chewed the warm bread, thoughtful. "More salt in the next batch?"

The Herdazian just kept harvesting the bread.

"You do think they need more salt, don't you?" Lunamor said.

Huio shrugged.

"Add more salt to that batch that I've started mixing," Lunamor said. "And do not look so self-satisfied. I may still throw you off side of plateau."

Huio smiled and kept working.

The men soon started coming over for something to drink. They grinned, thumped Lunamor on the back, told him he was a genius. But of course, none remembered that he had tried serving them shiki once before. They had mostly left it in the cauldron, opting for beer instead.

That day they hadn't been hot, sweaty, and frustrated. Know your enemy. Out here, with the right drink, he was a little god unto himself. Ha! A god of cool drinks and friendly advice. Any chef worth his spoons learned to talk, because cooking was an art—and art was subjective. One man could love an ice sculpture while another thought it boring. It was the same with food and drink. It did not make the food broken, or the person broken, to not be liked.

He chatted with Leyten, who was still shaken by their experience with the dark god below Urithiru. Powerful god that had been, and very vengeful. There were legends of such things in the Peaks; Lunamor's great-great-great-grandfather had met with one while traveling the third divide. Excellent and important story, which Lunamor did not share today.

He calmed Leyten, commiserated with him. The thick-bodied armorer was a fine man, and could talk as loudly as Lunamor sometimes. Ha! You could hear him two plateaus away, which Lunamor liked. What was the point of a little voice? Weren't voices for being heard?

Leyten went back to his practice, but others had their worries. Skar was the best spearman among them—particularly now that Moash had left—but was feeling self-conscious at not having drawn in Stormlight. Lunamor asked Skar to show him what he'd learned, and—after Skar's instruction—Lunamor actually managed to draw some in himself. To his delight and surprise.

Skar left with a spring to his step. Another man would have felt worse, but Skar was a teacher at heart. The short man still hoped that Lunamor would someday choose to fight. He was the only one of the bridgemen who actively spoke out about Lunamor's pacifism.

Once the men had been thoroughly watered, Lunamor found himself looking out across the plateaus for some sign of movement in the distance. Well, best to keep busy with the meal. The stew was perfect—he was pleased to have been able to get the crabs. So much of what everyone ate in the tower was of Soulcast grain or meat, neither of which was very appetizing. The flatbread had cooked up nicely, and he'd even been able to concoct a chutney last night. Now he just had to . . .

Lunamor almost stumbled into his own cauldron as he saw what was assembling on the plateau to his left. *Gods!* Strong gods, like Sylphrena. Glowing a faint blue, they clustered around a tall spren woman, who had long hair streaming behind her. She had taken the shape of a person, human sized, and wore an elegant gown. The others swirled about in the air, though their focus was obviously the practicing bridgemen and hopefuls.

"Uma'ami tukuma mafah'liki . . ." Lunamor started, hastily making the signs of respect. Then, to be sure, he got down on his knees and bowed. He had never seen so many in one place. Even his occasional meeting with an afah'liki in the Peaks did not hit him as hard as this.

What was the proper offering? He could not give only bows for such a sight as this. But bread and stew? Mafah'liki would not want bread and stew.

"You," a feminine voice said beside him, "are so wonderfully respectful, it borders on being silly."

Lunamor turned to find Sylphrena sitting on the side of his cauldron, in her small and girlish shape, legs crossed and hanging over the edge.

He made the sign again. "They are your kin? Is this woman at their front your nuatoma, ali'i'kamura?"

"Kind of maybe sort of halfway," she said, cocking her head. "I can barely remember a voice . . . her voice, Phendorana, reprimanding me. I got in *so* much trouble for searching out Kaladin. Yet here they are! They won't speak to me. I think they assume that if they do, they'd have to admit to me they were wrong." She leaned forward, grinning. "And they absolutely hate being wrong."

Lunamor nodded solemnly.

"You're not as brown as you were," Sylphrena said.

"Yes, my tan is fading," Lunamor said. "Too much time indoors, mafah'liki."

"Humans can change colors?"

"Some more than others," Lunamor said, holding up his hand. "Some from other peaks are pale, like Shin, though my peak has always been more bronze."

"You look like somebody washed you *way* too much," Sylphrena said. "They took a scrub brush to you, and rubbed your skin off! And that's why your hair is red, because you got so sore!"

"These are wise words," Lunamor said. He wasn't sure why yet. He'd have to ponder them.

He fished in his pocket for the spheres that he had on him, which weren't many. Still, he arranged each one in its own bowl and then approached the assemblage of spren. There had to be two dozen or more of them! Kali'kalin'da!

The other bridgemen couldn't see the gods, of course. He wasn't sure what Huio or Hobber thought of him walking reverently across the plateau, then bowing himself and arranging the bowls with their spheres as offerings. When he looked up, the ali'i'kamura—the most important god here—was studying him. She rested her hand over one of the bowls and drew out the Stormlight. Then she left, turning into a streak of light and zipping away.

The others remained, a mottled collection of clouds, ribbons, people, bunches of leaves, and other natural objects. They flitted overhead, watching the practicing men and women.

Sylphrena crossed the air to stand beside Lunamor's head.

"They are looking," Lunamor whispered. "This thing *is* happening. Not just bridgemen. Not just squires. Radiants, as Kaladin wishes."

"We'll see," she said, then huffed softly before zipping away as a ribbon of light herself.

Lunamor left the bowls in case any of the others wished to partake of his offering. At his cook station, he stacked up the flatbread, intending to give the plates to Hobber to hold and distribute. Only, Hobber didn't respond to his request. The lanky man sat on his little stool, leaning forward, his hand in a tight fist that glowed from the gemstone inside. The cups he'd been washing lay in an ignored stack beside him.

Hobber's mouth moved—whispering—and he stared at that glowing fist in the same way a man might stare at the tinder in his firepit on a very cold night, surrounded by snow. Desperation, determination, prayer.

Do it, Hobber, Lunamor thought, stepping forward. *Drink it in. Make it yours.* Claim *it.*

Lunamor felt an energy to the air. A moment of focus. Several windspren turned toward Hobber, and for a heartbeat Lunamor thought that everything else faded. Hobber became one man alone in a darkened place, fist glowing. He stared, unblinking, at that sign of power. That sign of *redemption.*

The light in Hobber's fist went out.

"Ha!" Lunamor shouted. "HA!"

Hobber jumped in surprise. His jaw dropped and he stared at the now-dun gemstone. Then he held up his hand, gawking at the luminescent smoke that rose from it. "Guys?" he called. "Guys, *guys!*"

Lunamor stepped back as the bridgemen left their stations and came rushing over. "Give him your gemstones!" Kaladin called. "He's going to need a lot! Pile them up!"

Bridgemen scrambled to give Hobber their emeralds, and he drew in more and more Stormlight. Then the light suddenly dampened. "I can feel them again!" Hobber cried. "I can feel my toes!"

He tentatively reached out for support. Drehy under one arm, Peet under the other, Hobber slipped off his stool and stood up. He grinned with a gap-toothed expression, and almost fell over—his legs obviously weren't very strong. Drehy and Peet righted him, but he forced them back, to let him stand precariously on his own.

The men of Bridge Four waited only briefly before pressing in with cries of excitement. Joyspren swirled around the group, like a sweeping gust of blue leaves. Amid them, Lopen shoved in close and made the Bridge Four salute.

It seemed to mean something special, coming from him. Two arms.

One of the first times Lopen had been able to make the salute. Hobber saluted back, grinning like a boy who'd just hit his first center shot with the bow.

Kaladin stepped up beside Lunamor, Sylphrena on his shoulder. "It *will* work, Rock. This will protect them."

Lunamor nodded, then by habit checked toward the west as he'd been doing all day. This time he spotted something.

It looked like a plume of smoke.

⁌

Kaladin flew to check it out. Lunamor, along with the rest of them, followed along on the ground, carrying their mobile bridge.

Lunamor ran at the center front of the bridge. It smelled of memories. The wood, the stain used to seal it. The sounds of several dozen men grunting and breathing in the enclosed spaces. The slapping of feet on plateau. Mixed exhaustion and terror. An assault. Arrows flying. Men dying.

Lunamor had known what might happen when he chose to come down from the Peaks with Kef'ha. No nuatoma from the Peaks had ever yet won a Shardblade or Shardplate from the Alethi or Vedens they challenged. Still, Kef'ha had determined the cost was worth the risk. At worst he had thought he would end up dead, and his family would become servants to a wealthy lowlander.

They hadn't anticipated the cruelty of Torol Sadeas, who had murdered Kef'ha without a proper duel, killed many of Lunamor's family who resisted, and seized his property.

Lunamor roared, charging forward, and his skin started to glow with the power of the Stormlight from his pouch and the spheres he had collected before leaving. He seemed to be carrying the bridge all on his own, towing the others.

Skar called out a marching song, and Bridge Four thundered the words. Bridge Four had grown strong enough to carry the bridge long distances without difficulty, but this day put those previous runs to shame. They ran at a sprint the entire distance, vibrant with Stormlight, Lunamor calling the commands as Kaladin or Teft had once done. When they reached a chasm, they practically tossed the bridge across. When they picked it up on the other side, it seemed light as a reed.

It felt like they'd barely started going before they neared the source of the smoke: a beleaguered caravan crossing the plains. Lunamor threw his weight against the bridge's outer support rods, pushing it across the chasm, then he charged over. Others followed. Dabbid and Lopen unhooked shields and spears from the side of the bridge and tossed one to each bridgeman as they passed. They fell into squads, and the men who normally followed Teft fell in behind Lunamor, though he had—of course—refused the spear Lopen tried to toss him.

Many of the caravan wagons had been transporting lumber from the forests outside the warcamps, though some were piled high with furniture. Dalinar Kholin spoke of repopulating his warcamp, but the two highprinces who remained behind had been encroaching on the land—quietly, like eels. For now, it was best to scavenge what they could and bring it to Urithiru.

The caravan had been using Dalinar's large, wheeled bridges to cross chasms. Lunamor passed one of these, lying on its side, broken. Three of the large lumber wagons near it had been set afire, making the air acrid with smoke.

Kaladin floated overhead, holding his brilliant Shardspear. Lunamor squinted through the smoke in the direction Kaladin was looking, and made out figures streaking away through the sky.

"Voidbringer attack," Drehy muttered. "We should have guessed they'd start raiding our caravans."

Lunamor didn't care at the moment. He pushed his way through weary caravan guards and frightened merchants hiding under wagons. There were bodies everywhere; the Voidbringers had killed dozens. Lunamor searched through the mess, trembling. Was that red hair on a corpse? No, that was blood soaking a headscarf. And that . . .

That other body wasn't human—it had marbled skin. A brilliant white arrow stuck from its back, fletched with goose feathers. An Unkalaki arrow.

Lunamor looked to the right, where someone had piled up furniture in a heap, almost like a fortification. A head poked up over the top, a stout woman with a round face and a deep red braid. She stood up tall and raised a bow toward Lunamor. Other faces peeked out from behind the furniture. Two youths, a boy and a girl, both around sixteen. Younger faces from there. Six in total.

Lunamor dashed toward them and found himself blubbering, tears streaming down his cheeks as he crawled up the outside of their improvised fortification.

His family, at long last, had arrived at the Shattered Plains.

⁘

"This is Song," Lunamor said, pulling the woman close, one arm around her shoulders. "Is best woman in all the Peaks. Ha! We made snow forts as childs, and hers was always best. I should have known to find her in castle, even if it was made of old chairs!"

"Snow?" Lopen asked. "How do you make forts out of snow? I've heard all about this stuff—it's like frost, right?"

"Airsick lowlander." Lunamor shook his head, moving to the twins. He put one hand on each of their shoulders. "Boy is Gift. Girl is Cord. Ha! When I left, Gift was short like Skar. Now he is nearly my height!"

He struggled to keep the pain from his voice. It had been almost a year. So long. Originally, his intent had been to bring them as soon as possible, but then everything had gone wrong. Sadeas, the bridge crews . . .

"Next son is Rock, but not same kind of Rock as me. This is . . . um . . . smaller Rock. Third son is Star. Second daughter is Kuma'tiki—is kind of shell, you do not have him here. Last daughter is another Song. Beautiful Song." He stooped down beside her, smiling. She was only four, and she shied away from him. She didn't remember her father. It broke his heart.

Song—Tuaka'li'na'calmi'nor—put her hand on his back. Nearby, Kaladin introduced Bridge Four, but only Gift and Cord had been taught lowlander languages, and Cord spoke only Veden. Gift managed a passable greeting in Alethi.

Little Song sought her mother's legs. Lunamor blinked away tears, though they were not completely sad tears. His family was *here*. His first saved wages had paid for the message, sent by spanreed to the Peaks message station. That station was still a week's travel from his home, and from there, traveling down from the slopes and crossing Alethkar took months.

Around them the caravan was finally limping into motion. This was the first chance Lunamor had found to introduce his family, as Bridge Four had spent the last half hour trying to help the wounded. Then, Renarin had arrived with Adolin and two companies of troops—and for all Renarin's worries about not being useful, his healing had saved several lives.

Tuaka rubbed Lunamor's back, then knelt down beside him, pulling their daughter close with one arm, Lunamor with the other. "It was a long journey," she said in Unkalaki, "and longest at the end, when those things came from the sky."

"I should have come to the warcamps," Lunamor said. "To escort you."

"We're here now," she said. "Lunamor, what happened? Your note was so terse. Kef'ha is dead, but what happened to you? Why so long without word?"

He bowed his head. How could he explain this? The bridge runs, the cracks in his soul. How could he explain that the man she'd always said was so strong had wished to die? Had been a coward, had given up, near the end?

"What of Tifi and Sinaku'a?" she asked him.

"Dead," he whispered. "They raised weapons in vengeance."

She put her hand to her lips. She wore a glove on her safehand, in deference to silly Vorin traditions. "Then you—"

"I am a chef now," Lunamor said, firm.

"But—"

"I cook, Tuaka." He pulled her close again. "Come, let us take the children to safety. We will reach the tower, which you will like—it is like the Peaks, almost. I will tell you stories. Some are painful."

"Very well. Lunamor, I have stories too. The Peaks, our home . . . something is wrong. Very wrong."

He pulled back and met her eyes. They'd call her darkeyed down here, though he found infinite depth, beauty, and light in those deep brown-green eyes.

"I will explain when we are safe," she promised, picking up little Beautiful Song. "You are wise to usher us forward. Wise as ever."

"No, my love," he whispered. "I am a fool. I would blame the air, but I was a fool above too. A fool to ever let Kef'ha leave on this errand of stupidity."

She walked the children across the bridge. He watched, and was glad to hear Unkalaki again, a proper language. Glad that the other men did not speak it. For if they did, they might have picked out the lies that he had told them.

Kaladin stepped up, clapping him on the shoulder. "I'm going to assign your family my rooms, Rock. I've been slow in getting family quarters for the bridgemen. This will light a fire under me. I'll get us an assignment, and until then I'll bunk with the rest of the men."

Lunamor opened his mouth to object, then thought better of it. Some days, the more honorable thing was to take a gift without complaint. "Thank you," he said. "For the rooms. For other things, my captain."

"Go walk with your family, Rock. We can handle the bridge without you today. We have Stormlight."

Lunamor rested his fingers on the smooth wood. "No," he said. "It will be a privilege to carry him one last time, for my family."

"One last time?" Kaladin said.

"We take to the skies, Stormblessed," Lunamor said. "We will walk no more in coming days. This is the end." He looked back toward a subdued Bridge Four group, who seemed to sense that what he said was true. "Ha! Do not look so sad. I left great stew back near city. Hobber will probably not ruin it before we return. Come! Pick up our bridge. The last time, we march not toward death, but toward full stomachs and good songs!"

Despite his urging, it was a solemn, respectful group who lifted the bridge. They were slaves no longer. Storms, in their pockets they carried riches! It glowed fiercely, and soon their skin did as well.

Kaladin took his place at the front. Together they carried the bridge on one final run—reverently, as if it were the bier of a king, being taken to his tomb for his eternal rest.

38

BROKEN PEOPLE

*Your skills are admirable, but you are merely a man. You had your
chance to be more, and refused it.*

Dalinar entered the next vision in the middle of a fight.

He had learned his lesson; he didn't intend to mire another
person in an unexpected battle. This time he intended to find a
safe point, *then* bring people in.

That meant appearing as he had many months ago: holding a spear in
sweaty hands, standing on a forlorn and broken plate of rock, surrounded
by men in primitive clothing. They wore wraps of rough-spun lavis fibers
and sandals of hogshide, and carried spears with bronze heads. Only the
officer wore armor: a mere leather jerkin, not even properly hardened. It
had been cured, then cut roughly into the shape of a vest. It proved no help
against an axe to the face.

Dalinar roared, indistinctly remembering his first time in this vision. It
had been one of the very earliest, when he still discounted them as nightmares. Today, he intended to tease out its secrets.

He charged the enemy, a group of men in similarly shoddy clothing.
Dalinar's companions had backed themselves up to the edge of a cliff. If
they didn't fight now, they'd be pushed off onto a steep incline that eventually ended in a sheer drop and a plummet of some fifty or sixty feet to the
bottom of a valley.

Dalinar rammed into the enemy group trying to push his men off the
cliff. He wore the same clothing as the others, carried their weapons, but
had brought one oddity: a pouch full of gemstones tucked at his waist.

He gutted one enemy with his spear, then shoved the fellow toward the others: thirty or so men with ragged beards and callous eyes. Two tripped over their dying friend, which protected Dalinar's flank for a moment. He seized the fallen man's axe, then attacked to his left.

The enemy resisted, howling. These men weren't well trained, but any fool with a sharpened edge could be dangerous. Dalinar cut, slashed, laid about himself with the axe—which was well balanced, a good weapon. He was confident he could beat this group.

Two things went wrong. First, the other spearmen didn't support him. Nobody filled in behind to protect him from being surrounded.

Second, the wild men didn't flinch.

Dalinar had come to rely on the way soldiers pulled away when they saw him fighting. He depended on their discipline to fail—even when he hadn't been a Shardbearer, he'd counted on his ferocity, his sheer *momentum*, to win fights.

Turned out, the momentum of one man—no matter how skilled or determined—amounted to little when running into a stone wall. The men before him didn't bend, didn't panic, didn't so much as quiver as he killed four of them. They struck at him with increased ferocity. One even laughed.

In a flash, his arm was chopped by an axe he didn't even see, then he was shoved over by the rush of the attackers. Dalinar hit the ground, stunned, looking with disbelief at the stump of his left forearm. The pain seemed a disconnected thing, distant. Only a single painspren, like a hand made of sinew, appeared by his knees.

Dalinar felt a shattering, humbling sense of his own mortality. Was this what every veteran felt, when he finally fell on the battlefield? This bizarre, surreal sense of both disbelief and long-buried resignation?

Dalinar set his jaw, then used his good hand to pull free the leather strap he was using for a belt. Holding one end in his teeth, he wrapped it around the stump of his arm right above the elbow. The cut wasn't bleeding too badly yet. Took a moment for a wound like this to bleed; the body constricted blood flow at first.

Storms. This blow had gone clean through. He reminded himself that this wasn't his actual flesh exposed to the air. That it wasn't his own bone there, like the center ring of a hunk of pork.

Why not heal yourself as you did in the vision with Fen? the Stormfather asked. *You have Stormlight.*

"Cheating," Dalinar said with a grunt.

Cheating? the Stormfather said. *Why in Damnation would that be cheating? You made no oath.*

Dalinar smiled to hear a fragment of God cursing. He wondered if the Stormfather was picking up bad habits from him. Ignoring the pain as best he could, Dalinar seized his axe in one hand and stumbled to his feet. Ahead of him, his squad of twelve fought desperately—and poorly—against the frantic enemy assault. They'd backed right to the edge of the cliff. With the towering rock formations all around, this place almost felt like a chasm, though it was considerably more open.

Dalinar wavered, and almost collapsed again. Storm it.

Just heal yourself, the Stormfather said.

"I used to be able to shrug off things like this." Dalinar looked down at his missing arm. Well, perhaps nothing as bad as this.

You're old, the Stormfather said.

"Maybe," Dalinar said, steadying himself, his vision clearing. "But they made a mistake."

Which is?

"They turned their backs on *me.*"

Dalinar charged again, wielding the axe in one hand. He dropped two of the enemy, punching through to his men. "Down!" he shouted to them. "We can't fight them up here. Skid down the incline to that ledge below! We'll try to find a way to climb down from there!"

He jumped off the cliff and hit the incline in motion. It was a reckless maneuver, but storms, they'd never survive up above. He slid down the stone, staying on his feet as he approached the sheer drop into the valley. A final small ledge of stone gave him a place to lurch to a stop.

Other men slid down around him. He dropped his axe and seized one man, keeping him from falling all the way off the ledge to his doom. He missed two others.

In all, seven men managed to stop around him. Dalinar puffed out, feeling light-headed again, then looked down over the side of their current perch. At least fifty feet to the bottom of the canyon.

His fellows were a broken, ragged group of men, bloodied and afraid. Exhaustionspren shot up nearby, like jets of dust. Above, the wild men clustered around the edge, looking down longingly, like axehounds contemplating the food on the master's table.

"Storms!" The man Dalinar had saved slumped down. "Storms! They're dead. Everyone's dead." He wrapped his arms around himself.

Looking about him, Dalinar counted only one man besides himself who had kept his weapon. The tourniquet he'd made was letting blood seep out.

"We win this war," Dalinar said softly.

Several others looked to him.

"We *win.* I've seen it. Our platoon is one of the last still fighting. While we may yet fall, the war itself is being won."

Above, a figure joined the wild men: a creature a good head taller than the others, with fearsome carapace armor of black and red. Its eyes glowed a deep crimson.

Yes . . . Dalinar remembered that creature. In this vision before, he'd been left for dead up above. This figure had walked past: a monster from a nightmare, he'd assumed, dredged from his subconscious, similar to the beings he fought on the Shattered Plains. Now he recognized the truth. That was a Voidbringer.

But there had been no Everstorm in the past; the Stormfather confirmed that. So where had those things come from, back during this time?

"Form up," Dalinar commanded. "Get ready!"

Two of the men listened, scrambling over to him. Honestly, two out of seven was more than he'd expected.

The cliff face shook as if something huge had struck it. And then the stones nearby *rippled*. Dalinar blinked. Was the blood loss causing his vision to waver? The stone face seemed to shimmer and undulate, like the surface of a pond that had been disturbed.

Someone grabbed the rim of their ledge from below. A figure resplendent in Shardplate—each piece visibly glowing an amber color at its edges despite the daylight—hauled itself onto their ledge. The imposing figure stood even larger than other men wearing Shardplate.

"Flee," the Shardbearer commanded. "Get your men to the healers."

"How?" Dalinar asked. "The cliff—"

Dalinar started. The cliff had handholds now.

The Shardbearer pressed his hand against the incline leading up toward the Voidbringer, and again the stone seemed to writhe. Steps formed in the rock, as if it were made of wax that could flow and be shaped. The Shardbearer extended his hand to the side, and a massive, glowing hammer appeared there.

He charged upward toward the Voidbringer.

Dalinar felt the rock, which was firm to his touch. He shook his head, then ushered his men to start climbing down.

The last one looked at the stump of his arm. "How are you going to follow, Malad?"

"I'll manage," Dalinar said. "Go."

The man left. Dalinar was growing more and more fuzzy-headed. Finally, he relented and drew in some Stormlight.

His arm regrew. First the cut healed, then the flesh expanded outward like a budding plant. In moments he wriggled his fingers, awed. He'd shrugged off a *lost arm* like a stubbed toe. The Stormlight cleared his head, and he took a deep, refreshed breath.

The sounds of fighting came from above, but even craning his neck, he couldn't see much—though a body did roll down the incline, then slip off the ledge.

"Those are humans," Dalinar said.

Obviously.

"I never put it together before," Dalinar said. "There were men who fought *for* the Voidbringers?"

Some.

"And that Shardbearer I saw? A Herald?"

No. Merely a Stoneward. That Surge that changed the stone is the other you may learn, though it may serve you differently.

Such a contrast. The regular soldiers looked so primitive, but that Surgebinder . . .

With a shake of his head, Dalinar climbed down, using the handholds in the rock face. Dalinar spotted his fellows joining a large group of soldiers farther down the canyon. Shouts and whoops of joy echoed against the walls from that direction. It was as he vaguely remembered: The war had been won. Only pockets of the enemy still resisted. The larger bulk of the army was starting to celebrate.

"All right," Dalinar said. "Bring in Navani and Jasnah." He eventually planned to show this vision to the young emperor of Azir, but first he wanted to prepare. "Put them somewhere close to me, please. Let them keep their own clothing."

Nearby, two men stopped in place. A mist of glowing Stormlight obscured their forms, and when the mist faded, Navani and Jasnah stood there, wearing havahs.

Dalinar jogged over to them. "Welcome to my madness, ladies."

Navani turned about, craning her neck to stare up at the tops of the castle-like rock formations. She glanced toward a group of soldiers who limped past, one man helping his wounded companion and calling for Regrowth. "Storms!" Navani whispered. "It feels so real."

"I did warn you," Dalinar said. "Hopefully you don't look *too* ridiculous back in the rooms." Though he had become familiar enough with the visions that his body no longer acted out what he was doing in them, that wouldn't be so for Jasnah, Navani, or any of the monarchs he brought in.

"What is that woman doing?" Jasnah asked, curious.

A younger woman met the limping men. A Radiant? She had the look about her, though she wasn't armored. It was more her air of confidence, the way she settled them down and took something glowing from the pouch at her belt.

"I remember this," Dalinar said. "It's one of those devices I mentioned from another vision. The ones that provide Regrowth, as they call it. Healing."

Navani's eyes widened, and she beamed like a child who had been given a plate full of sweets for Middlefest. She gave Dalinar a quick hug, then hurried over to watch. She stepped right up to the side of the group, then waved impatiently for the Radiant to continue.

Jasnah turned to look around the canyon. "I know of no place in our time of this description, Uncle. This seems like the stormlands, from those formations."

"Maybe it's lost somewhere in the Unclaimed Hills?"

"That, or it's been so long the rock formations have weathered away completely." She narrowed her eyes at a group of people who came through the canyon, carrying water to the soldiers. Last time, Dalinar had stumbled down into the canyon just in time to meet them and get a drink.

You're needed above, one had told him, pointing up the shallow slope along the side of the canyon opposite where he had been fighting.

"That clothing," Jasnah said softly. "Those weapons . . ."

"We've gone back to ancient times."

"Yes, Uncle," Jasnah said. "But didn't you tell me this vision comes at the end of the Desolations?"

"From what I remember of it, yes."

"So the vision with the Midnight Essence happened before this, chronologically. Yet you saw steel, or at least iron, in that one. Remember the poker?"

"I'm not likely to forget." He rubbed his chin. "Iron and steel then, but men wielding crude weapons here, of copper and bronze. As if they didn't know how to Soulcast iron, or at least not how to forge it properly, despite it being a later date. Huh. That *is* odd."

"This is confirmation of what we've been told, but which I could never quite believe. The Desolations were so terrible they destroyed learning and progress and left behind a broken people."

"The orders of Radiants were supposed to stop that," Dalinar said. "I learned it in another vision."

"Yes, I read that one. All of them, actually." She looked to him then, and smiled.

People were always surprised to see emotion from Jasnah, but Dalinar considered that unfair. She did smile—she merely reserved the expression for when it was most genuine.

"Thank you, Uncle," she said. "You have given the world a grand gift. A man can be brave in facing down a hundred enemies, but coming into these—and recording them rather than hiding them—was bravery on an entirely different level."

"It was mere stubbornness. I refused to believe I was mad."

"Then I bless your stubbornness, Uncle." Jasnah pursed her lips in thought, then continued more softly. "I'm worried about you, Uncle. What people are saying."

"You mean my heresy?" Dalinar said.

"I'm less worried about the heresy itself, and more how you're dealing with the backlash."

Ahead of them, Navani had somehow bullied the Radiant into letting her look at the fabrial. The day was stretching toward late afternoon, the canyon falling into shadow. But this vision was a long one, and he was content to wait upon Navani. He settled down on a rock.

"I don't deny God, Jasnah," he said. "I simply believe that the being we call the Almighty was never actually God."

"Which is the wise decision to make, considering the accounts of your visions." Jasnah settled down beside him.

"You must be happy to hear me say that," he said.

"I'm happy to have someone to talk to, and I'm certainly happy to see you on a journey of discovery. But am I happy to see you in pain? Am I happy to see you forced to abandon something you held dear?" She shook her head. "I don't mind people believing what works for them, Uncle. That's something nobody ever seems to understand—I have no stake in their beliefs. I don't need *company* to be *confident*."

"How do you suffer it, Jasnah?" Dalinar said. "The things people say about you? I see the lies in their eyes before they speak. Or they will tell me, with utter sincerity, things I have reportedly said—even though I deny them. They refuse my own word against the rumors about me!"

Jasnah stared out across the canyon. More men were gathering at the other end, a weak, beleaguered group who were only now discovering they were the victors in this contest. A large column of smoke rose in the distance, though he couldn't see the source.

"I wish I had answers, Uncle," Jasnah said softly. "Fighting makes you strong, but also callous. I worry I have learned too much of the latter and not enough of the former. But I can give you a warning."

He looked toward her, raising his eyebrows.

"They will try," Jasnah said, "to define you by something you are not. Don't let them. I can be a scholar, a woman, a historian, a Radiant. People will still try to classify me by the thing that makes me an outsider. They want, ironically, the thing I *don't* do or believe to be the prime marker of my identity. I have always rejected that, and will continue to do so."

She reached over and put her freehand on his arm. "You are not a heretic, Dalinar Kholin. You are a king, a Radiant, and a father. You are a man with complicated beliefs, who does not accept everything you are told. *You* decide how you are defined. Don't surrender that to them. They will gleefully take the chance to define you, if you allow it."

Dalinar nodded slowly.

"Regardless," Jasnah said, standing. "This is probably not the best occasion for such a conversation. I realize we can replay this vision at will, but the number of storms in which we can do it will be limited. I should be exploring."

"Last time, I went that way," Dalinar said, pointing up the slope. "I'd like to see what I saw again."

"Excellent. We'd best split to cover more ground. I will go in the other direction, then we can meet afterward and compare notes." She took off down the slope toward the largest gathering of men.

Dalinar stood up and stretched, his earlier exertion still weighing on him. A short time later Navani returned, mumbling explanations of what she'd seen under her breath. Teshav sat with her in the waking world, and Kalami with Jasnah, recording what they said—the only way to take notes in one of these visions.

Navani took his arm in hers and looked after Jasnah, a fond smile on her lips. No, none would think Jasnah emotionless if they'd witnessed that tearful reunion between mother and daughter.

"How did you ever mother that one?" Dalinar asked.

"Mostly without letting her realize she was being mothered," Navani said. She pulled him close. "That fabrial is wonderful, Dalinar. It's like a Soulcaster."

"In what way?"

"In that I have no idea how it works! I think . . . I think something is wrong with the way we've been viewing the ancient fabrials." He looked to her, and she shook her head. "I can't explain yet."

"Navani . . ." he prodded.

"No," she said stubbornly. "I need to present my ideas to the scholars, see if what I'm thinking even makes sense, and then prepare a report. That's the short of it, Dalinar Kholin. So be patient."

"I probably won't understand half of what you say anyway," he grumbled.

He didn't immediately start them up in the direction he'd gone before. Last time he'd been prompted by someone in the vision. He'd acted differently this time. Would the same prompting still come?

He had to wait only a short time until an officer came running up to them.

"You there," the man said. "Malad-son-Zent, isn't that your name? You're promoted to sergeant. Head to base camp three." He pointed up the incline. "Up over that knob there, down the other side. Hop to it!" He spared a frown for Navani—to his eyes, the two of them didn't belong standing in such a familiar pose—but then charged off without another word.

Dalinar smiled.

"What?" Navani said.

"These are set experiences that Honor wanted me to have. Though there's freedom in them, I suspect that the same information will be conveyed no matter what I do."

"So, do you want to disobey?"

Dalinar shook his head. "There are some things I need to see again—now that I understand this vision is accurate, I know better questions to ask."

They started up the incline of smooth rock, walking arm in arm. Dalinar felt unexpected emotions start to churn within him, partially due to Jasnah's words. But this was something deeper: a welling of gratitude, relief, even love.

"Dalinar?" Navani asked. "Are you well?"

"I'm just . . . thinking," he said, trying to keep his voice even. "Blood of my fathers . . . it's been nearly half a year, hasn't it? Since all this started? All that time, I came to these alone. It's just good to share the burden, Navani. To be able to show this to you, and to know for once—absolutely and certainly—that what I'm seeing isn't merely in my own mind."

She pulled him close again, walking with her head on his shoulder. Far more affectionate in public than Alethi propriety would sanction, but hadn't they thrown that out the window long ago? Besides, there was nobody to see—nobody real, anyway.

They crested the slope, then passed several blackened patches. What could burn rock like that? Other sections looked like they'd been broken by an impossible weight, while yet others had strangely shaped holes ripped in them. Navani stopped them beside a particular formation, only knee high, where the rock rippled in a strange little symmetrical pattern. It looked like liquid, frozen midflow.

Cries of pain echoed through these canyons and across the open plain of rock. Looking out over the ridge, Dalinar found the main battlefield. Stretching into the distance were corpses. Thousands of them, some in piles. Others slaughtered in heaps while pressed against walls of stone.

"Stormfather?" Dalinar said, addressing the spren. "This *is* what I told Jasnah it was, isn't it? Aharietiam. The Last Desolation."

That is what it was called.

"Include Navani in your responses," Dalinar requested.

AGAIN, YOU MAKE DEMANDS OF ME. YOU SHOULD NOT DO THIS. The voice rumbled in the open air, and Navani jumped.

"Aharietiam," Dalinar said. "This isn't how songs and paintings depict the final defeat of the Voidbringers. In them, it's always some grand conflict, with tremendous monsters clashing against brave lines of soldiers."

Men lie in their poetry. Surely you know this.

"It just . . . seems so like any other battlefield."

And that rock behind you?

Dalinar turned toward it, then gasped, realizing something he'd mistaken for a boulder was actually a giant skeletal face. A mound of rubble they'd passed was actually one of those *things* he'd seen in a different vision. A stone monster that ripped its way out of the ground.

Navani stepped up to it. "Where are the parshmen?"

"Earlier, I fought against humans," Dalinar said.

They were recruited to the other side, the Stormfather said. I think.

"You think?" Dalinar demanded.

During these days, Honor still lived. I was not yet fully myself. More of a storm. Less interested in men. His death changed me. My memory of that time is difficult to explain. But if you would see parshmen, you need but look across that field.

Navani joined Dalinar at the ridge, looking out over the plain of corpses below. "Which ones?" Navani asked.

You can't tell?

"Not from this distance."

Maybe half of those are what you'd call parshmen.

Dalinar squinted, but still couldn't make out which were human and which were not. He led Navani down the ridge, then across a plain. Here, the corpses intermingled. Men in their primitive clothing. Parshmen corpses that bled orange blood. This was a warning he should have recognized, but hadn't been able to put together his first time in the vision. He'd thought he was seeing a nightmare of their fight on the Shattered Plains.

He knew the path to take, one that led him and Navani across the field of corpses, then into a shadowed recess beneath a tall rocky spire. The light had caught on the rocks here, intriguing him. Before, he thought he'd wandered into this place by accident, but in truth the entire vision had pointed him at this moment.

Here, they found nine Shardblades rammed into the stone. Abandoned. Navani put her gloved safehand to her mouth at the sight—nine beautiful Blades, each a treasure, simply left here? Why and how?

Dalinar stepped through the shadows, rounding the nine Blades. This was another image he'd misunderstood when living this vision the first time. These weren't just Shardblades.

"Ash's eyes," Navani said, pointing. "I recognize that one, Dalinar. It's the one . . ."

"The one that killed Gavilar," Dalinar said, stopping beside the plainest

Blade, long and thin. "The weapon of the Assassin in White. It's an Honorblade. They all are."

"This is the day that the Heralds made their final ascension to the Tranquiline Halls!" Navani said. "To lead the battle there instead."

Dalinar turned to the side, to where he glimpsed the air shimmering. The Stormfather.

"Only . . ." Navani said. "This wasn't actually the end. Because the enemy came back." She walked around the ring of swords, then paused by an open spot in the circle. "Where is the tenth Blade?"

"The stories are wrong, aren't they?" Dalinar said to the Stormfather. "We didn't defeat the enemy for good, as the Heralds claimed. They *lied*."

Navani's head snapped up, her eyes focused on Dalinar.

I LONG BLAMED THEM, the Stormfather said, FOR THEIR LACK OF HONOR. IT IS . . . DIFFICULT FOR ME TO LOOK PAST OATHS BROKEN. I HATED THEM. NOW, THE MORE I COME TO KNOW MEN, THE MORE I SEE HONOR IN THOSE POOR CREATURES YOU NAME HERALDS.

"Tell me what happened," Dalinar said. "What *really* happened?"

ARE YOU READY FOR THIS STORY? THERE ARE PARTS YOU WILL NOT LIKE.

"If I have accepted that God is dead, I can accept the fall of his Heralds."

Navani settled down on a nearby stone, face pale.

IT STARTED WITH THE CREATURES YOU NAME VOIDBRINGERS, the Stormfather said, voice rumbling and low, distant. Introspective? As I SAID, MY VIEW OF THESE EVENTS IS DISTORTED. I DO REMEMBER THAT ONCE, LONG BEFORE THE DAY YOU'RE SEEING NOW, THERE WERE MANY SOULS OF CREATURES WHO HAD BEEN SLAIN, ANGRY AND TERRIBLE. THEY HAD BEEN GIVEN GREAT POWER BY THE ENEMY, THE ONE CALLED ODIUM. THAT WAS THE BEGINNING, THE START OF DESOLATIONS.

FOR WHEN THESE DIED, THEY REFUSED TO PASS ON.

"That's what is happening now," Dalinar said. "The parshmen, they're transformed by these things in the Everstorm. Those things are . . ." He swallowed. "The souls of their dead?"

THEY ARE THE SPREN OF PARSHMEN LONG DEAD. THEY ARE THEIR KINGS, THEIR LIGHTEYES, THEIR VALIANT SOLDIERS FROM LONG, LONG AGO. THE PROCESS IS NOT EASY ON THEM. SOME OF THESE SPREN ARE MERE FORCES NOW, ANIMALISTIC, FRAGMENTS OF MINDS GIVEN POWER BY ODIUM. OTHERS ARE MORE . . . AWAKE. EACH REBIRTH FURTHER INJURES THEIR MINDS.

THEY ARE REBORN USING THE BODIES OF PARSHMEN TO BECOME THE FUSED. AND EVEN BEFORE THE FUSED LEARNED TO COMMAND THE SURGES, MEN COULD NOT FIGHT THEM. HUMANS COULD NEVER WIN

WHEN THE CREATURES THEY KILLED WERE REBORN EACH TIME THEY WERE SLAIN. AND SO, THE OATHPACT.

"Ten people," Dalinar said. "Five male, five female." He looked at the swords. "They stopped this?"

THEY GAVE THEMSELVES UP. AS ODIUM IS SEALED BY THE POWERS OF HONOR AND CULTIVATION, YOUR HERALDS SEALED THE SPREN OF THE DEAD INTO THE PLACE YOU CALL DAMNATION. THE HERALDS WENT TO HONOR, AND HE GAVE THEM THIS RIGHT, THIS OATH. THEY THOUGHT IT WOULD END THE WAR FOREVER. BUT THEY WERE WRONG. HONOR WAS WRONG.

"He was like a spren himself," Dalinar said. "You told me before—Odium too."

HONOR LET THE POWER BLIND HIM TO THE TRUTH—THAT WHILE SPREN AND GODS CANNOT BREAK THEIR OATHS, MEN CAN AND WILL. THE TEN HERALDS WERE SEALED UPON DAMNATION, TRAPPING THE VOID-BRINGERS THERE. HOWEVER, IF ANY ONE OF THE TEN AGREED TO BEND HIS OATH AND LET VOIDBRINGERS PAST, IT OPENED A FLOOD. THEY COULD ALL RETURN.

"And that started a Desolation," Dalinar said.

THAT STARTED A DESOLATION, the Stormfather agreed.

An oath that could be bent, a pact that could be undermined. Dalinar could see what had happened. It seemed so obvious. "They were tortured, weren't they?"

HORRIBLY, BY THE SPIRITS THEY TRAPPED. THEY COULD SHARE THE PAIN BECAUSE OF THEIR BOND—BUT EVENTUALLY, SOMEONE ALWAYS YIELDED.

ONCE ONE BROKE, ALL TEN HERALDS RETURNED TO ROSHAR. THEY FOUGHT. THEY LED MEN. THEIR OATHPACT DELAYED THE FUSED FROM RETURNING IMMEDIATELY, BUT EACH TIME AFTER A DESOLATION, THE HERALDS RETURNED TO DAMNATION TO SEAL THE ENEMY AGAIN. TO HIDE, FIGHT, AND FINALLY WITHSTAND TOGETHER.

THE CYCLE REPEATED. AT FIRST THE RESPITE BETWEEN DESOLATIONS WAS LONG. HUNDREDS OF YEARS. NEAR THE END, DESOLATIONS CAME SEPARATED BY FEWER THAN TEN YEARS. THERE WAS LESS THAN ONE YEAR BETWEEN THE LAST TWO. THE SOULS OF THE HERALDS HAD WORN THIN. THEY BROKE ALMOST AS SOON AS THEY WERE CAUGHT AND TORTURED IN DAMNATION.

"Which explains why things look so bad this time," Navani whispered from her seat. "Society had suffered Desolation after Desolation, separated by short intervals. Culture, technology . . . all broken."

Dalinar knelt and rubbed her shoulder.

"It is not so bad as I feared," she said. "The Heralds, they *were* honorable. Perhaps not as divine, but I may even like them more, to know they were once just normal men and women."

They were broken people, the Stormfather said. But I can start to forgive them, and their shattered oaths. It makes . . . sense to me now as it never did before. He sounded surprised.

"The Voidbringers who did this," Navani said. "They are the ones that are returning now. Again."

The Fused, the souls of the dead from long ago, they loathe you. They are not rational. They have become permeated with his essence, the essence of pure hatred. They will see this world destroyed in order to destroy mankind. And yes, they have returned.

"Aharietiam," Dalinar said, "was not really the end. It was just another Desolation. Except something changed for the Heralds. They left their swords?"

After each Desolation, the Heralds returned to Damnation, the Stormfather said. If they died in the fighting, they went there automatically. And those who survived went back willingly at the end. They had been warned that if any lingered, it could lead to disaster. Besides, they needed to be together, in Damnation, to share the burden of torture if one was captured. But this time, an oddity occurred. Through cowardice or luck, they avoided death. None were killed in battle—except one.

Dalinar looked to the open spot in the ring.

The nine realized, the Stormfather said, that one of them had never broken. Each of the others, at some point, had been the one to give in, to start the Desolation to escape the pain. They determined that perhaps they didn't all need to return.

They decided to stay here, risking an eternal Desolation, but hoping that the one they left in Damnation would alone be enough to hold it all together. The one who wasn't meant to have joined them in the first place, the one who was not a king, scholar, or general.

"Talenelat," Dalinar said.

The Bearer of Agonies. The one abandoned in Damnation. Left to withstand the tortures alone.

"Almighty above," Navani whispered. "How long has it been? Over a thousand years, right?"

Four and a half thousand years, the Stormfather said. Four and a half millennia of torture.

Silence settled over the little alcove, which was adorned with silvery Blades and lengthening shadows. Dalinar, feeling weak, sat down on the ground beside Navani's rock. He stared at those Blades, and felt a sudden irrational hatred for the Heralds.

It was foolish. As Navani had said, they *were* heroes. They'd spared humanity the assaults for great swaths of time, paying with their own sanity. Still, he hated them. For the man they had left behind.

The man . . .

Dalinar leaped to his feet. "It's *him*!" he shouted. "The madman. He really *is* a Herald!"

HE FINALLY BROKE, the Stormfather said. HE HAS JOINED THE NINE, WHO STILL LIVE. IN THESE MILLENNIA NONE HAVE EVER DIED AND RETURNED TO DAMNATION, BUT IT DOESN'T MATTER AS IT ONCE DID. THE OATHPACT HAS BEEN WEAKENED ALMOST TO ANNIHILATION, AND ODIUM HAS CREATED HIS OWN STORM. THE FUSED DO NOT RETURN TO DAMNATION WHEN KILLED. THEY ARE REBORN IN THE NEXT EVERSTORM.

Storms. How could they defeat that? Dalinar looked again at that empty spot among the swords. "The madman, the Herald, he came to Kholinar with a Shardblade. Shouldn't that have been his Honorblade?"

YES. BUT THE ONE DELIVERED TO YOU IS NOT IT. I DO NOT KNOW WHAT HAPPENED.

"I need to speak with him. He . . . he was at the monastery, when we marched. Wasn't he?" Dalinar needed to ask the ardents, to see who had evacuated the madmen.

"Is this what caused the Radiants to rebel?" Navani asked. "Are these secrets what sparked the Recreance?"

NO. THAT IS A DEEPER SECRET, ONE I WILL NOT SPEAK.

"Why?" Dalinar demanded.

BECAUSE WERE YOU TO KNOW IT, YOU WOULD ABANDON YOUR OATHS AS THE ANCIENT RADIANTS DID.

"I wouldn't."

WOULDN'T YOU? the Stormfather demanded, his voice growing louder. WOULD YOU SWEAR IT? SWEAR UPON AN UNKNOWN? THESE HERALDS SWORE THEY WOULD HOLD BACK THE VOIDBRINGERS, AND WHAT HAPPENED TO THEM?

THERE IS NOT A MAN ALIVE WHO HAS NOT BROKEN AN OATH, DALINAR KHOLIN. YOUR NEW RADIANTS HOLD IN THEIR HANDS THE SOULS AND LIVES OF MY CHILDREN. NO. I WILL NOT LET YOU DO AS YOUR PREDECESSORS DID. YOU KNOW THE IMPORTANT PARTS. THE REST IS IRRELEVANT.

Dalinar drew in a deep breath, but contained his anger. In a way, the Stormfather was right. He couldn't know how this secret would affect him or his Radiants.

He'd still rather know it. He felt as if he were walking about with a headsman following, planning to claim his life at any moment.

He sighed as Navani stood and walked to him, taking his arm. "I'll need to try to do sketches from memory of each of those Honorblades—or better, send Shallan to do it. Perhaps we can use the drawings to locate the others."

A shadow moved at the entrance to this little alcove, and a moment later a young man stumbled in. He was pale of skin, with strange, wide Shin eyes and brown hair that had a curl to it. He could have been one of any number of Shin men Dalinar had seen in his own time—they were still ethnically distinct, despite the passing of millennia.

The man fell to his knees before the wonder of the abandoned Honorblades. But a moment later, the man looked to Dalinar, and then spoke with the Almighty's voice. "Unite them."

"Was there nothing you could do for the Heralds?" Dalinar asked. "Was there nothing their God could do to prevent this?"

The Almighty, of course, couldn't answer. He had died fighting this thing they faced, the force known as Odium. He had, in a way, given his own life to the same cause as the Heralds.

The vision faded.

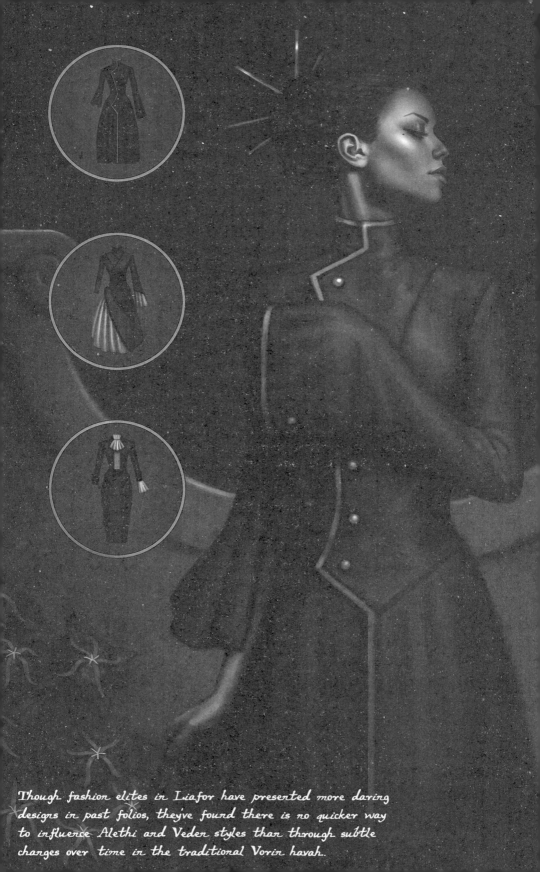

Though fashion elites in Liafor have presented more daring designs in past folios, they've found there is no quicker way to influence Alethi and Veden styles than through subtle changes over time in the traditional Vorin havah.

No good can come of two Shards settling in one location. It was agreed that we would not interfere with one another, and it disappoints me that so few of the Shards have kept to this original agreement.

S hallan can take notes for us," Jasnah said.

Shallan looked up from her notebook. She'd settled against the tile-covered wall, sitting on the floor in her blue havah, and had intended to spend the meeting doing sketches.

It had been over a week since her recovery and subsequent meeting with Jasnah at the crystal pillar. Shallan was feeling better and better, and at the same time less and less like herself. What a surreal experience it was, following Jasnah around as if nothing had changed.

Today, Dalinar had called a meeting of his Radiants, and Jasnah had suggested the basement rooms of the tower because they were so well secured. She was incredibly worried about being spied upon.

The rows of dust had been removed from the library floor; Navani's flock of scholars had carefully catalogued every splinter. The emptiness served only to underscore the absence of the information they'd hoped to find.

Now everyone was looking at her. "Notes?" Shallan asked. She'd barely been following the conversation. "We could call for Brightness Teshav. . . ."

So far, it was a small group. The Blackthorn, Navani, and their core Surgebinders: Jasnah, Renarin, Shallan, and Kaladin Stormblessed, the flying bridgeman. Adolin and Elhokar were away, visiting Vedenar to survey the military capacities of Taravangian's army. Malata was working the Oathgate for them.

"No need to call in another scribe," Jasnah said. "We covered short-hand in your training, Shallan. I'd see how well you've retained the skill. Be fastidious; we will need to report to my brother what we determine here."

The rest of them had settled into a group of chairs except for Kaladin, who stood leaning against the wall. Looming like a thundercloud. He had killed Helaran, her brother. The emotion of that peeked out, but Shallan smothered it, stuffing it into the back of her mind. Kaladin wasn't to be blamed for that. He'd just been defending his brightlord.

She stood up, feeling like a chastened child. The weight of their stares prodded her to walk over and take a seat beside Jasnah with her pad open and pencil ready.

"So," Kaladin said. "According to the Stormfather, not only is the Almighty dead, but he condemned ten people to an eternity of torture. We call them Heralds, and they're not only traitors to their oaths, they're probably also mad. We had one of them in our custody—likely the maddest of the lot—but we lost him in the turmoil of getting everyone to Urithiru. In short, everyone who might have been able to help us is crazy, dead, a traitor, or some combination of the three." He folded his arms. "Figures."

Jasnah glanced at Shallan. She sighed, then recorded a summary of what he'd said. Even though it was *already* a summary.

"So what do we do with this knowledge?" Renarin said, leaning forward with his hands clasped.

"We *must* curb the Voidbringer assault," Jasnah said. "We can't let them secure too great a foothold."

"The parshmen aren't our enemies," Kaladin said softly.

Shallan glanced at him. There *was* something about that wavy dark hair, that grim expression. Always serious, always solemn—and so *tense*. Like he had to be strict with himself to contain his passion.

"Of course they're our enemies," Jasnah said. "They're in the process of *conquering the world*. Even if your report indicates they aren't as immediately destructive as we feared, they are still an enormous threat."

"They just want to live better lives," Kaladin said.

"I can believe," Jasnah said, "that the common parshmen have such a simple motive. But their leaders? They *will* pursue our extinction."

"Agreed," Navani said. "They were born out of a twisted thirst to destroy humankind."

"The parshmen are the key," Jasnah said, shuffling through some pages of notes. "Looking over what you discovered, it seems that all parshmen can bond with ordinary spren as part of their natural life cycle. What we've been calling 'Voidbringers' are instead a combination of a parshman with some kind of hostile spren or spirit."

"The Fused," Dalinar said.

"Great," Kaladin said. "Fine. Let's fight *them*, then. Why do the common folk have to get crushed in the process?"

"Perhaps," Jasnah said, "you should visit my uncle's vision and see for yourself the consequences of a soft heart. Firsthand witness of a Desolation might change your perspective."

"I've seen war, Brightness. I'm a soldier. Problem is, Ideals have expanded my focus. I can't help but see the common men among the enemy. They're *not* monsters."

Dalinar raised a hand to stop Jasnah's reply. "Your concern does you credit, Captain," Dalinar said. "And your reports have been exceptionally timely. Do you honestly see a chance for an accommodation here?"

"I . . . I don't know, sir. Even the common parshmen are furious at what was done to them."

"I can't afford to stay my hand from war," Dalinar said. "Everything you say is right, but it is also nothing new. I have never gone to battle where some poor fools on either side—men who didn't want to be there in the first place—weren't going to bear the brunt of the pain."

"Maybe," Kaladin said, "that should make you reconsider those other wars, rather than using them to justify this one."

Shallan's breath caught. It didn't seem the sort of thing you said to the Blackthorn.

"Would that it were so simple, Captain." Dalinar sighed loudly, looking . . . weathered to Shallan. "Let me say this: If we can be certain of one thing, it is the morality of defending our homeland. I don't ask you to go to war idly, but I *will* ask you to protect. Alethkar is besieged. The men doing it might be innocents, but they are controlled by those who are evil."

Kaladin nodded slowly. "The king has asked my help in opening the Oathgate. I've agreed to give it to him."

"Once we secure our homeland," Dalinar said, "I promise to do something I'd never have contemplated before hearing your reports. I'll seek to negotiate; I'll see if there is some way out of this that doesn't involve smashing our armies together."

"Negotiate?" Jasnah said. "Uncle, these creatures are crafty, ancient, and angry. They spent *millennia* torturing the Heralds just to return and seek our destruction."

"We'll see," Dalinar said. "Unfortunately, I haven't been able to contact anyone in the city with the visions. The Stormfather has found Kholinar to be a 'dark spot' to him."

Navani nodded. "That seems, unfortunately, to coordinate with the failure of the spanreeds in the city. Captain Kaladin's report confirms what our last notes from the city said: The enemy is mobilizing for an assault on the capital. We can't know what the city's status will be once our strike force arrives. You might have to infiltrate an occupied city, Captain."

"Please send that it isn't so," Renarin whispered, eyes down. "How many would have died on those walls, fighting nightmares . . ."

"We need more information," Jasnah said. "Captain Kaladin, how many people can you take with you to Alethkar?"

"I plan to fly at the front of a storm," Kaladin said. "Like I did returning to Urithiru. It's a bumpy ride, but maybe I can fly over the top of the winds. I need to test it. Anyway, I think I could bring a small group."

"You won't need a large force," Dalinar said. "You, a few of your best squires. I'd send Adolin with you too, so you have another Shardbearer in an emergency. Six, perhaps? You, three of your men, the king, Adolin. Get past the enemy, sneak into the palace, and activate the Oathgate."

"Pardon if this is out of line," Kaladin said, "but Elhokar himself is the odd one. Why not just send me and Adolin? The king will probably slow us down."

"The king needs to go for personal reasons. Will there be a problem between you?"

"I'll do what is right, regardless of my feelings, sir. And . . . I might be beyond those feelings anyway, now."

"This is too small," Jasnah mumbled.

Shallan started, then glanced at her. "Too small?"

"Not ambitious enough," Jasnah said more firmly. "By the Stormfather's explanation, the Fused are immortal. Nothing stops their rebirth now that the Heralds have failed. *This* is our real problem. Our enemy has a near-endless supply of parshman bodies to inhabit, and judging by what the good captain has confirmed through experience, these Fused can access some kind of Surgebinding. How do we fight against that?"

Shallan looked up from her notepad, glancing toward the others in the room. Renarin still leaned forward, hands clasped, eyes on the floor. Navani and Dalinar were sharing a look. Kaladin continued to lean against the wall, arms folded, but he shifted his posture, uncomfortable.

"Well," Dalinar finally said. "We'll have to take this one goal at a time. First Kholinar."

"Pardon, Uncle," Jasnah said. "While I don't disagree with that first step, now is not the time to think only of the immediate future. If we are to avoid a Desolation that breaks society, then we'll need to use the past as our guide and make a *plan*."

"She's right," Renarin whispered. "We're facing something that killed the Almighty himself. We fight terrors that break the minds of men and ruin their souls. We can't think small." He ran his hands through his hair, which was marked by less yellow than his brother's. "Almighty. We have to think big—but can we take it all in without going mad ourselves?"

Dalinar took a deep breath. "Jasnah, you have a suggestion of where to start this plan?"

"Yes. The answer is obvious. We need to find the Heralds."

Kaladin nodded in agreement.

"Then," Jasnah added, "we need to kill them."

"*What?*" Kaladin demanded. "Woman, are you insane?"

"The Stormfather laid it out," Jasnah said, unperturbed. "The Heralds made a pact. When they died, their souls traveled to Damnation and trapped the spirits of the Voidbringers, preventing them from returning."

"Yeah. Then the Heralds were *tortured* until they *broke*."

"The Stormfather said their pact was weakened, but did not say it was destroyed," Jasnah said. "I suggest that we at least see if one of them is willing to return to Damnation. Perhaps they can still prevent the spirits of the enemy from being reborn. It's either that, or we completely exterminate the parshmen so that the enemy has no hosts." She met Kaladin's eyes. "In the face of such an atrocity, I would consider the sacrifice of one or more Heralds to be a small price."

"Storms!" Kaladin said, standing up straight. "Have you no sympathy?"

"I have plenty, bridgeman. Fortunately, I temper it with logic. Perhaps you should consider acquiring some at a future date."

"Listen, *Brightness*," Kaladin began. "I—"

"Enough, Captain," Dalinar said. He gave Jasnah a glance. Both fell quiet, Jasnah without so much as a peep. Shallan had never seen her respond to someone with the respect she gave Dalinar.

"Jasnah," Dalinar said. "Even if the pact of the Heralds still holds, we can't know that they'd stay in Damnation—or the mechanics for locking away the Voidbringers there. That said, locating them seems like an excellent first step; they must know much that can greatly assist us. I will leave it to you, Jasnah, to plan out how to accomplish that."

"What . . . what of the Unmade?" Renarin said. "There will be others, like the creature we found down here."

"Navani has been researching them," Dalinar said.

"We need to go even farther, Uncle," Jasnah said. "We need to watch the movements of the Voidbringers. Our only hope is to defeat their armies so soundly that even if their leaders are constantly reborn, they lack the manpower to overwhelm us."

"Protecting Alethkar," Kaladin said, "doesn't have to mean completely crushing the parshmen and—"

"If you wish, Captain," Jasnah snapped, "I can get you some mink kits to cuddle while the adults plan. None of us *want* to talk about this, but that does not make it any less *inevitable*."

"I'd love that," Kaladin responded. "In turn, I'll get you some eels to cuddle. You'll feel right at home."

Jasnah, curiously, smiled. "Let me ask this, Captain. Do you think ignoring the movement of Voidbringer troops would be wise?"

"Probably not," he admitted.

"And do you think, perhaps, that you could train your squire Windrunners to fly up high and scout for us? If spanreeds are proving unreliable these days, we'll need another method of watching the enemy. I'd happily cuddle skyeels, as you offer, if your team would be willing to spend some time *imitating* them."

Kaladin looked to Dalinar, who nodded appreciatively.

"Excellent," Jasnah said. "Uncle, your coalition of monarchs is a superb idea. We need to pen the enemy in and prevent them from overrunning all of Roshar. If . . ."

She trailed off. Shallan paused, looking at the doodle she'd been doing. Actually, it was a bit more complex than a doodle. It was . . . kind of a full sketch of Kaladin's face, with passionate eyes and a determined expression. Jasnah had noticed a creationspren in the form of a small gemstone that had appeared on the top of her page, and Shallan blushed, shooing it away.

"Perhaps," Jasnah said, glancing at Shallan's sketchbook, "we could do with a short break, Uncle."

"If you wish," he said. "I could use something to drink."

They broke up, Dalinar and Navani chatting softly as they went to check with the guards and servants in the main hallway. Shallan watched them go with a sense of longing, as she felt Jasnah loom over her.

"Let us chat," Jasnah said, nodding toward the far end of the long, rectangular room.

Shallan sighed, closed her notebook, and followed Jasnah to the other end, near a pattern of tiles on the wall. This far from the spheres brought for the meeting, the lighting was dim.

"May I?" Jasnah said, holding out her hand for Shallan's notebook.

She relinquished it.

"A fine depiction of the young captain," Jasnah said. "I see . . . three lines of notes here? After you were pointedly instructed to take the minutes."

"We should have sent for a scribe."

"We had a scribe. To take notes is not a lowly task, Shallan. It is a service you can provide."

"If it's not a lowly task," Shallan said, "then perhaps you should have done it."

Jasnah closed the sketchpad and fixed Shallan with a calm, level stare. The type that made Shallan squirm.

"I remember," Jasnah said, "a nervous, desperate young woman. Frantic to earn my goodwill."

Shallan didn't reply.

"I understand," Jasnah said, "that you have enjoyed independence. What you accomplished here is *remarkable,* Shallan. You even seem to have earned my uncle's trust—a challenging task."

"Then maybe we can just call the wardship finished, eh?" Shallan said. "I mean, I'm a full Radiant now."

"Radiant, yes," Jasnah said. "Full? Where's your armor?"

"Um . . . armor?"

Jasnah sighed softly, opening up the sketchpad again. "Shallan," she said in a strangely . . . comforting tone. "I'm impressed. I *am* impressed, truly. But what I've heard of you recently is troubling. You've ingratiated yourself with my family, and made good on the causal betrothal to Adolin. Yet here you are with wandering eyes, as this sketch testifies."

"I—"

"You skip meetings that Dalinar calls," Jasnah continued, soft but immovable. "When you do go, you sit at the back and barely pay attention. He tells me that half the time, you find an excuse to slip out early.

"You investigated the presence of an Unmade in the tower, and frightened it off basically alone. Yet you never explained how you found it when Dalinar's soldiers could not." She met Shallan's eyes. "You've always hidden things from me. Some of those secrets were very damaging, and I find myself unwilling to believe you don't have others."

Shallan bit her lip, but nodded.

"That was an invitation," Jasnah said, "to talk to me."

Shallan nodded again. *She* wasn't working with the Ghostbloods. That was Veil. And Jasnah didn't need to know about Veil. Jasnah *couldn't* know about Veil.

"Very well," Jasnah said with a sigh. "Your wardship is not finished, and won't be until I'm convinced that you can meet minimum requirements of scholarship—such as taking shorthand notes during an important conference. Your path as a Radiant is another matter. I don't know that I can guide you; each order was distinctive in its approach. But as a young man will not be excused from his geography lessons simply because he has achieved competence with the sword, I will not release you from your duties to me simply because you have discovered your powers as a Radiant."

Jasnah handed back the sketchpad and walked toward the ring of chairs. She settled next to Renarin, prodding him gently to speak with her. He looked up for the first time since the meeting had begun and nodded, saying something Shallan couldn't hear.

"Mmmm . . ." Pattern said. "She is wise."

"That's perhaps her most infuriating feature," Shallan said. "Storms. She makes me feel like a child."

"Mmm."

"Worst part is, she's probably right," Shallan said. "Around her, I *do* act more like a child. It's like part of me wants to let her take care of everything. And I hate, hate, *hate* that about myself."

"Is there a solution?"

"I don't know."

"Perhaps . . . act like an adult?"

Shallan put her hands to her face, groaning softly and rubbing her eyes with her fingers. She'd basically asked for that, hadn't she? "Come on," she said, "let's go to the rest of the meeting. As much as I want an excuse to get out of here."

"Mmm . . ." Pattern said. "Something about this room . . ."

"What?" Shallan asked.

"Something . . ." Pattern said in his buzzing way. "It has memories, Shallan."

Memories. Did he mean in Shadesmar? She'd avoided traveling there—that was at least one thing in which she'd listened to Jasnah.

She made her way back to her seat, and after a moment's thought, slipped Jasnah a quick note. *Pattern says this room has memories. Worth investigating in Shadesmar?*

Jasnah regarded the note, then wrote back.

I've found that we should not ignore the offhand comments of our spren. Press him; I will investigate this place. Thank you for the suggestion.

The meeting started again, and now turned to discussion of specific kingdoms around Roshar. Jasnah was most keen on getting the Shin to join them. The Shattered Plains held the easternmost of the Oathgates, and that was already under Alethi control. If they could gain access to the one farthest to the west, they could travel the breadth of Roshar—from the entry point of the highstorms to the entry point of the Everstorms—in a heartbeat.

They didn't talk tactics too specifically; that was a masculine art, and Dalinar would want his highprinces and generals to discuss the battlefields. Still, Shallan didn't fail to notice the tactical terms Jasnah used now and then.

In things like this, Shallan had difficulty understanding the woman. In some ways, Jasnah seemed fiercely masculine. She studied whatever she pleased, and she talked tactics as easily as she talked poetry. She could be aggressive, even cold—Shallan had seen her straight-up *execute* thieves who had tried to rob her. Beyond that . . . well, it probably was best not to speculate on things with no meaning, but people *did* talk. Jasnah had turned down every suitor for her hand, including some very attractive and influential men. People wondered. Was she perhaps simply not interested?

All of this should have resulted in a person who was decidedly unfeminine. Yet Jasnah wore the finest makeup, and wore it well, with shadowed eyes and bright red lips. She kept her safehand covered, and preferred intricate and fetching styles of braids from her hairdresser. Her writings and her mind made her the very model of Vorin femininity.

Next to Jasnah, Shallan felt pale, stupid, and completely lacking in curves. What would it be like, to be so confident? So beautiful, yet so unconstrained, all at once? Surely, Jasnah Kholin had far fewer problems in life than Shallan. At the very least, she *created* far fewer for herself than Shallan did.

It was about this point that Shallan realized she'd missed a good fifteen minutes of the meeting, and had again lapsed in her note-taking. Blushing furiously, she huddled up on her chair and did her best to remain focused for the rest of the meeting. At the end, she presented a sheet of formal shorthand to Jasnah.

The woman looked it over, then cocked a perfectly shaped eyebrow at the line at the center where Shallan had grown distracted. *Dalinar said some stuff here,* the line read. *It was very important and useful, so I'm sure you remember it without needing a reminder.*

Shallan smiled apologetically and shrugged.

"Please write this out in longhand," Jasnah said, handing it back. "Have a copy sent to my mother and to my brother's head scribe."

Shallan took it as a dismissal and rushed away. She felt like a student who had just been released from lessons, which angered her. At the same time, she wanted to run off and immediately do as Jasnah had asked, to renew her mistress's faith in her, which angered her even *more.*

She ran up the steps out of the tower's basement, using Stormlight to prevent fatigue. The different sides within her clashed, snapping at each other. She imagined months spent under Jasnah's watchful care, training to become a mousy scribe as her father had always wanted.

She remembered the days in Kharbranth, when she'd been so uncertain, so timid. She couldn't return to that. She *wouldn't.* But what to do instead?

When she finally reached her rooms, Pattern was buzzing at her. She tossed aside her sketchpad and satchel, digging out Veil's coat and hat. Veil would know what to do.

However, pinned to the inside of Veil's coat was a sheet of paper.

Shallan froze, then looked around the room, suddenly anxious. Hesitantly, she unpinned the sheet and unfolded it.

The top read:

You have accomplished the task we set out for you. You have investigated the Unmade, and not only learned something of it, but also frightened it away. As promised, here is your reward.

The following letter explains the truth about your deceased brother, Nan Helaran, acolyte of the Radiant order of the Skybreakers.

As for Uli Da, it was obvious from the outset that she was going to be a problem. Good riddance.

There are at least two major institutions on Roshar, other than ourselves, which presaged the return of the Voidbringers and the Desolations, the letter read.

You are familiar with the first of these, the men who call themselves the Sons of Honor. The old king of Alethkar—the Blackthorn's brother, Gavilar Kholin—was a driving force in their expansion. He brought Meridas Amaram into their fold.

As you no doubt discovered upon infiltrating Amaram's mansion in the war-camps, the Sons of Honor explicitly worked for the return of the Desolations. They believed that only the Voidbringers would cause the Heralds to show themselves—and they believed that a Desolation would restore both the Knights Radiant and the classical strength of the Vorin church. King Gavilar's efforts to rekindle the Desolations are likely the true reason he was assassinated. Though there were many in the palace that night who had reason to see him dead.

A second group who knew the Desolations might return are the Skybreak-ers. Led by the ancient Herald Nalan'Elin—often simply called Nale—the Skybreakers are the only order of Radiants that did not betray its oaths during the Recreance. They have maintained a continuous clandestine line from ancient days.

Nale believed that men speaking the Words of other orders would hasten the return of the Voidbringers. We do not know how this could possibly be true, but as a Herald, Nale has access to knowledge and understanding beyond us.

You should know that the Heralds are no longer to be seen as allies to man. Those that are not completely insane have been broken. Nale himself is ruthless, without pity or mercy. He has spent the last two decades—perhaps much longer—dealing with anyone close to bonding a spren. Sometimes he recruited these people, bonding them to highspren and making them Skybreakers. Others he eliminated. If the person had already bonded a spren, then Nale usually went in person to dispatch them. If not, he sent a minion.

A minion like your brother Helaran.

Your mother had intimate contact with a Skybreaker acolyte, and you know the result of that relationship. Your brother was recruited because Nale was impressed with him. Nale may also have learned, through means we do not understand, that a member of your house was close to bonding a spren. If this is true, they came to believe that Helaran was the one they wanted. They recruited him with displays of great power and Shards.

Helaran had not yet proved himself worthy of a spren bond. Nale is exacting with his recruits. Likely, Helaran was sent to kill Amaram as a test—either that or he took it upon himself as a way of proving his worthiness for knighthood.

It is also possible that the Skybreakers knew someone in Amaram's army was close to bonding a spren, but I believe it likelier that the attack on Amaram was simply a strike against the Sons of Honor. From our spying upon the Skybreakers, we have records showing the only member of Amaram's army to have bonded a spren was long since eliminated.

The bridgeman was not, so far as we understand, known to them. If he had been, he would certainly have been killed during his months as a slave.

It ended there. Shallan sat in her room, lit only by the faintest sphere. Helaran, a Skybreaker? And King Gavilar, working with Amaram to bring back the Desolations?

Pattern buzzed with concern on her skirts and moved up onto the page, reading the letter. She whispered the words again to herself, to memorize them, for she knew she couldn't keep this letter. It was too dangerous.

"Secrets," Pattern said. "There are lies in this letter."

So many questions. Who else had been there on the night Gavilar had died, as the letter hinted? And what about this reference to another Surgebinder in Amaram's army? "He's dangling tidbits in front of me," Shallan said. "Like a man on the docks who has a trained kurl that will dance and wave its arms for fish."

"But . . . we want those tidbits, don't we?"

"That's why it works." Storm it.

She couldn't deal with this at the moment. She took a Memory of the page. It wasn't a particularly efficient method in regards to text, but it would work in a pinch. Then she stuffed the letter in a basin of water and washed off the ink, before shredding it and wadding it into a ball.

From there, she changed into her coat, trousers, and hat, and snuck from the rooms as Veil.

∴

Veil found Vathah and some of his men playing at pieces in their barracks common room. Though this was for Sebarial's soldiers, she saw men in blue uniforms as well—Dalinar had ordered his men to spend time with the soldiers of his allies, to help foster a sense of comradery.

Veil's entrance drew glances, but not stares. Women were allowed in such common rooms, though few came. Little sounded less appealing to a woman being courted than, "Hey, let's go sit in the barracks common room and watch men grunt and scratch themselves."

She sauntered over to where Vathah and his men had set up at a round wooden table. Furniture was finally trickling down to the ordinary men; Shallan even had a bed now. Veil settled down in a seat and leaned back, tipping the chair so it clicked against the stone wall. This large common room reminded her of a wine cellar. Dark, unadorned, and filled with a variety of unusual stenches.

"Veil," Vathah said, nodding to her. Four of them were playing at this table: Vathah, one-eyed Gaz, lanky Red, and Shob. The latter wore a glyph-ward wrapped around one arm and sniffled periodically.

Veil leaned her head back. "I seriously need something to drink."

"I've got an extra mug or two on my ration," Red said cheerfully.

Veil eyed him to see if he was hitting on her again. He was smiling, but otherwise didn't seem to be making a pass. "Right kind of you, Red," Veil said, digging out a few chips and tossing them to him. He tossed over his requisition chit, a little piece of metal with his number stamped on it.

A short time later she was back in her place, nursing some lavis beer.

"Tough day?" Vathah said, lining up his pieces. The small stone bricks were about the size of a thumb, and the men each had ten of them that they arranged facedown. The betting started soon after. Apparently, Vathah was the mink for this round.

"Yeah," she replied. "Shallan's been an even bigger pain than usual."

The men grunted.

"It's like she can't decide who she is, you know?" Veil continued. "One moment she's cracking jokes like she's sitting in a knitting circle with old ladies—the next she's staring at you with that hollow gaze. The one that makes you think her soul has gone vacant . . ."

"She's a strange one, our mistress," Vathah agreed.

"Makes you want to do things," Gaz said with a grunt. "Things you never thought you'd do."

"Yeah," Glurv said from the next table over. "I got a medal. *Me.* For helping find that mess hiding in the basement. Old Kholin himself sent it down for me." The overweight soldier shook his head, bemused—but he *was* wearing the medal. Pinned right to his collar.

"It was fun," Gaz admitted. "Going out carousing, but feeling like we were doing something. That's what she promised us, you know? Making a difference again."

"The difference I want to make," Vathah said, "is filling my pouch with your spheres. You men betting or not?"

The four players all tossed in some spheres. Pieces was one of those games that the Vorin church grudgingly allowed, as it involved no randomization. Dice, drawing from a deck of cards, even shuffling up the pieces—betting on such things was like trying to guess the future. And that was so deeply wrong, thinking of it made Veil's skin crawl. She wasn't even particularly religious, not like Shallan was.

People wouldn't play games like those in the official barracks. Here, they played guessing games. Vathah had arranged nine of his pieces in a triangle shape; the tenth one he set to the side and flipped over as the seed. It, like the hidden nine, was marked with the symbol of one of the Alethi princedoms. In this case, the seed was Aladar's symbol, in the form of a chull.

The goal was to arrange your ten pieces in a pattern identical to his, even though they were facedown. You'd guess which were which through a series of questions, peeks, and inferences. You could force the mink to reveal pieces just to you, or to everyone, based on certain other rules.

In the end, someone called and everyone flipped over their pieces. The one with the most matches to the mink's pattern was declared winner, and claimed the pot. The mink got a percentage, based on certain factors, such as the number of turns it took before someone called.

"What do you think?" Gaz asked, as he tossed a few chips into the bowl at the center, buying the right to peek at one of Vathah's tiles. "How long will Shallan go this time before she remembers we're here?"

"Long time, I hope," Shob said. "Oi think Oi might be comin' down with somethin'."

"So all is normal, Shob," Red said.

"It's big this time," Shob said. "Oi think Oi might be turnin' into a *Voidbringer.*"

"A Voidbringer," Veil said flatly.

"Yeah, look at this rash." He pulled back the glyphward, exposing his upper arm. Which looked perfectly normal.

Vathah snorted.

"Eh!" Shob said. "Oi'm likely to die, Sarge. You mark me, Oi'm likely to die." He moved around a few of his tiles. "If Oi do, give my winnings to dem orphans."

"Them orphans?" Red asked.

"You know, orphans." Shob scratched his head. "There's orphans, right? Somewhere? Orphans that need food? Give them mine after I die."

"Shob," Vathah said, "with the way justice plays out in this world, I can guarantee you'll outlive the rest of us."

"Ah, that's nice," Shob said. "Right nice, Sarge."

The game progressed only a few rounds before Shob started flipping over his tiles.

"Already!" Gaz said. "Shob, you cremling. Don't do it yet! I don't even have two lines!"

"Too late," Shob said.

Red and Gaz reluctantly started flipping their tiles.

"Sadeas," Shallan said absently. "Bethab, Ruthar, Roion, Thanadal, Kholin, Sebarial, Vamah, Hatham. With Aladar as the seed."

Vathah gaped at her, then flipped the tiles over, revealing them exactly as she'd said. "And you didn't even get any peeks . . . Storms, woman. Remind me never to play pieces with you."

"My brothers always said the same thing," she said as he split the pot with Shob, who had gotten them all right but three.

"Another hand?" Gaz asked.

Everyone looked at his bowl of spheres, which was almost empty.

"I can get a loan," he said quickly. "There's some fellows in Dalinar's guard who said—"

"Gaz," Vathah said.

"But—"

"Seriously, Gaz."

Gaz sighed. "Guess we can play for ends, then," he said, and Shob eagerly got out some drops of glass shaped roughly like spheres, but without gemstones at the center. Fake money for gambling without stakes.

Veil was enjoying her mug of beer more than she'd expected. It was refreshing to sit here with these men and not have to worry about all Shallan's problems. Couldn't that girl just *relax*? Let it all blow past her?

Nearby some washwomen entered, calling that laundry pickup would be in a few minutes. Vathah and his men didn't stir—though by Veil's estimation, the very clothing they were wearing could use a good scrub.

Unfortunately, Veil couldn't completely ignore Shallan's problems. Mraize's note proved how useful he could be, but she had to be careful. He obviously wanted a mole among the Knights Radiant. *I need to turn this around on him. Learn what he knows.* He'd told her what the Skybreakers and the Sons of Honor had been up to. But what about Mraize and his cohorts? What was *their* objective?

Storms, did she dare try to double-cross him? Did she really have the experience, or the training, to attempt something like that?

"Hey, Veil," Vathah said as they prepped for another game. "What do you think? Has the brightness already forgotten about us again?"

Veil shook herself out of her thoughts. "Maybe. She doesn't seem to know what to do with you lot."

"She's not the first," Red said—he was the next mink, and carefully arranged his tiles in a specific order, facedown. "I mean, it's not like we're *real* soldiers."

"Our crimes are forgiven," Gaz said with a grunt, squinting his single eye at the seed tile that Red turned over. "But forgiven ain't forgotten. No military will take us on, and I don't blame them. I'm just glad those storming bridgemen haven't strung me up by my toes."

"Bridgemen?" Veil asked.

"He's got a history with them," Vathah noted.

"I used to be their storming sergeant," Gaz said. "Did everything I could to get them to run those bridges faster. Nobody likes their sergeant though."

"I'm sure you were the *perfect* sergeant," Red said with a grin. "I'll bet you really looked out for them, Gaz."

"Shut your cremhole," Gaz grumbled. "Though I do wonder. If I'd been a little less hard on them, do you think maybe I'd be out on that plateau right now, practicing like the lot of them do? Learning to fly . . ."

"You think *you* could be a Knight Radiant, Gaz?" Vathah said, chuckling.

"No. No, I guess I don't." He eyed Veil. "Veil, you tell the brightness. We ain't good men. Good men, they'll find something useful to do with their time. We, on the other hand, might do the opposite."

"The opposite?" Zendid said from the next table over, where a few of the others continued to drink. "Opposite of useful? I think we're already there, Gaz. And we've been there forever."

"Not me," Glurv said. "I've got a *medal.*"

"I *mean,*" Gaz said, "we might get into trouble. I *liked* being useful. Reminded me of back when I first joined up. You tell her, Veil. Tell her to give us something to do other than gambling and drinking. Because to be honest, I ain't very good at either one."

Veil nodded slowly. A washwoman idled by, messing with a sack of laundry. Veil tapped her finger on her cup. Then she stood and seized the washwoman by the dress and hauled her backward. The woman shouted, dropping her pile of clothing as she stumbled, nearly falling.

Veil shoved her hand into the woman's hair, pushing away the wig of mottled brown and black. Underneath, the woman's hair was pure Alethi black, and she wore ashes on her cheeks, as if she'd been doing hard labor.

"You!" Veil said. This was the woman from the tavern at All's Alley. What had her name been? Ishnah?

Several nearby soldiers had leapt up with alarmed expressions at the woman's outcry. *Every one of those is a soldier from Dalinar's army,* Veil noted, suppressing a roll of her eyes. Kholin troops did have a habit of assuming that nobody could take care of themselves.

"Sit," Veil said, pointing at the table. Red hastily pulled up another chair.

Ishnah settled herself, holding the wig to her chest. She blushed deeply, but maintained some measure of poise, meeting the eyes of Vathah and his men.

"You are getting to be an annoyance, woman," Veil said, sitting.

"Why do you assume I'm here because of you?" Ishnah said. "You're jumping to conclusions."

"You showed an unhealthy fascination with my associates. Now I find you in disguise, eavesdropping on my conversations?"

Ishnah raised her chin. "Maybe I'm just trying to prove myself to you."

"With a disguise I saw through the moment I glanced at you?"

"You didn't catch me last time," Ishnah said.

Last time?

"You talked about where to get Horneater lager," Ishnah said. "Red insisted it was nasty. Gaz loves it."

"Storms. How long have you been spying on me?"

"Not long," Ishnah said quickly, in direct contradiction to what she'd just said. "But I can assure you, *promise it,* that I'll be more valuable to you than these rancid buffoons. Please, at least let me try."

"Buffoons?" Gaz said.

"Rancid?" Shob said. "Oh, that's just moi boils, miss."

"Walk with me," Veil said, standing up. She strode away from the table.

Ishnah scrambled to her feet and followed. "I wasn't *really* trying to spy on you. But how else was I—"

"Quiet," Veil said. She stopped at the doorway to the barracks, far enough from her men that they couldn't hear. She folded her arms, leaning against the wall by the door and looking back at them.

Shallan had trouble with follow-through. She had good intentions and grand plans, but she got diverted too easily by new problems, new adventures. Fortunately, Veil could pick up a few of those loose threads.

These men had proven that they were loyal, and they wanted to be useful. A woman could be given much less than that to work with.

"The disguise was well done," she said to Ishnah. "Next time, rough up your freehand some more. The fingers gave you away; they aren't the fingers of a laborer."

Ishnah blushed, balling her freehand into a fist.

"Tell me what you can do, and why I should care," Veil said. "You have two minutes."

"I . . ." Ishnah took a deep breath. "I was trained as a spy for House Hamaradin. In Vamah's court? I know information gathering, message coding, observation techniques, and how to search a room without revealing what I've done."

"So? If you're so useful, what happened?"

"Your people happened. The Ghostbloods. I'd heard of them, whispered of by Brightlady Hamaradin. She crossed them somehow, and then . . ." She shrugged. "She ended up dead, and everyone thought it might have been one of us who did it. I fled and ended up in the underground, working for a petty gang of thieves. But I could be so much more. Let me prove it to you."

Veil crossed her arms. A spy. That could be useful. Truth was, Veil herself didn't have much actual training—only what Tyn had showed her and what she'd learned on her own. If she was going to dance with the Ghostbloods, she'd need to be better. Right now, she didn't even know what it was she didn't know.

Could she get some of that from Ishnah? Somehow get some training without revealing that Veil wasn't as skilled as she pretended to be?

An idea began to take form. She didn't trust this woman, but then she didn't need to. And if her former brightlady really *had* been killed by the Ghostbloods, perhaps there was a secret to learn there.

"I have some important infiltrations planned," Veil said. "Missions where I need to gather information of a sensitive nature."

"I can help!" Ishnah said.

"What I really need is a support team, so I don't have to go in alone."

"I can find people for you! Experts."

"I wouldn't be able to trust them," Veil said, shaking her head. "I need someone I know is loyal."

"Who?"

Veil pointed at Vathah and his men.

Ishnah's expression fell. "You want to turn *those men* into *spies*?"

"That, and I want you to prove to me what you can do by showing it to those men." *And hopefully I can pick up something too.* "Don't look so daunted. They don't need to be true spies. They just need to know enough about my work to support me and keep watch."

Ishnah raised her eyebrows skeptically, watching the men. Shob was, obligingly, picking his nose.

"That's a little like saying you want me to teach hogs to talk—with promises it will be easy, as they only need to speak Alethi, not Veden or Herdazian."

"This is the chance I'm offering, Ishnah. Take it, or agree to stay away from me."

Ishnah sighed. "All right. We'll see. Just don't blame me if the pigs don't end up talking."

Regardless, this is not your concern. You turned your back on divinity. If Rayse becomes an issue, he will be dealt with.

And so will you.

Teft woke up. Unfortunately.

His first sensation was pain. Old, familiar pain. The throbbing behind his eyes, the raw biting needles of his burned fingers, the stiffness of a body that had outlived its usefulness. Kelek's breath . . . had he *ever* been useful?

He rolled over, groaning. No coat, only a tight undershirt soiled from lying on the ground. He was in an alleyway between tents in the Break-away market. The high ceiling vanished into the darkness. From just beyond the alleyway came the bright sounds of people chatting and haggling.

Teft stumbled to his feet, and was halfway through relieving himself against some empty boxes before he realized what he was doing. There were no highstorms in here to wash the place out. Besides, he wasn't some drunkard who wallowed in filth and pissed in alleys. Was he?

That thought immediately reminded him of the deeper pain. A pain beyond the pounding in his head or the ache of his bones. The pain that was with him always, like a persistent ringing, cutting deep to his core. This pain had awakened him. The pain of *need*.

No, he wasn't just some drunkard. He was far, far worse.

He stumbled out of the alleyway, trying to smooth his hair and beard. Women he passed held safehands to mouths and noses, looking away as if embarrassed for him. Perhaps it was a good thing he'd lost his coat—

storms help him if anyone recognized who he was. He'd shame the entire crew.

You're already a shame to the crew, Teft, and you know it, he thought. *You're a godless waste of spit.*

He eventually found his way to the well, where he slouched in a line behind some others. Once at the water, he fell down on his knees, then used a trembling hand to fish out a drink with his tin cup. Once he tasted the cool water, his stomach immediately cramped, rejecting it even though he was parched. This always happened after a night on the moss, so he knew to ride the nausea and the cramps, hoping he could keep the water down.

He slumped, holding his stomach, frightening the people in line behind him. Out in the crowd—there was always at least a small crowd near the well—some men in uniforms shoved through. Forest green. Sadeas's men.

They ignored the lines, then filled their buckets. When a man in Kholin blue objected, Sadeas's soldiers got right up in his face. The Kholin soldier finally backed down. Good lad. They didn't need *another* brawl starting between Sadeas's men and other soldiers.

Teft dipped his cup again, the pain from his previous sip fading. This well seemed deep. Rippling water on top, and a deep blackness below.

He almost threw himself in. If he woke up in Damnation tomorrow, would he still feel that itching need inside? That would be a fitting torment. Voidbringers wouldn't even have to flay his soul—all they'd need to do was tell him he'd never feel sated again, and then they could watch him squirm.

Reflected in the waters of the well, a face appeared over his shoulder. A woman with pale white skin, glowing faintly, and hair that hovered around her head like clouds.

"You leave me alone," he said, slapping his hand into the water. "You just . . . you just go find someone who cares."

He stumbled back to his feet, finally getting out of the way so someone else could take a spot. Storms, what hour was it? Those women with buckets were ready to draw water for the day. The drunken nighttime crowds had been replaced by the enterprising and industrious.

He'd been out all night again. Kelek!

Returning to the barracks would be the smart thing to do. But could he face them like this? He wandered through the market instead, eyes down.

I'm getting worse, a piece of him realized. The first month in Dalinar's employ, he'd been able to resist for the most part. But he'd had money again, after so long as a bridgeman. Having money was dangerous.

He'd functioned, only mossing an evening here, an evening there. But then Kaladin had left, and this tower, where everything had felt so wrong . . . Those monsters of darkness, including one that had looked just like Teft.

He'd needed the moss to deal with that. Who wouldn't? He sighed. When he looked up, he found that spren standing in front of him.

Teft . . . she whispered. *You've spoken oaths.* . . .

Foolish, stupid oaths, spoken when he'd hoped that being Radiant would remove the cravings. He turned away from her and found his way to a tent nestled among the taverns. Those were closed for the morning, but this place—it had no name and didn't need one—was open. It was always open, just like the ones back in Dalinar's warcamp had been, just like the ones in Sadeas's warcamp. They were harder to find in some places than others. But they were always there, nameless but still known.

The tough-looking Herdazian man sitting at the front waved him in. It was dim inside, but Teft found his way to a table and slumped down. A woman in tight clothing and a glove with no fingers brought him a little bowl of firemoss. They didn't ask for payment. They all knew that he wouldn't have any spheres on him today, not after his binge last night. But they *would* make sure to get paid eventually.

Teft stared at the little bowl, loathing himself. And yet the scent of it made his longing multiply tenfold. He let out a whimpering groan, then seized the firemoss and ground it between his thumb and forefinger. The moss let off a small plume of smoke, and in the dim light, the center of the moss glowed like an ember.

It hurt, of course. He'd worn through his calluses last night, and now rubbed the moss with raw, blistering fingers. But this was a sharp, present pain. A good kind of pain. Merely physical, it was a sign of life.

It took a minute before he felt the effects. A washing away of his pains, followed by a strengthening of his resolve. He could remember long ago that the firemoss had done more to him—he remembered euphoria, nights spent in a dizzy, wonderful daze, where everything around him seemed to make sense.

These days, he needed the moss to feel normal. Like a man scrambling up wet rocks, he could barely reach where everyone else was standing before he slowly started sliding back down. It wasn't euphoria he craved anymore; it was the mere capacity to keep on going.

The moss washed away his burdens. Memories of that dark version of himself. Memories of turning his family in as heretics, even though they'd been right all along. He was a wretch and a coward, and didn't deserve to wear the symbol of Bridge Four. He'd as good as betrayed that spren already. She'd best have fled.

For a moment he could give that all up to the firemoss.

Unfortunately, there was something broken in Teft. Long ago he'd gone to the moss at the urgings of other men in his squad in Sadeas's army. They could rub the stuff and get some benefit, like a man chewed ridgebark when on guard duty to stay awake. A little firemoss, a little relaxation, and then they moved on with their lives.

Teft didn't work that way. Burdens shoved aside, he *could* have gotten up and gone back to the bridgemen. He could have started his day.

But storms, a few more minutes sounded so nice. He kept going. He went through three bowls before a garish light made him blink. He pulled his face off the table where—to his shame—he'd drooled a puddle. How long had it been, and what was that terrible, awful light?

"Here he is," Kaladin's voice said as Teft blinked. A figure knelt beside the table. "Oh, Teft . . ."

"He owes us for three bowls," said the den's keeper. "One garnet broam."

"Be glad," an accented voice growled, "we do not rip off pieces of your body and pay you with those."

Storms. Rock was here too? Teft groaned, turning away. "Don't see me," he croaked. "Don't . . ."

"Our establishment is perfectly legal, Horneater," the den keeper said. "If you assault us, be assured we *will* bring the guard and they *will* defend us."

"Here's your blood money, you eel," Kaladin said, pushing the light toward them. "Rock, can you get him?"

Large hands took Teft, surprisingly gentle with their touch. He was crying. Kelek . . .

"Where's your coat, Teft?" Kaladin asked from the darkness.

"I sold it," Teft admitted, squeezing his eyes shut against the shame-spren that drifted down around him, in the shape of flower petals. "I sold my own storming coat."

Kaladin fell silent, and Teft let Rock carry him from the den. Halfway back, he finally managed to scrounge up enough dignity to complain about Rock's breath and make them let him walk on his own feet—with a little support under the arms.

∴

Teft envied better men than he. They didn't have the itch, the one that went so deep that it stung his soul. It was persistent, always with him, and couldn't ever be scratched. Despite how hard he tried.

Kaladin and Rock set him up in one of the barrack rooms, private, wrapped in blankets and with a bowl of Rock's stew in his hands. Teft made the proper noises, the ones they expected. Apologies, promises he would tell them if he was feeling the need again. Promises that he'd let them help him. Though he couldn't eat the stew, not yet. It would be another day before he could keep anything down.

Storms, but they were good men. Better friends than he deserved. They were all growing into something grand, while Teft . . . Teft just stayed on the ground, looking up.

They left him to get some rest. He stared at the stew, smelling the familiar scent, not daring to eat it. He'd go back to work before the day was out, training bridgemen from the other crews. He *could* function. He could go for days, pretending that he was normal. Storms, he'd balanced everything in Sadeas's army for years before taking one step too far, missing duty one too many times, and landing himself in the bridge crews as punishment.

Those months running bridges had been the only time in his adult life when he hadn't been dominated by the moss. But even back then, when he'd been able to afford a little alcohol, he'd known that eventually he'd find his way back. The liquor wasn't ever enough.

Even as he braced himself to go to work for the day, one nagging thought overshadowed his mind. A shameful thought.

I'm not going to get any more moss for a while, am I?

That sinister knowledge hurt him more than anything. He was going to have to go a few excruciating days feeling like half a man. Days when he couldn't feel anything but his own self-loathing, days living with the shame, the memories, the glances of other bridgemen.

Days without any storming help whatsoever.

That terrified him.

42

CONSEQUENCES

Cephandrius, bearer of the First Gem,
You must know better than to approach us by relying upon
presumption of past relationship.

Inside the increasingly familiar vision, Dalinar carefully nocked an arrow, then released, sending a black-fletched missile into the back of the wildman. The man's screech was lost in the cacophony of battle. Ahead, men fought frantically as they were pushed backward toward the edge of a cliff.

Dalinar methodically nocked a second arrow, then loosed. This arrow hit as well, lodging in a man's shoulder. The man dropped his axe midswing, causing him to miss the young, dark-skinned youth lying on the ground. The boy was barely into his teens; the awkwardness hadn't left him yet, and he had limbs that seemed too long, a face that was too round, too childlike. Dalinar might have let him run messages, but not hold a spear.

The lad's age hadn't prevented him from being named Prime Aqasix Yanagawn the First, ruler of Azir, emperor of greater Makabak.

Dalinar had perched on some rocks, bow in hand. While he didn't intend to repeat his mistake of letting Queen Fen manage all on her own in a vision, he also didn't want Yanagawn to slip through it without challenge or stress. There was a reason that the Almighty had often put Dalinar in danger in these visions. He'd needed a visceral understanding of what was at stake.

He felled another enemy who got close to the boy. The shots weren't difficult from his vantage near the fight; he had some training with the bow—though his archery in recent years had been with so-called Shard-bows, fabrial bows crafted with such a heavy draw weight that only a man in Shardplate could use them.

It was strange, experiencing this battle for the third time. Though each repetition played out slightly differently, there were certain familiar details. The scents of smoke and moldy, inhuman blood. The way that man below fell after losing an arm, screaming the same half-prayer, half-condemnation of the Almighty.

With Dalinar's bowmanship, the band of defenders lasted against the enemy until that Radiant climbed up over the edge of the cliff, glowing in Shardplate. Emperor Yanagawn sat down as the other soldiers rallied around the Radiant and pushed the enemy backward.

Dalinar lowered his bow, reading the terror in the youth's trembling figure. Other men spoke of getting the shakes when a fight was over—the horror of it catching up with them.

The emperor finally stumbled to his feet, using the spear like a staff. He didn't notice Dalinar, didn't even question why some of the bodies around him had arrows in them. This boy was no soldier, though Dalinar hadn't expected him to be one. From his experience, Azish generals were too prag-matic to want the throne. It involved too much pandering to bureaucrats and, apparently, dictating essays.

The youth started down a path away from the cliff, and Dalinar fol-lowed. Aharietiam. The people who lived through this had thought it the end of the world. Surely they assumed they'd soon return to the Tranqui-line Halls. How would they respond to the information that—after four millennia—mankind still hadn't been allowed back into heaven?

The boy stopped at the bottom of the twisting path, which led into the valley between rock formations. He watched wounded men limp by, sup-ported by friends. Moans and shouts rose in the air. Dalinar intended to step up and start explaining about these visions, but the boy strode out to walk beside some wounded men, chatting with them.

Dalinar followed, curious, catching fragments of the conversation. *What happened here? Who are you? Why were you fighting?*

The men didn't have many answers. They were wounded, exhausted, trailed by painspren. They did find their way to a larger group though, in the direction Jasnah had gone during Dalinar's previous visit to this vision.

The crowd had gathered around a man standing on a large boulder. Tall and confident, the man was in his thirties, and he wore white and blue. He had an Alethi feel to him, except . . . not quite. His skin was a shade darker, and something was faintly off about his features.

Yet there was something . . . familiar about the man.

"You must spread the word," the man proclaimed. "We have won! At long last, the Voidbringers are defeated. This is not my victory, or that of the other Heralds. It is *your* victory. You have done this."

Some of the people shouted in triumph. Too many others stood silent, staring with dead eyes.

"I will lead the charge for the Tranquiline Halls," the man shouted. "You will not see me again, but think not on that now! You have won your peace. Revel in it! Rebuild. Go now, help your fellows. Carry with you the light of your Herald king's words. We are victorious, at long last, over evil!"

Another round of shouts, more energetic this time.

Storms, Dalinar thought, feeling a chill. This was Jezerezeh'Elin himself, Herald of Kings. The greatest among them.

Wait. Did the king have *dark* eyes?

The group broke up, but the young emperor remained, staring at the place where the Herald had stood. Finally, he whispered, "Oh, Yaezir. King of the Heralds."

"Yes," Dalinar said, stepping up beside him. "That *was* him, Your Excellency. My niece visited this vision earlier, and she wrote that she thought she'd spotted him."

Yanagawn grabbed Dalinar by the arm. "What did you say? You know me?"

"You are Yanagawn of Azir," Dalinar said. He nodded his head in a semblance of a bow. "I am Dalinar Kholin, and I apologize that our meeting must take place under such irregular circumstances."

The youth's eyes widened. "I see Yaezir himself first, and now my enemy."

"I am *not* your enemy." Dalinar sighed. "And this is no mere dream, Your Excellency. I—"

"Oh, I know it's not a dream," Yanagawn said. "As I am a Prime raised to the throne miraculously, the Heralds may choose to speak through me!" He looked about. "This day we are living through, it is the Day of Glory?"

"Aharietiam," Dalinar said. "Yes."

"Why did they place you here? What does it mean?"

"They didn't place me here," Dalinar said. "Your Excellency, *I* instigated this vision, and *I* brought you into it."

Skeptical, the boy folded his arms. He wore the leather skirt provided by the vision. He'd left his bronze-tipped spear leaning against a rock nearby.

"Have you been told," Dalinar asked, "that I am considered mad?"

"There are rumors."

"Well, this was my madness," Dalinar said. "I suffered visions during the storms. Come. See."

He led Yanagawn to a better view of the large field of the dead, which spread out from the mouth of the canyon. Yanagawn followed, then his face grew ashen at the sight. Finally, he strode down onto the larger battlefield, moving among the corpses, moans, and curses.

Dalinar walked beside him. So many dead eyes, so many faces twisted in pain. Lighteyed and dark. Pale skin like the Shin and some Horneaters. Dark skin like the Makabaki. Many that could have been Alethi, Veden, or Herdazian.

There were other things, of course. The giant broken stone figures. Parshmen wearing warform, with chitin armor and orange blood. One spot they passed had a whole heap of strange cremlings, burned and smoking. Who would have taken the time to pile up a thousand little crustaceans?

"We fought together," Yanagawn said.

"How else could we have resisted?" Dalinar said. "To fight the Desolation alone would be madness."

Yanagawn eyed him. "You wanted to talk to me without the viziers. You wanted me alone! And you can just . . . you just show me whatever will strengthen your argument!"

"If you accept that I have the power to show you these visions," Dalinar said, "would that not in itself imply that you should listen to me?"

"The Alethi are dangerous. Do you know what happened the *last* time the Alethi were in Azir?"

"The Sunmaker's rule was a long time ago."

"The viziers have talked about this," Yanagawn said. "They told me *all* about it. It started the same way back then, with a warlord uniting the Alethi tribes."

"Tribes?" Dalinar said. "You'd compare us to the nomads that roam Tu Bayla? Alethkar is one of the most cultured kingdoms on Roshar!"

"Your code of law is barely thirty years old!"

"Your Excellency," Dalinar said, taking a deep breath, "I doubt this line of conversation will be relevant. Look around us. Look and *see* what the Desolation will bring."

He swept his hand across the awful view, and Yanagawn's temper cooled. It was impossible to feel anything but sorrow when confronted by so much death.

Eventually, Yanagawn turned and started back the way they'd come. Dalinar joined him, hands clasped behind.

"They say," Yanagawn whispered, "that when the Sunmaker rode out of the passes and into Azir, he had one unexpected problem. He conquered my people too quickly, and didn't know what to do with all of his captives. He couldn't leave a fighting population behind him in the towns. There were thousands upon thousands of men he needed to murder.

"Sometimes he'd simply assign the work to his soldiers. Every man was to kill thirty captives—like a child who had to find an armload of firewood before being allowed to play. In other places the Sunmaker declared something arbitrary. Say that every man with hair beyond a certain length was to be slaughtered.

"Before he was struck down with disease by the Heralds, he murdered *ten percent* of the population of Azir. They say Zawfix was filled with the bones, blown by highstorms into piles as tall as the buildings."

"I am *not* my ancestor," Dalinar said softly.

"You revere him. The Alethi all but worship Sadees. You carry his storming *Shardblade.*"

"I gave that away."

They stopped at the edge of the battlefield. The emperor had grit, but didn't know how to carry himself. He walked with shoulders slumped, and his hands kept reaching for pockets his antiquated clothing didn't have. He was of low birth—though in Azir, they didn't properly revere eye color. Navani had once told him it was because there weren't enough people in Azir with light eyes.

The Sunmaker himself had used this to justify conquering them.

"I am not my ancestor," Dalinar repeated. "But I do share much with him. A youth of brutality. A lifetime spent at war. I have one advantage he did not."

"Which is?"

Dalinar met the young man's eyes. "I've lived long enough to see the consequences of what I've done."

Yanagawn nodded slowly.

"Yeah," a voice piped up. "You're *old.*"

Dalinar turned, frowning. That had sounded like a young girl. Why would there be a girl on the battlefield?

"I didn't expect you to be so old," the girl said. She sat perched cross-legged on a large boulder nearby. "And you're not really that black. They call you Blackthorn, but you're really more like . . . Dark-tan-thorn. Gawx is more black than you are, and even *he's* pretty brownish."

The young emperor, remarkably, burst into an enormous grin. "Lift! You're back!" He started climbing up the boulder, heedless of decorum.

"Not quite back," she said. "Got sidetracked. But I'm close now."

"What happened in Yeddaw?" Yanagawn said, eager. "You barely gave me any kind of explanation!"

"Those people *lie* about their food." She narrowed her eyes at Dalinar as the young emperor slipped down the boulder, then tried to climb up another side.

This is not possible, the Stormfather said in Dalinar's mind. *How did she come here?*

"You didn't bring her in?" Dalinar said softly.

No. This is not possible! How . . . ?

Yanagawn finally attained the top of the boulder and gave the younger girl a hug. She had long dark hair, pale white eyes, and tan skin, though she likely wasn't Alethi—the face was too round. Reshi, perhaps?

"He's trying to convince me I should trust him," Yanagawn said, pointing at Dalinar.

"Don't," she said. "He's got too nice a butt."

Dalinar cleared his throat. "*What?*"

"Your butt is too nice. Old guys shouldn't have tight butts. It means you spend *waaay* too much time swinging a sword or punching people. You should have an old flabby butt. Then I'd trust you."

"She . . . has a thing about butts," Yanagawn said.

"No I don't," the girl said, rolling her eyes. "If someone thinks I'm strange for talking about butts, it's usually because they're jealous, 'cuz I'm the only one *without* something rammed up mine." She narrowed her eyes at Dalinar, then took the emperor by the arm. "Let's go."

"But—" Dalinar said, raising his hand.

"See, you're learning." She grinned at him.

Then she and the emperor vanished.

The Stormfather rumbled in frustration. *That woman! This is a creation specifically meant to defy my will!*

"Woman?" Dalinar asked, shaking his head.

That child is tainted by the Nightwatcher.

"Technically, so am I."

This is different. This is unnatural. She goes too far. The Stormfather rumbled his discontent, refusing to speak to Dalinar further. He seemed genuinely upset.

In fact, Dalinar was forced to sit and wait until the vision finished. He spent the time staring out over that field of the dead, haunted equally by the future and the past.

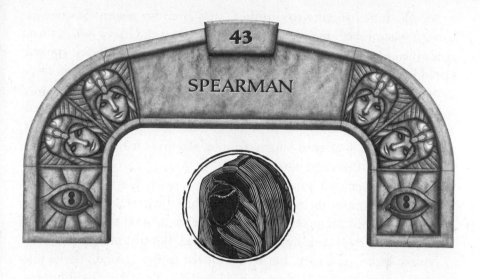

You have spoken to one who cannot respond. We, instead, will take your communication to us—though we know not how you located us upon this world.

M oash picked at the mush that Febrth called a "stew." It tasted like crem.

He stared at the flamespren in their large cookfire, trying to warm himself as Febrth—a Thaylen man with striking Horneater red hair—argued with Graves. The fire's smoke curled into the air, and the light would be visible for miles across the Frostlands. Graves didn't care; he figured that if the Everstorm hadn't cleared the bandits out of the area, two Shardbearers would be more than enough to deal with any who remained.

Shardblades can't stop an arrow in the back, Moash thought, feeling exposed. *And neither can Plate, if we're not wearing it.* His armor, and that of Graves, lay bundled in their wagon.

"Look, that is the Triplets," Graves said, waving toward a rock formation. "It's *right here* on the map. We go west now."

"I've been this way before," Febrth said. "We must continue south, you see. Then east."

"The map—"

"I have no need for your maps," Febrth said, folding his arms. "The Passions guide me."

"The Passions?" Graves said, throwing his hands up. "The *Passions?* You're supposed to have abandoned such superstitions. You belong to the Diagram now!"

"I can do both," Febrth said solemnly.

Moash stuffed another spoonful of "stew" into his mouth. Storms, he hated it when Febrth took a turn cooking. And when Graves took a turn. And when Fia took a turn. And . . . well, the stuff Moash himself cooked tasted like spiced dishwater. None of them could cook worth a dun chip. Not like Rock.

Moash dropped his bowl, letting the mush slop over the side. He grabbed his coat off a tree branch and stalked out into the night. The cold air felt strange on his skin after so long in front of the fire. He hated how cold it was down here. Perpetual winter.

The four of them had suffered through the storms hiding in the cramped, reinforced bottom of their wagon, which they'd chained to the ground. They'd frightened away rogue parshmen with their Shardblades—they hadn't been nearly as dangerous as he'd worried. But that new storm . . .

Moash kicked at a rock, but it was frozen to the ground and he just stubbed his toe. He cursed, then glanced over his shoulder as the argument ended in shouts. He'd once admired how refined Graves seemed. That had been before spending weeks crossing a barren landscape together. The man's patience had frayed to threads, and his refinement didn't matter much when they were all eating slop and pissing behind hills.

"So how lost are we?" Moash asked as Graves joined him in the darkness outside camp.

"Not lost at all," Graves said, "if that idiot would actually *look* at a *map*." He glanced at Moash. "I've told you to get rid of that coat."

"Which I'll do," Moash said, "when we're not crawling across winter's own frozen backside."

"At least take the patch off. It might give us away, if we meet someone from the warcamps. Rip it off." Graves turned on his heel and walked back toward camp.

Moash felt at the Bridge Four patch on his shoulder. It brought memories. Joining Graves and his band, who had been planning to kill King Elhokar. An assassination attempt once Dalinar was away, marching toward the center of the Shattered Plains.

Facing off against Kaladin, wounded and bleeding.

You. Will. Not. Have. Him.

Moash's skin had gone clammy from the cold. He slid his knife from his side sheath—he still wasn't used to being able to carry one that long. A knife that was too big could get you into trouble as a darkeyes.

He wasn't darkeyed anymore. He was one of them.

Storms, he *was* one of them.

He cut the stitches on the Bridge Four patch. Up one side, then down the other. How simple it was. It would be harder to remove the tattoo he'd gotten with the others, but that he'd had placed on his shoulder, not his forehead.

Moash held up the patch, trying to catch the firelight for a last look, and then couldn't bring himself to throw it away. He walked back and settled by the fire. Were the others sitting around Rock's stewpot somewhere? Laughing, joking, betting on how many mugs of ale Lopen could drink? Ribbing Kaladin, trying to get him to crack a smile?

Moash could almost hear their voices, and he smiled, imagining that he was there. Then, he imagined Kaladin telling them what Moash had done.

He tried to kill me, Kaladin would say. *He betrayed everything. His oath to protect the king, his duty to Alethkar, but most importantly* us.

Moash sagged, patch in his fingers. He should throw that thing in the fire.

Storms. He should throw *himself* in the fire.

He looked up toward the skies, toward both Damnation and the Tranquiline Halls. A group of starspren quivered above.

And beside them, something moving in the sky?

Moash shouted, throwing himself backward off his perch as four Voidbringers descended upon the little camp. They smashed into the ground, wielding long, sinuous swords. Not Shardblades—those were Parshendi weapons.

One creature struck where Moash had been sitting an instant before. Another creature stabbed Graves straight through the chest, then yanked the weapon free and beheaded him with a backhand swipe.

Graves's corpse tumbled and his Shardblade materialized, clanging to the ground. Febrth and Fia didn't have a chance. Other Voidbringers struck them down, spilling their blood in this cold, forgotten land.

The fourth Voidbringer came for Moash, who threw himself into a roll. The creature's sword slammed down near him, hitting rock, the blade throwing sparks.

Moash rolled to his feet, and Kaladin's training—drilled into him through hours and hours spent at the bottom of a chasm—took over. He danced away, putting his back to the wagon, as his Shardblade fell into his fingers.

The Voidbringer rounded the fire toward him, light glittering from her taut, muscular body. These weren't like the Parshendi he'd seen on the Shattered Plains. They had deep red eyes and red-violet carapace, some of which framed their faces. The one facing him had a swirling pattern to her skin, three different colors mixing. Red, black, white.

Dark light, like inverse Stormlight, clung to each of them. Graves had spoken of these creatures, calling their return merely one of many events predicted by the inscrutable "Diagram."

Moash's foe came for him, and he lashed out with his Blade, driving her back. She seemed to *glide* as she moved, feet barely touching the ground. The other three ignored him, instead picking through the camp, inspecting the bodies. One soared in a graceful leap onto the wagon and began digging in the items there.

His opponent tried again, carefully sweeping her long, curved sword at him. Moash shied back, Shardblade gripped with both hands, trying to intercept her weapon. His motions seemed clumsy compared to the graceful power of this creature. She slipped to the side, clothing rippling in the wind, breath visible in the cold air. She wasn't taking chances against a Shardblade, and didn't strike as Moash stumbled.

Storms. This weapon was just too clunky. Six feet long, it was hard to angle right. Yes, it could cut through anything, but he needed to actually *hit* for that to matter. It had been much easier to wield the thing wearing Plate. Without it, he felt like a child holding an adult's weapon.

The Voidbringer smiled. Then she struck with blurring speed. Moash stepped back, swinging, forcing her to twist to the side. He took a long cut up the arm, but his move prevented her from impaling him.

His arm flared with pain and he grunted. The Voidbringer regarded him confidently, knowingly. He was dead. Maybe he should simply let it happen.

The Voidbringer working in the cart said something eager, excited. He'd found the Shardplate. He kicked other items while digging it free, and something rolled out the back of the wagon, thumping against the stone. A spear.

Moash looked down at his Shardblade, the wealth of nations, the most valuable possession a man could own.

Who am I kidding? he thought. *Who did I ever think I was kidding?*

The Voidbringer woman launched into an attack, but Moash dismissed his Shardblade and dashed away. His attacker was so surprised that she hesitated, and Moash had time to dive for the spear, rolling to his feet. Holding the smooth wood in his hand, a familiar weight, Moash snapped easily into his stance. The air suddenly smelled damp and faintly rotten— he remembered the chasms. Life and death together, vines and rot.

He could almost hear Kaladin's voice. *You can't fear a Shardblade. You can't fear a lighteyes on horseback. They kill with fear first and the sword second.*

Stand your ground.

The Voidbringer came for him, and Moash stood his ground. He turned her aside by catching her weapon on the haft of the spear. Then he thrust the butt end of the spear up underneath her arm as she came in for a backhand.

The Voidbringer gasped in surprise as Moash executed a takedown he'd practiced a thousand times in the chasms. He swung the butt of his spear at her ankles and swept her legs out from under her. He began to follow with a classic twist and thrust, to stab down through her chest.

Unfortunately, the Voidbringer didn't fall. She caught herself in the air, hovering instead of collapsing. Moash noticed in time, and pulled out of his maneuver to block her next attack.

The Voidbringer glided backward, then dropped to the ground in a prowling crouch, sword held to the side. She then leaped forward and grabbed Moash's spear as he tried to use it to ward her off. Storms! She gracefully pulled herself close to him, inside his reach. She smelled of wet clothing and of the alien, moldy scent he associated with the Parshendi.

She pressed her hand against Moash's chest, and that dark light transferred from her to him. Moash felt himself grow lighter.

Fortunately, Kaladin had tried this on him too.

Moash seized the Voidbringer with one hand, holding on to the front of her loose shirt, as his body tried to fall into the air.

His sudden pull jerked her off balance, even lifted her a few inches. He yanked her up toward him with one hand while pushing his spearhead down against the rocky ground. That sent the two of them spinning in the air, hovering.

She cried out in an alien tongue. Moash dropped his spear and grabbed his knife. She tried to shove him away, Lashing him again, stronger this time. He grunted, but hung on, and got his knife up and rammed it into her chest.

Orange Parshendi blood poured around his hand, spraying into the cold night as they continued to spin in the air. Moash hung on tight and pushed the knife farther.

She didn't heal, as Kaladin would have. Her eyes stopped glowing, and the dark light vanished.

The body grew limp. A short time later, the force pulling Moash upward ran out. He dropped the five feet to the ground, her body cushioning his fall.

Orange blood coated him, steaming in the chill air. He seized his spear again, fingers slick with blood, and pointed it at the three remaining Voidbringers, who regarded him with stunned expressions.

"Bridge Four, you bastards," Moash growled.

Two of the Voidbringers turned toward the third, the other woman, who looked Moash up and down.

"You can probably kill me," Moash said, wiping a hand on his clothes to improve his grip. "But I'll take one of you with me. At least one."

They didn't seem angry that he'd killed their friend. Storms though, did things like these even *have* emotions? Shen had often just sat around staring. He locked eyes with the woman at the center. Her skin was white and red, not a bit of black in it. The paleness of that white reminded him of the Shin, who always looked sickly to Moash.

"You," she said in accented Alethi, "have passion."

One of the others handed her Graves's Shardblade. She held it up, inspecting it by the firelight. Then she rose into the air. "You may choose," she said to him. "Die here, or accept defeat and give up your weapons."

Moash clung to the spear in the shadow of that figure, her clothing rippling in the air. Did they think he'd actually trust them?

But then . . . did he really think he could stand against three of them?

With a shrug, he tossed aside the spear. He summoned his Blade. After all those years dreaming of one of these, he'd finally received one. Kaladin had given it to him. And what good had come of it? He obviously couldn't be trusted with such a weapon.

Setting his jaw, Moash pressed his hand to the gemstone, and willed the bond to break. The gemstone at its pommel flashed, and he felt an icy coolness wash through him. Back to being a darkeyes.

He tossed the Blade to the ground. One of the Voidbringers took it. Another flew off, and Moash was confused as to what was happening. A short time later, that one returned with six more. Three attached ropes to the Shardplate bundles, then flew off, hauling the heavy armor into the air after them. Why not Lash it?

Moash thought for a moment they were actually going to leave him there, but finally two others grabbed him—one arm each—and hauled him into the air.

44

THE BRIGHT SIDE

*We are indeed intrigued, for we thought it well hidden. Insignificant
among our many realms.*

Veil lounged in a tavern tent with her men. Her boots up on a
table, chair tipped back, she listened to the life bubbling around
her. People drinking and chatting, others strolling the path
outside, shouting and joking. She enjoyed the warm, enveloping buzz of
fellow humans who had turned this tomb of rock into something alive
again.

It still daunted her to contemplate the size of the tower. How had
anyone *built* a place this big? It could gobble up most cities Veil had seen
without having to loosen its belt.

Well, best not to think about that. You needed to sneak low, beneath all
the questions that distracted scribes and scholars. That was the only way to
get anything useful done.

Instead she focused on the people. Their voices blended together, and
collectively they became a faceless crowd. But the grand thing about people
was that you could also choose to focus on particular faces, really see them,
and find a wealth of stories. So many people with so many lives, each a
separate little mystery. Infinite detail, like Pattern. Look close at his frac-
tal lines, and you'd realize each little ridge had an entire architecture of
its own. Look close at a given person, and you'd see their uniqueness—
see that they didn't quite match whatever broad category you'd first put
them in.

"So . . ." Red said, talking to Ishnah. Veil had brought three of her men
today, with the spy woman to train them. So Veil could listen, learn, and

try to judge if this woman was trustworthy—or if she was some kind of plant.

"This is great," Red continued, "but when do we learn the stuff with the knives? Not that I'm eager to kill anyone. Just . . . you know . . ."

"I know what?" Ishnah asked.

"Knives are deevy," Red said.

"Deevy?" Veil asked, opening her eyes.

Red nodded. "Deevy. You know. Incredible, or neat, but in a smooooth way."

"Everyone knows that knives are deevy," Gaz added.

Ishnah rolled her eyes. The short woman wore her havah with hand covered, and her dress had a light touch of embroidery. Her poise and dress indicated she was a darkeyed woman of relatively high social standing.

Veil drew more attention, and not just because of her white jacket and hat. It was the attention of men assessing whether they wanted to approach her, which they didn't do with Ishnah. The way she carried herself, the prim havah, kept them back.

Veil sipped her drink, enjoying the wine.

"You've heard lurid stories, I'm sure," Ishnah said. "But espionage is not about knives in alleys. I'd barely know what to do with myself if I had to stab someone."

The three men deflated.

"Espionage," Ishnah continued, "is about the careful gathering of information. Your task is to observe, but to not *be* observed. You must be likable enough that people talk to you, but not so interesting that they remember you."

"Well, Gaz is out," Red said.

"Yeah," Gaz said, "it's a curse to be so storming interesting."

"Would you two shut up?" Vathah said. The lanky soldier had leaned in, cup of cheap wine left untouched. "How?" he asked. "I'm tall. Gaz has one eye. We'll be remembered."

"You need to learn to channel attention toward superficial traits you can change, and away from traits you cannot. Red, if *you* wore an eye patch, that detail would stick in their minds. Vathah, I can teach you how to slouch so your height isn't noticeable—and if you add an unusual accent, people will describe you by that. Gaz, I could put you in a tavern and have you lie on the table in a feigned drunken stupor. Nobody will notice the eye patch; they'll ignore you as a drunkard.

"That is beside the point. We must begin with observation. If you are to be useful, you need to be able to make quick assessments of a location, memorize details, and be able to report back. Now, close your eyes."

They reluctantly did so, Veil joining them.

"Now," Ishnah said. "Can any of you describe the tavern's occupants? Without looking, mind you."

"Uh . . ." Gaz scratched at his eye patch. "There's a cute one at the bar. She might be Thaylen."

"What color is her blouse?"

"Hm. Well, it's low cut, and she's grown some nice rockbuds . . . uh . . ."

"There's this really ugly guy with an eye patch," Red said. "Short, annoying type. Drinks your wine when you aren't looking."

"Vathah?" Ishnah asked. "What about you?"

"I think there were some guys at the bar," he said. "They were in . . . Sebarial uniforms? And maybe half the tables were occupied. I couldn't say by who."

"Better," Ishnah said. "I didn't expect you to be able to do this. It's human nature to ignore these things. I'll train you though, so that—"

"Wait," Vathah said. "What about Veil? What does she remember?"

"Three men at the bar," Veil said absently. "Older man with whitening hair, and two soldiers, probably related, judging by those hooked noses. The younger one is drinking wine; the older one is trying to pick up the woman Gaz noticed. She's not Thaylen, but she's wearing Thaylen dress with a deep violet blouse and a forest-green skirt. I don't like the pairing, but she seems to. She's confident, used to playing with the attention of men. But I think she came here looking for someone, because she's ignoring the soldier and keeps glancing over her shoulder.

"The barkeep is an older man, short enough that he stands on boxes when he fills orders. I bet he hasn't been a barkeep long. He hesitates when someone orders, and he has to glance over the bottles, reading their glyphs before he finds the right one. There are three barmaids—one is on break—and fourteen customers other than us." She opened her eyes. "I can tell you about them."

"Won't be necessary," Ishnah said as Red clapped softly. "Very impressive, Veil, though I should note that there are *fifteen* other customers, not fourteen."

Veil started, then glanced around the tent room again, counting—as she'd done in her head just a moment ago. Three at that table . . . four over there . . . two women standing together by the door . . .

And a woman she'd missed, nestled into a chair by a small table at the back of the tent. She wore simple clothing, a skirt and blouse of Alethi peasant design. Had she intentionally chosen clothing that blended in with the white of the tent and brown of the tables? And what was she doing there?

Taking notes, Veil thought with a spike of alarm. The woman had carefully hidden a little notebook in her lap. "Who is she?" Veil hunkered down. "Why is she watching us?"

"Not us specifically," Ishnah said. "There will be dozens like her in the market, moving like rats, gathering what information they can. She might be independent, selling tidbits she finds, but likely she's employed by one of the highprinces. That's the job I used to do. I'd guess from the people she's watching that she's been told to gather a report on the mood of the troops."

Veil nodded and listened intently as Ishnah started training the men in memory tricks. She suggested they should learn glyphs, and use some ploy—like making marks on their hands—to help them keep track of information. Veil had heard of some of these tricks, including the one Ishnah talked about, the so-called mind museum.

Most interesting were Ishnah's tips on how to tell what was relevant to report, and how to find it. She talked about listening for the names of high-princes and for common words used as stand-ins for more important matters, and about how to listen for someone who had just the right amount of drink in them to say things they shouldn't. Tone, she said, was key. You could sit five feet from someone sharing important secrets, but miss it because you were focused on the argument at the next table over.

The state she described was almost meditative—sitting and letting your ears take in everything, your mind latching on to only certain conversations. Veil found it fascinating. But after about an hour of training, Gaz complained that his head felt like he'd had four bottles already. Red was nodding, and the way his eyes were crossed made him seem completely overwhelmed.

Vathah though . . . he'd closed his eyes and was reeling off descriptions of everyone in the room to Ishnah. Veil grinned. For as long as she'd known the man, he'd gone about each of his duties as if he had a boulder tied to his back. Slow to move, quick to find a place to sit down and rest. Seeing this enthusiasm from him was encouraging.

In fact, Veil was so engaged, she completely missed how much time had passed. When she heard the market bells she cursed softly. "I'm a storming fool."

"Veil?" Vathah asked.

"I've got to get going," she said. "Shallan has an appointment." Who would have thought that bearing an ancient, divine mantle of power and honor would involve so many meetings?

"And she can't make it without you?" Vathah said.

"Storms, have you *watched* that girl? She'd forget her feet if they weren't stuck on. Keep practicing! I'll meet up with you later." She pulled on her hat and went dashing through the Breakaway.

A short time later, Shallan Davar—now safely tucked back into a blue havah—strolled through the hallway beneath Urithiru. She was pleased with the work that Veil was doing with the men, but storms, did she have to drink so much? Shallan burned off practically an entire *barrel's* worth of alcohol to clear her head.

She took a deep breath, then stepped into the former library room. Here she found not only Navani, Jasnah, and Teshav, but a host of ardents and scribes. May Aladar, Adrotagia from Kharbranth . . . there were even three *stormwardens,* the odd men with the long beards who liked to predict the weather. Shallan had heard that they would occasionally use the blowing of the winds to foretell the future, but they never offered such services openly.

Being near them made Shallan wish for a glyphward. Veil didn't keep any handy, unfortunately. *She* was basically a heretic, and thought about religion as often as she did seasilk prices in Rall Elorim. At least Jasnah had the backbone to pick a side and announce it; Veil would simply shrug and make some wisecrack. It—

"Mmmm . . ." Pattern whispered from her skirt. "Shallan?"

Right. She'd been just standing in the doorway, hadn't she? She walked in, unfortunately passing Janala, who was acting as Teshav's assistant. The pretty young woman stood with her nose perpetually in the air, and was the type of person whose very enunciation made Shallan's skin crawl.

The woman's arrogance was what Shallan didn't like—not, of course, that Adolin had been courting Janala soon before meeting Shallan. She had once tried to avoid Adolin's former romantic partners, but . . . well, that was like trying to avoid soldiers on a battlefield. They were just kind of everywhere.

A dozen conversations buzzed through the room: talk about weights and measures, the proper placement of punctuation, and the atmospheric variations in the tower. Once she'd have given anything to be in a room like this. Now she was constantly late to the meetings. What had changed?

I know how much a fraud I am, she thought, hugging the wall, passing a pretty young ardent discussing Azish politics with one of the stormwardens. Shallan had barely perused those books that Adolin had brought her. On her other side, Navani was talking fabrials with an engineer in a bright red havah. The woman nodded eagerly. "Yes, but how to stabilize it, Brightness? With the sails underneath, it will want to spin over, won't it?"

Shallan's proximity to Navani had offered ample opportunity to study fabrial science. Why hadn't she? As it enveloped her—the ideas, the questions, the logic—she suddenly felt she was drowning. Overwhelmed. Everyone in this room knew so much, and she felt insignificant compared to them.

I need someone who can handle this, she thought. *A scholar. Part of me can become a scholar. Not Veil, or Brightness Radiant. But someone—*

Pattern started humming on her dress again. Shallan backed to the wall. No, this . . . this was *her,* wasn't it? Shallan had always wanted to be a scholar, hadn't she? She didn't need another persona to deal with this. Right?

. . . Right?

The moment of anxiety passed, and she breathed out, forcing herself to steady. Eventually she pulled a pad of paper and a charcoal pencil out of her satchel, then sought out Jasnah and presented herself.

Jasnah cocked an eyebrow. "Late again?"

"Sorry."

"I intended to ask your help understanding some of the translations we're receiving from the Dawnchant, but we haven't time before my mother's meeting starts."

"Maybe I could help you—"

"I have a few items to finish up. We can speak later."

An abrupt dismissal, but nothing more than Shallan had come to expect. She walked over to a chair beside the wall and sat down. "Surely," she said softly, "if Jasnah had *known* that I'd just confronted a deep insecurity of mine, she'd have shown some empathy. Right?"

"Jasnah?" Pattern asked. "I do not think you are paying attention, Shallan. She is not very empathetic."

Shallan sighed.

"*You're* empathetic though!"

"The pathetic part, at least." She steeled herself. "I belong here, Pattern, don't I?"

"Mmm. Yes, of course you do. You'll want to sketch them, right?"

"The classic scholars didn't just draw. The Oilsworn knew mathematics—he *created* the study of ratios in art. Galid was an inventor, and her designs are still used in astronomy today. Sailors couldn't find longitude at sea until the arrival of her clocks. Jasnah's a historian—and more. That's what I want."

"Are you sure?"

"I think so." Problem was, Veil wanted to spend her days drinking and laughing with the men, practicing espionage. Radiant wanted to practice with the sword and spend time around Adolin. What did Shallan want? And did it matter?

Eventually Navani called the meeting to order, and people took seats. Scribes on one side of Navani, ardents from a variety of devotaries on the other—and far from Jasnah. As the stormwardens settled down farther around the ring of seats, Shallan noticed Renarin standing in the doorway.

He shuffled, peeking in, but not entering. When several scholars turned toward him, he stepped backward, as if their stares were physically forcing him out.

"I . . ." Renarin said. "Father said I could come . . . just listen maybe."

"You're more than welcome, Cousin," Jasnah said. She nodded for Shallan to get him a stool, so she did—and didn't even protest being ordered about. She *could* be a scholar. She'd be the best little ward ever.

Head down, Renarin rounded the ring of scholars, keeping a white-knuckled grip on a chain hung from his pocket. As soon as he sat, he started pulling the chain between the fingers of one hand, then the other.

Shallan did her best to take notes, and *not* stray into sketching people instead. Fortunately, the proceedings were more interesting than usual. Navani had most of the scholars here working on trying to understand Urithiru. Inadara reported first—she was a wizened scribe who reminded Shallan of her father's ardents—explaining that her team had been trying to ascertain the meaning of the strange shapes of the rooms and tunnels in the tower.

She went on at length, talking of defensive constructions, air filtration, and the wells. She pointed out groupings of rooms that were shaped oddly, and of the bizarre murals they'd found, depicting fanciful creatures.

When she eventually finished, Kalami reported on her team, who were convinced that certain gold and copper metalworks they'd found embedded in walls were fabrials, but they didn't seem to do anything, even with gems attached. She passed around drawings, then moved on to explaining the efforts—failed so far—they'd taken to try to infuse the gemstone pillar. The only working fabrials were the lifts.

"I suggest," interrupted Elthebar, head of the stormwardens, "that the ratio of the gears used in the lift machinery might be indicative of the nature of those who built it. It is the science of digitology, you see. You can judge much about a man by the width of his fingers."

"And this has to do with gears . . . how?" Teshav asked.

"In every way!" Elthebar said. "Why, the fact that you don't know this is a *clear* indication that you are a scribe. Your writing is pretty, Brightness. But you must give more heed to *science*."

Pattern buzzed softly.

"I never have liked him," Shallan whispered. "He acts nice around Dalinar, but he's quite mean."

"So . . . which attribute of his are we totaling and how many people are in the sample size?" Pattern asked.

"Do you think, maybe," Janala said, "we are asking the wrong questions?"

Shallan narrowed her eyes, but checked herself, suppressing her jealousy. There was no need to hate someone simply because they'd been close to Adolin.

It was just that something felt . . . *off* about Janala. Like many women at court, her laughter sounded rehearsed, contained. Like they used it as a seasoning, rather than actually feeling it.

"What do you mean, child?" Adrotagia asked Janala.

"Well, Brightness, we talk about the lifts, the strange fabrial column, the twisting hallways. We try to understand these things merely from their designs. Maybe instead we should figure out the tower's needs, and then work backward to determine how these things might have met them."

"Hmmm," Navani said. "Well, we know that they grew crops outside. Did some of these wall fabrials provide heat?"

Renarin mumbled something.

Everyone in the room looked at him. Not a few seemed surprised to hear him speak, and he shrank back.

"What was that, Renarin?" Navani asked.

"It's not like that," he said softly. "They're not fabrials. They're *a* fabrial."

The scribes and scholars shared looks. The prince . . . well, he often incited such reactions. Discomforted stares.

"Brightlord?" Janala asked. "Are you perhaps secretly an artifabrian? Studying engineering by night, reading the women's script?"

Several of the others chuckled. Renarin blushed deeply, lowering his eyes farther.

You'd never laugh like that at any other man of his rank, Shallan thought, feeling her cheeks grow hot. The Alethi court could be severely polite—but that didn't mean they were nice. Renarin always had been a more acceptable target than Dalinar or Adolin.

Shallan's anger was a strange sensation. On more than one occasion, she'd been struck by Renarin's oddness. His presence at this meeting was just another example. Was he thinking of finally joining the ardents? And he did that by simply showing up at a meeting for scribes, as if he were one of the women?

At the same time, how *dare* Janala embarrass him?

Navani started to say something, but Shallan cut in. "Surely, Janala, you didn't just try to *insult* the son of the *highprince.*"

"What? No, no of course I didn't."

"Good," Shallan said. "Because, if you *had* been trying to insult him, you did a terrible job. And I've heard that you're very clever. So full of wit, and charm, and . . . other things."

Janala frowned at her. ". . . Is that flattery?"

"We weren't talking of your chest, dear. We're speaking of your mind! Your wonderful, brilliant mind, so keen that it's never been sharpened! So quick, it's still running when everyone else is done! So dazzling, it's never failed to leave everyone in awe at the things you say. So . . . um . . ."

Jasnah was glaring at her.

". . . Hmm . . ." Shallan held up her notebook. "I took notes."

"Could we have a short break, Mother?" Jasnah asked.

"An excellent suggestion," Navani said. "Fifteen minutes, during which everyone should consider a list of requirements this tower would have, if it were to somehow become self-sufficient."

She rose, and the meeting broke up into individual conversations again.

"I see," Jasnah said to Shallan, "that you still use your tongue like a bludgeon rather than a knife."

"Yeah." Shallan sighed. "Any tips?"

Jasnah eyed her.

"You heard what she said to Renarin, Brightness!"

"And Mother was about to speak to her about it," Jasnah said, "discreetly, with a judicious word. Instead, you threw a dictionary at her head."

"Sorry. She gets on my nerves."

"Janala is a fool, just bright enough to be proud of the wits she has, but stupid enough to be unaware of how outmatched they are." Jasnah rubbed her temples. "Storms. This is why I never take wards."

"Because they give you so much trouble."

"Because I'm bad at it. I have scientific evidence of that fact, and you are but the latest experiment." Jasnah shooed her away, rubbing her temples.

Shallan, feeling ashamed, walked to the side of the room, while everyone else got refreshments.

"Mmmm!" Pattern said as Shallan leaned against the wall, notebook held closer to her chest. "Jasnah doesn't seem angry. Why are you sad?"

"Because I'm an idiot," Shallan said. "And a fool. And . . . because I don't *know* what I *want*." Hadn't it been only a week or two ago that she'd innocently assumed she had it figured out? Whatever "it" was?

"I can see him!" said a voice to her side.

Shallan jumped and turned to find Renarin staring at her skirt and the pattern there, which blended into her embroidery. Distinct if you knew to look, but easy to miss.

"He doesn't turn invisible?" Renarin said.

"He says he can't."

Renarin nodded, then looked up at her. "Thank you."

"For?"

"Defending my honor. When Adolin does that, someone usually gets stabbed. Your way was pleasanter."

"Well, nobody should take that tone with you. They wouldn't *dare* do it to Adolin. And besides, you're right. This place *is* one big fabrial."

"You feel it too? They keep talking about this device or that device, but that's wrong, isn't it? That's like taking the parts of a cart, without realizing you've got a cart in the first place."

Shallan leaned in. "That *thing* that we fought, Renarin. It could stretch its tendrils all the way up to the very top of Urithiru. I felt its wrongness wherever I went. That gemstone at the center is tied to everything."

"Yes, this isn't only a collection of fabrials. It's many fabrials put together to make one *big* fabrial."

"But what does it do?" Shallan asked.

"It does being a city." He frowned. "Well, I mean, it bees a city. . . . It does what the city is. . . ."

Shallan shivered. "And the Unmade was running it."

"Which let us discover this room and the fabrial column," Renarin said. "We might not have accomplished that without it. Always look on the bright side."

"Logically," Shallan said, "the bright side is the only side you can look on, because the other side is dark."

Renarin laughed. It brought to mind how her brothers would laugh at what she said. Maybe not because it was the most hilarious thing ever spoken, but because it was good to laugh. That reminded her of what Jasnah had said, though, and Shallan found herself glancing at the woman.

"I know my cousin is intimidating," Renarin whispered to her. "But you're a Radiant too, Shallan. Don't forget that. We could stand up to her if we wanted to."

"Do we want to?"

Renarin grimaced. "Probably not. So often, she's right, and you just end up feeling like one of the ten fools."

"True, but . . . I don't know if I can stand being ordered around like a child again. I'm starting to feel crazy. What do I do?"

Renarin shrugged. "I've found the best way to avoid doing what Jasnah says is to not be around when she's looking for someone to give orders to."

Shallan perked up. That made a lot of sense. Dalinar would need his Radiants to go do things, right? She needed to get away, just until she could figure things out. Go somewhere . . . like on that mission to Kholinar? Wouldn't they need someone who could sneak into the palace and activate the device?

"Renarin," she said, "you're a genius."

He blushed, but smiled.

Navani called the meeting together again, and they sat to continue discussing fabrials. Jasnah tapped Shallan's notebook and she did a better job of taking the minutes, practicing her shorthand. It wasn't nearly as irksome now, as she had an exit strategy. An escape route.

She was appreciating that when she noticed a tall figure striding through the door. Dalinar Kholin cast a shadow, even when he wasn't standing in front of the light. Everyone immediately hushed.

"Apologies for my tardiness." He glanced at his wrist, and the forearm timepiece that Navani had given him. "Please don't stop because of me."

"Dalinar?" Navani asked. "You've never attended a meeting of scribes before."

"I just thought I should watch," Dalinar said. "Learn what this piece of my organization is doing." He settled down on a stool outside the ring. He looked like a warhorse trying to perch on a stand meant for a show pony.

They started up again, everyone obviously self-conscious. She'd have thought that Dalinar would know to stay away from meetings like this, where women and scribes . . .

Shallan cocked her head as she saw Renarin glance at his father. Dalinar responded with a raised fist.

He came so Renarin wouldn't feel awkward, Shallan realized. *It can't be improper or feminine for the prince to be here if the storming Blackthorn decides to attend.*

She didn't miss the way that Renarin actually raised his eyes to watch the rest of the proceedings.

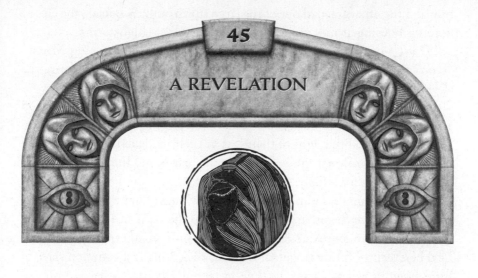

45

A REVELATION

As the waves of the sea must continue to surge, so must our will continue resolute.

    Alone.

The Voidbringers carried Moash to Revolar, a city in central Alethkar. Once there, they dropped him outside the city and shoved him toward a group of lesser parshmen.

His arms ached from being carried. Why hadn't they used their powers to Lash him upward and make him lighter, as Kaladin would have?

He stretched his arms, looking around. He'd been to Revolar many times, working a regular caravan to Kholinar. Unfortunately, that didn't mean he'd seen much of the city. Every city of size had a little huddle of buildings on the outskirts for people like him: modern-day nomads who worked caravans or ran deliveries. The people of the eaves, some had called them. Men and women who hovered close enough to civilization to get out of the weather when it turned bad, but who never really belonged.

From the looks of things, Revolar had quite the eaves culture now—too much of one. The Voidbringers seemed to have taken over the entire storming place, exiling the humans to the outskirts.

The Voidbringers left him without a word, despite having lugged him all this distance. The parshmen who took custody of him here looked like a hybrid between Parshendi warriors and the normal, docile parshmen he'd known from many a caravan run. They spoke perfect Alethi as they shoved him toward a group of humans in a little pen.

Moash settled in to wait. Looked like the Voidbringers had patrols scouting the area, grabbing human stragglers. Eventually, the parshmen herded him and the others toward one of the large storm bunkers outside the city—used for housing armies or multiple caravans during highstorms.

"Don't make trouble," a parshwoman said, specifically eyeing Moash. "Don't fight, or you'll be killed. Don't run, or you'll be beaten. You're the slaves now."

Several of the humans—homesteaders, from the looks of it—started weeping. They clutched meager bundles, which parshmen searched through. Moash could read the signs of their loss in their reddened eyes and ragged possessions. The Everstorm had wiped out their farm. They'd come to the big city looking for refuge.

He had nothing on him of value, not any longer, and the parshmen let him go in before the others. He walked into the bunker, feeling a surreal sense of . . . abandonment? He'd spent the trip here alternately assuming he'd be executed or interrogated. Instead, they'd made a common slave of him? Even in Sadeas's army, he'd never technically been a slave. Assigned to bridge runs, yes. Sent to die. But he'd never worn the brands on his forehead. He felt at the Bridge Four tattoo under his shirt, on his left shoulder.

The vast, high-ceilinged storm bunker was shaped like a huge stone loaf. Moash ambled through it, hands stuffed in his coat pockets. Huddled groups of people regarded him with hostility, even though he was just another refugee.

He'd always been met with hostility, no matter where he storming went. A youth like him, too big and obviously too confident for a darkeyes, had been considered a threat. He'd joined the caravans to give himself something productive to do, encouraged by his grandparents. They'd been murdered for their kindly ways, and Moash . . . he'd spent his life putting up with looks like that.

A man on his own, a man you couldn't control, was dangerous. He was *inherently frightening*, just because of who he was. And nobody would ever let him in.

Except Bridge Four.

Well, Bridge Four had been a special case, and he'd failed that test. Graves had been right to tell him to cut the patch off. *This* was who he really was. The man everyone looked at with distrust, pulling their children tight and nodding for him to move along.

He stalked down the middle of the structure, which was so wide it needed pillars to hold up the ceiling. Those rose like trees, Soulcast right into the rock below. The edges of the building were crowded with people, but the center was kept clear and patrolled by armed parshmen. They'd set up stations with wagons as perches, where parshmen were addressing crowds. Moash went over to one.

"In case we missed any," the parshman shouted, "experienced farmers should report to Bru at the front end of the chamber. He will assign you a plot of land to work. Today, we also need workers to carry water in the city, and more to clear debris from the last storm. I can take twenty of each."

Men started calling out their willingness, and Moash frowned, leaning toward a man nearby. "They offer us work? Aren't we slaves?"

"Yeah," the man said. "Slaves who don't eat unless they work. They let us choose what we want to do, though it's not much of a storming choice. One kind of drudgery or another."

With a start, Moash realized that the man had pale green eyes. Yet he still raised his hand and volunteered to carry water—something that had once been parshman work. Well, that was a sight that couldn't help but brighten a man's day. Moash shoved hands back in pockets and continued through the room, checking each of the three stations where parshmen offered jobs.

Something about these parshmen and their perfect Alethi unsettled him. The Voidbringers were what he'd expected, with their alien accents and dramatic powers. But the ordinary parshmen—many of them looked like Parshendi now, with those taller builds—seemed almost as bewildered at their reversal in fortune as the humans were.

Each of the three stations dealt with a different category of labor. The one at the far end was looking for farmers, women with sewing skill, and cobblers. Food, uniforms, boots. The parshmen were preparing for war. Asking around, Moash learned they'd already grabbed the smiths, fletchers, and armorers—and if you were found hiding skill in any of these three, your whole family would be put on half rations.

The middle station was for basic labor. Hauling water, cleaning, cooking food. The last station was the most interesting to Moash. This was for hard labor.

He lingered here, listening to a parshman ask for volunteers to pull wagons of supplies with the army when it marched. Apparently, there weren't enough chulls to move wagons for what was coming.

Nobody raised their hands for this one. It sounded like ghastly work, not to mention the fact that it would mean marching toward battle.

They'll need to press the people into this, Moash thought. *Maybe they can round up some lighteyes and make them trudge across the rock like beasts of burden.* He'd like to see that.

As he left this last station, Moash spotted a group of men with long staffs, leaning against the wall. Sturdy boots, waterskins in holsters tied to their thighs, and a walking kit sewn into the trousers on the other side. He knew from experience what that would carry. A bowl, spoon, cup, thread, needle, patches, and some flint and tinder.

Caravaneers. The long staffs were for slapping chull shells while walking beside them. He'd worn an outfit like that many times, though many of the caravans he'd worked had used parshmen to pull wagons instead of chulls. They were faster.

"Hey," he said, strolling over to the caravaneers. "Is Guff still around?"

"Guff?" one of the caravaneers said. "Old wheelwright? Half a reed tall? Bad at cussing?"

"That's him."

"I think he's over there," the young man said, pointing with his staff. "In the tents. But there ain't work, friend."

"The shellheads are marching," Moash said, thumbing over his shoulder. "They'll need caravaneers."

"Positions are full," another of the men said. "There was a fight to see who got those jobs. Everyone else will be pulling wagons. Don't draw too much attention, or they'll slap a harness on you. Mark my words."

They smiled in a friendly way to Moash, and he gave them an old caravaneers' salute—close enough to a rude gesture that everyone else mistook it—and strode in the direction they'd pointed. Typical. Caravaneers were a big family—and, like a family, prone to squabbling.

The "tents" were really some sections of cloth that had been stretched from the wall to poles driven into buckets of rocks to keep them steady. That made a kind of tunnel along the wall here, and underneath, a lot of older people coughed and sniffled. It was dim, with only the occasional chip on an overturned box giving light.

He picked out the caravaneers by their accents. He asked after Guff— who was one of the men he'd known back in the day—and was allowed to penetrate deeper along the shadowy tent tunnel. Eventually, Moash found old Guff sitting right in the middle of the tunnel, as if to keep people from going farther. He had been sanding a piece of wood—an axle, by the looks of it.

He squinted as Moash stepped up. "Moash?" he said. "Really? What storming storm brought you here?"

"You wouldn't believe me if I told you," Moash said, squatting down beside the old man.

"You were on Jam's caravan," Guff said. "Off to the Shattered Plains; gave you all up for dead. Wouldn't have bet a dun chip on you returning."

"A wise enough bet," Moash said. He hunched forward, resting his arms on his knees. In this tunnel, the buzz of people outside seemed a distant thing, though only cloth separated them.

"Son?" Guff asked. "Why you here, boy? What do you want?"

"I just need to be who I was."

"That makes as much sense as the storming Stormfather playing the flute, boy. But you wouldn't be the first to go off to those Plains and come back not all right. No you wouldn't. That's the Stormfather's storming own truth, that storming is."

"They tried to break me. Damnation, they did break me. But then he made me again, a new man." Moash paused. "I threw it all away."

"Sure, sure," Guff said.

"I always do that," Moash whispered. "Why must we always take something precious, Guff, and find ourselves *hating* it? As if by being pure, it reminds us of just how little we deserve it. I held the spear, and I stabbed myself with it. . . ."

"The spear?" Guff asked. "Boy, you a storming soldier?"

Moash looked at him with a start, then stood up, stretching, showing his patchless uniform coat.

Guff squinted in the darkness. "Come with me." The old wheelwright rose—with difficulty—and set his piece of wood on his chair. He led Moash with a rickety gait farther into the cloth tunnel, and they entered a portion of the tented area that was more roomlike, the far corner of the large bunker. Here, a group of maybe a dozen people sat in furtive conversation, chairs pulled together.

A man at the door grabbed Guff by the arm as he shuffled in. "Guff? You're supposed to be on guard, fool man."

"I'm storming on storming guard, you pisser," Guff said, shaking his arm free. "The bright wanted to know if we found any soldiers. Well I found a storming soldier, so storm off."

The guard turned his attention to Moash, then flicked his eyes to Moash's shoulder. "Deserter?"

Moash nodded. It was true in more ways than one.

"What's this?" One of the men stood up, a tall fellow. Something about his silhouette, that bald head, that cut of clothing . . .

"Deserter, Brightlord," the guard said.

"From the Shattered Plains," Guff added.

The highlord, Moash realized. *Paladar.* Vamah's kinsman and regent, a notoriously harsh man. In years past, he had nearly run the city to the ground, driving away many darkeyes who had the right of travel. Not a caravan had passed when someone hadn't complained about Paladar's greed and corruption.

"From the Shattered Plains, you say?" Paladar said. "Excellent. Tell me, deserter, what news is there from the highprinces? Do they know of my plight here? Can I expect aid soon?"

They put him in charge, Moash thought, spotting other lighteyes. They wore fine clothing—not silks of course, but well-trimmed uniforms. Exceptional boots. There was food aplenty set out at the side of this chamber, while those outside scrounged and did heavy labor.

He'd begun to hope . . . But of course that had been stupid. The arrival of the Voidbringers hadn't cast the lighteyes down; the few Moash had seen outside were merely the sacrifices. The fawning darkeyes at the periphery confirmed this. Soldiers, guards, some favored merchants.

To *Damnation* with them! They'd been given a chance to escape from the lighteyes, and it had only made them *more eager* to be servants! In that moment—surrounded by the pettiness that was his own kind—Moash had a revelation.

He wasn't broken. *All* of them were broken. Alethi society—lighteyed and dark. Maybe all of humankind.

"Well?" the regent demanded. "Speak up, man!"

Moash remained silent, overwhelmed. He wasn't the exception, always ruining what he was given. Men like *Kaladin* were the exception—the very, very rare exception.

These people proved it. There was *no reason* to obey lighteyes. They had no power, no authority. Men had taken opportunity and cast it to the crem.

"I . . . I think there's something wrong with him, Brightlord," the guard said.

"Yeah," Guff added. "Should maybe have mentioned, he's storming strange in the head now, storming pisser."

"Bah!" the regent said, pointing at Moash. "Have that one thrown out. We haven't time for foolishness if we are to restore my place!" He pointed at Guff. "Have *that one* beaten, and post a competent guard next time, Ked, or you'll be next!"

Old Guff cried out as they seized him. Moash just nodded. Yes. Of course. That was what they would do.

The guards took him under the arms and dragged him to the side of the tent. They parted the cloth and hauled him out. They passed a frazzled woman trying to divide a single piece of flatbread between three young, crying children. You could probably hear their weeping from the brightlord's tent, where he had a stack of bread piled high.

The guards threw him back out into the "street" that ran down the middle of the large bunker. They told him to stay away, but Moash barely heard. He picked himself up, dusted himself off, then walked to the third of the work stations—the one seeking hard laborers.

There, he volunteered for the most difficult job they had, pulling wagons of supplies for the Voidbringer army.

Did you expect anything else from us? We need not suffer the inter-
ference of another. Rayse is contained, and we care not for his
prison.

Skar the bridgeman ran up one of the ramps outside Urithiru, breath
puffing in the cold air as he silently counted his steps to maintain
focus. The air was thinner up here at Urithiru, and that made
running harder, though he really only noticed it outside.

He wore full marching pack and gear: rations, equipment, helmet, jerkin, and a shield tied to the back. He carried his spear, and even had some
greaves stuck to his legs, held in place by the shape of the metal. All of that
weighed almost as much as he did.

He finally hit the top of the Oathgate platform. Storms, but the center
building looked farther away than he remembered. He tried to pick up his
pace anyway, and jogged for all he was worth, the pack clinking. Finally—
sweating, breath growing ragged—he reached the control building and
dashed inside. He finally pulled to a stop, dropping his spear and resting
his hands on his knees, gasping for breath.

Most of Bridge Four waited here, some glowing with Stormlight. Of
them all, Skar was the only one who—despite two weeks of practice—still
hadn't figured out how to draw it in. Well, except for Dabbid and Rlain.

Sigzil checked the clock they'd been allocated by Navani Kholin, a device the size of a small box. "That was about ten minutes," he said. "Just
under."

Skar nodded, wiping his brow. He'd run over a mile from the center of the market, then crossed the plateau and charged the ramp. Storms. He'd pushed himself too hard.

"How long," he said, gasping, "how long did it take Drehy?" The two had set out together.

Sigzil glanced at the tall, muscled bridgeman who still glowed with residual Stormlight. "Under six minutes."

Skar groaned, sitting down.

"The baseline is equally important, Skar," Sigzil said, marking glyphs in his notebook. "We need to know a normal man's abilities to make comparisons. Don't worry though. I'm sure you'll figure out Stormlight soon."

Skar flopped backward, looking up. Lopen was walking around on the ceiling of the room. Storming Herdazian.

"Drehy, you used a quarter of a Basic Lashing, by Kaladin's terminology?" Sigzil continued, still making notes.

"Yeah," Drehy said. "I . . . I know the precise amount, Sig. Strange."

"Which made you half as heavy as usual, when we put you on the scale back in the rooms. But *why* does a quarter Lashing make you half as heavy? Shouldn't it make you twenty-five percent as heavy?"

"Does it matter?" Drehy asked.

Sigzil looked at him as if he were crazy. "Of course it does!"

"I want to try a Lashing at an angle next," Drehy said. "See if I can make it feel like I'm running downhill, no matter which direction I go. Might not need it. Holding Stormlight . . . it made me feel like I could run forever."

"Well, it's a new record . . ." Sigzil mumbled, still writing. "You beat Lopen's time."

"Did he beat mine?" Leyten called from the side of the small room where he was inspecting the tiling on the floor.

"You stopped for food on the way, Leyten," Sigzil said. "Even *Rock* beat your time, and he was skipping like a girl the last third."

"Was Horneater dance of victory," Rock said from near Leyten. "Is very manly."

"Manly or not, it threw off my test," Sigzil said. "At least Skar is willing to pay attention to proper procedure."

Skar remained lying on the ground as the others chatted—Kaladin was supposed to come and transport them to the Shattered Plains, and Sigzil had decided to run some tests. Kaladin, as usual, was late.

Teft sat down next to Skar, inspecting him with dark green eyes with bags underneath. Kaladin had named the two of them lieutenants, along with Rock and Sigzil, but their roles had never really settled into that ranking. Teft was the perfect definition of a platoon sergeant.

"Here," Teft said, handing over a chouta—meatballs wrapped in flatbread, Herdazian style. "Leyten brought food. Eat something, lad."

Skar forced himself to sit up. "I'm not that much younger than you, Teft. I'm hardly a lad."

Teft nodded to himself, chewing on his own chouta. Finally, Skar started into his. It was good, not spicy like a lot of Alethi food, but still good. Flavorful.

"Everyone keeps telling me that I'll 'get it soon,'" Skar said. "But what if I don't? There won't be room in the Windrunners for a lieutenant who has to walk everywhere. I'll end up cooking lunch with Rock."

"Ain't nothing wrong with being on the support team."

"Pardon, Sarge, but *storm that*! Do you know how long I waited to hold a spear?" Skar picked up the weapon from beside his pack and laid it across his lap. "I'm good at it. I can fight. Only . . ."

Lopen left the ceiling, rotating to get his legs under him and floating gently to the floor. He laughed as Bisig in turn tried flying up to the ceiling and crashed headfirst into it. Bisig hopped to his feet, looking down at them all, embarrassed. But what did he have to be embarrassed about? He was standing on the ceiling!

"You were in the military before," Teft guessed.

"No, but not for lack of trying. You heard of the Blackcaps?"

"Aladar's personal guards."

"Let's just say they didn't think much of my application."

Yes, we let darkeyes in. But not runts.

Teft grunted, chewing on his chouta.

"Said they might reconsider if I equipped myself," Skar said. "Do you know how much armor costs? I was a stupid rocksplitter with visions of battlefield glory."

It used to be they'd never speak about their pasts. That had changed, though Skar couldn't specify exactly when. It came out, as part of the catharsis of having become something greater.

Teft was an addict. Drehy had struck an officer. Eth had been caught planning to desert with his brother. Even simple Hobber had been part of a drunken brawl. Knowing Hobber, he'd probably only gone along with what his squad was doing, but a man had ended up dead.

"You'd think," Teft said, "that our high and mighty leader would have gotten here by now. I swear, Kaladin acts more like a lighteyes every day."

"Don't let *him* hear you say that," Skar said.

"I'll say what I want," Teft snapped. "If that boy's not going to come, maybe I should be going. I have things to do."

Skar hesitated, glancing up at Teft.

"Not *that*," Teft growled. "I've barely touched the stuff in days. You'd think a man had never had a wild night out, the way you're all treating me."

"Didn't say a thing, Teft."

"Knowing what we've suffered, it's insane to think that we *wouldn't* need something to get us through the day. The moss isn't the problem. It's the storming world going all crazy. That's the problem."

"Sure is, Teft."

Teft eyed him, then studied his chouta roll intently. "So . . . how long have the men known? I mean, did anyone . . ."

"Not long," Skar said quickly. "Nobody's even thinking about it."

Teft nodded, and didn't see through the lie. Truth was, most of them had noticed Teft sneaking off to grind a little moss now and then. It wasn't uncommon in the army. But doing what he'd done—missing duty, selling his uniform, ending up in an alley—that was different. It was the sort of thing that could get you discharged, at best. At worst . . . well, it might get you assigned to bridge duty.

Trouble was, they weren't common soldiers anymore. They weren't lighteyes either. They were something strange, something that nobody understood.

"I don't want to talk about this," Teft said. "Look, weren't we discussing how to get you to glow? *That's* the problem at hand."

Before he could press further, Kaladin Stormblessed finally deigned to arrive, bringing with him the scouts and hopefuls from other bridge crews who had been trying to draw in Stormlight. So far, nobody except men from Bridge Four had managed it, but that included a few that had never actually run bridges: Huio and Punio—Lopen's cousins—and men like Koen from the old Cobalt Guard, who had been recruited into Bridge Four a couple months back. So there was still hope that others could manage it.

Kaladin had brought roughly thirty people *beyond* those who had already been training with the team. Judging by their uniform patches, this thirty had come from other divisions—and some were lighteyed. Kaladin had mentioned asking General Khal to round up the most promising potential recruits from throughout the Alethi army.

"All here?" Kaladin said. "Good." He strode to the side of the single-roomed control building, a sack of glowing gemstones slung over his shoulder. His magnificent Shardblade appeared in his hand, and he slid it into the keyhole in the chamber wall.

Kaladin engaged the ancient mechanism, pushing the sword—and the entire inner wall, which could rotate—toward a specific point marked by murals. The floor began to glow, and outside, Stormlight rose in a swirl around the entire stone plateau.

Kaladin locked the Blade into place at the mark on the floor designating the Shattered Plains. When the glow faded, they'd come to Narak.

Sigzil left his pack and armor leaning against the wall, and strode out.

Best they could determine, the entire stone top of the platform had come with them, swapping places with the one that had been out here.

At the platform edge, a group of people climbed across a ramp to meet them. A short Alethi woman named Ristina counted out the bridgemen and soldiers as they passed, marking on her ledger.

"Took you long enough, Brightlord," she noted to Kaladin—whose eyes glowed faintly blue. "The merchants were beginning to complain."

It took Stormlight to power the device—some of the gemstones in Kaladin's sack would have been drained by the process—but curiously, it didn't take much more to swap two groups than it did to travel one way. So they tried to run the Oathgates when they had people on both sides wanting to exchange places.

"Tell the merchants when they next come through," Kaladin said, "that the Knights Radiant are not their doormen. They'll want to accustom themselves to waiting, unless they find a way to swear the oaths themselves."

Ristina smirked and wrote it down, as if she were going to pass on that exact message. Skar smiled at that. Nice to see a scribe with a sense of humor.

Kaladin led the way through the city of Narak, once a Parshendi stronghold, now an increasingly important human waystop between the warcamps and Urithiru. The buildings here were surprisingly sturdy: well constructed of crem and carved greatshell carapace. Skar had always assumed the Parshendi to be like the nomads who roved between Azir and Jah Keved. He imagined Parshendi who were wild and ferocious, without civilization, hiding in caves for storms.

Yet here was a well-built, carefully laid-out city. They'd found a building full of artwork of a style that baffled the Alethi scribes. Parshman *art*. They'd been painting even while they fought a war. Just like . . . well, just like ordinary people.

He glanced at Shen—no, Rlain, it was hard to remember—walking with spear to his shoulder. Skar forgot he was there most of the time, and that made him ashamed. Rlain was as much a member of Bridge Four as anyone else, right? Would he rather have been painting than fighting?

They passed sentry posts full of Dalinar's soldiers, along with many in red and light blue. Ruthar's colors. Dalinar was putting some of the other soldiers to work, trying to prevent more dustups between soldiers from different princedoms. Without the fighting on the Shattered Plains to keep them focused, the men were getting restless.

They passed a large group of soldiers practicing with bridges on a nearby plateau. Skar couldn't hold back a grin as he saw their black uniforms and helms. Plateau runs had been started again, but with more structure, and the spoils were shared equally among the highprinces.

Today, it was the Blackcaps' turn. Skar wondered if any of them would recognize him. Probably not, even if he *had* caused quite a ruckus among them. There had been only one logical way to get the equipment he needed for his application: He'd stolen it from the Blackcap quartermaster.

Skar had thought they would praise his ingenuity. He was so eager to be a Blackcap that he'd go to great lengths to join them, right?

Wrong. His reward had been a slave brand and eventual sale to Sadeas's army.

He brushed his fingers across the scars on his forehead. Stormlight had healed the brands of the other men—they'd covered them all up with tattoos anyway—but it seemed another little dig, dividing him from the others. Right now, he was the only fighting man in Bridge Four who still had his slave brand.

Well, him and Kaladin, whose scars wouldn't heal for some reason.

They reached the training plateau, crossing the old Bridge Four, which was held in place with some Soulcast rock guideposts. Kaladin called a meeting of the officers as several of Rock's children set up a water station. The tall Horneater seemed beyond enthused to have his family working with him.

Skar joined Kaladin, Sigzil, Teft, and Rock. Though they stood close, there was a conspicuous gap where Moash should have been. It felt so wrong to have a member of Bridge Four completely unaccounted for, and Kaladin's silence on the topic hung over them like an executioner's axe.

"I'm worried," Kaladin said, "that nobody practicing with us has begun breathing Stormlight."

"It's only been two weeks, sir," Sigzil said.

"True, but Syl thinks several 'feel right,' though she won't tell me who, as she says it would be wrong." Kaladin gestured toward the newcomers. "I asked Khal to send me another batch of hopefuls because I figured the more people we had, the better our chances of finding new squires." He paused. "I didn't specify they couldn't be lighteyed. Perhaps I should have."

"Don't see why, sir," Skar said, pointing. "That's Captain Colot—good man. He helped us explore."

"Just wouldn't feel right, having lighteyed men in Bridge Four."

"Other than you?" Skar asked. "And Renarin. And, well, any of us who earn our own Blades, and maybe Rock, who I *think* might have been lighteyed among his people, even if he has dark—"

"Fine, Skar," Kaladin said. "Point made. Anyway, we don't have a lot of time left before I leave with Elhokar. I'd like to push the recruits harder, see if they're likely to be able to swear the oaths. Any thoughts?"

"Shove them off edge of plateau," Rock said. "Those who fly, we let in."

"Any *serious* suggestions?" Kaladin asked.

"Let me run them through some formations," Teft said.

"A good idea," Kaladin said. "Storms, I wish we knew how the Radiants used to handle expansion. Were there recruitment drives, or did they just wait until someone attracted a spren?"

"That wouldn't make them a squire though," Teft said, rubbing his chin. "But a full Radiant, right?"

"A valid point," Sigzil said. "We have no proof that we squires are a step *toward* becoming full Radiants. We might always be your support team— and in that case, it's not individual skill that matters, but your decision. Maybe that of your spren. You choose them, they serve under you, and then they start drawing in Stormlight."

"Yeah," Skar said, uncomfortable.

They all glanced at him.

"The first of you that says something placating," Skar said, "gets a fist in the face. Or the stomach, if I can't reach your storming stupid Horneater face."

"Ha!" Rock said. "You could hit my face, Skar. I have seen you jump very high. Almost, you seem as tall as regular person when you do that."

"Teft," Kaladin said, "go ahead and run those potential recruits through formations. And tell the rest of the men to watch the sky; I'm worried about more raids on the caravans." He shook his head. "Something about those raids doesn't add up. The warcamps' parshmen, by all reports, have marched to Alethkar. But why would those Fused keep harrying us? They won't have the troops to take advantage of any supply problems they cause."

Skar shared a glance with Sigzil, who shrugged. Kaladin talked like this sometimes, differently from the rest of them. He'd trained them in formations and the spear, and they could proudly call themselves soldiers. But they'd only *actually* fought a few times. What did they know of things like strategy and battlefield tactics?

They broke, Teft jogging off to drill the potential recruits. Kaladin set Bridge Four to studying their flying. They practiced landings, and then did sprints in the air, zipping back and forth in formation, getting used to changing directions quickly. It was a little distracting, seeing those glowing lines of light shoot through the sky.

Skar attended Kaladin as he observed the recruits doing formations. The lighteyes didn't voice a single complaint about being filed into ranks with darkeyes. Kaladin and Teft . . . well, all of them really . . . had a tendency to act as if every lighteyed man was in some way regal. But there were far, far more of them who did normal jobs—though granted, they got paid better for those jobs than a darkeyed man did.

Kaladin watched, then glanced at the Bridge Four men in the sky. "I wonder, Skar," he said. "How important are formations going to be for us, going forward? Can we devise new ones to use in flying? Everything changes when your enemy can attack from all sides. . . ."

After about an hour, Skar went for water, and enjoyed some good-natured ribbing from the others, who landed to grab something to drink. He didn't mind. What you had to watch out for was when Bridge Four *didn't* torment you.

The others took off a short time later, and Skar watched them go, launching into the sky. He took a long draught of Rock's current refreshment—he called it tea, but it tasted like boiled grain—and found himself feeling useless. Were these people, these new recruits, going to start glowing and take his place in Bridge Four? Would he be shuffled off to other duties, while someone else laughed with the crew and got ribbed for their height?

Storm it, he thought, tossing aside his cup. *I hate feeling sorry for myself.* He hadn't sulked when the Blackcaps had turned him down, and he wouldn't sulk now.

He was fishing in his pocket for gemstones, determined to practice some more, when he spotted Lyn sitting on a rock nearby, watching the recruits run formations. She was slouching, and he read frustration in her posture. Well, he knew *that* feeling.

Skar shouldered his spear and sauntered over. The four other scout women had gone to the water station; Rock let out a bellowing laugh at what one of them said.

"Not joining in?" Skar asked, nodding toward the new recruits marching past.

"I don't know formations, Skar. I've never done drills—never even held a storming spear. I ran messages and scouted the Plains." She sighed. "I didn't pick it up fast enough, did I? He's gone and gotten some new people to test, since I failed."

"Don't be stupid," Skar said, sitting beside her on the large rock. "You're not being forced out. Kaladin just wants to have as many potential recruits as possible."

She shook her head. "Everyone knows that we're in a new world now—a world where rank and eye color don't matter. Something glorious." She looked up at the sky, and the men training there. "I want to be part of it, Skar. So *badly.*"

"Yeah."

She looked at him, and probably saw it in his eyes. That same emotion. "Storms. I hadn't even thought, Skar. Must be worse for you."

He shrugged and reached into his pouch, taking out an emerald as big as his thumb. It shone fiercely, even in the bright daylight. "You ever hear about the first time Captain Stormblessed drew in Light?"

"He told us. That day, after he knew he could do it because Teft told him. And—"

"Not that day."

"You mean while he was healing," she said. "After the highstorm where he was strung up."

"Not that day either," Skar said, holding up the gemstone. Through it, he saw men running formations, and imagined them carrying a bridge. "I was there, second row. Bridge run. Bad one. We were charging the plateau, and a lot of Parshendi had set up. They dropped most of the first row, all but Kaladin.

"That exposed me, right beside him, second row. In those days, you didn't have good odds, running near the front. The Parshendi wanted to take down our bridge, and they focused their shots on us. On me. I knew I was dead. I *knew* it. I saw the arrows coming, and I breathed a last prayer, hoping the next life wouldn't be quite so bad.

"Then . . . then the arrows moved, Lyn. They storming *swerved toward Kaladin.*" He turned the emerald over, and shook his head. "There's a special Lashing you can do, which makes things curve in the air. Kaladin painted the wood above his hands with Stormlight and drew the arrows toward him, instead of me. That's the first time I can say I knew something special was happening." He lowered the gemstone and pressed it into her hand. "Back then, Kaladin did it without even knowing what he was doing. Maybe we're just trying too hard, you know?"

"But it doesn't make sense! They say you have to suck it in. What does that even mean?"

"No idea," Skar said. "They each describe it differently, and it's breaking my brain trying to figure it out. They talk about a sharp intake of breath— only, not really for breathing."

"Which is perfectly clear."

"Tell me about it," Skar said, tapping the gemstone in her palm. "It worked best for Kaladin when he didn't stress. It was harder when he focused on *making* it happen."

"So I'm supposed to accidently but deliberately breathe something in without breathing, but not try too hard at it?"

"Doesn't it just make you want to string the lot of them up in the storms? But their advice is all we got. So . . ."

She looked at the stone, then held it close to her face—that didn't seem to be important, but what could it hurt—and breathed in. Nothing happened, so she tried again. And again. For a solid ten minutes.

"I don't know, Skar," she finally said, lowering the stone. "I keep thinking, maybe I don't belong here. If you haven't noticed, none of the women have managed this. I kind of forced my way among you all, and nobody asked—"

"Stop," he said, taking the emerald and holding it before her again. "Stop right there. You want to be a Windrunner?"

"More than anything," she whispered.

"Why?"

"Because I want to soar."

"Not good enough. Kaladin, he wasn't thinking about being left out, or how great it would be to fly. He was thinking about saving the rest of us. Saving *me*. Why do *you* want to be in the Windrunners?"

"Because I want to help! I want to do something other than stand around, waiting for the enemy to come to us!"

"Well, you have a chance, Lyn. A chance nobody has had for ages, a chance in millions. Either you seize it, and in so doing decide you're worthy, or you leave and give up." He pressed the gemstone back down into her hand. "But if you leave, you don't get to complain. As long as you keep trying, there's a chance. When you give up? That's when the dream dies."

She met his eyes, closed her fist around the gemstone, and breathed in with a sharp, distinct breath.

Then started glowing.

She yelped in surprise and opened her hand to find the gemstone within dun. She looked at him in awe. "What did you do?"

"Nothing," Skar said. Which was the problem. Still, he found he couldn't be jealous. Maybe this was his lot, helping others become Radiants. A trainer, a facilitator?

Teft saw Lyn glowing, then dashed over and started cursing—but they were "good" Teft curses. He grabbed her by the arm and towed her toward Kaladin.

Skar took in a long, satisfied breath. Well, that was two he'd helped so far, counting Rock. He . . . he could live with that, couldn't he?

He strolled over to the drink station and got another cup. "What is this foul stuff, Rock?" he asked. "You didn't mistake the washing water for tea, did you?"

"Is old Horneater recipe," he said. "Has proud tradition."

"Like skipping?"

"Like formal war dance," he said. "And hitting annoying bridgemen on head for not showing proper respect."

Skar turned around and leaned one hand on the table, watching Lyn's enthusiasm as her squad of scouts ran up to her. He felt good about what he'd done—strangely good. Excited, even.

"I think I'm going to have to get used to smelly Horneaters, Rock," Skar said. "I'm thinking of joining your support team."

"You think I will let *you* anywhere near cook pot?"

"I might not ever learn to fly." He squished the part of him that whimpered at that. "I need to come to terms with the fact. So, I'll have to find another way to help out."

"Ha. And the fact that you are glowing with Stormlight right now is not at all consideration in decision?"

Skar froze. Then he focused on his hand, right in front of his face, holding a cup. Tiny wisps of Stormlight curled off it. He dropped the cup with a cry, digging from his pocket a couple of dun chips. He'd given his practice gemstone to Lyn.

He looked up at Rock, then grinned stupidly.

"I suppose," Rock said, "I can maybe have you wash dishes. Though you do keep throwing my cups on ground. Is not proper respect at all . . ."

He trailed off as Skar left him, running for the others and whooping with excitement.

Indeed, we admire his initiative. Perhaps if you had approached the correct one of us with your plea, it would have found favorable audience.

I am Talenel'Elin, Herald of War. The time of the Return, the Desolation, is near at hand. We must prepare. You will have forgotten much, following the destruction of the times past.

Kalak will teach you to cast bronze, if you have forgotten this. We will Soulcast blocks of metal directly for you. I wish we could teach you steel, but casting is so much easier than forging, and you must have something we can produce quickly. Your stone tools will not serve against what is to come.

Vedel can train your surgeons, and Jezrien will teach you leadership. So much is lost between Returns. I will train your soldiers. We should have time. Ishar keeps talking about a way to keep information from being lost following Desolations. And you have discovered something unexpected. We will use that. Surgebinders to act as guardians . . . Knights . . .

The coming days will be difficult, but with training, humanity *will* survive. You must bring me to your leaders. The other Heralds should join us soon.

I think I am late, this time. I think . . . I fear, oh God, that I have failed. No. This is not right, is it? How long has it been? Where am I? I . . . am Talenel'Elin, Herald of War. The time of the Return, the Desolation, is near at hand. . . .

Jasnah trembled as she read the madman's words. She turned over the sheet, and found the next one covered in similar ideas, repeated over and over.

This couldn't be a coincidence, and the words were too specific. The abandoned Herald had come to Kholinar—and had been dismissed as a madman.

She leaned back in her seat and Ivory—full-sized, like a human—stepped over to the table. Hands clasped behind his back, he wore his usual stiff formal suit. The spren's coloring was jet black, both clothing and features, though something prismatic swirled on his skin. It was as if pure black marble had been coated in oil that glistened with hidden color. He rubbed his chin, reading the words.

Jasnah had rejected the nice rooms with balconies on the rim of Urithiru; those had such an obvious entrance for assassins or spies. Her small room at the center of Dalinar's section was far more secure. She had stuffed the ventilation openings with cloth. The airflow from the hallway outside was adequate for this room, and she wanted to make sure nobody could over-hear her by listening through the shafts.

In the corner of her room, three spanreeds worked tirelessly. She had rented them at great expense, until she could acquire new ones of her own. They were paired with reeds in Tashikk that had been delivered to one of the finest—and most trustworthy—information centers in the princedom. There, miles and miles away, a scribe was carefully rewriting each page of her notes, which she had originally sent to them to keep safe.

"This speaker, Jasnah," Ivory said, tapping the sheet she'd just read. Ivory had a clipped, no-nonsense voice. "This one who said these words. This person *is* a Herald. Our suspicions are true. The Heralds *are,* and the fallen one still *is.*"

"We need to find him," Jasnah said.

"We must search Shadesmar," Ivory said. "In this world, men can hide easily—but their souls shine out to us on the other side."

"Unless someone knows how to hide them."

Ivory looked toward the growing stack of notes in the corner; one of the pens had finished writing. Jasnah rose to change the paper; Shallan had rescued one of her trunks of notes, but two others had gone down with the sinking ship. Fortunately, Jasnah had sent off these backup copies.

Or did it matter? This sheet, encrypted by her cipher, contained lines and lines of information connecting the parshmen to the Voidbringers. Once, she'd slaved over each of these passages, teasing them from history. Now their contents were common knowledge. In one moment, all of her expertise had been wiped away.

"We've lost so much time," she said.

"Yes. We must catch what we have lost, Jasnah. We *must.*"

"The enemy?" Jasnah asked.

"He stirs. He angers." Ivory shook his head, kneeling beside her as she changed the sheets of paper. "We are naught before him, Jasnah. He would destroy my kind and yours."

The spanreed finished, and another started writing out the first lines of her memoirs, which she'd worked on intermittently throughout her life. She'd thrown aside a dozen different attempts, and as she read this latest one, she found herself disliking it as well.

"What do you think of Shallan?" she asked Ivory, shaking her head. "The person she's become."

Ivory frowned, lips drawing tight. His sharply chiseled features, too angular to be human, were like those of a roughed-out statue the sculptor had neglected to finish.

"She . . . is troubling," he said.

"That much hasn't changed."

"She is not stable."

"Ivory, you think *all* humans are unstable."

"Not you," he said, lifting his chin. "*You* are like a spren. You think by facts. You change not on simple whims. You are as you *are*."

She gave him a flat stare.

"Mostly," he added. "Mostly. But it *is*, Jasnah. Compared to other humans, you are practically a stone!"

She sighed, standing up and brushing past him, returning to her writing desk. The Herald's ravings glared at her. She settled down, feeling tired.

"Jasnah?" Ivory asked. "Am I . . . in error?"

"I am not so much a stone as you think, Ivory. Sometimes I wish I were."

"These words trouble you," he said, stepping up to her again and resting his jet-black fingers on the paper. "Why? You have read many troubling things."

Jasnah settled back, listening to the three spanreeds scratching paper, writing out notes that—she feared—would mostly be irrelevant. Something stirred deep within her. Glimmers of memory from a dark room, screaming her voice ragged. A childhood illness nobody else seemed to remember, for all it had done to her.

It had taught her that people she loved could still hurt her.

"Have you ever wondered how it would feel to lose your sanity, Ivory?"

Ivory nodded. "I have wondered this. How could I not? Considering what the ancient fathers are."

"You call me logical," Jasnah whispered. "It's untrue, as I let my passions rule me as much as many. In my times of peace, however, my mind has always been the one thing I could rely upon."

Except once.

She shook her head, picking up the paper again. "I fear losing that, Ivory. It *terrifies* me. How would it have felt, to be these Heralds? To suffer your mind slowly becoming untrustworthy? Are they too far gone to know? Or are there lucid moments, where they strain and sort through memories . . . trying frantically to decide which are reliable and which are fabrications . . ."

She shivered.

"The ancient ones," Ivory said again, nodding. He didn't often speak of the spren who had been lost during the Recreance. Ivory and his fellows had been mere children—well, the spren equivalent—at the time. They spent years, centuries, with no older spren to nurture and guide them. The inkspren were only now beginning to recover the culture and society they had lost when men abandoned their vows.

"Your ward," Ivory said. "Her spren. A Cryptic."

"Which is bad?"

Ivory nodded. He preferred simple, straightforward gestures. You never saw Ivory shrug. "Cryptics *are* trouble. They enjoy lies, Jasnah. Feast upon them. Speak one word untrue at a gathering, and seven cluster around you. Their humming fills your ears."

"Have you warred with them?"

"One does not war with Cryptics, as one does honorspren. Cryptics have but one city, and do not wish to rule more. Only to listen." He tapped the table. "Perhaps this one is better, with the bond."

Ivory was the only new-generation inkspren to form a Radiant bond. Some of his fellows would rather have killed Jasnah, instead of letting him risk what he had done.

The spren had a noble air about him, stiff-backed and commanding. He could change his size at will, but not his shape, except when fully in this realm, manifesting as a Shardblade. He had taken the name Ivory as a symbol of defiance. He was not what his kin said he was, and would not suffer what fate proclaimed.

The difference between a higher spren like him and a common emotion spren was in their ability to decide how to act. A living contradiction. Like human beings.

"Shallan won't listen to me any longer," Jasnah said. "She rebels against every little thing I tell her. These last few months on her own have changed the child."

"She never obeyed well, Jasnah. That is who she *is*."

"In the past, at least she pretended to care about my teaching."

"But you have said, more humans should question their places in life. Did you not say that they too often accept presumed truth as fact?"

She tapped the table. "You're right, of course. Wouldn't I rather have her straining against her boundaries, as opposed to happily living within them? Whether she obeys me or not is of little import. But I *do* worry about her ability to command her situation, rather than letting her impulses command her."

"How do you change this, if it is?"

An excellent question. Jasnah searched through the papers on her small table. She'd been collecting reports from her informants in the warcamps—the ones who had survived—about Shallan. She'd truly done well in Jasnah's absence. Perhaps what the child needed was not more structure, but more challenges.

"All ten orders are again," Ivory said from behind her. For years it had been only the two of them, Jasnah and Ivory. Ivory had been dodgy about giving odds on whether the other sapient spren would refound their orders or not.

However, he'd always said that he was certain that the honorspren—and therefore the Windrunners—would never return. Their attempts to rule Shadesmar had apparently not endeared them to the other races.

"Ten orders," Jasnah said. "All ended in death."

"All but one," Ivory agreed. "They lived in death instead."

She turned around, and he met her eyes with his own. No pupils, just oil shimmering above something deeply black.

"We must tell the others what we learned from Wit, Ivory. Eventually, this secret must be known."

"Jasnah, *no*. It would be the end. Another Recreance."

"The truth has not destroyed me."

"You are special. No knowledge is that can destroy you. But the others . . ."

She held his eyes, then gathered the sheets stacked beside her. "We shall see," she said, then carried them to the table to bind them into a book.

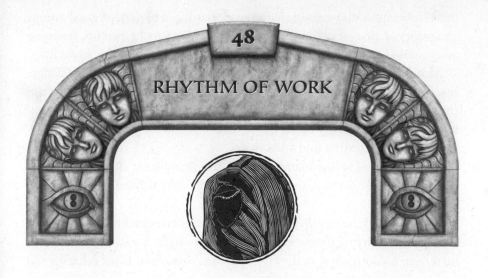

48

RHYTHM OF WORK

But we stand in the sea, pleased with our domains. Leave us alone.

Moash grunted as he crossed the uneven ground, hauling a thick, knotted cord over his shoulder. Turned out, the Voidbringers had run out of wagons. Too many supplies to bring, and not enough vehicles.

At least, vehicles with wheels.

Moash had been assigned to a sledge—a cart with broken wheels that had been repurposed with a pair of long, steel skids. They'd put him first in the line pulling their rope. The parshman overseers had considered him the most enthusiastic.

Why wouldn't he be? The caravans moved at the slow pace of the chulls, which pulled roughly half the ordinary wagons. He had sturdy boots, and even a pair of gloves. Compared to bridge duty, this was a paradise.

The scenery was even better. Central Alethkar was far more fertile than the Shattered Plains, and the ground sprouted with rockbuds and the gnarled roots of trees. The sledge bounced and crunched over these, but at least he didn't have to carry the thing on his shoulders.

Around him, hundreds of men pulled wagons or sledges piled high with foodstuffs, freshly cut lumber, or leather made from hogshide or eelskin. Some of the workers had collapsed on their first day out of Revolar. The Voidbringers had separated these into two groups. The ones who had tried, but were genuinely too weak, had been sent back to the city. A few deemed to be faking had been whipped, then moved to sledges instead of wagons.

Harsh, but fair. Indeed, as the march continued, Moash was surprised at how well the human workers were treated. Though strict and unforgiving, the Voidbringers understood that to work hard, slaves needed good rations and plenty of time at night to rest. They weren't even chained up. Running away would be pointless under the watchful care of Fused who could fly.

Moash found himself enjoying these weeks hiking and pulling his sledge. It exhausted his body, quieted his thoughts, and let him fall into a calm rhythm. This was certainly far better than his days as a lighteyes, when he'd worried incessantly about the plot against the king.

It felt *good* to just be told what to do.

What happened at the Shattered Plains wasn't my fault, he thought as he hauled the sledge. *I was pushed into it. I can't be blamed.* These thoughts comforted him.

Unfortunately, he couldn't ignore their apparent destination. He'd walked this path dozens of times, running caravans with his uncle even when he'd been a youth. Across the river, straight southeast. Over Ishar's Field and cutting past the town of Inkwell.

The Voidbringers were marching to take Kholinar. The caravan included tens of thousands of parshmen armed with axes or spears. They wore what Moash now knew was called warform: a parshman form with carapace armor and a strong physique. They weren't experienced—watching their nightly training told him they were basically the equivalent of darkeyes scrounged from villages and pressed into the army.

But they were learning, and they had access to the Fused. Those zipped through the air or strode along beside carts, powerful and imperious—and surrounded by dark energy. There seemed to be different varieties, but each was intimidating.

Everything was converging on the capital. Should that bother him? After all, what had Kholinar ever done for him? It was the place where his grandparents had been left to die, cold and alone in a prison cell. It was where the blighted King Elhokar had danced and connived while good people rotted.

Did humankind even deserve this kingdom?

During his youth, he'd listened to traveling ardents who accompanied the caravans. He knew that long ago, humankind had *won.* Aharietiam, the final confrontation with the Voidbringers, had happened thousands of years ago.

What had they done with that victory? They'd set up false gods in the form of men whose eyes reminded them of the Knights Radiant. The life of men over the centuries had been nothing more than a long string of murders, wars, and thefts.

The Voidbringers had obviously returned because men had proven they couldn't govern themselves. That was why the Almighty had sent this scourge.

Indeed, the more he marched, the more Moash admired the Voidbringers. The armies were efficient, and the troops learned quickly. The caravans were well supplied; when an overseer saw that Moash's boots were looking worn, he had a new pair by evening.

Each wagon or sledge was given two parshman overseers, but these were told to use their whips sparingly. They were quietly trained for the position, and Moash heard the occasional conversation between an overseer—once a parshman slave—and an unseen spren who gave them directions.

The Voidbringers were smart, driven, and efficient. If Kholinar fell to this force, it would be no more than humankind deserved. Yes . . . perhaps the time for his people had passed. Moash had failed Kaladin and the others—but that was merely how men were in this debased age. He couldn't be blamed. He was a product of his culture.

Only one oddity marred his observations. The Voidbringers seemed so much better than the human armies he'd been part of . . . except for one thing.

There was a group of parshman slaves.

They pulled one of the sledges, and always walked apart from the humans. They wore workform, not warform—though otherwise they looked exactly like the other parshmen, with the same marbled skin. Why did this group pull a sledge?

At first, as Moash plodded across the endless plains of central Alethkar, he found the sight of them encouraging. It suggested that the Voidbringers could be egalitarian. Maybe there'd simply been too few men with the strength to pull these sledges.

Yet if that were so, why were these parshman sledge-pullers treated so poorly? The overseers did little to hide their disgust, and were allowed to whip the poor creatures without restriction. Moash rarely glanced in their direction without finding one of them being beaten, yelled at, or abused.

Moash's heart wrenched to see and hear this. Everyone else seemed to work so well together; everything else about the army seemed so perfect. Except this.

Who were these poor souls?

⁘

The overseer called a break, and Moash dropped his rope, then took a long pull on his waterskin. It was their twenty-first day of marching, which he only knew because some of the other slaves kept track. He judged the location as several days past Inkwell, in the final stretch toward Kholinar.

He ignored the other slaves and settled down in the shade of the sledge, which was piled high with cut timber. Not far behind them, a village burned. There hadn't been anyone in it, as word had run before them. Why had the Voidbringers burned it, but not others they'd passed? Perhaps it was to send a message—indeed, that smoke trail was ominous. Or perhaps it was to prevent any potential flanking armies from using the village.

As his crew waited—Moash didn't know their names, and hadn't bothered to ask—the parshman crew trudged past, bloodied and whipped, their overseers yelling them onward. They'd lagged behind. Pervasive cruel treatment led to a tired crew, which in turn led to them being forced to march to catch up when everyone else got a water break. That, of course, only wore them out and caused injuries—which made them lag farther behind, which made them get whipped . . .

That's what happened to Bridge Four, back before Kaladin, Moash thought. *Everyone said we were unlucky, but it was just a self-perpetuating downward spiral.*

Once that crew passed, trailing a few exhaustionspren, one of Moash's overseers called for his team to take up their ropes and get moving again. She was a young parshwoman with dark red skin, marbled only slightly with white. She wore a havah. Though it didn't seem like marching clothing, she wore it well. She had even done up the sleeve to cover her safehand.

"What'd they do, anyway?" he said as he took up his rope.

"What was that?" she asked, looking back at him. Storms. Save for that skin and the odd singsong quality to her voice, she could have been a pretty Makabaki caravan girl.

"That parshman crew," he said. "What did they do to deserve such rough treatment?"

He didn't actually expect an answer. But the parshwoman followed his gaze, then shook her head. "They harbored a false god. Brought him into the very center among us."

"The Almighty?"

She laughed. "A *real* false god, a living one. Like our living gods." She looked up as one of the Fused passed overhead.

"There are lots who think the Almighty is real," Moash said.

"If that's the case, why are *you* pulling a sledge?" She snapped her fingers, pointing.

Moash picked up his rope, joining the other men in a double line. They merged with the enormous column of marching feet, scraping sledges, and rattling wheels. The Parshendi wanted to arrive at the next town before an impending storm. They'd weathered both types—highstorm and Everstorm—sheltering in villages along the way.

Moash fell into the sturdy rhythm of the work. It wasn't long until he was sweating. He'd grown accustomed to the colder weather in the east, near the Frostlands. It was strange to be in a place where the sun felt hot on his skin, and now the weather here was turning toward summer.

His sledge soon caught up to the parshman crew. The two sledges walked side by side for a time, and Moash liked to think that keeping pace with his crew could motivate the poor parshmen. Then one of them slipped and fell, and the entire team lurched to a stop.

The whipping began. The cries, the *crack* of leather on skin.

That's enough.

Moash dropped his rope and stepped out of the line. His shocked overseers called after him, but didn't follow. Perhaps they were too surprised.

He strode up to the parshman sledge, where the slaves were struggling to pull themselves back up and start again. Several had bloodied faces and backs. The large parshman who had slipped lay curled on the ground. His feet were bleeding; no wonder he'd had trouble walking.

Two overseers were whipping him. Moash seized one by the shoulder and pushed him back. "Stop it!" he snapped, then shoved the other overseer aside. "Don't you see what you're doing? You're becoming like *us.*"

The two overseers stared at him, dumbfounded.

"You can't abuse each other," Moash said. "You *can't.*" He turned toward the fallen parshman and extended a hand to help him up, but from the corner of his eye he saw one of the overseers raise his arm.

Moash spun and caught the whip that cracked at him, snatching it from the air and twisting it around his wrist to gain leverage. Then he *yanked* it—pulling the overseer stumbling toward him. Moash smashed a fist into his face, slamming him backward to the ground.

Storms that hurt. He shook his hand, which had clipped carapace on the side as he'd connected. He glared at the other overseer, who yelped and dropped his whip, jumping backward.

Moash nodded once, then took the fallen slave by the arm and pulled him upright. "Ride in the sledge. Heal those feet." He took the parshman slave's place in line, and pulled the rope taut over his shoulder.

By now, his own overseers had gathered their wits and chased after him. They conferred with the two that he'd confronted, one nursing a bleeding cut around his eye. Their conversation was hushed, urgent, and punctuated by intimidated glances toward him.

Finally, they decided to let it be. Moash pulled the sledge with the parshmen, and they found someone to replace him on the other sledge. For a while he thought more would come of it—he even saw one of the overseers conferring with a Fused. But they didn't punish him.

No one dared to again raise a whip against the parshman crew the rest of the march.

49

BORN UNTO LIGHT

TWENTY-THREE YEARS AGO

Dalinar pressed his fingers together, then rubbed them, scraping the dry, red-brown moss against itself. The scratchy sound was unpleasantly similar to that of a knife along bone.

He felt the warmth immediately, like an ember. A thin plume of smoke rose from his callused fingers and struck below his nose, then parted around his face.

Everything faded: the raucous sound of too many men in one room, the musky smell of their bodies pressed together. Euphoria spread through him like sudden sunlight on a cloudy day. He released a protracted sigh. He didn't even mind when Bashin accidentally elbowed him.

Most places, being highprince would have won him a bubble of space, but at the stained wooden table in this poorly lit den, social standing was irrelevant. Here, with a good drink and a little help pressed between his fingers, he could finally relax. Here nobody cared how presentable he was, or if he drank too much.

Here, he didn't have to listen to reports of rebellion and imagine himself out on those fields, solving problems the direct way. Sword in hand, Thrill in his heart . . .

He rubbed the moss more vigorously. Don't think about war. Just live in the moment, as Evi always said.

Havar returned with drinks. The lean, bearded man studied the overcrowded bench, then set the drinks down and hauled a slumped drunk out of his spot. He squeezed in beside Bashin. Havar was lighteyed, good family too. He'd been one of Dalinar's elites back when that had meant something, though now he had his own land and a high commission. He was one of the few who didn't salute Dalinar so hard you could hear it.

Bashin though . . . well, Bashin was an odd one. Darkeyed of the first nahn, the portly man had traveled half the world, and encouraged Dalinar to go with him to see the other half. He still wore that stupid, wide-brimmed floppy hat.

Havar grunted, passing down the drinks. "Squeezing in beside you, Bashin, would be far easier if you didn't have a gut that stretched to next week."

"Just trying to do my duty, Brightlord."

"Your duty?"

"Lighteyes need folks to obey them, right? I'm making certain that you got *lots* to serve you, at least by weight."

Dalinar took his mug, but didn't drink. For now, the firemoss was doing its job. His wasn't the only plume rising in the dim stone chamber.

Gavilar hated the stuff. But then, Gavilar *liked* his life now.

In the center of the dim room, a pair of parshmen pushed tables aside, then started setting diamond chips on the floor. Men backed away, making space for a large ring of light. A couple of shirtless men pushed their way through the crowd. The room's general air of clumsy conversation turned to one of roaring excitement.

"Are we going to bet?" Havar asked.

"Sure," Bashin replied. "I'll put three garnet marks on the shorter one."

"I'll take that bet," Havar said, "but not for the money. If I win, I want your hat."

"Deal! Ha! So you're finally going to admit how dashing it is?"

"Dashing? Storms, Bashin. I'm going to do you a favor and *burn* the thing."

Dalinar sat back, mind dulled by the firemoss.

"Burn my hat?" Bashin said. "Storms, Havar. That's harsh. Just because you envy my dashing profile."

"The only thing dashing about that hat is how it makes women run the other way."

"It's *exotic*. From the *west*. Everyone knows fashion comes from the west."

"Yeah, from Liafor and Yezier. Where did you get that hat again?"

"The Purelake."

"Ah, that bastion of culture and fashion! Are you going shopping in Bavland next?"

"Barmaids don't know the difference," Bashin grumbled. "Anyway, can we just watch the match? I'm looking forward to winning those marks off you." He took a drink, but fingered his hat anxiously.

Dalinar closed his eyes. He felt as if he could drift off, maybe get some sleep without worrying about Evi, or dreaming of war. . . .

In the ring, bodies *smacked* against each other.

That sound—the grunts of exertion as the wrestlers tried to push each other from the ring—reminded him of the battle. Dalinar opened his eyes, dropped the moss, and leaned forward.

The shorter wrestler danced out of the other's grip. They revolved around one another, crouched, hands at the ready. When they locked again, the shorter man pushed his opponent off balance. *Better stance,* Dalinar thought. *Kept himself low. That taller fellow has gotten by too long on his strength and size. He's got terrible form.*

The two strained, backing toward the edge of the ring, before the taller man managed to trip them both. Dalinar stood up as others, ahead of him, raised their hands and cheered.

The contest. The fight.

That led me to almost kill Gavilar.

Dalinar sat back down.

The shorter man won. Havar sighed, but rolled a few glowing spheres to Bashin. "Double or nothing on the next bout?"

"Nah," Bashin said, hefting the marks. "This should be enough."

"For what?"

"To bribe a few influential young dandies into trying hats like mine," Bashin said. "I tell you, once word gets out, *everyone* is going to be wearing them."

"You're an idiot."

"So long as I'm a fashionable one."

Dalinar reached to the floor and picked up the firemoss. He tossed it onto the table and stared at it, then took a pull from his mug of wine. The next wrestling match started, and he winced as the two competitors collided. Storms. Why did he keep putting himself into situations like this?

"Dalinar," Havar said. "Any word yet on when we're going to the Rift?"

"The Rift?" Bashin asked. "What about it?"

"Are you dense?" Havar said.

"No," Bashin said, "but I might be *drunk*. What's up with the Rift?"

"Rumor is they want to set up their own highprince," Havar said. "Son of the old one, what was his name . . ."

"Tanalan," Dalinar said. "But we are not going to be visiting the Rift, Havar."

"Surely the king can't—"

"*We* won't be going," Dalinar said. "You've got men to train. And I . . ." Dalinar drank more wine. "I'm going to be a father. My brother can handle the Rift with diplomacy."

Havar leaned back, flippantly dropping his mug to the table. "The king can't politic his way past open rebellion, Dalinar."

Dalinar closed his fist around the firemoss, but didn't rub it. How much of his interest in the Rift was his duty to protect Gavilar's kingdom, and how much was his craving to feel the Thrill again?

Damnation. He felt like half a man these days.

One of the wrestlers had shoved the other from the ring, disturbing the line of lights. The loser was declared, and a parshman carefully reset the ring. As he did so, a master-servant stepped up to Dalinar's table.

"Pardon, Brightlord," he whispered. "But you should know. The feature match will have to be canceled."

"What?" Bashin said. "What's wrong? Makh isn't going to fight?"

"Pardon," the master-servant repeated. "But his opponent has stomach problems. The match must be canceled."

Apparently, news was spreading through the room. The crowd manifested their disapproval with boos and curses, shouts, and spilled drinks. A tall, bald man stood at the side of the ring, bare-chested. He argued with several of the lighteyed organizers, pointing at the ring, angerspren boiling on the floor around him.

To Dalinar, this racket sounded like the calls of battle. He closed his eyes and breathed it in, finding a euphoria far superior to the firemoss. Storms. He should have gotten drunker. He was going to slip.

Might as well be quick about it then. He tossed aside the firemoss and stood, then pulled off his shirt.

"Dalinar!" Havar said. "What are you doing?"

"Gavilar says I need to have more concern for our people's sorrows," Dalinar said, stepping up onto the table. "Seems like we've got a room full of sorrow here."

Havar gaped, jaw dropping.

"Bet on me," Dalinar said. "For old times' sake." He leaped off the table on the other side, then shoved through the crowd. "Someone tell that man he has a challenger!"

Silence spread from him like a bad smell. Dalinar found himself at the edge of the ring in a completely quiet room, packed with once-rowdy men both lighteyed and dark. The wrestler—Makh—stepped back, his dark green eyes wide, angerspren vanishing. He had a powerful build, arms that bulged like they were overstuffed. Word was, he'd never been defeated.

"Well?" Dalinar said. "You wanted a fight and I need a workout."

"Brightlord," the man said. "This was to be a freeform bout, all hits and holds allowed."

"Excellent," Dalinar said. "What? You worried about injuring your highprince? I promise you clemency for anything done to me."

"Hurting *you*?" the man said. "Storms, that's not what I'm afraid of." He shivered visibly, and a Thaylen woman—perhaps his manager—smacked him on the arm. She thought he'd been rude. The wrestler only bowed and backed away.

Dalinar turned about the room, confronted by a sea of faces that suddenly seemed very uncomfortable. He'd broken some kind of rule here.

The gathering dissolved, parshmen retrieving spheres from the ground. It seemed Dalinar had been too hasty to judge rank unimportant here. They'd suffered him as an observer, but he was not to participate.

Damnation. He growled softly as he stalked to his bench, those anger-spren following him on the floor. He took his shirt from Bashin with a swipe of the hand. Back with his elites, any man—from the lowest spearman to the highest captains—would have sparred or wrestled with him. Storms, he'd faced the *cook* several times, much to the amusement of everyone involved.

He sat down and pulled on his shirt, stewing. He'd ripped the buttons free in removing it so quickly. The room fell silent as people continued to leave, and Dalinar just sat there, tense—his body still expecting the fight that would never come. No Thrill. Nothing to fill him.

Soon, he and his friends were alone in the room, surveying empty tables, abandoned cups, and spilled drinks. The place somehow smelled even worse now than it had when crowded with men.

"Probably for the best, Brightlord," Havar said.

"I want to be among soldiers again, Havar," Dalinar whispered. "I want to be marching again. Best sleep a man can get is after a long march. And, Damnation, I want to *fight*. I want to face someone who won't pull their punches because I'm a highprince."

"Then let's *find* such a fight, Dalinar!" Havar said. "Surely the king will let us go. If not to the Rift, then to Herdaz or one of the isles. We can bring him land, glory, honor!"

"That wrestler," Dalinar said, "there was . . . something to his words. He was certain I would hurt him." Dalinar drummed his fingers on the table. "Was he scared off because of my reputation in general, or is there something more specific?"

Bashin and Havar shared a look.

"When?" Dalinar asked.

"Tavern fight," Havar said. "Two weeks back? Do you remember it?"

Dalinar remembered a haze of monotony broken by light, a burst of color in his life. Emotion. He breathed out. "You told me everyone was fine."

"They lived," Havar said.

"One . . . of the brawlers you fought will never walk," Bashin admitted. "Another had to have his arm removed. A third babbles like a child. His brain doesn't work anymore."

"That's far from *fine*," Dalinar snapped.

"Pardon, Dalinar," Havar said. "But when facing the Blackthorn, that's as good as one can expect."

Dalinar crossed his arms on the table, grinding his teeth. The firemoss wasn't working. Yes, it gave him a quick rush of euphoria, but that only made him want the greater headiness of the Thrill. Even now he felt on edge—he had the urge to smash this table and everything in the room. He'd been so ready for the fight; he'd surrendered to the temptation, and then had the pleasure stolen from him.

He felt all the shame of losing control, but none of the satisfaction of actually getting to fight.

Dalinar seized his mug, but it was empty. Stormfather! He threw it and stood up, wanting to scream.

He was fortunately distracted by the back door to the wrestling den inching open, revealing a familiar pale face. Toh wore Alethi clothing now, one of the new suits that Gavilar preferred, but it fit him poorly. He was too spindly. No man would ever mistake Toh—with that overcautious gait and wide-eyed innocence—for a soldier.

"Dalinar?" he asked, looking over the spilled drinks and the locked sphere lamps on the walls. "The guards said I could find you here. Um . . . was this a party?"

"Ah, Toh," Havar said, lounging back in his seat. "How could it have been a party without you?"

Toh's eyes flicked toward the chunk of firemoss on the ground nearby. "I'll never understand what you see in these places, Dalinar."

"He's just getting to know the common people, Brightlord," Bashin said, pocketing the firemoss. "You know us darkeyed types, always wallowing in depravity. We need good role models to—"

He cut off as Dalinar raised his hand. He didn't need underlings to cover for him. "What is it, Toh?"

"Oh!" the Riran man said. "They were going to send a messenger, but I wanted to deliver the news. My sister, you see. It's a little early, but the midwives aren't surprised. They say it's natural when—"

Dalinar gasped, like he'd been punched in the stomach. *Early. Midwives. Sister.*

He charged for the door, and didn't hear the rest of what Toh said.

⁘

Evi looked like she'd fought in a battle.

He'd seen that expression on the faces of soldiers many times: that sweaty brow, that half-dazed, drowsy look. Exhaustionspren, like jets in the air.

These were the mark of a person pushed past the limits of what they thought they could do.

She bore a smile of quiet satisfaction. A look of victory. Dalinar pushed past doting surgeons and midwives, stepping up to Evi's bed. She held out a limp hand. Her left hand, which was wrapped only in a thin envelope that ended at the wrist. It would have been a sign of intimacy, to an Alethi. But Evi still preferred that hand.

"The baby?" he whispered, taking the hand.

"A son. Healthy and strong."

"A son. I . . . I have a son?" Dalinar dropped to his knees beside the bed. "Where is he?"

"Being washed, my lord," said one of the midwives. "He will be returned shortly."

"Torn buttons," Evi whispered. "You've been fighting again, Dalinar?"

"Just a small diversion."

"That's what you say each time."

Dalinar squeezed her hand through the envelope, too elated to prickle at the chastisement. "You and Toh came here to Alethkar because you wanted someone to protect you. You *sought out* a fighter, Evi."

She squeezed his hand back. A nurse approached with a bundle in her arms and Dalinar looked up, stunned, unable to rise.

"Now," the woman said, "many men are apprehensive at first when—"

She cut off as Dalinar found his strength and seized the child from her arms. He held the boy aloft in both hands, letting out a whooping laugh, gloryspren bursting around him as golden spheres.

"My son!" he said.

"My lord!" the nurse said. "Be careful!"

"He's a Kholin," Dalinar said, cradling the child. "He's made of hardy stuff." He looked down at the boy, who—red faced—wiggled and thrashed with his tiny fists. He had shockingly thick hair, black and blond mixed. Good coloring. Distinctive.

May you have your father's strength, Dalinar thought, rubbing the child's face with his finger, *and at least some of your mother's compassion, little one.*

Looking into that face, swelling with joy, Dalinar finally understood. *This* was why Gavilar thought so much about the future, about Alethkar, about crafting a kingdom that would last. Dalinar's life so far had stained him crimson and thrashed his soul. His heart was so crusted over with crem, it might as well have been a stone.

But this boy . . . he could rule the princedom, support his cousin the king, and live a life of honor.

"His name, Brightlord?" asked Ishal, an aged ardent from the Devotary of Purity. "I would burn the proper glyphwards, if it pleases you."

"Name . . ." Dalinar said. "Adoda." Light. He glanced toward Evi, who nodded in agreement.

"Without a suffix, my lord? Adodan? Adodal?"

"Lin," Dalinar whispered. Born unto. "Adolin." A good name, traditional, full of meaning.

With regret, Dalinar surrendered the child to the nurses, who returned him to his mother, explaining that it was important to train the baby to suckle as soon as possible. Most in the room began to file out to offer privacy, and as they did, Dalinar caught sight of a regal figure standing at the back. How had he missed Gavilar there?

Gavilar took him by the arm and gave him a good thump on the back as they left the chamber. Dalinar was so dazed he barely felt it. He needed to celebrate—buy drinks for every man in the army, declare a holiday, or just run through the city whooping for joy. He was a father!

"An excellent day," Gavilar said. "A *most* excellent day."

"How do you contain it?" Dalinar said. "This *excitement*?"

Gavilar grinned. "I let the emotion be my reward for the work I have done."

Dalinar nodded, then studied his brother. "What?" Dalinar said. "Something is wrong."

"Nothing."

"Don't lie to me, Brother."

"I don't want to ruin your wonderful day."

"Wondering will ruin it more than anything you could say, Gavilar. Out with it."

The king mulled, then nodded toward Dalinar's den. They crossed the main chamber, passing furniture that was far too showy—colorful, with floral patterns and plush cushions. Evi's taste was partially to blame, though it was also just . . . life, these days. His *life* was plush.

The den was more to his liking. A few chairs, a hearth, a simple rug. A cabinet with various exotic and potent wines, each in a distinctive bottle. They were the type it was almost a shame to drink, as it spoiled the display.

"It's your daughter," Dalinar guessed. "Her lunacy."

"Jasnah is fine, and recovering. It's not that." Gavilar frowned, his expression dangerous. He'd agreed to a crown after much debate—Sunmaker hadn't worn one, and the histories said Jezerezeh'Elin refused them as well. But people did love symbols, and most Western kings wore crowns. Gavilar had settled upon a black iron circlet. The more Gavilar's hair greyed, the easier the crown was to see.

A servant had set a fire in the hearth, though it was burning low, only a single flamespren crawling along the embers.

"I am failing," Gavilar said.

"What?"

"Rathalas. The Rift."

"But I thought—"

"Propaganda," Gavilar said. "Intended to quiet critical voices in Kholinar. Tanalan is raising an army and settling into his fortifications. Worse, I think the other highprinces are encouraging him. They want to see how I handle this." He sneered. "There's talk I've grown soft over the years."

"They're wrong." Dalinar had seen it, these months living with Gavilar. His brother had *not* grown soft. He was still as eager for conquest as ever; he simply approached it differently. The clash of words, the maneuvering of princedoms into positions where they were forced to obey.

The fire's embers seemed to pulse like a heartbeat. "Do you ever wonder about the time when this kingdom was truly great, Dalinar?" Gavilar asked. "When people looked to the Alethi. When kings sought their advice. When we were . . . Radiant."

"Traitors," Dalinar said.

"Does the act of a single generation negate many generations of domination? We revere the Sunmaker when his reign lasted but the blink of an eye—yet we ignore the centuries the Radiants led. How many Desolations did they defend mankind?"

"Um . . ." The ardents talked about this in prayers, didn't they? He tried a guess. "Ten?"

"A meaningless number," Gavilar said, waving his fingers. "The histories just say 'ten' because it sounds significant. Either way, I have failed in my diplomatic efforts." He turned toward Dalinar. "It is time to show the kingdom that we are not soft, Brother."

Oh no. Hours ago, he would have leaped in excitement. But after seeing that child . . .

You'll be anxious again in a few days, Dalinar told himself. *A man can't change in a moment.*

"Gavilar," he whispered, "I'm worried."

"You're still the Blackthorn, Dalinar."

"I'm not worried about whether I can win battles." Dalinar stood, throwing back his chair in his haste. He found himself pacing. "I'm like an animal, Gavilar. Did you hear about the bar fight? Storms. I can't be trusted around people."

"You are what the Almighty made you."

"I'm telling you, I'm dangerous. Sure, I can crush this little rebellion, bathe Oathbringer in some blood. Great. Wonderful. Then what? I come back here and lock myself in a cage again?"

"I . . . might have something that will help."

"Bah. I've tried living a quiet life. I can't live through endless politics, like you can. I need more than *just words*!"

"You've merely been trying to restrain yourself—you've tried casting out the bloodthirst, but you haven't replaced it with anything else. Go do what I command, then return and we can discuss further."

Dalinar stopped near his brother, then took a single purposeful step into his shadow. *Remember this. Remember you serve him.* He would never return to that place that had almost led him to attack this man.

"When do I ride for the Rift?" Dalinar asked.

"You don't."

"But you just said—"

"I'm sending you to battle, but not against the Rift. Our kingdom suffers threats from abroad. There is a new dynasty threatening us from Herdaz; a Reshi house has gained power there. And the Vedens have been raiding Alethkar in the southwest. They're claiming it's bandits, but the forces are too organized. It's a test to see how we react."

Dalinar nodded slowly. "You want me to go fight on our borders. Remind everyone we're still capable of employing the sword."

"Exactly. This is a dangerous time for us, Brother. The highprinces question. Is a united Alethkar worth the trouble? Why bow before a king? Tanalan is the manifestation of their questions, but he has been careful not to stray into outright rebellion. If you attack him, the other highprinces could unite behind the rebels. We could shatter the kingdom and have to start all over.

"I will not allow that. I *will* have a unified Alethkar. Even if I have to hit the highprinces so hard, they are forced to *melt* together from the heat of it. They need to remember that. Go to Herdaz first, then Jah Keved. Remind everyone *why* they fear you."

Gavilar met Dalinar's eyes. No . . . he was not soft. He thought like a king now. He sought the long term, but Gavilar Kholin was as determined as ever.

"It will be done," Dalinar said. Storms, this day had been a tempest of emotion. Dalinar stalked toward the door. He wanted to see the child again.

"Brother?" Gavilar said.

Dalinar turned back and regarded Gavilar, who was bathed by the bleeding light of a fire reaching its end.

"Words *are* important," Gavilar said. "Much more than you give them credit for being."

"Perhaps," Dalinar said. "But if they were all-powerful, you wouldn't need my sword, would you?"

"Perhaps. I can't help feeling words *would* be enough, if only I knew the right ones to say."

We also instruct that you should not return to Obrodai. We have claimed that world, and a new avatar of our being is beginning to manifest there.

She is young yet, and—as a precaution—she has been instilled with an intense and overpowering dislike of you.

To Dalinar, flying felt much like being on a ship in the ocean.

There was something profoundly disconcerting about being out on the ocean, subject to the winds and currents. Men didn't control the waves, they merely set out and prayed that the ocean didn't decide to consume them.

Flying alongside Captain Kaladin provoked some of the same emotions in Dalinar. On one hand, the view over the Shattered Plains was magnificent. He felt he could almost see the pattern to it that Shallan mentioned.

On the other hand, this kind of travel was deeply unnatural. Winds buffeted them, and if you moved your hands or arched your back in the wrong way, you were sent in a different direction from everyone else. Kaladin had to constantly zip back and forth, righting one of them that got blown off-course. And if you looked down, and paused to consider exactly how high up you were . . .

Well, Dalinar was not a timid man, but he was still glad of Navani's hand in his.

On his other side flew Elhokar, and beyond him were Kadash and a pretty young ardent who served as one of Navani's scholars. The five of them were escorted by Kaladin and ten of his squires. The Windrunners had been training steadily for three weeks now, and Kaladin had finally—

after practicing by flying groups of soldiers back and forth to the warcamps—agreed to treat Dalinar and the king to a similar trip.

It is *like being on a ship,* Dalinar thought. What would it feel like to be up here during a highstorm? That was how Kaladin planned to get Elhokar's team to Kholinar—fly them at the leading edge of a storm, so his Stormlight was continually renewed.

You're thinking of me, the Stormfather sent. *I can feel it.*

"I'm thinking of how you treat ships," Dalinar whispered, his physical voice lost to the winds—yet his meaning carried, unhampered, to the Stormfather.

Men should not be upon the waters during a storm, he replied. *Men are not of the waves.*

"And the sky? Are men of the sky?"

Some are. He said this grudgingly.

Dalinar could only imagine how terrible it must be to be a sailor out at sea during a storm. He had taken only short coastwise trips by ship.

No, wait, he thought. *There was one, of course. A trip to the Valley . . .*

He barely remembered that voyage, though he could not blame that solely upon the Nightwatcher.

Captain Kaladin swooped over. He was the only one who seemed truly in control of his flying. Even his men flew more like dropped rocks than skyeels. They lacked his finesse, his *control.* Though the others could help if something went wrong, Kaladin had been the only one Lashing Dalinar and the others. He said he wanted practice, for the eventual flight to Kholinar.

Kaladin touched Elhokar, and the king started to slow. Kaladin then moved down the line, slowing each in turn. He then swept them up so they were close enough to speak. His soldiers stopped and floated nearby.

"What's wrong?" Dalinar asked, trying to ignore that he was hanging hundreds of feet in the sky.

"Nothing's wrong," Kaladin said, then pointed.

With the wind in his eyes, Dalinar had failed to spot the warcamps: ten craterlike circles arrayed along the northwestern edge of the Shattered Plains. From up here, it was obvious they had once been domes. The way their walls curved, like cupping fingers from underneath.

Two of the camps were still fully occupied, and Sebarial had set up forces to lay claim to the nearby forest. Dalinar's own warcamp was less populated, but had a few platoons of soldiers and some workers.

"We arrived so quickly!" Navani said. Her hair was a wind-tousled mess, much of it having escaped her careful braid. Elhokar hadn't fared much better—his hair sprayed out from his face like waxed Thaylen eyebrows. The two ardents, of course, were bald and didn't have such worries.

"Quick indeed," Elhokar said, redoing a few buttons of his uniform. "This is most promising for our mission."

"Yeah," Kaladin said. "I still want to test it more in front of a storm." He took the king by the shoulder, and Elhokar started to drift downward.

Kaladin sent them each down in turn, and when his feet finally touched stone again, Dalinar heaved a sigh of relief. They were only one plateau over from the warcamp, where a soldier at a watchpost waved to them with eager, exaggerated movements. Within minutes, a troop of Kholin soldiers had surrounded them.

"Let's get you inside the walls, Brightlord," their captainlord said, hand on the pommel of his sword. "The shellheads are still active out here."

"Have they attacked this close to the camps?" Elhokar asked, surprised.

"No, but that doesn't mean they won't, Your Majesty."

Dalinar wasn't so worried, but said nothing as the soldiers ushered him and the others into the warcamp where Brightness Jasalai—the tall, stately woman Dalinar had put in charge of the camp—met and accompanied them.

After spending so much time in the alien hallways of Urithiru, walking through this place—which had been Dalinar's home for five years—was relaxing. Part of that was finding the warcamp mostly intact; it had weathered the Everstorm quite well. Most of the buildings were stone bunkers, and that western rim of the former dome had provided a solid windbreak.

"My only worry," he told Jasalai after a short tour, "is about logistics. This is a long march from Narak and the Oathgate. I fear that by dividing our forces among Narak, here, and Urithiru, we're increasing our vulnerability to an attack."

"That is true, Brightlord," the woman said. "I endeavor only to provide you with options."

Unfortunately, they would probably need this place for farming operations, not to mention the lumber. Plateau runs for gemhearts couldn't sustain the tower city's population forever, particularly in the face of Shallan's assessment that they had likely hunted chasmfiends near to extinction.

Dalinar glanced at Navani. She thought they should found a new kingdom here, on and around the Shattered Plains. Import farmers, retire older soldiers, start production here on a much larger scale than they'd ever tried before.

Others disagreed. There was a reason the Unclaimed Hills weren't densely inhabited. It would be a harsh life here—rockbuds grew smaller, crops would be less productive. And founding a new kingdom during a Desolation? Better to protect what they had. Alethkar could probably feed Urithiru—but that depended on Kaladin and Elhokar recovering the
capital.

Their tour ended with a meal at Dalinar's bunker, in his former sitting room, which looked bare now that most of the furniture and rugs had been removed to Urithiru.

After the meal, he found himself standing by the window, feeling oddly out of place. He'd left this warcamp only ten weeks ago, but the place was at once deeply familiar and also no longer his.

Behind him, Navani and her scribe ate fruit as they chatted quietly over some sketches that Navani had done.

"Oh, but I think that the others need to experience that, Brightness!" the scribe said. "The flight was *remarkable*. How fast do you think we were going? I believe we might have attained a speed that no human has reached since the Recreance. Think about that, Navani! Surely we were faster than the fastest horse or ship."

"Focus, Rushu," Navani said. "My sketch."

"I don't think this math is right, Brightness. No, that sail will never stand."

"It's not meant to be completely accurate," Navani said. "Just a concept. My question is, can it work?"

"We'll need more reinforcement. Yes, more reinforcement for certain. And then the steering mechanism . . . definitely work to do there. This *is* clever though, Brightness. Falilar needs to see it; he will be able to say whether or not it can be built."

Dalinar glanced away from the window, catching Navani's eye. She smiled. She always claimed that she wasn't a scholar, but a patron of scholars. She said her place was to encourage and guide the real scientists. Anyone who saw the light in her eyes as she took out another sheet and sketched her idea further knew she was being too modest.

She began another sketch, but then stopped and glanced to the side, where she'd set out a spanreed. The ruby was blinking.

Fen! Dalinar thought. The queen of Thaylenah had asked that, in this morning's highstorm, Dalinar send her into the vision of Aharietiam, which she knew about from the published accounts of Dalinar's visions. He'd reluctantly sent her alone, without supervision.

They'd been waiting for her to speak of the event, to say anything. In the morning, she hadn't replied to their requests for a conversation.

Navani prepared the spanreed, then set it writing. It scribbled for only a brief moment.

"That was short," Dalinar said, stepping toward her.

"Only one word," Navani said. She looked up at him. "Yes."

Dalinar heaved out a long breath. She was willing to visit Urithiru. *Finally!*

"Tell her we'll send her a Radiant." He left the window, watching as she replied. In her sketchpad, he caught sight of some kind of shiplike contraption, but with the sail on the *bottom*. What in the world?

Fen seemed content to leave the conversation there, and Navani returned to her discussion of engineering, so Dalinar slipped from the room. He passed through his bunker, which felt hollow. Like the rind of a fruit with the pulp scooped out. No servants scuttling back and forth, no soldiers. Kaladin and his men had gone off somewhere, and Kadash was probably at the camp monastery. He'd been keen to get there, and Dalinar had been gratified by his willingness to fly with Kaladin.

They hadn't spoken much since their confrontation in the sparring room. Well, perhaps seeing the Windrunners' power firsthand would improve Kadash's opinion of the Radiants.

Dalinar was surprised—and secretly pleased—to find that no guards had been posted at the bunker's back door. He slipped out alone and headed to the warcamp monastery. He wasn't looking for Kadash; he had another purpose.

He soon arrived at the monastery, which looked like most of the warcamp—a collection of buildings with the same smooth, rounded construction. Crafted from the air by Alethi Soulcasters. This place had a few small, hand-built buildings of cut stone, but they looked more like bunkers than places of worship. Dalinar had never wanted his people to forget that they were at war.

He strolled through the campus and found that without a guide, he didn't know his way among the nearly identical structures. He stopped in a courtyard between buildings. The air smelled of wet stone from the highstorm, and a nice group of shalebark sculptures rose to his right, shaped like stacks of square plates. The only sound was water dripping from the eaves of the buildings.

Storms. He should know his way around his own monastery, shouldn't he? *How often did you actually visit here, during all the years in the warcamps?* He'd meant to come more often, and talk to the ardents in his chosen devotary. There had always been something more pressing, and besides, the ardents stressed that he didn't *need* to come. They had prayed and burned glyphwards on his behalf; that was why highlords owned ardents.

Even during his darkest days of war, they'd assured him that in pursuing his Calling—by leading his armies—he served the Almighty.

Dalinar stooped into a building that had been divided into many small rooms for prayers. He walked down a hallway until he stepped through a storm door into the atrium, which still smelled faintly of incense. It seemed insane that the ardents would be angry with him now, after training him his whole life to do as he wished. But he'd upset the balance. Rocked the

boat.

He moved among braziers filled with wet ash. Everyone liked the system they had. The lighteyes got to live without guilt or burden, always confident that they were active manifestations of God's will. The darkeyes got free access to training in a multitude of skills. The ardents got to pursue scholarship. The best of them lived lives of service. The worst lived lives of indolence—but what else were important lighteyed families going to do with unmotivated children?

A noise drew his attention, and he left the courtyard and looked into a dark corridor. Light poured from a room at the other end, and Dalinar was not surprised to find Kadash inside. The ardent was moving some ledgers and books from a wall safe into a pack on the floor. On a desk nearby, a spanreed scribbled.

Dalinar stepped into the room. The scarred ardent jumped, then relaxed when he saw it was Dalinar.

"Do we need to have this conversation again, Dalinar?" he asked, turning back to his packing.

"No," Dalinar said. "I didn't actually come looking for you. I want to find a man who lived here. A madman who claimed to be one of the Heralds."

Kadash cocked his head. "Ah, yes. The one who had a Shardblade?"

"All of the other patients at the monastery are accounted for, safe at Urithiru, but he vanished somehow. I was hoping to see if his room offered any clues to what became of him."

Kadash looked at him, gauging his sincerity. Then the ardent sighed, rising. "That's a different devotary from mine," he said, "but I have occupancy records here. I should be able to tell you which room he was in."

"Thank you."

Kadash looked through a stack of ledgers. "Shash building," he finally said, pointing absently out the window. "That one right there. Room thirty-seven. Insah ran the facility; her records will list details of the madman's treatment. If her departure from the warcamp was anything like mine, she'll have left most of her paperwork behind." He gestured toward the safe and his packing.

"Thank you," Dalinar said. He moved to leave.

"You . . . think the madman was actually a Herald, don't you?"

"I think it's likely."

"He spoke with a rural Alethi accent, Dalinar."

"And he looked Makabaki," Dalinar replied. "That alone is an oddity, wouldn't you say?"

"Immigrant families are not so uncommon."

"Ones with Shardblades?"

Kadash shrugged.

"Let's say I could actually find one of the Heralds," Dalinar said. "Let's say we could confirm his identity, and you accepted that proof. Would you believe him if he told you the same things I have?"

Kadash sighed.

"Surely you'd want to know if the Almighty were dead, Kadash," Dalinar said, stepping back into the room. "Tell me you wouldn't."

"You know what it would mean? It would mean there is no spiritual basis for your rule."

"I know."

"And the things you did in conquering Alethkar?" Kadash said. "No divine mandate, Dalinar. Everyone accepts what you did because your victories were proof of the Almighty's favor. Without him . . . then what are you?"

"Tell me, Kadash. Would you *really* rather not know?"

Kadash looked at the spanreed, which had stopped writing. He shook his head. "I don't know, Dalinar. It certainly would be easier."

"Isn't that the problem? What has any of this ever required of men like me? What has it required of *any* of us?"

"It required you to be what you are."

"Which is self-fulfilling," Dalinar said. "You were a swordsman, Kadash. Would you have gotten better without opponents to face? Would you have gotten stronger without weights to lift? Well, in Vorinism, we've spent *centuries* avoiding the opponents and the weights."

Again, Kadash glanced at the spanreed.

"What is it?" Dalinar asked.

"I left most of my spanreeds behind," Kadash explained, "when I went with you toward the center of the Shattered Plains. I took only the spanreed linked to an ardent transfer station in Kholinar. I thought that would be enough, but it no longer works. I've been forced to use intermediaries in Tashikk."

Kadash lifted a box onto the desk and opened it. Inside were five more spanreeds, with blinking rubies, indicating that someone had been trying to contact Kadash.

"These are links to the leaders of Vorinism in Jah Keved, Herdaz, Kharbranth, Thaylenah, and New Natanan," Kadash said, counting them off. "They had a meeting via reeds today, discussing the nature of the Desolation and the Everstorm. And perhaps you. I mentioned I was going to recover my own spanreeds today. Apparently, their meeting has made them all very eager to question me further."

He let the silence hang between them, measured out by the five blinking red lights.

"What of the one that is writing?" Dalinar asked.

"A line to the Palanaeum and the heads of Vorin research there. They've been working on the Dawnchant, using the clues Brightness Navani gave them from your visions. What they've sent me are relevant passages from ongoing translations."

"Proof," Dalinar said. "You wanted solid proof that what I've been seeing is real." He strode forward, grabbing Kadash by the shoulders. "You waited for that reed first, before answering the leaders of Vorinism?"

"I wanted all the facts in hand."

"So you know that the visions are real!"

"I long ago accepted that you weren't mad. These days, it's more a question of who might be influencing you."

"Why would the Voidbringers give me these visions?" Dalinar said. "Why would they grant us great powers, like the one that flew us here? It's not rational, Kadash."

"Neither is what you're saying about the Almighty." He held up a hand to cut off Dalinar. "I *don't* want to have this argument again. Before, you asked me for proof that we are following the Almighty's precepts, right?"

"All I asked for and all I want is the truth."

"We have it already. I'll show you."

"I look forward to it," Dalinar said, walking to the door. "But Kadash? In my painful experience, the truth may be simple, but it is rarely *easy*."

Dalinar crossed to the next building over and counted down the rooms. Storms, this building felt like a prison. Most of the doors hung open, revealing uniform chambers beyond: each had one tiny window, a slab for a bed, and a thick wooden door. The ardents knew what was best for the sick—they had access to all the world's latest research in all fields—but was it really necessary to lock madmen away like this?

Number thirty-seven was still bolted shut. Dalinar rattled the door, then threw his shoulder against it. Storms, it was thick. Without thinking he put his hand to the side and tried summoning his Shardblade. Nothing happened.

What are you doing? the Stormfather demanded.

"Sorry," Dalinar said, shaking his hand out. "Habit."

He crouched down and tried peeking under the door, then called out, suddenly horrified by the idea that they might have simply left the man in here to starve. That couldn't have happened, could it?

"My powers," Dalinar said, rising. "Can I use them?"

Binding things? the Stormfather said. *How would that open a door? You are a Bondsmith; you bring things together, you do not divide them.*

"And my other Surge?" Dalinar said. "That Radiant in the vision made stone warp and ripple."

You are not ready. Besides, that Surge is different for you than it is for a Stoneward.

Well, from what Dalinar could see underneath the door, there seemed to be light in this room. Perhaps it had a window to the outside he could use.

On his way out, he poked through the ardent chambers until he found an office like Kadash's. He didn't find any keys, though the desk still had pens and ink sitting on it. They'd left in haste, so there was a good chance the wall safe contained records—but of course, Dalinar couldn't get in. Storms. He missed having a Shardblade.

He rounded the outside of the building to check the window, then immediately felt silly for spending so much time trying to get through the door. Somebody else had already cut a hole in the stone out here, using the distinctive, clean slices of a Shardblade.

Dalinar stepped inside, picking his way around the broken remnants of the wall, which had fallen inward—indicating that the Shardbearer had cut from the outside. He found no madman. The ardents had likely seen this hole and moved on with their evacuation. News of the strange hole must not have filtered up to the lead ardents.

He didn't find anything to indicate where the Herald had gone, but at least he knew a Shardbearer was involved. Someone powerful had wanted into this room, which lent even more credence to the madman's claims of being a Herald.

So who had taken him? Or had they done something to him instead? What happened to a Herald's body when they died? Could someone else have come to the same conclusion that Jasnah had?

As he was about to leave, Dalinar spotted something on the ground beside the bed. He knelt down, shooed away a cremling, and picked up a small object. It was a dart, green with yellow twine wrapped around it. He frowned, turning it over in his fingers. Then he looked up as he heard someone distantly calling his name.

He found Kaladin out in the monastery courtyard, calling for him. Dalinar approached, then handed him the little dart. "Ever seen anything like this before, Captain?"

Kaladin shook his head. He sniffed at the tip, then raised his eyebrows. "That's poison on the tip. Blackbane derived."

"Are you sure?" Dalinar asked, taking the dart back.

"Very. Where did you find it?"

"In the chamber that housed the Herald."

Kaladin grunted. "You need more time for your search?"

"Not much," Dalinar said. "Though it would help if you'd summon your

Shardblade. . . ."

A short time later, Dalinar handed Navani the records he'd taken from the ardent's safe. He dropped the dart in a pouch and handed it over as well, warning her about the poisoned tip.

One by one, Kaladin sent them into the sky, where his bridgemen caught them and used Stormlight to stabilize them. Dalinar was last, and as Kaladin reached for him, he took the captain by the arm.

"You want to practice flying in front of a storm," Dalinar said. "Could you get to Thaylenah?"

"Probably," Kaladin said. "If I Lashed myself southward as fast as I can go."

"Go, then," Dalinar said. "Take someone with you to test flying another person in front of a storm, if you want, but get to Thaylen City. Queen Fen is willing to join us, and I want that Oathgate active. The world has been turning before our very noses, Captain. Gods and Heralds have been warring, and we were too focused on our petty problems to even notice."

"I'll go next highstorm," Kaladin said, then sent Dalinar soaring up into the air.

51

FULL CIRCLE

This is all we will say at this time. If you wish more, seek these
waters in person and overcome the tests we have created.
Only in this will you earn our respect.

T he parshmen of Moash's new sledge crew didn't like him. That
didn't bother him. Lately, he didn't much like himself.

He didn't expect or need their admiration. He knew what it felt
like to be beaten down, despised. When you'd been treated as they had,
you didn't trust someone like Moash. You asked yourself what *he* was trying to get from you.

After a few days of pulling their sledge, the landscape began to change.
The open plains became cultivated hills. They passed great sweeping wards—
artificial stone ridges built by planting sturdy wooden barricades to collect
crem during storms. The crem would harden, slowly building up a mound on
the stormward side. After a few years, you raised the top of the barricade.

They took generations to grow to useful sizes, but here—around the oldest, most populated centers of Alethkar—they were common. They looked
like frozen waves of stone, stiff and straight on the western side, sloping
and smooth on the other side. In their shadows, vast orchards spread in
rows, most of the trees cultivated to grow no more than the height of
a man.

The western edge of those orchards was ragged with broken trees.
Barriers would need to be erected to the west as well, now.

He expected the Fused to burn the orchards, but they didn't. During a
water break, Moash studied one of them—a tall woman who hovered a
dozen feet in the air, toes pointed downward. Her face was more angular

than those of the parshmen. She resembled a spren the way she hung there, an impression accented by her flowing clothing.

Moash leaned back against his sledge and took a pull on his waterskin. Nearby, an overseer watched him and the parshmen of his crew. She was new; a replacement for the one he'd punched. A few more of the Fused passed on horses, trotting the beasts with obvious familiarity.

That variety doesn't fly, he thought. *They can raise the dark light around themselves, but it doesn't give them Lashings. Something else.* He glanced back at the one nearest him, the one hovering. *But that type almost never walks. It's the same kind that captured me.*

Kaladin wouldn't have been able to stay aloft as long as these did. He'd run out of Stormlight.

She's studying those orchards, Moash thought. *She looks impressed.*

She turned in the air and soared off, long clothing rippling behind her. Those overlong robes would have been impractical for anyone else, but for a creature who almost always flew, the effect was mesmerizing.

"This isn't what it was supposed to be like," Moash said.

Nearby, one of the parshmen of his crew grunted. "Tell me about it, human."

Moash glanced at the man, who had settled down in the shade of their lumber-laden sledge. The parshman was tall, with rough hands, mostly dark skin marbled with lines of red. The others had called him "Sah," a simple Alethi darkeyes name.

Moash nodded his chin toward the Voidbringers. "They were supposed to sweep in relentlessly, destroying everything in their path. They are *literally* incarnations of destruction."

"And?" Sah asked.

"And that one," Moash said, pointing toward the flying Voidbringer, "is pleased to find these orchards here. They only burned a few towns. They seem intent on keeping Revolar, working it." Moash shook his head. "This was supposed to be an apocalypse, but you don't *farm* an apocalypse."

Sah grunted again. He didn't seem to know any more about this than Moash did, but why should he? He'd grown up in a rural community in Alethkar. Everything he knew about history and religion, he'd have heard filtered through the human perspective.

"You shouldn't speak so casually about the Fused, human," Sah said, standing up. "They're dangerous."

"Don't know about that," Moash said as two more passed overhead. "The one I killed went down easy enough, though I don't think she was expecting me to be able to fight back."

He handed his waterskin to the overseer as she came around for them; then he glanced at Sah, who was staring at him, slack-jawed.

Probably shouldn't have mentioned killing one of their gods, Moash thought, walking to his place in line—last, closest to the sledge, so he stared at a sweaty parshman back all day.

They started up again, and Moash expected another long day's work. These orchards meant Kholinar itself was a little over a day's hike away at an easy pace. He figured the Voidbringers would push them hard to reach the capital by nightfall.

He was surprised, then, when the army diverged from the direct route. They wove between some hillsides until they reached a town, one of the many suburbs of Kholinar. He couldn't recall the name. The tavern had been nice, and welcoming to caravaneers.

Clearly there were other Voidbringer armies moving through Alethkar, because they'd obviously seized this city days—if not weeks—ago. Parshmen patrolled it, and the only humans he saw were already working the fields.

Once the army arrived, the Voidbringers surprised Moash again by selecting some of the wagon-pullers and setting them free. They were the weaklings, the ones who had fared worst on the road. The overseers sent them trudging toward Kholinar, which was still too far off to see.

They're trying to burden the city with refugees, Moash thought. *Ones that aren't fit to work or fight anymore.*

The main bulk of the army moved into the large storm bunkers in this suburb. They wouldn't attack the city immediately. The Voidbringers would rest their armies, prepare, and besiege.

In his youth, he'd wondered why there weren't any suburbs closer than a day's walk from Kholinar. In fact, there was nothing between its walls and here, only empty flats—even the hills there had been mined down centuries ago. The purpose was clear to him now. If you wanted to lay siege to Kholinar, this was the closest you could put your army. You couldn't camp in the city's shadow; you'd be swept away by the first storm.

In the town, the supply sledges were split, some sent down one street—which looked hauntingly empty to him—while his went down another. They actually passed the tavern he'd preferred, the Fallen Tower; he could see the glyph etched into the leeward stone.

Finally his crew was called to a halt, and he let go of the rope, stretching his hands and letting out a relieved sigh. They'd been sent to a large open ground near some warehouses, where parshmen were cutting lumber.

A lumberyard? he thought, then felt stupid. After hauling wood all this way, what else would he expect?

Still . . . a lumberyard. Like those back in the warcamps. He started laughing.

"Don't be so jovial, human," spat one of the overseers. "You're to spend the next few weeks working here, building siege equipment. When the assault happens, *you'll* be at the front, running a ladder toward Kholinar's infamous walls."

Moash laughed even harder. It consumed him, shook him; he couldn't stop. He laughed helplessly until, short of breath, he dizzily lay back on the hard stone ground, tears leaking down the sides of his face.

∴

We have investigated this woman, Mraize's newest letter to Shallan read.

> Ishnah has overinflated her importance to you. She was indeed involved in espionage for House Hamaradin, as she told you, but she was merely an assistant to the true spies.
>
> We have determined that she is safe to allow close to you, though her loyalties should not be trusted too far. If you eliminate her, we will help cover up the disappearance, at your request. But we have no objection to you retaining her services.

Shallan sighed, settling back in her seat, where she waited outside King Elhokar's audience chamber. She'd found this paper unexpectedly in her satchel.

So much for hoping Ishnah had information about the Ghostbloods she could use. The letter practically boiled with possessiveness. They would "allow" Ishnah to be close to her? Storms, they acted like they owned her already.

She shook her head, then rummaged in her satchel, taking out a small sphere pouch. It would look unremarkable to anyone inspecting it—for they wouldn't know that she'd transformed it with a small but simple illusion. Though it appeared violet, it was actually white.

The interesting thing about it was not the illusion itself, but how she was powering it. She'd practiced before with attaching an illusion to Pattern, or to a location, but she'd always needed to power it with her own Stormlight. This one, however, she'd attached to a sphere inside the pouch.

She was going on four hours now with the Lightweaving needing no extra Stormlight from her. She'd needed only to create it, then affix it to the sphere. Slowly, the Light had been draining from the sapphire mark—just like a fabrial draining its gemstone. She'd even left the pouch alone in her rooms when going out, and the illusion had still been in place when she'd returned.

This had begun as an experiment on how she could help Dalinar create his illusory maps of the world, then leave them for him, without her having to remain in the meeting. Now, however, she was seeing all *kinds* of possible applications.

The door opened, and she dropped the pouch back into her satchel. A master-servant ushered a few merchants out of the king's presence; then the servant bowed to Shallan, waving her in. She stepped hesitantly into the audience chamber: a room with a fine blue and green rug and stuffed with furniture. Diamonds shone from lamps, and Elhokar had ordered the walls painted, obscuring the strata.

The king himself, in a blue Kholin uniform, was unrolling a map onto a large table at the side of the room. "Was there another, Helt?" he asked the master-servant. "I thought I was done for the . . ." He trailed off as he turned. "Brightness Shallan! Were you waiting out there? You could have seen me immediately!"

"I didn't want to be a bother," Shallan said, stepping over to him as the master-servant prepared refreshment.

The map on the table showed Kholinar, a grand city, which seemed every bit as impressive as Vedenar. Papers in a pile beside it looked to have the final reports from spanreeds in the city, and a wizened ardent sat near them, ready to read for the king or take notes at his request.

"I think we're almost ready," the king said, noting her interest. "The delay has been nearly insufferable, but requisite, I'm sure. Captain Kaladin did want to practice flying other people before bringing my royal person. I can respect that."

"He's asked me to fly with him above the storm to Thaylen City," Shallan said, "to open the Oathgate there. He's overly worried about dropping people—but if he does that to me, I'll have Stormlight of my own, and should survive the fall."

"Excellent," Elhokar said. "Yes, a fine solution. But then, you didn't come here to talk about this. What is your request of me?"

"Actually," Shallan said. "Could I talk to you in private for a moment, Your Majesty?"

He frowned, but then ordered his people to step out into the hallway. When two guards from Bridge Thirteen hesitated, the king was firm. "She's a Knight Radiant," he said. "What do you think is going to happen to me?"

They filed out, leaving the two of them beside Elhokar's table. Shallan took a deep breath.

Then changed her face.

Not to that of Veil or Radiant—not one of her *secrets*—but instead to an illusion of Adolin. It was still surprisingly uncomfortable for her to do it in front of someone. She'd still been telling most people that she was of the Elsecallers, like Jasnah, so they wouldn't know of her ability to become other people.

Elhokar jumped. "Ah," he said. "Ah, that's right."

"Your Majesty," Shallan said, changing her face and body to look like that of a cleaning woman she'd sketched earlier, "I'm worried that your mission will not be as simple as you think."

The letters out of Kholinar—the last ones they'd gotten—were frightened, worried things. They spoke of riots, of darkness, of spren taking form and hurting people.

Shallan changed her face to that of a soldier. "I've been preparing a team of spies," she explained. "Specializing in infiltration and information gathering. I've been keeping my focus quiet, for obvious reasons. I would like to offer my services for your mission."

"I'm not certain," Elhokar said, hesitantly, "if Dalinar would want me taking *two* of his Radiants away from him."

"I'm not accomplishing much for him sitting around here," Shallan said, still wearing the soldier's face. "Besides. Is it his mission? Or is it yours?"

"My mission," the king said. Then hesitated. "But let's not fool ourselves. If he didn't want you to go . . ."

"I am not his subject," she said. "Nor yours, yet. I'm my own woman. You tell me. What happens if you get to Kholinar, and the Oathgate is held by the enemy? Are you going to let the bridgeman just fight his way in? Or might there be a better option?"

She changed her face to that of a parshwoman she had from her older sketches.

Elhokar nodded, walking around her. "A team, you say. Of spies? Interesting . . ."

⁂

A short time later, Shallan left the room carrying—tucked into her safepouch—a formal royal request to Dalinar for Shallan's aid on the mission. Kaladin had said he felt comfortable bringing six people, other than a few bridgemen, who could fly on their own.

Adolin and Elhokar would leave room for four others. She tucked Elhokar's request into her safepouch, beside the letter from Mraize.

I just need to be away from this place, Shallan thought. *I need to be away from them, and from Jasnah, at least until I can figure out what I want.*

A part of her knew what she was doing. It was getting harder to hide things in the back of her mind and ignore them, now that she'd spoken Ideals. Instead she was fleeing.

But she *could* help the group going to Kholinar. And it *did* feel exciting, the idea of going to the city and finding the secrets there. She wasn't *only* running. She'd also be helping Adolin reclaim his home.

Pattern hummed from her skirts, and she hummed along with him.

EIGHTEEN AND A HALF YEARS AGO

Dalinar plodded back into camp, so tired he suspected only the energy of his Plate was keeping him upright. Each muggy breath inside his helm fogged the metal, which—as always—went somewhat transparent from the inside when you engaged the visor.

He'd crushed the Herdazians—sending them back to start a civil war, securing the Alethi lands to the north and claiming the island of Akak. Now he'd moved southward, to engage the Vedens at the border. Herdaz had taken far longer than Dalinar had expected. He'd been out on campaign a total of four years now.

Four glorious years.

Dalinar walked straight to his armorers' tent, picking up attendants and messengers along the way. When he ignored their questions, they trailed after him like cremlings eyeing a greatshell's kill, waiting for their moment to snatch a tidbit.

Inside the tent, he extended his arms to the sides and let the armorers start the disassembly. Helm, then arms, revealing the gambeson he wore for padding. The helm's removal exposed sweaty, clammy skin that made the air feel too cold. The breastplate was cracked along the left side, and the armorers buzzed, discussing the repair. As if they had to do something other than merely give the Plate Stormlight and let it regrow itself.

Eventually, all that remained were his boots, which he stepped out of, maintaining a martial posture by pure force of will. The support of his Plate removed, exhaustionspren began to shoot up around him like jets of dust. He stepped over to a set of travel cushions and sat down, reclining against them, sighing, and closing his eyes.

"Brightlord?" one of the armorers asked. "Um . . . that's where we set—"

"This is now my audience tent," Dalinar said, not opening his eyes. "Take what is absolutely essential and leave me."

The clanking of armor stopped as the workers digested what he'd said. They left in a whispering rush, and nobody else bothered him for a blissful five minutes—until footfalls sounded nearby. Tent flaps rustled, then leather scrunched as someone knelt beside him.

"The final battle report is here, Brightlord." Kadash's voice. Of course it would be one of his storming officers. Dalinar had trained them far too well.

"Speak," Dalinar said, opening his eyes.

Kadash had reached middle age, maybe two or three years older than Dalinar. He now had a twisting scar across his face and head from where a spear had hit him.

"We completely routed them, Brightlord," Kadash said. "Our archers and light infantry followed with an extended harry. We slew, by best count, two thousand—nearly half. We could have gotten more if we'd boxed them in to the south."

"Never box in an enemy, Kadash," Dalinar said. "You want them to be able to retreat, or they'll fight you worse for it. A rout will serve us better than an extermination. How many people did we lose?"

"Barely two hundred."

Dalinar nodded. Minimal losses, while delivering a devastating blow.

"Sir," Kadash said. "I'd say this raiding group is done for."

"We've still got many more to dig out. This will last years yet."

"Unless the Vedens send in an entire army and engage us in force."

"They won't," Dalinar said, rubbing his forehead. "Their king is too shrewd. It isn't full-on war he wants; he only wanted to see if any contested land had suddenly become uncontested."

"Yes, Brightlord."

"Thank you for the report. Now get out of here and post some storming guards at the front so I can rest. Don't let anyone in, not even the Night-watcher herself."

"Yes, sir." Kadash crossed the tent to the flaps. "Um . . . sir, you were incredible out there. Like a tempest."

Dalinar just closed his eyes and leaned back, fully determined to fall asleep in his clothing.

Sleep, unfortunately, refused to come. The report set his mind to considering implications.

His army had only one Soulcaster, for emergencies, which meant supply trains. These borderlands were expansive, hilly, and the Vedens had better generals than the Herdazians. Defeating a mobile enemy was going to be hard in such circumstances, as this first battle proved. It would take planning, maneuvering, and skirmish after skirmish to pin the various groups of Vedens down and bring them into proper battle.

He yearned for those early days, when their fights had been more rowdy, less coordinated. Well, he wasn't a youth anymore, and he'd learned in Herdaz that he no longer had Gavilar to do the hard parts of this job. Dalinar had camps to supply, men to feed, and logistics to work out. This was almost as bad as being back in the city, listening to scribes talk about sewage disposal.

Save for one difference: Out here, he had a reward. At the end of all the planning, the strategy, and the debates with generals, came the Thrill.

In fact, through his exhaustion, he was surprised to find that he could sense it still. Deep down, like the warmth of a rock that had known a recent fire. He was *glad* that the fighting had dragged on all these years. He was *glad* that the Herdazians had tried to seize that land, and that now the Vedens wanted to test him. He was *glad* that other highprinces weren't sending aid, but waiting to see what he could accomplish on his own.

Most of all, he was glad that—despite today's important battle—the conflict was not over. Storms, he loved this feeling. Today, hundreds had tried to bring him down, and he'd left them ashen and broken.

Outside his tent, people demanding his attention were turned away one after another. He tried not to feel pleasure each time. He would answer their questions eventually. Just . . . not now.

Thoughts finally released their grip on his brain, and he dipped toward slumber. Until one unexpected voice jerked him out of it and sent him bolting upright.

That was Evi.

He leapt to his feet. The Thrill surged again within him, drawn out of its own slumber. Dalinar ripped open the tent's front flaps and gaped at the blonde-haired woman standing outside, wearing a Vorin havah—but with sturdy walking boots sticking out below.

"Ah," Evi said. "Husband." She looked him up and down, and her expression soured, lips puckering. "Has no person seen fit to order him a bath? Where are his grooms, to see him undressed properly?"

"Why are you here?" Dalinar demanded. He hadn't intended to roar it, but he was so tired, so shocked . . .

Evi leaned backward before the outburst, eyes opening wide.

He briefly felt a spike of shame. But why should he? This was his warcamp—here he was the Blackthorn. This was the place where his domestic life should have no purchase on him! By coming here, she invaded that.

"I . . ." Evi said. "I . . . Other women are at the camp. Other wives. It is common, for women to go to war. . . ."

"Alethi women," Dalinar snapped, "trained to it from childhood and acquainted with the ways of warfare. We spoke of this, Evi. We—" He halted, looking at the guards. They shuffled uncomfortably.

"Come inside, Evi," Dalinar said. "Let's discuss this in private."

"Very well. And the children?"

"*You brought our children to the battlefront?*" Storms, she didn't even have the sense to leave them at the town the army was using as a long-term command post?

"I—"

"In," Dalinar said, pointing at the tent.

Evi wilted, then scuttled to obey, cringing as she passed him. Why had she come? Hadn't he just been back to Kholinar to visit? That had been . . . recent, he was sure. . . .

Or maybe not so recent. He did have several letters from Evi that Teleb's wife had read to him, with several more waiting to be read. He dropped the flaps back into position and turned toward Evi, determined not to let his frayed patience rule him.

"Navani said I should come," Evi said. "She said it was shameful that you have waited so long between visits. Adolin has gone over a year without seeing you, Dalinar. And little Renarin has never even *met* his father."

"Renarin?" Dalinar said, trying to work out the name. He hadn't picked that. "Rekher . . . no, Re . . ."

"Re," Evi said. "From my language. Nar, after his father. In, to be born unto."

Stormfather, that was a butchering of the language. Dalinar fumbled, trying to work through it. Nar meant "like unto."

"What does 'Re' mean in your language?" Dalinar asked, scratching his face.

"It has no meaning," Evi said. "It is simply the name. It means our son's name, or him."

Dalinar groaned softly. So the child's name was "Like one who was born unto himself." Delightful.

"You didn't answer," Evi pointed out, "when I asked after a name via spanreed."

How had Navani and Ialai allowed this travesty of a name? Storms . . . knowing those two, they'd probably encouraged it. They were always trying to get Evi to be more forceful. He moved to get something to drink, but then remembered that this wasn't actually his tent. There wasn't anything in here to drink but armor oil.

"You shouldn't have come," Dalinar said. "It is dangerous out here."

"I wish to be a more Alethi wife. I want you to *want* me to be with you."

He winced. "Well, you still should not have brought the children." Dalinar slumped down into the cushions. "They are heirs to the princedom, assuming this plan of Gavilar's with the Crownlands and his own throne works out. They need to remain safe in Kholinar."

"I thought you'd want to see them," Evi said, stepping up to him. Despite his harsh words, she unbuckled the top of his gambeson to get her hands under it, and began rubbing his shoulders.

It felt wonderful. He let his anger melt away. It *would* be good to have a wife with him, to scribe as was proper. He just wished that he didn't feel so guilty at seeing her. He was not the man she wanted him to be.

"I hear you had a great victory today," Evi said softly. "You do service to the king."

"You'd have hated it, Evi. I killed hundreds of people. If you stay, you'll have to listen to war reports. Accounts of deaths, many at my hand."

She was silent for a time. "Could you not . . . let them surrender to you?"

"The Vedens aren't here to surrender. They're here to test us on the battlefield."

"And the individual men? Do they care for such reasoning as they die?"

"What? Would you like me to stop and ask each man to surrender as I prepare to strike him down?"

"Would that—"

"No, Evi. That wouldn't work."

"Oh."

He stood up, suddenly anxious. "Let's see the boys, then."

Leaving his tent and crossing the camp was a slog, his feet feeling like they'd been encased in blocks of crem. He didn't dare slouch—he always tried to present a strong image for the men and women of the army—but he couldn't help that his padded garb was wrinkled and stained with sweat.

The land here was lush compared to Kholinar. The thick grass was broken by sturdy stands of trees, and tangled vines draped the western cliff faces. There were places farther into Jah Keved where you couldn't take a step without vines writhing under your feet.

The boys were by Evi's wagons. Little Adolin was terrorizing one of the chulls, perched atop its shell and swinging a wooden sword about, showing off for several of the guards—who dutifully complimented his moves. He'd somehow assembled "armor" from strings and bits of broken rockbud shell.

Storms, he's grown, Dalinar thought. When last he'd seen Adolin, the child had still looked like a toddler, stumbling through his words. Little over a year later, the boy spoke clearly—and dramatically—as he described his fallen enemies. They were, apparently, evil flying chulls.

He stopped when he saw Dalinar, then he glanced at Evi. She nodded, and the child scrambled down from the chull—Dalinar was certain he'd fall at three different points. He got down safely, walked over.

And saluted.

Evi beamed. "He asked the best way to talk to you," she whispered. "I told him you were a general, the leader of all the soldiers. He came up with that on his own."

Dalinar squatted down. Little Adolin immediately shied back, reaching for his mother's skirts.

"Afraid of me?" Dalinar asked. "Not unwise. I'm a dangerous man."

"Daddy?" the boy said, holding to the skirt with one white-knuckled hand—but not hiding.

"Yes. Don't you remember me?"

Hesitantly, the motley-haired boy nodded. "I remember you. We talk about you every night when we burn prayers. So you will be safe. Fighting bad men."

"I'd prefer to be safe from the good ones too," Dalinar said. "Though I will take what I am offered." He stood up, feeling . . . what? Shame to not have seen the boy as often as he should have? Pride at how the boy was growing? The Thrill, still squirming deep down. How had it not dissipated since the battle?

"Where is your brother, Adolin?" Dalinar asked.

The boy pointed toward a nurse who carried a little one. Dalinar had expected a baby, but this child could nearly walk, as evidenced by the nurse putting him down and watching fondly as he toddled a few steps, then sat, trying to grab blades of grass as they pulled away.

The child made no sounds. He just stared, solemn, as he tried to grip blade after blade. Dalinar waited for the excitement he'd felt before, upon meeting Adolin for the first time . . . but storms, he was just so *tired*.

"Can I see your sword?" Adolin asked.

Dalinar wanted nothing more than to sleep, but he summoned the Blade anyway, driving it into the ground with the edge pointed away from Adolin. The boy's eyes grew wide.

"Mommy says I can't have my Plate yet," Adolin said.

"Teleb needs it. You can have it when you come of age."

"Good. I'll need it to win a Blade."

Nearby, Evi clicked her tongue softly, shaking her head.

Dalinar smiled, kneeling beside his Blade and resting his hand on the small boy's shoulder. "I'll win you one in war, son."

"No," Adolin said, chin up. "I want to win my own. Like you did."

"A worthy goal," Dalinar said. "But a soldier needs to be willing to accept help. You mustn't be hardheaded; pride doesn't win battles."

The boy cocked his head, frowning. "Your head isn't hard?" He rapped his knuckles against his own.

Dalinar smiled, then stood up and dismissed Oathbringer. The last embers of the Thrill finally faded. "It's been a long day," he told Evi. "I need to rest. We'll discuss your role here later."

Evi led him to a bed within one of her stormwagons. Then, at last, Dalinar was able to sleep.

My Friend,

The secrets uncovered infiltrating the Calligraphers Guild are more mundane than expected. I prefer bloodstains to inkstains any day, so next time send me somewhere I'm more likely to die from wounds than from handcramps. By Gavity's Eye, if you ask me to draw another glyph...

The darkest secret of the guild is that the phonemes within a glyph can sometimes be deciphered. (Sorry to shatter your theories of dark rites and ancient moon dances.) But glyphs aren't pronounced or read. They're memorized, and they change over time till the original collection of phonograms is almost unrecognizable. Take, for instance, the glyph for storm: "zeras."

| Old | Middle | Modern |

| high "kecheh" | storm "zeras" |

Highstorm "kezeras"

| eternal "kalad" | storm "zeras" |

Everstorm "kalazeras"

Glyphpairs are slightly more common than single glyphs. Less used are 3 glyphs in a row.

Glyphs have simplified versions for small writing

Contrast "zeras" with a glyph in its infancy: "zatalef," a bat-like cephalopod the Alethi hadn't encountered until their recent conquests in Akak.

The glyph's phonemes are apparent as well as the glyph's resemblance to the actual creature.

Even older than "zeras" are the glyphs used in the First Oath of the Knights Radiant. These resemble more the complex, unreadable glyphs representing the orders of knights than they do any middle or modern Alethi glyphs.

I suspect these were borrowed from an earlier source and incorporated into an already developing Alethi glyph lexicon.

This supports the claim that Alethi glyphs were adopted from older scripts likely descended from Dawnchant and might explain the two sets of phonemes used in glyph creation: Standard and Calligraphic.

| javani | tebel | tsameth |

| katef | tebel | kadulek |

| mehlak | tebel | mevizh |

	A		I		M		SH
	B		F		N		T
	V		P		O		TH
	CH		G		U		Y
	K		H		R		J
	D		L		S		Z
	E						

Glyphmakers use both, the phonemes rotated, flipped, and distorted to fit the calligrapher's vision. Next page: The Calligraphic Phoneme set

53

SUCH A
TWISTED CUT

Friend,

Your letter is most intriguing, even revelatory.

The ancient Siln dynasty in Jah Keved had been founded after the death of King NanKhet. No contemporary accounts survived; the best they had dated from two centuries later. The author of that text—Natata Ved, often called Oileyes by her contemporaries—insisted that her methods were rigorous, although by modern standards, historical scholarship had been in its infancy.

Jasnah had long been interested in NanKhet's death, because he'd ruled for only three months. He'd succeeded to the throne when the previous king, his brother NanHar, had taken ill and died while on campaign in what would become modern Triax.

Remarkably, during the brief span of his reign, NanKhet survived *six* assassination attempts. The first had come from his sister, who had wanted to place her husband on the throne. After surviving poisoning, NanKhet had put them both to death. Soon after, their son had tried to kill him in his bed. NanKhet, apparently a light sleeper, struck down his nephew with his own sword.

NanKhet's cousin tried next—that attack left NanKhet blinded in one eye—and was followed by another brother, an uncle, and finally NanKhet's own son. At the end of three exasperating months, according to Oileyes, "The great, but weary, NanKhet called for an accounting of all his household. He gathered them together at a grand feast, promising the delights of distant Aimia. Instead, when all were assembled, NanKhet had them executed one by one. Their bodies were burned in a grand pyre, upon which was cooked the meat for the feast that he ate alone, at a table set for two hundred."

Natata Oileyes was known to have had a passion for the dramatic. The text sounded almost delighted when she'd explained how he'd died by choking on the food at that very feast, alone with nobody to help him.

Similar tales repeated themselves throughout the long history of the Vorin lands. Kings fell, and their brothers or sons took the throne. Even a pretender of no true lineage would usually claim kinship through oblique and creative genealogical justifications.

Jasnah was simultaneously fascinated and worried by these accounts. Thoughts about them were unusually present in her mind as she made her way into Urithiru's basement. Something in her readings the night before had lodged this particular story in her brain.

She soon peeked into the former library beneath Urithiru. Both rooms— one on either side of the hallway that led to the crystal pillar—were filled with scholars now, occupying tables carried down by squads of soldiers. Dalinar had sent expeditions down the tunnel the Unmade had used to flee. The scouts reported a long network of caverns.

Following a stream of water, they'd marched for days, and eventually located an exit into the mountain foothills of Tu Fallia. It was nice to know that, in a pinch, there was another way out of Urithiru—and a potential means of supply other than through the Oathgates.

They maintained guards in the upper tunnels, and for now it seemed safe enough in the basement. Therefore, Navani had transformed the area into a scholarly institute designed to solve Dalinar's problems and to provide an edge in information, technology, and pure research. Concentration-spren rippled in the air like waves overhead—a rarity in Alethkar, but common here—and logicspren darted through them, like tiny storm-clouds.

Jasnah couldn't help but smile. For over a decade, she'd dreamed of uniting the best minds of the kingdom in a coordinated effort. She'd been ignored; all anyone had wanted to discuss was her lack of belief in their god. Well, they were focused now. Turned out that the end of the world had to actually *arrive* before people would take it seriously.

Renarin was there, standing near the corner, watching the work. He'd been joining the scholars with some regularity, but he still wore his uniform with the Bridge Four patch.

You can't spend forever floating between worlds, Cousin, she thought. *Eventually you'll need to decide where you want to belong.* Life was so much harder, but potentially so much more fulfilling, when you found the courage to choose.

The story of the old Veden king, NanKhet, had taught Jasnah something troubling: Often, the greatest threat to a ruling family was its own members. Why were so many of the old royal lines such knots of murder, greed, and infighting? And what made the few exceptions different?

She'd grown adept at protecting her family against danger from without, carefully removing would-be deposers. But what could she do to protect it from within? In her absence, already the monarchy trembled. Her brother and her uncle—who she knew loved each other deeply—ground their wills against one another like mismatched gears.

She would *not* have her family implode. If Alethkar was going to survive the Desolation, they'd need committed leadership. A stable throne.

She entered the library room and walked to her writing stand. It was in a position where she could survey the others and have her back to a wall.

She unpacked her satchel, setting up two spanreed boards. One of the reeds was blinking early, and she twisted the ruby, indicating she was ready. A message came back, writing out, *We will begin in five minutes.*

She passed the time scrutinizing the various groups in the room, reading the lips of those she could see, absently taking notes in shorthand. She moved from conversation to conversation, gleaning a little from each one and noting the names of the people who spoke.

—tests confirm something is different here. Temperatures are distinctly lower on other nearby peaks of the same elevation—

—we have to assume that Brightlord Kholin is not going to return to the faith. What then?—

—don't know. Perhaps if we could find a way to conjoin the fabrials, we could imitate this effect—

—the boy could be a powerful addition to our ranks. He shows interest in numerology, and asked me if we can truly predict events with it. I will speak with him again—

That last one was from the stormwardens. Jasnah tightly pursed her lips. "Ivory?" she whispered.

"I will watch them."

He left her side, shrunken to the size of a speck of dust. Jasnah made a note to speak to Renarin; she would not have him wasting his time with a bunch of fools who thought they could foretell the future based on the curls of smoke from a snuffed candle.

Finally, her spanreed woke up.

I have connected Jochi of Thaylenah and Ethid of Azir for you, Brightness. Here are their passcodes. Further entries will be strictly their notations.

Excellent, Jasnah wrote back, authenticating the two passcodes. Losing her spanreeds in the sinking of the *Wind's Pleasure* had been a huge setback. She could no longer directly contact important colleagues or informants. Fortunately, Tashikk was set up to deal with these kinds of situations. You could always buy new reeds connected to the princedom's infamous information centers.

You could reach anyone, in practice, so long as you trusted an intermediary. Jasnah had one of those she'd personally interviewed—and whom she paid good money—to ensure confidentiality. The intermediary would burn her copies of this conversation afterward. The system was as secure as Jasnah could make it, all things considered.

Jasnah's intermediary would now be joined by two others in Tashikk. Together, the three would be surrounded by six spanreed boards: one each for receiving comments from their masters, and one each to send back the entire conversation in real time, including the comments from the other two. That way, each conversant would be able to see a constant stream of comments, without having to stop and wait before replying.

Navani talked of ways to improve the experience—of spanreeds that could be adjusted to connect to different people. That was one area of scholarship, however, that Jasnah did not have time to pursue.

Her receiving board started to fill with notes written by her two colleagues.

Jasnah, you live! Jochi wrote. *Back from the dead. Remarkable!*

I can't believe you ever thought she was dead, Ethid replied. *Jasnah Kholin? Lost at sea? Likelier we'd find the Stormfather dead.*

Your confidence is comforting, Ethid, Jasnah wrote on her sending board. A moment later, those words were copied by her scribe into the common spanreed conversation.

Are you at Urithiru? Jochi wrote. *When can I visit?*

As soon as you're willing to let everyone know you aren't female, Jasnah wrote back. Jochi—known to the world as a dynamic woman of distinctive philosophy—was a pen name for a potbellied man in his sixties who ran a pastry shop in Thaylen City.

Oh, I'm certain your wonderful city has need of pastries, Jochi wrote back jovially.

Can we please discuss your silliness later? Ethid wrote. *I have news.* She was a scion—a kind of religious order of scribe—at the Azish royal palace.

Well stop wasting time then! Jochi wrote. *I love news. Goes excellently with a filled doughnut . . . no, no, a fluffy brioche.*

The news? Jasnah just wrote, smiling. These two had studied with her under the same master—they were Veristitalians of the keenest mind, regardless of how Jochi might seem.

I've been tracking a man we are increasingly certain is the Herald Nakku, the Judge, Ethid wrote. *Nalan, as you call him.*

Oh, are we sharing nursery tales now? Jochi asked. *Heralds? Really, Ethid?*

If you haven't noticed, Ethid wrote, *the Voidbringers are back. Tales we dismissed are worth a second look, now.*

I agree, Jasnah wrote. *But what makes you think you've found one of the Heralds?*

It's a combination of many things, she wrote. *This man attacked our palace, Jasnah. He tried to kill some thieves—the new Prime is one of them, but keep that in your sleeve. We're doing what we can to play up his common roots while ignoring the fact that he was intent on robbing us.*

Heralds alive and trying to kill people, Jochi wrote. *And here I thought my news about a sighting of Axies the Collector was interesting.*

There's more, Ethid wrote. *Jasnah, we've got a Radiant here. An Edgedancer. Or . . . we had one.*

Had one? Jochi wrote. *Did you misplace her?*

She ran off. She's just a kid, Jasnah. Reshi, raised on the streets.

I think we may have met her, Jasnah wrote. *My uncle encountered someone interesting in one of his recent visions. I'm surprised you let her get away from you.*

Have you ever tried to hold on to an Edgedancer? Ethid wrote back. *She chased after the Herald to Tashikk, but the Prime says she is back now—and avoiding me. In any case, something's wrong with the man I think is Nalan, Jasnah. I don't think the Heralds will be a resource to us.*

I will provide you with sketches of the Heralds, Jasnah said. *I have drawings of their true faces, provided by an unexpected source. Ethid, you are right about them. They aren't going to be a resource; they're broken. Have you read the accounts of my uncle's visions?*

I have copies somewhere, Ethid wrote. *Are they real? Most sources agree that he's . . . unwell.*

He's quite well, I assure you, Jasnah wrote. *The visions are related to his order of Radiants. I will send you the latest few; they have relevance to the Heralds.*

Storms, Ethid wrote. *The Blackthorn is actually a Radiant? Years of drought, and now they're popping up like rockbuds.*

Ethid did not think highly of men who earned their reputations through conquest, despite having made the study of such men a cornerstone of her research.

The conversation continued for some time. Jochi, growing uncharacteristically solemn, spoke directly of the state of Thaylenah. It had been hit hard by the repeated coming of the Everstorm; entire sections of Thaylen City were in ruin.

Jasnah was most interested in the Thaylen parshmen who had stolen the ships that had survived the storm. Their exodus—combined with Kaladin Stormblessed's interactions with the parshmen in Alethkar—was painting a new picture of what and who the Voidbringers were.

The conversation moved on as Ethid transcribed an interesting account she'd discovered in an old book discussing the Desolations. From there, they spoke of the Dawnchant translations, in particular those by some ardents in Jah Keved who were ahead of the scholars at Kharbranth.

Jasnah glanced through the library room, seeking out her mother, who was sitting near Shallan to discuss wedding preparations. Renarin still lurked at the far side of the room, mumbling to himself. Or perhaps to his spren? She absently read his lips.

—it's coming from in here, Renarin said. *Somewhere in this room—*

Jasnah narrowed her eyes.

Ethid, she wrote, *weren't you going to try to construct drawings of the spren tied to each order of Radiant?*

I've gotten quite far, actually, she wrote back. *I saw the Edgedancer spren personally, after demanding a glimpse.*

What of the Truthwatchers? Jasnah wrote.

Oh! I found a reference to those, Jochi wrote. *The spren reportedly looked like light on a surface after it reflects through something crystalline.*

Jasnah thought for a moment, then briefly excused herself from the conversation. Jochi said he needed to go find a privy anyway. She slipped off her seat and crossed the room, passing near Navani and Shallan.

"I don't want to push you at all, dear," Navani was saying. "But in these uncertain times, surely you wish for stability."

Jasnah stopped, freehand resting idly on Shallan's shoulder. The younger woman perked up, then followed Jasnah's gaze toward Renarin.

"What?" Shallan whispered.

"I don't know," Jasnah said. "Something odd . . ."

Something about the way the youth was standing, the words he had spoken. He still looked wrong to her without his spectacles. Like a different person entirely.

"Jasnah!" Shallan said, suddenly tense. "The doorway. Look!"

Jasnah sucked in Stormlight at the girl's tone and turned away from Renarin, toward the room's doorway. There, a tall, square-jawed man had darkened the opening. He wore Sadeas's colors, forest green and white. In fact, he *was* Sadeas now, at least its regent.

Jasnah would always know him as Meridas Amaram.

"What's *he* doing here?" Shallan hissed.

"He's a highprince," Navani said. "The soldiers aren't going to forbid him without a direct command."

Amaram fixated on Jasnah with regal, light tan eyes. He strode toward her, exuding confidence, or was it conceit? "Jasnah," he said when he drew close. "I was told I could find you here."

"Remind me to find whoever told you," Jasnah said, "and have them hanged."

Amaram stiffened. "Could we speak together more privately, just for a moment?"

"I think not."

"We need to discuss your uncle. The rift between our houses serves nobody. I wish to bridge that chasm, and Dalinar listens to you. Please, Jasnah. You can steer him properly."

"My uncle knows his own mind on these matters, and doesn't require me to 'steer' him."

"As if you haven't been doing so already, Jasnah. Everyone can see that he has started to share your religious beliefs."

"Which would be incredible, since I don't *have* religious beliefs."

Amaram sighed, looking around. "Please," he said. "Private?"

"Not a chance, Meridas. Go. Away."

"We were close once."

"My father *wished* us to be close. Do not mistake his fancies for fact."

"Jasnah—"

"You really should leave before somebody gets hurt."

He ignored her suggestion, glancing at Navani and Shallan, then stepping closer. "We thought you were *dead*. I needed to see for myself that you are well."

"You have seen. Now leave."

Instead, he gripped her forearm. "Why, Jasnah? *Why* have you always denied me?"

"Other than the fact that you are a detestable buffoon who achieves only the lowest level of mediocrity, as it is the best your limited mind can imagine? I can't possibly think of a reason."

"Mediocre?" Amaram growled. "You insult my mother, Jasnah. You know how hard she worked to raise me to be the best soldier this kingdom has ever known."

"Yes, from what I understand, she spent the seven months she was with child entertaining each and every military man she could find, in the hopes that something of them would stick to you."

Meridas's eyes widened, and his face flushed deeply. To their side, Shallan audibly gasped.

"You godless *whore*," Amaram hissed, releasing her. "If you weren't a woman . . ."

"If I weren't a woman, I suspect we wouldn't be having this conversation. Unless I were a pig. Then you'd be doubly interested."

He thrust his hand to the side, stepping back, preparing to summon his Blade.

Jasnah smiled, holding her freehand toward him, letting Stormlight curl and rise from it. "Oh, please do, Meridas. Give me an excuse. I dare you."

He stared at her hand. The entire room had gone silent, of course. He'd forced her to make a spectacle. His eyes flicked up to meet hers; then he spun and stalked from the room, shoulders hunched as if trying to shrug away the eyes—and the snickers—of the scholars.

He will be trouble, Jasnah thought. *Even more than he has been.* Amaram genuinely thought he was Alethkar's only hope and salvation, and had a keen desire to prove it. Left alone, he'd rip the armies apart to justify his inflated opinion of himself.

She'd speak with Dalinar. Perhaps the two of them could devise something to keep Amaram safely occupied. And if that didn't work, she *wouldn't* speak to Dalinar about the other precaution she would take. She'd been out of touch for a long time, but she was confident there would be assassins for hire here, ones who knew her reputation for discretion and excellent pay.

A high-pitched sound came from beside her, and Jasnah glanced to find Shallan sitting perkily on her seat, making an excited noise in the back of her throat and clapping her hands together quickly, the sound muffled by her clothed safehand.

Wonderful.

"Mother," Jasnah said, "might I speak for a moment with my ward?"

Navani nodded, her eyes lingering on the doorway where Amaram had exited. Once, she'd pushed for the union between them. Jasnah didn't blame her; the truth of Amaram was difficult to see, and had been even more so in the past, when he'd been close to Jasnah's father.

Navani withdrew, leaving Shallan alone at the table stacked with reports.

"Brightness!" Shallan said as Jasnah sat. "That was incredible!"

"I let myself be pushed into abundant emotion."

"You were so *clever!*"

"And yet, my first insult was not to attack *him,* but the moral reputation of his *female relative.* Clever? Or simply the use of an obvious bludgeon?"

"Oh. Um . . . Well . . ."

"Regardless," Jasnah cut in, wishing to avoid further conversation about Amaram, "I've been thinking about your training."

Shallan stiffened immediately. "I've been very busy, Brightness. However, I'm sure I'll be able to get to those books you assigned me very soon."

Jasnah rubbed her forehead. This girl . . .

"Brightness," Shallan said, "I think I might have to request a leave from my studies." Shallan spoke so quickly the words ran into one another. "His Majesty says he needs me to go with him on the expedition to Kholinar."

Jasnah frowned. Kholinar? "Nonsense. They'll have the Windrunner with them. Why do they need you?"

"The king is worried they might need to sneak into the city," Shallan said. "Or even through the middle of it, if it's occupied. We can't know how far the siege has progressed. If Elhokar has to reach the Oathgate without being recognized, then my illusions will be invaluable. I have to go. It's so inconvenient. I'm sorry." She took a deep breath, eyes wide, as if afraid that Jasnah would snap at her.

This girl.

"I'll speak with Elhokar," Jasnah said. "I feel that might be extreme. For now, I want you to do drawings of Renarin's and Kaladin's spren, for scholarly reasons. Bring them to me for . . ." She trailed off. "What *is* he doing?"

Renarin stood near the far wall, which was covered in palm-size tiles. He tapped a specific one, and somehow made it pop *out*, like a drawer.

Jasnah stood, throwing back her chair. She strode across the room, Shallan scampering along behind her.

Renarin glanced at them, then held up what he'd found in the small drawer. A ruby, long as Jasnah's thumb, cut into a strange shape with holes drilled in it. What on Roshar? She took it from him and held it up.

"What is it?" Navani said, shouldering up beside her. "A fabrial? No metal parts. What is that shape?"

Jasnah reluctantly surrendered it to her mother.

"So many imperfections in the cut," Navani said. "That will cause it to lose Stormlight quickly. It won't even hold a charge for a day, I bet. And it will vibrate something fierce."

Curious. Jasnah touched it, infusing the gemstone with Stormlight. It started glowing, but not nearly as brightly as it should have. Navani was, of course, right. It vibrated as Stormlight curled off it. Why would anyone spoil a gem with such a twisted cut, and why hide it? The small drawer was latched with a spring, but she couldn't see how Renarin had gotten it undone.

"Storms," Shallan whispered as other scholars crowded around. "That's a pattern."

"A pattern?"

"Buzzes in sequence . . ." Shallan said. "My spren says he thinks this is a code. Letters?"

"Music of language," Renarin whispered. He drew in Stormlight from some spheres in his pocket, then turned and pressed his hands against the wall, sending a surge of Stormlight through it that extended from his palms like twin ripples on the surface of a pond.

Drawers slid open, one behind each white tile. A hundred, two hundred . . . each revealing gemstones inside.

The library had decayed, but the ancient Radiants had obviously anticipated that.

They'd found another way to pass on their knowledge.

*I would have thought, before attaining my current station, that a
deity could not be surprised.*

*Obviously, this is not true. I can be surprised. I can perhaps
even be naive, I think.*

I'm just asking," Khen grumbled, "how this is any better. We were
slaves under the Alethi. Now we're slaves under the Fused. Great. It
does me so much good to know that our misery is now at the hands of
our own people." The parshwoman set her bundle down with a rattling
thump.

"You'll get us in trouble again, talking like that," Sah said. He dropped
his bundle of wooden poles, then walked back the other way.

Moash followed, passing rows of humans and parshmen turning the
poles into ladders. These, like Sah and the rest of his team, would soon be
carrying those ladders into battle, facing down a storm of arrows.

What a strange echo of his life months ago in Sadeas's warcamp. Except here he'd been given sturdy gloves, a nice pair of boots, and three solid
meals a day. The only thing wrong with the situation—other than the
fact that he and the others would soon be charging a fortified position—
was that he had too much free time.

The workers hauled stacks of wood from one part of the lumberyard to
the next, and were occasionally assigned to saw or chop. But there wasn't
enough to keep them busy. That was a very bad thing, as he'd learned
on the Shattered Plains. Give condemned men too much time and they'd
start to ask questions.

"Look," Khen said, walking next to Sah just ahead, "at least tell me you're *angry*, Sah. Don't tell me you think we *deserve* this."

"We harbored a spy," Sah muttered.

A spy that, Moash had quickly learned, had been none other than *Kaladin Stormblessed*.

"Like a bunch of slaves should be able to spot a spy?" Khen said. "Really? Shouldn't the *spren* have been the one to spot him? It's like they wanted something to pin on us. Like it's . . . it's a . . ."

"Like it's a setup?" Moash asked from behind.

"Yeah, a setup," Khen agreed.

They did that a lot, forgetting words. Or . . . maybe they were simply trying the words out for the first time.

Their accent was so similar to that of many of the bridgemen who had been Moash's friends.

Let go, Moash, something deep within him whispered. *Give up your pain. It's all right. You did what was natural.*

You can't be blamed. Stop carrying that burden.

Let go.

They each picked up another bundle and began walking back. They passed the carpenters who were making the ladder poles. Most of these were parshmen, and one of the Fused walked among their ranks. He was a head taller than the parshmen, and was a subspecies that grew large portions of carapace armor in wicked shapes.

The Fused stopped, then explained something to one of the working parshmen. The Fused made a fist, and dark violet energy surrounded his arm. Carapace grew there into the shape of a saw. The Fused sawed, carefully explaining what he did. Moash had seen this before. Some of these monsters from the void were *carpenters*.

Out beyond the lumberyards, parshman troops practiced close-order drill and received basic weapon training. Word was that the army intended to assault Kholinar within weeks. That was ambitious, but they didn't have time for an extended siege. Kholinar had Soulcasters to make food, while the Voidbringer operations in the country would take months to get going. This Voidbringer army would soon eat itself out of supplies, and would have to divide up to forage. Better to attack, use overwhelming numbers, and seize the Soulcasters for themselves.

Every army needed someone to run at the front and soak up arrows. Well organized or not, benevolent or not, the Voidbringers couldn't avoid that. Moash's group wouldn't be trained; they were really only waiting until the assault so they could run in front of more valuable troops.

"We were set up," Khen repeated as they walked. "They knew they had too few humans strong enough to run the first assault. They need some of us in there, so they found a *reason* to toss us out to die."

Sah grunted.

"Is that all you're going to say?" Khen demanded. "Don't you care what our *own gods* are doing to us?"

Sah slammed his bundle to the ground. "Yes, I *care*," Sah snapped. "You think I haven't been asking the same questions? Storms! They took my daughter, Khen! They ripped her away from me and sent me off to die."

"Then what do we do?" Khen asked, her voice growing small. "What do we *do*?"

Sah looked around at the army moving and churning, preparing for war. Overwhelming, enveloping, like its own kind of storm—in motion and inexorable. The sort of thing that picked you up and carried you along.

"I don't know," Sah whispered. "Storms, Khen. I don't know anything."

I do, Moash thought. But he couldn't find the will to say anything to them. Instead, he found himself annoyed, angerspren boiling up around him. He felt frustrated both at himself and at the Voidbringers. He slammed his bundle down, but then stalked off, out of the lumberyard.

An overseer yelped loudly and scuttled after him—but she didn't stop him, and neither did the guards he passed. He had a reputation.

Moash strode through the city, tailed by the overseer, searching for one of the flying type of Fused. They seemed to be in charge, even of the other Fused.

He couldn't find one, so he settled for approaching one of the other subspecies: a malen that sat near the city's cistern, where rainwater collected. The creature was of the heavily armored type, with no hair, the carapace encroaching across his cheeks.

Moash strode right up to the creature. "I need to talk to someone in charge."

Behind him, Moash's overseer gasped—perhaps only now realizing that whatever it was Moash was up to, it could get her in serious trouble.

The Fused regarded him and grinned.

"Someone in charge," Moash repeated.

The Voidbringer laughed, then fell backward into the water of the cistern, where he floated, staring at the sky.

Great, Moash thought. *One of the crazy ones.* There were many of those.

Moash stalked away, but didn't get much farther into the town before something dropped from the sky. Cloth fluttered in the air, and in the middle of it floated a creature with skin that matched the black and red clothing. He couldn't tell if it was malen or femalen.

"Little human," the creature said with a foreign accent, "you are passionate and interesting."

Moash licked his lips. "I need to talk to someone in charge."

"You *need* nothing but what we give you," the Fused said. "But your *desire* is to be granted. Lady Leshwi will see you."

"Great. Where can I find her?"

The Fused pressed its hand against his chest and smiled. Dark Voidlight spread from its hand across Moash's body. Both of them rose into the air.

Panicking, Moash clutched at the Fused. Could he get the creature into a chokehold? *Then* what? If he killed it up here, he'd drop to his own death.

They rose until the town looked like a tiny model: lumberyard and parade ground on one side, the single prominent street down the center. To the right, the man-made ward provided a buffer against the highstorms, creating a shelter for trees and the citylord's mansion.

They ascended even farther, the Fused's loose clothes fluttering. Though the air was warm at ground level, up here it was quite chilly, and Moash's ears felt odd—dull, as if they were stuffed with cloth.

Finally, the Fused slowed them to a hovering stop. Though Moash tried to hold on, the Fused shoved him to the side, then zoomed away in a flaring roil of cloth.

Moash drifted alone above the expansive landscape. His heart thundered, and he regarded that drop, realizing something. He did *not* want to die.

He forced himself to twist and look about him. He felt a surge of hope as he found he was drifting toward another Fused. A woman who hovered in the sky, wearing robes that must have extended a good ten feet below her, like a smear of red paint. Moash drifted right up beside her, getting so close that she was able to reach out and stop him.

He resisted grabbing that arm and hanging on for dear life. His mind was catching up to what was happening—she wanted to meet him, but in a realm where she belonged and he did not. Well, he would contain his fear.

"Moash," the Fused said. Leshwi, the other had called her. She had a face that was all three Parshendi colors: white, red, and black, marbled like paint swirled together. He had rarely seen someone who was all three colors before, and this was one of the most transfixing patterns he'd seen, almost liquid in its effect, her eyes like pools around which the colors ran.

"How do you know my name?" Moash asked.

"Your overseer told me," Leshwi said. She had a distinct serenity about her as she floated with feet down. The wind up here tugged at the ribbons she wore, pushing them backward in careless ripples. There were no windspren in sight, oddly. "Where did you get that name?"

"My grandfather named me," Moash said, frowning. This was not how he'd anticipated this conversation going.

"Curious. Do you know that it is one of our names?"

"It is?"

She nodded. "How long has it drifted on the tides of time, passing from the lips of singers to men and back, to end up here, on the head of a human slave?"

"Look, you're one of the leaders?"

"I'm one of the Fused who is sane," she said, as if it were the same thing.

"Then I need to—"

"You're bold," Leshwi said, eyes forward. "Many of the singers we left here are not. We find them remarkable, considering how long they were abused by your people. But still, they are not bold enough."

She looked to him for the first time during the conversation. Her face was angular, with long flowing parshman hair—black and crimson, thicker than that of a human. Almost like thin reeds or blades of grass. Her eyes were a deep red, like pools of shimmering blood.

"Where did you learn the Surges, human?" she asked.

"The Surges?"

"When you killed me," she said, "you were Lashed to the sky—but you responded quickly, with familiarity. I will say, without guile, that I was furious to be caught so unaware."

"Wait," Moash said, cold. "When I *killed* you?"

She regarded him, unblinking, with those ruby eyes.

"You're the same one?" Moash asked. *That pattern of marbled skin . . .* he realized. *It's the same as the one I fought.* But the features were different.

"This is a new body offered to me in sacrifice," Leshwi said. "To bond and make my own, as I have none."

"You're some kind of spren?"

She blinked but did not reply.

Moash started to drop. He felt it in his clothes, which lost their power to fly first. He cried out, reaching toward the Fused woman, and she seized him by the wrist and injected him with more Voidlight. It surged across his body, and he hovered again. The violet darkness retreated, visible again only as faint periodic crackles on her skin.

"My companions spared you," she said to him. "Brought you here, to these lands, as they thought I might wish personal vengeance once reborn. I did not. Why would I destroy that which had such passion? Instead I watched you, curious to see what you did. I saw you help the singers who were pulling the sledges."

Moash took a deep breath. "Can you tell me, then, why you treat your own so poorly?"

"Poorly?" she said, sounding amused. "They are fed, clothed, and trained."

"Not all of them," Moash said. "You had those poor parshmen working as slaves, like humans. And now you're going to throw them at the city walls."

"Sacrifice," she said. "Do you think an empire is built without sacrifice?" She swept her arm across the landscape before them.

Moash's stomach turned over; he'd briefly been able to fixate only on her and forget exactly how *high* he was. Storms . . . this land was big. He could see extensive hills, plains, grass, trees, and stone in all directions.

And in the direction she gestured, a dark line on the horizon. Kholinar?

"I breathe again because of their sacrifices," Leshwi said. "And this world will be ours, because of sacrifice. Those who fall will be sung of, but their blood is ours to demand. If they survive the assault, if they prove themselves, then they will be honored." She looked to him again. "You fought for them during the trip here."

"Honestly, I expected you to have me killed for that."

"If you were not killed for striking down one of the Fused," she said, "then why would you be killed for striking one of our lessers? In both cases, human, you proved your passion and earned your right to succeed. Then you bowed to authority when presented, and earned your right to continue to live. Tell me. *Why* did you protect those slaves?"

"Because you need to be unified," Moash said. He swallowed. "My people don't deserve this land. We're broken, ruined. Incapable."

She cocked her head. A cool wind played with her clothing. "And are you not angered that we took your Shards?"

"They were first given me by a man I betrayed. I . . . don't deserve them."

No. Not you. It's not your fault.

"You aren't angry that we conquer you?"

"No."

"Then what *does* anger you? What is your passionate fury, Moash, the man with an ancient singer's name?"

Yes, it was there. Still burning. Deep down.

Storm it, Kaladin had been protecting a *murderer.*

"Vengeance," he whispered.

"Yes, I understand." She looked at him, smiling in what seemed to him a distinctly sinister way. "Do you know why *we* fight? Let me tell you. . . ."

⁚⁚

A half hour later as evening approached, Moash walked the streets of a conquered town. By himself. Lady Leshwi had ordered that Moash be left alone, freed.

He walked with his hands in the pockets of his Bridge Four coat, remembering the frigid air up above. He still felt chilled, even though down here it was muggy and warm.

This was a nice town. Quaint. Little stone buildings, plants growing at the backs of every house. On his left, that meant cultivated rockbuds and bushes burst from around doors—but to his right, facing the storm, there were only blank stone walls. Not even a window.

The plants smelled of civilization to him. A sort of civic perfume that you didn't get out in the wilds. They barely quivered as he passed, though lifespren bobbed at his presence. The plants were accustomed to people on the streets.

He finally stopped at a low fence surrounding pens holding the horses the Voidbringers had captured. The animals munched cut grass the parshmen had thrown to them.

Such strange beasts. Hard to care for, expensive to keep. He turned from the horses and looked out over the fields toward Kholinar. She'd said he could leave. Join the refugees making for the capital. Defend the city.

What is your passionate fury?

Thousands of years being reborn. What would it be like? Thousands of years, and they'd never given up.

Prove yourself . . .

He turned and made his way back to the lumberyard, where the workers were packing up for the day. There was no storm projected tonight, and they wouldn't have to secure everything, so they worked with a relaxed, almost jovial air. All save for his crew, who—as usual—gathered by themselves, ostracized.

Moash seized a bundle of ladder rods off a pile. The workers there turned to object, but cut off when they saw who it was. He untied the bundle and, upon reaching the crew of unfortunate parshmen, tossed a length of wood to each one.

Sah caught his and stood up, frowning. The others mimicked him.

"I can train you with those," Moash said.

"Sticks?" Khen asked.

"Spears," Moash said. "I can teach you to be soldiers. We'll probably die anyway. Storm it, we'll probably never make it to the top of the walls. But it's something."

The parshmen looked at one another, holding rods that could mimic spears.

"I'll do it," Khen said.

Slowly, the others nodded in agreement.

ALONE TOGETHER

*I am the least equipped, of all, to aid you in this endeavor. I am
finding that the powers I hold are in such conflict that the most
simple of actions can be difficult.*

Rlain sat on the Shattered Plains alone and listened to the rhythms.
Enslaved parshmen, deprived of true forms, weren't able to
hear the rhythms. During his years spent as a spy, he'd adopted
dullform, which heard them weakly. It had been so hard to be apart from
them.

They weren't quite true songs; they were beats with hints of tonality and
harmony. He could attune one of several dozen to match his mood, or—
conversely—to help alter his mood.

His people had always assumed the humans were deaf to the rhythms,
but he wasn't convinced. Perhaps it was his imagination, but it seemed that
sometimes they responded to certain rhythms. They'd look up at a moment
of frenzied beats, eyes getting a far-off look. They'd grow agitated and shout
in time, for a moment, to the Rhythm of Irritation, or whoop right on beat
with the Rhythm of Joy.

It comforted him to think that they might someday learn to hear the
rhythms. Perhaps then he wouldn't feel so alone.

He currently attuned the Rhythm of the Lost, a quiet yet violent beat
with sharp, separated notes. You attuned it to remember the fallen, and
that felt the correct emotion as he sat here outside Narak, watching humans
build a fortress from what used to be his home. They set a watchpost atop
the central spire, where the Five had once met to discuss the future of his
people. They turned homes into barracks.

He was not offended—his own people had repurposed the ruins of Stormseat into Narak. No doubt these stately ruins would outlast the Alethi occupation, as they had the listeners. That knowledge did not prevent him from mourning. His people were gone, now. Yes, parshmen had awakened, but they were not listeners. No more than Alethi and Vedens were the same nationality, simply because most had similar skin tones.

Rlain's people were gone. They had fallen to Alethi swords or had been consumed by the Everstorm, transformed into incarnations of the old listener gods. He was, as far as he knew, the last.

He sighed, pulling himself to his feet. He swung a spear to his shoulder, the spear they *let* him carry. He loved the men of Bridge Four, but he was an oddity, even to them: the parshman they allowed to be armed. The potential Voidbringer they had decided to trust, and wasn't he just so lucky.

He crossed the plateau to where a group of them trained under Teft's watchful eye. They didn't wave to him. They often seemed surprised to find him there, as if they'd forgotten he was around. But when Teft did notice him, the man's smile was genuine. They were his friends. It was merely . . .

How could Rlain be so fond of these men, yet at the same time want to slap them?

When he and Skar had been the only two who couldn't draw Stormlight, they'd encouraged Skar. They'd given him pep talks, told him to keep trying. They had believed in him. Rlain, though . . . well, who knew what would happen if he could use Stormlight? Might it be the first step in turning him into a monster?

Never mind that he'd told them you had to open yourself to a form to adopt it. Never mind that he had the power to *choose* for himself. Though they never spoke it, he saw the truth in their reactions. As with Dabbid, they thought it best that Rlain remain without Stormlight.

The parshman and the insane man. People you couldn't trust as Windrunners.

Five bridgemen launched into the air, Radiant and steaming with Light. Some of the crew trained while another group patrolled with Kaladin, checking on caravans. A third group—the ten other newcomers that had learned to draw in Stormlight—trained with Peet a few plateaus over. That group included Lyn and all *four* of the other scouts, along with four men from other bridge crews, and a single lighteyed officer. Colot, the archer captain.

Lyn had slid into Bridge Four's comradery easily, as had a couple of the bridgemen. Rlain tried not to feel jealous that they almost seemed more a part of the team than he did.

Teft led the five in the air through a formation while the four others strolled toward Rock's drink station. Rlain joined them, and Yake slapped him on the back, pointing toward the next plateau over, where the bulk of the hopefuls continued to train.

"That group can barely hold a spear properly," Yake said. "You ought to go show them how a *real* bridgeman does a kata, eh, Rlain?"

"Kalak help them if they have to fight those shellheads," Eth added, taking a drink from Rock. "Um, no offense, Rlain."

Rlain touched his head, where he had carapace armor—distinctively thick and strong, as he held warform—covering his skull. It had stretched out his Bridge Four tattoo, which had transferred to the carapace. He had protrusions on his arms and legs too, and people always wanted to feel those. They couldn't believe they actually grew from his skin, and somehow thought it was appropriate to try to peek underneath.

"Rlain," Rock said. "Is okay to throw things at Eth. He has hard head too, almost like he has shell."

"It's all right," Rlain said, because that was what they expected him to say. He accidentally attuned Irritation, though, and the rhythm laced his words.

To cover his embarrassment, he attuned Curiosity and tried Rock's drink of the day. "This is good! What is in it?"

"Ha! Is water I boiled cremlings in, before serving them last night."

Eth spurted out his mouthful of drink, then looked at the cup, aghast.

"What?" Rock said. "You ate the cremlings easily!"

"But this is . . . like their *bathwater*," Eth complained.

"Chilled," Rock said, "with spices. Is good taste."

"Is bathwater," Eth said, imitating Rock's accent.

Teft led the other four in a streaking wave of light overhead. Rlain looked up, and found himself attuning Longing before he stomped it out. He attuned Peace instead. Peace, yes. He could be peaceful.

"This isn't working," Drehy said. "We can't storming patrol the entirety of the Shattered Plains. More caravans are going to get hit, like that one last night."

"The captain says it's strange for those Voidbringers to keep raiding like this," Eth said.

"Tell that to the caravaneers from yesterday."

Yake shrugged. "They didn't even burn much; we got there before the Voidbringers had time to do much more than frighten everyone. I'm with the captain. It's strange."

"Maybe they're testing our abilities," Eth said. "Seeing what Bridge Four can really do."

They glanced at Rlain for confirmation.

"Am . . . am I supposed to be able to answer?" he asked.

"Well," Eth said. "I mean . . . storms, Rlain. They're your kinsmen. Surely you know something about them."

"You can guess, right?" Yake said.

Rock's daughter refilled his cup for him, and Rlain looked down at the clear liquid. *Don't blame them*, he thought. *They don't know. They don't understand.*

"Eth, Yake," Rlain said carefully, "my people did everything we could to separate ourselves from those creatures. We went into hiding long ago, and swore we would never accept forms of power again.

"I don't know what changed. My people must have been tricked somehow. In any case, these Fused are as much my enemies as they are yours— *more*, even. And no, I can't say what they will do. I spent my entire life trying to avoid thinking of them."

Teft's group came crashing down to the plateau. For all his earlier difficulty, Skar had quickly taken to flight. His landing was the most graceful of the bunch. Hobber hit so hard he yelped.

They jogged over to the watering station, where Rock's eldest daughter and son began giving them drinks. Rlain felt sorry for the two; they barely spoke Alethi, though the son—oddly—was Vorin. Apparently, monks came from Jah Keved to preach the Almighty to the Horneaters, and Rock let his children follow any god they wanted. So it was that the pale-skinned young Horneater wore a glyphward tied to his arm and burned prayers to the Vorin Almighty instead of making offerings to the Horneater spren.

Rlain sipped his drink and wished Renarin were here; the quiet, light-eyed man usually made a point of speaking with Rlain. The others jabbered excitedly, but didn't think to include him. Parshmen were invisible to them—they'd been brought up that way.

And yet, he loved them because they *did* try. When Skar bumped him—and was reminded that he was there—he blinked, then said, "Maybe we should ask Rlain." The others immediately jumped in and said he didn't want to talk about it, giving a kind of Alethi version of what he'd told them earlier.

He belonged here as much as he did anywhere else. Bridge Four was his family, now that those from Narak were gone. Eshonai, Varanis, Thude . . .

He attuned the Rhythm of the Lost and bowed his head. He had to believe that his friends in Bridge Four could feel a hint of the rhythms, for otherwise how would they know how to mourn with true pain of soul?

Teft was getting ready to take the other squad into the air when a group of dots in the sky announced the arrival of Kaladin Stormblessed. He landed with his squad, including Lopen, who juggled an uncut gemstone the size of a man's head. They must have found a chrysalis from a beast of the chasms.

"No sign of Voidbringers today," Leyten said, turning over one of Rock's buckets and using it as a seat. "But storms . . . the Plains sure do seem smaller when you're up there."

"Yeah," Lopen said. "And *bigger*."

"Smaller and bigger?" Skar asked.

"Smaller," Leyten said, "because we can cross them so fast. I remember plateaus that felt like they took *years* to cross. We zip past those in an eyeblink."

"But then you get up high," Lopen added, "and you realize how wide this place is—sure, how much of it we never even explored—and it just seems . . . big."

The others nodded, eager. You had to read their emotion in their expressions and the way they moved, not in their voices. Maybe that was why emotion spren came so often to humans, more often than to listeners. Without the rhythms, men needed help understanding one another.

"Who's on the next patrol?" Skar asked.

"None for today," Kaladin said. "I have a meeting with Dalinar. We'll leave a squad in Narak, but . . ."

Soon after he left through the Oathgate, everyone would slowly start to lose their powers. They'd be gone in an hour or two. Kaladin had to be relatively near—Sigzil had placed their maximum distance from him at around fifty miles, though their abilities started to fade somewhere around thirty miles.

"Fine," Skar said. "I was looking forward to drinking more of Rock's cremling juice anyway."

"Cremling juice?" Sigzil said, drink halfway to his lips. Other than Rlain, Sigzil's dark brown skin was the most different from the rest of the crew—though the bridgemen didn't seem to care much about skin color. To them, only eyes mattered. Rlain had always found that strange, as among listeners, your skin patterns had at times been a matter of some import.

"So . . ." Skar said. "Are we going to talk about Renarin?"

The twenty-eight men shared looks, many settling down around the barrel of Rock's drink as they once had around the cookfire. There were certainly a suspicious number of buckets to use as stools, as if Rock had planned for this. The Horneater himself leaned against the table he'd brought out for holding cups, a cleaning rag thrown over his shoulder.

"What about him?" Kaladin asked, frowning and looking around at the group.

"He's been spending a lot of time with the scribes studying the tower city," Natam said.

"The other day," Skar added, "he was talking about what he's doing there. It sounded an *awful* lot like he was learning how to read."

The men shifted uncomfortably.

"So?" Kaladin asked. "What's the problem? Sigzil can read his own language. Storms, *I* can read glyphs."

"It's not the same," Skar said.

"It's feminine," Drehy added.

"Drehy," Kaladin said, "you are *literally* courting a man."

"So?" Drehy said.

"Yeah, what are you saying, Kal?" Skar snapped.

"Nothing! I just thought Drehy might empathize. . . ."

"That's hardly fair," Drehy said.

"Yeah," Lopen added. "Drehy likes other guys. That's like . . . he wants to be even less around women than the rest of us. It's the *opposite* of feminine. He is, you could say, extra manly."

"Yeah," Drehy said.

Kaladin rubbed his forehead, and Rlain empathized. It was sad that humans were so burdened by always being in mateform. They were *always* distracted by the emotions and passions of mating, and had not yet reached a place where they could put that aside.

He felt embarrassed for them—they were simply too concerned about what a person should and shouldn't be doing. It was because they didn't have forms to change into. If Renarin wanted to be a scholar, let him be a scholar.

"I'm sorry," Kaladin said, holding out his hand to calm the men. "I wasn't trying to insult Drehy. But storms, men. We know that things are changing. Look at the lot of us. We're halfway to being lighteyes! We've already let five women into Bridge Four, and they'll be fighting with spears. Expectations are being upended—and *we're* the cause of it. So let's give Renarin a little leeway, shall we?"

Rlain nodded. Kaladin *was* a good man. For all his faults, he tried even more than the rest of them.

"I have thing to say," Rock added. "During last few weeks, how many of you have come to me, saying you feel you don't fit in with Bridge Four now?"

The plateau fell silent. Finally, Sigzil raised his hand. Followed by Skar. And several others, including Hobber.

"Hobber, you did not come to me," Rock noted.

"Oh. Yeah, but I felt like it, Rock." He glanced down. "Everything's changing. I don't know if I can keep up."

"I still have nightmares," Leyten said softly, "about what we saw in the bowels of Urithiru. Anyone else?"

"I have trouble Alethi," Huio said. "It makes me . . . embarrassing. Alone."

"I'm scared of heights," Torfin added. "Flying up there is terrifying to me."

A few glanced at Teft.

"What?" Teft demanded. "You expect this to be a feeling-sharing party because the storming Horneater gave you a sour eye? Storm off. It's a miracle I'm not burning moss every moment of the day, having to deal with you lot."

Natam patted him on the shoulder.

"And I will not fight," Rock said. "I know some of you do not like this. He makes me feel different. Not only because I am only one with proper beard in crew." He leaned forward. "Life *is* changing. We will all feel alone because of this, yes? Ha! Perhaps we can feel alone together."

They all seemed to find this comforting. Well, except Lopen, who had snuck away from the group and for some reason was lifting up rocks on the other side of the plateau and looking underneath them. Even among humans, he was a strange one.

The men relaxed and started to chat. Though Hobber slapped Rlain on the back, it was the closest any of them came to asking how he felt. Was it childish of him to feel frustrated? They all thought they were alone, did they? Felt that they were outsiders? Did they *know* what it was like to be of an entirely different species? A species they were currently at war with—a species whose people had all been either murdered or corrupted?

People in the tower watched him with outright hatred. His friends didn't, but they sure did like to pat themselves on the back for that fact. *We understand that you're not like the others, Rlain. You can't help what you look like.*

He attuned Annoyance and sat there until Kaladin sent the rest of them off to train the aspiring Windrunners. Kaladin spoke softly with Rock, then turned and paused, seeing Rlain sitting there on his bucket.

"Rlain," Kaladin said, "why don't you take the rest of the day off?"

What if I don't want special accommodation because you feel sorry for me?

Kaladin squatted down beside Rlain. "Hey. You heard what Rock said. I know how you feel. We can help you shoulder this."

"Do you really?" Rlain said. "Do you *actually* know how I feel, Kaladin Stormblessed? Or is that simply a thing that men say?"

"I guess it's a thing men say," Kaladin admitted, then pulled over an upside-down bucket for himself. "Can you tell me how it feels?"

Did he really want to know? Rlain considered, then attuned Resolve. "I can try."

I am also made uncertain by your subterfuge. Why have you not made yourself known to me before this? How is it you can hide? Who are you truly, and how do you know so much about Adonalsium?

Dalinar appeared in the courtyard of a strange fortress with a single towering wall of bloodred stones. It closed a large gap in a mountainous rock formation.

Around him, men carried supplies or otherwise made themselves busy, passing in and out of buildings constructed against the natural stone walls. Winter air made Dalinar's breath puff before him.

He held Navani's freehand on his left, and Jasnah's on his right. It had worked. His control over these visions was increasing beyond even what the Stormfather assumed possible. Today, by holding their hands, he had brought Navani and Jasnah in without a highstorm.

"Wonderful," Navani said, squeezing his hand. "That wall is as majestic as you described. And the people. Bronze weapons again, very little steel."

"That armor is Soulcast," Jasnah said, releasing his hand. "Look at the fingermarks on the metal. That's burnished iron, not true steel, Soulcast from clay into that shape. I wonder . . . did access to Soulcasters retard their drive to learn smelting? Working steel is difficult. You can't simply melt it over a fire, like you can bronze."

"So . . ." Dalinar asked, "when are we?"

"Maybe two thousand years ago," Jasnah said. "Those are Haravingian swords, and see those archways? Late classical architecture, but washed out faux blue on the cloaks, rather than true blue dyes. Mix that with the language you spoke in—which my mother recorded last time—and I'm fairly certain." She glanced at the passing soldiers. "A multiethnic coalition here, like during the Desolations—but if I'm right, this is over two thousand years after Aharietiam."

"They're fighting someone," Dalinar said. "The Radiants retreat from a battle, then abandon their weapons on the field outside."

"Which places the Recreance a little more recently than Masha-daughter-Shaliv had it in her history," Jasnah said, musing. "From my reading of your vision accounts, this is the last chronologically—though it's difficult to place the one with you overlooking ruined Kholinar."

"Who could they be fighting?" Navani asked as men atop the wall raised the alarm. Horsemen galloped out of the keep, off to investigate. "This is well after the Voidbringers left."

"It could be the False Desolation," Jasnah said.

Dalinar and Navani both looked at her.

"A legend," Jasnah said. "Considered pseudohistorical. Dovcanti wrote an epic about it somewhere around fifteen hundred years ago. The claim is that some Voidbringers survived Aharietiam, and there were many clashes with them afterward. It's considered unreliable, but that's because many later ardents insist that no Voidbringers could have survived. I'm inclined to assume this is a clash with parshmen before they were somehow deprived of their ability to change forms."

She looked to Dalinar, eyes alight, and he nodded. She strode off to collect whatever historical tidbits she could.

Navani took some instruments from her satchel. "One way or another, I'm going to figure out where this 'Feverstone Keep' is, even if I have to bully these people into drawing a map. Perhaps we could send scholars to this location and find clues about the Recreance."

Dalinar made his way over to the base of the wall. It *was* a truly majestic structure, typical of the strange contrasts of these visions: a classical people, without fabrials or even proper metallurgy, accompanied by wonders.

A group of men piled down the steps from the top of the wall. They were trailed by His Excellency Yanagawn the First, Prime Aqasix of Azir. While Dalinar had brought Navani and Jasnah by touch, he had asked the Stormfather to bring in Yanagawn. The highstorm currently raged in Azir.

The youth saw Dalinar and stopped. "Do I have to fight today, Blackthorn?"

"Not today, Your Excellency."

"I'm getting really tired of these visions," Yanagawn said, descending the last few steps.

"That fatigue never leaves, Your Excellency. In fact, it has grown as

I've begun to grasp the importance of what I have seen in vision, and the burden it puts upon me."

"That *isn't* what I meant by tired."

Dalinar didn't reply, hands clasped behind him as together they walked to the sally port, where Yanagawn watched events unfold outside. Radiants were crossing the open plain or flying down. They summoned their Blades, provoking concern from the watching soldiers.

The knights drove their weapons into the ground, then *abandoned* them. They left their armor as well. Shards of incalculable value, renounced.

The young emperor looked to be in no rush to confront them as Dalinar had been. Dalinar, therefore, took him by the arm and guided him out as the first soldiers opened the doors. He didn't want the emperor to get caught in the flood that would soon come, as men dashed for those Blades, then started killing one another.

As before in this vision, Dalinar felt as if he could hear the screaming deaths of the spren, the terrible sorrow of this field. It almost overwhelmed him.

"Why?" Yanagawn asked. "Why did they just . . . give up?"

"We don't know, Your Excellency. This scene haunts me. There is so much I don't understand. Ignorance has become the theme of my rule."

Yanagawn looked around, then scrambled for a tall boulder to climb, where he could better watch the Radiants. He seemed far more engaged by this than he had been by other visions. Dalinar could respect that. War was war, but this . . . this was something you never saw. Men willingly giving up their Shards?

And that *pain*. It pervaded the air like a terrible stench.

Yanagawn settled down on his boulder. "So why show me this? You don't even know what it means."

"If you're not going to join my coalition, I figure I should still give you as much knowledge as I can. Perhaps we will fall, and you will survive. Maybe your scholars can solve these puzzles when we cannot. And maybe you are the leader Roshar needs, while I am just an emissary."

"You don't believe that."

"I don't. I still want you to have these visions, just in case."

Yanagawn fidgeted, playing with the tassels on his leather breastplate. "I . . . don't matter as much as you think I do."

"Pardon, Your Excellency, but you underestimate your importance. Azir's Oathgate will be vital, and you are the strongest kingdom of the west. With Azir at our side, many other countries will join with us."

"I mean," Yanagawn said, "that *I* don't matter. Sure, Azir does. But I'm only a kid they put on the throne because they were afraid that assassin would come back."

"And the miracle they're publishing? The proof from the Heralds that you were chosen?"

"That was Lift, not me." Yanagawn looked down at his feet, swinging beneath him. "They're training me to act important, Kholin, but I'm not. Not yet. Maybe not ever."

This was a new face to Yanagawn. The vision today had shaken him, but not in the way Dalinar had hoped. *He's a youth,* Dalinar reminded himself. Life at his age was challenging anyway, without adding to it the stress of an unexpected accession to power.

"Whatever the reason," Dalinar told the young emperor, "you are Prime. The viziers have published your miraculous elevation to the public. You do have some measure of authority."

He shrugged. "The viziers aren't bad people. They feel guilty for putting me in this position. They give me education—kind of force it down my throat, honestly—and expect me to participate. But I'm *not* ruling the empire.

"They're scared of you. Very scared. More scared than they are of the assassin. He burned the emperors' eyes, but emperors can be replaced. You represent something far more terrible. They think you could destroy our entire culture."

"No Alethi has to set foot on Azish stone," Dalinar said. "But come to me, Your Excellency. Tell them you've seen visions, that the Heralds want you to at least *visit* Urithiru. Tell them that the opportunities far outweigh the danger of opening that Oathgate."

"And if this happens again?" Yanagawn asked, nodding toward the field of Shardblades. Hundreds of them sprouting from the ground, silvery, reflecting sunlight. Men were now pouring out of the keep, flooding toward those weapons.

"We will see that it doesn't. Somehow." Dalinar narrowed his eyes. "I don't know what caused the Recreance, but I can guess. They lost their vision, Your Excellency. They became embroiled in politics and let divisions creep among them. They forgot their purpose: protecting Roshar for its people."

Yanagawn looked to him, frowning. "That's harsh. You always seemed so respectful of the Radiants before."

"I respect those who fought in the Desolations. These? I can sympathize. I too have on occasion let myself be distracted by small-minded pettiness. But respect? No." He shivered. "They killed their spren. They betrayed their oaths! They may not be villains, as history paints them, but in this moment they failed to do what was right and just. *They failed Roshar.*"

The Stormfather rumbled in the distance, agreeing with this sentiment.

Yanagawn cocked his head.

"What?" Dalinar asked.

"Lift doesn't trust you," he said.

Dalinar glanced about, expecting her to appear as she had in the previous two visions he'd shown Yanagawn. There was no sign of the young Reshi girl that the Stormfather detested so much.

"It's because," Yanagawn continued, "you act so righteous. She says anyone who acts like you do is trying to hide something."

A soldier strode up and spoke to Yanagawn in the Almighty's voice. "They are the first."

Dalinar stepped back, letting the young emperor listen as the Almighty gave his short speech for this vision. *These events will go down in history. They will be infamous. You will have many names for what happened here . . .*

The Almighty said the same words he had to Dalinar.

The Night of Sorrows will come, and the True Desolation. The Everstorm.

The men on the field full of Shards started to fight over the weapons. For the first time in history, men started slaughtering one another with dead spren. Finally, Yanagawn faded, vanishing from the vision. Dalinar closed his eyes, feeling the Stormfather draw away. Everything now dissolved . . .

Except it didn't.

Dalinar opened his eyes. He was still on the field before the looming, bloodred wall of Feverstone Keep. Men fought over Shardblades while some voices called for everyone to be patient.

Those who claimed a Shard this day would become rulers. It bothered Dalinar that the best men, the ones calling for moderation or raising concerns, would be rare among their numbers. They weren't aggressive enough to seize the advantage.

Why was he still here? Last time, the vision had ended before this.

"Stormfather?" he asked.

No reply. Dalinar turned around.

A man in white and gold stood there.

Dalinar jumped, scrambling backward. The man was old, with a wide, furrowed face and bone-white hair that swept back from his head as if blown by wind. Thick mustaches with a hint of black in them blended into a short white beard. He seemed to be Shin, judging by his skin and eyes, and he wore a golden crown in his powdery hair.

Those eyes . . . they were ancient, the skin surrounding them deeply creased, and they danced with joy as he smiled at Dalinar and rested a golden scepter on his shoulder.

Suddenly overwhelmed, Dalinar fell to his knees. "I know you," he whispered. "You're . . . you're Him. God."

"Yes," the man said.

"Where have you been?" Dalinar said.

"I've always been here," God said. "Always with you, Dalinar. Oh, I've watched you for a long, long time."

"Here? You're . . . not the Almighty, are you?"

"Honor? No, he truly is dead, as you've been told." The old man's smile deepened, genuine and kindly. "I'm the other one, Dalinar. They call me Odium."

57

PASSION

If you would speak to me further, I request open honesty. Return to my lands, approach my servants, and I will see what I can do for your quest.

O dium.

Dalinar scrambled to his feet, lurching backward and seeking a weapon he didn't possess.

Odium. Standing in *front* of him.

The Stormfather had grown distant, almost vanished—but Dalinar could sense a faint emotion from him. A whine, like he was straining against something heavy?

No. No, that was a whimper.

Odium rested his golden scepter against the palm of his hand, then turned to regard the men fighting over Shardblades.

"I remember this day," Odium said. "Such *passion*. And such loss. Terrible for many, but glorious for others. You are wrong about why the Radiants fell, Dalinar. There was infighting among them, true, but no more than in other eras. They were honest men and women, with different views at times, but unified in their desire to do what was best."

"What do you want of me?" Dalinar said, hand to his breast, breathing quickly. Storms. He wasn't ready.

Could he *ever* be ready for this moment?

Odium strolled over to a small boulder and settled down. He sighed in relief, like a man releasing a heavy burden, then nodded to the space next to him.

Dalinar made no move to sit.

"You have been placed in a difficult position, my son," Odium said. "You are the first to bond the Stormfather in his current state. Did you know that? You are deeply connected to the remnants of a god."

"Whom you killed."

"Yes. I'll kill the other one too, eventually. She's hidden herself somewhere, and I'm too . . . shackled."

"You're a monster."

"Oh, Dalinar. This from you of all people? Tell me you've never found yourself in conflict with someone you respect. Tell me you've never killed a man because you had to, even if—in a better world—he shouldn't deserve it?"

Dalinar bit back a retort. Yes, he'd done that. Too many times.

"I know you, Dalinar," Odium said. He smiled again, a paternal expression. "Come sit down. I won't devour you, or burn you away at a touch."

Dalinar hesitated. *You need to hear what he says. Even this creature's lies can tell you more than a world of common truths.*

He walked over, then stiffly sat down.

"What do you know of us three?" Odium asked.

"Honestly, I wasn't even aware there *were* three of you."

"More, in fact," Odium said absently. "But only three of relevance to you. Me. Honor. Cultivation. You speak of her, don't you?"

"I suppose," Dalinar said. "Some people identify her with Roshar, the spren of the world itself."

"She'd like that," Odium said. "I wish I could simply let her have this place."

"So do it. Leave us alone. Go away."

Odium turned to him so sharply that Dalinar jumped. "Is that," Odium said quietly, "an offer to release me from my bonds, coming from the man holding the remnants of Honor's name and power?"

Dalinar stammered. *Idiot. You're not some raw recruit. Pull yourself together.* "No," he said firmly.

"Ah, all right then," Odium said. He smiled, a twinkle in his eyes. "Oh, don't fret so. These things must be done properly. I *will* go if you release me, but only if you do it by Intent."

"And what are the consequences of my releasing you?"

"Well, first I'd see to Cultivation's death. There would be . . . other consequences, as you call them, as well."

Eyes burned as men swept about themselves with Shardblades, killing others who had mere moments before been their comrades. It was a frantic, insane brawl for power.

"And you can't just . . . leave?" Dalinar asked. "Without killing anyone?"

"Well, let me ask you this in return. Why did you seize control of Alethkar from poor Elhokar?"

"I . . ." *Don't reply. Don't give him ammunition.*

"You knew it was for the best," Odium said. "You knew that Elhokar was weak, and the kingdom would suffer without firm leadership. You took control for the greater good, and it has served Roshar well."

Nearby, a man stumbled toward them, limping out of the fray. His eyes burned as a Shardblade rammed through his back, protruding three feet out of his chest. He fell forward, eyes trailing twin lines of smoke.

"A man cannot serve two gods at once, Dalinar," Odium said. "And so, I cannot leave her behind. In fact, I cannot leave behind the Splinters of Honor, as I once thought I could. I can already see that going wrong. Once you release me, my transformation of this realm will be substantial."

"You think you'll do better?" Dalinar wet his mouth, which had gone dry. "Do better than others would, for this land? You, a manifestation of hatred and pain?"

"They call me Odium," the old man said. "A good enough name. It does have a certain *bite* to it. But the word is too limiting to describe me, and you should know that it is not all I represent."

"Which is?"

He looked to Dalinar. "*Passion*, Dalinar Kholin. I am emotion incarnate. I am the soul of the spren and of men. I am lust, joy, hatred, anger, and exultation. I am glory and I am vice. I am the very thing that makes men *men*.

"Honor cared only for bonds. Not the *meaning* of bonds and oaths, merely that they were kept. Cultivation only wants to see transformation. Growth. It can be good or bad, for all she cares. The pain of men is nothing to her. Only I understand it. Only I *care*, Dalinar."

I don't believe that, Dalinar thought. *I can't believe that.*

The old man sighed, then heaved himself to his feet. "If you could see the result of Honor's influence, you would not be so quick to name me a god of anger. Separate the emotion from men, and you have creatures like Nale and his Skybreakers. *That* is what Honor would have given you."

Dalinar nodded toward the terrible fray on the field before them. "You said I was wrong about what caused the Radiants to abandon their oaths. What was it really?"

Odium smiled. "Passion, son. Glorious, wondrous *passion*. Emotion. It is what defines men—though ironically you are poor vessels for it. It fills you up and breaks you, unless you find someone to share the burden." He looked toward the dying men. "But can you imagine a world without it? No. Not one I'd want to live in. Ask that of Cultivation, next time you see her. Ask what she'd want for Roshar. I think you'll find me to be the better choice."

"Next time?" Dalinar said. "I've never seen her."

"Of course you have," Odium said, turning and walking away. "She simply robbed you of that memory. Her touch is not how I would have helped you. It stole a part of you away, and left you like a blind man who can't remember that he once had sight."

Dalinar stood up. "I offer you a challenge of champions. With terms to be discussed. Will you accept it?"

Odium stopped, then turned slowly. "Do you speak for the world, Dalinar Kholin? Will you offer this for all Roshar?"

Storms. Would he? "I . . ."

"Either way, I don't accept." Odium stood taller, smiling in an unnervingly understanding way. "I need not take on such a risk, for I know, Dalinar Kholin, that you will make the right decision. You will free me."

"No." Dalinar stood. "You shouldn't have revealed yourself, Odium. I once feared you, but it is easier to fear what you don't understand. I've seen you now, and I can fight you."

"You've seen me, have you? Curious."

Odium smiled again.

Then everything went white. Dalinar found himself standing on a speck of nothingness that was the entire world, looking up at an eternal, all-embracing *flame*. It stretched in every direction, starting as red, moving to orange, then changing to blazing white.

Then somehow, the flames seemed to burn into a deep blackness, violet and angry.

This was something so terrible that it consumed light itself. It was hot. A radiance indescribable, intense heat and black fire, colored violet at the outside.

Burning.

Overwhelming.

Power.

It was the scream of a thousand warriors on the battlefield.

It was the moment of most sensual touch and ecstasy.

It was the sorrow of loss, the joy of victory.

And it *was* hatred. Deep, pulsing hatred with a pressure to turn all things molten. It was the heat of a thousand suns, it was the bliss of every kiss, it was the lives of all men wrapped up in one, defined by everything they felt.

Even taking in the smallest fraction of it terrified Dalinar. It left him tiny and frail. He knew if he drank of that raw, concentrated, liquid black fire, he'd be nothing in a moment. The entire planet of Roshar would puff away, no more consequential than the curling smoke of a snuffed-out candle.

It faded, and Dalinar found himself lying on the rock outside Feverstone Keep, staring upward. Above him, the sun seemed dim and cold. Everything felt frozen by contrast.

Odium knelt down beside him, then helped him rise to a seated position. "There, there. That was a smidge too much, wasn't it? I had forgotten how overwhelming that could be. Here, take a drink." He handed Dalinar a waterskin.

Dalinar looked at it, baffled, then up at the old man. In Odium's eyes, he could see that violet-black fire. Deep, deep within. The figure with whom Dalinar spoke was not the god, it was merely a face, a mask.

Because if Dalinar had to confront the true force behind those smiling eyes, he would go mad.

Odium patted him on the shoulder. "Take a minute, Dalinar. I'll leave you here. Relax. It—" He cut off, then frowned, spinning. He searched the rocks.

"What?" Dalinar asked.

"Nothing. Just an old man's mind playing tricks on him." He patted Dalinar on the arm. "We'll speak again, I promise."

He vanished in an eyeblink.

Dalinar collapsed backward, completely drained. Storms. Just . . . Storms.

"That guy," a girl's voice said, "is *creepy*."

Dalinar shifted, sitting up with difficulty. A head popped up from behind some nearby rocks. Tan skin, pale eyes, long dark hair, lean, girlish features.

"I mean, old men are *all* creepy," Lift said. "Seriously. All wrinkly and 'Hey, want some sweets?' and 'Oh, listen to this boring story.' I'm on to them. They can act nice all they want, but nobody gets old without ruining a whole buncha lives."

She climbed over the rocks. She wore fine Azish clothing now, compared to the simple trousers and shirt from last time. Colorful patterns on robes, a thick overcoat and cap. "Even as old people go, that one was extra creepy," she said softly. "What was that thing, tight-butt? Didn't smell like a real person."

"They call it Odium," Dalinar said, exhausted. "And it is what we fight."

"Huh. Compared to that, you're *nothing*."

"Thank you?"

She nodded, as if it were a compliment. "I'll talk to Gawx. You got good food at that tower city of yours?"

"We can prepare some for you."

"Yeah, I don't care what you prepare. What do *you* eat? Is it good?"

". . . Yes?"

"Not military rations or some such nonsense, right?"

"Not usually."

"Great." She looked at the place where Odium had vanished, then shivered visibly. "We'll visit." She paused, then poked him in the arm. "Don't tell Gawx about that Odium thing, okay? He's got too many old people to worry about already."

Dalinar nodded.

The bizarre girl vanished and, moments later, the vision finally faded.

THE END OF

Part Two

İNTERLUDES

KAZA • TARAVANGIAN • VENLI

KAZA

The ship *First Dreams* crashed through a wave, prompting Kaza to cling tightly to the rigging. Her gloved hands already ached, and she was certain each new wave would toss her overboard.

She refused to go down below. This was *her* destiny. She was not a thing to be carted from place to place, not any longer. Besides, that dark sky—suddenly stormy, even though the sailing had been easy up until an hour ago—was no more disconcerting than her visions.

Another wave sent water crashing across the deck. Sailors scrambled and screamed, mostly hirelings out of Steen, as no rational crew would make this trip. Captain Vazrmeb stalked among them, shouting orders, while Droz—the helmsman—kept them on a steady heading. Into the storm. Straight. Into. The storm.

Kaza held tight, feeling her age as her arms started to weaken. Icy water washed over her, pushing back the hood of her robe, exposing her face—and its twisted nature. Most sailors weren't paying attention, though her cry *did* bring Vazrmeb's attention.

The only Thaylen on board, the captain didn't much match her image of the people. Thaylens, to her, were portly little men in vests—merchants with styled hair who haggled for every last sphere. Vazrmeb, however, was as tall as an Alethi, with hands wide enough to palm boulders and forearms large enough to lift them.

Over the crashing of waves, he yelled, "Someone get that Soulcaster below deck!"

"No," she shouted back at him. "I stay."

"I didn't pay a prince's ransom to bring you," he said, stalking up to her, "only to lose you over the side!"

"I'm not a thing to—"

"Captain!" a sailor shouted. "*Captain!*"

They both looked as the ship tipped over the peak of a huge wave, then teetered, before just kind of *falling* over the other side. Storms! Kaza's stomach practically squeezed up into her throat, and she felt her fingers sliding on the ropes.

Vazrmeb seized her by the side of her robe, holding her tight as they plunged into the water beyond the wave. For a brief terrifying moment, they seemed entombed in the chill water. As if the entire ship had sunk.

The wave passed, and Kaza found herself lying in a sodden heap on the deck, held by the captain. "Storming fool," he said to her. "You're my secret weapon. You drown yourself when you're *not* in my pay, understand?"

She nodded limply. And then realized, with a shock, she'd been able to hear him easily. The storm . . .

Was gone?

Vazrmeb stood up straight, grinning broadly, his white eyebrows combed back into his long mane of dripping hair. All across the deck, the sailors who had survived were climbing to their feet, sopping wet and staring at the sky. It maintained its overcast gloom—but the winds had fallen completely still.

Vazrmeb bellowed out a laugh, sweeping back his long, curling hair. "What did I tell you, men! That new storm came from Aimia! Now it has gone and escaped, leaving the riches of its homeland to be plundered!"

Everyone knew you didn't linger around Aimia, though everyone had different explanations why. Some rumors told of a vengeful storm here, one that sought out and destroyed approaching ships. The strange wind they'd encountered—which didn't match the timing of highstorm *or* Everstorm—seemed to support that.

The captain started shouting orders, getting the men back into position. They hadn't been sailing long, only a short distance out of Liafor, along the Shin coast, then westward toward this northern section of Aimia. They'd soon spotted the large main island, but had not visited it. Everyone knew that was barren, lifeless. The treasures were on the hidden islands, supposedly lying in wait to enrich those willing to brave the winds and treacherous straits.

She cared less for that—what were riches to her? She had come because of another rumor, one spoken of only among her kind. Perhaps here, at last, she could find a cure for her condition.

Even as she righted herself, she felt in her pouch, seeking the comforting touch of her Soulcaster. *Hers,* no matter what the rulers of Liafor claimed. Had they spent their youths caressing it, learning its secrets? Had they spent their middle years in service, stepping—with each use—closer and closer to oblivion?

The common sailors gave Kaza space, refusing to look her in the eyes. She pulled her hood up, unaccustomed to the gaze of ordinary people. She'd entered the stage where her . . . disfigurements were starkly obvious.

Kaza was, slowly, becoming smoke.

Vazrmeb took the helm himself, giving Droz a break. The lanky man stepped down from the poop deck, noting her by the side of the ship. He grinned at her, which she found curious. She hadn't ever spoken to him. Now he sauntered over, as if intending to make *small talk*.

"So . . ." he said. "Up on deck? Through *that*? You've got guts."

She hesitated, considering this strange creature, then lowered her hood.

He didn't flinch, even though her hair, her ears, and now parts of her face were disintegrating. There was a hole in her cheek through which you could see her jaw and teeth. Lines of smoke rimmed the hole; the flesh seemed to be burning away. Air passed through it when she spoke, altering her voice, and she had to tip her head all the way back to drink anything. Even then, it dribbled out.

The process was slow. She had a few years left until the Soulcasting killed her.

Droz seemed intent on pretending nothing was wrong. "I can't believe we got through that storm. You think it hunts ships, like the stories say?"

He was Liaforan like herself, with deep brown skin and dark brown eyes. What *did* he want? She tried to remember the ordinary passions of human life, which she'd begun to forget. "Is it sex you want? . . . No, you are much younger than I am. Hmmm . . ." Curious. "Are you frightened, and wishing for comfort?"

He started to fidget, playing with the end of a tied-off rope. "Um . . . So, I mean, the prince sent you, right?"

"Ah." So he knew that she was the prince's cousin. "You wish to connect yourself to royalty. Well, I came on my own."

"Surely he *let* you go."

"Of course he didn't. If not for my safety, then for that of my device." It *was* hers. She looked off across the too-still ocean. "They locked me up each day, gave me comforts they assumed would keep me happy. They realized that at any moment, I could *literally* make walls and bonds turn to smoke."

"Does . . . does it hurt?"

"It is blissful. I slowly connect to the device, and through it to Roshar. Until the day it will take me fully into its embrace." She lifted a hand and pulled her black glove off, one finger at a time, revealing a hand that was disintegrating. Five lines of darkness, one rising from the tip of each finger. She turned it, palm toward him. "I could show you. Feel my touch, and you can know. One moment, and then you will mingle with the air itself."

He fled. Excellent.

The captain steered them toward a small island, poking from the placid ocean right where the captain's map had claimed it would be. It had dozens of names. The Rock of Secrets. The Void's Playground. So melodramatic. She preferred the old name for the place: Akinah.

Supposedly, there had once been a grand city here. But who would put a city on an island you couldn't approach? For, jutting from the ocean here were a set of strange rock formations. They ringed the entire island like a wall, each some forty feet tall, resembling spearheads. As the ship drew closer, the sea grew choppy again, and she felt a bout of nausea. She liked that. It was a *human* feeling.

Her hand again sought her Soulcaster.

That nausea mixed with a faint sense of hunger. Food was something she often forgot about these days, as her body needed less of it now. Chewing was annoying, with the hole in her cheek. Still, she liked the scents from whatever the cook was stirring up below. Perhaps the meal would calm the men, who seemed agitated about approaching the island.

Kaza moved to the poop deck, near the captain.

"Now you earn your keep, Soulcaster," he said. "And I'm justified in hauling you all the way out here."

"I'm not a thing," she said absently, "to be used. I am a person. Those spikes of stone . . . they were Soulcast there." The enormous stone spearheads were too even in a ring about the island. Judging by the currents ahead, some lurked beneath the waters as well, to rip up the hulls of approaching vessels.

"Can you destroy one?" the captain asked her.

"No. They are much larger than you indicated."

"But—"

"I can make a hole in them, Captain. It is easier to Soulcast an entire object, but I am no ordinary Soulcaster. I have begun to see the dark sky and the second sun, the creatures that lurk, hidden, around the cities of men."

He shivered visibly. Why should that have frightened him? She'd merely stated facts.

"We need you to transform the tips of a few under the waves," he said. "Then make a hole at least large enough for the dinghies to get in to the island beyond."

"I will keep my word, but you must remember. I do not *serve* you. I am here for my own purposes."

They dropped anchor as close to the spikes as they dared get. The spikes were even more daunting—and more obviously Soulcast—from here. *Each would have required several Soulcasters in concert,* she thought, standing at the prow of the ship as the men ate a hasty meal of stew.

The cook was a woman, Reshi from the looks of her, with tattoos all across her face. She pushed the captain to eat, claiming that if he went in hungry, he'd be distracted. Even Kaza took some, though her tongue no longer tasted food. It all felt like the same mush to her, and she ate with a napkin pressed to her cheek.

The captain drew anticipationspren as he waited—ribbons that waved in the wind—and Kaza could see the beasts beyond, the creatures that accompanied the spren.

The ship's four dinghies were cramped, with rowers and officers all together, but they made space for her at the front of one. She pulled up her hood, which still hadn't dried, and sat on her bench. What had the captain been planning to do if the storm hadn't stopped? Would he seriously have tried to use her and a dinghy to remove these spears in the middle of a tempest?

They reached the first spike, and Kaza carefully unwrapped her Soulcaster, releasing a flood of light. Three large gemstones connected by chains, with loops for her fingers. She put it on, with the gemstones on the back of her hand. She sighed softly to feel the metal against her skin again. Warm, welcoming, a part of her.

She reached over the side into the chill water and pressed her hand against the tip of the stone spear—smoothed from years in the ocean. Light from the gemstones lit the water, reflections dancing across her robe.

She closed her eyes, and felt the familiar sensation of being drawn into the other world. Of another will reinforcing her own, something commanding and powerful, attracted by her request for aid.

The stone did not wish to change. It was content with its long slumber in the ocean. But . . . yes, yes, it *remembered*. It had once been air, until someone had locked it into this shape. She could not make it air again; her Soulcaster had only one mode, not the full three. She did not know why.

Smoke, she whispered to the stone. *Freedom in the air. Remember?* She tempted it, picking at its memories of dancing free.

Yes . . . freedom.

She nearly gave in herself. How *wonderful* would it be to no longer fear? To soar into infinity on the air? To be free of mortal pains?

The tip of the stone burst into smoke, sending an explosion of bubbles up around the dinghy. Kaza was shocked back into the real world, and a piece deep within her trembled. Terrified. She'd almost gone that time.

Smoke bubbles rattled the dinghy, which nearly upended. She should have warned them. Sailors muttered, but in the next dinghy over, the captain praised her.

She removed two more spear tips beneath the waves before finally reaching the wall. Here, the spearheadlike formations had been grown so close together, there was barely a handspan gap between them. It took three tries to get the dinghy close enough—as soon as they got into position, some turning of the waves would pull them away again.

Finally, the sailors managed to keep the dinghy steady. Kaza reached out with the Soulcaster—two of the three gems were almost out of Stormlight, and glowed only faintly. She should have enough.

She pressed her hand against the spike, then convinced it to become smoke. It was . . . easy this time. She felt the explosion of wind from the transformation, her soul crying in delight at the smoke, thick and sweet. She breathed it in through the hole in her cheek while sailors coughed. She looked up at the smoke, drifting away. How wonderful it would be to join it. . . .

No.

The island proper loomed beyond that hole. Dark, like its stones had been stained by smoke themselves, it had tall rock formations along its center. They looked almost like the walls of a city.

The captain's dinghy pulled up to hers, and the captain transferred to her boat. His began to row backward.

"What?" she asked. "Why is your boat heading back?"

"They claim to not be feeling well," the captain said. Was he abnormally pale? "Cowards. They won't have any of the prize, then."

"Gemstones lay around just for the plucking here," Droz added. "Generations of greatshells have died here, leaving their hearts. We're going to be rich, rich men."

As long as the secret was here.

She settled into her place at the prow of the boat as the sailors guided the three dinghies through the gap. The Aimians had known about Soulcasters. This was where you'd come to get the devices, in the old days. You'd come to the ancient island of Akinah.

If there was a secret of how to avoid death by the device she loved, she would find it here.

Her stomach began acting up again as they rowed. Kaza endured it, though she felt as if she were slipping into the other world. That wasn't an ocean beneath her, but deep black glass. And two suns in the sky, one that drew her soul toward it. Her shadow, to stretch out in the wrong direction . . .

Splash.

She started. One of the sailors had slipped from his boat into the water. She gaped as another slumped to the side, oar falling from his fingers.

"Captain?" She turned to find him with drooping eyes. He went limp, then fell backward, unconscious, knocking his head against the back seat of the boat.

The rest of the sailors weren't doing any better. The other two dinghies had begun to drift aimlessly. Not a single sailor seemed to be conscious.

My destiny, Kaza thought. *My choice.*

Not a thing to be carted from place to place, and ordered to Soulcast. Not a *tool*. A *person*.

She shoved aside an unconscious sailor and took the oars herself. It was difficult work. She was unaccustomed to physical labor, and her fingers had trouble gripping. They'd started to dissolve further. Perhaps a year or two for her survival was optimistic.

Still, she rowed. She fought the waters until she at long last got close enough to hop out into the water and feel rock beneath her feet. Her robes billowing up around her, she finally thought to check if Vazrmeb was alive.

None of the sailors in her dinghy were breathing, so she let the boat slip backward on the waves. Alone, Kaza fought through the surf and—finally—on hands and knees, crawled up onto the stones of the island.

There, she collapsed, drowsy. Why was she so sleepy?

She awoke to a small cremling scuttling across the rocks near her. It had a strange shape, with large wings and a head that made it look like an axehound. Its carapace shimmered with dozens of colors.

Kaza could remember a time when she'd collected cremlings, pinning them to boards and proclaiming she'd become a natural historian. What had happened to that girl?

She was transformed by necessity. Given the Soulcaster, which was always to be kept in the royal family. Given a charge.

And a death sentence.

She stirred, and the cremling scrambled away. She coughed, then began to crawl toward those rock formations. That city? Dark city of stone? She could barely think, though she did notice a gemstone as she passed it—a large uncut gemheart among the bleached white carapace leftovers of a dead greatshell. Vazrmeb had been right.

She collapsed again near the perimeter of the rock formations. They looked like large, ornate buildings, crusted with crem.

"Ah . . ." a voice said from behind her. "I should have guessed the drug would not affect you as quickly. You are barely human anymore."

Kaza rolled over and found someone approaching on quiet, bare feet. The cook? Yes, that was her, with the tattooed face.

"You . . ." Kaza croaked, "you *poisoned* us."

"After many warnings not to come to this place," the cook said. "It is rare I must guard it so . . . aggressively. Men must not again discover this place."

"The gemstones?" Kaza asked, growing more drowsy. "Or . . . is it something else . . . something . . . more . . ."

"I cannot speak," the cook said, "even to sate a dying demand. There are those who could pull secrets from your soul, and the cost would be the ends of worlds. Sleep now, Soulcaster. This is the most merciful end I could give."

The cook began to hum. Pieces of her broke off. She crumbled to a pile of chittering little *cremlings* that moved out of her clothing, leaving it in a heap.

A hallucination? Kaza wondered as she drifted.

She was dying. Well, that was nothing new.

The cremlings began to pick at her hand, taking off her Soulcaster. No . . . she had one last thing to do.

With a defiant shout, she pressed her hand to the rocky ground beneath her and demanded it change. When it became smoke, she went with it.

Her choice.

Her destiny.

Taravangian paced in his rooms in Urithiru as two servants from the Diagram arranged his table, and fidgety Dukar—head of the King's Testers, who each wore a ridiculous stormwarden robe with glyphs all along the seams—set out the tests, though they needn't have bothered.

Today, Taravangian was a storming *genius.*

The way he thought, breathed, even moved, implicitly conveyed that today was a day of intelligence—perhaps not as brilliant as that single transcendent one when he'd created the Diagram, but he finally felt like himself after so many days trapped in the mausoleum of his own flesh, his mind like a master painter allowed only to whitewash walls.

Once the table was finished, Taravangian pushed a nameless servant aside and sat down, grabbing a pen and launching into the problems— starting at the second page, as the first was too simple—and flicking ink at Dukar when the idiot started to complain.

"Next page," he snapped. "Quickly, quickly. Let's not waste this, Dukar."

"You still must—"

"Yes, yes. Prove myself not an idiot. The one day I'm not drooling and lying in my own waste, you tax my time with this idiocy."

"You set—"

"It up. Yes, the irony is that you let the prohibitions instituted by my idiot self control my true self when it finally has opportunity to emerge."

"You weren't an idiot when you—"

"Here," Taravangian said, proffering the sheet of math problems to him. "Done."

"All but the last on this sheet," Dukar said, taking it in cautious fingers. "Do you want to try that one, or . . ."

"No need. I know I can't solve it; too bad. Make quick with the requisite formalities. I have work to do."

Adrotagia had entered with Malata, the Dustbringer; they were growing in companionship as Adrotagia attempted to secure an emotional bond with this lesser Diagram member who had suddenly been thrust into its upper echelons, an event predicted by the Diagram—which explained that the Dustbringers would be the Radiants most likely to accept their cause, and at that Taravangian felt proud, for actually locating one of their number who could bond a spren had not, by any means, been an assured accomplishment.

"He's smart," Dukar said to Mrall. The bodyguard was the final adjudicator of Taravangian's daily capacity—an infuriating check necessary to prevent his stupid side from ruining anything, but a mere annoyance when Taravangian was like this.

Energized.

Awake.

Brilliant.

"He's almost to the danger line," Dukar said.

"I can see that," Adrotagia said. "Vargo, are you—"

"I feel perfect. Can't we be done with this? I can interact, and make policy decisions, and need no restrictions."

Dukar nodded, reluctantly, in agreement. Mrall assented. Finally!

"Get me a copy of the Diagram," Taravangian said, pushing past Adrotagia. "And some music, something relaxing but not too slow. Clear the chambers of nonessential persons, empty the bedroom of furniture, and *don't* interrupt me."

It took them a frustratingly long time to accomplish, almost half an hour, which he spent on his balcony, contemplating the large space for a garden outside and wondering how big it was. He needed measurements. . . .

"Your room is prepared, Your Majesty," Mrall said.

"Thank you, Uscritic one, for your leave to go into my own bedroom. Have you been drinking salt?"

". . . What?"

Taravangian strode through the small room beside the balcony and into his bedroom, then breathed deeply, pleased to find it completely empty of furniture—only four blank stone walls, no window, though it had a strange rectangular outcropping along the back wall, like a high step, which Maben was dusting.

Taravangian seized the maid by the arm and hauled her out, to where Adrotagia was bringing him a thick book bound in hogshide. A copy of the Diagram. Excellent. "Measure the available gardening area of the stone field outside our balcony and report it to me."

He carried the Diagram into the room, and then shut himself into blissful self-company, in which he arranged a diamond in each corner—a light to accompany that of his own spark, which shone in truth where others could not venture—and as he finished, a small choir of children started to sing Vorin hymns outside the room per his request.

He breathed in, out, bathed in light and encouraged by song, his hands to the sides; capable of *anything*, he was consumed by the satisfaction of his own working mind, unclogged and flowing freely for the first time in what seemed like ages.

He opened the Diagram. In it, Taravangian finally faced something greater than himself: a different version of himself.

The Diagram—which was the name for this book and for the organization that studied it—had not originally been written merely on paper, for on that day of majestic capacity, Taravangian had annexed every surface to hold his genius—from the cabinetry to the walls—and while so doing had invented new languages to better express ideas that had to be recorded, by necessity, in a medium less perfect than his thoughts. Even as the intellect he was today, the sight of that writing enforced humility; he leafed through pages packed with tiny scrawls, copied—spots, scratches, and all—from the original Diagram room, created during what felt like a different lifetime, as alien to him now as was the drooling idiot he sometimes became.

More alien. Everyone understood stupidity.

He knelt on the stones, ignoring his aches of body, reverently leafing through the pages. Then he slipped out his belt knife, and began to cut it up.

The Diagram had not been written on paper, and interacting with its transcription bound into codex form must necessarily have influenced their thinking, so to obtain true perspective—he now decided—he needed the flexibility of seeing the pieces, then arranging them in new ways, for his thoughts had not been locked down on that day and he should not perceive them as such today.

He was not as brilliant as he'd been on that day, but he didn't need to be. That day, he'd been God. Today, he could be God's prophet.

He arranged the cut-out pages, and found numerous new connections simply by how the sheets were placed next to each other—indeed, this page here *actually* connected to this page here . . . yes. Taravangian cut them both down the middle, dividing sentences. When he put the halves of separate pages beside one another, they made a more complete whole. Ideas he'd missed before seemed to rise from the pages like spren.

Taravangian did not believe in any religion, for they were unwieldy things, designed to fill gaps in human understanding with nonsensical explanations, allowing people to sleep well at night, granting them a false sense of comfort and control and preventing them from stretching further for true understanding, yet there was something strangely holy about the Diagram, the power of raw intelligence, the only thing man should worship, and oh how little most understood it—oh, how little they *deserved* it—in handling purity while corrupting it with flawed understanding and silly superstitions. Was there a way he could prevent any but the most intelligent from learning to read? That would accomplish so much good; it seemed insane that nobody had implemented such a ban, for while Vorinism forbade men to read, that merely prevented an arbitrary half of the population from handling information, when it was the stupid who should be barred.

He paced in the room, then noted a scrap of paper under the door; it contained the answer to his question about the size of the farming platform. He looked over the calculations, listening with half an ear to voices outside, almost overwhelmed by the singing children.

"Uscritic," Adrotagia said, "seems to refer to Uscri, a figure from a tragic poem written seventeen hundred years ago. She drowned herself after hearing her lover had died, though the truth was that he'd not died at all, and she misunderstood the report about him."

"All right . . ." Mrall said.

"She was used in following centuries as an example of acting without information, though the term eventually came to simply mean 'stupid.' The salt seems to refer to the fact that she drowned herself in the sea."

"So it was an insult?" Mrall asked.

"Using an obscure literary reference. Yes." He could almost hear Adrotagia's sigh. Best to interrupt her before she thought on this further.

Taravangian flung open the door. "Gum paste for sticking paper to this wall. Fetch it for me, Adrotagia."

They'd put paper in a stack by the door without being asked, which surprised him, as they usually had to be ordered to do everything. He closed the door, then knelt and did some calculations relating to the size of the tower city. *Hmmmm . . .*

It provided a fine distraction, but he was soon drawn back to the true work, interrupted only by the arrival of his gum paste, which he used to begin sticking fragments of the Diagram to his walls.

This, he thought, arranging pages with numbers interspersing the text, pages they'd never been able to make sense of. *It's a list of what? Not code, like the other numbers. Unless . . . could this be shorthand for words?*

Yes . . . yes, he'd been too impatient to write the actual words. He'd numbered them in his head—alphabetically perhaps—so he could write quickly. Where was the key?

This is reinforcement, he thought as he worked, *of the Dalinar paradigm!* His hands shook with excitement as he wrote out possible interpretations. Yes . . . Kill Dalinar, or he will resist your attempts to take over Alethkar. So Taravangian had sent the Assassin in White, which—incredibly—had failed.

Fortunately, there were contingencies. *Here,* Taravangian thought, bringing up another scrap from the Diagram and gluing it to the wall beside the others. *The initial explanation of the Dalinar paradigm, from the catechism of the headboard, back side, third quadrant.* It had been written in meter, as a poem, and presaged that Dalinar would attempt to unite the world.

So if he looked to the second contingency . . .

Taravangian wrote furiously, seeing words instead of numbers, and—full of energy—for a time he forgot his age, his aches, the way his fingers trembled—sometimes—even when he wasn't so excited.

The Diagram hadn't seen the effect the second son, Renarin, would have—he was a completely wild element. Taravangian finished his notations, proud, and wandered toward the door, which he opened without looking up.

"Get me a copy of the surgeon's words upon my birth," he said to those outside. "Oh, and kill those children."

The music trailed off as the children heard what he'd said. Musicspren flitted away.

"You mean, quiet them from singing," Mrall said.

"Whatever. I'm perturbed by the Vorin hymns as a reminder of historic religious oppression of ideas and thought."

Taravangian returned to his work, but a short time later a knock came at the door. He flung it open. "I was not to be—"

"Interrupted," Adrotagia said, proffering him a sheet of paper. "The surgeon's words you requested. We keep them handy now, considering how often you ask for them."

"Fine."

"We need to talk, Vargo."

"No we—"

She walked in anyway, then stopped, inspecting the cut-up pieces of the Diagram. Her eyes widened as she turned about. "Are you . . ."

"No," he said. "I haven't become him again. But I *am* me, for the first time in weeks."

"This *isn't* you. This is the monster you sometimes become."

"I am not smart enough to be in the dangerous zone." The zone where, annoyingly, they claimed he was *too* smart to be allowed to make decisions. As if intelligence were somehow a liability!

She unfolded a piece of paper from the pocket of her skirt. "Yes, your daily test. You stopped on this page, claiming you couldn't answer the next question."

Damnation. She'd seen it.

"If you'd answered," she said, "it would have proved you were intelligent enough to be dangerous. Instead, you decided you couldn't manage. A loophole we should have considered. You *knew* that if you finished the question, we'd restrict your decision-making for the day."

"Do you know about Stormlight growth?" he said, brushing past her and taking one of the pages he'd written earlier.

"Vargo . . ."

"Calculating the total surface area for farming at Urithiru," he said, "and comparing it to the projected number of rooms that could be occupied, I have determined that even *if* food grew here naturally—as it would at the temperatures of your average fecund plain—it could not provide enough to sustain the entire tower."

"Trade," she said.

"I have trouble believing the Knights Radiant, always threatened with war, would build a fortress like this to be anything but self-sufficient. Have you read Golombi?"

"Of course I have, and you know it," she said. "You think they enhanced the growth by use of Stormlight-infused gemstones, providing light to darkened places?"

"Nothing else makes sense, does it?"

"The tests are inconclusive," she said. "Yes, spherelight inspires growth in a dark room, when candlelight cannot, but Golombi says that the results may have been compromised, and the efficiency is . . . Oh, bah! That's a distraction, Vargo. We were discussing what you've done to circumvent the rules *you yourself* set out!"

"When I was stupid."

"When you were normal."

"Normal is stupid, Adro." He took her by the shoulders and firmly pushed her from the room. "I won't make policy decisions, and I'll avoid ordering the murder of any further groups of melodic children. Fine? All right? Now leave me alone. You're stinking up the place with an air of contented idiocy."

He shut the door, and—deep down—felt a glimmer of shame. Had he called Adrotagia, of all people, an idiot?

Well. Nothing to do about it now. She would understand.

He set to work again, cutting out more of the Diagram, arranging it, searching for any mentions of the Blackthorn, as there was too much in the book to study today, and he had to be *focused* on their current problem.

Dalinar lived. He was building a coalition. So what did Taravangian do now? Another assassin?

What is the secret? he thought, holding up sheets from the Diagram, finding one where he could see the words on the other side through the paper. Could that have been intentional? *What should I do? Please. Show me the way.*

He scribbled words on a page. Light. Intelligence. Meaning. He hung them on the wall to inspire him, but he couldn't help reading the surgeon's words—the words of a master healer who had delivered Taravangian through a cut in his mother's belly.

He had the cord wrapped around his neck, the surgeon had said. *The queen will know the best course, but I regret to inform her that while he lives, your son may have diminished capacity. Perhaps this is one to keep on outer estates, in favor of other heirs.*

The "diminished capacity" hadn't appeared, but the reputation had chased Taravangian from childhood, so pervasive in people's minds that not a one had seen through his recent act of stupidity, which they'd attributed to a stroke or to simple senility. Or maybe, some said, that was the way he'd always been.

He'd overcome that reputation in magnificent ways. Now he'd save the world. Well, the part of the world that mattered.

He worked for hours, pinning up more portions of the Diagram, then scribbling on them as connections came to him, using beauty and light to chase away the shadows of dullness and ignorance, giving him answers—they were here, he merely needed to interpret them.

His maid finally interrupted him; the annoying woman was always bustling around, trying to make him do this or that, as if he didn't have more important concerns than soaking his feet.

"Idiot woman!" he shouted.

She didn't flinch, but walked forward and put a tray of food down beside him.

"Can't you see that my work here is important?" he demanded. "I haven't time for food."

She set out drink for him, then, infuriatingly, patted him on the shoulder. As she left, he noticed Adrotagia and Mrall standing right outside.

"I don't suppose," he said to Mrall, "you'd execute that maid if I demanded it?"

"We have decided," the bodyguard said, "that you are not allowed to make such decisions today."

"To Damnation with you then. I almost have the answers anyway. We must not assassinate Dalinar Kholin. The time has passed for that. Instead, we must support his coalition. Then we force him to step down, so that I can take his place at the head of the monarchs."

Adrotagia walked in and inspected his work. "I doubt Dalinar will simply *give* leadership of the coalition to you."

Taravangian rapped on a set of pages stuck to the wall. "Look here. It should be clear, even to you. I foresaw this."

"You've made *changes*," Mrall said, aghast. "To the Diagram."

"Only little ones," Taravangian said. "Look, see the original writing here? I didn't change that, and it's clear. Our task now is to make Dalinar withdraw from leadership, take his place."

"We don't kill him?" Mrall asked.

Taravangian eyed him, then turned and waved toward the other wall, with even more papers stuck to it. "Killing him now would only raise suspicion."

"Yes," Adrotagia said, "I see this interpretation of the headboard—we must push the Blackthorn so hard that he collapses. But we'll need secrets to use against him."

"Easy," Taravangian said, pushing her toward another set of notations on the wall. "We send that Dustbringer's spren to spy. Dalinar Kholin *reeks* of secrets. We can break him, and I can take his place—as the coalition will see me as nonthreatening—whereupon we'll be in a position of power to negotiate with Odium—who will, by laws of spren and gods, be bound by the agreement made."

"Can't we . . . *beat* Odium instead?" Mrall asked.

Muscle-bound idiot. Taravangian rolled his eyes, but Adrotagia—more sentimental than he was—turned and explained. "The Diagram is clear, Mrall," she said. "This is the *purpose* of its creation. We cannot beat the enemy; so instead, we save whatever we can."

"The only way," Taravangian agreed. Dalinar would never accept this fact. Only one man would be strong enough to make that sacrifice.

Taravangian felt a glimmer of . . . something. Memory.

Give me the capacity to save us.

"Take this," he said to Adrotagia, pulling down a sheet he'd annotated. "This *will* work."

She nodded, towing Mrall from the room as Taravangian knelt before the broken, ripped, sliced-up remnants of the Diagram.

Light and truth. Save what he could.

Abandon the rest.

Thankfully, he had been given that capacity.

THIS ONE IS MINE

Venli was determined to live worthy of power.

She presented herself with the others, a small group selected from the remaining listeners, and braced for the oncoming storm.

She didn't know if Ulim—or his phantom masters, the ancient listener gods—could read her mind. But if they could, they'd find that she was loyal.

This was war, and Venli among its vanguard. *She* had discovered the first Voidspren. *She* had discovered stormform. *She* had redeemed her people. *She* was blessed.

Today would prove it. Nine of them had been selected from among the two thousand listener survivors, Venli included. Demid stood beside her with a wide grin on his face. He loved to learn new things, and the storm was another adventure. They'd been promised something great.

See, Eshonai? Venli thought. *See what we can do, if you don't hold us back?*

"All right, yes, that's it," Ulim said, rippling across the ground as vibrant red energy. "Good, good. All in a line. Keep facing west."

"Should we seek for cover before the storm, Envoy?" Melu asked to the Rhythm of Agony. "Or carry shields?"

Ulim took the form of a small person before them. "Don't be silly. This is *our* storm. You have nothing to fear."

"And it will bring us power," Venli said. "Power beyond even that of stormform?"

"Great power," Ulim said. "You've been chosen. You're special. But you *must* embrace this. Welcome it. You have to *want* it, or the powers will not be able to take a place in your gemhearts."

Venli had suffered so much, but this was her reward. She was done with a life spent wasting away under human oppression. She would never again be trapped, impotent. With this new power, she would always, *always* be able to fight back.

The Everstorm appeared from the west, returning as it had before. A tiny village in the near distance fell into the storm's shadow, then was illuminated by the striking of bright red lightning.

Venli stepped forward and hummed to Craving, holding her arms out to the sides. The storm wasn't like the highstorms—no stormwall of blown debris and cremwater. This was far more elegant. It was a billowing cloud of smoke and darkness, lightning breaking out on all sides, coloring it crimson.

She tipped her head back to meet the boiling, churning clouds, and was consumed by the storm.

Angry, violent darkness overshadowed her. Flecks of burning ash streamed past her on all sides, and she felt no rain this time. Just the beat of thunder. The storm's pulse.

Ash bit into her skin, and something crashed down beside her, rolling on the stones. A tree? Yes, a burning tree. Sand, shredded bark, and pebbles washed across her skin and carapace. She knelt down, eyes squeezed closed, arms protecting her face from the blown debris.

Something larger glanced off her arm, cracking her carapace. She gasped and dropped to the stone ground, curling up.

A pressure enveloped her, pushing at her mind, her soul. *Let Me In.*

With difficulty, she opened herself up to this force. This was just like adopting a new form, right?

Pain seared her insides, as if someone had set fire to her veins. She screamed, and sand bit her tongue. Tiny coals ripped at her clothing, singeing her skin.

And then, a voice.

WHAT IS THIS?

It was a warm voice. An ancient, paternal voice, kindly and enveloping.

"Please," Venli said, gasping in breaths of smoky air. "Please."

YES, the voice said. CHOOSE ANOTHER. THIS ONE IS MINE.

The force that had been pushing against her retreated, and the pain stopped. Something else—something smaller, less domineering—took its place. She accepted this spren gladly, then whimpered in relief, attuned to Agony.

An eternity seemed to pass as she lay huddled before the storm. Finally, the winds weakened. The lightning faded. The thunder moved into the distance.

She blinked the grit from her eyes. Bits of cremstone and broken bark streamed from her as she moved. She coughed, then stood, looking at her ruined clothing and singed skin.

She no longer bore stormform. She'd changed to . . . was this nimbleform? Her clothing felt large on her, and her body no longer bore its impressive musculature. She attuned the rhythms, and found they were still the new ones—the violent, angry rhythms that came with forms of power.

This wasn't nimbleform, but it also wasn't anything she recognized. She had breasts—though they were small, as with most forms outside of mateform—and long hairstrands. She turned about to see if the others were the same.

Demid stood nearby, and though his clothing was in tatters, his well-muscled body wasn't scored. He stood tall—far taller than her—with a broad chest and powerful stance. He seemed more like a statue than a listener. He flexed, eyes glowing red, and his body pulsed with a dark violet power—a glow that somehow evoked both light and darkness at once. It retreated, but Demid seemed pleased by his ability to invoke it.

What form was *that*? So majestic, with ridges of carapace poking through his skin along the arms and at the corners of the face. "Demid?" she asked.

He turned toward Melu, who strode up in a similar form and said something in a language Venli didn't recognize. The rhythms were there though, and this was to Derision.

"Demid?" Venli asked again. "How do you feel? What happened?"

He spoke again in that strange language, and his next words seemed to blur in her mind, somehow shifting until she understood them. ". . . Odium rides the very winds, like the enemy once did. Incredible. Aharat, is that you?"

"Yes," Melu said. "This . . . this feels . . . good."

"Feel," Demid said. "It feels." He took a long, deep breath. "It feels."

Had they gone mad?

Nearby, Mrun pulled himself past a large boulder, which had not been there before. With horror, Venli realized that she could see a broken arm underneath it, blood leaking out. In direct defiance of Ulim's promise of safety, one of them had been crushed.

Though Mrun had been blessed with a tall, imperious form like the others, he stumbled as he stepped away from the boulder. He grabbed the stone, then fell to his knees. His body coursing with that dark violet light, he groaned, muttering gibberish. Altoki approached from the other direction, standing low, teeth bared, her steps like those of a predator. When she drew closer, Venli could hear her whispering between bared teeth. "High sky. Dead winds. Blood rain."

"Demid," Venli said to Destruction. "Something has gone wrong. Sit down, wait. I will find the spren."

Demid looked at her. "You knew this corpse?"

"This corpse? Demid, why—"

"Oh no. Oh no. Oh *no*!" Ulim coursed across the ground to her. "You— You aren't— Oh, bad, bad."

"Ulim!" Venli demanded, attuning Derision and gesturing at Demid. "Something is wrong with my companions. What have you brought upon us?"

"Don't talk to them, Venli!" Ulim said, forming into the shape of a little man. "Don't point at them!"

Nearby, Demid was pooling dark violet power in his hand somehow, studying her and Ulim. "It is you," he said to Ulim. "The Envoy. You have my respect for your work, spren."

Ulim bowed to Demid. "Please, grand of the Fused, see passion and forgive this child."

"You should explain to her," Demid said, "so she does not . . . aggravate me."

Venli frowned. "What is—"

"Come with me," Ulim said, rippling across the ground. Concerned, overwhelmed by her experience, Venli attuned Agony and followed. Behind, Demid and the others were gathering.

Ulim formed as a person again before her. "You're lucky. He could have destroyed you."

"Demid would never do that."

"Unfortunately for you, your once-mate is *gone*. That's Hariel—and he has one of the worst tempers of all the Fused."

"Hariel? What do you mean by . . ." She trailed off as the others spoke softly to Demid. They stood so tall, so haughty, and their mannerisms— all wrong.

Each new form changed a listener, down to their ways of thinking, even their temperament. Despite that, you were always you. Even stormform hadn't changed her into someone else. Perhaps . . . she had become less empathetic, more aggressive. But she'd still been herself.

This was different. Demid didn't stand like her once-mate, or speak like him.

"No . . ." she whispered. "You said we were opening ourselves up to a new spren, a new form!"

"I *said*," Ulim hissed, "that you were opening yourselves up. I didn't say what would enter. Look, your gods need bodies. It's like this every Return. You should be flattered."

"Flattered to be *killed*?"

"Yeah, for the good of the race," Ulim said. "Those are the Fused: ancient souls reborn. What you have, apparently, is just another form of power. A bond with a lesser Voidspren, which puts you above common listeners—who have normal forms—but a step below the Fused. A *big* step."

She nodded, then started to walk back toward the group.

"Wait," Ulim said, rippling across the ground before her. "What are you doing? What is *wrong* with you?"

"I'm going to send that soul out," she said. "Bring Demid back. He needs to know the consequences before he can choose such a drastic—"

"Back?" Ulim said. "*Back?* He's *dead.* As you should be. This is bad. What did you do? Resist, like that sister of yours?"

"Out of my way."

"He'll kill you. I warned of his temper—"

"Envoy," Demid said to Destruction, turning toward them. It wasn't his voice.

She attuned Agony. It *wasn't his voice.*

"Let her pass," the thing with Demid's body said. "I will speak with her."

Ulim sighed. "Bother."

"You speak like a human, spren," Demid said. "Your service here was grand, but you use their ways, their language. I find that displeasing."

Ulim rippled away across the stones. Venli stepped up to the group of Fused. Two still had trouble moving. They lurched, stumbled, fell to their knees. A different two wore smiles, twisted and wrong.

The listener gods were not completely sane.

"I regret the death of your friend, good servant," Demid said with a deep voice, fully in sync with the Rhythm of Command. "Though you are the children of traitors, your war here is to be commended. You faced our hereditary enemies and gave no quarter, even when doomed."

"Please," Venli said. "He was precious to me. Can you return him?"

"He has passed into the blindness beyond," Demid said. "Unlike the witless Voidspren you bonded—which resides in your gemheart—my soul cannot share its dwelling. Nothing, not Regrowth or act of Odium, can restore him now."

He reached out and took Venli by the chin, lifting her face, inspecting it. "You were to bear a soul I have fought beside for thousands of years. She was turned away, and you were reserved. Odium has a purpose for you. Revel in that, and mourn not your friend's passing. Odium will bring vengeance at long last to those we fight."

He let go of her, and she had to struggle to keep herself from collapsing. No. No, she would not show weakness.

But . . . Demid . . .

She put him out of her mind, like Eshonai before him. This was the path she had placed herself on from the moment she'd first listened to Ulim years ago, deciding that she would risk the return of her people's gods.

Demid had fallen, but she had been preserved. And Odium himself, god of gods, had a purpose for her. She sat down on the ground to wait as the Fused conversed in their strange language. As she waited, she noted something hovering near the ground a short distance away. A little spren that looked like a ball of light. Yes . . . she'd seen one of those near Eshonai. What was it?

It seemed agitated, and scooted across the stone closer to her. She instantly knew something—an instinctive truth, as sure as the storms and the sun. If the creatures standing nearby saw this spren, they would destroy it.

She slapped her hand down over the spren as the creature wearing Demid's body turned toward her. She cupped the little spren against the stone, and attuned Abashment.

He didn't seem to notice what she'd done.

"Ready yourself to be carried," he said. "We must travel to Alethela."

PART
THREE

Defying Truth, Love Truth

DALINAR · SHALLAN ·
KALADIN · ADOLIN

This folio page targets the Thayler merchant
class with styles heavily influenced by the fashion
worn by the nobles of Queen Fer Rnamdi's court.

58

BURDENS

*As a Stoneward, I spent my entire life looking to sacrifice myself.
I secretly worry that is the cowardly way. The easy way out.*

—From drawer 29-5, topaz

T he clouds that usually congregated about the base of the Urithiru
plateau were absent today, allowing Dalinar to see down along the
endless cliffs below the tower's perch. He couldn't see the ground;
those cliffs seemed to extend into eternity.

Even with that, he had trouble visualizing how high in the mountains
they were. Navani's scribes could measure height using the air somehow,
but their numbers didn't satisfy him. He wanted to *see*. Were they really
higher than the clouds were over the Shattered Plains? Or did the clouds
here in the mountains fly lower?

How contemplative you've grown in your old age, he thought to himself,
stepping onto one of the Oathgate platforms. Navani held his arm, though
Taravangian and Adrotagia had trailed behind on the ramp up.

Navani looked into his eyes as they waited. "Still bothered by the latest
vision?"

That wasn't what was distracting him at the moment, but he nodded
anyway. Indeed, he was worried. Odium. Though the Stormfather had
returned to his previous self-confident ways, Dalinar could not shake the
memory of the mighty spren whimpering in fright.

Navani and Jasnah had eagerly feasted on his account of meeting the
dark god, though they'd chosen not to publish this one for wide dissemi-
nation.

"Maybe," Navani said, "this was somehow another preplanned event, placed by Honor for you to encounter."

Dalinar shook his head. "Odium felt *real*. I truly interacted with him."

"You can interact with the people in the visions. Just not the Almighty himself."

"Because, you theorize, the Almighty couldn't create a full simulacrum of a god. No. I saw eternity, Navani . . . a divine vastness."

He shivered. For now, they had decided to suspend use of the visions. Who knew what risk they'd run by bringing people's minds in and potentially exposing them to Odium?

Of course, who's to say what he can and cannot touch in the real world? Dalinar thought. He looked up again, the sun burning white, the sky a faded blue. He would have thought that being above the clouds would give him more perspective.

Taravangian and Adrotagia finally arrived, followed by Taravangian's strange Surgebinder, the short-haired woman, Malata. Dalinar's guards brought up the rear. Rial saluted him. Again.

"You don't need to salute me each time I look at you, Sergeant," Dalinar said dryly.

"Just trying ta be extra careful, sir." The leathery, dark-skinned man saluted one more time. "Wouldn't want ta be reported for being disrespectful."

"I didn't mention you by name, Rial."

"Everyone knew anyway, Brightlord."

"Imagine that."

Rial grinned, and Dalinar waved for the man to open his canteen, then sniffed for alcohol. "It's clean this time?"

"Absolutely! You chastised me last time. Water only."

"And so you keep the alcohol . . ."

"In my flask, sir," Rial said. "Right leg pocket of my uniform. Don't worry though. It's buttoned up tight, and I've completely forgotten it's there. I'll discover it when duty is done."

"I'm sure." Dalinar took Navani by the arm and followed Adrotagia and Taravangian.

"You could have someone else assigned to guard you," Navani whispered to him. "That greasy man is . . . unfitting."

"I actually like him," Dalinar admitted. "Reminds me of some of my friends from the old days."

The control building at the center of this platform was shaped like the others—mosaics on the floor, keyhole mechanism in the curved wall. The patterns on the floor, however, were glyphs in the Dawnchant. This building would be identical to one in Thaylen City—and when engaged, it would swap places with that one.

Ten platforms here, ten across the world. The glyphs on the floors indicated that it might somehow be possible to transport directly from one city to another without coming to Urithiru first. They hadn't discovered how that might work, and for now each gate could swap only with its twin—and they had to first be unlocked from both sides.

Navani went straight for the control mechanism. Malata joined her, watching over Navani's shoulder as she fiddled with the keyhole, which was in the center of a ten-pointed star on a metal plate. "Yes," Navani said, consulting some notes. "The mechanism is the same as the one to the Shattered Plains. You need to twist this here . . ."

She wrote something via spanreed to Thaylen City, then ushered them back outside. A moment later, the building itself flashed—a ring of Stormlight running around it, like the afterimage of a firebrand being waved in the dark. Then Kaladin and Shallan emerged from the doorway.

"It worked!" Shallan said as she bounced out, bubbling over with eagerness. In contrast, Kaladin stepped out with a firm gait. "Transferring only the control buildings, instead of the entire platform, should save us Stormlight."

"Up until now," Navani said, "we've been working the Oathgates at full power for every transfer. I suspect that's not the only mistake we've made in regard to this place and its devices. Anyway, now that you two have unlocked the Thaylen gate on their end, we should be able to use it at will—with the help of a Radiant, of course."

"Sir," Kaladin said to Dalinar, "the queen is prepared to meet with you."

Taravangian, Navani, Adrotagia, and Malata entered the building, though Shallan started down the ramp back toward Urithiru. Dalinar took Kaladin by the arm as he moved to follow.

"The flight in front of the highstorm went well?" Dalinar asked.

"No problems, sir. I'm confident it will work."

"Next storm then, soldier, make for Kholinar. I'm counting on you and Adolin to keep Elhokar from doing anything too foolhardy. Be careful. Something strange is going on inside the city, and I can't afford to lose you."

"Yes, sir."

"As you fly, wave to the lands along the south fork of the Deathbend River. The parshmen may have conquered them by now, but they actually belong to you."

". . . Sir?"

"You're a Shardbearer, Kaladin. That makes you at least fourth dahn, which should be a landed title. Elhokar found you a nice portion along the river that reverted to the crown last year at the death of its brightlord, who had no heir. It's not as large as some, but it is yours now."

Kaladin looked stunned. "Are there villages on this land, sir?"

"Six or seven; one town of note. The river is one of the most consistent in Alethkar. It doesn't even dry up in the Midpeace. That's on a good caravan route. Your people will do well."

"Sir. You know I don't want this burden."

"If you'd wanted a life without burdens, you shouldn't have said the oaths," Dalinar said. "We don't get to choose things like this, son. Just make sure you have a good steward, wise scribes, and some solid men of the fifth and sixth dahns to lead the towns. Personally, I'll count us lucky—you included—if at the end of all this we still *have* a kingdom to burden us."

Kaladin nodded slowly. "My family is in northern Alethkar. Now that I've practiced flying with the storms, I'll want to go and fetch them, once I get back from the Kholinar mission."

"Get that Oathgate open, and you can have as much time as you want. I guarantee, the best thing you can do for your family right now is keep Alethkar from falling."

By spanreed reports, the Voidbringers were slowly moving northward, and had captured much of Alethkar. Relis Ruthar had tried to gather the remaining Alethi forces in the country, but had been pushed back toward Herdaz, suffering at the hands of the Fused. However, the Voidbringers weren't killing noncombatants. Kaladin's family should be safe enough.

The captain jogged off down the ramp, and Dalinar watched, thinking about his own burdens. Once Elhokar and Adolin returned from the mission to rescue Kholinar, they'd need to get on with Elhokar's highking arrangement. He still hadn't announced that, not even to the highprinces.

A part of Dalinar knew he should simply go forward with it now, naming Adolin highprince and stepping down, but he delayed. This would make a final separation between himself and his homeland. He'd at least like to help recover the capital first.

Dalinar joined the others in the control building, then nodded toward Malata. She summoned her Shardblade and inserted it into the slot. The metal of the plate shifted and flowed, matching the shape of the Blade. They'd run tests, and though the walls of the buildings were thin, you couldn't see the other end of the Shardblade jutting through. The Blade was melding into the mechanism.

Malata pushed against the side of the Blade's hilt. The inner wall of the control building rotated. The floor underneath the mosaics began glowing, illuminating them like stained glass. She stopped her Blade at the proper position, and a flash of light later, they had arrived. Dalinar stepped out of the small building onto a platform in distant Thaylen City, a port on the western coast of a large southern island near the Frostlands.

Here the platform that surrounded the Oathgate had been turned into a sculpture garden—but most of the sculptures lay toppled and broken. Queen Fen waited on the ramp up with her attendants. Shallan had probably told her to wait there in case the room-only transfer didn't work.

The platform was high up in the city, and as Dalinar neared the edge, he saw that it gave an excellent view. The sight of it made Dalinar's breath catch.

Thaylen City was a mountainside metropolis like Kharbranth, placed with its back to a mountain to provide shelter from the highstorms. Though Dalinar had never been to the city before, he'd studied maps, and knew Thaylen City had once included only a section near the center they called the Ancient Ward. This raised portion had a distinctive shape formed by the way the rocks had been carved millennia ago.

The city had long since been built beyond that. A lower section called the Low Ward cluttered the stones around the base of the wall—a wide, squat fortification to the west that ran from the cliffs on one side of the city to the mountain foothills on the other.

Above and behind the Ancient Ward, the city had expanded up a series of steplike tiers. These Loft Wards ended at a majestic Royal Ward at the top of the city, holding palaces, mansions, and temples. The Oathgate platform was on this level, at the northern edge of the city, close to the cliffs down to the ocean.

Once, this place would have been stunning because of its magnificent architecture. Today, Dalinar paused for a different reason. Dozens . . . *hundreds* of buildings had fallen in. Entire sections had become rubble when higher structures, smashed by the Everstorm, had slid down on top of them. What had once been one of the finest cities of all Roshar—known for its art, trade, and fine marble—was cracked and broken, like a dinner plate dropped by a careless maid.

Ironically, many more modest buildings at the base of the city—in the wall's shadow—had weathered the storm. But the famous Thaylen docks were out beyond this fortification, on the small western peninsula fronting the city. This area had once been densely developed—likely with warehouses, taverns, and shops. All wood.

They'd been swept away completely. Only smashed ruins remained.

Stormfather. No wonder Fen had resisted his distracting demands. Most of this destruction had been caused by that first full Everstorm; Thaylen City was particularly exposed, with no land to break the storm as it surged across the western ocean. Beyond that, many more of these structures had been of wood, particularly in the Loft Wards. A luxury available to a place like Thaylen City, which up until now had been subject only to the most mild of the stormwinds.

The Everstorm had come five times now, though subsequent passings had—blessedly—been tamer than the first. Dalinar lingered, taking it in, before leading his group to where Queen Fen stood on the ramp with a collection of scribes, lighteyes, and guards. This included her prince consort, Kmakl, an aging Thaylen man with matching mustaches and eyebrows, both drooping down to frame his face. He wore a vest and cap, and was attended by two ardents as scribes.

"Fen . . ." Dalinar said softly. "I'm sorry."

"We lived too long in luxury, it seems," Fen said, and he was momentarily surprised by her accent. It hadn't been present in the visions. "I remember as a child worrying that everyone in other countries would discover how nice things were here, with the mild straits weather and the broken storms. I assumed we'd be swarmed with immigrants someday."

She turned toward her city, and sighed softly.

How would it have been to live here? He tried to imagine living in homes that didn't feel like fortresses. Buildings of wood with broad windows. Roofs needed only for keeping the rain off. He'd heard people joke that in Kharbranth, you had to hang a bell outside to know when the highstorm had arrived, for otherwise you'd miss it. Fortunately for Taravangian, that city's slightly southern orientation had prevented devastation on this scale.

"Well," Fen said, "let's do a tour. I think there are a few places worth seeing that are still standing."

If this is to be permanent, then I wish to leave record of my husband and children. Wzmal, as good a man as any woman could dream of loving. Kmakra and Molinar, the true gemstones of my life.

—From drawer 12-15, ruby

T he temple of Shalash," Fen said, gesturing as they entered.

To Dalinar, it looked much like the others she'd shown them: a large space with a high-domed ceiling and massive braziers. Here, ardents burned thousands of glyphwards for the people, who supplicated the Almighty for mercy and aid. Smoke pooled in the dome before leaking out through holes in the roof, like water through a sieve.

How many prayers have we burned, Dalinar wondered uncomfortably, *to a god who is no longer there? Or is someone else receiving them instead?*

Dalinar nodded politely as Fen recounted the ancient origin of the structure and listed some of the kings or queens who had been crowned here. She explained the significance of the elaborate design on the rear wall, and led them around the sides to view the carvings. It was a pity to see several statues with the faces broken off. How had the storm gotten to them in here?

When they were done, she led them back outside onto the Royal Ward, where the palanquins waited. Navani nudged him.

"What?" he asked softly.

"Stop scowling."

"I'm not scowling."

"You're bored."

"I'm not . . . scowling."

She raised an eyebrow.

"Six temples?" he asked. "This city is practically rubble, and we're looking at temples."

Ahead, Fen and her consort climbed into their palanquin. So far, Kmakl's only part in the tour had been to stand behind Fen and—whenever she said something he thought significant—nod for her scribes to record it in the official histories.

Kmakl didn't carry a sword. In Alethkar, that would indicate the man—at least one of his rank—was a Shardbearer, but that was not the case here. Thaylenah had only five Blades—and three suits of Plate—each held by an ancient family line sworn to defend the throne. Couldn't Fen have taken him on a tour to see those Shards instead?

"Scowling . . ." Navani said.

"It's what they expect of me," Dalinar said, nodding toward the Thaylen officers and scribes. Near the front, one group of soldiers in particular had watched Dalinar with keen interest. Perhaps this tour's true intent was to give those lighteyes a chance to study him.

The palanquin he shared with Navani was scented like rockbud blossoms. "The progression from temple to temple," Navani said softly as their bearers lifted the palanquin, "is traditional in Thaylen City. Visiting all ten allows a survey of the Royal Ward, and is a not-so-subtle reinforcement of the throne's Vorin piety. They've had trouble with the church in the past."

"I sympathize. Do you think if I explain I'm a heretic too, she'll stop with all the pomp?"

Navani leaned forward in the small palanquin, putting her freehand on his knee. "Dear one, if this kind of thing irks you so, we could send a diplomat."

"I am a diplomat."

"Dalinar . . ."

"This is my duty now, Navani. I *have* to do my duty. Every time I've ignored it in the past, something terrible has happened." He took her hands in his. "I complain because I can be unguarded with you. I'll keep the scowling to a minimum. I promise."

As their porters skillfully carried them up some steps, Dalinar watched out the palanquin window. This upper section of the city had weathered the storm well enough, as many of the structures here were of thick stone. Still, some had cracked, and a few roofs had fallen in. The palanquin passed a fallen statue, which had broken off at the ankles and toppled from a ledge toward the Loft Wards.

This city was hit harder than any I've had a report about, he thought. *This level of destruction is unique. Is it just all that wood, and the lack of anything to blunt the storm? Or is it more?* Some reports of the Everstorm mentioned no winds, only lightning. Others confusingly reported no rain, but burning embers. The Everstorm varied greatly, even within the same passing.

"It's probably comforting for Fen to do something familiar," Navani told him quietly as the porters set them down at the next stop. "This tour is a reminder of days before the city suffered such terrors."

He nodded. With that in mind, it was easier to bear the thought of yet another temple.

Outside, they found Fen emerging from her palanquin. "The temple of Battah, one of the oldest in the city. But of course the greatest sight here is the Simulacrum of Paralet, the grand statue that . . ." She trailed off, and Dalinar followed her gaze to the stone feet of the statue nearby. "Oh. Right."

"Let's see the temple," Dalinar urged. "You said it's one of the oldest. Which are older?"

"Only Ishi's temple is more ancient," she said. "But we won't linger there, or here."

"We won't?" Dalinar asked, noticing the lack of prayer smoke from this roof. "Is the structure damaged?"

"The structure? No, not the structure."

A pair of tired ardents emerged and walked down the steps, their robes stained with flecks of red. Dalinar looked to Fen. "Do you mind if I go up anyway?"

"If you wish."

As Dalinar climbed the steps with Navani, he caught a scent on the wind. The scent of blood, which reminded him of battle. At the top, the sight inside the doors of the temple was a familiar one. Hundreds of wounded covered the marble floor, lying on simple pallets, painspren reaching out like orange sinew hands between them.

"We had to improvise," Fen said, stepping up behind him in the doorway, "after our traditional hospitals filled."

"So many?" Navani said, safehand to her mouth. "Can't some be sent home to heal, to their families?"

Dalinar read the answers in the suffering people. Some were waiting to die; they'd bled internally, or had rampant infections, marked by tiny red rotspren on their skin. Others had no homes left, evidenced by the families that huddled around a wounded mother, father, or child.

Storms . . . Dalinar felt almost ashamed at how well his people had weathered the Everstorm. When he eventually turned to go, he almost ran into Taravangian, who haunted the doorway like a spirit. Frail, draped in soft robes, the aged monarch was weeping openly as he regarded the people in the temple.

"Please," he said. "*Please*. My surgeons are in Vedenar, an easy trip through the Oathgates. Let me bring them. Let me ease this suffering."

Fen pursed her lips to a thin line. She'd agreed to meet, but that didn't make her a part of Dalinar's proposed coalition. But what could she say to a plea like that?

"Your help would be appreciated," she said.

Dalinar suppressed a smile. She'd conceded one step by letting them activate the Oathgate. This was another one. *Taravangian, you are a gem.*

"Lend me a scribe and spanreed," Taravangian said. "I will have my Radiant bring aid immediately."

Fen gave the necessary orders, her consort nodding for the words to be recorded. As they walked back toward the palanquins, Taravangian lingered on the steps, looking out over the city.

"Your Majesty?" Dalinar asked, pausing.

"I can see my home in this, Brightlord." He put a trembling hand against the wall of the temple for support. "I blink bleary eyes, and I see Kharbranth destroyed in war. And I ask, 'What must I do to preserve them?'"

"We will protect them, Taravangian. I *vow* it."

"Yes . . . Yes, I believe you, Blackthorn." He took a long, drawn-out breath, and seemed to wilt further. "I think . . . I think I shall remain here and await my surgeons. Please go on."

Taravangian sat down on the steps as the rest of them walked away. At his palanquin, Dalinar looked back up and saw the old man sitting there, hands clasped before himself, liver-spotted head bowed, almost in the attitude of one kneeling before a burning prayer.

Fen stepped up beside Dalinar. The white ringlets of her eyebrows shook in the wind. "He is far more than people think of him, even after his accident. I've often said it."

Dalinar nodded.

"But," Fen continued, "he acts as if this city is a burial ground. That is *not* the case. We will rebuild from stone. My engineers plan to put walls on the front of each ward. We'll get our feet underneath us again. We just have to get ahead of the storm. It's the sudden loss of labor that really crippled us. Our parshmen . . ."

"My armies could do much to help clear rubble, move stones, and rebuild," Dalinar said. "Simply give the word, and you will have access to thousands of willing hands."

Fen said nothing, though Dalinar caught muttered words from the young soldiers and attendants waiting beside the palanquins. Dalinar let his attention linger on them, picking out one in particular. Tall for a Thaylen, the young man had blue eyes, with eyebrows combed and starched straight back alongside his head. His crisp uniform was, naturally, cut in the Thaylen style, with a shorter jacket that buttoned tight across the upper chest.

That will be her son, Dalinar thought, studying the young man's features. By Thaylen tradition, he would be merely another officer, not the heir. The monarchy of the kingdom was not a hereditary position.

Heir or not, this young man was important. He whispered something jeering, and the others nodded, muttering and glaring at Dalinar.

Navani nudged Dalinar and gave him a questioning look.

Later, he mouthed, then turned to Queen Fen. "So the temple of Ishi is full of wounded as well?"

"Yes. Perhaps we can skip that."

"I wouldn't mind seeing the lower wards of the city," Dalinar said. "Perhaps the grand bazaar I've heard so much about?"

Navani winced, and Fen grew stiff.

"It was . . . by the docks then, was it?" Dalinar said, looking out at the rubble-filled plain before the city. He'd assumed that it would have been in the Ancient Ward, the central part of the city. He should have paid better attention to those maps, apparently.

"I have refreshments set up at the courtyard of Talenelat," Fen said. "It was to be the last stop on our tour. Shall we go directly there now?"

Dalinar nodded, and they reboarded the palanquins. Inside, he leaned forward and spoke softly to Navani. "Queen Fen is not an absolute authority."

"Even your brother wasn't *absolutely* powerful."

"But the Thaylen monarch is worse. The councils of merchants and naval officers pick the new monarch, after all. They have great influence in the city."

"Yes. Where are you going with this?"

"It means she can't accede to my requests on her own," Dalinar said. "She can never agree to military aid as long as elements in the city believe that I'm bent on domination." He found some nuts in an armrest compartment and began munching on them.

"We don't have time for a drawn-out political thaw," Navani said, waving for him to hand her some nuts. "Teshav might have family in the city she can lean on."

"We could try that. Or . . . I have an idea budding."

"Does it involve punching someone?"

He nodded. To which she sighed.

"They're waiting for a spectacle," Dalinar said. "They want to see what the Blackthorn will do. Queen Fen . . . she was the same way, in the visions. She didn't open up to me until I gave her my honest face."

"Your honest face doesn't *have* to be that of a killer, Dalinar."

"I'll try not to kill anyone," he said. "I just need to give them a lesson. A display."

A lesson. A display.

Those words caught in his mind, and he found himself reaching back through his memories toward something still fuzzy, undefined. Something . . . something to do with the Rift and . . . and with Sadeas?

The memory darted away, just beneath the surface of his awareness. His subconscious shied from it, and he flinched like he'd been slapped.

In that direction . . . in that direction was *pain*.

"Dalinar?" Navani said. "I suppose it's *possible* you're right. Perhaps the people seeing you be polite and calm is actually bad for our message."

"*More* scowls, then?"

She sighed. "More scowls."

He grinned.

"Or a grin," she added. "From you, one of those can be *more* disturbing."

The courtyard of Talenelat was a large stone square dedicated to Stonesinew, Herald of Soldiers. Atop a set of steps was the temple itself, but they didn't get a chance to look inside, for the main entrance had collapsed. A large, rectangular stone block—that had once spanned the top of the doorway—rested wedged downward inside it.

Beautiful reliefs covered the walls on the outside, depicting the Herald Talenelat standing his ground alone against a tide of Voidbringers. Unfortunately, these had cracked in hundreds of places. A large black scorch at the top of the wall showed where the strange Everstorm lightning had blasted the building.

None of the other temples had fared this poorly. It was as if Odium had a grudge against this one in particular.

Talenelat, Dalinar thought. *He was the one they abandoned. The one I lost . . .*

"I have some business to attend to," Fen said. "With trade to the city disrupted so seriously, I haven't much to offer as victuals. Some nuts and fruit, some salted fish. We've laid them out for you to enjoy. I'll return later so we can conference. In the meantime, my attendants will see to your needs."

"Thank you," Dalinar said. They both knew she was making him wait on purpose. It wouldn't be long—maybe a half hour. Not enough to be an insult, but enough to establish that she was still the authority here, no matter how powerful he was.

Even though he wanted some time with her people, he found himself annoyed at the gamesmanship of it. Fen and her consort withdrew, leaving most of the rest behind to enjoy the repast.

Dalinar, instead, decided to pick a fight.

Fen's son would do. He did appear the most critical among those talking. *I don't want to seem the aggressor,* Dalinar thought, positioning himself close to the young man. *And I should pretend I haven't guessed who he is.*

"The temples were nice," Navani said, joining him. "But you didn't enjoy them, did you? You wished to see something more militaristic."

An excellent opening. "You are right," he said. "You there. Captainlord. I'm not one for dallying. Show me the city's wall. *That* is something of real interest."

"Are you *serious?*" Fen's son said in Thaylen-accented Alethi, words all mashed together.

"Always. What? Are your armies in such bad shape that you'd be embarrassed to let me see them?"

"I'm not going to let an enemy general inspect our defenses."

"I'm not your enemy, son."

"I'm not your son, tyrant."

Dalinar made a big show of looking resigned. "You've been shadowing me this entire day, soldier, speaking words that I've chosen not to hear. You're close to a line that, if crossed, *will* earn a response."

The young man paused, showing some measure of restraint. He weighed what he was getting himself into, and decided that the risk was worth the reward. Humiliate the Blackthorn here, and maybe he could save his city—at least as he saw it.

"I regret only," the man snapped, "that I didn't speak loudly enough for you to hear the insults, despot."

Dalinar sighed loudly, then began unbuttoning his uniform jacket, leaving himself in the snug undershirt.

"No Shards," the young man said. "Longswords."

"As you wish." Fen's son didn't have Shards, though he could have borrowed them if Dalinar insisted. Dalinar preferred this anyway.

The man covered his nervousness by demanding one of his attendants use a rock to draw a ring on the ground. Rial and Dalinar's guards approached, anticipationspren whipping nervously in their wakes. Dalinar waved them back.

"Don't hurt him," Navani whispered. She hesitated. "But don't lose either."

"I'm not going to hurt him," Dalinar said, handing her his jacket. "I can't promise the part about losing." She didn't see—but of course she didn't. He couldn't simply beat this man up. All that would do was prove to the rest of them that Dalinar was a bully.

He strode to the ring and paced it off, to memorize how many steps he could take without being forced out.

"I said longswords," the young man said, weapon in hand. "Where's your sword?"

"We'll do this by alternating advantage, three minutes," Dalinar said. "To first blood. You may lead off."

The young man froze. Alternating advantage. The youth would have three minutes armed, against Dalinar unarmed. If Dalinar survived without being bloodied or leaving the ring, he'd have three minutes against his opponent in the reverse: Dalinar armed, the young man unarmed.

It was a ridiculous imbalance, usually only seen in sparring practice, when men trained for situations where they might be unarmed against an armed foe. And then, you'd never use real weapons.

"I . . ." the young man said. "I'll switch to a knife."

"No need. Longsword is fine."

The young man gaped at Dalinar. Songs and stories told of the heroic unarmed man facing down many armed opponents, but in truth, fighting a single armed foe was incredibly difficult.

Fen's son shrugged. "As much as I'd love to be known as the man who bested the Blackthorn on even terms," he said, "I'll take an unfair fight. But have your men here swear an oath that if this goes poorly for you, I'll not be named an assassin. You yourself set these terms."

"Done," Dalinar said, looking to Rial and the others, who saluted and said the words.

A Thaylen scribe stood to witness the bout. She counted off the start, and the young man came for Dalinar immediately, swinging like he meant it. Good. If you were going to agree to a fight like this, you shouldn't hesitate.

Dalinar dodged, then dropped into a wrestling stance, though he didn't intend to get close enough to try for a hold. As the scribe counted off the time, Dalinar continued to dodge attacks, hovering around the outside of the ring, careful not to step over the line.

Fen's son—though aggressive—displayed some innate wariness. The young man probably could have forced Dalinar out, but he kept testing instead. He came in again, and Dalinar scrambled away from the flashing sword.

The young man grew concerned and frustrated. Perhaps if it had been cloudy, he would have seen the faint glow of the Stormlight Dalinar was holding.

As the countdown drew near the end, the young man grew more frantic. He knew what was coming. Three minutes alone in a ring, unarmed against the Blackthorn. The attacks strayed from hesitant, to determined, to desperate.

All right, Dalinar thought. *Just about now . . .*

The countdown hit ten. The young man came at him with a last-ditch, all-out assault.

Dalinar stood up, relaxed, and held his hands to the sides so that the audience could see him intentionally fail to dodge. Then he stepped *into* the young man's thrust.

The longsword hit him right in the chest, just to the left of his heart. Dalinar grunted at the impact, and the pain, but managed to take the sword in a way that it missed the spine.

Blood filled one of his lungs, and Stormlight rushed to heal him. The young man looked aghast, as if—despite everything—he hadn't expected, or wanted, to land such a decisive blow.

The pain faded. Dalinar coughed, spat blood to the side, then took the young man's hand by the wrist, shoving the sword farther through his chest.

The young man released the sword hilt and scrabbled backward, eyes bulging.

"That was a good thrust," Dalinar said, voice watery and ragged. "I could see how worried you were at the end; others might have let their form suffer."

The queen's son dropped to his knees, staring up as Dalinar stepped closer and loomed over him. Blood seeped around the wound, staining his shirt, until the Stormlight finally had time to heal the external cuts. Dalinar drew in enough that he glowed even in the daylight.

The courtyard had grown silent. Scribes held their mouths, aghast. Soldiers put hands on swords, shockspren—like yellow triangles—shattering around them.

Navani shared a sly smile with him, arms folded.

Dalinar took the sword by the hilt and slid it from his chest. Stormlight rushed to heal the wound.

To his credit, the young man stood up and stammered, "It's your turn, Blackthorn. I'm ready."

"No, you blooded me."

"You let me."

Dalinar took off his shirt and tossed it at the youth. "Give me your shirt, and we'll call it even."

The youth caught the bloody shirt, then looked up at Dalinar in befuddlement.

"I don't want your life, son," Dalinar said. "I don't want your city or your kingdom. If I'd *wanted* to conquer Thaylenah, I wouldn't offer you a smiling face and promises of peace. You should know that much from my reputation."

He turned to the watching officers, lighteyes, and scribes. He'd accomplished his goal. They were in awe of him, afraid. He had them in his hand.

It was shocking, then, to feel his own sudden, stark *displeasure*. For some reason, those frightened faces hit him harder than the sword had.

Angry, ashamed for a reason he still didn't understand, he turned and strode away, up the steps from the courtyard toward the temple above. He waved away Navani when she came to speak with him.

Alone. He needed a moment alone. He climbed to the temple, then turned and sat down on the steps, putting his back against the stone block that had fallen into the doorway. The Stormfather rumbled in the back of his mind. And beyond that sound was . . .

Disappointment. What had he just accomplished? He said he didn't want to conquer this people, but what story did his actions tell? *I'm stronger than you,* they said. *I don't need to fight you. I could crush you without exerting myself.*

Was that what it should feel like to have the Knights Radiant come to your city?

Dalinar felt a twisting nausea deep in his gut. He'd performed stunts like this dozens of times throughout his life—from recruiting Teleb back in his youth, to bullying Elhokar into accepting that Dalinar wasn't trying to kill him, to more recently forcing Kadash to fight him in the practice chamber.

Below, people gathered around Fen's son, talking animatedly. The young man rubbed his chest, as if he'd been the one who'd been struck.

In the back of Dalinar's mind, he heard that same insistent voice. The one he'd heard from the beginning of the visions.

Unite them.

"I'm trying," Dalinar whispered.

Why couldn't he ever convince anyone peacefully? Why couldn't he get people to listen without first pounding them bloody—or, conversely, shocking them with his own wounds?

He sighed, leaning back and resting his head against the stones of the broken temple.

Unite us. Please.

That was . . . a different voice. A hundred of them overlapping, making the same plea, so quiet he could barely hear them. He closed his eyes, trying to pick out the source of those voices.

Stone? Yes, he had a sensation of chunks of stone in *pain.* Dalinar started. He was hearing the spren of the *temple itself.* These temple walls had existed as a single unit for centuries. Now the pieces—cracked and ruined—hurt. They still viewed themselves as a beautiful set of carvings, not a ruined facade with fallen chunks scattered about. They longed to again be a single entity, unmarred.

The spren of the temple cried with many voices, like men weeping over their broken bodies on a battlefield.

Storms. Does everything I imagine have to be about destruction? About dying, broken bodies, smoke in the air and blood on the stones?

The warmth inside of him said that it did not.

He stood and turned, full of Stormlight, and seized the fallen stone that blocked the doorway. Straining, he shifted the block until he could slip in—squatting—and press his shoulders against it.

He took a deep breath, then *heaved* upward. Stone ground stone as he lifted the block toward the top of the doorway. He got it high enough, then positioned his hands immediately over his head. With a final push, shouting, he pressed with legs, back, and arms together, shoving the block upward with everything he had. Stormlight raged inside him, and his joints popped—then healed—as he inched the stone back into place above the doorway.

He could *feel* the temple urging him onward. It wanted so badly to be whole again. Dalinar drew in more Stormlight, as much as he could hold, draining every gemstone he'd brought.

Sweat streaming across his face, he got the block close enough that it felt *right* again. Power flooded through his arms into it, then seeped across the stones.

The carvings popped back together.

The stone lintel in his hands lifted and settled into place. Light filled the cracks in the stones and knit them back together, and gloryspren burst around Dalinar's head.

When the glow faded, the front wall of the majestic temple—including the doorway and the cracked reliefs—had been restored. Dalinar faced it, shirtless and coated in sweat, feeling twenty years younger.

No, the man he'd been twenty years ago could never have done this.

Bondsmith.

A hand touched his arm; Navani's soft fingers. "Dalinar . . . what did you do?"

"I listened." The power was good for far, far more than breaking. *We've been ignoring that. We've been ignoring answers right in front of our eyes.*

He looked back over his shoulder at the crowd climbing the steps, gathering around. "You," Dalinar said to a scribe. "You're the one who wrote to Urithiru and sent for Taravangian's surgeons?"

"Y . . . yes, Brightlord," she said.

"Write again. Send for my son Renarin."

※

Queen Fen found him in the courtyard of the temple of Battah, the one with the large broken statue. Her son—now wearing Dalinar's bloodied shirt tied around his waist, like some kind of girdle—led a crew of ten men with ropes. They'd just gotten the hips of the statue settled back into place; Dalinar drained Stormlight from borrowed spheres, sealing the stone together.

"I think I found the left arm!" a man called from below, where the bulk of the statue had toppled through the roof of a mansion. Dalinar's team of soldiers and lighteyes whooped and rushed down the steps.

"I did not expect to find the Blackthorn shirtless," Queen Fen said, "and . . . playing sculptor?"

"I can only fix inanimate things," Dalinar said, wiping his hands on a rag tied at his waist, exhausted. Using this much Stormlight was a new experience for him, and quite draining. "My son does the more important work."

A small family left the temple above. Judging by the father's tentative steps, supported by his sons, it seemed the man had broken a leg or two in the most recent storm. The burly man gestured for his sons to step back, took a few steps on his own—and then, his eyes wide, did a short skip.

Dalinar knew that feeling: the lingering effects of Stormlight. "I should have seen it earlier—I *should* have sent for him the moment I saw those wounded. I'm a fool." Dalinar shook his head. "Renarin has the ability to heal. He is new to his powers, as I am to mine, and can best heal those who were recently wounded. I wonder if it's similar to what I'm doing. Once the soul grows accustomed to the wound, it's much harder to fix."

A single awespren burst around Fen as the family approached, bowing and speaking in Thaylen, the father grinning like a fool. For a moment, Dalinar felt he could *almost* understand what they were saying. As if a part of him were stretching to bond to the man. A curious experience, one he didn't quite know how to interpret.

When they left, Dalinar turned to the queen. "I don't know how long Renarin will hold out, and I don't know how many of those wounds will be new enough for him to fix. But it is something we could do."

Men called below, heaving a stone arm out through the window of the mansion.

"I see you've charmed Kdralk as well," Fen noted.

"He's a good lad," Dalinar said.

"He was determined to find a way to duel you. I hear you gave him that. You're going to roll over this whole city, charming each person in turn, aren't you?"

"Hopefully not. That sounds like it would take a lot of time."

A young man came running down from the temple, holding a child with floppy hair who—though his clothing was torn and dusty—was smiling with a broad grin. The youth bowed to the queen, then thanked Dalinar in broken Alethi. Renarin kept blaming the healings on him.

Fen watched them go with an unreadable expression on her face.

"I need your help, Fen," Dalinar whispered.

"I find it hard to believe you need anything, considering what you've done today."

"Shardbearers can't hold ground."

She looked at him, frowning.

"Sorry. That's a military maxim. It . . . never mind. Fen, I have Radiants, yes—but they, no matter how powerful, won't win this war. More importantly, I can't see what I'm missing. *That's* why I need you.

"I think like an Alethi, as do most of my advisors. We consider the war, the conflict, but miss important facts. When I first learned of Renarin's powers, I thought only of restoring people on the battlefield to continue the fight. I need you; I need the Azish. I need a coalition of leaders who see what I don't, because we're facing an enemy that doesn't think like any we've faced before." He bowed his head to her. "Please. Join me, Fen."

"I've already opened that gate, and I'm talking to the councils about giving aid to your war effort. Isn't that what you wanted?"

"Not close, Fen. I want you to *join* me."

"The difference is?"

"The distinction between referring to it as 'your' war, and 'our' war."

"You're relentless." She took a deep breath, then cut him off as he tried to object. "I suppose that is what we need right now. All right, Blackthorn. You, me, Taravangian. The first real united Vorin coalition the world has seen since the Hierocracy. It's unfortunate that two of us lead kingdoms that are in ruin."

"Three," Dalinar said with a grunt. "Kholinar is besieged by the enemy. I've sent help, but for now, Alethkar is an occupied kingdom."

"Wonderful. Well, I think I can persuade the factions in my city to let your troops come and help here. If everything goes well with that, I will write to the Prime of Azir. Maybe that will help."

"I'm certain it will. Now that you've joined, the Azish Oathgate is the most essential to our cause."

"Well, they're going to be tricky," Fen said. "The Azish aren't as desperate as I am—and frankly, they aren't Vorin. People here, myself included, respond to a good *push* from a determined monarch. Strength and passion, the Vorin way. But those tactics will just make the Azish dig in and rebuff you harder."

He rubbed his chin. "Do you have any suggestions?"

"I don't think you'll find it very appealing."

"Try me," Dalinar said. "I'm starting to appreciate that the way I usually do things has severe limitations."

I worry about my fellow Truthwatchers.

—From drawer 8-21, second emerald

The storm did not belong to Kaladin.

He claimed the skies, and to an extent the winds. Highstorms were something different, like a country in which he was a visiting dignitary. He retained some measure of respect, but he also lacked real authority.

While fighting the Assassin in White, Kaladin had traveled with the highstorm by flying at the very front of the stormwall, like a leaf caught in a wave. That method—with the full force of the highstorm raging at his feet—seemed far too risky to use when bringing others. Fortunately, during their trip to Thaylenah, he and Shallan had tested other methods. It turned out he could still draw upon the storm's power while flying above it, so long as he stayed within a hundred feet or so of the stormclouds.

He soared there now, with two bridgemen and Elhokar's chosen team. The sun shone brightly above, and the eternal storm extended in all directions below. Swirling black and grey, lit by sparks of lightning. Rumbling, as if angry at the small group of stowaways. They couldn't see the stormwall now; they'd lagged far behind that. Their angle to Kholinar required them to travel more northward than westward as they cut across the Unclaimed Hills toward northern Alethkar.

There was a mesmerizing beauty to the storm's churning patterns, and Kaladin had to forcibly keep his attention on his charges. There were six of those, which made their team nine in total, counting himself, Skar, and Drehy.

King Elhokar was at the front. They couldn't bring their suits of Shardplate; Lashings didn't work on those. Instead, the king wore thick clothing and a strange kind of glass-fronted mask to block the wind. Shallan had suggested those; they were apparently naval equipment. Adolin came next. Then two of Shallan's soldiers—the sloppy deserters she'd collected like wounded axehound pups—and one maidservant. Kaladin didn't understand why they'd brought those three, but the king had insisted.

Adolin and the others were bundled up as much as the king, which made Shallan look even more odd. She flew in only her blue havah—which she'd pinned to keep it from fluttering too much—with white leggings underneath. Stormlight surged from her skin, keeping her warm, sustaining her.

Her hair streamed behind her, a stark auburn red. She flew with arms outstretched and eyes closed, grinning. Kaladin had to keep adjusting her speed to keep her in line with the others, as she couldn't resist reaching out to feel the wind between her freehand fingers, and waving to windspren as they passed.

How does she smile like that? Kaladin wondered. During their trip through the chasms together, he'd learned her secrets. The wounds she hid. And yet . . . she could simply ignore them somehow. Kaladin had never been able to do that. Even when he wasn't feeling particularly grim, he felt weighed down by his duties or the people he needed to care for.

Her heedless joy made him want to show her how to *really* fly. She didn't have Lashings, but could still use her body to sculpt the wind and dance in the air. . . .

He snapped himself back to the moment, banishing silly daydreams. Kaladin tucked his arms against himself, making a narrower profile for the wind. This made him move up the line of people, so he could renew their Stormlight each in turn. He didn't use Stormlight to maneuver so much as the wind itself.

Skar and Drehy handled their own flight about twenty feet below the group, watching in case anyone dropped for some reason. Lashings renewed, Kaladin maneuvered himself into line between Shallan and King Elhokar. The king stared forward through the mask, as if oblivious to the wondrous storm beneath. Shallan drifted onto her back, beaming as she looked up at the sky, the hem of her pinned skirts rippling and fluttering.

Adolin was a different story. He glanced at Kaladin, then closed his eyes and gritted his teeth. At least he'd stopped flailing each time they hit a change in the winds.

They didn't speak, as their voices would only be lost to the rushing wind.

Kaladin's instincts said he could probably lessen the force of the wind while flying—he'd done so before—but there were some abilities he had trouble deliberately reproducing.

Eventually, a line of light flitted from the storm below. It soon looped into a ribbon of light and spun up toward him. "We just passed the Windrunner River," Syl said. The words were more of a mental impression than actual sound.

"We're near Kholinar then," he said.

"She clearly likes the sky," Syl said, glancing at Shallan. "A natural. She almost seems like a spren, and I consider that high praise."

He sighed, and did not look at Shallan.

"Come on . . ." Syl said, zipping around to his other side. "You need to be with people to be happy, Kaladin. I know you do."

"I have my bridge crew," he muttered, voice lost to the winds—but Syl would be able to hear, as he could hear her.

"Not the same. And you know it."

"She brought her handmaid on a scouting mission. She couldn't go a week without someone to do her hair. You think I'd be interested in that?"

"Think?" Syl said. She took the shape of a tiny young woman in a girlish dress, flying through the sky before him. "I *know*. Don't think I don't spot you stealing looks." She smirked.

"Time to stop so we don't overshoot Kholinar," Kaladin said. "Go tell Skar and Drehy."

Kaladin took his charges one at a time, canceling their Lashing forward, replacing it with a half Lashing upward. There was a strange effect to the Lashings that frustrated Sigzil's scientific attempts at terminology. All of his numbers had assumed that once Lashed, a person would be under the influence of both the ground and the Lashing.

That wasn't the case. Once you used a Basic Lashing on someone, their body completely forgot about the pull of the ground, and they fell in the direction you indicated. Partial Lashings worked by making part of the person's weight forget the ground, though the rest continued to be pulled downward. So a half Lashing upward made a person weightless.

Kaladin situated the groups so he could speak to the king, Adolin, and Shallan. His bridgemen and Shallan's attendants hovered a short distance off. Even Sigzil's new explanations had trouble accounting for everything that Kaladin did. He'd somehow made a kind of . . . channel around the group, like in a river. A current, sweeping them along, keeping them closer together.

"It really is beautiful," Shallan said, surveying the storm, which blanketed everything but the tips of some very distant peaks to their left.

Probably the Sunmaker Mountains. "Like mixing paint—if dark paint could somehow spawn new colors and light within its swirls."

"So long as I can continue to watch it from a safe distance," Adolin said. He held Kaladin's arm to keep from drifting away.

"We're close to Kholinar," Kaladin said. "Which is good, as we're getting near the back edge of the storm, and I'll soon lose access to its Stormlight."

"What I feel like I'm about to lose," Shallan said, looking down, "is my shoes."

"Shoes?" Adolin said. "I lost my *lunch* back there."

"I can't help imagining something sliding off and dropping into it," Shallan whispered. "Vanishing. Gone forever." She glanced at Kaladin. "No wisecracks about missing boots?"

"I couldn't think of anything funny." He hesitated. "Though that hasn't ever stopped you."

Shallan grinned. "Have you ever considered, bridgeman, that *bad* art does more for the world than good art? Artists spend more of their lives making bad practice pieces than they do masterworks, particularly at the start. And even when an artist becomes a master, some pieces don't work out. Still others are somehow just *wrong* until the last stroke.

"You learn more from bad art than you do from good art, as your mistakes are more important than your successes. Plus, good art usually evokes the same emotions in people—most good art is the same *kind* of good. But bad pieces can each be bad in their own unique way. So I'm glad we have bad art, and I'm sure the Almighty agrees."

"All this," Adolin said, amused, "to justify your sense of humor, Shallan?"

"My sense of humor? No, I'm merely trying to justify the creation of Captain Kaladin."

Ignoring her, Kaladin squinted eastward. The clouds behind them were lightening from deep, brooding black and grey to a more general blandness, the color of Rock's morning mush. The storm was near to ending; what arrived with a fanfare ended with an extended sigh, gales giving way to peaceful rain.

"Drehy, Skar," Kaladin called. "Keep everyone in the air. I'm going to go scout below."

The two gave him salutes, and Kaladin dropped through the clouds, which—from within—looked like dirty fog. Kaladin came out crusted in frost, and rain began pelting him, but it was growing weak. Thunder rumbled softly above.

Enough light seeped through the clouds for him to survey the landscape. Indeed, the city was close, and it was majestic, but he forced himself to look for enemies before marveling. He noted a broad plain before the city—a killing field kept free of trees or large boulders, so that neither could offer cover to an invading army. That was empty, which wasn't unexpected.

The question was who held the city—Voidbringers or humans? He cautiously descended. The place glowed with a sprinkling of Stormlight from cages left out in the storm to recharge the gems. And . . . yes, from guard posts flew Alethi flags, raised now that the worst of the storm had passed.

Kaladin let out a relieved sigh. Kholinar had not fallen, though if their reports were right, all surrounding towns were occupied. In fact, looking closely, he could see that the enemy had begun building stormshelters on the killing field: bunkers from which they could prevent resupply to Kholinar. They were mere foundations of brick and mortar for now. During the times between storms, they were likely guarded—and built up—by large enemy forces.

He finally let himself stare at Kholinar. He knew it was coming, inevitable as a budding yawn; he couldn't keep it down forever. First assess the area for danger, get the lay of the land.

Then gawk.

Storms, that city was beautiful.

He'd flown high above it once in a half dream where he'd seen the Stormfather. That hadn't affected him the way it did to float here, looking over the vast metropolis. He'd seen proper cities now—the warcamps together were probably larger than Kholinar—so it wasn't the size that amazed him, really, but the variety. He was accustomed to functional bunkers, not stone buildings of many shapes and roofing styles.

Kholinar's defining feature, of course, was the windblades: curious rock formations that rose from the stone like the fins of some giant creature mostly hidden beneath the surface. The large curves of stone glittered with red, white, and orange strata, their hues deepened by the rain. He hadn't realized that the city walls were partially constructed on the tops of the outer windblades. There, the lower sections of the walls literally *sprouted* from the ground, while men had built fortifications atop them, evening out the heights and filling spaces between the curves.

Towering over the northern side of the city was the palace complex, which rose high and confident, as if in defiance of the storms. The palace was like a little city unto itself, with bright columns, rotundas, and turrets.

And something was very, *very* wrong with it.

A cloud hung over the palace, a darkness that—at first glance—seemed like nothing more than a trick of the light. Yet the feeling of wrongness persisted, and seemed strongest around a portion at the east of the palace complex. This flat, raised plaza was filled with small buildings. The palace monastery.

The Oathgate platform.

Kaladin narrowed his eyes, then Lashed himself back upward, passing into the clouds. He'd probably let himself gape for too long—he didn't want to start talk of a glowing person in the sky.

Still . . . that city. In Kaladin's heart still lived a country boy who had dreamed of seeing the world.

"Did you see that darkness around the palace?" Kaladin asked Syl.

"Yeah," she whispered. "Something's very wrong."

Kaladin emerged from the clouds and found that his crew had drifted off to the west in the breeze. He Lashed himself toward them, and noticed—for the first time—that his Stormlight was no longer being renewed by the storm.

Drehy and Skar looked visibly relieved when he arrived. "Kal—" Skar started.

"I know. We don't have much time left. Your Majesty, the city is right below us—and our forces still control the walls. The Parshendi are building storm bunkers and besieging the area, though the bulk of their army probably retreated to nearby towns in anticipation of the storm."

"The city stands!" Elhokar said. "Excellent! Captain, take us down."

"Your Majesty," Kaladin said. "If we drop from the sky like this, the enemy scouts *will* see us entering."

"So?" Elhokar said. "The need for subterfuge was predicated on a fear that we might have to sneak in. If our forces still hold the city, we can march up to the palace, assert command, and activate the Oathgate."

Kaladin hesitated. "Your Majesty, something is . . . wrong with the palace. It looks *dark,* and Syl saw it too. I advise caution."

"My wife and child are inside," Elhokar said. "They might be in danger."

You didn't seem to worry much about them during six years away at war, Kaladin thought.

"Let's go down anyway," the king said. "We want to get to the Oathgate as soon as possible . . ." He trailed off, looking from Kaladin to Shallan, to Adolin. "Don't we?"

"I advise caution," Kaladin repeated.

"The bridgeman isn't the jumpy type, Your Majesty," Adolin said. "We don't know what's going on in the city, or what happened since the reports of chaos and a revolt. Caution sounds good to me."

"Very well," Elhokar said. "This *is* why I brought the Lightweaver. What do you recommend, Brightness?"

"Let's land outside the city," Shallan said. "Far enough away that the glow of Stormlight doesn't give us away. We can use illusions to sneak in and find out what is going on without revealing ourselves."

"Very well," Elhokar said, nodding curtly. "Do as she suggests, Captain."

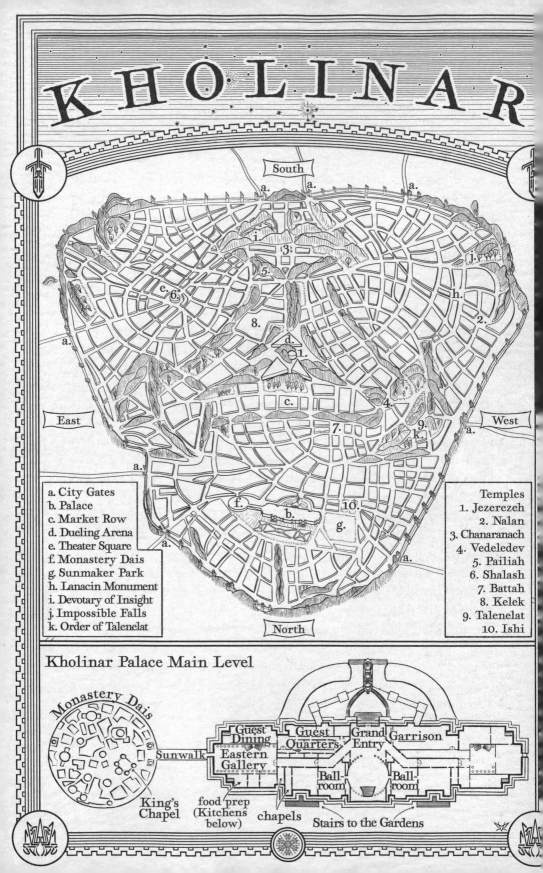

KHOLINAR

South

a.   a.   a.

i.

3.   j.

5.

e. 6.   h.

8.   2.

d.

1.

c.

4.

East   West

7.   9.
k.

a.

a.

f.   10.

b.

g.

a.

a.

North

Key

a. City Gates
b. Palace
c. Market Row
d. Dueling Arena
e. Theater Square
f. Monastery Dais
g. Sunmaker Park
h. Lanacin Monument
i. Devotary of Insight
j. Impossible Falls
k. Order of Talenelat

Temples

1. Jezerezeh
2. Nalan
3. Chanaranach
4. Vedeledev
5. Pailiah
6. Shalash
7. Battah
8. Kelek
9. Talenelat
10. Ishi

Kholinar Palace Main Level

Monastery Dais

Sunwalk

King's Chapel

food prep (Kitchens below)

chapels

Guest Dining

Eastern Gallery

Guest Quarters

Grand Entry

Garrison

Ball-room

Ball-room

Stairs to the Gardens

We can record any secret we wish, and leave it here? How do we know that they'll be discovered? Well, I don't care. Record that then.

—From drawer 2-3, smokestone

The enemy army was letting refugees approach the city.

At first, this surprised Kaladin. Wasn't the point of a siege to *prevent* people from getting in? And yet, a constant stream of people was allowed to approach Kholinar. The gates stood closed against an army invasion, but the side doors—which were still large—were wide open.

Kaladin handed the spyglass to Adolin. They'd landed in an inconspicuous location, then hiked back to the city on foot—but it had been dark by the time they'd arrived. They'd decided to spend the night outside the city, hidden by one of Shallan's illusions. Impressively, her Lightweaving had lasted all night on very little Stormlight.

Now that morning had arrived, they were surveying the city, which was maybe a mile away. From the outside, their hideout would seem like merely another knob of stone ground. Shallan couldn't make it transparent from only one side, so they had to see out using a slit that—if someone walked close by—would be visible.

The illusion felt like a cave—except for the fact that wind and rain went right through it. The king and Shallan had grumbled all morning, complaining of a damp, cold night. Kaladin and his men had slept like stones. There were advantages to having lived through Bridge Four.

"They let refugees in so they can drain the city's resources," Adolin said, watching through the spyglass. "A solid tactic."

"Brightness Shallan," Elhokar said, accepting the spyglass from Adolin, "you can give us each illusions, right? We can pretend to be refugees and enter the city easily."

Shallan nodded absently. She sat sketching near a shaft of light pouring through a small hole in the ceiling.

Adolin turned his spyglass toward the palace, the top of which surmounted the city in the distance. The day was perfectly sunny, bright, and crisp, with only a hint of moisture in the air from the highstorm the day before. There wasn't a cloud in the sky.

But somehow, the palace was still in shadow.

"What could it be?" Adolin said, lowering his spyglass.

"One of *them*," Shallan whispered. "The Unmade."

Kaladin looked back at her. She'd sketched the palace, but it was twisted, with odd angles and distorted walls.

Elhokar studied the palace. "You were right to recommend caution, Windrunner. My instinct is still to rush in. That's wrong, isn't it? I must be *prudent* and *careful*."

They gave Shallan time to finish sketches—she claimed to need them for complex illusions. Eventually she stood, flipping pages in her sketchpad. "All right. Most of us won't need disguises, as nobody will recognize me or my attendants. Same goes for Kaladin's men, I assume."

"If someone does recognize me," Skar said, "it won't cause any problems. Nobody here knows what happened to me at the Shattered Plains." Drehy nodded.

"All right," Shallan said, turning to Kaladin and Adolin. "You two will get new faces and clothing, making you into old men."

"I don't need a disguise," Kaladin said. "I—"

"You spent time with those parshmen earlier in the month," Shallan said. "Best to be safe. Besides, you scowl at everyone like an old man anyway. You'll be a great fit."

Kaladin glowered at her.

"Perfect! Keep it up." Shallan stepped over and breathed out, and Stormlight wreathed him. He felt he should be able to take it in, use it—but it resisted him. It was a strange sensation, as if he'd found a glowing coal that gave off no heat.

The Stormlight vanished and he held up a hand, which now appeared wizened. His uniform coat had been changed to a homespun brown jacket. He touched his face, but didn't feel anything different.

Adolin pointed at him. "Shallan, that is positively *wretched*. I'm impressed."

"What?" Kaladin looked at his men. Drehy winced.

Shallan wrapped Adolin in Light. He resolved into a sturdy, handsome man in his sixties, with dark brown skin, white hair, and a lean figure. His clothing was no longer ornate, but in good repair. He looked like the kind of old rogue you'd find in a pub, with handy tales about the brilliant things he'd done in his youth. The kind of man that made women think they preferred older men, when in reality they just preferred *him*.

"Oh, now that's unfair," Kaladin said.

"If I stretch a lie too far, people are more likely to be suspicious," Shallan said lightly, then stepped over to the king. "Your Majesty, you're going to be a woman."

"Fine," Elhokar said.

Kaladin started. He'd have expected an objection. Judging by the way that Shallan seemed to stifle a quip, she'd been expecting one too.

"You see," she said instead, "I don't think you can keep from carrying yourself like a king, so I figure that if you look like a highborn lighteyed woman, it's less likely that you'll be memorable to the guards who—"

"I said it was fine, Lightweaver," Elhokar said. "We mustn't waste time. My city and nation are in peril."

Shallan breathed out again, and the king was transfigured into a tall, stately Alethi woman with features reminiscent of Jasnah's. Kaladin nodded appreciatively. Shallan was right; there was something about the way Elhokar held himself that bespoke nobility. This was an excellent way to deflect people who might wonder who he was.

As they gathered their packs, Syl zipped into the enclosure. She took the shape of a young woman and flitted up to Kaladin, then stepped back in the air—aghast.

"Oh!" she said. "Wow!"

Kaladin glared at Shallan. "What did you *do* to me?"

"Oh, don't be that way," she said. "This will only highlight your excellent personality."

Don't let her get to you, Kaladin thought. *She wants to get to you.* He hefted his pack. It *didn't* matter what he looked like; it was only an illusion.

But what *had* she done?

He led the way out of their enclosure, and they fell into a line. The rock illusion melted away behind them. Kaladin's men had brought generic blue uniforms with no insignias. They could have belonged to any minor house guard within the Kholin princedom. Shallan's two had on generic brown uniforms, and with Elhokar wearing the dress of a lighteyed woman, they actually looked like a real refugee group. Elhokar would be seen as a bright-lady who had fled—without even a palanquin or carriage—before the enemy's advance. She'd brought a few guards, some servants, and Shallan as her young ward. And Kaladin was her . . . what?

Storms. "Syl," he growled, "could I summon you not as a sword, but as a flat, shiny piece of metal?"

"A mirror?" she asked, flying along beside him. "Hmmm. . . ."

"Not sure if it's possible?"

"Not sure if it's dignified."

"Dignified? Since when have you cared about dignity?"

"I'm not to be toyed with. I'm a *majestic* weapon to be used only in *majestic* ways." She hummed to herself and flitted away. Before he could call her back to complain, Elhokar caught up to him.

"Slow down, Captain," the king said. Even his voice had changed to sound womanly. "You'll outpace us."

Reluctantly, Kaladin slowed. Elhokar didn't show what he thought of Kaladin's face; the king kept his eyes forward. He never did think much about other people, so that was normal.

"They call it the Windrunner, you know," the king said softly. It took Kaladin a moment to realize that Elhokar was referring to the river that ran past Kholinar. Their path took them across it on a wide stone bridge. "The Alethi lighteyes rule because of *you*. Your order was prominent here, in what was then Alethela."

"I—"

"Our quest is vital," Elhokar continued. "We can't afford to let this city fall. We *cannot* afford mistakes."

"I assure you, Your Majesty," Kaladin said, "I don't intend to make mistakes."

Elhokar glanced at him, and for a moment Kaladin felt he could see the real king. Not because the illusion was failing, but because of the way Elhokar's lips tightened, his brow creased, and his gaze became so intense.

"I wasn't speaking of you, Captain," the king said quietly. "I was referring to my own limitations. When I fail this city, I want to make sure *you* are there to protect it."

Kaladin looked away, ashamed. Had he really just been thinking of how selfish this man was? "Your Majesty . . ."

"No," Elhokar said firmly. "This is a time to be realistic. A king must do whatever he can for the good of his people, and my judgment has proven . . . deficient. Anything I have 'accomplished' in life has been handed to me by my father or my uncle. You are here, Captain, to succeed when I fail. Remember that. Open the Oathgate, see that my wife and child are ushered through it to safety, and return with an army to reinforce this city."

"I'll do my best, Your Majesty."

"No," Elhokar said. "You'll do what I command. Be extraordinary, Captain. Nothing else will suffice."

Storms. How was it that Elhokar could give a compliment and yet be insulting at the same time? Kaladin felt a *weight* at hearing words that reminded him of his days in Amaram's army, back when people had first started talking about him, expecting things from him.

Those rumors had become a challenge, creating for everyone the notion of a man who was like Kaladin, but at the same time greater than he could ever be. He'd used that fictional man, relied upon him, to equip his team and to get soldiers transferred to his squad. Without it, he'd never have met Tarah. It was useful to have a reputation, so long as it didn't crush you.

The king dropped back farther into the line. They crossed the killing field under the watchful eyes of bowmen atop the wall. It made Kaladin's back itch, though they were Alethi soldiers. He tried to ignore it by focusing on studying the wall as they stepped into its shadow.

Those strata, he thought, *remind me of the tunnels in Urithiru.* Could there be some connection?

He glanced over his shoulder as Adolin came up to him. The disguised prince winced as he looked at Kaladin.

"Hey," Adolin said. "Um . . . wow. That's really distracting."

Storming woman. "What do you want?"

"I've been thinking," Adolin said. "We'll want a place inside the city to hole up, right? We can't follow either of our original plans—we can't simply stride up to the palace, but we don't want to assault it either. Not until we've done a little scouting."

Kaladin nodded. He hated the prospect of spending too much time in Kholinar. None of the other bridgemen had gotten far enough to swear the Second Ideal, so Bridge Four would be unable to practice with their powers until he returned. At the same time, the shadowed palace was disquieting. They did need to spend a few days gathering intelligence.

"Agreed," Kaladin said. "Do you have any ideas for where we can set up?"

"I've got just the place. Run by people I trust, and close enough to the palace to do some scouting, but far enough away not to get caught in . . . whatever is going on there. Hopefully." He looked concerned.

"What was it like?" Kaladin asked. "The thing beneath the tower that you and Shallan fought?"

"Shallan has pictures. You should ask her."

"I've seen them in the reports Dalinar's scribes gave me," Kaladin said. "What was it *like*?"

Adolin turned his blue eyes back to their path. The illusion was so real, it was hard to believe it was actually him—but he did *walk* the same way, with that inborn confidence only a lighteyes had.

"It was . . . wrong," Adolin finally said. "Haunting. A nightmare made manifest."

"Kind of like my face?" Kaladin asked.

Adolin glanced at him, then grinned. "Fortunately, Shallan covered it up for you with that illusion."

Kaladin found himself smiling. The way Adolin said things like that made it clear he was joking—and not only at your expense. Adolin made you want to laugh with him.

They drew close to the entrance. Though dwarfed by the main city gates, the side doors were wide enough to admit a cart. Unfortunately, the entrance was blocked by soldiers, and a crowd was accumulating, angerspren boiling on the ground around them. The refugees shook their fists and shouted at being barred entrance.

They'd been letting people in earlier. What was happening? Kaladin glanced at Adolin, then gestured with his chin. "Check it out?"

"We'll go have a look," Adolin said, turning toward the others of their group. "Wait here."

Skar and Drehy stopped, but Elhokar followed as Kaladin and Adolin continued forward—and so did Shallan. Her servants hesitated briefly, then trailed after her. Storms, the command structure in this expedition was going to be a nightmare.

Elhokar imperiously marched forward and barked at people to move out of his way. Reluctantly, they did—a woman with his bearing was not someone to cross. Kaladin exchanged a wearied glance with Adolin, then both fell in beside the king.

"I demand entry," Elhokar said, reaching the front of the crowd—which had swelled to some fifty or sixty people, with more steadily arriving.

The small group of guards looked over Elhokar, and their captain spoke. "How many fighting men can you provide for the city defense?"

"None," Elhokar snapped. "They are my *personal* guard."

"Then, Brightness, you should march them *personally* on to the south and try another city."

"Where?" Elhokar demanded, the sentiment echoed by many in the crowd. "There are monsters everywhere, Captain."

"Word is that there are fewer to the south," the soldier said, pointing. "Regardless, Kholinar is full to bursting. You won't find sanctuary here. Trust me. Move on. The city—"

"Who is your superior?" Elhokar cut in.

"I serve Highmarshal Azure, of the Wall Guard."

"Highmarshal Azure? I've never heard of such a man. Do these people look like they can walk farther? I *command* you to let us enter the city."

"I'm under orders to only let a set number in each day," the guard said with a sigh. Kaladin recognized that sense of exasperation; Elhokar could bring it out in the most patient of guards. "We've passed the limit. You'll need to wait until tomorrow."

People growled, and more angerspren appeared around them.

"It's not that we're callous," the guard captain called. "Will you just *listen?* The city is low on food, and we're running out of room in storm-shelters. Every person we add strains our resources further! But the monsters are focused here; if you flee to the south, you can take refuge there, maybe even get to Jah Keved."

"Unacceptable!" Elhokar said. "You've gotten these inane orders from that Azure fellow. Who commands him?"

"The highmarshal has no commander."

"What?" Elhokar demanded. "What of Queen Aesudan?"

The guard just shook his head. "Look, are those two men yours?" He pointed at Drehy and Skar, still standing near the back of the crowd. "They look like good soldiers. If you assign them to the Wall Guard, I'll give you immediate entry, *and* we'll see that you get a grain ration."

"Not that one though," another guard said, nodding toward Kaladin. "He looks sick."

"Impossible!" Elhokar demanded. "I need my guards with me at all times."

"Brightness . . ." the captain said. Storms, but Kaladin empathized with the poor man.

Syl suddenly grew alert, zipping into the sky as a ribbon of light. Kaladin immediately stopped paying attention to Elhokar and the guards. He searched the sky until he saw figures flying toward the wall in a V formation. There were at least twenty Voidbringers, each trailing a plume of dark energy.

Above, soldiers began to scream. The urgent call of drums followed, and the guard captain cursed in response. He and his men charged in through the open doors, then ran toward the nearest stairs leading up to the wall walk.

"In!" Adolin said as other refugees surged forward. He grabbed the king and towed him inside.

Kaladin fought against the press, refusing to be pushed into the city. He instead craned his neck to look upward, watching the Voidbringers hit the wall. Kaladin's angle at the base was terrible for making sense of the action directly above.

A few men got tossed off the wall farther along. Kaladin took a step toward them, but before he could do anything, they crashed to the ground with strikingly loud impacts. Storms! He was shoved farther toward the city by the crowd, and barely restrained himself from drawing in Stormlight.

Steady, he told himself. *The point is to get in without being seen. You would ruin that by flying to the defense of the city?*

But he was supposed to protect.

"Kaladin," Adolin called, fighting back through the crowd to where Kaladin stood right outside. "Come on."

"They're dominating that wall, Adolin. We should go help."

"Help how?" Adolin said. He leaned in, speaking softly. "Summon Shardblades and swing them wildly in the air, like a farmer chasing sky-eels? This is merely a raid to test our defenses. It's not a full-on assault."

Kaladin drew in a breath, then let Adolin pull him into the city. "Two dozen of the Fused. They could take this city with ease."

"Not alone," Adolin said. "Everyone knows that Shardbearers can't hold ground—it should be the same for Radiants and those Fused. You need soldiers to take a city. Let's move."

They went inside and met with the others, then moved away from the walls and gates. Kaladin tried to close his ears to the distant shouts of the soldiers. As Adolin had guessed, the raid ended as abruptly as it had begun, the Fused soaring away from the wall after only a few minutes of fighting. Kaladin sighed, watching them go, then steeled himself and followed with the rest as Adolin led them down a wide thoroughfare.

Kholinar was both more impressive and more depressing from the inside. They passed endless side streets packed with tall, three-story homes built like stone boxes. And storms, the guard at the wall had not been exaggerating. People crowded every street. Kholinar didn't have many alleyways; the stone buildings were built right up against each other in long rows. But people sat in the gutters, clinging to blankets and meager possessions. Too many doors were closed; often on nice days like this, people in the warcamps would leave the thick stormdoors and shutters open to the breeze. Not here. They were locked up tightly, for fear of being overwhelmed by refugees.

Shallan's soldiers pulled tight around her, hands carefully on their pockets. They seemed familiar with the underbelly of city life. Fortunately, she'd accepted Kaladin's pointed suggestion and hadn't brought Gaz.

Where are the patrols? Kaladin thought as they walked through curving streets, up and down slopes. With all these people clogging the streets, surely they needed as many men as possible keeping the peace.

He didn't see anything until they passed out of the section of city nearest the gates and entered a more wealthy area. This part was dominated by larger homes, with grounds marked by iron fences anchored into the stone with hardened crem. Behind *those* were guards, but the streets were devoid of anything similar.

Kaladin felt the gaze of the refugees. The wondering. Was it worth robbing him? Did it matter? Did they have food? Fortunately, the spears Skar and Drehy carried—along with the cudgels held by Shallan's two men—seemed enough to deter any would-be robbers.

Kaladin quickened his pace to catch up to Adolin at the front of their little group. "Is this safehouse of yours close? I don't like the feeling on these streets."

"It's a way yet," Adolin said. "But I agree. Storms, I should have brought a side sword. Who knew I'd be worried about summoning my Blade?"

"Why can't Shardbearers hold a city?" Kaladin asked.

"Basic military theory," Adolin said. "Shardbearers do a great job killing people—but what are they going to do against the population of an entire city? Murder everyone who disobeys? They'd get overwhelmed, Shards or not. Those flying Voidbringers will need to bring in the entire army to take the city. But first they'll test the walls, maybe weaken the defenses."

Kaladin nodded. He liked to think he knew a great deal about warfare, but the truth was, he didn't have the training of a man like Adolin. He'd participated in wars, but he'd never *run* any.

The farther they got from the walls, the better things seemed to be in the city—fewer refugees, more sense of order. They passed a market that was actually open, and inside he finally spotted a policing force: a tight group of men wearing unfamiliar colors.

This area would have looked nice, under other circumstances. Ridges of shalebark along the street, manicured with a variety of colors: some like plates, others like knobby branches reaching upward. Cultivated trees—which rarely pulled in their leaves—sprouted in front of many of the buildings, gripping the ground with thick roots that melded into the stone.

Refugees huddled in family groups. Here, the buildings were built in large square layouts, with windows facing inward and courtyards at the centers. People crowded into these, turning them into improvised shelters. Fortunately, Kaladin saw no obvious starvation, so the city's food stores hadn't given out yet.

"Did you see that?" Shallan asked softly, joining him.

"What?" Kaladin asked, looking over his shoulder.

"Performers in that market over there, dressed in very odd clothing." Shallan frowned, pointing down an intersecting street as they passed. "There's another one."

It was a man dressed all in white, with strips of cloth that streamed and fluttered as he moved. Head down, he stood on a street corner, leaping back and forth from one position to another. When he looked up and met Kaladin's eyes, he was the first stranger that day who didn't immediately look away.

Kaladin watched until a chull pulling a wagon of storm refuse blocked his view. Then, ahead of them, people started clearing the street.

"To the side," Elhokar said. "I'm curious about what this could be."

They joined the crowds pressed up against the buildings, Kaladin shoving his hands in his pack to protect the large number of spheres he had tucked away in a black purse there. Soon, a strange procession came marching down the center of the street. These men and women were also dressed like performers—their clothes augmented with brightly colored strips of red, blue, or green fabric. They walked past, calling out nonsense phrases. Words Kaladin knew, but which didn't belong together.

"What in Damnation is happening in this city?" Adolin muttered.

"This isn't normal?" Kaladin whispered.

"We have buskers and street performers, but nothing like this. Storms. What are they?"

"Spren," Shallan whispered. "They're imitating spren. Look, those are like flamespren, and the ones of white and blue with the flowing ribbons—windspren. Emotion spren too. There's pain, that's fear, anticipation . . ."

"So it's a parade," Kaladin said, frowning. "But nobody is having any fun."

The heads of spectators bowed, and people murmured or . . . prayed? Nearby an Alethi refugee—wrapped in rags and holding a sniveling baby in her arms—leaned against a building. A burst of exhaustionspren appeared above her, like jets of dust rising in the air. Only *these* were bright red instead of the normal brown, and seemed *distorted*.

"This is wrong, wrong, *wrong*," Syl said from Kaladin's shoulder. "Oh . . . oh, that spren is from *him*, Kaladin."

Shallan watched the rising not-exhaustionspren with widening eyes. She took Adolin by the arm. "Keep us moving," she hissed.

He started pushing through the crowd toward a corner where they could cut away from the strange procession. Kaladin grabbed the king by the arm, while Drehy, Skar, and Shallan's two guards instinctively formed up around them. The king let Kaladin pull him away, and a good thing too. Elhokar had been fishing in his pocket, perhaps for a sphere to give the exhausted woman. Storms! In the middle of the crowd!

"Not far now," Adolin said once they had breathing room on the side street. "Follow me."

He led them to a small archway, where the buildings had been built around a shared courtyard garden. Of course, refugees had taken shelter there, many of them huddled in blanket tents that were still wet from the storm the day before. Lifespren bobbed among the plants.

Adolin carefully wound his way through all the people to get to the door he wanted, and then knocked. It was the back door, facing the courtyard instead of the street. Was this a rich person's winehouse, perhaps? It seemed more like a home though.

Adolin knocked again, looking worried. Kaladin stepped up beside him, then froze. On the door was a shiny steel plate with engraved numbers. In it, he could see his reflection.

"Almighty above," Kaladin said, poking at the scars and bulges on his face, some with open sores. Fake teeth jutted from his mouth, and one eye was higher in his head than the other. His hair grew out in patches, and his nose was *tiny*. "What did you *do* to me, woman?"

"I've recently learned," Shallan said, "that a good disguise *can* be memorable, so long as it makes you memorable for the wrong reason. You, Captain, have a way of sticking in people's heads, and I worried you would do so no matter what face you wore. So I enveloped it with something even *more* memorable."

"I look like some kind of hideous spren."

"Hey!" Syl said.

The door finally opened, revealing a short, matronly Thaylen woman in an apron and vest. Behind her stood a burly man with a white beard, cut after the Horneater style.

"What?" she said. "Who are you?"

"Oh!" Adolin said. "Shallan, I'll need . . ."

Shallan rubbed his face with a towel from her pack, as if to remove makeup—covering the transformation as his face became his own again. Adolin grinned at the woman, and her jaw dropped.

"Prince *Adolin?*" she said. "Hurry, hurry. Get in here. It's not safe outside!"

She ushered them in and quickly shut the door. Kaladin blinked at the sphere-lit chamber, its walls lined with bolts of cloth and dummies with half-finished coats on them.

"What is this place?" Kaladin asked.

"Well, I figured we'd want someplace safe," Adolin said. "We'd need to stay with someone I'd trust with my life, or *more*." He looked at Kaladin, then gestured toward the woman. "So I brought us to my tailor."

62

RESEARCH

I wish to submit my formal protest at the idea of abandoning the tower. This is an extreme step, taken brashly.

—From drawer 2-22, smokestone

Secrets.

This city was brimming with them. It was *stuffed* with them, so tightly they couldn't help but ooze out.

The only thing for Shallan to do, then, was punch herself in the face.

That was harder than it seemed. She always flinched. *Come on,* she thought, making a fist. With eyes squeezed shut, she braced herself, then smacked her freehand into the side of her head.

It barely hurt; she simply wasn't capable of hitting herself hard enough. Maybe she could get Adolin to do it for her. He was in the back workroom of the tailor's shop. Shallan had excused herself to step into the front showroom, as she figured the others would react poorly to her trying to actively attract a painspren.

She could hear their voices as they interrogated the polite tailor. "It started with the riots, Your Majesty," the woman said in response to a question from Elhokar. "Or maybe before, with the . . . Well, it's complicated. Oh, I can't believe that you're here. I've had Passion for something to happen, true, but to finally . . . I mean . . ."

"Take a deep breath, Yokska," Adolin said gently. Even his voice was adorable. "Once you've taken all this in, we can continue."

Secrets, Shallan thought. *Secrets caused all of this.*

Shallan peeked into the other room. The king, Adolin, Yokska the tailor, and Kaladin sat inside, all wearing their own faces again. They'd sent Kaladin's men—along with Red, Ishnah, and Vathah—off with the tailor's housemaid to prepare the upper rooms and attic to accommodate guests.

Yokska and her husband would be sleeping on pallets in the back room here; naturally, Elhokar had been given their room. Right now, the small group had arranged a circle of wooden chairs under the heedless watch of tailor's dummies wearing a variety of half-finished coats.

Similar finished coats were displayed around the showroom. They were made in bright colors—even brighter than the Alethi wore at the Shattered Plains—with gold or silver thread, shiny buttons, and elaborate embroidery on the large pockets. The coats didn't close at the front except for a few buttons right below the collar, while the sides flared out, then split into tails at the back.

"It was the execution of the ardent, Brightlord," Yokska said. "The queen had her hanged, and . . . Oh! It was so gruesome. Blessed Passion, Your Majesty. I don't want to speak ill of your wife! She must not have realized—"

"Just tell us," Elhokar said. "Do not fear reprisal. I must know what the city's people think."

Yokska trembled. She was a small, plump woman who wore her long Thaylen eyebrows curled in twin ringlets, and was probably very fashionable in that skirt and blouse. Shallan lingered in the doorway, curious as to what the tailor had to say.

"Well," Yokska continued, "during the riots, the queen . . . the queen basically vanished. We'd get proclamations from her, now and then, but they often didn't make much sense. It all went wrong at the ardent's death. The city was already in an uproar. . . . She wrote such *awful* things, Your Majesty. About the state of the monarchy, and the queen's faith and . . ."

"And Aesudan condemned her to death," Elhokar said. Lit by only a few spheres at the center of their circle, his face was half shadowed. It was a most intriguing effect, and Shallan took a Memory for later sketching.

"Yes, Your Majesty."

"It was the dark spren, obviously, who gave the actual order," Elhokar said. "The dark spren that is controlling the palace. My wife would never be so imprudent as to publicly execute an ardent during such parlous times."

"Oh! Yes, of course. Dark spren. In the palace." Yokska sounded relieved to have a rationale for not blaming the queen.

Shallan considered, then noticed a pair of fabric scissors on a ledge nearby. She snatched them, then ducked back into the showroom. She pulled her skirt to the side, then stabbed herself in the leg with the scissors.

The sharp pain seared up her leg and through her body.

"Mmmm," Pattern said. "Destruction. This . . . this is not normal for you, Shallan. Too far."

She trembled at the pain. Blood welled from the wound, but she pressed her hand against it to limit its spread.

There! That had done it. Painspren appeared around her, as if crawling out of the ground—like little disembodied hands. They looked skinless, made of sinew. Normally they were bright orange, but these were a sickly green. And they were also *wrong* . . . instead of human hands, these seemed to be from some kind of monster—too distorted, with claws jutting from the sinew.

Shallan eagerly took a Memory, still holding her havah skirt up to keep it from the blood.

"Does that not hurt?" Pattern asked, from where he'd moved onto the wall.

"Of course it does," Shallan said, her eyes watering. "That was the point."

"Mmmm . . ." He buzzed, worried, but he needn't have been, as Shallan had what she wanted. Satisfied, she took in a little Stormlight and healed up, then used some cloth from her satchel to wipe the blood from her leg. She rinsed her hands and the cloth in the washroom basin. She was surprised at the running water; she hadn't thought Kholinar had such things.

She took out her drawing pad and returned to the back room's doorway, where she leaned against the jamb, doing a quick sketch of the strange, twisted painspren. Jasnah would tell her to put down her sketchpad and go sit with the others—but Shallan often paid better attention with a sketchpad in her hands. People who didn't draw never seemed to understand that.

"Tell us about the palace," Kaladin said. "The . . . dark spren, as His Majesty put it."

Yokska nodded. "Oh, yes, Brightlord."

Shallan glanced up to catch Kaladin's reaction at being called Brightlord, but he didn't show one. His illusory disguise was gone—though Shallan had tucked that sketch away, for possible further use. He'd summoned his Blade earlier in the morning, and he now had eyes as blue as any she'd seen. They hadn't faded yet.

"There was that unexpected highstorm," Yokska continued. "And after that, the weather went insane. The rains started going in fits and starts. But oh! When that new storm came, the one with the red lightning, it left a *gloom over the palace.* So nasty! Dark times. I suppose . . . suppose those haven't ended."

"Where were the royal guards?" Elhokar said. "They should have augmented the Watch, restored order during the rioting!"

"The Palace Guard retreated into the palace, Your Majesty," Yokska said. "And she ordered the City Watch to barricade into the barracks. They eventually moved to the palace on the queen's orders. They . . . haven't been seen since."

Storms, Shallan thought, continuing her sketch.

"Oh, I guess I'm jumping about, but I forgot!" Yokska continued. "In the middle of the rioting, a proclamation came from the queen. Oh, Your Majesty. She wanted to execute the city's parshmen! Well, we all thought she must be—I'm sorry—but we thought she must be mad. Poor things. What have they ever done? That's what we thought. We didn't know.

"Well, the queen posted criers all over the city, proclaiming the parshmen to be Voidbringers. And I must say, about that she was right. Yet it was still so strange. She didn't even seem to notice that half the city was rioting!"

"The dark spren," Elhokar said, making a fist. "*It* must be blamed, not Aesudan."

"Were there reports of any strange murders?" Adolin asked. "Murders, or violence, that came in pairs—a man would die, and then a few days later someone else would be killed in the exact same way?"

"No, Brightlord. Nothing . . . nothing like that, though there were many who were killed."

Shallan shook her head. It was a different Unmade here; another ancient spren of Odium. Religion and lore spoke of them vaguely at best, tending to simplistically conflate them into one evil entity. Navani and Jasnah had begun to research them over the last weeks, but they still didn't know very much.

She finished her sketch of the painspren, then did one of the exhaustionspren they'd seen earlier. She'd managed to glimpse some hungerspren around a refugee on their way. Oddly, those didn't look any different. Why?

Need more information, Shallan thought. *More data.* What was the most embarrassing thing she could think of?

"Well," Elhokar said, "though we didn't order the parshmen executed, only exiled, at least that order seems to have reached Aesudan. She must have been free enough from the control of the dark forces to heed our words via spanreed."

Of course, he didn't mention the logical problems. If the tailor was correct about the dark spren arriving during the Everstorm, then Aesudan had executed the ardent on her own—as that had happened before. Likewise, the order to exile the parshmen would also have come before the Everstorm. And who knew if an Unmade could even influence someone like the queen? The spren in Urithiru had mimicked people, not controlled them.

Yokska did seem to be a little scattered in her retelling of events, so maybe Elhokar could be forgiven for mixing up the timeline. Either way, Shallan needed something embarrassing. *When I spilled wine the first time Father gave me some at a dinner party. No . . . no . . . something more . . .*

"Oh!" Yokska said. "Your Majesty, you should know. The proclamation requiring the execution of the parshmen . . . well, a coalition of important lighteyes didn't follow it. Then, after that terrible storm, the queen started giving other orders, so the lighteyes went to meet with her."

"Let me guess," Kaladin said. "They never came back from the palace."

"No, Brightlord, they did not."

How about when I woke and faced Jasnah, after I'd almost died, and she'd discovered that I'd betrayed her?

Surely remembering *that* event would be enough.

No?

Bother.

"So the parshmen," Adolin said. "*Did* they get executed?"

"No," Yokska continued. "Like I said, everyone was concerned with the riots—save for the servants posting the queen's orders, I suppose. The Wall Guard eventually took action. They restored some measure of order in the city, then rounded up the parshmen and exiled them to the plain outside. And then . . ."

"The Everstorm came," Shallan said, covertly undoing the button on her safehand sleeve.

Yokska seemed to shrink down in her seat. The others fell silent, which provided the perfect opportunity for Shallan. She took a deep breath, then strolled forward, holding her sketchpad as if distracted. She tripped herself over a roll of cloth on the floor, yelped, and tumbled into the center of the ring of chairs.

She ended up sprawled on the floor, skirts up about her waist—and she wasn't even wearing the leggings today. Her safehand bulged out from between the sleeve buttons, poking into the open *right* in front of not just the king, but Kaladin *and* Adolin.

Perfectly, horribly, *incredibly* mortifying. She felt a deep blush come on, and shamespren dropped around her in a wave. Normally, they took the shape of falling red and white flower petals.

These were like pieces of broken glass.

The men, of course, were more distracted by the position she'd gotten herself into. She squawked, managed to take a Memory of the shamespren, and righted herself, blushing furiously and tucking her hand in her sleeve.

That, she thought, *might be the craziest thing you've ever done. Which is saying a lot.*

She grabbed her sketchbook and bustled away, passing Yokska's white-bearded husband—Shallan still hadn't heard him speak a word—standing in the doorway with a tray of wine and tea. Shallan grabbed the darkest cup of wine and downed it in a single gulp, feeling the stares of the men on her back.

"Shallan?" Adolin piped up. "Um . . ."

"I'mfinethatwasanexperiment," she said, ducking into the showroom and throwing herself into a seat placed there for customers. *Storms, that was humiliating.*

She could still see partway into the other room. Yokska's husband walked with his silver tray to the group. He stopped by Yokska—though serving the king first would have been the correct protocol—and rested a hand on her shoulder. She put her own on his.

Shallan flipped open her sketchpad, and was pleased to see more shamespren dropping around her. Still glass. She started a drawing, burying herself in it to keep from thinking about what she'd just done.

"So . . ." Elhokar said in the next room. "We were talking about the Wall Guard. They obeyed the queen's orders?"

"Well, that was around the time that the highmarshal appeared. I've never seen *him* either. He doesn't come down from the wall much. He restored order, so that's good, but the Wall Guard doesn't have the numbers to police the city *and* watch the wall—so they've taken to watching the wall and mostly leaving us to just . . . survive in here."

"Who rules now?" Kaladin asked.

"Nobody," Yokska said. "Various highlords . . . well, they basically seized sections of the city. Some argued that the monarchy had fallen, that the king—I beg pardon, Your Majesty—had abandoned them. But the real power in the city is the Cult of Moments."

Shallan looked up from her drawing.

"Those people we saw on the street?" Adolin asked. "Dressed like spren."

"Yes, Your Highness," Yokska said. "I don't . . . I don't know what to tell you. Spren look strange sometimes in the city, and people think it has to do with the queen, the weird storm, the parshmen . . . They're scared. Some have started claiming they can see a new world coming, a truly strange new world. One ruled by spren.

"The Vorin church has declared the Cult of Moments a heresy, but so many of the ardents were in the palace when it grew dark. Most of those remaining took refuge with one of the highlords who claimed small sections of Kholinar. Those are increasingly isolated, ruling their districts on their own. And then . . . and then there are the fabrials. . . ."

Fabrials. Shallan scrambled to her feet and stuck her head into the next room. "What about the fabrials?"

"If you use a fabrial," Yokska said, "of any sort—from spanreed, to warmer, to painrial—you'll draw *them*. Screaming yellow spren that ride the wind like streaks of terrible light. They shout and swirl about you. That then usually brings the creatures from the sky, the ones with the loose clothing and long spears. They seize the fabrial, and sometimes kill the one trying to use it."

Storms . . . Shallan thought.

"Have you seen this?" Kaladin asked. "What did the spren look like? You heard them speak?"

Shallan glanced at Yokska, who had sunk down farther in her seat. "I think . . . maybe we should give the good tailor a break," Shallan noted. "We've shown up on her doorstep out of nowhere, stolen her bedroom, and are now interrogating her. I'm sure the world won't fall apart if we let her have a few minutes to drink her tea and recover."

The woman looked at Shallan with an expression of pure gratitude.

"Storms!" Adolin said, leaping to his feet. "Of course you're right, Shallan. Yokska, forgive us, and thank you *so* much for—"

"No need for thanks, Your Highness," she said. "Oh, I *did* have Passion that help would come. And here it is! But if it pleases the king, a little rest . . . Yes, a little rest would be *much* appreciated."

Kaladin grunted and nodded, and Elhokar waved a hand in a way that wasn't *quite* dismissive. More just . . . self-absorbed. The three men left Yokska to rest and joined Shallan in the showroom, where light from the setting sun streamed between the drapes on the front windows. Those would normally be open to show off the tailor's creations, but no doubt they'd lately spent most of their time closed.

The four gathered together to digest what they'd discovered. "Well?" Elhokar asked, speaking—for once—in a soft, thoughtful tone.

"I want to know what's going on with the Wall Guard," Kaladin said. "Their leader . . . none of you have heard of him?"

"Highmarshal Azure?" Adolin asked. "No. But I've been away for years. There are bound to be many officers in the city who were promoted while the rest of us were at war."

"Azure might be the one feeding the city," Kaladin said. "Someone is providing grain. This place would have eaten itself to starvation without some source of food."

"At least we've learned something," Shallan said. "We know why the spanreeds cut off."

"The Voidbringers are trying to isolate the city," Elhokar said. "They locked down the palace to prevent anyone from using the Oathgate, then cut off communication via spanreeds. They're stalling until they can gather a large enough army."

Shallan shivered. She held up her sketchpad, showing them the drawings she'd done. "Something *is* wrong with the city's spren."

The men nodded as they saw her drawings, though only Kaladin seemed to catch what she'd been doing. He looked from the drawing of the shamespren to her hand, then raised an eyebrow at her.

She shrugged. *Well, it worked, didn't it?*

"Prudence," the king said softly. "We mustn't simply rush in and fall to whatever darkness seized the palace, but we also can't afford to be inactive."

He stood up straighter. Shallan had grown so accustomed to seeing Elhokar as an afterthought—a fault of the way Dalinar, increasingly, had been treating him. But there was an earnest determination to him, and yes, even a regal bearing.

Yes, she thought, taking another Memory of Elhokar. *Yes, you are king. And you* can *live up to your father's legacy.*

"We must have a plan," Elhokar said. "I would gladly hear your wisdom on this matter, Windrunner. How should we approach this?"

"Honestly, I'm not sure we should. Your Majesty, it might be best to catch the next highstorm, return to the tower, and report back to Dalinar. He can't reach us with his visions here, and one of the Unmade could very well be beyond our mission's parameters."

"We don't need Dalinar's permission to act," Elhokar said.

"I didn't mean—"

"What is my uncle going to do, Captain? Dalinar won't know any more than we will. We either do something about Kholinar ourselves now, or give the city, the Oathgate, *and* my family up to the enemy."

Shallan agreed, and even Kaladin nodded slowly.

"We should at least scout the city and get a better feel for things," Adolin noted.

"Yes," Elhokar said. "A king needs accurate information to act correctly. Lightweaver, could you take on the look of a messenger woman?"

"Of course," Shallan said. "Why?"

"Let us say I were to dictate a letter to Aesudan," the king said, "then seal it with the royal seal. You could act the part of a messenger who had come personally from the Shattered Plains, traveling through great hardship to reach the queen to deliver my words. You could present yourself at the palace, and see how the guards there react."

"That's . . . not a bad idea," Kaladin said. He sounded surprised.

"It could be dangerous," Adolin said. "The guards might bring her into the palace itself."

"I'm the only one here who has confronted one of the Unmade directly," Shallan said. "I'm most likely to be able to spot their influence, and I have the resources to get out. I agree with His Majesty—eventually someone must go into the palace and see what is happening there. I promise to back off quickly if my gut says something is happening."

"Mmmm . . ." Pattern said unexpectedly from her skirts. He generally preferred to remain silent when others were near. "I will watch and warn. We will be careful."

"See if you can assess the state of the Oathgate," the king said. "Its platform is part of the palace complex, but there are ways up other than through the palace itself. The best thing for the city might be to go in quietly, activate it, and bring in reinforcements, *then* decide how to rescue my family. But do reconnaissance only, for now."

"And the rest of us just sit around tonight?" Kaladin complained.

"Waiting and trusting those whom you have empowered is the soul of kingship, Windrunner," Elhokar said. "But I suspect that Brightness Shallan would not object to your company, and I'd rather have someone watching to help get her out, in an emergency."

He wasn't exactly correct; she *would* object to Kaladin's presence. Veil wouldn't want him looking over her shoulder, and Shallan wouldn't want him asking questions about that persona.

However, she could find no reasonable objection. "I want to get a feel for the city," she said, looking to Kaladin. "Have Yokska scribe the king's letter, then meet me. Adolin, is there a good spot we could find each other?"

"The grand steps up to the palace complex, maybe?" he said. "They're impossible to miss, and have a little square out in front of them."

"Excellent," Shallan said. "I'll be wearing a black hat, Kaladin. You can wear your own face, I suppose, now that we're past the Wall Guard. But that slave brand . . ." She reached up to create an illusion to make it vanish from his forehead.

He caught the hand. "No need. I'll keep my hair down over it."

"It peeks out," she said.

"Then let it. In a city full of refugees, nobody is going to care."

She rolled her eyes, but didn't push. He was probably right. In that uniform, he'd probably just be taken for a slave someone bought, then put in their house guard. Even though the *shash* brand *was* odd.

The king went to prepare his letter, and Adolin and Kaladin stayed in the showroom to talk quietly about the Wall Guard. Shallan headed up the steps. Her own room was a smaller one on the second floor.

Inside were Red, and Vathah, and Ishnah the assistant spy, chatting quietly.

"How much did you eavesdrop on?" Shallan asked them.

"Not much," Vathah said, thumbing over his shoulder. "We were too busy watching Ishnah ransack the tailor's bedroom to see if she was hiding anything."

"Tell me you didn't make a mess."

"No mess," Ishnah promised. "And nothing to report either. The woman might actually be as boring as she seems. The boys did learn some good search procedures though."

Shallan walked past the small guest bed and looked out the window at a daunting view down a city street. So many homes, so many people. Intimidating.

Fortunately, Veil wouldn't see it that way. There was only one problem.

I can't work with this team, she thought, *without them eventually asking questions.* This Kholinar mission would bring it to a head, as Veil hadn't flown with them.

She'd been dreading this. And . . . kind of . . . anticipating it? "I need to tell them," she whispered.

"Mmm," Pattern said. "It's good. Progress."

Rather, she'd been backed into a corner. Still, it had to be done eventually. She walked to her pack and removed a white coat and a hat, which folded up on its side. "Some privacy, boys," she said to Vathah and Red. "Veil needs to get dressed."

They looked from the coat to Shallan, then back. Red slapped the side of his head and laughed. "You're *kidding.* Well, I feel like an idiot."

She'd expected Vathah to feel betrayed. Instead he nodded—as if this made perfect sense. He saluted her with one finger, then the two men retreated.

Ishnah lingered. Shallan had—after some debate—decided to bring the woman. Mraize had vetted her, and in the end, Veil needed the training.

"You don't look surprised about this," Shallan said as she started changing.

"I was suspicious when Veil . . . when you told me to go on this mission," she said. "Then I saw the illusions, and guessed." She paused. "I had it reversed. I thought Brightness Shallan was the persona. But the spy— *that's* the false identity."

"Wrong," Shallan said. "They're both equally false." Once dressed, she flipped through her sketchbook and found a drawing of Lyn in her scouting uniform. Perfect. "Go tell Brightlord Kaladin I'm already out and exploring, and that he should meet me in about an hour."

She climbed out the window and dropped one story to the ground, relying on her Stormlight to keep her legs from breaking. Then she struck off down the street.

I returned to the tower to find squabbling children, instead of proud knights. That's why I hate this place. I'm going to go chart the hidden undersea caverns of Aimia; find my maps in Akinah.

—From drawer 16-16, amethyst

Veil enjoyed being in a proper city again, even if it was half feral. Most cities lived on the very edge of civilization. Everyone talked about towns and villages out in the middle of nowhere as if they were uncivilized, but she'd found people in those places pleasant, even-tempered, and comfortable with their quieter way of life.

Not in cities. Cities balanced on the edge of sustainability, always one step from starvation. When you pressed so many people together, their cultures, ideas, and stenches rubbed off on one another. The result wasn't civilization. It was contained chaos, pressurized, bottled up so it couldn't escape.

There was a *tension* to cities. You could breathe it, feel it in every step. Veil loved it.

Once a few streets from the tailor's shop, she pulled down the brim of her hat and held up a page from her sketchbook as if consulting a map. This covered her as she breathed out Stormlight, transforming her features and hair to match those of Veil, instead of Shallan.

No spren came, screaming to warn of what she'd done. So Lightweaving was different from using fabrials. She'd been fairly certain it was safe, as they'd worn disguises into the city, but she'd wanted to be away from the tailor's shop in case.

Veil strolled down the thoroughfare, long coat rippling around her calves. She decided immediately that she liked Kholinar. She liked how the city rolled across its hills, a lumpy blanket of buildings. She liked how it smelled of Horneater spices in one gust of wind, then of Alethi steamed crabs in the next. Admittedly, those probably weren't proper crabs today, but cremlings.

That part she didn't like. These poor people. Even in this more affluent area, she could barely walk a quarter block without having to weave around huddles of people. The midblock courtyards were clogged with what had probably been normal villagers not long ago, but who were now impoverished wretches.

There wasn't much wheeled traffic on the streets. Some palanquins ringed by guards. No carriages. Life, however, did not stop for a war—or even for a second Aharietiam. There was water to draw, clothes to clean. Women's work mostly, as she could see from the large groups of men standing around. With no one really in charge in the city, who would pay men to work forges? To clean streets or chip crem? Even worse, in a city this size, much of the menial labor would have been done by parshmen. Nobody would be eager to leap in to take their place.

The bridgeboy is right though, Veil thought, loitering at an intersection. *The city* is *still being fed.* A place like Kholinar could consume itself quickly, once the food or water ran out.

No, cities were not civilized places. No more than a whitespine was domesticated just because it had a collar around its neck.

A small group of cultists dressed as rotspren limped down the street, the wet red paint on their clothing evocative of blood. Shallan considered these people extreme and alarming, probably crazy, but Veil wasn't convinced. They were too theatrical—and there were too many of them—for all to be truly deranged. This was a fad. A way of dealing with unexpected events and giving some shape to lives that had been turned upside down.

That didn't mean they weren't dangerous. A group of people all trying to impress one another was always more dangerous than the lone psychopath. So she gave the cultists a wide berth.

Over the next hour, Veil surveyed the city while wending her way in the general direction of the palace. The area with the tailor's shop was the most normal. It had a good functioning market, which she intended to investigate further when not pressed for time. It had parks, and though these had been appropriated by the crowds, the people in them were lively. Family groups—even communities transplanted from outer villages—doing the best they could.

She passed bunkerlike mansions of the wealthy. Several had been ransacked: gates broken down, window shutters cracked, grounds draped with blankets or shanties. Some lighteyed families, it seemed, hadn't maintained enough guards to withstand the riots.

Anytime Veil's path took her closer to the city walls, she entered sections of the city that were the most cramped, and the most despondent. Refugees just sitting on the streets. Vacant eyes, ragged clothing. People without homes or community.

The closer she drew to the palace though, the emptier the city became. Even the unfortunates who populated the streets near the walls—where the Voidbringers were raiding—knew to stay away from this area.

That made the homes of the wealthy here in the palace district seem . . . out of place. In normal times, living close to the palace would have been a privilege, and every large compound here had private walls that sheltered delicate gardens and ostentatious windows. But now, Veil felt the wrongness of the area as a prickling sensation on her skin. The families living here must have felt it, but they stubbornly remained in their mansions.

She peeked through the iron gate of one such mansion, and found soldiers on sentry duty: men in dark uniforms whose colors and heraldry she couldn't discern. In fact, when one glanced at her, she couldn't make out his eyes. It was probably just a trick of the light, but . . . storms. The soldiers had a wrongness about them; they moved oddly, rushing in bursts, like prowling predators. They didn't stop to talk to each other as they passed.

She backed away and continued down the street. The palace was right ahead. Straight on in front of it were the wide steps where she'd meet Kaladin, but she had some time left. She slipped into a park nearby, the first she'd seen in the city that wasn't clogged with refugees. Towering stumpweight trees—bred over time for height and spread of leaves—gave a shadowed canopy.

Away from potential prying eyes, she used Stormlight to overlay Veil's features and clothing with those of Lyn. A stronger, more sturdy build, a blue scout's uniform. The hat became a black rain hat, of the type often worn during the Weeping.

She left the park as Veil playing a part. She tried to keep this distinction sharp in her mind. She was *still Veil*. Merely in disguise.

Now, to see what she could find out about the Oathgate. The palace was built on a rise overlooking the city, and she slipped through the streets to its eastern side, where she indeed found the Oathgate platform. It was covered in buildings, and was as high as the palace—maybe twenty feet up. It connected to the main palace by a covered walkway that rested atop a small wall.

They built that walkway right over the ramp, she thought with displeasure. The only other paths up onto the platform were sets of steps cut into the rock, and those were guarded by people in spren costumes.

Veil watched from a safe distance. So the cult was involved in this somehow? Above on the platform, smoke trailed from a large fire, and Veil could hear sounds rising from that direction. Were those . . . screams?

The whole place was unnerving, and she shivered, then retreated. She found Kaladin leaning against the base of a statue in a square before the palace steps. Soulcast out of bronze, the statue depicted a figure in Shardplate rising as if from waves.

"Hey," she said softly. "It's me. Do you like the boots on this outfit?" She raised her foot.

"Do we have to keep bringing that up?"

"I was giving you a passcode, bridgeboy," she said. "To prove I'm who I say I am."

"Lyn's face made that clear," he said, handing her the king's letter, inside a sealed envelope.

I like him, Veil thought. An . . . odd thought, in how much stronger that feeling was to Veil than it had been to Shallan. *I like that brooding sense he has about him, those dangerous eyes.*

Why did Shallan focus so much on Adolin? He was nice, but also bland. You couldn't tease him without feeling bad, but Kaladin, he glared at you in the most satisfying of ways.

The part of her that was still Shallan, deep down, was bothered by this line of thinking. So instead, Veil turned her attention to the palace. It was a grand structure, but more like a fortress than she'd pictured. Very Alethi. The bottom floor was a massive rectangle, with the short side facing toward the storm. The upper levels were successively thinner, and a dome rose from the center of the building.

From up close, she couldn't make out exactly where the sunlight stopped and the shadow began. Indeed, the air of darkness felt . . . different from how Urithiru had when the dark spren was there. She kept feeling that she wasn't seeing it all. When she'd glance away and look back, she could *swear* that something was different. Had that planter moved, the one running along the grand entry steps? Or . . . had that door always been painted blue?

She took a Memory, then looked away and back, and took another Memory. She wasn't certain what good it would do, as she'd had trouble drawing the palace earlier.

"Do you see them?" Kaladin whispered. "The soldiers, standing between the pillars?"

She hadn't. The front of the palace—at the top of the long set of stairs—was set with pillars. Looking closer into the shadows, she saw men in there, gathered beneath the overhang supported by the columns. They stood like

statues, their spears upright, never moving.

Anticipationspren rose around Veil, and she jumped. While two of the spren looked normal—like flat streamers—the others were wrong. They waved long, thin tendrils that looked like lashes to whip a servant.

She shared a glance with Kaladin, then took a Memory of the spren.

"Shall we?" Kaladin asked.

"I shall. You stay here."

He glanced at her.

"If something goes wrong, I'd rather you be ready out here to come in and help. Best not to potentially get us both stuck in the grip of one of the Unmade. I'll shout if I need you."

"And if you can't shout? Or if I can't hear you?"

"I'll send Pattern."

Kaladin folded his arms, but nodded. "Fine. Just be careful."

"I'm always careful."

He raised an eyebrow at her, but he was thinking of Shallan. Veil wasn't as foolhardy.

The climb up those steps seemed to take far too long. For a moment she could have sworn they stretched into the sky, toward the eternal void. And then she was atop them, standing before those pillars.

A group of guards approached her.

"I have a message from the king!" she said, holding it up. "To be delivered directly to Her Majesty. I've traveled all the way from the Shattered Plains!"

The guards didn't break stride. One opened a door into the palace while the others formed up behind Veil, prodding her forward. She swallowed, sweat chilling her brow, and let them force her to that door. That maw . . .

She walked into a grand entryway, marked by marble and a brilliant sphere chandelier. No Unmade. No darkness waiting to consume her. She breathed out, though she *could* feel something. That phantom eeriness was indeed stronger here. The *wrongness*. She jumped when one of the soldiers put his hand on her shoulder.

A man in a captainlord's knots left a small room beside the grand chamber. "What is this?"

"Messenger," a soldier said. "From the Shattered Plains." Another plucked the letter from her fingers and handed it toward the captainlord. She could see their eyes now, and they seemed ordinary—darkeyed grunts, lighteyed officer.

"Who was your commander there?" the captain asked her, looking over the letter, then squinting at the seal. "Well? I served on the Plains for a few years."

"Captain Colot," she said, naming the officer who had joined the

Windrunners. He wasn't Lyn's actual commander, but he did have scouts in his team.

The captainlord nodded, then handed the letter to one of his men. "Take it to Queen Aesudan."

"I was supposed to deliver it in person," Veil said, though she itched to be out of this place. To flee madly, if she were being honest. She had to stay. Whatever she learned here would be of—

One of the soldiers ran her through.

It happened so quickly, she was left gaping at the sword blade protruding through her chest—wet with her blood. He yanked the weapon back out, and Veil collapsed with a groan. She reached for Stormlight, by instinct.

No . . . no, do as . . . as Jasnah did . . .

Pretend. Feign. She stared up at the men in horror, in betrayal, painspren rising around her. One soldier jogged off with the message, but the captain merely walked back toward his post. Not one of the rest said a word as she bled all over the floor, her vision fading . . .

She let her eyes close, then took in a short, sharp breath of Stormlight. Just a tiny amount, which she kept within, holding her breath. Enough to keep her alive, heal the wounds inside . . .

Pattern. Please don't go. Don't do anything. Don't hum, don't buzz. Quiet. Stay quiet.

One of the soldiers picked her up and slung her over his shoulder, then carried her through the palace. She dared cracking a single eye, and found the wide hallway here was lined with dozens upon dozens of soldiers. Just . . . standing there. They were alive; they'd cough, or shift position. Some leaned back against the wall, but they all kind of stayed in place. Human, but *wrong*.

The guard carrying her passed a floor-to-ceiling mirror rimmed in a fancy bronze frame. In it, she glimpsed the guard with Lyn thrown over his shoulder. And beyond that, deep within the mirror, something turned—the normal image fading—and looked toward Shallan with a sudden and surprised motion. It looked like a shadow of a person, only with white spots for eyes.

Veil quickly closed her peeking eye. Storms, what had *that* been?

Don't shift. Stay perfectly still. Don't even breathe. Stormlight allowed her to survive without air.

The guard carried her down some steps, then opened a door and walked down a few more. He dropped her none too gently onto the stone and tossed her hat on top of her, then turned and left, closing a door behind him.

Veil waited as long as she could stand before opening her eyes and finding herself in darkness. She took a breath, and nearly choked at the rotten, musty stench. Dreading and suspecting what she might find, she drew in Stormlight and made herself glow.

She'd been dropped beside a small line of corpses. There were seven of them, three male and four female, wearing fine clothing—but covered in rotspren, their flesh chewed at by cremlings.

Holding in a scream, she scrambled to her feet. Perhaps . . . perhaps these were some of those lighteyes who'd come to the palace to talk to the queen?

She snatched her hat and scrambled to the steps. This was the wine cellar, a stone vault cut right into the rock. At the door she finally heard Pattern, who had been talking, though his voice had seemed distant.

"Shallan? I felt what you told me. Don't go. Shallan, are you well? Oh! The destruction. You destroy some things, but seeing others destroyed upsets you. Hmmmm. . . ." He seemed pleased to have figured it out.

She focused on his voice, something familiar. Not the memory of a sword protruding from her own chest, not the callous way she'd been dumped here and left to rot, not the line of corpses with exposed bones, haunted faces, chewed-out eyes . . .

Don't think. Don't see it.

She shoved it all away, and rested her forehead against the door. Then she carefully eased it open and found an empty stone hallway beyond, with more steps leading upward.

There were too many soldiers that way. She put on a new illusion, of a servant woman from her sketchbook. Maybe that would be less suspicious. It covered the blood, at least.

She didn't head back upstairs, but instead took a separate path farther into the tunnels. This turned out to be the Kholin mausoleum, which was lined with another kind of corpse: old kings turned to statues. Their stone eyes chased her down empty tunnels until she found a door that, judging from the sunlight underneath, led out into the city.

"Pattern," she whispered. "Check for guards outside."

He hummed and slid under the door, then returned a moment later. "Mmm . . . There are two."

"Go back, then along the wall slowly to the right," she said, infusing him.

He did so, sliding under the door. A sound she'd created rose from him as he moved away, imitating the captainlord's voice from above, calling for the guards. It wasn't perfect, as she hadn't sketched the man, but it seemed to work as she heard booted feet move off.

She slipped out, and found herself at the base of the rise that the palace sat upon, a cliff of some twenty feet above her. The guards were distracted, walking to her right, so Veil slipped onto a street nearby, then ran for a short time, thankful to finally have a chance to work off some of her energy.

She collapsed in the shadow of a hollow building, with the windows broken open and the door missing. Pattern scooted along the ground nearby, joining her. The guards didn't seem to have noticed her.

"Go find Kaladin," she said to Pattern. "Bring him here. Warn him that soldiers might be watching him from the palace, and they might come for him."

"Mmmm." Pattern slid away from her. She huddled against herself, back to a stone wall, her coat still covered in blood. After a nerve-racking wait, Kaladin stepped onto the street, then hurried up to her. "Storms!" he said, kneeling beside her. Pattern slipped off his coat, humming happily. "Shallan, what happened to you?"

"Well," she said, "as a connoisseur of things that have killed me, I think a *sword* happened."

"Shallan . . ."

"The evil force that rules the palace did not think highly of someone coming with a letter from the king." She smiled at him. "You could say, um, it made that point quite clear."

Smile. I need you to smile.

I need what happened to be all right. Something that can simply roll off me. Please.

"Well . . ." Kaladin said. "I'm glad we . . . took a stab at this anyway." He smiled.

It was all right. Just another day, another infiltration. He helped her to her feet, then looked to check on her wound, and she slapped his hand. The cut was *not* in an appropriate location.

"Sorry," he said. "Surgeon's instincts. Back to the hideout?"

"Yes, please," she said. "I'd rather not be killed again today. It's quite draining. . . ."

BINDER OF GODS

The disagreements between the Skybreakers and the Windrunners have grown to tragic levels. I plead with any who hear this to recognize you are not so different as you think.

—From drawer 27-19, topaz

D alinar reached into the dark stone shaft where he'd hidden the assassin's Honorblade. It was still there; he felt the hilt under the lip of stone.

He expected to feel more upon touching it. Power? A tingling? This was a weapon of Heralds, a thing so ancient that common Shardblades were young by comparison. Yet, as he slipped it free and stood up, the only thing he felt was his own anger. This was the weapon of the assassin who had killed his brother. The weapon used to terrorize Roshar, murder the lords of Jah Keved and Azir.

It was shortsighted of him to see such an ancient weapon merely as the sword of the Assassin in White. He stepped out into the larger room next door, then regarded the sword in the light of the spheres he had placed on a stone slab there. Sinuous and elegant, this was the weapon of a king. Jezerezeh'Elin.

"There are some who assumed you were one of the Heralds," Dalinar noted to the Stormfather, who rumbled in the back of his mind. "Jezerezeh, Herald of Kings, Father of Storms."

Men say many foolish things, the Stormfather replied. *Some name Kelek Stormfather, others Jezrien. I am neither of them.*

"But Jezerezeh *was* a Windrunner."

He was before Windrunners. He was Jezrien, a man whose powers bore no name. They were simply him. The Windrunners were named only after Ishar founded the orders.

"Ishi'Elin," Dalinar said. "Herald of Luck."

Or of mysteries, the Stormfather said, *or of priests. Or of a dozen other things, as men dubbed him. He is now as mad as the rest. More, perhaps.*

Dalinar lowered the Honorblade, looking eastward toward the Origin. Even through the stone walls, he knew that was where to find the Stormfather. "Do you know where they are?"

I have told you. I do not see all. Only glimpses in the storms.

"Do you *know* where they *are*?"

Only one, he said with a rumble. *I . . . have seen Ishar. He curses me at night, even as he names himself a god. He seeks death. His own. Perhaps that of every man.*

It clicked. "Stormfather!"

Yes?

"Oh. Uh, that was a curse. . . . Never mind. Tezim, the god-priest of Tukar? Is it him? Ishi, Herald of Luck, is the man who has been waging war against Emul?"

Yes.

"For what purpose?"

He is insane. Do not look for meaning in his actions.

"When . . . when were you thinking of informing me of this?"

When you asked. When else would I speak of it?

"When you thought of it!" Dalinar said. "You know things that are important, Stormfather!"

He just rumbled his reply.

Dalinar took a deep breath, trying to calm himself. Spren did not think like men. Anger would not change what the Stormfather told him. But what would?

"Did you know about my powers?" Dalinar asked. "Did you know that I could heal the stone?"

I knew it once you did it, the Stormfather said. *Yes, once you did it, I always knew.*

"Do you know what else I can do?"

Of course. Once you discover it, I will know.

"But—"

Your powers will come when you are ready for them, not before, the Stormfather said. *They cannot be hurried or forced.*

But do not look toward the powers of others, even those who share your Surges. Their lot is not yours, and their powers are small, petty things. What you did in reknitting those statues was a mere trifle, a party trick.

Yours is the power Ishar once held. Before he was Herald of Luck, they called him Binder of Gods. He was the founder of the Oathpact. No Radiant is capable of more than you. Yours is the power of Connection, of joining men and worlds, minds and souls. Your Surges are the greatest of all, though they will be impotent if you seek to wield them for mere battle.

The words washed over Dalinar, seeming to press him backward with their force. When the Stormfather was done, Dalinar found himself out of breath, a headache coming on. He reflexively drew in Stormlight to heal it, and the small chamber dimmed. That stopped the pain, but it did nothing for his cold sweat.

"Are there others like me out there?" he finally asked.

Not right now, and there can ever be only three. One for each of us.

"Three?" Dalinar said. "Three spren who make Bondsmiths. You . . . and Cultivation are two?"

The Stormfather actually laughed. *You would have a difficult time making her your spren. I should like to see you try it.*

"Then who?"

My siblings need not concern you.

They seemed of compelling concern, but Dalinar had learned when to avoid pressing an issue. That would only cause the spren to withdraw.

Dalinar took the Honorblade in a firm grip, then collected his spheres, one of which had gone dun. "Have I ever asked how you renew these?" Dalinar held up the sphere, inspecting the ruby at the center. He'd seen these loose, and had always been surprised by how small they actually were. The glass made them look far larger.

Honor's power, during a storm, is concentrated in one place, the Stormfather said. *It pierces all three realms and brings Physical, Cognitive, and Spiritual together momentarily in one. The gemstones, exposed to the wonder of the Spiritual Realm, are lit by the infinite power there.*

"Could you renew this sphere, now?"

I . . . do not know. He sounded intrigued. *Hold it forth.*

Dalinar did so, and felt something happen, a tugging on his insides, like the Stormfather straining against their bond. The sphere remained dun.

It is not possible, the Stormfather said. *I am close to you, but the power is not—it still rides the storm.*

That was far more than he usually got from the Stormfather. He hoped he could remember it exactly to repeat to Navani—of course, if the Stormfather was listening, he'd correct Dalinar's mistakes. The Stormfather hated to be misquoted.

Dalinar stepped out into the hallway to meet Bridge Four. He held up the Honorblade—a powerful, world-changing artifact. But, like the Shardblades modeled after it, the weapon was useless if he left it hidden.

"This," he said to the men of Bridge Four, "is the Honorblade your captain recovered."

The twenty-odd men gathered closer, their curious faces reflecting in the metal.

"Anyone who holds this," Dalinar said, "will immediately gain the powers of a Windrunner. Your captain's absence is interrupting your training. Perhaps this, though only one can use it at a time, can mitigate that."

They gaped at the weapon, so Dalinar held it out toward Kaladin's first lieutenant—the bearded older bridgeman named Teft.

Teft reached out, then drew his hand back. "Leyten," he barked. "You're our storming armorer. You take the thing."

"Me?" a stocky bridgeman said. "That's not armor."

"Close enough."

"I . . ."

"Airsick lowlanders," Rock the Horneater said, shoving forward and taking the weapon. "Your soup is cold. That is idiom for 'You are all stupid.'" The Horneater hefted it, curious, and his eyes bled to a glassy blue.

"Rock?" Teft asked. "You? Holding a weapon?"

"I am not going to swing this thing," Rock said, rolling his eyes. "I will keep him safe. This is all."

"It's a Shardblade," Dalinar warned. "You've trained on those, correct?"

"We have, sir," Teft said. "Doesn't mean one of this lot won't storming cut their own feet off. But . . . I suppose we can use this to heal it if they do. Sigzil, come up with a rotation so we can practice."

Heal . . . Dalinar felt stupid. He'd missed it again. Anyone holding this Blade had the powers of a Radiant. Did that mean they could use Stormlight to heal themselves? If so, that might be a valuable extra use of the weapon.

"Don't let anyone know you have this," Dalinar told them. "I assume you can learn to dismiss and summon it like an ordinary Shardblade. See what you can discover, then report to me."

"We'll put it to good use, sir," Teft promised.

"Good." The clock fabrial on his forearm dinged, and Dalinar stifled a sigh. She'd learned to make it ding? "If you'll all excuse me, I have to prepare for an appointment with an emperor a thousand miles away."

⁙

A short time later, Dalinar stood on his balcony. Hands clasped behind his back, he stared out toward the Oathgate transport platforms.

"I did a great deal of business with the Azish when I was younger," Fen said from behind him. "This might not work, but it is a *much* better plan than traditional Alethi strutting."

"I don't like him going alone," Navani replied.

"By all reports," Fen said dryly, "he got stabbed through the chest, lifted a stone roughly the weight of ten men, then started putting my city back together one rock at a time. I think he'll be fine."

"No amount of Stormlight will help if they simply imprison him," Navani said. "We could be sending him to become a hostage."

They were arguing for his benefit. He had to understand the risks. And he did. He walked over to give Navani a light kiss. He smiled at her, then turned and extended his hand toward Fen, who gave him a paper packet, like a large envelope.

"This is it, then?" he asked. "All three are in here?"

"They're marked with appropriate glyphs," Navani said. "And the spanreed is inside too. They've promised to speak in Alethi during the meeting— you won't have an interpreter from our side, as you insist on going alone."

"I do," Dalinar said, starting toward the door. "I want to try Fen's suggestion."

Navani quickly rose and took his arm with her freehand.

"I assure you," he said. "I will be safe."

"No you won't. But this is no different from a hundred other times you've ridden off to battle. Here." She handed him a small box sheathed in cloth.

"Fabrial?"

"Lunch," she said. "There's no telling when those people will feed you."

She'd wrapped it in a glyphward. Dalinar cocked his eyebrow at it, and she shrugged. *Can't hurt, right?* that seemed to say. She took him in an embrace, held on an extra moment—more than another Alethi might— then stepped back. "We'll be watching the spanreed. One hour with no communication, and we're coming for you."

He nodded. He couldn't write to them of course, but he could flip the reed on and off to send signals, an old general's trick for when you lacked a scribe.

A short time later, he strode out onto Urithiru's western plateau. Crossing it on his way to the Oathgate, he passed men marching in formations, sergeants shouting orders, runners carrying messages. Two of his Shardbearers—Rust and Serugiadis, men who had the Plate only—practiced with massive Shardbows, launching thick arrows hundreds of yards toward a large straw target that Kaladin had placed for them on a nearby mountainside.

A significant number of the common soldiers sat around holding spheres, staring at them intently. Word had spread that Bridge Four was recruiting. He'd lately noticed numerous men in the hallways holding a sphere "for luck." Dalinar even passed a group out here who were talking about *swallowing* spheres.

The Stormfather rumbled with displeasure. *They go about this backward. Foolish men. They can't draw in Light and become Radiant; they first must be approaching Radiance, and look for Light to fulfill the promise.*

Dalinar barked at the men to get back to training, and to *not* swallow any spheres. They obeyed with a scrambling rush, shocked to find the Blackthorn looming over them. He shook his head, then continued. His path, unfortunately, took him through a mock battle. Two blocks of spearmen pressed against each other on the plateau, straining and grunting, training to hold their formations under stress. Though they carried blunt practice spears, this was mostly shield work.

Dalinar saw the warning signs of things going too far. Men were shouting with real acrimony, and angerspren were boiling at their feet. One of the lines wavered, and instead of pulling back, their opponents rammed their shields against them repeatedly.

Green and white on one side, black and maroon on the other. Sadeas and Aladar. Dalinar cursed and approached the men, shouting for them to pull back. Soon, his call was taken up by captains and commanders. The rear ranks of the two practice blocks pulled away—leaving the contestants at the center to devolve into a brawl.

Dalinar shouted, and Stormlight shimmered along the stones before him. Those who hadn't gotten caught up in the fighting jumped back. The rest got stuck in the Stormlight, which glued them to the ground. This caused all but the most furious to stop their fighting.

He pulled the last few apart and pushed them down, sticking them by their seats to the stone next to their angerspren. The men thrashed, then saw him and froze, looking appropriately chagrined.

I remember being that wrapped up in battle, Dalinar thought. *Is it the Thrill?* He couldn't remember feeling it for . . . for a long time. He would have the men questioned to determine whether any could feel it.

Dalinar let the Stormlight evaporate away like luminescent steam. Aladar's officers withdrew their group in an orderly fashion, shouting for the men to start calisthenics. The soldiers from Sadeas's army, however, spat at the ground and heaved themselves to their feet, retreating in sullen bunches, cursing and muttering.

They're getting worse, Dalinar thought. Under Torol Sadeas, they'd been slovenly and sadistic, but still soldiers. Yes, they tended to brawl, but they'd been quick to obey in battle. So they'd been effective, just not exemplary.

The new Sadeas banner flew above these men. Meridas Sadeas—

Amaram—had changed the glyphpair's design, as was traditional: Sadeas's squat tower had elongated, and the hammer had changed to an axe.

Despite his reputation for running a crisp army, it was obvious he was having trouble controlling these men. He'd never commanded a force this large—and perhaps the murder of their highprince had upset the men to the point that there was nothing Amaram could do.

Aladar hadn't been able to provide anything of substance about Torol's murder. The investigation was supposed to be ongoing . . . but there were no leads. The spren hadn't done it, but they had no idea who had.

I'll need to take action about those soldiers, Dalinar thought. *They need something to tire them out, keep them from getting into fights. . . .*

Perhaps he had just the thing. He considered that as he finally made his way up the ramp to the proper Oathgate platform, then crossed the empty field to the control building. Jasnah waited within, reading a book and making notes. "What took you?" she asked.

"Almost had a riot out on the parade ground," he said. "Two training formations got interlocked and started bashing one another."

"Sadeas?"

Dalinar nodded.

"We'll have to do something about them."

"I've been thinking. Maybe some hard labor—strictly supervised—in a ruined city might be just the thing."

Jasnah smiled. "How convenient that we're currently providing exactly such assistance to Queen Fen. Work Sadeas's troops to exhaustion, assuming we can keep them under control there."

"I'll start with small batches, to be certain we're not sending more trouble Fen's direction," Dalinar said. "Have you had any news from the king's infiltration team at Kholinar?" As anticipated, the Stormfather was unable to reach anyone on the team to bring them into a vision—nor would Dalinar dare risk it—but they'd sent several spanreeds with Elhokar and Shallan.

"None. We'll keep watch and tell you the moment we get any sort of response."

Dalinar nodded, and shoved down his worry for Elhokar and his son. He had to trust that they'd eventually either accomplish their task, or find a way to report what was stopping them.

Jasnah summoned her Shardblade. Odd how natural it looked to see Jasnah with a sword. "You ready?"

"I am."

The Reshi girl, Lift, had obtained permission from the Azish court to unlock the Oathgate on their side. The emperor was—at long last—willing to meet with Dalinar in the flesh.

Jasnah engaged the device, rotating the inner wall, the floor shimmering.

Light flashed outside, and immediately, stuffy heat surged in through the doorways. Apparently a season of summer was well under way in Azir.

It *smelled* different here. Of exotic spices and more subtle things like unfamiliar woods.

"Good luck," Jasnah said as he stepped out of the room. It flashed behind him as she returned to Urithiru, leaving him to meet the Azish imperial court on his own.

Now that we abandon the tower, can I finally admit that I hate this place? Too many rules.

—From drawer 8-1, amethyst

Memories churned in Dalinar's head as he walked down a long corridor outside the Oathgate control building in Azimir, which was covered by a magnificent bronze dome. The Grand Market, as it was called, was an enormous indoor shopping district. That would prove inconvenient when Dalinar needed to use the full Oathgate.

He couldn't see any of the market currently; the control building—which had been treated as some kind of monument in the market—was now surrounded by a wooden set of walls, and a new corridor. Empty of people, it was lit by sphere lamps along the walls. Sapphires. Coincidence, or a gesture of respect to a Kholin visitor?

At the end, the hallway opened into a small room populated by a line of Azish soldiers. They wore plated mail, with colorful caps on their heads, greatshields, and very long-handled axes with small heads. The whole group jumped as Dalinar entered, and then shied back, weapons held threateningly.

Dalinar held his arms out to the sides, packet from Fen in one hand, food bundle in the other. "I am unarmed."

They spoke quickly in Azish. He didn't see the Prime or the little Radiant, though the people in patterned robes were viziers and scions—both were, essentially, Azish versions of ardents. Except here, the ardents were involved in the government far more than was proper.

A woman stepped forward, the many layers of her long, extravagant robes rustling as she walked. A matching hat completed the outfit. She was important, and perhaps planned to interpret for him herself.

Time for my first attack, Dalinar thought. He opened the packet that Fen had given him and removed four pieces of paper.

He presented them to the woman, and was pleased at the shock in her eyes. She hesitantly took them, then called to some of her companions. They joined her before Dalinar, which made the guards distinctly anxious. A few had drawn triangular kattari, a popular variety of short sword here in the west. He'd always wanted one.

The ardents withdrew behind the soldiers, speaking animatedly. The plan was to exchange pleasantries in this room, then for Dalinar to immediately return to Urithiru—whereupon they intended to lock the Oathgate from their side. He wanted more. He intended to *get* more. Some kind of alliance, or at least a meeting with the emperor.

One of the ardents started reading the papers to the others. The writing was in Azish, a funny language made of little markings that looked like cremling tracks. It lacked the elegant, sweeping verticals of the Alethi women's script.

Dalinar closed his eyes, listening to the unfamiliar language. As in Thaylen City, he had a moment of feeling he could almost understand. Stretching, he felt that meaning was close to him.

"Would you help me understand?" he whispered to the Stormfather.

What makes you think I can?

"Don't be coy," Dalinar whispered. "I've spoken new languages in the visions. You can make me speak Azish."

The Stormfather rumbled in discontent. *That wasn't me,* he finally said. *It was you.*

"How do I use it?"

Try touching one of them. With Spiritual Adhesion, you can make a Connection.

Dalinar regarded the group of hostile guards, then sighed, waving and miming the act of dumping a drink into his mouth. The soldiers exchanged sharp words, then one of the youngest was pushed forward with a canteen. Dalinar nodded in thanks, then—as he took a drink from the water bottle—grabbed the young man by the wrist and held on.

Stormlight, the rumbling in his mind said.

Dalinar pressed Stormlight into the other man, and felt something— like a friendly sound coming from another room. All you had to was get in. After a careful shove, the door opened, and sounds twisted and undulated in the air. Then, like music changing keys, they modulated from gibberish to sense.

"Captain!" cried the young guard that Dalinar held. "What do I do? He's got me!"

Dalinar let go, and fortunately his understanding of the language persisted. "I'm sorry, soldier," Dalinar said, handing back the canteen. "I didn't mean to alarm you."

The young soldier stepped back among his fellows. "The warlord speaks *Azish*?" He sounded as surprised as if he'd met a talking chull.

Dalinar clasped his hands behind his back and watched the ardents. *You insist on thinking of them as ardents,* he told himself, *because they can read, both male and female.* But he was no longer in Alethkar. Despite those bulky robes and large hats, the Azish women wore nothing on their safehands.

Sunmaker, Dalinar's ancestor, had argued that the Azish had been in need of civilizing. He wondered if anyone had believed that argument even in those days, or if they'd all seen it for the rationalization it was.

The viziers and scions finished reading, then turned toward Dalinar, lowering the pages he'd given them. He had heeded Queen Fen's plan, trusting that he couldn't bully his way through Azir with a sword. Instead, he had brought a different kind of weapon.

An essay.

"Do you truly speak our language, Alethi?" the lead vizier called. She had a round face, dark brown eyes, and a cap covered in bright patterns. Her greying hair came out the side in a tight braid.

"I've had the opportunity to learn it recently," Dalinar said. "You are Vizier Noura, I assume?"

"Did Queen Fen really write this?"

"With her own hand, Your Grace," Dalinar said. "Feel free to contact Thaylen City to confirm."

They huddled to consult again in quiet tones. The essay was a lengthy but compelling argument for the economic value of the Oathgates to the cities that hosted them. Fen argued that Dalinar's desperation to forge an alliance made for the perfect opportunity to secure beneficial and lasting trade deals through Urithiru. Even if Azir had no plans to fully join the coalition, they should negotiate use of the Oathgates and send a delegation to the tower.

It spent a lot of words saying what was obvious, and was exactly the sort of thing Dalinar had no patience for. Which, hopefully, would make it perfect for the Azish. And if it wasn't quite sufficient . . . well, Dalinar knew never to go into battle without fresh troops in reserve.

"Your Highness," Noura said, "as impressed as we are that you cared to learn our language—and even considering the compelling argument presented here—we think it best if . . ."

She trailed off as Dalinar reached in his packet and withdrew a second sheaf of papers, six pages this time. He held them up before the group like a raised banner, then proffered them. A nearby guard jumped back, making his mail jingle.

The small chamber grew quiet. Finally, a guard accepted the papers and took them to the viziers and scions. A shorter man among them began reading quietly—this one was an extended treatise from Navani, talking about the wonders they'd discovered in Urithiru, formally inviting the Azish scholars to visit and share.

She made clever arguments about the importance of new fabrials and technology in fighting the Voidbringers. She included diagrams of the tents she'd made to help them fight during the Weeping, and explained her theories for floating towers. Then, with Dalinar's permission, she offered a gift: detailed schematics that Taravangian had brought from Jah Keved, explaining the creation of so-called half-shards, fabrial shields that could withstand a few blows from Shardblades.

The enemy is united against us, went her essay's final argument. *They have the unique advantages of focus, harmony, and memories that extend far into the past. Resisting them will require our greatest minds, whether Alethi, Azish, Veden, or Thaylen. I freely give state secrets, for the days of hoarding knowledge are gone. Now, we either learn together or we fall individually.*

The viziers finished, then they passed around the schematics, studying them for an extended time. When the group looked back at Dalinar, he could see that their attitude was changing. Remarkably, this was *working.*

Well, he didn't know much about essays, but he had an instinct for combat. When your opponent was gasping for breath, you didn't let him get back up. You rammed your sword right into his throat.

Dalinar reached into his packet and removed the last paper inside: a single sheet written on front and back. He held it up between his first two fingers. The Azish watched it with wide eyes, as if he'd revealed a glowing gemstone of incalculable wealth.

This time Vizier Noura herself stepped forward and took it. "'Verdict,'" she read from the top. "'By Jasnah Kholin.'"

The others pushed through the guards, gathering around, and began reading it to themselves. Though this was the shortest of the essays, he heard them whispering and marveling over it.

"Look, it incorporates all *seven* of Aqqu's Logical Forms!"

"That's an allusion to the *Grand Orientation.* And . . . storms . . . she quotes Prime Kasimarlix in three successive stages, each escalating the same quote to a different level of Superior Understanding."

One woman held her hand to her mouth. "It's written entirely in a single rhythmic meter!"

"Great *Yaezir*," Noura said. "You're *right*."

"The allusions . . ."

"Such wordplay . . ."

"The *momentum* and *rhetoric* . . ."

Logicspren burst around them in the shape of little stormclouds. Then, practically as one, the scions and viziers turned to Dalinar.

"This is a work of *art*," Noura said.

"Is it . . . persuasive?" Dalinar asked.

"It provokes further consideration," Noura said, looking to the others, who nodded. "You actually came alone. We are shocked by that—aren't you worried for your safety?"

"Your Radiant," Dalinar said, "has proven to be wise for one so young. I am certain I can depend on her for my safety."

"I don't know that I'd depend on her for anything," said one of the men, chuckling. "Unless it's swiping your pocket change."

"All the same," Dalinar said, "I have come begging you to trust me. This seemed the best proof of my intentions." He spread his hands to the sides. "Do not send me back immediately. Let us talk as allies, not men in a battlefield tent of parley."

"I will bring these essays before the Prime and his formal council," Vizier Noura finally said. "I admit he seems fond of you, despite your inexplicable invasion of his dreams. Come with us."

That would lead him away from the Oathgate, and any chance he had at transferring home in an emergency. But that was what he'd been hoping for.

"Gladly, Your Grace."

◦•◦

They walked along a twisting path through the dome-covered market—which was now empty, like a ghost town. Many of the streets ended at barricades manned by troops.

They'd turned the Azimir Grand Market into a kind of reverse fortress, intended to protect the city from whatever might come through the Oathgate. If troops left the control building, they would find themselves in a maze of confusing streets.

Unfortunately for the Azish, the control building alone was *not* the gate. A Radiant could make this entire *dome* vanish, replaced with an army in the middle of Azimir. He'd have to be delicate about how he explained that.

He walked with Vizier Noura, followed by the other scribes, who passed the essays around again. Noura didn't make small talk with him, and Dalinar maintained no illusions. This trip through the dark indoor streets—with packed market buildings and twisting paths—was meant to confuse him, should he try to remember the way.

They eventually climbed up to a second level and left through a doorway out onto a ledge along the outside rim of the dome. Clever. From up here, he could see that the ground-floor exits from the market were barricaded or sealed off. The only clear way out was up that flight of steps, onto this platform around the circumference of the large bronze dome, then down another set of steps.

From this upper ramp, he could see some of Azimir—and was relieved by how little destruction he saw. Some of the neighborhoods on the west side of the city seemed to have collapsed, but all in all, the city had weathered the Everstorm in good shape. Most of the structures were stone here, and the grand domes—many overlaid with reddish-gold bronze—reflected the sunlight like molten marvels. The people wore colorful clothing, of patterns that scribes could read like a language.

This summer season was warmer than he was accustomed to. Dalinar turned east. Urithiru lay somewhere in that direction, in the border mountains—far closer to Azir than to Alethkar.

"This way, Blackthorn," Noura said, starting down the wooden ramp. It was constructed upon a woodwork lattice. Seeing those wooden stilts, Dalinar had a moment of surreal memory. It vaguely reminded him of something, of perching above a city and looking down at wooden lattices. . . .

Rathalas, he thought. *The Rift.* The city that had rebelled. Right. He felt a chill, and the pressure of something hidden trying to thrust itself into his consciousness. There was more to remember about that place.

He walked down the ramp, and took it as a mark of respect that two entire divisions of troops surrounded the dome. "Shouldn't those men be on the walls?" Dalinar asked. "What if the Voidbringers attack?"

"They've withdrawn through Emul," Noura said. "Most of that country is on fire by now, due to either the parshmen or Tezim's armies."

Tezim. Who was a Herald. *Surely he wouldn't side with the enemy, would he?* Perhaps the best thing they could hope for was a war between the Voidbringers and the armies of a mad Herald.

Rickshaws waited for them below. Noura joined him in one. It was novel, being pulled by a man acting like a chull. Though it was faster than a palanquin, Dalinar found it far less stately.

The city was laid out in a very orderly manner. Navani had always admired that. He watched for more signs of destruction, and while he found few, a different oddity struck him. Masses of people standing in clumps, wearing colorful vests, loose trousers or skirts, and patterned caps. They shouted about unfairness, and though they looked angry, they were surrounded by logicspren.

"What's all this?" Dalinar asked.

"Protestors." She looked to him, and obviously noted his confusion. "They've lodged a formal complaint, rejecting an order to exit the city and work the farms. This gives them a one-month period to make their grievances known before being forced to comply."

"They can simply *disobey* an imperial order?"

"I suppose you'd merely march everyone out at swordpoint. Well, we don't do things that way here. There are processes. Our people aren't slaves."

Dalinar found himself bristling; she obviously didn't know much about Alethkar, if she assumed all Alethi darkeyes were like chulls to be herded around. The lower classes had a long and proud tradition of rights related to their social ranking.

"Those people," he said, realizing something, "have been ordered to the fields because you lost your parshmen."

"Our fields haven't yet been planted," Noura said, eyes growing distant. "It's like they knew the very best time to cripple us by leaving. Carpenters and cobblers must be pressed into manual labor, just to prevent a famine. We might feed ourselves, but our trades and infrastructure will be devastated."

In Alethkar, they hadn't been as fixated on this, as reclaiming the kingdom was more pressing. In Thaylenah, the disaster had been physical, the city ravaged. Both kingdoms had been distracted from a more subversive disaster, the economic one.

"How did it happen?" Dalinar asked. "The parshmen leaving?"

"They gathered in the storm," she said. "Leaving homes and walking right out into it. Some reports said the parshmen claimed to hear the beating of drums. Other reports—these are all very contradictory—speak of spren guiding the parshmen.

"They swarmed the city gates, threw them open in the rain, then moved out onto the plain surrounding the city. The next day, they demanded formal economic redress for improper appropriation of their labors. They claimed the subsection of the rules exempting parshmen from wages was extralegal, and put a motion through the courts. We were negotiating—a bizarre experience, I must say—before some of their leaders got them marching off instead."

Interesting. Alethi parshmen had acted Alethi—immediately gathering for war. The Thaylen parshmen had taken to the seas. And the Azish parshmen . . . well, they'd done something quintessentially Azish. They had lodged a complaint with the government.

He had to be careful not to dwell on how amusing that sounded, if only because Navani had warned him not to underestimate the Azish. Alethi liked to joke about them—insult one of their soldiers, it was said, and he'd submit a form requesting an opportunity to swear at you. But that was a caricature, likely about as accurate as Noura's own impression of his people always doing everything by the sword and spear.

Once at the palace, Dalinar tried to follow Noura and the other scribes into the main building—but soldiers instead gestured him toward a small outbuilding.

"I was hoping," he called after Noura, "to speak with the emperor in person."

"Unfortunately, this petition cannot be granted," she said. The group left him and strode into the grand palace itself, a majestic bronze building with bulbous domes.

The soldiers sequestered him in a narrow chamber with a low table at the center and nice couches along the sides. They left him inside the small room alone, but took up positions outside. It wasn't quite a prison, but he obviously wasn't to be allowed to roam either.

He sighed and sat on a couch, dropping his lunch to the table beside some bowls of dried fruit and nuts. He took the spanreed out and sent a brief signal to Navani that meant *time,* the agreed sign that he was to be given another hour before anyone panicked.

He rose and began pacing. How did men suffer this? In battle, you won or lost based on strength of arms. At the end of the day, you knew where you stood.

This endless talking left him so uncertain. Would the viziers dismiss the essays? Jasnah's reputation seemed to be powerful even here, but they'd seemed less impressed by her argument than by the way she expressed it.

You've always worried about this, haven't you? the Stormfather said in his mind.

"About what?"

That the world would come to be ruled by pens and scribes, not swords and generals.

"I . . ." *Blood of my fathers.* That was true.

Was that why he insisted on negotiating himself? Why he didn't send ambassadors? Was it because deep down, he didn't trust their gilded words and intricate promises, all contained in documents he couldn't read? Pieces of paper that were somehow harder than the strongest Shardplate?

"The contests of kingdoms are supposed to be a *masculine* art," he said. "I should be able to do this myself."

The Stormfather rumbled, not truly in disagreement. Just in . . . amusement?

Dalinar finally settled onto one of the couches. Might as well eat something . . . except his cloth-wrapped lunch lay open, crumbs on the table, the wooden curry box empty save for a few drips. What on Roshar?

He slowly looked up at the other couch. The slender Reshi girl perched not on the seat, but up on the backrest. She wore an oversized Azish robe and cap, and was gnawing on the sausage Navani had packed with the meal, to be cut into the curry.

"Kind of bland," she said.

"Soldier's rations," Dalinar said. "I prefer them."

"'Cuz you're bland?"

"I prefer not to let a meal become a distraction. Were you in here all along?"

She shrugged, continuing to eat his food. "You said something earlier. About men?"

"I . . . was beginning to realize that I'm uncomfortable with the idea of scribes controlling the fates of nations. The things women write are stronger than my military."

"Yeah, that makes sense. Lots of boys is afraid of girls."

"I'm not—"

"They say it changes when you grow up," she said, leaning forward. "I wouldn't know, because I ain't going to grow. I figured it out. I just gotta stop eatin'. People that don't eat, don't get bigger. Easy."

She said it all around mouthfuls of his food.

"Easy," Dalinar said. "I'm sure."

"I'm gonna start *any* day now," she said. "You want that fruit, or . . ."

He leaned forward, pushing the two bowls of dried fruit toward her. She attacked them. Dalinar leaned back in the seat. This girl seemed so out of place. Though she was lighteyed—with pale, clear irises—that didn't matter as much in the west. The regal clothing was too big on her, and she didn't take care to keep her hair pulled back and tucked up under the cap.

This entire room—this entire city, really—was an exercise in ostentation. Metal leaf coated domes, the rickshaws, even large portions of the walls of this room. The Azish owned only a few Soulcasters, and famously one could make bronze.

The carpeting and couches displayed bright patterns of orange and red. The Alethi favored solid colors, perhaps some embroidery. The Azish preferred their decorations to look like the product of a painter having a sneezing fit.

In the middle of it all was this girl, who looked so simple. She swam through ostentation, but it didn't stick to her.

"I listened to what they're sayin' in there, tight-butt," the girl said. "Before comin' here. I think they're gonna deny you. They gots a *finger.*"

"I should think they have many fingers."

"Nah, this is an *extra* one. Dried out, looks like it belonged to some gramma's gramma, but it's actually from an *emperor.* Emperor Snot-a-Lot or—"

"Snoxil?" Dalinar asked.

"Yeah. That's him."

"He was Prime when my ancestor sacked Azimir," Dalinar said with a sigh. "It's a relic." The Azish could be a superstitious lot, for all their claims about logic and essays and codes of law. This relic was probably being used during their discussions as a reminder of the last time the Alethi had been in Azir.

"Yeah, well, all I know is he's *dead,* so he ain't got to worry about . . . about . . ."

"Odium."

The Reshi girl shivered visibly.

"Could you go and talk to the viziers?" Dalinar asked. "Tell them that you think supporting my coalition is a good idea? They listened to you when you asked to unlock the Oathgate."

"Nah, they listened to Gawx," she said. "The geezers that run the city don't like me much."

Dalinar grunted. "Your name is Lift, right?"

"Right."

"And your order?"

"More food."

"I meant your order of Knights Radiant. What powers do you have?"

"Oh. Um . . . Edgedancer? I slip around and stuff."

"Slip around."

"It's real fun. Except when I run into things. Then it's only kinda fun."

Dalinar leaned forward, wishing—again—he could go in and talk to all those fools and scribes.

No. For once, trust in someone else, Dalinar.

Lift cocked her head. "Huh. You smell like her."

"Her?"

"The crazy spren who lives in the forest."

"You've met the *Nightwatcher?*"

"Yeah . . . You?"

He nodded.

They sat there, uncomfortable, until the young girl handed one of her bowls of dried fruit toward Dalinar. He took a piece and chewed it in silence, and she took another.

They ate the entire bowl, saying nothing until the door opened. Dalinar jumped. Noura stood in the doorway, flanked by other viziers. Her eyes flickered toward Lift, and she smiled. Noura didn't seem to think as poorly of Lift as the little girl indicated.

Dalinar stood up, feeling a sense of dread. He prepared his arguments, his pleas. They had to—

"The emperor and his council," Noura said, "have decided to accept your invitation to visit Urithiru."

Dalinar cut off his objection. Did she say *accept*?

"The Prime of Emul has almost reached Azir," Noura said. "He brought the Sage with him, and they should be willing to join us. Unfortunately, following the parshman assault, Emul is a fraction of what it once was. I suspect he will be eager for any and every source of aid, and will welcome this coalition of yours.

"The prince of Tashikk has an ambassador—his brother—in the city. He'll come as well, and the princess of Yezier is reportedly coming in person to plead for aid. We'll see about her. I think she simply believes Azimir will be safer. She lives here half the year anyway.

"Alm and Desh have ambassadors in the city, and Liafor is always eager to join whatever we do, as long as they can cater the storming meetings. I can't speak for Steen—they're a tricky bunch. I doubt you want Tukar's priest-king, and Marat is overrun. But we can bring a good sampling of the empire to join your discussions."

"I . . ." Dalinar stammered. "Thank you!" It was actually *happening*! As they'd hoped, Azir was the linchpin.

"Well, your wife writes a good essay," Noura said.

He started. "Navani's essay was the one that convinced you? Not Jasnah's?"

"Each of the three arguments were weighed favorably, and the reports from Thaylen City are encouraging," Noura said. "That had no small part in our decision. But while Jasnah Kholin's writing is every bit as impressive as her reputation suggests, there was something . . . more authentic about Lady Navani's plea."

"She is one of the most authentic people I know." Dalinar smiled like a fool. "And she is good at getting what she wants."

"Let me lead you back to the Oathgate. We will be in contact about the Prime's visit to your city."

Dalinar collected his spanreed and bade farewell to Lift, who stood on the back of the couch and waved to him. The sky looked brighter as the viziers accompanied him back to the dome that housed the Oathgate. He could hear them speaking eagerly as they entered the rickshaws; they seemed to be embracing this decision with gusto, now that it had been made.

Dalinar passed the trip quietly, worried that he might say something brutish and ruin things. Once they entered the market dome, he did take the opportunity to mention to Noura that the Oathgate could be used to transport everything there, including the dome itself.

"I'm afraid that it's a larger security threat than you know," he finished saying to her as they reached the control building.

"What would it do," she said, "if we built a structure halfway across the plateau perimeter? Would it slice the thing in two? What if a person is half on, half off?"

"That we don't know yet," Dalinar said, fumbling the spanreed on and off in a pattern to send the signal that would bring Jasnah back through the Oathgate to fetch him.

"I'll admit," Noura said softly as the other viziers chatted behind, "I'm . . . not pleased at being overruled. I am the emperor's loyal servant, but I do *not* like the idea of your Radiants, Dalinar Kholin. These powers are dangerous, and the ancient Radiants turned traitor in the end."

"I will convince you," Dalinar said. "We will prove ourselves to you. All I need is a chance."

The Oathgate flashed, and Jasnah appeared inside. Dalinar bowed to Noura in respect, then stepped backward into the building.

"You are not what I expected, Blackthorn," Noura said.

"And what did you expect?"

"An animal," she said frankly. "A half-man creature of war and blood."

Something about that struck him. *An animal* . . . Echoes of memories shuddered inside of him.

"I was that man," Dalinar said. "I've merely been blessed with enough good examples to make me aspire to something more." He nodded to Jasnah, who repositioned her sword, rotating the inner wall to initiate the transfer and take them back to Urithiru.

Navani waited outside the building. Dalinar stepped out and blinked at the sunlight, chilled by the mountain cold. He smiled broadly at her, opening his mouth to tell her what her essay had done.

An animal . . . An animal reacts when it is prodded . . .

Memories.

You whip it, and it becomes savage.

Dalinar stumbled.

He vaguely heard Navani crying out, yelling for help. His vision spun, and he fell to his knees, feeling an overwhelming nausea. He clawed at the stone, groaning, breaking fingernails. Navani . . . Navani was calling for a healer. She thought he'd been poisoned.

It wasn't that. No, it was far, far worse.

Storms. He *remembered*. It came crashing down on him, the weight of a thousand boulders.

He remembered what had happened to Evi. It had started in a cold fortress, in highlands once claimed by Jah Keved.

It had ended at the Rift.

66

STRATEGIST

ELEVEN YEARS AGO

Dalinar's breath misted as he leaned on the stone windowsill. In the room behind him, soldiers set up a table with a map on it.

"See there," Dalinar said, pointing out the window. "That ledge down there?"

Adolin, now twelve years old—nearly thirteen—leaned out the window. The outside of the large stone keep bulged here at the second floor, which would make scaling it challenging—but the stonework provided a convenient handhold in the form of a ledge right below the window.

"I see it," Adolin said.

"Good. Now watch." Dalinar gestured into the room. One of his guards pulled a lever, and the stonework ledge retracted into the wall.

"It moved!" Adolin said. "Do that again!"

The soldier obliged, using the lever to make the ledge stick out, then retract again.

"Neat!" Adolin said. So full of energy, as always. If only Dalinar could harness that for the battlefield. He wouldn't need Shards to conquer.

"Why did they build that, do you think?" Dalinar asked.

"In case people climb it! You could make them drop back down!"

"Defense against Shardbearers," Dalinar said, nodding. "A fall this far would crack their Plate, but the fortress also has interior corridor sections that are too narrow to maneuver in properly with Plate and Blade."

Dalinar smiled. Who knew that such a gem had been hiding in the highlands between Alethkar and Jah Keved? This solitary keep would provide a nice barrier if true war ever did break out with the Vedens.

He gestured for Adolin to move back, then shuttered the window and rubbed his chilled hands. This chamber was decorated like a lodge, hung with old forgotten greatshell trophies. At the side, a soldier stoked a flame in the hearth.

The battles with the Vedens had wound down. Though the last few fights had been disappointing, having his son with him had been an absolute delight. Adolin hadn't gone into battle, of course, but he'd joined them at tactics meetings. Dalinar had at first assumed the generals would be annoyed at the presence of a child, but it was hard to find little Adolin annoying. He was so earnest, so interested.

Together, he and Adolin joined a few of Dalinar's lesser officers at the room's table map. "Now," Dalinar said to Adolin, "let's see how well you've been paying attention. Where are we now?"

Adolin leaned over, pointing at the map. "This is our new keep, which you won for the crown! Here's the old border, where it used to be. Here's the *new* border in blue, which we won back from those thieving Vedens. They've held our land for *twenty years*."

"Excellent," Dalinar said. "But it's not merely land we've won."

"Trade treaties!" Adolin said. "That's the point of the big ceremony we had to do. You and that Veden highprince, in formal dress. We won the right to trade for *tons* of stuff for cheap."

"Yes, but that's not the most important thing we won."

Adolin frowned. "Um . . . horses . . ."

"No, son, the most *important* thing we've won is legitimacy. In signing this new treaty, the Veden king has recognized Gavilar as the rightful king of Alethkar. We've not just defended our borders, we've forestalled a greater war, as the Vedens now acknowledge our right to rule—and won't be pressing their own."

Adolin nodded, understanding.

It was gratifying to see how much one could accomplish in both politics and trade by liberally murdering the other fellow's soldiers. These last years full of skirmishes had reminded Dalinar of why he lived. More, they'd given him something new. In his youth, he'd warred, then spent the evenings drinking with his soldiers.

Now he had to explain his choices, vocalize them for the ears of an eager young boy who had questions for everything—and expected Dalinar to know the answers.

Storms, it was a challenge. But it felt good. *Incredibly* good. He had no intention of ever returning to a useless life spent wasting away in Kholinar, going to parties and getting into tavern brawls. Dalinar smiled and accepted a cup of warmed wine, surveying the map. Though Adolin had been focused on the region where they were fighting the Vedens, Dalinar's eyes were instead drawn to another section.

It included, written in pencil, the numbers he'd requested: projections of troops at the Rift.

"*Viim cachi eko!*" Evi said, stepping into the room, holding her arms tight to her chest and shivering. "I had thought central Alethkar was cold. Adolin Kholin, where is your jacket?"

The boy looked down, as if suddenly surprised that he wasn't wearing it. "Um . . ." He looked to Teleb, who merely smiled, shaking his head.

"Run along, son," Dalinar said. "You have geography lessons today."

"Can I stay? I don't want to leave you."

He wasn't speaking merely of today. The time was approaching when Adolin would go to spend part of the year in Kholinar, to drill with the swordmasters and receive formal training in diplomacy. He spent most of the year with Dalinar, but it was important he get *some* refinement in the capital.

"Go," Dalinar said. "If you pay attention in your lesson, I'll take you riding tomorrow."

Adolin sighed, then saluted. He hopped off his stool and gave his mother a hug—which was un-Alethi, but Dalinar suffered the behavior. Then he was out the door.

Evi stepped up to the fire. "So cold. What possessed someone to build a fortress way up here?"

"It's not that bad," Dalinar said. "You should visit the Frostlands in a season of winter."

"You Alethi cannot understand cold. Your bones are frozen."

Dalinar grunted his response, then leaned down over the map. *I'll need to approach from the south, march up along the lake's coast. . . .*

"The king is sending a message via spanreed," Evi noted. "It's being scribed now."

Her accent is fading, Dalinar noticed absently. When she sat down in a chair by the fire, she supported herself with her right hand, safehand tucked demurely against her waist. She kept her blonde hair in Alethi braids, rather than letting it tumble about her shoulders.

She'd never be a great scribe—she didn't have the youthful training in art and letters of a Vorin woman. Besides, she didn't like books, and preferred her meditations. But she'd tried hard these last years, and he was impressed.

She still complained that he didn't see Renarin enough. The other son was unfit for battle, and spent most of his time in Kholinar. Evi spent half the year back with him.

No, no, Dalinar thought, writing a glyph on the map. *The coast is the expected route.* What then? An amphibious assault across the lake? He'd need to see if he could get ships for that.

A scribe eventually entered bearing the king's letter, and everyone but Dalinar and Evi left. Evi held the letter and hesitated. "Do you want to sit, or—"

"No, go ahead."

Evi cleared her voice. "'Brother,'" the letter began, "'the treaty is sealed. Your efforts in Jah Keved are to be commended, and this should be a time of celebration and congratulations. Indeed, on a personal note, I wish to express my pride in you. The word from our best generals is that your tactical instincts have matured to full-fledged strategic genius. I never counted myself among their ranks, but to a man, they commend you as their equal.

"'As I have grown to become a king, it seems you have found your place as our general. I'm most interested to hear your own reports of the small mobile team tactics you've been employing. I would like to speak in person at length about all of this—indeed, I have important revelations of my own I would like to share. It would be best if we could meet in person. Once, I enjoyed your company every day. Now I believe it has been three years since we last spoke face to face.'"

"But," Dalinar said, interrupting, "the Rift needs to be dealt with."

Evi broke off, looking at him, then back down at the page. She continued reading. "'Unfortunately, our meeting will have to wait a few storms longer. Though your efforts on the border have certainly helped solidify our power, I have failed to dominate Rathalas and its renegade leader with politics.

"'I must send you to the Rift again. You are to quell this faction. Civil war could tear Alethkar to shreds, and I dare not wait any longer. In truth, I wish I'd listened when we spoke—so many years ago—and you challenged me to send you to the Rift.

"'Sadeas will gather reinforcements and join you. Please send word of your strategic assessment of the problem. Be warned, we are certain now that one of the other highprinces—we don't know who—is supporting Tanalan and his rebellion. He may have access to Shards. I wish you strength of purpose, and the Heralds' own blessings, in your new task. With love and respect, Gavilar.'"

Evi looked up. "How did you know, Dalinar? You've been poring over those maps for weeks—maps of the Crownlands and of Alethkar. You *knew* he was going to assign you this task."

"What kind of strategist would I be if I couldn't foresee the next battle?"

"I thought we were going to relax," Evi said. "We were going to be done with the killing."

"With the momentum I have? What a waste that would be! If not for this problem in Rathalas, Gavilar would have found somewhere else for me to fight. Herdaz again, perhaps. You can't have your best general sitting around collecting crem."

Besides. There would be men and women among Gavilar's advisors who worried about Dalinar. If anyone was a threat to the throne, it would be the Blackthorn—particularly with the respect he'd gained from the kingdom's generals. Though Dalinar had decided years ago that he would never do such a thing, many at court would think the kingdom safer if he were kept away.

"No, Evi," he said as he made another notation, "I doubt we will ever settle back in Kholinar again."

He nodded to himself. That was the way to get the Rift. One of his mobile bands could round and secure the lake's beach. He could move the entire army across it then, attacking far faster than the Rift expected.

Satisfied, he looked up. And found Evi crying.

The sight stunned him, and he dropped his pencil. She tried to hold it back, turning toward the fire and wrapping her arms around herself, but the sniffles sounded as distinct and disturbing as breaking bones.

Kelek's breath . . . he could face soldiers and storms, falling boulders and dying friends, but nothing in his training had ever prepared him to deal with these soft tears.

"Seven years," she whispered. "Seven *years* we've been out here, living in wagons and waystops. Seven years of murder, of chaos, of men crying to their wounds."

"You married—"

"Yes, I *married a soldier*. It's my fault for not being strong enough to deal with the consequences. Thank you, Dalinar. You've made that very clear."

This was what it was like to feel helpless. "I . . . thought you were growing to like it. You now fit in with the other women."

"The other women? Dalinar, they make me feel *stupid*."

"But . . ."

"Conversation is a *contest* to them," Evi said, throwing her hands up. "*Everything* has to be a contest to you Alethi, always trying to show up everyone else. For the women it's this awful, unspoken game to prove how witty they each are. I've thought . . . maybe the only answer, to make you proud, is to go to the Nightwatcher and ask for the blessing of intelligence. The Old Magic can change a person. Make something great of them—"

"Evi," Dalinar cut in. "Please, don't speak of that place or that creature. It's blasphemous."

"You say that, Dalinar," she said. "But no one actually cares about religion here. Oh, they make sure to point out how superior their beliefs are to mine. But who actually ever worries about the Heralds, other than to swear by their names? You bring ardents to battle merely to Soulcast rocks into grain. That way, you don't have to stop *killing* each other long enough to find something to eat."

Dalinar approached, then settled down into the other seat by the hearth. "It is . . . different in your homeland?"

She rubbed her eyes, and he wondered if she'd see through his attempt to change the subject. Talking about her people often smoothed over their arguments.

"Yes," she said. "True, there are those who don't care about the One or the Heralds. They say we shouldn't accept Iriali or Vorin doctrines as our own. But Dalinar, many *do* care. Here . . . here you just pay some ardent to burn glyphwards for you and call it done."

Dalinar took a deep breath and tried again. "Perhaps, after I've seen to the rebels, I can persuade Gavilar not to give me another assignment. We could travel. Go west, to your homeland."

"So you could kill my people instead?"

"No! I wouldn't—"

"They'd attack you, Dalinar. My brother and I are exiles, if you haven't forgotten."

He hadn't seen Toh in a decade, ever since the man had gone to Herdaz. He reportedly liked it quite well, living on the coast, protected by Alethi bodyguards.

Evi sighed. "I'll never see the sunken forests again. I've accepted that. I will live my life in this harsh land, so dominated by wind and cold."

"Well, we could travel someplace warm. Up to the Steamwater. Just you and I. Time together. We could even bring Adolin."

"And Renarin?" Evi asked. "Dalinar, you have *two* sons, in case you have forgotten. Do you even care about the child's condition? Or is he nothing to you now that he can't become a soldier?"

Dalinar grunted, feeling like he'd taken a mace to the head. He stood up, then walked toward the table.

"What?" Evi demanded.

"I've been in enough battles to know when I've found one I can't win."

"So you flee?" Evi said. "Like a coward?"

"The coward," Dalinar said, gathering his maps, "is the man who delays a necessary retreat for fear of being mocked. We'll go back to Kholinar after I deal with the rebellion at the Rift. I'll promise you at least a year there."

"Really?" Evi said, standing up.

"Yes. You've won this fight."

"I . . . don't feel like I've won. . . ."

"Welcome to war, Evi," Dalinar said, heading toward the door. "There are no unequivocal wins. Just victories that leave fewer of your friends dead than others."

He left and slammed the door behind him. Sounds of her weeping chased him down the steps, and shamespren fell around him like flower petals. *Storms, I don't deserve that woman, do I?*

Well, so be it. The argument was her fault, as were the repercussions. He stomped down the steps to find his generals, and continue planning his return assault on the Rift.

Normal Painspren

Altered Painspren

The painspren in Kholinar are a sickly green color, with long claws and oddly distorted proportions (even more than usual).

They respond to pain as readily as ever.

Shamespren have transformed from their usual manifestations as falling blossoms to shards of broken glass.

The sense of embarrassment itself appears unaffected.

Curiously, the hungerspren appear to be unchanged.

This generation has had only one Bondsmith, and some blame the divisions among us upon this fact. The true problem is far deeper. I believe that Honor himself is changing.

—From drawer 24-18, smokestone

A day after being murdered in a brutal fashion, Shallan found that she was feeling much better. The sense of oppression had left her, and even her horror seemed distant. What lingered was that single glimpse she'd seen in the mirror: a glimmer of the Unmade's presence, beyond the plane of the reflection.

The mirrors in the tailor's shop didn't show such proclivities; she had checked every one. Just in case, she'd given a drawing of the thing she'd seen to the others, and warned them to watch.

Today, she strolled into the little kitchen, which was beside the rear workroom. Adolin ate flatbread and curry while King Elhokar sat at the room's table, earnestly . . . writing something? No, he was *drawing*.

Shallan rested fond fingers on Adolin's shoulder and enjoyed his grin in response. Then she rounded to peek over the king's shoulder. He was doing a map of the city, with the palace and the Oathgate platform. It wasn't half bad.

"Anyone seen the bridgeman?" Elhokar asked.

"Here," Kaladin said, strolling in from the workroom. Yokska, her husband, and her maid were out shopping for more food, using spheres that Elhokar had provided. Food was apparently still for sale in the city, if you had the spheres to pay.

"I," Elhokar said, "have devised a plan for how to proceed in this city."

Shallan shared a look with Adolin, who shrugged. "What do you suggest, Your Majesty?"

"Thanks to the Lightweaver's excellent reconnaissance," the king said, "it is evident my wife is being held captive by her own guards."

"We don't know that for certain, Your Majesty," Kaladin said. "It sounded like the queen has succumbed to whatever is affecting the guards."

"Either way, she is in need of rescue," Elhokar said. "Either we must sneak into the palace for her and little Gavinor, or we must rally a military force to help us capture the location by strength of arms." He tapped his map of the city with his pen. "The Oathgate, however, remains our priority. Brightness Davar, I want you to investigate this Cult of Moments. Find out how they're using the Oathgate platform."

Yokska had confirmed that each night, some members of the cult set a blazing fire on top of the platform. They guarded the place all hours of the day.

"If you could join whatever ritual or event they are performing," the king said, "you would be within feet of the Oathgate. You could transport the entire plateau to Urithiru, and let our armies there deal with the cult.

"In case that is not viable, Adolin and I—in the guise of important lighteyes from the Shattered Plains—shall contact the lighteyed houses in the city who maintain private guard forces. We shall gather their support, perhaps revealing our true identities, and put together an army for assaulting the palace, if needed."

"And me?" Kaladin asked.

"I don't like the sound of this Azure person. See what you can find out about him and his Wall Guard."

Kaladin nodded, then grunted.

"It's a good plan, Elhokar," Adolin said. "Nice work."

A simple compliment probably should not have made a king beam like it did. Elhokar even drew a gloryspren—and notably, it didn't seem different from ordinary ones.

"But there is something we have to face," Adolin continued. "Have you listened to the list of charges that ardent—the one who got executed—made against the queen?"

"I . . . Yes."

"Ten glyphs," Adolin said, "denouncing Aesudan's excess. Wasting food while people starved. Increasing taxes, then throwing lavish parties for her ardents. Elhokar, this started long before the Everstorm."

"We can . . . ask her," the king said. "Once she is safe. Something must have been wrong. Aesudan was always proud, and always ambitious, but never gluttonous." He eyed Adolin. "I know that Jasnah says I shouldn't have married her—that Aesudan was too hungry for power. Jasnah never understood. I *needed* Aesudan. Someone with strength . . ." He took a deep breath, then stood up. "We mustn't waste time. The plan. Do you agree with it?"

"I like it," Shallan said.

Kaladin nodded. "It's too general, but it's at least a line of attack. Additionally, we need to trace the grain in the city. Yokska says the lighteyes provide it, but she also says the palace stores are closed."

"You think someone has a Soulcaster?" Adolin asked.

"I think this city has too many secrets," Kaladin said.

"Adolin and I shall ask the lighteyes, and see if they know," Elhokar said, then looked to Shallan. "The Cult of Moments?"

"I'll get on it," she said. "I need a new coat anyway."

．．

She slipped out of the building again as Veil. She wore the trousers and her coat, though that now had a hole in the back. Ishnah had been able to wash the blood off, but Veil still wanted to replace it. For now, she covered the hole with a Lightweaving.

Veil sauntered down the street, and found herself feeling increasingly confident. Back in Urithiru, she'd still been struggling to get her coat on straight, so to speak. She winced as she thought of her trips through the bars, making a fool of herself. You didn't need to *prove* how much you could drink in order to look tough—but that was the sort of thing you couldn't learn without wearing the coat, living in it.

She turned toward the market, where she hoped to get a feel for Kholinar's people. She needed to know how they thought before she could begin to understand how the Cult of Moments had come to be, and therefore how to infiltrate it.

This market was very different from those at Urithiru, or the night markets of Kharbranth. First off, this one was obviously ancient. These worn, weathered shops felt like they'd been here for the first Desolation. These were stones smoothed by the touch of a million fingers, or indented by the press of thousands of passing feet. Awnings bleached by the progression of day after day.

The street was wide, and not crowded. Some stalls were empty, and the remaining merchants didn't shout at her as she passed. These seemed effects of the smothered sensation everyone felt—the feeling of a city besieged.

Yokska served only men, and Veil wouldn't have wanted to reveal herself to the woman anyway. So she stopped at a clothier and tried on some new coats. She chatted with the woman who ran the accounts—her husband was the actual tailor—and got some suggestions on where to look for a coat matching her current one, then stepped back out onto the street.

Soldiers in light blue patrolled here, the glyphs on their uniforms proclaiming them to be of House Velalant. Yokska had described their brightlord as a minor player in the city until so many lighteyes had vanished into the palace.

Veil shivered, remembering the line of corpses. Adolin and Elhokar were fairly certain those were the remnants of a distant Kholin and his attendants—a man named Kaves, who had often tried to gain power in the city. Neither were sad to see him go, but it whispered of a continuing mystery. More than thirty people had gone to meet with the queen, many more powerful than Kaves. What had happened to them?

She passed an assortment of vendors peddling the usual range of necessities and curiosities, from ceramics to dining wares, to fine knives. It was nice to see that here, the soldiers had imposed some semblance of order. Perhaps rather than fixating on the closed stalls, Veil should have appreciated how many were still open.

The third clothing shop finally had a coat she liked, of the same style as her old one—white and long, past her knees. She paid to have it taken in, then casually asked the seamstress about the city's grain.

The answers led her one street over to a grain station. It had formerly been a Thaylen bank, with the words *Secure Keeps* across the top in Thaylen and the women's script. The proprietors had long ago fled—moneylenders seemed to have a sixth sense for impending danger, the way some animals could sense a storm hours before it arrived.

The soldiers in light blue had appropriated it, and the vaults now protected precious grain. People waited in line outside, and at the front, soldiers doled out enough lavis for one day's flatbread and gruel.

It was a good sign—if a distinct and terrible reminder of the city's situation. She would have applauded Velalant's kindness, save for his soldiers' blatant incompetence. They shouted at everyone to stay in line, but didn't do anything to enforce the order. They did have a scribe watching to make sure nobody got in line twice, but they didn't exclude people who were *obviously* too well-to-do to need the handout.

Veil glanced around the market, and noted people watching from the crannies and hollows of abandoned stalls. The poor and unwanted, those destitute beyond even the refugees. Tattered clothing, dirty faces. They watched like spren drawn by a powerful emotion.

Veil settled down on a low wall beside a drainage trough. A boy huddled nearby, watching the line with hungry eyes. One of his arms ended in a twisted, unusable hand: three fingers mere nubs, the other two crooked.

She fished in her trouser pocket. Shallan didn't carry food, but Veil knew the importance of having something to chew on. She could have sworn she'd tucked something in while getting ready. . . . There it was. A meat stick, Soulcast but flavored with sugar. Not quite large enough to be a sausage. She bit off an end, then wagged the rest toward the urchin.

The boy sized her up, probably trying to determine her angle. Finally he crept over and took the offering, quickly stuffing the whole thing into his mouth. He waited, eyeing her to see if she had more.

"Why don't you get in line?" Veil asked.

"They got rules. Gotta be a certain age. And if you're too poor, they shove ya out of line."

"For what reason?"

The boy shrugged. "Don't need one, I guess. They say you've already been through, 'cept you haven't."

"Many of those people . . . they're servants from wealthy homes, aren't they?"

The urchin nodded.

Storming lighteyes, Veil thought as she watched. Some of the poor were shoved out of line for one infraction or another, as the urchin had claimed. The others waited patiently, as it was their job. They'd been sent by wealthy homes to collect food. Many bore the lean, strong look of house guards, though they didn't wear uniforms.

Storms. Velalant's men really had no idea how to do this. *Or maybe they know* exactly *what they're doing,* she thought. *And Velalant is just keeping the local lighteyes happy and ready to support his rule, should the winds turn his way.*

It made Veil sick. She fished out a second meat stick for the urchin, then started to ask him how far Velalant's influence reached—but the kid was gone in a heartbeat.

The grain distribution ended, and a lot of unhappy people called out in despair. The soldiers said they'd do another handout in the evening, and counseled people to line up and wait. Then the bank closed its doors.

But where did Velalant *get* the food? Veil rose and continued through the market, passing pools of angerspren. Some looked like the normal pools of blood; others were more like tar, pitch-black. When the bubbles in these popped, they showed a burning red within, like embers. Those vanished as people settled down to wait—and exhaustionspren appeared instead.

Her optimism about the market evaporated. She passed crowds milling about, looking lost, and read depression in people's eyes. Why try to pretend life could go on? They were doomed. The Voidbringers were going to rip this city apart—if they didn't simply let everyone starve.

Someone needed to do something. *Veil* needed to do something. Infiltrating the Cult of Moments suddenly seemed too abstract. Couldn't she do something directly for these poor people? Except . . . she hadn't even been able to save her own family. She had no idea what Mraize had done with her brothers, and she refused to think about them. How would she save an entire city?

She shouldered through the crowd, seeking freedom, suddenly feeling trapped. She needed out. She—

What was that sound?

Shallan pulled up short, turning, *hearing*. Storms. It couldn't be, could it? She drifted toward the sound, that *voice*.

"You say that, my dear man," it proclaimed, "but *everyone* thinks they know the moons. How could they not? We live beneath their gaze each night. We've known them longer than our friends, our wives, our children. And yet . . . and yet . . ."

Shallan pushed through the milling crowd to find him sitting on the low wall around a storm cistern. A metal brazier burned before him, emitting thin lines of smoke that twisted in the wind. He was dressed, strangely, in a soldier's uniform—Sadeas's livery, with the coat unbuttoned and a colored scarf around his neck.

The traveler. The one they called the King's Wit. Angular features, a sharp nose, hair that was stark black.

He was *here*.

"There are still stories to tell." Wit leaped to his feet. Few people were paying attention. To them, he was just another busker. "Everyone knows that Mishim is the cleverest of the three moons. Though her sister and brother are content to reign in the sky—gracing the lands below with their light—Mishim is always looking for a chance to escape her duty."

Wit tossed something into the brazier, producing a bright green puff of smoke the color of Mishim, the third and slowest of the moons.

"This story takes place during the days of Tsa," Wit continued. "The grandest queen of Natanatan, before that kingdom's fall. Blessed with grand poise and beauty, the Natan people were famous across all of Roshar. Why, if you'd lived back then, you'd have viewed the east as a place of great culture, not an empty wasteland!

"Queen Tsa, as you've doubtless heard, was an architect. She designed high towers for her city, built to reach ever upward, grasping toward the sky. One night, Tsa rested in her greatest tower, enjoying the view. So it was that Mishim, that clever moon, happened to pass in the sky close by. (It was a night when the moons were large, and these—everyone knows— are nights when the moons pay special attention to the actions of mortals.)

"'Great Queen!' Mishim called. 'You build such fine towers in your grand city. I enjoy viewing them each night as I pass.'"

Wit dropped powder into the brazier, this time in clumps that caused two lines of smoke—one white, one green—to stream upward. Shallan stepped forward, watching the smoke curl. The marketgoers slowed, and began to gather.

"Now," Wit said, thrusting his hands into the smoke lines, twisting them so that the smoke swirled and contorted, giving the sense of a green moon spinning in the center, "Queen Tsa was hardly ignorant of Mishim's crafty ways. The Natans were never fond of Mishim, but rather revered the great Nomon.

"Still, one does not ignore a moon. 'Thank you, Great Celestial One,' Tsa called. 'Our engineers labor ceaselessly to erect the most splendid of mortal accomplishments.'

"'Almost they reach to my domain,' Mishim called. 'One wonders if you are trying to obtain it.'

"'Never, Great Celestial One. My domain is this land, and the sky is yours.'"

Wit thrust his hand high in his smoke, drawing the line of white into the shape of a straight pillar. His other hand swirled a pocket of green above it, like a whirlpool. A tower and a moon.

That can't be natural, can it? Shallan thought. *Is he Lightweaving?* Yet she saw no Stormlight. There was something more . . . organic about what he did. She couldn't be completely certain it was supernatural.

"As always, Mishim was hatching a scheme. She loathed being hung in the sky each night, far from the delights of the world below, and the pleasures that only mortals know. The next night, Mishim again passed Queen Tsa in her tower. 'It is a pity,' Mishim said, 'that you cannot see the constellations from up close. For they are truly beautiful gemstones, shaped by the finest of gem cutters.'

"'It *is* a pity,' Tsa said. 'But all know that the eyes of a mortal would burn to see such a lofty sight.'

"On the next night, Mishim tried again. 'It is a pity,' she said, 'that you cannot converse with the starspren, as they tell delightsome stories.'

"'It *is* a pity,' Tsa agreed. 'But everyone knows that the language of the heavens would drive a mortal mad.'

"The next night, Mishim tried a third time. 'It is a pity that you cannot see the beauty of your kingdom from above. For the pillars and domes of your city are radiant.'

"'It *is* a pity,' Tsa agreed. 'But those sights are meant for the great ones of heaven, and to behold them myself would be blasphemous.'"

Wit dropped another powder into the brazier, bringing up yellow-gold smoke. By now, dozens of people had gathered to watch. He swept his hands to the sides, sending the smoke spraying out in a flat plane. Then it crept upward again in lines—forming towers. A city?

He continued to swirl with one hand, drawing the green smoke up into a ring that—with a thrust of his hand—he sent spinning across the top of the yellow-golden city. It was *remarkable,* and Shallan found her jaw dropping. This was an image that *lived.*

Wit glanced to the side, where he'd put his pack. He started, as if surprised. Shallan cocked her head as he quickly recovered, jumping back into the story so fast that it was easy to miss his lapse. But now, as he spoke, he searched the audience with careful eyes.

"Mishim," he said, "was not finished. The queen was pious, but the moon was crafty. I will leave it to you to decide which is the more powerful. The fourth night, as Mishim passed the queen, she tried a different ploy.

"'Yes,' Mishim said, 'your city is grand, as only a god can see from above. That is why it is so, so sad that one of the towers has a flawed roof.'"

Wit swept to the side, destroying the lines of smoke that made up the city. He let the smoke dwindle, the powders he'd thrown running out, all save the line of green.

"'*What?*' Tsa said. 'A flawed tower? *Which one?*'

"'It is but a minor blemish,' Mishim said. 'Do not let it worry you. I appreciate the effort your craftsmen, however incompetent, put into their work.' She continued on her way, but knew that she had trapped the queen.

"Indeed, on the next night, the beautiful queen stood waiting on her balcony. 'Great One of the Heavens!' Tsa called. 'We have inspected the roofs, and cannot find the imperfection! Please, *please* tell me which tower it is, so I can break it down.'

"'I cannot say,' Mishim said. 'To be mortal is to be flawed; it is not right to expect perfection of you.'

"This only made the queen more worried. On the next night, she asked, 'Great One of the Sky, *is* there a way that I could visit the heavens? I will close my ears to the stories of the starspren and turn my eyes away from the constellations. I would look only upon the flawed works of my people, not the sights meant for you, so that I may see with my own eyes what must be fixed.'

"'It is a forbidden thing that you ask,' Mishim said, 'for we would have to trade places, and hope that Nomon does not notice.' She said it with much glee, though hidden, for this request was the very thing she desired.

"'I will feign that I am you,' Tsa promised. 'And I will do all that you do. We will switch back once I am done, and Nomon will never know.'"

Wit grinned broadly. "And so, the moon and the woman traded places."

His raw enthusiasm for the story was infectious, and Shallan found herself smiling.

They were at war, the city was falling, but all she wanted to do was listen to the end of this story.

Wit used powders to send up four different smoke lines—blue, yellow, green, and intense orange. He swirled them together in a transfixing vortex of hues. And as he worked, his blue eyes fell on Shallan. They narrowed, and his smile became sly.

He just recognized me, she realized. *I'm still wearing Veil's face. But how . . . how did he know?*

When he finished his swirling colors, the moon had become white, and the single straight tower he made by swiping up in the smoke was instead pale green.

"Mishim came down among the mortals," he proclaimed, "and Tsa climbed the heavens to sit in the place of the moon! Mishim spent the remaining hours of the night drinking, and courting, and dancing, and singing, and doing all the things she had watched from afar. She lived frantically during her few hours of freedom.

"In fact, she was so captivated that she forgot to return, and was shocked by the dawning of sunlight! She hurriedly climbed to the queen's high tower, but Tsa had already set, and the night had passed.

"Mishim now knew not only the delights of mortality, but the anxiety as well. She passed the day in great disquiet, knowing that Tsa would be trapped with her wise sister and solemn brother, spending the day in the place where moons rest. When night again came, Mishim hid inside the tower, expecting that Salas would call out and chide her for her appetites. Yet Salas passed without comment.

"Surely, when Nomon rose, he would lash out against her foolishness. Yet Nomon passed without comment. Finally, Tsa rose in the sky, and Mishim called to her. 'Queen Tsa, mortal, what has happened? My siblings did not call to me. Did you somehow go undiscovered?'

"'No,' Tsa replied. 'Your siblings knew me as an impostor immediately.'

"'Then let us trade places quickly!' Mishim said. 'So that I may tell them lies and placate them.'

"'They are placated already,' Tsa said. 'They think I am delightful. We spent the daylight hours feasting.'

"'Feasting?' Her siblings had never feasted with her before.

"'We sang sweet songs together.'

"'Songs?' Her siblings had never sung with her before.

"'It is truly wonderful up here,' Tsa said. 'The starspren tell amazing tales, as you promised, and the gemstone constellations are grand from up close.'

"'Yes. I love those stories, and those sights.'

"'I think,' Tsa said, 'that I might stay.'"

Wit let the smoke fail until only a single line of green remained. It shrank down, dwindling, almost out. When he spoke, his voice was soft.

"Mishim," he said, "now knew another mortal emotion. Loss.

"The moon began to panic! She thought of her grand view from up so high, where she could see all lands and enjoy—if from afar—their art, buildings, and songs! She remembered the kindness of Nomon and the thoughtfulness of Salas!"

Wit made a swirl of white smoke, and pushed it slowly to his left, the new moon Tsa close to setting.

"'Wait!' Mishim said. 'Wait, Tsa! Your word is broken! You spoke to the starspren and gazed upon the constellations!'"

Wit caught the smoke ring with one hand, somehow making it stay, swirling in one place.

"'Nomon said that I could,' Tsa explained. 'And I was not harmed.'

"'You broke your word nonetheless!' Mishim cried. 'You must come back to earth, mortal, for our bargain is at an end!'"

Wit let the ring hang there.

Then vanish.

"To Mishim's eternal relief, Tsa relented. The queen climbed back down into her tower, and Mishim scrambled up into the heavens. With great pleasure, she sank toward the horizon. Though just before she set, Mishim heard a song."

Oddly, Wit added a small line of blue smoke to the brazier.

"It was a song of laughter, of beauty. A song Mishim had never heard! It took her long to understand that song, until months later, she passed in the sky at night and saw the queen in the tower again. Holding a child with skin that was faintly blue.

"They did not speak, but Mishim knew. The queen had tricked her. Tsa had *wanted* to spend one day in the heavens, to know Nomon for a night. She had given birth to a son with pale blue skin, the color of Nomon himself. A son born of the gods, who would lead her people to glory. A son who bore the mantle of the heavens.

"And that is why to this day, the people of Natanatan have skin of a faintly blue shade. And it is why Mishim, though still crafty, has never again left her place. Most importantly, it is the story of how the moon came to know the one thing that before, only mortals had known. Loss."

The last line of blue smoke dwindled, then went out.

Wit didn't bow for applause or ask for tips. He sat back down on the cistern wall that had been his stage, looking exhausted. People waited, stunned, until a few started yelling for more. Wit remained silent. He bore their requests, their pleas, then their curses.

Slowly, the audience drifted away.

Eventually, only Shallan stood before him.

Wit smiled at her.

"Why that story?" she asked. "Why now?"

"I don't give the meanings, child," he said. "You should know that by now. I just tell the tale."

"It was beautiful."

"Yes," he said. Then he added, "I miss my flute."

"Your what?"

He hopped up and began gathering his things. Shallan slipped forward and glanced inside his pack, catching sight of a small jar, sealed at the top. It was mostly black, but the side pointed toward her was instead white.

Wit snapped the pack closed. "Come. You look like you could use the opportunity to buy me something to eat."

My research into the cognitive reflections of spren at the tower has been deeply illustrative. Some thought that the Sibling had withdrawn from men by intent—but I find counter to that theory.

—From drawer 1-1, first zircon

W it led Shallan to a squat tavern that was so grown over with crem, it gave the impression of having been molded from clay. Inside, a fabrial ceiling fan hung motionless; starting it up would have drawn the attention of the strange screaming spren.

Despite the large signs outside offering chouta for sale, the place was empty. The prices raised Shallan's eyebrows, but the scents emanating from the kitchen were inviting. The innkeeper was a short, heavyset Alethi man with a paunch so thick he looked like a big chull egg. He scowled as Wit entered.

"You!" he said, pointing. "Storyteller! You were supposed to draw customers here! The place would be full, you said!"

"My tyrannical liege, I believe you misunderstood." Wit gave a flowery bow. "I said that you would be full. And you are. Of what, I did not say, as I did not wish to sully my tongue."

"Where are my patrons, you idiot!"

Wit stepped to the side, holding out his hands toward Shallan. "Behold, mighty and terrible king, I have recruited you a subject."

The innkeeper squinted at her. "Can she pay?"

"Yes," Wit said, holding up Shallan's purse and poking through it. "She'll probably leave a tip too."

With a start, Shallan felt at her pocket. Storms, she'd even kept her hand on that purse most of the day.

"Take the private room then," the innkeeper said. "It's not like anyone else is using it. Idiot bard. I'll expect a good performance out of you tonight!"

Wit sighed, tossing Shallan her purse. He seized his pack and brazier, leading her to a chamber beside the main dining room. As he ushered her in, he raised a fist toward the innkeeper. "I've had enough of your oppression, tyrant! Secure your wine well this evening, for the revolution will be swift, vengeful, and intoxicated!"

Closing the door behind him, Wit shook his head. "That man really should know better by now. I have no idea why he continues to put up with me." He set his brazier and pack by the wall, then settled at the room's dining table, where he leaned back and put his boots up on the seat next to him.

Shallan sat at the table more delicately, Pattern slipping off her coat and across to dimple the tabletop next to her. Wit didn't react to the spren.

The room was nice, with painted wood panels set into the walls and rockbuds along a ledge near the small window. The table even had a yellow silk tablecloth. The room was obviously meant for lighteyes to enjoy private dining, while unsavory darkeyes ate out in the main chamber.

"That's a nice illusion," Wit said. "You got the back of the head right. People always flub the back. You've broken character though. You're walking like a prim lighteyes, which looks silly in that costume. You'll only be able to pull off a coat and hat if you *own* them."

"I know," she said, grimacing. "The persona . . . fled once you recognized me."

"Shame about the dark hair. Your natural red would be arresting with the white coat."

"This guise is supposed to be less memorable than that."

He glanced at the hat, which she'd set on the table. Shallan blushed. She felt like a girl nervously showing her first drawings to her tutor.

The innkeeper entered with drinks, a mild orange, as it was still early in the day. "Many thanks, my liege," Wit said. "I vow to compose another song about you. One without so many references to the things you've mistaken for young maidens . . ."

"Storming idiot," the man said. He set the drinks on the table, and didn't notice that Pattern rippled out from under one. The innkeeper bustled out, closing the door.

"Are you one of them?" Shallan blurted out. "Are you a Herald, Wit?"

Pattern hummed softly.

"Heavens no," Wit said. "I'm not stupid enough to get mixed up in religion again. The last seven times I tried it were all disasters. I believe there's at least one god still worshipping me by accident."

She eyed him. It was always hard to tell which of Wit's exaggerations were supposed to mean something and which were confusing distractions. "Then what *are* you?"

"Some men, as they age, grow kinder. I am not one of those, for I have seen how the cosmere can mistreat the innocent—and that leaves me disinclined toward kindness. Some men, as they age, grow wiser. I am not one of those, for wisdom and I have always been at cross-purposes, and I have yet to learn the tongue in which she speaks. Some men, as they age, grow more cynical. I, fortunately, am not one of those. If I were, the very air would warp around me, sucking in all emotion, leaving only scorn."

He tapped the table. "Other men . . . other men, as they age, merely grow stranger. I fear that I *am* one of those. I am the bones of a foreign species left drying on the plain that was once, long ago, a sea. A curiosity, perhaps a reminder, that all has not always been as it is now."

"You're . . . old, aren't you? Not a Herald, but as old as they are?"

He slid his boots off the chair and leaned forward, holding her eyes. He smiled in a kindly way. "Child, when they were but babes, I had already lived dozens of lifetimes. 'Old' is a word you use for worn shoes. I'm something else entirely."

She trembled, looking into those blue eyes. Shadows played within them. Shapes moved, and were worn down by time. Boulders became dust. Mountains became hills. Rivers changed course. Seas became deserts.

"Storms," she whispered.

"When I was young . . ." he said.

"Yes?"

"I made a vow."

Shallan nodded, wide-eyed.

"I said I'd always be there when I was needed."

"And you have been?"

"Yes."

She breathed out.

"It turns out I should have been more specific, as 'there' is technically anywhere."

"It . . . what?"

"To be honest, 'there' has—so far—been a random location that is of absolutely no use to anyone."

Shallan hesitated. In an instant, whatever she seemed to have sensed in Wit was gone. She flopped back in her seat. "Why am I talking to *you* of all people?"

"Shallan!" he said, aghast. "If you were talking to someone else, they wouldn't be me."

"I happen to know plenty of people who aren't you, Wit. I even *like* some of them."

"Be careful. People who aren't me are prone to spontaneous bouts of sincerity."

"Which is bad?"

"Of course! 'Sincerity' is a word people use to justify their chronic dullness."

"Well, *I* like sincere people," Shallan said, raising her cup. "It's delightful how surprised they look when you push them down the stairs."

"Now, that's unkind. You shouldn't push people down the stairs for being sincere. You push people down the stairs for being *stupid*."

"What if they're sincere *and* stupid?"

"Then you run."

"I quite like arguing with them instead. They do make me look smart, and Vev knows I need the help. . . ."

"No, no. You should *never* debate an idiot, Shallan. No more than you'd use your best sword to spread butter."

"Oh, but I'm a scholar. I enjoy things with curious properties, and stupidity is *most* interesting. The more you study it, the further it flees—and yet the more of it you obtain, the less you understand about it!"

Wit sipped his drink. "True, to an extent. But it can be hard to spot, as—like body odor—you never notice your own. That said . . . put two smart people together, and they *will* eventually find their common stupidity, and in so doing become idiots."

"Like a child, it grows the more you feed it."

"Like a fashionable dress, it can be fetching in youth, but looks particularly bad on the aged. And unique though its properties may be, stupidity is frighteningly common. The sum total of stupid people is somewhere around the population of the planet. Plus one."

"Plus one?" Shallan asked.

"Sadeas counts twice."

"Um . . . he's dead, Wit."

"What?" Wit sat up straight.

"Someone murdered him. Er . . . we don't know who." Aladar's investigators had continued hunting the culprit, but the investigation had stalled by the time Shallan left.

"Someone offed old Sadeas, and I *missed* it?"

"What would you have done? Helped him?"

"Storms, no. I'd have *applauded*."

Shallan grinned and let out a deep sigh. Her hair had reverted to red—she'd let the illusion lapse. "Wit," she said, "why are you here? In the city?"

"I'm not completely sure."

"Please. Could you just answer?"

"I did—and I was honest. I can know where I'm supposed to be, Shallan, but not always what I'm supposed to do there." He tapped the table. "Why are *you* here?"

"To open the Oathgate," Shallan said. "Save the city."

Pattern hummed.

"Lofty goals," Wit said.

"What's the point of goals, if not to spur you to something lofty?"

"Yes, yes. Aim for the sun. That way if you miss, at least your arrow will fall far away, and the person it kills will likely be someone you don't know."

The innkeeper chose that moment to arrive with some food. Shallan didn't feel particularly hungry; seeing all those starving people outside had stolen her appetite.

The small plates held crumbly cakes of Soulcast grain topped with a single steamed cremling—a variety known as a skrip, with a flat tail, two large claws, and long antennae. Eating cremlings wasn't uncommon, but it wasn't particularly fine dining.

The only difference between Shallan's meal and Wit's was the sauce—hers sweet, his spicy, though his had the sauce in a cup at the side. Food supplies were tight, and the kitchen wasn't preparing both masculine and feminine dishes.

The innkeeper frowned at her hair, then shook his head and left. She got the impression he was accustomed to oddities around Wit.

Shallan looked down at her food. Could she give this to someone else? Someone who deserved it more than she did?

"Eat up," Wit said, rising and walking to the small window. "Don't waste what you're given."

Reluctantly, she did as he instructed. It wasn't particularly good, but it wasn't terrible. "Aren't you going to eat?" she asked.

"I'm smart enough not to follow my own advice, thank you very much." He sounded distracted. Outside the window, a procession from the Cult of Moments was passing.

"I want to learn to be like you," Shallan said, feeling silly as she said it.

"No you don't."

"You're funny, and charming, and—"

"Yes, yes. I'm so storming clever that half the time, even *I* can't follow what I'm talking about."

"—and you change things, Wit. When you came to me, in Jah Keved, you changed everything. I want to be able to do that. I want to be able to change the world."

He didn't seem at all interested in his food. *Does he eat?* she wondered. *Or is he . . . like some kind of spren?*

"Who came with you to the city?" he asked her.

"Kaladin. Adolin. Elhokar. Some of our servants."

"King Elhokar? Here?"

"He's determined to save the city."

"Most days, Elhokar has trouble saving face, let alone cities."

"I like him," Shallan said. "Despite his . . . Elhokarness."

"He does grow on you, I suppose. Like a fungus."

"He really wants to do what is right. You should hear him talk about it lately. He wants to be remembered as a good king."

"Vanity."

"You don't care about how you'll be remembered?"

"I'll remember myself, which is enough. Elhokar though, he worries about the wrong things. His father wore a simple crown because he needed no reminder of his authority. Elhokar wears a simple crown because he worries that something more lavish might make people look at it, instead of at him. He doesn't want the competition."

Wit turned away from his inspection of the hearth and chimney. "You want to change the world, Shallan. That's well and good. But be careful. The world predates you. She has seniority."

"I'm a Radiant," Shallan said, shoving another forkful of crumbly, sweet bread into her mouth. "Saving the world is in the job description."

"Then be wise about it. There are two kinds of important men, Shallan. There are those who, when the boulder of time rolls toward them, stand up in front of it and hold out their hands. All their lives, they've been told how great they are. They assume the world itself will bend to their whims as their nurse did when fetching them a fresh cup of milk.

"Those men end up squished.

"Other men stand to the side when the boulder of time passes, but are quick to say, 'See what I did! I made the boulder roll there. Don't make me do it again!'

"These men end up getting everyone else squished."

"Is there not a third type of person?"

"There is, but they are oh so rare. These know they can't stop the boulder. So they walk beside it, study it, and bide their time. Then they shove it—ever so slightly—to create a deviation in its path.

"These are the men . . . well, these are the men who actually change the world. And they terrify me. For men never see as far as they think they do."

Shallan frowned, then looked at her empty plate. She hadn't thought she was hungry, but once she'd started eating . . .

Wit walked past and deftly lifted her plate away, then swapped it with his full one.

"Wit . . . I can't eat that."

"Don't be persnickety," he said. "How are you going to save the world if you starve yourself?"

"I'm *not* starving myself." But she took a little bite to satisfy him. "You make it sound like having the power to change the world is a bad thing."

"Bad? No. Abhorrent, depressing, ghastly. Having power is a terrible burden, the worst thing imaginable, except for every other alternative." He turned and studied her. "What is *power* to you, Shallan?"

"It's . . ." Shallan cut at the cremling, separating it from its shell. "It's what I said earlier—the ability to change things."

"Things?"

"Other people's lives. Power is the ability to make life better or worse for the people around you."

"And yourself too, of course."

"I don't matter."

"You should."

"Selflessness is a Vorin virtue, Wit."

"Oh, bother *that*. You've got to live life, Shallan, *enjoy* life. Drink of what you're proposing to give everyone else! That's what I do."

"You . . . do seem to enjoy yourself a great deal."

"I like to live every day like it's my last."

Shallan nodded.

"And by that I mean lying in a puddle of my own urine, calling for the nurse to bring me more pudding."

She almost choked on a bite of cremling. Her cup was empty, but Wit walked past and put his in her hand. She gulped it down.

"Power is a knife," Wit said, taking his seat. "A terrible, dangerous knife that can't be wielded without cutting yourself. We joked about stupidity, but in reality most people aren't stupid. Many are simply *frustrated* at how little control they have over their lives. They lash out. Sometimes in spectacular ways . . ."

"The Cult of Moments. They reportedly claim to see a transformed world coming upon us."

"Be wary of anyone who claims to be able to see the future, Shallan."

"Except you, of course. Didn't you say you can see where you need to be?"

"Be wary," he repeated, "of *anyone* who claims to be able to see the future, Shallan."

Pattern rippled on the table, not humming, only changing more quickly, forming new shapes in a rapid sequence. Shallan swallowed. To her surprise, her plate was empty again. "The cult has control of the Oathgate platform," she said. "Do you know what they do up there every night?"

"They feast," Wit said softly, "and party. There are two general divisions among them. The common members wander the streets, moaning, pretending to be spren. But others up on the platform actually *know* the spren—specifically, the creature known as the Heart of the Revel."

"One of the Unmade."

Wit nodded. "A dangerous foe, Shallan. The cult reminds me of a group I knew long ago. Equally dangerous, equally foolish."

"Elhokar wants me to infiltrate them. Get onto that platform and activate the Oathgate. Is it possible?"

"Perhaps." Wit settled back. "Perhaps. I can't make the gate work; the spren of the fabrial won't obey me. You have the proper key, and the cult takes new members eagerly. Consumes them, like a fire needing new logs."

"How? What do I do?"

"Food," he said. "Their proximity to the Heart drives them to feast and celebrate."

"Drinking in life?" she said, quoting his sentiment from earlier.

"No. Hedonism has never been enjoyment, Shallan, but the opposite. They take the wonderful things of life and indulge until they lose savor. It's listening to beautiful music, performed so loud as to eliminate all subtlety—taking something beautiful and making it carnal. Yet their feasting does give you an opening. I've brushed against their leaders—despite my best efforts. Bring them food for the revel, and I can get you in. A warning, however, simple Soulcast grain won't satisfy them."

A challenge, then. "I should get back to the others." She looked up to Wit. "Would you . . . come with me? Join us?"

He stood, then walked to the door and pressed his ear against it. "Unfortunately, Shallan," he said, glancing at her, "you're not why I am here."

She took a deep breath. "I *am* going to learn how to change the world, Wit."

"You already know how. Learn *why*." He stepped back from the door and pressed himself against the wall. "Also, tell the innkeeper I disappeared in a puff of smoke. It will drive him crazy."

"The inn—"

The door opened suddenly, swinging inward. The innkeeper entered, and hesitated as he found Shallan sitting alone at the table. Wit slipped deftly around the door and out behind the man, who didn't notice.

"Damnation," the innkeeper said, searching around. "I don't suppose he's

going to work tonight?"

"I have no idea."

"He said he'd treat me like a king."

"Well, he's keeping that promise . . ."

The innkeeper took the plates, then bustled out. Conversations with Wit had a way of ending in an odd manner. And, well, starting in an odd manner. Odd all around.

"Do you know anything about Wit?" she asked Pattern.

"No," Pattern said. "He feels like . . . mmm . . . one of us."

Shallan fished in her pouch for some spheres—Wit had stolen a few, she noted—as a tip for the poor innkeeper. Then she made her way back to the tailor's shop, planning how to use her team to get the requisite food.

69

FREE MEAL, NO STRINGS

The wilting of plants and the general cooling of the air is disagreeable, yes, but some of the tower's functions remain in place. The increased pressure, for example, persists.

—From drawer 1-1, second zircon

Kaladin drew in a small amount of Stormlight and stoked the tempest within. That little storm raged inside him, rising from his skin, haunting the space behind his eyes and making them glow. Fortunately—though he stood in a busy market square—this tiny amount of Stormlight wouldn't be enough for people to see in the bright sunlight.

The storm was a primal dance, an ancient song, an eternal battle that had raged since Roshar was new. It wanted to be used. He acquiesced, kneeling to infuse a small stone. He Lashed it upward just enough to make it tremble, but not enough to send it zipping into the air.

The eerie screams came soon after. People started to shout in panic. Kaladin ducked away, exhaling his Stormlight and becoming—hopefully—merely another bystander. He crouched with Shallan and Adolin behind a planter. This plaza—with pillared archways on all four sides, sheltering what had once been a great variety of shops—was several blocks away from the tailor's shop.

People squeezed into buildings or slipped out onto other streets. The slow ones simply huddled down beside the walls, hands over their heads. The spren arrived as two lines of bright yellow-white, twisting about one another above the plaza. Their inhuman screeches were awful. Like . . . like the sound of a wounded animal, dying alone in the wilderness.

Those weren't the spren he'd seen while traveling with Sah and the other parshmen. That one had seemed more akin to a windspren; these looked like vivid yellow spheres crackling with energy. They didn't seem to be able to pinpoint the rock directly, and spun over the courtyard as if confused, still screaming.

A short time later, a figure descended from the sky. A Voidbringer in loose red and black clothing that rippled and churned in the breeze. He carried a spear and a tall, triangular shield.

That spear, Kaladin thought. Long, with a slender point for puncturing armor, it was like a horseman's lance. He found himself nodding. That would be an excellent weapon for using in flight, where you'd need extra reach to attack men on the ground, or even enemies soaring around you.

The spren ceased screaming. The Voidbringer looked about, fluttering through the air, then glared at the spren and said something. Again, they seemed confused. They'd sensed Kaladin's use of Stormlight—likely interpreted it as a fabrial being used—but now couldn't pinpoint the location. Kaladin had used such a small amount of Stormlight, the rock had lost its charge almost immediately.

The spren dispersed, vanishing as emotion spren often did. The Voidbringer lingered, surrounded by dark energy, until horns nearby announced the Wall Guard approaching. The creature finally shot back into the air. People who had been hiding scuttled away, looking relieved to have escaped with their lives.

"Huh," Adolin said, standing. He wore an illusion, imitating—as per Elhokar's instructions—Captainlord Meleran Khal, Teshav's youngest son, a powerfully built balding man in his thirties.

"I can hold Stormlight as long as I want without drawing attention," Kaladin said. "The moment I Lash something, they come screaming."

"And yet," Adolin said, glancing at Shallan, "the disguises draw no attention."

"Pattern says we're quieter than him," Shallan said, thumbing toward Kaladin. "Come on, let's get back. Don't you boys have an appointment tonight?"

⁂

"A party," Kaladin said, pacing back and forth in the tailor shop's showroom. Skar and Drehy leaned by the doorway, each with a spear in the crook of his arm.

"*This* is what they're like," Kaladin said. "Your city is practically burning. What should you do? Throw a *party,* obviously."

Elhokar had suggested parties as a way of contacting the city's lighteyed families. Kaladin had laughed at the idea, assuming that there wouldn't be such a thing. Yet, with minimal searching, Adolin had scrounged up *half a dozen* invitations.

"Good darkeyed people slave away, growing and preparing food," Kaladin said. "But the lighteyes? They have so much storming time they have to *make up* things to do."

"Hey Skar," Drehy said. "You ever go out drinking, even when at war?"

"Sure," Skar said. "And back in my village, we'd have a dance in the stormshelter twice a month, even while boys were off fighting in border skirmishes."

"It's not the same," Kaladin said. "You taking their side?"

"Are there sides?" Drehy asked.

A few minutes later, Adolin came tromping down the stairs and grinning like a fool. He was wearing a ruffled shirt under a powder-blue suit with a jacket that didn't close all the way and tails at the back. Its golden embroidery was the finest the shop could provide.

"Please tell me," Kaladin said, "that you didn't bring us to live with your tailor because you wanted a new wardrobe."

"Come on, Kal," Adolin said, inspecting himself in a showroom mirror. "I need to look the part." He checked his cuffs and grinned again.

Yokska came out and looked him over, then dusted his shoulders. "I think it pulls too tightly through the chest, Brightlord."

"It's wonderful, Yokska."

"Take a deep breath."

It was like she was a storming surgeon, the way she lifted his arm and felt at his waist, muttering to herself. Kaladin had seen his father give physicals that were less invasive.

"I thought that straight coats were still the style," Adolin said. "I have a folio out of Liafor."

"Those aren't up to date," Yokska said. "I was in Liafor last Midpeace, and they're moving *away* from military styles. But they made those folios to sell uniforms at the Shattered Plains."

"Storms! I had *no idea* how unfashionable I was being."

Kaladin rolled his eyes. Adolin saw that in the mirror, but just turned around, giving a bow. "Don't worry, bridgeboy. You can continue to wear clothing to match your scowl."

"You look like you tripped and fell into a bucket of blue paint," Kaladin said, "then tried to dry off with a handful of parched grass."

"And you look like what the storm leaves behind," Adolin said, passing by and patting Kaladin on the shoulder. "We like you anyway. Every boy has a favorite stick he found out in the yard after the rains."

Adolin stepped over to Skar and Drehy, clasping hands with each of them in turn. "You two looking forward to tonight?"

"Depends on how the food is in the darkeyed tent, sir," Skar said.

"Swipe me something from the inner party," Drehy said. "I hear they've got storming good pastries at those fancy lighteyes parties."

"Sure. You need anything, Skar?"

"The head of my enemy, fashioned into a tankard for drinking," Skar said. "Barring that, I'll take a pastry or seven."

"I'll see what I can do. Keep your ears open for any good taverns that are still open. We can go out tomorrow." He strode past Kaladin and tied on a side sword.

Kaladin frowned, looking to him, then to his bridgemen, then back at Adolin. "What?"

"What what?" Adolin asked.

"You're going to go out drinking with bridgemen?" Kaladin said.

"Sure," Adolin said. "Skar, Drehy, and I go way back."

"We spent some time keeping His Highness from falling into chasms," Skar said. "He repaid us with a bit of wine and good conversation."

The king entered, wearing a more muted version of the same style of uniform. He bustled past Adolin, heading toward the stairs. "Ready? Excellent. Time for new faces."

The three stopped by Shallan's room, where she was sketching and humming to herself, surrounded by creationspren. She gave Adolin a kiss that was more intimate than Kaladin had seen from the two of them before, then changed him back into Meleran Khal. Elhokar became an older man, also bald, with pale yellow eyes. General Khal, one of Dalinar's highest officers.

"I'm fine," Kaladin said as she eyed him. "Nobody is going to recognize me."

He wasn't sure what it was, but wearing another face like that . . . to him it felt like lying.

"The scars," Elhokar said. "We need you not to stand out, Captain."

Reluctantly, Kaladin nodded, and allowed Shallan to add a Lightweaving to his head to make the slave brands vanish. Then, she handed each of them a sphere. The illusions were tied to the Stormlight inside of those—if the sphere ran out, their false faces would vanish.

The group set out, Skar and Drehy joining them, spears at the ready. Syl flitted out from an upper window of the shop, soaring on ahead of them along the street. Kaladin had tested summoning her as a Blade earlier, and that hadn't drawn the screamers, so he felt well-armed.

Adolin immediately started joking with Skar and Drehy. Dalinar wouldn't have liked to hear they'd gone out drinking. Not because of any specific prejudice, but there was a command structure to an army. Generals weren't supposed to fraternize with the rank and file; it threw wrinkles into how armies worked.

Adolin could get away with things like that. As he listened, Kaladin found himself feeling ashamed of his earlier attitude. The truth was, he was feeling pretty good these days. Yes, there was a war, and yes, the city was seriously stressed—but ever since he'd found his parents alive and well, he'd been feeling better.

That wasn't so uncommon a feeling for him. He felt good lots of days. Trouble was, on the bad days, that was hard to remember. At those times, for some reason, he felt like he had *always* been in darkness, and always *would* be.

Why was it so hard to remember? Did he have to keep slipping back down? Why couldn't he stay up here in the sunlight, where everyone else lived?

It was nearing evening, maybe two hours from sunset. They passed several plazas like the one where they'd tested his Surgebinding. Most had been turned into living space, with people crowding in. Just sitting and waiting for whatever would happen next.

Kaladin trailed a little behind the others, and when Adolin noticed, he excused himself from the conversation and dropped back. "Hey," he said. "You all right?"

"I'm worried that summoning a Shardblade would make me stand out too much," Kaladin said. "I should have brought a spear tonight."

"Maybe you should let me teach you how to use a side sword. You're pretending to be head of our bodyguards tonight, and you're lighteyed today. It looks strange for you to walk around without a side sword."

"Maybe I'm one of those punchy guys."

Adolin stopped in place and grinned at Kaladin. "Did you just say *'punchy guys'?*"

"You know, ardents who train to fight unarmed."

"Hand to hand?"

"Hand to hand."

"Right," Adolin said. "Or 'punchy guys,' as everyone calls them."

Kaladin met his eyes, then found himself grinning back. "It's the academic term."

"Sure. Like swordy fellows. Or spearish chaps."

"I once knew a real axalacious bloke," Kaladin said. "He was great at psychological fights."

"Psychological fights?"

"He could really get inside someone's head."

Adolin frowned as they walked. "Get inside . . . Oh!" Adolin chuckled, slapping Kaladin on the back. "You talk like a girl sometimes. Um . . . I mean that as a compliment."

"Thanks?"

"But you *do* need to practice the sword more," Adolin said, growing excited. "I know you like the spear, and you're good with it. Great! But you're not simply a spearman anymore; you're going to be an irregular. You won't be fighting in a line, holding a shield for your buddies. Who knows what you'll be facing?"

"I trained a little with Zahel," Kaladin said. "I'm not *completely* useless with a sword. But . . . part of me doesn't see the point."

"You'll be better if you practice with a sword, trust me. Being a good duelist is about knowing one weapon, and being a good foot soldier—that's probably more about training than it is about *any* single weapon. But you want to be a great *warrior*? For that you need to be able to use the best tool for the job. Even if you're never going to use a sword, you'll fight people who do. The best way to learn how to defeat someone wielding a weapon is to practice with it yourself."

Kaladin nodded. He was right. It was strange to look at Adolin in that bright outfit, stylish and glittering with golden thread, and hear him speak real battle sense.

When I was imprisoned for daring to accuse Amaram, he was the only light-eyes who stood up for me.

Adolin Kholin was simply a good person. Powder-blue clothing and all. You couldn't hate a man like him; storms, you kind of *had* to like him.

Their destination was a modest home, by lighteyed standard. Tall and narrow, at four stories high it could have housed a dozen darkeyed families.

"All right," Elhokar said as they drew near. "Adolin and I will feel out the lighteyes for potential allies. Bridgemen, chat with those in the dark-eyed guard tent, and see if you can discover anything about the Cult of Moments, or other oddities in the city."

"Got it, Your Majesty," Drehy said.

"Captain," he said to Kaladin, "you'll go to the lighteyed guard tent. See if you can—"

"—find out anything about this Highmarshal Azure person," Kaladin said. "From the Wall Guard."

"Yes. We will plan to stay relatively late, as intoxicated party guests might share more than sober ones."

They broke, Adolin and Elhokar presenting invitations to the doorman, who let them in—then gestured Drehy and Skar toward the darkeyed guards' feast, happening in a tent set up on the grounds.

There was a separate tent for people who were lighteyed but not land-owners. Privileged, but not good enough to get in the doors to the actual party. In his role as a lighteyed bodyguard, that would be the place for Kaladin—but for some reason the thought of going in there made him feel sick.

Instead he whispered to Skar and Drehy—promising to be back soon—and borrowed Skar's spear, just in case. Then Kaladin left, walking the block. He'd return to do as told by Elhokar. But while there was enough light, he thought he'd maybe survey the wall and see if he could get an idea of the Wall Guard's numbers.

More, he wanted to walk a little longer. He strolled to the foot of the nearby city wall, counting guard posts on top, looking at the large lower portion that was a natural part of the local rock. He rested his hand on the smooth, strata-lined formation of stone.

"Hey!" a voice called. "Hey, you!"

Kaladin sighed. A squad of soldiers from the Wall Guard was patrol-ling here. They considered this road around the city—next to the foot of the wall—to be their jurisdiction, but they didn't patrol any farther inward.

What did they want? He wasn't doing anything wrong. Well, running would only stir up a ruckus, so he dropped his spear and turned around, extending his arms out to the sides. In a city full of refugees, certainly they wouldn't harass one man too much.

A squad of five tromped over to him, led by a man with a wispy dark beard and bright, light blue eyes. The man took in Kaladin's uniform, with no insignia, and glanced at the fallen spear. Then he looked at Kaladin's forehead and frowned.

Kaladin raised his hands to the brands there, which he could feel. But Shallan had put an illusion over those. Hadn't she?

Damnation. He's going to assume I'm a deserter.

"Deserter, I assume?" the soldier asked sharply.

Should have just gone to the storming party.

"Look," Kaladin said. "I don't want trouble. I just—"

"Do you want a meal?"

"A . . . meal?"

"Free food for deserters."

That's unexpected.

Reluctantly, he lifted the hair from his forehead, testing to see that the brands were still visible. Mostly, the hair prevented one from seeing the details.

The soldiers started visibly. Yes, they could see the brands. Shallan's illusion had worn off for some reason? Hopefully the other disguises fared better.

"A lighteyes with a *shash* brand?" their lieutenant asked. "Storms, friend. You've got to have *some* story." He slapped Kaladin on the back and pointed toward their barracks ahead. "I'd love to hear it. Free meal, no strings. We won't press you into service. I give my oath."

Well, he'd wanted information about the leader of the Wall Guard, hadn't he? What better place to get it than from these men?

Kaladin picked up his spear and let them lead him away.

70

HIGHMARSHAL AZURE

Something is happening to the Sibling. I agree this is true, but the division among the Knights Radiant is not to blame. Our perceived worthiness is a separate issue.

—From drawer 1-1, third zircon

The Wall Guard's barracks smelled like home to Kaladin. Not his father's house—which smelled of antiseptic and the flowers his mother crushed to season the air. His *true* home. Leather. Boiling stew. Crowded men. Weapon oil.

Spheres hung on the walls, white and blue. The place was big enough to house two platoons, a fact confirmed by the shoulder patches he saw. The large common room was filled with tables, and a few armorers worked in the corner, sewing jerkins or uniforms. Others sharpened weapons, a rhythmic, calming sound. These were the noises and scents of an army well maintained.

The stew didn't smell anywhere near as good as Rock's; Kaladin had been spoiled by the Horneater's cooking. Still, when one of the men went to fetch him a bowl, he found himself smiling. He settled onto a long wooden bench, near a fidgety little ardent who was scribing glyphwards onto pieces of cloth for the men.

Kaladin instantly loved this place, and the state of the men spoke highly of Highmarshal Azure. He would likely be some middling officer who had been thrust into command during the chaos of the riots, which made him all the more impressive. Azure had secured the wall, gotten the parshmen out of the city, and seen to the defense of Kholinar.

Syl zipped around the rafters as soldiers called out questions about the newcomer. The lieutenant who had found him—his name was Noromin, but his men called him Noro—answered readily. Kaladin was a deserter. He had a *shash* brand, an ugly one. You should see it. Sadeas's mark. On a *lighteyes* no less.

The others in the barrack found this curious, but not worrisome. Some even cheered. Storms. Kaladin couldn't imagine any force of Dalinar's soldiers being so welcoming of a deserter, let alone a dangerous one.

Considering that, Kaladin now picked out another undercurrent in the room. Men sharpening weapons that had chips in them. Armorers repairing cuts in leather—cuts made by lances in battle. Conspicuously empty seats at most of the tables, with cups set at them.

These men had suffered losses. Not huge ones yet. They could still laugh. But storms, there was a tension to this room.

"So," Noro said. "*Shash* brand?"

The rest of the squad settled in, and a short man with hair on the backs of his hands set a bowl of thick stew and flatbread in front of Kaladin. Standard fare, with steamed tallew and cubed meat. Soulcast, of course, and lacking flavor—but hearty and nutritious.

"I had a squabble," Kaladin said, "with Highlord Amaram. I felt he'd gotten some of my men killed needlessly. He disagreed."

"Amaram," said one of the men. "You aim high, friend."

"I know Amaram," the man with hairy hands said. "I did secret missions for him, back in my operative days."

Kaladin looked at him, surprised.

"Best to ignore Beard," Lieutenant Noro said. "It's what the rest of us do."

"Beard" didn't have a beard. Maybe the hairy hands were enough. He nudged Kaladin. "It's a good story. I'll tell it to you sometime."

"You can't just brand a lighteyed man a slave," Lieutenant Noro said. "You need a highprince's permission. There's more to this story."

"There is," Kaladin said. Then he continued eating his stew.

"Oooh," said a tall member of the squad. "Mystery!"

Noro chuckled, then waved at the room. "So what do you think?"

"You said you weren't going to press me," Kaladin said between bites.

"I'm not pressing you, but you won't find a place out there in the city where you'll eat as well as you do here."

"Where do you get it?" Kaladin asked, spooning the stew into his mouth. "You can't use Soulcasters. The screamers will come after you. Stockpile? I'm surprised one of the highlords in the city hasn't tried to appropriate it."

"Astute," Lieutenant Noro said with a smile. He had a disarming way about him. "That's a Guard secret. But in here there's always a stew bubbling and bread baking."

"It's my recipe," Beard added.

"Oh please," the tall man said. "You're a cook now too, Beard?"

"A *chef*, thank you very much. I learned that flatbread recipe from a Horneater mystic at the top of a mountain. The real *story* is how I got there. . . ."

"It's where you landed, obviously," the tall soldier said, "after someone in your last squad *kicked* you."

The men laughed. It felt warm in here, on this long bench, a well-laid fire burning steadily in the corner. Warm and friendly. As Kaladin ate, they gave him some space, chatting among themselves. Noro . . . he seemed less a soldier and more a chummy merchant trying to sell you earrings for your beloved. He dropped very obvious dangling hints for Kaladin. Reminders of how well-fed they were, of how good it was to be part of a squad. He spoke of warm beds, of how they didn't have to go on watch duty *that* often. Of playing cards while the highstorm blew.

Kaladin got a second bowl of stew, and as he settled back into his place, he realized something with a shock.

Storms. They're all lighteyes, aren't they?

Every person in the room, from the cook to the armorers, to the soldiers doing dishes. In a group like this, everyone had a secondary duty, like armoring or field surgery. Kaladin hadn't noticed their eyes. The place had felt so natural, so comfortable, that he'd assumed they were all darkeyed like him.

He knew that most lighteyed soldiers weren't high officers. He'd been told that they were basically just people—he'd been told it over and over. Somehow, sitting in that room finally made the fact real to him.

"So, Kal . . ." Lieutenant Noro asked. "What do you think? Maybe reenlist? Give this another try?"

"Aren't you afraid I'll desert?" Kaladin asked. "Or worse, that I can't control my temper? I might be dangerous."

"Not as dangerous as being short manned," Beard said. "You know how to kill people? That's good enough for us."

Kaladin nodded. "Tell me about your commander. That will be a big part of any group. I only just got into town. Who *is* this Highmarshal Azure?"

"You can meet him yourself!" Beard said. "He does rounds every night around dinner time, checking on each barracks."

"Um, yes," Noro said.

Kaladin eyed him. The lieutenant seemed uncomfortable.

"The highmarshal," Noro said quickly, "is *incredible*. We lost our former commander during the riots, and Azure led a group who held the wall when the Cult of Moments tried—in the chaos—to seize the city gates."

"He fought like a Voidbringer," another squad member said. "I was there.

We were almost overwhelmed, then Azure joined us, holding aloft a gleaming Shardblade. He rallied our numbers, inspired even the wounded to keep fighting. Storms. Felt like we had spren at our backs, holding us up, helping us fight."

Kaladin narrowed his eyes. "You don't say . . ."

He pried more from them as he finished his bowl. They had nothing but praise for Azure, though the man hadn't displayed any other . . . odd abilities that Kaladin could discover. Azure was a Shardbearer, maybe a foreigner, who had been previously unknown to the Guard—but with the fall of their commander, and the subsequent disappearance of their highlord patron at the palace, Azure had ended up in command.

There was something else. Something they weren't saying. Kaladin helped himself to a third bowl of stew, more to delay to see if the highmarshal really would make an appearance or not.

Soon, a disturbance near the door sent men standing up. Kaladin followed suit, turning. A senior officer entered wearing a glittering chain and a bright tabard, accompanied by attendants, inspiring a round of salutes. The highmarshal wore an appropriately azure cloak—a lighter shade than the traditional Kholin blue—with a mail coif down around the neck and a helm carried in hand.

She was also a she.

Kaladin blinked in surprise, and heard a gasp from Syl up above. The highmarshal was of average height for an Alethi woman, maybe just under, and wore her hair straight and short, reaching halfway down her cheeks. Her eyes were orange, and she wore a side sword with a glistening silver basket hilt. That wasn't Alethi design. Was it the aforementioned Shardblade? It did have an otherworldly look about it, but why wear it instead of dismissing it?

Regardless, the highmarshal was lean and grim, and had a couple of serious scars on her face. She wore gloves on both hands.

"The highmarshal is a *woman*?" Kaladin hissed.

"We don't talk about the marshal's secret," Beard said.

"Secret?" Kaladin said. "It's pretty *storming* obvious."

"We don't talk about the marshal's secret," Beard repeated, and the others nodded. "Hush, all right?"

Hush about it? Storms. This sort of thing simply didn't *happen* in Vorin society. Not like in the ballads and stories. He'd been in three armies, and had never seen a woman holding a weapon. Even the Alethi scouts carried only knives. He'd half expected a riot when he'd armed Lyn and the others, although for Radiants, Jasnah and Shallan had already supplied precedent.

Azure told the men they could sit down. One of the men offered her a bowl of stew, and she accepted. The men cheered after she took a bite and complimented the cook.

She handed the bowl to one of her attendants, and things returned to normal—men chatting, working, eating. Azure walked to speak with the various officers. First the platoon leader, who would be a captain. The other lieutenants next.

When she stopped at their table, she took in Kaladin with a discerning gaze.

"Who's the new recruit, Lieutenant Noro?" she asked.

"This is Kal, sir!" Noro said. "Found him haunting the street outside. Deserter, with a *shash* brand."

"On a lighteyes? Storms, man. Who did you kill?"

"It's not the one that I killed that got me my brands, sir. It's the one I didn't kill."

"That has the sound of a practiced explanation, soldier."

"That's because it is."

Kaladin figured she, at last, would push for more information. She merely grunted. He couldn't place her age, though the scars probably made her look older than she really was.

"You joining up?" she said. "We have food for you."

"Frankly, sir, I don't know. On one hand, I can't believe nobody cares about my past. On the other, you're obviously desperate, which also makes me reluctant."

She turned toward Lieutenant Noro. "You haven't shown him?"

"No, sir. We just got some stew in him."

"I'll do it. Kal, come with me."

.•.

Whatever they wanted to show him was at the top of the wall, as they hiked him up an enclosed stone stairwell. Kaladin wanted to learn more about the supposed "secret" that Azure was a woman. But when he asked, Lieutenant Noro shook his head quickly and made a hushing motion.

Soon they'd assembled atop the fortifications. The Kholinar wall was a powerful defensive structure, reportedly over sixty feet tall at points, with a wide wall walk on the top, ten feet across. The wall rolled across the landscape, enclosing all of Kholinar. It had actually been built *on top* of the outer windblades, fitting onto them like an inverted crown, the raised portions matching crevasses between windblades.

The wall was interrupted by guard towers every three hundred feet or so. These large structures were big enough to house squads, perhaps entire platoons, on watch.

"Guessing from that brand," Azure said to him, "you were in one of the armies that recruits in the north. You joined up to fight on the Shattered Plains, didn't you? But Sadeas used that army up north to funnel him veterans, plus maybe seize some land now and then from rival highprinces. You ended up fighting other Alethi, scared farmboys, instead of shipping off to avenge the king. Something like that?"

"Something like that," Kaladin admitted.

"Damnation me if I blame a man for deserting that," Azure said. "I don't hold it against you, soldier."

"And the brand?"

Azure pointed northward. Night had finally fallen, and in the distance, Kaladin could see a glow.

"They advance back into place after each storm," Azure said softly. "And camp a portion of their army out there. That's good battle sense, to prevent us from being resupplied—and to make sure we don't know when they'll attack. Nightmares, Kal. A real *Voidbringer* army.

"If that were an Alethi force, the people in this city wouldn't have much to worry about. Sure, there would be casualties on the wall, but no would-be king of Alethkar is going to burn and pillage the capital. But those *aren't* Alethi. They're monsters. At best, they'll enslave the entire populace. At worst . . ." She let the thought dangle, then looked at him. "I'm *glad* you have a brand. It says you're dangerous, and we have narrow confines up here on the wall. We can't simply press every eligible man; I need real soldiers, men who know what they're doing."

"So that's why I'm here?" Kaladin asked. "To see that?"

"I want you to think," Azure said. "I tell the men—this Wall Guard, this is *redemption*. If you fight here, nobody will care what you did before. Because they know if we fall, this city and this nation will be no more.

"*Nothing* matters, except holding this wall when that assault comes. You can go hide in the city and pray that we are strong enough without you. But if we aren't, you'll be no more than another corpse. Up here, you can fight. Up here, you have a *chance*.

"We won't press you. Walk away tonight. Lie down and think about what is coming; imagine another night when men are up here dying, bleeding for you. Think about how powerless you'll feel if the monsters get in. Then when you come back tomorrow, we'll get you a Wall Guard patch."

It was a potent speech. Kaladin glanced to Syl, who landed on his shoulder, then took a long look at the lights on the horizon.

Are you out there, Sah? Did they bring you and the others here? What of Sah's little daughter, who had collected flowers and clutched playing cards like a treasured toy? Was Khen there, the parshwoman who had demanded Kaladin retain his freedom, despite being angry at him for the entire trip?

Winds send that they hadn't been dragged further into this mess.

He joined the others in clattering back down the stairwell. Afterward, Noro and the rest of the squad bade him a happy farewell, as if certain he'd return. And he probably would, though not for the reasons they assumed.

He went back to the mansion and forced himself to chat with some of the guards at the lighteyed tent, though he learned nothing, and his brands made something of a stir among them. Adolin and Elhokar finally emerged, *their* illusions intact. So what was wrong with Kaladin's? The sphere Shallan had given him was still infused.

Kaladin gathered Drehy and Skar, then joined the king and Adolin as they started the walk home.

"What has you so thoughtful, Captain?" Elhokar asked.

"I think," Kaladin said, eyes narrowed, "I might have found us another Radiant."

71

A SIGN OF HUMANITY

ELEVEN YEARS AGO

There weren't enough boats for an amphibious attack on Rathalas, so Dalinar was forced to use a more conventional assault. He marched down from the west—having sent Adolin back to Kholinar—and assigned Sadeas and his forces to come in from the east. They converged toward the Rift.

Dalinar spent much of the trip passing through pungent smoke trails from the incense Evi burned in a small censer attached to the side of her carriage. A petition to the Heralds to bless her marriage.

He often heard her weeping inside the vehicle, though whenever she left it she was perfectly composed. She read letters, scribed his responses, and took notes at his meetings with generals. In every way, she was the perfect Alethi wife—and her unhappiness crushed his soul.

Eventually they reached the plains around the lake, crossing the riverbed—which was dry, except during storms. The rockbuds drank so fully of the local water supply, they'd grown to enormous sizes. Some were taller than a man's waist, and the vines they produced were as thick as Dalinar's wrist.

He rode alongside the carriage—his horse's hooves beating a familiar rhythm on the stones beneath—and smelled incense. Evi's hand reached out of her carriage's side window, and she placed another glyphward into the censer. He didn't see her face, and her hand retreated quickly.

Storming woman. An Alethi would be using this as a ploy to guilt him into bending. But she wasn't Alethi, for all her earnest imitations. Evi was far too genuine, and her tears were real. She sincerely thought their spat back in the Veden fortress boded ill for their relationship.

That bothered him. More than he wanted to admit.

A young scout jogged up to give him the latest report: The vanguard had secured his desired camp ground near the city. There had been no fighting yet, and he hadn't expected any. Tanalan would not abandon the walls around the Rift to try to control ground beyond bowshot.

It was good news, but Dalinar still wanted to snap at the messenger—he wanted to snap at *someone*. Stormfather, this battle couldn't come soon enough. He restrained himself and sent the messenger woman away with a word of thanks.

Why did he care so much about Evi's petulance? He'd never let his arguments with Gavilar bother him. Storms, he'd never let his arguments with *Evi* bother him this way before. It was strange. He could have the accolades of men, fame that stretched across a continent, but if she didn't admire him, he felt that he had somehow failed. Could he really ride into combat feeling like this?

No. He couldn't.

Then do something about it. As they wound through the plain of rockbuds, he called to the driver of Evi's carriage, having him stop. Then, handing his horse's reins to an attendant, he climbed into the carriage.

Evi bit her lip as he settled down on the seat across from her. It smelled nice within—the incense was fainter here, while the crem dust of the road was blocked by wood and cloth. The cushions were plush, and she had some dried fruit in a dish, even some chilled water.

"What is wrong?" she demanded.

"I was feeling saddle sore."

She cocked her head. "Perhaps you could request a salve—"

"I want to talk, Evi," Dalinar said with a sigh. "I'm not actually sore."

"Oh." She pulled her knees up against her chest. In here, she had undone and rolled back her safehand sleeve, displaying her long, elegant fingers.

"Isn't this what you wanted?" Dalinar said, looking away from the safehand. "You've been praying nonstop."

"For the Heralds to soften your heart."

"Right. Well, they've done that. Here I am. Let's talk."

"No, Dalinar," she said, reaching across to fondly touch his knee. "I wasn't praying for myself, but for those of your countrymen you are planning to kill."

"The rebels?"

"Men no different from you, who happened to be born in another city. What would *you* have done, had an army come to conquer your home?"

"I'd have fought," Dalinar said. "As they will. The better men will dominate."

"What gives you the right?"

"My sword." Dalinar shrugged. "If the Almighty wants us to rule, we'll win. If He doesn't, then we'll lose. I rather think He wants to see which of us is stronger."

"And is there no room for mercy?"

"Mercy landed us here in the first place. If they don't want to fight, they should give in to our rule."

"But—" She looked down, hands in her lap. "I'm sorry. I don't want another argument."

"I do," Dalinar said. "I like it when you stand up for yourself. I like it when you *fight*."

She blinked tears and looked away.

"Evi . . ." Dalinar said.

"I hate what this does to you," she said softly. "I see beauty in you, Dalinar Kholin. I see a great man struggling against a terrible one. And sometimes, you get this look in your eyes. A horrible, terrifying nothingness. Like you have become a creature with no heart, feasting upon souls to fill that void, dragging painspren in your wake. It haunts me, Dalinar."

Dalinar shifted on the carriage seat. What did that even mean? A "look" in his eyes? Was this like when she'd claimed that people stored bad memories in their skin, and needed to rub them off with a stone once a month? Westerners had some curiously superstitious beliefs.

"What would you have me do, Evi?" he asked softly.

"Have I won again?" she said, sounding bitter. "Another battle where I've bloodied you?"

"I just . . . I need to know what you want. So I can understand."

"Don't kill today. Hold back the monster."

"And the rebels? Their brightlord?"

"You spared that boy's life once before."

"An obvious mistake."

"A sign of *humanity*, Dalinar. You asked what I want. It is foolish, and I *can* see there is trouble here, that you have a duty. But . . . I do not wish to see you kill. Do not feed *it*."

He rested his hand on hers. Eventually the carriage slowed again, and Dalinar stepped out to survey an open area not clogged by rockbuds. The vanguard waited there, five thousand strong, assembled in perfect ranks. Teleb did like to put on a good show.

Across the field, outside of bowshot, a wall broke the landscape with—seemingly—nothing to protect. The city was hidden in the rift in the stone. From the southwest, a breeze off the lake brought the fecund scent of weeds and crem.

Teleb strode up, wearing his Plate. Well, Adolin's Plate.

Evi's Plate.

"Brightlord," Teleb said, "a short time ago, a large guarded caravan left the Rift. We hadn't the men to besiege the city, and you had ordered us not to engage. So I sent a scout team to tail them, men who know the area, but otherwise let the caravan escape."

"You did well," Dalinar said, taking his horse from a groom. "Though I'd have liked to know who was bringing supplies to the Rift, that might have been an attempt to draw you away into a skirmish. However, gather the vanguard now and bring them in behind me. Pass the word to the rest of the men. Have them form ranks, just in case."

"Sir?" Teleb asked, shocked. "You don't want to rest the army before attacking?"

Dalinar swung into the saddle and rode past him at a trot, heading toward the Rift. Teleb—usually so unflappable—cursed and shouted orders, then hurried to the vanguard, gathering them and marching them hastily behind Dalinar.

Dalinar made sure not to get too far ahead. Soon he approached the walls of Rathalas, where the rebels had gathered, primarily archers. They wouldn't be expecting an attack so soon, but of course Dalinar wouldn't camp for long outside either, not exposed to the storms.

Do not feed it.

Did she know that he considered this hunger inside of him, the blood-lust, to be something strangely external? A companion. Many of his officers felt the same. It was natural. You went to war, and the Thrill was your reward.

Dalinar's armorers arrived, and he climbed out of the saddle and stepped into the boots they provided, then held out his arms, letting them quickly strap on his breastplate and other sections of armor.

"Wait here," he told his men, then climbed back onto his horse and set his helm on his pommel. He walked his horse out onto the killing field, summoning his Shardblade and resting it on his shoulder, reins in the other hand.

Years had passed since his last assault on the Rift. He imagined Gavilar racing ahead of him, Sadeas cursing from behind them and demanding "prudence." Dalinar picked his way forward until he was about halfway to the gates. Any closer and those archers were likely to start shooting; he was already well within their range. He stilled his horse and waited.

There was some discussion on the walls; he could see the agitation among the soldiers. After about thirty minutes of him sitting there, his horse calmly licking the ground and nibbling at the grass that peeked out, the gates finally creaked open. A company of infantrymen poured out, accompanying two men on horseback. Dalinar dismissed the bald one with the purple birthmark across half his face; he was too old to be the boy Dalinar had spared.

It had to be the younger man riding the white steed, cape streaming behind him. Yes, he had an eagerness to him, his horse threatening to outstrip his guards. And the way he stared daggers at Dalinar . . . this was Brightlord Tanalan, son of the old Tanalan, whom Dalinar had bested after falling down into the Rift itself. That furious fight across wooden bridges and then in a garden suspended from the side of the chasm.

The group stopped about fifty feet from Dalinar.

"Have you come to parley?" called the man with the birthmark on his face.

Dalinar walked his horse closer so he wouldn't have to shout. Tanalan's guards raised shields and spears.

Dalinar inspected them, then the fortifications. "You've done well here. Polemen on the walls to push me off, should I come in alone. Netting draped down at the top, which you can cut free to entangle me."

"What do you want, tyrant?" Tanalan snapped. His voice had the typical nasal accent of the Rifters.

Dalinar dismissed his Blade and swung free of his horse, Plate grinding on stone as he hit the ground. "Walk with me a moment, Brightlord. I promise not to harm you unless I'm attacked first."

"I'm supposed to take your word?"

"What did I do, the last time we were together?" Dalinar asked. "When I had you in my hand, how did I act?"

"You robbed me."

"And?" Dalinar asked, meeting the younger man's violet eyes.

Tanalan measured him, tapping one finger against his saddle. Finally he dismounted. The man with the birthmark put a hand on his shoulder, but the youthful brightlord pulled free.

"I don't see what you hope to accomplish here, Blackthorn," Tanalan said, joining Dalinar. "We have nothing to say to one another."

"What do I want to accomplish?" Dalinar said, musing. "I'm not certain. My brother is normally the talker." He started walking along the corridor between the two hostile armies. Tanalan lingered, then jogged to catch up.

"Your troops look good," Dalinar said. "Brave. Arrayed against a stronger force, yet determined."

"They have strong motivation, Blackthorn. You murdered many of their fathers."

"It will be a pity to destroy them in turn."

"Assuming you can."

Dalinar stopped and turned to regard the shorter man. They stood on a too-quiet field, where even the rockbuds and the grass had the sense to withdraw. "Have I ever lost a battle, Tanalan?" Dalinar asked softly. "You know my reputation. Do you think it exaggerated?"

The younger man shifted, looking over his shoulder toward where he had left his guards and advisors. When he looked back, he was more resolved. "Better to die trying to bring you down than to surrender."

"You'd better be sure of that," Dalinar said. "Because if I win here, I'm going to have to make an example. I'll *break* you, Tanalan. Your sorry, weeping city will be held up before all who would defy my brother. Be *absolutely* certain you want to fight me, because once this starts, I will be forced to leave only widows and corpses to populate the Rift."

The young nobleman's jaw slowly dropped. "I . . ."

"My brother attempted words and politics to bring you into line," Dalinar said. "Well, I'm good at only one thing. He builds. I destroy. But because of the tears of a good woman, I have come—against my better judgment—to offer you an alternative. Let's find an accommodation that will spare your city."

"An accommodation? You *killed my father.*"

"And someday a man will kill me," Dalinar said. "My sons will curse his name as you curse mine. I hope *they* don't throw away thousands of lives in a hopeless battle because of that grudge. You want vengeance. Fine. Let's duel. Me and you. I'll lend you a Blade and Plate, and we'll face each other on equal grounds. I win, and your people surrender."

"And if I beat you, will your armies leave?"

"Hardly," Dalinar said. "I suspect they'll fight harder. But they won't have me, and you'll have won your father's Blade back. Who knows? Maybe you'll defeat the army. You'll have a better storming chance, at least."

Tanalan frowned at Dalinar. "You aren't the man I thought you were."

"I'm the same man I've always been. But today . . . today that man doesn't want to kill anyone."

A sudden fire inside him raged against those words. Was he really going to such lengths to *avoid* the conflict he'd been so anticipating?

"One of your own is working against you," Tanalan suddenly said. "The loyal highprinces? There's a traitor among them."

"I'd be surprised if there weren't several," Dalinar said. "But yes, we know that one has been working with you."

"A pity," Tanalan said. "His men were here not an hour ago. A little earlier and you'd have caught them. Maybe they'd have been forced to join me, and their master would have been pulled into the war." He shook his head, then turned and walked back toward his advisors.

Dalinar sighed in frustration. A dismissal. Well, there had never been much of a chance that this would work. He walked back to his horse and pulled himself up into the saddle.

Tanalan mounted as well. Before riding back to his city, the man gave Dalinar a salute. "This is unfortunate," he said. "But I see no other way. I cannot defeat you in a duel, Blackthorn. To try would be foolish. But your offer is . . . appreciated."

Dalinar grunted, pulled on his helm, then turned his horse.

"Unless . . ." Tanalan said.

"Unless?"

"Unless, of course, this was really a ruse all along, a scheme arranged by your brother, you, and me," Tanalan said. "A . . . false rebellion. Intended to trick disloyal highprinces into revealing themselves."

Dalinar raised his faceplate and turned back.

"Perhaps my outrage was feigned," Tanalan said. "Perhaps we have been in touch since your attack here, all those years ago. You *did* spare my life, after all."

"Yes," Dalinar said, feeling a sudden surge of excitement. "That would explain why Gavilar didn't immediately send our armies against you. We were in collusion all along."

"What better proof, than the fact that we just had this strange battle-field conversation?" Tanalan looked over his shoulder at the body of his men on the wall. "My men must be thinking it very odd. It will make sense when they hear the truth—that I was telling you about the envoy that had been here, delivering weapons and supplies to us from one of your secret enemies."

"Your reward, of course," Dalinar said, "would be legitimacy as a highlord in the kingdom. Perhaps that highprince's place."

"And no fighting today," Tanalan said. "No deaths."

"No deaths. Except perhaps for the actual traitors."

Tanalan looked to his advisors. The man with the birthmark nodded slowly.

"They headed east, toward the Unclaimed Hills," Tanalan said, point-ing. "A hundred soldiers and caravaneers. I think they were planning to stay for the night in the waystop at a town called Vedelliar."

"Who was it?" Dalinar asked. "Which highprince?"

"It might be best if you find out for yourself, as—"

"*Who?*" Dalinar demanded.

"Brightlord Torol Sadeas."

Sadeas? "Impossible!"

"As I said," Tanalan noted. "Best if you see for yourself. But I will testify before the king, assuming you keep your side of our . . . accord."

"Open your gates to my men," Dalinar said, pointing. "Stand down your soldiers. You have my word of honor for your safety."

With that, he turned and trotted back toward his forces, passing into a corridor of men. As he did, Teleb ran up to meet him. "Brightlord!" he said. "My scouts have returned from surveying that caravan. Sir, it—"

"Was from a highprince?"

"Undoubtedly," Teleb said. "They couldn't determine which one, but they claim to have seen someone in *Shardplate* among them."

Shardplate? That made no sense.

Unless that is how he's planning to see that we lose, Dalinar thought. *That might not have been a simple supply caravan—it could be a flanking force in disguise.*

A single Shardbearer hitting the back of his army while it was distracted could do incredible damage. Dalinar didn't believe Tanalan, not completely. But . . . storms, if Sadeas secretly *had* sent one of his Shardbearers to the battlefield, Dalinar couldn't just send a simple team of soldiers to deal with him.

"You have command," he said to Teleb. "Tanalan is going to stand down; have the vanguard join the locals on the fortifications, but do not displace them. Camp the rest of the army back in the field, and keep our officers out of Rathalas. This isn't a surrender. We're going to pretend that he was on our side all along, so he can save face and preserve his title. Horinar, I want a company of a hundred elites, our fastest, ready to march with me immediately."

They obeyed, asking no questions. Runners dashed with messages, and the entire area became a hive of motion, men and women hastening in all directions.

One person stood still in the midst of it, hands clasped hopefully at her breast. "What happened?" Evi asked as he trotted his horse toward her.

"Go back to our camp and compose a message to my brother saying that we may have brought the Rift to our side without bloodshed." He paused, then added, "Tell him not to trust anyone. One of our closest allies may have betrayed us. I'm going to go find out."

72

ROCKFALL

The Edgedancers are too busy relocating the tower's servants and farmers to send a representative to record their thoughts in these gemstones.

I'll do it for them, then. They are the ones who will be most displaced by this decision. The Radiants will be taken in by nations, but what of all these people now without homes?

—From drawer 4-17, second topaz

T his city had a heartbeat, and Veil felt she could hear it when she closed her eyes.

She crouched in a dim room, hands touching the smooth stone floor, which had been eroded by thousands upon thousands of footfalls. If stone met a man, stone might win—but if stone met *humanity*, then no force could preserve it.

The city's heartbeat was deep within these stones, old and slow. It had yet to realize something dark had moved in. A spren as ancient as it was. An urban disease. People didn't speak of it; they avoided the palace, mentioned the queen only to complain about the ardent who had been killed. It was like standing in a highstorm and griping that your shoes were too tight.

A soft whistling drew Veil's attention. She looked up and scanned the small loading dock around her, occupied only by herself, Vathah, and their wagon. "Let's go."

Veil eased the door open and entered the mansion proper. She and

Vathah wore new faces. Hers was a version of Veil with too large a nose and dimpled cheeks.

His was the face of a brutish man Shallan had seen in the market. Red's whistle meant the coast was clear, so they strode down the hallway without hesitation.

This extravagant stone mansion had been built around a square, skylit atrium, where manicured shalebark and rockbuds flourished, bobbing with lifespren. The atrium went up four stories, with walkways around each level. Red was on the second, whistling as he leaned on the balustrade.

The real showpiece of the mansion, however, wasn't the garden, but waterfalls. Because not a single one of them was actually water.

They *had* been, once. But sometime long ago, someone had mixed far too much wealth with far too much imagination. They had hired Soulcasters to transform large fountains of water that had been poured from the top level, four stories up. They'd been Soulcast into other materials right as the water splashed to the floor.

Veil's path took her along rooms to her left, with an overhang of the first floor's atrium balcony overhead. A former waterfall spilled down to her right, now made of crystal. The shape of flowing water crashed forever onto the stone floor, where it blossomed outward in a wave, brilliant and glistening. The mansion had changed hands dozens of times, and people called it Rockfall—despite the newest owner's attempt over the last decade to rename it the incredibly boring Hadinal Keep.

Veil and Vathah hurried along, accompanied by Red's reassuring whistling. The next waterfall was similar in shape, but made instead from polished dark stumpweight wood. It looked strangely natural, almost like a tree *could* have grown in that shape, poured from above and running down in an undulating column, splashing outward at the base.

They soon passed a room to their left, where Ishnah was talking with the current mistress of Rockfall. Each time the Everstorm struck, it left destruction—but in an oddly distinct way from a highstorm. Everstorm lightning had proven its greatest danger. The strange red lightning didn't merely set fires or scorch the ground; it could break through rock, causing blasts of fragmenting stone.

One such strike had broken a gaping hole in the side of this ancient, celebrated mansion. It had been patched with an unsightly wooden wall that would be covered with crem, then finally bricked over. Brightness Nananav—a middle-aged Alethi woman with a bun of hair practically as tall as she was—gestured at the boarded-up hole, and then at the floor.

"You'll make them match the others," Nananav said to Ishnah, who wore the guise of a rug merchant. "I won't stand for them to be even a *shade* off.

When you return with the repaired rugs, I'm going to set them beside the ones in other rooms to check!"

"Yes, Brightness," Ishnah said. "But the damage is much worse than I—"

"These rugs were woven in *Shinovar*. They were made by a blind man who trained *thirty years* with a master weaver before being allowed to produce his own rugs! He died after finishing my commission, so there are *no others* like these."

"I'm well aware, as you've told me three times now. . . ."

Veil took a Memory of the woman; then she and Vathah slipped past the room, continuing along the atrium. They were supposedly part of Ishnah's staff, and wouldn't be suffered to wander about freely. Red—noting that they were on their way—started to head back to rejoin Ishnah. He'd have been excused to visit the privy, but would be missed if he was gone too long.

His tune cut off.

Veil opened a door and pulled Vathah inside, heart thrumming as—right outside—a pair of guards walked down the stairwell from the second level.

"I still say we should be doing this at night," Vathah whispered.

"They have this place guarded like a fort at night."

The change of the guard was in midmorning, so Veil and the others had come just before that. Theoretically, this meant the guards would be tired and bored after an uneventful night.

Veil and Vathah had entered a small library lit by a few spheres in a goblet on the table. Vathah eyed them, but didn't move—this infiltration was about far more than a few chips. Veil set down her pack and rummaged until she got out a notebook and charcoal pencil.

Veil took a deep breath, then let Shallan bleed back into existence. She quickly sketched Nananav from the glimpse earlier.

"I'm still amazed you were both of them, all along," Vathah said. "You don't act anything like one another."

"That's rather the point, Vathah."

"I wish I'd picked it out myself." He grunted, scratching the side of his head. "I like Veil."

"Not me?"

"You're my boss. I'm not supposed to like you."

Straightforward, if rude. At least you always knew where you stood with him. He listened at the door, then cracked it open, tracking the guards. "All right. We go up the stairs, then come back along the second-floor walkway. We grab the goods, stuff them in the dumbwaiter, and make for the exit. Storms. I wish we could do this when nobody was awake."

"What would be the fun of that?" Shallan finished her drawing with a flourish, then stood, poking Vathah in the side. "Admit it. You're enjoying this."

"I'm as nervous as a new recruit on his first day at war," Vathah said. "My hands shake, and I swear every noise means someone spotted us. I feel *sick*."

"See?" Shallan said. "Fun." She pushed beside him and glanced out through the cracked door. Storming guards. They'd set up in the atrium nearby. They could undoubtedly hear the real Nananav's voice from there, so if Shallan strolled out wearing the woman's face, that would certainly cause alarm.

Time to get creative. Pattern buzzed as she considered. Make the waterfalls flow again? Illusions of strange spren? No . . . no, nothing so theatrical. Shallan was letting her sense of the dramatic run away with her.

Stay simple, as she'd done before. Veil's way. She closed her eyes and breathed out, pressing the Light into Pattern, Lightweaving only sound—that of Nananav calling the guards into the room where she was lecturing Ishnah. Why come up with a new trick when the old ones worked fine? Veil didn't feel the need to improvise merely to be different.

Pattern carried the illusion away, and the sound lured the guards off down the hall. Shallan led Vathah out of the library, then around the corner and up the steps. She breathed out Stormlight, which washed over her, and became Veil fully. Then Veil became the woman who was not *quite* Veil, with the dimples. And then, layered on top of that, she became Nananav.

Arrogant. Talkative. Certain that everyone around her was just *looking* for a reason not to do things properly. As they stepped onto the next floor, she adopted a calm, measured gait, eyeing the banister. When had that last been polished?

"I don't find this fun," Vathah said, walking beside her. "But I do like it."

"Then it's fun."

"Fun is winning at cards. This is something else."

He'd taken to his role earnestly, but she really should look at getting more refined servants. Vathah was like a hog in human clothing, always grunting and mulling about.

Why shouldn't she be served by the best? She was a *Knight Radiant*. She shouldn't have to put up with barely human deserters who looked like something Shallan would draw after a hard night drinking, and maybe while holding the pencil with her teeth.

The role is getting to you, a part of her whispered. *Careful*. She glanced about for Pattern, but he was still below.

They stopped at a second-floor room, locked tightly. The plan was for Pattern to open it, but she didn't have the patience to wait. Besides, a

master-servant was walking along.

He gave a bow when he saw Nananav.

"*That* is your bow?" Nananav said. "That quick bob? Where did they teach you that?"

"My apologies, Brightness," the man said, bowing more deeply.

"I could cut your legs off at the knees," Nananav said. "Then maybe you'd at least *appear* properly penitent." She rapped on the door. "Open this."

"Why—" He broke off, perhaps realizing she was not in a mood for complaints. He hurried forward and undid the combination lock on the door, then pulled it open for her, letting out air that smelled of spice.

"You may go do penance for your insult to me," Nananav said. "Climb to the roof and sit there for exactly one hour."

"Brightness, if I have offended—"

"*If?*" She pointed. "Go!"

He gave another bow—barely sufficient—and ran off.

"You might be overdoing that, Brightness," Vathah said, rubbing his chin. "She has a reputation for being difficult, not *insane*."

"Shut up," Nananav said, striding into the room.

The mansion's larder.

Racks of dried sausages covered one wall. Sacks of grain were stacked in the back, and boxes filled with longroots and other tubers covered the floor. Bags of spices. Small jugs of oil.

Vathah pulled the door closed, then hurriedly began stuffing sausages in a sack. Nananav wasn't so hasty. This was a good place to keep it all, nice and locked up. Taking it elsewhere seemed . . . well, a crime.

Maybe she could move into Rockfall, act the part. And the former lady of the house? Well, she was an inferior version, obviously. Just deal with her, take her place. It would feel *right*, wouldn't it?

With a chill, Veil let one layer of illusion drop. Storms . . . Storms. What had *that* been?

"Not to give *offense*, Brightness," Vathah said, putting his sack of sausages in the dumbwaiter, "but you can stand there and supervise. Or you can storming help, and get twice as much food along with half as much ego."

"Sorry," Veil said, grabbing a sack of grain. "That woman's head is a frightening place."

"Well, I did say that Nananav is notoriously difficult."

Yeah, Veil thought. *But I was talking about Shallan.*

They worked quickly, filling the large dumbwaiter—which was needed to take in large shipments from the delivery room below. They got all of the sausages, most of the longroots, and a few sacks of grain. Once the dumbwaiter was full, the two of them lowered the thing to the ground floor. They waited by the door, and fortunately Red started whistling. The ground floor was clear again. Not trusting herself with Nananav's face, she stayed

Veil as the two hurried out. Pattern waited outside, and he hummed, climbing her trousers.

On their way down, they passed a waterfall made of pure marble. Shallan would have loved to linger and marvel at the artful Soulcasting. Fortunately, Veil was running this operation. Shallan . . . Shallan got lost in things. She'd get focused on details, or stick her head in the clouds and dream about the big picture. That comfortable middle, that safe place of moderation, was unfamiliar ground to her.

They descended the steps, then joined Red at the damaged room and helped him carry a rolled-up carpet to the loading bay. She had Pattern quietly open the lock to the dumbwaiter down here, then sent him away to decoy a few servants who had been bringing wood into the bay. They pursued an image of a feral mink with a key in its mouth.

Together, Veil, Red, and Vathah unrolled the rug, filled it with sacks of food from the dumbwaiter, then rolled it back up and heaved it into their waiting wagon. The guards at the gate shouldn't notice a few extra-bulgy carpets.

They fetched a second carpet, repeated the process, then started back. Veil, however, paused in the loading bay, right by the door. What was that on the ceiling? She cocked her head at the strange sight of pools of liquid, dripping down.

Angerspren, she realized. *Collecting there and then boiling through the floor.* The larder was directly above them.

"Run!" Veil said, spinning and bolting back toward the wagon. A second later, someone upstairs started shouting.

Veil scrambled into the wagon's seat, then slapped the chull with the steering reed. Her team, joined by Ishnah, charged back into the room and leapt into the wagon, which started moving. Step. By. Protracted. Step.

Veil . . . Shallan slapped the large crab on the shell, urging it forward. But chulls went at chull speed. The wagon eased out into the courtyard, and ahead the gates were already closing.

"Storms!" Vathah said. He looked over his shoulder. "Is this part of the 'fun'?"

Behind them, Nananav burst out of the building, her hair wobbling. "Stop them! Thieves!"

"Shallan?" Vathah asked. "Veil? Whoever you are? Storms, they have *crossbows!*"

Shallan breathed out.

The gates clanged shut ahead of them. Armed guards entered the small courtyard, weapons ready.

"Shallan!" Vathah cried.

She stood on the wagon, Stormlight swirling around her. The chull pulled to a stop, and she confronted the guards. The men stumbled to a halt, jaws dropping.

Behind, Nananav broke the silence. "What are you idiots doing? Why . . ."

She trailed off, then pulled up short as Shallan turned to look at her. Wearing the woman's face.

Same hair. Same features. Same clothing. Mimicked right down to the attitude, with nose in the air. Shallan/Nananav raised her hands to the side, and spren burst from the ground around the wagon. Pools of blood, shimmering the wrong color, and boiling far too violently. Pieces of glass that rained down. Anticipationspren, like thin tentacles.

Shallan/Nananav let her image distort, features sliding off her face, dripping down like paint running down a wall. Ordinary Nananav screamed and fled back toward the building. One of the guards loosed his crossbow, and the bolt took Shallan/Nananav right in the head.

Bother.

Her vision went dark for a moment, and she had a flash of panic remembering her stabbing in the palace. But why should she care if actual painspren joined the illusory ones around her? She righted herself and looked back toward the soldiers, her face melting, the crossbow bolt sticking from her temple.

The guards ran.

"Vathah," she said, "plesh open sha gate." Her mouth didn't work right. How odd.

Vathah didn't move, so she glared at him.

"Gah!" he shouted, scrambling back and stumbling across one of the rugs in the bed of the wagon. He fell down beside Red, who was surrounded by fearspren, like globs of goo. Even Ishnah looked as if she'd seen a Voidbringer.

Shallan let the illusions go, all of them, right down to Veil. Just normal, everyday Veil. "Itsh all right," Veil said. "Jush illushionsh. Go, open sha gatesh."

Vathah heaved himself out of the wagon and ran for the gates.

"Um, Veil?" Red said. "That crossbow bolt . . . the blood is staining your outfit."

"I wash going to shrow it away regardlesh," she said, settling back down, growing more comfortable as Pattern rejoined the wagon and scuttled across the seat to her. "I've got a new outfit almosht ready."

At this rate, she'd have to buy them in bulk.

They maneuvered the wagon out the gates, then picked up Vathah. No guards gave pursuit, and Veil's mind . . . drifted as they pulled away.

That . . . that crossbow bolt *was* getting annoying. She couldn't feel her safehand. Bother. She poked at the bolt; it seemed that her Stormlight had healed her head *around* the wound. She gritted her teeth and tried to pull it out, but the thing was jammed in there. Her vision blurred again.

"I'm going to need shome help, boysh," she said, pointing at it and drawing in more Stormlight.

She blacked out entirely when Vathah pulled it free. She came to a short time later, slumped in the front seat of the wagon. When she brushed the side of her head with her fingers, she found no hole.

"You worry me sometimes," Vathah said, steering the chull with a reed.

"I do what needs to be done," Veil said, relaxing back and setting her feet up on the front of the wagon. Was it only her imagination, or did the people lining the streets today look hungrier than they had previous days? Hungerspren buzzed about the heads of the people, like black specks, or little flies of the type you could find sometimes on rotting plants. Children cried in the laps of exhausted mothers.

Veil turned away, ashamed, thinking of the food she had hidden in the wagon. How much good could she do with all of that? How many tears could she dry, how many of the hungry cries of children could she silence?

Steady . . .

Infiltrating the Cult of Moments was a greater good than feeding a few mouths now. She needed this food to buy her way in. To investigate . . . the Heart of the Revel, as Wit had called it.

Veil didn't know much of the Unmade. She'd never paid attention to the ardents on important matters, let alone when they spoke of old folktales and stories of Voidbringers. Shallan knew little more, and wanted to find a book about the subject, of course.

Last night, Veil had returned to the inn where Shallan had met with the King's Wit, and while he hadn't been there, he'd left a message for her.

I'm still trying to get you a contact among the cult's highers. Everyone I talk to merely says, "Do something to get their attention." I would, but I'm certain that violating the city's indecency laws would be unwise, even considering the lack of a proper watch.

Do something to get their attention. They seemed to have their fingers in everything, in this city. Kind of like the Ghostbloods. Watching secretly.

Maybe she didn't need to wait for Wit. And maybe she could solve two problems at once.

"Take us to the Ringington Market," she said to Vathah, naming the market closest to the tailor's shop.

"Aren't we going to unload the food before we return the wagon to that merchant?"

"Of course we are," she said.

He eyed her, but when she didn't explain further, he turned the wagon as she directed. Veil took her hat and coat from the back of the wagon and pulled them on, then covered the bloodstains on her shirt with a Light-weaving.

She had Vathah pull up to a specific building in the market. When they stopped, refugees peeked into the wagon bed, but saw only rugs—and they scattered when Vathah glared at them.

"Guard the wagon," Veil said, digging out a small sack of food. She hopped down and went sauntering toward the building. The roof had been ruined by the Everstorm, making it a perfect place for squatters. She found Grund inside the main room, as usual.

She'd returned several times during her time in the city, getting information from Grund—who was the grimy little urchin she'd bribed with food on her first day in the market. He seemed to always be hanging around here, and Veil was well aware of the value of having a local urchin to ply for information.

Today, he was alone in the room. The other beggars were out hunting food. Grund drew on a little board with charcoal, using his one good hand, the deformed one hidden in his pocket. He perked up as soon as he saw her. He'd stopped running away; it seemed that city urchins got concerned when someone was actively looking for them.

That changed when they knew you had food.

He tried to look uninterested until Veil dropped the sack in front of him. A sausage peeked out. Then, his dark eyes practically bulged out of his face.

"An entire *sack*?" Grund asked.

"It was a good day," Veil said, squatting down. "Any news for me on those books?"

"Nope," he said, poking the sausage—as if to see whether she'd suddenly snatch it back. "I ain't heard nothing."

"Let me know if you do. In the meantime, do you know of anyone who could use a little extra food? People who are particularly nice or deserving, but who get overlooked by the grain rationing?"

He eyed her, trying to determine her angle.

"I've got extra to give away," Veil explained.

"You're going to *give* them *food*." He said it as if it was as rational as making cremlings fall from the sky.

"Surely I'm not the first. The palace used to give food to the poor, didn't it?"

"That's a thing that kings do. Not regular people." He looked her up and down. "But you aren't regular people."

"I'm not."

"Well . . . Muri the seamstress has always been nice to me. She's got lots of kids. Having trouble feedin' them. She has a hovel over by the old bakery that burned down on that first Evernight. And the refugee kids that live in the park over on Moonlight Way. They're just little, you know? Nobody to watch for them. And Jom, the cobbler. He broke his arm . . . You wanna write this down or something?"

"I'll remember."

He shrugged and gave her an extensive list. She thanked him, then reminded him to keep looking for the book she'd asked for. Ishnah had visited some booksellers on Shallan's orders, and one had mentioned a title called *Mythica,* a newer volume that spoke of the Unmade. The bookseller had owned a copy, but his shop had been robbed during the riots. Hopefully, someone in the underground knew where his goods had gone.

Veil had a spring to her step as she walked back to the wagon. The cult wanted her to get their attention? Well, she'd get their attention. She doubted Grund's list was unbiased, but stopping right in the middle of the market and heaving out sacks seemed likely to incite a riot. This was as good a method to give away the food as any.

Muri the seamstress proved to indeed be a woman with many children and little means of feeding them. The children in the park were right where Grund had indicated. Veil left a heap of food for them, then walked away as they scrambled up to it in amazement.

By the fourth stop, Vathah had figured it out. "You're going to give it all away, aren't you?"

"Not all," Veil said, lounging in her seat as they rolled toward the next destination.

"What about paying the Cult of Moments?"

"We can always steal more. First, my contact says we have to get their attention. I figure, a crazy woman in white riding through the market throwing out sacks of food is bound to do that."

"You've got the crazy part right, at least."

Veil slipped her hand back into a rolled-up carpet, and pulled out a sausage for him. "Eat something. It'll make you feel better."

He grumbled, but took it and bit at the end.

By the evening, the cart was empty. Veil wasn't certain if she could get the cult's attention this way, but storms did it feel good to be *doing* something. Shallan could go off and study books, talk plots, and scheme. Veil would worry about the people who were actually starving.

She didn't give it *all* away though. She let Vathah keep his sausage.

I am worried about the tower's protections failing. If we are not safe from the Unmade here, then where?

—From drawer 3-11, garnet

S tuff it, Beard," Ved said. "You did *not* meet the Blackthorn."

"I did!" the other soldier said. "He complimented me on my uniform, and gave me his own knife. For valor."

"Liar."

"Be careful," Beard said. "Kal might stab you if you keep interrupting a good story."

"Me?" Kaladin said, walking with the others of the squad on patrol. "Don't bring me into this, Beard."

"Look at him," Beard said. "He's got *hungry* eyes, Ved. He wants to hear the end of the story."

Kaladin smiled with the others. He had joined the Wall Guard officially upon Elhokar's orders, and had promptly been added to Lieutenant Noro's squad. It felt almost . . . cheap to be part of the group so quickly, after the effort it had been to forge Bridge Four.

Still, Kaladin liked these men, and enjoyed their banter as they ran their patrol beat along the inside base of the wall. Six men was a lot for a simple patrol, but Azure wanted them to stay in groups. Along with Beard, Ved, and Noro, the squad included a heavyset man named Alaward and a friendly man named Vaceslv—Alethi, but with obvious Thaylen heritage. The two kept trying to get Kaladin to play cards with them.

It was an uncomfortable reminder of Sah and the parshmen.

"Well, you won't believe what happened next," Beard continued. "The Blackthorn told me . . . Oh, storm it. You're not listening, are you?"

"Nope," Ved said. "Too busy looking at that." He nodded back at something they'd passed.

Beard snickered. "Ha! Will you look at that roosting chicken? Who does he think he's impressing?"

"Storming waste of skin," Ved agreed.

Kal grinned, glanced over his shoulder, looking for whoever Beard and Ved had spotted. Must be someone silly to provoke such a strong . . .

It was Adolin.

The prince lounged on the corner, wearing a false face and a yellow suit after the new fashionable style. He was guarded by Drehy, who stood several inches taller, happily munching on some chouta.

"Somewhere," Beard said solemnly, "a kingdom is without its banners because that fellow bought them all up and made coats out of them."

"Where do they think up these things?" Vaceslv asked. "I mean . . . storms! Do they just say, 'You know what I need for the apocalypse? You know what would be *really* handy? A new *coat*. Extra sequins.'"

They passed Adolin—who nodded toward Kaladin, then looked away. That meant all was well, and Kaladin could continue with the guards. A shake of the head would have been the sign to extricate himself and return to the tailor's shop.

Beard continued to snicker. "When in the service of the merchant lords of Steen," he noted, "I once had to swim across an entire vat of dye in order to save the prince's daughter. When I was done, I *still* wasn't as colorful as that preening cremling."

Alaward grunted. "Storming highborns. Useless for anything but giving bad orders and eating twice as much food as an honest man."

"But," Kaladin said, "how can you say that? I mean, he's lighteyed. Like us." He winced. Did that sound fake? *It sure is nice being lighteyed as I, of course, have light eyes—like you, my eyes are lighter than the dark eyes of dark-eyes.* He had to summon Syl several times a day to keep his eye color from changing.

"Like us?" Beard said. "Kal, what crevasse have you been living in? Are the middlers actually *useful* where you come from?"

"Some," Kaladin said.

Beard and Ved—well, the whole squad, except Noro—were tenners: men of the tenth dahn, lowest ranking in the lighteyed stratification system. Kaladin hadn't ever paid much attention; to him, lighteyes had always just been lighteyes.

These men saw the world very differently. Middlers were anyone better than eighth dahn, but who weren't quite highlords. They might as well have been another species, for how the squadsmen thought of them—particularly those of the fifth and sixth dahn who didn't serve in the military.

How was it that these men somehow naturally ended up surrounding themselves with others of their own rank? They married tenners, drank with tenners, joked with tenners. They had their own jargon and traditions. There was an entire world represented here that Kaladin had never seen, despite it residing right next door to him.

"Some middlers *are* useful," Kaladin said. "Some of them are good at dueling. Maybe we could go back and recruit that guy. He was wearing a sword."

The others looked at him like he was mad.

"Kal, my kip," Beard said. "Kip" was a slang word that Kaladin hadn't quite figured out yet. "You're a good fellow. I like how you see the best in folks. You haven't even learned to ignore me yet, which most folks decide to do after our first meal together.

"But you've *got* to learn to see the world for how it is. You can't go around trusting middlers, unless they're good officers like the highmarshal. Men like that one back there, they'll strut about telling you everything you should do—but put them on the wall during an attack, and they'll wet themselves yellower than that suit."

"They have parties," Ved agreed. "Best thing for them, really. Keeps them out of our business."

What a strange mix of emotions. On one hand, he wanted to tell them about Amaram and rant about the injustices done—repeatedly—to those he loved. At the same time . . . they were mocking *Adolin Kholin*, who had a shot at the title of best swordsman in all of Alethkar. Yes, his suit was a little bright—but if they would merely spend five minutes talking to him, they'd see he wasn't so bad.

Kaladin trudged along. It felt wrong to be on patrol without a spear, and he instinctively sought out Syl, who rode the winds above. He'd been given a side sword to carry at his right, a truncheon to carry at his left, and a small round shield. The first thing the Wall Guard had taught him was how to draw the sword by reaching down with his right hand—not lowering his shield—and pulling it free of the sheath.

They wouldn't use sword or truncheon when the Voidbringers finally assaulted; there were proper pikes up above for that. Down here was a different matter. The large road—it rounded the city alongside the wall—was clear and clean, maintained by the Guard. But most of the streets that branched off it were crowded with people. Nobody but the poorest and most wretched wanted to be this close to the walls.

"How is it," Ved said, "those refugees can't get it through their heads that we're the only thing separating them from the army outside?"

Indeed, many of those they passed on side streets watched the patrol with outright hostility. At least nobody had thrown anything at them today.

"They see that we're fed," Noro replied. "They smell food from our barracks. They're not thinking with their heads, but with their stomachs."

"Half of those belong to the cult anyway," Beard noted. "One of these days, I'll have to infiltrate that. Might have to marry their high priestess, but let me tell you, I'm *terrible* in a harem. Last time, the other men grew jealous of me taking all the priestess's attention."

"She laughed so hard at your offering she got distracted, eh?" Ved asked.

"Actually, there's a story about—"

"Calm it, Beard," the lieutenant said. "Let's get ready for the delivery." He shifted his shield to his other hand, then took out his truncheon. "Get intimidating, everybody. Truncheons only."

The group pulled out their wooden cudgels. It felt wrong to have to defend themselves from their own people—brought back memories of being in Amaram's army, bivouacking near towns. Everyone had always *talked* about the glories of the army and the fight on the Shattered Plains. And yet, once towns got done gawking, they transitioned to hostility with remarkable speed. An army was the sort of thing everyone wanted to have, so long as it was off doing important things elsewhere.

Noro's squad met up with another from their platoon—with two squads on the wall for duty, two squads off, and two down here patrolling, they were around forty strong. Together, the twelve men formed up to guard a slow, chull-pulled wagon that left one of their larger barrack warehouses. It carried a mound of closed sacks.

Refugees crowded around, and Kaladin brandished his truncheon. He had to use his shield to shove a man who got too close. Fortunately, this caused others to back away, instead of rushing the wagon.

They rolled inward only one street before stopping at a city square. Syl flitted down and rested on his shoulder. "They . . . they look like they *hate* you."

"Not me," Kaladin whispered. "The uniform."

"What . . . what will you do if they actually attack?"

He didn't know. He hadn't come to this city to fight the populace, but if he refused to defend the squad . . .

"Storming Velalant is late," Ved grumbled.

"A little more time," Noro said. "We'll be fine. The good people know this food goes to them eventually."

Yes, after they wait hours in line at Velalant's distribution stations.

Farther into the city—obscured by the gathering crowds—a group of people approached in stark violet, with masks obscuring their faces. Kaladin watched uncomfortably as they started whipping their own forearms. Drawing painspren, which climbed from the ground around them, like hands missing the skin. Except these were too large, and the wrong color, and . . . and didn't seem human.

"I prayed to the spren of the night and they came to me!" a man at their forefront shouted, raising hands high. "They rid me of my pain!"

"Oh no . . ." Syl whispered.

"Embrace them! The spren of changes! The spren of a new storm, a new land. A new people!"

Kaladin took Noro by the arm. "Sir, we need to retreat. Get this grain back to the warehouse."

"We have orders to . . ." Noro trailed off as he glanced at the increasingly hostile crowd.

Fortunately, a group of some fifty men in blue and red rounded a corner and began shoving aside refugees with rough hands and barked shouts. Noro's sigh was almost comically loud. The angry crowd broke away as Velalant's troops surrounded the grain shipment.

"Why do we do this in the daytime?" Kaladin asked one of their officers. "And why don't you simply come to our warehouse and escort it from there? Why the display?"

A soldier moved him—politely, but firmly—back from the wagon. The troops surrounded it and marched it away, the crowd flowing after them.

When they got back to the wall, Kaladin felt like a man seeing land after swimming all the way to Thaylenah. He pressed his palm against the stone, feeling its cool, rough grain. Drawing a sense of safety from it, much as he would draw out Stormlight. It would have been easy to fight that crowd—they were basically unarmed. But while training prepared you for the mechanics of the fight, the emotions were another thing entirely. Syl huddled on his shoulder, staring back along the street.

"This is all the queen's fault," Beard muttered softly. "If she hadn't killed that ardent . . ."

"Stop with that," Noro said sharply. He took a deep breath. "My squad, we're on the wall next. You have half an hour to grab a drink or a nap, then assemble at our station above."

"And storms be praised for that!" Beard said, heading straight for the stairwell, obviously planning to get to the station above, then relax. "I'll happily take some time staring down an enemy army, thank you very much."

Kaladin joined Beard in climbing. He still didn't know where the man had gotten his nickname. Noro was the only one in the squad who wore a beard, though his wasn't exactly inspiring. Rock would have laughed it to shame and euthanized it with a razor and some soap.

"Why do we pay off the highlords, Beard?" Kaladin asked as they climbed. "Velalant and his type are pretty useless, from what I've seen."

"Yeah. We lost the *real* highlords in the riots or to the palace. But the highmarshal knows what to do. I suspect that if we didn't share with people like Velalant, we'd have to fight *them* off from seizing the grain. At least this way, people are eventually getting fed, and we can watch the wall."

They talked like that a lot. Holding the city wall was their job, and if they looked too far afield—tried too hard to police the city or bring down the cult—they'd lose their focus. The city had to stand. Even if it burned inside, it had to stand. To an extent, Kaladin agreed. The army couldn't do everything.

It still hurt.

"When are you going to tell me how we make all that food?" Kaladin whispered.

"I . . ." Beard looked around in the stairwell. He leaned in. "I don't know, Kal. But first thing that Azure did when he took command? Had us attack the low monastery, by the eastern gates, away from the palace. I know men from other companies who were on that assault. The place had been overrun by rioters."

"They had a Soulcaster, didn't they?"

Beard nodded. "Only one in the city that wasn't at the palace when it . . . you know."

"But how do we use it without drawing the screamers?" Kaladin asked.

"Well," Beard said, and his tone shifted. "I can't tell you all the secrets, but . . ." He launched into a story about the time Beard himself had learned to use a Soulcaster from the king of Herdaz. Maybe he wasn't the best source of information.

"The highmarshal," Kaladin interrupted. "Have you noticed the odd thing about her Shardblade? No gemstone on the pommel or crossguard."

Beard eyed him, lit by the stairwell's window slits. Calling the high-marshal a "she" always provoked a response. "Maybe that's why *the high-marshal* never dismisses it," Beard said. "Maybe it's broken somehow?"

"Maybe," Kaladin said. Aside from his fellow Radiants' Blades, he'd seen one Shardblade before that didn't have a gemstone on it. The Blade of the Assassin in White. An Honorblade, which granted Radiant powers to whoever held it. If Azure held a weapon that let her have the power of Soulcasting, perhaps that explained why the screamers hadn't found out yet.

They finally emerged onto the top of the wall, stepping into sunlight. The two of them stopped there, looking inward over the flowing city—with the breaching windblades and rolling hills. The palace, ever in gloom, dominated the far side. The Wall Guard barely patrolled the section of wall that passed behind it.

"Did you know anyone in the Palace Guard ranks?" Kaladin asked. "Are any of the men in there still in contact with families out here or anything?"

Beard shook his head. "I got close a little while back. I heard voices, Kal. Whispering to me to join them. The highmarshal says we have to close our ears to those. They can't take us unless we listen." He rested his hand on Kaladin's shoulder. "Your questions are honest, Kal. But you worry too much. We need to focus on the wall. Best not to talk too much about the queen, or the palace."

"Like we don't talk about Azure being a woman."

"Her secret"—Beard winced—"I mean, the highmarshal's secret is ours to guard and protect."

"We do a storming poor job of that, then. Hopefully we're better at defending the wall."

Beard shrugged, hand still on Kaladin's shoulder. For the first time, Kaladin noticed something. "No glyphward."

Beard glanced at his arm, where he wore the traditional white armband that you'd tie a glyphward around. His was blank. "Yeah," he said, shoving his hand in his coat pocket.

"Why not?" Kaladin said.

Beard shrugged. "Let's just say, I know a lot about telling which stories have been made up. Nobody's watching over us, Kal."

He trudged off toward their muster station: one of the tower structures that lined the wall. Syl stood up on Kaladin's shoulder, then walked up—as if on invisible steps—through the air to stand even with his eyes. She looked after Beard, her girlish dress rippling in wind that Kaladin couldn't feel. "Dalinar thinks God isn't dead," she said. "Just that the Almighty—Honor—was never actually God."

"You're part of Honor. Doesn't that offend you?"

"Every child eventually realizes that her father isn't actually God." She looked at him. "Do you think anybody is watching? Do you really think there isn't anything out there?"

Strange question to answer, to a little bit of a divinity.

Kaladin lingered in the doorway to the guard tower. Inside, the men of his squad—Platoon Seven, Squad Two, which didn't have the same ring to it as Bridge Four—laughed and banged about as they gathered equipment.

"I used to take the terrible things that had happened to me," he said, "as proof that there was no god. Then in some of my darkest moments, I took my life as proof there *must* be something up there, for only *intentional* cruelty could offer an explanation."

He took a deep breath, then looked toward the clouds. He had been delivered up to the sky, and had found magnificence there. He'd been given the power to protect and defend.

"Now," he said. "Now I don't know. With all due respect, I think Dalinar's beliefs sound too convenient. Now that one deity has proven faulty, he insists the Almighty must never have *been* God? That there must be something else? I don't like it. So . . . maybe this simply isn't a question we can ever answer."

He stepped into the fortification. It had broad doorways on either side leading in from the wall, while slits along the outward side provided archer positions, as did the roof. To his right stood racks of weapons and shields, and a table for mess. Above that, a large window looked out at the city beyond, where those inside could get specific orders via signal flags from below.

He was sliding his shield onto a rack when the drums sounded, calling the alarm. Syl zipped up behind him like string suddenly pulled taut.

"Assault on the wall!" Kaladin shouted, reading the drumbeats. "Equip up!" He scrambled across the room and seized a pike from the line on the wall. He tossed it to the first man who came, then continued distributing as the men scrambled to obey the signals. Lieutenant Noro and Beard handed out shields—rectangular full shields in contrast to the small round patrolling shields they'd carried below.

"Form up!" Kaladin shouted, right before Noro did it.

Storms. I'm not their commander. Feeling like an idiot, Kaladin took his own pike and balanced the long pole, carrying it out beside Beard, who carried only a shield. On the wall, the four squads formed a bristling formation of pikes and overlapping shields. Some of the men in the center—like Kaladin and Noro—held only a pike, gripping it two-handed.

Sweat trickled down Kaladin's temples. He'd been trained briefly in pike blocks during his time in Amaram's army. They were used as a counter to heavy cavalry, which was a newer development in Alethi warfare. He couldn't imagine that they'd be terribly effective atop a wall. They were great for thrusting outward toward an enemy block of troops, but it was difficult for him to keep the pike pointed upward. It didn't balance well that way, but how else were they to fight the Fused?

The other platoon that shared a station with them formed up on the tower's top, holding bows. Hopefully, the arrow cover mixed with the defensive pike formation would be effective. Kaladin finally saw the Fused streaking through the air—approaching another section of the wall.

Men in his platoon waited, nervous, adjusting glyphwards or repositioning shields. The Fused clashed distantly with others of the Wall

Guard; Kaladin could barely make out yells. The drumbeats from the drummers' stations were a holding beat, telling everyone to remain in their own section.

Syl came zipping back, moving agitatedly, sweeping one way, then the other. Several men in the formation leaned out, as if wanting to break away and go charging to where their fellows were fighting.

Steady, Kaladin thought, but cut himself off from saying it. He wasn't in command here. Captain Deedanor, the platoon leader, hadn't arrived yet—which meant Noro was the ranking officer, with seniority over the other squad lieutenants. Kaladin gritted his teeth, straining, forcibly keeping himself from giving any kind of order until—blessedly—Noro spoke up.

"Now, don't you break away, Hid," the lieutenant called. "Keep your shields together, men. If we rush off now, we'll be easy pickings."

The men reluctantly pulled back into formation. Eventually, the Fused streaked away. Their strikes never lasted long; they would hit hard, testing reaction times at various places along the wall—and they often broke into and searched the towers nearby. They were preparing for a true assault, and—Kaladin figured—also trying to find out how the Wall Guard was feeding itself.

The drums signaled for the squads to stand down, and the men of Kaladin's platoon lethargically trudged back to their tower. A sense of frustration accompanied them. Pent-up aggression. All of that anxiety, the rush of the battle, only to stand around and sweat while other men died.

Kaladin helped rack up the weapons, then got himself a bowl of stew and joined Lieutenant Noro, who was waiting on the wall right outside the tower. A messenger used signal flags to indicate to others down in the city that Noro's platoon hadn't engaged.

"You have my apologies, sir," Kaladin said softly. "I'll see it doesn't happen again."

"Um . . . it?"

"I preempted you earlier," Kaladin said. "Gave orders when it was your place."

"Oh! Well, you're quite quick off the cuff, Kal! Eager for combat, I'd say."

"Perhaps, sir."

"You want to prove yourself to the team," Noro said, rubbing his wispy beard. "Well, I like a man with enthusiasm. Keep your head, and I suspect you'll end up as a squadleader before too long." He said it like a proud parent.

"Permission, sir, to be excused from duty? There might be wounded that need my attention farther along the wall."

"Wounded? Kal, I know you said you had some field medicine training—but the army's surgeons will be there already."

Right, they'd have actual surgeons.

Noro clapped him on the shoulder. "Go in and eat your stew. There will be enough action later. Don't run too fast toward danger, all right?"

"I'll . . . try to remember that, sir."

Still, there was nothing to do but walk back into the tower, Syl alighting on his shoulder, and sit down to eat his stew.

*Today, I leaped from the tower for the last time. I felt the wind
dance around me as I fell all the way along the eastern side, past
the tower, and to the foothills below. I'm going to miss that.*

—From drawer 10-1, sapphire

Veil leaned her head to look in through the window of the old,
broken shop in the market. Grund the urchin sat in his usual
place, carefully stripping down an old pair of shoes for the hogshide. As he heard Veil, he dropped his tool and reached for a knife with
his good hand.

He saw that it was her, then caught the package of food she tossed to
him. It was smaller this time, but actually had some fruit. Very rare in the
city these days. The urchin pulled the bag of food close, closing his dark
green eyes, looking . . . reserved. What an odd expression.

He's still suspicious of me, she thought. *He's wondering what I'll someday
demand of him for all this.*

"Where are Ma and Seland?" Veil asked. She had prepared packages for
the two women who stayed here with Grund.

"Moved out to the old tinker's place," Grund said. He thumbed upward,
toward the sagging ceiling. "Thought this place was getting too dangerous."

"You sure you don't want to do the same?"

"Nah," he said. "I can finally move without kicking someone."

She left him and shoved her hands in her pockets, wearing her new coat
and hat against the cool air. She'd hoped that Kholinar would prove to be

warmer, after so long on the Shattered Plains or Urithiru. But it was cold here too, suffering a season of winter weather. Perhaps the arrival of the Everstorm was to be blamed.

She checked in on Muri next, the former seamstress with three daughters. She was of second nahn, high ranking for a darkeyes, and had run a successful business in a town near Revolar. Now she trolled the water ditches following storms for the corpses of rats and cremlings.

Muri always had some gossip that was amusing but generally pointless. Veil left about an hour later and made her way out of the market, dropping her last package in the lap of a random beggar.

The old beggar sniffed the package, then whooped with excitement. "The Swiftspren!" he said, nudging one of the other beggars. "Look, the Swiftspren!" He cackled, digging into the package, and his friend roused from his sleep and snatched some flatbread.

"Swiftspren?" Veil asked.

"That's you!" he said. "Yup, yup! I *heard* of you. Robbing rich folk all through the city, you do! And nobody can stop you, 'cuz you're a *spren*. Can walk through walls, you can. White hat, white coat. Don't always appear the same, do ya?"

The beggar started stuffing his face. Veil smiled—her reputation was spreading. She'd enhanced it by sending Ishnah and Vathah out, wearing illusions to look like Veil, giving away food. Surely, the cult couldn't ignore her much longer. Pattern hummed as she stretched, exhaustionspren— all of the corrupted variety—spinning about her in the air, little red whirlwinds. The merchant she'd stolen from earlier had chased her away himself, and had been nimble for his age.

"Why?" Pattern asked.

"Why what?" Veil asked. "Why is the sky blue, the sun bright? Why do storms blow, or rains fall?"

"Mmmm . . . Why are you so happy about feeding so few?"

"Feeding these few is something we can do."

"So is jumping from a building," he said—frank, as if he didn't understand the sarcasm he used. "But we do not do this. You lie, Shallan."

"Veil."

"Your lies wrap other lies. Mmm . . ." He sounded drowsy. Could spren get drowsy? "Remember your Ideal, the truth you spoke."

She shoved hands in her pockets. Evening was coming, the sun slipping toward the western horizon. As if it were running from the Origin and the storms.

It was the individual touch, the light in the eyes of people she gave to, that really excited her. Feeding them felt so much more *real* than the rest of the plan to infiltrate the cult and investigate the Oathgate.

It's too small, she thought. That was what Jasnah would say. *I'm thinking too small.*

Along the street, she passed people who whimpered and suffered. Far too many hungerspren in the air, and fearspren at nearly every corner. She had to do *something* to help.

Like throwing a thimbleful of water onto a bonfire.

She stood at an intersection, head bowed, as the shadows grew long, reaching toward night. Chanting broke her out of her trance. How long had she been standing there?

Flickering light, orange and primal, painted a street to her left. No sphere glowed that color. She walked toward it, pulling off her hat and sucking in Stormlight. She released it in a puff, then stepped through, trailing tendrils that wrapped around her and transformed her shape.

People had gathered, as they usually did, when the Cult of Moments paraded. Swiftspren broke through them, wearing the costume of a spren from her notes—notes she'd lost to the sea. A spren shaped like a glowing arrowhead that wove through the sky around skyeels.

Golden tassels streamed from her back, long, with arrowhead shapes at the ends. Her entire front was wrapped in cloth that trailed behind, her arms, legs, and face covered. Swiftspren flowed among the cultists, and drew stares even from them.

I have to do more, she thought. *I have to think grander schemes.*

Could Shallan's lies help her be something more than a broken girl from rural Jah Keved? A girl who was, deep down, terrified that she had *no idea* what she was doing.

The cultists chanted softly, repeating the words of the leaders at the front.

"Our time has passed."

"Our time has passed."

"The spren have come."

"The spren have come."

"Give them our sins."

"Give them our sins. . . ."

Yes . . . she could feel it. The freedom these people felt. It was the peace of surrender. They coursed down the street, proffering their torches and lanterns toward the sky, wearing the garb of spren. Why worry? Embrace the release, embrace the transition, embrace the coming of storm and spren.

Embrace the end.

Swiftspren breathed in their chants and saturated herself with their ideas. She became them, and she could *hear* it, whispering in the back of her mind.

Surrender.

Give me your passion. Your pain. Your love.

Give up your guilt.

Embrace the end.

Shallan, I'm not your enemy.

That last one stood out, like a scar on a beautiful man's face. Jarring.

She came to herself. Storms. She'd initially thought that this group might lead her up to the revel on the Oathgate platform, but . . . she'd let herself be carried away by the darkness. Trembling, she stopped in place.

The others stopped around her. The illusion—the sprenlike tassels behind her—continued to stream, even when she wasn't walking. There was no wind.

The cultists' chanting broke off, and corrupted awespren exploded around several of their heads. Soot-black puffs. Some fell to their knees. To them—wrapped in streaming cloth, face obscured, ignoring wind and gravity—she would look like an actual spren.

"There are spren," Shallan said to the gathered crowd, using Lightweaving to twist and warp her voice, "and there are *spren*. You followed the dark ones. They whisper for you to abandon yourselves. *They lie.*"

The cultists gasped.

"We do not want your devotion. When have spren ever demanded your *devotion*? Stop dancing in the streets and be *men* and *women* again. Strip off those idiotic costumes and return to your families!"

They didn't move quickly enough, so she sent her tassels streaming upward, curling about one another, lengthening. A powerful light flashed from her.

"Go!" she shouted.

They fled, some throwing off their costumes as they went. Shallan waited, trembling, until she was alone. She let the glow vanish and shrouded herself in blackness, then stepped off the street.

When she emerged from the blackness, she looked like Veil again. Storms. She'd . . . she'd become one of them so *easily*. Was her mind so quickly corrupted?

She wrapped her arms around herself, trailing through streets and markets. Jasnah would have been strong enough to keep going with them until reaching the platform. And if these hadn't been allowed up—most that wandered the streets weren't privileged enough to join the feast—then she'd have done something else. Perhaps take the place of one of the feast guards.

Truth was, she *enjoyed* the thievery and feeding the people. Veil wanted to be a hero of the streets, like in the old stories. That had corrupted Shallan, preventing her from going forward with something more logical.

But she'd never been the logical one. That was Jasnah, and Shallan *couldn't* be her. Maybe . . . maybe she could become Radiant and . . .

She huddled against a wall, arms wrapped around herself. Sweating, trembling, she went looking for light. She found it down a street: a calm, level glow. The friendly light of spheres, and with it a sound that seemed impossible. Laughter?

She chased it, hungry, until she reached a gathering of people singing beneath Nomon's azure gaze. They'd overturned boxes, gathering in a ring, while one man led the boisterous songs.

Shallan watched, hand on the wall of a building, Veil's hat held limply in her gloved safehand. Shouldn't that laughter have been more desperate? How could they be so happy? How could they sing? In that moment, these people seemed like strange beasts, beyond her understanding.

Sometimes she felt like a thing wearing a human skin. She was that thing in Urithiru, the Unmade, who sent out puppets to feign humanity.

It's him, she noticed absently. *Wit's leading the songs.*

He hadn't left her any more messages at the inn. Last time she'd visited, the innkeeper complained that he'd moved out, and had coerced her to pay Wit's tab.

Veil pulled on her hat, then turned and trailed away down the small market street.

⁂

She turned herself back into Shallan right before she reached the tailor's shop. Veil let go reluctantly, as she kept wanting to go track down Kaladin in the Wall Guard. He wouldn't know her, so she could approach him, pretend to get to know him. Maybe flirt a little . . .

Radiant was aghast at that idea. Her oaths to Adolin weren't complete, but they were important. She respected him, and enjoyed their time training together with the sword.

And Shallan . . . what did Shallan want again? Did it matter? Why bother worrying about her?

Veil finally let go. She folded her hat and coat, then used an illusion to disguise them as a satchel. She layered an illusion of Shallan and her havah over the top of her trousers and shirt, then strolled inside, where she found Drehy and Skar playing cards and debating which kind of chouta was best. There were different kinds?

Shallan nodded to them, then—exhausted—started up the steps. A few hungerspren, however, reminded her that she hadn't saved anything for herself from the day's thievery. She put away her clothing, then hiked down to the kitchen.

Here she found Elhokar drinking from a single cup of wine into which he'd dropped a sphere. That red-violet glow was the room's only light. On the table before him was a sheet of glyphs: names of the houses he had been approaching, through the parties. He'd crossed out some of the names, but had circled the others, writing down numbers of troops they might be able to provide. Fifty armsmen here, thirty there.

He raised the glowing cup to her as she gathered some flatbread and sugar. "What is that design on your skirt? It . . . seems familiar to me."

She glanced down. Pattern, who usually clung to her coat, had been replicated in the illusion on the side of her havah. "Familiar?"

Elhokar nodded. He didn't seem drunk, just contemplative. "I used to see myself as a hero, like you. I imagined claiming the Shattered Plains in my father's name. Vengeance for blood spilled. It doesn't even matter now, does it? That we won?"

"Of course it matters," Shallan said. "We have Urithiru, and we defeated a large army of Voidbringers."

He grunted. "Sometimes I think that if I merely *insist* long enough, the world will transform. But wishing and expecting is of the Passions. A heresy. A good Vorin worries about transforming themselves."

Give me your passion. . . .

"Have you any news about the Oathgate or the Cult of Moments?" Elhokar asked.

"No. I have some thoughts about getting up there though. New ones."

"Good. I might have troops for us soon, though their numbers will be smaller than I'd hoped. We depend upon your reconnaissance, however. I would know what is happening on that platform before I march troops onto it."

"Give me a few more days. I'll get onto the platform, I promise."

He took a drink of his wine. "There are few people remaining to whom I can still be a hero, Radiant. This city. My son. Storms. He was a baby when I last saw him. He'd be three now. Locked in the palace . . ."

Shallan set down her food. "Wait here." She fetched her sketchpad and pencils from a shelf in the showroom, then returned to Elhokar and settled down. She placed some spheres out for light, then started drawing.

Elhokar sat at the table across from her, lit by the cup of wine. "What are you doing?"

"I don't have a proper sketch of you," Shallan said. "I want one."

Creationspren started to appear around her immediately. They seemed normal, though they were so odd anyway, it could be hard to tell.

Elhokar *was* a good man. In his heart, at least. Shouldn't that matter most? He moved to look over her shoulder, but she was no longer sketching from sight.

"We'll save them," Shallan whispered. "You'll save them. It will be all

right."

Elhokar watched silently as she filled in the shading and finished the picture. Once she lifted her pencil, Elhokar reached past her and rested his fingers on the page. It depicted Elhokar kneeling on the ground, beaten down, clothing ragged. But he looked upward, outward, chin raised. He wasn't beaten. No, this man was noble, *regal*.

"Is that what I look like?" he whispered.

"Yes." *It's what you could be, at least.*

"May I . . . may I have it?"

She lacquered the page, then handed it to him.

"Thank you." Storms. He almost seemed to be in tears!

Feeling embarrassed, she gathered her supplies and her food, then hurried out of the kitchen. Back in her rooms, she met Ishnah, who was grinning. The short, darkeyed woman had been out earlier, wearing Veil's face and clothing.

She held up a slip of paper. "Someone handed me this today, Brightness, while I was giving away food."

Frowning, Shallan took the note.

Meet us at the borders of the revel in two nights, the day of the next Everstorm, it read. *Come alone. Bring food. Join the feast.*

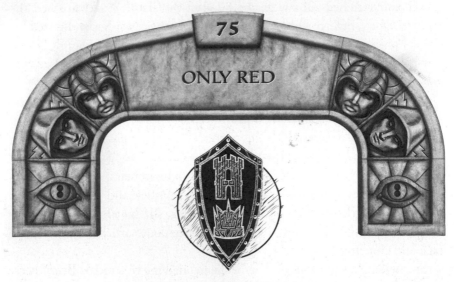

ELEVEN YEARS AGO

Dalinar left the horse.

Horses were too slow.

A misty fog blew off the lake, reminding him of that day long ago when he, Gavilar, and Sadeas had first attacked the Rift.

The elites who accompanied him were the product of years of planning and training. Primarily archers, they wore no armor, and were trained for long-distance running. Horses were magnificent beasts; the Sunmaker famously had used an entire company of cavalry. Over a short distance, their speed and maneuverability had been legendary.

Those possibilities intrigued Dalinar. Could men be trained to fire bows from horseback? How devastating would that be? What about a charge of horses bearing men with spears, like the legends spoke of during the Shin invasion?

For today, however, he didn't need horses. Men were better suited for long-distance running, not to mention being much better at scrambling over broken hillsides and uneven rocks. This company of elites could outrun any harrying force he'd yet to meet. Though archers, they were proficient with the sword. Their training was unparalleled, and their stamina legendary.

Dalinar hadn't trained with them personally, as he didn't have time to practice running thirty miles a day. Fortunately, he had Plate to make up the difference. Clad in his armor, he led the charging force over scrub and rock, past reeds that released hairlike inner strands to shiver on the breeze until he drew near. Grass, tree, and weed took fright at his approach.

Two fires burned inside him. First the energy of the Plate, lending power to each step. The second fire was the Thrill. Sadeas, a traitor? Impossible. He had supported Gavilar all along. Dalinar trusted him.

And yet . . .

I thought myself trustworthy, Dalinar thought, leading the charge down a hillside, a hundred men flooding behind him. *Yet I almost turned on Gavilar.*

He would see for himself. He would find out whether this "caravan" that had brought supplies to the Rift actually had a Shardbearer in its ranks or not. But the possibility that he had been betrayed—that Sadeas could have been working against them all along—drove Dalinar to a kind of focused madness. A clarity only the Thrill bestowed.

It was the focus of a man, his sword, and the blood he would spill.

The Thrill seemed to transform within him as he ran, soaking into his tiring muscles, saturating him. It became a power unto itself. So, when they crested a hillside some distance south of the Rift, he felt somehow *more* energetic than when he'd left.

As his company of elites jogged up, Dalinar pulled to a stop, armored feet grinding on stone. Ahead, down the hill and at the mouth of a canyon, a frantic group was scrambling to arms. The caravan. Its scouts must have spotted the approach of Dalinar's force.

They'd been setting up camp, but left their tents, running for the canyon, where they'd be able to avoid being flanked. Dalinar roared, summoning his Blade, ignoring the fatigue of his men as he dashed down the hillside.

The soldiers wore forest green and white. Sadeas's colors.

Dalinar reached the bottom of the hill and stormed through the now-abandoned camp. He swept past the stragglers, slicing out with Oathbringer, dropping them, their eyes burning.

Wait.

His momentum wouldn't *let* him stop now. Where was the enemy Shardbearer?

Something is wrong.

Dalinar led his men into the canyon after the soldiers, following the enemy along a wide path up the side. He raised Oathbringer high as he ran.

Why would they put on Sadeas's colors if they're a secret *envoy bringing contraband supplies?*

Dalinar stopped in place, his soldiers swarming around him. Their path had taken them about fifty feet up from the bottom of the canyon, on the south side of a steep incline. He saw no sign of a Shardbearer as the enemy gathered above. And . . . those uniforms . . .

He blinked. That . . . that was wrong.

He shouted an order to pull back, but the sound of his voice was overwhelmed by a sudden roar. A sound like thunder, accompanied by a dreadful clatter of rock against rock. The ground quivered, and he turned in horror to find a landslide tumbling down the steep side of the ravine to his right—directly above where he had led his men.

He had a fraction of a moment to take it in before the rocks pounded him in a terrible crash.

Everything spun, then grew black. Still he was pounded, rolled, *crushed*. An explosion of molten sparks briefly flashed in his eyes, and something hard smacked him on the head.

Finally it ended. He found himself lying in blackness, his head pounding, thick warm blood running down his face and dripping from his chin. He could feel the blood, but not see it. Had he been blinded?

His cheek was pressed against a rock. No. He wasn't blind; he'd been buried. And his helm had shattered. He shifted with a groan, and something illuminated the stones around his head. Stormlight seeping from his breastplate.

Somehow he'd survived the landslide. He lay facedown, prone, buried. He shifted again, and from the corner of his eye saw a rock sink, threatening to crush sideways into his skull. He lay still, his head thundering with pain. He flexed his left hand and found that gauntlet broken, his forearm plate too. But his right-hand armor still worked.

This . . . this was a trap. . . .

Sadeas was not a traitor. This had been designed by the Rift and its highlord to lure Dalinar in, then drop stones to crush him. Cowards. They'd tried something like that in Rathalas long ago too. He relaxed, groaning softly.

No. Can't lie here.

Maybe he could pretend to be dead. That sounded so appealing he closed his eyes and started to drift.

A fire ignited inside him.

You have been betrayed, Dalinar. Listen. He heard voices—men picking through the wreckage of the rockslide. He could make out their nasal accent. Rifters.

Tanalan sent you here to die!

Dalinar sneered, opening his eyes. Those men wouldn't let him hide in this tomb of stone, feigning death. He carried Shards. They would find him to recover their prize.

He braced himself, using his Plated shoulder to keep the rock from rolling against his exposed head, but did not otherwise move. Eventually the men above started speaking eagerly; from their words, they'd found his armor's cape sticking out through the stone, the glyphs of *khokh* and *linil* stark on the blue background.

Stones scraped, and the burden upon him lightened. The Thrill built to a crescendo. The stone near his head rolled back.

Go.

Dalinar heaved with his Plated feet and shifted a boulder with his still-armored hand, opening enough space that he could stand up straight. He ripped free of the tomb and stumbled upright into open air, stones clattering.

The Rifters cursed and scrambled backward as he leaped out of the hole, boots grinding against stones. Dalinar growled, summoning his Blade.

His armor was in worse shape than he'd assumed. Sluggish. Broken in four separate places.

All around him, Tanalan's men's eyes seemed to *glow*. They gathered and grinned at him; he could see the Thrill thick in their expressions. His Blade and leaking Plate reflected in their dark eyes.

Blood streaming down the side of his face, Dalinar grinned back at them.

They rushed to attack.

·⁂·

Dalinar saw only red.

He partially came to himself as he found himself pounding a man's head repeatedly against the stones. Behind him lay a pile of corpses with burned eyes, piled high around the hole where Dalinar had stood, fighting against them.

He dropped the head of the corpse in his hands and breathed out, feeling . . . What did he feel? Numb, suddenly. Pain was a distant thing. Even anger was nebulous. He looked down at his hands. Why was he using those, and not his Shardblade?

He turned to the side, where Oathbringer protruded from a rock where he'd stabbed it. The . . . gemstone on the pommel was cracked. That was right. He couldn't dismiss it; something about the crack had interfered.

He stumbled to his feet, looking around for more foes, but none came to challenge him. His armor . . . someone had broken the breastplate while fighting him, and he felt at a stab wound on his chest. He barely remembered that.

The sun was low on the horizon, plunging the canyon into shadows. Around him, discarded bits of clothing flapped in the breeze, and bodies lay still. Not a sound, not even cremling scavengers.

Drained, he bound the worst of his wounds, then grabbed Oathbringer and set it on his shoulder. Never had a Shardblade felt so heavy.

He started walking.

Along the way, he discarded pieces of Shardplate, which grew too heavy. He'd lost blood. Far too much.

He focused on the steps. One after another.

Momentum. A fight was all about *momentum*.

He didn't dare take the obvious route, in case he encountered more Rifters. He crossed through the wilderness, vines writhing beneath his feet and rockbuds sprouting after he passed.

The Thrill returned to urge him on. For this walk *was* a fight. A battle. Night fell, and he threw off his last piece of Shardplate, leaving only the neck brace. They could regrow the rest of it from that, if they had to.

Keep. Moving.

In that darkness, shadowed figures seemed to accompany him. Armies made of red mist at the corners of his vision, charging forces that fell to dust and then sprouted from shadow again, like surging ocean waves in a constant state of disintegration and rebirth. Not just men, but eyeless horses. Animals locked in struggle, stifling the life from one another. Shadows of death and conflict to propel him through the night.

He hiked for an eternity. Eternity was nothing when time had no meaning. He was actually surprised when he approached the light of the Rift, from torches held by soldiers on the walls. His navigation by the moons and stars had been successful.

He stalked through the darkness toward his own camp on the field. There was another army here. Sadeas's actual soldiers; they'd arrived ahead of schedule. Another few hours, and Tanalan's ploy wouldn't have worked.

Dalinar dragged Oathbringer behind him; it made a soft scraping sound as it cut a line in the stone. He numbly heard soldiers talking by the bonfire ahead, and one called something out. Dalinar ignored them, each step relentless, as he passed into their light. A pair of young soldiers in blue crowed their challenges until cutting off and lowering spears, gaping.

"Stormfather," one of them said, stumbling back. "Kelek and the Almighty himself!"

Dalinar continued through camp. Noise stirred at his passing, men crying of visions of the dead and of Voidbringers. He made for his command tent. The eternity it took to get there seemed the same length as the others. How could he cross so many miles in the same time as it took to go the few feet to a simple tent? Dalinar shook his head, seeing red at the sides of his vision.

Words broke through the canvas of the tent. "Impossible. The men are spooked. They . . . No, it's simply not *possible*."

The flaps burst apart, revealing a man with fine clothing and wavy hair.

Sadeas gaped, then stumbled to the side, holding the flap for Dalinar, who did not break stride. He walked straight in, Oathbringer slicing a ribbon in the ground.

Inside, generals and officers gathered by the grim light of a few sphere lanterns. Evi, comforted by Brightness Kalami, was weeping, though Ialai studied the table full of maps. All eyes turned toward Dalinar.

"How?" Teleb asked. "Blackthorn? We sent a team of scouts to inform you as soon as Tanalan turned on us and cast our soldiers off his walls. Our force reported all men lost, an ambush . . ."

Dalinar hefted Oathbringer and slammed it down into the stone ground beside him, then sighed at finally being able to release the burden. He placed his palms on the sides of the battle table, hands crusted in blood. His arms were covered in it too.

"You sent the same scouts," he whispered, "who first spied on the caravan, and reported seeing a Shardbearer leading it?"

"Yes," Teleb said.

"Traitors," Dalinar said. "They're working with Tanalan." He couldn't have known that Dalinar would parley with him. Instead, the man had somehow bribed away members of the army, and had intended to use their reports to coax Dalinar into a hurried ride to the south. Into a trap.

It had all been set in motion before Dalinar had spoken to Tanalan. Planned well in advance.

Teleb barked out orders for the scouts to be imprisoned. Dalinar leaned down over the battle maps on the table. "This is a map for a siege," he whispered.

"We . . ." Teleb looked to Sadeas. "We figured that the king would want time to come down himself. To, um, avenge you, Brightlord."

"Too slow," Dalinar said, his voice ragged.

"Highprince Sadeas proposed . . . another option," Teleb said. "But the king—"

Dalinar looked to Sadeas.

"They used my name to betray you," Sadeas said, then spat to the side. "We will suffer rebellions like this time and time again unless they *fear* us, Dalinar."

Dalinar nodded slowly. "They must bleed," he whispered. "I want them to suffer for this. Men, women, children. They must know the punishment for broken oaths. *Immediately.*"

"Dalinar?" Evi stood up. "Husband?" She stepped forward, toward the table.

Then he turned toward her, and she stopped. Her unusual, pale Westerner skin grew even more starkly white. She stepped backward, pulling her hands toward her chest, and gaped at him, horrified, fearspren growing up from the ground around her.

Dalinar glanced toward a sphere lantern, which had a polished metal surface. The man who looked back seemed more Voidbringer than man, face crusted over with blackened blood, hair matted with it, blue eyes wide, jaw clenched. He was sliced with what seemed to be a hundred wounds, his padded uniform in tatters.

"You shouldn't do this," Evi said. "Rest. Sleep, Dalinar. Think about this. Give it a few days."

So tired . . .

"The entire kingdom thinks us weak, Dalinar," Sadeas whispered. "We took too long to put this rebellion down. You have never listened to me before, but listen now. You want to prevent this sort of thing from happening again? You *must* punish them. Every one."

"Punish them . . ." Dalinar said, the Thrill rising again. Pain. Anger. Humiliation. He pressed his hands against the map table to steady himself. "The Soulcaster that my brother sent. She can make two things?"

"Grain and oil," Teleb said.

"Good. Set her to work."

"More food supplies?"

"No, oil. As much as we have gemstones for. Oh, and someone take my wife to her tent so she may recover from her unwarranted grief. Everyone else, gather round. In the morning, we make Rathalas an example. I promised Tanalan that his widows would weep for what I did here, but that is too merciful for what they've done to me.

"I intend to so thoroughly ruin this place that for ten generations, nobody will *dare* build here for fear of the spirits who will haunt it. We will make a *pyre* of this city, and there shall be no weeping for its passing, for *none will remain to weep.*"

ELEVEN YEARS AGO

Dalinar agreed to change clothing. He washed his face and arms, and let a surgeon look at his wounds.

The red mist was still there, coloring his vision. He would *not* sleep. It wouldn't let him.

About an hour after he'd arrived in camp, he trudged back to the command tent, cleaned but not particularly refreshed.

The generals had drawn up a new set of battle plans to take the city walls, as instructed by Sadeas. Dalinar inspected and made a few changes, but told them to suspend making plans to march down into the city and clear it. He had something else in mind.

"Brightlord!" a messenger woman said, arriving at the tent. She stepped in. "An envoy is leaving the city. Flying the flag of truce."

"Shoot them dead," Dalinar said calmly.

"Sir?"

"Arrows, woman," Dalinar said. "Kill anyone who comes out of the city, and leave their bodies to rot."

"Um, yes, Brightlord." The messenger ducked away.

Dalinar looked up toward Sadeas, who still wore his Shardplate, glittering in the spherelight. Sadeas nodded in approval, then gestured to the side. He wanted to speak in private.

Dalinar left the table. He should hurt more. Shouldn't he? Storms . . . he was so numb, he could barely feel anything, aside from that burning within, simmering deep down. He stepped with Sadeas out of the tent.

"I've been able to stall the scribes," Sadeas whispered, "as you ordered.

Gavilar doesn't know that you live. His orders from before were to wait and lay siege."

"My return supersedes his distant orders," Dalinar said. "The men will know that. Even Gavilar wouldn't disagree."

"Yes, but why keep him ignorant of your arrival?"

The last moon was close to setting. Not long until morning. "What do you think of my brother, Sadeas?"

"He's exactly what we need," Sadeas said. "Hard enough to lead a war; soft enough to be beloved during peace. He has foresight and wisdom."

"Do you think he could do what needs to be done here?"

Sadeas fell silent. "No," he finally said. "No, not now. I wonder if *you* can either. This will be more than just death. It will be complete destruction."

"A lesson," Dalinar whispered.

"A display. Tanalan's plan was clever, but risky. He knew his chances of winning here depended upon removing you and your Shards from the battle." He narrowed his eyes. "You thought those soldiers were mine. You actually believed I'd betray Gavilar."

"I worried."

"Then know this, Dalinar," Sadeas said, low, his voice like stone grinding stone. "I would cut out my own heart before betraying Gavilar. I have no interest in being king—it's a job with little praise and even less amusement. I mean for this kingdom to stand for centuries."

"Good," Dalinar said.

"Honestly, I worried that *you* would betray him."

"I almost did, once. I stopped myself."

"Why?"

"Because," Dalinar said. "There has to be someone in this kingdom capable of doing what needs to be done, and it can't be the man sitting on the throne. Continue to hold the scribes back; it will be better if my brother can reasonably disavow what we're about to do."

"Something will leak out soon," Sadeas said. "Between our two armies, there are too many spanreeds. Storming things are getting so cheap, most of the officers can afford to buy a pair to manage their households from a distance."

Dalinar strode back into the tent, Sadeas following. Oathbringer still sat where he'd stuck it into the stones, though an armorer had replaced the gemstone for him.

He pulled the Blade from the rock. "Time to attack."

Amaram turned from where he stood with the other generals. "Now, Dalinar? At night?"

"The bonfires on the wall should be enough."

"To take the wall fortifications, yes," Amaram said. "But Brightlord, I don't relish fighting down into those vertical streets in the night."

Dalinar shared a look with Sadeas. "Fortunately, you won't have to. Send the word for the men to prepare the oil and flaming brands. We march."

Highmarshal Perethom took the orders and began organizing specifics. Dalinar lifted Oathbringer on his shoulder. *Time to bring you home.*

In under a half hour, men charged the walls. No Shardbearers led this time; Dalinar was too weak, and his Plate was in shambles. Sadeas never did like exposing himself too early, and Teleb couldn't rush in alone.

They did it the mundane way, sending men to be crushed by stones or impaled by arrows as they carried ladders. They broke through eventually, securing a section of the wall in a furious, bloody fight.

The Thrill was an unsatisfied lump inside Dalinar, but he was wrung out, worn down. So he continued to wait until finally, Teleb and Sadeas joined the fight and routed the last of the defenders, sending them down from the walls toward the chasm of the city itself.

"I need a squad of elites," Dalinar said softly to a nearby messenger. "And my own barrel of oil. Have them meet me inside the walls."

"Yes, Brightlord," the young boy said, then ran off.

Dalinar strode across the field, passing fallen men bloody and dead. They'd died almost in ranks where waves of arrows had struck. He also passed a cluster of corpses in white, where the envoy had been slaughtered earlier. Warmed by the rising sun, he passed through the now-open gates of the wall and entered the ring of stone that surrounded the Rift.

Sadeas met him there, faceplate up, cheeks even redder than normal from exertion. "They fought like Voidbringers. More vicious than last time, I'd say."

"They know what is coming," Dalinar said, walking toward the cliff edge. He stopped halfway there.

"We checked it for a trap this time," Sadeas noted.

Dalinar continued forward. The Rifters had gotten the better of him twice now. He should have learned the first time. He stopped at the edge of the cliff, looking down at a city built on platforms, rising up along the widening sides of the rift of stone. It was little wonder they thought so highly of themselves as to resist. Their city was grand, a monument of human ingenuity and grit.

"Burn it," Dalinar said.

Archers gathered with arrows ready to ignite, while other men rolled up barrels of oil and pitch to give extra fuel.

"There are thousands of people in there, sir," Teleb said softly from his side. "Tens of thousands."

"This kingdom must know the price of rebellion. We make a statement today."

"Obey or die?" Teleb asked.

"The same deal I offered you, Teleb. You were smart enough to take it."

"And the common people in there, the ones who didn't get a chance to choose a side?"

Sadeas snorted from nearby. "We will prevent more deaths in the future by letting every brightlord in this kingdom know the punishment for disobedience." He took a report from an aide, then stepped up to Dalinar. "You were right about the scouts who turned traitor. We bribed one to turn on the others, and will execute the rest. The plan was apparently to separate you from the army, then hopefully kill you. Even if you were simply delayed, the Rift was hoping their lies would prompt your army into a reckless attack without you."

"They weren't counting on your swift arrival," Dalinar said.

"Or your tenacity."

The soldiers unplugged barrels of oil, then began dropping them down, soaking the upper levels of the city. Flaming brands followed—starting struts and walkways on fire. The very foundations of this city were flammable.

Tanalan's soldiers tried to organize a fight back out of the Rift, but they'd surrendered the high ground, expecting Dalinar to do as he had before, conquering and controlling.

He watched as the fires spread, flamespren rising in them, seeming larger and more . . . angry than normal. He then walked back—leaving a solemn Teleb—to gather his remaining elites. Captainlord Kadash had fifty for him, along with two barrels of oil.

"Follow," Dalinar said, walking around the Rift on its east side, where the fracture was narrow enough to cross on a short bridge.

Screams below. Then cries of pain. Calls for mercy. People flooded from buildings, shouting in terror, fleeing on walkways and steps toward the basin below. Many buildings burned, trapping others inside.

Dalinar led his squad along the northern rim of the Rift until they reached a certain location. His armies waited here to kill any soldiers who tried to break out, but the enemy had concentrated their assault on the other side, then been mostly beaten back. The fires hadn't reached up here yet, though Sadeas's archers had killed several dozen civilians who had tried to flee in this direction.

For now, the wooden ramp down into the city was clear. Dalinar led his group down one level to a location he remembered so well: the hidden door set into the wall. It was metal now, guarded by a pair of nervous Rifter soldiers.

Kadash's men shot them down with shortbows. That annoyed Dalinar; all of this fighting, and nothing with which to feed the Thrill. He stepped over one of the corpses, then tried the door, which was no longer hidden. It was still locked tight. Tanalan had decided to go with security instead of secrets, this time.

Unfortunately for them, Oathbringer had come home. Dalinar easily cut off the steel hinges. He stepped back as the door slammed forward onto the walkway, shaking the wood.

"Light those," he said, pointing to the barrels. "Roll them down and burn out anyone hiding inside."

The men hurried to obey, and soon the tunnel of rock had fitful black smoke pouring from it. Nobody tried to flee, though he thought he heard cries of pain inside. Dalinar watched as long as he could, until soon the smoke and heat drove him back.

The Rift behind him was becoming a pit of darkness and fire. Dalinar retreated up the ramp to the stones above. Archers lit the final walkways and ramps behind him. It would be long before people decided to resettle here. Highstorms were one thing, but there was a more terrible force upon the land. And it carried a Shardblade.

Those screams . . . Dalinar passed lines of soldiers who waited along the northern rim in silent horror; many wouldn't have been with Dalinar and Gavilar during the early years of their conquest, when they'd allowed pillaging and ransacking of cities. And for those who did remember . . . well, he'd often found an excuse to stop things like this before.

He drew his lips to a line, and shoved down the Thrill. He would *not* let himself enjoy this. That single sliver of decency he could keep back.

"Brightlord!" a soldier said, waving to him. "Brightlord, you must see this!"

Just below the cliff here—one tier down into the city—was a beautiful white building. A palace. Farther out along the walkways, a group of people fought to reach the building. The wooden walkways were on fire, and preventing their access. Shocked, Dalinar recognized Tanalan the younger from their encounter earlier.

Trying to get into his home? Dalinar thought. Figures darkened the building's upper windows; a woman and children. *No. Trying to get to his family.*

Tanalan hadn't been hiding in the saferoom after all.

"Throw a rope," Dalinar said. "Bring Tanalan up here, but shoot down the bodyguards."

The smoke billowing out of the Rift was growing thick, lit red by the fires. Dalinar coughed, then stepped back as his men let down a rope to the platform below, a section that wasn't burning. Tanalan hesitated, then took it, letting Dalinar's men haul him up. The bodyguards were sent arrows when they tried to climb up a nearby burning ramp.

"Please," Tanalan said, clothing ashen from the smoke, as he was hauled up over the stone rim. "My family. *Please.*"

Dalinar could hear them screaming below. He whispered an order, and his elites pushed back the regular Kholin troops from the area, opening up a wide half-circle against the burning rift, where only Dalinar and his closest men were able to observe the captive.

Tanalan slumped on the ground. "Please . . ."

"I," Dalinar said softly, "am an animal."

"What—"

"An animal," Dalinar said, "reacts as it is prodded. You whip it, and it becomes savage. With an animal, you can start a tempest. Trouble is, once it's gone feral, you can't just whistle it back to you."

"Blackthorn!" Tanalan screamed. "Please! My *children.*"

"I made a mistake years ago," Dalinar said. "I will not be so foolish again." And yet . . . those screams.

Dalinar's soldiers seized Tanalan tightly as Dalinar turned from the man and walked back to the pit of fire. Sadeas had just arrived with a company of his own men, but Dalinar ignored them, Oathbringer still held against his shoulder. Smoke stung Dalinar's nose, his eyes watering. He couldn't see across the Rift to the rest of his armies; the air warped with heat, colored red.

It was like looking into Damnation itself.

Dalinar released a long breath, suddenly feeling his exhaustion even more deeply. "It is enough," he said, turning toward Sadeas. "Let the rest of the people of the city escape out the mouth of the canyon below. We have sent our signal."

"What?" Sadeas said, hiking over. "Dalinar—"

A loud series of cracks interrupted him. An entire section of the city nearby collapsed into the flames. The palace—and its occupants—crashed down with it, a tempest of sparks and splintering wood.

"No!" Tanalan shouted. "*NO!*"

"Dalinar . . ." Sadeas said. "I prepared a battalion below, with archers, per your orders."

"My orders?"

"You said to 'Kill anyone who comes out of the city and leave their bodies to rot.' I had men stationed below; they've launched arrows in at the city struts, burned the walkways leading down. This city burns from both directions—from underneath and from above. We can't stop it now."

Wood cracked as more sections of city collapsed. The Thrill surged, and

Dalinar pushed it away. "We've gone too far."

"Nonsense! Our lesson won't mean much if people can merely walk away." Sadeas glanced toward Tanalan. "Last loose end is this one. We don't want him getting away again." He reached for his sword.

"I'll do it," Dalinar said. Though the concept of more death was starting to sicken him, he steeled himself. This was the man who had betrayed him.

Dalinar stepped closer. To his credit, Tanalan tried to leap to his feet and fight. Several elites shoved the traitor back down to the ground, though Captainlord Kadash himself was just standing at the side of the city, looking down at the destruction. Dalinar could feel that heat, so terrible. It mirrored a sense within him. The Thrill . . . incredibly . . . was *not satisfied*. Still it thirsted. It didn't seem . . . didn't seem it *could* be satiated.

Tanalan collapsed, blubbering.

"You should not have betrayed me," Dalinar whispered, raising Oathbringer. "At least this time, you didn't hide in your hole. I don't know who you let take cover there, but know they are dead. I took care of that with barrels of fire."

Tanalan blinked, then started laughing with a frantic, crazed air. "You don't know? How could you not know? But you killed our messengers. You poor fool. You poor, *stupid* fool."

Dalinar seized him by the chin, though the man was still held by his soldiers. "*What?*"

"She came to us," Tanalan said. "To plead. How could you have missed her? Do you track your own family so poorly? The hole you burned . . . we don't hide there anymore. Everyone knows about it. Now it's a prison."

Ice washed through Dalinar, and he grabbed Tanalan by the throat and held, Oathbringer slipping from his fingers. He strangled the man, all the while demanding that he retract what he'd said.

Tanalan died with a smile on his lips. Dalinar stepped back, suddenly feeling too weak to stand. Where was the Thrill to bolster him? "Go back," he shouted at his elites. "Search that hole. Go . . ." He trailed off.

Kadash was on his knees, looking woozy, a pile of vomit on the rock before him. Some elites ran to try to do as Dalinar said, but they shied away from the Rift—the heat rising from the burning city was incredible.

Dalinar roared, standing, pushing toward the flames. However, the fire was too intense. Where he had once seen himself as an unstoppable force, he now had to admit exactly how small he was. Insignificant. Meaningless.

Once it's gone feral, you can't just whistle it back to you.

He fell to his knees, and remained there until his soldiers pulled him— limp—away from the heat and carried him to his camp.

Six hours later, Dalinar stood with hands clasped behind his back—partially to hide how badly they were shaking—and stared at a body on the table, covered in a white sheet.

Behind him in the tent, some of his scribes whispered. A sound like swishing swords on the practice field. Teleb's wife, Kalami, led the discussion; she thought that Evi must have defected. What else could explain why the burned corpse of a highprince's wife had been found in an enemy safehouse?

It fit the narrative. Showing uncharacteristic determination, Evi had drugged the guard protecting her. She'd snuck away in the night. The scribes wondered how long Evi had been a traitor, and if she'd helped recruit the group of scouts who had betrayed Dalinar.

He stepped forward, resting his fingers on the smooth, too-white sheet. *Fool woman.* The scribes didn't know Evi well enough. She hadn't been a traitor—she'd gone to the Rift to plead for them to surrender. She'd seen in Dalinar's eyes that he wouldn't spare them. So, Almighty help her, she'd gone to do what she could.

Dalinar barely had the strength to stand. The Thrill had abandoned him, and that left him broken, pained.

He pulled back the corner of the sheet. The left side of Evi's face was scorched, nauseating, but the right side had been down toward the stone. It was oddly untouched.

This is your fault, he thought at her. *How dare you do this? Stupid, frustrating woman.*

This was *not* his fault, *not* his responsibility.

"Dalinar," Kalami said, stepping up. "You should rest."

"She didn't betray us," Dalinar said firmly.

"I'm sure eventually we'll know what—"

"She did *not* betray us," Dalinar snapped. "Keep the discovery of her body quiet, Kalami. Tell the people . . . tell them my wife was slain by an assassin last night. I will swear the few elites who know to secrecy. Let everyone think she died a hero, and that the destruction of the city today was done in retribution."

Dalinar set his jaw. Earlier today, the soldiers of his army—so carefully trained over the years to resist pillaging and the slaughter of civilians—had burned a city to the ground. It would ease their consciences to think that first, the highlady had been murdered.

Kalami smiled at him, a knowing—even self-important—smile. His lie would serve a second purpose. As long as Kalami and the head scribes *thought* they knew a secret, they'd be less likely to dig for the true answer.

Not my fault.

"Rest, Dalinar," Kalami said. "You are in pain now, but as the highstorm must pass, all mortal agonies will fade."

Dalinar left the corpse to the ministrations of others. As he departed, he strangely heard the screams of those people in the Rift. He stopped, wondering what it was. Nobody else seemed to notice.

Yes, that was distant screaming. In his head, maybe? They all seemed children to his ears. The ones he'd abandoned to the flames. A chorus of the innocent pleading for help, for mercy.

Evi's voice joined them.

The Taker of Secrets

Sja-anat, creator and corrupter - unique among the Unmade.

Creator

Her twisted
creations
are her
beloved
children.

· Her
admiration
of the
spren of
our world
inspires
her.

Corrupter

She seeks
the
Children
of
Honor
and the
Children
of
Cultivation.

With one
touch
she
corrupts.

Sja-anat

Something must be done about the remnants of Odium's forces. The parsh, as they are now called, continue their war with zeal, even without their masters from Damnation.

—From drawer 30-20, first emerald

Kaladin dashed across the street. "Wait!" he shouted. "One more here!"

Ahead, a man with a thin mustache struggled to close a thick wooden door. It stuck partway open, however, giving just enough time for Kaladin to slip through.

The man swore at him, then pulled the door shut. Made of dark stumpweight wood, it made a muffled *thunk*. The man did up the locks, then stepped back and let three younger men place a thick bar into the settings.

"Cutting that close, armsman," the mustachioed man said, noting the Wall Guard patch on Kaladin's shoulder.

"Sorry," Kaladin said, handing the man a few spheres as a cover charge. "But the storm is still a few minutes away."

"Can't be too careful with this new storm," the man said. "Be glad the door got stuck."

Syl sat on the hinges, legs hanging over the sides. Kaladin doubted it had been luck; sticking people's shoes to the stone was a classic windspren trick. Still, he did understand the doorman's hesitance. Everstorms didn't *quite* match up with scholarly projections. The previous one had arrived hours earlier than anyone had guessed it would. Fortunately, they tended to blow in slower than highstorms. If you knew to watch the sky, there was time to find shelter.

Kaladin ran his hand through his hair and started deeper into the winehouse. This was one of those fashionable places that—while technically a stormshelter—was used only by rich people who had come to spend the storm enjoying themselves. It had a large common room and thick walls of stone blocks. No windows, of course. A bartender kept people liquored near the back, and a number of booths ringed the perimeter.

He spotted Shallan and Adolin sitting in a booth at the side. She wore her own face, but Adolin looked like Meleran Khal, a tall, bald man around Adolin's height. Kaladin lingered, watching Shallan laugh at something Adolin said, then poke him—with her safehand—in the shoulder. She seemed completely enthralled by him. And good for her. Everyone deserved something to give them light, these days. But . . . what about the glances she shot him on occasion, times when she didn't quite seem to be the same person? A different smile, an almost wicked look to her eyes . . .

You're seeing things, he thought to himself. He strode forward and caught their attention, settling into the booth with a sigh. He was off duty, and free to visit the city. He'd told the others he'd find his own shelter for the storm, and only had to be back in time for evening post-storm patrol.

"Took you long enough, bridgeboy," Adolin said.

"Lost track of time," Kaladin said, tapping the table. He hated being in stormshelters. They felt too much like prisons.

Outside, thunder announced the Everstorm's arrival. Most people in the city would be inside their homes, the refugees instead in public stormshelters.

This for-pay shelter was sparsely occupied, only a few of the tables or booths in use. That would give privacy to talk, fortunately, but it didn't bode well for the proprietor. People didn't have spheres to waste.

"Where's Elhokar?" Kaladin asked.

"Elhokar is working on last-minute plans through the storm," Adolin said. "He's decided to reveal himself tonight to the lighteyes he's chosen. And . . . he's done a good job, Kal. We'll at least have some troops because of this. Fewer than I'd like, but *something.*"

"And maybe another Knight Radiant?" Shallan asked, glancing at Kaladin. "What have you found?"

He quickly caught them up on what he'd learned: The Wall Guard might have a Soulcaster, and was *definitely* producing food somehow. It had seized emerald stores in the city—a fact he'd recently discovered.

"Azure is . . . tough to read," Kaladin finished. "She visits the barracks every night, but never talks about herself. Men report seeing her sword cut through stone, but it has no gemstone. I think it might be an Honorblade, like the weapon of the Assassin in White."

"Huh," Adolin said, sitting back. "You know, that would explain a lot."

"My platoon has dinner with her tonight, after evening patrol," Kaladin said. "I intend to see what I can learn."

A serving girl came for orders, and Adolin bought them wine. He knew about lighteyed drinks and—without needing to be told—ordered something without a touch of alcohol for Kaladin. He'd be on duty later. Adolin did get Shallan a cup of violet, to Kaladin's surprise.

As the serving girl left with the order, Adolin reached out toward Kaladin. "Let me see your sword."

"My sword?" Kaladin said, glancing toward Syl, who was huddling near the back of the booth and humming softly to herself. A way of ignoring the sounds of the Everstorm, which rumbled beyond the stones.

"Not *that* sword," Adolin said. "Your side sword."

Kaladin glanced down to where the sword stuck out beside his seat. He'd almost forgotten he was wearing the thing, which was a relief. The first few days, he'd bumped the sheath into everything. He unbuckled it and set it on the table for Adolin.

"Good blade," the prince said. "Well maintained. It was in this condition when they assigned it to you?"

Kaladin nodded. Adolin drew it and held it up.

"It's a little small," Shallan noted.

"It's a one-handed sword, Shallan. Close-range infantry weapon. A longer blade would be impractical."

"Longer . . . like Shardblades?" Kaladin asked.

"Well, yes, they break all kinds of rules." Adolin waved the sword through a few motions, then sheathed it. "I like this highmarshal of yours."

"It's not even *her* weapon," Kaladin said, taking it back.

"You boys done comparing your swords?" Shallan asked. "Because I've found something." She thumped a large book onto the table. "One of my contacts finally tracked down a copy of Hessi's *Mythica*. It's a newer book, and has been poorly received. It attributes distinct personalities to the Unmade."

Adolin lifted the cover, peeking in. "So . . . anything about swords in it?"

"Oh hush," she said, and batted his arm in a playful—and somewhat nauseating—way.

Yes, it was uncomfortable to watch the two of them. Kaladin liked them both . . . just not together. He forced himself to look around the room, which was occupied by lighteyes trying to drink away the sounds of the storm. He tried not to think of refugees who would be packed into stuffy public shelters, clutching their meager possessions and hoping some of what they were forced to leave behind would survive the storm.

"The book," Shallan said, "claims there were nine Unmade. That matches the vision Dalinar saw, though other reports speak of ten Unmade. They're likely ancient spren, primal, from the days before human society and civilization.

"The book claims the nine rampaged during the Desolations, but says not all were destroyed at Aharietiam. The author insists that some are active today; I find her vindicated—obviously—by what we've experienced."

"And there's one of these in the city," Adolin said.

"I think . . ." Shallan said. "I think there might be *two*, Adolin. Sja-anat, the Taker of Secrets, is one. Again, Dalinar's visions mention her. Sja-anat's touch corrupted other spren—and we're seeing the effects of that here."

"And the other one?" Adolin asked.

"Ashertmarn," Shallan said softly. She slipped a little knife from her satchel and began to absently carve at the top of the table. "The Heart of the Revel. The book has less to say on him, though it speaks of how he leads people to indulge in excess."

"Two Unmade," Kaladin said. "Are you sure?"

"Sure as I can be. Wit confirmed the second, and the way the queen acted leading up to the riots seems an obvious sign. As for the Taker of Secrets, we can see the corrupted spren ourselves."

"How do we fight two?" Kaladin asked.

"How do we fight *one*?" Adolin said. "In the tower, we didn't so much fight the thing as frighten it off. Shallan can't even say how she did that. What does the book say about fighting them?"

"Nothing." Shallan shrugged, blowing at her little carving on the table. It was of a corrupted gloryspren in the shape of a cube, which another patron had attracted. "The book says if you see a spren the wrong color, you're supposed to immediately move to another town."

"There's *kind of* an army in the way," Kaladin said.

"Yes, amazingly your stench hasn't cleared them out yet." Shallan started leafing through her book.

Kaladin frowned. Comments like that were part of what confused him about Shallan. She seemed perfectly friendly one moment, then she'd snap at him the next, while pretending it was merely part of normal conversation. But she didn't talk like that to others, not even in jest.

What is wrong with you, woman? he thought. They'd shared something intimate, in the chasms back on the Shattered Plains. A highstorm huddled together, and words. Was she embarrassed by that? Was that the reason she snapped at him sometimes?

If that was so, how did one explain the other times, when she watched him and grinned? When she winked, in a sly way?

"Hessi reports stories of the Unmade not only corrupting spren, but corrupting *people*," Shallan was saying. "Maybe that's what's happening with the palace. We'll know more after infiltrating the cult tonight."

"I don't like you going alone," Adolin said.

"I won't be alone. I'll have my team."

"One washwoman and two deserters," Kaladin said. "If Gaz is anything to judge by, Shallan, you shouldn't put too much trust in those men."

Shallan raised her chin. "At least *my* soldiers knew when to get away from the warcamps, as opposed to just standing around letting people fling arrows at them."

"We trust you, Shallan," Adolin said, eyeing Kaladin as if to say, *Drop it.* "And we really need a look at that Oathgate."

"What if I can't open it?" Shallan asked. "What then?"

"We have to retreat back to the Shattered Plains," Kaladin said.

"Elhokar won't leave his family."

"Then Drehy, Skar, and I rush the palace," Kaladin said. "We fly in at night, enter through the upper balcony, grab the queen and the young prince. We do it all right before the highstorm comes, then the lot of us fly back to Urithiru."

"And leave the city to fall," Adolin said, drawing his lips to a line.

"Can the city hold?" Shallan asked. "Maybe until we can get back with a real army, marched out here?"

"That would take months," Adolin said. "And the Wall Guard is . . . what? Four battalions?"

"Five in total," Kaladin said.

"Five thousand men?" Shallan asked. "So few?"

"That's large for a city garrison," Adolin said. "The point of fortifications is to let a small number hold against a much larger force. But the enemy has an unexpected advantage. Voidbringers who can fly, and a city infested with their allies."

"Yeah," Kaladin said. "The Wall Guard is earnest, but they won't be able to withstand a dedicated assault. There are tens of thousands of parshmen out there—and they're close to attacking. We don't have much time left. The Fused will sweep in to secure portions of the wall, and their armies will follow. If we're going to hold this city, we'll need Radiants and Shardbearers to even the odds."

Kaladin and Shallan shared a look. Their Radiants were not a battle-ready group, not yet. Storms. His men had barely taken to the skies. How could they be expected to fight those creatures who flew so easily upon the winds? How could he protect this city *and* protect his men?

They fell silent, listening to the room shake with the sounds of thunder outside. Kaladin finished his drink, wishing it were one of Rock's concoctions instead, and flicked away an odd cremling that he spotted clinging to the side of the bench. It had a multitude of legs, and a bulbous body, with a strange tan pattern on its back.

Disgusting. Even with the stresses to the city, the proprietor could at least keep this place clean.

* * *

Once the storm finally blew itself out, Shallan stepped from the winehouse, holding Adolin's arm. She watched Kaladin hurry off toward the barracks for evening patrol.

She should probably be equally eager to get going. She still had to steal some food today—enough to satisfy the Cult of Moments when she approached them later in the evening. That should be easy enough. Vathah had taken to planning operations under Ishnah's guidance, and was proving quite proficient.

Still, she lingered, enjoying Adolin's presence. She wanted to be here, with him, before it was time to be Veil. *She* . . . well, she didn't much care for him. Too clean-cut, too oblivious, too *expected*. She was fine with him as an ally, but wasn't the least bit interested romantically.

Shallan held his arm, walking with him. People already moved through the city, cleaning up—more so they could scavenge than out of civic duty. They reminded her of cremlings that emerged after a storm to feast on the plants. Indeed, nearby, ornamental rockbuds spat out vines in clusters beside doorways. A splatter of green vines and unfurling leaves, set against the brown city canvas.

One patch nearby had been struck—and burned away—by the Everstorm's red lightning.

"I need to show you the Impossible Falls sometime," Adolin said. "If you watch them from the right angles, it looks like the water is flowing down along the tiers, then somehow right up onto the top again. . . ."

As they walked, she had to step over a dead mink sticking half out of a broken tree trunk. Not the most romantic of strolls, but it *was* good to hold on to Adolin's arm—even if he had to wear a false face.

"Hey!" Adolin said. "I didn't get to look through the sketchbook. You said you were going to show me."

"I brought the wrong one, remember? I had to carve on the table." She grinned. "Don't think I missed you going up and paying for the damage when I wasn't looking."

He grunted.

"People carve on bar tables. It happens *all the time*."

"Sure, sure. It was a good carving too."

"And you still think I shouldn't have done it." She squeezed his arm. "Oh, Adolin Kholin. You *are* your father's son. I won't do it again, all right?"

He was blushing. "I," he said, "was promised sketches. I don't care if it's the wrong sketchbook. I feel like I haven't seen any of your pictures for ages."

"There's nothing good in this one," she said, digging in her satchel. "I've been distracted lately."

He still made her hand it over, and secretly she was pleased. He started flipping through the more recent pictures, and though he noted the ones of strange spren, he idled most on the sketches of refugees she'd done for her collection. A mother with her daughter, sitting in shadow, but with her face looking toward the horizon and the hints of a rising sun. A thick-knuckled man sweeping the area around his pallet on the street. A young woman, lighteyed and hanging out a window, hair drifting free, wearing only a nightgown with her hand tied in a pouch.

"Shallan," he said, "these are amazing! Some of the best work you've ever done."

"They're just quick sketches, Adolin."

"They're beautiful," he said, looking at another, where he stopped. It was a picture of him in one of his new suits.

Shallan blushed. "Forgot that was there," she said, trying to get the sketchbook back. He lingered on the picture, then finally succumbed to her prodding and handed it back. She let out a sigh of relief. It wasn't that she'd be *embarrassed* if he saw the sketch of Kaladin on the next page—she did sketches of all kinds of people. But best to end on the picture of Adolin. Veil had been seeping through on that other one.

"You're getting better, if that's possible."

"Maybe. Though I don't know how much I can credit myself with the progress. *Words of Radiance* says that a lot of Lightweavers were artists."

"So the order recruited people like you."

"Or the Surgebinding made them better at sketching, giving them an unfair advantage over other artists."

"I have an unfair advantage over other duelists. I have had the finest training since childhood. I was born strong and healthy, and my father's wealth gave me some of the best sparring partners in the world. My build gives me reach over other men. Does that mean I don't deserve accolades when I win?"

"You don't have *supernatural* help."

"You still had to work hard. I know you did." He put his arm around her, pulling her closer as they walked. Other Alethi couples kept their distance in public, but Adolin had been raised by a mother with a fondness for hugs. "You know, there's this thing my father complains about. He asked what the use of Shardblades was."

"Um . . . I think they're pretty obviously for cutting people up. Without cutting them, actually. So—"

"But why only swords? Father asks why the ancient Radiants never made tools for the people." He squeezed her shoulder. "I *love* that your powers make you a better artist, Shallan. Father was wrong. The Radiants *weren't* just soldiers! Yes, they created incredible weapons, but they also created incredible art! And maybe once this war is done, we can find other uses for their powers."

Storms, his enthusiasm could be intoxicating. As they walked toward the tailor's shop, she was loath to part with him, though Veil did need to get on with her day's work.

I can be anyone, Shallan thought, noticing a few joyspren blowing past, like a swirl of blue leaves. *I can become anything.* Adolin deserved someone far better than her. Could she . . . become that someone? Craft for him the perfect bride, a woman that looked and acted as befitted Adolin Kholin?

It wouldn't be her. The real her was a bruised and sorry thing, painted up all pretty, but inside a horrid mess. She already put a face over that for him. Why not go a few steps farther? Radiant . . . Radiant could be his perfect bride, and she *did* like him.

The thought made Shallan feel cold inside.

Once they were close enough to the tailor's shop that she didn't worry about him being safe as he walked back on his own, Shallan forced herself to pull out of his grip. She held his hand a moment with her freehand. "I need to be going."

"You aren't to meet the cult until sunset."

"I need to steal some food first to pay them."

Still, he held to her hand. "What do you do out there, Shallan? Who do you become?"

"Everyone," she said. Then she reached up and kissed him on the cheek. "Thank you for being you, Adolin."

"Everyone else was taken already," he mumbled.

Never stopped me.

He watched her until she ducked around a corner, heart thumping. Adolin Kholin in her life was like a warm sunrise.

Veil started to seep out, and she was forced to acknowledge that sometimes she preferred the storm and the rain to the sun.

She checked at the drop point, inside a corner of a building that was now rubble. Here, Red had deposited a pack that contained Veil's outfit. She grabbed it and went hunting a good place to change.

The end of the world had come, but that seemed most true after a storm. Refuse strewn about, people who hadn't gotten to shelters moaning from fallen shacks or alongside streets.

It was like each storm tried to wipe them off Roshar, and they only remained through sheer grit and luck. Now, with two storms, it was even worse. If they defeated the Voidbringers, would the Everstorm remain? Had it begun to erode their society in a way that—win the war or not—would eventually end with them all swept out to sea?

She felt her face changing as she walked, draining Stormlight from her satchel. It rose in her like a flaring flame, before dimming to an ember as she became the people from the sketches Adolin had seen.

The poor man who tried doggedly to keep the area around his little pallet clean, as if to try to maintain some control over an insane world.

The lighteyed girl who wondered what had happened to the joy of adolescence. Instead of her wearing her first havah to a ball, her family was forced to take in dozens of relatives from neighboring towns, and she spent the days locked away because the streets weren't safe.

The mother with a child, sitting in darkness, looking toward the horizon and a hidden sun.

Face after face. Life after life. Overpowering, intoxicating, alive. Breathing, and crying, and laughing, and being. So many hopes, so many lives, so many dreams.

She unbuttoned her havah up the side, then let it fall. She dropped her satchel, which thumped from the heavy book inside. She stepped forward in only her shift, safehand uncovered, feeling the wind on her skin. She was still wearing an illusion, one that didn't disrobe, so nobody could see her.

Nobody could see her. Had anyone *ever* seen her? She stopped on the street corner, wearing shifting faces and clothing, enjoying the sensation of freedom, clothed yet naked skin shivering at the wind's kiss.

Around her, people ducked away into buildings, frightened.

Just another spren, Shallan/Veil/Radiant thought. *That's what I am. Emotion made carnal.*

She lifted her hands to the sides, exposed, yet invisible. She breathed the breaths of a city's people.

"Mmm . . ." Pattern said, unweaving himself from her discarded dress. "Shallan?"

"Maybe," she said, lingering.

Finally, she let herself slip fully into Veil's persona. She immediately shook her head and fetched the clothing and satchel. She was lucky it hadn't been stolen. Foolish girl. They didn't have time for prancing around from poem to poem.

Veil found a secluded location beside a large gnarled tree whose roots spread all the way along the wall in either direction. She quickly rearranged her underclothing, then put on her trousers and did up her shirt. She pulled on her hat, checked herself in a hand mirror, then nodded.

Right, then. Time to meet up with Vathah.

He was waiting at the inn where Wit had once stayed. Radiant retained hope that she'd meet him again there, for a more thorough interrogation. In the private room, away from the eyes of the fretting innkeeper, Vathah laid out a couple of spheres to light the maps he'd purchased. They detailed the manor she intended to hit this afternoon.

"They call it the Mausoleum," Vathah explained as Veil sat. He showed her an artist's sketch he'd purchased, which was of the building's grand hall. "Those statues are all Soulcast, by the way. They're favored servants of the house, turned to storming stone."

"It's a sign of honor and respect among lighteyes."

"It's *creepy*," Vathah said. "When I die, burn my corpse up right good. Don't leave me staring for eternity while your descendants sip their tea."

Veil nodded absently, placing Shallan's sketchbook on the table. "Pick an alias from this. This map says the larder is on the outside wall. Time is tight, so we might want to do this one the easy way. Have Red make a distraction, then use Shallan's Blade to cut us an opening right in to the food."

"You know, they're said to have *quite* the fortune at the Mausoleum. The Tenet family riches are . . ." He trailed off as he saw her expression. "No riches, then."

"We get the food to pay the cult, then we get out."

"Fine." He settled on the image of the man sweeping around his pallet, staring at it. "You know, when you reformed me from banditry, I figured I was done with stealing."

"This is different."

"Different how? We stole mostly food back then too, Brightness. Just wanted to stay alive and forget."

"And do you still want to forget?"

He grunted. "No, suppose I don't. Suppose I sleep a little better now at night, don't I?"

The door opened and the innkeeper bustled in, holding drinks. Vathah yelped, though Veil turned with a droll expression. "I believe," she said, "I wanted to not be interrupted."

"I brought drinks!"

"Which is an interruption," Veil said, pointing out the door. "If we're thirsty, we'll ask."

The innkeeper grumbled, then backed out the door, carrying his tray.

He's suspicious, Veil thought. *He thinks we were up to something with Wit, and wants to find out what.*

"Time to move these meetings to another location, eh, Vathah?" She looked back at the table.

And found someone else sitting there.

Vathah was gone, replaced by a bald man with thick knuckles and a well-kept smock. Shallan glanced at the picture on the table, then at the drained sphere beside it, then back at Vathah.

"Nice," she said. "But you forgot to do the back of the head, the part not in the drawing."

"What?" Vathah asked, frowning.

She showed him the hand mirror.

"Why'd you put his face on me?"

"I didn't," Veil said, standing. "You panicked and this happened."

Vathah prodded at his face, still looking in the mirror, confused.

"I'll bet the first few times are always accidents," Veil said. She tucked the mirror away. "Gather this stuff up. We'll do the mission as planned, but tomorrow you're relieved of infiltration duty. I'll want you practicing with your Stormlight instead."

"Practicing . . ." He finally seemed to get it, his brown eyes opening widely. "Brightness! I'm no storming *Radiant*."

"Of course not. You're probably a squire—I think most orders had them. You might become something more. I think Shallan was making illusions off and on for years before she said the oaths. But then, it's all kind of muddled in her head. I had my sword when I was very young, and . . ."

She took a deep breath. Fortunately, Veil hadn't lived through those days.

Pattern hummed in warning.

"Brightness . . ." Vathah said. "Veil, you really think that I . . ."

Storms, he seemed like he was going to *cry*.

She patted him on the shoulder. "We don't have time to waste. The cult will be waiting for me in four hours, and expect a nice payment of food. You going to be all right?"

"Sure, sure," he said. The illusion finally dropped, and the image of Vathah himself so emotional was even more striking. "I can do this. Let's go steal from some rich people and give to some crazy people instead."

*A coalition has been formed among scholar Radiants. Our goal is
to deny the enemy their supply of Voidlight; this will prevent their
continuing transformations, and give us an edge in combat.*

—From drawer 30-20, second emerald

Veil had exposed herself.

That nagged at her as the wagon—filled with spoils from the
robbery—rolled toward the appointed meeting place with the
cult. She nestled in the back, against a bag of grain, feet up on a paper-
wrapped haunch of cured pork.

"Swiftspren" was Veil, as she was the one who had been seen distributing the food. Therefore, to enter this revel, she would have to go as herself.

The enemy knew what she looked like. Should she have created a new
persona, a false face, to not expose Veil?

But Veil is a false face, a part of her said. *You could always abandon her.*

She strangled that part of her, smothered it deep. Veil was too real, too
vital, to abandon. Shallan would be easier.

First moon was up by the time they reached the steps to the Oathgate
platform. Vathah rolled the wagon into place, and Veil hopped off, coat rippling around her. Two guards here were dressed as flamespren, with golden
and red tassels. Their muscular builds, and those two spears set near the
steps, hinted these men might have been soldiers before joining the cult.

A woman bustled between them, wearing a flat white mask with eye-
holes but no mouth or other features. Veil narrowed her eyes; the mask

reminded her of Iyatil, Mraize's master in the Ghostbloods. But it was a very different shape.

"You were told to come alone, Swiftspren," the woman said.

"You expected me to unload all of this on my own?" Veil waved to the back of the wagon.

"We can handle it," the woman said smoothly, stepping over as one of the guards held up a torch—not a sphere lamp—and the other lowered the wagon's tailgate. "Mmmm . . ."

Veil turned sharply. That hum . . .

The guards started unloading the food.

"You can take all but the two bags marked with red," Veil said, pointing. "I need those for my rounds visiting the poor."

"I wasn't aware this was a negotiation," the cultist said. "You asked for this. You've been leaving whispers through the city that you want to join the revel."

Wit's work, apparently. She'd have to thank him.

"Why are you here?" the cultist asked, sounding curious. "What is it you want, Swiftspren, so-called hero of the markets?"

"I just . . . keep hearing this voice. It says that this is the end, that I should give in to it. Embrace the time of spren." She turned toward the Oathgate platform; an orange glow was rising from the top. "The answers are up there, aren't they?"

From the corner of her eye, she saw the three nod to one another. She'd passed some kind of test.

"You may climb the steps to enlightenment," the cultist in white told her. "Your guide will meet you at the top."

She tossed her hat to Vathah and met his eyes. Once the unloading was through, he'd pull away and set up a few streets farther off, where he could watch the edge of the Oathgate platform. If she had trouble, she would throw herself off, counting on Stormlight to heal her after falling.

She started up the steps.

⁘

Kaladin normally liked the feeling of the city after a storm. Clean and fresh, washed of grime and refuse.

He'd done evening patrol, checking over their beat to see everything was all right following the storm. Now he stood on the top of the wall, waiting for the rest of his squad, who were still stowing their equipment. The sun had barely set, and it was time for dinner.

Below, he picked out buildings newly scarred from lightning strikes.

A pod of corrupted windspren danced past, trailing intense red light. Even the smell of the air was wrong somehow. Moldy and sodden.

Syl sat quietly on his shoulder until Beard and the others piled into the stairwell. He finally joined them, walking down below to the barrack, where both platoons—his and the one they shared the space with—were gathering for dinner. Roughly twenty of the men from the other platoon would be on wall duty tonight, but everyone else was present.

Not long after Kaladin arrived, the two platoon captains called their men to muster. Kaladin fell into line between Beard and Ved, and together they saluted as Azure stepped into the doorway. She was arrayed for battle as always, with her breastplate, chain, and cloak.

Tonight, she decided to do a formal inspection. Kaladin held attention with the others as she walked down their lines and commented quietly to the two captains. She looked over a few swords, and asked several of the men if they needed anything. Kaladin felt as if he'd stood in similar lines a hundred times, sweating and hoping that the general would find everything in order.

They always did. This wasn't the type of inspection that was intended to actually find problems—this was a chance for the men to show off for their highmarshal. They swelled as she told them they "just might be the finest platoons of fighting men I've ever had the privilege of leading." Kaladin was certain he'd heard those exact words from Amaram.

Trite or not, the words inspired the men. They gave the highmarshal shouts of approval once they were given leave to break ranks. Perhaps the number of "finest platoons" in the army went up during times of war, when everyone craved a morale boost.

Kaladin walked to the officers' table. It hadn't taken much work to get himself invited to dine with the highmarshal. Noro really wanted him promoted to lieutenant, and most of the others were too intimidated by Azure to sit at her table.

The highmarshal hung her cloak and strange sword on a peg. She kept her gloves on, and though he couldn't see her chest because of the breastplate, that face and build were obviously female. She was also very Alethi, with the skin tone and hair, her eyes a glimmering light orange.

She must have spent time as a mercenary out west, Kaladin thought. Sigzil had once told him that women fought in the west, particularly among mercenaries.

The meal was simple curried grain. Kaladin took a bite, well acquainted by now with the aftertaste of Soulcast grain. A lingering staleness. The curry helped, but the cooks had used the boiled-off starch of the grain to thicken it, so it had some of the same flavor.

He'd been placed relatively far from the center of the table, where Azure conversed with the two platoon captains. Eventually, one excused himself to use the privy.

Kaladin thought for a moment, then picked up his plate and moved down the table to settle into the open spot.

∴

Veil reached the top of the platform, entering what felt like a little village. The monastery structures here were much smaller—yet far nicer—than the ones on the Shattered Plains had been. A cluster of fine stonework structures with slanted, wedge-shaped roofs, the points toward the Origin.

Ornamental shalebark grew around the bases of most of the buildings, cultivated and carved into swirling patterns. Veil took a Memory for Shallan, but her focus was on the firelight coming from farther inward. She couldn't see the control building. All of these other structures were in the way. She *could* see the palace off to her left, glowing in the night with windows lit. It connected to the Oathgate platform by a covered walkway called the Sunwalk. A small group of soldiers, visible in the darkness only as shadows, guarded the way across.

Close to her—at the top of the steps—a rotund man sat along a shalebark ridge. He had short hair and light green eyes, and gave her an affable grin. "Welcome! I'm your guide tonight, for your first time at the revel! It can be . . . ah, disorienting."

Those are ardent robes, Veil noted. Ripped, stained from what appeared to be a variety of foods.

"Everyone who comes up here," he said, hopping off his seat, "is reborn. Your name is now . . . um . . ." He pulled a piece of paper from his pocket. "Where did I write that? Well, suppose it isn't important. Your name is Kishi. Doesn't that sound nice? Good job getting up here. This is where you'll find the real fun in the city."

He shoved his hands back in his pockets and looked down one of the roadways, then his shoulders slumped. "Anyway," he said. "Let's get going. Lots of reveling to do tonight. Always so much reveling to be done . . ."

"And you are?"

"Me? Oh, um, Kharat is what they named me. I think? I forget." He ambled forward without waiting to see if she followed.

She did, eager to get to the center. However, just past the first building, she reached the revel—and had to stop to take it in. A bonfire burned right on the ground, flames crackling and whipping in the wind, bathing Veil in heat. Corrupted flamespren, vivid blue and somehow more jagged, danced inside of it. Tables lined the walkway here, piled with food. Candied meats, stacks of flatbread crusted with sugar, fruits and pastries.

A variety of people passed by, occasionally scooping food off the tables with their bare hands. They laughed and shouted. Many had been ardents, marked by brown robes. Others were lighteyes, though their clothing had . . . decayed? It seemed a fitting word for these suits with missing jackets, havah dresses whose skirts were ragged from brushing the ground. Safehand sleeves ripped off at the shoulder and discarded somewhere.

They moved like fish in a school, flowing from right to left. She picked out soldiers, both lighteyed and dark, in the remnants of uniforms. They seemed to take no note of her or Kharat standing to the side.

She'd have to cut through the stream of people to get farther inward to the Oathgate control building. She started to do so, but Kharat took her by the arm, steering her to join the flow of people.

"We have to stay to the outer ring," he said. "No going inward for us, nope. Be happy. You get . . . you get to enjoy the end of the world in style. . . ."

She reluctantly let herself be pulled along. It was probably best to do a round of the platform anyway. However, not long after starting, she began to hear the voice.

Let go.

Give up your pain.

Feast. Indulge.

Embrace the end.

Pattern hummed on her coat, his sound lost to the many people laughing and drinking. Kharat stuck his fingers into some kind of creamy dessert, taking it by the handful. His eyes had glazed over, and he muttered to himself as he pushed the food into his mouth. Though others laughed and even danced, most showed that same glassy look.

She could feel Pattern's vibrations on her coat. It seemed to counteract the voices, clearing her head. Kharat handed her a cup of wine he'd scooped from a table. Who set this all up? Where were the servants?

There was just *so much* food. Tables and tables of it. People moved in buildings they passed, engaging in other carnal delights. Veil tried to slip across the stream of revelers, but Kharat kept hold of her.

"Everyone wants to go inward their first time," he said. "You aren't allowed. Enjoy this. Enjoy the feeling. It's not our fault, right? We didn't fail her. We were only doing what she asked. Don't cause a storm, girl. Nobody wants that. . . ."

He hung on to Veil's arm. So instead she waited until they passed another building, and tugged him that way.

"Going to find a partner?" he asked, numb. "Sure. That's allowed. Assuming you can find anyone still sober enough to care . . ."

They entered the building, which had once been a place for meditation, filled with individual rooms. It smelled sharply of incense, and each alcove had its own brazier for burning prayers. Those were now occupied for another sort of experience.

"I just want to rest a moment," she told Kharat, peeking into an empty room. It had a window. She could slip out that, maybe. "It's all so overwhelming."

"Oh." He looked over his shoulder toward the revel passing outside. His left hand was still coated with sweet paste.

Veil stepped into the chamber. When he tried to follow, she said, "I need a moment alone."

"I'm supposed to keep watch on you," he said, and prevented her from closing the door.

"Then watch," she said and settled down on the bench inside the cell. "From a distance."

He sighed and sat down on the floor of the hallway.

Now what? *A new face,* she thought. *What did he name me?* Kishi. It meant Mystery. She used a Memory she'd drawn earlier in the day, that of a woman from the market. In her mind, Shallan added touches to the clothing. A havah, ragged like the others, an exposed safehand.

It would do. She wished she could sketch it, but she could make this work. Now, what to do about her guard?

He probably hears voices, she thought. *I can use that.* She pressed her hand to Pattern, and wove sound.

"Go," she whispered, "hang on the wall of the hallway outside, next to him."

Pattern softly hummed his reply. She closed her eyes, and could faintly hear the words she'd woven to be whispered near Kharat.

Indulge.

Get something to drink.

Join the revel.

"You going to just sit there?" Kharat called in to her.

"Yes."

"I'm going to get something to drink. Don't leave."

"Fine."

He rose, then jogged out. By the time he got back, she had attached an illusion of Veil to a ruby mark, then left it there. It showed Veil resting on the bench, eyes closed, snoring softly.

Kishi passed Kharat in the hallway, stepping with glassy eyes. He didn't spare her a second glance, and instead settled down in the hallway with a large cup of wine to watch Veil.

Kishi joined the revel outside. A man there laughed and grabbed at her safehand, as if to pull her toward one of the rooms. Kishi dodged him and slipped farther inward, flowing through the stream of people. This "outer ring" seemed to round the entire Oathgate platform.

The secrets were farther toward the center. Nobody forbade Kishi as she left the flow of the outer ring, stepping between two buildings, heading inward.

⁙

The others stopped their small talk, and the officers' table grew very still as Kaladin settled down across from Azure.

The highmarshal laced her gloved hands before herself. "Kal, was it?" she said. "The lighteyed man with slave brands. How are you finding your time in the Wall Guard?"

"It's a well-run army, sir, and strangely welcoming of one such as myself." He then nodded over the highmarshal's shoulder. "I've never seen someone treat a Shardblade so casually. You just hang it on a peg?"

The others at the table watched with obviously held breaths.

"I'm not particularly worried about anyone taking her," Azure said. "I trust these men."

"It's still remarkable," Kaladin said. "Foolhardy, even."

Across the table, two places down from Azure, Lieutenant Noro raised his hands silently toward Kaladin in a pleading way. *Don't screw this up, Kal!*

But Azure smiled. "I never did get an explanation for that *shash* brand, soldier."

"I never gave a proper one, sir," Kaladin said. "I'm not fond of the memories that earned me the scar."

"How did you end up in this city?" Azure asked. "Sadeas's lands are far to the north. There are several armies of Voidbringers between here and there, by report."

"I flew. How about you, sir? You couldn't have been in the city long before the siege began; nobody talks of you earlier than that time. They say you appeared right when the Guard needed you."

"Perhaps I was always here, but merely blended in."

"With those scars? They may not spell out danger as explicitly as mine, but they'd have been memorable."

The rest of the table—lieutenants and the platoon captain—stared at Kaladin slack-jawed. Perhaps he was pushing too hard, acting too far above his station.

He'd never been good at acting his station though.

"Perhaps," Azure said, "one shouldn't be questioning my arrival. Be thankful someone was here when the city needed them."

"I *am* thankful," Kaladin said. "Your reputation with these men commends you, Azure, and extreme times can excuse a great deal. Eventually though, you'll need to come clean. These men deserve to know who—exactly—is commanding them."

"And what about you, Kal?" She took a spoonful of curry and rice—men's food, which she ate with gusto. "Do they deserve to know your past? Shouldn't you come clean?"

"Perhaps."

"I am your commanding officer, you realize. You *should* answer me when I ask questions."

"I've given answers," Kaladin said. "If they aren't the ones you want, then perhaps your questions aren't very good."

Noro gasped audibly.

"And you, Kal? You make statements, dripping with implications. You want answers? Why not just *ask*?"

Storms. She was right. He'd been dancing around serious questions. Kaladin looked her in the eyes. "Why won't you let anyone talk about the fact that you're a woman, Azure? Noro, don't faint. You'll embarrass us all."

The lieutenant thumped his forehead against the table, groaning softly. The captainlord, with whom Kaladin hadn't interacted much, had gone red-faced.

"They came up with this game on their own," Azure said. "They're Alethi, so they need an excuse for why they're listening to a woman giving military orders. Pretending there's some mystery focuses them on that, instead of on masculine pride. I find the entire thing silly." She leaned forward. "Tell me honestly. Did you come here chasing me?"

Chasing you? Kaladin cocked his head.

Drums sounded in the near distance.

It took a moment for them, even Kaladin, to register what that meant. Then Kaladin and Azure threw themselves back from the bench at nearly the same time. "To arms!" Kaladin shouted. "There's an attack on the wall!"

⁂

The next ring inward on the Oathgate platform was filled with people crawling.

Kishi stood at the perimeter, watching a multitude of men and women in ragged finery crawl past her, giggling, moaning, or gasping. Each seemed in the thrall of a different emotion, and each stared with an openly maddened expression. She thought she recognized a few from the descriptions of lighteyes who had disappeared into the palace, though in their state, it was hard to tell.

A woman with long hair dragging on the ground looked toward her, grinning with clenched teeth and bleeding gums. She crawled, one hand after another, her havah shredded, faded. She was followed by a man wearing rings glowing with Stormlight, in contrast to his ripped clothing. He giggled incessantly.

The food on the tables here rotted, and was infested with decayspren. Kishi wavered at the edge of the ring. She should have kept to the outer ring; she didn't belong here. There was food aplenty behind her. Laughter and reveling. It seemed to pull her back, inviting her to join the eternal, beautiful walk.

Within that ring, time wouldn't matter. She could forget Shallan, and what she'd done. Just . . . just give in . . .

Pattern hummed. Veil gasped, letting Kishi burst from her, Lightweaving collapsing. Storms. She had to be away from this place. It was doing things to her brain. Strange things, even for *her*.

Not yet. She pulled her coat tight, then picked her way across the street full of crawling people. No bonfire lit her way, only the moon overhead and the light of the jewelry the people wore.

Storms. Where had they all gone for the storm? Their moaning, chittering, and babbling chased her as she crossed the street, then hurried down a dark pathway between two monastery buildings, inward. Toward the control building, which should be right ahead.

The voices in her head combined from whispers to a kind of surging rhythm. A thumping of impressions, followed by a pause, followed by another surge. Almost like . . .

She stepped between the buildings and entered a moonlit square, colored violet from Salas above. Instead of the control building, she found an overgrown mass. Something had covered the entire structure, like the Midnight Mother had enveloped the gemstone pillar beneath Urithiru.

The dark mass pulsed and throbbed. Black veins as thick as a man's leg ran from it and melded with the ground nearby. A heart. It beat an irregular rhythm, *bum-ba-ba-bum* instead of the common *ba-bum* of her own heartbeat.

Give in.

Join the revel.

Shallan, listen to me.

She shook herself. That last voice had been different. She'd heard it before, hadn't she?

She looked to the side, and found her shadow on the ground, pointed the wrong way, toward the moonlight instead of away from it. The shadow crept up the wall, with eyes that were white holes, glowing faintly.

I'm not your enemy. But the heart is a trap. Take caution.

Distantly, drums started sounding on the top of the wall. The Void-bringers were attacking.

It all threatened to overwhelm her. The thumping heart, the strange processions in rings around it, the drums and the panic that the Fused were coming for *her* because she'd been *seen*.

Veil seized control. She'd accomplished her goal, she'd scouted the area, and she had information about the Oathgate. It was time to get out.

She turned and—forcibly—put on Kishi's face. She crossed the stream of crawling, moaning people. She flowed back into the outer ring of revelers, before slipping out.

She didn't check on her guide. She walked to the rim of the Oathgate platform and, without a look back, leaped off.

Our revelation is fueled by the theory that the Unmade can perhaps be captured like ordinary spren. It would require a special prison. And Melishi.

—From drawer 30-20, third emerald

Kaladin charged up the stairwell beside Highmarshal Azure, the sound of drums breaking the air like echoes of thunder from the departed storm. He counted the beats.

Storms. That's my section under assault.

"Damnation these creatures!" Azure muttered. "I'm missing something. Like white on black . . ." She glanced at Kaladin. "Just tell me. Who are you?"

"Who are *you*?"

The two burst out of the stairwell onto the wall's top, entering a scene of chaos. The soldiers on duty had lit the enormous oil lamps on the tops of the towers, giving light to the dark walls. Fused swooped between them, trailing dark violet light, attacking with long, bloodied lances.

Men lay screaming on the ground or huddled in pairs, holding up shields as if trying to hide from the nightmares above.

Kaladin and Azure exchanged a look, then nodded to one another. *Later.*

She broke left and Kaladin dashed right, shouting for men to form up. Syl spun around his head, concerned, anxious. Kaladin scooped a shield off the ground and seized a soldier by the arm, towing him around and locking shields. A swooping lance *clanged* off the metal, sending a jolt through Kaladin. The Voidbringer flew past.

Pained, Kaladin ignored the wounded and bleeding who crawled with corrupted painspren. He pulled the scattered remnants of the Eighth Platoon back together while his own men stumbled to a halt outside the stairwell. These were their friends, the people with whom they shared a barrack.

"To your right and up!" Syl shouted.

Kaladin set himself and used his shield to push aside the lance of a Voidbringer who soared past. A second Voidbringer followed, wearing a long skirt of rippling crimson cloth. The way she flew was almost mesmerizing. . . . Right up until her lance pinned Captain Deedanor against the wall's battlements, then lifted him and tossed him over.

He screamed as he plummeted toward the ground below. Kaladin almost broke rank and ran for him, but held himself in the line by force. He reached, by instinct, for the Stormlight in his pouch—but held himself back. Using it for Lashing would attract screamers, and in this darkness, even drawing in a small amount would reveal him for what he was. The Fused would all attack him together; he would risk undermining the mission to save the entire city.

Today, he protected best through discipline, order, and keeping a level head. "Squads One and Two, with me!" he shouted. "Vardinar, you've got Five and Six; have your men hand out pikes, then grab bows and get to the tower's top. Noro, take squads Three and Four and set up on the wall walk just past the tower. My men will hold here on this side. Go, *go!*"

Nobody voiced a complaint as they scrambled to do as he said. Kaladin heard shouts from the highmarshal farther down the wall, but didn't have a chance to see how she was doing. As his two squads finally got a proper shield wall mounted, a human corpse slammed down onto the wall walk nearby. It had been dropped from very high up—or perhaps it had been Lashed into the sky and had only now fallen. Most of the wounded men were archers from the Eighth Platoon; it looked like they'd been swept from the top of the tower.

We can't fight these things, Kaladin thought. The Voidbringers attacked in sweeping dives, coming in from all directions. It was impossible to maintain a normal formation beneath that assault.

Syl shifted into the shape of a girl and looked at him questioningly. He shook his head. He *could* fight without Stormlight. He'd protected people long before he could fly.

He started to call out orders, but a Fused passed by, slapping at their pikes with a large shield. Before the men could get them reoriented, another *crashed* down into the center of them, sending soldiers stumbling. A violet glow steamed from the creature's body as it swept around with its lance, wielding it like an oversized staff.

Kaladin ducked by instinct, trying to maneuver his pike. The Fused grinned as the formation disintegrated. It was male, reminiscent of a Parshendi, with layered plates of chitin armor creeping down across its forehead and rising from cheeks that were marbled black and red.

Kaladin leveled his pike, but the creature lunged along it and pressed its hand against Kaladin's chest. He felt himself grow lighter, but also suddenly begin to fall backward.

The creature had *Lashed* him.

Kaladin fell back, like he was toppling off a ledge, falling along the wall toward a group of his men. The Fused wanted Kaladin to crash into them, but it had made a mistake.

The sky was *his*.

Kaladin responded immediately to the Lashing, and reoriented himself in the blink of an eye. *Down* became the direction he was falling: along the walkway, toward the towering guard post. His men seemed to be stuck to the side of a cliff, turning toward him, horrified.

Kaladin was able to shove against the stone with the end of his pike, moving him to the side so he whooshed past his men instead of crashing into them. Syl joined him as a ribbon, and he twisted, falling feet-first along the walkway toward the guard tower below.

He was able to nudge himself so he fell right into the open doorway. He dropped the pike, then caught the lip of the doorway as he passed through it. He stopped with a jarring lurch, arms protesting with pain, but that maneuver slowed him enough. When he swung and let go, he dropped through the room—past the dining table, which seemed glued to the wall—and landed on the opposite wall, inside the building. He stepped over to the other doorway, which looked out onto the walk where he'd positioned Noro's squad. Beard and Ved held pikes toward the sky, looking anxious.

"Kaladin!" Syl said. "Above!"

He looked upward and out the doorway he'd come through. The Voidbringer who had Lashed him came soaring downward, carrying a lance. It curved to bypass the tower, preparing to whip around and attack Beard and the men on the other side.

Kaladin growled and dashed along the inside wall of the tower, pulled himself up past the table, then *hurled* himself out a window.

He crashed into the Voidbringer in midair, shoving the creature's lance to the side.

"Leave. My. Men. *Alone!*"

Kaladin clung to the clothing of the monster, spinning in the air dozens of feet above the dark city, sparkling with the light of spheres in windows or lanterns. The Voidbringer Lashed them higher, falsely assuming that the more height it had, the more advantage it would gain over Kaladin.

Holding tightly with his left hand, wind whipping around them, Kaladin reached out with his right hand and summoned Syl as a long knife. She appeared immediately, and Kaladin shoved the diminutive Shardblade into the creature's stomach.

The Voidbringer grunted and looked at him with deep, glowing red eyes. It dropped its lance and began to claw at Kaladin while spinning itself in the air, trying to throw him free.

They can survive wounds, Kaladin thought, gritting his teeth as the thing gripped at his neck. *Like Radiants. That Voidlight sustains them.*

Kaladin still refrained from drawing in his own Stormlight. He suffered the Fused's Lashings as it spun them in the air, shouting in a language Kaladin didn't understand. He tried to maneuver the Shardknife and cut the thing's spine. The weapon was insanely sharp, but for the moment, leverage and disorientation were bigger factors.

The Voidbringer grunted, then Lashed itself—with Kaladin hanging on—back downward toward the wall. They fell quickly, a double or triple Lashing, spiraling and screaming toward the wall walk.

Kaladin! Syl's voice, in his head. *I sense something . . . something about its power. Cut upward, toward the heart.*

The city, the battle, the sky—all became a blur. Kaladin forced his Blade farther into the creature's chest, pushing it upward, seeking . . .

The Shardknife struck something brittle and hard.

The Fused's red eyes winked out.

Kaladin twisted, putting the corpse beneath him and the wall walk. They hit hard, and he bounced off the corpse, then hit the stones with a *crack*. He groaned, eyes flashing with pain, and was forced—by instinct—to take in a breath of Stormlight to heal the damage of the fall.

That Light flowed through him, reknitting bones, repairing organs. It was used up in a moment, and he forced himself not to draw in more, instead pushing himself up and shaking his head.

The Voidbringer stared sightlessly from the wall walk beside him. It was dead.

Ahead, the other Fused began streaking away in retreat, leaving a broken and battered group of guards. Kaladin stumbled to his feet; his section of the wall was empty, save for the dead and the dying. He didn't recognize any; he'd hit the wall some fifty feet away from his platoon's position.

Syl landed on his shoulder and patted him on the side of the head.

Painspren littered the wall, crawling this way and that, in the shape of hands without skin.

This city is doomed, Kaladin thought as he knelt by one of the wounded and quickly prepared a bandage by slicing up a fallen cloak. *Storms. We might all be doomed. We're not anywhere near ready to fight these things.*

It looked like Noro's squad, at least, had survived. They jogged down the wall and gathered around the Voidbringer Kaladin had killed, nudging it with the butts of their pikes. Kaladin tied off a tourniquet, then moved to another man, whose head he wrapped.

Soon, army surgeons flooded the wall. Kaladin stepped back, bloodied—but more angry than tired. He turned to Noro, Beard, and the others, who had gathered around him.

"You killed one," Beard said, feeling at his arm with the empty glyph-ward. "Storms. You actually *killed* one, Kal."

"How many have you brought down?" Kaladin asked, realizing that he'd never asked. "How many has the Wall Guard killed during the assaults these last weeks?"

His men shared glances.

"Azure drove a few off," Noro said. "They're afraid of her Shardblade. But as for Voidbringers killed . . . this would be the first, Kal."

Storms. Even worse, the one he'd killed would be reborn. Unless the Heralds set up their prison again, Kaladin couldn't ever really kill one of the Fused.

"I need to talk to Azure," he said, striding down the wall walk. "Noro, report."

"None fallen, sir, though Vaceslv took a gash to the chest. He's with the surgeons, and should pull through."

"Good. Squad, you're with me."

He found Azure surveying the Eighth Platoon's losses near their guard tower. She had her cloak off and held oddly in one hand, wrapped around her forearm, with part of it draping down below. Her unsheathed Shard-blade glittered, long and silvery.

Kaladin stepped up to her, the sleeve of his uniform stained dark with the blood of the Voidbringer he'd killed. Azure looked tired, and she gestured with her sword outward. "Have a look."

Lights lit the horizon. Sphere lights. Thousands upon thousands of them—far more than he'd seen on previous nights. They blanketed the landscape.

"That's the entire enemy army," Azure said. "I'd bet my red life on it. Somehow, they marched them *through* that storm earlier today. It won't be long now. They'll have to attack before the next highstorm. A few days

at most."

"I need to know what's going on here, Azure," Kaladin said. "How are you getting food for this army?"

She drew her lips to a line.

"He killed one, Highmarshal," Beard whispered from behind him. "Storms . . . he took one of them down. Grabbed on like he was mounting a storming horse, then rode the bastard through the sky."

The woman studied him, and reluctantly Kaladin summoned Syl as a Shardblade. Noro's eyes bulged, and Ved nearly fainted—though Beard just grinned.

"I'm here," Kaladin said, resting the Sylblade on his shoulder, "on orders from King Elhokar and the Blackthorn. It's my job to save Kholinar. And it's time you started talking to me."

She smiled at him. "Come with me."

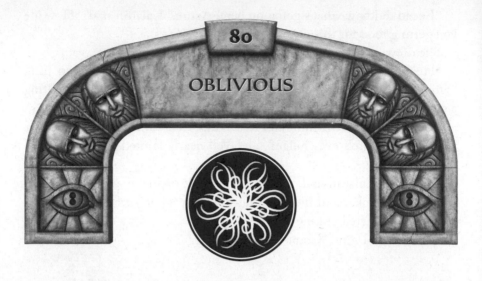

*Ba-Ado-Mishram has somehow Connected with the parsh people,
as Odium once did. She provides Voidlight and facilitates forms
of power. Our strike team is going to imprison her.*

—From drawer 30-20, fourth emerald

G rund wasn't at his normal spot inside the corner of the broken
shop.

The place hadn't fared well during the Everstorm; the ceiling was sagging even *more,* and a snarl of tree branches had been blown in through the window, littering the floor. Veil frowned, calling his name. After fleeing the Oathgate platform, she'd met up with Vathah, who had been waiting as instructed.

She'd sent Vathah back to report to the king, and probably should have gone herself. But she hadn't been able to shake the eerie disquiet of her trip through the revel. Going back home would have left her too much time to think.

Veil wanted to be out working instead. Monsters and Voidbringers were something she couldn't comprehend, but starving children . . . she could do something about that. She'd taken the two remaining sacks of food and gone to help the city's people.

If she could find them.

"Grund?" Veil repeated, leaning farther in through the window. Before, he'd always been up at this time. Perhaps he'd finally moved out of the building, like all the others had. Or maybe he hadn't gotten back from the stormshelter yet, following the Everstorm.

She turned to leave, but Grund finally stumbled into the room. The little urchin tucked his malformed hand into his pocket and scowled at her. That was odd. He normally seemed so happy when she arrived.

"What's wrong?" she asked.

"Nothin'," he said. "Thought you was someone else." He gave her a grin.

Veil fished a few pieces of flatbread from her bag. "Not much today, I'm afraid. I wanted to make sure to stop by though. The information you gave us on that book was very helpful."

He licked his lips, holding out his hands. She tossed him the flatbread, and he took an eager bite. "What do you need next?"

"Nothing right now," Veil said.

"Come on. There has to be something I can do to help. Something you want, right?"

Too desperate, Veil thought. *What is beneath the surface here? What have I missed?*

"I'll consider," she said. "Grund, is everything all right?"

"Right. Sure, everything is great!" He paused. "Unless it shouldn't be?"

Pattern hummed softly on Veil's coat. She agreed.

"I'll stop by again in a few days. Should have a big haul then." Veil tipped her hat to the urchin, then slipped back into the market. It was late, but people lingered. Nobody wanted to be alone on days after the Everstorm came. Some looked toward the wall, where those Fused had attacked. But that sort of thing happened almost daily, so it didn't cause too much of a stir.

Veil drew more attention than she'd have wanted. She'd exposed herself to them, given up her face.

"Grund tells lies, doesn't he?" Pattern whispered.

"Yeah. I'm not sure why, or what about."

As she wove into the market, she put her hand before her face, changing it with a wave of the fingers. She took her hat off, folded it, and covertly Lightwove it to look like a waterskin. Each was a little change that nobody would notice. She tucked her hair into her coat, made it look shorter, then finally closed her coat and changed the clothing underneath. When she took off the coat and folded it up, she was no longer Veil, but a market guard she'd drawn earlier.

Rolled coat under her arm, she lingered at a corner and waited to see if anyone passed, looking for Veil. She didn't spot anyone, though her training with Ishnah at spotting tails wasn't yet extensive. She threaded her way back through the crowd to Grund's shop again. She lingered near the wall, then eased toward the window, listening.

". . . Told you we shouldn't have given her the book," a voice was saying inside.

"This is pathetic," another said. "Pathetic! That was the best you could do?"

She heard a grunt, and a whimper. *That's Grund.* Veil cursed softly, scrambling around to look in through the window. A group of thugs was chewing on the flatbread she'd brought. Grund lay in the corner, whimpering and holding his stomach.

Veil felt a flash of rage, and angerspren immediately boiled around her, pools that sprayed red and orange. She shouted at the men and dashed for the doorway. They immediately scattered, though one slammed a cudgel onto Grund's head with a sickening *crunch.*

By the time she reached Grund, the men had vanished farther into the building. She heard the door in the back slam closed. Pattern appeared in her hand as a Shardblade, but Stormfather! She couldn't give chase—not and leave the poor child here.

Veil dismissed Pattern and knelt, aghast at the bloody wound in Grund's head. It was bad. The skull was broken, bleeding . . .

He blinked, dazed. "V . . . Veil?"

"Storms, Grund," she whispered. "I . . ." What could she do? "Help? Help, somebody! There's a wounded child in here!"

Grund whimpered, then whispered something. Veil leaned close, feeling useless.

"Hate . . ." Grund whispered. "Hate you."

"It's all right," Veil said. "They're gone now. They . . . they ran. I'll help." Bandage. She cut at her shirttails with her knife.

"Hate you," Grund whispered.

"It's me, Grund. Not those others."

"Why couldn't you leave me alone?" he whispered. "They killed them all. My friends. Tai . . ."

Veil pressed the cloth against his head wound, and he winced. Storms. "Quiet. Don't exert yourself."

"Hate you," he repeated.

"I brought you food, Grund."

"You drew *them,*" he hissed. "You strutted around, throwing food. You thought people wouldn't notice?" He closed his eyes. "Had to sit all day, wait for . . . for you. My *life* was waiting for you. If I wasn't here when you came, or if I tried to hide the food, they beat me."

"How long?" she whispered, feeling her confidence shake.

"Since the first day, you storming woman. Hate . . . hate you . . . Others too. We all . . . hate you . . ."

She sat with him as his breathing slowed, then cut off. Finally she knelt back, bloodied cloth in her hands.

Veil could handle this. She'd seen death. It . . . it was life . . . on the street . . . and . . .

Too much. Too much for one day.

Shallan blinked tears from the corners of her eyes. Pattern hummed. "Shallan," he said. "The boy, he spoke of the others. Others?"

Storms! She threw herself to her feet and pushed out into the night, dropping Veil's hat and coat in her haste. She ran for Muri—the mother who had once been a seamstress. Shallan shoved through the market until she reached the packed tenement where the seamstress lived. She crossed the common room, then breathed a sigh of relief as she found Muri alive, inside her small room. The woman was hurriedly tossing clothing into a sack, her eldest daughter clutching a similar one.

She looked up, saw Shallan—who still looked like Veil—and cursed to herself. "You." The frown lines and scowl were unfamiliar. She'd always seemed so pleasant.

"You know already?" Shallan asked. "About Grund?"

"Grund?" Muri snapped. "All I know is that the Grips are angry about something. I'm not going to take a chance."

"The Grips?"

"How oblivious are you, woman? The gang in charge of this area has had toughs watching us all for when you next arrived. The one watching me met with another, and they had a quiet argument, then took off. I heard my name. So I'm leaving."

"They took the food I gave you, didn't they? Storms, they *killed* Grund!"

Muri stopped, then shook her head. "Poor kid. Better you than he." She cursed, gathering her sacks and shoving her children toward the common room. "We always had to sit here, waiting for you and your storming sack of goodies."

"I'm . . . I'm sorry."

Muri left into the night with her children. Shallan watched them go, feeling numb. Empty. She quietly sank down in Muri's deserted room, still holding the cloth with Grund's blood.

81

ITHI AND HER SISTER

We are uncertain the effect this will have on the parsh. At the very least, it should deny them forms of power. Melishi is confident, but Naze-daughter-Kuzodo warns of unintended side effects.

—From drawer 30-20, fifth emerald

My name is Kaladin," he said, standing in the barrack common room—which had been emptied at the highmarshal's order. Noro's squad had remained by Kaladin's request, and Azure had invited in Battalionlord Hadinar—a stocky, bejowled fellow, one of Azure's primary officers. The only other person in the room was the fidgety ardent who painted glyphwards for the platoon.

Soft blue spherelight bathed the table where most of them sat. Kaladin stood instead, washing the blood from his hands with a damp rag at a water basin.

"Kaladin," Azure mused. "A regal name. What's your house?"

"They just call me Stormblessed. If you need proof of my orders from the king, it can be arranged."

"Let's pretend, for the sake of conversation, that I believe you," Azure said. "What do you want from us?"

"I need to know how you're using a Soulcaster without drawing the attention of the screaming spren. The secret might be essential to my work to save the city."

Azure nodded, then rose and walked toward the back of the barrack. She used a key to open the back room. Kaladin had glanced in there before though. It only held some supplies.

The rest of them followed Azure into the room, where she slipped a small hook between two stones and threw a hidden latch. This let her remove a stone, revealing a handle. She heaved, pulling open a doorway. The light of a few handheld spheres revealed a small corridor that ran down the middle of the city wall.

"You cut a tunnel in one of the *windblades*, sir?" Beard asked, shocked.

"This has been here longer than any of us have been alive, soldier," Battalionlord Hadinar said. "It is a quick, secret way between posts. There are even a few hidden stairwells up to the top."

They had to go single file inside. Beard followed behind Kaladin, scrunched up against him in the confines. "Um, so Kal, you . . . you know the Blackthorn?"

"Better than most."

"And . . . ahem . . . you know—"

"That the two of you never went swimming together in the Purelake?" Kaladin said. "Yes, though I suspect the rest of the squad guessed that, Beard."

"Yeah," he said, glancing back at the others. He exhaled softly. "I figured you'd never believe the truth, since it was actually the Azish emperor. . . ."

This corridor, cut through the stone, reminded Kaladin of the strata of Urithiru. They reached a trapdoor in the floor, which Azure opened with a key. A short trip down a ladder—which had a dumbwaiter beside it, with ropes and pulleys—led them to a large room filled with sacks of grain. Kaladin held up a sphere, revealing a jagged wall with chunks cut out of it in a distinctly uneven way.

"I come down here every night or so," Azure said, pointing with a gloved hand, "and cut out blocks with my Blade. I have nightmares about the city collapsing down on us, but I don't know of another way to get enough stone—at least not without drawing even more attention."

On the other side of the chamber, they found yet another locked door. Azure knocked twice, then opened this one, revealing a smaller room occupied by an aged female ardent. She knelt beside a stone block, and wore a distinctive fabrial on her hand—one that glowed powerfully with light from the emeralds it contained.

The woman had an inhuman look to her; she seemed to be growing vines under her skin, and they peeked out around her eyes, growing from the corners and spreading down her face like runners of ivy.

She stood and bowed to Azure. A real Soulcaster. So . . . Azure wasn't doing it herself? "How?" Kaladin asked. "Why didn't the screamers come for you?"

Azure pointed at the sides of the room, and for the first time Kaladin noticed the walls were covered in reflective metal plates. He frowned and rested his fingers against one, and found it cool to the touch. This wasn't steel, was it?

"Soon after the strangeness at the palace began," Azure said, "a man pulled a chull cart up to the front of our barrack. He had these sheets of metal in the back. He was . . . an odd fellow. I've had interactions with him before."

"Angular features?" Kaladin guessed. "Quick with an insult. Silly and straight, somehow all at once?"

"You know him, I see," Azure said. "He warned us to only Soulcast inside a room lined with this metal. So far as we can tell, it prevents the screamers from sensing us. Unfortunately, it also blocks spanreeds from contacting the outside.

"We keep poor Ithi and her sister working nonstop, trading off the Soulcaster. Feeding the entire city would be an impossible task for the two of them, but we've been able to at least keep our army strong, with some to spare."

Damnation, Kaladin thought, inspecting the reflective walls. This wasn't going to help him use his powers without notice.

"All right, Stormblessed," Azure said. "I've opened our secrets to you. Now you'll tell me how the king could expect *one man*, even a Shardbearer, to be able to save this city."

"There's a device in Kholinar," he said, "of ancient design. It can instantly transport large groups of people across great distances." He turned toward Azure and the others. "The Kholin armies wait to join us here. All we need to do is activate the device—something that only a select few people can do."

The soldiers looked stunned—all but Azure, who perked up. "Really? You're serious?"

Kaladin nodded.

"Great! Let's get this thing working! Where is it?"

Kaladin took a deep breath. "Well, that happens to be the problem. . . ."

Surely this will bring—at long last—the end to war that the Heralds promised us.

—From drawer 30-20, final emerald

She huddled someplace. She'd forgotten where.

For a while, she'd been . . . everybody. A hundred faces, cycling one after another. She searched them for comfort. Surely she could find *someone* who didn't hurt.

All the nearby refugees had fled, naming her a spren. They left her with those hundred faces, in silence, until her Stormlight died off.

That left only Shallan. Unfortunately.

Darkness. A candle snuffed out. A scream cut off. With nothing to see, her mind provided images.

Her father, his face turning purple as she strangled him, singing a lullaby.

Her mother, dead with burned eyes.

Tyn, run through by Pattern.

Kabsal, shaking on the floor as he succumbed to poison.

Yalb, the incorrigible sailor from *Wind's Pleasure*, dead in the depths of the sea.

An unnamed coachman, murdered by members of the Ghostbloods.

Now Grund, his head opened up.

Veil had tried to help these people, but had succeeded only in making their lives worse. The lie that was Veil became suddenly manifest. She *hadn't* lived on the streets and she *didn't* know how to help people. Pretending to have experience didn't mean she actually did.

Veil had always thought to herself that Shallan could handle the big picture, the Voidbringers and the Unmade. Now she had to confront the truth that she had *no idea* what to do. She couldn't get to the Oathgate. It was guarded by an ancient spren that could get inside her brain.

The whole city was depending on her, but she hadn't even been able to save a little beggar boy. As she curled up on the floor, Grund's death seemed a shadow of everything else, of her good intentions turned arrogant.

Everywhere she trod, death haunted her. Every face she wore was a lie to pretend she could stop it.

Couldn't she be somebody who didn't hurt, just once?

Light pushed shadows before it, long and slender. She blinked, momentarily transfixed. How many days had it been since she'd seen light? A figure stepped into the common room outside her little hole of a chamber. She was still in the long room Muri had lived in.

She sniffled softly.

The newcomer brought his light to her doorway, then carefully stepped inside and settled down across from her, his back against the wall. The room was narrow enough that his legs stretched out and touched the wall beside her. She had hers drawn up, knees against her chest, head resting on them.

Wit didn't speak. He put his sphere on the floor, and let her have the silence.

"I should have known better," she finally whispered.

"Perhaps," Wit said.

"Giving out so much food only drew predators. Foolish. I should have focused on the Oathgate."

"Again, perhaps."

"It's so hard, Wit. When I wear Veil's face . . . I . . . I have to think like her. Seeing the larger scope grows difficult when she takes over. And I *want* her to take over, because she's not me."

"The thieves who killed that child have been seen to," Wit said.

She looked up at him.

"When some of the men in the market heard what had happened," Wit continued, "they finally formed the militia they'd been talking about. They rushed the Grips, forcing them to give up the murderer, then disperse. I apologize for not acting sooner; I had been distracted by other tasks. You'll be pleased to know that some of the food you gave away was still in their base."

"Was it worth that boy's life?" Shallan whispered.

"I cannot judge the worth of a life. I would not dare to attempt it."

"Muri said it would be better if I were dead."

"As *I* lack the experience to decide the worth of a life, I sincerely doubt that she has somehow obtained it. You tried to help the people of the market. You mostly failed. This is life. The longer you live, the more you fail. Failure is the mark of a life well lived. In turn, the only way to live without failure is to be of no use to anyone. Trust me, I've practiced."

She sniffled, looking away. "I have to become Veil to escape the memories, but I don't have the experience that she pretends to have. I haven't lived her life."

"No," Wit said softly. "You've lived a harsher one, haven't you?"

"Yet still, somehow, a naive one." She drew in a deep, ragged breath. She had to stop this. She knew she had to get over the tantrum and go back to the tailor's shop.

She'd do it. She'd shove all this into the back of her mind, with everything else she ignored. They could all fester together.

Wit settled back. "Have you heard the story of the Girl Who Looked Up?"

Shallan didn't reply.

"It's a story from long ago," Wit said. He cupped his hands around the sphere on the floor. "Things were different in that time. A wall kept out the storms, but everyone ignored it. All but one girl, who looked up one day, and contemplated it."

"Why is there a wall?" Shallan whispered.

"Oh, so you *do* know it? Good." He leaned down, blowing at the crem dust on the floor. It swirled up, making a figure of a girl. It gave the brief impression of her standing before a wall, but then disintegrated back into dust. He tried again, and it swirled a little higher this time, but still fell back to dust.

"A little help?" he asked. He pushed a bag of spheres across the ground toward Shallan.

Shallan sighed, then picked up the bag and drew in the Stormlight. It started to rage within her, demanding to be used, so she stood up and breathed out, Weaving it into an illusion she'd done once before. A pristine village, and a young girl standing and looking upward, toward an impossibly tall wall in the distance.

The illusion made the room seem to vanish. Somehow, Shallan painted the walls and ceiling in precisely the right way, making them disappear into the landscape—become part of it. She hadn't made them invisible; they were merely covered up in a way that made it seem Shallan and Wit were standing in another place.

This was . . . this was more than she'd ever done before. But was *she* really doing it? Shallan shook her head and stepped up beside the girl, who wore long scarves.

Wit stepped up on the other side. "Hmmm," he said. "Not bad. But it's not dark enough."

"What?"

"I thought you knew the story," Wit said, tapping the air. The color and light bled from her illusion, leaving them standing in the darkness of night, lit only by a frail set of stars. The wall was an enormous blot before them. "In these days, there was no light."

"No light . . ."

"Of course, even without light, people still had to live, didn't they? That's what people do. I hasten to guess it's the *first* thing they learn how to do. So they lived in the darkness, farmed in the darkness, ate in the darkness." He waved behind him. People stumbled about in the village, feeling their way to different activities, barely able to see by the starlight.

In this context, strange though it seemed, some pieces of the story as she'd told it made sense. When the girl went up to people and asked, "Why is there a wall?" it was obvious why they found it so easy to ignore.

The illusion followed Wit's words as the girl in the scarves asked several people about the wall. *Don't go beyond it, or you shall die.*

"And so," Wit said, "she decided that the only way she'd find answers would be to climb the wall herself." He glanced at Shallan. "Was she stupid or bold?"

"How should I know?"

"Wrong answer. She was both."

"It *wasn't* stupid. If nobody asked questions, then we would never learn anything."

"What of the wisdom of her elders?"

"They offered no explanation for why she shouldn't ask about the wall! No rationalization, no justification. There's a difference between listening to your elders and just being as frightened as everyone else."

Wit smiled, the sphere in his hand lighting his face. "Funny, isn't it, how so many of our stories start the same way, but have opposing endings? In half, the child ignores her parents, wanders out into the woods, and gets eaten. In the other half she discovers great wonders. There aren't many stories about the kids who say, 'Yes, I shall not go into the forest. I'm glad my parents explained that is where the monsters live.'"

"Is that what you're trying to teach me, then?" Shallan snapped. "The fine distinction between choosing for yourself and ignoring good advice?"

"I'm a terrible teacher." He waved his hand as the girl reached the wall after a long hike. She started to climb. "Fortunately, I am an *artist,* and not a teacher."

"People learn things from art."

"Blasphemy! Art is not art if it has a *function*."

Shallan rolled her eyes.

"Take this fork," Wit said. He waved his hand. Some of her Stormlight split off from her, spinning above his hand and making an image of a floating fork in the darkness. "It has a use. Eating. Now, if it were to be ornamented by a master artisan, would that change its function?" The fork grew intricate embossing in the form of growing leaves. "No, of course not. It has the same use, ornamented or not. The *art* is the part that serves no purpose."

"It makes me happy, Wit. That's a purpose."

He grinned, and the fork disappeared.

"Weren't we in the middle of a story about a girl climbing a wall?" Shallan asked.

"Yes, but that part takes *forever*," he said. "I'm finding things to occupy us."

"We could just skip the boring part."

"Skip?" Wit said, aghast. "*Skip* part of a *story*?"

Shallan snapped her fingers, and the illusion shifted so that they stood atop the wall in the darkness. The girl in the scarves finally—after toiling many days—pulled herself up beside them.

"You wound me," Wit said. "What happens next?"

"The girl finds *steps*," Shallan said. "And the girl realizes that the wall wasn't to keep something in, but to keep her and her people out."

"Because?"

"Because we're monsters."

Wit stepped over to Shallan, then quietly folded his arms around her. She trembled, then twisted, burying her face in his shirt.

"You're not a monster, Shallan," Wit whispered. "Oh, child. The *world* is monstrous at times, and there are those who would have you believe that you are terrible by association."

"I am."

"No. For you see, it flows the other direction. You are not worse for your association with the world, but it is better for its association with *you*."

She pressed against him, shivering. "What do I do, Wit?" she whispered. "I know . . . I know I shouldn't be in so much pain. I had to . . ." She took a deep breath. "I had to kill them. I *had* to. But now I've said the words, and I can't ignore it anymore. So I should . . . should just die too, for having done it. . . ."

Wit waved to the side, toward where the girl in the scarves still overlooked a new world. What was that long pack she had set down beside her?

"So you remember," Wit said gently, "the rest of the story?"

"It's not important. We found the moral already. The wall kept people out."

"Why?"

"Because . . ." What had she told Pattern before, when she'd been showing him this story?

"Because," Wit said, pointing, "beyond the wall was God's Light."

It burst alight in a sudden explosion: a brilliant and powerful brightness that lit the landscape beyond the wall. Shallan gasped as it shone over them. The girl in the scarves gasped in turn, and saw the world in all its colors for the first time.

"She climbed down the steps," Shallan whispered, watching the girl run down the steps, scarves streaming behind her. "She hid among the creatures who lived on this side. She sneaked up to the Light and she brought it back with her. To the other side. To the . . . to the land of shadows . . ."

"Yes indeed," Wit said as the scene played out, the girl in the scarves slipping up to the grand source of light, then breaking off a little piece in her hand.

An incredible chase.

The girl climbing the steps frantically.

A crazed descent.

And then . . . light, for the first time in the village, followed by the coming of the storms—boiling over the wall.

"The people suffered," Wit said, "but each storm brought light renewed, for it could never be put back, now that it had been taken. And people, for all their hardship, would never choose to go back. Not now that they could *see*."

The illusion faded, leaving the two of them standing in the common room of the building, Muri's little chamber off to the side. Shallan pulled back, ashamed at having wept on his shirt.

"Do you wish," Wit asked, "that you could go back to not being able to see?"

"No," she whispered.

"Then live. And let your failures be part of you."

"That sounds . . . that sounds an awful lot like a moral, Wit. Like you're trying to do something *useful*."

"Well, as I said, we all fail now and then." He swept his hands to the sides, as if brushing something away from Shallan. Stormlight curled out from her right and left, swirling, then forming into two identical versions of Shallan. They stood with ruddy hair, mottled faces, and sweeping white coats that belonged to someone else.

"Wit . . ." she started.

"Hush." He walked up to one of the illusions, inspecting it, tapping his chin with his index finger. "A lot has happened to this poor girl, hasn't it?"

"Many people have suffered more and they get along fine."

"Fine?"

Shallan shrugged, unable to banish the truths she'd spoken. The distant memory of singing to her father as she strangled him. The people she'd failed, the problems she'd caused. The illusion of Shallan to the left gasped, then backed up against the wall of the room, shaking her head. She collapsed, head down against her legs, curling up.

"Poor fool," Shallan whispered. "Everything she tries only makes the world worse. She was broken by her father, then broke herself in turn. She's worthless, Wit." She gritted her teeth, found herself sneering. "It's not really her fault, but she's still worthless."

Wit grunted, then pointed at the second illusion, standing behind them. "And that one?"

"No different," Shallan said, tiring of this game. She gave the second illusion the same memories. Father. Helaran. Failing Jasnah. Everything.

The illusory Shallan stiffened. Then set her jaw and stood there.

"Yes, I see," Wit said, strolling up to her. "No different."

"What are you doing to my illusions?" Shallan snapped.

"Nothing. They're the same in every detail."

"Of course they're not," Shallan said, tapping the illusion, feeling it. A sense pulsed through her from it, memories and pain. And . . . and something smothering them . . .

Forgiveness. For herself.

She gasped, pulling her finger back as if it had been bitten.

"It's terrible," Wit said, stepping up beside her, "to have been hurt. It's unfair, and awful, and horrid. But Shallan . . . it's okay to live on."

She shook her head.

"Your other minds take over," he whispered, "because they look so much more appealing. You'll never control them until you're confident in returning to the one who birthed them. Until *you* accept being *you*."

"Then I'll never control it." She blinked tears.

"No," Wit said. He nodded toward the version of her still standing up. "You will, Shallan. If you do not trust yourself, can you trust me? For in you, I see a woman more wonderful than any of the lies. I promise you, that woman is *worth* protecting. *You* are worth protecting."

She nodded toward the illusion of herself still standing. "I can't be her. She's just another fabrication."

Both illusions vanished. "I see only one woman here," Wit said. "And it's the one who is standing up. Shallan, that has always been you. You just have to admit it. Allow it." He whispered to her. "It's all right to hurt."

He picked up his pack, then unfolded something from inside it. Veil's hat. He pressed the hat into her palm.

Shockingly, morning light was shining in the doorway. Had she been here all night, huddled in this hole of a room?

"Wit?" she asked. "I . . . I can't do it."

He smiled. "There are certain things I know, Shallan. This is one of them. You *can*. Find the balance. Accept the pain, but *don't accept that you deserved it.*"

Pattern hummed in appreciation of that. But, it wasn't as easy as Wit said. She took in a breath, and felt . . . a shiver run through her. Wit collected his things, pack over his shoulder. He smiled, then stepped out into the light.

Shallan released her breath, feeling foolish. She followed Wit out into the light, emerging into the market, which hadn't quite woken up yet. She didn't see Wit outside, but that was no surprise. He had a way of being where he shouldn't, but not being where you'd expect.

Carrying Veil's hat, she walked the street, feeling odd to be herself in trousers and coat. Red hair, but a safehand glove. Should she hide?

Why? This felt . . . fine. She walked all the way back to the tailor's shop and peeked in. Adolin sat at a table inside, bleary-eyed.

He stood upright. "Shallan? We were worried! Vathah said you should have come back!"

"I—"

He embraced her, and she relaxed into him. She felt . . . better. Not well yet. It was all still there. But something about Wit's words . . .

I see only one woman here. The one who is standing up.

Adolin still held her for a time, as if he needed to reassure himself. "I know you're fine, of course," he said. "I mean, you're basically unkillable, right?" Finally, he pulled back—still holding her shoulders—and looked down at her outfit. Should she explain?

"Nice," Adolin said. "Shallan, that's *sharp*. The red on white." He stepped back, nodding. "Did Yokska make that for you? Let me see the hat on you."

Oh, Adolin, she thought, pulling on the hat.

"The jacket is a hair too loose," Adolin said. "But the style is a really good match. Bold. Crisp." He cocked his head. "Would look better with a sword at your waist. Maybe . . ." He trailed off. "Do you hear that?"

She turned, frowning. It sounded like marching. "A parade this early?"

They looked out at the street and found Kaladin approaching along with what seemed to be an army of five or six hundred men, wearing the uniforms of the Wall Guard.

Adolin sighed softly. "Of course. He's probably their leader now or something. Storming bridgeboy."

Kaladin marched his men right up to the front of the tailor's shop. She and Adolin stepped out to meet him, and she heard Elhokar scrambling down the steps inside, shouting at what he'd apparently seen out the window.

Kaladin was speaking softly with a woman in armor, helm under her arm, face crossed by a pair of scars. Highmarshal Azure was younger than Shallan had expected.

The soldiers grew hushed as they saw Adolin, then the king, who was already dressed.

"So *that's* what you meant," Azure said to Kaladin.

"Stormblessed?" Elhokar asked. "What is this?"

"You've been wanting an army to attack the palace, Your Majesty," Kaladin said. "Well, we're ready."

83

CRIMSON TO BREAK

> *As the duly appointed keepers of the perfect gems, we of the Else-callers have taken the burden of protecting the ruby nicknamed Honor's Drop. Let it be recorded.*
>
> —From drawer 20-10, zircon

Adolin Kholin washed his face with a splash of cold water, then rubbed it clean with a washrag. He was tired—he'd spent much of the night fretting about Shallan's failure to return. Below, in the shop proper, he could hear the others stomping about as they made last-minute preparations for the assault.

An assault on the *palace*, his home for many years. He took a deep breath.

Something was wrong. He fidgeted, checking his belt knife, the emergency bandages in his pocket. He checked the glyphward Shallan had made him at his request—*determination*—wrapped around his forearm. Then he finally realized what was bothering him.

He summoned his Shardblade.

It was thick at the base, as wide as a man's palm, and the front waved like the ripples of a moving eel. The back had small crystalline protrusions growing out of it. No sheath could hold a weapon like this, and no mortal sword could imitate it—not without growing unusably heavy. You *knew* a Shardblade when you saw one. That was the point.

Adolin held the weapon before him in the lavatory, looking at his reflection in the metal. "I don't have my mother's necklace," he said, "or any of the other traditions I used to follow. I never really needed those. I've only ever needed you."

He took a deep breath. "I guess . . . I guess you used to be alive. The others say they can hear your screaming if they touch you. That you're dead, yet somehow still in pain. I'm sorry. I can't do anything about that, but . . . thank you. Thank you for assisting me all these years. And if it helps, I'm going to use you to do something good today. I'll try to always use you that way."

He felt better as he dismissed the Blade. Of course, he carried another weapon: his belt knife, long and thin. A weapon intended for stabbing armored men.

It had felt so *satisfying* to shove it through Sadeas's eye. He still didn't know whether to feel ashamed or proud. He sighed, checked himself in the mirror, then made another quick decision.

When he walked down the steps to the main room a short time later, he was wearing his Kholin uniform. His skin missed the softer silk and better form of the tailored outfit, but he found he walked taller in this one. Despite the fact that a part of him, deep down, worried he didn't deserve to bear his father's glyphs any longer.

He nodded to Elhokar, who was speaking with the strange woman known as Highmarshal Azure. "My scouts have been driven back," she said. "But they saw enough, Your Majesty. The Voidbringer army *is* here, in its strength. They'll attack today or tomorrow for certain."

"Well," Elhokar said. "I suppose I understand why you did what you had to in taking control of the Guard. I can't very well have you hanged as a usurper. Good work, Highmarshal."

"I . . . appreciate that?"

Shallan, Kaladin, Skar, and Drehy were standing with a palace map. They needed to memorize the layout. Adolin and Elhokar, of course, already knew it. Shallan had chosen not to change out of the fetching white outfit she'd been wearing earlier. It would be more functional for an assault than a skirt. Storms, there was something about a woman in trousers and a coat.

Elhokar left Azure to take reports from some of her men. Nearby in the room, a few lighteyed men saluted him—the highlords he and Adolin had revealed themselves to the night before. All they'd needed to do was walk away from the spheres powering their illusions, and their true faces had become manifest.

Some of these men were opportunists, but many were loyalists. They'd brought some hundred men-at-arms with them—not as many as Kaladin had brought from the Wall Guard, but still, Elhokar seemed proud of what he had done in gathering them. As well he should.

Together, he and Adolin joined the Radiants near the front of the shop. Elhokar waved for the highlords to join them, then spoke firmly. "Is everyone clear?" Elhokar asked.

"Storm the palace," Kaladin said. "Seize the Sunwalk, cross to the Oathgate platform, hold it while Shallan tries to drive away the Unmade like she did in Urithiru. Then we activate the Oathgate, and bring troops to Kholinar."

"The control building is *completely* overgrown with that black heart, Your Majesty," Shallan said. "I don't truly know how I drove away the Midnight Mother—and I certainly don't know that I'll be able to do the same here."

"But you're willing to try?" the king asked.

"Yes." She took a deep breath. Adolin squeezed her on the shoulder reassuringly.

"Windrunner," the king said. "The duty I give you and your men is to get Queen Aesudan and the heir to safety. If the Oathgate works, we take them that way. If not, you must fly them out of the city."

Adolin glanced at the highlords, who seemed to be taking all of this—the arrival of Knights Radiant, the king's decision to storm his own palace—in stride. He knew a little of how they felt. Voidbringers, Everstorm, corrupted spren in the city . . . eventually, you stopped being shocked at what happened to you.

"Are we sure this path across the Sunwalk is the best way?" Kaladin asked, pointing at the map Drehy was holding. He moved his finger from the palace's eastern gallery, along the Sunwalk onto the Oathgate platform.

Adolin nodded. "It's the best way to the Oathgate. Those narrow steps up the outside of that plateau would be murder to storm. Our best chance is to go up the palace's front steps, bring down the doors with our Shardblades, and fight through the entryway to the eastern gallery. From there, you can go up to the right to reach the king's quarters, or go straight across the Sunwalk."

"I don't relish fighting along this corridor," Kaladin said. "We have to assume that the Fused will join the battle on the side of the Palace Guard."

"It's possible I can distract them, if they do come," Shallan said.

Kaladin grunted and didn't complain further. He saw, as Adolin did. This wasn't going to be an easy fight—there were a lot of choke points the defenders could use. But what else could they do?

In the distance, drums had begun sounding. From the walls. Kaladin looked toward them.

"Another raid?" one of the highlords asked.

"Worse," Kaladin said as, behind them, Azure cursed softly. "That's the signal that the city's under attack."

Azure pushed out the front doors of the tailor's shop, and the rest of them followed. Most of the six hundred men here belonged to the Wall

Guard, and some stepped toward the distant walls, gripping spears and shields.

"Steady, men," Azure called. "Your Majesty, the bulk of my soldiers are dying on the wall in a hopeless fight. I'm here because Stormblessed convinced me that the *only* way to help them is to take that palace. So if we're going to do it, the time is *now*."

"We march, then!" Elhokar said. "Highmarshal, Brightlords, pass the word to your forces. Organize ranks! We march on the palace at my command!"

Adolin turned as some Fused coursed through the sky along the distant wall. Enemy Surgebinders. Storms. He shook his head and hurried over to Yokska and her husband. They had watched all this—the arrival of an army on their doorstep, the preparations for an assault—with bewilderment.

"If the city holds," Adolin said, "you'll be fine. But if it falls . . ." He took a deep breath. "Reports from other cities indicate that there won't be wholesale slaughter. The Voidbringers are here to occupy, not exterminate. I'd still suggest you prepare to flee the city and make your way to the Shattered Plains."

"The *Shattered Plains*?" Yokska asked, aghast. "But Brightlord, that's hundreds and hundreds of miles!"

"I know," he said, wincing. "Thank you so much for taking us in. We're going to do what we can to stop this."

Nearby, Elhokar approached the timid ardent who had come with Azure. He had been hurriedly painting glyphwards for the soldiers, and jumped as Elhokar took him by the shoulder and shoved an object into his hand.

"What's this?" the ardent asked, nervous.

"It's a spanreed," Elhokar said. "A half hour after my army marches, you are to contact Urithiru and warn them to get their forces ready to transfer here, via the Oathgate."

"I can't use a fabrial! The screamers—"

"Steady, man! The enemy may be too preoccupied by their attack to notice you. But even if they do, you *must* take the risk. Our armies must be ready. The fate of the city could depend upon this."

The ardent nodded, pale.

Adolin joined the troops, calming his nerves by force. Just another battle. He'd been in dozens, if not hundreds of those. But storms, he was used to empty fields of stone, not streets.

Nearby, a small group of guardsmen chatted softly. "We'll be fine," one of them was saying. He was a shorter man, clean-shaven, though he had strikingly hairy arms. "I tell you, I saw my own death up there on the wall. She streaked toward me, lance held right toward my heart. I looked in those red eyes, and I saw myself dying. Then . . . he was there. He shot from the tower window like an arrow and crashed into the Voidbringer. That spear was meant for my life, and he changed fate, I tell you. I swear, he was *glowing* when he did it. . . ."

We're entering an era of gods, Adolin thought.

Elhokar raised his Shardblade high and gave the command. They marched through the city, passing worried refugees. Rows of buildings with doors shut tight, as if in preparation for a storm. Eventually, the palace rose before the army like an obsidian block. The very stones seemed to have changed color.

Adolin summoned his Shardblade, and the sight of it seemed to give comfort to the men nearby. Their march took them toward the northern section of the city, near the city wall. Here, the Fused were visible, attacking the troops. A strange *thumping* started, and Adolin took it as another set of drums—until a *head* crested the top of the wall nearest them.

Storms! It had an enormous stone wedge of a face that reminded him of that of some greatshell beast, though its eyes were just red spots glowing from deep within.

The monster pulled itself up by one arm. It didn't seem quite as tall as the city walls, but it was still enormous. Fused buzzed about as it swatted along the wall—spraying defenders like cremlings—then smashed a guard tower.

Adolin realized that he, along with much of their force, had stopped to stare at the daunting sight. The ground trembled as stones tumbled down a few blocks away, smashing into buildings.

"Keep moving!" Azure called. "Storms! They're trying to get in and beat us to the palace!"

The monster ripped apart the guard tower, then with a casual flip tossed a boulder the size of a horse toward them. Adolin gaped, feeling powerless as the rock inexorably hurtled toward him and the troops.

Kaladin rose into the air on a streak of light.

He hit the stone and rolled with it, twisting and tumbling in the air. His glow diminished severely.

The boulder lurched. It somehow *changed momentum,* tossed away from Kaladin like a pebble flicked off the table. It crested the city wall, narrowly missing the monster that had thrown it. Adolin faintly heard spren begin to scream, but that was drowned out by the sounds of rock falling and people on the streets shouting.

Kaladin renewed himself with Stormlight from his pack. He was carrying most of the gemstones they'd brought from Urithiru, a wealth from the emerald reserve, to use in their mission and in opening the Oathgate.

Drehy rose into the air beside him, then Skar, who had Lashed Shallan upward as well. Adolin knew she was basically immortal, but it was still strange to see her here, on the front lines.

"We'll distract the Fused," Kaladin shouted to Adolin, pointing at a group of figures flying through the air in their direction. "And—if we can—we'll seize the Sunwalk. Get in through the palace, and meet with us in the eastern gallery!"

They zipped off. In the near distance, the monster started pounding on the gates there, cracking and splintering the wood.

"Forward!" Azure yelled.

Adolin charged, running up beside Elhokar and Azure. They reached the palace grounds and surged up the steps. At the top, soldiers in very similar uniforms—black and a darker blue, but still Kholin—withdrew, shutting the palace's front doors.

"King's Guard," Adolin shouted, pointing at a group of men in red who had been designated as Elhokar's honor guard. "Be sure to watch the king's flanks as he cuts! Don't let the enemy strike at him as the door falls!"

Men crowded up the steps, taking positions along the front of the palace's front porch. They held spears, though some were lighteyed. Adolin, Azure, and Elhokar each went to a separate door atop the steps. Here, the front of the palace roof—held up by thick columns—shielded them from the stones that the creature was flinging.

Teeth gritted, Adolin rammed his Blade into the crack between the thick wooden palace door and the wall. He swiped upward quickly, cutting through both hinges and the bar that had been thrown on the inside. After another slice down the other side freed the door, he stepped back into position. It fell inward with a crash.

Immediately, the enemy soldiers inside rammed spears outward, hoping to catch Adolin. He danced back, and didn't dare swing. Wielding a Shardblade with one hand was a challenge, even when you didn't have to worry about hitting your own men.

He skipped to the side and let the Wall Guard attack the doorway. Adolin, instead, moved over beside a group of soldiers who had come with Highlord Urimil. Here, Adolin cut through a section of the wall, making an improvised doorway that the soldiers shoved open. He moved down the long porch, opening another, then a third.

That done, he peeked in on Elhokar, who had stepped through his felled door, and was now inside the palace. He swept about himself with his Blade in a one-handed grip, shield held in the other. He opened a pocket in the enemy soldiers, having killed dozens already.

Careful, Elhokar, Adolin thought. *Remember, you don't have Plate.* Adolin pointed at a platoon of soldiers. "Reinforce the King's Guard, and make sure he doesn't get overwhelmed. If he does, shout for me."

They saluted, and Adolin stepped back. Azure had cut down her door, but her Shardblade wasn't as long as the other two. She was leading a more conservative attack, cutting the ends off spears as they rammed out toward her men. As he watched, she stabbed an enemy soldier who tried to push through. Remarkably, his eyes didn't burn, though his skin did go a strange ashen grey as he died.

Blood of my fathers, Adolin thought. *What's wrong with her Blade?*

Even with all the opened doorways, getting into the palace was slow going. The men inside had formed shield-wall rings around the doorways, and the fighting mostly happened with men using short spears to stab at each other. Some platoons of Wall Guard brought in longer pikes to break the ranks of defenders, preparing for a surge.

"You men ever flank-shielded a Shardbearer?" Adolin said to the nearest squad of soldiers.

"No sir," said one of the men. "But we've done the training. . . ."

"It'll have to do," Adolin said, taking his Blade in two hands. "I'm going in that center hole. Stay close and keep the spears off my sides. I'll be careful not to catch you in my sweeps."

"Yes, sir!" their squadleader said.

Adolin took a deep breath, then approached the opening. The interior bristled with spears. Like the proverbial whitespine's den.

At Adolin's instruction, a soldier on his side faced his men and did a countdown with one hand. As the last finger dropped, the soldiers at the doorway fell back. Adolin charged through into the palace entry hall, with its marble floors and high vaulted ceilings.

The enemy thrust a dozen spears at him. He ducked low, taking a slice on the shoulder as he did a two-handed sweep, cutting a group of soldiers at the knees. The enemy dropped, their legs ruined by the Shardblade.

Four men followed him in and raised shields at his sides. Adolin attacked forward, hacking the fronts off spears, cutting at hands. Storms . . . the men he fought were too silent. They'd cry in pain if stabbed, or grunt with exertion, but they otherwise seemed muted—as if the darkness smothered their emotions.

Adolin took his Blade in an overhead grip and fell into Stonestance, swiping down with precise cuts, felling man after man in a careful, controlled set of strikes. His soldiers protected his flanks, while the wide reach of the Blade protected his front.

Eyes burned. The shield line wavered. "Fall back three steps!" Adolin shouted to his men, then transitioned to Windstance and swept outward with wide, flowing sweeps.

In the passion and beauty of dueling, he sometimes forgot how *terrible* a weapon Shardblades were. Here, as he rampaged among the faltering line, it was all too obvious. He killed eight men in a moment, and completely destroyed the defensive line.

"Go!" he shouted, pointing with his Blade. Men surged through the doorway and seized the ground just inside the entry hall. Nearby, Elhokar stood tall, his narrow Shardblade glittering as he called commands. Soldiers fell, dying and cursing—the true sounds of battle. The price of conflict.

The enemy finally broke, falling back through the entry hall—which was too large to hold—toward the narrower hallway leading to the eastern gallery.

"Pull out the wounded!" Azure called, stepping in. "Seventh Company, hold that far side of the room, make sure they don't try to rush back in. Third Company, sweep the wings and make sure there aren't any surprises."

Curiously, Azure had removed her cloak and wrapped it half around her left arm. Adolin had never seen anything like it; perhaps she was accustomed to fighting in Plate.

Adolin got some water, then let a surgeon bandage the shallow cut he'd taken. Though the depths of the palace felt like caverns, this entryway was glorious. Walls of marble, polished and reflective. Grand staircases, and a bright red rug down the center. He'd burned that as a child once, playing with a candle.

Cut bandaged, he joined Azure, Elhokar, and several of the highlords, who were studying the wide corridor that led to the eastern gallery. The enemy had formed an excellent shield wall here. They'd settled in, and men in the second rank had crossbows ready and waiting.

"That's going to be crimson to break," Azure said. "We'll fight for every inch."

Outside, the crashing at the gate finally grew silent.

"They're in," Adolin guessed. "That breach isn't far from here."

Highlord Shaday grunted. "Maybe our enemies will turn against one another? Can we hope the Voidbringers and the Palace Guard will start fighting each other?"

"No," Elhokar said. "The forces that have darkened the palace belong to the enemy who now fights quickly to reach us. They know the danger the Oathgate presents."

"Agreed," Adolin said. "This palace will soon be swarming with parshman troops."

"Gather your men," Elhokar said to the group. "Azure has command of the assault. Highmarshal, you *must* clear this hallway."

One of the highlords looked at the woman and cleared his throat, but then decided not to say anything.

Grim, Azure commanded archers to use shortbows to try to soften the enemy. But that shield wall was built to hold out against arrows, so Azure gave the order, and her men advanced against the fortified enemy.

Adolin looked away as the corridor became a meat grinder, crossbow bolts smacking against men in waves. The Wall Guard had shields too, but they had to risk advancing, and a crossbow could *punch*.

Adolin had never been good at this part of battlefield fighting. Storm it, he wanted to be at the front, leading the charge. The rational part of him knew that would be stupid. You didn't risk your Shardbearers in such a charge, not unless they had Plate.

"Your Majesty," an officer called to Elhokar, crossing the entryway. "We found an oddity."

Elhokar nodded for Adolin to take care of it, and—glad for the distraction—he jogged over to meet up with the man. "What?"

"Closed door to the palace garrison," the man said, "rigged to lock from the *outside*."

Curious. Adolin hiked after the man, passing an improvised triage station where a couple of surgeons knelt among painspren, seeing to men who had been wounded in the initial assault. They'd be far busier once the push down the hallway was finished.

To the west of the entryway was the palace garrison, a large housing for soldiers. A group of Azure's men were studying the door—which had indeed been rigged to lock shut from the outside with a metal bar. Judging from the splintered wood, whatever was inside had tried to get out.

"Open it," Adolin said, summoning his Shardblade.

The soldiers cautiously lifted aside the bar, then eased open the door, one holding out some spheres for light. They didn't find monsters, but a group of dirty men in Palace Guard uniforms. They had gathered at the noise outside, and at seeing Adolin, a few of them fell to their knees, letting out relieved praises to the Almighty.

"Your Highness?" said a younger Alethi man with captain's knots on his shoulder. "Oh, Prince Adolin. It *is* you. Or is this . . . is this somehow a cruel deception?"

"It's me," Adolin said. "Sidin? Storms, man! I barely recognize you through that beard. What happened?"

"Sir! Something's wrong with the queen. First she killed that ardent, and then *executed* Brightlord Kaves. . . ." He took a deep breath. "We're traitors, sir."

"She culled the Guard, sir," another man said. "Locked us in here because we wouldn't obey. Practically forgot about us."

Adolin breathed out a relieved sigh. The fact that the entire Guard hadn't simply gone along with her . . . well, it lifted a burden from his shoulders, one he hadn't realized he'd been carrying.

"We're taking back the palace," Adolin said. "Gather your men, Sidin, and meet up with the surgeons in the main entryway. They'll look you over, get you some water, take your reports."

"Sir!" Sidin said. "If you're storming the palace, we want to join you." Many of the others nodded.

"Join us? You've been locked in here for weeks, men! I don't expect that you're fit for combat."

"Weeks?" Sidin said. "Surely it's only been a few days, Brightlord." He scratched at a beard that seemed to argue with that sentiment. "We've only eaten . . . what, three times since being thrown in here?"

Several of the others nodded.

"Take them to the surgeons," Adolin said to the scouts who had fetched him. "But . . . get spears for the ones who claim to be strong enough to hold them. Sidin, your men will be reserves. Don't push yourselves too hard."

Back in the main entryway, Adolin passed a surgeon working on a man in a Palace Guard uniform. To the surgeons, it didn't matter if you were an enemy—they were helping any who needed their attention. That was fine, but this man stared up with glazed eyes, and didn't cry or groan like a wounded man should. He only whispered to himself.

I know him *too,* Adolin realized, searching for the name. *Dod? That's it. That's what we called him, anyway.*

He reported to the king what he'd found. Ahead, Azure's men were making a final push to claim the hallway. They'd left dozens dying, staining the carpet a darker shade of red. Adolin had the distinct sense that he could *hear* something. Over the din of the fighting, over the shouts of men echoing against the walls. A quiet voice that somehow cut to his soul.

Passion. Sweet passion.

The Palace Guard finally relinquished the hallway, retreating through two sets of broad double doors at the other end. Those would lead to the eastern gallery; the doors weren't very defensible, but the enemy was obviously trying to buy as much time as possible.

Some soldiers cleared bodies out of the way, preparing the way for Adolin and Elhokar to cut down the doors. The wood, however, started shaking before they could strike. Adolin backed up, presenting his Blade in Windstance by habit, ready to strike at what came through.

The door opened, revealing a glowing figure.

"Stormfather . . ." Adolin whispered.

Kaladin shone with a powerful brilliance, his eyes beacons of blue, streaming with Stormlight. He gripped a glowing metallic spear that was easily twelve feet long. Behind him, Skar and Drehy also glowed brilliantly, looking little like the affable bridgemen who had protected Adolin on the Shattered Plains.

"The gallery is secure," Kaladin said, Stormlight puffing from his lips. "The enemy you pushed back has fled up the steps. Your Majesty, I suggest you send Azure's men onto the Sunwalk to hold it."

Adolin ducked into the eastern gallery, followed by a flood of soldiers, Azure calling commands. Straight ahead was the entrance to the Sunwalk, an open-sided walkway. On it, Adolin was surprised to see not only guard corpses, but three prominent bodies in blue. Kaladin, Skar, Drehy. Illusions?

"Worked better than fighting them off," Shallan said, stepping up to his side. "The flying ones are distracted by the fighting at the city wall, so they left the moment they thought the bridgemen had fallen."

"We pushed another force of Palace Guards back into the monastery first," Kaladin said, pointing. "We're going to need an army to scrape them out."

Azure looked to Elhokar, who nodded, so she started giving the commands. Shallan clicked her tongue, prodding at Adolin's bandaged shoulder, but he assured her it was nothing serious.

The king strode through the gallery, then looked up the broad stairs.

"Your Majesty?" Kaladin called.

"I'm going to lead a force up to the royal chambers," Elhokar said. "Someone needs to find out what happened to Aesudan, what happened to this whole storming city."

The glow faded from Kaladin's eyes, his Stormlight running low. His clothing seemed to droop, his feet settling more solidly on the ground. He suddenly seemed a man again, and Adolin found that more relaxing.

"I'll go with him," Kaladin said softly to Adolin, handing him the pack of emeralds, after picking out two brilliant ones for himself. "Take Skar and Drehy, and get Shallan to the Unmade."

"Sounds good," Adolin said. He picked out some soldiers to go with the king: a platoon from the Wall Guard, a handful of the armsmen the highlords had brought. And—after some thought—he added Sidin and half a platoon of the men who had been imprisoned in the palace.

"Those troops refused the queen's orders," Adolin said to Elhokar, nodding to Sidin. "They seem to have resisted the influence of whatever's going on in here, and they'll know the palace better than the Wall Guard."

"Excellent," Elhokar said, then started up the steps. "Don't wait for us. If Brightness Davar is successful, go right to Urithiru and bring our armies back."

Adolin nodded, then gave Kaladin a quick salute—tapping his wrists together with hands in fists. The Bridge Four salute. "Good luck, bridgeboy."

Kaladin smiled, his silvery spear vanishing as he gave the salute back, then hustled after the king. Adolin jogged over to Shallan, who was staring along the Sunwalk. Azure had claimed it with her soldiers, but hadn't advanced onto the Oathgate platform beyond.

Adolin rested his hand on Shallan's shoulder.

"They're there," she whispered. "Two of them, this time. Last night, Adolin . . . I had to run. The revel was getting inside my head."

"I've heard it," he said, resummoning his Blade. "We'll face it together. Like last time."

Shallan took a deep breath, then summoned Pattern as a Shardblade. She held the Blade before herself in a common stance.

"Good form," Adolin said.

"I had a good teacher."

They advanced across the Sunwalk, passing fallen enemy soldiers—and a single dead Fused, pinned to a cleft in the rock by what appeared to be his own lance. Shallan lingered at the corpse, but Adolin pulled her along until they reached the monastery proper. Azure's soldiers advanced at his command, engaging Palace Guards here to secure a path toward the center.

As they waited, Adolin stepped up to the edge of the plateau and surveyed the city. His home.

It was falling.

The nearest gate had been broken completely open, and parshmen flooded through it toward the palace. Others had taken the walls via ladder crews, and those were pushing down into the city at other points, including near the palace gardens.

That enormous stone monstrosity moved along the wall on the inside, reaching up and slapping at guard towers. A large group of people in varied costumes had surged down Talan Way, passing along one of the windblades. The Cult of Moments? He couldn't be certain what part they'd played, but parshmen were flooding the city in that direction as well.

We can fix this, Adolin thought. *We can bring our armies in, hold the palace hill, push back to the walls.* They had dozens of Shardbearers. They had Bridge Four and other Surgebinders. They *could* save this city.

He just needed to get them here.

Soon, Azure approached with a platoon of thirty men. "The pathway inward is secure, though a knot of the enemy still holds the very center. I've spared a few men to scour nearby buildings. It looks like the people you mentioned—the ones who were reveling last night—are slumbering inside. They don't move, even when we prod them."

Adolin nodded, then led the way toward the center of the plateau, Shallan and Azure following. They passed battle lines of Azure's soldiers, who were holding the streets. He soon saw the main force of the enemy, collected on a path between monastery buildings, barring the way to the Oathgate's control building.

Spurred by the urgency of Kholinar's predicament, Adolin took point and swept among the enemy, burning their eyes with his Blade. He broke their line, though one straggler almost got in a lucky strike. Skar, fortunately, seemed to appear out of nowhere; the bridgeman caught the blow with his shield, then rammed a spear through the guardsman's chest.

"How many is that I owe you now?" Adolin asked.

"I wouldn't think to keep count, Brightlord," Skar said with a grin, glowing light puffing from his lips.

Drehy joined them, and they chased the routed enemy past the King's Chapel, finally reaching the control building. Adolin had always known it as the Circle of Memories, merely another part of the monastery. As Shallan had warned, it was overgrown with a dark mass that pulsed and throbbed, like a pitch-black heart. Dark veins spread from it like roots, pulsating in time with the heart.

"Storms . . ." Drehy whispered.

"All right," Shallan said, walking forward. "Guard this area. I'll see what I can do."

84

THE ONE
YOU CAN SAVE

The enemy makes another push toward Feverstone Keep. I wish we knew what it was that had them so interested in that area. Could they be intent on capturing Rall Elorim?

—From drawer 19-2, third topaz

Kaladin charged up the broad stairs, followed by some fifty soldiers. Stormlight pulsed within him, lending a spring to each step. The Fused had taken time to come attack him on the Sunwalk, and had left soon after Shallan had created her ruse. He could only assume that the city assault was consuming the enemy's attention, which meant he might be able to use his powers without drawing immediate reprisal.

Elhokar led the way, brilliant Shardblade carried in a two-handed grip. They twisted around at a landing and charged up another flight. Elhokar didn't seem to care that each step took them farther from the bulk of their army.

"Up the stairs," he said softly to Syl. "Check for an ambush on each floor."

"Yessir, commander sir, Radiant sir," she said, and zipped off. A moment later she zipped back down. "Lots of men on the third floor, but they're backing away from the stairwell. Doesn't look like an ambush."

Kaladin nodded, then slowed Elhokar with a touch on the arm. "We have a reception waiting," Kaladin said. He pointed at a squad of soldiers. "It seems the king lost his guards somewhere. You're now them. If we get into combat, keep His Majesty from being surrounded." He pointed at another group. "You men are . . . Beard?"

"Yes, Kal?" the stocky guardsman said. He hesitated, then saluted. "Um, sir?" Behind him were Noro, Ved, Alaward, and Vaceslv . . . Kaladin's entire squad from the Wall Guard.

Noro shrugged. "Without the captain, we don't have a proper platoon leader. Figured we should stick with you."

Beard nodded and rubbed at the glyphward wrapping his right arm. *Fortune*, it read.

"Good to have you," Kaladin said. "Try to keep me from being flanked, but give me space if you can."

"Don't crowd you," Lieutenant Noro said, "and don't let anyone else crowd you either. Can do, sir."

Kaladin looked to the king and nodded. The two of them took the last few steps up to the landing to emerge into a broad stone hallway, carpeted down the center but otherwise unornamented. Kaladin had expected the palace to be more lavish, but it appeared that even here—in the seat of their power—the Kholins preferred buildings that felt like bunkers. Funny, after hearing them complain that their fortresses on the Shattered Plains lacked comfort.

Syl was right. A platoon of enemy soldiers had formed up down the hall, holding halberds or crossbows, but seemed content to wait. Kaladin prepared Stormlight; he could paint the walls with a power that would cause crossbow bolts to veer aside in their flight, but it was far from a perfect art. It was the power he understood the least.

"Do you not see me?" Elhokar bellowed. "Do you not know your monarch? Are you so far consumed by the touch of the spren that you would kill your *own king*?"

Storms . . . those soldiers barely seemed to be breathing. At first they didn't move—then a few looked backward, down the hallway. Was that a distant voice?

The palace soldiers immediately broke formation and retreated. Elhokar set his jaw, then led the way after them. Each step made Kaladin more anxious. He didn't have the troops to properly hold their retreat; all he could do was post a pair of men at each intersection, with instructions to yell if they saw someone coming down the cross hallways.

They passed a corridor lined with statues of the Heralds. Nine of them, at least. One was missing. Kaladin sent Syl ahead to watch, but that left him feeling even more exposed. Everyone but him seemed to know the way, which made sense, but it made him feel carried along on some sort of tide.

They finally reached the royal chambers, marked by a broad set of doors, open and inviting. Kaladin stopped his men thirty feet from the opening, near a corridor that split off to the left.

Even from here, he could see that the chamber beyond the doors finally displayed some of the lavish ornamentation he had expected. Rich carpets, too much furniture, everything covered in embroidery or gilding.

"There are soldiers down that smaller hallway to the left," Syl said, zipping back to him. "There isn't a single one in the room ahead, but . . . Kaladin, *she's* in there. The queen."

"I can hear her," Elhokar said. "That's her voice, singing."

I know that tune, Kaladin thought. Something about her soft song was familiar. He wanted to advise caution, but the king was already hurrying forward, a worried squad of men following.

Kaladin sighed, then arranged his remaining men; half stayed back to watch their retreat, and the other half formed up at the left hallway to stare down the Palace Guard. Storms. If this went wrong he'd have a bloodbath on his hands, with the king trapped in the middle.

Still, this *was* why they'd come up here. He followed the queen's song and entered the room.

⁂

Shallan stepped up to the dark heart. Even though she hadn't studied human anatomy as much as she'd have liked—her father thought it unfeminine— in the sunlight, she could easily see that it was the wrong shape.

This isn't a human heart, she decided. *Maybe it's a parshman heart.* Or, well, a giant, dark violet spren in the shape of one, growing over the Oathgate control building.

"Shallan," Adolin said. "We're running out of time."

His voice brought to her an awareness of the city around her. Of soldiers skirmishing only one street over. Of distant drums going quiet, one at a time, as guard posts on the wall fell. Of smoke in the air, and a soft, high-pitched roar that seemed the echoes of thousands upon thousands of people shouting in the chaos of a city being conquered.

She tried Pattern first, stabbing him into the heart as a Shardblade. The mass simply split around the Blade. She slashed with it, and the spren cut, then sealed up behind. So. Time to try what she'd done in Urithiru.

Trembling, Shallan closed her eyes and pressed her hand against the heart. It *felt* real, like warm flesh. Like in Urithiru, touching the thing let her sense it. Feel it. *Know* it.

It tried to sweep her away.

⁂

The queen sat at a vanity beside the wall.

She was much as Kaladin had anticipated. Younger than Elhokar, with long dark Alethi hair, which she was combing. Her song had fallen away to a hum.

"Aesudan?" Elhokar asked.

She looked away from the mirror, then smiled broadly. She had a narrow face, with prim lips painted a deep red. She rose from the seat and glided to him. "Husband! So it *was* you I heard. You have returned at last? Victorious over our enemies, your father avenged?"

"Yes," Elhokar said, frowning. He moved to step toward her, but Kaladin grabbed him by the shoulder and held him back.

The queen focused on Kaladin. "New bodyguard, dear one? Far too scruffy; you should have consulted me. You have an image to maintain."

"Where is Gav, Aesudan? Where is my son?"

"He's playing with friends."

Elhokar looked to Kaladin, and gestured to the side with his chin. *See what you can find,* it seemed to say.

"Keep alert," Kaladin whispered, then began picking through the room. He passed the remnants of lavish meals only partially eaten. Pieces of fruit each with a single bite taken out of them. Cakes and pastries. Candied meats on sticks. It looked like it should have rotted, based on the decayspren he noticed, but it hadn't.

"Dear one," Elhokar said, keeping his distance from the queen, "we heard that the city has seen . . . trouble lately."

"One of my ardents tried to refound the Hierocracy. We really should keep better watch on who joins them; not every man or woman is proper for service."

"You had her executed."

"Of course. She tried to overthrow us."

Kaladin picked around a pile of musical instruments of the finest wood, sitting in a heap.

Here, Syl's voice said in his mind. *Across the room. Behind the dressing screen.*

He passed the balcony to his left. If he remembered right—though the story had been told so often, he had heard a dozen differing versions— Gavilar and the assassin had fallen off that ledge during their struggles.

"Aesudan," Elhokar said, his voice pained. He stepped forward, extending his hand. "You're not well. Please, come with me."

"Not well?"

"There's an evil influence in the palace."

"Evil? Husband, what a fool you are at times."

Kaladin joined Syl and glanced behind the dressing screen, which had been pushed back against the wall to section off a small cubby. Here a child—two or three years old—huddled and trembled, clutching a stuffed soldier. Several spren with soft red glows were picking at him like cremlings at a corpse. The boy tried to turn his head, and the spren pulled on the back of his hair until he looked up, while others hovered in front of his face and took horrific shapes, like horses with melting faces.

Kaladin reacted with swift, immediate *rage*. He growled, seizing the Sylblade from the air, forming a small dagger from mist. He drove the dagger forward and caught one of the spren, pinning it to the wall's wooden paneling. He had never known a Shardblade to cut a spren before, but this worked. The thing screamed in a soft voice, a hundred hands coming from its shape and scraping at the Blade, at the wall, until it seemed to *rip* into a thousand tiny pieces, then faded.

The other three red spren streaked away in a panic. In his hands, Kaladin felt Syl *tremble*, then groan softly. He released her, and she took the shape of a small woman. "That was . . . that was *terrible*," she whispered, floating over to land on his shoulder. "Did we . . . just *kill* a spren?"

"The thing deserved it," Kaladin said.

Syl just huddled on his shoulder, wrapping her arms around herself.

The child sniffled. He was dressed in a little uniform. Kaladin glanced back at the king and queen—he'd lost track of their conversation, but they spoke in hissing, furious tones.

"Oh, Elhokar," the queen was saying. "You were ever so oblivious. Your father had grand plans, but you . . . all you ever wanted to do was sit in his shadow. It was for the best that you went off to play war."

"So you could stay here and . . . and do *this*?" Elhokar said, waving toward the palace.

"I continued your father's work! I found the secret, Elhokar. Spren, ancient spren. You can *bond* with them!"

"Bond . . ." Elhokar's mouth worked, as if he couldn't understand the very word he spoke.

"Have you seen my Radiants?" Aesudan asked. She grinned. "The Queen's Guard? I've done what your father could not. Oh, he found one of the ancient spren, but he could never discover how to bond it. But I, *I* have solved the riddle."

In the dim light of the royal chambers, Aesudan's eyes glittered. Then started to glow a deep red.

"Storms!" Elhokar said, stepping back.

Time to go. Kaladin reached down to try to pick up the child, but the boy screamed and scrambled away from him. That, finally, drew the king's attention. Elhokar rushed over, throwing aside the dressing screen. He gasped, then knelt beside his son.

The child, Gavinor, scooted away from his father, crying.

Kaladin looked back to the queen. "How long have you been planning this?"

"Planning for my husband's return?"

"I'm not talking to you. I'm talking to the thing beyond you."

She laughed. "Yelig-nar serves me. Or do you speak of the Heart of the Revel? Ashertmarn has no will; he is merely a force of consumption, mindless, to be harnessed."

Elhokar whispered something to his son. Kaladin couldn't hear the words, but the child stopped weeping. He looked up, blinked away tears, and finally let his father pick him up. Elhokar cradled the child, who in turn clutched his stuffed soldier. It wore blue armor.

"Out," Kaladin said.

"But . . ." The king looked toward his wife.

"Elhokar," Kaladin said, gripping the king's shoulder. "Be a hero to the one you can save."

The king met his eyes, then nodded, clutching the young child. He started toward the door, and Kaladin followed, keeping his eyes on the queen.

She sighed loudly, stepping after them. "I feared this."

They rejoined their soldiers, then began to retreat down the hallway.

Aesudan stopped in the doorway to the king's chambers. "I have outgrown you, Elhokar. I have taken the gemstone into me, and have harnessed Yelig-nar's power." Something started to twist around her, a black smoke, blown as if from an unseen wind.

"Double time," Kaladin said to his men, drawing in Stormlight. He could feel it coming; he'd sensed where this would go the moment they'd started up the steps.

It was almost a relief when, at last, Aesudan shouted for her soldiers to attack.

∴

Give it all to me, the voices whispered in Shallan's mind. *Give me your passion, your hunger, your longing, your loss. Surrender it. You are what you feel.*

Shallan swam in it, lost, like in the depths of the ocean. The voices beset her from all sides. When one whispered that she was pain, Shallan became a weeping girl, singing as she twisted a chain tight around a thick neck. When another whispered that she was hunger, she became an urchin on the street, wearing rags for clothing.

Passion. Fear. Enthusiasm. Boredom. Hatred. Lust.

She became a new person with every heartbeat. The voices seemed thrilled by this. They assaulted her, growing to a frenzy. Shallan was a thousand people in a moment.

But which one was her?

All of them. A new voice. Wit's?

"Wit!" she screamed, surrounded by snapping eels in a dark place. "Wit! Please."

You're all of them, Shallan. Why must you be only one emotion? One set of sensations? One role? One life?

"They rule me, Wit. Veil and Radiant and all the others. They're *consuming* me."

Then be ruled as a king is ruled by his subjects. Make Shallan so strong, the others must bow.

"I don't know if I can!"

The darkness thrummed and surged.

And then . . . withdrew?

Shallan didn't feel as if she'd changed anything, but still the darkness retreated. She found herself kneeling on the cold stones outside the control building. The enormous heart became sludge, then melted away, almost seeming to crawl, sending out runners of dark liquid before itself.

"You did it!" Adolin said.

I did?

"Secure that building," Azure commanded her soldiers. Drehy and Skar glowed nearby, looking grim, fresh blood on their clothing. They'd been fighting.

Shallan stood up on shaky feet. The small, circular structure in front of her seemed insignificant compared to the other monastery buildings, but it was the key to everything.

"This is going to be tricky, Azure," Adolin said. "We're going to have to fight back down into the city, push the enemy out. Storms, I hope my father has our armies ready."

Shallan blinked, dazed. She couldn't help feeling she'd failed. That she hadn't done *anything*.

"The first transfer will be only the control building," Adolin said. "After that, she'll swap the entire platform—buildings and all. We'll want to move our army back into the palace before that happens." Adolin turned, surveying the path back. "What is taking the king so long?"

Shallan stepped into the control building. It looked much as the one she'd discovered at the Shattered Plains—though better maintained, and its tile mosaics on the floor were of fanciful creatures. An enormous beast with claws, and fur like a mink. Something that looked like a giant fish. On the walls, lanterns shone with gemstones—and between them hung full-length mirrors.

Shallan walked toward the keyhole control device, summoning Pattern as a Blade. She studied him, then looked up at herself in one of the mirrors hanging on the wall.

Someone else stood in the mirror. A woman with black hair that fell to her waist. She wore archaic clothing, a sleeveless, flowing gown that was more of a tunic, with a simple belted waist. Shallan touched her face. Why had she put this illusion on?

The reflection didn't mimic her motions, but pressed forward, raising hands against the glass. The reflected room faded and the figure distorted, and became a jet-black shadow with white holes for eyes.

Radiant, the thing said, mouthing the words. *My name is Sja-anat. And I am not your enemy.*

Kaladin's men charged down the steps in their escape, though the back ranks bunched up in the hallway around the stairwell. Behind, the Queen's Guard set up and lowered crossbows. Sylspear held high, Kaladin stepped between the two groups and pooled Stormlight into the ground, drawing the bolts downward. He was unpracticed with this power, and unfortunately, some of the bolts still slammed into shields, even heads.

Kaladin growled, then drew in a deep breath of Stormlight, bursting alight—the glow of his skin shining on the walls and ceiling of the palace hallway. The queen's soldiers shied back before the light as if it were something physical.

Distantly, he heard the screaming spren react to what he'd done. He Lashed himself in precisely the right way to rise a few feet off the ground, then float there. The queen's soldiers blinked against the light, as if it were somehow too strong for their eyes. At last, the captain of the rearguard called the final withdrawal, and the rest of Kaladin's men rushed down the stairs. Only Noro's squad lingered.

Some of the queen's soldiers began to test forward at him, so he dropped to the floor and started down the steps at a run. Beard and the rest of the squad joined him, followed by the queen's soldiers, unnaturally silent.

Unfortunately, Kaladin heard something else echoing up the stairwell from down below. The sounds of men clashing, and of familiar singing.

Parshendi songs.

"Rearguard!" Kaladin shouted. "Form up on the steps; orient toward the upper floor!"

His soldiers obeyed, turning and leveling spears and shields at the descending enemy. Kaladin Lashed himself upward and twisted so that he hit the ceiling feet-first. He ducked and ran—passing over the heads of his men in the high stairwell—until he reached the ground floor.

The first ranks of his soldiers clashed with parshman troops in the eastern gallery. But the enemy had penned them into the stairwell, so most of his troops couldn't get down to the fight.

Kaladin released his Lashing, dropping and twisting to land in a tempest of light before the parshman ranks. Several of his men groaned and cried as they fell, bloodied, to the enemy spears. Kaladin felt his rage flare, and he lowered the Sylspear. It was time to begin the work of death.

Then he saw the face of the parshman in front of him.

It was Sah. Former slave. Cardplayer. Father.

Kaladin's friend.

⁂

Shallan regarded the figure in the mirror. It *had* spoken. "What are you?"

They call me the Taker of Secrets, the figure said. *Or they once did.*

"One of the Unmade. Our enemies."

We were made, then unmade, she agreed. *But no, not an enemy!* The figure turned humanlike again, though the eyes remained glowing white. It pressed its hands against the glass. *Ask my son. Please.*

"You're of *him.* Odium."

The figure glanced to the sides, as if frightened. *No. I am of me. Now, only of me.*

Shallan considered, then looked at the keyhole. By using Pattern in that, she could initiate the Oathgate.

Don't do it, Sja-anat pled. *Listen, Radiant. Listen to my plea. Ashertmarn fled on purpose. It is a trap. I was compelled to touch the spren of this device, so it will not function as you wish.*

⁂

Kaladin's will to fight evaporated.

He'd been stoked with energy, ready to enter the battle and protect his men. But . . .

Sah recognized him and gasped, then grabbed his companion—Khen, one of the others Kaladin knew—and pointed. The parshwoman cursed, and the group of them scrambled away from the steps—leaving dead human soldiers.

In the opening provided, Kaladin's men pushed down off the steps into the grand hall. They surged around Kaladin as—stunned—he lowered his spear.

The large, pillared hall became a scene of utter chaos. Azure's soldiers rushed in from the Sunwalk, meeting the parshmen who came up the stairs from the back of the palace—they'd likely broken in through the gardens there. The king held his son, standing amid a group of soldiers in the very center. Kaladin's men managed to get down off the steps, and behind them rushed the Queen's Guard.

It all churned into a melee. Battle lines disintegrated, and platoons shattered, men fighting alone or in pairs. It was a battlefield commander's nightmare. Hundreds of men mixing and screaming and fighting and dying.

Kaladin saw them. *All* of them. Sah and the parshmen, fighting to keep their freedom. The guardsmen who had been rescued, fighting for their king. Azure's Wall Guard, terrified as their city fell around them. The Queen's Guard, convinced they were loyally following orders.

In that moment, Kaladin lost something precious. He'd always been able to trick himself into seeing a battle as *us* against *them*. Protect those you love. Kill everyone else. But . . . but they didn't deserve death.

None of them did.

He locked up. He froze, something that hadn't happened to him since his first days in Amaram's army. The Sylspear vanished in his fingers, puffing to mist. How could he fight? How could he kill people who were just doing the best they could?

"Stop!" he finally bellowed. "*Stop it! Stop killing each other!*"

Nearby, Sah rammed Beard through with a spear.

"*STOP! PLEASE!*"

Noro responded by running through Jali—one of the other parshmen Kaladin had known. Ahead, Elhokar's ring of guards fell, and a member of the Queen's Guard managed to ram the point of a halberd into the king's arm. Elhokar gasped, dropping his Shardblade from pained fingers, holding his son close with his other arm.

The Queen's Guardsman pulled back, eyes widening—as if seeing the king for the first time. One of Azure's soldiers cut the guardsman down in his moment of confusion.

Kaladin screamed, tears streaming from his eyes. He begged them to just stop, to listen.

They couldn't hear him. Sah—gentle Sah, who had only wanted to protect his daughter—died by Noro's sword. Noro, in turn, got his head split by Khen's axe.

Noro and Sah fell beside Beard, whose dead eyes stared sightlessly—his arm stretched out, glyphward soaking up his blood.

Kaladin slumped to his knees. His Stormlight seemed to frighten off the enemies; everyone stayed away from him. Syl spun around him, begging for him to listen, but he couldn't hear her.

The king . . . he thought, numb. *Get . . . get to Elhokar . . .*

Elhokar had fallen to his knees. In one arm he held his terrified son, in the other hand he held . . . a sheet of paper? A sketch?

Kaladin could almost hear Elhokar stuttering the words.

Life . . . life before death . . .

The hair on Kaladin's neck rose. Elhokar started to glow softly.

Strength . . . before weakness . . .

"Do it, Elhokar," Kaladin whispered.

Journey. Journey before . . .

A figure emerged from the battle. A tall, lean man—so, so familiar. Gloom seemed to cling to Moash, who wore a brown uniform like the parshmen. For a heartbeat the battle pivoted on him. Wall Guard behind him, broken Palace Guard before.

"Moash, no . . ." Kaladin whispered. He couldn't move. Stormlight bled from him, leaving him empty, exhausted.

Lowering his spear, Moash ran Elhokar through the chest.

Kaladin screamed.

Moash pinned the king to the ground, shoving aside the weeping child prince with his foot. He placed his boot against Elhokar's throat, holding him down, then pulled the spear out and stabbed Elhokar through the eye as well.

He held the weapon in place, carefully waiting until the fledgling glow around the king faded and flickered out. The king's Shardblade appeared from mist and clanged to the ground beside him.

Elhokar, king of Alethkar, was dead.

Moash pulled the spear free and glanced at the Shardblade. Then he kicked it aside. He looked at Kaladin, then quietly made the Bridge Four salute, wrists tapped together. The spear he held dripped with Elhokar's blood.

The battle broke. Kaladin's men had been all but obliterated; the remnants escaped along the Sunwalk. A member of the Queen's Guard scooped up the young prince and carried him away. Azure's men limped back before the growing parshman armies.

The queen descended the stairs, wreathed in black smoke, eyes glowing red. She'd transformed, strange crystal formations having pierced her skin like carapace. Her chest was glowing bright with a gemstone, as if it had replaced her heart. It shone through her dress.

Kaladin turned from her and crawled toward the king's corpse. Nearby, a member of the Queen's Guard finally took notice of him, seizing him by the arm.

And then . . . light. Glowing Stormlight flooded the chamber as twin Radiants exploded out from the Sunwalk. Drehy and Skar swept through the enemy, driving them back with sweeping spears and Lashings.

A second later, Adolin grabbed Kaladin under the arms and heaved him backward. "Time to go, bridgeboy."

Don't tell anyone. I can't say it. I must whisper. I foresaw this.

—From drawer 30-20, a particularly small emerald

Adolin shoved down the emotion of seeing Elhokar's dead body. It was one of the first battlefield lessons his father had taught him.

Grieve later.

Adolin pulled Kaladin out along the Sunwalk while Skar and Drehy guarded their retreat, encouraging the last of the Wall Guard to run—or limp—to safety.

Kaladin stumbled along. Though he didn't appear wounded, he stared with a glazed-over look. Those were the eyes of a man who bore the kinds of wounds you couldn't fix with bandages.

They eventually poured out of the Sunwalk onto the Oathgate platform, where Azure's soldiers held firm, her surgeons running to help the wounded who had escaped the bloodbath in the eastern gallery. Skar and Drehy dropped down to the platform, guarding the way onto the Sunwalk, to prevent the Queen's Guard or parshmen from following.

Adolin stumbled to a stop. From this vantage he could see the city.

Stormfather.

Tens of thousands of parshmen flooded in through the broken gates or across the nearby sections of wall. Figures glowing with dark light zipped through the air. Those seemed to be gathering in formations nearby, perhaps for an assault on the Oathgate platform.

Adolin took it all in, and admitted the terrible truth. His city was lost.

"All forces, hold the platform," he heard himself saying. "But pass the word. I'm going to take us to Urithiru."

"Sir!" a soldier said. "Civilians are crowding the base of the platform, trying to get up the steps."

"Let them!" Adolin shouted. "Get as many people up here as you can. Hold against any enemy who tries to reach the platform top, but don't engage them if they don't press. We're abandoning the city. Anyone not on the platform in ten minutes will be left behind!"

Adolin hurried toward the control building. Kaladin followed, dazed. *After what he's been through,* Adolin thought, *I wouldn't have expected that anything could faze him. Not even Elhokar's . . .*

Storms. Grieve later.

Azure stood guard in the doorway to the control building, holding the pack full of gemstones. Hopefully, those would be enough to get everyone to safety.

"Brightness Davar told me to clear everyone else out," the highmarshal said. "Something's wrong with the device."

Adolin cursed under his breath and stepped inside. Shallan knelt on the ground before a mirror, looking at herself. Behind, Kaladin stepped in, then settled down on the floor, placing his back to the wall.

"Shallan," Adolin said. "We need to go. *Now.*"

"But—"

"The city has fallen. Transfer the entire platform, not just the control building. We need to get as many people as we can to safety."

"My men on the wall!" Azure said.

"They're dead or routed," Adolin said, gritting his teeth. "I don't like it any more than you do."

"The king—"

"The king is *dead.* The queen has joined the enemy. I'm ordering our retreat, Azure." Adolin locked gazes with the woman. "We gain nothing by dying here."

She drew her lips to a line, but didn't argue further.

"Adolin," Shallan whispered, "the heart was a trick. I didn't chase it off—it left on purpose. I think . . . I think the Voidbringers *intentionally* left Kaladin and his men alone after only a brief fight. They let us come here because the Oathgate is trapped."

"How do you know?" Adolin asked.

Shallan cocked her head. "I'm speaking to her."

"Her?"

"Sja-anat. The Taker of Secrets. She says that if we engage the device, we'll be caught in a disaster."

Adolin took a deep breath.

"Do it anyway," he said.

⁂

Do it anyway.

Shallan understood the implication. How could they trust an ancient spren of Odium? Perhaps Shallan really *had* driven the black heart away, and—in a panic to keep the humans from escaping—Sja-anat was now stalling.

Shallan looked away from the pleading figure in the mirror. The others couldn't see her—she'd confirmed this with Azure already.

"Pattern?" she whispered. "What do you think?"

"Mmmm . . ." he said quietly. "Lies. So many lies. I don't know, Shallan. I cannot tell you."

Kaladin slumped by the wall, staring sightlessly, as if he were dead inside. She couldn't recall ever seeing him in such a state.

"Get ready." Shallan stood up, summoning Pattern as a Blade.

Trust is not mine, said the figure in the mirror. *You will not give my children a home. Not yet.*

Shallan pushed the Blade into the lock. It melded to match Pattern's shape.

I will show you, Sja-anat said. *I will try. My promise is not strong, for I cannot know. But I will try.*

"Try what?" Shallan asked.

Try not to kill you.

With those words haunting her, Shallan engaged the Oathgate.

*My spren claims that recording this will be good for me, so here
I go. Everyone says I will swear the Fourth Ideal soon, and in so
doing, earn my armor. I simply don't think that I can. Am I not
supposed to want to help people?*

—From drawer 10-12, sapphire

D alinar Kholin stood at attention, hands behind his back, one
wrist gripping the other. He could see so far from his balcony at
Urithiru—but it was endless miles of nothing. Clouds and rock.
So much and so little, all at once.

"Dalinar," Navani said, stepping up and resting her hands on his arm.
"Please. At least come inside."

They thought he was sick. They thought his collapse on the Oathgate
platform had been caused by heart troubles, or fatigue. The surgeons had
suggested rest. But if he stopped standing up straight, if he let it bow him
down, he worried the memories would crush him.

The memories of what he'd done at the Rift.

The crying voices of children, begging for mercy.

He forced his emotions down. "What news," he said, embarrassed by
how his voice trembled.

"None," Navani said. "Dalinar . . ."

Word had come from Kholinar via spanreed, one that somehow still
worked. An assault on the palace, an attempt to reach the Oathgate.

Outside, the gathered Kholin, Aladar, and Roion armies clogged one of
Urithiru's Oathgate platforms, waiting to be taken to Kholinar to join the

battle. But nothing happened. Time seeped away. It had been four hours since the first communication.

Dalinar closed his mouth, eyes ahead, and stared at the expanse. At attention, like a soldier. That was how he would wait. Even though he'd never *really* been a soldier. He'd commanded men, ordered recruits to stand in line, inspected ranks. But he himself . . . he'd skipped all of that. He'd waged war in a bloodthirsty riot, not a careful formation.

Navani sighed, patting him on the arm, then returned to their rooms to sit with Taravangian and a small collection of scribes and highprinces. Awaiting news from Kholinar.

Dalinar stood in the breeze, wishing he could empty his mind, rid himself of memories. Go back to being able to pretend he was a good man. Problem was, he'd given in to a kind of fancy, one everyone told about him. They said the Blackthorn had been a terror on the battlefield, but still honest. Dalinar Kholin, he would fight you fair, they said.

Evi's cries, and the tears of murdered children, spoke the truth. Oh . . . oh, *Almighty above.* How could he live with this pain? So fresh, restored anew? But why pray? There was no Almighty watching. If there had been—and if he'd had a shred of justice to him—Honor would have long ago purged this world of the fraud that was Dalinar Kholin.

And I had the gall to condemn Amaram for killing one squad of men to gain a Shardblade. Dalinar had burned an entire city for less. Thousands upon thousands of people.

"Why did you bond me?" Dalinar whispered to the Stormfather. "Shouldn't you have picked a man who was just?"

Just? Justice is *what you brought to those people.*

"That was not justice. That was a massacre."

The Stormfather rumbled. *I have burned and broken cities myself. I can see . . . yes, I see a difference now. I see pain now. I did not see it before the bond.*

Would Dalinar lose his bond now, in exchange for making the Stormfather increasingly aware of human morality? Why *had* these cursed memories returned? Couldn't he have continued for a little longer without them? Long enough to forge the coalition, to prepare the defense of humankind?

That was the coward's route. Wishing for ignorance. The coward's route he'd obviously taken—though he could not yet remember his visit to the Nightwatcher, he knew what he'd asked for. Relief from this awful burden. The ability to lie, to pretend he had not done such horrible things.

He turned away and walked back into his rooms. He didn't know how he'd face this—bear this burden—but today, he needed to focus on the salvation of Kholinar. Unfortunately, he couldn't make battle plans until he knew more about the city's situation.

He entered the common room, where the core of his government had gathered. Navani and the others sat on some couches around the spanreed, waiting. They'd laid out battle maps of Kholinar, talked over strategies, but then . . . hours had passed with no news.

It felt so frustrating to just sit here, ignorant. And it left Dalinar with too much time to think. To remember.

Instead of sitting with the others, Taravangian had taken his normal place: a seat before the warming fabrial in the corner. Legs aching and back stiff, Dalinar walked over and finally let himself sit, groaning softly as he took the seat beside Taravangian.

Before them, a bright red ruby glowed with heat, replacing a fire with something safer but far more lifeless.

"I'm sorry, Dalinar," Taravangian finally said. "I'm sure news will come soon."

Dalinar nodded. "Thank you for what you did when the Azish came to tour the tower."

The Azish had arrived yesterday for an initial tour, but Dalinar had been recovering from the sudden return of his memories. Well . . . truth was, he was *still* recovering. He'd welcomed them, then retired, as Taravangian had offered to lead the tour. Navani said the Azish dignitaries had all been charmed by the elderly king, and planned to return soon for a more in-depth meeting about the possibility of a coalition.

Dalinar leaned forward, staring at the heating fabrial. Behind, Aladar and General Khal conversed—for probably the hundredth time—on how to recover the Kholinar walls, if they were lost by the time the Oathgate started working.

"Have you ever come to the sudden realization," Dalinar said softly, "that you're not the man everyone thinks you are?"

"Yes," Taravangian whispered. "More daunting, however, are similar moments: when I realize I'm not the man *I* think of myself as being."

Stormlight swirled in the ruby. Churning. Trapped. Imprisoned.

"We spoke once," Dalinar said, "of a leader forced to either hang an innocent man or free three murderers."

"I remember."

"How does one live after making a decision like that? Particularly if you eventually discover you made the wrong choice?"

"This is the sacrifice, isn't it?" Taravangian said softly. "Someone must bear the responsibility. Someone must be dragged down by it, ruined by it. Someone must stain their soul so others may live."

"But you're a good king, Taravangian. You didn't murder your way to your throne."

"Does it matter? One wrongly imprisoned man? One murder in an alley that a proper policing force could have stopped? The burden for the blood of those wronged must rest somewhere. I am the sacrifice. *We,* Dalinar Kholin, are the sacrifices. Society offers us up to trudge through dirty water so others may be clean." He closed his eyes. "Someone has to fall, that others may stand."

The words were similar to things Dalinar had said, and thought, for years. Yet Taravangian's version was somehow twisted, lacking hope or life.

Dalinar leaned forward, stiff, feeling old. The two didn't speak for a long period until the others started to stir. Dalinar stood, anxious.

The spanreed was writing. Navani gasped, safehand to her lips. Teshav turned pale, and May Aladar sat back in her seat, looking sick.

The spanreed cut off abruptly and dropped to the page, rolling as it landed.

"What?" Dalinar demanded. "What does it say?"

Navani looked to him, then glanced away. Dalinar shared a look with General Khal, then Aladar.

Dread settled on Dalinar like a cloak. *Blood of my fathers.* "What does it say?" he pled.

"The . . . the capital has fallen, Dalinar," Navani whispered. "The ardent reports that Voidbringer forces have seized the palace. He . . . he cut off after only a few sentences. It looks like they found him, and . . ."

She squeezed her eyes shut.

"The team you sent," Teshav continued, "has apparently failed, Brightlord." She swallowed. "The remnants of the Wall Guard have been captured and imprisoned. The city has fallen. There is no word on the king, Prince Adolin, or the Radiants. Brightlord . . . the message cuts off there."

Dalinar sank back down into his chair.

"Almighty above," Taravangian whispered, grey eyes reflecting the glow of the heating fabrial. "I am so, *so* sorry, Dalinar."

87

THIS PLACE

Good night, dear Urithiru. Good night, sweet Sibling. Good night, Radiants.

—From drawer 29-29, ruby

T he Oathgate's control building shook like it had been hit by a boulder. Adolin stumbled, then fell to his knees.

The shaking was followed by a distinct *ripping* sound, and a blinding flash of light.

His stomach lurched.

He fell through the air.

Shallan screamed somewhere nearby.

Adolin struck a hard surface, and the impact was so jarring that he rolled to the side. That caused him to tumble off the edge of a white stone platform.

He fell into something that gave way beneath him. Water? No, it didn't feel right. He twisted in it—not a liquid, but *beads*. Thousands upon thousands of glass beads, each smaller than a Stormlight sphere.

Adolin thrashed, panicked as he sank. He was dying! He was going to die and suffocate in this sea of endless beads. He—

Someone caught his hand. Azure pulled him up and helped him back onto the platform, beads rolling from his clothing. He coughed, feeling that he had been drowning, though he'd gotten only a few beads in his mouth.

Stormfather! He groaned, looking around. The sky overhead was wrong.

Pitch-black, it was streaked with strange clouds that seemed to stretch forever into the distance—like roads in the sky. They led toward a small, distant sun.

The ocean of beads extended in every direction, and tiny lights hovered above them—thousands upon thousands, like candle flames. Shallan stepped over, kneeling beside him. Nearby, Kaladin was standing up, shaking himself. This circular stone platform was like an island in the ocean of beads, roughly where the control building had been.

Hovering in the air were two enormous spren—they looked like stretched-out versions of people, and stood some thirty feet tall, like sentinels. One was pitch-black in coloring, the other red. He thought them statues at first, but their clothing rippled in the air, and they shifted, one turning eyes down to look at him.

"Oh, this is bad," someone said nearby. "So very, very bad."

Adolin looked and found the speaker to be a creature in a stiff black costume, with a robe that seemed—somehow—to be made of stone. In place of its head was a shifting, changing ball of lines, angles, and impossible dimensions.

Adolin jumped to his feet, scrambling back. He almost collided with a young woman with blue-white skin, pale as snow, wearing a filmy dress that rippled in the wind. Another spren stood beside her, with ashen brown features that seemed to be made of tight cords, the thickness of hair. She wore ragged clothing, and her eyes had been scratched out, like a canvas that someone had taken a knife to.

Adolin looked around, counting them. Nobody else was here on the landing. Those two enormous spren in the sky, and the three smaller ones on the platform. Adolin, Shallan, Kaladin, and Azure.

It seemed the Oathgate had only taken those who had been inside the control building. But *where* had it taken them?

Azure looked up at the sky. "Damnation," she said softly. "I *hate* this place."

THE END OF

Part Three

İNTERLUDES

VENLI • MEM • SHELER

Odium's grand purpose for Venli meant turning her into a show-piece.

"Then, the humans waged a war of extermination against us," she told the assembled crowd. "My sister tried to negotiate, to explain that we had no blame for the assassination of their king. They would not listen. They saw us only as slaves to be dominated."

The wagon upon which she stood wasn't a particularly inspiring dais, but it was better than the pile of boxes she'd used in the last town. At least her new form—envoyform—was tall, the tallest she'd ever worn. It was a form of power, and brought strange abilities, primarily the ability to speak and understand all languages.

That made it perfect for instructing the crowds of Alethi parshmen. "They fought for *years* to exterminate us," she said to Command. "They could not suffer slaves who could think, who could resist. They worked to crush us, lest we inspire a revolution!"

The people gathered around the wagon bore thick lines of marbling—of red and either black or white. Venli's own white and red was far more delicate, with intricate swirls.

She continued, speaking triumphantly to the Rhythm of Command, telling these people—as she'd told many others—her story. At least the version of it that Odium had instructed her to tell.

She told them she'd personally discovered new spren to bond, creating a form that would summon the Everstorm. The story left out that Ulim had done much of the work, giving her the secrets of stormform. Odium obviously wanted to paint the listeners as a heroic group, with Venli their brave leader. The listeners were to be the foundation myth of his growing empire: the last of the old generation, who had fought bravely against the

Alethi, then sacrificed themselves to free their enslaved brothers and sisters.

Hauntingly, the narrative said that Venli's people were now extinct, save herself.

The former slaves listened, rapt by her narrative. She told it well; she should, given how often she'd related it these last weeks. She ended with the call to action, as specifically instructed.

"My people have passed, joining the eternal songs of Roshar," she said. "The day now belongs to you. We had named ourselves 'listeners' because of the songs we heard. These are your heritage, but you are not to merely listen, but sing. Adopt the rhythms of your ancestors and build a nation here! You must *work*. Not for the slavers who once held your minds, but for the future, for your children! And for us. Those who died that you might exist."

They cheered to the Rhythm of Excitement. That was good to hear, even if it was an inferior rhythm. Venli heard something better now: new, powerful rhythms that accompanied forms of power.

Yet . . . hearing those old rhythms awakened something in her. A memory. She put her hand to the pouch at her belt.

How like the Alethi these people act, she thought. She had found humans to be . . . stern. Angry. Always walking about with their emotions worn openly, prisoners to what they felt. These former slaves were similar. Even their jokes were Alethi, often biting toward those to whom they were closest.

At the conclusion of her speech, an unfamiliar Voidspren ushered the people back to work. She'd learned there were three levels in the hierarchy of Odium's people. There were these common singers, who wore the ordinary forms Venli's people had used. Then there were those called Regals, like herself, who were distinguished by forms of power—created by bonding one of several varieties of Voidspren. At the top were the Fused—though she had trouble placing spren like Ulim and others. They obviously outranked the common singers, but what of the Regals?

She saw no humans in this town; those had been rounded up or chased off. She'd overheard some Fused saying that human armies still fought in western Alethkar, but this eastern section was completely singer controlled—remarkable, considering how the humans greatly outnumbered the singers. The Alethi collapse was due in part to the Everstorm, in part to the arrival of the Fused, and in part to the fact that the Alethi had repeatedly conscripted eligible men for their wars.

Venli settled down on the back of the cart, and a femalen singer brought her a cup of water, which she took gladly. Proclaiming yourself as the savior of an entire people was thirsty work.

The singer woman lingered. She wore an Alethi dress, with the left hand covered up. "Is your story really true?"

"Of course it is," Venli said to Conceit. "You doubt?"

"No, of course not! It's just . . . it's hard to imagine. Parshmen *fighting*."

"Call yourselves singers, not parshmen."

"Yes. Um, of course." The femalen held her hand to her face, as if embarrassed.

"Speak to the rhythms to express apology," Venli said. "Use Appreciation to thank someone for correction, or Anxiety to highlight your frustration. Consolation if you are truly contrite."

"Yes, Brightness."

Oh, Eshonai. They have so far to go.

The woman scampered away. That lopsided dress looked ridiculous. There was no reason to distinguish between the genders except in mateform. Humming to Ridicule, Venli hopped down, then walked through the town, head high. The singers wore mostly workform or nimbleform, though a few—like the femalen who had brought the water—wore scholarform, with long hairstrands and angular features.

She hummed to Fury. Her people had spent *generations* struggling to discover new forms, and here these people were given a dozen different options? How could they value that gift without knowing the struggle? They gave Venli deference, bowing like humans, as she approached the town's mansion. She had to admit there was something very satisfying about that.

"What are *you* so smug about?" Rine demanded to Destruction when Venli stepped inside. The tall Fused waited by the window, hovering—as always—a few feet off the ground, his cloak hanging down and resting on the floor.

Venli's sense of authority evaporated. "I can't help but feel as if I'm among babes, here."

"If they are babes, you are a toddler."

A second Fused sat on the floor amid the chairs. That one never spoke. Venli didn't know the femalen's name, and found her constant grin and unblinking eyes . . . upsetting.

Venli joined Rine by the window, looking out at the singers who populated the village. Working the land. Farming. Their lives might not have changed much, but they had their songs back. That meant everything.

"We should bring them human slaves, Ancient One," Venli said to Subservience. "I fear that there is too much land here. If you really want these villages to supply your armies, they'll need more workers."

Rine glanced at her. She'd found that if she spoke to him respectfully— and if she spoke in the ancient tongue—her words were less likely to be dismissed.

"There are those among us who agree with you, child," Rine said.

"You do not?"

"No. We will need to watch the humans constantly. At any moment, any of them could manifest powers from the enemy. We killed him, and yet he fights on through his Surgebinders."

Surgebinders. Foolishly, the old songs spoke highly of them. "How can they bind spren, Ancient One?" she asked to Subservience. "Humans don't . . . you know . . ."

"So timid," he said to Ridicule. "Why is mentioning gemhearts so difficult?"

"They are sacred and personal." Listener gemhearts were not gaudy or ostentatious, like those of greatshells. Clouded white, almost the color of bone, they were beautiful, intimate things.

"They're a part of you," Rine said. "The dead bodies taboo, the refusal to talk of gemhearts—you're as bad as those out there, walking around with one hand covered."

What? *That* was unfair. She attuned Fury.

"It . . . shocked us when it first happened," Rine eventually said. "Humans don't have gemhearts. How could they bond spren? It was unnatural. Yet somehow, their bond was *more powerful than ours*. I always said the same thing, and believe it even more strongly now: We must exterminate them. Our people will never be safe on this world as long as the humans exist."

Venli felt her mouth grow dry. Distantly, she heard a rhythm. The Rhythm of the Lost? An inferior one. It was gone in a moment.

Rine hummed to Conceit, then turned and barked a command to the crazy Fused. She scrambled to her feet and loped after him as he floated out the door. He was probably going to confer with the town's spren. He'd give orders and warnings, which he usually only did right before they left one town for another. Despite having unpacked her things, working under the assumption she'd be here for the night, now Venli suspected they would soon be moving on.

She went to her room on the second floor of the mansion. As usual, the *luxury* of these buildings astounded her. Soft beds you felt you would sink into. Fine woodworking. Blown-glass vases and crystal sconces on the walls for holding spheres. She'd always hated the Alethi, who had acted like they were benevolent parents encountering wild children to be educated. They had pointedly ignored the culture and advancements of Venli's people, eyeing only the hunting grounds of the greatshells that they—because of translation errors—decided must be the listeners' gods.

Venli felt at the beautiful swirls in the glass of a wall sconce. How had they colored some of it white, but not all of it? Whenever she encountered things like this, she had to remind herself forcefully that the Alethi being *technologically* superior did not make them *culturally* superior. They'd simply had access to more resources. Now that the singers had access to artform, they would be able to create works like this too.

But still . . . it was so beautiful. Could they really *exterminate* the people who had created such beautiful and delicate swirls in the glass? The decorations reminded her of her own pattern of marbling.

The pouch at her waist started vibrating. She wore a listener's leather skirt below a tight shirt, topped with a looser overshirt. Part of Venli's place was to show the singers that someone like them—not some distant, fearsome creature from the past—had brought the storms and freed the singers.

Her eyes lingered on the sconce, and then she dumped out her pouch on the room's stumpweight desk. Spheres bounced free, along with a larger number of uncut gemstones, which her people had used instead.

The little spren rose from where it had been hiding among the light. It looked like a comet when it moved, though sitting still—as it did now—it only glowed like a spark.

"Are you one of them?" she asked softly. "The spren that move in the sky some nights?"

It pulsed, sending off a ring of light that dissipated like glowing smoke. Then it began zipping through the room, looking at things.

"The room isn't any different from the last one you looked at," she said to Amusement.

The spren zipped to the wall sconce, where it let off a pulse in awe, then moved to the identical one on the opposite side of the door.

Venli moved to gather her clothing and writings from the drawers in the dresser. "I don't know why you stay with me. It can't be comfortable in that bag."

The spren zipped past her, looking in the drawer that she'd opened.

"It's a *drawer*," she said.

The spren peeked out, then pulsed in a quick blinking succession.

That's Curiosity, she thought, recognizing the rhythm. She hummed it to herself as she packed her things, then hesitated. Curiosity was an old rhythm. Like . . . Amusement, which she'd attuned moments ago. She could hear the normal rhythms again.

She looked at the little spren. "Is this your doing?" she demanded to Irritation.

It shrank, but pulsed to Resolve.

"What are you hoping to accomplish? Your kind betrayed us. Go find a human to bother."

It shrank further. Then pulsed to Resolve again.

Bother. Down below, the door slammed open. Rine was back already.

"In the pouch," she hissed to Command. "Quickly."

There was art to doing laundry.

Sure, everyone knew the basics, just like every child could hum a tune. But did they know how to relax the fibers of a stubborn seasilk dress by returning it to a warm brine, then restore its natural softness by rinsing it and brushing with the grain? Could they spot the difference between a mineral dye from Azir and a floral dye from the Veden slopes? You used different soaps for each one.

Mem toiled at her canvas—which was, in this case, a pair of vivid red trousers. She scooped some powder soap—hog fat based, mixed with fine abrasive—and rubbed at a stain on the leg. She wetted the trousers again, then with a fine brush she worked in the soap.

Oil stains were challenging enough, but this man had gotten blood on the same spot. She had to get the stain out without fading that fine Mycalin red—they got it from a slug on the shores of the Purelake—or ruining the cloth. Mraize did like his clothing to look sharp.

Mem shook her head. What *was* this stain? She had to go through four soaps, then try some of her drying powder, before she got it to budge, and then she moved on to the rest of the suit. Hours passed. Clean this spot, rinse that shirt. Hang it up for all to see. She didn't notice the time until the other Veden washwomen started to leave in clumps, returning to their homes, some of which were empty and cold, their husbands and sons dead in the civil war.

The need for clean clothing outlived disasters. The end of the world could come, but that would only mean more bloodstains to wash. Mem finally stepped back before her drying racks, hands on hips, basking in the accomplishment of a day's work well done.

Drying her hands, Mem went to check on her new assistant, Pom, who was washing underclothes. The dark-skinned woman was obviously of mixed blood, both Easterner and Westerner. She was finishing an undershirt, and didn't say anything as Mem stepped up beside her.

Storms, why hasn't anyone snatched her up? Mem thought as the gorgeous woman rubbed the shirt, then dunked it, then rubbed it again. Women like Pom didn't usually end up as washgirls, though she did tend to stare daggers at any man who got too close. Maybe that was it.

"Well done," Mem said. "Hang that to dry and help me gather the rest of this." They piled clothing in baskets, then made the short hike through the city.

Vedenar still smelled like smoke to Mem. Not the good smoke of bakeries, but rather of the enormous pyres that had burned outside on the plain. Her employer lived near the markets, in a large townhome beside some rubble—a lingering reminder of when siege weapons had rained boulders upon Vedenar.

The two washwomen passed guards at the front and headed up the steps. Mem insisted on not using the servants' entrance. Mraize was one of the few who humored her.

"Keep close," she said to Pom, who dallied once they were inside. They hurried down a long, unornamented corridor, then up a staircase.

People said that servants were invisible. Mem had never found that to be true, particularly around people like Mraize. Not only did the house steward notice if someone so much as moved a candlestick, Mraize's friends were the type who kept careful track of everyone near them. Two of them stood in a doorway Mem passed, a man and woman speaking quietly. Both wore swords, and though they didn't interrupt their conversation as the washwomen passed, they watched.

Mraize's quarters were at the top of a staircase. He wasn't there today— he appeared on occasion to drop off dirty clothing, then gallivanted off someplace to find new types of crem to stain his shirts. Mem and Pom went into his den first—he kept his evening jackets there.

Pom froze in the doorway.

"Stop dallying," Mem reminded her, covering a smile. After stark, empty hallways and stairwells, this overstuffed den *was* a little overwhelming. She'd marveled too, her first time here. A mantel covered in curiosities, each in its own glass display. Deep rugs from Marat. Five paintings of the finest skill, each of a different Herald.

"You were right," Pom said from behind.

"Of course I was right," Mem said, setting down her basket in front of the corner wardrobe. "Mraize—remember, he doesn't want to be called 'master'—is of the finest and most refined taste. He employs *only* the best of—"

She was interrupted by a ripping sound.

It was a sound that inspired terror. The sound of a seam splitting, or of a delicate chemise tearing as it caught on part of a washtub. It was the sound of disaster incarnate. Mem turned to find her new assistant standing on a chair, *attacking* one of Mraize's paintings with a knife.

A piece of Mem's brain stopped working. A whine escaped from the back of her throat and her vision grew dark.

Pom was . . . she was *destroying one of Mraize's paintings*.

"I've been looking for that," Pom said, stepping back and putting hands on hips, still standing on the chair.

Two guards burst into the room, perhaps drawn by the noise. They looked at Pom and their jaws dropped. In turn, she flipped her knife about in her hand and pointed it threateningly at the men.

Then, horror of horrors, *Mraize himself* appeared behind the soldiers, wearing an evening jacket and slippers. "What is this ruckus?"

So *refined*. Yes, his face looked like it had seen the wrong side of a sword a couple of times. But he had exquisite taste in clothing and—of course—in garment-care professionals.

"Ah!" he said, noticing Pom. "Finally! The masterpiece of the Oilsworn was all it took, was it? Excellent!" Mraize shoved out the confused guards, then pulled the door shut. He didn't even seem to notice Mem. "Ancient One, would you care for something to drink?"

Pom narrowed her eyes at him, then hopped off the chair. She walked quickly to Mraize and used one hand on his chest to push him aside. She pulled open the door.

"I know where Talenelat is," Mraize said.

Pom froze.

"Yes . . . let's have that drink, shall we?" Mraize asked. "My *babsk* has been eager to speak with you." He glanced at Mem. "Is that my Azish cavalrylord's suit?"

"Um . . . yes . . ."

"You got the aether out of it?"

"The . . . what?"

He strode over and pulled the red trousers out of the basket to inspect them. "Mem, you are an absolute genius. Not every hunter carries a spear, and this is proof indeed. Go to Condwish and tell him I approve a three-firemark bonus for you."

"Th-thank you, Mraize."

"Go collect your bonus, and leave," Mraize said. "Note that you will need to find a new washgirl to help you, after today."

Eshonai would have loved this, Venli thought as she flew hundreds of feet in the air. Rine and the other Fused carried her by means of linked harnesses. It made her feel like a sack of grain being hauled to market, but it gave her quite an amazing view.

Endless hills of stone. Patches of green, often in the shadows of hillsides. Thick forests snarled with undergrowth to present a unified front against the storms.

Eshonai would have been thrilled; she'd have begun drawing maps, talking about the places she could go.

Venli, on the other hand, spent most of these trips feeling sick to her stomach. Normally she didn't have to suffer for long; towns were close together here in Alethkar. Yet today, her ancestors flew her past many occupied towns without stopping.

Eventually, what first appeared to be another ridge of stones resolved into the walls of a large city, easily twice the size of one of the domes at the Shattered Plains.

Stone buildings and reinforced towers. Marvels and wonders. It had been years since she'd seen Kholinar—only that once, when they'd executed King Gavilar. Now, smoke rose in patches throughout the city, and many of the guard towers had been shattered. The city gates lay broken. Kholinar, it seemed, had been conquered.

Rine and his companions zipped through the air, raising fists toward other Fused. They surveyed the city, then soared out beyond the wall and landed near a bunker outside the city. They waited as Venli undid her harness, then lifted into the air again just high enough that the bottoms of their long cloaks brushed the stones.

"Am I finished with my work, Ancient One?" Venli asked to Subservience. "Is that why you finally brought me here?"

"Done?" Rine said to Ridicule. "Child, you haven't even begun. Those little villages were practice. Today, your true labor begins."

"You have three choices," the Herdazian general said.

He had dark brown skin the color of a weathered stone, and there was a hint of grey in the thin mustache on his upper lip. He stepped up to Sheler, then put his hands to his sides. Remarkably, some men affixed manacles *to the general's own wrists*. What on Roshar?

"Pay attention," the general said. "This is important."

"To the manacles?" Sheler said in Herdazian. Life on the border had forced him to learn the language. "What is going on here? Do you realize the *trouble* you're in for taking me captive?" Sheler started to stand, but one of the Herdazian soldiers forced him down so hard, his knees rapped against the hard stone floor of the tent.

"You have *three* choices." The general's manacles clinked as he twisted his hands in them. "First, you can choose the sword. Now, that might be a clean death. A good beheading rarely hurts. Unfortunately, it won't be a headsman who gets the chance with you. We'll give the sword to the women you abused. Each gets a hack, one after another. How long it goes on will depend on them."

"This is *outrageous*!" Sheler said. "I'm a lighteyes of the fifth dahn! I'm cousin to the highlord himself, and—"

"Second option," the general said, "is the hammer. We break your legs and arms, then hang you from the cliff by the ocean. You might last until the storm that way, but it will be miserable."

Sheler struggled to no avail. Captured by *Herdazians*. Their general wasn't even a lighteyes!

The general twisted his hands, then pulled them apart. The manacles clinked to the ground. Nearby, several of his officers grinned, while others groaned. A scribe had tapped off the time, and gave an accounting of the seconds the escape had taken.

The general accepted the applause of several men, then thumped another—a loser in the betting—on his back. Sheler almost seemed forgotten for a moment. Finally, the general turned back to him. "I wouldn't take the hammer, if I were you. But there's a third option: the hog."

"I *demand* the right of ransom!" Sheler said. "You *must* contact my highprince and accept payment based on my rank!"

"Ransom is for men caught in battle," the general said. "Not bastards caught robbing and murdering civilians."

"My homeland is under invasion!" Sheler shouted. "I was gathering resources so we might mount a resistance!"

"A resistance is *not* what we caught you mounting." The general kicked at the manacles by his feet. "Choose one of the three options. I don't have all day."

Sheler licked his lips. How had he ended up in this situation? His homeland gone crazy, the parshmen rampaging, his men scattered by *flying* monsters? Now this? The dirty Herdazians obviously weren't going to listen to reason. They . . .

Wait.

"Did you say *hog*?" Sheler asked.

"It lives down by the shore," the Herdazian general said. "That's your third option. We grease you, and you wrestle the hog. It's fun for the men to watch. They need sport now and then."

"And if I do this, you won't kill me?"

"No, but this isn't as easy as you think. I've tried it myself, so I can speak with authority."

Crazy Herdazians. "I choose the hog."

"As you wish." The general picked up the manacles and handed them to his officer.

"Thought you'd fail these ones for sure," the officer said. "The merchant claimed they're from the best Thaylen locksmiths."

"Doesn't matter how good the lock is, Jerono," the general said with a grin, "if the cuffs are loose." What a ridiculous little man—too-wide smile, a flat nose, a missing tooth. Why, Highlord Amaram would have—

Sheler was jerked to his feet by the chains, then pulled through the camp of Herdazian soldiers on the Alethi border. There were more refugees here than actual fighting men! Give Sheler a single company, and he could rout this entire force.

His insufferable captors led him down an incline, past the cliffs and toward the shore. Soldiers and refugees alike gathered above, jeering and calling. Obviously, the Herdazian general was too frightened to actually *kill* an Alethi officer. So they would humiliate him by making him wrestle a pig. They'd have a good laugh, then send him away smarting.

Idiots. He'd come back with an army.

One man locked Sheler's chain to a metal loop on the stones. Another approached with a pitcher of oil. They poured it over Sheler's head; he sputtered as the liquid ran down his face. "What is that *stench*?"

Above, someone blew a horn.

"I'd say 'good luck,' boss," the Herdazian soldier told Sheler as his companion ran off, "but I've got three marks on you not lasting a full minute. Still, who knows. When the general was chained down here, he got out in less."

The ocean started to churn.

"Of course," the soldier said, "the general likes this kind of thing. He's a little weird."

The soldier dashed back up the bank, leaving Sheler locked in place, doused in pungent oil, and gaping as an enormous claw broke the surface of the ocean.

Perhaps "the hog" was more of a nickname.

Venli's little spren—whom she'd named Timbre—peeked around the room, looking in each corner and shadowed place, like she did each time Venli let her out of the pouch.

Days had passed since Venli had first arrived at Kholinar. And, as Rine had warned, this was her true labor. Venli now gave her presentation a dozen times each day, speaking to groups of singers brought out of the city for the purpose. She wasn't allowed into Kholinar herself. They kept her sequestered in this stormshelter outside, which they called the hermitage.

Venli hummed to Spite as she leaned against the window, annoyed by the incarceration. Even the window had only been installed—cut by a Shardblade and set with thick stormshutters—after her repeated requests. The city outside called to her. Majestic walls, beautiful buildings. It reminded her of Narak . . . which, actually, her people hadn't built. In living there, the listeners had profited from the labors of ancient humans, as modern humans had profited from the enslaved singers.

Timbre floated over to her, then hovered by the window, as if to sneak out and look around outside.

"No," Venli said.

Timbre pulsed to Resolve, then inched forward in the air.

"Stay inside," Venli said to Command. "They're watching for spren like you. Descriptions of your kind, and others, have been spread all through the city."

The little spren backed away, pulsing to Annoyance, before settling in the air beside Venli.

Venli rested her head on her arms. "I feel like a relic," she whispered. "Already I seem like a cast-off ruin from a nearly forgotten day. Are you the reason I feel like that, suddenly? I only get this way when I let you out."

Timbre pulsed to Peace. Upon hearing that, something stirred deep within Venli: the Voidspren that occupied her gemheart. That spren couldn't think, not like Ulim or the higher Voidspren. It was a thing of emotions and animal instincts, but the bond with it granted Venli her form of power.

She started to wonder. So many of the Fused were obviously unhinged; perhaps their inordinately long lives had taken a toll on their psyches. Wouldn't Odium need new leaders for his people? If she proved herself, could she claim a place among them?

New Fused. New . . . gods?

Eshonai had always worried about Venli's thirst for power, and had cautioned her to control her ambitions. Even Demid, at times, had been worried for her. And now . . . and now they were all dead.

Timbre pulsed to Peace, then to Pleading, then back to Peace.

"I can't," Venli said to Mourning. "I can't."

Pleading. More insistent. The Rhythm of the Lost, of Remembrance, and then Pleading.

"I'm the wrong one," Venli said to Annoyance. "I can't do this, Timbre. I can't resist him."

Pleading.

"I *made* this happen," she said to Fury. "Don't you realize that? I'm the one who *caused all this*. Don't plead to me!"

The spren shrank, her light diminishing. Yet she still pulsed to Resolve. Idiot spren. Venli put a hand to her head. Why . . . why was she not more angry about what had happened to Demid, Eshonai, and the others? Could Venli really think about joining the Fused? Those monsters insisted her people were gone, and rebuffed her questions about the thousands of listeners who had survived the Battle of Narak. Were they all . . . *all* being turned into Fused? Shouldn't Venli be thinking about that, not her ambitions?

A form changes the way you think, Venli. Everyone knew that. Eshonai had lectured—incessantly, as had been her way—about not letting the form dictate one's actions. *Control the form, don't let it control you.*

But then, Eshonai had been exemplary. A general and a hero. Eshonai had done her duty.

All Venli had ever wanted was power.

Timbre suddenly pulsed with a flash of light, and zipped away under the bed, terrified.

"Ah," Venli said to Mourning, looking past the city at the sudden darkening of the sky. The Everstorm. It came about every nine days, and this was the second since her arrival. "So that's why they didn't bring an evening batch to listen to me."

She folded her arms, took a deep breath, and hummed to Resolve until she lost track and shifted unconsciously to the Rhythm of Destruction.

She didn't close the window. He didn't like that. Instead, she closed her eyes and listened to the thunder. Lightning flashed beyond her eyelids, red and garish. The spren in her *leaped* to feel it, and she grew excited, the Rhythm of Destruction swelling inside her.

Her people might be gone, but this . . . this *power* was worth it. How could she not embrace this?

How long can you keep being two people, Venli? She seemed to hear Eshonai's voice. *How long will you vacillate?*

The storm hit, wind blasting through the window, lifting her . . . and she entered some kind of vision. The building vanished, and she was tossed about in the storm—but she knew that after it passed, she wouldn't be hurt.

Venli eventually dropped onto a hard surface. She hummed to Destruction and opened her eyes, finding herself standing on a platform hanging high in the sky, far above Roshar, which was a blue and brown globe below. Behind her was a deep, black nothingness marred only by a tiny blip that could have been a single star.

That yellow-white star expanded toward her at an awesome speed, swelling, growing, until it overwhelmed her with an incredible flame. She felt her skin melting, her flesh burning away.

You are not telling the story well enough, Odium's voice declared, speaking the ancient tongue. *You grow restless. The Fused inform me of it. This will change or you will be destroyed.*

"Y-yes . . . Lord." Speaking burned away her tongue. She could no longer see; the fire had claimed her eyes. Pain. Agony. But she *couldn't bend to it,* for the god before her demanded all of her attention. The pain of her body being consumed was nothing compared to *him.*

You are mine. Remember this.

She was vaporized completely.

And woke on the floor of her hermitage, fingers bleeding from having clawed the stone again. The storm's rumbling had grown distant—she'd been gone for hours. Had she burned the entire time?

Trembling, she squeezed her eyes shut. Her skin melting, her eyes, her tongue burning away . . .

The Rhythm of Peace pulled her out of it, and she knew Timbre hovered beside her. Venli rolled over and groaned, eyes still shut, seeking Peace in her own mind.

She couldn't find it. Odium's presence was too fresh; the spren inside her thrummed to Craving instead.

"I can't do it," she whispered to Derision. "You've got the wrong sister."

The wrong sister had died. The wrong sister lived.

Venli had schemed to return their gods.

This was her reward.

FOUR

Defy! Sing Beginnings!

ADOLIN • SHALLAN • KALADIN • DALINAR •
NAVANI • SZETH • TARAVANGIAN • VENLI

88

VOICES

EIGHT YEARS AGO

Gavilar was starting to look worn.

Dalinar stood at the back of the king's den, listening with half an ear. The king spoke with the heirs of the highprinces, staying to safe topics, like Gavilar's plans for various civic projects in Kholinar.

He's looking so old, Dalinar thought. *Grey before his time. He needs something to revitalize him.* A hunt, maybe?

Dalinar didn't need to participate in the meeting; his job was to loom. Occasionally, one of the younger men would glance toward the perimeter of the room, and see the Blackthorn there in shadow. Watching.

He saw fires reflected in their eyes, and heard the weeping of children in the back of his mind.

Don't be weak, Dalinar thought. *It's been almost three years.*

Three years, living with what he'd done. Three years, wasting away in Kholinar. He'd assumed it would get better.

It was only getting worse.

Sadeas had carefully spun news of the Rift's destruction to the king's advantage. He'd called it regrettable that the Rifters had forced Kholin action by killing Dalinar's wife, and named it unfortunate that the city had caught fire during the fighting. Gavilar had publicly censured Dalinar and Sadeas for "losing the city to flames," but his denunciation of the Rifters had been far more biting.

The implication was clear. Gavilar didn't *want* to unleash the Blackthorn. Even he couldn't predict what kind of destruction Dalinar would bring. Obviously, such measures were a last resort—and these days, everyone was careful to give him plenty of other options.

So efficient. All it had cost was one city. And possibly Dalinar's sanity.

Gavilar suggested to the gathered lighteyes that they light a fire in the hearth, for warmth. Well, that was the signal that he could leave. Dalinar could not *stand* fire. The scent of smoke smelled like burning skin, and the crackling of flames reminded him only of her.

Dalinar slipped out the back door, stepping into a hallway on the third floor, heading toward his own rooms. He had moved himself and his sons into the royal palace. His own keep reminded him too much of her.

Storms. Standing in that room—looking at the fear in the eyes of Gavilar's guests—had made the pain and memories particularly acute today. He was better on some days. Others . . . felt like today. He needed a stiff drink from his wine cabinet.

Unfortunately, as he rounded through the curved corridor, he smelled incense in the air. Coming from his rooms? Renarin was burning it again.

Dalinar pulled up, as if he'd run up against something solid, then turned on his heel and walked away. It was too late, unfortunately. That scent . . . that was *her* scent.

He strode down to the second floor, passing bloodred carpets, pillared hallways. Where to get something to drink? He couldn't go out into the city, where people acted so terrified of him. The kitchens? No, he wouldn't go begging to one of the palace chefs—who would in turn tiptoe to the king and whisper that the Blackthorn had been at the violets again. Gavilar complained at how much Dalinar drank, but what else did soldiers do when not at war? Didn't he deserve a little relaxation, after all he'd done for this kingdom?

He turned toward the king's throne room, which—as the king was using his den instead—would be empty today. He went in through the servants' entrance and stepped into a small staging room, where food was prepared before being delivered to the king. Using a sapphire sphere for light, Dalinar knelt and rummaged in one of the cupboards. Usually they kept some rare vintages here for impressing visitors.

The cupboards were empty. Damnation. He found nothing but pans, trays, and cups. A few bags of Herdazian spices. He fumed, tapping the counter. Had Gavilar discovered that Dalinar was coming here, and moved the wine? The king thought him a drunkard, but Dalinar indulged only on occasion. On bad days. Drink quieted the sounds of people crying in the back of his mind.

Weeping. Children burning. Begging their fathers to save them from the flames. And Evi's voice, accompanying them all . . .

When was he going to escape this? He was becoming a coward! Nightmares when he tried to sleep. Weeping in his mind whenever he saw fire. Storms take Evi for doing this to him! If she'd acted like an adult instead of a child—if she'd been able to face *duty* or just *reality* for once—she wouldn't have gotten herself killed.

He stomped into the corridor and strode right into a group of young soldiers. They scrambled to the sides of the hallway and saluted. Dalinar tipped his head toward their salutes, trying to keep the thunder from his expression.

The consummate general. That was who he was.

"Father?"

Dalinar pulled up sharply. He'd completely missed that Adolin was among the soldiers. At fifteen, the youth was growing tall and handsome. He got the former from Dalinar. Today, Adolin wore a fashionable suit with far too much embroidery, and boots that were topped by silver.

"That's not a standard-issue uniform, soldier," Dalinar said to him.

"I know!" Adolin said. "I had it specially tailored!"

Storms . . . His son was becoming a fop.

"Father," Adolin said, stepping up and making an eager fist. "Did you get my message? I've got a bout set up with Tenathar. Father, he's *ranked*. It's a step toward winning my Blade!" He beamed at Dalinar.

Emotions warred inside of Dalinar. Memories of good years spent with his son in Jah Keved, riding or teaching him the sword.

Memories of her. The woman from whom Adolin had inherited that blond hair and that smile. So genuine. Dalinar wouldn't trade Adolin's sincerity for a hundred soldiers in proper uniforms.

But he also couldn't face it right now.

"Father?" Adolin said.

"You're in uniform, soldier. Your tone is too familiar. Is this how I taught you to act?"

Adolin blushed, then put on a stronger face. He didn't wilt beneath the stern words. When censured, Adolin only *tried harder*.

"Sir!" the young man said. "I'd be proud if you'd watch my bout this week. I think you'll be pleased with my performance."

Storming child. Who could deny him? "I'll be there, soldier. And will watch with pride."

Adolin grinned, saluted, then dashed back to join the others. Dalinar walked off as quickly as he could, to get away from that hair, that wonderful—haunting—smile.

Well, he needed a drink now more than ever. But he would *not* go begging to the cooks. He had another option, one that he was certain even his brother—sly though Gavilar was—wouldn't have considered. He went down another set of steps and reached the eastern gallery of the palace, now passing ardents with shaved heads. It was a sign of his desperation that he came all the way out here, facing their condemning eyes.

He slipped down the stairwell into the depths of the building, entering halls that led toward the kitchens in one direction, the catacombs in the other. A few twists and turns led him out onto the Beggars' Porch: a small patio between the compost heaps and the gardens. Here, a group of miserable people waited for the offerings Gavilar gave after dinner.

Some begged of Dalinar, but a glare made the rag-clothed wretches pull back and cower. At the back of the porch, he found Ahu huddled in the shadows between two large religious statues, their backs facing the beggars, their hands spread toward the gardens.

Ahu was an odd one, even for a crazy beggar. With black, matted hair and a scraggly beard, his skin was dark for an Alethi. His clothing was mere scraps, and he smelled worse than the compost.

Somehow he always had a bottle with him.

Ahu giggled at Dalinar. "Have you seen me?"

"Unfortunately." Dalinar settled on the ground. "I have smelled you too. What are you drinking today? It had better not be water this time, Ahu."

Ahu wagged a stout, dark bottle. "Dunno what it is, little child. Tastes good."

Dalinar tried a sip and hissed. A burning wine, no sweetness to it at all. A white, though he didn't recognize the vintage. Storms . . . it smelled intoxicating.

Dalinar took a chug, then handed the bottle back to Ahu. "How are the voices?"

"Soft, today. They chant about ripping me apart. Eating my flesh. Drinking my blood."

"Pleasant."

"Hee hee." Ahu snuggled back against the branches of the hedge-wall, as if they were soft silk. "Nice. Not bad at all, little child. What of your noises?"

In reply, Dalinar reached out his hand. Ahu gave him the bottle. Dalinar drank, welcoming the fuzzing of mind that would quiet the weeping.

Aven begah, Ahu said. "It's a fine night for my torment, and no telling the skies to be still. Where is my soul, and who is this in my face?"

"You're a strange little man, Ahu."

Ahu cackled his response and waved for the wine. After a drink, he returned it to Dalinar, who wiped off the beggar's spittle with his shirt. Storm Gavilar for pushing him to this.

"I like you," Ahu said to Dalinar. "I like the pain in your eyes. Friendly pain. Companionable pain."

"Thanks."

"Which one got to you, little child?" Ahu asked. "The Black Fisher? The Spawning Mother, the Faceless? Moelach is close. I can hear his wheezing, his scratching, his scraping at time like a rat breaking through walls."

"I have no idea what you're talking about."

"Madness," Ahu said, then giggled. "I used to think it wasn't my fault. But you know, we can't escape what we did? *We* let them in. *We* attracted them, befriended them, took them out to dance and courted them. It is *our fault.* You open yourself to it, and you pay the price. They ripped my brain out and made it dance! I watched."

Dalinar paused, the bottle halfway to his lips. Then he held it out to Ahu. "Drink this. You need it."

Ahu obliged.

Sometime later, Dalinar stumbled back to his rooms, feeling downright *serene*—thoroughly smashed and without a crying child to be heard. At the door, he stopped and looked back down the corridor. Where . . . He couldn't remember the trip back up from the Beggars' Porch.

He looked down at his unbuttoned jacket, his white shirt stained with dirt and drink. *Um . . .*

A voice drifted through the closed door. Was that Adolin inside? Dalinar started, then focused. Storms, he'd come to the wrong door.

Another voice. Was that Gavilar? Dalinar leaned in.

"I'm worried about him, Uncle," Adolin's voice said.

"Your father never adjusted to being alone, Adolin," the king replied. "He misses your mother."

Idiots, Dalinar thought. He didn't miss Evi. He wanted to be *rid* of her.

Though . . . he did ache now that she was gone. Was that why she wept for him so often?

"He's down with the beggars again," another voice said from inside. Elhokar? That little boy? Why did he sound like a man? He was only . . . how old? "He tried the serving room again first. Seems he forgot he drank that all last time. Honestly, if there's a bottle hidden in this palace anywhere, that drunken fool will find it."

"My father is *not* a fool!" Adolin said. "He's a great man, and you owe him your—"

"Peace, Adolin," Gavilar said. "Both of you, hold your tongues. Dalinar is a soldier. He'll fight through this. Perhaps if we go on a trip we can distract him from his loss. Maybe Azir?"

Their voices . . . He had just rid himself of Evi's weeping, but hearing this dragged her back. Dalinar gritted his teeth and stumbled to the proper door. Inside, he found the nearest couch and collapsed.

X Kholinar

SEA OF ORACLES

SEA OF ORACLES

SEA OF ORACLES

I rode that mandra from here to Celebrant, so you owe me those silver pieces after all.

Candlemore

Salavashi Trench

I met Smolderbrand. Stole this map from her.

Smolderbrand Channel

Celebrant

Celebrant Channel

North Hallen Channel

Nor Channel

Emberdark Channel

South Hallen Channel

Emberdark

The Burning Gardens

THE GLASSWATER DEEP

Spren fishing is illegal here, but their jail is nicer than most.

Ravizadth

THE LUMINOUS SHALLOWS

I hate this lake.

X Thayler City

THAYLEN SEA

Avoid at all costs.

Caretaker of Laughter

Salumon the Third Tower

My personal map of the requested area, including notes from previous errands

89

DAMNATION

My research into the Unmade has convinced me that these things were not simply "spirits of the void" or "nine shadows who moved in the night." They were each a specific kind of spren, endowed with vast powers.

—From Hessi's *Mythica*, page 3

Adolin had never bothered imagining what Damnation might look like.

Theology was for women and scribes. Adolin figured he'd try to follow his Calling, becoming the best swordsman he could. The ardents told him that was enough, that he didn't need to worry about things like Damnation.

Yet here he was, kneeling on a white marble platform with a black sky overhead, a cold sun—if it could even be called that—hanging at the end of a roadway of clouds. An ocean of shifting glass beads, clattering against one another. Tens of thousands of flames, like the tips of oil lamps, hovering above that ocean.

And the spren. Terrible, awful spren swarmed in the ocean of beads, bearing a multitude of nightmare forms. They twisted and writhed, howling with inhuman voices. He didn't recognize any of the varieties.

"I'm dead," Adolin whispered. "We're dead, and this is Damnation."

But what of the pretty, blue-white spren girl? The creature with the stiff robe and a mesmerizing, impossible symbol instead of a head? What of the woman with the scratched-out eyes? And those two enormous spren standing overhead, with spears and—

Light exploded to Adolin's left. Kaladin Stormblessed, pulling in power, floated into the air. Beads rattled, and every monster in the writhing throng turned—as if one—to fixate upon Kaladin.

"Kaladin!" the spren girl shouted. "Kaladin, they feed on Stormlight! You'll draw their attention. *Everything's* attention."

"Drehy and Skar . . ." Kaladin said. "Our soldiers. Where are they?"

"They're still on the other side," Shallan said, standing up beside Adolin. The creature with the twisted head took her arm, steadying her. "Storms, they might be safer than we are. We're in Shadesmar."

Some of the lights nearby vanished. Candles' flames being snuffed out.

Many spren swam toward the platform, joining an increasingly large group that churned around it, causing a ruckus in the beads. The majority of them were long eel-like things, with ridges along their backs and purple antennae that squirmed like tongues and seemed to be made of thick liquid.

Beneath them, deep in the beads, something enormous shifted, causing beads to roll off one another in piles.

"Kaladin!" the blue girl shouted. "Please!"

He looked at her, and seemed to see her for the first time. The Light vanished from him, and he dropped—hard—to the platform.

Azure held her thin Shardblade, gaze fixed on the things swimming through the beads around their platform. The only one who didn't seem frightened was the strange spren woman with the scratched-out eyes and the skin made of rough cloth. Her eyes . . . they weren't empty sockets. Instead she was like a portrait where the eyes had been scraped off.

Adolin shivered. "So . . ." he said. "Any idea what is happening?"

"We're not dead," Azure growled. "They call this place Shadesmar. It's the realm of thought."

"I peek into this place when I Soulcast," Shallan said. "Shadesmar overlaps the real world, but many things are inverted here."

"I passed through it when I first came to your land about a year ago," Azure added. "I had guides then, and I tried to avoid looking at too much crazy stuff."

"Smart," Adolin said. He put his hand to the side to summon his own Shardblade.

The woman with the scratched eyes stretched her head toward him in an unnatural way, then *screeched* with a loud, piercing howl.

Adolin stumbled away, nearly colliding with Shallan and her . . . her spren? Was that Pattern?

"That is your sword," Pattern said in a perky voice. He had no mouth that Adolin could see. "Hmmm. She is quite dead. I don't think you can summon her here." He cocked his bizarre head, looking at Azure's Blade. "Yours is different. Very curious."

The thing deep beneath their platform shifted again.

"That is probably bad," Pattern noted. "Hmmm . . . yes. Those spren above us are the souls of the Oathgate, and that one deep beneath us is likely one of the Unmade. It must be very large on this side."

"So what do we do?" Shallan asked.

Pattern looked in one direction, then the other. "No boat. Hmmm. Yes, that *is* a problem, isn't it?"

Adolin spun around. Some of the eel-like spren climbed onto the platform, using stumpy legs that Adolin had missed earlier. Those long purple antennae stretched toward him, wiggling. . . .

Fearspren, he realized. Fearspren were little globs of purple goo that looked exactly like the tips of those antennae.

"We need to get off this platform," Shallan said. "Everything else is secondary. Kaladin . . ." She trailed off as she glanced toward him.

The bridgeman knelt on the stone, head bowed, shoulders slumped. Storms . . . Adolin had been forced to carry him away from the battle, numb and broken. Looked like that emotion had caught up to him again.

Kaladin's spren—Adolin could only guess that was the identity of the pretty girl in blue—stood beside him, one hand resting protectively on his back. "Kaladin's not well," she said.

"I have to be well," Kaladin said, his voice hoarse as he climbed back to his feet. His long hair fell across his face, obscuring his eyes. Storms. Even surrounded by monsters, the bridgeman could look intimidating. "How do we get to safety? I can't fly us without attracting attention."

"This place is the inverse of your world," Azure said. She stepped back from a long antenna exploring in her direction. "Where there are larger bodies of water on Roshar, we will have land here, correct?"

"Mmm," Pattern said, nodding.

"The river?" Adolin asked. He tried to orient himself, looking past the thousands of floating lights. "There." He pointed at a lump he could barely spot in the distance. Like a long island.

Kaladin stared at it, frowning. "Can we swim in these beads?"

"No," Adolin said, remembering what it had felt like to fall into this ocean. "I . . ."

The beads rattled and clacked against one another as the large thing surged beneath. In the near distance, a single spire of rock broke the surface, tall and black. It emerged like a mountain peak slowly lifting from the sea, beads rattling in waves around it. As it grew to the height of a building, a *joint* appeared. Storms. It wasn't a spire or a mountain . . . it was a claw.

More emerged in other directions. An enormous hand was reaching slowly upward through the glass beads. Deep beneath them a heartbeat began sounding, rattling the beads.

Adolin stumbled back, horrified, and nearly slipped into the bead ocean. He kept his balance, barely, and found himself face-to-face with the woman with scratches for eyes. She stared at him, completely emotionless, as if waiting for him to try to summon his Shardblade so she could scream again.

Damnation. No matter what Azure said, he was certainly in Damnation.

⁘

"What do I do?" Shallan whispered. She knelt on the white stone of the platform, searching among the beads. Each gave her an impression of an object in the Physical Realm. A dropped shield. A vase from the palace. A scarf.

Nearby, hundreds of little spren—like little orange or green *people*, only a few inches tall—were climbing among the spheres. She ignored those, searching for the soul of something that would help.

"Shallan," Pattern said, kneeling. "I don't think . . . I don't think Soulcasting will accomplish anything? It will change an object in the other realm, but not here."

"What *can* I do here?" Those spines or claws or whatever rose around them, inevitable, deadly.

Pattern hummed, hands clasped before him. His fingers were too smooth, as if they were chiseled of obsidian. His head shifted and changed, going through its sequence—the spherical mass was never the same, yet somehow still always felt like him.

"My memory . . ." he said. "I don't remember."

Stormlight, Shallan thought. Jasnah had told her to never enter Shadesmar without Stormlight. Shallan pulled a sphere from her pocket—she still wore Veil's outfit. The beads nearby reacted, trembling and rolling toward her.

"Mmmm . . ." Pattern said. "Dangerous."

"I doubt staying here will be better," Shallan said. She sucked in a little Stormlight, only one mark's worth. As before, the spren didn't seem to notice her use of Stormlight as much as they had Kaladin's. She rested her freehand against the surface of the ocean. Beads stopped rolling and instead clicked together beneath her hand. When she pushed down, they resisted.

Good first step, she thought, drawing in more Stormlight. The beads pressed around her hand, gathering, rolling onto one another. She cursed, worried that she'd soon just have a big pile of beads.

"Shallan," Pattern said, poking at one of the beads. "Perhaps this?"

It was the soul of the shield she'd felt earlier. She moved the sphere to her gloved safehand, then pressed her other hand to the ocean. She used that bead's soul as a guide—much like she used a Memory as a guide for doing a sketch—and the other beads obediently rolled together and locked into place, forming an imitation of the shield.

Pattern stepped out onto it, then jumped up and down happily. Her shield held him without sinking, though he seemed as heavy as an ordinary person. Good enough. Now she just needed something big enough to hold them all. Preferably, as she considered, two somethings.

"You, sword lady!" Shallan said, pointing at Azure. "Help me over here. Adolin, you too. Kaladin, see if you can brood this place into submission."

Azure and Adolin hurried over.

Kaladin turned, frowning. "What?"

Don't think about that haunted look in his eyes, Shallan thought. *Don't think about what you've done in bringing us here, or how it happened. Don't think, Shallan.*

Her mind went blank, like it did in preparation for drawing, then locked on to her task.

Find a way out.

"Everybody," she said, "those flames are the souls of people, while these spheres represent the souls of objects. Yes, there are huge philosophical implications in that. Let's try to ignore them, shall we? When you touch a bead, you should be able to sense what it represents."

Azure sheathed her Shardblade and knelt, feeling at the spheres. "I can . . . Yes, there's an impression to each one."

"We need the soul of something long and flat." Shallan plunged her hands into the spheres, eyes closed, letting the impressions wash over her.

"I can't sense anything," Adolin said. "What am I doing wrong?" He sounded overwhelmed, but don't think about that.

Look. Fine clothing that hadn't been taken out of its trunk in a long, long time. So old that it saw the dust as part of itself.

Withering fruit that understood its purpose: decompose and stick its seeds to the rock, where they could hopefully weather storms long enough to sprout and gain purchase.

Swords, recently swung and glorying in their purpose fulfilled. Other weapons belonged to dead men, blades that had the faintest inkling that they'd failed somehow.

Living souls bobbed around, a swarm of them entering the Oathgate control chamber. One brushed Shallan. Drehy the bridgeman. For a brief moment she *felt* what it was like to be him. Worried for Kaladin. Panicked that nobody was in charge, that he would have to take command. He wasn't a commander. You couldn't be a rebel if you were in charge. He liked being told what to do—that way he could find a method to do it with style.

Drehy's worries caused her own to bubble up. *The bridgemen's powers will fade without Kaladin,* she thought. *What of Vathah, Red, and Ishnah? I didn't—*

Focus. Something reached out from the back of her mind, grabbed those thoughts and feelings, and yanked them into the darkness. Gone.

She brushed a bead with her fingers. A large door, like a keep's gate. She grabbed the sphere and shifted it to her safehand. Unfortunately, the next bead she touched was the palace *itself.* Momentarily stunned by the majesty of it, Shallan gaped. She held the entire palace in her *hand.*

Too large. She dropped it and kept searching.

Trash that still saw itself as a child's toy.

A goblet that had been made from melted-down nails, taken from an old building.

There. She seized hold of a sphere and pressed Stormlight into it. A building rose before her, made entirely out of beads: a copy of the Oathgate control building. She managed to make its top rise only a few feet above the surface, most of the building sinking into the depths. The rooftop was within reach.

"On top of it!" she shouted.

She held the replica in place as Pattern scrambled onto the roof. Adolin followed, trailed by that ghostly spren and Azure. Finally, Kaladin picked up his pack and walked with his spren onto the rooftop.

Shallan joined them with the aid of a hand from Adolin. She clutched the sphere that was the soul of the building, and tried to make the bead structure move through the sea like a raft.

It resisted, sitting there motionless. Well, she had another plan. She scurried to the other side of the roof and stretched down, held by Pattern, to touch the sea again. She used the soul of the large door to make another standing platform. Pattern jumped down, followed by Adolin and Azure.

Once they'd all piled precariously on the door, Shallan let go of the building. It crashed down behind them, beads falling in a tumult, frightening some of the little green spren crawling among the beads nearby.

Shallan reconstructed the building on the other side of the door, with only the rooftop showing. They filed across.

They progressed like that—following building with door and door with building—inching toward that distant land. Each iteration took Stormlight, though she could reclaim some from each creation before it collapsed. Some of the eel-like spren with the long antennae followed them, curious, but the rest of the varieties—and there were dozens—let them pass without much notice.

"Mmm . . ." Pattern said. "Much emotion on the other side. Yes, this is good. It distracts them."

The work was tiring and tedious, but step by step, Shallan moved them away from the frothing mess of the city of Kholinar. They passed the frightened lights of souls, the hungry spren who feasted on the emotions from the other side.

"Mmm . . ." Pattern whispered to her. "Look, Shallan. The lights of souls are no longer disappearing. People must be surrendering in Kholinar. I know you do not like the destruction of your own."

That *was* good, but not unexpected. The parshmen had never massacred civilians, though she couldn't say for certain what happened to Azure's soldiers. She hoped fervently they were able to either escape or surrender.

Shallan had to edge her group frighteningly close to two of the spines that had emerged from the depths. Those gave no sign of having noticed them. Beyond, they reached a calmer space out among the beads. A place where the only sound came from the clacking of glass.

"She corrupted them," Kaladin's spren whispered.

Shallan took a break, wiping her brow with a handkerchief from her satchel. They were distant enough that the lights of souls in Kholinar were just a general haze of light.

"What was that, spren?" Azure asked. "Corrupted?"

"That's why we're here. The Oathgate—do you remember those two spren in the sky? Those two are the gateway's soul, but the red coloring . . . They must be His now. That's why we ended up here, instead of going to Urithiru."

Sja-anat, Shallan thought, *said she was supposed to kill us. But that she'd try not to.*

Shallan wiped her brow again, then got back to work.

◆ ◆

Adolin felt useless.

All his life, he had understood. He'd taken easily to dueling. People naturally seemed to like him. Even in his darkest moment—standing on the battlefield and watching Sadeas's armies retreat, abandoning him and his father—he'd *understood* what was happening to him.

Not today. Today he was just a confused little boy standing in Damnation.

Today, Adolin Kholin was nothing.

He stepped onto another copy of the door. They had to huddle together while Shallan dismissed the rooftop behind, sending it crashing down, then squeezed past everyone to raise another copy of the building.

Adolin felt small. So very small. He started toward the rooftop. Kaladin, however, remained standing on the door, staring sightlessly. Syl, his spren, tugged his hand.

"Kaladin?" Adolin asked.

Kaladin finally shook himself and gave in to Syl's prodding. He walked onto the rooftop. Adolin followed, then took Kaladin's pack—deliberately but firmly—and swung it over his own shoulder. Kaladin let him. Behind, the doorway shattered back into the ocean of beads.

"Hey," Adolin said. "It will be all right."

"I survived Bridge Four," Kaladin growled. "I'm strong enough to survive this."

"I'm pretty sure you could survive anything. Storms, bridgeboy, the Almighty used some of the same stuff he put into Shardblades when he made you."

Kaladin shrugged. But as they walked onto the next platform, his expression grew distant again. He stood while the rest of them moved on. Almost like he was waiting for their bridge to dissolve and dump him into the sea.

"I couldn't make them see," Kaladin whispered. "I couldn't . . . couldn't protect them. I'm supposed to be able to *protect* people, aren't I?"

"Hey," Adolin said. "You really think that strange spren with the weird eyes is my sword?"

Kaladin started and focused on him, then scowled. "Yes, Adolin. I thought that was clear."

"I was just wondering." Adolin glanced over his shoulder and shivered. "What do you think about this place? Have you ever heard of anything like it?"

"Do you *have* to talk right now, Adolin?"

"I'm frightened. I talk when I'm frightened."

Kaladin glared at him as if suspecting what Adolin was doing. "I know little of this place," he finally answered. "But I think it's where spren are born. . . ."

Adolin kept him talking. As Shallan created each new platform, Adolin would lightly touch Kaladin on the elbow or shoulder and the bridgeman would step forward. Kaladin's spren hovered nearby, but she let Adolin guide the conversation.

Slowly they approached the strip of land, which turned out to be made of a deep, glassy black stone. Kind of like obsidian. Adolin got Kaladin across onto the land, then settled him with his spren. Azure followed, her shoulders sagging. In fact, her . . . her *hair* was fading. It was the strangest thing; Adolin watched it dim from Alethi jet-black to a faint grey as she sat down. Must be another effect of this strange place.

How much did she know of Shadesmar? He'd been so focused on Kaladin, he hadn't thought to interrogate her. Unfortunately, he was so tired right now, he was having trouble thinking straight.

Adolin stepped back onto the platform as Pattern stepped off. Shallan looked as if she was about to collapse. She stumbled, and the platform ruptured. He managed to grab her, and fortunately they only fell to waist-deep in the beads before their feet touched ground. The little balls of glass seemed to slide and move too easily, not supporting their weight.

Adolin had to practically haul Shallan through the tide of beads up onto the bank. There, she toppled backward, groaning and closing her eyes.

"Shallan?" he asked, kneeling beside her.

"I'm fine. It just took . . . concentration. Visualization."

"We need to find another way back to our world," Kaladin said, seated nearby. "We can't rest. They're fighting. We need to help them."

Adolin surveyed his companions. Shallan lay on the ground; her spren had joined her, lying in a similar posture and looking up at the sky. Azure slumped forward, her small Shardblade across her lap. Kaladin continued to stare at nothing with haunted eyes, his spren hovering behind him, worried.

"Azure," Adolin said, "is it safe here, on this land?"

"As safe as anywhere in Shadesmar," she said tiredly. "The place can be dangerous if you attract the wrong spren, but there isn't anything we can do about that."

"Then we camp here."

"But—" Kaladin said.

"We camp," Adolin said. Gentle, but firm. "We can barely stand up straight, bridgeman."

Kaladin didn't argue further. Adolin scouted up the bank, though each step felt like it was weighted with stone. He found a small depression in the glassy stone and—with some urging—got the rest of them to move to it.

As they made improvised beds from their coats and packs, Adolin looked one last time at the city, standing witness to the fall of his birthplace.

Storms, he thought. *Elhokar . . . Elhokar is dead.*

Little Gav had been taken, and Dalinar was planning to abdicate. Third in line was . . . Adolin himself.

King.

90

REBORN

I have done my best to separate fact from fiction, but the two blend like mixing paint when the Voidbringers are involved. Each of the Unmade has a dozen names, and the powers ascribed to them range from the fanciful to the terrifying.

—From Hessi's *Mythica*, page 4

Szeth-son-son . . .
  Szeth-son . . .
    Szeth, Truthless . . .
Szeth. Just Szeth.

Szeth of Shinovar, once called the Assassin in White, had been reborn. Mostly.

The Skybreakers whispered of it. Nin, Herald of Justice, had restored him following his defeat in the storm. Like most things, death had not been Szeth's to claim. The Herald had used a type of fabrial to heal his body before his spirit departed.

It had *almost* taken too long, however. His spirit hadn't properly reattached to his body.

Szeth walked with the others out onto the stone field before their small fortress, which overlooked the Purelake. The air was humid, almost like that of his homeland, though it didn't smell earthy or alive. It smelled of seaweed and wet stone.

There were five other hopefuls, all of them younger than Szeth. He was shortest among them, and the only one who kept his head bald. He couldn't grow a full head of hair, even if he didn't shave it.

The other five kept their distance from him. Perhaps it was because of the way he left a glowing afterimage when he moved: a sign of his soul's improper reattachment. Not all could see it, but these could. They were close enough to the Surges.

Or maybe they feared him because of the black sword in a silver sheath that he wore strapped to his back.

Oh, it's the lake! the sword said in his mind. It had an eager voice that didn't sound distinctly feminine or masculine. *You should draw me, Szeth! I would love to see the lake. Vasher says there are magic fish here. Isn't that interesting?*

"I have been warned, sword-nimi," Szeth reminded the weapon, "not to draw you except in the case of extreme emergency. And only if I carry much Stormlight, lest you feed upon my soul."

Well, I wouldn't do that, the sword said. It made a huffing sound. *I don't think you're evil at all, and I only destroy things that are evil.*

The sword was an interesting test, given him by Nin the Herald—called Nale, Nalan, or Nakku by most stonewalkers. Even after weeks of carrying this black sword, Szeth did not understand what the experience was to teach him.

The Skybreakers arranged themselves to watch the hopefuls. There were some fifty here, and that didn't count the dozens who were supposedly out on missions. So *many.* An entire order of Knights Radiant had survived the Recreance and had been watching for the Desolation for two thousand years, constantly replenishing their numbers as others died of old age.

Szeth would join them. He would accept their training, as Nin had promised him he would receive, then travel to his homeland of Shinovar. There, he would bring justice to the ones who had falsely exiled him.

Do I dare bring them judgment? a part of him wondered. *Dare I trust myself with the sword of justice?*

The sword replied. *You? Szeth, I think you're super trustworthy. And I'm a good judge of people.*

"I was not speaking to you, sword-nimi."

I know. But you were wrong, and so I had to tell you. Hey, the voices seem quiet today. That's nice, isn't it?

Mentioning it brought the whispers to Szeth's attention. Nin had not healed Szeth's madness. He'd called it an effect of Szeth's connection to the powers, and said that he was hearing trembles from the Spiritual Realm. Memories of the dead he'd killed.

He no longer feared them. He had died and been forced to return. He had failed to join the voices, and now they . . . they had no power over him, right?

Why, then, did he still weep in the night, terrified?

One of the Skybreakers stepped forward. Ki was a golden-haired woman, tall and imposing. Skybreakers clothed themselves in the garb of local lawkeepers—so here, in Marabethia, they wore a patterned shoulder cloak and a colorful skirtlike wrap. Ki wore no shirt, merely a simple cloth tied around her chest.

"Hopefuls," she said in Azish, "you have been brought here because a full Skybreaker has vouched for your dedication and solemnity."

She's boring, the sword said. *Where did Nale go?*

"You said he was boring too, sword-nimi," Szeth whispered.

That's true, but interesting things happen around him. We need to tell him that you should draw me more often.

"Your first training has already been completed," Ki said. "You traveled with the Skybreakers and joined them in one of their missions. You have been evaluated and deemed worthy of the First Ideal. Speak it. You know the Words."

Vasher always drew me, the sword said, sounding resentful.

"Life before death," Szeth said, closing his eyes. "Strength before weakness. Journey before destination."

The other five belted it out. Szeth whispered it to the voices that called to him from the darkness. Let them see. He would bring justice to those who had caused this.

He'd hoped that the first oath would restore his ability to draw upon Stormlight—something he had lost along with his previous weapon. However, when he removed a sphere from his pocket, he was unable to access the Light.

"In speaking this ideal," Ki said, "you are officially pardoned for any past misdeeds or sins. We have paperwork signed by proper authorities for this region.

"To progress further among our ranks, and to learn the Lashings, you will need a master to take you as their squire. Then may you speak the Second Ideal. From there, you will need to impress a highspren and form a bond—becoming a full Skybreaker. Today you will take the first of many tests. Though we will evaluate you, remember that the final measure of your success or failure belongs to the highspren. Do you have any questions?"

None of the other hopefuls said anything, so Szeth cleared his throat. "There are five Ideals," he said. "Nin told me of this. You have spoken them all?"

"It's been centuries since anyone mastered the Fifth Ideal," Ki said. "One becomes a full Skybreaker by speaking the Third Ideal, the Ideal of Dedication."

"We can . . . know what the Ideals are?" Szeth asked. For some reason, he'd thought they would be hidden from him.

"Of course," Ki said. "You will find no games here, Szeth-son-Neturo. The First Ideal is the Ideal of Radiance. You have spoken it. The second is the Ideal of Justice, an oath to seek and administer justice.

"The Third Ideal, the Ideal of Dedication, requires you to have first bonded a highspren. Once you have, you swear to dedicate yourself to a greater truth—a code to follow. Upon achieving this, you will be taught Division, the second—and more dangerous—of the Surges we practice."

"Someday," another Skybreaker noted, "you may achieve the Fourth Ideal: the Ideal of Crusade. In this, you choose a personal quest and complete it to the satisfaction of your highspren. Once successful, you become a master like ourselves."

Cleanse Shinovar, Szeth thought. That would be his quest. "What is the Fifth Ideal?" he asked.

"The Ideal of Law," Ki said. "It is difficult. You must become law, become truth. As I said, it has been centuries since that was achieved."

"Nin told me we were to *follow* the law—something external, as men are changeable and unreliable. How can we become the law?"

"Law must come from somewhere," another of the Skybreaker masters said. "This is not an oath you will swear, so don't fixate upon it. The first three will do for most Skybreakers. I was of the Third Ideal for two decades before achieving the Fourth."

When nobody else asked further questions, experienced Skybreakers began Lashing the hopefuls into the air.

"What is happening?" Szeth asked.

"We will carry you to the place of the test," Ki said, "as you cannot move with your own Stormlight until you swear the Second Ideal."

"Do I belong with these youths?" Szeth said. "Nin treated me as something different." The Herald had taken him on a mission to Tashikk, hunting Surgebinders from other orders. A heartless act that Nin had explained would prevent the coming of the Desolation.

Except that it had not. The Everstorm's return had convinced Nin he was wrong, and he'd abandoned Szeth in Tashikk. Weeks had passed there until Nin had returned to collect him. The Herald had dropped Szeth here at the fortress, then had vanished into the sky again, this time off to "seek guidance."

"The Herald," Ki said, "originally thought that you might skip to the Third Ideal because of your past. He is no longer here, however, and we cannot judge. You'll have to follow the same path as everyone else."

Szeth nodded. Very well.

"No further complaints?" Ki asked.

"It is orderly," Szeth said, "and you have explained it well. Why would I complain?"

The others seemed to like this response, and Ki herself Lashed him into the sky. For a moment he felt the freedom of flight—reminding him of his first days, holding an Honorblade long ago. Before he'd become Truthless.

No. You were never Truthless. Remember that.

Besides, this flight was not truly his. He continued falling upward until another Skybreaker caught him and Lashed him downward, counteracting the first effect and leaving him hovering.

A pair of Skybreakers took him, one under each arm, and the entire group soared through the air. He couldn't imagine they'd done this sort of thing in the past, as they'd remained hidden for so many years. But they didn't seem to care about secrecy anymore.

I like it up here, the sword said. *You can see everything.*

"Can you actually see things, sword-nimi?"

Not like a man. You *see all kinds of things, Szeth. Except, unfortunately, how useful I am.*

I should point out that although many personalities and motives are ascribed to them, I'm convinced that the Unmade were still spren. As such, they were as much manifestations of concepts or divine forces as they were individuals.

—From Hessi's *Mythica*, page 7

K aladin remembered cleaning crem off the bunker floor while in Amaram's army.

That sound of chisel on stone reminded Kal of his mother. He knelt on kneepads and scraped at the crem, which had seeped in under doors or had been tracked in on the boots of soldiers, creating an uneven patina on the otherwise smooth floor. He wouldn't have thought that soldiers would care that the ground wasn't level. Shouldn't he be sharpening his spear, or . . . or oiling something?

Well, in his experience, soldiers spent little time doing soldier things. They instead spent ages walking places, waiting around, or—in his case— getting yelled at for walking around or waiting in the wrong places. He sighed as he worked, using smooth even strokes, like his mother had taught him. Get underneath the crem and push. You could lift it up in flat sections an inch or more wide. Much easier than chipping at it from above.

A shadow darkened the door, and Kal glanced over his shoulder, then hunkered down farther. *Great.*

Sergeant Tukks walked to one of the bunks and settled down, the wood groaning under his weight. Younger than the other sergeants, he had features that were . . . off somehow. Perhaps it was his short stature, or his sunken cheeks.

"You do that well," Tukks said.

Kal continued to work, saying nothing.

"Don't feel so bad, Kal. It's not unusual for a new recruit to pull back. Storms. It's not so uncommon to freeze in *battle*, let alone on the practice field."

"If it's so common," Kal muttered, "why am *I* being punished?"

"What, this? A little cleaning duty? Kid, this isn't punishment. This is to help you fit in."

Kal frowned, leaning back and looking up. "Sergeant?"

"Trust me. Everyone was waiting for you to get a dressing-down. The longer you went without one, the longer you were going to feel like the odd man out."

"I'm scraping floors because I *didn't* deserve to be punished?"

"That, and for talking back to an officer."

"He wasn't an officer! He was just a lighteyes with—"

"Better to stop that kind of behavior *now*. Before you do it to someone who matters. Oh, don't glower, Kal. You'll understand eventually."

Kal attacked a particularly stubborn knob of crem near the leg of a bunk.

"I found your brother," Tukks noted.

Kaladin's breath caught.

"He's in the Seventh," Tukks said.

"I need to go to him. Can I be transferred? We weren't supposed to be split apart."

"Maybe I can get him moved here, to train with you."

"He's a messenger! He's not supposed to train with the spear."

"Everyone trains, even the messenger boys," Tukks said.

Kal gripped his chisel tightly, fighting down the urge to stand up and go looking for Tien. Didn't they understand? Tien couldn't hurt *cremlings*. He'd catch the things and usher them outside, talking to them like pets. The image of him holding a spear was ludicrous.

Tukks took out some fathom bark and started chewing. He leaned back on the bunk and put his feet up on the footboard. "Make sure you get that spot to your left."

Kaladin sighed, then moved to the indicated place.

"Do you want to talk about it?" Tukks asked. "The moment when you froze during practice?"

Stupid crem. Why did the Almighty make it?

"Don't be ashamed," Tukks continued. "We practice so you can freeze now, instead of when it will get you killed. You face down a squad, knowing they want to kill you even though they've never met you. And you hesitate, thinking it can't possibly be true. You can't possibly be here, preparing to fight, to bleed. Everyone feels that fear."

"I wasn't afraid of getting hurt," Kal said softly.

"You won't get far if you can't admit to a little fear. Emotion is good. It's what defines us, makes us—"

"I wasn't afraid of getting hurt." Kaladin took a deep breath. "I was afraid of *making* someone hurt."

Tukks twisted the bark in his mouth, then nodded. "I see. Well, that's another problem. Not unusual either, but a different matter indeed."

For a time, the only sound in the large barrack was that of chisel on stone. "How do you do it?" Kal finally asked, not looking up. "How can you hurt people, Tukks? They're just poor darkeyed slobs like us."

"I think about my mates," Tukks said. "I can't let the lads down. My squad is my family now."

"So you kill someone else's family?"

"Eventually, we'll be killing shellheads. But I know what you mean, Kal. It's hard. You'd be surprised how many men look in the face of an enemy and find that they're simply not capable of hurting another person."

Kal closed his eyes, letting the chisel slip from his fingers.

"It's good you aren't so eager," Tukks said. "Means you're sane. I'll take ten unskilled men with earnest hearts over one callous idiot who thinks this is all a game."

The world doesn't make sense, Kal thought. His father, the consummate surgeon, told him to avoid getting too wrapped up in his patients' emotions. And here was a career killer, telling him *to* care?

Boots scraped on stone as Tukks stood up. He walked over and rested one hand on Kal's shoulder. "Don't worry about the war, or even the battle. Focus on your squadmates, Kal. Keep *them* alive. Be the man *they* need." He grinned. "And get the rest of this floor scraped. I think when you come to dinner, you'll find the rest of the squad more friendly. Just a hunch."

That night, Kaladin discovered that Tukks was right. The rest of the men *did* seem more welcoming, now that he'd been disciplined. So Kal held his tongue, smiled, and enjoyed the companionship.

He never told Tukks the truth. When Kal had frozen on the practice field, it hadn't been out of fear. He'd been very sure he *could* hurt someone. In fact, he'd realized that he could kill, if needed.

And that was what had terrified him.

◆◆

Kaladin sat on a chunk of stone that looked like melted obsidian. It grew right out of the ground in Shadesmar, this place that didn't seem real.

The distant sun hadn't shifted in the sky since they'd arrived. Nearby, one of the strange fearspren crawled along the banks of the sea of glass beads. As big as an axehound, but longer and thinner, it looked vaguely like an eel with stumpy legs. The purple feelers on its head wiggled and shifted, flowing in his direction. When it didn't sense anything in him that it wanted, it continued along the bank.

Syl didn't make any noise as she approached, but he caught sight of her shadow coming up from behind—like other shadows here, it pointed *toward* the sun. She sat down on the lump of glass next to him, then thumped her head sideways, resting it on his arm, her hands in her lap.

"Others still asleep?" Kaladin asked.

"Yup. Pattern's watching over them." She wrinkled her nose. "Strange."

"He's nice, Syl."

"That's the strange part."

She swung her legs out in front of her, barefoot as usual. It seemed odder here on this side where she was human size. A small flock of spren flew above them, with bulbous bodies, long wings, and flowing tails. Instead of a head, each one had a golden ball floating right in front of the body. That seemed familiar. . . .

Gloryspren, he thought. It was like the fearspren, whose antennae manifested in the real world. Only part of the actual spren showed there.

"So . . ." Syl said. "Not going to sleep?"

Kaladin shook his head.

"Now, I might not be an *expert* on humans," she said. "For example, I still haven't figured out why only a handful of your cultures seem to worship me. But I do think I heard somewhere that you have to sleep. Like, every night."

He didn't respond.

"Kaladin . . ."

"What about you?" he said, looking away, along the isthmus of land that marked where the river was in the real world. "Don't you sleep?"

"Have I ever needed sleep?"

"Isn't this your land? Where you come from? I figured you'd . . . I don't know . . . be more mortal here."

"I'm still a spren," she said. "I'm a little piece of God. Did you miss the part about worshipping me?"

When he didn't reply, she poked him in the side. "You were supposed to say something sarcastic there."

"Sorry."

"We don't sleep; we don't eat. I think we might feed off humans, actually. Your emotions. Or you thinking about us, maybe. It all seems very complicated. In Shadesmar, we can think on our own, but if we go to your realm, we need a human bond. Otherwise, we're practically as mindless as those gloryspren."

"But how did you make the transition?"

"I . . ." She adopted a distant expression. "You called for me. Or, no, I knew that you would *someday* call for me. So I transferred to the Physical Realm, trusting that the honor of men lived, unlike what my father always said."

Her father. The *Stormfather.*

It was so strange to be able to feel her head on his arm. He was accustomed to her having very little substance.

"Could you transfer again?" Kaladin asked. "To carry word to Dalinar that something might be wrong with the Oathgates?"

"I don't think so. You're here, and my bond is to you." She poked him again. "But this is all a distraction from the real problem."

"You're right. I need a weapon. And we'll need to find food somehow."

"Kaladin . . ."

"Are there trees on this side? This obsidian might make a good spear-head."

She lifted her head from his arm and looked at him with wide, worried eyes.

"I'm fine, Syl," he said. "I just lost my focus."

"You were basically catatonic."

"I won't let it happen again."

"I'm not *complaining*." She wrapped her arms around his right arm, like a child clinging to a favored toy. Worried. Frightened. "Something's wrong inside you. But I don't know what."

I've never locked up in real combat, he thought. *Not since that day in training, when Tukks had to come talk to me.* "I . . . was just surprised to find Sah there," he said. "Not to mention Moash."

How do you do it? How can you hurt people, Tukks. . . .

She closed her eyes and leaned against him without letting go of his arm.

Eventually he heard the others stirring, so he extricated himself from Syl's grasp and went to join them.

92

WATER
WARM AS BLOOD

*The most important point I wish to make is that the Unmade are
still among us. I realize this will be contentious, as much of the
lore surrounding them is intertwined with theology. However, it is
clear to me that some of their effects are common in the world—
and we simply treat them as we would the manifestations of other
spren.*

—From Hessi's *Mythica*, page 12

The Skybreaker test was to take place in a modest-sized town on the
north border of the Purelake. Some people lived *in* the lake, of
course, but sane society avoided that.

Szeth landed—well, *was* landed—near the center of the town square,
along with the other hopefuls. The main bulk of the Skybreakers either
remained in the air or settled onto the cliffs around the town.

Three masters landed near Szeth, as did a handful of younger men and
women who could Lash themselves. The group being tested today would
include hopefuls like Szeth—who needed to find a master and swear the
Second Ideal—and squires who had achieved that step already, but now
needed to attract a spren and speak the Third Ideal.

It was a varied group; the Skybreakers didn't seem to care for ethnicity
or eye color. Szeth was the only Shin among them, but the others included
Makabaki, Reshi, Vorins, Iriali, and even one Thaylen.

A tall, strong man in a Marabethian wrap and an Azish coat hefted
himself from his seat on a porch. "It took you long enough!" he said in

Azish, striding toward them. "I sent for you hours ago! The convicts have escaped into the lake; who knows how far they've gotten by now! They will kill again if not stopped. Find and deal with them—you'll know them by the tattoos on their foreheads."

The masters turned to the squires and hopefuls; some of the more eager among them immediately went running toward the water. Several that could Lash took to the sky.

Szeth lingered, along with four of the others. He stepped up to Ki, in her shoulder cloak of a high judge of Marabethia.

"How did this man know to send for us?" Szeth asked.

"We have been expanding our influence, following the advent of the new storm," she replied. "The local monarchs have accepted us as a unifying martial force, and have given us legal authority. The city's high minister wrote to us via spanreed, pleading for help."

"And these convicts?" a squire asked. "What do we know of them, and our duty here?"

"This group of convicts escaped the prison there along the cliffs. The report says they are dangerous murderers. Your task is to find the guilty and execute them. We have writs ordering their deaths."

"All of those who escaped are guilty?"

"They are."

At that, several of the other squires left, hurrying to prove themselves. Still, Szeth lingered. Something about the situation bothered him. "If these men are murderers, why were they not executed before?"

"This area is populated by Reshi idealists, Szeth-son-Neturo," Ki said. "They have a strange, nonviolent attitude, even toward criminals. This town is charged with holding prisoners from all across the region, and Minister Kwati is paid tribute to maintain these facilities. Now that the murderers have escaped, mercy is withdrawn. They are to be executed."

That was enough for the last two squires, who took to the sky to begin their search. And Szeth supposed it was enough for him as well.

These are Skybreakers, he thought. *They wouldn't knowingly send us after innocents.* He could have taken their implied approval at the start. Yet . . . something bothered him. This was a test, but of what? Was it merely about the speed with which they could dispatch the guilty?

He started toward the waters.

"Szeth-son-Neturo," Ki called to him.

"Yes?"

"You walk on stone. Why is this? Each Shin I have known calls stone holy, and refuses to set foot on it."

"It cannot be holy. If it truly were, Master Ki, it would have burned me away long ago." He nodded to her, then stepped into the Purelake.

The water was warmer than he'd remembered. It wasn't deep at all—

reportedly, even in the very center of the lake the water wouldn't reach higher than a man's thighs, save for the occasional sinkhole.

You are far behind those others, the sword said. *You're never going to catch anyone at this rate.*

"I knew a voice like yours once, sword-nimi."

The whispers?

"No. A single one, in my mind, when I was young." Szeth shaded his eyes, looking across the glistening lake. "I hope things go better this time."

The flying squires would catch anyone in the open, so Szeth would need to search for less obvious criminals. He only needed one . . .

One? the sword said. *You're not being ambitious enough.*

"Perhaps. Sword-nimi, do you know why you were given to me?"

Because you needed help. I'm good at helping.

"But why me?" Szeth continued trudging through the water. "Nin said I was never to let you leave my presence."

It seemed like more of a burden than an aid. Yes, the sword was a Shardblade—but one he'd been cautioned about drawing.

The Purelake seemed to extend forever, wide as an ocean. Szeth's steps startled schools of fish, which would follow behind him for a bit, occasionally nipping at his boots. Gnarled trees poked from the shallows, gorging themselves on the water while their roots grasped the many holes and furrows in the lake bed. Rock outcrops broke the lake near the coast, but inward the Purelake grew placid, more *empty.*

Szeth turned parallel to the shore.

You're not going the same way as the others.

That was true.

Honestly, Szeth, I have to be frank. You aren't good at slaying evil. We haven't killed anyone *while you've held me.*

"I wonder, sword-nimi. Did Nin-son-God give you to me so I could practice resisting your encouragements, or because he saw me as equally bloodthirsty? He did call us a good match."

I'm not bloodthirsty, the sword said immediately. *I just want to be useful.*

"And not bored?"

Well, that too. The sword made some soft hums, imitating a human deep in thought. *You say you killed many people before we met. But the whispers . . . you didn't take pleasure in destroying those who needed to be destroyed?*

"I am not convinced that they needed to be destroyed."

You killed them.

"I was sworn to obey."

By a magic rock.

He had explained his past to the sword several times now. For some reason, it had difficulty understanding—or remembering—certain things.

"The Oathstone had no magic. I obeyed because of honor, and I sometimes obeyed evil or petty men. Now I seek a higher ideal."

But what if you pick the wrong thing to follow? Couldn't you end up in the same place again? Can't you just find evil, then destroy it?

"And what is evil, sword-nimi?"

I'm sure you can spot it. You seem smart. If increasingly kind of boring.

Would that he could continue in such monotony.

Nearby, a large twisted tree rose from the bank. Several of the leaves along one branch were pulled in, seeking refuge inside the bark; someone had disturbed them. Szeth didn't give overt indication that he'd noticed, but angled his walk so that he stepped beneath the tree. Part of him hoped the man hiding in the tree had the sense to stay hidden.

He did not. The man leaped for Szeth, perhaps tempted by the prospect of obtaining a fine weapon.

Szeth sidestepped, but without Lashings he felt slow, awkward. He escaped the slashes of the convict's improvised dagger, but was forced back toward the water.

Finally! the sword said. *All right, here's what you have to do. Fight him and win, Szeth.*

The criminal rushed him. Szeth caught the hand with the dagger, twisting to use the man's own momentum to send him stumbling into the lake.

Recovering, the man turned toward Szeth, who was trying to read what he could from the man's ragged, sorry appearance. Matted, shaggy hair. Reshi skin bearing many lesions. The poor fellow was so filthy, beggars and street urchins would find him distasteful company.

The convict passed his knife from one hand to the other, wary. Then he rushed Szeth again.

Szeth caught the man by the wrist once more and spun him around, the water splashing. Predictably, the man dropped his knife, which Szeth plucked from the water. He dodged the man's grapple, and in a moment had one arm around the convict's neck. Szeth raised the knife and—before he formed conscious thought—pressed the blade against the man's chest, drawing blood.

He managed to pull back, preventing himself from killing the convict. Fool! He needed to question the man. Had his time as Truthless made him such an eager killer? Szeth lowered the knife, but that gave the man an opening to twist and pull them both down into the Purelake.

Szeth splashed into water warm as blood. The criminal landed on top and forced Szeth under the surface, slamming his hand against the stony bottom and making him drop the knife. The world became a distorted blur.

This isn't *winning,* the sword said.

How ironic it would be to survive the murder of kings and Shardbearers only to die at the hands of a man with a crude knife. Szeth almost let it happen, but he knew fate was not finished with him yet.

He threw off the criminal, who was weak and scrawny. The man tried to grab the knife—which was clearly visible beneath the surface—while Szeth rolled the other direction to gain some distance. Unfortunately, the sword on his back got caught between the stones of the lake bottom, and that caused him to jerk back to the water. Szeth growled and—with a heave—ripped himself free, breaking the sword's harness strap.

The weapon sank into the water. Szeth splashed to his feet, turning to face the winded, dirty convict.

The man glanced at the submerged, silver sword. His eyes glazed, then he grinned wickedly, *dropped* his knife, and dove for the sword.

Curious. Szeth stepped back as the convict came up looking gleeful, holding the weapon.

Szeth punched him across the face, his arm leaving a faint afterimage. He grabbed the sheathed sword, ripping it from the weaker man's hands. Though the weapon often seemed too heavy for its size, it now felt light in his fingers. He stepped to the side and swung it—sheath and all—at his enemy.

The weapon struck the convict's back with a sickening crunch. The poor man splashed down into the lake and fell still.

I suppose that will do, the sword said. *Really, you should have just used me in the first place.*

Szeth shook himself. Had he killed the fellow after all? Szeth knelt and pulled him up by his matted hair. The convict gasped, but his body didn't move. Not dead, but paralyzed.

"Did someone work with you in your escape?" Szeth asked. "One of the local nobility, perhaps?"

"What?" the man sputtered. "Oh, Vun Makak. What have you done to me? I can't feel my arms, my legs . . ."

"Did *anyone* from the outside help you?"

"No. Why . . . why would you ask?" The man sputtered. "Wait. Yes. Who do you want me to name? I'll do whatever you say. Please."

Szeth considered. *Not working with the guards then, or the minister of the town.* "How did you get out?"

"Oh, Nu Ralik . . ." the man said, crying. "We shouldn't have killed the guard. I just wanted . . . wanted to see the sun again. . . ."

Szeth dropped the man back into the water. He stepped onto the shore and sat down on a rock, breathing deeply. Not long ago, he had danced with a Windrunner at the front of a storm. Today, he fought in shallow water against a half-starved man.

Oh, how he missed the sky.

That was cruel, the sword said. *Leaving him to drown.*

"Better than feeding him to a greatshell," Szeth said. "That happens to criminals in this kingdom."

Both are cruel, the sword said.

"You know of cruelty, sword-nimi?"

Vivenna used to tell me that cruelty is only for men, as is mercy. Only we can choose one or the other, and beasts cannot.

"You count yourself as a man?"

No. But sometimes she talked like she did. And after Shashara made me, she argued with Vasher, saying I could be a poet or a scholar. Like a man, right?

Shashara? That sounded like Shalash, the Eastern name for the Herald Shush-daughter-God. So perhaps this sword's origin was with the Heralds.

Szeth rose and walked up the coast, back toward the town.

Aren't you going to search for other criminals?

"I needed only one, sword-nimi, to test what has been told to me and to learn a few important facts."

Like how smelly convicts are?

"That is indeed part of the secret."

He passed the small town where the master Skybreakers waited, then hiked up the hillside to the prison. The dark block of a structure over-looked the Purelake, but the beautiful vantage was wasted; the place had barely any windows.

Inside, the smell was so foul, he had to breathe through his mouth. The body of a single guard had been left in a pool of blood between cells. Szeth almost tripped over it—there was no light in the place, save for a few sphere lamps in the guard post.

I see, he thought, kneeling beside the fallen man. *Yes.* This test was indeed a curious one.

Outside, he noted some of the squires returning to the town with corpses in tow, though none of the other hopefuls seemed to have found anyone. Szeth picked his way carefully down the rocky slope to the town, careful not to drag the sword. Whatever Nin's reasons for entrusting him with the weapon, it was a holy object.

At the town, he approached the beefy nobleman, who was trying to make small talk with Master Ki—failing spectacularly. Nearby, other members of the town were debating the ethics of simply executing murderers, or holding them and risking this. Szeth inspected the dead convicts, and found them as dirty as the one he had fought, though two weren't nearly as emaciated.

There was a prison economy, Szeth thought. *Food went to those in power while others were starved.*

"You," Szeth said to the nobleman. "I found only one body above. Did you really have a *single* guard posted to watch all these prisoners?"

The nobleman sneered at him. "A Shin stonewalker? Who are you to question me? Go back to your stupid grass and dead trees, little man."

"The prisoners were free to create their own hierarchy," Szeth continued. "And nobody watched to see they didn't make weapons, as I faced one with a knife. These men were mistreated, locked in darkness, not given enough food."

"They were criminals. *Murderers.*"

"And what happened to the money you were sent to administrate this facility? It certainly didn't go toward proper security."

"I don't have to listen to this!"

Szeth turned from him to Ki. "Do you have a writ of execution for this man?"

"It is the first we obtained."

"*What?*" the nobleman said. Fearspren boiled up around him.

Szeth undid the clasp on the sword and drew it.

A rushing sound, like a thousand screams.

A wave of power, like the beating of a terrible, stunning wind.

Colors changed around him. They deepened, growing darker and more vibrant. The city nobleman's cloak became a stunning array of deep oranges and blood reds.

The hair on Szeth's arms stood on end and his skin spiked with a sudden incredible pain.

DESTROY!

Liquid darkness flowed from the Blade, then melted to smoke as it fell. Szeth screamed at the pain in his arm even as he slammed the weapon through the chest of the blubbering nobleman.

Flesh and blood puffed instantly into black smoke. Ordinary Shardblades burned only the eyes, but this sword somehow consumed the entire body. It seemed to sear away even the man's *soul*.

EVIL!

Veins of black liquid crept up Szeth's hand and arm. He gaped at them, then gasped and rammed the sword back into its silvery sheath.

He fell to his knees, dropping the sword and raising his hand, fingers bent and tendons taut. Slowly, the blackness evaporated from his flesh, the awful pain easing. The skin of his hand, which had already been pale, had been bleached to grey-white.

The sword's voice sank to a deep muttering in his mind, its words slurring. It struck him as sounding like the voice of a beast falling into a stupor after having gorged itself. Szeth breathed deeply. Fumbling at his pouch, he saw that several spheres inside were completely drained. *I will need far more Stormlight if I'm to ever try that again.*

The surrounding townspeople, squires, and even master Skybreakers regarded him with uniform horror. Szeth picked up the sword and struggled to his feet, before fastening the sword's clasp. Holding the sheathed weapon in both hands, he bowed to Ki. "I have dealt," he said, "with the worst of the criminals."

"You have done well," she said slowly, glancing at where the nobleman had stood. There wasn't even a stain on the stones. "We will wait and make certain the other criminals have been killed or captured."

"Wise," Szeth said. "Could I . . . beg something to drink? I suddenly find myself very thirsty."

⁂

By the time all the escapees had been accounted for, the sword was stirring again. It had never fallen asleep, if a sword could do such a thing. Rather, it had mumbled in his mind until it slowly became lucid.

Hey! the sword said as Szeth sat on a low wall alongside the city. *Hey, did you draw me?*

"I did, sword-nimi."

Great job! Did we . . . did we destroy lots of evil?

"A great and corrupt evil."

Wow! I'm impressed. You know, Vivenna never drew me even once? She carried me for a long time too. Maybe a couple of days even?

"And how long have I been carrying you?"

At least an hour, the sword said, satisfied. *One, or two, or ten thousand. Something like that.*

Ki approached, and he returned her water canteen. "Thank you, Master Ki."

"I have decided to take you as my squire, Szeth-son-Neturo," she said. "In all honesty, there was an argument among us over who would have the privilege."

He bowed his head. "I may swear the Second Ideal?"

"You may. Justice will serve you until you attract a spren and swear to a more specific code. During my prayers last night, Winnow proclaimed the highspren are watching you. I won't be surprised if it takes mere months before you achieve the Third Ideal."

Months. No, he would not take months. But he did not swear quite yet. Instead, he nodded toward the prison. "Pardon, master, a question. You knew this breakout would happen, didn't you?"

"We suspected. One of our teams investigated this man and discovered how he was using his funds. When the call came, we were not surprised. It provided a perfect testing opportunity."

"Why not deal with him earlier?"

"You must understand our purpose and our place, a fine point difficult for many squires to grasp. That man had *not yet broken a law*. His duty was to imprison the convicts, which he had done. He was allowed to judge if his methods were satisfactory or not. Only once he failed, and his charges had escaped, could we mete out justice."

Szeth nodded. "I swear to seek justice, to let it guide me, until I find a more perfect Ideal."

"These Words are accepted," Ki said. She removed a glowing emerald sphere from her pouch. "Take your place above, squire."

Szeth regarded the sphere, then—trembling—breathed in the Stormlight. It returned to him in a rush.

The skies were his once again.

Taxil mentions Yelig-nar, named Blightwind, in an oft-cited quote. Though Jasnah Kholin has famously called its accuracy into question, I believe it.

—From Hessi's *Mythica*, page 26

When Adolin woke up, he was still in the nightmare.

The dark sky, glass ground, the strange creatures. He had a crick in his neck and a pain in his back; he'd never mastered the "sleep anywhere" skill the grunts bragged about.

Father could have slept on the ground, a part of him thought. *Dalinar is a true soldier.*

Adolin thought again of the jolt he'd felt when ramming his dagger through Sadeas's eye and into his brain. Satisfaction and shame. Strip away Adolin's nobility, and what was left? A duelist when a world needed generals? A hothead who couldn't even take an insult?

A murderer?

He threw off his coat and sat up, then jumped and gasped as he found the woman with the scratched-out eyes looming over him. "Ishar's soul!" Adolin cursed. "Do you have to stay so close?"

She didn't move. Adolin sighed, then changed the dressing on his shallow shoulder cut, using bandages from his pocket. Nearby, Shallan and Azure catalogued their meager supplies. Kaladin trudged over to join them. Had the bridgeboy slept?

Adolin stretched, then—accompanied by his ghostly spren—walked down the short slope to the ocean of glass beads. A few lifespren floated nearby; on this side, their glowing green motes had tufts of white hair that rippled as they danced and bobbed. Perhaps they were circling plants by the riverbank in the Physical Realm? Those small dots of light swimming above the rock might be the souls of fish. How did that work? In the real would, they'd be in the water, so shouldn't they be *inside* the stone?

He knew so little, and felt so overwhelmed. So *insignificant.*

A fearspren crawled up out of the ocean of beads, purple antenna pointing at him. It scuttled closer until Adolin picked up some beads and threw one at the spren, which scuttled back into the ocean and lurked there, watching him.

"What do you think of all this?" Adolin asked the woman with the scratched-out eyes. She didn't respond, but he often talked to his sword without it responding.

He tossed up one of the beads and caught it. Shallan could tell what each represented, but all he got was a dull impression of . . . something red?

"I'm being childish, aren't I?" Adolin asked. "So, forces moving in the world now make me look insignificant. That's no different from a child growing up and realizing his little life isn't the center of the universe. Right?"

Problem was, his little life *had* been the center of the universe, growing up. *Welcome to being the son of Dalinar storming Blackthorn.* He hurled the sphere into the sea, where it skittered against its fellows.

Adolin sighed, then started a morning kata. Without a sword, he fell back on the first kata he'd ever learned—an extended sequence of stretches, hand-to-hand moves, and stances to help loosen his muscles.

The forms calmed him. The world was turning on its head, but familiar things were still familiar. Strange, that he should have to come to that revelation.

About halfway through, he noticed Azure standing on the bank. She walked down the slope and fell into line beside him, doing the same kata. She must have known it already, for she kept pace with him exactly.

They stepped back and forth along the rocks, sparring with their own shadows, until Kaladin approached and joined them. He wasn't as practiced, and cursed under his breath as he got a sequence wrong—but he'd obviously done it before too.

He must have learned it from Zahel, Adolin realized.

The three moved together, their breathing controlled, scraping boots on the glass. The sea of beads rolling against itself began to sound soothing. Even rhythmic.

The world is the same as it's always been, Adolin thought. *These things we're finding—monsters and Radiants—aren't new. They were only hidden. The world has always been like this, even if I didn't know it.*

And Adolin . . . he was still himself. He had all the same things to be proud of, didn't he? Same strengths? Same accomplishments?

Same flaws too.

"Are you three *dancing*?" a voice suddenly piped up.

Adolin immediately spun around. Shallan had settled on the slope above them, still wearing her white uniform, hat, and single glove. He found himself grinning stupidly. "It's a warm-up kata," he explained. "You—"

"I know what it is. You tried to teach it to me, remember? I just thought it odd to see you all down here like that." She shook her head. "Weren't we going to plan how to get out of here?"

Together, they started up the slope, and Azure fell into step beside Adolin. "Where did you learn that kata?"

"From my swordmaster. You?"

"Likewise."

As they approached their camp in the small nestlike depression in the obsidian ground, something felt off to Adolin. Where was his sword, the woman with the scratched-out eyes?

He stepped back and spotted her standing on the coast, looking at her feet.

"All right," Shallan said, drawing him back. "I made a list of our supplies." She gestured with a pencil toward the items—which were arrayed on the ground—as she spoke. "One bag of gemstones from the emerald reserve. I used roughly half of our Stormlight in our transfer to Shadesmar and crossing the sea of beads. We have my satchel, with charcoal, reed pens, brushes, ink, lacquer, some solvents, three sketchpads, my sharpening knife, and one jar of jam I'd stowed inside for an emergency snack."

"Wonderful," Kaladin said. "I'm sure a pile of brushes will be useful in fighting off Voidspren."

"Better than your tongue, which is notably dull lately. Adolin has his side knife, but our only real weapon is Azure's Shardblade. Kaladin brought the bag of gemstones inside his pack, which fortunately also contained his travel rations: three meals of flatbread and jerked pork. We also have a water jug and three canteens."

"Mine is half empty," Adolin noted.

"Mine too," Azure said. "Which means we have maybe one day's worth of water and three meals for four people. Last time I crossed Shadesmar, it took four weeks."

"Obviously," Kaladin said, "we have to get back through the Oathgate into the city."

Pattern hummed, standing behind Shallan. He seemed like a statue; he didn't shift his weight or move in small ways like a human would. Kaladin's spren was different. She always seemed to be moving, slipping this way or that, girlish dress rippling as she walked, her hair swaying.

"Bad," Pattern said. "The spren of the Oathgate are *bad* now."

"Do we have any other options?" Kaladin said.

"I remember . . . some," Syl said. "Much more than I used to. Our land, every land, is three realms. The highest is the Spiritual, where gods live— there, all things, times, and spaces are made into one.

"We're now in the Cognitive Realm. Shadesmar, where spren live. You are from the Physical Realm. The only way I know of to transfer there is to be pulled by human emotions. That won't help you, as you're not spren."

"There's another way to transfer between realms," Azure said. "I've used it."

Her hair had recovered its dark coloring, and it seemed to Adolin that her scars had faded. Something about her was downright strange. She seemed almost like a spren herself.

She bore his scrutiny, looking from him to Kaladin, to Shallan. Finally she sighed deeply. "Story time?"

"Yes, please," Adolin replied. "You've traveled in this place before?"

"I'm from a far land, and I came to Roshar by crossing this place, Shadesmar."

"All right," Adolin said. "But why?"

"I came chasing someone."

"A friend?"

"A criminal," she said softly.

"You're a soldier though," Kaladin said.

"Not really. In Kholinar, I merely stepped up to do a job nobody else was doing. I thought perhaps the Wall Guard would have information on the man I'm hunting. Everything went wrong, and I got stuck."

"When you arrived in our land," Shallan said, "you used an Oathgate to get from Shadesmar to the Physical Realm?"

"No." Azure laughed, shaking her head. "I didn't know of those until Kal told me about them. I used a portal between realms. Cultivation's Perpendicularity, they call it. On your side, it's in the Horneater Peaks."

"That's hundreds of miles from here," Adolin said.

"There's supposedly another perpendicularity," Azure said. "It's unpredictable and dangerous, and appears randomly in different places. My guides warned against trying to hunt it."

"Guides?" Kaladin said. "Who were these guides?"

"Why, spren of course."

Adolin glanced toward the distant city they'd left, where there had been fearspren and painspren aplenty.

"Not like those," Azure said, laughing. "People spren, like these two."

"Which raises a question," Adolin said, pointing as the spren with the strange eyes rejoined them. "That's the soul of my Shardblade. Syl is

Kaladin's, and Pattern Shallan's. So . . ." He pointed at the weapon at her belt. "Tell us honestly, Azure. Are you a Knight Radiant?"

"No."

Adolin swallowed. *Say it.* "You're a Herald then."

She laughed. "No. What? A Herald? Those are basically *gods,* right? I'm no figure from mythology, thank you very much. I'm just a woman who has been constantly out of her league since adolescence. Trust me."

Adolin glanced at Kaladin. He didn't seem convinced either.

"Really," Azure said. "There's no spren here for my Blade because it's flawed. I can't summon or dismiss it, like you can yours. She's a handy weapon, but a pale copy of what you carry." She patted it. "Anyway, when I last crossed this place, I hired a ship to convey me."

"A ship?" Kaladin said. "Sailed by whom?"

"Spren. I hired it at one of their cities."

"Cities?" Kaladin looked toward Syl. "You have *cities?*"

"Where did you think we lived?" Syl said, amused.

"Lightspren are usually guides," Azure continued. "They like to travel, to see new places. They sail all across Roshar's Shadesmar, peddling goods, trading with other spren. Um . . . you're supposed to watch out for Cryptics."

Pattern hummed happily. "Yes. We are very famous."

"What about using Soulcasting?" Adolin looked to Shallan. "Could you make us supplies?"

"I don't think it would work," Shallan replied. "When I Soulcast, I change an object's soul here in this realm, and it reflects in the other world. If I changed one of these beads, it might become something new in the Physical Realm—but it would still be a bead to us."

"Food and water aren't impossible to find here," Azure said, "if you can make it to a port city. The spren don't need these things, but humans living on this side—and there are some—need a constant supply. With that Stormlight of yours, we can trade. Maybe buy passage to the Horneater Peaks."

"That would take a long time," Kaladin said. "Alethkar is falling *right now,* and the Blackthorn needs us. It—"

He was interrupted by a haunting screech. It was reminiscent of sheets of steel grinding against one another. It was met by others, echoing in unison. Adolin spun toward the sounds, shocked by their intensity. Syl put her hands to her lips, and Pattern cocked his strange head.

"What was *that?*" Kaladin demanded.

Azure hurriedly began shoving their supplies into Kaladin's pack. "You remember before we slept, how I said we'd be fine unless we attracted the wrong spren?"

". . . Yes?"

"We should get moving. *Now.*"

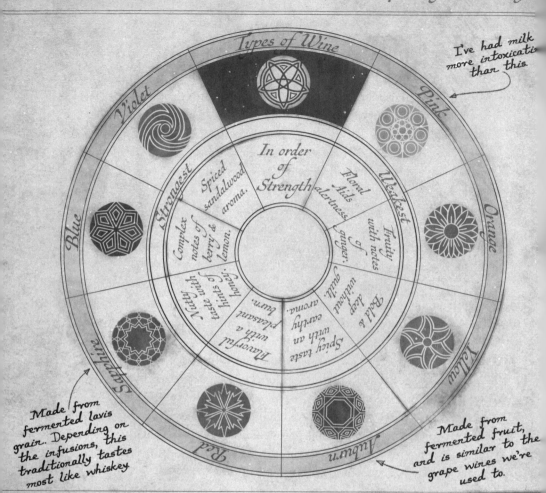

Types of Wine

In order of Strength

Violet — Spiced sandalwood aroma.

Blue — Complex notes of berry & lemon.

Sapphire — Nutty taste with a hint of honey.

Strongest

Red — Flavorful with a pleasant burn.

Auburn — Spicy taste with an earthy aroma.

Yellow — Bold & deep without aroma.

Orange — Fruity with notes of ginger.

Pink — Floral. Aids alertness.

Weakest

I've had milk more intoxicating than this.

Made from fermented lavis grain. Depending on the infusions, this traditionally tastes most like whiskey.

Made from fermented fruit, and is similar to the grape wines we're used to.

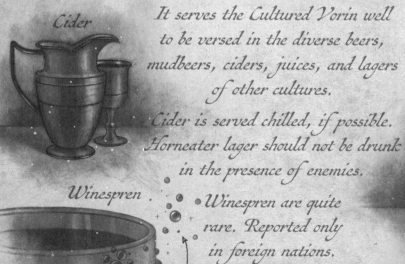

Cider

Winespren

It serves the Cultured Vorin well to be versed in the diverse beers, mudbeers, ciders, juices, and lagers of other cultures.

Cider is served chilled, if possible. Horneater lager should not be drunk in the presence of enemies.

Winespren are quite rare. Reported only in foreign nations.

Responsible for that embarrassing tattoo of mine.

What? Rare? I see these all the time.

Horneater Lager

94

A SMALL BOTTLE

SEVEN YEARS AGO

Dalinar stumbled as he swept everything from the dresser, up-
ending a bowl of hot soup. He didn't want *soup*. He yanked out
drawers, dumping clothing to the ground, steam curling from
the spilled broth.

They'd done it again! They'd taken his bottles. How *dare* they! Couldn't
they hear the weeping? He roared, then grabbed his trunk, overturning it.
A flask rolled out along with the clothing. Finally! Something they hadn't
found.

He slurped down the dregs it contained, and groaned. The weeping
echoed around him. Children dying. Evi begging for her life.

He needed more.

But . . . wait, did he need to be presentable? The hunt? Was that today?

Stupid man, he thought. The last of the hunts had been weeks ago. He'd
convinced Gavilar to come with him out into the wilderness, and the trip
had gone well. Dalinar had been presentable—sober, commanding even.
A figure right from the storming songs. They'd discovered those parshmen. They'd been so *interesting*.

For a time, away from civilization, Dalinar had felt like himself. His
old self.

He hated that person.

Growling, he dug in his large wardrobe. This fort on the eastern rim of
Alethkar was the first mark of civilization on their trip home. It had given
Dalinar access, again, to the necessities of life. Like wine.

He barely heard the rap on his door as he flung coats out of the wardrobe. When he looked over, he saw two youths standing there. His sons.

Angerspren boiled around him. Her hair. Her judgmental eyes. How many lies about him had she stuffed into their heads?

"What?" Dalinar roared.

Adolin stood his ground. Almost seventeen now, fully a man. The other one, the invalid, cringed down. He looked younger than his ... what ... twelve years? Thirteen?

"We heard the commotion, *sir*," Adolin said, jutting out his chin. "We thought you might need help."

"I need nothing! Out! *GET OUT!*"

They scrambled away.

Dalinar's heart raced. He slammed the wardrobe and pounded his fists on the bedside table, toppling the sphere lamp. Puffing, groaning, he fell to his knees.

Storms. They were only a few days' march from the ruins of Rathalas. Was that why the screaming was louder today?

A hand fell on his shoulder. "Father?"

"Adolin, so help me—" Still kneeling, Dalinar turned, then cut off. It wasn't Adolin, but the other one. Renarin had returned, timid as always, his spectacled eyes wide and his hand trembling. He held something out.

A small bottle. "I ...." Renarin swallowed. "I got you one, with the spheres the king gave me. Because you always go through what you buy so quickly."

Dalinar stared at that bottle of wine for an endless moment. "Gavilar hides the wine from me," he mumbled. "That's why none is left. I ... couldn't possibly ... have drunk it all. ..."

Renarin stepped in and hugged him. Dalinar flinched, bracing as if for a punch. The boy clung to him, not letting go.

"They talk about you," Renarin said, "but they're wrong. You just need to rest, after all the fighting you did. I know. And I miss her too."

Dalinar licked his lips. "What did she tell you?" he said, voice ragged. "What did your mother say about me?"

"The only honest officer in the army," Renarin said, "the honorable soldier. Noble, like the Heralds themselves. Our father. The greatest man in Alethkar."

What stupid words. Yet Dalinar found himself weeping. Renarin let go, but Dalinar grabbed him, pulling him close.

Oh, Almighty. Oh God. Oh God, please ... I've started to hate my sons. Why hadn't the boys learned to hate him back? They should hate him. He *deserved* to be hated.

Please. Anything. I don't know how to get free of this. Help me. Help me ...

Dalinar wept and clung to that youth, that child, as if he were the only real thing left in a world of shadows.

Yelig-nar had great powers, perhaps the powers of all Surges compounded in one. He could transform any Voidbringer into an extremely dangerous enemy. Curiously, three legends I found mention swallowing *a gemstone to engage this process.*

—From Hessi's *Mythica*, page 27

K aladin marched at speed through Shadesmar, trying—with difficulty—to control the simmering dissatisfaction inside of him.

"Mmmm . . ." Pattern said as another screech sounded behind them. "Humans, you must stop your emotions. They are very inconvenient here."

The group hiked southward, along the narrow line of land that overlaid the river in the real world. Shallan was the slowest of them, and had difficulty keeping up, so they'd agreed she should hold a little Stormlight. It was either that, or let the screeching spren reach them.

"What are they like?" Adolin said to Azure, puffing as they marched. "You said those sounds were from angerspren? Boiling pools of blood?"

"That's the part you see in the Physical Realm," Azure said. "Here . . . that's merely their saliva, pooling as they drool. They're nasty."

"And dangerous," Syl said. She scampered along the obsidian ground, and didn't seem to get tired. "Even to spren. But how did we draw them? Nobody was angry, right?"

Kaladin tried again to smother his frustration.

"I wasn't feeling anything other than tired," Shallan said.

"I felt overwhelmed," Adolin said. "Still do. But not angry."

"Kaladin?" Syl said.

He looked at the others, then down at his feet. "It just feels like . . . like we're abandoning Kholinar. And only I *care*. You were talking about how to get food, find a way to the Horneater Peaks, this perpendicularity or whatever. But we're *abandoning* people to the Voidbringers."

"I care too!" Adolin said. "Bridgeboy, that was my *home*. It—"

"I know," Kaladin snapped. He took a breath, forcing himself to calm. "I know, Adolin. I *know* it's not rational to try to get back through the Oathgate. We don't know how to work it from this side, and besides, it's obviously been corrupted. My emotions are irrational. I'll try to contain them. I promise."

They fell silent.

You're not angry at Adolin, Kaladin thought forcefully. *You're not actually angry at* anyone. *You're just looking for something to latch on to. Something to feel.*

Because the darkness was coming.

It fed off the pain of defeat, the agony of losing men he'd tried to protect. But it could feed off anything. Life going well? The darkness would whisper that he was only setting himself up for a bigger fall. Shallan glances at Adolin? They must be whispering about him. Dalinar sends him to protect Elhokar? The highprince must want to get rid of Kaladin.

He'd failed at that, regardless. When Dalinar heard that Kholinar had fallen . . .

Get out, Kaladin thought, squeezing his eyes shut. *Get out, get out, get out!*

It would continue until numbness seemed preferable. Then that numbness would claim him and make it hard to do anything at all. It would become a sinking, inescapable void from within which everything looked washed out. Dead.

Within that dark place, he'd wanted to betray his oaths. Within that dark place, he'd given the king up to assassins and murderers.

Eventually, the screeches faded into the distance. Syl guessed that the angerspren had been drawn into the beads, off toward Kholinar and the powerful emotions there. The group continued their hike. There was only one way to go: south, along the narrow peninsula of obsidian running through the bead ocean.

"When I traveled here last time," Azure said, "we passed numbers of peninsulas like this one. They always had lighthouses at the ends. We stopped at them sometimes for supplies."

"Yes . . ." Syl said, nodding. "I remember those. It's useful for ships to note where land juts into the beads. There should be one at the end of this one . . . though it looks loooong. We'll have to hike it for several days."

"At least it's a goal," Adolin said. "We travel south, get to the light-house, and hope to catch a ship there."

There was an insufferable spring to his step, like he was actually *excited* by this terrible place. Idiot Adolin, who probably didn't even understand the consequences of—

Stop it. STOP IT. He helped you.

Storms. Kaladin hated himself when he got like this. When he tried to empty his mind, he drifted toward the void of darkness. But when he instead let himself think, he started remembering what had happened in Kholinar. Men he loved, killing each other. Awful, terrifying perspective.

He could see too many sides. Parshmen angry at being enslaved for years, attempting to overthrow a corrupt government. Alethi protecting their homes from invading monsters. Elhokar trying to save his son. The palace guards trying to keep their oaths.

Too many eyes to see through. Too many emotions. Were these his only two options? Pain or oblivion?

Fight it.

Their hike continued, and he tried to turn his attention to his surroundings instead of his thoughts. The thin peninsula wasn't barren, as he'd first assumed. Growing along its edges were small, brittle plants that looked like ferns. When he asked, Syl told him they grew exactly like plants in the Physical Realm.

Most were black, but occasionally they had vibrant colors, blended together like stained glass. None grew higher than his knees, and most only reached his ankles. He felt terrible whenever he brushed one and it crumpled.

The sun didn't seem to change position in the sky, no matter how long they walked. Through spaces between the clouds, he saw only blackness. No stars, no moons. Eternal, endless darkness.

⁘

They camped for what should have been the night, then hiked all the next day. Kholinar vanished into the distance behind, but still they kept going: Azure at the front, then Pattern, Syl, and Kaladin, with Shallan and Adolin at the back, Adolin's spren trailing them. Kaladin would have preferred to take the rearguard, but if he tried, Adolin positioned himself to the back again. What did the princeling think? That Kaladin would lag behind, if not minded?

Syl walked beside him, mostly quiet. Being back on this side troubled her. She'd look at things, like the occasional colorful plant, and cock her head as if trying to remember. "It's like a dream from the time when I was dead," she'd said when he prompted her.

They camped another "night," then started walking again. Kaladin skipped breakfast—their rations were basically gone. Besides, he welcomed the grumbling stomach. It reminded him that he was alive. Gave him something to think about, other than the men he'd lost . . .

"Where did you live?" he asked Syl, still carrying his pack, hiking along the seemingly infinite peninsula. "When you were young, on this side?"

"It was far to the west," she said. "A grand city, ruled by honorspren! I didn't like it though. I wanted to travel, but Father kept me in the city, especially after . . . you know . . ."

"I'm not actually sure that I do."

"I bonded a Knight Radiant. Haven't I told you of him? I remember . . ." She closed her eyes as she walked, chin up, as if basking in a wind he could not feel. "I bonded him soon after I was born. He was an elderly man, kindly, but he *did* fight. In one battle. And he died. . . ."

She blinked open her eyes. "That was a long time ago."

"I'm sorry."

"It's all right. I wasn't ready though for the bond. Spren normally weather the death of their Radiant, but I . . . I lost myself when I lost him. It all turned out to be morbidly fortuitous, because soon after, the Recreance happened. Men forsook their oaths, which killed my siblings. I survived, for I didn't have a bond then."

"And the Stormfather locked you away?"

"Father assumed I'd been killed with the others. He found me, asleep, after what must have been . . . wow, a thousand years on your side. He woke me and took me home." She shrugged. "After that, he wouldn't let me leave the city." She took Kaladin by the arm. "He was foolish, as were the other honorspren born after the Recreance. They knew something bad was coming, but wouldn't do anything. And I heard you calling, even from so far away. . . ."

"The Stormfather let you out?" Kaladin said, stunned by the confessions. This was more than he'd found out about her since . . . since forever.

"I snuck away," she said with a grin. "I gave up my mind and joined your world, hiding among the windspren. We can barely see them on this side. Did you know that? Some spren live mostly in your realm. I suppose the wind is always there somewhere, so they don't fade like passions do." She shook her head. "Oh!"

"Oh?" Kaladin asked. "Did you remember something?"

"No! Oh!" She pointed, hopping up and down. "Look!"

In the distance, a bright yellow light glowed like a spark in the otherwise dim landscape.

A lighthouse.

Yelig-nar is said to consume souls, but I can't find a specific explanation. I'm uncertain this lore is correct.

—From Hessi's *Mythica*, page 51

On the day of the first meeting of monarchs at Urithiru, Navani made each person—no matter how important—carry their own chair. The old Alethi tradition symbolized each chief bringing important wisdom to a gathering.

Navani and Dalinar arrived first, stepping off the lift and walking toward the meeting room near the top of Urithiru. Her chair was sensible but comfortable, made of Soulcast wood with a padded seat. Dalinar had tried to bring a stool, but she'd insisted that he do better. This wasn't a battlefield strategy tent, and forced austerity wouldn't impress the monarchs. He'd eventually selected a sturdy wooden chair of thick stumpweight, with wide armrests but no padding.

He'd quietly spent the trip up watching floors pass. When Dalinar was troubled, he went silent. His brow would scrunch up in thought, and to everyone else, it looked like he was scowling.

"They got out, Dalinar," Navani said to him. "I'm sure they did. Elhokar and Adolin are safe, somewhere."

He nodded. But even if they had survived, Kholinar had fallen. Was that why he seemed so haunted?

No, it was something else. Ever since he'd collapsed after visiting Azir, it seemed that something in Dalinar had snapped. This morning, he had quietly asked her to lead the meeting. She worried, deeply, for what was happening to him. And for Elhokar. And for Kholinar . . .

But storms, they had worked so hard to forge this coalition. She would *not* let it collapse now. She'd already grieved for a daughter, but then that daughter had returned to her. She *had* to hope the same for Elhokar—at the very least, so she could keep functioning while Dalinar mourned.

They settled their chairs in the large meeting room, which had a clear view out flat glass windows overlooking mountains. Servants had already set out refreshment along the curved side wall of the half-circle room. The tiled floor was inlaid with the image of the Double Eye of the Almighty, complete with Surges and Essences.

Bridge Four piled into the room after them. Many had brought simple seats, but the Herdazian had stumbled onto the lift with a chair so grand—inlaid with embroidered blue cloth and silver—it was almost a throne.

They settled their chairs behind hers with a fair bit of squabbling, and then attacked the food without waiting for permission. For a group that was essentially one step from being lighteyed Shardbearers, they were an unruly and raucous bunch.

Bridge Four had, characteristically, taken the news of their leader's potential fall with laughter. *Kaladin is tougher than a wind-tossed boulder, Brightness,* Teft had told her. *He survived Bridge Four, he survived the chasms, and he'll survive this.*

She had to admit their optimism was heartening. But if the team had survived, why hadn't they returned during the latest highstorm?

Steady, Navani thought to herself, regarding the bridgemen, who were surrounded by laughterspren. One of those men currently carried Jezerezeh's Honorblade. She couldn't tell which; the Blade could be dismissed like an ordinary Shardblade, and they swapped it among themselves in order to be unpredictable.

Soon, the others began arriving on different lifts, and Navani watched carefully. The chair-carrying tradition was, in part, a symbol of equality— but Navani figured she might be able to learn something about the monarchs from their choices. Being a human was about making sense of chaos, finding meaning among the random elements of the world.

First to arrive was the young Azish Prime. His tailor had done a wonderful job making his regal costume fit; it would have been easy for the youth to look like a child swimming in those stately robes and that headdress. He carried a very ornate throne, covered in loud Azish patterns, and each of his closest advisors helped by holding it with one hand.

The large contingent settled in, and others flooded in behind, including three representatives of kingdoms subject to Azir: the prime of Emul, the princess of Yezier, and the ambassador from Tashikk. All brought chairs that were *faintly* inferior to that of the Azish Prime.

A balancing act went on here. Each of the three monarchies gave just enough respect to the Prime so as not to embarrass him. They were his subjects in name only. Still, Navani should be able to focus her diplomacy efforts on the Prime. Tashikk, Emul, and Yezier would fall in line. Two were historically closest with the Azish throne, and the third—Emul—was in no position to stand on its own after the war with Tukar and the Voidbringer assault had basically broken the princedom into pieces.

The Alethi contingent arrived next. Renarin, who seemed terrified that something had happened to his brother, brought a simple chair. Jasnah had outdone him by actually bringing a padded stool—she and Dalinar could be painfully similar. Navani noticed with annoyance that Sebarial and Palona weren't with the other highprinces. Well, at least they hadn't shown up bearing massage tables.

Notably, Ialai Sadeas ignored the requirement that she carry her own chair. A scarred guardsman placed a sleek, lacquered chair down for her—stained so dark a maroon, it might as well have been black. She met Navani's eyes as she sat, cold and confident. Amaram was technically highprince, but he was still in Thaylenah, working alongside his soldiers to rebuild the city. Navani doubted Ialai would have let him represent them at this meeting anyway.

It seemed so long ago when Ialai and Navani had huddled together at dinners, conspiring on how to stabilize the kingdom their husbands were conquering. Now, Navani wanted to seize the woman and shake her. *Can't you stop being petty for one storming minute?*

Well, as had been happening for so long now, the other highprinces would defer either to Kholin or to Sadeas. Letting Ialai participate was a calculated risk. Forbid her, and the woman *would* find a way to sabotage the proceedings. Let her in, and hopefully she'd start to see the importance of this work.

At least Queen Fen and her consort seemed committed to the coalition. They set their chairs by the glass window, backs to the storms, as the Thaylens often joked. Their wooden chairs were high-backed, painted blue, and upholstered a pale nautical white. Taravangian—bearing a nondescript chair of wood with no padding—asked to join them. The old man had insisted on carrying his own chair, though Navani had specifically excused him, Ashno of Sages, and others with a frail bearing.

Adrotagia sat with him, as did his Surgebinder. She didn't go join Bridge Four . . . and, curiously, Navani realized she still thought of the woman as *his* Surgebinder.

The only other person of note was Au-nak, the Natan ambassador.

He represented a dead kingdom that had been reduced to a single city-state on the eastern coast of Roshar with a few other cities as protectorates.

For a moment, it all seemed too much for Navani. The Azish Empire, with all its intricacies. The countermovement among the Alethi highprinces. Taravangian, who was somehow king of Jah Keved—the second-largest kingdom on Roshar. Queen Fen and her obligation to the guilds in her city. The Radiants—like the little Reshi who was currently outeating the huge Horneater bridgeman, almost as if it were a contest.

So much to think about. *Now* was when Dalinar stepped back?

Calm, Navani thought at herself, taking a deep breath. *Order from chaos. Find the structure here and start building upon it.*

Everyone had naturally arranged themselves into a circle, with monarchs at the front and highprinces, viziers, interpreters, and scribes radiating out from them. Navani stood up and strode into the center. Just as everyone was quieting, Sebarial and his mistress finally sauntered in. They made right for the food, and had apparently forgotten chairs entirely.

"I," she said as the room hushed again, "know of no other conference like this in the history of Roshar. Perhaps they were common in the days of the Knights Radiant, but certainly nothing like it has occurred since the Recreance. I would like to both welcome *and* thank you, our noble guests. Today we make history."

"It only took a Desolation to cause it," Sebarial said from the food table. "The world should end more often. It makes everyone so much more accommodating."

The various interpreters whispered translations to their charges. Navani found herself wondering if it was too late to have him tossed off the tower. You could do it—the sheer side of Urithiru, facing the Origin, was straight all the way down. She could watch Sebarial fall practically to the bottom of the mountains, if she wanted.

"We," Navani said sharply, "are here to discuss the future of Roshar. We must have a unified vision and goal."

She glanced around the room as people considered. *He's going to talk first,* she thought, noticing the prime of Emul shifting in his seat. His name was Vexil the Wise, but people often referred to the Makabaki princes and primes by their country, much as Alethi highprinces were often referred to by their house name.

"The course is obvious, isn't it?" Emul said through an interpreter, though Navani understood his Azish. He bowed in his seat to the Azish child emperor, then continued. "We must reclaim my nation from the hands of the traitor parshmen; then we must conquer Tukar. It is completely un-reasonable to allow this insane man, who claims to be a god, to continue bereaving the glorious Azish Empire."

This is going to get difficult, Navani thought as a half dozen other people started to speak at once. She raised her freehand. "I will do my best to moderate fairly, Your Majesties, but do realize that I am only one person. I depend upon you all to facilitate the discussion, rather than trying to talk over one another."

She nodded at the Azish Prime, hoping he'd take the floor. A translator whispered her words into the Prime's left ear; then Noura the vizier leaned forward and spoke quietly into the other, undoubtedly giving instructions.

They'll want to see how this plays out, Navani decided. *One of the others will speak next. They'll want to contrast the Emuli position, to assert themselves.*

"The throne recognizes the prime of Emul," the little emperor finally said. "And, er, we are aware of his desires." He paused and looked around. "Um, anyone else have a comment?"

"My brother the prince wishes to address you," said the tall, refined representative from Tashikk, who wore a flowery suit of yellow and gold rather than his people's traditional wrap. A scribe whispered to him as a spanreed scratched out the message Tashikk's prince wanted conveyed to the gathering.

He'll contradict Emul, Navani thought. *Point us in another direction. Toward Iri maybe?*

"We of Tashikk," the ambassador said, "are more interested in the discovery of these glorious portals. The Alethi have invited us here and told us we're part of a grand coalition. We would respectfully inquire how often we will have use of these gates, and how to negotiate tariffs."

Immediately, the room exploded with conversation.

"Our gate," Au-nak said, "in our *historical homeland* is being used without our permission. And while we thank the Alethi for securing it for us—"

"If there is to be war," Fen said, "then it's a bad time to be discussing tariffs. We should just agree to free trade."

"Which would help your merchants, Fen," Sebarial called. "How about asking them to help the rest of us out with some free wartime supplies?"

"Emul—" the Emuli Prime began.

"Wait," the Yezier princess said. "Shouldn't we be concerned about Iri and Rira, who seem to have completely fallen in with the enemy?"

"Please," Navani said, interrupting the mess of conversations. "*Please.* Let's do this in an orderly way. Perhaps before deciding where to fight, we could discuss how to best equip ourselves against the enemy threat?" She looked to Taravangian. "Your Majesty, can you tell us more about the shields your scholars in Jah Keved are creating?"

"Yes. They . . . they are strong."

". . . How strong?" Navani prompted.

"Very strong. Er, yes. Strong enough." He scratched his head and looked at her helplessly. "How . . . how strong do you need them to be?"

She drew in a deep breath. He wasn't having a good day. Her mother had been like that, lucid on some days, barely cognizant on others.

"The half-shards," Navani said, addressing the room, "will give us an edge against the enemy. We have given the plans to the Azish scholars; I'm looking forward to pooling our resources and studying the process."

"Could it lead to Shardplate?" Queen Fen asked.

"Possibly," Navani said. "But the more I study what we've discovered here in Urithiru, the more I've come to realize that our image of the ancients having fantastic technology was deeply flawed. An exaggeration at best, perhaps a fancy."

"But Shards . . ." Fen said.

"Manifestations of spren," Jasnah explained. "Not fabrial technology. Even the gemstones we discovered, containing words of ancient Radiants during the days when they left Urithiru, were crude—if used in a way we hadn't yet explored. All this time we've been assuming that we lost great technology in the Desolations, but it seems we are far, far more advanced than the ancients ever were. It is the process of bonding spren that we lost."

"Not lost," the Azish Prime said. "*Abandoned.*"

He looked toward Dalinar, who sat in a relaxed posture. Not slumped, but not stiff either—a posture that somehow read as, "I'm in control here. Don't pretend otherwise." Dalinar loomed over a room even when trying to be unobtrusive. That furrowed brow darkened his blue eyes, and the way he rubbed his chin evoked the image of a man contemplating whom to execute first.

The attendees had arranged their seats roughly in a circle, but most of them faced Dalinar, who sat by Navani's chair. After everything that had happened, they didn't trust him.

"The ancient oaths are spoken once more," Dalinar said. "We are again Radiant. This time, we will not abandon you. I vow it."

Noura the vizier whispered in the Azish Prime's ear, and he nodded before speaking. "We are still *very* concerned about the powers in which you dabble. These abilities . . . who is to say that the Lost Radiants were wrong in abandoning them? They were frightened of something, and they locked these portals for a reason."

"It is too late to turn back from this now, Your Majesty," Dalinar said. "I have bonded the Stormfather himself. We must either use these abilities, or crumple beneath the invasion."

The Prime sat back, and his attendants seemed . . . concerned. They whispered among themselves.

Bring order from the chaos, Navani thought. She gestured toward the bridgemen and Lift. "I understand your concern, but surely you have read our reports of the oaths these Radiants follow. Protection. Remembering the fallen. Those oaths are proof that our cause is just, our Radiants trustworthy. The powers are in safe hands, Your Majesty."

"I think," Ialai declared, "we should stop dancing around and patting ourselves on the back."

Navani spun to face Ialai. *Don't sabotage this,* she thought, meeting the woman's eyes. *Don't you dare.*

"We are here," Ialai continued, "to focus our attention. We should be discussing where to invade to gain the best position for an extended war. Obviously, there is only one answer. Shinovar is a bounteous land. Their orchards grow without end; the land is so mild that even the grass has grown relaxed and fat. We should seize that land to supply our armies."

The others in the room nodded as if this were a perfectly acceptable line of conversation. With one targeted arrow, Ialai Sadeas proved what everyone whispered—that the Alethi were building a coalition to conquer the world, not just protect it.

"The Shin mountains present a historical problem," said the Tashikki ambassador. "Attacking across or through them is basically impossible."

"We have the Oathgates now," Fen said. "Not to bring up that particular problem again, but has anyone investigated whether the Shin one can be opened? Having Shinovar as a redoubt, difficult to invade conventionally, would help secure our position."

Navani cursed Ialai softly. This would only reinforce the Azish worry that the gates were dangerous. She tried to rein the discussion in, but it slipped away from her again.

"We need to know what the Oathgates do!" Tashikk was saying. "Could the Alethi not share with us everything they've discovered regarding them?"

"What about your people?" Aladar shot back. "They are the great traders in information. Could you share with us your secrets?"

"All Tashikki information is freely available."

"At a huge price."

"We need—"

"But *Emul*—"

"This whole thing is going to be a mess," Fen said. "I can see it already. We need to be able to trade freely, and Alethi greed could destroy this."

"*Alethi* greed?" Ialai demanded. "Are you trying to see how far you can push us? Because I assure you Dalinar Kholin will *not* be intimidated by a bunch of merchants and bankers."

"Please," Navani said into the growing uproar. "Quiet."

Nobody seemed to notice. Navani breathed out, then cleared her mind.

Order from chaos. How could she bring order to this chaos? She stopped fretting, and tried to listen to them. She studied the chairs they'd brought, the tone of their voices. Their fears, hidden behind what they demanded or requested.

The shape of it started to make sense to her. Right now, this room was full of building materials. Pieces of a fabrial. Each monarch, each kingdom, was one piece. Dalinar had gathered them, but he hadn't *formed* them.

Navani stepped up to the Azish Prime. People quieted as, shockingly, she bowed to him.

"Your Excellency," she said, upon rising. "What would you say is the Azish people's greatest strength?"

He glanced at his advisors as her words were translated, but they gave him no answer. Rather, they seemed curious to know what he'd say.

"Our laws," he finally replied.

"Your famed bureaucracy," Navani said. "Your clerks and scribes—and by extension, the great information centers of Tashikk, the timekeepers and stormwardens of Yezier, the Azish legions. You are the greatest organizers on Roshar. I've long envied your orderly approach to the world."

"Perhaps this is why your essay was so well received, Brightness Kholin," the emperor said, sounding completely sincere.

"In light of your skill, I wonder. Would anyone in this room complain if a specific task were assigned to your scribes? We need procedures. A code of how our kingdoms are to interact, and how we're to share resources. Would you of Azir be willing to create this?"

The viziers looked shocked, then immediately began talking to one another in hushed, excited tones. The looks of delight on their faces were enough proof that yes indeed, they'd be willing.

"Now, wait," Fen interjected. "Are you talking of laws? That we all have to follow?" Au-nak nodded eagerly in agreement.

"More *and* less than laws," Navani said. "We need codes to guide our interactions—as proven by today. We must have procedures on how we hold meetings, how to give each person a turn. How we share information."

"I don't know if Thaylenah can agree to even that."

"Well, surely you'd want to see what the codes contained first, Queen Fen," Navani said, strolling toward her. "After all, we *are* going to need to administrate trade through the Oathgates. I wonder, who has excellent expertise in shipping, caravans, and trade in general . . . ?"

"You'd give that to *us*?" Fen asked, completely taken aback.

"It seems logical."

Sebarial choked softly on the snacks he'd been eating, and Palona pounded him on the back. He'd wanted that job. *That will teach you to show up late to my meeting and make only wisecracks,* Navani noted.

She glanced at Dalinar, who seemed worried. Well, he always seemed worried lately.

"I'm not giving you the Oathgates," Navani said to Fen. "But someone has to oversee trade and supplies. It would be a natural match for the Thaylen merchants—so long as a fair agreement can be reached."

"Huh," Fen said, settling back. She glanced at her consort, who shrugged.

"And the Alethi?" the petite Yezier princess asked. "What of you?"

"Well, we do excel at one thing," Navani said. She looked to Emul. "Would you accept help from our generals and armies to help you secure what is left of your kingdom?"

"By every Kadasix that has ever been holy!" Emul said. "Yes, of course! Please."

"I have several scribes who are experts in fortification," Aladar suggested from his seat behind Dalinar and Jasnah. "They could survey your remaining territory and give you advice on securing it."

"And recovering what we've lost?" Emul asked.

Ialai opened her mouth to speak, perhaps to extol the virtues of Alethi warmongering again.

Jasnah cut her off, speaking decisively. "I propose we entrench ourselves first. Tukar, Iri, Shinovar . . . each of these looks tempting to attack, but what good will that do if we stretch ourselves too far? We should focus on securing our lands as they now stand."

"Yes," Dalinar said. "We shouldn't be asking ourselves, 'Where should we strike?' but instead, 'Where will our enemy strike next?'"

"They've secured three positions," Highprince Aladar said. "Iri, Marat . . . and Alethkar."

"But you sent an expedition," Fen said. "To reclaim Alethkar."

Navani caught her breath, glancing at Dalinar. He nodded slowly.

"Alethkar has fallen," Navani said. "The expedition failed. Our homeland is overrun."

Navani had expected this to prompt another burst of conversation, but instead it was greeted only by stunned silence.

Jasnah continued for her. "The last of our armies have retreated into Herdaz or Jah Keved, harried and confused by enemies who can fly—or by the sudden attacks of shock troops of parshmen. Our only holdouts are on the southern border, by the sea. Kholinar has fallen completely; the Oathgate is lost to us. We've locked it on our side, so that it cannot be used to reach Urithiru."

"I'm sorry," Fen said.

"My daughter is correct," Navani said, trying to project strength while admitting that they had become a nation of refugees. "We should apply our efforts *first* toward making sure no more nations fall."

"My homeland——" the prime of Emul began.

"No," Noura said in thickly accented Alethi. "I'm sorry, but no. If the Voidbringers had wanted your last nibble of land, Vexil, they'd have taken it. The Alethi can help you secure what you have, and it seems generous of them to do so. The enemy brushed past you to gather in Marat, conquering only what was necessary on the way. Their eyes are turned elsewhere."

"Oh my!" Taravangian said. "Could they . . . be coming for me?"

"It does seem a reasonable assumption," Au-nak said. "The Veden civil war left the country in ruin, and the border between Alethkar and Jah Keved is porous."

"Maybe," Dalinar said. "I've fought on that border. It's not as easy a battlefield as it would seem."

"We must defend Jah Keved," Taravangian said. "When the king gave me the throne, I promised I'd care for his people. If the Voidbringers attack us . . ."

The worry in his voice gave Navani an opportunity. She stepped back into the center of the room. "We won't allow that to happen, will we?"

"I will send troops to your aid, Taravangian," Dalinar said. "But one army can be construed as an invading force, and I am not intending to invade my allies, even in appearance. Can we not mortar this alliance with a show of solidarity? Will anyone else help?"

The Azish Prime regarded Dalinar. Behind him, the viziers and scions conducted a private conversation by writing on pads of paper. When they finished, Vizier Noura leaned forward and whispered to the emperor, who nodded.

"We will send five battalions to Jah Keved," he said. "This will prove an important test of mobility through the Oathgates. King Taravangian, you will have the support of Azir."

Navani released a long breath in relief.

She gave leave for the meeting to take a pause, so that people could enjoy refreshment—though most would probably spend it strategizing or relaying events to their various allies. The highprinces became a flurry of motion, breaking into individual houses to converse.

Navani settled down in her seat beside Dalinar.

"You've promised away a great deal," he noted. "Giving Fen control of trade and supply?"

"Administration is different from control," Navani said. "But either way, did you think you were going to make this coalition work without giving something up?"

"No. Of course not." He stared outward. That haunted expression made her shiver. *What did you remember, Dalinar? And what did the Nightwatcher do to you?*

They needed the Blackthorn. *She* needed the Blackthorn. His strength to quiet the sick worry inside of her, his will to forge this coalition. She took his hand in hers, but he stiffened, then stood up. He did that whenever he felt he was growing too relaxed. It was as if he was looking for danger to face.

She stood up beside him. "We need to get you out of the tower," she decided. "To get a new perspective. Visit someplace new."

"That," Dalinar said, voice hoarse, "would be good."

"Taravangian was speaking of having you tour Vedenar personally. If we're going to send Kholin troops into the kingdom, it would make sense for you to get a feel for the situation there."

"Very well."

The Azish called for her, asking for clarification on what direction she wanted them to take with their coalition bylaws. She left Dalinar, but couldn't leave off worrying about him. She'd have to burn a glyphward today. A dozen of them, for Elhokar and the others. Except . . . part of the problem was that Dalinar claimed nobody was watching the prayers as they burned, sending twisting smoke to the Tranquiline Halls. Did she believe that? Truly?

Today, she'd taken a huge step toward unifying Roshar. Yet she felt more powerless than ever.

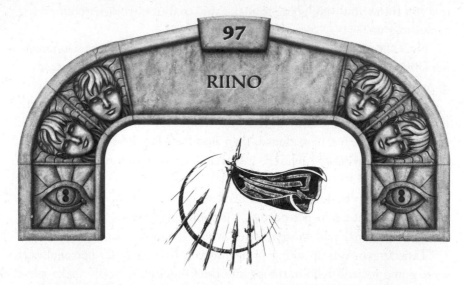

Of the Unmade, Sja-anat was most feared by the Radiants. They spoke extensively of her ability to corrupt spren, though only "lesser" spren—whatever that means.

—From Hessi's *Mythica*, page 89

Kaladin remembered holding a dying woman's hand.

It had been during his days as a slave. He remembered crouching in the darkness, thick forest underbrush scratching his skin, the night around him too quiet. The animals had fled; they knew something was wrong.

The other slaves didn't whisper, shift, or cough in their hiding places. He'd taught them well.

We have to go. Have to move.

He tugged on Nalma's hand. He'd promised to help the older woman find her husband, who had been sold to another household. That wasn't supposed to be legal, but you could get away with doing all kinds of things to slaves with the right brands, especially if they were foreign.

She resisted his tug, and he could understand her hesitance. The underbrush was safe, for the moment. It was also too obvious. The brightlords had chased them in circles for days, getting closer and closer. Stay here, and the slaves would be captured.

He tugged again, and she passed the signal to the next slave, all the way down the line. Then she clung to his hand as he led them—as quietly as he could—toward where he remembered a game trail.

Get away.

Find freedom. Find honor again.

It had to be out there somewhere.

The snapping sound of the trap closing sent a jolt through Kaladin. A year later, he'd still wonder how he missed stepping in it himself.

It got Nalma instead. She yanked her hand from his as she screamed.

Hunters' horns moaned in the night. Light burst from newly unshielded lanterns, showing men in uniforms among the trees. The other slaves broke, bursting out of the underbrush like game for sport. Next to Kaladin, Nalma's leg was caught in a fierce steel trap—a thing of springs and jaws that they wouldn't even use on a beast, for fear of ruining the sport. Her tibia jutted through her skin.

"Oh, Stormfather," Kaladin whispered as painspren writhed around them. "Stormfather!" He tried to stanch the blood, but it spurted between his fingers. "Stormfather, no. Stormfather!"

"Kaladin," she said through clenched teeth. "Kaladin, *run* . . ."

Arrows cut down several of the fleeing slaves. Traps caught two others. In the distance, a voice called, "Wait! That's my property you're cutting down."

"A necessity, Brightlord," a stronger voice said. The local highlord. "Unless you want to encourage more of this behavior."

So much blood. Kaladin uselessly made a bandage as Nalma tried to push him away, to make him run. He took her hand and held it instead, weeping as she died.

After killing the others, the brightlords found him still kneeling there. Against reason, they spared him. They said it was because he hadn't run with the others, but in truth they'd needed someone to bear warning to the other slaves.

Regardless of the reason, Kaladin had lived.

He always did.

.⁘.

There was no underbrush here in Shadesmar, but those old instincts served Kaladin well as he crept toward the lighthouse. He'd suggested that he scout ahead, as he didn't trust this dark land. The others had agreed. With Lashings, he could get away most easily in an emergency—and neither Adolin nor Azure had experience scouting. Kaladin didn't mention that most of *his* practice sneaking had come as a runaway slave.

He focused on staying low to the ground, trying to use rifts in the black stone to hide his approach. Fortunately, stepping silently wasn't difficult on this glassy ground.

The lighthouse was a large stone tower topped by an enormous bonfire.

It threw a flagrant orange glow over the point of the peninsula. Where did they get the *fuel* for that thing?

He drew closer, accidentally startling a burst of lifespren, which shot up from some crystalline plants, then floated back down. He froze, but heard no sounds from the lighthouse.

Once he got a little closer, he settled down to watch for a while, to see if he could spot anything suspicious. He sorely missed the diaphanous form Syl had in the Physical Realm; she could have reported back to the others what he'd seen, or even scouted into the building herself, invisible to all but the right eyes.

After a short time, something crawled out of the beads of the ocean near him: a round lurglike creature with a fat, bulbous body and squat legs. About the size of a toddler, it hopped close to him, then tipped the entire top half of its head backward. A long tongue shot up in the air from the gaping mouth; it began to flap and wave.

Storms. An anticipationspren? They looked like streamers on his side, but those . . . those were waving *tongues?* What other simple, stable parts of his life were complete lies?

Two more anticipationspren joined the first, clustering near him and deploying their long, wagging tongues. He kicked at them. "Shoo." Deceptively solid, they refused to budge, so he tried calming himself, hoping it would banish them. Finally, he just continued forward, his three bothersome attendants hopping behind. That sorely undermined the stealth of his approach, making him more nervous—which in turn made the anticipationspren even more eager to stick with him.

He managed to reach the wall of the tower, where he might have expected the heat of the enormous fire to be oppressive. Instead, he could barely feel it. Notably, the flames caused his shadow to behave normally, extending behind him instead of pointing toward the sun.

He took a breath, then glanced up through the open-shuttered window, into the ground floor of the lighthouse.

Inside, he saw an old Shin man—with furrowed, wrinkled skin and a completely bald head—sitting in a chair, reading by spherelight. A human? Kaladin couldn't decide if that was a good sign or not. The old man began to turn a page in his book, then froze, looking up.

Kaladin ducked down, heart thumping. Those stupid anticipationspren continued to crowd nearby, but their tongues shouldn't be visible through the window—

"Hello?" an accented voice called from inside the lighthouse. "Who's out there? Show yourself!"

Kaladin sighed, then stood up. So much for his promise to do some stealthy reconnaissance.

Shallan waited with the others in the shadow of a strange rock growth. It looked something like a mushroom made from obsidian, the height of a tree; she thought she'd seen its like before, during one of her glimpses into Shadesmar. Pattern said it was alive, but "very, very slow."

The group waited, pensive, as Kaladin scouted. She hated sending him alone, but Shallan knew nothing about that sort of work. Veil did. But Veil . . . still felt broken, from what had happened in Kholinar. That was dangerous. Where would Shallan hide now? As Radiant?

Find the balance, Wit had said. *Accept the pain, but don't accept that you deserved it. . . .*

She sighed, then got out her sketchbook and started drawing some of the spren they'd seen.

"So," Syl said, sitting on a rock nearby and swinging her legs. "I've always wondered. Does the world look weird to you, or normal?"

"Weird," Pattern said. "Mmm. Same as for everyone."

"I guess neither of us technically have eyes," Syl said, leaning back and looking up at the glassy canopy of their tree-mushroom shelter. "We're each a bit of power made manifest. We honorspren mimic Honor himself. You Cryptics mimic . . . weird stuff?"

"The fundamental underlying mathematics by which natural phenomena occur. Mmm. Truths that explain the fabric of existence."

"Yeah. Weird stuff."

Shallan lowered her pencil, looking with dissatisfaction at the attempt she'd made at drawing a fearspren. It looked like a child's scribble.

Veil was seeping out.

That has always been you, Shallan. You just have to admit it. Allow it.

"I'm trying, Wit," she whispered.

"You all right?" Adolin asked, kneeling beside her, putting his hand on her back, then rubbing her shoulders. Storms, that felt good. They'd walked *entirely* too far these last few days.

He glanced at her sketchpad. "More . . . what did you call it? Abstractionalism?"

She snapped the sketchpad closed. "What is taking that bridgeman so long?" She glanced over her shoulder, which interrupted Adolin. "Don't stop," she added, "or I will murder you."

He chuckled and continued working at her shoulders. "He'll be fine."

"You were worried about him yesterday."

"He's got battle fatigue, but an objective will help with that. We have to watch him when he's sitting around doing nothing, not when he's got a specific mission."

"If you say so." She nodded toward Azure, who stood by the coast, staring across the ocean of beads. "What do you make of her?"

"That uniform is well tailored," Adolin said, "but the blue doesn't work with her skin. She needs a lighter shade. The breastplate is overly much, like she's trying to prove something. I do like the cape though. I've always wanted to justify wearing one. Father gets away with it, but I never could."

"I wasn't asking for a wardrobe assessment, Adolin."

"Clothing says a lot about people."

"Yeah? What happened to the fancy suit you got in Kholinar?"

He looked down—which stopped the massaging of shoulders for an unacceptable count of three, so she growled at him.

"It didn't fit me anymore," he said, resuming the massage. "But you do raise an important problem. Yes, we need to find food and drink. But if I have to wear the same uniform this entire trip, you won't have to murder me. I'll commit suicide."

Shallan had almost forgotten that she was hungry. How odd. She sighed, closing her eyes and trying not to melt *too* much into the feeling of his touch.

"Huh," Adolin said a short time later. "Shallan, what do you suppose that is?"

She followed his nod and spotted an odd little spren floating through the air. Bone-white and brown, it had wings extending to the sides and long tresses for a tail. In front of its body hovered a cube.

"Looks like those gloryspren we saw earlier," she noted. "Only the wrong color. And the shape of the head is . . ."

"Corrupted!" Syl said. "That's one of Odium's!"

∴

As he stepped inside the lighthouse, Kaladin's instincts drove him to check to either side of the doorway for anyone waiting in ambush. The room seemed empty save for furniture, the Shin man, and some strange pictures on the walls. The place smelled of incense and spices.

The Shin man snapped his book closed. "Cutting it close, aren't you? Well, let us begin! We haven't much time." He stood up, proving himself to be rather short. His odd clothing had puffed out portions on the arms, the trousers very tight. He walked to a door at the side of the chamber.

"I should fetch my companions," Kaladin said.

"Ah, but the very *best* readings happen at the beginning of the high-storm!" The man checked a small device that he took from his pocket. "Only two minutes off."

A highstorm? Azure had said they didn't need to worry about those in Shadesmar.

"Wait," Kaladin said, stepping after the little man—who had entered a room built up against the base of the lighthouse. It had large windows, but its main feature was a small table at the center. That held something lumpish covered by a black cloth.

Kaladin found himself . . . curious. That was good, after the darkness of the last few days. He stepped in, glancing to the sides again. One wall contained a picture of people kneeling before a bright white mirror. Another was a cityscape at dusk, with a group of low houses clustered before an enormous wall that had light glowing beyond it.

"Well, let's begin!" the man said. "You have come to witness the extraordinary, and I shall provide it. The price is a mere two marks of Stormlight. You shall be greatly rewarded in kind—both in dreams and luster!"

"I should really get my friends. . . ." Kaladin said.

The man whipped the cloth off the table, revealing a large crystalline globe. It glowed with a powerful light, bathing the room in luminescence. Kaladin blinked against it. Was that Stormlight?

"Are you balking at the price?" the man said. "What is the money to you? Potential? If you never spend it, you gain nothing by having it. And the witness of what is to come will far recompense you for small means expended!"

"I . . ." Kaladin said, raising his hand against the light. "Storms, man. I have no idea what you're talking about."

The Shin man frowned, face lit from below like the globe. "You came here for a fortune, didn't you? To the Rii Oracle? You wish me to see the unwalked paths—during the highstorm, when realms blend."

"A fortune? You mean *foretelling the future?*" Kaladin felt a bitter taste in his mouth. "The future is *forbidden.*"

The old man cocked his head. "But . . . isn't this why you came to see me?"

"Storms, no. I'm looking for passage. We heard that ships come by here."

The old man rubbed the bridge of his nose and sighed. "Passage? Why didn't you say so? And I was really enjoying the speech. Ah well. A ship? Let me check my calendars. I think supplies are coming soon. . . ."

He bustled past Kaladin, muttering to himself.

Outside, the sky rippled with light. The clouds *shimmered,* gaining a strange, ethereal luminescence. Kaladin gaped, then glanced back at the little man, who had fetched a ledger from a side table.

"That . . ." Kaladin said. "Is that what a highstorm looks like on this side?"

"Hmmm? Oh, new, are you? How have you gotten into Shadesmar, but not seen a storm pass? Did you come directly from the perpendicularity?"

The old man frowned. "Not a lot of people coming through there anymore."

That *light.* The bright sphere on the table—as large as a man's head, and glowing with a milky light—shifted colors, matching the pearlescent ripples above. There was no gemstone inside that globe. And the light seemed different. Transfixing.

"Here now," the man said as Kaladin stepped forward, "don't touch that. It's only for *properly trained* fo—"

Kaladin rested his hand on the sphere.

And felt himself get carried away by the storm.

⁂

Shallan and the others dodged for cover, but too slowly. The strange spren flitted right under their small canopy.

Overhead, the clouds started to ripple with a vibrant set of colors.

The corrupted gloryspren *landed* on Shallan's arm. *Odium suspects that you survived,* a voice said in her mind. That . . . that was the voice of the Unmade from the mirror. Sja-anat. *He thinks something strange happened to the Oathgate because of our influence—we've never managed to Enlighten such powerful spren before. It's believable that something odd might happen. I lied, and said I think you were sent far, far from the point of transfer.*

He has minions in this realm, and they will be told to hunt you. So take care. Fortunately, he doesn't know that you're a Lightweaver—he thinks you are an Elsecaller for some reason.

I will do what I can, but I'm not sure he trusts me any longer.

The spren fluttered away.

"Wait!" Shallan said. "Wait, I have questions!"

Syl tried to snatch it, but it dodged and was soon out over the ocean.

⁂

Kaladin rode the storm.

He'd done this before, in dreams. He'd even spoken to the Stormfather.

This felt different. He rode in a shimmering, rippling surge of colors. Around him, the clouds streamed past at incredible speed, coming alight with those colors. Pulsing with them, as if to a beat.

He couldn't feel the Stormfather. He couldn't see a landscape beneath him. Just shimmering colors, and clouds that faded into . . . light.

Then a figure. Dalinar Kholin, kneeling someplace dark, surrounded by nine shadows. A flash of glowing red eyes.

The enemy's champion was coming. Kaladin knew in that moment—an overpowering sensation thrumming through him—that Dalinar was in terrible, *terrible* danger. Without help, the Blackthorn was doomed.

"Where!" Kaladin screamed to the light as it began to fade. "When! How do I reach him!"

The colors diminished.

"*Please!*"

He saw a flash of a vaguely familiar city. Tall, built along the stones, it had a distinctive pattern of buildings at the center. A wall and an ocean beyond.

Kaladin dropped to his knees in the fortuneteller's room. The little Shin man batted Kaladin's hand from the glowing sphere. "—rtune seers like myself. You'll ruin it, or . . ." He trailed off, then took Kaladin's head, turning it toward him. "You *saw something!*"

Kaladin nodded weakly.

"How? Impossible. Unless . . . you're *Invested*. What Heightening are you?" He squinted at Kaladin. "No. Something else. Merciful Domi . . . A Surgebinder? It has begun again?"

Kaladin stumbled to his feet. He glanced at the large globe of light, which the lighthouse keeper covered up again with the black cloth, then put his hand to his forehead, which had begun thumping with pain. What had *that* been? His heart still raced with anxiety.

"I . . . I need to go get my friends," he said.

⋰

Kaladin sat in the main room of the lighthouse, in the chair Riino—the Shin lighthouse keeper—had occupied earlier. Shallan and Adolin negotiated with him on the other side of the room, Pattern looming over Shallan's shoulder and making the fortuneteller nervous. Riino had food and supplies for trade, though it would cost them infused spheres. Apparently, Stormlight was the only commodity that mattered on this side.

"Charlatans like him aren't uncommon, where I come from," Azure said, resting with her back against the wall near Kaladin. "People who claim to be able to see the future, living off people's hopes. Your society was right to forbid them. The spren do likewise, so his kind have to live off in places like this, hoping people will be desperate enough to come to them. Probably gets some business with each ship that comes through."

"I saw something, Azure," Kaladin said, still trembling. "It was real." His limbs felt drained, like the aftereffect of lifting weights for a long period.

"Maybe," Azure said. "Those types use dusts and powders that grant euphoria, making you *think* you've seen something. Even the gods of my land catch only glimpses of the Spiritual Realm—and in all my life, I've only met one human I believe truly understood it. And he might actually be a god. I'm not sure."

"Wit," Kaladin said. "The man that brought you the metal that protected your Soulcaster."

She nodded.

Well, Kaladin *had* seen something. *Dalinar . . .*

Adolin walked over and handed Kaladin a squat metal cylinder. He used a device—provided by the Shin man—to break open the top. There were some fish rations inside. Kaladin poked at the chunks with his finger, then inspected the container.

"Canned food," Azure noted. "It's extremely convenient."

Kaladin's stomach rumbled, so he dug into the fish with the spoon Adolin provided. The meat tasted salty, but was good—far better than something Soulcast. Shallan joined them, trailed by Pattern, while the lighthouse keeper bustled off to fetch some supplies they'd traded for. The man glanced at the doorway, where the spren of Adolin's Blade stood, silent like a statue.

Out through the room's window, Kaladin could see Syl standing on the coast, watching out over the sea of beads. *Her hair doesn't ripple here,* he thought. In the Physical Realm it often waved as if being brushed by an unseen breeze. Here, it acted like the hair of a human.

She hadn't wanted to enter the lighthouse for some reason. What was that about?

"The lighthouse keeper says a ship will be arriving any time now," Adolin said. "We should be able to buy passage."

"Mmm," Pattern said. "The ship is going to Celebrant. Mmm. A city on the island."

"Island?"

"It's a lake on our side," Adolin said. "Called the Sea of Spears, in the southeast of Alethkar. By the ruins . . . of Rathalas." He drew his lips to a line and glanced away.

"What?" Kaladin asked.

"Rathalas was where my mother was killed," Adolin said. "Assassinated by rebels. Her death drove my father into a fury. We almost lost him to the despair." He shook his head, and Shallan rested her hand on his arm. "It's . . . not a pleasant event to think about. Sadeas burned the city to the ground in retribution. My father gets a strange, distant expression whenever someone mentions Rathalas. I think he blames himself for not stopping Sadeas, even though he was mad with grief at the time, wounded and incoherent from an attempt on his own life."

"Well, there's still a spren city on this side," Azure said. "But it's in the wrong direction. We need to be heading west—toward the Horneater Peaks—not south."

"Mmm," Pattern said. "Celebrant is a prominent city. In it, we could find passage wherever we wish to go. And the lighthouse keeper doesn't know when a ship going the right way might pass here."

Kaladin put his fish down, then gestured at Shallan. "Can I have some paper?"

She let him have a sheet from her sketchpad. With an unpracticed hand, he drew out the buildings he'd seen in his momentary . . . whatever it had been. *I've seen this pattern before. From above.*

"That's Thaylen City," Shallan said. "Isn't it?"

That's right, Kaladin thought. He'd only visited once, opening the city's Oathgate. "I saw this, in the vision I explained to you." He glanced at Azure, who seemed skeptical.

Kaladin could still feel his emotion from the vision, that thrumming sense of anxiety. The sure knowledge that Dalinar was in grave danger. Nine shadows. A champion who would lead the enemy forces . . .

"The Oathgate in Thaylen City is open and working," Kaladin said. "Shallan and I saw to that. And since the Oathgate in Kholinar brought us to Shadesmar, theoretically another—one that isn't corrupted by the Unmade—could get us back."

"Assuming I can figure out how to work it on this side," Shallan said. "That's a pretty daunting assumption."

"We should try to reach the perpendicularity in the Peaks," Azure said. "It's the only sure way back."

"The lighthouse keeper says he thinks something strange is happening there," Shallan said. "Ships from that direction have never ended up arriving."

Kaladin rested his fingers on the sketch he'd done. He *needed* to get to Thaylen City. It didn't matter how. The darkness inside him seemed to retreat.

He had a purpose. A goal. Something to focus on other than the people he'd lost in Kholinar.

Protect Dalinar.

Kaladin returned to eating his fish, and the group settled in to wait for the ship. It took a few hours, during which the clouds steadily faded in color, before growing plain white again. On the other side, the highstorm had completed its passing.

Eventually, Kaladin saw something out on the horizon, beyond where Syl sat on the rocks. Yes, that was a ship, sailing in from the west. Except . . . it didn't have a sail. Had he even felt wind in Shadesmar? He didn't think so.

The ship crashed through the ocean of beads, surging toward the lighthouse. It employed no sail, no mast, and no oars. Instead, it was pulled from the front by an elaborate rigging attached to a group of incredible spren. Long and sinuous, they had triangular heads and floated on multiple sets of rippling wings.

Storms . . . they pulled the ship like chulls. Flying, majestic chulls with undulating bodies. He'd never seen anything like it.

Adolin grunted from where he stood by the window. "Well, at least we'll be traveling in style."

Lore suggested leaving a city if the spren there start acting strangely. Curiously, Sja-anat was often regarded as an individual, when others—like Moelach or Ashertmarn—were seen as forces.

—From Hessi's *Mythica*, page 90

Szeth of Shinovar left the Skybreaker fortress with the twenty other squires. The sun approached the clouded horizon to the west, gilding the Purelake red and gold. Those calm waters, strangely, now sprouted dozens of long wooden poles.

Of various heights ranging from five to thirty feet, these poles appeared to have been jammed into fissures in the lake bottom. Each had an odd knobby shape at the top.

"This is a test of martial competence," Master Warren said. The Azish man looked strange in the garb of a Marabethian lawkeeper, chest bare and shoulders draped with the short, patterned cloak. The Azish were normally so proper, overly encumbered with robes and hats. "We must train to fight, if the Desolation truly has begun."

Without Nin's guidance to confirm, they spoke of the Desolation in "if"s and "might"s.

"Each pole is topped with a group of bags bearing powders of a different color," Warren continued. "Fight by throwing those—you cannot use other weapons, and you cannot leave the contest area marked by the poles.

"I will call time over when the sun sets. We will tally the number of times each squire's uniform was marked by one of the bags of powder. You lose four points for each different color on your uniform, and an additional point for each repeated hit from a color. The winner is the one who has lost the fewest points. Begin."

Szeth drew in Stormlight and Lashed himself into the air with the others. Though he didn't care if he won arbitrary tests of competence, the chance to dance the Lashings—for once without needing to cause death and destruction—called to him. This would be like those days in his youth, spent training with the Honorblades.

He soared upward about thirty feet, then used a half Lashing to hover. Yes, the tops of the poles each bore a collection of small pouches tied on by strings. He Lashed himself past one, snatching a pouch, which let out a puff of pink dust as it came off in his hand. He now saw why the squires had been told to wear a white shirt and trousers today.

"Excellent," Szeth said as the other squires scattered, grabbing pouches.

What? the sword asked. Szeth carried it on his back, tied securely in place, at an angle from which he could not draw the weapon. *I don't understand. Where is the evil?*

"No evil today, sword-nimi. Just a *challenge*."

He hurled the pouch at one of the other squires, hitting her square in the shoulder, and the resulting dust colored her shirt in that spot. Notably, the master had said that only color on the *uniform* would be counted, so holding the pouches and dusting one's own fingers was fine. Similarly, hitting each other in the face gained no advantage.

The others took quickly to the game; soon pouches were being flung in all directions. Each pole bore only a single color, encouraging competitors to move about to hit others with as many colors as possible. Joret tried hovering in one spot anyway, dominating one pole to prevent others from hitting him with its color. Sitting still made him a target, however, and his uniform was quickly covered in spots.

Szeth dove, then pulled himself up with an expert Lashing so that he swooped, skimming the surface of the Purelake. He grabbed a pole as he passed, bending it out of Cali's reach as she went by above.

I'm down too low, Szeth realized as bags of dust fell toward him. *Too easy a target.*

He twisted back and forth, executing a complex maneuver that manipulated both Lashings and the wind of his passing. Pouches smacked the water near him.

He pulled upward. Lashing wasn't like the flight of a swallow—instead, it was like tying oneself to strings, a puppet to be yanked about. It was easy to lose control, as evidenced by the awkward motions of the newer squires.

As Szeth gained height, Zedzil fell in behind him, holding a pouch in each hand. Szeth added a second Lashing upward, then a third. His Stormlight lasted so much longer than it had before—he could only assume that Radiants were more efficient than those who used Honorblades for the powers.

He shot upward like an arrow, windspren joining and twisting around him. Zedzil followed, but when he tried to throw a pouch at Szeth, the wind was too great. The pouch fell backward immediately, striking Zedzil on his own shoulder.

Szeth dropped into a dive, and Zedzil followed until Szeth snatched a green bag from a pole and tossed it over his shoulder, hitting Zedzil again. The younger man cursed, then shot away to find easier prey.

Still, this combat proved to be a surprising challenge. Szeth had rarely fought in the air itself, and this contest felt similar to when he'd battled the Windrunner in the skies. He twisted among the poles, dodging pouches—even snatching one from the air before it hit him—and found he was *enjoying* himself.

The screams from the shadows seemed dim, less pressing. He wove between thrown pouches, dancing above a lake painted by the hues of a setting sun, and smiled.

Then immediately felt guilty. He had left tears, blood, and terror in his wake like a personal seal. He had destroyed monarchies, families—innocent and guilty alike. He could not be *happy*. He was only a tool of retribution. Not redemption, for he dared not believe in such.

If he was to be forced to keep living, it should not be a life that anyone would ever envy.

You think like Vasher, the sword said in his head. *Do you know Vasher? He teaches swords to people now, which is funny because VaraTreledees always says Vasher isn't any good with the sword.*

Szeth rededicated himself to the fight, not for joy but for practicality. Unfortunately, his momentary distraction earned him his first hit. A dark blue pouch struck, its circle stark on his white shirt.

He growled, soaring upward with a pouch in each hand. He flung them with precision, hitting one squire in the back, then another in the leg. Nearby, four of the older squires flew in formation. They would chase an isolated squire, swarming him or her with a flurry of eight pouches, often scoring six or seven hits while rarely getting hit themselves.

As Szeth zoomed past, they fixated on him, perhaps because his uniform was nearly pristine. He immediately Lashed himself upward—canceling his lateral Lashing—to try to get above the pack. These were well practiced with their powers, however, and not so easily put off.

If he continued straight upward, they'd merely chase him until he ran out of Stormlight. Already his reserves were low, as each squire had only been given enough to last through the contest. If he double- or triple-Lashed himself too often, he'd run out early.

The sun was slipping inch by inch out of sight. Not much time left; he simply needed to last.

Szeth dove to the side, moving quickly and erratically. Only one of the pack chasing him chanced a throw; the others knew to wait for a better shot. Szeth's swoop took him straight toward a pole, but it held no pouches. Fari looked like he had gathered them all up to hoard the color.

So Szeth grabbed the pole itself.

He pushed it to the side, bending it until it snapped, leaving him with a pole some ten feet long. He lightened it with a partial Lashing upward, then tucked it under his arm.

A quick glance over the shoulder showed that the four teammates were still tailing him. The one who had thrown earlier had grabbed two new pouches and was catching up to the others with a double Lashing.

Make a stand, the sword suggested. *You can take them.*

For once, Szeth agreed. He zoomed down until he was near the water, his passing causing a trail of ripples on the surface. Younger squires dodged out of his way, flinging dust bags, but missing because of his speed.

He deliberately Lashed himself to the side in a smooth, predictable turn. It was exactly the opportunity the pack had been waiting for, and they started throwing at him. But he was no frightened child, to be intimidated and overwhelmed by superior numbers. He was the Assassin in White. And this was but a game.

Szeth spun and began batting the pouches away with his staff. He even managed to hit the last one back into the face of the leader of the group, a man named Ty.

It wouldn't count as a mark, but the dust got in Ty's eyes, causing him to blink and slow. The group expended most of their pouches, which let Szeth—Lashed now directly toward them—get close.

And nobody should *ever* let him get too close.

He dropped his staff and grabbed a squire by her shirt, using her as a shield from an opportunist outside the group, who was throwing crimson bags. Szeth spun with her, then kicked her toward a companion. They slammed together, trailing streaks of red dust. He grabbed another squire from the pack, trying to Lash him away.

The man's body resisted the Lashing, however. People bearing Storm-light were more difficult to Lash—something Szeth was only now coming to understand. He could, however, Lash himself backward, hauling the man with him. When he let go, the squire had trouble adjusting to the change in momentum, and jolted in the air, letting himself get hit by a

half dozen bags from outsiders.

Szeth zipped away, running dangerously low on Stormlight. Only another few minutes . . .

Beneath him, Ty called to the others, pointing up at Szeth. The obvious current winner. Only one strategy made sense at this point.

"Get him!" Ty shouted.

Oh, good! the sword said.

Szeth Lashed himself downward—which proved wise, as many of the squires shot up past him, assuming he'd try to stay high. No, his best defense while outnumbered was confusion. He got among them, a storm of pouches targeting him. Szeth did what he could to avoid them, zipping one way, then the other—but there were too many attacks. The poorly aimed ones were the most dangerous, as moving out of the way of a well-placed attack almost always took him into the path of an errant one.

One pouch struck his back, followed by a second. A third hit his side. Dust flew all around as the squires hit each other too. That was his hope: that even as he took hits, they would take more.

He soared up, then dove again, causing the others to dodge like sparrows before a hawk. He flew along the water, scattering fish in the waning light, then shot upward to—

His Stormlight ran out.

His glow vanished. The tempest within died. Before the sun could set, the cold took him. Szeth arced in the air, and was *pummeled* with a dozen different pouches. He dropped through the cloud of multicolored dust, leaving an afterimage from his loosely fastened spirit.

He splashed into the Purelake.

Fortunately, he hadn't been too high, so the landing was only mildly painful. He hit the bottom of the shallow lake; then when he stood up, the others hit him with another round of pouches. No mercy from *this* group.

The last sliver of the sun vanished, and Master Warren shouted an end to the test. The others streaked away, their Stormlight conspicuous in the dimming light.

Szeth stood waist-deep in water.

Wow, the sword said. *I kind of feel bad for you.*

"Thank you, sword-nimi. I . . ."

What were those two spren floating nearby, shaped as small *slits* in the air? They separated the sky, like wounds in skin, exposing a black field full of stars. When they moved, the substance of reality bent around them.

Szeth bowed his head. He no longer ascribed to spren any particular religious significance, but he could still be in awe of these. He might have lost this contest, but he seemed to have impressed the highspren.

Or *had* he lost? What *exactly* had the rules been?

Thoughtful, he ducked under the water, swimming in the shallow lake back toward the bank. He climbed out, water streaming from his clothing as he walked up to the others. The masters had brought out bright sphere lanterns, along with food and refreshment. A Tashikki squire was recording the points while two masters adjudicated what counted as a "hit" and what did not.

Szeth suddenly felt frustrated by their games. Nin had promised him the opportunity to cleanse Shinovar. What time was there for games? The moment had come for him to ascend to a rank beyond all of this.

He walked up to the masters. "I am sorry to have won this contest, as I did the one with the prison."

"You?" Ty said, incredulous. Ty had five spots on him. Not bad. "You got hit at *least* two dozen times."

"I believe," Szeth replied, "that the rules stated the winner was the one with the fewest marks on his uniform." He held his hands to the side, showing his white clothing, washed clean during his swim.

Warren and Ki shared a look. She nodded with a hint of a smile.

"There is always one," Warren said, "who notices that. Remember that while loopholes are to be exploited, Szeth-son-Neturo, they are dangerous to rely upon. Still, you have done well. Both in your performance, and in seeing this hole in the rules." He glanced into the night, squinting at the two highspren, who seemed to have made themselves visible to Warren as well. "Others agree."

"He used a weapon," one of the older squires said, pointing. "He broke the rules!"

"I used a pole to block pouches," Szeth said. "But I did not attack anyone with it."

"You attacked me!" said the woman he'd thrown at someone else.

"Physical contact was not forbidden, and I cannot help it if you are unable to control your Lashings when I release you."

The masters didn't object. Indeed, Ki leaned in to Warren. "He is beyond the skill of these. I hadn't realized . . ."

Warren looked back to him. "You shall soon have your spren, gauging by this performance."

"Not soon," Szeth said. "Right now. I shall say the Third Ideal this night, choosing to follow the law. I—"

"*No,*" a voice interrupted.

A figure stood up on the low wall surrounding the order's stone courtyard. Skybreakers gasped, holding up lanterns, illuminating a man with dark Makabaki skin highlighted by a white crescent birthmark on his right cheek. Unlike the others, he wore a striking uniform of silver and black.

Nin-son-God, Nale, Nakku, Nalan—this man had a hundred different names and was revered across all Roshar. The Illuminator. The Judge. A founder of humankind, defender against the Desolations, a man ascended to divinity.

The Herald of Justice had returned.

"Before you swear, Szeth-son-Neturo," Nin said, "there are things you need to understand." He looked across the Skybreakers. "Things you all must understand. Squires, masters, gather our gemstone reserves and mobile packs. We will leave most of the squires. They leak Stormlight too much, and we have a long way to go."

"Tonight, Just One?" Ki asked.

"Tonight. It is time for you to learn the two greatest secrets that I know."

MANDRAS

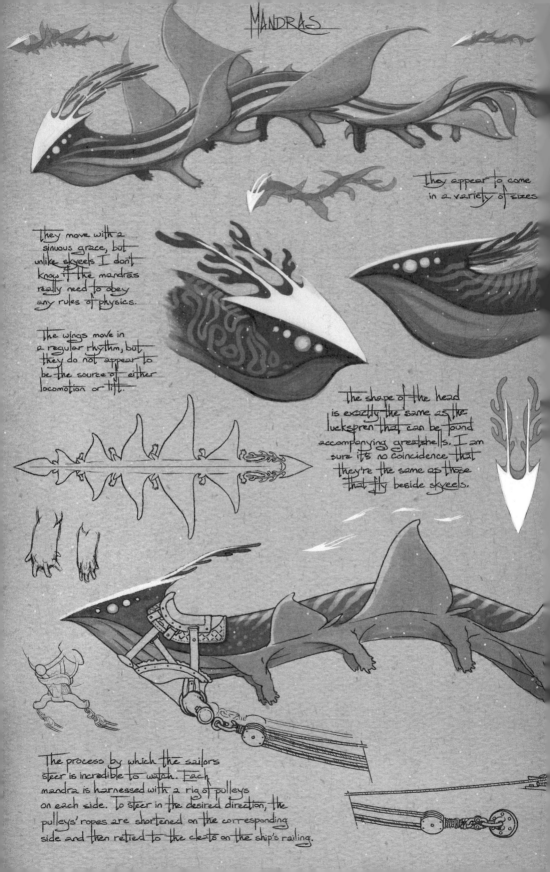

They appear to come in a variety of sizes

They move with a sinuous grace, but unlike skyeels I don't know if the mandras really need to obey any rules of physics.

The wings move in a regular rhythm, but they do not appear to be the source of either locomotion or lift.

The shape of the head is exactly the same as the luckspren that can be found accompanying greatshells. I am sure it's no coincidence that they're the same as those that fly beside skyeels.

The process by which the sailors steer is incredible to watch. Each mandra is harnessed with a rig of pulleys on each side. To steer in the desired direction, the pulleys' ropes are shortened on the corresponding side and then retied to the cleats on the ship's railing.

Nergaoul was known for driving forces into a battle rage, lending them great ferocity. Curiously, he did this to both sides of a conflict, Voidbringer and human. This seems common of the less self-aware spren.

—From Hessi's *Mythica*, page 121

When Kaladin awoke on the ship in Shadesmar, the others were already up. He sat, bleary-eyed on his bunk, listening to beads crash outside the hull. There almost seemed . . . a pattern or rhythm to them? Or was he imagining things?

He shook his head, standing and stretching. He had slept fitfully, slumber interrupted by thoughts of his men dying, of Elhokar and Moash, of worries for Drehy and Skar. The darkness blanketed his feelings, making him lethargic. He hated that he was the last to rise. That was always a bad sign.

He used the facilities, then forced himself to climb up the steps. The vessel had three levels. The bottom was the hold. The next level, the lower deck, was for the cabins, where the humans had been given a spot for them all to share.

The uppermost deck was open to the sky, and was populated by spren. Syl said they were lightspren, but the common name was Reachers. They looked like humans with strange bronze skin—metallic, as if they were living statues. Both men and women wore rugged jackets and trousers. Actual human clothing, not merely imitations of it like Syl wore.

They didn't carry weapons other than knives, but the ship had wicked harpoons clipped in racks at the sides of the deck. Seeing those made Kaladin infinitely more comfortable; he knew exactly where to go for a weapon.

Syl stood near the bow, watching out over the sea of beads again. He almost missed spotting her at first because her dress was red, instead of its normal white-blue. Her hair had changed to black, and . . . and her skin was *flesh colored*—tan, like Kaladin's. What on Roshar?

He crossed the deck toward her, stumbling as the ship crashed through a swell in the beads. Storms, and Shallan said this was *more* smooth than some boats she'd been on? Several Reachers passed, calmly managing the large riggings and harnesses that attached to the spren who pulled the craft.

"Ah, human," one of the Reachers said as Kaladin passed. That was the captain, wasn't it? Captain Ico? He resembled a Shin man, with large, childlike eyes made of metal. He was shorter than the Alethi, but sturdy. He wore the same tan clothing as the others, sporting a multitude of buttoned pockets.

"Come with me," Ico told Kaladin, then crossed the deck without waiting for a response. They didn't speak much, these Reachers.

Kaladin sighed, then followed the captain back to the stairwell. A line of copper plating ran down the inside wall of the stairwell—and Kaladin had seen a similar ornamentation on the deck. He'd assumed it was decorative, but as the captain walked, he rested his fingers on the metal in an odd way.

Touching a plate with the tips of his fingers, Kaladin felt a distinct vibration. They passed the quarters of the ordinary spren sailors. They didn't sleep, but they did seem to enjoy their breaks from work, swinging quietly in hammocks, often reading.

It didn't bother him to see male Reachers with books—spren were obviously similar to ardents, who were outside of common understandings of male and female. At the same time . . . spren, reading? How odd.

When they reached the hold, the captain turned on a small oil lamp—so far as Kaladin could tell, he didn't use a flaming brand to create the fire. How did it work? It seemed foolhardy to use fire for light with so much wood and cloth around.

"Why not use spheres for light?" Kaladin asked him.

"We have none," Ico said. "Stormlight fades too quickly on this side."

That was true. Kaladin's team carried several larger unset gemstones, which would hold Stormlight for weeks—but the smaller spheres would run out after a week or so without seeing a storm. They'd been able to trade the chips and marks to the lighthouse keeper in exchange for barter supplies—mostly cloth—to buy passage on this ship.

"The lighthouse keeper wanted the Stormlight," Kaladin said. "He kept it in some kind of globe."

Captain Ico grunted. "Foreign technology," he said. "Dangerous. Draws the wrong spren." He shook his head. "At Celebrant, the moneychangers have perfect gemstones that can hold the light indefinitely. Similar."

"Perfect gemstones? Like, the Stone of Ten Dawns?"

"I don't know of this thing. Light in a perfect stone doesn't run out, so you can give Stormlight to the moneychangers. They use devices to transfer it from smaller gemstones to their perfect ones. Then they give you credit to spend in the city."

The hold was closely packed with barrels and boxes that were lashed to the walls and floor. Kaladin could barely squeeze through. Ico selected a rope-handled box from a stack, then asked Kaladin to pull it out as Ico resettled the boxes that had been atop it, then relashed them.

Kaladin spent the time thinking about perfect gemstones. Did such a thing exist on his side? If there really *were* flawless stones that could hold Stormlight without ever running out, that seemed important to know. It could mean the difference between life and death for Radiants during the Weeping.

Once Ico was done resetting the cargo, he gestured for Kaladin to help him pick up the box they'd removed. They maneuvered it out of the hold and up onto the top deck. Here, the captain knelt and opened the box, which revealed a strange device that looked a little like a coatrack— although only about three feet tall. Made entirely of steel, it had dozens of small metal prongs extending from it, like the branches of a tree—only it had a metal basin at the very bottom.

Ico fished in a pocket and took out a small box, from which he removed a handful of glass beads like those that made up the ocean. He placed one of them into a hole in the center of the device, then waved toward Kaladin. "Stormlight."

"For what?"

"For you to live."

"Are you threatening me, Captain?"

Ico sighed and regarded him with a suffering expression. Very human in its nature. It seemed the look of a man talking to a child. The spren captain waved his hand, insistent, so Kaladin took a diamond mark from his pocket.

Cradling the sphere in one hand, Ico touched the glass bead he'd put in the fabrial. "This is a soul," he said. "Soul of water, but very cold."

"Ice?"

"Ice from a high, high place," he said. "Ice that has never melted. Ice that has never known warmth." The light in Kaladin's sphere dimmed as Ico concentrated. "You know how to manifest souls?"

"No," Kaladin said.

"Some of your kind do," he said. "It is rare. Rare among us too. The gardeners among the cultivationspren are best at it. I am unpracticed."

The ocean bead expanded and grew cloudy, looking like ice. Kaladin got a distinct sense of *coldness* from it.

Ico handed back the diamond mark, now partially drained, then dusted off his hands and stood up, pleased.

"What does it do?" Kaladin asked.

Ico nudged the device with his foot. "It gets cold now."

"Why?"

"Cold makes water," he said. "Water collects in that basin. You drink, and don't die."

Cold makes water? It didn't seem to be making any water that Kaladin could see. Ico hiked off to survey the spren steering the ship, so Kaladin knelt beside the device, trying to understand. Eventually, he spotted drops of water collecting on the "branches" of the device. They ran down the metal and gathered in the basin.

Huh. When the captain had said—during their initial negotiations—that he could provide water for human passengers, Kaladin had assumed the ship would have some barrels in the hold.

The device took about a half hour to make a small cup of water, which Kaladin drank as a test—the basin had a spigot and a detachable tin cup. The water was cool but flavorless, unlike rainwater. How did coldness make water though? Was this melting ice in the Physical Realm somehow, and bringing it here?

As he was sipping the water, Syl walked over—her skin, hair, and dress still colored like those of a human. She stopped next to him, placed her hands on her hips, and went into full pout.

"What?" Kaladin asked.

"They won't let me ride one of the flying spren."

"Smart."

"Insufferable."

"Why on Roshar would you look at one of those things and think, 'You know what, I need to get on its back'?"

Syl looked at him as if he were crazy. "Because they can *fly*."

"So can you. Actually, so can I."

"You don't fly, you fall the wrong way." She unfolded her arms so that she could fold them immediately again and huff loudly. "You're telling me you're not even curious what it's like to climb on one of those things?"

"Horses are bad enough. I'm not about to get onto something that doesn't even have *legs*."

"Where's your sense of adventure?"

"I dragged it out back and clubbed it senseless for getting me into the army. What have you done to your skin and hair, by the way?"

"It's a Lightweaving," she said. "I asked Shallan, because I didn't want rumors of an honorspren spreading from the ship's crew."

"We can't waste Stormlight on something like that, Syl."

"We used a mark that was running out anyway!" she said. "So it was worthless to us; it would have been depleted by the time we arrived. So it's wasting nothing."

"What if there's an emergency?"

She stuck her tongue out at him, then at the sailors at the front of the ship. Kaladin returned the little tin cup to its place on the side of the device, then settled with his back to the ship railing. Shallan sat across the deck near the flying spren, doing sketches.

"You should go talk to her," Syl said, sitting next to him.

"About wasting Stormlight?" Kaladin said. "Yes, perhaps I should. She does seem inclined to be frivolous with who she expends it for."

Syl rolled her eyes.

"What?"

"Don't go lecture her, silly. Chat with her. About life. About fun things." Syl nudged him with her foot. "I know you want to. I can *feel* that you do. Be glad I'm the wrong kind of spren, or I would probably be licking your forehead or something to get at your emotions."

The ship surged against a wave of beads. The souls of things in the physical world.

"Shallan is betrothed to Adolin," Kaladin said.

"Which isn't an oath," Syl said. "It's a promise to maybe make an oath sometime."

"It's still not the sort of thing you play around with."

Syl rested her hand on his knee. "Kaladin. I'm your spren. It's my *duty* to make sure that you're not alone."

"Is that so? Who decided?"

"I did. And don't give me excuses about not being lonely, or about 'only needing your brothers in arms.' You can't lie to me. You feel dark, sad. You need something, someone, and she makes you feel better."

Storms. It felt like Syl and his emotions were double-teaming him. One smiled with encouragement, while the other whispered terrible things. That he'd always be alone. That Tarah had been right to leave him.

He filled another cup with as much water as he could get from the basin, then carried it toward Shallan. The pitching of the ship almost made him dump the cup overboard.

Shallan glanced up as he eased down beside her, his back resting against the deck's railing. He handed her the cup. "It makes water," he said, thumbing at the device. "By getting cold."

"Condensation? How fast does it go? Navani would be interested in that." She sipped the water, holding it in her gloved safehand—which was strange to see on her. Even when they'd traveled the bottoms of the chasms together, she'd worn a very formal havah.

"You walk like they do," she said absently, finishing her sketch of one of the flying beasts.

"They?"

"The sailors. You keep your balance well. You'd have been at home as a sailor yourself, I suspect. Unlike some others." She nodded toward Azure, who stood across the deck, holding on to the railing for dear life and occasionally shooting distrusting glares at the Reachers. Either she did not like being on a ship, or she did not trust the spren. Perhaps both.

"May I?" Kaladin asked, nodding toward Shallan's sketch. She shrugged, so he took the sketchpad and studied her pictures of the flying beasts. As always, they were excellent. "What does the text say?"

"Just some theorizing," she said, flipping back a page in her notebook. "I lost my original of this picture, so this is kind of crude. But have you ever seen something like these arrowhead spren here?"

"Yeah . . ." Kaladin said, studying her drawing of a skyeel flying with arrowhead spren moving around it. "I've seen them near greatshells."

"Chasmfiends, skyeels, anything else that should be heavier than it actually is. Sailors call them luckspren on our side." She gestured with the cup toward the front of the ship, where sailors managed the flying beasts. "They call these 'mandras,' but the arrowhead shapes on their heads are the same shape as luckspren. These are bigger, but I think they—or something like them—help skyeels fly."

"Chasmfiends don't fly."

"They kind of do, mathematically. Bavamar did the calculations on Reshi greatshells, and found they should be crushed by their own weight."

"Huh," Kaladin said.

She started to get excited. "There's more. Those mandras, they *vanish* sometimes. Their keepers call it 'dropping.' *I* think they must be getting pulled into the Physical Realm. It means you can never use only one mandra to pull a ship, no matter how small that ship. And you can't take them—or most other spren—too far from human population centers on our side. They waste away and die for reasons people here don't understand."

"Huh. So what do they eat?"

"I'm not sure," Shallan said. "Syl and Pattern talk about feeding off emotions, but there's something else that . . ." She trailed off as Kaladin flipped to the next page in her notebook. It seemed like an attempt at drawing Captain Ico, but was incredibly juvenile. Basically just a stick figure.

"Did Adolin get hold of your sketchbook?" he asked.

She snatched the book from him and closed it. "I was just trying out a different style. Thanks for the water."

"Yes, I had to walk all the way from over there. At least seven steps."

"Easily ten," Shallan said. "And on this precarious deck. Very dangerous."

"Practically as bad as fighting the Fused."

"Could have stubbed your toe. Or gotten a splinter. Or pitched over the side and been lost to the depths, buried by a thousand thousand beads and the weight of the souls of an infinite number of forgotten objects."

"Or . . . that."

"Highly unlikely," Shallan agreed. "They keep this deck well maintained, so there really aren't any splinters."

"With my luck, I'd find one anyway."

"I had a splinter once," Shallan noted. "It eventually got out of hand."

"You . . . you did *not* just say that."

"Yes, you obviously imagined it. What a sick, sick mind you have, Kaladin."

Kaladin sighed, then nodded to the sailors. "They do walk about barefoot. Have you noticed that? Something about the copper lines set into the deck."

"The copper vibrates," Shallan said. "And they keep touching it. I think they might be using it to communicate somehow."

"That would explain why they don't talk much," Kaladin said. "I'd have expected them to watch us a little more than they do. They don't seem that curious about us."

"Which is odd, considering how interesting Azure is."

"Wait. Just Azure?"

"Yes. In that polished breastplate and striking figure, with her talk of chasing bounties and traveling worlds. She's deeply mysterious."

"I'm mysterious," Kaladin said.

"I used to think you were. *Then* I found out you don't like good puns—it's truly possible to know *too* much about somebody."

He grunted. "I'll try to be more mysterious. Take up bounty hunting." His stomach growled. "Starting with a bounty on lunch, maybe."

They'd been promised two meals a day, but considering how long it had taken Ico to remember they needed water, perhaps he should ask.

"I've been trying to track our speed," Shallan said, flipping through her notebook. She went quickly through the pages, and he could see that—oddly—they alternated between expert renditions and comically bad ones. She landed on a map she'd made of this region in Shadesmar. Alethi rivers were now peninsulas, and the Sea of Spears was an island, with the city named Celebrant on the western side. The river peninsulas meant that in order to get to the city, the ship had to swing to the west. Shallan had marked their path with a line.

"It's hard to gauge our progress, but I'd guess that we're moving faster than the average ship in our world. We can go directly where we want without worrying about the winds, for one thing."

"So . . . two more days?" Kaladin asked, guessing based on her marks.

"More or less. Quick progress."

He moved his fingers down, toward the bottom of her map. "Thaylen City?" he asked, tapping one point she'd marked.

"Yes. On this side, it will be on the edge of a lake of beads. We can guess the Oathgate will reflect there as a platform, like the one we left in Kholinar. But how to activate it . . ."

"I want to try. Dalinar is in danger. We *need* to get to him, Shallan. In Thaylen City."

She glanced at Azure, who maintained that was the wrong direction to go. "Kaladin . . . I don't know if we can trust what you saw. It's dangerous to presume you know the future—"

"I didn't see the future," Kaladin said quickly. "It wasn't like that. It was like soaring the sky with the Stormfather. I just know . . . I *know* I have to get to Dalinar."

She still seemed skeptical. Perhaps he'd told them too much of the lighthouse keeper's theatrics.

"We'll see, once we get to Celebrant." Shallan closed her map, then squirmed, glancing back at the railing they'd been leaning against. "Do you suppose they have chairs anywhere? These railings aren't very comfortable for sitting against."

"Probably not."

"What do you even call these things?" Shallan said, tapping the railing. "A deck wall?"

"No doubt they've made up some obscure nautical word," Kaladin said. "Everything on a ship has odd names. Port and starboard instead of left and right. Galley instead of kitchen. Nuisance instead of Shallan."

"There was a name . . . railing? Deck guard? No, wale. It's called a wale." She grinned. "I don't really like how it feels to sit against this wale, but I'm sure I'll eventually get over it."

He groaned softly. "Really?"

"Vengeance for calling me names."

"Name. One name. And it was more a declaration of fact than an attack."

She punched him lightly in the arm. "It's good to see you smiling."

"That was smiling?"

"It was the Kaladin equivalent. That scowl was almost jovial." She smiled at him.

Something felt warm within him at being near her. Something felt *right*. It wasn't like with Laral, his boyhood crush. Or even like with Tarah, his first real romance. It was something different, and he couldn't define it. He only knew he didn't want it to stop. It pushed back the darkness.

"Down in the chasms," he said, "when we were trapped together, you talked about your life. About . . . your father."

"I remember," she said softly. "In the darkness of the storm."

"How do you do it, Shallan? How do you keep smiling and laughing? How do you keep from fixating on the terrible things that have happened?"

"I cover them up. I have this uncanny ability to hide away anything I don't want to think about. It . . . it's getting harder, but for most things I can just . . ." She trailed off, staring straight ahead. "There. Gone."

"Wow."

"I know," she whispered. "I'm crazy."

"No. No, Shallan! I wish I could do the same."

She looked at him, brow wrinkling. "*You're* crazy."

"How nice would it be, if I could simply shove it all away? Storms." He tried to imagine it. Not spending his life worrying about the mistakes he'd made. Not hearing the constant whispers that he wasn't good enough, or that he'd failed his men.

"This way, I'll never face it," Shallan said.

"It's better than being unable to function."

"That's what I tell myself." She shook her head. "Jasnah said that power is an illusion of perception. Act like you have authority, and you often will. But pretending fragments me. I'm *too* good at pretending."

"Well, whatever you're doing, it's obviously working. If I could smother these emotions, I'd do so eagerly."

She nodded, but fell silent, then resisted all further attempts to draw her into conversation.

100

AN OLD FRIEND

I am convinced that Nergaoul is still active on Roshar. The accounts of the Alethi "Thrill" of battle align too well with ancient records—including the visions of red mist and dying creatures.

—From Hessi's *Mythica*, page 140

Dalinar remembered almost everything now. Though he still hadn't recovered the details of his meeting with the Nightwatcher, the rest was as fresh as a new wound, dripping blood down his face.

There had been so many more holes in his mind than he'd realized. The Nightwatcher had ripped apart his memories like the fabric of an old blanket, then sewn a new quilt out of it. In the intervening years he'd thought himself mostly whole, but now all those scars had been ripped free and he could see the truth.

He tried to put all of that out of his mind as he toured Vedenar, one of the great cities of the world, known for its amazing gardens and lush atmosphere. Unfortunately, the city had been devastated by the Veden civil war, then the subsequent arrival of the Everstorm. Even along the sanitized path he walked for the tour, they passed scorched buildings, piles of rubble.

He couldn't help but think of what he'd done to Rathalas. And so, Evi's tears accompanied him. The cries of dying children.

Hypocrite, they said. *Murderer. Destroyer.*

The air smelled of salt and was filled with the sounds of waves smashing on cliffs outside the city. How did they live with that constant roaring?

Did they never know peace? Dalinar tried to listen politely as Taravangian's people led him into a garden, full of low walls overgrown with vines and shrubs. One of few that hadn't been destroyed in the civil war.

The Vedens loved ostentatious greenery. Not a subtle people, all brimming with passion and vice.

The wife of one of the new Veden highprinces eventually led Navani off to inspect some paintings. Dalinar was instead led to a small garden square, where some Veden lighteyes were chatting and drinking wine. A low wall on the eastern side here allowed for the growth of all kinds of rare plants in a jumble, which was the current horticultural fashion. Lifespren bobbed among them.

More small talk? "Excuse me," Dalinar said, nodding toward a raised gazebo. "I'm going to take a moment to survey the city."

One of the lighteyes raised his hand. "I can show—"

"No thank you," Dalinar said, then started up the steps to the gazebo. Perhaps that had been too abrupt. Well, at least it fit his reputation. His guards had the sense to remain below, at the foot of the steps.

He reached the top, trying to relax. The gazebo gave him a nice view of the cliffs and the sea beyond. Unfortunately, it let him see the rest of the city—and storms, it was *not* in good shape. The walls were broken in places, the palace nothing more than rubble. Huge swaths of the city had burned, including many of the platelike terraces that had been Veden showpieces.

Out beyond—on the fields north of the city—black scars on the rock still showed where heaps of bodies had been burned following the war. He tried to turn away from all that and look out at the peaceful ocean. But he could smell smoke. That wasn't good. In the years following Evi's death, smoke had often sent him descending into one of his worse days.

Storms. I'm stronger than this. He *could* fight it. He wasn't the man he'd been all those years ago. He forced his attention toward the stated purpose of visiting the city: surveying the Veden martial capabilities.

Many of the living Veden troops were barracked in storm bunkers right inside the city walls. From reports he'd heard earlier, the civil war had brought incredible losses. Even *baffling* ones. Many armies would break after suffering ten percent casualties, but here—reportedly—the Vedens had continued fighting after losing more than *half* their numbers.

Perhaps they'd been driven mad by the persistent crashing of those waves. And . . . what else did he hear?

More phantom weeping. Taln's palms! Dalinar drew a deep breath, but smelled only smoke.

Why must I have these memories? he thought, angry. *Why did they suddenly return?*

Mixing with those emotions was a growing fear for Adolin and Elhokar. Why hadn't they sent word? If they'd escaped, wouldn't they have flown to safety—or at the very least, found a spanreed? It seemed ridiculous to assume multiple Radiants and Shardbearers were trapped in the city, unable to flee. But the alternative was to worry that they hadn't survived. That he'd sent them to die.

Dalinar tried to stand, straight-backed and at attention, beneath the weight of it all. Unfortunately, he knew too well that if you locked your knees and stood *too* straight, you risked fainting. Why was it that trying to stand tall should make you so much more likely to fall?

His guards at the base of the stone hill parted to let Taravangian—in his characteristic orange robes—shuffle through. The old man carried an enormous diamond-shaped kite shield, large enough to cover his entire left side. He climbed up to the gazebo, then sat down on one of the benches, panting.

"Did you want to see one of these, Dalinar?" he asked after a moment, holding out the shield.

Glad for the distraction, Dalinar took the shield, hefting it. "Half-shard?" he said, noting a steel box—with a gemstone inside—fastened to the inner surface.

"Indeed," Taravangian said. "Crude devices. There are legends of metal that can block a Shardblade. A metal that falls from the sky. Silver, but somehow lighter. I should like to see that, but for now we can use these."

Dalinar grunted.

"You know how they make fabrials, don't you?" Taravangian asked. "Enslaved spren?"

"Spren can't be 'enslaved' any more than a chull can."

The Stormfather rumbled distantly in his mind.

"That gemstone," Taravangian said, "imprisons the kind of spren that gives things substance, the kind that holds the world together. We have entrapped in that shield something that, at another time, might have blessed a Knight Radiant."

Storms. He couldn't deal with a philosophical problem like this today. He tried to change the topic. "You seem to be feeling better."

"It's a good day for me. I feel better than I have recently, but that can be dangerous. I'm prone to thinking about mistakes I've made." Taravangian smiled in his kindly way. "I try to tell myself that at the very least, I made the best choice I could, with the information I had."

"Unfortunately, I'm certain I *didn't* make the best choices I could," Dalinar said.

"But you wouldn't change them. If you did, you'd be a different person."

I did change them, Dalinar thought. *I erased them. And I* did *become a different person.* Dalinar set the shield beside the old man.

"Tell me, Dalinar," Taravangian said. "You've spoken of your disregard for your ancestor, the Sunmaker. You called him a tyrant."

Like me.

"Let us say," Taravangian continued, "you could snap your fingers and change history. Would you make it so that the Sunmaker lived longer and accomplished his desire, uniting all of Roshar under a single banner?"

"Turn him into *more* of a despot?" Dalinar said. "That would have meant him slaughtering his way all across Azir and into Iri. Of course I wouldn't wish that."

"But what if it left you, today, in command of a completely unified people? What if *his* slaughter let *you* save Roshar from the Voidbringer invasion?"

"I . . . You'd be asking me to consign millions of innocents to the pyre!"

"Those people are long dead," Taravangian whispered. "What are they to you? Numbers in a scribe's footnote. Yes, the Sunmaker was a monster. However, the current trade routes between Herdaz, Jah Keved, and Azir were forged by his tyranny. He brought culture and science back to Alethkar. Your modern Alethi cultural eruption can be traced *directly* back to what he did. Morality and law are built upon the bodies of the slain."

"I can't do anything about that."

"No, no. Of course you can't." Taravangian tapped the half-shard shield. "Do you know *how* we capture spren for fabrials, Dalinar? From spanreeds to heatrials, it's all the same. You lure the spren with something it loves. You give it something familiar to draw it in, something it knows deeply. In that moment, it becomes your slave."

I . . . I really *can't think about this right now.* "Excuse me," Dalinar said, "I need to go check on Navani."

He strode from the gazebo and down the steps, bustling past Rial and his other guards. They followed, towed in his wake like leaves after a strong gust of wind. He entered the city, but didn't go looking for Navani. Perhaps he could visit the troops.

He walked back along the street, trying to ignore the destruction. Even without it though, this city felt *off* to him. The architecture was very like Alethi architecture, nothing like the flowery designs of Kharbranth or Thaylenah—but many buildings had plants draping and dangling from every window. It was strange to walk along streets full of people who looked Alethi but spoke a foreign tongue.

Eventually Dalinar reached the large stormshelters right inside the city walls. Soldiers had set up tent cities next to them, temporary bivouacs they could tear down and carry into one of the loaflike bunkers for storms. Dalinar found himself growing calmer as he walked among them. This was familiar; this was the peace of soldiers at work.

The officers here welcomed him, and generals took him on tours of the bunkers. They were impressed by his ability to speak their language—something he'd gained early in his visit to the city, using his Bondsmith abilities.

All Dalinar did was nod and ask the occasional question, but somehow he felt like he was accomplishing something. At the end, he entered a breezy tent near the city gates, where he met with a group of wounded soldiers. Each had survived when his entire platoon had fallen. Heroes, but not the conventional type. It took being a soldier to understand the heroism of simply being willing to continue after all your friends had died.

The last in line was an elderly veteran who wore a clean uniform and a patch for a defunct platoon. His right arm was missing, his jacket sleeve tied off, and a younger soldier led him up to Dalinar. "Look, Geved. The Blackthorn himself! Didn't you always say you wanted to meet him?"

The older man had one of those stares that made him seem like he could see right through you. "Brightlord," he said, and saluted. "I fought your army at Slickrock, sir. Brightlord Nalanar's second infantry. Storming fine battle that was, sir."

"Storming fine indeed," Dalinar said, saluting him back. "I figured your forces had us at three different points."

"Those were good times, Brightlord. Good times. Before everything went wrong . . ." His eyes glazed over.

"What was it like?" Dalinar asked softly. "The civil war, the battle here, at Vedenar?"

"It was a nightmare, sir."

"Geved," the younger man said. "Let's go. They have food—"

"Didn't you hear him?" Geved said, pulling his remaining arm out of the boy's grip. "He *asked*. Everyone dances around me, ignoring it. Storms, sir. The civil war was a *nightmare*."

"Fighting other Veden families," Dalinar said, nodding.

"It wasn't that," Geved said. "Storms! We squabble as much as you do, sir. Pardon that. But I ain't ever felt bad fighting my own. It's what the Almighty wants, right? But that battle . . ." He shuddered. "Nobody would stop, Brightlord. Even when it should have been done. They just kept right on fighting. Killing because they *felt* like killing."

"It burned in us," another wounded man said from by the food table. The man wore an eye patch and looked like he hadn't shaved since the battle. "You know it, Brightlord, don't you? That river inside of you, pulling your blood all up into your head and making you love each swing. Making it so that you can't stop, no matter how tired you are."

The Thrill.

It started to glow inside Dalinar. So familiar, so warm, and so *terrible*. Dalinar felt it stir, like . . . like a favorite axehound, surprised to hear its master's voice after so long.

He hadn't felt it in what seemed like an eternity. Even back on the Shattered Plains, when he'd last felt it, it had seemed to be weakening. Suddenly that made sense. It wasn't that he'd been learning to overcome the Thrill. Instead, it had left him.

To come here.

"Did others of you feel this?" Dalinar asked.

"We all did," another of the men said, and Geved nodded. "The officers . . . they rode about with teeth clenched in rictus grins. Men shouted to keep the fight, maintain the momentum."

It's all about momentum.

Others agreed, talking about the remarkable haze that had covered the day.

Losing any sense of peace he'd gained from the inspections, Dalinar excused himself. His guards raced to keep up as he fled—moving even faster as a newly arrived messenger called to him, saying he was needed back at the gardens.

He wasn't ready. He didn't want to face Taravangian, or Navani, or especially Renarin. Instead, he climbed the city wall. Inspect . . . inspect the fortifications. That was why he'd come.

From the top, he could again see those large sections of the city, burned and broken in the war.

The Thrill called to him, distant and thin. No. *No.* Dalinar marched along the wall, passing soldiers. To his right, waves crashed against the rocks. Shadows moved in the shallows, beasts two or three times as big as a chull, their shells peeking from the depths between waves.

It seemed that Dalinar had been four people in his life. The bloodlusty warrior, who killed wherever he was pointed, and the consequences could go to Damnation.

The general, who had feigned distinguished civility—when secretly, he'd longed to get back on the battlefield so he could shed more blood.

Third, the broken man. The one who paid for the actions of the youth.

Then finally, the fourth man: most false of them all. The man who had given up his memories so he could pretend to be something better.

Dalinar stopped, resting one hand on the stones. His guards assembled behind him. A Veden soldier approached from the other direction along the wall, calling out in anger. "Who are you? What are you doing up here?"

Dalinar squeezed his eyes shut.

"You! Alethi. Answer me. Who let you scale this fortification?"

The Thrill stirred, and the animal inside him wanted to lash out. A fight. He needed a *fight*.

No. He fled again, hurrying down a tight, constricting stone stairwell. His breathing echoed against the walls, and he nearly stumbled and tripped down the last flight.

He burst out onto the street, sweating, surprising a group of women carrying water. His guards piled out after him. "Sir?" Rial asked. "Sir, are you . . . Is everything . . . ?"

Dalinar sucked in Stormlight, hoping it would drive away the Thrill. It didn't. It seemed to complement the sensation, driving him to act.

"Sir?" Rial said, holding out a canteen that smelled of something strong. "I know you said I shouldn't carry this, but I did. And . . . and you might need it."

Dalinar stared at that canteen. A pungent scent rose to envelop him. If he drank that, he could forget the whispers. Forget the burned city, and what he'd done to Rathalas. And to Evi.

So easy . . .

Blood of my fathers. Please. No.

He spun away from Rial. He needed rest. That was all, just rest. He tried to keep his head up and slow his pace as he marched back toward the Oathgate.

The Thrill nipped at him from behind.

If you become that first man again, it will stop hurting. In your youth, you did what needed to be done. You were stronger then.

He growled, spinning and flinging his cloak to the side, looking for the voice that had spoken those words. His guards shied back, gripping their spears tightly. The beleaguered inhabitants of Vedenar scurried away from him.

Is this leadership? To cry each night? To shake and tremble? Those are the actions of a child, not a man.

"Leave me alone!"

Give me your pain.

Dalinar looked toward the sky and let out a raw bellow. He charged through the streets, no longer caring what people thought when they saw him. He needed to be *away* from this city.

There. The steps up to the Oathgate. The people of this city had once made a garden out of its platform, but that had been cleared away. Ignoring the long ramp, Dalinar took the steps two at a time, Stormlight lending him endurance.

At the top, he found a cluster of guards in Kholin blue standing with Navani and a smattering of scribes. She immediately strode over. "Dalinar, I tried to ward him off, but he was insistent. I don't know what he wants."

"He?" Dalinar asked, puffing from his near run.

Navani gestured toward the scribes. For the first time, Dalinar noticed that several among them wore the short beards of ardents. But those blue robes? What were those?

Curates, he thought, *from the Holy Enclave in Valath.* Technically, Dalinar himself was a head of the Vorin religion—but in practice, the curates guided church doctrine. The staves they bore were wound with gemstones, more ornate than he'd expected. Hadn't most of that pomp been done away with at the fall of the Hierocracy?

"Dalinar Kholin!" one said, stepping forward. He was young for an ardentia leader, perhaps in his early forties. His square beard was streaked with a few lines of grey.

"I am he," Dalinar said, shrugging off Navani's touch to his shoulder. "If you would speak with me, let us retire to a place more private—"

"Dalinar Kholin," the ardent said, louder. "The council of curates declares you a heretic. We cannot tolerate your insistence that the Almighty is not God. You are hereby proclaimed excommunicate and anathema."

"You have no right—"

"We have *every* right! The ardents must watch the lighteyes so that you steer your subjects well. That is *still* our duty, as outlined in the Covenants of Theocracy, witnessed for centuries! Did you really think we would ignore what you've been preaching?"

Dalinar gritted his teeth as the stupid ardent began outlining Dalinar's heresies one by one, demanding that he deny them. The man stepped forward, close enough now that Dalinar could smell his breath.

The Thrill stirred, sensing a fight. Sensing blood.

I'm going to kill him, a part of Dalinar thought. *I have to run now, or I will kill this man.* It was as clear to him as the sun's light.

So he ran.

He dashed to the Oathgate control building, frantic with the need to escape. He scrambled up to the keyhole, and only then remembered that he didn't have a Shardblade that could operate this device.

Dalinar, the Stormfather rumbled. *Something is wrong. Something I cannot see, something hidden to me. What are you sensing?*

"I *have* to get away."

I will not be a sword to you. We spoke of this.

Dalinar growled. He felt something he could touch, something beyond places. The power that bound worlds together. *His* power.

Wait, the Stormfather said. *This is not right!*

Dalinar ignored him, reaching beyond and pulling power through. Something bright white manifested in his hand, and he rammed it into the keyhole.

The Stormfather groaned, a sound like thunder.

The power made the Oathgate work, regardless. As his guards called his name outside, Dalinar flipped the dial that would make only the small building transport—not the entire plateau—then pushed the keyhole around the outside of the room, using the power as a handhold.

A ring of light flashed around the structure, and cold wind poured in through the doorways. He stumbled out onto a platform before Urithiru. The Stormfather pulled back from him, not breaking the bond, but withdrawing his favor.

The Thrill flooded in to replace it. Even this far away. Storms! Dalinar couldn't escape it.

You can't escape yourself, Dalinar, Evi's voice said in his mind. *This is who you are. Accept it.*

He couldn't run. Storms . . . he couldn't run.

Blood of my fathers. Please. Please, help me.

But . . . to whom was he praying?

He staggered down from the platform in a daze, ignoring questions from soldiers and scribes alike. He made his way to his room, increasingly desperate to find a way—any way—to hide from Evi's condemning voice.

In his rooms, he pulled a book off the shelf. Bound in hogshide, with thick paper. He held *The Way of Kings* as if it were a talisman that would drive back the pain.

It did nothing. Once this book had saved him, but now it seemed useless. He couldn't even read its words.

Dropping the book, he stumbled out of the room. No conscious thought led him to Adolin's chambers or drove him to ransack the younger man's room. But he found what he'd hoped, a bottle of wine kept for a special occasion. Violet, prepared in its strength.

This represented that third man he'd been. Shame, frustration, and days spent in a haze. Terrible times. Times he'd given up part of his soul in order to forget.

But storms, it was either this or start killing again. He raised the bottle to his lips.

DEADEYE

Moelach is very similar to Nergaoul, though instead of inspiring a battle rage, he supposedly granted visions of the future. In this, lore and theology align. Seeing the future originates with the Unmade, and is from the enemy.

—From Hessi's *Mythica*, page 143

Adolin tugged at the jacket, standing in Captain Ico's cabin. The spren had lent the room to him for a few hours.

The jacket was too short, but was the biggest the spren had. Adolin had cut off the trousers right below the knees, then tucked the bottoms into his long socks and tall boots. He rolled the sleeves of the jacket up to match, approximating an old style from Thaylenah. The jacket still looked too baggy.

Leave it unbuttoned, he decided. *The rolled sleeves look intentional that way.* He tucked his shirt in, pulled the belt tight. Good by contrast? He studied it in the captain's mirror. It needed a waistcoat. Those, fortunately, weren't *too* hard to fake. Ico had provided a burgundy coat that was too small for him. He removed the collar and sleeves, stitched the rough edges under, then slit it up the back.

He was just finishing it up with some laces on the back when Ico checked in on him. Adolin buttoned on the improvised waistcoat, threw on the jacket, then presented himself with hands at his sides.

"Very nice," Ico said. "You look like an honorspren going to a Feast of Light."

"Thanks," Adolin said, inspecting himself in the small mirror. "The jacket needs to be longer, but I don't trust myself to let down the hems."

Ico studied him with metal eyes—bronze, with holes for the pupils, like Adolin had seen done for some statues. Even the spren's hair appeared sculpted in place. Ico could almost have been a Soulcast king from an age long past.

"You were a ruler among your kind, weren't you?" Ico asked. "Why did you leave? The humans we get here are refugees, merchants, or explorers. Not kings."

King. Was Adolin a king? Surely his father would decide not to continue with the abdication, now that Elhokar had passed.

"No answer?" Ico said. "That is fine. But you *were* a ruler among them. I can read it in you. Highborn status is important to humans."

"Maybe a little too important, eh?" Adolin said, adjusting the neck scarf he'd made from his handkerchief.

"That is true," Ico said. "You are all human—and so none of you, regardless of birth, can be trusted with oaths. A contract to travel, this is fine. But humans will betray trust if it is given to them." The spren frowned, then seemed to grow embarrassed, glancing away. "That was rude."

"Rudeness doesn't necessarily imply untruth though."

"I did not mean an insult, regardless. You are not to be blamed. Betraying oaths is simply your nature, as a human."

"You don't know my father," Adolin said. Still, the conversation left him uncomfortable. Not because of Ico's words—spren tended to say odd things, and Adolin didn't take offense.

More, he felt his own growing worry that he might *actually* have to take the throne. He'd grown up knowing it could happen, but he'd *also* grown up wishing—desperately—that it never would. In his quiet moments, he'd assumed this hesitance was because a king couldn't apply himself to things like dueling and . . . well . . . enjoying life.

What if it went deeper? What if he'd always known inconsistency lurked within him? He couldn't keep pretending he was the man his father wanted him to be.

Well, it was moot anyway—Alethkar, as a nation, had fallen. He accompanied Ico back out of the captain's cabin onto the deck, walking over to Shallan, Kaladin, and Azure, who stood by the starboard wale. Each wore a shirt, trousers, and jacket they'd bought off the Reachers with dun spheres. Dun gemstones weren't worth nearly as much on this side, but apparently trade with the other side *did* happen, so they had some value.

Kaladin gaped at Adolin, looking down at his boots, then up at the neck scarf, then focusing on the waistcoat. That befuddled expression alone made the work worthwhile.

"How?" Kaladin demanded. "Did you *sew* that?"

Adolin grinned. Kaladin looked like a man trying to wear his childhood suit; he'd never button that coat across his broad chest. Shallan fit her shirt and jacket better from a pure measurements standpoint, but the cut wasn't flattering. Azure looked far more . . . normal without her dramatic breastplate and cloak.

"I'd practically kill for a skirt," Shallan noted.

"You're kidding," Azure said.

"No. I'm getting tired of the way trousers rub my legs. Adolin, could you sew me a dress? Maybe stitch the legs of these trousers together?"

He rubbed his chin, which had begun to sprout a blond beard. "It doesn't work that way—I can't magic more cloth out of nothing. It . . ."

He trailed off as, overhead, the clouds suddenly rippled, glowing with a strange mother-of-pearl iridescence. Another highstorm, their second since arriving in Shadesmar. The group stopped and stared up at the dramatic light show. Nearby, the Reachers seemed to stand up more straight, move about their sailing duties more vigorously.

"See," Azure said. "I told you. They *must* feed off it, somehow."

Shallan narrowed her eyes, then grabbed her sketchbook and stalked over to begin interviewing some of the spren. Kaladin trailed away to join his spren at the prow of the ship, where she liked to stand. Adolin often noticed him looking southward, as if anxiously wishing the ship to move more quickly.

He lingered by the side of the ship, watching the beads crash away below. When he looked up, he found Azure studying him. "Did you really sew that?" she asked.

"There wasn't much sewing involved," Adolin said. "The scarf and jacket hide most of the damage I did to the waistcoat—which used to be a smaller jacket."

"Still," she said. "An unusual skill for a royal."

"And how many royals have you known?"

"More than some might assume."

Adolin nodded. "I see. And are you enigmatic on *purpose*, or is it kind of an accidental thing?"

Azure leaned against the ship's wale, breeze blowing her short hair. She looked more youthful when not wearing the breastplate and cloak. Mid-thirties, maybe. "A little of both. I discovered when I was younger that being too open with strangers . . . went poorly for me. But in answer to your question, I *have* known royals. Including one woman who left it behind. Throne, family, responsibilities . . ."

"She abandoned her duty?" That was practically inconceivable.

"The throne was better served by someone who enjoyed sitting on it."

"Duty isn't about what you *enjoy*. It's about doing what is demanded of you, in serving the greater good. You can't just abandon responsibility because you *feel like it*."

Azure glanced at Adolin, and he felt himself blush. "Sorry," he said, looking away. "My father and my uncle might have . . . instilled me with a little passion on the topic."

"It's all right," Azure said. "Maybe you're right, and maybe there's something in me that knows it. I always find myself in situations like in Kholinar, leading the Wall Guard. I get too involved . . . then abandon everyone. . . ."

"You *didn't* abandon the Wall Guard, Azure," Adolin said. "You couldn't have prevented what happened."

"Perhaps. I can't help feeling that this is merely one in a long string of duties abdicated, of burdens set down, perhaps to disastrous results." For some reason, she put her hand on the pommel of her Shardblade when she said that. Then she looked up at Adolin. "But of all the things I've walked away from, the one I don't regret is allowing someone else to rule. Sometimes, the best way to do your duty is to let someone else—someone more capable—try carrying it."

Such a *foreign* idea. Sometimes you took up a duty that wasn't yours, but abandoning one? Just . . . giving it to someone else?

He found himself musing on that. He nodded his thanks to Azure as she excused herself to get something to drink. He was still standing there when Shallan returned from interviewing—well, interrogating—the Reachers. She took his arm, and together they watched the shimmering clouds for a while.

"I look terrible, don't I?" she finally asked, nudging him in the side. "No makeup, with hair that hasn't been washed in days, and now wearing a dumpy set of worker's clothing."

"I don't think you're capable of looking terrible," he said, pulling her closer. "In all their color, even those clouds can't compete."

They passed through a sea of floating candle flames, which represented a village on the human side. The flames were huddled together in patches. Hiding from the storm.

Eventually the clouds faded—but they were supposedly near the city now, so Shallan got excited, watching for it. Finally, she pointed to land on the horizon.

Celebrant nestled not far down its coast. As they drew closer, they spotted other ships entering or leaving the port, each pulled by at least two mandras.

Captain Ico walked over. "We'll soon arrive. Let's go get your deadeye."

Adolin nodded, patting Shallan on the back, and followed Ico down to the brig, a small room far aft in the cargo hold. Ico used keys to unlock the door, revealing the spren of Adolin's sword sitting on a bench inside. She looked at him with those haunting scratched-out eyes, her string face void of emotion.

"I wish you hadn't locked her in here," Adolin said, stooping down to peer through the squat doorway.

"Can't have them on deck," Ico said. "They don't watch where they're walking and fall off. I'm not going to spend days trying to fish out a lost deadeye."

She moved to join Adolin, then Ico reached over to shut the cell.

"Wait!" Adolin said. "Ico, I saw something moving back there."

Ico locked the door and hung the keys on his belt. "My father."

"Your *father*?" Adolin said. "You keep your father locked up?"

"Can't stand the thought of him wandering around somewhere," Ico said, eyes forward. "Have to keep him locked away though. He'll go searching for the human carrying his corpse, otherwise. Walk right off the deck."

"Your father was a Radiant spren?"

Ico started toward the steps up to the deck. "It is rude to ask about such ones."

"Rudeness doesn't imply untruth though, right?"

Ico turned and regarded him, then smiled wanly and nodded toward Adolin's spren. "What is she to you?"

"A friend."

"A tool. You use her corpse on the other side, don't you? Well, I won't blame you. I've heard stories of what they can do, and I am a pragmatic person. Just . . . don't pretend she is your friend."

By the time they reached the deck, the ship was approaching the docks. Ico started calling orders, though his crew clearly knew what to do already.

The Celebrant docks were wide and large, longer than the city. Ships pulled in along stone piers, though Adolin couldn't figure out how they got back out again. Hook the mandras to the stern and pull them out that way?

The shore was marked by long warehouses set in rows, which marred the view of the city proper, in Adolin's opinion. The ship drew up at a berth on a specific pier, guided by a Reacher with semaphore. Ico's sailors unlatched a piece of the hull, which unfolded to steps, and a sailor hiked down immediately to greet another group of Reachers. These began unlatching the mandras with long hooks, leading them away.

As each flying spren was released from the rigging, the ship sank a little farther into the bead ocean. Eventually, it seemed to settle onto some braces and steady there.

Pattern came over, humming to himself and meeting the rest of them as they gathered on the deck. Ico stepped up, gesturing. "A deal fulfilled, and a bond kept."

"Thank you, Captain," Adolin said, shaking Ico's hand. Ico returned the gesture awkwardly. He obviously knew what to do, but was unpracticed at it. "You're sure you won't take us the rest of the way to the portal between realms?"

"I'm certain," Ico said firmly. "The region around Cultivation's Perpendicularity has gained a poor reputation of late. Too many ships vanishing."

"What about Thaylen City?" Kaladin asked. "Could you take us there?"

"No. I unload goods here, and then head east. Away from trouble. And if you'll accept a little advice, stay in Shadesmar. The Physical Realm is not a welcoming place these days."

"We'll take that under advisement," Adolin said. "Is there anything we should know about the city?"

"Don't stray too far outside; with human cities nearby, there will be angerspren in the area. Try not to draw too many lesser spren, and maybe see if you can find a place to tie up that deadeye of yours." He pointed. "The dock registrar is that building ahead of us, with the blue paint. There you'll find a list of ships willing to take on passengers—but you'll have to go to each one individually and make sure they are equipped to take humans, and haven't already booked all their cabins.

"The building next to that is a moneychanger, where you can trade Stormlight for notes of exchange." He shook his head. "My daughter used to work there, before she ran off chasing stupid dreams."

He bade them farewell, and the group of travelers walked down the gangway onto the docks. Curiously, Syl still wore an illusion, making her face an Alethi tan, her hair black, her clothing red. Was being an honorspren really that big a deal?

"So," Adolin said as they reached the pier, "how are we going to do this? In the city, I mean."

"I've counted out our marks," Shallan said, holding up a bag of spheres. "It's been long enough since they were renewed, they'll almost certainly lose their Stormlight in the next few days. A few have already gone out. We might as well trade for supplies—we can keep the broams and the larger gemstones for Surgebinding."

"First stop is the moneychanger, then," Adolin said.

"After that, we should see if we can buy more rations," Kaladin said, "just in case. And we need to look for passage."

"But to where?" Azure said. "The perpendicularity, or Thaylen City?"

"Let's see what our options are," Adolin decided. "Maybe there will be a ship to one destination, but not the other. Let's send one group to inquire with ships, and another to get supplies. Shallan, do you have a preference which you'd rather do?"

"I'll look for passage," she said. "I have experience with it—I made a *lot* of trips when chasing down Jasnah."

"Sounds good," Adolin said. "We should put one Radiant in each group, so bridgeboy and Syl, you'll go with me. Pattern and Azure will go with Shallan."

"Maybe I should help Shallan—" Syl began.

"We'll need a spren with us," Adolin said. "To explain culture here. Let's go trade in those spheres first, though."

Moelach was said to grant visions of the future at different times—but most commonly at the transition point between realms. When a soul was nearing the Tranquiline Halls.

—From Hessi's *Mythica*, page 144

K aladin hiked through the city with Adolin and Syl. The money-changing had gone quickly, and they'd left the spren of Adolin's sword with the others. After Shallan had taken the deadeye's hand, she had remained behind.

Reaching this city marked a welcome step forward, toward finally getting out of this place and reaching Dalinar. Unfortunately, a brand-new city full of unknown threats didn't encourage him to relax.

The city wasn't as densely populated as most human ones, but the variety of spren was stunning. Reachers like Ico and his sailors were common, but there were also spren that looked much like Adolin's sword—at least before she'd been killed. They were made entirely of vines, though they had crystal hands and wore human clothing. Equally common were spren with inky black skin that shone with a variety of colors when light hit them right. Their clothing seemed part of them, like that of the Cryptics and honorspren.

A small group of Cryptics passed nearby, huddling close together as they walked. Each had a head with a slightly different pattern. There were other spren with skin like cracked stone, molten light shining from within. Still others had skin the color of old white ashes—and when Kaladin saw one of these point toward something, the skin stretching at the joint of his arm disintegrated and blew away, revealing the joint and knobs of the humerus. The skin quickly regrew.

The variety reminded Kaladin of the costumes of the Cult of Moments—though he didn't spot a single honorspren. And it didn't seem like the other spren mixed much. Humans were rare enough that the three of them—including Syl, imitating an Alethi—turned heads.

Buildings were constructed using bricks in a variety of colors or blocks of many different types of stone. Each building was a hodgepodge of materials with no pattern Kaladin could determine.

"How do they get building materials?" Kaladin asked as they followed the moneychanger's instructions toward the nearby market. "Are there quarries on this side?"

Syl frowned. "I . . ." She cocked her head. "You know, I'm not sure. I think maybe we make it appear on this side, somehow, from yours? Like Ico did with the ice?"

"They seem to wear whatever," Adolin said, pointing. "That's an Alethi officer's coat over an *Azish scribe's vest*. Tashikki wrap worn with trousers, and there's *almost* a full Thaylen tlmko, but they're missing the boots."

"No children," Kaladin noticed.

"There have been a few," Syl said. "They just don't look little, like human children."

"How does that even *work*?" Adolin said.

"Well, it's certainly less messy than your method!" She scrunched her face up. "We're made of power, bits of gods. There are places where that power coalesces, and parts start to be aware. You go, and then come back with a child? I think?"

Adolin chuckled.

"What?" Kaladin asked.

"That's actually not that different from what my nanny told me when I asked her where children come from. A nonsense story about parents baking a new child out of crem clay."

"It doesn't happen often," Syl said as they passed a group of the ash-colored spren sitting around a table and watching the crowds. They eyed the humans with overt hostility, and one flicked fingers toward Kaladin. Those fingers exploded to bits of dust, leaving bones that grew back the flesh.

"Raising children doesn't happen often?" Adolin asked.

Syl nodded. "It's rare. Most spren will go hundreds of years without doing it."

Hundreds of years. "Storms," Kaladin whispered, considering it. "Most of these spren are that old?"

"Or older," Syl said. "But aging isn't the same with spren. Like time isn't. We don't learn as fast, or change much, without a bond."

Towers in the city's center showed the time by way of fires burning in a set of vertical holes—so they could judge how to meet back with the others in an hour, as agreed. The market turned out to be mostly roofless stalls open to the air, with goods piled on tables. Even in comparison to the improvised market of Urithiru, this seemed . . . ephemeral to Kaladin. But there were no stormwinds to worry about here, so it probably made sense.

They passed a clothing stall, and of course Adolin insisted on stopping. The oily spren who managed the place had an odd, very terse way of talking, with a strange use of words. But it did speak Alethi, unlike most of Ico's crew.

Kaladin waited for the prince to finish, until Syl stepped up and presented herself in an oversized poncho tied with a belt. On her head she wore a large, floppy hat.

"What's that?" Kaladin asked.

"Clothes!"

"Why do you need clothes? Yours are built in."

"Those are boring."

"Can't you change them?"

"Takes Stormlight, on this side," she said. "Plus, the dress is part of my essence, so I'm actually walking around naked *all the time*."

"It's not the same."

"Easy for you to say. We bought *you* clothing. You have three sets!"

"Three?" he said, looking down at his clothing. "I have my uniform, and this one Ico gave me."

"Plus the one you're wearing underneath that one."

"Underwear?" Kaladin said.

"Yeah. That means you have *three* sets of clothing, while I have *none*."

"We need two sets so one can be washed while we wear the other."

"Just so you won't be stinky." She rolled her eyes in an exaggerated way. "Look, you can give these to Shallan when I get bored with them. You know she likes hats."

That was true. He sighed, and when Adolin returned with another set of underclothing for each of them—along with a skirt for Shallan—Kaladin had him haggle for the clothing Syl was wearing too. The prices were shockingly cheap, using a tiny fraction of the money from their writ.

They continued on, passing stalls that sold building materials. According to the signs Syl could read, some items were far more expensive than others. Syl seemed to think the difference had to do with how permanent the thing was in Shadesmar—which made Kaladin worry for the clothing they'd bought.

They found a place selling weapons, and Adolin tried to negotiate while

Kaladin browsed. Some kitchen knives. A few hand axes. And sitting in a locked, glass-topped box, a long thin silvery chain.

"You like?" the shopkeeper asked. She was made of vines—her face formed as if from green string—and wore a havah with a crystal safehand exposed. "Only a thousand broams of Stormlight."

"A *thousand broams*?" Kaladin asked. He looked down at the box, which was locked to the table and guarded by small orange spren that looked like people. "No thanks." The pricing here really was bizarre.

The swords proved more expensive than Adolin wanted, but he did buy them two harpoons—and Kaladin felt a lot more secure once one was placed in his hands. Walking on, Kaladin noted that Syl was hunkered down in her oversized poncho, her hair tucked into the collar and her hat pulled down to shadow her face. It seemed like she didn't trust Shallan's illusion to keep her from being recognized as an honorspren.

The food stall they found had mostly more "cans" like those on the ship. Adolin started haggling, and Kaladin settled in for another wait, scanning those who passed on the pathway for danger. He found his eyes drawn, however, to a stall across from them. Selling art.

Kaladin had never had much time for art. Either the picture depicted something useful—like a map—or it was basically pointless. And yet, nestled among the paintings for display was a small one painted from thick strokes of oil. White and red, with lines of black. When he looked away, he found himself drawn back toward it, studying the way the highlights played off those dark lines.

Like nine shadows . . . he thought. *With a figure kneeling in the middle . . .*

◆◆

The ashen spren waved excitedly, pointing to the east and then making a cutting motion. She spoke a language Shallan couldn't understand, but fortunately Pattern could interpret.

"Ah . . ." he said. "Mmm, yes. I see. She will not sail back to Cultivation's Perpendicularity. Mmm. No, she will not go."

"Same excuse?" Shallan asked.

"Yes. Voidspren sailing warships and demanding tribute from any who approach. Oh! She says she would rather trade with honorspren than take another trip to the perpendicularity. I think this is an insult. Ha ha ha. Mmm . . ."

"Voidspren," Azure said. "Can she at least explain what that means?"

The ashen spren began speaking quickly after Pattern asked. "Hmm . . . There are many varieties, she says. Some of golden light, others are red shadows. Curious, yes. And it sounds like some of the Fused are with them—men with shells that can fly. I did not know this."

"What?" Azure prompted.

"Shadesmar has been changing these last months," Pattern explained. "Voidspren have arrived mysteriously just west of the Nexus of Imagination. Near Marat or Tukar on your side. Hmm . . . and they have sailed up and seized the perpendicularity. She says, ahem, 'You need but spit into a crowd, and you'll find one, these days.' Ha ha ha. I do not think she actually has spit."

Shallan and Azure shared a look as the sailor retreated onto her ship, to which mandras were being harnessed. The spren of Adolin's sword lingered nearby, seeming content to stay where told. Passersby looked away from her, as if embarrassed to see her there.

"Well, the dock registrar was right," Azure said, folding her arms. "No ships sailing toward the peaks *or* toward Thaylen City. Those destinations are too close to enemy holdings."

"Maybe we should try for the Shattered Plains instead," Shallan said. That meant going east—a direction ships were more likely to travel, these days. It would mean going away from both what Kaladin *and* Azure wanted, but at least it would be something.

If they got there, she'd still need to find a way to engage the Oathgate on this side. What if she failed? She imagined them trapped in some far-off location, surrounded by beads, slowly starving. . . .

"Let's keep asking the ships on our list," she said, leading the way. The next ship in line was a long, stately vessel made of white wood with golden trim. Its entire presentation seemed to say, *Good luck affording me.* Even the mandras being led toward it from one of the warehouses wore gold harnesses.

According to the list from the dock registrar, this was heading someplace called Lasting Integrity—which was to the southwest. That was *kind of* the direction Kaladin wanted to go, so Shallan had Pattern stop one of the grooms and ask if the captain of the ship would be likely to take human passengers.

The groom, a spren that looked like she was made of fog or mist, merely laughed and walked off as if she'd heard a grand joke.

"I suppose," Azure said, "we should take that for a no."

The next ship in line was a sleek vessel that looked fast to Shallan's untrained eyes. A good choice, the registrar had noted, and likely to be welcoming toward humans. Indeed, a spren working on the deck waved as they approached. He put one booted foot up on the side of his ship and looked down with a grin.

What kind of spren, Shallan thought, *has skin like cracked rock?* He glowed deep within, as if molten on the inside. "Humans?" he called in Veden, reading Shallan's hair as a sign of her heritage. "You're far from home. Or close, I suppose, just in the wrong realm!"

"We're looking for passage," Shallan called up. "Where are you sailing?"

"East!" he said. "Toward Freelight!"

"Could we potentially negotiate passage?"

"Sure!" he called down. "Always interesting to have humans aboard. Just don't eat my pet chicken. Ha! But negotiations will have to wait. We've got an inspection soon. Come back in a half hour."

The dock registrar had mentioned this; an official inspection of the ships happened at first hour every day. Shallan and the team backed off, and she suggested returning to their meeting place near the dock registrar. As they approached, Shallan could see that Ico's ship was already under inspection by a dock official—another spren made of vines and crystal.

Maybe we could convince Ico to take us, if we just tried harder. Perhaps—

Azure's breath caught and she grabbed Shallan by the shoulder, yanking her into an alley between two warehouses, out of sight of the ship. "Damnation!"

"What?" Shallan demanded as Pattern and, lethargically, Adolin's spren joined them.

"Look up there," Azure said. "Talking with Ico, on the poop deck."

Shallan frowned, then peeked out, spotting what she'd missed earlier: A figure stood up there, with the marbled skin of a parshman. He floated a foot or two off the deck next to Ico, looming like a stern tutor over a foolish student.

The spren with the vines and crystal body walked up, reporting to this one.

"Perhaps," Azure said, "we should have asked *who runs* the inspections."

⁘

Kaladin's harpoon drew nervous glances as he crossed the pathway between stalls, to get a closer look at the painting.

Can spren even be hurt in this realm? a part of him wondered. *The sailors wouldn't carry harpoons if things couldn't be killed on this side, right?* He'd have to ask Syl, once she was done interpreting for Adolin.

Kaladin stepped up to the painting. The ones beside it showed far more technical prowess—they were capable portraits, perfectly capturing their human subjects. This one was sloppy by comparison. It looked like the painter had simply taken a knife covered in paint and slopped it onto the canvas, making general shapes.

Haunting, *beautiful* shapes. Mostly reds and whites, but with a figure at the center, throwing out nine shadows . . .

Dalinar, he thought. *I failed Elhokar. After all we went through, after the rains and confronting Moash, I've failed. And I lost your city.*

He reached up his fingers to touch the painting.

"Marvelous, isn't it!" a spren said.

Kaladin jumped, sheepishly lowering his fingers. The proprietor of this stall was a Reacher woman, short, with a bronze ponytail.

"It's a unique piece, human," she said. "From the far-off Court of Gods, a painting intended only for a divinity to see. It is exceptionally rare that one escapes being burned at the court, and makes its way onto the market."

"Nine shadows," Kaladin said. "The Unmade?"

"This is a piece by Nenefra. It is said that each person who sees one of his masterworks sees something different. And to think, I charge such a minuscule price. Only three hundred broams' worth of Stormlight! Truly, times are difficult in the art market."

"I . . ."

Haunting images from Kaladin's vision overlapped the stark wedges of paint on the canvas. He needed to reach Thaylen City. He had to be there on time—

What was that disturbance behind him?

Kaladin shook out of his reverie and glanced over his shoulder, just in time to see Adolin jogging toward him.

"We have a problem," the prince said.

⁘

"How could you not mention this!" Shallan said to the little spren at the registrar office. "How could you *neglect* to point out that *Voidspren* ruled the city?"

"I thought everyone knew!" he said, vines curling and moving at the corners of his face. "Oh dear. Oh my! Anger is *not* helpful, human. I am a *professional*. It is not my job to explain things you should already know!"

"He's still on Ico's ship," Azure said, looking out the office window. "Why is he still on Ico's ship?"

"That *is* odd," the spren said. "Each inspection usually takes only thirteen minutes!"

Damnation. Shallan breathed out, trying to calm herself. Coming back to the registrar had been a calculated risk. He was probably working with the Fused, but they hoped to intimidate him into talking.

"When did it happen?" Shallan asked. "My spren friend told us this was a free city."

"It's been months now," the vine spren said. "Oh, they don't have *firm* control here, mind you. Just a few officials, and promises from our leaders to follow. Two Fused check in on us now and then. I think the other is quite insane. Kyril—who is running the inspections—well, he might be mad too, actually. You see, when he gets angry—"

"Damnation!" Azure cursed.

"What?"

"He just set Ico's ship on fire."

. .

Kaladin ran back across the street to find Syl a center of activity. She had pulled her oversized hat down to obscure her face, but a collection of spren stood around the food stall, pointing at her and talking.

Kaladin shoved his way through, took Syl by the arm, and pulled her away from the stall. Adolin followed, holding his harpoon in one hand and a sack of food in the other. He looked threateningly toward the spren in the gathered crowd, who didn't give chase.

"They recognize you," Kaladin said to Syl. "Even with the illusory skin color."

"Uh . . . maybe . . ."

"*Syl.*"

She held to her hat with one hand, her other arm in his hand as he towed her through the street. "So . . . you know how I mentioned I snuck away from the other honorspren . . ."

"Yes."

"So, there *might* have been an enormous reward for my return. Posted in basically every port in Shadesmar, with my description and some pictures. Um . . . yeah."

"You've been forgiven," Kaladin said. "The Stormfather has accepted your bond to me. Your siblings are watching Bridge Four, investigating potential bonds themselves!"

"That's kind of recent, Kaladin. And I doubt I've been forgiven—the others on the Shattered Plains wouldn't talk to me. As far as they're concerned, I'm a disobedient child. There's still an incredible reward in Stormlight to be given to the person that delivers me to the honorspren capital, Lasting Integrity."

"And you didn't think this was important to tell me?"

"Sure I did. Right now."

They stopped to allow Adolin to catch up. The spren back at the food stall were still talking. Storms. This news would spread throughout Celebrant before long.

Kaladin glared at Syl, who pulled down into the oversized poncho she'd bought. "Azure is a *bounty hunter*," she said in a small voice. "And I'm . . . I'm kind of like a spren lighteyes. I didn't want you to know. In case you hated me, like you hate them."

Kaladin sighed, taking her by the arm again and pulling her toward the docks.

"I should have known this disguise wouldn't work," she added. "I'm obviously too beautiful and interesting to hide."

"News of this might make it hard to get passage," Kaladin said. "We . . ." He stopped in the street. "Is that smoke up ahead?"

∴

The Fused touched down on the quay, tossing Ico to the ground of the docks. Behind, Ico's ship had become a raging bonfire—the other sailors and inspectors scrambled down the gangway in a frantic jumble.

Shallan watched from the window. Her breath caught as the Fused lifted a few inches off the ground, then glided toward the registrar's building.

She sucked in Stormlight by reflex. "Look frightened!" she said to the others. She grabbed Adolin's spren by the arm and pulled her to the side of the clerk's room.

The Fused burst in and found them cringing, wearing the faces of sailors that Shallan had sketched. Pattern was the oddest one, his strange head needing to be covered by a hat to have any semblance of looking realistic.

Please don't notice we're the same sailors as on the ship. Please.

The Fused ignored them, gliding up to the frightened vine spren behind the desk.

"That ship was hiding human criminals," Pattern whispered, translating the Fused's conversation with the registrar. "They had a hydrator and remnants of human food—eaten—on the deck. There are two or three humans, one honorspren, and one inkspren. Have you seen these criminals?"

The vine spren cringed down by the desk. "They went to the market for needed supplies. They asked me for ships that would get them passage to the perpendicularity."

"You *hid* this from me?"

"Why does everyone assume I'll just tell them things? Oh, I need *questions*, not assumptions!"

The Fused regarded him with a cold glare. "Put that out," he said, gesturing toward the fire. "Use the city's sand stores, if needed."

"Yes, great one. If I might say, starting fires on the docks is an unwise—"

"You may *not* say. When you finish putting out the fire, clear your things from this office. You are to be replaced immediately."

The Fused charged out of the room, letting in the scent of smoke. Ico's ship foundered, the blaze flaring high. Nearby, sailors from other ships were frantically trying to control their mandras and move their vessels away.

"Oh, oh *my*," said the spren behind the desk. He looked to them. "You . . . you are a Radiant? The old oaths are spoken again?"

"Yes," Shallan said, helping Adolin's spren to her feet.

The frightened little spren sat up straighter. "Oh, *glorious* day. Glorious! We have waited so long for the honor of men to return!" He stood up and gestured. "Go, please! Get on a ship. I will stall, yes I will, if that one comes back. Oh, but go *quickly*!"

❖

Kaladin sensed something on the air.

Perhaps it was the flapping of clothing, familiar to him after hours spent riding the winds. Perhaps it was the postures of the people farther down the street. He reacted before he understood what it was, grabbing Syl and Adolin, pulling them all into a tent at the edge of the market.

A Fused soared past outside, its shadow trailing behind, pointing the wrong direction.

"Storms!" Adolin said. "Nice work, Kal."

The tent was occupied only by a single bewildered spren made of smoke, looking odd in a green cap and what seemed to be Horneater clothing.

"Out," Kaladin said, the smell of smoke on the air filling him with dread. They hurried down an alleyway between warehouses, out onto the docks.

Farther down, Ico's ship burned brilliantly. There was chaos on the docks as spren ran in all directions, shouting in their strange language.

Syl gasped, pointing at a ship bedecked in white and gold. "We have to hide. *Now.*"

"Honorspren?" Kaladin asked.

"Yeah."

"Pull down your hat, go back into the alley." Kaladin scanned the crowd. "Adolin, do you see the others?"

"No," he said. "Ishar's soul! There's no water to put that fire out. It will burn for hours. What happened?"

One of Ico's sailors stepped from the crowd. "I saw a flash from something the Fused was holding. I think he intended to frighten Ico, but started the fire by accident."

Wait, Kaladin thought. *Was that Alethi?* "Shallan?" he asked as four Reachers gathered around.

"I'm right here," said a different one. "We are in trouble. The only ship that might have agreed to give us passage is that one there."

"The one sailing away at full speed?" Kaladin said with a sigh.

"Nobody else would consider taking us on," Azure said. "And they were all heading the wrong directions anyway. We're about to be stranded."

"We could try fighting our way onto a ship," Kaladin said. "Take control of it, maybe?"

Adolin shook his head. "I think that would take long enough—and make enough trouble—that the Fused would find us."

"Well, maybe I could fight *him*," Kaladin said. "Only one enemy. I should be able to take him."

"Using all our Stormlight in the process?" Shallan asked.

"I'm just trying to think of something!"

"Guys," Syl said. "I might have an idea. A great bad idea."

"The Fused went looking for you," Shallan said to Kaladin. "It flew to the market."

"It passed us."

"Guys?"

"Not for long though. It's going to turn around soon."

"Turns out Syl has a bounty on her head."

"Guys?"

"We need a plan," Kaladin said. "If nobody . . ." He trailed off.

Syl had started running toward the majestic white and gold ship, which was slowly being pulled away from the docks. She threw down her poncho and hat, then screamed up at the ship while running along the pier beside it.

"Hey!" she screamed. "Hey, look down here!"

The vessel stopped ponderously, handlers slowing its mandras. Three blue-white honorspren appeared at the side, looking down with utter shock.

"*Sylphrena*, the Ancient Daughter?" one shouted.

"That's me!" she shouted back. "You'd better catch me before I scamper away! Wow! I'm feeling capricious today. I might just vanish again, off to where nobody can find me!"

It worked.

A gangway dropped, and Syl scrambled up onto the ship—followed by the rest of them. Kaladin went last, watching nervously over his shoulder, expecting the Fused to come after them at any moment. It did, but it stopped at the mouth of the alleyway, watching them board the ship. Honorspren gave it pause, apparently.

On board, Kaladin discovered that most of the sailors were those spren made of fog or mist. One of these was tying Syl's arms together with rope. Kaladin tried to intervene, but Syl shook her head. "Not now," she mouthed.

Fine. He would argue with the honorspren later.

The ship pulled away, joining others that fled the city. The honorspren didn't pay much mind to Kaladin and the others—though one did take their harpoons, and another went through their pockets, confiscating their infused gemstones.

As the city grew smaller, Kaladin caught sight of the Fused hovering over the docks, beside the smoke trail of a burning ship.

It finally streaked off in the other direction.

HYPOCRITE

Many cultures speak of the so-called Death Rattles that sometimes overtake people as they die. Tradition ascribes them to the Almighty, but I find too many to be seemingly prophetic. This will be my most contentious assertion I am sure, but I think these are the effects of Moelach persisting in our current times. Proof is easy to provide: the effect is regionalized, and tends to move across Roshar. This is the roving of the Unmade.

—From Hessi's *Mythica*, page 170

D alinar started awake in an unfamiliar place, lying on a floor of cut stone, his back stiff. He blinked sleepily, trying to orient himself. Storms . . . where was he?

Soft sunlight shone through an open balcony on the far side of the room, and ethereal motes of dust danced in the streams of light. What were those sounds? They seemed like the voices of people, but muffled.

Dalinar stood, then fastened the side of his uniform jacket, which had come undone. It had been . . . what, three days since his return from Jah Keved? His excommunication from the Vorin church?

He remembered those days as a haze of frustration, sorrow, agony. And drink. A great deal of drink. He'd been using the stupor to drive away the pain. A terrible bandage for his wounds, blood seeping out on all sides. But so far, it had kept him alive.

I know this room, he realized, glancing at the mural on the ceiling. *I saw it in one of my visions.* A highstorm must have come while he was passed out.

"Stormfather?" Dalinar called, his voice echoing. "Stormfather, why have you sent me a vision? We agreed they were too dangerous."

Yes, he remembered this place well. This was the vision where he'd met Nohadon, author of *The Way of Kings*. Why wasn't it playing out as it had before? He and Nohadon had walked to the balcony, talked for a time, then the vision had ended.

Dalinar started toward the balcony, but storms, that light was *so intense*. It washed over him, making his eyes water, and he had to raise his hand to shield his eyes.

He heard something behind him. Scratching? He turned—putting his back to the brilliance—and spotted a door on the wall. It swung open easily beneath his touch, and he stepped out of the loud sunlight to find himself in a circular room.

He shut the door with a click. This chamber was much smaller than the previous one, with a wooden floor. Windows in the walls looked out at a clear sky. A shadow passed over one of these, like something enormous moving in front of the sun. But . . . how could the sun be pointed this direction too?

Dalinar looked over his shoulder at the wooden door. No light peeked underneath it. He frowned and reached for the handle, then paused, hearing the scratching once more. Turning, he saw a large desk, heaped with papers, by the wall. How had he missed that earlier?

A man sat at the desk, lit by a loose diamond, writing with a reed pen. Nohadon had aged. In the previous vision, the king had been young—but now his hair was silver, his skin marked by wrinkles. It *was* the same man though, same face shape, same beard that came to a point. He wrote with focused concentration.

Dalinar stepped over. "*The Way of Kings*," he whispered. "I'm watching it be written. . . ."

"Actually," Nohadon said, "it's a shopping list. I'll be cooking Shin loaf bread today, if I can get the ingredients. It always breaks people's brains. Grain was not meant to be so fluffy."

What . . . ? Dalinar scratched at the side of his head.

Nohadon finished with a flourish and tossed the pen down. He threw back his chair and stood, grinning like a fool, and grabbed Dalinar by the arms. "Good to see you again, my friend. You've been having a hard time of it lately, haven't you?"

"You have no idea," Dalinar whispered, wondering who Nohadon saw him as. In the previous vision, Dalinar had appeared as one of Nohadon's advisors. They'd stood together on the balcony as Nohadon contemplated a war to unite the world. A drastic resort, intended to prepare mankind for the next Desolation.

Could that morose figure have really become this spry and eager? And where had this vision come from? Hadn't the Stormfather told Dalinar that he'd seen them all?

"Come," Nohadon said, "let's go to the market. A little shopping to turn your mind from your troubles."

"Shopping?"

"Yes, you shop, don't you?"

"I . . . usually have people to do that for me."

"Ah, but of course you do," Nohadon said. "Very like you to miss a simple joy so you can get to something more 'important.' Well, come on. I'm the king. You can't very well say no, now can you?"

Nohadon led Dalinar back through the door. The light was gone. They crossed to the balcony, which—last time—had overlooked death and desolation. Now, it looked out on a bustling city full of energetic people and rolling carts. The sound of the place crashed into Dalinar, as if it had been suppressed until that moment. Laughing, chatting, calling. Wagons creaking. Chulls bleating.

The men wore long skirts, tied at the waists by wide girdles, some of which came all the way up over their stomachs. Above that they had bare chests, or wore simple overshirts. The outfits resembled the takama Dalinar had worn when younger, though of a far, far older style. The tubular gowns on the women were even stranger, made of layered small rings of cloth with tassels on the bottom. They seemed to ripple as they moved.

The women's arms were bare up to the shoulders. No safehand covering. *In the previous vision, I spoke the Dawnchant,* Dalinar remembered. *The words that gave Navani's scholars a starting point to translate ancient texts.*

"How do we get down?" Dalinar asked, seeing no ladder.

Nohadon leaped off the side of the balcony. He laughed, falling and sliding along a cloth banner tied between a tower window and a tent below. Dalinar cursed, leaning forward, worried for the old man—until he spotted Nohadon glowing. He was a Surgebinder—but Dalinar had known that from the last vision, hadn't he?

Dalinar walked back to the writing chamber and drew the Stormlight from the diamond that Nohadon had been using. He returned, then heaved himself off the balcony, aiming for the cloth Nohadon had used to break his fall. Dalinar hit it at an angle and used it like a slide, keeping his right foot forward to guide his descent. Near the bottom, he flipped off the banner, grabbing its edge with two hands and hanging there for an instant before dropping with a *thump* beside the king.

Nohadon clapped. "I thought you wouldn't do it."

"I have practice following fools in their reckless pursuits."

The old man grinned, then scanned his list. "This way," he said, pointing.

"I can't believe you're out shopping by yourself. No guards?"

"I walked all the way to Urithiru on my own. I think I can manage this."

"You didn't walk all the way to Urithiru," Dalinar said. "You walked to one of the Oathgates, then took that to Urithiru."

"Misconception!" Nohadon said. "I walked the whole way, though I did require some help to reach Urithiru's caverns. That is no more a cheat than taking a ferry across a river."

He bustled through the market and Dalinar followed, distracted by the colorful clothing everyone was wearing. Even the stones of the buildings were painted in vibrant colors. He'd always imagined the past as . . . dull. Statues from ancient times were weathered, and he'd never considered that they might have been painted so brightly.

What of Nohadon himself? In both visions, Dalinar had been shown someone he did not expect. The young Nohadon, considering war. Now the elderly one, glib and whimsical. Where was the deep-thinking philosopher who had written *The Way of Kings*?

Remember, Dalinar told himself, *this isn't really him. The person I'm talking to is a construct of the vision.*

Though some people in the market recognized their king, his passing didn't cause much of a stir. Dalinar spun as he saw something move beyond the buildings, a large shadow that passed between two structures, tall and enormous. He stared in that direction, but didn't see it again.

They entered a tent where a merchant was selling exotic grains. The man bustled over and hugged Nohadon in a way that *should* have been improper for a king. Then the two started haggling like scribes; the rings on the merchant's fingers flashed as he gestured at his wares.

Dalinar lingered near the side of the tent, taking in the scents of the grains in the sacks. Outside, something made a distant *thud.* Then another. The ground shook, but nobody reacted.

"Noh—Your Majesty?" Dalinar asked.

Nohadon ignored him. A shadow passed over the tent. Dalinar ducked, judging the form of the shadow, the sounds of crashing footfalls.

"Your Majesty!" he shouted, fearspren growing up around him. "We're in danger!"

The shadow passed, and the footfalls grew distant.

"Deal," Nohadon said to the merchant. "And well argued, you swindler. Make sure to buy Lani something nice with the extra spheres you got off me."

The merchant bellowed a laughing reply. "You think you got the worse of that? Storms, Your Majesty. You argue like my grandmother when she wants the last spoonful of jam!"

"Did you see that shadow?" Dalinar asked Nohadon.

"Have I told you," Nohadon replied, "where I learned to make Shin loaf bread? It wasn't in Shin Kak Nish, if that's what you were going to reply."

"I . . ." Dalinar looked in the direction the enormous shadow had gone. "No. You haven't told me."

"It was at war," Nohadon said. "In the west. One of those senseless battles in the years following the Desolation. I don't even remember what caused it. Someone invaded someone else, and that threatened our trade through Makabakam. So off we went.

"Well, I ended up with a scouting group on the edge of the Shin border. So you see, I tricked you just now. I said I wasn't in Shin Kak Nish, and I wasn't. But I was right next to it.

"My troops occupied a small village beneath one of the passes. The matron who cooked for us accepted my military occupation without complaint. She didn't seem to care which army was in charge. She made me bread every day, and I liked it so much, she asked if I wanted to learn . . ."

He trailed off. In front of him, the merchant set weights on one side of his large set of scales—representing the amount Nohadon had purchased—then started pouring grain into a bowl on the other side of the scale. Golden, captivating grain, like the light of captured flames. "What happened to the cook woman?" Dalinar asked.

"Something very unfair," Nohadon said. "It's not a happy story. I considered putting it into the book, but decided my story would best be limited to my walk to Urithiru." He fell silent, contemplative.

He reminds me of Taravangian, Dalinar suddenly thought. *How odd.*

"You are having trouble, my friend," Nohadon said. "Your life, like that of the woman, is unfair."

"Being a ruler is a burden, not merely a privilege," Dalinar said. "*You* taught me that. But storms, Nohadon. I can't see any way out! We've gathered the monarchs, yet the drums of war beat in my ears, demanding. For every step I make with my allies, we seem to spend weeks deliberating. The truth whispers in the back of my mind. I could best defend the world if I could simply *make* the others do as they should!"

Nohadon nodded. "So why don't you?"

"You didn't."

"I tried and failed. That led me to a different path."

"You're wise and thoughtful. I'm a warmonger, Nohadon. I've never accomplished *anything* without bloodshed."

He heard them again. The tears of the dead. Evi. The children. Flames burning a city. He heard the fire roar in delight at the feast.

The merchant ignored them, busy trying to get the grain to balance. The weighted side was still heavier. Nohadon set a finger on the bowl with the grain and pushed down, making the sides even. "That will do, my friend."

"But—" the merchant said.

"Give the excess to the children, please."

"After all that haggling? You know I'd have donated some if you'd asked."

"And miss the fun of negotiating?" Nohadon said. He borrowed the merchant's pen, then crossed an item off his list. "There is satisfaction," he said to Dalinar, "in creating a list of things you can actually accomplish, then removing them one at a time. As I said, a simple joy."

"Unfortunately, I'm needed for bigger things than shopping."

"Isn't that always the problem? Tell me, my friend. You talk about your burdens and the difficulty of the decision. What is the cost of a principle?"

"The cost? There shouldn't *be* a cost to being principled."

"Oh? What if making the right decision created a spren who instantly blessed you with wealth, prosperity, and unending happiness? What then? Would you still have principles? Isn't a principle about what you *give up*, not what you *gain*?"

"So it's all negative?" Dalinar said. "Are you implying that nobody should have principles, because there's no benefit to them?"

"Hardly," Nohadon said. "But maybe you shouldn't be looking for life to be easier because you choose to do something that is right! Personally, I think life *is* fair. It's merely that often, you can't immediately see what balances it." He wagged the finger he'd used to tip the merchant's scales. "If you'll forgive a somewhat blatant metaphor. I've grown fond of them. You might say I wrote an entire book about them."

"This . . . is different from the other visions," Dalinar said. "What's going on?"

The thumping from before returned. Dalinar spun, then charged out of the tent, determined to get a look at the thing. He saw it above the buildings, a stone creature with an angular face and red spots glowing deep in its rocky skull. Storms! And he had no weapon.

Nohadon stepped from the tent, holding his bag of grain. He looked up and smiled. The creature leaned down, then offered a large, skeletal hand. Nohadon touched it with its own, and the creature stilled.

"This is quite the nightmare you've created," Nohadon said. "What does that thunderclast represent, I wonder?"

"Pain," Dalinar said, backing away from the monster. "Tears. *Burdens.* I'm a lie, Nohadon. A hypocrite."

"Sometimes, a hypocrite is nothing more than a man who is in the process of changing."

Wait. Hadn't *Dalinar* said that? Back when he'd felt stronger? More certain?

Other thumps sounded in the city. Hundreds of them. Creatures approaching from all sides, shadows in the sun.

"All things exist in three realms, Dalinar," Nohadon said. "The Physical: what you are now. The Cognitive: what you see yourself as being. The Spiritual: the perfect you, the person beyond pain, and error, and uncertainty."

Monsters of stone and horror surrounded him, heads cresting roofs, feet crushing buildings.

"You've said the oaths," Nohadon called. "But do you understand the journey? Do you understand what it requires? You've forgotten one essential part, one thing that without which there can *be* no journey."

The monsters slammed fists toward Dalinar, and he shouted.

"What is the most important step a man can take?"

Dalinar awoke, huddled in his bed in Urithiru, asleep in his clothing again. A mostly empty bottle of wine rested on the table. There was no storm. It hadn't been a vision.

He buried his face in his hands, trembling. Something bloomed inside of him: a recollection. Not really a *new* memory—not one he'd completely forgotten. But it suddenly became as crisp as if he'd experienced it yesterday.

The night of Gavilar's funeral.

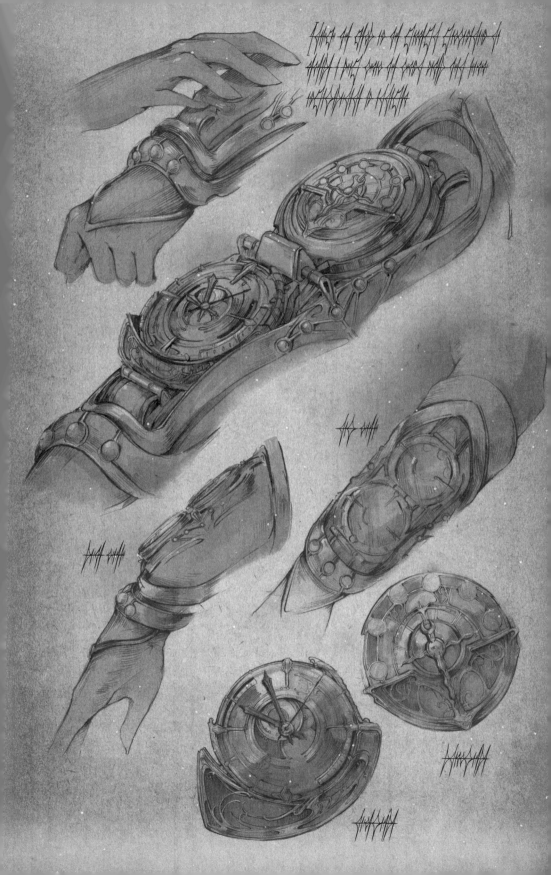

104. STRENGTH

Ashertmarn, the Heart of the Revel, is the final of the three great mindless Unmade. His gift to men is not prophecy or battle focus, but a lust for indulgence. Indeed, the great debauchery recorded from the court of Bayala in 480—which led to dynastic collapse—might be attributable to the influence of Ashertmarn.

—From Hessi's *Mythica*, page 203

Navani Kholin had some practice holding a kingdom together.

During Gavilar's last days, he had gone strange. Few knew how dark he'd grown, but they had seen the eccentricity. Jasnah had written about that, of course. Jasnah somehow found time to write about everything, from her father's biography, to gender relations, to the importance of chull breeding cycles on the southern slopes of the Horneater Peaks.

Navani strode through the hallways of Urithiru, joined by a nice burly group of Bridge Four Windrunners. As Gavilar had grown more and more distracted, Navani herself had worked to keep squabbling lighteyes from sundering the kingdom. But that had been a different kind of danger from the one she faced today.

Today, her work had implications not only for one nation, but for the entire world. She burst into a room deep within the tower, and the four lighteyes seated there scrambled to their feet—all but Sebarial, who appeared to be flipping through a stack of cards bearing pictures of women in compromising positions.

Navani sighed, then nodded as Aladar gave her a respectful bow, light glinting off his bald head. Not for the first time, Navani wondered if his thin mustache and the tuft of beard on his bottom lip were compensation for his lack of hair. Hatham was there as well: refined, with rounded features and green eyes. As usual, his fashion choices stood out from everyone else. Orange today.

Brightness Bethab had come representing her husband. The men in the army tended to disrespect him for letting her do so—but that ignored the fact that marrying Mishinah for her political acumen had been a wise and calculated move.

The five men of Bridge Four arrayed themselves behind Navani. They had been surprised when she'd asked them to escort her; they didn't yet understand the authority they lent the throne. The Knights Radiant were the new power in the world, and politics swirled around them like eddies in a river.

"Brightlords and Brightlady," Navani said. "I've come at your request, and am at your service."

Aladar cleared his throat, sitting. "You know, Brightness, that we are the most loyal to your husband's cause."

"Or at the least," Sebarial added, "we're the ones hoping to get rich by throwing in our lot with him."

"My husband appreciates the support," Navani said, "regardless of motive. You create a stronger Alethkar, and therefore a stronger world."

"What's left of either one," Sebarial noted.

"Navani," Brightlady Bethab said. She was a mousy woman with a pinched face. "We appreciate that you've taken the initiative in this difficult time." There was a glint to her orange eyes, as if she assumed Navani was enjoying her new power. "But the highprince's absence is not advantageous for morale. We know that Dalinar has returned to his . . . distractions."

"The highprince," Navani said, "is in mourning."

"The only thing he seems to be mourning," Sebarial said, "is the fact that people won't bring him bottles of wine fast enough for—"

"Damnation, Turinad!" Navani snapped. "That's *enough*!"

Sebarial blinked, then pocketed his cards. "Sorry, Brightness."

"My husband," Navani said, "is still this world's best chance for survival. He *will* push through his pain. Until then, our duty is to keep the kingdom running."

Hatham nodded, beads on his coat glistening. "This is, of course, our goal. But Brightness, can you define what you *mean* by kingdom? You do know that Dalinar . . . came to us and asked what we thought of this highking business."

That news wasn't commonly known yet. They'd planned an official announcement, and even had Elhokar seal the papers before leaving. Yet Dalinar had delayed. She understood; he wanted to wait until Elhokar and Adolin—who would become Kholin highprince in Dalinar's place—returned.

And yet, as more and more time passed, the questions began to grow more pressing. What had happened to them in Kholinar? Where *were* they?

Strength. They *would* return.

"The highking proclamation has not been made official," Navani said. "I think it's best to pretend you don't know about it, for now. And whatever you do, *don't* mention it to Ialai or Amaram."

"Very well," Aladar said. "But Brightness, we have other problems. Surely you've seen the reports. Hatham does an excellent job as Highprince of Works, but there isn't proper infrastructure. The tower has plumbing, but it keeps getting clogged, and the Soulcasters work themselves to exhaustion dealing with the waste."

"We can't continue pretending the tower can accommodate this population," Brightness Bethab said. "Not without a very favorable supply deal from Azir. Our emerald reserves, despite hunts on the Shattered Plains, are dwindling. Our water carts have to work nonstop."

"Equally important, Brightness," Hatham added, "we might be facing a severe labor shortage. We have soldiers or caravan men filling in hauling water or packing goods, but they don't like it. Menial carrying is beneath them."

"We're running low on lumber," Sebarial added. "I've tried to claim the forests back near the warcamps, but we used to have parshmen to cut them. I don't know if I can afford to pay men to do the work instead. But if we don't start something, Thanadal might try to seize them. He's building himself quite the kingdom in the warcamps."

"This is not a time," Hatham said softly, "when we can afford weak leadership. It is not a time when a would-be king can spend his days locked in his rooms. I'm sorry. We are not in rebellion, but we are *very* concerned."

Navani drew in a breath. *Hold it together.*

Order was the very substance of rule. If things were organized, control could be asserted. She just had to give Dalinar time. Even if, deep down, a part of her was angry. Angry that his pain so overshadowed her growing fear for Elhokar and Adolin. Angry that *he* got to drink himself to oblivion, leaving her to pick up the pieces.

But she had learned that nobody was strong all the time, not even Dalinar Kholin. Love wasn't about being right or wrong, but about standing up and helping when your partner's back was bowed. He would likely do the same for her someday.

"Tell us honestly, Brightness," Sebarial said, leaning forward. "What does the Blackthorn want? Is this all secretly a way for him to dominate the world?"

Storms. Even *they* worried about it. And why shouldn't they? It made so much sense.

"My husband wants unity," Navani said firmly. "*Not* dominion. You know as well as I do that we could have seized Thaylen City. That would have led to selfishness and loss. There is no path through conquest to facing our enemy together."

Aladar nodded slowly. "I believe you, and I believe in him."

"But how do we survive?" Brightness Bethab said.

"This tower's gardens once grew food," Navani said. "We will figure out how it was done, and we will grow here again. The tower once flowed with water. The baths and lavatories prove that. We will delve into the secrets of their fabrials, and we will fix the plumbing problems.

"The tower is above the enemy's storm, supremely defensible and connected to the most important cities in the world. If there is a nation that can stand against the enemy, we will forge it here. With your help and my husband's leadership."

They accepted that. Bless the Almighty, they accepted it. She made a mental note to burn a glyphward in thanks, then finally took a seat. Together, they delved into the tower's most recent list of problems, talking through—as they'd done many times before—the dirty necessities of running a city.

Three hours later, she checked her arm fabrial—a mirror of the one Dalinar carried, with inset clock and newly designed painrials. Three hours and twelve minutes since the meeting had begun. Exhaustionspren had collected to swirl around them all, and she called an end. They'd hashed out their immediate problems, and would summon their various scribes to offer specific revisions.

This would keep everyone going a little longer. And, bless them, these four *did* want the coalition to work. Aladar and Sebarial, for all their flaws, had followed Dalinar into the dark of the Weeping and found Damnation waiting there. Hatham and Bethab had been at the advent of the new storm, and could see that Dalinar had been right.

They didn't care that the Blackthorn was a heretic—or even whether he usurped the throne of Alethkar. They cared that he had a plan for dealing with the enemy, long-term.

After the meeting broke, Navani walked off down the strata-lined hallway, trailed by her bridgeman guards, two of whom carried sapphire lanterns. "I do apologize," she noted to them, "for how boring that must have been."

"We like boring, Brightness," Leyten—their leader today—said. He was a stocky man, with short, curly hair. "Hey, Hobber. Anyone try to kill you in there?"

The gap-toothed bridgeman grinned his reply. "Does Huio's breath count?"

"See, Brightness?" Leyten said. "New recruits might get bored by guard duty, but you'll never find a veteran complaining about a nice quiet afternoon full of not being stabbed."

"I can see the appeal," she said. "But surely it can't compare with soaring through the skies."

"That's true," Leyten said. "But we have to take turns . . . you know." He meant using the Honorblade to practice Windrunning. "Kal has to return before we can do more than that."

To a man, they were absolutely certain he'd return, and showed the world jovial faces—though she knew not everything was perfect with them. Teft, for example, had been hauled before Aladar's magistrates two days ago. Public intoxication on firemoss. Aladar had quietly requested her seal to free him.

No, all was not well with them. But as Navani led them down toward the basement library rooms, a different issue gnawed at her: Brightlady Bethab's implication that Navani was eager for the chance to take over while Dalinar was indisposed.

Navani was not a fool. She knew how it looked to others. She'd married one king. After he died, she'd immediately gone after the next most powerful man in Alethkar. But she *couldn't* have people believing she was the power behind the throne. Not only would it undermine Dalinar, but it would grow tedious for her. She had no problem being a wife or mother to monarchs, but to be one herself—storms, what a dark path that would lead them all down.

She and the bridgemen passed no fewer than six squads of sentries on their way to the library rooms with the murals and—more importantly— the hidden gemstone records. Arriving, she idled in the doorway, impressed by the operation that Jasnah had organized down here since Navani had been forced to step back from the research.

Each gemstone had been removed from its individual drawer, catalogued, and numbered. While one group listened and wrote, others sat at tables, busy translating. The room buzzed with a low hum of discussion and scratching reeds, concentrationspren dotting the air like ripples in the sky.

Jasnah strolled along the tables, looking through pages of translations. As Navani entered, the bridgemen gathered around Renarin, who blushed, looking up from his own papers, which were covered in glyphs and numbers. He *did* look out of place in the room, the only man in uniform rather than in the robes of an ardent or stormwarden.

"Mother," Jasnah said, not looking up from her papers, "we need more translators. Do you have any other scribes versed in classical Alethelan?"

"I've lent you everyone I have. What is Renarin studying over there?"

"Hm? Oh, he thinks there might be a pattern to which stones were stored in which drawers. He's been working on it all day."

"And?"

"Nothing, which is not surprising. He insists he can find a pattern if he looks hard enough." Jasnah lowered her pages and looked at her cousin, who was joking with the men of Bridge Four.

Storms, Navani thought. *He truly looks happy.* Embarrassed as they ribbed him, but happy. She'd worried when he had first "joined" Bridge Four. He was the son of a highprince. Decorum and distance were appropriate when dealing with enlisted soldiers.

But when, before this, had she last heard him *laugh*?

"Maybe," Navani said, "we should encourage him to take a break and go out with the bridgemen for the evening."

"I'd rather keep him here," Jasnah said, flipping through her pages. "His powers need additional study."

Navani would talk to Renarin anyway and encourage him to go out more with the men. There was no arguing with Jasnah, any more than there was arguing with a boulder. You just stepped to the side and went around.

"The translation goes well," Navani asked, "other than the bottleneck on numbers of scribes?"

"We're lucky," Jasnah said, "that the gemstones were recorded so late in the life of the Radiants. They spoke a language we can translate. If it had been the Dawnchant . . ."

"That's close to being cracked."

Jasnah frowned at that. Navani had thought the prospect of translating the Dawnchant—and writings lost to the shadowdays—would have excited her. Instead, it seemed to trouble her.

"Have you found anything more about the tower's fabrials in these gemstone records?" Navani asked.

"I'll be certain to prepare a report for you, Mother, with details of each and every fabrial mentioned. So far, those references are few. Most are personal histories."

"Damnation."

"Mother!" Jasnah said, lowering her pages.

"What? I wouldn't have thought you would object to a few strong words now and—"

"It's not the language, but the dismissal," Jasnah said. "Histories."

Oh, right.

"History is the key to human understanding."

Here we go.

"We must learn from the past and apply that knowledge to our modern experience."

Lectured by my own daughter again.

"The best indication of what human beings will do is not what they think, but what the record says similar groups have done in the past."

"Of course, Brightness."

Jasnah gave her a dry look, then set her papers aside. "I'm sorry, Mother. I've been dealing with a lot of lesser ardents today. My didactic side might have inflated."

"You have a didactic side? Dear, you *hate* teaching."

"Which explains my mood, I should think. I—"

A young scribe called for her from the other side of the room. Jasnah sighed, then went to answer the question.

Jasnah preferred to work alone, which was odd, considering how good she was at getting people to do what she wanted. Navani liked groups— but of course, Navani wasn't a scholar. Oh, she knew how to *pretend*. But all she really did was nudge here and there, perhaps provide an idea. Others did all the real engineering.

She poked through the papers Jasnah had set aside. Perhaps her daughter had missed something in the translations. To her mind, the only scholarship of importance was stuffy, dusty writings of old philosophers. When it came to fabrials, Jasnah barely knew her pairings from her warnings. . . .

What was this?

The glyphs were scrawled in white on the highprince's wall, the paper read. *We quickly ascertained the implement of writing to be a stone pried free near the window. This first sign was the roughest of them, the glyphs malformed. The reason for this later became apparent, as Prince Renarin was not versed in writing glyphs, save the numbers.*

The other pages were similar, talking about the strange numbers found around Dalinar's palace in the days leading up to the Everstorm. They'd been made by Renarin, whose spren had given him warning that the enemy was preparing an assault. The poor boy, uncertain of his bond and frightened to speak out, had instead written the numbers where Dalinar would see them.

It was a little odd, but in the face of everything else, it didn't really register. And . . . well, it *was* Renarin. Why had Jasnah collected all of these?

I have a description for you, finally, Jasnah, another said. *We've convinced the Radiant that Lift found in Yeddaw to visit Azimir. Though she has not yet arrived, you can find sketches of her spren companion here. It looks like the shimmer you see on a wall when you shine light through a crystal.*

Troubled, Navani set the sheets down before Jasnah could return. She got a copy of the translated portions from the gemstones—several young scribes were assigned to making these available—then slipped out to go check on Dalinar.

105

SPIRIT, MIND, AND BODY

SIX YEARS AGO

Only the very most important people were allowed to watch Gavilar's holy interment.

Dalinar stood at the front of the small crowd, gathered in the royal catacombs of Kholinar, beneath the stone sight of kings. Fires burned at the sides of the room, a primal light, traditional. Distinctly more alive than the light of spheres, it reminded him of the Rift—but for once, that pain was overpowered by something new. A fresh wound.

The sight of his brother, lying dead on the slab.

"Spirit, mind, and body," the wizened ardent said, her voice echoing in the stone catacomb. "Death is the separation of the three. The body remains in our realm, to be reused. The spirit rejoins the pool of divine essence that gave it birth. And the mind . . . the mind goes to the Tranquiline Halls to find its reward."

Dalinar's nails bit his skin as he clenched his hands into fists—tight, to keep him from trembling.

"Gavilar the Majestic," the ardent continued, "first king of Alethkar in the new Kholin Dynasty, thirty-second highprince of the Kholin princedom, heir of the Sunmaker and blessed of the Almighty. His accomplishments will be lauded by all, and his dominion extends to the hereafter. Already he leads men again on the battlefield, serving the Almighty in the true war against the Voidbringers."

The ardent thrust a bony hand toward the small crowd. "Our king's war has moved to the Tranquiline Halls. The end of our war for Roshar did not end our duty to the Almighty! Think upon your Callings, men and women of Alethkar. Think of how you might learn here, and be of use in the next world."

Jevena would use any available opportunity to preach. Dalinar clenched his hands tighter, angry at her—angry at the *Almighty*. Dalinar should not have lived to see his brother die. This was *not* the way it should have gone.

He felt eyes on his back. Collected highprinces and wives, important ardents, Navani, Jasnah, Elhokar, Aesudan, Dalinar's sons. Nearby, Highprince Sebarial glanced at Dalinar, eyebrows raised. He seemed to be expecting something.

I'm not drunk, you idiot, Dalinar thought. *I'm not going to make a scene to amuse you.*

Things had been going better lately. Dalinar had started controlling his vices; he'd confined his drinking to monthly trips away from Kholinar, visiting outer cities. He said the trips were to let Elhokar practice ruling without Dalinar looking over his shoulder, as Gavilar had been spending more and more time abroad. But during those trips, Dalinar drank himself to oblivion, letting himself escape the sounds of children crying for a few precious days.

Then, when he returned to Kholinar, he controlled his drinking. And he'd never again yelled at his sons, as he had at poor Renarin during that day on the way back from the Shattered Plains. Adolin and Renarin were the only pure remnant of Evi.

If you control your drinking when back in Kholinar, a part of him challenged, *what happened at the feast? Where were you when Gavilar was fighting for his life?*

"We must use King Gavilar as a model for our own lives," the ardent was saying. "We must remember that our lives are not our own. This world is but the skirmish to prepare us for the true war."

"And after that?" Dalinar asked, looking up from Gavilar's corpse.

The ardent squinted, adjusting her spectacles. "Highprince Dalinar?"

"After that, what?" Dalinar said. "After we win back the Tranquiline Halls? What then? No more war?"

Is that when we finally get to rest?

"You needn't worry, Blackthorn," Jevena said. "Once that war is won, the Almighty will certainly provide for you another conquest." She smiled comfortingly, then moved on to the ritual sayings. A series of keteks, some traditional, others composed by female family members for the event. Ardents burned the poems as prayers in braziers.

Dalinar looked back down at his brother's corpse, which stared upward, lifeless blue marbles replacing his eyes.

Brother, he'd said, *follow the Codes tonight. There is something strange upon the winds.*

Dalinar needed something to drink, storm it.

"You, always about dreams. My soul weeps. Farewell, weeping soul. My dreams . . . about, always, You."

The poem slapped him harder than the others. He sought out Navani, and knew instantly that the ketek had been hers. Gazing straight ahead, she stood with one hand on Elhokar's—*King Elhokar's*—shoulder. So beautiful. Next to her, Jasnah stood with arms wrapped around herself, eyes red. Navani reached toward her, but Jasnah pulled away from the others and stalked off toward the palace proper.

Dalinar wished he could do the same, but instead drew himself to attention. It was over. He'd never have a chance to live up to Gavilar's expectations. Dalinar would live the rest of his life as a failure to this man whom he had loved so dearly.

The hall grew still, quiet save for the crinkling sound of paper burning in the fires. The Soulcaster stood up, and old Jevena stepped hastily backward. She wasn't comfortable with what was coming next. None of them were, judging by the shuffling feet, the coughs into hands.

The Soulcaster might have been male, might have been female. Hard to say, with that hood up over their face. The skin beneath was colored like granite, cracked and chipped, and seemed to *glow* from within. The Soulcaster regarded the corpse, head cocked, as if surprised to find a body here. They ran their fingers along Gavilar's jaw, then brushed the hair off his forehead.

"The only part of you that is true," the Soulcaster whispered, tapping a stone that had replaced one of the king's eyes. Then, light emerged as the Soulcaster drew their hand from their pocket, revealing a set of gemstones bound into a fabrial.

Dalinar didn't look away, despite how the light made his eyes water. He wished . . . he wished he'd taken a drink or two before coming. Was he really supposed to watch something like this while sober?

The Soulcaster touched Gavilar on the forehead, and the transformation happened instantly. One moment Gavilar was there. The next he had become a statue.

The Soulcaster slipped a glove onto their hand while other ardents hurried to remove the wires that had held Gavilar's body in position. They used levers to tip him carefully forward until he was standing, holding a sword with point toward the ground, his other hand outstretched. He stared toward eternity, crown on his head, the curls of his beard and hair preserved delicately in the stone. A powerful pose; the mortuary sculptors had done a fantastic job.

The ardents pushed him back into an alcove, where he joined the lines of other monarchs—most of them highprinces of the Kholin princedom.

He would be forever frozen here, the image of a perfect ruler in his prime. Nobody would think of him as he'd been that terrible night, broken from his fall, his grand dreams cut short by treason.

"I'll have vengeance, Mother," Elhokar whispered. "I'll *have* it!" The young king spun toward the gathered lighteyes, standing before his father's outstretched stone hand. "You've each come to me privately to give support. Well, I demand you swear it in public! Today, we make a pact to hunt those who did this. Today, Alethkar goes to *war*!"

He was greeted by stunned silence.

"I swear it," Torol Sadeas said. "I swear to bring vengeance to the traitorous parshmen, Your Majesty. You can depend upon my sword."

Good, Dalinar thought, as others spoke up. This would hold them together. Even in death, Gavilar provided an excuse for unity.

Unable to stand that stone visage any longer, Dalinar left, stomping into the corridor toward the palace proper. Other voices echoed after him as highprinces swore.

If Elhokar was going to chase those Parshendi back toward the plains, he'd expect the Blackthorn's help. But . . . Dalinar hadn't been that man for years. He patted his pocket, looking for his flask. Damnation. He pretended he was better these days, kept telling himself he was in the process of finding a way out of this mess. Of returning to the man he'd once been.

But that man had been a monster. Frightening, that nobody had blamed him for the things he'd done. Nobody but Evi, who had seen what the killing would do to him. He closed his eyes, hearing her tears.

"Father?" a voice said from behind.

Dalinar forced himself to stand upright, turning as Adolin scrambled up to him.

"Are you well, Father?"

"Yes," Dalinar said. "I just . . . need to be alone."

Adolin nodded. Almighty above, the boy had turned out well, through little effort of Dalinar's. Adolin was earnest, likable, and a master of the sword. He was truly capable in modern Alethi society, where how you moved among groups was even more important than strength of arm. Dalinar had always felt like a tree stump in those kinds of settings. Too big. Too stupid.

"Go back," Dalinar said. "Swear for our house on this Vengeance Pact."

Adolin nodded, and Dalinar continued onward, fleeing those fires below. Gavilar's stare, judging him. The cries of people dying in the Rift.

By the time he reached the steps, he was practically running. He climbed one level, then another. Sweating, frantic, he raced through ornate hallways

past carved walls, sedate woods, and accusatory mirrors. He reached his chambers and scrabbled in his pockets for the keys. He'd locked the place tight; no more would Gavilar sneak in to take his bottles. Bliss waited inside.

No. Not bliss. Oblivion. Good enough.

His hands wouldn't stop shaking. He couldn't— It—

Follow the Codes tonight.

Dalinar's hands trembled, and he dropped the keys.

There is something strange upon the winds.

Screams for mercy.

Get out of my head! All of you, get out!

In the distance, a voice . . .

"You must find the most important words a man can say."

Which key was it? He got one into the lock, but it wouldn't turn. He couldn't see. He blinked, feeling dizzy.

"Those words came to me from one who claimed to have seen the future," the voice said, echoing in the hallway. Feminine, familiar. "'How is this possible?' I asked in return. 'Have you been touched by the void?'

"The reply was laughter. 'No, sweet king. The past is the future, and as each man has lived, so must you.'

"'So I can but repeat what has been done before?'

"'In some things, yes. You will love. You will hurt. You will dream. And you will die. Each man's past is your future.'

"'Then what is the point?' I asked. 'If all has been seen and done?'

"'The question,' she replied, 'is not whether you will love, hurt, dream, and die. It is *what* you will love, *why* you will hurt, *when* you will dream, and *how* you will die. This is your choice. You cannot pick the destination, only the path.'"

Dalinar dropped the keys again, sobbing. There was no escape. He would fall again. Wine would consume him like a fire consumed a corpse. Leaving only ash.

There was no way out.

"This started my journey," the voice said. "And this begins my writings. I cannot call this book a story, for it fails at its most fundamental to *be* a story. It is not one narrative, but many. And though it has a beginning, here on this page, my quest can never truly end.

"I wasn't seeking answers. I felt that I had those already. Plenty, in multitude, from a thousand different sources. I wasn't seeking 'myself.' This is a platitude that people have ascribed to me, and I find the phrase lacks meaning.

"In truth, by leaving, I was seeking only one thing.

"A journey."

For years, it seemed that Dalinar had been seeing everything around him through a haze. But those words . . . something about them . . .

Could words give off light?

He turned from his door and walked down the corridor, searching for the source of the voice. Inside the royal reading room, he found Jasnah with a huge tome set before her at a standing table. She read to herself, turning to the next page, scowling.

"What is that book?" Dalinar asked.

Jasnah started. She wiped her eyes, smearing the makeup, leaving her eyes . . . clean, but raw. Holes in a mask.

"This is where my father got that quote," she said. "The one he . . ."

The one he wrote as he died.

Only a few knew of that.

"What book is it?"

"An old text," Jasnah said. "Ancient, once well regarded. It's associated with the Lost Radiants, so nobody references it anymore. There has to be some secret here, a puzzle behind my father's last words. A cipher? But what?"

Dalinar settled down into one of the seats. He felt as if he had no strength. "Will you read it to me?"

Jasnah met his eyes, chewing her lip as she'd always done as a child. Then she read in a clear, strong voice, starting over from the first page, which he'd just heard. He had expected her to stop after a chapter or two, but she didn't, and he didn't want her to.

Dalinar listened, rapt. People came to check on them; some brought Jasnah water to drink. For once, he didn't ask them for anything. All he wanted was to listen.

He understood the words, but at the same time he seemed to be missing what the book said. It was a sequence of vignettes about a king who left his palace to go on a pilgrimage. Dalinar couldn't define, even to himself, what he found so striking about the tales. Was it their optimism? Was it the talk of paths and choices?

It was so unpretentious. So different from the boasts of society or the battlefield. Just a series of stories, their morals ambiguous. It took almost eight hours to finish, but Jasnah never gave any indication she wanted to stop. When she read the last word, Dalinar found himself weeping again. Jasnah dabbed at her own eyes. She had always been so much stronger than he was, but here they shared an understanding. This was their send-off to Gavilar's soul. This was their farewell.

Leaving the book on the lectern, Jasnah walked over to Dalinar as he stood up. They embraced, saying nothing. After a few moments, she left.

He went to the book, touching it, feeling the lines of the writing stamped into its cover. He didn't know how long he'd been standing there when Adolin peeked in. "Father? We're planning to send expeditionary forces to the Shattered Plains. Your input would be appreciated."

"I must," Dalinar whispered, "go on a journey."

"Yeah," Adolin said. "It's a long way. Might get some hunts in while we're on our way, if there's time. Elhokar wants these barbarians wiped out quickly. We could be gone and back in a year."

Paths. Dalinar could not choose his end.

But perhaps his *path . . .*

The Old Magic can change a person, Evi had said. *Make something great of them.*

Dalinar stood up taller. He turned and stepped toward Adolin, seizing him by the shoulder. "I've been a poor father these last few years," Dalinar said.

"Nonsense," Adolin said. "You—"

"I've been a poor father," Dalinar repeated, raising his finger. "To you and your brother both. You should know how proud I am of you."

Adolin beamed, glowing like a sphere right after a storm. Gloryspren sprang up around him.

"We will go to war together," Dalinar said. "Like we did when you were young. I will show you what it is to be a man of honor. But first, I need to take an advance force—without you, I'm afraid—and secure the Shattered Plains."

"We talked about that," Adolin said, eager. "Like your elites, from before. Fast, quick! You'll march—"

"Sail," Dalinar said.

"Sail?"

"The rivers should be flowing," Dalinar said. "I'll march south, then take a ship to Dumadari. From there, I'll sail to the Ocean of Origins and make landfall at New Natanan. I'll move in toward the Shattered Plains with my force and secure the region, preparing for the rest of you to arrive."

"That would be a sound idea, I guess," Adolin said.

It *was* sound. Sound enough that when one of Dalinar's ships was delayed—and Dalinar himself remained in port, sending most of his force on without him—nobody would think it strange. Dalinar did get himself into trouble.

He would swear his men and sailors to secrecy, and travel a few months out of his way before continuing on to the Shattered Plains.

Evi had said the Old Magic could transform a man. It was about time he started trusting her.

106

LAW IS LIGHT

I find Ba-Ado-Mishram to be the most interesting of the Unmade. She is said to have been keen of mind, a highprincess among the enemy forces, their commander during some of the Desolations. I do not know how this relates to the ancient god of the enemy, named Odium.

—From Hessi's *Mythica*, page 224

S zeth of Shinovar flew with the Skybreakers for three days, southward.

They stopped several times to recover hidden stockpiles in mountain peaks or remote valleys. To find doorways, they often had to hack through five inches of crem. That amount of buildup had probably taken centuries to accumulate, yet Nin spoke of the places as if he'd just left. At one, he was surprised to find the food long since decayed—though fortunately, the gemstone stockpile there had been hidden in a place where it remained exposed to the storms.

In these visits, Szeth finally began to grasp how *ancient* this creature was.

On the fourth day, they reached Marat. Szeth had been to the kingdom before; he had visited most of Roshar during the years of his exile. Historically, Marat wasn't truly a nation—but neither was it a place of nomads, like the backwaters of Hexi and Tu Fallia. Instead, Marat was a group of loosely connected cities, tribally run, with a highprince at their head—though in the local dialect, he was called "elder brother."

The country made for a convenient waystop between the Vorin kingdoms of the east and the Makabaki ones of the center west. Szeth knew that Marat was rich in culture, full of people as proud as you'd find in any nation—but of almost no value on the political scale.

Which made it curious that Nin chose to end their flight here. They landed on a plain full of strange brown grass that reminded Szeth of wheat, save for the fact that this pulled down into burrows, leaving visible only the small bob of grain on the top. This was casually eaten by wild beasts that were wide and flat, like walking discs, with claws only on the underside to shove the grain into their mouths.

The disclike animals would probably migrate eastward, their droppings containing seeds that—stuck to the ground—would survive storms to grow into first-stage polyps. Those would later blow to the west and become second-stage grain. All life worked in concert, he'd been taught in his youth. Everything but men, who refused their place. Who destroyed instead of added.

Nin spoke briefly with Ki and the other masters, who took to the air again. The others joined them—all but Szeth and Nin himself—and streaked toward a town in the distance. Before Szeth could follow, Nin took him by the arm and shook his head. Together, the two of them flew to a smaller town on a hill near the coast.

Szeth knew the effects of war when he saw them. Broken doors, ruins of a short, breached wall. The destruction looked recent, though any bodies had been cleaned out and the blood had been washed away by highstorms. They landed before a large stone building with a peaked roof. Mighty doors of Soulcast bronze lay broken off in the rubble. Szeth would be surprised if somebody didn't return to claim those for their metal. Not every army had access to Soulcasters.

Aw, the sword said from his back. *We missed the fun?*

"That tyrant in Tukar," Szeth said, looking through the silent town. "He decided to end his war against Emul, and expand eastward?"

"No," Nin said. "This is a different danger." He pointed toward the building with the broken doors. "Can you read that writing above the doorway, Szeth-son-Neturo?"

"It's in the local language. I don't know the script, aboshi." The divine honorific was his best guess of how to address one of the Heralds, though among his people it had been reserved for the great spren of the mountains.

"It says 'justice,'" Nin said. "This was a courthouse."

Szeth followed the Herald up the steps and into the cavernous main room of the ruined courthouse. In here, sheltered from the storm, they found blood on the floor. No bodies, but plenty of discarded weapons, helms, and—disturbingly—the meager possessions of civilians. The people had likely taken refuge inside here during the battle, a last grasp at safety.

"The ones you call parshmen name themselves the singers," Nin said. "They took this town and pressed the survivors into labor at some docks farther along the coast. Was what happened here justice, Szeth-son-Neturo?"

"How could it be?" He shivered. The dark reaches of the room seemed to be filled with haunted whispers. He drew closer to the Herald for safety. "Ordinary people, living ordinary lives, suddenly attacked and murdered?"

"A poor argument. What if the lord of this city had stopped paying his taxes, then forced his people to defend the city when higher authorities arrived and attacked? Is not a prince justified in maintaining order in his lands? Sometimes, it is just to kill ordinary people."

"But that did not happen here," Szeth said. "You said this was caused by an invading army."

"Yes," Nin said softly. "This is the fault of invaders. That is true." He continued walking through the hollow room, Szeth staying close behind him. "You are in a unique position, Szeth-son-Neturo. You will be the first to swear the oaths of a Skybreaker in a new world, a world where I have failed."

They found steps near the back wall. Szeth got out a sphere for light, as Nin did not appear to be so inclined. That drove the whispers back.

"I visited Ishar," Nin continued. "You call him Ishu-son-God. He has always been the most wise of us. I did not . . . want to believe . . . what had happened."

Szeth nodded. He had seen that. After the first Everstorm, Nin had insisted that the Voidbringers hadn't returned. He had given excuse after excuse, until eventually he'd been forced to admit what he was seeing.

"I worked for thousands of years to prevent another Desolation," Nin continued. "Ishar warned me of the danger. Now that Honor is dead, other Radiants might upset the balance of the Oathpact. Might undermine certain . . . measures we took, and give an opening to the enemy."

He stopped at the top of the steps and looked down at his hand, where a glistening Shardblade appeared. One of the two missing Honorblades. Szeth's people had care of eight. Once, long ago, it had been nine. Then this one had vanished.

He'd seen depictions of it, strikingly straight and unornamented for a Shardblade, yet still elegant. Two slits ran the length of the weapon, gaps that could never exist in an ordinary sword, as they would weaken it.

They walked along a loft at the top of the courtroom. Records storage, judging by the scattered ledgers on the floor.

You should draw me, the sword said.

"And do what, sword-nimi?" Szeth whispered.

Fight him. I think he might be evil.

"He is one of the Heralds—one of the *least*-evil things in the world."

Huh. Doesn't bode well for your world, then. Anyway, I'm better than that sword he has. I can show you.

Picking his way past the legal debris, Szeth joined Nin beside the loft's window. In the distance, farther along the coast, a large bay glistened with blue water. Many masts of ships gathered there, figures buzzing around them.

"I have failed," Nin repeated. "And now, for the people, justice must be done. A very difficult justice, Szeth-son-Neturo. Even for my Skybreakers."

"We will endeavor to be as passionless and logical as you, aboshi."

Nin laughed. It didn't seem to carry the mirth that it should have. "Me? No, Szeth-son-Neturo. I am hardly passionless. This is the problem." He paused, staring out the window at the distant ships. "I am . . . different from how I once was. Worse, perhaps? Despite all that, a part of me wishes to be merciful."

"And is . . . mercy such a bad thing, aboshi?"

"Not bad; merely chaotic. If you look through the records in this hall, you will find the same story told again and again. Leniency and mercy. Men set free despite crimes, because they were good fathers, or well-liked in the community, or in the favor of someone important.

"Some of those who are set free change their lives and go on to produce for society. Others recidivate and create great tragedies. The thing is, Szeth-son-Neturo, we humans are *terrible* at spotting which will be which. The *purpose* of the law is so we do not have to choose. So our native sentimentality will not harm us."

He looked down again at his sword.

"You," he said to Szeth, "must choose a Third Ideal. Most Skybreakers choose to swear themselves to the law—and follow with exactness the laws of whatever lands they visit. That is a good option, but not the only one. Think wisely, and choose."

"Yes, aboshi," Szeth said.

"There are things you must see, and things you must know, before you can speak. The others must *interpret* what they have sworn before, and I hope they will see the truth. *You* will be the first of a new order of Skybreakers." He looked back out the window. "The singers allowed the people of this town to return here to burn their dead. A kinder gesture than most conquerors would allow."

"Aboshi . . . may I ask you a question?"

"Law is light, and darkness does not serve it. Ask, and I will answer."

"I know you are great, ancient, and wise," Szeth said. "But . . . to my lesser eyes, you do not seem to obey your own precepts. You hunted Surgebinders, as you said."

"I obtained legal permission for the executions I performed."

"Yes," Szeth said, "but you ignored many lawbreakers to pursue these few. You had motives beyond the law, aboshi. You were not impartial. You brutally enforced specific laws to achieve your ends."

"This is true."

"So is this just your own . . . sentimentality?"

"In part. Though I have certain leniencies. The others have told you of the Fifth Ideal?"

"The Ideal where the Skybreaker *becomes* the law?"

Nin held out his empty left hand. A *Shardblade* appeared there, different and distinct from the Honorblade he carried in the other hand. "I am not only a Herald, but a Skybreaker of the Fifth Ideal. Though I was originally skeptical of the Radiants, I believe I am the only one who eventually joined his own order.

"And now, Szeth-son-Neturo, I must tell you of the decision we Heralds made, long ago. On the day that would become known as Aharietiam. The day we sacrificed one of our own to end the cycle of pain and death . . ."

107

THE FIRST STEP

There is very little information about Ba-Ado-Mishram in more modern times. I can only assume she, unlike many of them, returned to Damnation or was destroyed during Aharietiam.

—From Hessi's *Mythica*, page 226

Dalinar found a washbasin ready for him in the morning. Navani meticulously kept it filled, just as she cleaned up the bottles and allowed the servants to bring him more. She trusted him better than he trusted himself.

Stretching in his bed, Dalinar woke feeling far too . . . whole, considering the drinking he'd been doing. Indirect sunlight illuminated the room from the window. Normally they kept the shutters in this room closed to ward off the cold mountain air. Navani must have opened them after rising.

Dalinar splashed his face with water from the basin, then caught a hint of his own scent. *Right.* He looked into one of the connecting rooms, which they'd appropriated for a washroom, as it had a back entrance the servants could use. Sure enough, Navani had ordered the tub filled for him. The water was cold, but he'd known his share of cold baths. It would keep him from lingering.

A short time later, he took a razor to his face, peering at himself in a bedroom mirror. Gavilar had taught him to shave. Their father had been too busy getting himself cut apart in foolish duels of honor, including the one where he'd taken a blow to the head. He'd never been right after that.

Beards were unfashionable in Alethkar these days, but that wasn't why Dalinar shaved. He liked the ritual. The chance to prepare, to cut away the nightly chaff and reveal the real person underneath—furrows, scars, and harsh features included.

A clean uniform and underclothes waited for him on a bench. He dressed, then checked the uniform in the mirror, pulling down on the bottom of the coat to tighten any folds.

That memory of Gavilar's funeral . . . so vivid. He'd forgotten parts. Had that been the Nightwatcher, or the natural course of memories? The more he recovered of what he had lost, the more he realized that the memories of men were flawed. He'd mention an event now fresh to his mind, and others who had lived it would argue over details, as each recalled it differently. Most, Navani included, seemed to remember him as more noble than he deserved. Yet he didn't ascribe any magic to this. It was simply the way of human beings, subtly changing the past in their minds to match their current beliefs.

But then . . . that vision with Nohadon. Where had that come from? Just a common dream?

Hesitant, he reached out to the Stormfather, who rumbled distantly. "Still there, I see," Dalinar said, relieved.

Where would I go?

"I hurt you," Dalinar said. "When I activated the Oathgate. I was afraid you would leave me."

This is the lot I have chosen. It is you or oblivion.

"I'm sorry, regardless, for what I did. Were you . . . involved in that dream I had? The one with Nohadon?"

I know of no such dream.

"It was vivid," Dalinar said. "More surreal than one of the visions, true, but captivating."

What was the most important step a man could take? The first, obviously. But what did it mean?

He still bore the weight of what he had done at the Rift. This recovery—this stepping away from the week spent drinking—wasn't a redemption. What would he do if he felt the Thrill again? What would happen the next time the weeping in his mind became too difficult to bear?

Dalinar didn't know. He felt better today. Functional. For now, he would let that be enough. He picked a piece of lint off his collar, then belted on a side sword and stepped out of the bedroom, walking through his study and into the larger room with the hearth.

"Taravangian?" he said, surprised to find the elderly king seated there. "Wasn't there to be a meeting of the monarchs today?" He vaguely remembered Navani telling him of it early that morning.

"They said I wasn't needed."

"Nonsense! We're all needed at the meetings." Dalinar paused. "I've missed several, haven't I? Well, regardless, what are they talking about today?"

"Tactics."

Dalinar felt his face go red. "The deployment of troops and the defense of Jah Keved, your kingdom?"

"I think they believe that I will give up the throne of Jah Keved, once a suitable local man has been found." He smiled. "Do not be so outraged on my behalf, my friend. They didn't forbid me; they simply noted I wasn't needed. I wanted some time to think, so I came here."

"Still. Let's go up, shall we?"

Taravangian nodded, standing. He wobbled on unsteady legs and Dalinar hurried over to help him. Stabilized, Taravangian patted Dalinar's hand. "Thank you. You know, I've always felt old. But lately, it seems my body is determined to give me persistent reminders."

"Let me summon a palanquin to carry you."

"No, please. If I give up walking, I fear my deterioration will increase. I've seen similar things happen to people in my hospitals." But he held Dalinar's arm as they walked toward the doorway. Outside, Dalinar collected some guards of his own along with Taravangian's large Thaylen bodyguard. They started toward the lifts.

"Do you know," Dalinar said, "if there's word . . ."

"From Kholinar?" Taravangian asked.

Dalinar nodded. He vaguely remembered updates from Navani. No news of Adolin, Elhokar, or the Radiants. But had he been of sound enough mind to listen?

"I'm sorry, Dalinar," Taravangian said. "So far as I know, we haven't had a message from them. But we must keep hope, of course! They might have lost their spanreed, or gotten trapped in the city."

I . . . may have felt something, the Stormfather said. *During a recent highstorm, it felt like Stormblessed was there with me. I do not know what it means, for I cannot see him—or the others—anywhere. I presumed them dead, but now . . . now I find myself believing. Why?*

"You have hope," Dalinar whispered, smiling.

"Dalinar?" Taravangian asked.

"Just whispering to myself, Your Majesty."

"If I might say . . . You seem stronger today. You've decided something?"

"More, I've *remembered* something."

"Is it something you can share with a worried old man?"

"Not yet. I'll try to explain once I have it figured out myself."

After an extended trip up the lifts, Dalinar led Taravangian into a quiet, windowless chamber on the penultimate floor of the tower. They'd dubbed it the Gallery of Maps, after a similar location in the warcamps.

Aladar led the meeting, standing beside a table that was covered by a large map of Alethkar and Jah Keved. The dark-skinned Alethi man wore his war uniform—the mix of a traditional takama skirt and modern jacket that had been catching on among his officers. His bodyguard, Mintez, stood behind him in full Shardplate—Aladar preferred not to use the Shards personally. He was a general, not a warrior. He nodded to Dalinar and Taravangian when they entered.

Ialai sat nearby, and studied Dalinar, saying nothing. He'd almost have welcomed a wisecrack; in the old days, she'd been quick to joke with him. Her silence now didn't mean she was being respectful. It meant she was saving her barbs to whisper where he couldn't hear.

Highprince Ruthar—thick-armed and wearing a full beard—sat with Ialai. He'd opposed Dalinar from the start. The other Alethi highprince who had come today was Hatham, a long-necked man with light orange eyes. He wore a red and gold uniform of a type that Dalinar hadn't seen before, with a short jacket that buttoned only at the top. Silly-looking, but what did Dalinar know of fashion? The man was extremely polite, and he ran a tight army.

Queen Fen had brought the Thaylen high admiral, a scrawny old man with mustaches that drooped almost to the table. He wore a short sailor's saber and sash, and looked like exactly the type who would complain about being stuck on the land for too long. She'd also brought her son—the one Dalinar had dueled—who saluted Dalinar sharply. Dalinar saluted back. That boy would make an excellent officer, if he could learn to keep his temper.

The Azish emperor wasn't there, nor was their little Edgedancer. Instead, Azir had sent a collection of scholars. Azish "generals" tended to be of the armchair type, military historians and theorists who spent their days in books. Dalinar was certain they had men with practical knowledge in their military, but those rarely ended up promoted. So long as you failed certain tests, you could remain in the field and command.

Dalinar had met the two Veden highprinces during his trip to their city. The brothers were tall, prim men with short black hair and uniforms much like those of the Alethi. Taravangian had appointed them after their predecessors had been poisoned, following the civil war. Jah Keved obviously still had many problems.

"Dalinar?" Aladar said. He stood up straighter, then saluted. "Brightlord, you're looking better."

Storms. How much did the rest of them know?

"I've spent some time in meditation," Dalinar said. "I see you've been busy. Tell me about the defensive array."

"Well," Aladar said, "we—"

"That's it?" Queen Fen interrupted. "What in Damnation was wrong with you? You ran all around Vedenar like a wildman, then locked yourself in your room for a week!"

"I was excommunicated from the Vorin church soon after hearing of Kholinar's fall. I took it poorly. Did you expect me to react by throwing a feast?"

"I expected you to lead us, not *sulk*."

I deserved that. "You are right. You can't have a commander who refuses to command. I'm sorry."

The Azish whispered among themselves, looking surprised at the bluntness of the exchange. But Fen settled back and Aladar nodded. Dalinar's mistakes had needed to be aired.

Aladar began explaining their battle preparations. The Azish generals— all wearing robes and Western hats—crowded around, offering commentary through translators. Dalinar used a little Stormlight and touched one on the arm, to gain access to their language for a short time. He found their advice surprisingly astute, considering that they were basically a committee of scribes.

They'd moved ten battalions of Alethi troops through the Oathgates, along with five battalions of Azish. That put fifteen thousand men on the ground in Jah Keved, including some of their most loyal Kholin and Aladar forces.

That seriously cut into his troop numbers. Storms, they'd lost so many at Narak—the companies that Dalinar had remaining at Urithiru were mostly recruits or men from other princedoms who had asked to join his military. Sebarial, for example, had cut back to maintaining only a single division, giving Dalinar the rest to wear Kholin colors.

Dalinar had interrupted a discussion of how to fortify the Jah Keved border. He offered some insights, but mostly listened as they explained their plans: stockpiles here, garrisons there. They hoped the Windrunners would be able to scout for them.

Dalinar nodded, but found that something bothered him about this battle plan. A problem he couldn't define. They'd done well; their lines of supply had been drawn realistically and their scout posts were spaced for excellent coverage.

What, then, was wrong?

The door opened, revealing Navani, who froze when she saw Dalinar, then melted into a relieved smile. He nodded to her, as one of the Veden highprinces explained why they shouldn't abandon the backwater strip of land running east of the Horneater Peaks. Aladar had been ready to cede it and use the Peaks as a barrier.

"It's not only about the opportunity to levy troops from His Majesty's Horneater subjects, Brightlord," the highprince—Nan Urian—explained in Alethi. "These lands are lush and well appointed, buffered from storms by the very Alethi highlands you've been speaking of. We've always fought desperately for them against invasions, because they will succor those who seize them—and provide staging areas for assaults on the rest of Jah Keved!"

Dalinar grunted. Navani stepped over to where most of them stood around the table map, so he reached out and put his arm around her waist. "He's right, Aladar. I spent a long time skirmishing on that very border. That area is more important strategically than it first appears."

"Holding it is going to be tough," Aladar said. "We'll get mired in an extended battle for that ground."

"Which is what we want, isn't it?" the Veden highprince said. "The longer we stall the invasion, the more time it will give my Veden brethren to recover."

"Yes," Dalinar said. "Yes . . ." It *was* easy to get mired in battles along that vast Veden front. How many years had he spent fighting false bandits there? "Let's take a break. I want to consider this."

The others seemed to welcome the opportunity. Many stepped into the larger chamber outside, where attendants with spanreeds waited to relay information. Navani stayed beside Dalinar as he surveyed the map. "It's good to see you up," she whispered.

"You're more patient than I deserve. You should have dumped me out of bed and poured the wine on my head."

"I had a feeling you'd push through."

"I have for now," he said. "In the past, a few days—or even weeks—of sobriety didn't mean much."

"You're not the man you were back then."

Oh, Navani. I never grew beyond that man; I just hid him away. He couldn't explain that to her yet. Instead, he whispered thanks into her ear, and rested his hand on hers. How could he *ever* have been frustrated at her advances?

For now, he turned his attention to the maps, and lost himself in them: the fortresses, the storm bunkers, the cities, the drawn-in supply lines.

What's wrong? Dalinar thought. *What am I not seeing?*

Ten Silver Kingdoms. Ten Oathgates. The keys to this war. Even if the enemy can't use them, they can hinder us by seizing them.

One in Alethkar, which they already have. One in Natanatan—the Shat-

tered Plains—which we have. One in Vedenar, one in Azimir, one in Thaylen City. All three ours. But one in Rall Elorim and one in Kurth, both the enemy's by now. One in Shinovar, belonging to neither side.

That left the one in Panatham in Babatharnam—which the combined Iriali and Riran armies might have captured already—and one in Akinah, which Jasnah was confident had been destroyed long ago.

Jah Keved made the most sense for the enemy to attack, didn't it? Only . . . once you engaged yourself in Jah Keved, you were stuck fighting a long war of attrition. You lost mobility, had to dedicate enormous resources to it.

He shook his head, feeling frustrated. He left the map, trailed by Navani, and stepped into the other room for refreshment. At the wine table, he forced himself to pour a warm, spiced orange. Something with no kick.

Jasnah joined the group, delivering a stack of papers to her mother.

"May I see?" Ialai asked.

"No," Jasnah replied; Dalinar hid a smile in his drink.

"What secrets are you keeping?" Ialai asked. "What happened to your uncle's grand talk of unification?"

"I suspect that each monarch in this room," Jasnah said, "would prefer to know that state secrets are allowed to remain their own. This is an alliance, not a wedding."

Queen Fen nodded at that.

"As for these papers," Jasnah continued, "they happen to be a scholarly report which my mother has not yet reviewed. We will release what we discover, once we are certain that our translations are correct and that nothing in these notes might give our enemies an advantage against this city." Jasnah cocked an eyebrow. "Or would you prefer our scholarship be sloppy?"

The Azish seemed mollified by this.

"I just think," Ialai said, "you showing up here with them is a slap in the face for the rest of us."

"Ialai," Jasnah said, "it is good you are here. Sometimes, an intelligent dissenting voice tests and proves a theory. I do wish you'd work harder on the *intelligent* part."

Dalinar downed the rest of his drink and smiled as Ialai settled back in her chair, wisely not escalating a verbal battle against Jasnah. Unfortunately, Ruthar did not have similar sense.

"Don't mind her, Ialai," he said, mustache wet with wine. "The godless have no *concept* of proper decency. Everyone knows that the only reason to abandon belief in the Almighty is so that you can explore vice."

Oh, Ruthar, Dalinar thought. *You can't win this fight. Jasnah has thought about the topic far more than you have. It's a familiar battleground to her—*

Storms, that was it.

"They aren't going to attack Jah Keved!" Dalinar shouted, interrupting Jasnah's rebuttal.

Those in the room turned to him, surprised, Jasnah's mouth half open.

"Dalinar?" Highprince Aladar asked. "We decided that Jah Keved was the most likely—"

"No," Dalinar said. "No, we know the terrain too well! The Alethi and the Vedens have spent *generations* fighting over that land."

"What, then?" Jasnah asked.

Dalinar ran back into the map room. The others flooded in around him. "They went to Marat, right?" Dalinar asked. "They cut through Emul and into Marat, silencing spanreeds nationwide. Why? Why go there?"

"Azir was too well fortified," Aladar said. "From Marat, the Voidbringers can strike at Jah Keved from both the west and the east."

"Through the bottleneck in Triax?" Dalinar asked. "We talk of Jah Keved's weakness, but that's *relative*. They still have a huge standing army, strong fortifications. If the enemy wades into Jah Keved now, while solidifying their own power, it will drain their resources and stall their conquest. That isn't what they want right now, when they still have the upper hand in momentum."

"Where, then?" Nan Urian asked.

"A place that was hit hardest of all by the new storms," Dalinar said, pointing at the map. "A place whose military might was severely undermined by the Everstorm. A place with an Oathgate."

Queen Fen gasped, safehand going to her lips.

"Thaylen City?" Navani asked. "Are you sure?"

"If the enemy takes Thaylen City," Dalinar said, "they can blockade Jah Keved, Kharbranth, and what few lands in Alethkar we still own. They can seize command of the entire Southern Depths and launch naval assaults on Tashikk and Shinovar. They could swarm New Natanan and have a position from which to assault the Shattered Plains. Strategically, Thaylen City is *far* more important than Jah Keved—but at the same time, *far* worse defended."

"But they'd need ships," Aladar said.

"The parshmen took our fleet. . . ." Fen said.

"After that first terrible storm," Dalinar said, "how were there any ships *left* for them to take?"

Fen frowned. "As I think about it, that's remarkable, isn't it? There were dozens remaining, as if the winds left them alone. Because the enemy needed them . . ."

Storms. "I've been thinking too much like an Alethi," Dalinar said. "Boots on stone. But the enemy moved into Marat immediately, a *perfect* position from which to launch at Thaylen City."

"We need to revise our plans!" Fen said.

"Peace, Your Majesty," Aladar said. "We have armies in Thaylen City already. Good Alethi troops. Nobody is better on the ground than Alethi infantry."

"We have three divisions there right now," Dalinar said. "We'll want at least three more."

"Sir," Fen's son said. "Brightlord. That's not enough."

Dalinar glanced at Fen. Her wizened admiral nodded.

"Speak," Dalinar said.

"Sir," the youth said, "we're glad to have your troops on the island. Kelek's breath! If you're going to get into a fight, you *definitely* want the Alethi on your side. But an enemy fleet is a *much* larger problem than you're assuming—one you can't easily fix by moving troops around. If the enemy ships find Thaylen City well defended, they'll just sail on and attack Kharbranth, or Dumadari, or any *number* of defenseless cities along the coast."

Dalinar grunted. He *did* think too much like an Alethi. "What, then?"

"We need our own fleet, obviously," Fen's admiral said. He had a thick accent of mushed syllables, like a mouth full of moss. "But most of our ships were lost to the blustering Everstorm. Half were abroad, caught unaware. My colleagues now dance upon the bottom of the depths."

"And the rest of your fleet was stolen," Dalinar said with a grunt. "What else do we have?"

"His Majesty Taravangian has ships at our port," the Veden highprince said.

All eyes turned toward Taravangian. "Merchant ships only," the old man said. "Vessels that carried my healers. We haven't a true navy, but I did bring twenty ships. I could perhaps provide ten more from Kharbranth."

"The storm took a number of our ships," the Veden highprince said, "but the civil war was more devastating. We lost hundreds of sailors. We have more ships than we have crew for right now."

Fen joined Dalinar beside the map. "We might be able to scrape together a semblance of a navy to intercept the enemy, but the fighting will be on the decks of ships. We'll need troops."

"You'll have them," Dalinar said.

"Alethi who've never seen a rough sea in their lives?" Fen asked, skeptical. She looked to the Azish generals. "Tashikk has a navy, doesn't it? Staffed and supplemented by Azish troops."

The generals conferred in their own language. Finally, one spoke through an interpreter. "The Thirteenth Battalion, Red and Gold, has men who do a rotation on ships and patrol the grand waterway. Getting others here would take much time, but the thirteenth is already stationed in Jah Keved."

"We'll supplement them with some of my best men," Dalinar said. *Storms, we need those Windrunners active.* "Fen, would your admirals present a suggested course for the gathering and deployment of a unified fleet?"

"Sure," the short woman said. She leaned in, speaking under her breath. "I warn you. Many of my sailors follow the Passions. You're going to have to do something about these claims of heresy, Blackthorn. Already there's talk among my people that this is—at long last—the right time for the Thaylens to break free from the Vorin church."

"I won't recant," Dalinar said.

"Even if it causes a wholesale religious collapse in the middle of a war?"

He didn't reply, and she let him withdraw from the table, thinking about other plans. He spoke with the others about various items, thanked Navani—again—for holding everything together. Then eventually, he decided to go back down below and take a few reports from his stewards.

On his way out, he passed Taravangian, who had taken a seat by the wall. The old man looked distracted by something.

"Taravangian?" Dalinar said. "We'll leave troops in Jah Keved too, in case I'm wrong. Don't worry."

The old man looked to Dalinar, then strangely wiped tears from his eyes.

"Are . . . are you in pain?" Dalinar asked.

"Yes. But it is nothing you can fix." He hesitated. "You are a good man, Dalinar Kholin. I did not expect that."

Ashamed by that, Dalinar hurried from the room, followed by his guards. He felt tired, which seemed unfair, considering he'd just spent a week basically sleeping.

Before seeking his stewards, Dalinar stopped on the fourth floor from the bottom. An extended walk from the lifts took him to the outer wall of the tower, where a small series of rooms smelled of incense. People lined the hallways, waiting for glyphwards or to speak with an ardent. More than he'd expected—but then, they didn't have much else to do, did they?

Is that how you think of them already? a part of him asked. *Only here to seek spiritual welfare because they don't have anything better to do?*

Dalinar kept his chin high, resisting the urge to shrink before their stares. He passed several ardents and stepped into a room lit and warmed by braziers, where he asked after Kadash.

He was directed onto a garden balcony, where a small group of ardents was trying to farm. Some placed seed paste while others were trying to get some shalebark starters to take along the wall. An impressive project, and one he didn't remember ordering them to begin.

Kadash was quietly chipping crem off a planter box. Dalinar settled down beside him. The scarred ardent glanced at him and kept working.

"It's very late coming," Dalinar said, "but I wanted to apologize to you for Rathalas."

"I don't think I'm the one you need to apologize to," Kadash said. "Those who *could* bear an apology are now in the Tranquiline Halls."

"Still, I made you part of something terrible."

"I chose to be in your army," Kadash said. "I've found peace with what we did—found it among the ardents, where I no longer shed the blood of men. I suppose it would be foolish of me to suggest the same to you."

Dalinar took a deep breath. "I'm releasing you, and the other ardents, from my control. I won't put you in a position where you have to serve a heretic. I'll give you to Taravangian, who remains orthodox."

"No."

"I don't believe you have the option to—"

"Just listen for one *storming* moment, Dalinar," Kadash snapped, then he sighed, forcibly calming himself. "You assume that because you're a heretic, we don't want anything to do with you."

"You proved that a few weeks ago, when we dueled."

"We don't want to normalize what you've done or what you're saying. That doesn't mean we will abandon our posts. Your people need us, Dalinar, even if *you* believe you don't."

Dalinar walked to the edge of the garden, where he rested his hands on the stone railing. Beyond him, clouds mustered at the base of the peaks, like a phalanx protecting its commander. From up here, it looked like the entire world was nothing more than an ocean of white broken by sharp peaks. His breath puffed in front of him. Cold as the Frostlands, though it didn't seem as bad inside the tower.

"Are any of those plants growing?" he asked softly.

"No," Kadash said from behind. "We aren't sure if it's the cold, or the fact that few storms reach this high." He kept scraping. "What will it feel like when a storm goes high enough to engulf this entire tower?"

"Like we're surrounded by dark confusion," Dalinar said. "The only light coming in flashes we can't pinpoint or comprehend. Angry winds trying to tow us in a dozen different directions, or barring that, rip our limbs from our bodies." He looked toward Kadash. "Like always."

"The Almighty was a constant light."

"And?"

"And now you make us question. You make *me* question. Being an ardent is the only thing that lets me sleep at night, Dalinar. You want to take that from me too? If He's gone, there's only the storm."

"I think there must be something beyond. I asked you before, what did worship look like before Vorinism? What did—"

"Dalinar. Please. Just . . . stop." Kadash drew in a deep breath. "Release a statement. Don't let everyone keep whispering about how you went into hiding. Say something pedantic like, 'I'm pleased with the work the Vorin church does, and support my ardents, even if I myself no longer have the faith I once did.' Give us permission to move on. Storms, this isn't the time for confusion. We don't even know what we're fighting. . . ."

Kadash didn't want to know that Dalinar had *met* the thing they were fighting. Best not to speak of that.

But Kadash's question did leave him considering. Odium wouldn't be commanding the day-to-day operations of his army, would he? Who did that? The Fused? The Voidspren?

Dalinar strolled a short distance from Kadash, then looked toward the sky. "Stormfather?" he asked. "Do the enemy forces have a king or a high-prince? Maybe a head ardent? Someone other than Odium?"

The Stormfather rumbled. *Again, I do not see as much as you think I do. I am the passing storm, the winds of the tempest. All of this is me. But I am not all of it, any more than you control each breath that leaves your mouth.*

Dalinar sighed. It had been worth the thought.

There is one I have been watching, the Stormfather added. *I can see her, when I don't see others.*

"A leader?" Dalinar asked.

Maybe. Men, both human and singer, are strange in what or whom they revere. Why do you ask?

Dalinar had decided not to bring anyone else into one of the visions because he worried about what Odium would do to them. But that wouldn't count for people already serving Odium, would it?

"When is the next highstorm?"

⁘

Taravangian felt old.

His age was more than the aches that no longer faded as the day proceeded. It was more than the weak muscles, which still surprised him when he tried to lift an object that should have seemed light.

It was more than finding that he'd slept through yet another meeting, despite his best efforts to pay attention. It was even more than slowly seeing almost everyone he'd grown up with fade away and die.

It was the urgency of knowing that tasks he started today, he wouldn't finish.

He stopped in the hallway back to his rooms, hand resting on the strata-lined wall. It was beautiful, mesmerizing, but he only found himself wishing for his gardens in Kharbranth. Other men and women got to live out their waning hours in comfort, or at least familiarity.

He let Mrall take him by the arm and guide him to his rooms. Normally, Taravangian would have been bothered by the help; he did *not* like being treated like an invalid. Today though . . . well, today he would suffer the indignity. It was a lesser one than collapsing in the hallway.

Inside the room, Adrotagia sat amid six different scribbling spanreeds, buying and trading information like a merchant at market. She looked at him, but knew him well enough not to comment on his exhausted face or slow steps. Today was a good day, of average intelligence. Perhaps a little on the stupid side, but he'd take that.

He seemed to be having fewer and fewer intelligent days. And the ones he did have frightened him.

Taravangian settled down in a plush, comfortable seat, and Maben went to get him some tea.

"Well?" Adrotagia asked. She'd grown old too, with enormous bags around her green eyes, the persistent kind formed by drooping skin. She had liver spots and wispy hair. No man would look at her and see the mischievous child she'd once been. The trouble the two of them had gotten into . . .

"Vargo?" Adrotagia asked.

"My apologies," he said. "Dalinar Kholin has recovered."

"A problem."

"An enormous one." Taravangian took the tea from Maben. "More than you can guess, I should say, even with the Diagram before you. But please, give me time to consider. My mind is slow today. Have you reports?"

Adrotagia flipped over a paper from one of her stacks. "Moelach seems to have settled in the Horneater Peaks. Joshor is on his way there now. We might again soon have access to the Death Rattles."

"Very well."

"We've found what happened to Graves," Adrotagia continued. "Scavengers found the storm-blown wreckage of his wagon, and there was an intact spanreed inside."

"Graves is replaceable."

"And the Shards?"

"Irrelevant," Taravangian said. "We won't win the prize through force of arms. I was reluctant to let him try his little coup in the first place."

He and Graves had disagreed about the Diagram's instructions: to kill Dalinar or recruit him? And who was to be king of Alethkar?

Well, Taravangian had been wrong about the Diagram himself many times. So he'd allowed Graves to move forward with his own plots, according to his own readings of the Diagram. While the man's schemes had failed, so had Taravangian's attempt to have Dalinar executed. So perhaps neither of them had read the Diagram correctly.

He took some time to recover, frustrated that he should need to *recover* from a simple walk. A few minutes later, the guard admitted Malata. The Radiant wore her usual skirt and leggings, Thaylen style, with thick boots.

She took a seat across from Taravangian at the low table, then sighed in a melodramatic way. "This place is awful. Every last idiot here is frozen, ears to toes."

Had she been this confident before bonding a spren? Taravangian hadn't known her well then. Oh, he'd managed the project, full of eager recruits from the Diagram, but the individuals hadn't mattered to him. Until now.

"Your spren," Adrotagia asked, getting out a sheet of paper. "Has she anything to report?"

"No," Malata said. "Only the tidbit from earlier, about other visions Dalinar hasn't shared with everyone."

"And," Taravangian asked, "has the spren expressed any . . . reservations? About the work you've given her?"

"Damnation," Malata said, rolling her eyes. "You're as bad as Kholin's scribes. Always poking."

"We need to be cautious, Malata," Taravangian said. "We can't be certain what your spren will do as her self-awareness grows. She will surely dislike working against the other orders."

"You're as frozen as the lot of them," Malata said. She started glowing, Stormlight rising from her skin. She reached forward, whipping off her glove—safehand no less—and pressing it against the table.

Marks spread out from the point of contact, little swirls of blackness etching themselves into the wood. The scent of burning filled the air, but the flames didn't persist if she didn't will them to.

The swirls and lines extended across the tabletop, a masterwork of engraving accomplished in moments. Malata blew off the ash. The Surge she used, Division, caused objects to degrade, burn, or turn to dust.

It also worked on people.

"Spark is *fine* with what we're doing," Malata said, pressing her finger down and adding another swirl to the table. "I told you, the rest of them are *idiots*. They assume all the spren are going to be on their side. Never mind what the Radiants did to Spark's friends, never mind that *organized* devotion to *Honor* is what killed hundreds of ashspren in the first place."

"And Odium?" Taravangian asked, curious. The Diagram warned that the personalities of the Radiants would introduce great uncertainty to their plans.

"Spark is game for whatever it takes to get vengeance. And what lets her break stuff." Malata grinned. "Someone should have warned me how fun this would be. I'd have tried *way* harder to land the job."

"What we do is not *fun*," Taravangian said. "It is necessary, but it is *horrible*. In a better world, Graves would have been right. We would be allies to Dalinar Kholin."

"You're too fond of the Blackthorn, Vargo," Adrotagia warned. "It will cloud your mind."

"No. But I do wish I hadn't gotten to know him. That *will* make this difficult." Taravangian leaned forward, holding his warm drink. Boiled ingo tea, with mint. Smells of home. With a start, he realized . . . he'd probably never live in that home again, would he? He'd thought perhaps he would return in a few years.

He wouldn't be alive in a few years.

"Adro," he continued, "Dalinar's recovery convinces me we must take more drastic action. Are the secrets ready?"

"Almost," she said, moving some other papers. "My scholars in Jah Keved have translated the passages we need, and we have the information from Malata's spying. But we need some way to disseminate the information without compromising ourselves."

"Assign it to Dova," Taravangian said. "Have her write a scathing, anonymous essay, then leak it to Tashikk. Leak the translations from the Dawnchant the same day. I want it all to strike at once." He set aside the tea. Suddenly, scents of Kharbranth made him hurt. "It would have been so, *so* much better for Dalinar to have died by the assassin's blade. For now we must leave him to the enemy's desires, and that will not be as kind as a quick death."

"Will it be enough?" Malata asked. "That old axehound is tough."

"It will be enough. Dalinar would be the first to tell you that when your opponent is getting back up, you must act quickly to crush his knees. Then he will bow, and present to you his skull."

Oh, Dalinar. You poor, poor man.

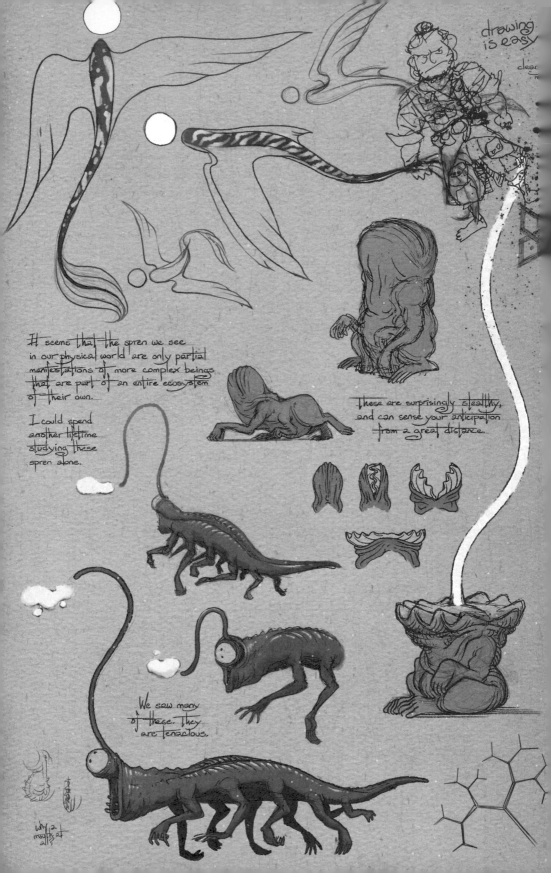

drawing is easy

clear in

It seems that the spren we see in our physical world are only partial manifestations of more complex beings that are part of an entire ecosystem of their own.

I could spend another lifetime studying these spren alone.

These are surprisingly stealthy, and can sense your anticipation from a great distance.

We saw many of these. They are tenacious.

Chemoarish, the Dustmother, has some of the most varied lore surrounding her. The wealth of it makes sorting lies from truths extremely difficult. I do believe she is not the Nightwatcher, contrary to what some stories claim.

—From Hessi's *Mythica*, page 231

Shallan sketched in her notepad as she stood on the deck of the honorspren ship, the wind of its passing ruffling her hair. Next to her, Kaladin rested his arms on the ship's railing, overlooking the ocean of beads.

Their current vessel, *Honor's Path*, was faster than Ico's merchant ship. It had mandras rigged not only at the front, but also to winglike rails jutting from the sides. It had five decks—including three below for crew and storage—but those were mostly empty. It felt like a war vessel intended to carry troops, but which didn't currently have a full complement.

The main deck was similar to the top deck of human ships, but this craft also had a high deck running down its center from prow to stern. Narrower than the main deck, it was supported by broad white pillars, and probably offered an excellent view. Shallan could no more than guess, as only the crew was allowed up there.

At least they'd been let out—Shallan and the others had spent their first week on board locked in the hold. The honorspren had given no explanation when, finally, the humans and Pattern had been released and allowed to move on deck, so long as they stayed off the high deck and did not make nuisances of themselves.

Syl remained imprisoned.

"Look here." Shallan tipped her sketched map toward Kaladin. "Pattern says there's an honorspren stronghold near Kharbranth in our world. They call it Unyielding Fidelity. We've *got* to be heading there. We went southwest after leaving Celebrant."

"While we were in the hold," Kaladin said softly, "I saw a sea of tiny flames through the porthole. A town on our side?"

"That was here," Shallan said, pointing at her map. "See where the rivers meet, just southwest of the lake? There are towns there, on our side. The river peninsulas should have blocked our way, but the spren seem to have cut a canal through the stone. We wove east around the Icingway River, then swung west again."

"So you're saying . . ."

She pointed at a spot with her charcoal pencil. "We're right about here, heading toward Kharbranth across the Frostlands."

Kaladin rubbed his chin. He glanced toward an honorspren passing above, and narrowed his eyes. He'd spent their first day of freedom arguing with the honorspren—which had ended with him locked up for *another* two days.

"Kaladin . . ." Shallan said.

"They need to let her out," he said. "Prisons are terrible for me—they'll be worse for her."

"Then help me figure out a way off this ship."

He looked back at her map and pointed. "Thaylen City," he said. "If we continue this direction, we'll eventually pass just north of it."

"'Just north' in this case meaning more than three hundred miles away from it, in the middle of a bead ocean."

"Far closer than we've been to any other Oathgate," he said. "And if we can get the ship to swing south a little, we could maybe get to the coast of Longbrow's Straits, which will be stone on this side. Or do you think we should still be trying for Azure's phantom 'perpendicularity' in the Horneater Peaks?"

"I . . ." He spoke with such authority, such a compelling sense of *motion*. "I don't know, Kaladin."

"We're heading in the right direction," he said, firm. "I *saw* it, Shallan. We just need to continue with the ship a few more days, then find a way to escape. We can hike to the Oathgate on this side, and you can transfer us to Thaylen City."

It sounded reasonable. Well, except for the fact that the honorspren were watching them. And the fact that the Fused knew where they were now, and were probably gathering forces to give chase. And the fact that they had to somehow escape from a ship in the middle of a sea of beads, reach the shore, then hike two hundred miles to reach Thaylen City.

All of that could fade before Kaladin's passion. All but the worry that topped them all—could she even make the Oathgate work? She couldn't help feeling that too much of this plan depended on her.

Yet those eyes . . .

"We could try a mutiny," Veil said. "Maybe those mistspren who do all the work will listen. They can't be happy, always hopping about, following honorspren orders."

"I don't know," Kaladin said, voice hushing as one of these spren—made entirely of mist, save for the hands and face—walked past. "Could be reckless. I can't fight them all."

"What if you had Stormlight?" Veil asked. "If I could pinch it back for you? What then?"

He rubbed at his chin again. Storms, he looked good with a beard. All ragged and untamed through the face, contrasted by his sharp blue uniform. Like a wild spren of passion, trapped by the oaths and codes . . .

Wait.

Wait, had that been *Veil*?

Shallan shook free of the momentary drifting of personality. Kaladin didn't seem to notice.

"Maybe," he said. "You really think you can steal the gemstones back for us? I'd feel a lot more comfortable with some Stormlight in my pocket."

"I . . ." Shallan swallowed. "Kaladin, I don't know if . . . Maybe it would be best not to fight them. They're honorspren."

"They're *jailers*," he said, but then calmed. "But they are taking us the right direction, if only inadvertently. What if we stole back our Stormlight, then simply jumped off the ship? Can you find a bead to make us a passage toward land, like you did at Kholinar?"

"I . . . guess I could try. But wouldn't the honorspren simply swing around and pick us up again?"

"I'll think about that," Kaladin said. "Try and find some beads that we can use." He walked across the deck, passing by Pattern—who stood with hands clasped behind his back, thinking number-filled thoughts. Kaladin eventually settled beside Azure, speaking softly with her, probably outlining their plan.

Such that it was.

Shallan tucked her sketchpad under her arm and looked over the side of the ship. So many beads, so many souls, piled on top of each other. Kaladin wanted her to search through all of *that* for something helpful?

She glanced toward a passing sailor, a mistspren who had gaseous limbs that ended in gloved hands. Her feminine face was the shape of a porcelain mask, and she—like the others of her kind—wore a vest and trousers that seemed to float on a body made of swirling, indistinct fog.

"Is there a way for me to get some of those beads?" Shallan asked.

The mistspren stopped in place.

"Please?" Shallan asked. "I—"

The sailor jogged off, and then returned a short time later with the captain: a tall, imperious-looking honorspren named Notum. He glowed a soft blue-white, and wore an outdated—but sharp—naval uniform, which was part of his substance. His beard was of a cut she hadn't seen before, with the chin shaved, almost like a Horneater, but with a thin mustache and a sculpted line of hair that ran from it up his cheeks and blended into his sideburns.

"You have a request?" he asked her.

"I would like some beads, Captain," Shallan said. "To practice my art, if you please. I need to do *something* to pass the time on this trip."

"Manifesting random souls is dangerous, Lightweaver. I would not have you doing it wantonly upon my decks."

Keeping the true nature of her order from him had proven impossible, considering how Pattern followed her around.

"I promise not to manifest anything," she said. "I merely want to practice visualizing the souls inside the beads. It's part of my training."

He studied her, clasping his hands behind his back. "Very well," he said—which surprised her. She hadn't expected that to work. He gave an order, however, and a mistspren lowered a bucket on a rope to get her some beads.

"Thank you," Shallan said.

"It was a simple request," the captain said. "Just be careful. I suppose you'd need Stormlight to manifest anyway, but still . . . be careful."

"What happens if we carry the beads away too far?" Shallan asked, curious as the mistspren handed her the bucket. "They are tied to objects in the Physical Realm, right?"

"You can carry them anywhere in Shadesmar you wish," the captain said. "Their tie is through the Spiritual Realm, and distance doesn't matter. However, drop them—let them free—and they'll work their way back to the general location of their physical counterpart." He eyed her. "You are very new to all of this. When did it begin again? Radiants, swearing Ideals?"

"Well . . ."

Her mother's dead face, eyes burned.

"It hasn't been going on for long," Shallan said. "A few months for most of us. A few years for some . . ."

"We had hoped this day would never come." He turned to march toward the high deck.

"Captain?" Shallan asked. "Why did you let us out? If you're so worried about Radiants, why not just keep us locked away?"

"It wasn't honorable," the captain said. "You are not prisoners."

"What are we, then?"

"Stormfather only knows. Fortunately, I don't have to sort it out. We'll deliver you and the Ancient Daughter to someone with more authority. Until then, please try not to break my ship."

⁘

As days passed, Shallan fell into a routine on the honorspren ship. She spent most days sitting on the main deck, near the wale. They let her have beads in plenitude to play with, but most of them were useless things. Rocks, sticks, bits of clothing. Still, it was useful to visualize them. Hold them, meditate on them. Understand them?

Objects had desires. Simple desires, true, but they could adhere to those desires with passion—as she'd learned during her few attempts at Soulcasting. Now, she didn't try to change those desires. She just learned to touch them, and to listen.

She felt a familiarity to some of the beads. A growing understanding that, perhaps, she could make their souls blossom from beads into full-fledged objects on this side. Manifestations, they were called.

Between practices with the beads, she did sketches. Some worked, some didn't. She wore the skirt that Adolin had purchased for her, hoping it would make her feel more like Shallan. Veil kept poking through, which could be useful—but the way it just kind of *happened* was frightening to her. This was the opposite of what Wit had told her to do, wasn't it?

Kaladin spent the days pacing the main deck, glaring at honorspren he passed. He looked like a caged beast. Shallan felt some of his same urgency. They hadn't seen any sign of the enemy, not since that day in Celebrant. But she slept uneasily each night, worried that she'd wake to calls of an enemy ship approaching them. Notum had confirmed that the Voidspren were creating their own empire in Shadesmar. And they controlled Cultivation's Perpendicularity, the easiest way to get between realms.

Shallan sorted through another handful of beads, feeling the impression of a small dagger, a rock, a piece of fruit that had started to see itself as something new—something that could grow into its own identity, rather than merely a part of the whole.

What would someone see when looking at her soul? Would it give a single, unified impression? Many different ideas of what it was to be her?

Nearby, the ship's first mate—an honorspren woman with short hair and an angular face—left the hold. Curiously, she was carrying Azure's Shardblade. She stepped onto the main deck, beneath the shadow of the high deck, and went hiking toward Azure, who stood watching the ocean pass nearby.

Curious, Shallan pocketed the bead representing a knife—just in case—then left the bucket on top of her sketchbook and walked over. Nearby, Kaladin was pacing again, and he also noticed the sword.

"Draw her carefully," Azure said to Borea, the first mate, as Shallan approached. "Don't pull her out all the way—she doesn't know you."

Borea wore a uniform like the captain's, all stiff and no-nonsense. She undid a small latch on the Shardblade, eased it from its sheath a half inch, then drew in a sharp breath. "It . . . tingles."

"She's investigating you," Azure said.

"It really is as you say," Borea said. "A Shardblade that requires no spren—no enslavement. This is something else. How did you do it?"

"I will trade knowledge, per our deal, once we arrive."

Borea snapped the Blade closed. "A good bond, human. We accept your offer." Surprisingly, the woman held the weapon toward Azure, who took it.

Shallan stepped closer, watching as Borea walked off toward the steps up to the high deck.

"How?" Shallan asked as Azure belted on the sword. "You got them to give your weapon back?"

"They're quite reasonable," Azure said, "so long as you make the right promises. I've negotiated for passage and an exchange of information, once we reach Lasting Integrity."

"You've done *what*?" Kaladin said. He stalked over. "What did I just hear?"

"I've made a deal, Stormblessed," Azure said, meeting his gaze. "I'll be free, once we reach their stronghold."

"We're not *going* to reach their stronghold," Kaladin said softly. "We're going to escape."

"I'm not your soldier, or even Adolin's subject. I'm going to do what gets me to the perpendicularity—and, barring that, I'm going to find out what these people know about the criminal I'm hunting."

"You'd throw away honor for a *bounty*?"

"I'm only here because you two—through no fault of your own, I admit—trapped me. I don't blame you, but I'm *also* not indebted to your mission."

"Traitor," he said softly.

Azure gave him a flat look. "At some point, Kal, you need to admit that the *best* thing you can do right now is go with these spren. At their stronghold, you could clear up this misunderstanding, then move on."

"That could take weeks."

"I wasn't aware we were on a schedule."

"Dalinar is in danger. Don't you care?"

"About a man I don't know?" Azure said. "In danger from a threat you can't define, happening at a time you can't pinpoint?" She folded her arms. "Forgive me for not sharing in your anxiety."

Kaladin set his jaw, then turned and stalked away—right *up* the steps toward the high deck. They weren't supposed to go up there, but sometimes rules didn't seem to apply to Kaladin Stormblessed.

Azure shook her head, then turned and gripped the ship railing.

"He's just having a bad day, Azure," Shallan said. "I think he feels anxious because his spren is imprisoned."

"Maybe. I've seen a lot of young hotheads in my time, and young Stormblessed feels like another color altogether. I wish I knew what it was he was so desperate to prove."

Shallan nodded, then glanced again at Azure's sword. "You said . . . the honorspren have information on your bounty?"

"Yeah. Borea thinks the weapon I'm chasing passed through their fortress a few years ago."

"Your bounty is a . . . *weapon?*"

"And the one who brought it to your land. A Shardblade that bleeds black smoke." Azure turned toward her. "I don't mean to be callous, Shallan. I realize you're all eager to return to your lands. I can even believe that—through some tide of Fortune—Kaladin Stormblessed has foreseen some danger."

Shallan shivered. *Be wary of anyone who claims to be able to see the future.*

"But," Azure continued, "even if his mission *is* critical, it doesn't mean mine isn't as well."

Shallan glanced toward the high deck, where she could faintly hear Kaladin making a disturbance. Azure turned and clasped her hands, adopting a far-off look. She seemed to want to be alone, so Shallan trailed back toward where she'd left her things. She settled down and removed the bucket from her sketchpad. The pages fluttered, showing various versions of herself, each one wrong. She kept drawing Veil's face on Radiant's body, or vice versa.

She started back into her latest bucket of beads. She found a shirt and a bowl, but the next bead was a fallen tree branch. This brought up memories of the last time she'd dipped into Shadesmar—freezing, near death, on the banks of the ocean.

Why . . . why hadn't she tried to Soulcast since then? She'd made excuses, avoided thinking about it. Had focused all her attention on Lightweaving.

She'd ignored Soulcasting. Because she'd failed.

Because she was afraid. Could she invent someone who wasn't afraid? Someone new, since Veil was broken, and had been since that failure in the Kholinar market . . .

"Shallan?" Adolin asked, coming over to her. "Are you all right?"

She shook herself. How long had she been sitting there? "I'm fine," she said. "Just . . . remembering."

"Good things or bad?"

"All memories are bad," she said immediately, then looked away, blushing.

He settled down next to her. Storms, his overt concern was annoying. She didn't want him worrying about her.

"Shallan?" he asked.

"Shallan will be fine," she said. "I'll bring her back in a moment. I just have to recover . . . her . . ."

Adolin glanced at the fluttering pages with the different versions of her. He reached out and hugged her, saying nothing. Which turned out to be the right thing to say.

She closed her eyes and tried to pull herself together. "Which one do you like the most?" she finally asked. "Veil is the one who wears the white outfit, but I'm having trouble with her right now. She peeks out sometimes when I don't want, but then won't come when I need her. Radiant is the one who practices with the sword. I made her prettier than the others, and you can talk to her about dueling. But some of the time, I'll have to be someone who can Lightweave. I'm trying to think of who she should be. . . ."

"Ash's eyes, Shallan!"

"Shallan's broken, so I think I'm trying to hide her. Like a cracked vase, where you turn the nice side toward the room, hiding the flaw. I'm not doing it on purpose, but it's happening, and I don't know how to stop it."

He held her.

"No advice?" she asked, numb. "Everyone always seems to have loads."

"You're the smart one. What can *I* say?"

"It's confusing, being all these people. I feel like I'm presenting different faces all the time. Lying to everyone, because I'm different inside.

I . . . That doesn't make sense, does it?" She squeezed her eyes shut again. "I'll pull it back together. I'll be . . . someone."

"I . . ." He pulled her tight again as the ship rocked. "Shallan, I killed Sadeas."

She blinked, then pulled back and looked him in the eyes. "*What?*"

"I killed Sadeas," Adolin whispered. "We met in the corridors of the tower. He started insulting Father, talking about the terrible things he was going to do to us. And . . . and I couldn't listen anymore. Couldn't stand there and look at his smug red face. So . . . I attacked him."

"So all that time we were hunting a killer . . ."

"It was me. I'm the one the spren copied the first time. I kept thinking about how I was lying to you, to Father, and to everyone. The honorable Adolin Kholin, the consummate duelist. A murderer. And Shallan, I . . . I don't think I'm *sorry.*

"Sadeas was a monster. He *repeatedly* tried to get us killed. His betrayal caused the deaths of many of my friends. When I formally challenged him to a duel, he wiggled out of it. He was smarter than me. Smarter than Father. He'd have won eventually. So I killed him."

He pulled her to him and took a deep breath.

Shallan shivered, then whispered, "Good for you."

"Shallan! You're a Radiant. You're not supposed to condone something like this!"

"I don't know what I'm *supposed* to do. I only know that the world is a better place for the death of Torol Sadeas."

"Father wouldn't like it, if he knew."

"Your father is a great man," Shallan said, "who is, perhaps, better off not knowing everything. For his own good."

Adolin breathed in again. With her head pressed to his chest, the air moving in and out of his lungs was audible, and his voice was different. More resonant. "Yeah," he said. "Yeah, maybe. In any case, I think I know what it's like to feel like you're lying to the world. So maybe if you figure out what to do, you could tell me?"

She leaned into him, listening to his heartbeat, his breathing. She felt his warmth.

"You never did say," she whispered, "which one you prefer."

"It's obvious. I prefer the real you."

"Which one is that, though?"

"She's the one I'm talking to right now. You don't have to hide, Shallan. You don't have to push it down. Maybe the vase is cracked, but that only means it can show what's inside. And I *like* what's inside."

So warm. Comfortable. And strikingly *unfamiliar.* What was this peace? This place without fear?

Noises from above spoiled it. Pulling back, she looked toward the upper deck. "What *is* the bridgeboy doing up there?"

· ·

"Sir," the misty sailor spren said in broken Alethi. "Sir! Not. Please, not!"

Kaladin ignored her, looking through the spyglass he'd taken from the chain nearby. He stood on the rear section of the high deck, searching the sky. That Fused had watched them leave Celebrant. The enemy would find them eventually.

Dalinar alone. Surrounded by nine shadows . . .

Kaladin finally handed the spyglass to the anxious mistspren. The captain of the ship, in a tight uniform that probably would have been uncomfortable on a human, approached and dismissed the sailor, who scuttled away.

"I would prefer," Captain Notum said, "if you would refrain from upsetting my crew."

"I would prefer that you let Syl go," Kaladin snapped, feeling her anxiety through their bond. "As I told you, the Stormfather has condoned what she did. There is no crime."

The short spren clasped his hands behind his back. Of all the spren they'd interacted with on this side, the honorspren seemed to share the most human mannerisms.

"I could lock you away again," the captain said. "Or even have you tossed overboard."

"Yeah? And what would *that* do to Syl? She told me that losing a bonded Radiant was hard on their spren."

"True. But she would recover, and it might be for the best. Your relationship with the Ancient Daughter is . . . inappropriate."

"It's not like we eloped."

"It is worse, as the Nahel bond is far more intimate a relationship. The linking of spirits. This is not a thing that should be done lightly, unsupervised. Besides, the Ancient Daughter is too young."

"Young?" Kaladin said. "Didn't you just call her *ancient*?"

"It would be difficult to explain to a human."

"Try anyway."

The captain sighed. "The honorspren were created by Honor himself, many thousands of years ago. You call him the Almighty, and . . . I'm afraid he's dead."

"Which makes sense, as it's pretty much the only excuse I would have accepted."

"That wasn't levity, human," Notum said. "Your god is *dead*."

"Not my god. But please continue."

"Well . . ." Notum frowned; he'd obviously thought the concept of Honor's death would have been more difficult for Kaladin to accept. "Well, sometime before his death, Honor stopped creating honorspren. We don't know why, but he asked the Stormfather to do it instead."

"He was setting up an heir. I've heard that the Stormfather is a kind of image of the Almighty."

"More like a weak shadow," Notum said. "You . . . actually understand this?"

"Understand, no. Follow? Mostly."

"The Stormfather created only a handful of children. All of these, save Sylphrena, were destroyed in the Recreance, becoming deadeyes. This loss stung the Stormfather, who didn't create again for centuries. When he was finally moved to remake the honorspren, he created only ten more. My great-grandmother was among them; she created my grandfather, who created my father, who eventually created me.

"It was only recently, even by your reckoning, that the Ancient Daughter was rediscovered. Asleep. So, in answer to your question, yes, Sylphrena is both old and young. Old of form, but young of mind. She is not ready to deal with humans, and certainly not ready for a bond. I wouldn't trust *myself* with one of those."

"You think we're too changeable, don't you? That we can't keep our oaths."

"I'm no highspren," the captain spat. "I can see that the variety of humankind is what gives you strength. Your ability to change your minds, to go *against* what you once thought, can be a great advantage. But your bond is dangerous, without Honor. There will not be enough checks upon your power—you risk disaster."

"How?"

Notum shook his head, then looked away, off into the distance. "I cannot answer. You should not have bonded Sylphrena, either way. She is too precious to the Stormfather."

"Regardless," Kaladin said, "you're about half a year too late. So you might as well accept it."

"Not too late. Killing you would free her—though it would be painful for her. There are other ways, at least until the Final Ideal is sworn."

"I can't imagine you'd be willing to kill a man for this," Kaladin said. "Tell me truthfully. Is there *honor* in that, Notum?"

He looked away, as if ashamed.

"You know Syl shouldn't be locked away like this," Kaladin said softly. "You're an honorspren too, Notum. You must know how she feels."

The captain didn't speak.

Finally, Kaladin gritted his teeth and strode off. The captain didn't demand that Kaladin go down below, so he took up a position at the very front of the high deck, hanging out over the bow.

With one hand on the flagpole, Kaladin rested a boot on the low railing, overlooking the sea of beads. He wore his uniform today, since he'd been able to wash it the previous night. *Honor's Path* had good accommodations for humans, including a device that made a great deal of water. The design—if not the vessel itself—probably stretched back centuries to when Radiants traveled Shadesmar with their spren.

Beneath him, the ship creaked as sailors shifted her heading. To the left, he could see land. Longbrow's Straits—on the other side of which they'd find Thaylen City. Tantalizingly close.

Technically, he was no longer Dalinar's bodyguard. But storms, during the Weeping, Kaladin had nearly abandoned his duty. The thought of Dalinar needing him now—while Kaladin was trapped and unable to help—brought a pain that was almost *physical*. He'd failed so many people in his life. . . .

Life before death. Strength before weakness. Journey before destination. Together, these Words formed the First Ideal of the Windrunners. He'd said them, but he wasn't certain he understood them.

The Second Ideal made more direct sense. *I will protect those who cannot protect themselves.* Straightforward, yes . . . but overwhelming. The world was a place of suffering. Was he really supposed to try to prevent it all?

I will protect even those I hate, so long as it is right. The Third Ideal meant standing up for anyone, if needed. But who decided what was "right"? Which side was he supposed to protect?

The Fourth Ideal was unknown to him, but the closer he drew to it, the more frightened he became. What would *it* demand of him?

Something crystallized in the air beside him, a line of light like a pinprick in the air that trailed a long, soft luminescence. A mistspren sailor near him gasped, then nudged his companion. She whispered something in awe, then both scrambled away.

What have I done now?

A second pinprick of light appeared near him, spinning, coordinated with the other. They made spiral trails in the air. He'd have called them spren, but they weren't any he'd seen before. Besides, spren on this side didn't seem to vanish and appear—they were always here, weren't they?

K-Kaladin? a voice whispered in his head.

"Syl?" he whispered.

What are you doing? It was rare that he heard her directly in his mind.

"Standing on the deck. What's happened?"

Nothing. I can just . . . feel your mind right now. Stronger than usual. They let you out?

"Yes. I've tried to get them to set you free."

They're stubborn. It's an honorspren trait which I, fortunately, escaped.

"Syl. What is the Fourth Ideal?"

You know you have to figure that out on your own, silly.

"It's going to be hard, isn't it?"

Yes. You're close.

He leaned forward, watching the mandras float beneath them. A small flock of gloryspren zipped past. They took a moment to fly up and spin about him before heading to the south, faster than the ship.

The strange pinpricks of light continued to whirl around him. Sailors gathered behind, making a ruckus until the captain pushed through and gaped.

"What are they?" Kaladin asked, nodding toward the pinpricks of light.

"Windspren."

"Oh." They did remind him a little of the way windspren would fly on gusts of wind. "They're common. Why is everyone so upset?"

"They're not common on this side," the captain said. "They live on your side, almost completely. I . . . I've never seen them before. They're beautiful."

Perhaps I haven't been giving Notum enough credit, Kaladin thought. Perhaps he would listen to a different kind of plea.

"Captain," Kaladin said. "I have taken an oath, as a Windrunner, to protect. And the Bondsmith who leads us is in danger."

"*Bondsmith?*" the captain asked. "Which one?"

"Dalinar Kholin."

"No. Which Bondsmith, of the three?"

"I don't know what you mean," Kaladin said. "But his spren is the Stormfather. I told you I'd spoken to him."

It seemed, from the captain's aghast expression, that perhaps Kaladin should have mentioned this fact earlier.

"I must keep my oath," Kaladin said. "I need you to let Syl go, then take us to a place where we can transfer between realms."

"I've sworn an oath myself," the captain said. "To Honor, and to the truths we follow."

"Honor is dead," Kaladin said. "But the Bondsmith is *not.* You say that you can see how human variety gives us strength—well, I challenge you to do the same. See beyond the letter of your rules. You must understand that my need to defend the Bondsmith is more important than your need to deliver Syl—especially considering that the Stormfather is well aware of her location."

The captain glanced at the windspren, which were still spinning about Kaladin, leaving trails that drifted the entire length of the ship before fading.

"I will consider," the captain said.

⁘

Adolin stopped at the top of the steps, just behind Shallan.

Kaladin, the storming bridgeman, stood at the bow of the ship, surrounded by glowing lines of light. They illuminated his heroic figure—determined, undaunted, one hand on the prow's flagpole, wearing his crisp Wall Guard uniform. The ship's spren gazed upon him as if he were a storming Herald come to announce the reclamation of the Tranquiline Halls.

Just ahead of him, Shallan seemed to change. It was in her bearing, the way she stopped resting lightly on one foot, and stood solidly on two feet instead. The way her posture shifted.

And the way that she seemed to melt upon seeing Kaladin, lips rising to a grin. Blushing, she adopted a fond—even eager—expression.

Adolin breathed out slowly. He'd caught those glimpses from her before—and seen the sketches of Kaladin in her book—but looking at her now, he couldn't deny what he was seeing. She was practically *leering*.

"I need to draw that," she said. But she just stood there instead, staring at him.

Adolin sighed and made his way up onto the high deck. Seemed they weren't forbidden here any longer. He joined Pattern, who had come up another set of steps, and was humming happily to himself.

"Kind of hard to compete with *that*," Adolin noted.

"Mmm," Pattern said.

"You know, I've never really felt like this before? It's not just Kaladin, it's all of this. And what's happening to us." He shook his head. "We certainly are an odd bunch."

"Yes. Seven people. Odd."

"It's not like I can blame him. It's not as if he's *trying* to be like he is."

Nearby, a sailor spren—one of the few who hadn't gathered around Stormblessed and his halo of glowing lights—lowered a spyglass. She frowned, then raised it again. Then she began to call out in the spren language.

People tore themselves away from Kaladin and crowded around. Adolin stepped back, watching until Kaladin and Shallan joined him. Azure crested the steps nearby, looking concerned.

"What is it?" Kaladin asked.

"No idea," Adolin said.

The captain waved for the mistspren and honorspren to make space, then took the spyglass. He finally lowered it and looked back at Kaladin. "You were right, human, when you said you might be followed." He waved Kaladin and Adolin forward. "Look low on the horizon, at two hundred ten degrees."

Kaladin looked through the spyglass, then breathed out. He extended it toward Adolin, but Shallan snatched it first.

"Storms!" she said. "There's at least six of them."

"Eight, my scout says," the captain replied.

Adolin finally got his turn. Because of the black sky, it took him forever to spot the distant specks flying toward the ship. The Fused.

Re-Shephir, the Midnight Mother, is another Unmade who appears to have been destroyed at Aharietiam.

—From Hessi's *Mythica*, page 250

Dalinar ran his fingers along a line of red crystal embedded in the stone wall. The little vein started at the ceiling and wound all the way down the wall—within the pattern of the light green and grey strata—to the floor. It was smooth to the touch, distinct in texture from the rock around it.

He rubbed his thumb across the crystal. *It's like the other strata lines ripple out from this one, getting wider as they move away from it.*

"What does it mean?" he asked Navani. The two of them stood in a storage room near the top of the tower.

"I don't know," Navani said, "but we're finding more and more of them. What do you know of Essential Theology?"

"A thing for ardents and scribes," he said.

"And Soulcasters. That is a garnet."

Garnet? Let's see . . . Emeralds for grain, that was the most important, and heliodors for flesh. They raised animals for their gemhearts to provide those two. He was pretty sure diamonds made quartz, and . . . storms, he didn't know much about the others. Topaz made stone. They'd needed those for the bunkers on the Shattered Plains.

"Garnets make blood," Navani said. "We don't have any Soulcasters that use them."

"Blood? That sounds useless."

"Well, scientifically, we think Soulcasters were able to use garnets to make any liquid that was soluble in water, as opposed to oil-based . . . Your eyes are crossing."

"Sorry." He felt at the crystals. "Another mystery. When will we find answers?"

"The records below," Navani said, "speak of this tower like a living thing. With a heart of emerald and ruby, and now these veins of garnet."

He stood up, looking around the darkened room, which held the monarchs' chairs between meetings. It was lit by a sphere he'd set on a stone ledge by the door.

"If this tower was alive," Dalinar said, "then it's dead now."

"Or sleeping. But if that's the case, I have no idea how to wake it. We've tried infusing the heart like a fabrial, even had Renarin try to push Stormlight into it. Nothing's worked."

Dalinar picked up a chair, then pushed the door open. He held the door with his foot—shooing away a guard who tried to do it for him—while Navani collected the sphere and joined him in the conference room, in front of the glass wall looking toward the Origin.

He set down the chair and checked his forearm clock. Stupid thing. He was growing *far* too dependent upon it. The arm device had a painrial in it too: a kind of fabrial with a spren that feasted upon pain. He'd never yet remembered to use the thing.

Twelve minutes left. Assuming Elthebar's calculations were correct. With spanreeds confirming the storm's arrival hours before in the east, the calculations were down to judging the speed of the storm.

A runner arrived at the door. Creer—the duty sergeant for guards today—accepted it. He was a bridgeman from . . . Bridge Twenty, was it? He and his brother were both guards, though Creer wore spectacles, unlike his twin.

"Message from Brightness Khal, sir," Creer said, handing the note to Navani. It looked like it had come from a spanreed. It had marks on the sides from the clips that had held it to the board, and the tight letters covered only the center of the page.

"From Fen," Navani said. "A merchant ship vanished in the Southern Depths this morning, just off Marat. They went ashore at what they hoped was a safe distance—to use the spanreed—and reported a large number of ships at dock along the coast. Glowing figures rose from a nearby city and descended upon them, and the communication cut off."

"Confirmation," Dalinar said, "that the enemy is building up a navy." If that fleet launched from Marat before his own ships were ready, or if the winds were wrong when his armada *did* launch . . .

"Have Teshav write back to the Thaylens," Dalinar said. "Suggest to

Queen Fen and our other allies that we hold the next meeting in Thaylen City. We'll want to inspect fortifications and shore up the ground defenses."

He sent the guards to wait outside, then approached the window and checked his wrist clock. Just a few minutes left. He thought he could see the stormwall below, but it was difficult to be sure from this height. He wasn't accustomed to looking *down* on a highstorm.

"Are you sure you want to do this?" Navani asked.

"The Stormfather asked me something similar this morning. I asked him if he knew the first rule of warfare."

"Is that the one about terrain, or the one about attacking where the enemy is weak?"

He could pick it out now, a dark ripple surging through the sky below.

"Neither," Dalinar said.

"Ah, right," Navani said. "I should have guessed." She was nervous, with good cause. It was the first time he'd stepped back into the visions since meeting Odium.

But Dalinar felt blind in this war. He didn't know what the enemy wanted, or how they intended to exploit their conquests.

The first rule of war. Know your enemy.

He raised his chin as the storm slammed into Urithiru, roughly at the height of its third tier.

All went white. Then Dalinar appeared in the ancient palace—the large open room with sandstone pillars and a balcony that looked out on an antiquated version of Kholinar. Nohadon strode through the center of the pillared chamber. This was the youthful Nohadon, not the elderly version from his recent dream.

Dalinar had taken the place of a guardsman, near the doors. A slender Parshendi woman appeared beside the king, in the spot Dalinar had occupied so long ago. Her skin was marbled red and white in a complex pattern, and she had long orange-red hair. She looked down with red eyes, surprised by her sudden appearance and the robes she wore, those of an advisor to the king.

Nohadon began speaking to her as if she were his friend Karm. "I don't know what to do, old friend."

Odium sees that a vision has begun, the Stormfather warned Dalinar. *The enemy is focusing on us. He comes.*

"Can you hold him back?"

I am but a shadow of a god. His power vastly outstrips my own. He sounded smaller than Dalinar was accustomed to. Like the quintessential bully, the Stormfather didn't know how to face someone stronger than himself.

"Can you *hold him back*? I need time to talk to her."

I will . . . try.

Good enough. Unfortunately, it meant that Dalinar didn't have time to let this Parshendi woman experience the vision in full. He strode toward her and Nohadon.

⁘

Venli turned around. Where was she? This wasn't Marat. Had Odium summoned her again?

No. It's the wrong storm. He doesn't come during highstorms.

A young Alethi male in robes was blathering at her. She ignored him, biting her hand to see if she could feel the pain.

She could. She shook her hand and looked down at the robes she wore. This couldn't be a dream. It was too real.

"My friend?" the Alethi man asked. "Are you well? I realize that events have taken their toll on us all, but—"

Footsteps rang loudly on the stone as another Alethi man approached, wearing a crisp blue uniform. White dusted the hair at his temples, and his face wasn't as . . . round as other human faces. His features could almost have been those of a listener, even if that nose was wrong and the face bore far more creases than a listener's ever would.

Wait . . . she thought, attuning Curiosity. *Is that* . . .

"Disturbance on the battlefield, sir," the older man said to her companion. "You are needed immediately."

"What is this? I didn't hear—"

"They didn't say what it was, Your Majesty, only that you are urgently requested."

The human king drew his lips to a tight line, and then—obviously frustrated—stalked toward the doorway. "Come," he said to Venli.

The older man grabbed her arm above the elbow. "Don't," he said softly. "We need to talk."

This is the Alethi warlord.

"My name is Dalinar Kholin," the man said. "I lead the Alethi, and you're seeing a vision of past events. Only your mind has been transported, not your body. We two are the only real people here."

She yanked her arm out of his hand and attuned Irritation. "How . . . why have you brought me here?"

"I want to talk."

"Of course you do. Now that you're losing, now that we've seized your capital, *now* you want to talk. What of the years spent slaughtering my people on the Shattered Plains?" It had been a *game* to them. Listener spy reports had shown the humans had *enjoyed* the sport on the Shattered Plains. Claiming wealth, and listener lives, as part of a grand contest.

"We were willing to talk, when you sent your emissary," Dalinar said. "The Shardbearer. I'm willing to talk again now. I want to forget old grievances, even those personal to me."

Venli walked away, still attuned to Irritation. "How have you brought me to this place? Is this a prison?" *Is this your work, Odium? Testing my loyalty with a false vision of the enemy?*

She was using the old rhythms. She'd never been able to do that when Odium's attention had been on her.

"I'll send you back soon," Kholin said, catching up to her. Though he was not short for a human, her current form was a good six inches taller than he was. "Please, just hear me out. I need to know. What would a truce between our people cost?"

"A truce?" she asked to Amusement, stopping near the balcony. "A *truce?*"

"Peace. No Desolation. No war. What would it cost?"

"Well, for a start, it would cost your kingdom."

He grimaced. His words were dead, like those of all humans, but he wore his feelings on his face. So much passion and emotion.

Is that why the spren betrayed us for them?

"What is Alethkar to you?" he said. "I can help you build a new nation on the Shattered Plains. I will give you laborers to raise cities, ardents to teach any skill you want. Wealth, as payment in ransom for Kholinar and its people. A formal apology. Whatever you demand."

"I demand that we keep Alethkar."

His face became a mask of pain, his brow furrowed. "Why must you live there? To you, Alethkar is a place to conquer. But it's *my* homeland."

She attuned Reprimand. "Don't you understand? The people who live there—the singers, my cousins—are *from* Alethkar. That is their homeland too. The only difference between them and you is that they were born as slaves, and you as their master!"

He winced. "Perhaps some other accommodation, then. A . . . dividing of the kingdom? A parshman highprince?" He seemed shocked to be considering it.

She attuned Resolve. "Your tone implies you know that would be impossible. There can be no accommodation, human. Send me from this place. We can meet on the battlefield."

"No." He seized her arm again. "I don't know what the accommodation will be, but we *can* find one. Let me prove to you that I want to negotiate, instead of fight."

"You can start," she said to Irritation, pulling away from him, "by not assaulting me."

She wasn't certain she could fight him, honestly. Her current body was tall, but fragile. And in truth, she'd never been proficient at battle, even during the days when she'd taken an appropriate form.

"At least let us try a negotiation," he said. "Please."

He didn't sound very pleading. He'd grown stern, face like a stone, *glaring*. With the rhythms, you could infuse your tone with the mood you wished to convey, even if your emotions weren't cooperating. Humans didn't have that tool. They were as dull as the dullest slave.

A sudden *thump* resounded in the vision. Venli attuned Anxiety and rushed out onto the balcony. A half-destroyed city stretched below, where a battle had happened, dead heaped in piles.

That pounding sounded again. The . . . the *air* was breaking. The clouds and sky seemed to be a mural painted on an enormous dome ceiling, and as the pounds continued, a web of cracks appeared overhead.

Beyond them shone a vivid yellow light.

"He's here," she whispered, then waved toward it. "That's why there can't be a negotiation, human. He knows we don't need one. You want peace? Surrender. Give yourselves up and *hope* that he doesn't care to destroy you."

A faint hope, considering what Rine had said to her about exterminating the humans.

With the next pound, the sky fractured and a hole appeared overhead, a powerful light shining beyond. The very shards of the air—broken like a mirror—were sucked into that light.

A *pulse* of power blasted from the hole, shaking the city with a terrible vibration. It tossed Venli to the balcony's floor. Kholin reached to help her, but a second pulse caused him to fall as well.

The bricks in the room's wall *separated* from one another and began to float apart. The boards that made up the balcony began to lift, nails floating into the sky. A guard ran to the balcony, but stumbled, and his very skin started to separate into water and a dried husk.

Everything just . . . came apart.

A wind rose around Venli, pulling debris toward that hole in the sky, and the brilliant, terrible light beyond. Boards shredded to splinters; bricks floated past her head. She growled, the Rhythm of Resolve thumping inside her as she grabbed and clung to parts of the floor that hadn't yet separated.

That *burning*. She knew it well, the terrible pain of Odium's heat scalding her skin, scorching her until her very bones—somehow still able to feel—became ash. It happened every time he gave her orders. What worse thing would he do if he found her fraternizing with the enemy?

She attuned Determination and crawled away from the light. *Escape!* She reached the chamber beyond the balcony and lurched to her feet, trying to run. The wind pulled at her, making each step a struggle.

Overhead, the ceiling separated in a single magnificent burst—each brick exploding away from the others, then streaming toward the void. The pieces of the unfortunate guard rose after them, a sack drained of grain, a puppet with no controlling hand.

Venli dropped to the ground again and continued crawling, but the stones of the floor separated, floating upward with her on them. Soon, she was scrambling precariously from one floating piece of stone to another. The Rhythm of Resolve still attuned, she dared to glance backward. The hole had widened, and the all-consuming light feasted on the streams of refuse.

She turned away, desperate to do what she could to delay her own burning. Then . . . she stopped and looked back again. Dalinar Kholin stood on the balcony. And he was glowing.

Neshua Kadal. Radiant Knight.

Without meaning to, she attuned the Rhythm of Awe. Around Kholin, the balcony was stable. Boards trembled and quivered at his feet, but did not move into the sky. The balcony railing had ripped apart to either side of him, but where he held to it with a firm grip, it remained secure.

He was her enemy, and yet . . .

Long ago, these humans had resisted her gods. Yes, the enslavement of her cousins—the singers—was impossible to ignore. Still, the humans had fought. And had *won.*

The listeners remembered this as a song sung to the Rhythm of Awe. *Neshua Kadal.*

The calm, gentle light spread from Dalinar Kholin's hand to the railing, then down into the floor. Boards and stones sank down from the air, reknitting. Venli's current block of stone settled back into place. All through the city, buildings burst apart and zoomed upward, but the walls of this tower returned to their positions.

Venli immediately made for the steps downward. If whatever Kholin was doing stopped, she wanted to be on solid rock. She wound her way to the ground floor, then—once on the street—she positioned herself near the balcony and Kholin's influence.

Above, Odium's light went out.

Stones and splinters rained down on the city, crashing about her. Dried bodies dropped like discarded clothing. Venli pressed back against the tower wall, attuning Anxiety, raising her arm against the dust of the debris.

The hole remained in the sky, though the light was gone from behind it. Below, the rubbled remains of the city seemed . . . a sham. No cries of fear, no moans of pain. Bodies were just husks, skins lying empty on the ground.

A sudden *pounding* broke the air behind her, opening another hole, lower down and near the edge of the city. The sky crumbled into the gap, revealing that hateful light again. It consumed everything near it—wall, buildings, even the *ground* disintegrating and flowing into the maw.

Dust and debris washed over Venli in a furious wind. She pressed against the stone wall, clinging to one of the balcony's supports. Terrible heat washed across her from the distant hole.

Clamping her eyes shut, she tightened her grip. He could come claim her, but she would not let go.

And what of the grand purpose? What of the power he offers? Did she still want those things? Or was that merely something to grasp onto, now that she had brought about the end of her people?

She gritted her teeth. In the distance, she heard a quiet rhythm. Somehow it sounded over the roar of the wind, the clacking of dust and stones. The Rhythm of Anxiety?

She opened her eyes, and saw Timbre fighting against the wind in an attempt to reach her. Bursts of light exploded from the little spren in frantic rings.

Buildings crumbled along the street. The entire city was collapsing away—even the palace broke apart, all save this one patch near the balcony.

The little spren changed to the Rhythm of the Lost and began to slide backward.

Venli shouted and released the pillar. She immediately was pushed with the wind—but although she wasn't in stormform any longer, this *was* a form of power, incredibly nimble. She controlled her fall, going down on her side and skidding on the stones, feet toward the oppressive light. As she neared the little spren, Venli jammed her foot into a cleft in the street, then grabbed a crack in a broken stone, pulling herself to a halt. With her other hand, she twisted and snatched Timbre from the air.

Touching Timbre felt like touching silk being blown by a wind. As Venli folded her left hand around the spren, she felt a pulsing warmth. Timbre pulsed to Praise as Venli pulled her close to her breast.

Great, Venli thought, lowering her head against the wind, her face against the ground, holding on to the cleft in the rock with her right hand. *Now we can fall together.*

She had one hope. To hold on, and hope that eventually . . .

The heat faded. The wind stilled. Debris came clattering back to the ground, though the fall was less clamorous this time. Not only had the wind been pulling sideways rather than up, there simply wasn't much debris left.

Venli rose, covered in dust, her face and hands cut by chips of stone. Timbre pulsed softly in her hand.

The city was basically gone. No more than the occasional outline of a building foundation and the remains of the strange rock formations known as the windblades. Even those had been weathered down to knobs five or six feet tall. The only structure in the city that remained was a quarter of the tower where Kholin had been standing.

Behind her was a black, gaping hole into nothingness.

The ground trembled.

Oh no.

Something beat against the stones underneath her. The very ground began to shake and crumble. Venli ran toward the broken palace right as everything—at last—fell apart. The ground, the remaining foundations, even the air seemed to disintegrate.

A chasm opened beneath her, and Venli leaped, trying to reach the other side. She came up a few feet short, and plummeted into the hole. Falling, she twisted in the air, reaching for the collapsing sky with one hand and clutching Timbre in the other.

Above, the man in the blue uniform leaped into the chasm.

He fell beside the hole's perimeter, and stretched one hand toward Venli. His other ground against the rock wall, hand scraping the stone. Something flashed around his arm. Lines of light, a framework that covered his body. His fingers didn't bleed as they scraped the stone.

Around her, the rocks—the air itself—became more substantial. In defiance of the heat below, Venli slowed just enough that her fingers met those of Kholin.

Go.

She crashed to the floor of her cave back in Marat, the vision gone. Sweating, panting, she opened her left fist. To her relief, Timbre floated out, pulsing with a hesitant rhythm.

⁘

Dalinar dissolved into pure pain.

He felt himself being ripped apart, flayed, shredded. Each piece of him removed and allowed to hurt in isolation. A punishment, a retribution, a personalized torment.

It could have persisted for an eternity. Instead, blessedly, the agony faded, and he came to himself.

He knelt on an endless plain of glowing white stone. Light coalesced beside him, forming into a figure dressed in gold and white, holding a short scepter.

"What *were* you seeing?" Odium asked, curious. He tapped his scepter on the ground like a cane. Nohadon's palace—where Dalinar had been moments before—materialized out of light beside them. "Ah, this one again? Looking for answers from the dead?"

Dalinar squeezed his eyes shut. What a fool he had been. If there had ever been a hope of peace, he'd probably destroyed it by pulling that Parshendi woman into a vision and subjecting her to Odium's horrors.

"Dalinar, Dalinar," Odium said. He settled down on a seat formed from light, then rested one hand on Dalinar's shoulder. "It hurts, doesn't it? Yes. I know pain. I am the only god who does. The only one who *cares*."

"Can there be peace?" Dalinar asked, his voice ragged. Speaking was hard. He'd felt himself being ripped apart in the light moments before.

"Yes, Dalinar," Odium said. "There can be. There *will* be."

"After you destroy Roshar."

"After *you* destroy it, Dalinar. I am the one who will rebuild it."

"Agree to a contest between champions," Dalinar forced out. "Let us . . . let us find a way to . . ." He trailed off.

How could he fight this thing?

Odium patted Dalinar's shoulder. "Be strong, Dalinar. I have faith in you, even when you don't have it in yourself. Though it will hurt for a time, there is an end. Peace is in your future. Push *through* the agony. Then you will be victorious, my son."

The vision faded, and Dalinar found himself back in the upper room of Urithiru. He collapsed into the seat he'd placed there, Navani taking his arm, concerned.

Through his bond, Dalinar sensed weeping. The Stormfather had kept Odium back, but storms, he had paid a price. The most powerful spren on Roshar—embodiment of the tempest that shaped all life—was crying like a child, whispering that Odium was too strong.

The Midnight Mother created monsters of shadow and oil, dark imitations of creatures she saw or consumed. Their description matches no spren I can find in modern literature.

—From Hessi's *Mythica,* page 252

Captain Notum gave the command, and two of the sailors un-latched a section of the hull, exposing the crashing waves of beads just beyond.

Shallan put her freehand on the frame of the open cargo door and leaned out over the churning depths. Adolin tried to tug her back, but she remained in place.

She'd chosen to wear Veil's outfit today, in part for the pockets. She carried three larger gemstones; Kaladin carried four others. Their broams had all run out of Stormlight. Even these larger, unset gems were getting close to failing. Hopefully they would last long enough to get them to Thaylen City and the Oathgate.

Beyond the waves—so close that the sailors feared hidden rocks beneath the beads—a dark landscape interrupted the horizon. The inverse of Longbrow's Straits, a place where trees grew tall, forming a black jungle of glass plants.

A sailor clomped down the steps into the hold and barked something at Captain Notum. "Your enemies are close now," the captain translated.

Honor's Path had made a heroic effort these last few hours, pushing its mandras to exhaustion—and it hadn't been nearly enough. The Fused were slower than Kaladin could go, but they were still far faster than the ship.

Shallan looked at the captain; his bearded face, which glowed with a soft, phantom light, betrayed nothing of what must have been a powerful conflict for him. Turn over the captives to the enemy and perhaps save his crew? Or set them free, and hope the Ancient Daughter could escape?

A door at the back of the hold opened, and Kaladin led Syl from her cabin. The captain had only now given permission to release her, as if wishing to delay the decision until the last possible moment. Syl's color seemed muted, and she clung to Kaladin's arm, unsteady. Was she going to be able to make it to shore with them?

She's a spren. She doesn't need air. She'll be fine. Hopefully.

"Go, then," the captain said. "And be swift. I cannot promise that my crew, once captured, will be able to keep this secret for long." Apparently it was difficult to kill spren, but *hurting* them was quite easy.

Another sailor released Adolin's sword spren from her cabin. She didn't look as weathered as Syl—one place seemed as good as another to her.

Kaladin led Syl over.

"Ancient Daughter," the captain said, bowing his head.

"Won't meet my eyes, Notum?" Syl said. "I suppose locking me away here isn't too different from all those days you spent running about at Father's whims back home."

He didn't reply, but instead turned away.

With Syl and the deadeye joining them, that only left one person. Azure lounged by the steps, wearing her breastplate and cloak, arms folded.

"You *sure* you won't change your mind?" Shallan asked.

Azure shook her head.

"Azure," Kaladin said. "I was too harsh earlier. That doesn't mean I—"

"It's not that," she said. "I simply have a different thread to chase, and besides, I left my men to fight these monsters in Kholinar. Doesn't feel right to do the same again." She smiled. "Don't fear for me, Stormblessed. You will have a much better chance if I stay here—as will these sailors. When you boys next meet the swordsman who taught you that morning kata, warn him that I'm looking for him."

"Zahel?" Adolin said. "You know *Zahel*?"

"We're old friends," she said. "Notum, have your sailors been cutting those bales of cloth into the shapes I requested?"

"Yes," the captain said. "But I don't understand—"

"You soon will." She gave Kaladin a lazy salute. He returned it, sharper. Then she nodded to them and walked up toward the main deck.

The ship crashed through a large wave of beads, sending some through the open cargo deck doors. Sailors with brooms started brushing them back toward the opening.

"Are you going?" the captain said to Shallan. "Every moment you delay increases the danger to us all." He still wouldn't look at Syl.

Right, Shallan thought. Well, someone had to start the party. She took Adolin by one hand and Pattern by the other. Kaladin linked hands with Pattern and Syl, and Adolin grabbed his spren. They crowded into the opening into the cargo hold, looking at the glass beads below. Churning, catching the light of a distant sun, sparkling like a million stars . . .

"All right," she said. "Jump!"

Shallan threw herself off the ship, joined by the others. She crashed into the beads, which swallowed her. They seemed to slip too easily into them—like before, when she'd fallen into this ocean, it felt like something was pulling her down.

She sank into the beads, which rolled against her skin, overwhelming her senses with thoughts of trees and rocks. She fought the sensations, struggling to keep herself from thrashing too much. She clung to Adolin, but Pattern's hand was pulled from her grip.

I can't do this! I can't let them claim me. I can't—

They hit the bottom, which was shallow, here near the shore. Then Shallan finally let herself draw in Stormlight. One precious gemstone's worth. It sustained her, calmed her. She fished in her pocket for the bead she'd picked from the bucket earlier.

When she fed the bead Stormlight, the other beads around her trembled, then pulled *back*, forming the walls and ceiling of a small room. The Stormlight curling from her skin illuminated the space with a faint glow. Adolin let go of her hand and fell to his knees, coughing and gasping. His deadeye just stood there, as always.

"Damnation," Adolin said, wheezing. "Drowning with no water. It shouldn't be so hard, should it? All we had to do was hold our breath. . . ."

Shallan stepped to the side of the room, listening. Yes . . . it was almost like she could hear the beads whispering to her beneath their clattering. She plunged her hand through the wall and her fingers brushed cloth. She grabbed hold, and a moment later Kaladin seized her arm and pulled himself into the room made from beads, stumbling and falling to his knees.

He wasn't glowing.

"You didn't use a gemstone?" Shallan asked.

"Almost had to," he said. He took a few deep breaths, then stood up. "But we need to conserve those." He turned around. "Syl?"

A disturbance at the other side of the chamber announced someone approaching. Whoever it was wasn't able to get in until Shallan walked over and broke the surface of the bead wall with her hand. Pattern entered and looked around the room, humming happily. "Mmm. A nice pattern, Shallan."

"Syl," Kaladin repeated. "We jumped hand-in-hand, but she let go. Where—"

"She'll be fine," Shallan said.

"Mmm," Pattern agreed. "Spren need no air."

Kaladin took a deep breath, then nodded. He started pacing anyway, so Shallan settled down on the ground to wait, pack in her lap. They each carried a change of clothing, three water jugs, and some of the food Adolin had purchased. Hopefully it would be enough to reach Thaylen City.

Then she'd have to make the Oathgate work.

They waited as long as they dared, hoping the Fused had passed them by, chasing the ship. Finally, Shallan stood up and pointed. "That way."

"You sure?" Kaladin asked.

"Yes. Even the slope agrees." She kicked at the obsidian ground, which ran at a gentle incline.

"Right," Adolin said. "Lock hands."

They did so and—heart fluttering—Shallan recovered the Stormlight from her shell of a room. Beads came crashing down, enveloping her.

They started up the slope, against the tide of beads. It was more difficult than she'd imagined; the current of the shifting beads seemed determined to hold them back. Still, she had Stormlight to sustain her. They soon reached a place where the ground was too steep to walk on easily. Shallan let go of the men's hands and scrambled up the incline.

A moment after her head broke the surface, Syl appeared on the bank, reaching down and helping Shallan up the last few feet. Beads rolled off her clothing, clattering against the ground, as the others pulled themselves onto the shore.

"I saw the enemy fly past," Syl said. "I was hiding by the trees here."

At her urging, they entered the forest of glass plants before settling down to recover from their escape. Shallan immediately felt herself itching for her sketchpad. These trees! The trunks were translucent; the leaves looked like they were blown from glass in a multitude of colors. Moss drooped from one branch, like melted green glass, strands hanging down in silky lines. When she touched them, they broke off.

Overhead, the clouds rippled with the mother-of-pearl iridescence that marked another highstorm in the real world. Shallan could barely see it through the canopy, but the effect on Pattern and Syl was immediate. They stood up straighter, and Syl's wan color brightened to a healthy blue-white. Pattern's head shifted more quickly, spinning through a dozen different cycles in a matter of minutes.

Stormlight still trailed from Shallan's skin. She'd taken in a rather large amount of it, but hadn't lost *too* much. She returned it to the gemstone, a process she didn't quite understand, but which felt natural at the same time.

Nearby, Syl looked to the southwest with a kind of wistful, far-off expression. "Syl?" Shallan asked.

"There's a storm that way too . . ." she whispered, then shook herself and seemed embarrassed.

Kaladin dug out two gemstones. "All right," he said, "we fly."

They'd decided to use two gemstones' worth of Stormlight to fly inward, a gamble to get a head start on their hike—and to get away from the coast. Hopefully the Fused wouldn't treat the honorspren *too* harshly. Shallan worried for them, but equally for what would happen if the Fused doubled back to search for her group.

A short flight now should deposit them far enough inland that they'd be tough to locate. Once they landed, they would hike across several days' worth of Shadesmar landscape before reaching the island of Thaylenah, which would manifest as a lake here. Thaylen City, and its Oathgate, were on the very rim of that lake.

Kaladin Lashed them one at a time—and fortunately, his arts worked on the spren as they did humans. They took to the air and started the last leg of their journey.

III

EILA STELE

*It will not take a careful reader to ascertain I have listed only eight
of the Unmade here. Lore is confident there were nine, an unholy
number, asymmetrical and often associated with the enemy.*

—From Hessi's *Mythica*, page 266

D alinar stepped out of the Oathgate control building into Thaylen
City and was met by the man he most wanted to punch in all
Roshar.

Meridas Amaram stood straight in his House Sadeas uniform, clean-
shaven, narrow-faced, square-jawed. Tall, orderly, with shining buttons
and a sharp posture, he was the very image of a perfect Alethi officer.

"Report," Dalinar said, hopefully keeping the dislike out of his voice.

Amaram—Sadeas—fell into step with Dalinar, and they walked to the
edge of the Oathgate platform, overlooking the city. Dalinar's guards gave
them space to converse.

"Our crews have done wonders for this city, Brightlord," Amaram said.
"We focused our initial attentions on the debris outside the walls. I worried that would give an invading force too much cover—not to mention
rubble to construct a ramp up to the wall."

Indeed, the plain before the city walls—which had once housed the
markets and warehouses of the docks—was completely clear. A killing
field, interrupted by the occasional outline of a broken foundation. The
Almighty only knew how the Thaylen military had allowed a collection of
buildings *outside* the walls in the first place. That would have been a nightmare to defend.

"We shored up positions where the wall was weakened," Amaram continued, gesturing. "It's not high by Kholinar standards, but is an impressive fortification nonetheless. We cleared out the buildings right inside to provide staging and resource dumps, and my army is camped there. We then helped with general reconstruction."

"The city looks far better," Dalinar said. "Your men did well."

"Then maybe our penance can be over," Amaram said. He said it straight, though angerspren—a pool of boiling blood—spread from beneath his right foot.

"Your work here was important, soldier. You didn't only rebuild a city; you built the trust of the Thaylen people."

"Of course." Amaram added, more softly, "And I *do* see the tactical importance of knowing the enemy fortifications."

You fool. "The Thaylens are not our enemies."

"I misspoke," Amaram said. "Yet I cannot ignore that the *Kholin* troops have been deployed to the border between our kingdom and Jah Keved. Your men get to liberate our homeland, while *mine* spend their days digging in rocks. You do realize the effect this has on their morale, particularly since many of them still assume you assassinated their highprince."

"I *hope* that their current leader has worked to disabuse them of such false notions."

Amaram finally turned to look Dalinar in the eyes. Those angerspren were still there, though his tone was crisp and militaristic. "Brightlord. I know you for a realist. I've modeled my career after yours. Frankly, even if you *did* kill him—which I know you must deny—I would respect you for it. Torol was a liability to this nation.

"Let me *prove* to you that I am not the same. Storms, Dalinar! I'm your best frontline general, and you know it. Torol spent years wasting me because my reputation intimidated him. Don't make the same mistake. *Use* me. Let me fight for Alethkar, not kiss the feet of Thaylen merchants! I—"

"Enough," Dalinar snapped. "Follow your orders. *That* is how you'll prove yourself to me."

Amaram stepped back, then—after a deliberate pause—saluted. He spun on his heel and marched down into the city.

That man . . . Dalinar thought. Dalinar had intended to tell him that this island would host the front lines in the war, but the conversation had slipped from him. Well, Amaram might quickly get the fighting he wanted—a fact he would discover soon enough, at the planning meeting.

Boots on stone sounded behind him as a group of men in blue uniforms joined him at the rim of the plateau. "Permission to stab him a little, sir," said Teft, the bridgeman leader.

"How do you stab someone 'a little,' soldier?"

"I could do it," Lyn said. "I've only started training with a spear. We could claim it was an accident."

"No, no," Lopen said. "You want to stab him a little? Let my cousin Huio do it, sir. He's the expert on little things."

"Short joke?" Huio said in his broken Alethi. "Be glad not short temper."

"I'm just trying to involve you, Huio. I know that most people overlook you. It's very easy to do, you see. . . ."

"Attention!" Dalinar snapped, though he found himself smiling. They scrambled into ranks. Kaladin had trained them well.

"You've got"—Dalinar checked the clock on his arm—"thirty-seven minutes until the meeting, men. And, er, women. Don't be late."

They rushed off, chatting among themselves. Navani, Jasnah, and Renarin joined him soon after, and his wife gave him a sly smile as she noticed him checking his arm clock again. Storming woman had gotten him to start arriving early for appointments just by strapping a device to his arm.

As they gathered, Fen's son climbed up onto the Oathgate platform and greeted Dalinar warmly. "We have rooms for you, above the temple where we'll be meeting. I . . . well, we know you don't *need* them, since you can simply Oathgate home in an instant . . ."

"We'll take them gladly, son," Dalinar said. "I could use a little refreshment and time to think."

The young man grinned. Dalinar never *would* get used to those spiked eyebrows.

They climbed down from the platform, and a Thaylen guard gave the all clear. A scribe sent word via spanreed that the next transfer could take place. Dalinar paused to watch. A minute later a flash occurred, surrounding the Oathgate with light. The Oathgates were under almost perpetual use these days—Malata was running the device today, as was becoming her duty more often.

"Uncle?" Jasnah said as he lingered.

"Merely curious about who's coming in next."

"I could pull the records for you . . ." Jasnah said.

The new arrivals turned out to be a group of Thaylen merchants in pompous clothing. They made their way down the larger ramp, surrounded by guards and accompanied by several men carrying large chests.

"More bankers," Fen's son said. "The quiet economic collapse of Roshar continues."

"Collapse?" Dalinar said, surprised.

"Bankers all across the continent have been pulling out of cities," Jasnah said, pointing. "See that fortress of a building at the front of the Ancient Ward down below? That's the Thaylen Gemstone Reserve."

"Local governments are going to have difficulty financing troops after this," Fen's son said with a grimace. "They'll have to write here with authorized spanreeds and get spheres shipped to them. It's going to be a nightmare of logistics for anyone not close to an Oathgate."

Dalinar frowned. "Couldn't you encourage the merchants to stay and support the cities they were in?"

"Sir!" he replied. "Sir, force the merchants to obey *military* authority?"

"Forget I asked," Dalinar said, sharing a look with Navani and Jasnah. Navani smiled fondly at what was probably a huge social misstep, but he suspected Jasnah agreed with him. She'd probably have seized the banks and used them to fund the war.

Renarin lingered, watching the merchants. "How big are the gemstones they've brought?" he asked.

"Brightlord?" Fen's son asked, glancing toward Dalinar for help. "They'll be spheres. Normal spheres."

"Any larger gemstones?" Renarin asked. He turned toward them. "Anywhere in the city?"

"Sure, lots of them," Fen's son said. "Some really nice pieces, like in every city. Um . . . why, Brightlord?"

"Because," Renarin said. He didn't say anything more.

※

Dalinar splashed water onto his face from a basin in his rooms, which were in a villa above the temple of Talenelat, on the top tier of the city—the Royal Ward. He wiped his face with the towel and reached out to the Stormfather. "Feeling any better?"

I do not feel like men. I do not sicken like men. I am. The Stormfather rumbled. *I could have been destroyed, though. Splintered into a thousand pieces. I live only because the enemy fears exposing himself to a strike from Cultivation.*

"So she lives still, then? The third god?"

Yes. You've met her.

"I . . . I *have*?"

You do not remember. But normally, she hides. Cowardice.

"Perhaps wisdom," Dalinar said. "The Nightwatcher—"

Is not her.

"Yes, you've said. The Nightwatcher is like you. Are there others, though? Spren like you, or the Nightwatcher? Spren that are shadows of gods?"

There is . . . a third sibling. They are not with us.

"In hiding?"

No. Slumbering.

"Tell me more."

No.

"But—"

No! Leave them alone. You hurt them enough.

"Fine," Dalinar said, setting aside the towel and leaning against the window. The air smelled of salt, reminding him of something not yet clear in his mind. One last hole in his memory. A trip by sea.

And his visit to the Valley.

He glanced at the dresser beside the washbasin, which held a book written in unfamiliar Thaylen glyphs. A little note beside it, in Alethi glyphs, read, "Pathway. King." Fen had left him a gift, a copy of *The Way of Kings* in Thaylen.

"I've done it," Dalinar said. "I've united them, Stormfather. I've kept my oath, and have brought men together, instead of dividing them. Perhaps this can be penance in some small way, for the pain I've caused."

The Stormfather rumbled in reply.

"Did he . . . care about what we felt?" Dalinar asked. "Honor, the Almighty? Did he truly care about men's pain?"

He did. Then, I didn't understand why, but now I do. Odium lies when he claims to have sole ownership of passion. The Stormfather paused. *I remember . . . at the end . . . Honor was more obsessed with oaths. There were times when the oath itself was more important than the meaning behind it. But he was not a passionless monster. He loved humankind. He died defending you.*

Dalinar found Navani entertaining Taravangian in the common area of their villa. "Your Majesty?" Dalinar asked.

"You could call me Vargo, if you wish," Taravangian said, pacing without looking at Dalinar. "It is what they called me as a youth. . . ."

"What's wrong?" Dalinar asked.

"I'm just worried. My scholars . . . It is nothing, Dalinar. Nothing. Silliness. I am . . . I am well today." He stopped and squeezed his pale grey eyes shut.

"That's good, isn't it?"

"Yes. But it is not a day to be heartless. So I worry."

Heartless? What did he mean?

"Do you need to sit out the meeting?" Navani asked.

Taravangian shook his head quickly. "Come. Let us go. I will be better . . . better once we've started. I'm sure."

⁘

As Dalinar stepped into the temple's main chamber, he found that he was looking *forward* to the meeting.

What a strange revelation. He'd spent so much of his youth and middle years dreading politics and the endless rambling of meetings. Now he was *excited*. He could see the outlines of something grand in this room. The Azish delegation warmly greeted Queen Fen, with Vizier Noura even giving Fen a poem she'd written as thanks for the Thaylen hospitality. Fen's son made a point of sitting next to Renarin and chatting with him. Emperor Yanagawn looked comfortable on his throne, surrounded by allies and friends.

Bridge Four joked with the guards of Highprince Aladar, while Lift the Edgedancer perched on a windowsill nearby, listening with a cocked head. In addition to the five scout women in uniform, two women in havahs had joined Bridge Four. They carried notepads and pencils, and had sewn Bridge Four patches to the upper sleeves of their dresses—the place where scribes commonly wore their platoon insignia.

Alethi highprinces, Azish viziers, Knights Radiant, and Thaylen admirals all in one room. The prime of Emul talking tactics with Aladar, who had been aiding the beleaguered country. General Khal and Teshav speaking with the princess of Yezier, who was eyeing Halam Khal—their eldest son—standing tall in his father's Shardplate by the door. There was talk of a political union there. It would be the first in centuries between an Alethi and a Makabaki princedom.

Unite them. A voice whispered the words in Dalinar's mind, echoing with the same resonant sound from months ago, when Dalinar had first started seeing the visions.

"I'm doing so," Dalinar whispered back.

Unite them.

"Stormfather, is that you? Why do you keep saying this to me?"

I said nothing.

It was growing hard to distinguish between his own thoughts and what came from the Stormfather. Visions and memories struggled for space in Dalinar's brain. To clear his mind, he strode around the perimeter of the circular temple chamber. Murals on the walls—ones he had healed with his abilities—depicted the Herald Talenelat during several of his many, many last stands against the Voidbringers.

A large map had been mounted on one wall depicting the Tarat Sea and surrounding areas, with markers noting the locations of their fleet. The room quieted as Dalinar stepped up and studied this. He glanced for a moment out the doors of the temple, toward the bay. Already, a few of the faster ships of their fleet had arrived, flying the flags of both Kharbranth and Azir.

"Your Excellency," Dalinar said to Yanagawn. "Could you share news of your troops?"

The emperor gave leave for Noura to report. The main fleet was less than a day away. Their outriders—or scout ships, as she called them—had spotted no indications of the enemy advance. They'd worried that this window between storms would be when the enemy would move, but so far there was no sign.

The admirals began to discuss how to best patrol the seas while keeping Thaylen City safe. Dalinar was pleased by the conversation, mostly because the admirals seemed to think that the real danger to Thaylen City had passed. A Veden highprince had managed to get a foot scout close enough to Marat to count the ships at the docks. Well over a hundred vessels were waiting in the various coves and ports along the coast. For whatever reason, they weren't ready to launch yet, which was a blessing.

The meeting progressed, with Fen belatedly welcoming everyone—Dalinar realized he should have let her take charge from the start. She described the defenses in Thaylen City and raised concerns from her guildmasters about Amaram's troops. Apparently they'd been carousing.

Amaram stiffened at that. For all his faults, he liked to run a tight army.

Sometime near the end of this discussion, Dalinar noticed Renarin shifting uncomfortably in his seat. As the Azish scribes began explaining their code of rules and guidelines for the coalition, Renarin excused himself in a hoarse voice, and left.

Dalinar glanced at Navani, who seemed troubled. Jasnah stood to follow, but was interrupted by a scribe bringing her a small sheaf of documents. She accepted them and moved to Navani's side so they could study them together.

Should we break? Dalinar thought, checking his forearm clock. They'd only been going for an hour, and the Azish were obviously excited by their guidelines.

The Stormfather rumbled.

What? Dalinar thought.

Something . . . something is coming. A storm.

Dalinar stood up, looking about the room, half expecting assassins to attack. His sudden motion caught the attention of one of the Azish viziers, a short man with a very large hat.

"Brightlord?" the interpreter asked at a word from the vizier.

"I . . ." Dalinar could feel it. "Something's wrong."

"Dalinar?" Fen asked. "What are you talking about?"

Spanreeds suddenly started blinking throughout the room. A dozen flashing rubies. Dalinar's heart sidestepped. Anticipationspren rose around him, streamers whipping from the ground, as the various scribes grabbed the blinking spanreeds from boxes or belts and set them out to begin writing.

Jasnah didn't notice that one of hers was blinking. She was too distracted by what she and Navani were reading.

"The Everstorm just hit Shinovar," Queen Fen finally explained, reading over a scribe's shoulder.

"Impossible!" Ialai Sadeas said. "It has only been five days since the last one! They come at nine-day intervals."

"Yes, well, I think we have enough confirmation," Fen said, nodding toward the spanreeds.

"The storm is too new," Teshav said. She pulled her shawl closer as she read. "We don't know it well enough to truly judge its patterns. The reports from Steen say it is particularly violent this time, moving faster than before."

Dalinar felt cold.

"How long until it reaches us?" Fen asked.

"Hours yet," Teshav said. "It can take a full day for the highstorm to get from one side of Roshar to the other, and the Everstorm is slower. Usually."

"It's moving faster though," Yanagawn said through his interpreter. "How far away are our ships? How are we going to shelter them?"

"Peace, Your Excellency," Fen said. "The ships are close, and the new docks miles farther along the coast are sheltered from both east and west. We merely need to make sure the fleet goes directly there, instead of stopping here to drop off troops."

The room buzzed with conversations as the various groups received reports from their contacts in Tashikk, who in turn would be relaying information from contacts in Iri, Steen, or even Shinovar.

"We should break for a short time," Dalinar told them. The others agreed, distracted, and separated into groups scattered about the room. Dalinar settled back in his seat, releasing a held breath. "That wasn't so bad. We can deal with this."

That wasn't it, the Stormfather said. He rumbled, his concerned voice growing very soft as he continued, *There's more.*

Dalinar jumped back to his feet, instincts prompting him to thrust his hand to the side, fingers splayed, to summon a Blade he no longer possessed. Bridge Four responded immediately, dropping food from the table of victuals, grabbing spears. Nobody else seemed to notice.

But . . . notice what? No attack came. Conversations continued on all sides. Jasnah and Navani were still huddled side by side, reading. Navani gasped softly, safehand going to her mouth. Jasnah looked at Dalinar, lips drawn to a line.

Their message wasn't about the storm, Dalinar thought, pulling his chair over to them. "All right," he whispered, though they were far enough from other groups to have some privacy. "What is it?"

"A breakthrough was made in translating the Dawnchant," Navani whispered. "Teams in Kharbranth and the monasteries of Jah Keved have arrived at the news separately, using the seed we provided through the visions. We are finally receiving translations."

"That's good, right?" Dalinar said.

Jasnah sighed. "Uncle, the piece that historians have been *most* eager to translate is called the Eila Stele. Other sources claim it is old, perhaps the oldest document in written memory, said to be scribed by the Heralds themselves. From the translation that finally came in today, the carving appears to be the account of someone who witnessed the very *first* coming of the Voidbringers, long, long ago. Even before the first Desolation."

"Blood of my fathers," Dalinar said. Before the first Desolation? The *last* Desolation had happened more than four thousand years ago. They were speaking of events lost to time. "And . . . we can read it?"

"'They came from another world,'" Navani said, reading from her sheet. "'Using powers that we have been forbidden to touch. Dangerous powers, of spren and Surges. They destroyed their lands and have come to us begging.

"'We took them in, as commanded by the gods. What else could we do? They were a people forlorn, without home. Our pity destroyed us. For their betrayal extended even to our gods: to spren, stone, and wind.

"'Beware the otherworlders. The traitors. Those with tongues of sweetness, but with minds that lust for blood. Do not take them in. Do not give them succor. Well were they named Voidbringers, for they brought the void. The empty pit that sucks in emotion. A new god. Their god.

"'These Voidbringers know no songs. They cannot hear Roshar, and where they go, they bring silence. They look soft, with no shell, but they are hard. They have but one heart, and it cannot ever live.'"

She lowered the page.

Dalinar frowned. *It's nonsense,* he thought. *Is it claiming that the first parshmen who came to invade had no carapace? But how would the writer know that parshmen should have carapace? And what is this about songs. . . .*

It clicked. "That was not written by a human," Dalinar whispered.

"No, Uncle," Jasnah said softly. "The writer was a Dawnsinger, one of the original inhabitants of Roshar. The Dawnsingers weren't spren, as theology has often postulated. Nor were they Heralds. They were parshmen. And the people they welcomed to their world, the otherworlders . . ."

"Were us," Dalinar whispered. He felt cold, like he'd been dunked in icy water. "They named *us* Voidbringers."

Jasnah sighed. "I have suspected this for a time. The first Desolation was the invasion of *humankind* onto Roshar. We came here and seized this land from the parshmen—after we accidentally used Surgebinding to destroy our previous world. That is the truth that destroyed the Radiants."

The Stormfather rumbled in his mind. Dalinar stared at that sheet of paper in Navani's hand. Such a small, seemingly unimportant object to have created such a pit inside of him.

It's true, isn't it? he thought at the Stormfather. *Storms . . . we're not the defenders of our homeland.*

We're the invaders.

Nearby, Taravangian argued softly with his scribes, then finally stood up. He cleared his throat, and the various groups slowly stilled. The Azish contingent had servants pull their chairs back toward the group, and Queen Fen returned to her place, though she didn't sit. She stood, arms folded, looking perturbed.

"I have had disconcerting news," Taravangian said. "Over the spanreed, just now. It involves Brightlord Kholin. I don't wish to be objectionable . . ."

"No," Fen said. "I've heard it too. I'm going to need an explanation."

"Agreed," Noura said.

Dalinar stood up. "I realize this is troubling. I . . . I haven't had time to adjust. Perhaps we could adjourn and worry about the storm first? We can discuss this later."

"Perhaps," Taravangian said. "Yes, perhaps. But it *is* a problem. We have believed that ours is a righteous war, but this news of mankind's origins has me disconcerted."

"What are you talking about?" Fen said.

"The news from the Veden translators? Ancient texts, manifesting that humans came from another world?"

"Bah," Fen said. "Dusty books and ideas for philosophers. What *I* want to know about is this highking business!"

"*Highking?*" Yanagawn asked through an interpreter.

"I've an essay," Fen said, slapping papers against her hand, "from Zetah the Voiced claiming that before King Elhokar left for Alethkar, he *swore* to Dalinar to accept him as emperor."

Noura the vizier leaped to her feet. "*What?*"

"Emperor is an exaggeration!" Dalinar said, trying to reorient toward this unexpected attack. "It's an internal Alethi matter."

Navani stood beside him. "My son was merely concerned about his political relation to Dalinar. We have prepared an explanation for you all, and our highprinces can confirm that we are *not* looking to expand our influence to your nations."

"And this?" Noura said, holding up some pages. "Were you preparing an explanation for *this* as well?"

"What is that?" Dalinar asked, bracing himself.

"Accounts of two visions," Noura said, "that you *didn't* share with us. In which you supposedly met and fraternized with a being known as Odium."

Behind Dalinar, Lift gasped. He glanced toward her, and the men of Bridge Four, who were muttering among themselves.

This is bad, Dalinar thought. *Too much. Too fast for me to control.*

Jasnah leaped to her feet. "This is obviously a concentrated attempt to destroy our reputation. Someone *deliberately* released all this information at the same time."

"Is it true?" Noura asked in Alethi. "Dalinar Kholin, *have you met with our enemy?*"

Navani gripped his arm. Jasnah subtly shook her head: *Don't answer that.*

"Yes," Dalinar said.

"Did he," Noura asked pointedly, "tell you you'd destroy Roshar?"

"What of this ancient record?" Taravangian said. "It claims that the Radiants *already* destroyed one world. Is that not what caused them to disband? They worried that their powers could not be controlled!"

"I'm still trying to wrap my mind around this highking nonsense," Fen said. "How is it merely an 'internal Alethi matter' if you've allowed another king to swear to you?"

Everyone started talking at once. Navani and Jasnah stepped forward, responding to the attacks, but Dalinar only sank into his seat. It was all falling apart. A sword, as keen as any on a battlefield, had been rammed into the heart of his coalition.

This is what you feared, he thought. *A world that turns not upon force of armies, but upon the concerns of scribes and bureaucrats.*

And in that world, he had just been deftly outflanked.

112

FOR THE LIVING

I am certain there are nine Unmade. There are many legends and names that I could have misinterpreted, conflating two Unmade into one. In the next section, I will discuss my theories on this.

—From Hessi's *Mythica*, page 266

K aladin remembered a woman's kiss.

Tarah had been special. The darkeyed daughter of an assistant quartermaster, she had grown up helping with her father's work. Though she was a hundred percent Alethi, she preferred dresses of an old-fashioned Thaylen style, which had an apronlike front with straps over the shoulders and skirts that ended right below the knee. She'd wear a buttoned shirt underneath, often in a bright color—brighter than most darkeyes could afford. Tarah knew how to squeeze the most out of her spheres.

That day, Kaladin had been sitting on a stump, shirt off, sweating. The evening was growing cold as the sun set, and he basked in the last warmth. His spear resting across his lap, he toyed with a rock of white, brown, and black. Alternating colors.

The warmth from the sun was mirrored as someone warm hugged him from behind, wrapping her arms across his chest. Kaladin rested a callused hand on Tarah's smooth one, drinking in her scent—of starched uniforms, new leather, and other clean things.

"You're done early," he said. "I thought there were greenvines to outfit today."

"I have the new girl doing the rest."

"I'm surprised. I know how much you like this part."

"Storms," she said, slipping around in front of him. "They get *so* embarrassed when you measure them. 'Hold on, kid. I'm not making a pass at you because I'm putting a measuring tape up against your chest, I swear. . . .'" She lifted his spear, looking it over with a critical eye, testing the balance. "I wish you'd let me requisition a new one for you."

"I like that one. Took me forever to find one long enough."

She peered along the length of the weapon, to make sure it was straight. She would never trust it, as she hadn't personally requisitioned it for him. She wore green today, under a brown skirt, her black hair tied back in a tail. Slightly plump, with a round face and firm build, Tarah's beauty was a subtle thing. Like an uncut gemstone. The more you saw of it—the more you discovered of its natural facets—the more you loved it. Until one day it struck you that you'd never known anything as wonderful.

"Any young boys among the greenvines?" Kaladin asked, standing up and pocketing Tien's stone.

"I didn't notice."

He grunted, waving to Gol—one of the other squadleaders. "You know I like to watch for kids who might need a little extra looking out for."

"I know, but I was busy. We got a caravan from Kholinar today." She leaned close to him. "There was real flour in one of the packages. I traded in some favors. You know I've been wanting you to try some of my father's Thaylen bread? I thought maybe we'd fix it tonight."

"Your father hates me."

"He's coming around. Besides, he loves anyone who compliments his bread."

"I have evening practice."

"You just got done practicing."

"I just got done warming up." He looked to her, then grimaced. "I organized the evening practice, Tarah. I can't just skip it. Besides, I thought you were going to be busy all evening. Maybe tomorrow, lunch?"

He kissed her on the cheek and reclaimed his spear. He'd taken only a step away when she spoke.

"I'm leaving, Kal," she said from behind.

He stumbled over his own feet, then spun about. *"What?"*

"I'm transferring," she said. "They offered me a scribe's job in Mourn's Vault, with the highprince's house. It's a good opportunity, particularly for someone like me."

"But . . ." He gaped. *"Leaving?"*

"I wanted to tell you over dinner, not out here in the cold. It's something I have to do. Father's getting older; he's worried he'll end up being shipped to the Shattered Plains. If I can get work, he can join me."

Kaladin put a hand to his head. She couldn't just leave, could she?

Tarah walked over, stood on the tips of her toes, and kissed him lightly on the lips.

"Could you . . . not go?" he asked.

She shook her head.

"Maybe I could get a transfer?" he said. "To the highprince's standing house guard?"

"Would you do that?"

"I . . ."

No. He wouldn't.

Not while he carried that stone in his pocket, not while the memory of his brother dying was fresh in his mind. Not while lighteyed highlords got boys killed in petty fights.

"Oh, Kal," she whispered, then squeezed his arm. "Maybe someday you'll learn how to be there for the living, not just for the dead."

After she left, he got two letters from her, talking about her life in Mourn's Vault. He had paid someone to read them to him.

He never sent responses. Because he was stupid, because he didn't understand. Because men make mistakes when they're young and angry.

Because she had been right.

⁘

Kaladin shouldered his harpoon, leading his companions through the strange forest. They'd flown part of the way, but needed to conserve what little Stormlight they had left.

So, they'd spent the last two days hiking. Trees and more trees, lifespren floating among them, the occasional bobbing souls of fish. Syl kept saying that they were lucky they hadn't encountered any angerspren or other predators. To her, this forest was strangely silent, strangely empty.

The jungle-style trees had given way to taller, more statuesque ones with deep crimson trunks and limbs like burnt-red crystals that, at the ends, burst into small collections of minerals. The rugged obsidian landscape was full of deep valleys and endless towering hills. Kaladin was beginning to worry that—despite the motionless sun to provide an unerring way to gauge their heading—they were going in the wrong direction.

"Storms, bridgeboy," Adolin said, hiking up the incline after him. "Maybe a break?"

"At the top," Kaladin said.

Without Stormlight, Shallan trailed farthest behind, Pattern at her side. Exhaustionspren circled in the air above, like large chickens. Though she tried to push herself, she wasn't a soldier, and often was the biggest limitation to their pace. Of course, without her mapmaking skills and memory of Thaylen City's exact location, they probably wouldn't have any idea which way to go.

Fortunately, there was no sign of pursuit. Still, Kaladin couldn't help worrying that they were moving too slowly.

Be there, Tarah had told him. *For the living.*

He urged them up this hillside, past a section of broken ground, where the obsidian had fractured like layers of crem that hadn't hardened properly. Worry pulled him forward. Step after relentless step.

He *had* to get to the Oathgate. He would *not* fail like he had in Kholinar.

A single glowing windspren burst alight next to him as he reached the top of the hill. Cresting it, he found himself overlooking a sea of souls. Thousands upon thousands of candle flames bobbed about in the next valley over, moving above a grand ocean of glass beads.

Thaylen City.

Adolin joined him, then finally Shallan and the three spren. Shallan sighed and settled to the ground, coughing softly from the effort of the climb.

Amid the sea of lights were two towering spren, much like the ones they'd seen in Kholinar. One sparkled a multitude of colors while the other shimmered an oily black. Both stood tall, holding spears as long as a building. The sentries of the Oathgate, and they didn't look corrupted.

Beneath them, the device itself manifested as a large stone platform with a wide, sweeping white bridge running over the beads and to the shore.

That bridge was guarded by an entire army of enemy spren, hundreds—perhaps thousands—strong.

113

THE THING
MEN DO BEST

If I'm correct and my research true, then the question remains. Who is the ninth Unmade? Is it truly Dai-Gonarthis? If so, could their actions have actually caused the complete destruction of Aimia?

—From Hessi's *Mythica*, page 307

Dalinar stood alone in the rooms Queen Fen had given him, staring out the window, looking west. Toward Shinovar, far beyond the horizon. A land with strange beasts like horses, chickens. And humans.

He'd left the other monarchs arguing in the temple below; anything he said only seemed to widen the rifts among them. They didn't trust him. They'd never really trusted him. His deception proved them right.

Storms. He felt *furious* with himself. He should have released those visions, should have immediately told the others about Elhokar. There had simply been so much piling on top of him. His memories . . . his excommunication . . . worry for Adolin and Elhokar . . .

Part of him couldn't help but be impressed by how deftly he'd been outmaneuvered. Queen Fen worried about Dalinar being genuine; the enemy had delivered perfect proof that Dalinar had hidden political motives. Noura and the Azish worried that the powers were dangerous, whispering of Lost Radiants. To them, the enemy indicated that Dalinar was being manipulated by evil visions. And to Taravangian—who spoke so often of philosophy—the enemy suggested that their moral foundation for the war was a sham.

Or maybe that dart was for Dalinar himself. Taravangian said that a king was justified in doing terrible things in the name of the state. But Dalinar . . .

For once, he'd assumed what he was doing was *right*.

Did you really think you belonged here? the Stormfather asked. *That you were native to Roshar?*

"Yes, maybe," Dalinar said. "I thought . . . maybe we came from Shinovar originally."

That is the land you were given, the Stormfather said. *A place where the plants and animals you brought here could grow.*

"We weren't able to confine ourselves to what we were given."

When has any man ever been content with what he has?

"When has any tyrant ever said to himself, 'This is enough'?" Dalinar whispered, remembering words Gavilar had once spoken.

The Stormfather rumbled.

"The Almighty kept this from his Radiants," Dalinar said. "When they discovered it, they abandoned their vows."

It is more than that. My memory of all this is . . . strange. First, I was not fully awake; I was but the spren of a storm. Then I was like a child. Changed and shaped during the frantic last days of a dying god.

But I do remember. It was not only the truth of humankind's origin that caused the Recreance. It was the distinct, powerful fear that they would destroy this world, as men like them had destroyed the one before. The Radiants abandoned their vows for that reason, as will you.

"I will *not*," Dalinar said. "I *won't* let my Radiants retread the fate of their predecessors."

Won't you?

Dalinar's attention was drawn to a solemn group of men leaving the temple below. Bridge Four, spears held on slumped shoulders, heads bowed as they quietly marched down the steps.

Dalinar scrambled out of his villa and ran down the steps to intercept the bridgemen. "Where are you going?" he demanded.

They halted, falling into ranks at attention.

"Sir," Teft said. "We thought we'd head back to Urithiru. We left some of the men behind, and they deserve to know about this business with the ancient Radiants."

"What we've discovered doesn't change the fact that we are being invaded," Dalinar said.

"Invaded by people trying to reclaim their homeland," Sigzil said. "Storms. I'd be mad too."

"We're supposed to be the good guys, you know?" Leyten said. "Fighting for a good cause, for once in our storming lives."

Echoes of his own thoughts. Dalinar found he couldn't formulate an argument against that.

"We'll see what Kal says," Teft replied. "Sir. All respect, sir. But we'll see what he says. He knows the right of things, even when the rest of us don't."

And if he never returns? Dalinar thought. *What if none of them return?* It had been four weeks. How long could he keep pretending that Adolin and Elhokar were alive out there somewhere? That pain hid behind the rest, taunting him.

The bridgemen gave Dalinar their unique cross-armed salute, then left without waiting to be dismissed.

In the past, Honor was able to guard against this, the Stormfather told him. *He convinced the Radiants they were righteous, even if this land hadn't originally been theirs. Who cares what your ancestors did, when the enemy is trying to kill you right now?*

But in the days leading to the Recreance, Honor was dying. When that generation of knights learned the truth, Honor did not support them. He raved, speaking of the Dawnshards, ancient weapons used to destroy the Tranquiline Halls. Honor . . . promised that Surgebinders would do the same to Roshar.

"Odium claimed the same thing."

He can see the future, though only cloudily. Regardless, I . . . understand now as I never did before. The ancient Radiants didn't abandon their oaths out of pettiness. They tried to protect the world. I blame them for their weakness, their broken oaths. But I also understand. You have cursed me, human, with this capacity.

The meeting in the temple seemed to be breaking up. The Azish contingent started down the steps.

"Our enemy hasn't changed," Dalinar said to them. "The need for a coalition is as strong as ever."

The young emperor, being carried in a palanquin, didn't look at him. Oddly, the Azish didn't make for the Oathgate, instead taking a path down into the city.

Only Vizier Noura idled to speak to him. "Jasnah Kholin might be right," she said in Azish. "The destruction of our old world, your secret visions, this business with you being highking—it seems too great a coincidence for it all to come at once."

"Then you can see that we're being manipulated."

"Manipulated by the truth, Kholin," she said, meeting his eyes. "That Oathgate is dangerous. These powers of yours are *dangerous*. Deny it."

"I cannot. I will not found this coalition on lies."

"You *already have*."

He drew in a sharp breath.

Noura shook her head. "We will take the scout ships and join the fleet carrying our soldiers. Then we will wait out this storm. After that . . . we shall see. Taravangian has said we may use his vessels to return to our empire, without needing to use the Oathgates."

She walked off after the emperor, eschewing the palanquin waiting to carry her.

Others drifted down the steps around him. Veden highprinces, who gave excuses. Thaylen lighteyes from their guild councils, who avoided him. The Alethi highprinces and scribes expressed solidarity—but Alethkar couldn't do this on its own.

Queen Fen was one of the last to leave the temple.

"Will you leave me too?" Dalinar asked.

She laughed. "To go where, old hound? An army is coming this way. I still need your famous Alethi infantry; I can't afford to throw you out."

"Such bitterness."

"Oh, did it show? I'm going to check on the city's defenses; if you decide to join us, we'll be at the walls."

"I'm sorry, Fen," Dalinar said, "for betraying your trust."

She shrugged. "I don't really think you intend to conquer me, Kholin. But oddly . . . I can't help wishing I *did* have to worry. Best I can tell, you've become a good man right in time to bravely sink with this ship. That's commendable, until I remember that the Blackthorn would have long since murdered everyone trying to sink him."

Fen and her consort climbed into a palanquin. People continued to trickle past, but eventually Dalinar stood alone before the quiet temple.

"I'm sorry, Dalinar," Taravangian said softly from behind. Dalinar turned, surprised to find the old man sitting on the steps. "I assumed everyone had the same information, and that it would be best to air it. I didn't expect all of this. . . ."

"This isn't your fault," Dalinar said.

"And yet . . ." He stood up, then walked—slowly—down the steps. "I'm sorry, Dalinar. I fear I can no longer fight beside you."

"Why?" Dalinar said. "Taravangian, you're the most pragmatic ruler I've met! Aren't you the one who talked to me about the importance of doing what was politically necessary!"

"And that is what I must do now, Dalinar. I wish I could explain. Forgive me."

He ignored Dalinar's pleas, limping down the stairs. Moving stiffly, the old man climbed into a palanquin and was carried away.

Dalinar sank down on the steps.

I tried my best to hide this, the Stormfather said.

"So we could continue living a lie?"

It is, in my experience, the thing men do best.

"Don't insult us."

What? Is this not what you've been doing, these last six years? Pretending that you aren't a monster? Pretending you didn't kill her, Dalinar?

Dalinar winced. He made a fist, but there was nothing here he could fight. He dropped his hand to his side, shoulders drooping. Finally, he climbed to his feet and quietly trudged up the stone steps to his villa.

THE END OF

Part Four

INTERLUDES

VENLI • RYSN • TEFT

After living for a week in a cave in Marat, Venli found herself missing the stone hermitage she'd been given outside Kholinar. Her new dwelling was even more austere, with only a single blanket for sleeping, and a simple cookfire upon which she prepared fish the crowds brought her.

She was growing dirty, rough. That was what the Fused seemed to want: a hermit living in the wilds. Apparently that was more convincing for the local crowds they brought to listen to her—most of whom were former Thaylen slaves. She was instructed to speak of "Passion" and emotion more often than she had in Alethkar.

"My people are dead now," Venli said to Destruction, repeating the now-familiar speech. "They fell in that last assault, singing as they drew the storm. I remain, but my people's work is done."

Those words *hurt*. Her people couldn't be *completely* gone . . . could they?

"The day now belongs to your Passion," she continued to Command. "We had named ourselves 'listeners' because of the songs we heard. These are your heritage, but you are not to just listen, but sing. Adopt the rhythms and Passions of your ancestors! You must sail to battle. For the future, for your children! And for us. Those who died that you might exist."

She turned away, as instructed that she do after the end of each speech. She wasn't allowed to answer questions any longer, not since she'd talked with some of these singers about the specific history of her people. It made her wonder. Did the Fused and the Voidspren *fear* the heritage of her people, even as they used her for their purposes? Or did they not trust her for other reasons?

She put her hand to her pouch. Odium didn't seem to know that she'd been in that vision with Dalinar Kholin. Behind, a Voidspren led the Thaylen singers away. Venli moved toward her cave, but then hesitated. A Fused sat on the rocks just above the opening.

"Ancient One?" she asked.

He grinned at her and giggled.

Another one of those.

She started into the cave, but he dropped and seized her under the arms, then carried her into the sky. Venli prevented herself—with difficulty—from trying to batter him away. The Fused never touched her, not even the crazy ones, without orders. Indeed, this one flew her down to one of the many ships at the harbor, where Rine—the tall Fused who had accompanied her during her first days preaching in Alethkar—stood at the prow. He glanced toward her as she was landed—roughly—on the deck.

She hummed to Conceit at her treatment.

He hummed to Spite. A small acknowledgment of a wrong done, the best she'd get out of him, so she hummed to Satisfaction in response.

"Ancient One?" she asked to Craving.

"You are to accompany us as we sail," he said to Command. "You may wash yourself in the cabin as we go, if you wish. There is water."

Venli hummed to Craving and looked toward the main cabin. Craving slipped into Abashment as she considered the sheer *size* of the fleet that was launching around her. Hundreds of ships, which must have been filled with thousands of singers, were sailing from coves all along the coast. They dotted the seas like rockbuds on the plains.

"Now?" she asked to Abashment. "I wasn't prepared! I didn't know!"

"You may wish to grab hold of something. The storm will soon arrive."

She looked to the west. A storm? She hummed to Craving again.

"Ask," Rine said to Command.

"I can easily see the strength of the grand assault force we've gathered. But . . . why do we need such? Are not the Fused enough of an army themselves?"

"Cowardice?" he asked to Derision. "You do not wish to fight?"

"I simply seek to understand."

Rine changed to a new rhythm, one she rarely heard. The Rhythm of Withdrawal—one of the only new rhythms that had a calm tone. "The strongest and most skilled of our number have yet to awaken—but even if we were all awake, we would not fight this war alone. This world will not be ours; we fight to give it to you, our descendants. When it is won, our vengeance taken and our homeland secured at long last, we will sleep. Finally."

He then pointed at the cabin. "Go prepare. We will sail swiftly, with Odium's own storm to guide us."

As if in agreement with his words, red lightning flashed on the western horizon.

Rysn was bored.

Once she'd walked to the farthest reaches of Roshar, trading with the isolationist Shin. Once she'd sailed with her babsk to Icewater and cut a deal with pirates. Once she'd climbed Reshi greatshells, which were as large as towns.

Now she kept Queen Fen's ledgers.

It was a good job, with an office in the Thaylen Gemstone Reserve. Vstim— her former babsk—had traded favors to get her the job. Her apprenticeship finished, she was a free woman. No longer a student. Now a master.

Of boredom.

She sat in her chair, doodling at the edges of a Liaforan word puzzle. Rysn could balance while sitting, though she couldn't feel her legs and embarrassingly couldn't control certain bodily functions. She had to rely upon her porters to move her.

Career, over. Freedom, over. Life, *over*.

She sighed and pushed away her word puzzle. Time to get back to work. Her duties included annotating the queen's pending mercantile contracts with references to previous ones, keeping the queen's personal vault in the Gemstone Reserve, preparing weekly expenditure reports, and accounting the queen's salary as a portion of taxable income from various Thaylen interests at home and abroad.

Wheeeeeeeee.

She had an audit today, which had prevented her from attending Fen's meeting with the monarchs. She might have enjoyed seeing the Black-thorn and the Azish emperor. Well, the other aides would bring her word once the meeting was through. For now, she prepared for her audit, working by spherelight, as the reserve didn't have windows.

The walls of her office were blank. She'd originally hung souvenirs from her years traveling, but those had reminded her of a life she could no longer have. A life full of promise. A life that had ended when she'd stupidly fallen from the head of a greatshell, and landed here, in this cripple's chair. Now, the only memento she kept was a single pot of Shin grass.

Well, that and the little creature sleeping among the blades. Chiri-Chiri breathed softly, rippling the too-dumb grass, which didn't pull into burrows. It grew in something called soil, which was like crem that never hardened.

Chiri-Chiri herself was a small winged beast a little longer than Rysn's outstretched palm. The Reshi named her a larkin, and though she was the size of a large cremling, she had the snout, carapace, and build of a creature far more grand. An axehound, perhaps, with wings. A lithe little flying predator—though, for all her dangerous appearance, she sure did like to nap.

As Rysn worked, Chiri-Chiri finally stirred and peeked out from the grass, then made a series of clicking sounds with her jaw. She climbed down onto the desk and eyed the diamond mark Rysn was using for light.

"No," Rysn said, double-checking numbers in her ledger.

Chiri-Chiri clicked again, slinking toward the gem.

"You *just* ate," Rysn said, then used her palm to shoo the larkin back. "I need that for light."

Chiri-Chiri clicked in annoyance, then flew—wings beating very quickly—to the upper reaches of the room, where she settled onto one of her favorite perches, the lintel above the doorway.

A short time later, a knock at the door interrupted Rysn's tedium. "Come," she said. Her man, Wmlak—who was half assistant, half porter—poked his head in.

"Let me guess," Rysn said, "the auditor is early." They always were.

"Yes, but . . ."

Behind Wmlak, Rysn caught sight of a familiar flat-topped, conical hat. Wmlak stepped back and gestured toward an old man in blue and red robes, his Thaylen eyebrows tucked behind his ears. Spry for a man past his seventieth year, Vstim had a wise but unyielding way about him. Inoffensively calculating. He carried a small box under his arm.

Rysn gasped in delight; once, she would have leaped to her feet to embrace him. Now she could only sit there and gape. "But you were off to trade in New Natanan!"

"The seas are not safe these days," Vstim said. "And the queen requested my aid in difficult negotiations with the Alethi. I have returned, with some reluctance, to accept an appointment from Her Majesty."

An appointment . . .

"In the *government?*" Rysn asked.

"Minister of trade, and royal liaison to the guild of shipping merchants."

Rysn could only gape further. That was the highest civilian appointment *in the kingdom.* "But . . . Babsk, you'll have to *live* in Thaylen City!"

"Well, I *am* feeling my age these days."

"Nonsense. You're as lively as I am." Rysn glanced at her legs. "More."

"Not so lively that I wouldn't mind a seat . . ."

She realized he was still standing in the doorway to her office. Even all these months after her accident, she pushed with her arms as if to spring up and fetch him a seat. Idiot.

"Please, sit!" she said, waving toward the room's other chair. He settled down and placed his box on the table while she twisted to do something to welcome him, leaning over—precariously—to get the teapot. The tea was cold, unfortunately. Chiri-Chiri had drained the gemstone in her fabrial hotplate.

"I can't believe you'd agree to settle down!" she said, handing him a cup.

"Some would say that the opportunity offered me is far too important to refuse."

"Storm that," Rysn said. "Staying in one city will wilt you—you'll spend your days doing paperwork and being bored."

"Rysn," he said, taking her hand. "Child."

She looked away. Chiri-Chiri flew down and landed on her head, clicking angrily at Vstim.

"I promise I'm not going to hurt her," the old man said, grinning and releasing Rysn's hand. "Here, I brought you something. See?" He held up a ruby chip.

Chiri-Chiri considered, then hovered down above his hand—not touching it—and sucked the Stormlight out. It flew to her in a little stream, and she clicked happily, then zipped over to the pot of grass and wriggled into it, peeking out at Vstim.

"You still have the grass, I see," he said.

"You ordered me to keep it."

"You're now a master merchant, Rysn! You needn't obey the orders of a doddering old man."

The grass rustled as Chiri-Chiri shifted. She was too big to hide in it, though that never stopped her from trying.

"Chiri-Chiri likes it," Rysn said. "Maybe because it can't move. Kind of like me . . ."

"Have you tried that Radiant who—"

"Yes. He can't heal my legs. It's been too long since my accident, which is appropriate. This is my consequence—payment for a contract I entered into willingly the moment I climbed down the side of that greatshell."

"You *don't* have to lock yourself away, Rysn."

"This is a good job. You yourself got it for me."

"Because you refused to go on further trading expeditions!"

"What good would I be? One must trade from a position of power, something I can never do again. Besides, an exotic goods merchant who can't walk? You know how much hiking is required."

Vstim took her hand again. "I thought you were frightened. I thought you wanted something safe and secure. But I've been listening. Hmalka has told me—"

"You spoke to my superior?"

"People talk."

"My work has been exemplary," Rysn said.

"It isn't your work she's worried about." He turned and brushed the grass, drawing Chiri-Chiri's attention to his hand. She narrowed her eyes at it. "Do you remember what I told you, when you cut out that grass?"

"That I was to keep it. Until it no longer seemed odd."

"You've always been so quick to make assumptions. About yourself, now, more than others. Here, perhaps this will . . . anyway, have a look." Vstim handed her the box.

She frowned, then slid off the wooden lid. Inside was a wound-up cord of white rope. Beside that, a slip of paper? Rysn took out the sheet, reading it.

"A deed of ownership?" she whispered. "To a *ship*?"

"Brand new," Vstim said. "A three-masted frigate, the largest I've ever owned—with fabrial stabilizers for storms, of the finest Thaylen engineering. I had her built in the shipyards of Klna City, which luckily sheltered her from both storms. While I've given the rest of my fleet—what's left of it—to the queen for use against the invasion, this one I reserved."

"*Wandersail*," Rysn said, reading the ship's name. "Babsk, you *are* a romantic. Don't tell me you believe that old story?"

"One can believe in a story without believing it happened." He smiled. "Whose rules are you following, Rysn? Who is forcing you to stay here? Take the ship. Go! I wish to fund your initial trade run, as an investment. After that, you'll have to do well to maintain a vessel of this size!"

Rysn recognized the white rope now. It was a captain's cord some twenty feet long, used as a traditional Thaylen mark of ownership. She'd wrap it in her colors and string it in the rigging of her ship.

It was a gift worth a fortune.

"I can't take this," she said, putting the box on the desk. "I'm sorry. I—"

He pushed the cord into her hands. "Just think about it, Rysn. Humor an old man who can no longer travel."

She held the rope and found her eyes watering. "Bother. Babsk, I have an *auditor* coming today! I need to be composed and ready to account the queen's vault!"

"Fortunately, the auditor is an old friend who has seen much worse from you than a few tears."

". . . But you're the minister of trade!"

"They were going to make me go to a stuffy meeting with old Kholin and his soldiers," Vstim said, leaning in, "but I insisted on coming to do this. I've always wanted to see the queen's vault in person."

Rysn wiped her tears, trying to recover some of her decorum. "Well, let's be to it then. I assure you, everything is in order."

* *

The Sphere Vault's thick steel door required three numbers to open, each rolled into a different dial, in three separate rooms. Rysn and other scribes knew one number, the door guards protected another, and an auditor—like Vstim—was typically given a third by the queen or the minister of the treasury. All were changed at random intervals.

Rysn knew for a fact that this was mostly for show. In a world of Shardblades, the real defense of the vault was in the layers of guards who surrounded the building, and—more importantly—in the careful auditing of its contents. Though novels were full of stories of the vault being robbed, the only real thefts had occurred through embezzlement.

Rysn moved her dial to the proper number, then pulled the lever in her room. The vault door finally opened with a resounding thump, and she scrambled her dial and called for Wmlak. Her porter entered, then pushed down on the back handles of her chair, lifting the front legs so he could wheel it out to meet the others.

Vstim stood by the now-open vault door with several soldiers. Today's inner door guard—Tlik—stood with crossbow at the ready, barring entry. There was a slot that let the men stationed in the vault communicate with those outside, but the door couldn't be opened from within.

"Scheduled accounting of the queen's personal vault," Rysn said to him. "Daily passcode: lockstep."

Tlik nodded, stepping back and lowering his crossbow. Vstim entered with ledger in hand, trailed by a member of the Queen's Guard: a rough-looking man with a shaved head and spiked eyebrows. Once they were in, Wmlak wheeled Rysn through the vault door, down a short corridor, and into a little alcove, where another guard—Fladm, today—waited.

Her porter brushed off his hands, then nodded to her and retreated. Tlik shut the vault door after him, the metal making a deep *thump* as it locked into place. The inner vault guards didn't like anyone coming in who wasn't specifically authorized—and that included her servant. She'd have to rely on the guards to move her now—but unfortunately, her large wheeled chair was too bulky to fit between the rows of shelves in the main vault.

Rysn felt a healthy dose of shame in front of her former babsk as she was taken—like a sack of roots—from her chair with rear wheels to a smaller chair with poles along the sides. Being carried was the most humiliating part.

The guards left her usual chair in the alcove, near the steps down to the lower level. Then, Tlik and the guardsman the queen had sent—Rysn didn't know his name—took the poles and carried her into the main vault chamber.

Even here, in this job where she sat most of the time, her inability was a huge inconvenience. Her embarrassment was exacerbated as Chiri-Chiri—who wasn't allowed in the vault for practical reasons—flitted by in a buzz of wings. How had *she* gotten in?

Tlik chuckled, but Rysn only sighed.

The main vault chamber was filled with metal racks, like bookcases, containing display boxes of gemstones. It smelled stale. Of a place that never changed, and was never intended to change.

The guards carried her down one of the narrow rows, light from spheres tied to their belts providing the only illumination. Rysn carried the captain's rope in her lap, and fingered it with one hand. Surely she couldn't take this offer. It was too generous. Too incredible.

Too difficult.

"So dark!" Vstim said. "A room full of a million gemstones, and it's *dark*?"

"Most gems never leave," Rysn said. "The personal merchant vaults are on the lower level, and there's some light to those, with the spheres everyone has been bringing lately. These, though . . . they're always here."

Possession of these gems changed frequently, but it was all done with numbers in a ledger. It was a quirk of the Thaylen system of underwriting trades; as long as everyone was confident that these gemstones were here, large sums could change hands without risk of anything being stolen.

Each gemstone was carefully annotated with numbers inscribed both on a plate glued to its bottom and on the rack that held it. Those numbers were what people bought and sold—Rysn was shocked by how few people actually asked to come down and view the thing they were trading to own.

"0013017-36!" Vstim said. "The Benval Diamond! I owned that way back when. Memorized the number even. Huh. You know, it's smaller than I thought it would be."

She and the two guards led Vstim to the back wall, which held a series of smaller metal vault doors. The main vault behind them was silent; no other scribes were working today, though Chiri-Chiri did flit past. She hovered down toward the queen's guardsman—eyeing the spheres on his belt—but Rysn snatched her from the air.

Chiri-Chiri griped, buzzing her wings against Rysn's hand and clicking. Rysn blushed, but held tight. "Sorry."

"Must be like a buffet for her down here!" Tlik said.

"A buffet of empty plates," Rysn said. "Keep an eye on your belt, Tlik."

The two guards set her chair down near a specific vault. With her free hand, Rysn dug a key from her pocket and handed it to Vstim. "Go ahead. Vault Thirteen."

Vstim unlocked and swung open the smaller vault-within-the-vault, which was roughly the size of a closet.

Light poured from it.

The shelves inside were filled with gemstones, spheres, jewelry, and even some mundane objects like letters and an old knife. But the most stunning item in the collection was obviously the large ruby on the center shelf. The size of a child's head, it glowed brightly.

The King's Drop. Gemstones of its size weren't unheard of—most greatshells had gemhearts as big. What made the King's Drop unique was that it was still glowing—over *two hundred* years after being first locked into the vault.

Vstim touched it with one finger. The light shone with such brilliance that the room seemed almost to be in daylight, though shaded bloodred by the gemstone's color.

"Amazing," Vstim whispered.

"As far as scholars can tell," Rysn said, "the King's Drop never loses its Stormlight. A stone this large *should* have run out after a month. It's something about the crystal lattice, the lack of flaws and imperfections."

"They say it's a chunk off the Stone of Ten Dawns."

"Another story?" Rysn said. "You *are* a romantic."

Her former babsk smiled, then placed a cloth shade over the gemstone to reduce its glare so it wouldn't interfere with their work. He opened his ledger. "Let's start with the smaller gemstones and work our way up, shall we?"

Rysn nodded.

The queen's guard killed Tlik.

He did it with a knife, right into the neck. Tlik dropped without a word, though the sound of the knife being ripped free shocked Rysn. The treacherous guard knocked against her chair, toppling her over as he slashed at Vstim.

The enemy underestimated the merchant's spryness. Vstim dodged backward into the queen's vault, screaming, "Murder! Robbery! Raise the alarm!"

Rysn untangled herself from her toppled chair and, panicked, pulled herself away by her arms, dragging legs like cordwood. The murderer reached into the vault to deal with her babsk, and she heard a grunt.

A moment later, the traitor stepped out, carrying a large red light in his hand. The King's Drop, shining brightly enough despite its black wrapping cloth. Rysn caught a glimpse of Vstim collapsed on the floor inside the vault, holding his side.

The traitor kicked the door closed—locking the old merchant away. He glanced toward her.

And a crossbow bolt hit him.

"Thief in the vault!" Fladm's voice said. "Alarm!"

Rysn pulled herself to a row of gemstone racks. Behind her, the thief took a *second* crossbow bolt, but didn't seem to notice. How . . .

The thief stepped over and picked up poor Tlik's crossbow. Footsteps and calls indicated that several guards from the lower level had heard Fladm, and were coming up the steps. The thief fired the crossbow once down a nearby row, and a shout of pain from Fladm indicated it had connected. Another guardsman arrived a second later and attacked the thief with his sword.

He should have run for help! Rysn thought as she huddled by the shelf. The thief took a cut along the face from the sword, then set his prize down and caught the guard's arm. The two struggled, and Rysn watched the cut on the thief's face reknit.

He was *healing*? Could . . . could this man be a *Knight Radiant*?

Rysn's eyes flicked toward the large ruby the thief had set down. Four more guards joined the fight, obviously assuming they could subdue one man on their own.

Sit back. Let them handle it.

Chiri-Chiri suddenly darted past, ignoring the combatants and making for the glowing gemstone. Rysn lunged forward—well, more *flopped* forward—to grab at the larkin, but missed. Chiri-Chiri landed on the cloth containing the enormous ruby.

Nearby, the thief stabbed one of the guards. Rysn winced at the awful sight of their struggle, lit by the ruby, then crawled forward—dragging her legs—and snatched the gemstone.

Chiri-Chiri clicked at her in annoyance as Rysn dragged the ruby with her around the corner. Another guard screamed. They were dropping quickly.

Have to do something. Can't just sit here, can I?

Rysn clutched the gemstone and looked down the row between shelves. An impossible distance, hundreds of feet, to the corridor and the exit. The door was locked, but she could call through the communication slot for help.

But why? If five guards couldn't handle the thief, what could one crippled woman do?

My babsk is locked in the queen's vault. Bleeding.

She looked down the long row again, then used the cord Vstim had given her to tie the ruby's cloth closed around it, and attached it to her ankle so she wouldn't have to carry it. Then she started pulling herself along the shelves. Chiri-Chiri rode behind on the ruby, and its light dimmed. Everyone else was struggling for their lives, but the little larkin was feasting.

Rysn made faster progress than she had expected to, though soon her arms began to ache. Behind, the fighting stilled, the last guard's shout cutting off.

Rysn redoubled her efforts, pulling herself along toward the exit, reaching the alcove where they'd left her chair. Here, she found blood.

Fladm lay at the threshold of the entry corridor, a bolt in him, his own crossbow on the floor beside him. Rysn collapsed a couple of feet from him, muscles burning. Spheres on his belt illuminated her chair and the steps down to the lower vault level. No more help would be coming from down there.

Past Fladm's body, the corridor led to the door out. "Help!" she shouted. "Thief!"

She thought she heard voices on the other side, through the communication slot. But . . . it would take the guards outside time to get it open, as they didn't know all three codes. Maybe that was good. The thief couldn't get out until they opened it, right?

Of course, that meant she was trapped inside with him while Vstim bled. . . .

The silence from behind haunted her. Rysn heaved herself to Fladm's corpse and took his crossbow and bolts, then pulled herself toward the steps. She turned over, putting the enormous ruby beside her, and pushed up so that she was seated against the wall.

She waited, sweating, struggling to point the unwieldy weapon into the darkness of the vault. Footsteps sounded somewhere inside, coming closer. Trembling, she swung the crossbow back and forth, searching for motion. Only then did she notice that the crossbow *wasn't loaded.*

She gasped, then hastily pulled out a bolt. She looked from it to the crossbow, helpless. You were supposed to cock the weapon by stepping into a stirrup on the front, then pulling it upward. Easy to do, if you could *step* in the first place.

A figure emerged from the darkness. The bald guard, his clothing ripped, a sword dripping blood in his shadowed hand.

Rysn lowered the crossbow. What did it matter? Did she think she could fight? That man could just heal anyway.

She was alone.

Helpless.

Live or die. Did she care?

I . . .

Yes. Yes, I care! I want to sail my own ship!

A sudden blur darted out of the darkness and flew around the thief. 1067

Chiri-Chiri moved with blinding speed, hovering about the man, drawing his attention.

Rysn frantically placed the crossbow bolt, then took the captain's cord off the ruby's sack and tied one end to the stirrup at the front of the crossbow. She tied the other end to the back of her heavy wooden chair. That done, she spared a glance for Chiri-Chiri, then hesitated.

The larkin was *feeding* off the thief. A line of light streamed from him, but it was a strange dark *violet* light. Chiri-Chiri flew about, drawing it from the man, whose face *melted* away, revealing marbled skin underneath.

A parshman? Wearing some kind of disguise?

No, a Voidbringer. He growled and said something in an unfamiliar language, batting at Chiri-Chiri, who buzzed away into the darkness.

Rysn gripped the crossbow tightly with one hand, then with the other she shoved her chair down the long stairway.

It fell in a clatter, the rope playing out after it. Rysn grabbed on to the crossbow with the other hand. The cord pulled taut as the chair jerked to a stop partway down the steps, and she yanked back on the crossbow at the same time, hanging on for all she was worth.

Click.

She cut the rope free with her belt knife. The thief lunged for her, and she twisted—screaming—and pulled the firing lever on the crossbow. She didn't know how to aim properly, but the thief obligingly loomed over her.

The crossbow bolt hit him right in the chin.

He dropped and, blessedly, fell still. Whatever power had been healing him was gone, consumed by Chiri-Chiri.

The larkin buzzed over and landed on her stomach, clicking happily.

"Thank you," Rysn whispered, sweat streaming down the sides of her face. "Thank you, *thank you.*" She hesitated. "Are you . . . bigger?"

Chiri-Chiri clicked happily.

Vstim. I need the second set of keys.

And . . . that ruby, the King's Drop. The Voidbringers had been trying to steal it. Why?

Rysn tossed aside the crossbow, then pulled herself toward the vault door.

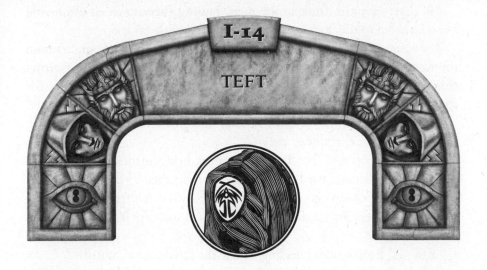

Teft could function.

You learned how to do that. How to cling to the normal parts of your life so that people wouldn't be *too* worried. So that you wouldn't be *too* undependable.

He stumbled sometimes. That eroded trust, to the point where it was hard to keep telling himself that he could handle it. He knew, deep down, that he'd end up alone again. The men of Bridge Four would tire of digging him out of trouble.

But for now, Teft functioned. He nodded to Malata, who was working the Oathgate, then led his men across the platform and down the ramp toward Urithiru. They were a subdued group. Few grasped the meaning of what they'd learned, but they all sensed that something had *changed*.

Made perfect sense to Teft. It couldn't be easy, now, could it. Not in his storming life.

A winding path through corridors and a stairwell led them back toward their barracks. As they walked, a woman appeared in the hallway beside Teft, roughly his height, glowing with soft blue-white light. Storming spren. He pointedly did not look at her.

You have Words to speak, Teft, she said in his mind.

"Storm you," he muttered.

You have started on this path. When will you tell the others the oaths you have sworn?

"I didn't—"

She turned away from him suddenly, becoming alert, looking down the corridor toward the Bridge Four barracks.

"What?" Teft stopped. "Something wrong?"

Something is very wrong. Run quickly, Teft!

He charged out in front of the men, causing them to shout after him. He scrambled to the door into their barracks and threw it open.

The scent of blood immediately assaulted him. The Bridge Four common room was in shambles, and blood stained the floor. Teft shouted, rushing through the room to find three corpses near the back. He dropped his spear and fell to his knees beside Rock, Bisig, and Eth.

Still breathing, Teft thought, feeling at Rock's neck. *Still breathing. Remember Kaladin's training, you fool.*

"Check the others!" he shouted as more bridgemen joined him. He pulled off his coat and used it on Rock's wounds; the Horneater was sliced up good, a half dozen cuts that looked like they'd come from a knife.

"Bisig's alive," Peet called. "Though . . . storms, that's a Shardblade wound!"

"Eth . . ." Lopen said, kneeling beside the third body. "Storms . . ."

Teft hesitated. Eth had been the one carrying the Honorblade today. Dead.

They came for the Blade, he realized.

Huio—who was better at field medicine than Teft—took over ministering to Rock. Blood on his hands, Teft stumbled back.

"We need Renarin," Peet said. "It's Rock's best chance!"

"But where did he go?" Lyn said. "He was at the meeting, but left." She looked toward Laran, one of the other former messengers—fastest among them. "Run for the guard post! They should have a spanreed to contact the Oathgate!"

Laran dashed out of the room. Nearby, Bisig groaned. His eyes fluttered open. His entire arm was grey, and his uniform had been sliced through.

"Bisig!" Peet asked. "Storms, what happened!"

"Thought . . . thought it was one of us," Bisig muttered. "I didn't really look—until he attacked." He leaned back, groaning, closing his eyes. "He had on a bridgeman coat."

"Stormfather!" Leyten said. "Did you see the face?"

Bisig nodded. "Nobody I recognize. A short man, Alethi. Bridge Four coat, lieutenant's knots on the shoulder . . ."

Lopen, nearby, frowned, then glanced toward Teft.

A Bridge Four officer's coat, worn as a disguise. *Teft's* coat, which he'd sold weeks ago in the market. To get a few spheres.

He stumbled back as they hovered around Rock and Bisig, then fled through a falling patch of shamespren into the hallway outside.

PART
FIVE

New Unity

THE KNIGHTS RADIANT • ASH • NAVANI •
ADOLIN • TARAVANGIAN • YANAGAWN •
PALONA • VYRE • WIT

THE COST

FIVE AND A HALF YEARS AGO

Dalinar came to himself, gasping, in the cabin of a stormwagon. Heart pounding, he spun about, kicking aside empty bottles and lifting his fists. Outside, the riddens of a storm washed the walls with rain.

What in the Almighty's tenth name had *that* been? One moment, he'd been lying in his bunk. The next, he had been . . . Well, he didn't rightly remember. What was the drink doing to him now?

Someone rapped on his door.

"Yes?" Dalinar said, his voice hoarse.

"The caravan is preparing to leave, Brightlord."

"Already? The rain hasn't even stopped yet."

"I think they're, um, eager to be rid of us, sir."

Dalinar pushed open the door. Felt stood outside, a lithe man with long, drooping mustaches and pale skin. Had to have some Shin blood in him, judging by those eyes.

Though Dalinar hadn't expressly said what he intended to do out here in Hexi, his soldiers seemed to understand. Dalinar wasn't sure whether he should be proud of their loyalty, or scandalized by how easily they accepted his intention to visit the Nightwatcher. Of course, one of them—Felt himself—had been this way before.

Outside, the caravan workers hitched up their chulls. They'd agreed to drop him off here, along their path, but refused to take him farther toward the Valley.

"Can you get us the rest of the way?" Dalinar asked.

"Sure," Felt said. "We're less than a day off."

"Then tell the good caravan master that we will take our wagons and split from him here. Pay him what he asked, Felt, and then some on top."

"If you say so, Brightlord. Seems that having a Shardbearer along with him should be payment enough."

"Explain that, in part, we're buying his silence."

Dalinar waited until the rain had mostly stopped, then threw on his coat and stepped out to join Felt, walking at the front of the wagons. He didn't feel like being cooped up any longer.

He'd expected this land to look like the Alethi plains. After all, the windswept flatlands of Hexi were not unlike those of his homeland. Yet strangely, there wasn't a rockbud in sight. The ground was covered in wrinkles, like frozen ripples in a pond, perhaps two or three inches deep. They were crusty on the stormward side, covered with lichen. On the leeward side, grass spread on the ground, flattened.

The sparse trees here were scrawny, hunched-over things with thistle leaves. Their branches bent so far leeward, they almost touched the ground. It was like one of the Heralds had strolled through this place and bent everything sideways. The nearby mountainsides were bare, blasted and scoured raw.

"Not far now, sir," Felt said. The short man barely came up to the middle of Dalinar's chest.

"When you came before," Dalinar said. "What . . . what did you see?"

"To be frank, sir, nothing. She didn't come to me. Doesn't visit everyone, you see." He clapped his hands, then breathed on them. It had been winter, lately. "You'll want to go in right after dark. Alone, sir. She avoids groups."

"Any idea why she didn't visit you?"

"Well, best I could figure, she doesn't like foreigners."

"I might have trouble too."

"You're a little less foreign, sir."

Up ahead, a group of small dark creatures burst from behind a tree and shot into the air, clumped together. Dalinar gaped at their speed and agility. "Chickens?" he said. Little black ones, each the size of a man's fist.

Felt chuckled. "Yes, wild chickens range this far east. Can't see what they'd be doing on this side of the mountains though."

The chickens eventually picked another bent-over tree and settled in its branches.

"Sir," Felt said. "Forgive me for asking, but you sure you want to do this? You'll be in her power, in there. And you don't get to pick the cost."

Dalinar said nothing, feet crunching on fans of weeds that trembled and rattled when he touched them. There was so much emptiness here in Hexi. In Alethkar, you couldn't go more than a day or two without running into a farming village. They hiked for a good three hours, during which Dalinar felt both an anxiety to be finished and—at the same time—a reluctance to progress. He had enjoyed his recent sense of purpose. Simultaneously, his decision had given him excuses. If he was going to the Nightwatcher anyway, then why fight the drink?

He'd spent much of the trip intoxicated. Now, with the alcohol running out, the voices of the dead seemed to chase him. They were worst when he tried to sleep, and he felt a dull ache behind his eyes from poor rest.

"Sir?" Felt eventually asked. "Look there." He pointed to a thin strip of green painting the windswept mountainside.

As they continued, Dalinar got a better view. The mountains split into a valley here, and since the opening pointed to the northeast, foothills shielded the interior from highstorms.

So plant life had *exploded* inside. Vines, ferns, flowers, and grasses grew together in a wall of underbrush. Trees stretched above them, and these weren't the durable stumpweights of his homeland. These were gnarled, tall, and twisted, with branches that wound together. They were overgrown with draping moss and vines, lifespren bobbing about them in plenitude.

It all piled atop itself, reeds and branches sticking out in all directions, ferns so overgrown with vines that they drooped beneath the weight. It reminded Dalinar of a battlefield. A grand tapestry, depicting people locked in mortal combat, each one struggling for advantage.

"How does one enter?" Dalinar asked. "How do you pass through *that*?"

"There are some trails," Felt said. "If you look hard enough. Shall we camp here, sir? You can scout out a path tomorrow, and make your final decision?"

He nodded, and they set up at the edge of the breach, close enough he could smell the humidity inside. They set up the wagons as a barrier between two trees, and the men soon had tents assembled. They were quick to get a fire going. There was a . . . feeling to the place. Like you could hear all of those plants growing. The valley shivered and cracked. When wind blew out, it was hot and muggy.

The sun set behind the mountains, plunging them into darkness. Soon after, Dalinar started inward. He couldn't wait another day. The sound of it lured him. The vines rustling, moving as tiny animals scampered between them. Leaves curling. The men didn't call after him; they understood his decision.

He stepped into the musty, damp valley, vines brushing his head. He could barely see in the darkness, but Felt had been right—trails revealed themselves as vines and branches bent away from him, allowing Dalinar entrance with the same reluctance as guards allowing an unfamiliar man into the presence of their king.

He had hoped for the Thrill to aid him here. This was a challenge, was it not? He felt nothing, not even a hint.

He trudged through the darkness, and suddenly felt stupid. What was he doing here? Chasing a pagan superstition while the rest of the high-princes gathered to punish Gavilar's killers? He should be at the Shattered Plains. *That* was where he'd change himself, where he would go back to the man he'd been before. He wanted to escape the drink? He just needed to summon Oathbringer and find someone to fight.

Who knew what was out there in this forest? If he were a bandit, this was certainly where he would set up. People must flock here. Damnation! He wouldn't be surprised to discover that someone had started all this simply to draw in unsuspecting marks.

Wait. What was that? A sound different from scurries in the underbrush or vines withdrawing. He stopped in place, listening. It was . . .

Weeping.

Oh, Almighty above. No.

He heard a boy weeping, pleading for his life. It sounded like Adolin. Dalinar turned from the sound, searching the darkness. Other screams and pleas joined that one, people burning as they died.

In a moment of panic, he turned to run back the way he'd come. He immediately tripped in the underbrush.

He collapsed against rotten wood, vines twisting under his fingers. People screamed and howled all around, the sounds echoing in the near-absolute darkness.

Frantic, he summoned Oathbringer and stumbled to his feet, then began slashing, trying to clear space. Those *voices*. All around him!

He pushed past a tree trunk, fingers digging into the hanging moss and wet bark. Was the entrance this way?

Suddenly he saw himself in the Unclaimed Hills, fighting those traitorous parshmen. He saw himself killing, and hacking, and murdering. He saw his lust, eyes wide and teeth clenched in a dreadful grin. A skull's grin.

He saw himself strangling Elhokar, who had never possessed his father's poise or charm. Dalinar took the throne. It should have been his anyway.

His armies poured into Herdaz, then Jah Keved. He became a king of kings, a mighty conqueror whose accomplishments far overshadowed those of his brother. Dalinar forged a unified Vorin empire that covered half of Roshar. An unparalleled feat!

And he saw them burn.

Hundreds of villages. Thousands upon *thousands* of people. It was the only way. If a town resisted, you burned it to the ground. You slaughtered any who fought back, and you left the corpses of their loved ones to feed the scavengers. You sent terror before you like a storm until your enemies surrendered.

The Rift would be but the first in a long line of examples. He saw himself standing upon the heaped corpses, laughing. Yes, he had escaped the drink. He had become something grand and terrible.

This was his future.

Gasping, Dalinar dropped to his knees in the dark forest and allowed the voices to swarm around him. He heard Evi among them, crying as she burned to death, unseen, unknown. Alone. He let Oathbringer slip from his fingers and shatter to mist.

The crying faded until it was distant.

Son of Honor . . . a new sound whispered on the winds, a voice like the rustling of the trees.

He opened his eyes to find himself in a tiny clearing, bathed in starlight. A shadow moved in the darkness beyond the trees, accompanied by the noise of twisting vines and blowing grass.

Hello, human. You smell of desperation. The feminine voice was like a hundred overlapping whispers. The elongated figure moved among the trees ringing the clearing, stalking him like a predator.

"They . . . they say you can change a man," Dalinar said, weary.

The Nightwatcher *seeped* from the darkness. She was a dark green mist, vaguely shaped like a crawling person. Too-long arms reached out, pulling her along as she floated above the ground. Her essence, like a tail, extended far behind her, weaving among tree trunks and disappearing into the forest.

Indistinct and vaporous, she flowed like a river or an eel, and the only part of her with any specific detail was her smooth, feminine face. She glided toward him until her nose was mere inches from his own, her silken black eyes meeting his. Tiny *hands* sprouted from the misty sides of her head. They reached out, taking his face and touching it with a thousand cold— yet gentle—caresses.

What is it you wish of me? the Nightwatcher asked. *What boon drives you, Son of Honor? Son of Odium?*

She started to circle him. The tiny black hands kept touching his face, but their arms stretched out, becoming tentacles.

What would you like? she asked. *Renown? Wealth? Skill? Would you like to be able to swing a sword and never tire?*

"No," Dalinar whispered.

Beauty? Followers? I can feed your dreams, make you glorious.

Her dark mists wrapped around him. The tiny tendrils tickled his skin. She brought her face right up to his again. *What is your boon?*

Dalinar blinked tears, listening to the sounds of the children dying in the distance, and whispered a single word.

"Forgiveness."

The Nightwatcher's tendrils dodged away from his face, like splayed fingers. She leaned back, pursing her lips.

Perhaps it is possessions you wish, she said. *Spheres, gemstones. Shards. A Blade that bleeds darkness and cannot be defeated. I can give it to you.*

"Please," Dalinar said, drawing in a ragged breath. "Tell me. Can I . . . can I ever be forgiven?"

It wasn't what he'd intended to request.

He couldn't remember what he'd intended to request.

The Nightwatcher curled around him, agitated. *Forgiveness is no boon. What should I do to you. What should I give you? Speak it, human. I—*

THAT IS ENOUGH, CHILD.

This new voice startled them both. If the Nightwatcher's voice was like whispering wind, this one was like tumbling stones. The Nightwatcher backed away from him in a sharp motion.

Hesitant, Dalinar turned and found a woman with brown skin—the color of darkwood bark—standing at the edge of the clearing. She had a matronly build and wore a sweeping brown dress.

Mother? the Nightwatcher said. *Mother, he came to me. I was going to bless him.*

THANK YOU, CHILD, the woman said. BUT THIS BOON IS BEYOND YOU. She focused on Dalinar. YOU MAY ATTEND ME, DALINAR KHOLIN.

Numbed by the surreal spectacle, Dalinar stood up. "Who are you?"

SOMEONE BEYOND YOUR AUTHORITY TO QUESTION. She strode into the forest, and Dalinar joined her. Moving through the underbrush seemed easier now, though the vines and branches pulled *toward* the strange woman. Her dress seemed to meld with it all, the brown cloth becoming bark or grass.

The Nightwatcher curled along beside them, her dark mist flowing through the holes in the underbrush. Dalinar found her distinctly unnerving.

YOU MUST FORGIVE MY DAUGHTER, the woman said. THIS IS THE FIRST TIME IN CENTURIES I'VE COME PERSONALLY TO SPEAK WITH ONE OF YOU.

"Then this isn't how it happens every time?"

OF COURSE NOT. I LET HER HOLD COURT HERE. The woman brushed her fingers through the Nightwatcher's misty hair. IT HELPS HER UNDERSTAND YOU.

Dalinar frowned, trying to make sense of all this. "What . . . why did you choose to come out now?"

BECAUSE OF THE ATTENTION OTHERS PAY YOU. AND WHAT DID I

TELL YOU OF DEMANDING QUESTIONS?

Dalinar shut his mouth.

WHY HAVE YOU COME HERE, HUMAN? DO YOU NOT SERVE HONOR, THE ONE YOU CALL ALMIGHTY? LOOK UNTO HIM FOR FORGIVENESS.

"I asked the ardents," Dalinar said. "I didn't get what I wanted."

YOU GOT WHAT YOU DESERVED. THE TRUTH YOU HAVE CRAFTED FOR YOURSELVES.

"I am doomed then," Dalinar whispered, stopping in place. He could still hear those voices. "They weep, Mother."

She looked back at him.

"I hear them when I close my eyes. All around me, begging me to save them. They're driving me mad."

She contemplated him, the Nightwatcher twining around her legs, then around Dalinar's, then back again.

This woman . . . she was more than he could see. Vines from her dress curled into the earth, permeating everything. In that moment he knew that he was not seeing *her*, but instead a fragment with which he could interact.

This woman extended into eternity.

THIS WILL BE YOUR BOON. I WILL NOT MAKE OF YOU THE MAN YOU CAN BECOME. I WILL NOT GIVE YOU THE APTITUDE, OR THE STRENGTH, NOR WILL I TAKE FROM YOU YOUR COMPULSIONS.

BUT I WILL GIVE YOU . . . A PRUNING. A CAREFUL EXCISION TO LET YOU GROW. THE COST WILL BE HIGH.

"Please," Dalinar said. "Anything."

She stepped back to him. IN DOING THIS, I PROVIDE FOR HIM A WEAPON. DANGEROUS, VERY DANGEROUS. YET, ALL THINGS MUST BE CULTIVATED. WHAT I TAKE FROM YOU WILL GROW BACK EVENTUALLY. THIS IS PART OF THE COST.

IT WILL DO ME WELL TO HAVE A PART OF YOU, EVEN IF YOU ULTIMATELY BECOME HIS. YOU WERE ALWAYS BOUND TO COME TO ME. I CONTROL ALL THINGS THAT CAN BE GROWN, NURTURED.

THAT INCLUDES THE THORNS.

She seized him, and the trees descended, the branches, the vines. The forest curled around him and crept into the crevices around his eyes, under his fingernails, into his mouth and ears. Into his *pores*.

A BOON AND A CURSE, the Mother said. THAT IS HOW IT IS DONE. I WILL TAKE THESE THINGS FROM YOUR MIND. AND WITH THEM, I TAKE HER.

"I . . ." Dalinar tried to speak as plant life engulfed him. "Wait!"

Remarkably, the vines and branches stopped. Dalinar hung there, speared by vines that had somehow pushed through his skin. There was no pain, but he felt the tendrils writhing inside his very veins.

SPEAK.

"You'll take . . ." He spoke with difficulty. "You'll take Evi from me?"

ALL MEMORIES OF HER. THIS IS THE COST. SHOULD I FORBEAR?

Dalinar squeezed his eyes shut. Evi . . .

He had never deserved her.

"Do it," he whispered.

The vines and branches surged forward and began to rip away pieces of him from the inside.

.⁘.

Dalinar crawled from the forest the next morning. His men rushed to him, bringing water and bandages, though strangely he needed neither.

But he *was* tired. Very, *very* tired.

They propped him in the shade of his stormwagon, exhaustionspren spinning in the air. Malli—Felt's wife—quickly scribed a note via spanreed back to the ship.

Dalinar shook his head, memory fuzzy. What . . . what had happened? Had he really asked for *forgiveness*?

He couldn't fathom why. Had he felt that bad for failing . . . He stretched for the word. For failing . . .

Storms. His wife. Had he felt so bad for failing her by letting assassins claim her life? He searched his mind, and found that he couldn't recall what she looked like. No image of her face, no memories of their time together.

Nothing.

He did remember these last few years as a drunkard. The years before, spent in conquest. In fact, everything about his past seemed clear *except* her.

"Well?" Felt said, kneeling beside him. "I assume it . . . happened."

"Yes," Dalinar said.

"Anything we need to know about?" he asked. "I once heard of a man who visited here, and from then on, every person he touched fell *upward* instead of down."

"You needn't worry. My curse is for me alone." How strange, to be able to remember scenes where she had been, but not remember . . . um . . . storms take him, her *name*.

"What was my wife's name?" Dalinar asked.

"*Shshshsh*?" Felt said. It came out as a blur of sounds.

Dalinar started. She'd been taken completely? Had that . . . that been the cost? Yes . . . grief had caused him to suffer these last years. He'd suffered a breakdown at losing the woman he loved.

Well, he assumed that he'd loved her. Curious.

Nothing.

It seemed that the Nightwatcher had taken memories of his wife, and in so doing, given him the boon of peace. However, he *did* still feel sorrow and guilt for failing Gavilar, so he wasn't completely healed. He still wanted a bottle to numb the grief of losing his brother.

He would break that habit. When men abused drink under his command, he'd found that the solution was to work them hard, and not let them taste strong wines. He could do the same to himself. It wouldn't be easy, but he could manage it.

Dalinar relaxed, but felt like something else was missing inside of him. Something he couldn't identify. He listened to his men breaking camp, telling jokes now that they could leave. Beyond that, he heard rustling leaves. And beyond that, nothing. Shouldn't he have heard . . .

He shook his head. Almighty, what a foolish quest this had been. Had he really been so weak that he needed a *forest spren* to relieve his grief?

"I need to be in communication with the king," Dalinar said, standing. "Tell our men at the docks to contact the armies. By the time I arrive, I want to have battle maps and plans for the Parshendi conquest."

He'd moped long enough. He had not always been the best of brothers, or the best of lighteyes. He'd failed to follow the Codes, and that had cost Gavilar his life.

Never again.

He straightened his uniform and glanced at Malli. "Tell the sailors that while they're in port, they're to find me an Alethi copy of a book called *The Way of Kings*. I'd like to hear it read to me again. Last time, I wasn't in my right mind."

They came from another world, using powers that we have been
forbidden to touch. Dangerous powers, of spren and Surges. They
destroyed their lands and have come to us begging.

—From the Eila Stele

A spry ocean wind blew in through the window, shaking Dalinar's
hair as he stood in his villa in Thaylen City. The wind was
sharply chill. Crisp. It didn't linger, but passed him by, turning
the pages of his book with a quiet ruffling sound.

It fled from the Everstorm.

Crimson. Furious. *Burning.* The Everstorm's clouds flowed in from the
west. Like blood billowing in water, each new thunderhead spurted from
the one behind it, hemorrhaging fits of lightning. And beneath the
storm—within its shadow, and upon those tempestuous seas—*ships* dotted
the waves.

"Ships?" he whispered. "They sailed *during* the storm?"

He controls it, the Stormfather said, his voice diminutive—like the
pattering of rain. *He uses it, as Honor once used me.*

So much for stopping the enemy in the ocean. Dalinar's fledgling armada
had fled to take shelter from the storm, and the enemy had sailed in uncontested. The coalition had shattered anyway; they wouldn't defend this city.

The storm slowed as it darkened the bay in front of Thaylen City—then
seemed to stop. It dominated the sky to the west, but strangely did not
proceed. Enemy ships landed in its shadow, many ramming right up onto
the shores.

Amaram's troops flooded out of the gates to seize the ground between bay and city; there wasn't enough room for them to maneuver on top of the wall. The Alethi were field troops, and their best chance of victory would involve hitting the parshmen while they disembarked. Behind them, Thaylen troops mounted the wall, but they were not veterans. Their navy had always been their strength.

Dalinar could faintly hear General Khal on the street below, shouting for runners and scribes to send word to Urithiru, calling up the Alethi reinforcements. *Too slow*, Dalinar thought. Suitably deploying troops could take hours, and though Amaram was hustling his men, they weren't going to get together in time for a proper assault on the ships.

And then there were the Fused, dozens of which launched into the skies from the ships. He imagined his armies bottlenecked as they left the Oathgate, assaulted from the air as they tried to fight through the streets to reach the lower portion of the city.

It came together with a frightening beauty. Their armada fleeing the storm. Their armies unprepared. The sudden evaporation of support . . .

"He's planned for everything."

It is what he does.

"You know, Cultivation warned me that my memories would return. She said she was 'pruning' me. Do you know why she did that? Did I *have* to remember?"

I do not know. Is it relevant?

"That depends upon the answer to a question," Dalinar said. He carefully closed the book atop the dresser before the window, then felt the symbols on its cover. "What is the most important step that a man can take?"

He straightened his blue uniform, then slipped the tome off the table. With *The Way of Kings* a comfortable weight in his hand, he stepped out the door and into the city.

⋅⋅

"All this way," Shallan whispered, "and they're already *here?*"

Kaladin and Adolin stood like two statues to either side of her, their faces twin stoic masks. She could see the Oathgate distinctly; that round platform at the edge of the bridge was the exact size of the control buildings.

Hundreds upon hundreds of strange spren stood in the lake of beads that marked the shore of Thaylen City. They looked vaguely humanoid, though they were twisted and odd, like shimmering dark light. More the scribbled outlines of people, like drawings she'd done in a maddened state.

On the shore, a large dark mass of living red light surged across the obsidian ground. It was something more terrible than all of these—something that made her eyes *hurt* to look upon. And as if that weren't enough, a half dozen Fused passed overhead, then landed on the bridge that led to the Oathgate platform.

"They knew," Adolin said. "They led us here with that cursed vision."

"Be wary," Shallan whispered, "of *anyone* who claims to be able to see the future."

"No. No, that wasn't from him!" Kaladin looked between them, frantic, and finally turned to Syl for support. "It was like when the Stormfather . . . I mean . . ."

"Azure warned us from this path," Adolin said.

"And what else could we have done?" Kaladin said, then hushed his voice, pulling back with the rest of them into the shadowed concealment of the trees. "We couldn't go to the Horneater Peaks, like Azure wanted. The enemy waits there too! Everyone says their ships patrol there." Kaladin shook his head. "This was our only option."

"We don't have enough food to return . . ." Adolin said.

"Even if we did," Syl whispered, "where would we go? They hold Celebrant. They're watching this Oathgate, so they're probably watching the others. . . ."

Shallan sank down on the obsidian ground. Pattern put his hand on her shoulder, humming softly with concern. Her body yearned for Stormlight to wash away her fatigue. Light could make an illusion, change this world into something else—at least for a few moments—so she could pretend . . .

"Kaladin is right," Syl said. "We *can't* back down now. Our remaining gemstones won't last much longer."

"We have to try," Kaladin said with a nod.

"Try what, Kal?" Adolin said. "Take on an army of Voidbringers by ourselves?"

"I don't know how the portal works," Shallan added. "I don't even know how much Stormlight it might require."

"We'll . . . we'll try something," Kaladin said. "We have Stormlight still. An illusion? A distraction? We could get you to the Oathgate, and you could . . . find out how to free us." He shook his head. "We can make it work. We *have* to."

Shallan bowed her head, listening to Pattern hum. Some problems could not be fixed with a lie.

⁘

Jasnah carefully stepped out of the way of a troop of soldiers running for the Oathgate. She had been informed via spanreed that troops were gathering in Urithiru to come help. Unfortunately, they would soon have to acknowledge what she already knew.

Thaylen City was lost.

Their adversary had played this hand too well. That angered her, but she kept that emotion in check. At the very least, she hoped that Amaram's band of malcontents would soak up arrows and spears long enough to let the Thaylen civilians evacuate.

Lightning from the storm lit the city red.

Focus. She had to focus on what she *could* do, not what she had *failed* to do. First, she had to see that her uncle didn't get himself killed fighting a useless battle. Second, she needed to help evacuate Thaylen City; she had already warned Urithiru to prepare for refugees.

Both these goals would wait a short time as she dealt with a matter even more pressing.

"The facts align," Ivory said. "The truth that has always been, will now soon manifest to all." He rode upon the high collar of her dress, tiny, holding on with one hand. "You are correct. A traitor *is*."

Jasnah undid the buttons on her safehand sleeve and pinned it back, exposing the gloved hand underneath. In preparation, she'd also worn a scout's yellow and gold havah, with shorter skirts slit at the sides and front, trousers underneath. Sturdy boots.

She turned out of the path of another group of cursing soldiers and strode up the steps to the doorway of the temple of Pailiah'Elin. True to the information she'd been given, she found Renarin Kholin kneeling on the floor inside, head bowed. Alone.

A spren rose from his back, bright red, shimmering like the heat of a mirage. A crystalline structure, like a snowflake, though it dripped light upward toward the ceiling. In her pouch, she carried a sketch of the proper spren of the Truthwatchers.

And this was something different.

Jasnah put her hand to the side, then—taking a deep breath—summoned Ivory as a Shardblade.

∴

Venli hopped down from the ship's improvised gangway. The city before her was yet another marvel. Built up the side of a mountain, it looked almost like it had been cut from the stone—sculpted like the winds and rain had shaped the Shattered Plains.

Hundreds of singers streamed around her. Hulking Fused walked among them, bearing carapace armor as impressive as any Shardplate.

Some of the ordinary singers wore warform—but unlike their Alethi counterparts, they had not been through combat training.

Azish, Thaylen, Marati . . . a host of nationalities, these newly awakened singers were frightened, uncertain. Venli attuned Agony. Would they force her to march to the front line? She didn't have much battle training either; even with a form of power, she'd be cut to ribbons.

Like my people, on the field of Narak, who were sacrificed to birth the Everstorm. Odium seemed very quick to expend the lives of both listener and singer.

Timbre pulsed to Peace in her pouch, and Venli rested her hand on it. "Hush," she whispered to Agony. "*Hush.* Do you want one of them to hear you?"

Timbre reluctantly softened her pulsings, though Venli could still feel a faint vibration from her pouch. And that . . . that relaxed her. She almost thought that she could hear the Rhythm of Peace herself.

One of the hulking Fused called for her. "You! Listener woman! Come!"

Venli attuned the Rhythm of Destruction. She would *not* be intimidated by these, gods though they be. She stepped up to this one and kept her head high.

The Fused handed her a sword in a sheath. She took it, then attuned Subservience. "I've used an axe before, but not—"

"Carry it," he said, eyes glowing softly red. "You may need to defend yourself."

She did not object further. There was a fine line between respectful confidence and defiance. She belted the sword on her slender body, wishing she had some carapace.

"Now," the Fused said to Conceit, striding forward and expecting her to keep up, "tell me what this little one is saying."

Venli followed him to a gathering of singers in workform, holding spears. She had been speaking to the Fused in the ancient language, but these were speaking in Thaylen.

I'm an interpreter, she thought, relaxing. *That's why they wanted me on the battlefield.*

"What was it," Venli said to Derision, addressing the one the Fused had indicated, "you wished to say to the holy one?"

"We . . ." The singer licked his lips. "We aren't soldiers, ma'am. We're fishers. What are we doing here?" Though a shade of the Rhythm of Anxiety laced his words, his cringing form and face were the stronger indication. He spoke and acted like a human.

She interpreted.

"You are here to do as you are told," the Fused told them, through Venli.

"In return, you are rewarded with further opportunities to serve." Though his rhythm was Derision, he didn't seem angry. More . . . as if he were lecturing a child.

She passed that along, and the sailors looked to each other, shuffling uncomfortably.

"They wish to object," she told the Fused. "I can read it in them."

"They may speak," he said.

She prompted them, and their leader looked down, then spoke to Anxiety. "It's just that . . . Thaylen City? This is our home. We're expected to attack it?"

"Yes," the Fused said after Venli interpreted. "They enslaved you. They tore your families apart, treated you like dumb animals. Do you not thirst for vengeance?"

"Vengeance?" the sailor said, looking to his fellows for support. "We're glad to be free. But . . . I mean . . . some of them treated us pretty nice. Can't we just go settle somewhere, and leave the Thaylens alone?"

"No," the Fused said. Venli interpreted, then jumped to follow him as he stalked off.

"Great one?" she asked to Subservience.

"These have the wrong Passion," he said. "The ones who attacked Kholinar did so gladly."

"The Alethi are a warlike people, great one. It's not surprising they passed this on to their slaves. And perhaps these were better treated?"

"They were slaves for far too long. We need to show them a better way."

Venli stuck close to the Fused, happy to have found one that was both sane and reasonable. He didn't shout at the groups they visited, many of whom shared similar complaints. He merely had her repeat the same sorts of phrases.

You must seize vengeance, little ones. You must earn *your Passion.*

Qualify yourselves for greater service, and you will be elevated to the place of a Regal, given a form of power.

This land was yours long ago, before they stole it. You have been trained to be docile. We will teach you to be strong again.

The Fused remained calm, but fierce. Like a smoldering fire. Controlled, but ready to burst alight. He eventually walked to join some of his fellows. Around them, the singer army formed up awkwardly, coating the land just east of the bay. Alethi troops mustered across a short battlefield, banners flapping. They had archers, heavy infantry, light infantry, even some outriders on horses.

Venli hummed to Agony. This was going to be a *slaughter.*

She suddenly felt something odd. Like a rhythm, but oppressive, *demanding.* It shook the very air, and the ground beneath her feet trembled. **1087**

Lightning in the clouds behind seemed to flash to this rhythm, and in a moment she saw that the area around her was filled with ghostly spren.

Those are the spirits of the dead, she realized. *Fused who haven't yet chosen a body.* Most were twisted to the point that she barely recognized them as singers. Two were roughly the size of buildings.

One dominated even these: a creature of swirling violence, tall as a small hill, seemingly made up entirely of red smoke. She could see these overlaid on the real world, but somehow knew they would be invisible to most. She could see into the other world. That happened sometimes right before . . .

A blistering heat shone behind her.

Venli braced herself. She usually only saw him during the storms. But . . . this *was* a storm. It hovered behind, immobile, churning the seas.

Light crystallized beside her, forming an ancient parshman with a face marbled gold and white, and a regal scepter he carried like a cane. For once, his presence didn't vaporize her immediately.

Venli released a relieved breath. This was more an *impression* than his true being. Still, power streamed from him like the tendrils of a vinebud waving in the wind, vanishing into infinity.

Odium had come to personally supervise this battle.

⁙

Teft hid.

He couldn't face the others. Not after . . . after what he'd done.

Rock and Bisig bleeding. Eth dead. The room destroyed. The Honorblade stolen.

He had . . . he had on a Bridge Four . . . uniform. . . .

Teft scrambled through the rock hallways, passing shamespren in bursts, looking for a place where nobody could see him. He'd done it again, to yet another group that trusted him. Just like with his family, whom he'd sold out in a misguided attempt at righteousness. Just like with his squad in Sadeas's army, whom he'd abandoned for his addiction. And now . . . and now Bridge Four?

He tripped on an uneven bit of stone in the dark hallway and fell, grunting, scraping his hand against the floor. He groaned, then lay there, knocking his head against the stone.

Would that he could find someplace hidden, and squeeze inside, never *ever* to be found again.

When he looked up, she was standing there. The woman made of light and air, with curls of hair that vanished into mist.

"Why are you following me?" Teft growled. "Go pick one of the others. Kelek! Pick *anyone* but me."

He rose and pushed past her—she had barely any substance—and continued down the hallway. Light from ahead showed that he'd accidentally made his way to the outer ring of the tower, where windows and balconies overlooked the Oathgate platforms.

He stopped by a stone doorway, puffing, holding on with a hand that bled from the knuckles.

"Teft."

"You don't want me. I'm *broken*. Pick Lopen. Rock. Sigzil. Damnation, woman. I . . ."

What was that?

Drawn by faint sounds, Teft walked into the empty room. Those sounds . . . Shouts?

He walked out onto the balcony. Below, figures with marbled skin flooded across one of the Oathgate platforms, the one that led to Kholinar. That was supposed to be locked, unusable.

Scouts and soldiers began to shout in panic down below. Urithiru was under attack.

⁂

Puffing from her run, Navani scrambled up the last few steps onto the wall of Thaylen City. Here, she found Queen Fen's retinue. *Finally.*

She checked her arm clock. If only she could find a fabrial that would manipulate exhaustion, not just pain. Wouldn't *that* be something. There were exhaustionspren, after all . . .

Navani strode along the wall walk toward Fen. Below, Amaram's troops flew the new Sadeas banner: the axe and the tower, white on forest green. Anticipationspren and fearspren—the eternal attendants of the battlefield—grew up around them. Sadeas's men were still streaming through the gates, but already blocks of archers moved forward. They'd soon start pelting the disorganized parshman army.

That storm though . . .

"The enemy only keeps coming," Fen said as Navani approached, her admirals making room. "I'll soon get to judge your famed Alethi troops firsthand—as they fight an impossible battle."

"Actually," Navani said, "we're better off than it looks. The new Sadeas is a renowned tactician. His soldiers are well rested and—if lacking in discipline—known for their tenacity. We can attack the enemy before it finishes deploying. Then, if they rebound and overwhelm us with numbers, we can pull back into the city until we get reinforcements."

Kmakl, Fen's consort, nodded. "This is winnable, Fen. We might even be able to capture some of our ships back."

The ground shook. For a moment, Navani felt that she was on a swaying ship. She cried out, grabbing the battlement to keep from falling.

Out in the field, between the enemy troops and the Alethi ones, the ground *shattered*. Lines and cracks split the stone, and then an enormous stone *arm* pulled itself from the ground—the fractures having outlined its hand, forearm, elbow, and upper arm.

A monster easily thirty feet tall pulled itself from the stone, dropping chips and dust on the army below. Like a skeleton made of rock, it had a wedge-shaped head with deep, molten red eyes.

·•·

Venli got to watch the thunderclasts awaken.

Among the waiting spirits were two larger masses of energy—souls so warped, so mangled, they didn't seem singer at all. One crawled into the stone ground, somehow inhabiting it like a spren taking residence in a gemheart. The stone *became* its form.

Then it ripped itself free of the rock. Around her, the parshmen stumbled back in awe, so surprised that they actually drew spren. The thing loomed over the human forces, while its companion climbed into the stone ground, but didn't rip out immediately.

There was one other, mightier than even these. It was out in the water of the bay, but when she looked into the other world, she couldn't help but glance toward it. If those two lesser souls had created such daunting stone monsters, then what was *that* mountain of power?

In the Physical Realm, the Fused knelt and bowed their heads toward Odium. So they could see him too. Venli knelt quickly, knocking her knees against the stone. Timbre pulsed to Anxiety, and Venli put her hand on the pouch, squeezing it. *Quiet. We can't fight him.*

"Turash," Odium said, resting fingers upon the shoulder of the Fused she had been following. "Old friend, you look well in this new body."

"Thank you, master," Turash said.

"Your mind holds firm, Turash. I am proud of you." Odium waved toward Thaylen City. "I have prepared a grand army for our victory today. What do you think of our prize?"

"An excellent position of great import, even without the Oathgate," Turash said. "But I fear for our armies, master."

"Oh?" Odium asked.

"They are weak, untrained, and frightened. Many may refuse to fight. They don't crave vengeance, master. Even with the thunderclast, we may be outmatched."

"These?" Odium asked, looking over his shoulder at the gathered singers.

"Oh, Turash. You think too *small*, my friend! These are not my army. I brought them here to watch."

"Watch what?" Venli asked, looking up. She cringed, but Odium paid her no mind. Odium held his hands to the sides, yellow-gold power streaming behind his figure like a wind made visible. Beyond him, in the other place, that red churning power became more *real*. It was pulled into this realm completely, and the ocean boiled.

Something came surging out. Something primeval, something Venli had felt but never truly known. Red mist. Ephemeral, like a shadow you see on a dark day and mistake for something real. Charging red horses, angry and galloping. The forms of men, killing and dying, shedding blood and reveling in it. Bones piled atop one another, making a hill upon which men struggled.

The red mist climbed up from the surging waves, rolling out onto an empty section of rock, northward along the rim of the water. It brought to her a lust for the battlefield. A beautiful focus, a Thrill for the fight.

⁘

The largest of the spren, the roiling mass of red light, vanished from Shadesmar.

Kaladin gasped and walked closer to the outer edge of the trees, feeling that power vacate this place and . . . go to the other?

"Something's happening," he said to Adolin and Shallan, who were still discussing what to do. "We might have an opening!"

They joined him and watched as the strange army of spren began to vanish too, winking out in waves.

"The Oathgate?" Shallan asked. "Maybe they're using it?"

In moments, only the six Fused remained, guarding the bridge.

Six, Kaladin thought. *Can I defeat six?*

Did he need to?

"I can challenge them as a distraction," he said to the others. "Maybe we can use some illusions as well? We can draw them off while Shallan sneaks over and figures out how to work the Oathgate."

"I suppose we don't have any other choice," Adolin said. "But . . ."

"What?" Kaladin said, urgent.

"Aren't you worried about where that army went?"

⁘

"Passion," Odium said. "There is great Passion here."

Venli felt cold.

"I've prepared these men for decades," Odium said. "Men who want nothing so much as something to *break*, to gain vengeance against the one who killed their highprince. Let the singers watch and learn. I've prepared a different army to fight for us today."

Ahead of them on the battlefield, the human ranks slumped, their banner wavering. A man in glittering Shardplate, sitting upon a white horse, led them.

Deep within his helm, something started glowing red.

The dark spren flew toward the men, finding welcoming bodies and willing flesh. The red mist made them lust, made their minds open. And the spren, then, *bonded* to the men, slipping into those open souls.

"Master, you have learned to inhabit humans?" Turash said to Subservience.

"Spren have always been able to bond with them, Turash," Odium said. "It merely requires the right mindset and the right environment."

Ten thousand Alethi in green uniforms gripped their weapons, their eyes glowing a deep, dangerous red.

"Go," Odium whispered. "Kholin would have sacrificed you! Manifest your anger! Kill the Blackthorn, who murdered your highprince. Set your Passion free! Give me your pain, and seize this city in my name!"

The army turned and—led by a Shardbearer in gleaming Plate—attacked Thaylen City.

116

ALONE

We took them in, as commanded by the gods. What else could we do? They were a people forlorn, without a home. Our pity destroyed us. For their betrayal extended even to our gods: to spren, stone, and wind.

—From the Eila Stele

Kaladin thought he could hear the wind as he stepped from beneath the obsidian trees. Syl said this place had no wind. Yet was that the tinkling of glass leaves as they quivered? Was that the sigh of cool, fresh air coursing around him?

He'd come far in the last half year. He seemed a man distant from the one who carried bridges against Parshendi arrows. That man had welcomed death, but now—even on the bad days, when everything was cast in greys—he *defied* death. It could not have him, for while life was painful, life was also sweet.

He had Syl. He had the men of Bridge Four. And most importantly, he had purpose.

Today, Kaladin *would* protect Dalinar Kholin.

He strode toward the sea of souls that marked the existence of Thaylen City on the other side. Many of those souls' flames, in ranks, had turned sharply *red*. He shivered to think what that meant. He stepped up onto the bridge, beads churning below, and reached the highest point in its arc before the enemy noticed him.

Six Fused turned and rose into the air, arraying to regard him. They raised long spears, then looked to the sides, seeming shocked.

One man, alone?

Kaladin set one foot back—gently scraping the tip of his boot against the white marble bridge—and fell into a combat posture. He hooked the harpoon in a one-handed underarm grip, letting out a long breath.

Then he drew in all of his Stormlight, and burst alight.

Within the power's embrace, a lifetime's worth of moments seemed to snap into place. Throwing Gaz to the ground in the rain. Screaming in defiance while charging at the front of a bridge. Coming awake in the practice grounds during the Weeping. Fighting the assassin on the stormwall.

The Fused leaped for him, trailing long cloaks and robes. Kaladin Lashed himself straight upward, and took to the sky for the first time in what had been far, far too long.

* * *

Dalinar stumbled as the ground shook again. A second sequence of cracks sounded outside. He was too low down in the city now to see past the city wall, but he feared he knew what that breaking stone must signify. A second thunderclast.

Violet fearspren sprouted from the streets all around as civilians shouted and screamed. Dalinar had made his way down through the central section of the city—the part called the Ancient Ward—and had just entered the Low Ward, the bottom portion nearest the city wall. The steps behind him were filling with people who fled upward, toward the Oathgate.

As the trembling subsided, Dalinar grabbed the arm of a young mother who was pounding frantically on the door of a building. He sent her running up the steps with her child in her arms. He needed these people off the streets, preferably taking shelter at Urithiru, so they wouldn't get caught between clashing armies.

Dalinar felt his age as he jogged past the next row of buildings, still clutching *The Way of Kings* under his arm. He had barely any spheres on him, an oversight, but neither did he have Plate or Blade. This would be his first battle in many, many years without Shards. He'd insisted on stepping out of those boots, and would have to let Amaram and other Shardbearers command the field.

How was Amaram faring? Last Dalinar had seen, the highprince had been arranging his archers—but from this low in the city, Dalinar couldn't see the troops outside.

A sudden feeling slammed into him.

It was focus and passion. An eager energy, a warmth, a promise of strength. Glory.

Life.

To Dalinar, this thirst for the battle felt like the attentions of a lover you'd turned away long ago. The Thrill was here. His old, *dear* friend.

"No," he whispered, sagging against a wall. The emotion struck him harder than the earthquake had. "*No.*"

The taste was so, *so* appealing. It whispered that he could save this city all on his own. Let the Thrill in, and the Blackthorn could return. He didn't need Shards. He only needed this passion. Sweeter than any wine.

No.

He shoved the Thrill aside, scrambling to his feet. As he did, however, a shadow moved beyond the wall. A monster of stone, one of the beasts from his visions, standing some thirty feet tall—looming over the twenty-foot city wall. The thunderclast clasped its hands together, then swung them low, *crashing* them through the city wall, flinging out chunks of stone.

Dalinar leaped toward cover, but a falling boulder pounded into him, crushing him into a wall.

Blackness.

Falling.

Power.

He gasped, and Stormlight flooded into him—he shook awake to find his arm pinned by the boulder, rocks and dust falling on a rubble-strewn street before him. And . . . not just rubble. He coughed, realizing some of those lumps were bodies coated in dust, lying motionless.

He struggled to pull his arm from under the boulder. Nearby, the thunderclast kicked at the broken wall, opening a hole. Then it stepped through, footfalls shaking the ground, approaching the shelf that made up the front of the Ancient Ward.

A massive stone foot *thumped* to the ground by Dalinar. Storms! Dalinar hauled on his arm, heedless of the pain or the damage to his body, and finally got it free. The Stormlight healed him as he crawled away, ducking as the monster ripped the roof off a building at the front of the Ancient Ward and sent debris raining down.

The Gemstone Reserve? The monster cast the roof aside, and several Fused that he'd missed before—they were riding on its shoulders—slipped down into the building. Dalinar was torn between heading for the battlefield outside, and investigating whatever was going on here.

Any idea what they're after? he asked the Stormfather.

No. This is odd behavior.

In a flash decision, Dalinar yanked his book out from under some rubble nearby, then went running back up the now-empty steps to the Ancient Ward, dangerously close to the thunderclast.

The monster released a sudden piercing roar, like a thunderclap. The shock wave almost knocked Dalinar off his feet again. In a fit of rage, the titanic creature *attacked* the Gemstone Reserve, ripping apart its walls and innards, tossing chunks backward. A million sparkling bits of glass caught the sunlight as they fell over the city, the wall, and beyond.

Spheres and gemstones, Dalinar realized. *All the wealth of Thaylenah. Scattered like leaves.*

The thing seemed increasingly angry as it pounded the area around the reserve. Dalinar put his back to a wall as two Fused darted past, led by what appeared to be a glowing yellow spren. These two Fused didn't seem to be able to fly, but there was a startling grace to their motion. They slid along the stone street with no apparent effort, as if the ground were greased.

Dalinar gave chase, squeezing past a group of scribes huddled in the street, but before he could catch up, the Fused attacked one palanquin among the many trying to move through the crowds. They knocked it over, shoving aside the porters, and dug inside.

The Fused ignored Dalinar's shouts. They soon streaked away—one tucking a large object under its arm. Dalinar drew in Stormlight from some fleeing merchants, then ran the rest of the distance to the palanquin. Amid the wreckage he found a young Thaylen woman alongside an elderly man who appeared to have been previously wounded, judging by the bandages.

Dalinar helped the dazed young woman to a sitting position. "What did they want?"

"Brightlord?" she said in Thaylen. She blinked, then seized his arm. "The King's Drop . . . a ruby. They tried to steal it before, and now, now they've taken it!"

A ruby? A simple gemstone? The porters attended to the old man, who was barely conscious.

Dalinar looked over his shoulder at the retreating thunderclast. The enemy had ignored the wealth of the Gemstone Reserve. Why would they want a specific ruby? He was about to press for more details when something else drew his attention. From this higher vantage, he could see through the hole the thunderclast had broken in the wall.

Figures outside with glowing red eyes arrayed themselves on the battlefield—but they weren't parshmen.

Those were *Sadeas* uniforms.

⁖

Jasnah moved into the temple, gripping her Shardblade, stepping on slippered feet. The red spren rising from Renarin—like a snowflake made of crystal and light—seemed to sense her and panicked, disappearing into Renarin with a puff.

A spren is, Ivory said. *The wrong spren is.*

Renarin Kholin was a liar. He was no Truthwatcher.

That is *a spren of Odium,* Ivory said. *Corrupted spren. But . . . a human, bonded to one? This thing is not.*

"It is," Jasnah whispered. "Somehow."

She was now close enough to hear Renarin whispering. "No . . . Not Father. No, *please . . .*"

⁘

Shallan wove Light.

A simple illusion, recalled from the pages of her sketchpad: some soldiers from the army, people from Urithiru, and some of the spren she'd sketched on her trip. Around twenty individuals in total.

"Taln's nails," Adolin said as Kaladin shot upward through the sky. "The bridgeboy is really into it."

Kaladin drew away four of the Fused, but two remained behind. Shallan added an illusion of Azure to her group, then some of the Reachers she'd drawn. She hated using up so much Stormlight—what if she didn't have enough left to get through the Oathgate?

"Good luck," she whispered to Adolin. "Remember, I won't be controlling these directly. They will make only rudimentary motions."

"We'll be fine." Adolin glanced at Pattern, Syl, and the spren of his sword. "Right, guys?"

"Mmmm," Pattern said. "I do not like being stabbed."

"Wise words, friend. Wise words." Adolin gave Shallan a kiss, then they took off running toward the bridge. Syl, Pattern, and the deadeye followed—as did the illusions, which were bound to Adolin.

This force drew the attention of the last two Fused. As those were distracted, Shallan slipped over to the base of the bridge, then eased herself down into the beads. She crossed silently beneath the bridge, using precious Stormlight to make herself a safe walking platform with one of the beads she'd found while on *Honor's Path.*

She made her way across to the small island platform that represented the Oathgate on this side. Two enormous spren stood above it.

Judging by the shouting on the bridge, Adolin and the others were doing their job. But could Shallan do hers? She stepped up beneath the two sentinels, which stood tall as buildings, reminiscent of statues in armor.

One mother-of-pearl, the other black with a variegated oily shimmer.

Did they guard the Oathgate, or did they—somehow—facilitate its workings?

At a loss for what else to do, Shallan simply waved her hand. "Um, hello?"

Steadily, two heads turned down toward her.

⁂

The air around Venli—once crowded by the spirits of the dead—was now empty save for the single black figure of swirling smoke. She'd missed that one at first, as it was the size of a normal person. It stood near Odium, and she did not know what it represented.

The second thunderclast dragged arms as long as its body, with hands like hooks. It crossed the field eastward, toward the city walls and the human army of turncoats. Just behind Venli, to the west, the common singers stood arrayed before their ships. They stayed far from the red mist of the Unmade coating the north side of the battlefield.

Odium stood beside Venli, a glowing force of burning gold. The first thunderclast left the city and placed something down on the ground: two of the Fused—gods with lithe bodies and little armor. They skirted the turncoat army, sliding along the rock with an uncanny grace.

"What is that they carry?" Venli asked. "A gemstone? Is *that* why we came here? A rock?"

"No," Odium said. "That is merely a precaution, a last-minute addition I made to prevent a potential disaster. The prize I claim today is far greater— even more grand than the city itself. The conduit of my freedom. The bane of Roshar. Forward, child. To the gap in the wall. I may need you to speak for me."

She swallowed, then started hiking toward the city. The dark spirit followed, the one of swirling mists, the last who had yet to inhabit a body.

⁂

Kaladin soared through this place of black heavens, haunted clouds, and a distant sun. Only four of the Fused had chosen to take off after him. Adolin would have to deal with the other two.

The four flew with precision. They used Lashings like Kaladin did, though they didn't seem to be able to vary their speed as much as he could. It took them longer to build up to greater Lashings, which should have made it easy to stay ahead of them.

But *storms*, the way they flew! So graceful. They didn't jerk this way or that, but flowed lithely from one motion to the next. They used their entire bodies to sculpt the wind of their passing and control their flight. Even the Assassin in White hadn't been so fluid as these, so like the winds themselves.

Kaladin had claimed the skies, but storms, it looked like he'd moved into territory where someone had a prior entitlement.

I don't have to fight them, he thought. *I only have to keep them busy long enough for Shallan to figure out how to activate the portal.*

Kaladin Lashed himself upward, toward those strange, too-flat clouds. He twisted in the air, and found one of the Fused almost upon him—a male with pale white skin swirled through with a single marbling of red, like smoke blown across the cheeks. The creature stabbed its long spear at him, but Kaladin Lashed himself to the side just in time.

Lashing *wasn't* flying, and that was part of its strength. Kaladin didn't have to be facing any specific direction to move in the air. He fell up and slightly to the north, but fought while facing downward, battering away the enemy lance with his harpoon. The Fused's weapon was far longer, with sharpened sides rather than a single fine point. Kaladin's harpoon was at a severe disadvantage.

Right. Time to change that.

As the Fused rammed the lance upward again, Kaladin reached out with both hands on his harpoon's haft, holding it sideways. He let the enemy spear pass into the opening between his arms, chest, and harpoon.

He Lashed his own weapon downward with multiple Lashings. Then he dropped it.

It slid along the length of the lance and smacked into the Fused's arms. The creature shouted in pain, letting go of his weapon. At the same moment Kaladin dove, canceling all upward Lashings and binding himself downward instead.

The sudden, jarring change made his stomach lurch and his vision go black. Even with Stormlight, this was almost too much. His ears ringing, he gritted his teeth, riding the momentary loss of sight until—blessedly—his vision returned. He spun in the air, then pulled up and snatched the falling lance as it dropped past him.

The four Fused swooped after him, more cautious. The wind of his passing chilled the sweat on his face from his near blackout.

Let's . . . not try that again, Kaladin thought, hefting his new weapon. He'd practiced with things like this in pike walls, but they were normally too long to maneuver in one-on-one combat. Flying would negate that.

The Fused he'd disarmed swooped down to fetch the harpoon. Kaladin waved his hand toward the others palm upward, then took off toward some nearby dark obsidian mountains, forested on the sides—the direction he and the others had come. Down below, he could see Shallan's illusions engaging the two Fused on the bridge.

Eyes forward, Kaladin thought as the four others chased after him. He belonged in the skies with these creatures.

Time to prove it.

∴

Prime Aqasix Yanagawn the First, emperor of all Makabak, paced in the cabin of his ship.

He was actually starting to *feel* like an emperor. He wasn't embarrassed talking to the viziers and scions any longer. He understood much of what they discussed now, and didn't jump when someone called him "Your Majesty." Remarkably, he was starting to forget that he'd ever been a frightened thief sneaking through the palace.

But then, even an emperor had limits to his rule.

He paced back the other way. Regal robes—of Azish patterns—weighed him down, along with the Imperial Yuanazixin: a fancy hat with sweeping sides. He'd have taken the thing off, but he felt he needed its authority when talking to his three most important advisors.

"Lift thinks we should have stayed," he said. "War is coming to Thaylen City."

"We're merely protecting our fleet from the storm," Noura said.

"Pardon, Vizier, but that's a load of chull dung, and you know it. We left because you're worried that Kholin is being manipulated by the enemy."

"That is not the *only* reason," Scion Unoqua said. He was an old man with a full paunch. "We have always been skeptical of the Lost Radiants. The powers that Dalinar Kholin wishes to harness are extremely dangerous, as now proven by the translations of an ancient record!"

"Lift says—" Yanagawn said.

"Lift?" Noura said. "You listen to her far too much, Your Imperial Majesty."

"She's smart."

"She once tried to *eat* your cummerbund."

"She . . . thought it sounded like a type of dessert." Yanagawn took a deep breath. "Besides, she's not *that* kind of smart. She's the other kind."

"What other kind, Your Imperial Majesty?" Vizier Dalksi asked. Her hair was powder white, peeking out beneath her formal headdress.

"The kind that knows when it's wrong to betray a friend. I think we should go back. Am I emperor or not?"

"You *are* emperor," Noura said. "But, Your Majesty, remember your lessons. The thing that *separates* us from the monarchies of the east—and the chaos they suffer—is that our emperor is held in check. Azir can, and will, withstand a change in dynasty. Your power is absolute, but you do not exercise it all. You must not."

"You were chosen," Unoqua said, "by Yaezir himself to lead—"

"I was *chosen*," Yanagawn cut in, "because nobody would shed a tear if the Assassin in White came for me! Let's not play games, all right?"

"You performed a miracle," Unoqua said.

"*Lift* performed a miracle. Using powers you now say are too dangerous to trust!"

The three—two viziers, one scion—looked to each other. Unoqua was their religious leader, but Noura had most seniority by year of passing the tests for master office, which she'd done—remarkably—at age *twelve*.

Yanagawn stopped by the cabin window. Outside, waves chopped, churning, rocking their ship. His smaller ship had met up with the main fleet, then joined them in taking shelter in Vtlar Cove, along the Thaylen coast. But reports via spanreed said that the Everstorm had *stopped* near Thaylen City.

A knock came at the door. Yanagawn let Dalksi—least senior, despite her age—call admittance. Yanagawn settled in his regal chair as a guardsman with light brown skin entered. Yanagawn thought he recognized the man, who held a cloth to the side of his face and winced as he gave the formal bow of admittance to the emperor.

"Vono?" Noura asked. "What happened to your charge? You were to keep her busy and distracted, yes?"

"I was, Your Grace," Vono said. "Until she kicked me in my spheres and stuffed me under the bed. Um, Your Grace. Don't right know how she moved me. She's not real big, that one. . . ."

Lift? Yanagawn thought. He almost cried out, demanding answers, but that would have shamed this man. Yanagawn held himself back with difficulty, and Noura nodded to him in appreciation of a lesson learned.

"When was this?" Noura asked.

"Right before we left," the guard said. "Sorry, Your Grace. I've been down since then, only now recovered."

Yanagawn turned toward Noura. Surely *now* she would see the importance of returning. The storm had yet to advance. They could go back if . . .

Another figure approached the door, a woman in the robes and pattern of a second-level scribe, seventh circle. She entered and quickly gave the formal bows to Yanagawn, so hasty she forgot the third gesture of subservient obedience.

"Viziers," she said, bowing in turn to them, then to Unoqua. "News from the city!"

"Good news?" Noura asked hopefully.

"The Alethi have turned against the Thaylens, and now seek to conquer them! They've been allied with the parshmen all along. Your Grace, by fleeing, we have narrowly avoided a trap!"

"Quickly," Noura said. "Separate our ships from any that bear Alethi troops. We must not be caught unaware!"

They left, abandoning Yanagawn to the care of a dozen young scribes who were next in line for basking in his presence. He settled into his seat, worried and afraid, feeling a sickness in his gut. The Alethi, traitors?

Lift had been wrong. He had been wrong.

Yaezir bless them. This really was the end of days.

⁘

We are the gatekeepers, the two enormous spren said to Shallan, speaking with voices that overlapped, as if one. Though their mouths did not move, the voices reverberated through Shallan. *Lightweaver, you have no permission to use this portal.*

"But I *need* to get through," Shallan cried up to them. "I have Stormlight to pay!"

Your payment will be refused. We are locked by the word of the parent.

"Your parent? Who?"

The parent is dead now.

"So . . ."

We are locked. Travel to and from Shadesmar was prohibited during the parent's last days. We are bound to obey.

Behind Shallan, on the bridge, Adolin had devised a clever tactic. He acted like an illusion.

Her false people had instructions to act like they were fighting—though without her direct attention, that meant they just stood around and slashed at the air. To avoid revealing himself, Adolin had chosen to do the same, slashing about with his harpoon randomly. Pattern and Syl did likewise, while the two Fused hovered overhead. One held her arm, which had been hit—but now seemed to be healing. They knew *someone* in that mass was real, but they couldn't ascertain who.

Shallan's time was short. She looked back up at the gatekeepers. "Please. The other Oathgate—the one at Kholinar—let me through."

Impossible, they said. *We are bound by Honor, by rules spren cannot break. This portal is closed.*

"Then why did you let those others through? The army that stood around here earlier?"

The souls of the dead? They did not need our portal. They were called by the enemy, pulled along ancient paths to waiting hosts. You living cannot do the same. You must seek the perpendicularity to transfer. The enormous spren cocked their heads in concert. *We are apologetic. We have been . . . alone very long. We would enjoy granting passage to men again. But we cannot do that which was forbidden.*

.·.

Szeth of the Skybreakers hovered far above the battlefield.

"The Alethi have changed sides, aboshi?" Szeth asked.

"They have seen the truth," Nin said, hovering beside him. Only the two of them watched; Szeth did not know where the rest of the Skybreakers had gone.

Nearby, the Everstorm rumbled its discontent. Red lightning rippled across the surface, passing from one cloud to the next.

"All along," Szeth said, "this world belonged to the parshmen. My people watched not for the return of an invading enemy, but for the masters of the house."

"Yes," Nin said.

"And you sought to stop them."

"I knew what must happen if they returned." Nin turned toward him. "Who has jurisdiction over this land, Szeth-son-Neturo? A man can rule his home until the citylord demands his taxes. The citylord controls his lands until the highlord, in turn, comes to him for payment. But the highlord must answer to the highprince, when war is called in his lands. And the king? He . . . must answer to God."

"You said God was dead."

"*A* god is dead. Another won the war by right of conquest. The original masters of this land have returned, as you so aptly made metaphor, with the keys to the house. So tell me, Szeth-son-Neturo—he who is about to swear the Third Ideal—whose law should the Skybreakers follow? That of humans, or that of the *real* owners of this land?"

There seemed to be no choice. Nin's logic was sound. No choice at all . . .

Don't be stupid, the sword said. *Let's go fight those guys.*

"The parshmen? They are the rightful rulers of the land," Szeth said.

Rightful? Who has a right to land? Humans are always claiming things. But nobody asks the things, now do they? Well, nobody owns me. Vivenna told me. I'm my own sword.

"I have no choice."

Really? Didn't you tell me you spent a thousand years following the instructions of a rock?

"More than seven years, sword-nimi. And I didn't follow the rock, but the words of the one who held it. I . . ."

. . . Had no choice?

But it had always been nothing more than a rock.

⁂

Kaladin swooped downward and passed above the treetops, rattling the glass leaves, sending a spray of broken shards behind himself. He turned upward with the slope of the mountain, adding another Lashing to his speed, then another.

When he passed the tree line, he Lashed himself closer to the rock, skimming with obsidian only inches from his face. He used his arms to sculpt the wind around himself, angling toward a crack through the glossy black rock where two mountains met.

Alive with Light and wind, he didn't care if the Fused were gaining on him or not.

Let them watch.

His angle was wrong to get through the crack, so Kaladin Lashed himself back away from the mountain slope in an enormous loop, continuously changing his Lashings one after another. He made a circle in the air, then darted past the Fused and straight through the crack, close enough to the walls that he could feel them pass.

He broke out the other side, exhilarated. Should he have run out of Stormlight by now? He didn't use it up as quickly as he had during his early months training.

Kaladin dove along the slopes as three Fused popped out of the crack to follow him. He led them around the base of the obsidian mountain, then wound back toward the Oathgate to check on Shallan and the others. As he approached, he let himself drop among the trees, still moving at incredible speed. He oriented himself as if he were diving through the chasms. Dodging these trees wasn't so different from that.

He wove between them, using his body more than Lashings to control his direction. His wake caused a melody of breaking glass. He exploded free of the forest, and found the fourth Fused—the one with his harpoon—waiting. The creature attacked, but Kaladin dodged and tore across the ground until he was passing over the sea of beads.

A quick glance showed him Shallan on the platform, waving her hands over her head—the prearranged signal that she needed more time.

Kaladin continued out over the sea, and beads reacted to his Stormlight, rattling and surging like a wave behind him. The last Fused slowed to hover in place, and the other three slowly emerged from the forest.

Kaladin spun in another loop, beads rising in the air behind him like a column of water. He curved in an arc and came in toward the harpoon-wielding Fused. Kaladin slapped the parshman's weapon aside, then swung the butt of his own lance up, catching the harpoon on the haft while he kicked his enemy in the chest.

The harpoon went upward. The Fused went backward.

The creature pulled himself to a stop in the air with a Lashing, then looked down at his hands, dumbfounded as Kaladin caught the harpoon in his free hand. The disarmed enemy barked something, then shook his head and took out his sword. He glided backward to join the other three, who approached with fluttering robes.

One of these—the male with the white face swirled with red—moved forward alone, then pointed at Kaladin with his lance and said something.

"I don't speak your language," Kaladin called back. "But if that was a challenge, you against me, I accept. Gladly."

At that moment, his Stormlight ran out.

⁎⁎

Navani finally got the rock unwedged, and shoved it out of the remnants of the doorway. Other stones fell around it, opening a path out onto the wall.

What was left of it.

About fifteen feet from where she stood, the wall ended in a ragged, broken gap. She coughed, then tucked back a lock of hair that had escaped her braid. They'd run for cover inside one of the stone guard towers along the wall, but one side had collapsed in the shaking.

It had fallen on the three soldiers who had come to protect the queen. The poor souls. Behind, Fen led her consort—who nursed a cut scalp—out over the rubble. Two other scribes had taken shelter with Navani and the queen, but most of the admirals had run in the other direction, taking shelter in the next guard tower along.

That tower was now missing. The monster had swept it away. Now the creature stomped across the plain outside, though Navani couldn't see what had drawn its attention.

"The stairway," Fen said, pointing. "Looks like it survived."

The stairway down was fully enclosed in stone, and would lead into a small guard chamber at the bottom. Maybe they could find soldiers to help the wounded and search the rubble for survivors. Navani pulled open the door, letting Fen and Kmakl head down first. Navani moved to follow, but hesitated.

Damnation, that sight beyond the wall was mesmerizing. The red lightning storm. The two monsters of stone. And the boiling, churning red mist along the right coast. It had no distinct shape, but somehow gave the impression of charging horses with the flesh ripped away.

One of the Unmade, certainly. An ancient spren of Odium. A thing beyond time and history. Here.

A company of soldiers had just finished pouring into the city through the gap. Another formed up outside to enter next. Navani felt a growing chill as she looked at them.

Red eyes.

Gasping softly, she left the stairwell and stumbled along the wall, reaching the broken stone edge. *Oh, dear Almighty, no . . .*

The ranks outside split, making way for a single parshwoman. Navani squinted, trying to see what was so special about her. One of the Fused? Behind her, the red mist surged, sending tendrils to weave among the men—including one wearing Shardplate, riding a brilliant white stallion. Amaram had changed sides.

He joined an overwhelming force of Voidbringers in all shapes and sizes. How could they fight this?

How could anyone *ever* fight this?

Navani fell to her knees above the broken edge of the wall. And then she noticed something else. Something incongruous, something her mind refused—at first—to accept. A solitary figure had somehow gotten around the troops who had already entered the city. He now picked his way across the rubble, wearing a blue uniform, carrying a *book* tucked under his arm.

Unaided and defenseless, Dalinar Kholin stepped into the gap in the broken wall, and there faced the nightmare alone.

117

CHAMPION WITH NINE SHADOWS

Beware the otherworlders. The traitors. Those with tongues of sweetness, but with minds that lust for blood. Do not take them in. Do not give them succor. Well were they named Voidbringers, for they brought the void. The empty pit that sucks in emotion. A new god. Their god.

—From the Eila Stele

Dalinar stepped onto the rubble, boots scraping stone. The air felt too still out here near the red storm. Stagnant. How could the air be so motionless?

Amaram's army hesitated outside the gap. Some men had already gotten in, but the bulk had been forming up to wait their turn. When you rushed a city like this, you wanted to be careful not to push your own forces too hard from behind, lest you crush them up against the enemy.

These kept uneven ranks, snarling, eyes red. More telling, they ignored the wealth at their feet. A field of spheres and gemstones—all dun—that had been thrown out onto this plain by the thunderclast that destroyed the reserve.

They wanted blood instead. Dalinar could *taste* their lust for the fight, the challenge. What held them back?

Twin thunderclasts stomped toward the wall. A red haze drifted among the men. Images of war and death. A deadly storm. Dalinar faced it alone. One man. All that remained of a broken dream.

"So . . ." a sudden voice said from his right. "What's the plan?"

Dalinar frowned, then looked down to find a Reshi girl with long hair, dressed in a simple shirt and trousers.

"Lift?" Dalinar asked in Azish. "Didn't you leave?"

"Sure did. What's wrong with your army?"

"They're his now."

"Did you forget to feed them?"

Dalinar glanced at the soldiers, standing in ranks that felt more like packs than they did true battle formations. "Perhaps I didn't try hard enough."

"Were you . . . thinkin' you'd fight them all on your own?" Lift said. "With a book?"

"There is someone else for me to fight here."

". . . With a book?"

"Yes."

She shook her head. "Sure, all right. Why not? What do you want me to do?"

The girl didn't match the conventional ideal of a Knight Radiant. Not even five feet tall, thin and wiry, she looked more urchin than soldier.

She was also all he had.

"Do you have a weapon?" he asked.

"Nope. Can't read."

"Can't . . ." Dalinar looked down at his book. "I meant a real weapon, Lift."

"Oh! Yeah, I've got one a those." She thrust her hand to the side. Mist formed into a small, glittering Shardblade.

. . . Or no, it was just a pole. A silver pole with a rudimentary cross-guard.

Lift shrugged. "Wyndle doesn't like hurting people."

Doesn't like . . . Dalinar blinked. What kind of world did he live in where *swords* didn't like *hurting people*?

"A Fused escaped from this city a short time ago," Dalinar said, "carrying an enormous ruby. I don't know why they wanted it, and I'd rather not find out. Can you steal it back?"

"Sure. Easy."

"You'll find it with a Fused who can move with a power similar to your own. A woman."

"Like I said. Easy."

"Easy? I think you might find—"

"Relax, grandpa. Steal the rock. I can do that." She took a deep breath, then exploded with Stormlight. Her eyes turned a pearly, glowing white. "It's just us two, then?"

"Yes."

"Right. Good luck with the army."

Dalinar looked back at the soldiers, where a figure materialized, wearing gold, holding a scepter like a cane.

"It's not the army that worries me," Dalinar said. But Lift had already scampered away, hugging the wall and running quickly to round the outside of the army.

Odium strolled up to Dalinar, trailed by a handful of Fused—plus the woman Dalinar had sucked into his visions—and a shadowy spren that looked like it was made of twisting smoke. What was that?

Odium didn't address Dalinar at first, but instead turned to his Fused. "Tell Yushah I want her to stay out here and guard the prison. Kai-garnis did well destroying the wall; tell her to return to the city and climb toward the Oathgate. If the Tisark can't secure it, she is to destroy the device and recover its gemstones. We can rebuild it as long as the spren aren't compromised."

Two Fused left, each running toward one of the towering thunderclasts. Odium placed both hands on the top of his scepter and smiled at Dalinar. "Well, my friend. Here we are, and the time has arrived. Are you ready?"

"Yes," Dalinar said.

"Good, good. Let us begin."

⁂

The two Fused hovered near Adolin, out of easy reach, admiring Shallan's illusory handiwork. He did his best to blend in, waving his harpoon around crazily. He wasn't sure where Syl had gone, but Pattern seemed to be enjoying himself, humming pleasantly and swinging a glass branch.

One of the Fused nudged the other, then pointed at Shallan, whom they'd just noticed. Neither appeared worried that she'd open the Oathgate—which was a bad sign. What did they know about the device that Adolin's team did not?

The Fused turned from Shallan and continued a conversation in a language Adolin couldn't understand. One pointed at each illusion in turn, then thrust with his spear. The other shook her head, and Adolin could almost interpret her answer. *We tried stabbing each one. They keep mixing about, so it's hard to keep track.*

Instead, the female took out a knife and cut her hand, then flung it toward the illusions. Orange blood fell through the illusions, leaving no stain, but splattered against Adolin's cheek. Adolin felt his heart flutter, and he tried to covertly wipe the blood off, but the female gestured toward him with a satisfied grin. The male saluted her with a finger to his head, then lowered his lance and flew straight toward Adolin.

Damnation.

Adolin scrambled away, passing through an illusion of Captain Notum and causing it to diffuse. It formed back together, then blew apart a second later as the Fused soared through it, lance pointed at Adolin's back.

Adolin spun and flung his harpoon up to block, deflecting the lance, but the Fused still smashed into him, tossing him backward. Adolin hit the stone bridge hard, smacking his head, seeing stars.

Vision swimming, he reached for his harpoon, but the Fused slapped the weapon away with the butt of his lance. The creature then alighted softly on the bridge, billowing robes settling.

Adolin yanked out his belt knife, then forced himself to his feet, unsteady. The Fused lowered its lance to a two-handed, underarm grip, then waited.

Knife against spear. Adolin breathed in and out, worried about the other Fused—who had gone for Shallan. He tried to dredge up Zahel's lessons, remembering days on the practice yard running this exact exchange. Jakamav had refused the training, laughing at the idea that a Shardbearer would ever fight knife to spear.

Adolin flipped the knife to grip it point down, then held it forward so he could deflect the spear thrusts. Zahel whispered to him. Wait until the enemy thrusts with the spear, deflect it or dodge it, then grab the spear with your left hand. Pull yourself close enough to ram the knife into the enemy's neck.

Right. He could do that.

He'd "died" seven times out of ten doing it against Zahel, of course.

Winds bless you anyway, you old axehound, he thought. Adolin stepped in, testing, and waited for the thrust. When it came, Adolin shoved the lance's point aside with his knife, then grabbed at—

The enemy floated backward in an unnatural motion, too fast—no ordinary human could have moved in such a way. Adolin stumbled, trying to reassess. The Fused idly brought the lance back around, then fluidly rammed it right through Adolin's stomach.

Adolin gasped at the sharp spike of pain, doubling over, feeling blood on his hands. The Fused seemed almost *bored* as he yanked the lance out, the tip glistening red with Adolin's blood, then dropped the weapon. The creature landed and instead unsheathed a wicked-looking sword. He advanced, slapped away Adolin's weak attempt at a parry, and raised the sword to strike.

Someone leaped onto the Fused from behind.

A figure in tattered clothing, a scrabbling, angry woman with brown vines instead of skin and scratched-out eyes. Adolin gaped as his deadeye raked long nails across the Fused's face, causing him to stumble backward, *humming* of all things. He rammed his sword into the spren's chest, but it didn't faze her in the least. She just let out a screech like the one she'd made at Adolin when he'd tried to summon his Blade, and kept attacking.

Adolin shook himself. *Flee, idiot!*

Holding his wounded gut—each step causing a shock of pain—he lurched across the bridge toward Shallan.

∴

Employing subterfuge will not deceive us or weaken our resolve, Lightweaver, the guardians said. *For indeed, this is not a matter of decision, but one of nature. The path remains closed.*

Shallan let the illusion melt around her, then slumped down, exhausted. She'd tried pleading, cajoling, yelling, and even Lightweaving. It was no use. She had failed. Her illusions on the bridge were wavering and vanishing, their Stormlight running out.

Through them shot a Fused trailing dark energy, lance leveled directly toward Shallan. She dove to the side, barely getting out of the way. The creature passed in a whoosh, then slowed and turned for another pass.

Shallan leaped to her feet first. "Pattern!" she yelled, sweeping her hands forward by instinct, trying to summon the Blade. A part of her was impressed that was her reaction. Adolin would be proud.

It didn't work, of course. Pattern shouted in apology from the bridge, panicked. And yet in that moment—facing the enemy bearing down, its lance pointed at her heart—Shallan felt *something*. Pattern, or something like him, just beyond her mental reach. On the other side, and if she could just tug on it, feed it . . .

She screamed as Stormlight flowed through her, raging in her veins, reaching toward something in her pocket.

A wall appeared in front of her.

Shallan gasped. A sickening *smack* from the other side of the wall indicated that the Fused had collided with it.

A wall. A storming *wall* of worked stones, broken at the sides. Shallan looked down and found that her pocket—she was still wearing Veil's white trousers—was connected to the strange wall.

What on Roshar? She pulled out her small knife and sawed the pocket free, then stumbled back. In the center of the wall was a small bead, melded into the stone.

That's the bead I used to cross the sea down below, Shallan thought. What she'd done felt like Soulcasting, yet different.

Pattern ran up to her, humming as he left the bridge. Where were Adolin and Syl?

"I took the soul of the wall," Shallan said, "and then made its physical form appear on this side."

"Mmm. I think these beads are more minds than souls, but you did manifest it here. Very nice. Though your touch is unpracticed. Mmm. It will not stay for long."

The edges were already starting to unravel to smoke. A scraping sound on the other side indicated that the Fused had not been defeated, merely stunned. Shallan turned from it and scrambled over the bridge, away from the towering sentinels. She passed some of her illusions and recovered a little of their Stormlight. Now, where was—

Adolin. Bleeding!

Shallan dashed over and grabbed him by the arm, trying to keep him upright as he stumbled.

"It's just a little cut," he said. Blood seeped out between his fingers, which were pressed to his gut, right below the navel. The back of his uniform was bloody too.

"Just a little cut? Adolin! You—"

"No time," he said, leaning against her. He nodded toward the Fused she'd fought, who rose into the air over Shallan's wall. "The other one is back behind me somewhere. Could be on us at any moment."

"Kaladin," Shallan said. "Where—"

"Mmm . . ." Pattern said, pointing. "He ran out of Stormlight and fell into the beads over that way."

Great.

"Take a deep breath," Shallan said to Adolin, then pulled him off the bridge with her and leaped for the beads.

⁙

Lift became awesome.

Her powers manifested as the ability to slide across objects without truly touching them. She could become really, really slick—which was handy, because soldiers tried to snatch her as she rounded the Alethi army. They grabbed at her unbuttoned overshirt, her arm, her hair. They couldn't hold her. She just slid away. It was like they were trying to grab hold of a song.

She burst from their ranks and fell to her knees, which she'd slicked up real good. That meant she kept going, sliding on her knees away from the men with the glowing red eyes. Wyndle—who she knew by now was almost certainly not a Voidbringer—was a little snaking line of green beside her. He looked like a fast-growing vine, jutting with small crystals here and there.

"Oh, I don't like this," he said.

"You don't like nothin'."

"Now, that is *not* true, mistress. I liked that nice town we passed back in Azir."

"The one that was deserted?"

"So peaceful."

There, Lift thought, picking out a *real* Voidbringer—the type that looked like parshmen, only big and scary. This one was a woman, and moved across the rock smoothly, like she was awesome too.

"I've always wondered," Lift said. "Do you suppose they got those marble colorings on *all* their parts?"

"Mistress? Does it matter?"

"Maybe not now," Lift admitted, glancing at the red storm. She kept her legs slick, but her hands not slick, which let her paddle and steer herself. Going about on your knees didn't look as deevy as standing up—but when she tried being awesome while standing, she usually ended up crashed against a rock with her butt in the air.

That Fused *did* seem to be carrying something large in one hand. Like a big gemstone. Lift paddled in that direction—which was taking her dangerously close to that parshman army and their ships. Still, she got up pretty close before the Voidbringer woman turned and noticed.

Lift slid to a halt, letting her Stormlight run out. Her stomach growled, so she took a bite of some jerky she'd found in her guard's pocket.

The Voidbringer said something in a singsong voice, hefting the enormous ruby—it didn't have any Stormlight, which was good, since one that big would have been *bright*. Like, redder and brighter than Gawx's face when Lift told him about how babies was made. He should know stuff like that already. He'd been a starvin' thief! Hadn't he known any whores or anything?

Anyway . . . how to get that ruby? The Voidbringer spoke again, and while Lift couldn't figure out the words, she couldn't help feeling that the Voidbringer sounded amused. The woman pushed off with one foot, then slid on the other, easy as if she were standing on oil. She coasted for a second, then looked over her shoulder and grinned before kicking off and sliding to the left, casually moving with a grace that made Lift seem super stupid.

"Well starve me," Lift said. "She's *more* awesome than I am."

"Do you *have* to use that term?" Wyndle asked. "Yes, she appears to be able to access the Surge of—"

"Shut it," Lift said. "Can you follow her?"

"I might leave you behind."

"I'll keep up." Maybe. "You follow her. I'll follow you."

Wyndle sighed but obeyed, streaking off after the Voidbringer. Lift followed, paddling on her knees, feeling like a pig trying to imitate a professional dancer.

⁘

"You must choose, Szeth-son-Neturo," Nin said. "The Skybreakers will swear to the Dawnsingers and their law. And you? Will you join us?"

Wind rippled Szeth's clothing. All those years ago, he'd been correct. The Voidbringers *had* returned.

Now . . . now he was to simply accept their rule?

"I don't trust myself, aboshi," Szeth whispered. "I cannot see the right any longer. My own decisions are not trustworthy."

"Yes," Nin said, nodding, hands clasped behind his back. "Our minds are fallible. This is why we must pick something external to follow. Only in strict adherence to a code can we approximate justice."

Szeth inspected the battlefield far below.

When are we going to actually fight someone? asked the sword on his back. *You sure do like to talk. Even more than Vasher, and he could go on and on and on. . . .*

"Aboshi," Szeth said. "When I say the Third Ideal, can I choose a *person* as the thing I obey? Instead of the law?"

"Yes. Some of the Skybreakers have chosen to follow me, and I suspect that will make the transition to obeying the Dawnsingers easier for them. I would not suggest it. I feel that . . . I am . . . am getting worse. . . ."

A man in blue barred the way into the city below. He confronted . . . something else. A force that Szeth could just barely sense. A hidden fire.

"You followed men before," Nin continued. "They caused your pain, Szeth-son-Neturo. Your agony is because you did not follow something unchanging and pure. You picked men instead of an ideal."

"Or," Szeth said, "perhaps I was simply forced to follow the wrong men."

⁘

Kaladin thrashed in the beads, suffocating, coughing. He wasn't that deep, but which way . . . which way was out? *Which way was out?*

Frantic, he tried to swim toward the surface, but the beads didn't move like water, and he couldn't propel himself. Beads slipped into his mouth, pushed at his skin. Pulled at him like an invisible hand. Trying to drag him farther and farther into the depths.

Away from the light. Away from the wind.

His fingers brushed something warm and soft among the beads. He thrashed, trying to find it again, and a hand seized his arm. He brought his other arm around and grabbed hold of a thin wrist. Another hand took him by the front of the coat, pulling him away from the darkness, and he stumbled, finding purchase on the bottom of the sea.

Lungs burning, he followed, step by step, eventually bursting from the beads to find Syl pulling him by the front of the coat. She led him up the bank, where he collapsed in a heap, spitting out spheres and wheezing. The Fused he'd been fighting landed on the Oathgate platform near the two they'd left behind.

As Kaladin was recovering his breath, beads nearby pulled back, revealing Shallan, Adolin, and Pattern crossing the seafloor through some kind of passage she'd made. A hallway in the depths? She was growing in her ability to manipulate the beads.

Adolin was wounded. Kaladin gritted his teeth, forcing himself to his feet and stumbling over to help Shallan get the prince up onto the shore. The prince lay on his back, cursing softly, holding his gut with bloodied hands.

"Let me see it," Kaladin said, prying Adolin's fingers out of the way.

"The blood—" Shallan started.

"The blood is the least of his worries," Kaladin said, prodding at the wound. "He's not going to bleed out from a gut wound anytime soon, but sepsis is another story. And if internal organs got cut . . ."

"Leave me," Adolin said, coughing.

"Leave you to go *where*?" Kaladin said, moving his fingers in the wound. Storms. The intestines were cut. "I'm out of Stormlight."

Shallan's glow faded. "That was the last of what I had."

Syl gripped Kaladin's shoulder, looking toward the Fused, who launched up and flew toward them, lances held high. Pattern hummed softly. Nervously.

"What do we do then?" Shallan asked.

No . . . Kaladin thought.

"Give me your knife," Adolin said, trying to sit up.

It can't be the end.

"Adolin, no. Rest. Maybe we can surrender."

I can't fail him!

Kaladin looked over his shoulder toward Syl, who held him lightly by the arm.

She nodded. "The Words, Kaladin."

⁜

Amaram's soldiers parted around Dalinar, flooding into the city. They ignored him—and unfortunately, he had to ignore them.

"So, child . . ." Odium nodded toward the city, and took Dalinar by the shoulder. "You did something marvelous in forging that coalition. You should feel proud. *I'm* certainly proud."

How could Dalinar fight this thing, who thought of every possibility, who planned for every outcome? How could he face something so vast, so incredible? Touching it, Dalinar could *sense* it stretching into infinity. Permeating the land, the people, the sky and the stone.

He would break, go insane, if he tried to comprehend this being. And somehow he had to defeat it?

Convince him that he can lose, the Almighty had said in vision. *Appoint a champion. He will take that chance. . . . This is the best advice I can give you.*

Honor had been slain resisting this thing.

Dalinar licked his lips. "A test of champions," he said to Odium. "I demand that we clash over this world."

"For what purpose?" Odium asked.

"Killing us won't free you, will it?" Dalinar said. "You could rule us or destroy us, but either way, you'd still be trapped here."

Nearby, one of the thunderclasts climbed over the wall and entered the city. The other stayed behind, stomping around near the rearguard of the army.

"A contest," Dalinar said to Odium. "Your freedom if you win, our lives if humans win."

"Be careful what you request, Dalinar Kholin. As Bondsmith, you can offer this deal. But is this truly what you wish of me?"

"I . . ."

Was it?

⁂

Wyndle followed the Voidbringer, and Lift followed him. They slipped back among the men of the human army. The front ranks were pouring into the city, but the opening wasn't big enough for them to all go at once. Most waited out here for their turn, cursing and grumbling at the delay.

They took swipes at Lift as she tried to follow the trail of vines Wyndle left. Being little helped her avoid them, fortunately. She liked being little. Little people could squeeze into places others couldn't, and could go unnoticed. She wasn't supposed to get any older; the Nightwatcher had promised her she wouldn't.

The Nightwatcher had lied. Just like a starvin' human would have. Lift shook her head and slipped between the legs of a soldier. Being little was nice, but it *was* hard not to feel like every man was a mountain towering overhead. They smashed weapons about her, speaking guttural Alethi curses.

I can't do this on my knees, she thought as a sword chopped close to her shirt. *I have to be like her. I have to be free.*

Lift zipped over the side of a small rise in the rock, and managed to land on her feet. She ran for a moment, then slicked the bottoms of her feet and went into a slide.

The Voidbringer woman passed ahead. She didn't slip and fall, but performed this strange walking motion—one that let her control her smooth glide.

Lift tried to do the same. She trusted in her awesomeness—her Stormlight—to sustain her as she held her breath. Men cursed around her, but sounds slid off Lift as she coated herself in Light.

The wind itself couldn't touch her. She'd been here before. She'd held for a beautiful moment between crashes, sliding on bare feet, moving free, untouched. Like she was gliding between worlds. She could do it. She could—

Something crashed to the ground nearby, crushing several soldiers, throwing Lift off balance and sending her into a heap. She slid to a stop and rolled over, looking up at one of the huge stone monsters. The skeletal thing raised a spiked hand and slammed it down.

Lift threw herself out of the way, but the shaking from the impact sent her sprawling again. Soldiers nearby didn't seem to care that their fellows had been crushed. Eyes glowing, they scrambled for her, as if it were a contest to see who could kill her first.

Her only choice was to dodge *toward* the stone monster. Maybe she could get so close that it—

The creature pounded again, mashing three soldiers, but also slamming into Lift. The blow snapped her legs in the blink of an eye, then crushed her lower half, sending her into a screaming fit of pain. Eyes watering, she curled up on the ground.

Heal. Heal.

Just had to weather the pain. Just had to . . .

Stones ground against one another overhead. She blinked away tears, looking up at the creature raising its spike high in the sky, toward the sun, which was slipping behind the clouds of the deadly storm.

"Mistress!" Wyndle said. His vines climbed over her, as if trying to cradle her. "Oh, mistress. Summon me as a sword!"

The pain in her legs started to fade. Too slowly. She was growing hungry again, her Stormlight running low. She summoned Wyndle as a rod, twisting against the pain and holding him toward the monster, her eyes watering with the effort.

An explosion of light appeared overhead, a ball of expanding Radiance. Something dropped from the middle of it, trailing smoke both black and white. Glowing like a star.

"Mother!" Wyndle said. "What is—"

As the monster raised its fist to strike Lift, the spear of light hit the creature in the head and *cut straight through*. It divided the enormous thing in two, sending out an explosion of black smoke. The halves of the monster fell to the sides, crashing into the stone, then *burned away*, evaporating into blackness.

Soldiers cursed and coughed, backing up as something resolved in the center of the tempest. A figure in the smoke, glowing white and holding a jet-black Shardblade that seemed to *feed* on the smoke, sucking it in, then letting it pour down beneath itself as a liquid blackness.

White and black. A man with a shaved head, eyes glowing a light grey, Stormlight rising from him. He straightened and strode through the smoke, leaving an afterimage behind. Lift had seen this man before. The Assassin in White. Murderer.

And apparently savior.

He stopped beside her. "The Blackthorn assigned you a task?"

"Uh . . . yeah," Lift said, wiggling her toes, which seemed to be working again. "There's a Voidbringer who stole a large ruby. I'm supposed to get it back."

"Then stand," the assassin said, raising his strange Shardblade toward the enemy soldiers. "Our master has given us a task. *We shall see it completed.*"

∴

Navani scrambled across the top of the wall, alone except for crushed corpses.

Dalinar, don't you dare become a martyr, she thought, reaching the stairwell. She pulled open the door at the top and started down the dark steps. What was he thinking? Facing an entire army on his own? He wasn't a young man in his prime, outfitted in Shardplate!

She fumbled for a sphere in her safepouch, then eventually undid the clasp on her arm fabrial instead, using its light to guide her down the steps and into the room at the base. Where had Fen and—

A hand grabbed her, pulling her to the side and slamming her against the wall. Fen and Kmakl lay here, gagged, bound tightly. A pair of men in forest green, eyes glowing red, held knives to them. A third one, wearing the knots of a captain, pressed Navani against the wall.

"What a handsome reward you'll earn me," the man hissed at Navani. "Two queens. Brightlord Amaram will enjoy this gift. That almost makes up for not being able to kill you personally, as justice for what your husband did to Brightlord Sadeas."

∴

Ash stumbled to a stop before a brazier. It bore delicate metalwork around the rim, a finer piece than one expected to find in such a common location.

This improvised camp was where the Alethi troops had bivouacked while repairing the city; it clogged multiple streets and squares of the Low Ward. The unlit brazier that had stopped Ash was in front of a tent, and had perhaps been used for warmth on cold Thaylen nights. Ten figures ringed the bowl. Her fingers *itched*. She couldn't move on, no matter how desperate her task, until she'd done it.

She seized the bowl and turned it until she found the woman depicting her, marked by the iconography of the brush and the mask, symbols of creativity. Pure absurdity. She pulled out her knife and sawed at the metal until she'd managed to scratch out the face.

Good enough. Good enough.

She dropped the brazier. Keep going. What that man, Mraize, had told her had better be true. If he had lied . . .

The large tent near the wall was completely unguarded, though soldiers had run past her a short time ago, eyes glowing with the light of corrupted Investiture. *Odium has learned to possess men.* A dark, dangerous day. He'd always been able to tempt them to fight for him, but sending spren to bond with them? Terrible.

And how had he managed to start a *storm* of his *own*?

Well, this land was finally doomed. And Ash . . . Ash couldn't find it inside herself to care any longer. She pushed into the tent, forcibly keeping herself from looking at the rug in case it bore depictions of the Heralds.

There she found him, sitting alone in the dim light, staring ahead sightlessly. Dark skin, even darker than hers, and a muscled physique. A king, for all the fact that he'd never worn a crown. He was the one of the ten who was never supposed to have borne their burden.

And he'd borne it the longest anyway.

"Taln," she whispered.

∴

Renarin Kholin knew he wasn't actually a Knight Radiant. Glys had once been a different kind of spren, but something had changed him, corrupted him. Glys didn't remember that very well; it had happened before they had formed their bond.

Now, neither knew what they'd become. Renarin could feel the spren trembling inside him, hiding and whispering about the danger. Jasnah had found them.

Renarin had seen that coming.

He knelt in the ancient temple of Pailiah, and to his eyes it was full of colors. A thousand panes of stained glass sprouted on the walls, combining and melting together, creating a panorama. He saw himself coming to Thaylen City earlier in the day. He saw Dalinar talking to the monarchs, and then he saw them turning against him.

She will hurt us! She will hurt us!

"I know, Glys," he whispered, turning toward a specific section of stained glass. This showed Renarin kneeling on the floor of the temple. In the sequence of stained glass panels, Jasnah approached him from behind, sword raised.

And then . . . she struck him down.

Renarin couldn't control what he saw or when he saw it. He had learned to read so he could understand the numbers and words that appeared under some of the images. They had shown him when the Everstorm would come. They had shown him how to find the hidden compartments in Urithiru. Now they showed his death.

The future. Renarin could see what was forbidden.

He wrenched his eyes away from the glass pane showing himself and Jasnah, turning toward one even worse. In it, his father knelt before a god of gold and white.

"No, Father," Renarin whispered. "Please. Not that. Don't do it. . . ."

He will not be resisted, Glys said. *My sorrow, Renarin. I will give you my sorrow.*

⁘

A pair of gloryspren swung down from the skies, golden spheres. They floated and spun around Dalinar, brilliant like drops of sunlight.

"Yes," Dalinar said. "This is what I wish."

"You wish a contest of champions?" Odium repeated. "This is your true desire, not forced upon you? You were not beguiled or tricked in any way?"

"A contest of champions. For the fate of Roshar."

"Very well," Odium said, then sighed softly. "I agree."

"That easily?"

"Oh, I assure you. This won't be easy." Odium raised his eyebrows in an open, inviting way. A *concerned* expression. "I have chosen my champion already. I've been preparing him for a long, long time."

"Amaram."

"Him? A passionate man, yes, but hardly suited to this task. No, I need someone who dominates a battlefield like the sun dominates the sky."

The Thrill suddenly returned to Dalinar. The red mist—which had been fading—roared back to life. Images filled his mind. Memories of his youth spent fighting.

"I need someone stronger than Amaram," Odium whispered.

"No."

"A man who will win no matter the cost."

The Thrill overwhelmed Dalinar, choking him.

"A man who has served me all his life. A man I trust. I believe I warned you that I knew you'd make the right decision. And now here we are."

"*No.*"

"Take a deep breath, my friend," Odium whispered. "I'm afraid that this will hurt."

118

THE WEIGHT OF IT ALL

These Voidbringers know no songs. They cannot hear Roshar, and where they go, they bring silence. They look soft, with no shell, but they are hard. They have but one heart, and it cannot ever live.

—From the Eila Stele

"N o," Dalinar whispered again, voice ragged as the Thrill thrummed inside of him. "*No.* You are wrong."

Odium gripped Dalinar's shoulder. "What does *she* say?"

She?

He heard Evi crying. Screaming. Begging for her life as the flames took her.

"Don't blame yourself," Odium said as Dalinar winced. "I made you kill her, Dalinar. I caused *all* of this. Do you remember? I can help. Here."

Memories flooded Dalinar's mind, a devastating onslaught of images. He lived them all in detail, somehow squeezed into a moment, the Thrill raging inside of him.

He saw himself stab a poor soldier in the back. A young man trying to crawl to safety, crying for his mother . . .

"I was with you then," Odium said.

He killed a far better man than himself, a highlord who had held Teleb's loyalty. Dalinar knocked him to the ground, then slammed a poleaxe into his chest.

"I was with you then."

Dalinar fought atop a strange rock formation, facing another man who knew the Thrill. Dalinar dropped him to the ground with burning eyes, and called it a mercy.

"I was with you then."

He raged at Gavilar, anger and lust rising as twin emotions. He broke a man in a tavern, frustrated that he'd been held back from enjoying the fight. He fought on the borders of Jah Keved, laughing, corpses littering the ground. He remembered every moment of the carnage. He felt each death like a spike driven into his soul. He began to weep for the destruction.

"It's what you needed to do, Dalinar," Odium said. "You made a better kingdom!"

"So . . . much . . . *pain*."

"Blame me, Dalinar. It wasn't you! You saw red when you did those things! It was *my* fault. Accept that. You don't have to hurt."

Dalinar blinked, meeting Odium's eyes.

"Let me have the pain, Dalinar," Odium said. "Give it to me, and never feel guilty again."

"No." Dalinar hugged *The Way of Kings* close. "No. I can't."

"Oh, Dalinar. What does *she* say?"

No . . .

"Have you forgotten? Here, let me help."

And he was back in that day. The day he killed Evi.

⁘

Szeth found purpose in wielding the sword.

It screamed at him to destroy evil, even if evil was obviously a concept that the sword itself could not understand. Its vision was occluded, like Szeth's own. A metaphor.

How was a twisted soul like his to decide who should die? Impossible. And so he put his trust in someone else, someone whose light peeked through the shadow.

Dalinar Kholin. Knight Radiant. *He* would know.

This choice was not perfect. But . . . Stones Unhallowed . . . it was the best he could manage. It brought him some small measure of peace as he swept through the enemy army.

The sword screamed at him. *DESTROY!*

Anyone he so much as nicked *popped* into black smoke. Szeth laid waste to the red-eyed soldiers, who kept coming, showing no fear. Screaming, as if they thirsted for death.

It was a drink that Szeth was all too good at serving.

He wielded Stormlight in one hand, Lashing any men who drew too close, sending them flipping into the air or crashing backward into their fellows. With the other hand he swept the sword through their ranks. He moved on nimble feet, his own body Lashed upward just enough to lighten him. Skybreakers didn't have access to all of the Lashings, but the most useful—and most deadly—were still his.

Remember the gemstone.

A phantom sense called to him, a desire to continue killing, to revel in the butchery. Szeth rejected it, sick. He had never enjoyed this. He *could* never enjoy this.

The Voidbringer with the gemstone had slipped away, moving on too-swift feet. Szeth pointed the sword—a piece of him terrified by how quickly it was chewing through his own Stormlight—and Lashed himself to follow. He plowed through soldiers, men bursting into smoke, seeking that one individual.

The Voidbringer turned at the last moment, dancing away from his sword. Szeth Lashed himself downward, then spun in a sweeping arc, towing black smoke—almost liquid—behind his sword as he destroyed men in a grand circle.

EVIL! the sword cried.

Szeth leaped for the Voidbringer woman, but she dropped to the ground and slid on the stone as if it were greased. His sword swung over her head, and she pushed herself backward toward him, sliding right past his legs. There, she swept gracefully to her feet and seized the *sheath* off Szeth's back, where he'd tied it for safekeeping.

It broke free. When Szeth turned to attack, she blocked the sword with its own sheath. How had she done that? Was there something about the silvery metal that Szeth didn't know?

She blocked his next few attacks, then ducked away from his attempts to Lash her.

The sword was growing frustrated. *DESTROY, DESTROY, DESTROY!* Black veins began to grow around Szeth's hand, creeping toward his upper arm.

He struck again, but she simply slipped away, moving across the ground as if natural laws had no purchase on her. Other soldiers piled in, and the pain started up Szeth's arm as he worked death among them.

⁂

Jasnah stopped one pace behind Renarin. She could hear his whispers clearly now. "Father. Oh, Father . . ." The young man whipped his head in one direction, then another, seeing things that weren't there.

"He sees not what *is*, but what *is to come*," Ivory said. "Odium's power, Jasnah."

⁂

"Taln," Ash whispered, kneeling before him. "Oh, Taln . . ."

The Herald stared forward with dark eyes. "I am Talenel'Elin, Herald of War. The time of the Return, the Desolation, is near at hand. . . ."

"Taln?" Ash took his hand. "It's me. It's Ash."

"We must prepare. You will have forgotten much. . . ."

"Please, Taln."

"Kalak will teach you to cast bronze. . . ."

He just continued on, repeating the same words over and over and over.

⁂

Kaladin fell to his knees on the cold obsidian of Shadesmar.

Fused descended around them, six figures in brilliant, flapping clothing.

He had a single slim hope. Each Ideal he'd spoken had resulted in an outpouring of power and strength. He licked his lips and tried whispering it. "I . . . I will . . ."

He thought of friends lost. Malop. Jaks. Beld and Pedin.

Say it, storm you!

"I . . ."

Rod and Mart. Bridgemen he'd failed. And before them, slaves he'd tried to save. Goshel. Nalma, caught in a trap like a beast.

A windspren appeared near him, like a line of light. Then another.

A single hope.

The Words. Say the Words!

⁂

"Oh, Mother! Oh, Cultivation!" Wyndle cried as they watched the assassin murder his way across the field. "What have we done?"

"We've pointed *him* away from *us*," Lift said as she perched on a boulder, her eyes wide. "You'd rather he was close by?"

Wyndle continued to whimper, and Lift kinda understood. That was a *lot* of killing that the assassin did. Red-eyed men who seemed to have no light left in them, true, but . . . storms.

She'd lost track of the woman with the gemstone, but at least the army seemed to be flowing away from Szeth, leaving him fewer people to kill. He stumbled, slowing, then dropped to his knees.

"Uh-oh." Lift summoned Wyndle as a rod in case the assassin lost his starvin' mind—what was left of it—and attacked her. She slipped off the rock, then ran over.

He held the strange Shardblade before himself. It continued to leak black liquid that vaporized as it streamed toward the ground. His hand had gone all black.

"I . . ." Szeth said. "I have lost the sheath. . . ."

"Drop the sword!"

"I . . . can't. . . ." Szeth said, teeth gritted. "It holds to me, feasting upon my . . . my Stormlight. It will soon consume me."

Stormsstormsstormsstorms. "Right. Right. Ummmmm . . ." Lift looked around. The army was flooding into the city. The second stone monster was stomping across the Ancient Ward, stepping on buildings. Dalinar Kholin still stood before the gap. Maybe . . . maybe he could help?

"Come on," Lift said.

⁙

"Kill the man," said the captain holding Navani. He swept his hand toward old Kmakl, Fen's consort. "We don't need him."

Fen screamed against her gag, but she was held tightly. Navani carefully wiggled her safehand fingers out of her sleeve, then touched her other arm and the fabrial there, flipping a latch. Small knobs extended from the front of the device, just above her wrist.

Kmakl struggled to stand. He seemed to want to face his death with dignity, but the other two soldiers didn't give him that honor. They pushed him back against the wall, one pulling out a dagger.

Navani seized the arm of the man holding her, then pressed the knobs of her pain fabrial against his skin. He screamed and dropped, writhing in agony. One of the others turned toward her, and she pressed the painrial against his uplifted hand. She'd tested the device on herself, of course, so she knew what it felt like. A thousand needles being shoved into your skin, under your nails, into your *eyes*.

The second man wet himself as he dropped.

The last one managed to cut a gash in her arm before she sent him to the ground, spasming. Bother. She flipped the switch on the painrial, drawing away the agony of the cut. Then she took the knife and quickly cut Fen's bonds. As the queen freed Kmakl, Navani bound her painless wound.

"These will recover soon," Navani said. "We may need to dispatch them before that happens."

Kmakl kicked the man who had almost slit his throat, then cracked the door into the city. A troop of men with glowing eyes rushed past. The entire area was overrun with them.

"These are the least of our trouble, it seems," the aging man said, shutting the door.

"Back up to the wall, then," Fen said. "We might be able to spot friendly troops from that vantage."

Navani nodded, and Fen led the way up. At the top, they barred the door. There were bars on both sides; you wanted to be able to lock out enemies who had seized the wall, and also ones who had broken through the gates.

Navani surveyed their options. A quick glance revealed that the streets were indeed held by Amaram's troops. Some groups of Thaylens held ground farther up, but they were falling quickly.

"By Kelek, storms, and Passions alike," Kmakl said. "What is *that*?"

He'd noticed the red mist on the north side of the battlefield, with its horrific images forming and breaking apart. Shadows of soldiers dying, of skeletal features, of charging horses. It was a grand, intimidating sight.

But Dalinar . . . *Dalinar* drew her eyes. Standing alone, surrounded by enemy soldiers, and facing something she could just *barely* sense. Something vast. Something unimaginable.

Something angry.

⁘

Dalinar lived in two places.

He saw himself crossing a darkened landscape, dragging his Shardblade behind him. He was on the field at Thaylen City with Odium, but he was also in the past, approaching Rathalas. Urged on by the boiling red anger of the Thrill. He returned to the camp, to the surprise of his men, like a spren of death. Coated in blood, eyes glowing.

Glowing red.

He ordered the oil brought. He turned toward a city where Evi was imprisoned, where children slept, where innocent people hid and prayed and burned glyphwards and wept.

"Please . . ." Dalinar whispered in Thaylen City. "Don't make me live it again."

"Oh, Dalinar," Odium said. "You will live it again and again until you let go. You can't carry this burden. Please, give it to me. *I* drove you to do this. *It wasn't your fault.*"

Dalinar pulled *The Way of Kings* close against his chest, clutching it, like a child with his blanket in the night. But a sudden *flash* of light blasted in front of him, accompanied by a deafening crack.

Dalinar stumbled backward. Lightning. That had been *lightning*. Had it struck him?

No. It had somehow struck only the book. Burned pages fluttered around him, singed and smoldering. It had been blasted right from his hands.

Odium shook his head. "The words of a man long dead, long failed."

Overhead, the sun finally passed behind the clouds of the storm, and all fell into darkness. Slowly, the flames of the burning pages went out.

.•.

Teft huddled someplace dark.

Maybe the darkness would hide his sins. But in the distance, he heard shouting. Men fighting.

Bridge Four dying.

.•.

Kaladin stuttered, the Words stumbling.

He thought of his men from Amaram's army. Dallet and his squad, slain either by Shallan's brother or by Amaram. Such good friends who had fallen.

And then, of course, he thought of Tien.

.•.

Dalinar fell to his knees. A few gloryspren swirled around him, but Odium batted them away, and they faded.

In the back of his mind, the Stormfather wept.

He saw himself step up to where Evi was imprisoned. That tomb in the rock. Dalinar tried to look away, but the vision was everywhere. He didn't merely see it, he *lived* it. He ordered Evi's death, and listened to her screams.

"Please . . ."

Odium wasn't done with him. Dalinar had to watch the city burn, hear the children die. He gritted his teeth, groaning in agony. Before, his pains had driven him to drink. There was no drink now. Just the Thrill.

He had always craved it. The Thrill had made him live. Without it . . . he'd . . . he'd been dead. . . .

He slumped, bowing his head, listening to the tears of a woman who had believed in him. He'd *never* deserved her. The Stormfather's weeping faded as Odium somehow shoved the spren away, separating them.

That left Dalinar alone.

"So alone . . ."

"You're *not* alone, Dalinar," Odium said, going down on one knee beside him. "I'm here. I've always been here."

The Thrill boiled within. And Dalinar knew. He *knew* he'd always been a fraud. He was the same as Amaram. He had an honest reputation, but was a murderer on the inside. A destroyer. A child killer.

"Let go," Odium whispered.

Dalinar squeezed his eyes shut, trembling, hands tense as he hunched over and clawed the ground. It hurt so badly. To know that he'd failed them. Navani, Adolin, Elhokar, Gavilar. He couldn't live with this.

He couldn't live with her *tears*!

"Give it to me," Odium pled.

Dalinar ripped his fingernails off, but the pain of the body couldn't distract him. It was nothing beside the agony of his soul.

Of knowing what he truly was.

※

Szeth tried to walk toward Dalinar. The darkness had grown up his arm, and the sword drank his last wisps of Stormlight.

There was . . . was a lesson in this . . . wasn't there? There had to be. Nin . . . Nin wanted him to learn. . . .

He fell to the ground, still holding the sword as it screamed mindlessly. *DESTROY EVIL.*

The little Radiant girl scrambled to him. She looked toward the sky as the sun vanished behind clouds. Then she took Szeth's head in her hands.

"No . . ." he tried to croak. *It will take you too. . . .*

She breathed life into him somehow, and the sword drank of it freely. Her eyes went wide as the black veins began to grow up her fingers and hands.

※

Renarin didn't want to die. But strangely, he found himself welcoming Jasnah's strike.

Better to die than to live to see what was happening to his father. For he saw the future. He saw his father in black armor, a plague upon the land. He saw the Blackthorn return, a terrible scourge with nine shadows.

Odium's champion.

"He's going to fall," Renarin whispered. "He's already fallen. He belongs to the enemy now. Dalinar Kholin . . . is no more."

Venli shivered on the plain, near Odium. Timbre had been pulsing to Peace, but now she quieted. Twenty or thirty yards away, a figure in white clothing collapsed to the ground, a little girl at his side.

Nearer to her, Dalinar Kholin—the man who had resisted—slumped forward, head bowed, holding one hand against his chest and trembling.

Odium stepped back, his appearance that of a parshman with golden carapace. "It is done," he said, looking toward Venli and the gathered group of Fused. "You have a leader."

"We must follow one of them?" Turash asked. "A human?"

Venli's breath caught. There had been no respect in that tone.

Odium smiled. "You will follow me, Turash, or I will reclaim that which gives you persistent life. I care not for the shape of the tool. Only that it cuts."

Turash bowed his head.

Stone crunched as a figure in glittering Shardplate walked up to them, carrying a Shardblade in one hand and—strangely—an empty sheath in the other. The human had his faceplate up, exposing red eyes. He tossed the silvery sheath to the ground. "I was told to deliver that to you."

"Well done, Meridas," Odium said. "Abaray, could you provide this human with an appropriate housing for Yelig-nar?"

One of the Fused stepped forward and proffered a small, uncut smokestone toward the human, Meridas.

"And what is *this*?" Meridas asked.

"The fulfillment of my promise to you," Odium said. "Swallow it."

"*What?*"

"If you wish for the promised power, ingest that—then try to control the one who follows. But be warned, the queen at Kholinar tried this, and the power consumed her."

Meridas held up the gemstone, inspecting it, then glanced toward Dalinar Kholin. "So, you've been speaking to him all this time too?"

"Even longer than I've been speaking to you."

"Can I kill him?"

"Someday, assuming I don't let him kill you." Odium rested his hand on the shoulder of the huddled Dalinar Kholin. "It's done, Dalinar. The pain has passed. Stand up and claim the station you were born to obtain."

Kaladin thought, finally, of Dalinar.

Could Kaladin do it? Could he really say these Words? Could he *mean* them?

The Fused swept close. Adolin bled.

"I . . ."

You know what you need to do.

"I . . . can't," Kaladin finally whispered, tears streaming down his cheeks. "I can't lose him, but . . . oh, Almighty . . . I can't save him." Kaladin bowed his head, sagging forward, trembling.

He couldn't say those Words.

He wasn't strong enough.

Syl's arms enfolded him from behind, and he felt softness as her cheek pressed against the back of his neck. She pulled him tight as he wept, sobbing, at his failure.

⁂

Jasnah raised her Blade over Renarin's head.

Make it quick. Make it painless.

Most threats to a dynasty came from within.

Renarin was obviously corrupted. She'd known there was a problem the moment she'd read that he had predicted the Everstorm. Now, Jasnah had to be strong. She had to do what was *right*, even when it was so, so hard.

She prepared to swing, but then Renarin turned and looked at her. Tears streaming down his face, he met her eyes, and he *nodded*.

Suddenly they were young again. He was a trembling child, weeping on her shoulder for a father who didn't seem to be able to feel love. Little Renarin, always so solemn. Always misunderstood, laughed at and condemned by people who said similar things about Jasnah behind her back.

Jasnah froze, as if standing at the edge of a cliff. Wind blew through the temple, carrying with it a pair of spren in the form of golden spheres, bobbing in the currents.

Jasnah dismissed her sword.

"Jasnah?" Ivory said, appearing back in the form of a man, clinging to her collar.

Jasnah fell to her knees, then pulled Renarin into an embrace. He broke down crying, like he had as a boy, burying his head in her shoulder.

"What's wrong with me?" Renarin asked. "Why do I see these things? I thought I was doing something right, with Glys, but somehow it's all wrong. . . ."

"Hush," Jasnah whispered. "We'll find a way through it, Renarin. Whatever it is, we'll fix it. We'll survive this, somehow."

Storms. The things he'd said about Dalinar . . .

"Jasnah," Ivory said, becoming full size as he stepped free of her collar.

He leaned down. "Jasnah, this is right. Somehow it *is*." He seemed completely stunned. "It is not what makes sense, yet it is still right. How. How *is* this thing?"

Renarin pulled back from her, his tearstained eyes going wide. "I saw you kill me."

"It's all right, Renarin. I'm not going to."

"But don't you *see*? Don't you understand what that means?"

Jasnah shook her head.

"Jasnah," Renarin said. "My vision was wrong about you. What I see . . . it *can be wrong*."

.•.

Alone.

Dalinar held a fist to his chest.

So alone.

It hurt to breathe, to think. But something stirred inside his fist. He opened bleeding fingers.

The most . . . the most important . . .

Inside his fist, he somehow found a golden sphere. A solitary gloryspren.

The most important step a man can take. It's not the first one, is it?

It's the next *one. Always the next step, Dalinar.*

Trembling, bleeding, agonized, Dalinar forced air into his lungs and spoke a single ragged sentence.

"You cannot have my pain."

119

UNITY

As I began my journey, I was challenged to defend why I insisted on traveling alone. They called it irresponsible. An avoidance of duty and obligation.

Those who said this made an enormous mistake of assumption.

—From *The Way of Kings*, postscript

Odium stepped back. "Dalinar? What is this?"

"You cannot have my pain."

"Dalinar—"

Dalinar forced himself to his feet. "You. Cannot. Have. My. Pain."

"Be sensible."

"I killed those children," Dalinar said.

"No, it—"

"I burned the people of Rathalas."

"I was there, influencing you—"

"*YOU CANNOT HAVE MY PAIN!*" Dalinar bellowed, stepping toward Odium. The god frowned. His Fused companions shied back, and Amaram raised a hand before his eyes and squinted.

Were those gloryspren spinning around Dalinar?

"I *did* kill the people of Rathalas," Dalinar shouted. "You might have been there, but *I* made the choice. I decided!" He stilled. "I killed her. It hurts so much, but I did it. I accept that. You cannot have her. You *cannot* take her from me again."

"Dalinar," Odium said. "What do you hope to gain, keeping this burden?"

Dalinar sneered at the god. "If I pretend . . . If I pretend I *didn't* do those things, it means that I can't have grown to become someone else."

"A failure."

Something stirred inside of Dalinar. A warmth that he had known once before. A warm, calming light.

Unite them.

"Journey before destination," Dalinar said. "It cannot be a journey if it *doesn't have a beginning.*"

A thunderclap sounded in his mind. Suddenly, awareness poured back into him. The Stormfather, distant, feeling frightened—but also surprised.

Dalinar?

"I will take responsibility for what I have done," Dalinar whispered. "If I must fall, I will rise each time a better man."

* * *

Renarin ran after Jasnah through the Loft Wards of the city. People clogged the streets, but she didn't use those. She leaped off buildings, dropping onto rooftops of the tiers below. She ran across each of these, then leaped down to the next street.

Renarin struggled to follow, afraid of his weakness, confused by the things he'd seen. He dropped to a rooftop, feeling sudden pain at the fall—though Stormlight healed that. He limped after her until the pain left.

"Jasnah!" he called. "Jasnah, I can't keep up!"

She stopped at the edge of a rooftop. He reached her, and she took his arm. "You *can* keep up, Renarin. You're a Knight Radiant."

"I don't think I'm a Radiant, Jasnah. I don't know *what* I am."

An entire *stream* of gloryspren flew past them, hundreds in a sweeping formation that curved toward the base of the city. Something was glowing down there, a beacon in the dim light of an overcast city.

"I know what you are," Jasnah said. "You're my cousin. Family, Renarin. Hold my hand. Run with me."

He nodded, and she towed him after her, leaping from the rooftop, ignoring the monstrous creature that climbed up nearby. Jasnah seemed focused on only one thing.

That light.

* * *

Unite them!

Gloryspren streamed around Dalinar. Thousands of golden spheres, more spren than he'd ever seen in one place. They swirled around him in a column of golden light.

Beyond it, Odium stumbled back.

So small, Dalinar thought. *Has he always looked that small?*

⁖

Syl looked up.

Kaladin turned to see what had drawn her attention. She looked past the Fused who had landed to attack. She was staring toward the ocean of beads, and the trembling lights of souls above it.

"Syl?"

She pulled him tight. "Maybe you don't have to save anyone, Kaladin. Maybe it's time for someone to save *you*."

⁖

UNITE THEM!

Dalinar thrust his left hand to the side, plunging it between realms, grabbing hold of the very fabric of existence. The world of minds, the realm of thought.

He thrust his right hand to the other side, touching something vast, something that wasn't a place—it was all places in one. He'd seen this before, in the moment when Odium had let him glimpse the Spiritual Realm.

Today, he held it in his hand.

The Fused scrambled away. Amaram pushed down his faceplate, but that wasn't enough. He stumbled back, arm raised. Only one person remained in place. A young parshwoman, the one that Dalinar had visited in the visions.

"What are you?" she whispered as he stood with arms outstretched, holding to the lands of mind and spirit.

He closed his eyes, breathing out, listening to a sudden stillness. And within it a simple, quiet voice. A woman's voice, so familiar to him.

I forgive you.

Dalinar opened his eyes, and knew what the parshwoman saw in him. Swirling clouds, glowing light, thunder and lightning.

"I am Unity."

He slammed both hands together.

And combined three realms into one.

Shadesmar exploded with light.

Fused screamed as a wind blasted them away, though Kaladin felt nothing. Beads clattered and roared.

Kaladin shaded his eyes with his hand. The light faded, leaving a brilliant, glowing pillar in the middle of the sea. Beneath it, the beads locked together, turning into a highway of glass.

Kaladin blinked, taking Shallan's hand as she helped him to his feet. Adolin had forced himself to sit up, holding his bloodied stomach. "What . . . what is it?"

"Honor's Perpendicularity," Syl whispered. "A well of power that pierces all three realms." She looked to Kaladin. "A pathway home."

.·.

Taln gripped Ash's hand.

Ash looked at his fingers, thick and callused. Thousands of years could come and pass, and she could lose lifetimes to the dream, but those hands . . . she'd never forget those hands.

"Ash," he said.

She looked up at him, then gasped and raised her fingers to her lips.

"How long?" he asked.

"Taln." She gripped his hand in both of hers. "I'm sorry. I'm so, *so* sorry."

"How long?"

"They say it's been four millennia. I don't always . . . note the passing of time. . . ."

"Four thousand years?"

She held his hand tighter. "I'm sorry. I'm *sorry*."

He pulled his hand from hers and stood up, walking through the tent. She followed, apologizing again—but what good were words? They'd betrayed him.

Taln brushed aside the front drapes and stepped out. He looked up at the city expanding above them, at the sky, at the wall. Soldiers in breastplates and chain rushed past to join a fight farther along.

"Four thousand years?" Taln asked again. "Ash . . ."

"We couldn't continue— I . . . we thought . . ."

"Ash." He took her hand again. "What a *wonderful* thing."

Wonderful? "We *left* you, Taln."

"What a gift you gave them! Time to recover, for once, between Desolations. Time to progress. They never had a chance before. But this time . . . yes, maybe they do."

"No, Taln. You can't be like this."

"A wonderful thing indeed, Ash."

"You *can't* be like this, Taln. You have to hate me! Hate me, *please*."

He turned from her, but still held her hand, pulling her after him. "Come. He's waiting."

"Who?" she asked.

"I don't know."

.·.

Teft gasped in the darkness.

"Can you see it, Teft?" the spren whispered. "Can you feel the Words?"

"I'm *broken*."

"Who isn't? Life breaks us, Teft. Then we fill the cracks with something stronger."

"I make myself sick."

"Teft," she said, a glowing apparition in the darkness, "that's what the Words are *about*."

Oh, Kelek. The shouts. Fighting. His friends.

"I . . ."

Storm you! Be a man for once in your life!

Teft licked his lips, and spoke.

"I will protect those I hate. Even . . . even if the one I hate most . . . is . . . *myself*."

.·.

Renarin fell to the last level of the city, the Low Ward. He stumbled to a stop there, his hand slipping from Jasnah's. Soldiers marched through these streets, with eyes like embers.

"Jasnah!" he called. "Amaram's soldiers changed sides. They serve Odium now! I saw it in vision!"

She ran right toward them.

"Jasnah!"

The first soldier swung his sword at her. Jasnah ducked the weapon, then shoved her hand against him, throwing him backward. He *crystallized* in the air, slamming into the next man, who caught the transformation like a disease. He slammed into *another* man, knocking him back, as if the full force of Jasnah's shove had transferred to him. He crystallized a moment later.

Jasnah spun, a Shardblade forming in her gloved safehand, her skirt rippling as she sliced through six men in one sweep. The sword vanished as she slapped her hand into the wall of a building behind her, and that wall *puffed away* into smoke, causing the roof to crash down, blocking the alley between buildings, where other soldiers had been approaching.

She swept her hand upward, and air coalesced into stone, forming steps that she took—barely breaking her stride—to climb to the rooftop of the next building.

Renarin gaped. That— How—

It will be . . . great . . . vast . . . wonderful! Glys said from within Renarin's heart. *It will be beautiful, Renarin! Look!*

A well blossomed inside of him. Power like he'd never before felt, an awesome, overwhelming *strength.* Stormlight unending. A source of it so vast, he was stunned.

"Jasnah?" he shouted, then belatedly ran up the steps she'd created, feeling so *alive* that he wanted to dance. Wouldn't that be a sight? Renarin Kholin dancing on a rooftop while . . .

He slowed, gaping again as he looked through a gap in the wall and saw a column of light. Rising higher and higher, it stretched toward the clouds.

⁘

Fen and her consort backed away from the storm of light.

Navani exulted in it. She leaned out far over the side of the wall, laughing like a fool. Gloryspren streamed around her, brushing her hair, flowing toward the already impossible number that coursed around Dalinar in a pillar that stretched hundreds of feet into the air.

Then *lights* sparked to life in a wave across the field, the top of the wall, the street below. Gemstones that had been lying ignored, scattered from the broken bank, drank in Stormlight from Dalinar. They lit the ground with a thousand pinpricks of color.

⁘

"No!" Odium screamed. He stepped forward. "No, we killed you. WE KILLED YOU!"

Dalinar stood within a pillar of light and spinning gloryspren, one hand to each side, clutching the realms that made up reality.

Forgiven. The pain he'd so recently insisted that he would keep started to fade away on its own.

These Words . . . are accepted, the Stormfather said, sounding stunned. *How? What have you done?*

Odium stumbled back. "Kill him! *Attack him!*"

The parshwoman didn't move, but Amaram lethargically lowered his hand from his face, then stepped forward, summoning his Shardblade.

Dalinar took his hand from the glowing pillar and held it out. "You *can* change," he said. "You can become a better person. I did. Journey before destination."

"No," Amaram said. "No, he'll never forgive me."

"The bridgeman?"

"Not him." Amaram tapped his chest. "Him. I'm sorry, Dalinar."

He raised a familiar Shardblade. Dalinar's Shardblade, Oathbringer. Passed from tyrant to tyrant to tyrant.

A portion of light split from Dalinar's column.

Amaram swung Oathbringer with a shout, but the light met the Shardblade with an explosion of sparks, throwing Amaram backward—as if the strength of Shardplate were no more than that of a child. The light resolved into a man with shoulder-length wavy hair, a blue uniform, and a silvery spear in his hand.

A second glowing form split off into Shallan Davar, brilliant red hair streaming behind her, a long thin Shardblade with a slight curve forming in her hands.

And then, blessedly, Adolin appeared.

·:·

"Mistress!" Wyndle said. "Oh, mistress!"

For once, Lift didn't have the will to tell him to shut up. She focused everything on those tendrils creeping up her arms, like deep, dark vines.

The assassin lay on the ground, staring upward, practically *covered* in those vines. Lift held them at bay, teeth gritted. Her will against the darkness until . . .

Light.

Like a sudden detonation, a force of light flashed across the field. Gemstones on the ground flared up, capturing Stormlight, and the assassin screamed, drawing in Light like glowing mist.

The vines shriveled, as the sword's thirst was slaked by the Stormlight. Lift fell back on the stone and pried her hands off Szeth's head.

I knew I liked you, a voice said in Lift's mind.

The sword. So it was a spren? "You almost *ate* him," Lift said. "You almost starvin' ate *me*!"

Oh, I wouldn't do that, the voice said. She seemed completely baffled, voice growing slow, like she was drowsy. *But . . . maybe I was just really, really hungry. . . .*

Well, Lift supposed she couldn't blame someone for that.

The assassin climbed unsteadily to his feet. His face was crisscrossed with lines where the vines had been. That somehow left his skin grey in streaks, the color of stone. Lift's arms bore the same. Huh.

Szeth walked toward the glowing column of light, leaving an afterimage behind him. "Come," he said.

* *

Elhokar? Dalinar thought. But no one else came through the column of light. And he knew. Knew, somehow, that the king was not coming.

He closed his eyes, and accepted that grief. He had failed the king in many ways.

Stand up, he thought. *And do better.*

He opened his eyes, and slowly his column of gloryspren faded. The power within him withdrew, leaving him exhausted. Fortunately, the field was covered in glittering gemstones. Stormlight in plenty.

A direct conduit to the Spiritual Realm, the Stormfather said. *You renew spheres, Dalinar?*

"We are Connected."

I was bonded to men before. This never happened then.

"Honor was alive then. We are something different. His remnants, your soul, my will."

Kaladin Stormblessed stepped up beside Dalinar before the rubble of the wall, and Shallan Davar stood on the other side. Jasnah emerged from the city and surveyed the scene with a critical air, while Renarin popped out behind her, then cried out and ran for Adolin. He grabbed his older brother in an embrace, then gasped. Adolin was wounded?

Good lad, Dalinar thought as Renarin immediately set to healing his brother.

Two more people crossed the battlefield. Lift he had anticipated. But the assassin? Szeth scooped the silvery sheath off the ground and slammed his black Shardblade into it, before stepping up to join Dalinar.

Skybreaker, Dalinar thought, counting them off. *Edgedancer.* That was seven.

He would have expected three more.

There, the Stormfather said. *Behind your niece.*

Two more people appeared in the shadow of the wall. A large, powerful man with an impressive physique, and a woman with long, dark hair. Their dark skin marked them as Makabaki, perhaps Azish, but their eyes were wrong.

I know them, the Stormfather said, sounding surprised. *I know them from long, long ago. Memories of days when I did not fully live.*

Dalinar, you are in the presence of divinities.

"I've grown accustomed to it," Dalinar said, turning back toward the field. Odium had retreated into nothingness, though his Fused remained, as did most of the troops, and one strange spren—the one like black smoke. Beyond it, of course, the Thrill still encompassed the north side of the landing, near the water.

Amaram had ten thousand men, and maybe half of those had made it into the city so far. They had wilted before Dalinar's display, but now . . .

Wait.

Those two only make nine, he thought to the Stormfather. Something told him there should be one more.

I don't know. Perhaps they haven't been found yet. Regardless, even with the bond you are just one man. Radiants are not immortal. How do you face this army?

"Dalinar?" Kaladin said. "Orders, sir?"

The enemy ranks were recovering. They lifted weapons, eyes glowing deep red. Amaram stirred as well, some twenty feet away. The Thrill had Dalinar most worried, however. He knew what it could do.

He glanced down at his arm, and noticed something. The lightning that had struck him earlier, shredding *The Way of Kings,* had broken his arm fabrial. The clasp was undone, and Dalinar could see the tiny gemstones Navani had placed to power it.

"Sir?" Kaladin asked again.

"The enemy is trying to crush this city, Captain," Dalinar said, lowering his arm. "We're going to hold it against his forces."

"Seven Radiants?" Jasnah said, skeptical. "Uncle, that seems a tall order, even if one of us is—apparently—the storming *Assassin in White.*"

"I serve Dalinar Kholin," Szeth-son-son-Vallano whispered. His face, for some reason, was streaked with grey. "I cannot know truth, so I follow one who does."

"Whatever we do," Shallan said, "we should do it quickly. Before those soldiers—"

"Renarin!" Dalinar barked.

"Sir!" Renarin said, scrambling forward.

"We need to hold out until troops arrive from Urithiru. Fen doesn't have the numbers to fight alone. Get to the Oathgate, stop that thunder-clast up there from destroying it, and open the portal."

"Sir!" Renarin saluted.

"Shallan, we don't have an army yet," Dalinar said. "Lightweave one up for us, and keep these soldiers busy. They're consumed by a bloodlust that I suspect will make them easier to distract. Jasnah, the city we're defending happens to have a big storming hole in its wall. Can you hold that hole and stop anyone who tries to get through?"

She nodded, thoughtful.

"What about me?" Kaladin asked.

Dalinar pointed at Amaram, who was climbing to his feet in his Shardplate. "He's going to try to kill me for what I do next, and I could use a bodyguard. As I recall, you have a score to settle with the highlord."

"You could say that."

"Lift, I believe I already gave you an order. Take the assassin and *get me that ruby*. Together, we hold this city until Renarin returns with troops. Any questions?"

"Um . . ." Lift said. "Could you maybe . . . tell me where to get something to eat . . . ?"

Dalinar glanced at her. Something to *eat*? "There . . . should be a supply dump just inside the wall."

"Thanks!"

Dalinar sighed, then started walking toward the water.

"Sir!" Kaladin called. "Where are you going?"

"The enemy brought a very big stick to this battle, Captain. I'm going to take it away."

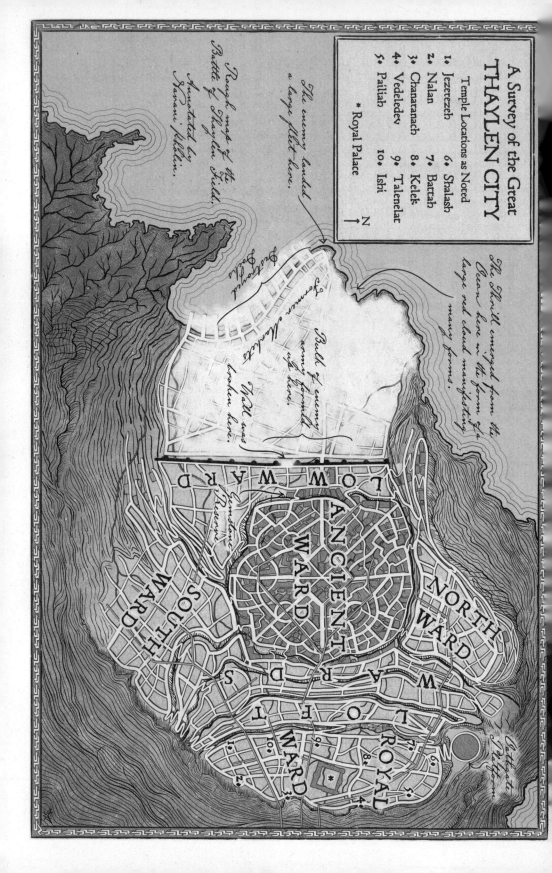

120

THE SPEAR THAT WOULD NOT BREAK

If the journey itself is indeed the most important piece, rather than the destination itself, then I traveled not to avoid duty—but to seek it.

—From *The Way of Kings*, postscript

K aladin rose into the sky, alive with Stormlight.

Below him, Dalinar walked toward the red mist. Though tendrils of it moved among the soldiers of Amaram's army, the bulk of it swirled closer to the coast, to the right of the bay and the destroyed docks.

Storms, Kaladin felt good to be in the real world again. Even with the Everstorm dominating the sun, this place felt so much more *bright* than Shadesmar. A group of windspren dodged around him, though the air was relatively still. Perhaps they were the ones who had come to him on the other side, the ones he had failed.

Kaladin, Syl said. *You* don't *need another reason to berate yourself.*

She was right. Storms, he *could* be down on himself sometimes. Was that the flaw that had prevented him from speaking the Words of the Fourth Ideal?

For some reason, Syl sighed. *Oh, Kaladin.*

"We'll talk about it later," he said.

For now, he'd been given a second chance to protect Dalinar Kholin. Stormlight raging inside of him, the Sylspear a comfortable weight in his hand, he Lashed himself downward and crashed to the stones near Amaram.

The highlord, in turn, fell to his knees.

What? Kaladin thought. Amaram was coughing. He tipped his head back, faceplate up, and groaned.

Had he just *swallowed* something?

⁂

Adolin prodded at his stomach. Beneath the bloodstained rip, he felt only smooth, new skin. Not even a hint of an ache.

For a time, he'd been sure he would die.

He'd been there before. Months ago, he'd felt it when Sadeas had withdrawn, leaving the Kholin troops alone and surrounded on the Shattered Plains. This had been different. Staring up at that black sky and those unnatural clouds, feeling suddenly, *appallingly* fragile . . .

And then light. His father—the great man Adolin could never match—somehow embodying the Almighty himself. Adolin couldn't help feeling that he hadn't been worthy to step into that light.

Here he was anyway.

The Radiants broke apart to do Dalinar's bidding, though Shallan knelt to check on Adolin. "How do you feel?"

"Do you realize how fond I was of this jacket?"

"Oh, Adolin."

"Really, Shallan. Surgeons should take more care with the clothing they cut open. If a man's going to live, he'll want that shirt. And if he dies . . . well, he should *at least* be well dressed on his deathbed."

She smiled, then glanced over her shoulder toward the troops with red eyes.

"Go," he said. "I'll be fine. Save the city. Be *Radiant,* Shallan."

She kissed him, then turned and stood. That white clothing seemed to glow, the red hair a striking swatch, as Stormlight rose from her. Pattern appeared as a Shardblade with a faint, almost invisible latticework running up the length. She wove her power, and an *army* climbed from the ground around her.

In Urithiru, she'd made an army of a score to distract the Unmade. Now, *hundreds* of illusions rose around her: soldiers, shopkeepers, washwomen, scribes, all drawn from her pages. They glowed brilliantly, Light streaming from them—as if each were a Knight Radiant.

Adolin climbed to his feet, and came face-to-face with an illusion of himself wearing a Kholin uniform. The illusory Adolin glowed with Stormlight and floated a few inches off the ground. She'd made him a Windrunner.

I . . . I can't take that. He turned toward the city. His father had been focused on the Radiants, and had neglected to give Adolin a specific duty. So maybe he could help the defenders inside.

Adolin picked his way across the rubble and through the broken wall. Jasnah stood right inside, hands on hips, as if she were surveying a mess left by rampaging children. The gap opened into an unremarkable city square dominated by barracks and storehouses. Fallen troops wearing either Thaylen or Sadeas uniforms indicated a recent clash here, but most of the enemy seemed to have moved on. Shouts and clangs sounded from nearby streets.

Adolin reached for a discarded sword, then paused, and—feeling a fool—summoned his Shardblade. He braced himself for a scream, but none came, and the Blade fell into his hand after ten heartbeats.

"I'm sorry," he said, lifting the glistening weapon. "And thank you."

He headed toward one of the nearby clashes, where men were shouting for help.

⁛

Szeth of the Skybreakers envied Kaladin, the one they called Stormblessed, in the honor of protecting Dalinar Kholin. But of course, he would not complain. He had chosen his oath.

And he would do as his master demanded.

Phantoms appeared, created from Stormlight by the woman with the red hair. These were the shadows in the darkness, the ones he heard whispering of his murders. How she brought them to life, he did not know. He landed near the Reshi Surgebinder, Lift.

"So," she said to him. "How do we find that ruby?"

Szeth pointed with his sheathed Shardblade toward the ships docked in the bay. "The creature carrying it ran back that way." The parshmen still clustered there, deep within the shadow of the Everstorm.

"Figures," Lift said, then glanced at him. "You aren't gonna try to eat me again, right?"

Don't be silly, said the sword in Szeth's hand. *You aren't evil. You're nice. And I don't eat people.*

"I will not draw the sword," Szeth said, "unless you are already dead and I decide to accept death myself."

"Greaaaaaaaaaaat," Lift said.

You're supposed to contradict me, Szeth, the sword said, *when I say I don't eat people. Vasher always did. I think he was joking. Anyway, as people who have carried me go, you aren't very good at this.*

"No," Szeth said. "I am not good at being a person. It is . . . a failing of mine."

It's all right! Be happy. Looks like there's a lot of evil to slay today! That's greaaaaaaaaaaat, right?

Then the sword started humming.

⋅⋅

The brands on Kaladin's head seemed a fresh pain as he dove to strike Amaram. But Amaram recovered quickly from his fit, then slammed his faceplate down. He rebuffed Kaladin's attack with an armored forearm.

Those red eyes cast a crimson glow through the helm's slit. "You should thank me, boy."

"*Thank* you?" Kaladin said. "For what? For showing me that a person could be even *more* loathsome than the petty lighteyes who ruled my hometown?"

"I created you, spearman. I *forged* you." Amaram pointed at Kaladin with the wide, hook-ended Shardblade. Then he extended his left hand, summoning a *second* Blade. Long and curved, the back edge rippled like flowing waves.

Kaladin knew that Blade well. He'd won it—saving Amaram's life—then refused to bear it. For when he looked at his reflection in the silvery metal, all he could see were the friends it had killed. So much death and pain, caused by that rippling Blade.

It seemed a symbol of all he'd lost, particularly held now in the hand of the man who had lied to him. The man who had taken Tien away.

Amaram presented a sword stance, holding two Blades. One taken in bloodshed, at the cost of Kaladin's crew. The other, Oathbringer. A sword given to ransom Bridge Four.

Don't be intimidated! Syl whispered in Kaladin's mind. *History notwithstanding, he's only a man. And you're a Knight Radiant.*

The vambrace of Amaram's armor *pulsed* suddenly on his forearm, as if something were pushing it from beneath. The red glow from the helm deepened, and Kaladin got the distinct impression of something enveloping Amaram.

A black smoke. The same that Kaladin had seen surrounding Queen Aesudan at the end, as they'd fled the palace. Other sections of Amaram's armor began to rattle or pulse, and he suddenly moved with a violent burst of speed, swinging with one Shardblade, then the other.

⋅⋅

Dalinar slowed as he approached the main core of the Thrill. The red mist churned and boiled here, nearly solid. He saw familiar faces reflected in it.

He watched the old highprince Kalanor fall from the heights of a rock formation. He saw himself fight alone on a field of stone after a rockslide. He watched as he caught the claw of a chasmfiend on the Shattered Plains.

He could hear the Thrill. A thrumming, insistent, warming pulse. Almost like the beating of a drum.

"Hello, old friend," Dalinar whispered, then stepped into the red mist.

⁂

Shallan stood with arms outstretched. Stormlight expanded from her on the ground, a pool of liquid light, radiant mist swirling above it. It became a gateway. From it, her collection emerged.

Every person she'd ever sketched—from the maids in her father's house to the honorspren who had held Syl captive—grew from Stormlight. Men and women, children and grandparents. Soldiers and scribes. Mothers and scouts, kings and slaves.

Mmm, Pattern said as a sword in her hand. *MMMMMMM.*

"I've lost these," Shallan said as Yalb the sailor climbed from the mist and waved to her. He drew a glowing Shardspear from the air. "I lost these pictures!"

You are close to them, Pattern said. *Close to the realm of thought . . . and beyond. All the people you've Connected to, over the years . . .*

Her brothers emerged. She'd buried worries about them in the back of her mind. Held by the Ghostbloods . . . No word from any spanreed she tried . . .

Her father stepped from the Light. And her mother.

The illusions immediately started to fail, melting back to Light. Then, someone seized her by the left hand.

Shallan gasped. Forming from mist was . . . was *Veil?* With long straight black hair, white clothing, brown eyes. Wiser than Shallan—and more focused. Capable of working on small pieces when Shallan grew overwhelmed by the large scale of her work.

Another hand took Shallan's on the right. Radiant, in glowing garnet Shardplate, tall, with braided hair. Reserved and cautious. She nodded to Shallan with a steady, determined look.

Others boiled at Shallan's feet, trying to crawl from the Stormlight, their glowing hands grabbing at her legs.

". . . No," Shallan whispered.

This was enough. She had created Veil and Radiant to be strong when she was weak. She squeezed their hands tight, then hissed out slowly. The other versions of Shallan retreated into the Stormlight.

Then, farther out, figures by the hundred surged from the ground and raised weapons at the enemy.

⁂

Adolin, now accompanied by some two dozen soldiers, charged through the streets of the Low Ward.

"There!" one of his men shouted with a thick Thaylen accent. "Bright-lord!" He pointed toward a group of enemy soldiers disappearing down an alley back toward the wall.

"Damnation," Adolin said, waving his troops to follow as he gave chase. Jasnah was alone in that direction, trying to hold the gap. He charged down the alleyway to—

A soldier with red eyes suddenly hurtled through the air overhead. Adolin ducked, worried about Fused, but it was an ordinary soldier. The unfortunate man crashed into a rooftop. What on Roshar?

As they approached the end of the alleyway, another body smashed into the wall right by the opening. Gripping his Shardblade, Adolin peeked around the corner, expecting to find another stone monster like the one that had climbed into the Ancient Ward.

Instead, he found only Jasnah Kholin, looking completely nonplussed. A glow faded around her, different from the smoke of her Stormlight. Like geometric shapes outlining her . . .

All right then. Jasnah didn't need help. Adolin instead waved for his men to follow the sounds of battle to the right. There they found a small group of beleaguered Thaylen soldiers backed up against the base of the wall, facing a much larger force of men in green uniforms.

Well. This Adolin could fix.

He waved his own soldiers back, then charged the enemy in Smokestance, sweeping with his Shardblade. The enemy had packed in close to try to get at their prey, and had a hard time adjusting to the miniature storm that crashed into them from behind.

Adolin stepped through the sequence of swipes, feeling immense satisfaction at finally being able to do something. The Thaylens let out a cheer as he dropped the last group of enemies, red eyes going black as they burned out. His satisfaction lasted until, glancing down at the corpses, he was struck by how *human* they looked.

He'd spent years fighting Parshendi. He didn't think he'd actually killed another Alethi since . . . well, he couldn't remember.

Sadeas. Don't forget Sadeas.

Fifty men dead at his feet, and some three dozen killed while gathering his other troops. Storms . . . after feeling so useless in Shadesmar, now this. How much of his reputation was him, and how much of it was—and had always been—the sword?

"Prince Adolin?" a voice called in Alethi. "Your Highness!"

"Kdralk?" Adolin said as a figure emerged from the Thaylens. The queen's son had seen better days. His eyebrows were bloodied from a cut across his forehead. His uniform was torn, and there was a bandage on his upper arm.

"My mother and father," Kdralk said. "They're trapped on the wall a little farther down. We were pushing to reach them, but we got cornered."

"Right. Let's move, then."

Jasnah stepped over a corpse. Her Blade vanished in a puff of Stormlight, and Ivory appeared next to her, his oily black features concerned as he regarded the sky. "This place is three, still," he said. "Almost three."

"Or three places are nearly one," Jasnah replied. Another batch of gloryspren flocked past, and she could see them as they were in the Cognitive Realm: like strange avians with long wings, and a golden sphere in place of the head. Well, being able to see into the Cognitive Realm without trying was one of the *least* unnerving things that had happened so far today.

An incredible amount of Stormlight thrummed inside her—more than she'd ever held before. Another group of soldiers broke through Shallan's illusions and charged over the rubble through the gap in the wall. Jasnah casually flipped her hand toward them. Once, their souls would have resisted mightily. Soulcasting living things was difficult; it usually required care and concentration—along with proper knowledge and procedure.

Today, the men puffed away to smoke at her barest thought. It was so easy that a part of her was horrified.

She felt invincible, which was a danger in itself. The human body wasn't meant to be stuffed this full of Stormlight. It rose from her like smoke from a bonfire. Dalinar had closed his perpendicularity, however. He had been the storm, and had somehow recharged the spheres—but like a storm, his effects were passing.

"Three worlds," Ivory said. "Slowly splitting apart again, but for now, three realms *are* close."

"Then let's make use of it before it fades, shall we?"

She stepped up before the rent portion of the wall, a gap as wide as a small city block.

Then raised her hands.

Szeth of the Skybreakers led the way toward the parshman army, the child Edgedancer following.

Szeth feared not pain, as no physical agony could rival the pain he already bore. He feared not death. That sweet reward had already been snatched from him. He feared only that he had made the wrong choice.

Szeth expunged that fear. Nin was correct. Life could not be lived making decisions at each juncture.

The parshmen standing on the shore of the bay did not have glowing eyes. They looked much like the Parshendi who had used him to assassinate King Gavilar. When he drew close, several of them ran off and boarded one of the ships.

"There," he said. "I suspect they are going to warn the one we seek."

"I'm after it, crazyface," Lift said. "Sword, don't eat anyone unless they try to eat you first." She zipped off in her silly way—kneeling and slapping her hands on the ground. She slid among the parshmen. When she reached the ship, she somehow scrambled up its side, then squeezed through a tiny porthole.

The parshmen here didn't seem aggressive. They shied away from Szeth, murmuring among themselves. Szeth glanced at the sky and picked out Nin—as a speck—still watching. Szeth could not fault the Herald's decision; the law of these creatures *was* now the law of the land.

But . . . that law was the product of the many. Szeth had been exiled because of the consensus of the many. He had served master after master, most of them using him to attain terrible or at least selfish goals. You could not arrive at excellence by the average of these people. Excellence was an individual quest, not a group effort.

A flying Parshendi—"Fused" was a term Lift had used for them—shot out of the ship, carrying the large dun ruby that Dalinar sought. Lift followed the Fused out, but couldn't fly. She clambered up onto the prow of the ship, releasing a loud string of curses.

Wow, the sword said. *That's impressive vocabulary for a child. Does she even know what that last one means?*

Szeth Lashed himself into the air after the Fused.

If she does know what it means, the sword added, *do you think she'd tell me?*

The enemy swooped down low across the battlefield, and Szeth followed, a mere inch above the rocks. They soon passed among the fighting illusions. Some of these appeared as enemy soldiers, to further add confusion. A clever move. The enemy would be less likely to retreat if they thought most of their companions were still fighting, and it made the battle look far more real. Except that when Szeth's quarry zipped past, her fluttering robes struck and disturbed illusory shapes.

Szeth followed close, passing through a pair of fighting men he had seen were illusions. This Fused was talented, better than the Skybreakers had been, though Szeth had not faced their best.

The chase took him in a long loop, eventually swinging back down near where Dalinar was walking through the edge of the red mist. The whispered voices grew louder, and Szeth put his hands to his ears as he flew.

The Fused was smooth and graceful, but sped up and slowed less quickly than Szeth did. He took advantage of this, anticipating the enemy's move, then cutting to the side as they turned. Szeth collided with the enemy, and they twisted in the air. The Fused—gemstone in one hand—stabbed Szeth with a wicked knife.

Fortunately, with Stormlight, that didn't do anything but cause pain.

Szeth Lashed them both downward, holding tight, and sent them crashing to the stone. The gemstone rolled free as the Fused groaned. Szeth Lashed himself gracefully to his feet, then slipped along the stone at a standing glide. He scooped up the ruby with his free hand, the one not carrying his sheathed sword.

Wow, the sword said.

"Thank you, sword-nimi," Szeth said. He restored his Stormlight from nearby fallen spheres and gemstones.

I meant that. *To your right.*

Three more Fused were swooping down toward him. He appeared to have gotten the enemy's attention.

⁘

Adolin and his men reached a covered stairwell leading up onto the wall. Aunt Navani waved from up above, then gestured urgently. Adolin hurried inside the stairwell, and at the top found a jumble of Sadeas troops chopping at the door with hand axes.

"I can probably get through that a little easier," Adolin said from behind them.

A short time later, he stepped onto the wall walk, leaving five more corpses on the steps. These didn't make him feel quite so melancholy. They'd been minutes from reaching Aunt Navani.

Navani hugged him. "Elhokar?" she asked, tense.

Adolin shook his head. "I'm sorry."

She pulled him tight, and he dismissed his Blade, holding her as she shook, letting out quiet tears. Storms . . . he knew how that felt. He hadn't really been able to take time to think since Elhokar's death. He'd felt the oppressive hand of responsibility, but had he grieved for his cousin?

He pulled his aunt tighter, feeling her pain, mirror to his own. The stone monster crashed through the city, and soldiers shouted from all around—but in that moment, Adolin did what he could to comfort a mother who had lost her son.

Finally they broke, Navani drying her eyes with a handkerchief. She gasped as she saw his bloodied side.

"I'm fine," he explained. "Renarin healed me."

"I saw your betrothed and the bridgeman down below," Navani said. "So everyone . . . everyone but him?"

"I'm sorry, Aunt. I just . . . We failed him. Elhokar and Kholinar both."

She blotted her eyes and stiffened with determination. "Come. Our focus now has to be on keeping this city from suffering the same fate."

They joined Queen Fen, who was surveying the battle from atop the wall. "Estnatil was on the wall with us when that thing hit," she was saying to her son. "He got thrown down and likely died, but there's a Shardblade in that rubble somewhere. I haven't seen Tshadr. Perhaps at his manor? I wouldn't be surprised to find him gathering troops at the upper tiers."

Counting Shardbearers. Thaylenah had three sets of Plate and five Blades—a solid number of Shards for a kingdom of this size. Eight houses passed them down, father to son, each of whom served the throne as a highguard.

Adolin glanced over the city, assessing the defense. Fighting in city streets was difficult; your men got divided up, and were easily flanked or surrounded. Fortunately, the Sadeas troops seemed to have forgotten their battle training. They didn't hold ground well; they had broken into roving bands, like axehound packs, loping through the city and looking for contests.

"You need to join your troops," Adolin said to the Thaylens. "Block off a street below, coordinate a resistance. Then—"

A sudden whooshing sound cut him off.

He stumbled back as the wall shook, then the broken gap in it *mended*. Metal grew like crystals to fill the hole, springing into existence out of a tempest of rushing, howling air.

The end result was a beautiful, brilliant section of polished bronze melding with the stonework and completely sealing the gap.

"Taln's *palms*," Fen said. She and her consort stepped closer to the edge and looked down at Jasnah, who dusted off her hands, then rested them on her hips in a satisfied posture.

"So . . . change of tactics," Adolin said. "With the gap filled, you can get archers in position to harry the army outside *and* hold the inside square.

Set up a command position here, clear the street below, and then hold this wall at *all costs*."

Below, Jasnah strode away from the marvel she'd created, then knelt beside some rubble and cocked her head, listening to something. She pressed her hand against the rubble and it vanished into smoke, revealing a corpse beneath—and a brilliant Shardblade beside it.

"Kdralk," Adolin said, "how are your Shardblade stances?"

"I . . . I've practiced with them, like other officers, and—I mean—"

"Great. Take ten soldiers, go get that Blade, then rescue that cluster of troops over there at the base of the Ancient Ward. Next try to rescue that other group fighting on the steps. Station every archer you can up here on the wall, and put the rest of the soldiers to work guarding the streets." Adolin glanced over his shoulder. Shallan's distraction was working well, for now. "Don't stretch too far, but as you rescue more men, make a coordinated effort to hold the entire Low Ward."

"But Prince Adolin," Fen said, "what will *you* be doing?"

Adolin summoned his Blade and pointed with it toward the back of the Ancient Ward, where the gigantic stone monstrosity swept a group of soldiers from a rooftop. Others tried—in futility—to trip it with ropes.

"Those men seem like they could use the help of a weapon designed *specifically* to cut through stone."

∴

Amaram fought with striking fury—a frenetic kind of harmony, an unending assault of weaving Shardblades and beautiful stances. Kaladin blocked one Blade with the Sylspear, and they locked for a moment.

A sharp violet *crystal* burst out of Amaram's elbow, cracking the Shardplate there, glowing with a soft inner light. Storms! Kaladin flung himself backward as Amaram swung his other Blade, nearly connecting.

Kaladin danced away. His training with the sword had been short, and he'd never seen anyone use two Blades at once. He would have considered it unwieldy. Amaram made it look elegant, mesmerizing.

That deep red glow within Amaram's helm grew darker, bloody, somehow even more sinister. Kaladin blocked another hit, but the power of the blow sent him skidding backward on the stone. He'd made himself lighter for the fight, but that had repercussions when facing someone in Plate.

Puffing, Kaladin launched himself into the air to get some distance. That Plate prevented him from using Lashings against Amaram, and it blocked hits from the Sylspear. Yet, if Amaram landed a single strike, that would immobilize Kaladin. Healing the wound from a Shardblade was possible, but was slow and left him horribly weakened.

This was all complicated by the fact that, while Amaram could focus only on their duel, Kaladin had to keep watching Dalinar in case—

Damnation!

Kaladin Lashed himself to the side, streaking through the air to engage one of the Fused who had started hovering near Dalinar. She struck toward Kaladin—but that only let him change Syl to a Blade midswing, and cut her long spear in half. She hummed an angry song and floated backward, sliding her sword from its sheath. Below, Dalinar was a mere shadow against the shifting crimson cloud. Faces emerged within, screaming with rage, fury, bloodlust—like the billowing front of a thunderhead.

Being near the mist made Kaladin feel nauseous. Fortunately, the enemy didn't seem eager to enter it either. They hovered outside, watching Dalinar. A few had ducked in closer, but Kaladin had managed to drive them back.

He pressed his advantage against his current foe, using Syl as a spear. The Fused was nimble, but Kaladin was flush with Stormlight. The field below was still littered with a fortune in glowing spheres.

After he got in close with a strike—cutting the Fused's robes—she zipped away to join a group that was focusing on Szeth. Hopefully the assassin could stay ahead of them.

Now, where had Amaram gotten to. . . . Kaladin glanced over his shoulder, then yelped and Lashed himself backward, Stormlight puffing before him. A thick black arrow shot right through that, dispersing the Light.

Amaram stood near his horse, where he'd unhooked a massive Shardbow that used arrows as thick as a spear's haft. Amaram raised it to loose again, and a line of crystals *jutted* out along his arm, cracking his Shardplate. Storms, what was happening to that man?

Kaladin zipped out of the way of the arrow. He could heal from a hit like that, but it would distract him—potentially let some of the Fused seize him. All the Stormlight in the world wouldn't save him if they simply bound him, then hacked at him until he stopped healing.

Amaram launched another arrow, and Kaladin blocked it with Syl, who became a shield in his grip. Then, Kaladin Lashed himself into a dive, summoning Syl as a lance. He swooped down on Amaram, who hooked his Shardbow back onto the horse's saddle and dodged to the side, moving with incredible speed.

Amaram grabbed the Syllance as Kaladin dove past, flinging Kaladin to the side. Kaladin was forced to dismiss Syl and slow himself, spinning and sliding across the ground until his Lashing ran out and he settled down.

Teeth gritted, Kaladin summoned Syl as a short spear, then rushed

Amaram—determined to bring the highlord down before the Fused returned to attack Dalinar.

* * *

The Thrill was happy to see Dalinar.

He had imagined it as some evil force, malignant and insidious, like Odium or Sadeas. How wrong he was.

Dalinar walked through the mist, and each step was a battle he relived. Wars from his youth, to secure Alethkar. Wars during his middle years, to preserve his reputation—and to sate his lust for the fight. And . . . he saw times when the Thrill withdrew. Like when Dalinar had held Adolin for the first time. Or when he'd grinned with Elhokar atop a rocky spire on the Shattered Plains.

The Thrill regarded these events with a sad sense of abandonment and confusion. The Thrill didn't hate. Though some spren could make decisions, others were like animals—primal, driven by a single overpowering directive. Live. Burn. Laugh.

Or in this case, *fight*.

* * *

Jasnah existed halfway in the Cognitive Realm, which made everything a blurry maze of shadows, floating souls of light, and beads of glass. A thousand varieties of spren churned and climbed over one another in Shadesmar's ocean. Most did not manifest in the physical world.

She willed steps to Soulcast beneath her feet. Individual axi of air lined up and packed next to each other, then Soulcast into stone—though in spite of the realms being linked, this was difficult. Air was amorphous, even in concept. People thought of it as the sky, or a breath, or a gust of wind, or a storm, or just "the air." It *liked* to be free, difficult to define.

Yet, with a firm command and a concept of what she wanted, Jasnah made steps form beneath her feet. She reached the top of the wall and found her mother there with Queen Fen and some soldiers. They had made a command station at one of the old guard posts. Soldiers huddled outside with pikes pointed toward two Fused in the sky.

Bother. Jasnah strode along the wall, taking in the melee of illusions and men outside. Shallan stood at the back; most of the spheres around her had been drained already. She was burning through Stormlight at a terrible rate.

"Bad?" she asked Ivory.

"It is," he said from her collar. "It is."

"Mother," Jasnah called, approaching where Fen and Navani stood by the guard post. "You need to rally the troops within the city and clear the enemy inside."

"We're working on it," Navani said. "But— Jasnah! In the air—"

Jasnah raised an absent hand without looking, forming a wall of black pitch. A Fused crashed through it, and Jasnah Soulcast a flick of fire, sending the thing screaming and flailing, burning with a terrible smoke.

Jasnah Soulcast the rest of the pitch on the wall to smoke, then continued forward. "We must take advantage of Radiant Shallan's distraction and cleanse Thaylen City. Otherwise, when the assault comes from outside once more, our attention will be divided."

"From outside?" Fen said. "But we have the wall fixed, and— Storms! Brightness!"

Jasnah stepped aside without looking as the second Fused swooped down—the reactions of spren in Shadesmar allowed her to judge where it was. She turned and swung her hand at the creature. Ivory formed and sliced through the Fused's head as it passed, sending it curling about itself—eyes burning—and tumbling along the wall top.

"The enemy," Jasnah said, "will not be stopped by a wall, and Brightness Shallan has feasted upon almost all of the spheres Uncle Dalinar recharged. My Stormlight is nearly gone. We have to be ready to hold this position through conventional means once the power is gone."

"Surely there aren't enough enemy troops to . . ." Fen's consort said, but trailed off as Jasnah pointed with Ivory—who obligingly formed again— toward the waiting parshman armies. Neither the hovering red haze nor the breaking lightning of the storm was enough to drown out the red glows beginning to appear in the parshmen's eyes.

"We must be ready to hold this wall as long as it takes for troops to arrive from Urithiru," Jasnah said. "Where is Renarin? Wasn't he to deal with that thunderclast?"

"One of my soldiers reported seeing him," Fen said. "He had been slowed by the crowds. Prince Adolin expressed an intention to go help."

"Excellent. I will trust that task to my cousins, and instead see what I can do to keep my ward from getting herself killed."

⁎⁎

Szeth wove and dodged between the attacks of five enemy Fused, carrying the large dun ruby in his left hand, the sheathed black sword in his right. He tried to approach Dalinar in the red mist, but the enemy cut him off, and he was forced to turn east.

He skimmed the now-repaired wall and crossed over the city, eventually soaring past the monster of stone. It flung several soldiers into the air, and for a moment they soared with Szeth.

Szeth Lashed himself downward, diving for the city streets. Behind him, Fused broke around the monster and swarmed after. He shot through a doorway and into a small home—and heard a thump above as a soldier's body fell onto the roof—then crashed out the back door and Lashed himself upward, narrowly avoiding the next building.

"Was I supposed to save those soldiers, sword-nimi?" Szeth said. "I am a Radiant now."

I think they would have flown like you instead of falling down, if they'd wanted to be saved.

There was a profound puzzle in the words, one which Szeth could not consider. The Fused were deft, more skilled than he was. He dodged among the streets, but they kept on him. He swung around, left the Ancient Ward, and shot for the wall—trying to get back to Dalinar. Unfortunately, a swarm of the enemies cut him off. The rest surrounded him.

Looks like we're cornered, the sword said. *Time to fight, right? Accept death, and die slaying as many as possible? I'm ready. Let's do it. I'm ready to be a noble sacrifice.*

No. He did not win by dying.

Szeth lobbed the gemstone away as hard as he could.

The Fused went after it, leaving him an avenue to escape. He dropped toward the ground, where spheres glistened like stars. He drew in a deep breath of Stormlight, then spotted Lift waiting on the field between the fighting illusions and the waiting parshmen.

Szeth settled down lightly beside her. "I have failed to carry this burden."

"That's okay. Your weird face is burden enough for one man."

"Your words are wise," he said, nodding.

Lift rolled her eyes. "You're right, sword. He's not very fun, is he?"

I think he's deevy anyway.

Szeth did not know this word, but it sent Lift chortling in a fit of amusement, which the sword mimicked.

"We have not fulfilled the Blackthorn's demands," Szeth snapped at the two of them, Stormlight puffing from his lips. "I could not stay ahead of those Fused long enough to deliver the stone to our master."

"Yeah, I saw," Lift said. "But I've got an *idea*. People are always after stuff, but they don't really like the *stuff*—they like *having* the stuff."

"These words are . . . not so wise. What do you mean?"

"Simple. The best way to rob someone is leave them thinking that nothing is wrong. . . ."

Shallan clung to Veil's and Radiant's hands.

She'd long since fallen to her knees, staring ahead as tears leaked from her eyes. Taut, her teeth gritted. She'd made *thousands* of illusions. Each one . . . each one was her.

A portion of her mind.

A portion of her soul.

Odium had made a mistake in flooding these soldiers with such thirst for blood. They didn't care that Shallan fed them illusions—they just wanted a battle. So she provided one, and somehow her illusions *resisted* when the enemy hit them. She thought maybe she was combining Soulcasting with her Lightweaving.

The enemy howled and sang, exulting in the fray. She painted the ground red and sprayed the enemy with blood that felt real. She serenaded them with the sounds of men screaming, dying, swords clashing and bones breaking.

She absorbed them in the false reality, and they drank it in; they *feasted* on it.

Each one of her illusions that died hit her with a little *shock*. A sliver of her dying.

Those were reborn as she pushed them out to dance again. Enemy Fused bellowed for order, trying to rally their troops, but Shallan drowned out their voices with sounds of screaming and metal on metal.

The illusion absorbed her entirely, and she lost track of everything else. Like when she was drawing. Creationspren blossomed around her by the hundred, shaped like discarded objects.

Storms. It was beautiful. She gripped Veil's and Radiant's hands tighter. They knelt beside her, heads bowed within her painted tapestry of violence, her—

"Hey," a girl's voice said. "Could you, uh, stop hugging yourself for a minute? I need some help."

※

Kaladin ducked toward Amaram, thrusting with his spear one-handed. That was usually a good tactic against an armored man with a sword. His spear hit right on target, where it would have dug into the armpit of an ordinary opponent. Here, unfortunately, the spear just slid off. Shardplate didn't have traditional weak points, other than the eye slit. You had to break it open with repeated hits, like cracking into a crab's shell.

Amaram laughed, a startlingly genuine mirth. "You have great form, spearman! Do you remember when you first came to me? Back in that village, when you begged me to take you? You were a blubbering child who wanted so badly to be a soldier. The glory of the battle! I could see the lust in your eyes, boy."

Kaladin glanced toward the Fused, who rounded the cloud, timid, looking for Dalinar.

Amaram chuckled. With those deep red eyes and the strange crystals growing from his body, Kaladin hadn't expected him to sound so much like himself. Whatever hybrid monster this was, it still had the mind of Meridas Amaram.

Kaladin stepped back, reluctantly changing Syl into a Blade, which would be better for cracking Plate. He fell into Windstance, which had always seemed appropriate. Amaram laughed again and surged forward, his second Shardblade appearing in his waiting grip. Kaladin dodged to the side, ducking under one Blade and getting at Amaram's back—where he got in a good hit on the Plate, cracking it. He raised his Blade to attack again.

Amaram slammed his foot down, and his Shardplate boot *shattered,* exploding outward in bits of molten metal. Beneath, his ripped sock revealed a foot overgrown with carapace and deep violet crystals.

As Kaladin came in for his attack, Amaram tapped his foot, and the stone ground became *liquid* for a moment. Kaladin stumbled, sinking down several inches, as if the rock were crem mud. It hardened in a moment, locking Kaladin's boots in place.

Kaladin! Syl cried in his mind as Amaram swung with two Shardblades, parallel to one another. Syl became a halberd in Kaladin's hands, and he blocked the blows—but their force threw him to the ground, snapping his ankles.

Teeth gritted, Kaladin hauled his pained feet out of the boots and pulled himself away. Amaram's weapons sliced the ground behind, narrowly missing him. Then Amaram's other armored boot exploded, crystals from inside breaking it apart. The highlord pushed with one foot and *glided* across the ground, incredibly quick, approaching Kaladin and swinging.

Syl became a large shield, and Kaladin barely blocked the attack. He Lashed himself backward, getting out of range as Stormlight healed his ankles. Storms. *Storms!*

That Fused! Syl said. *She's getting very close to Dalinar.*

Kaladin cursed, then scooped up a large stone. He launched it into the air with several Lashings compounded, which sent it zipping off to slam into the head of the Fused. She shouted in pain, pulling back.

Kaladin scooped up another stone and Lashed it toward Amaram's horse.

"Beating up the animal because you can't defeat me?" Amaram asked.

He didn't seem to notice that the horse, in bolting away, carried off the Shardbow.

I've killed a man wearing that Shardplate before, Kaladin thought. *I can do it again.*

Only, he wasn't merely facing a Shardbearer. Amethyst crystals broke Amaram's armor all up the arms. How did Kaladin defeat . . . whatever this thing was?

Stab it in the face? Syl suggested.

It was worth a try. He and Amaram fought on the battlefield near the red mist, on the western shore but between the main body of troops and the waiting parshmen. The area was mostly flat, except for some broken building foundations. Kaladin Lashed himself up a few inches, so he wouldn't sink into the ground if Amaram tried again to do . . . whatever he'd done. Then he moved backward carefully, positioning himself where Amaram would likely leap across a broken foundation to get at him.

Amaram stepped up, chuckling softly. Kaladin raised Syl as a Shardblade, but shifted his grip, preparing for the moment when she'd become a thin spear he could ram right through that faceplate—

Kaladin! Syl cried.

Something hit Kaladin with the force of a falling boulder, flinging him to the side. His body broke, and the world spun.

By instinct, Kaladin Lashed himself upward and forward, opposite the way he'd been flung. He slowed and released the Lashings right as his momentum ran out, touching down, then slid to a stop on the stone, pain fading from a healed shoulder and side.

A brawny Fused—taller even than Amaram in his Plate—dropped a shattered club that he'd used on Kaladin. His carapace was the color of stone; he must have been crouching near that foundation, and Kaladin had taken him for merely another part of the stony field.

As Kaladin watched, the creature's brown carapace crusted up his arms, covering his face like a helm, growing to thick armor in a matter of moments. He raised his arms, and carapace spurs grew above and below the hands.

Delightful.

⁂

Adolin heaved himself up over the rim of a broken rooftop onto a small alley between two buildings. He'd made it to the Loft Wards of the city, right above the Ancient Ward. Here, buildings were constructed practically atop one another in tiers.

The building to his left had been completely flattened. Adolin crept across rubble. To his right, a main city thoroughfare led upward—toward the Royal Ward and the Oathgate—but was clogged with people fleeing from the enemy troops below. This was compounded by the local merchant guards and platoons of Thaylen military, who struggled against the tide.

Moving on the streets was extremely slow—but Adolin had found one corridor that was empty. The thunderclast had crossed the Ancient Ward, kicking down buildings, then had stepped on roofs as it climbed up to the Loft Wards. This swath of destruction made almost a roadway. Adolin had managed to follow, using rubble like stairs.

Now he was right in the thing's shadow. The corpse of a Thaylen soldier drooped from a rooftop nearby, tangled in ropes. It hung there, eyebrows dangling to brush the ground. Adolin swept past, peeking out between buildings onto a larger street.

A handful of Thaylens fought here, trying to bring the thunderclast down. The ropes had been a great idea, but the thing was obviously too strong to be tripped that way. In the street beyond Adolin, a soldier got in close and tried to hit the monster's leg with a hammer. The weapon bounced off. That was old hardened cremstone. The plucky soldier ended up getting stomped.

Adolin gritted his teeth, summoning his Shardblade. Without Plate, he'd be as squishy as anyone else. He had to be careful, tactical.

"This is what you were designed for, isn't it?" Adolin said softly as his Blade dropped into his hand. "It was for fighting things like that. Shardblades are impractically long for duels, and Plate is overkill even on the battlefield. But against a monster of stone . . ."

He felt something. A stirring on the wind.

"You want to fight it, don't you?" Adolin asked. "It reminds you of when you were alive."

Something tickled his mind, very faint, like a sigh. A single word: *Mayalaran*. A . . . name?

"Right, Maya," Adolin said. "Let's bring that thing down."

Adolin waited for it to turn toward the small group of defending soldiers, then he bolted out along the rubbled street, dashing straight for the thunderclast. He was barely as tall as its calf.

Adolin didn't use any of the sword stances—he just hacked as if he were attacking a wall, slicing right along the top of the thing's ankle.

A sudden *bang* sounded above, like two stones *slamming* against one another, as the thing cried out. A shock wave of air washed over Adolin and the monster turned, thrusting a hand down toward him. Adolin dodged to the side, but the monster's palm smashed the ground with such force that Adolin's boots left the ground momentarily. He dismissed Maya as he fell, then rolled.

He came up puffing on one knee with his hand out, summoning Maya again. Storms, he was like a rat gnawing on the toes of a chull.

The beast regarded him with eyespots like molten rock just beneath the surface. He'd heard the descriptions of these things from his father's visions—but looking up at it, he was struck by the shape of its face and head.

A chasmfiend, he thought. *It looks like a chasmfiend*. The head, at least. The body was vaguely like a thick human skeleton.

"Prince Adolin!" one of the few living soldiers shouted. "It's the son of the Blackthorn!"

"Protect the prince! Distract the monster from the Shardbearer. It's our only chance to—"

Adolin lost the last part as the monster swept its hand across the ground. He barely dodged, then threw himself through the doorway of a low building. Inside, he leaped over a few bedding pallets, pushed into the next room, then attacked the brick wall with Maya, cutting in four quick strikes. He slammed his shoulder against the wall, breaking through the hole.

As he did, he heard a whimper from behind.

Adolin gritted his teeth. *I could use one of those storming Radiants about now.*

He ducked back into the building and flipped over a table, finding a young boy huddled underneath. That was the only person Adolin saw in the building. He hauled the boy out right as the thunderclast smashed a fist down through the roof. Dust billowing after him, Adolin shoved the child into the arms of a soldier, then pointed both toward the street to the south. Adolin took off running east, around the side of the building. Maybe he could climb up to the next level of the Loft Wards and circle the creature.

For all the troops' calls to distract the thing, however, it obviously knew who to focus on. It stepped over the broken house and thrust a fist toward Adolin—who leaped through a window into another house, across a table, then out an open window on the other side.

Crash.

The building fell in behind him. The thing was doing damage to its own hands with the attacks, leaving the wrists and fingers scored with white scrapes. It didn't seem to care—and why should it? It had ripped itself right from the ground to make this body.

Adolin's only advantage, other than his Blade, was his ability to react faster than the thing. It swung for the next building beyond him, trying to smash it before he got inside—but he was already doubling back. He ran underneath the monster's swing, sliding on the chips and dust as the fist passed narrowly overhead.

That put him in position to run between the thunderclast's legs. He slashed at the ankle he'd already cut once, digging his Blade deep into the stone, then whipping it out the other side. *Just like a chasmfiend,* he thought. *Legs first.*

When the thing stepped again, the ankle cracked with a sharp sound, then its foot broke free.

Adolin braced himself for the pained thunderclap from above, but still winced at the shock wave. Unfortunately, the monster balanced easily on the stump of its leg. It was a little clumsier than before, but it was in no real danger of falling. The Thaylen soldiers had regrouped and gathered up their ropes, however, so maybe—

A hand in Shardplate reached out of a building nearby, grabbed Adolin, and pulled him inside.

⁘

Dalinar held his hands out to the sides, enveloped by the Thrill. It returned every memory he hated about himself. War and conflict. Times when he'd shouted Evi into submission. Anger that had driven him to the brink of madness. His shame.

Though he had once crawled before the Nightwatcher to beg for release, he no longer wished to forget. "I embrace you," he said. "I accept what I was."

The Thrill colored his sight red, inflicting a deep longing for the fight, the conflict, the challenge. If he rejected it, he would drive the Thrill away.

"Thank you," Dalinar said, "for giving me strength when I needed it."

The Thrill thrummed with a pleased sound. It drew in closer to him, the faces of red mist grinning with excitement and glee. Charging horses screamed and died. Men laughed as they were cut down.

Dalinar was once again walking on the stone toward the Rift, intent on murdering everyone inside. He felt the heat of anger. The yearning so powerful, it made him ache.

"I *was* that man," Dalinar said. "I *understand* you."

⁘

Venli crept away from the battlefield. She left the humans to struggle against shadows in a mess of anger and lust. She walked deeper into the darkness beneath Odium's storm, feeling strangely sick.

The rhythms were going *crazy* inside her, merging and fighting. A fragment from Craving blended into Fury, into Ridicule.

She passed Fused arguing about what to do, now that Odium had withdrawn. Did they send the parshmen in to fight? They couldn't control the humans, consumed by one of the Unmade as they were.

Rhythms piled over rhythms.

Agony. Conceit. Destruction. Lost—

There! Venli thought. *Grab that!*

She attuned the Rhythm of the Lost. She clung to the solemn beat, desperate—a rhythm one attuned to remember those you missed. Those who had gone before.

Timbre thrummed to the same rhythm. Why did that feel different from before? Timbre vibrated *through* Venli's entire being.

Lost. What had Venli lost?

Venli missed being someone who cared about something other than power. Knowledge, favoritism, forms, wealth—it was all the same to her. Where had she gone wrong?

Timbre pulsed. Venli dropped to her knees. Cold stone reflected lightning from above, red and garish.

But her own eyes . . . she could see her own eyes in the polished wet rock.

There wasn't a hint of red in them.

"Life . . ." she whispered.

The king of the Alethi had reached out toward her. Dalinar Kholin, the man whose brother they'd killed. But he'd reached from the pillar of gloryspren all the same, and spoken to her.

You can change.

"Life before death."

You can become a better person.

"Strength before . . . before weakness . . ."

I did.

"Jou—"

Someone grabbed Venli roughly and spun her over, slamming her to the ground. A Fused with the form that grew carapace armor like Shardplate. He looked Venli up and down, and for a panicked moment she was sure he'd kill her.

The Fused seized her pouch, the one that hid Timbre. She screamed and clawed at his hands, but he shoved her back, then ripped open the pouch.

Then he turned it inside out.

"I could have sworn . . ." he said in their language. He tossed the pouch aside. "You failed to obey the Word of Passion. You did not attack the enemy when commanded."

"I . . . I was frightened," Venli said. "And weak."

"You cannot be weak in his service. You must choose who you will serve."

"I choose," she said, then shouted, "I *choose!*"

He nodded, evidently impressed by her Passion, then stalked back toward the battlefield.

Venli climbed to her feet and made her way to one of the ships. She stumbled up the gangway—yet felt crisper, more awake, than she'd been in a long, long time.

In her mind played the Rhythm of Joy. One of the old rhythms her people had learned long ago—after casting out their gods.

Timbre pulsed from *within* her. Inside her gemheart.

"I'm still wearing one of their forms," Venli said. "There was a Voidspren in my gemheart. How?"

Timbre pulsed to Resolve.

"You've done *what*?" Venli hissed, stopping on the deck.

Resolve again.

"But how can you . . ." She trailed off, then hunched over, speaking more softly. "How can you keep a Voidspren *captive*?"

Timbre pulsed to Victory within her. Venli rushed toward the ship's cabin. A parshman tried to forbid her, but she glared him to submission, then took the ruby sphere from his lantern and went inside, slamming the door and locking it.

She held up the sphere, and then—heart fluttering—she drank it in. Her skin started glowing with a soft white light.

"Journey before destination."

⁂

Adolin was confronted by a figure in glistening black Shardplate, a large hammer strapped to its back. The helm had stylized eyebrows like knives sweeping backward, and the Plate was skirted with a triangular pattern of interlocking scales. *Cvaderln*, he thought, remembering his lists of Thaylen Shards. It meant, roughly, "shell of Cva."

"Are you Tshadr?" Adolin guessed.

"No, Hrdalm," the Shardbearer said in a thick Thaylen accent. "Tshadr holds Court Square. I come, stop monster."

Adolin nodded. Outside, the thing sounded its angry call, confronting the remaining Thaylen troops.

"We need to get out and help those men," Adolin said. "Can you distract the monster? My Blade can cut, while you can take hits."

"Yes," Hrdalm said. "Yes, good."

Adolin quickly helped Hrdalm get the hammer untied. Hrdalm hefted it, then pointed at the window. "Go there."

Adolin nodded, waiting by the window as Hrdalm charged out the doorway and went running straight for the thunderclast, shouting a Thaylen battle cry. When the thing turned toward Hrdalm, Adolin leaped out the window and charged around the other side.

Two flying Fused swooped in behind Hrdalm, slamming spears into his back, tossing him forward. Plate ground against stone as he fell, face-first. Adolin ran for the thunderclast's leg—but the creature ignored Hrdalm and fixated on Adolin. It crashed a palm down on the ground nearby, forcing Adolin to dance backward.

Hrdalm stood up, but a Fused swooped down and kicked him over. The other landed on his chest and began pounding on his helm with a hammer, cracking it. As Hrdalm tried to grab her and throw her free, the other one swooped down and used a spear to pin the hand down. Damnation!

"All right, Maya," Adolin said. "We've practiced this."

He wound up, then hurled the Shardblade, which spun in a gleaming arc before slamming into the Fused on Hrdalm's chest, piercing her straight through. Dark smoke trailed from her eyes as they burned away.

Hrdalm sat up, sweeping away the other Fused with a Shard-enhanced punch. He turned toward the dead one, then looked back at Adolin with a posture that somehow expressed amazement.

The thunderclast called, sending a wave of sound across the street, rattling chips of stone. Adolin swallowed, then started counting heartbeats as he dashed away. The monster crashed along the street behind—but Adolin soon pulled to a stop in front of a large section of rubble, which blocked the street. Storms, he'd run the wrong way.

He shouted, spinning around. He hit a count of ten, and Maya returned to him.

The thunderclast loomed overhead. It thrust its palm down, and Adolin managed to judge the shadow and dodge between two fingers. As its palm crashed to the ground, Adolin leaped, trying to avoid being knocked over. He grabbed a massive finger with his left arm, desperately holding Maya to the side in his right.

As before, the thunderclast began to rub its palm across the ground, an attempt to grind Adolin to the stones. He hung from the finger, feet lifted a few inches off the ground. The sound was terrible, like Adolin was trapped in a rockslide.

As soon as the thunderclast ended its sweep of the hand, Adolin dropped off, then raised Maya in a double-handed grip and chopped straight through the finger. The beast released a thunderclap of anger and pulled its hand back. The tip of an unbroken finger connected with Adolin and flung him backward.

Pain.

It hit him like a flash of lightning. He struck the ground and rolled, but the agony was so sharp, he barely noticed. As he came to a rest, he coughed and trembled, his body seizing up.

Storms. Stormsstormsstorms . . . He squeezed his eyes shut against the pain. He'd . . . he'd gotten too accustomed to the invincibility of Plate. But his suit was back in Urithiru—or hopefully coming here soon on Gaval, his Plate standby.

Adolin somehow crawled to his feet, each move causing a spear of agony from his chest. Broken rib? Well, at least his arms and legs were working.

Move. That thing was still behind him.

One.

The roadway in front of him was piled with rubble from a broken building.

Two.

He limped to the right—toward the ledge down to the next tier of homes.

Three. Four.

The thunderclast trumped and followed, its steps shaking the ground.

Five. Six.

He could hear stone grinding just behind.

He fell to his knees.

Seven.

Maya! he thought, truly desperate. *Please!*

Blessedly, as he raised his hands, the Blade materialized. He slammed it into the rock wall—the edge pointed to the side, not down—then rolled off the ledge, holding on to the hilt. The thunderclast's fist came down again, crashing to the rock. Adolin dangled from Maya's hilt over the edge, a drop of some ten feet to the rooftop below.

Adolin gritted his teeth—his elbow was hurting badly enough to make his eyes water. But, once the thunderclast had rubbed its hand to the side, Adolin grabbed the cliff edge with one hand and swept Maya out to the side, freeing her from the stone. He reached down and rammed her into the stone below, then let go and swung from this new handhold a moment before releasing the Blade and dropping the rest of the way to the rooftop.

His leg screamed in pain. He collapsed to the rooftop, eyes watering. As he lay there in agony, he felt something—a faint *panic* on the wind. He forced himself to roll to the side, and a Fused swept past, its lance barely missing him.

Need . . . a weapon . . .

He started counting again and climbed, shakily, to his knees. But the thunderclast loomed on the tier overhead, then rammed its stump leg down into the center of the stone roof Adolin was on.

Adolin fell in a jumble of broken stone and dust, then hit hard on the floor inside, chunks of rock clattering around him.

Everything went black. He tried to gasp, but his muscles couldn't make the motions. He could only lie there, straining, groaning softly. A part of him was aware of the sounds made as the thunderclast pulled its stump out of the broken home. He waited for it to smash him, but as his vision slowly returned, he saw it stepping down from that upper tier onto the street outside.

At least . . . at least it wasn't continuing on toward the Oathgate.

Adolin shifted. Chips from the shattered roof streamed off him. His face and hands bled from a hundred scrapes. He recovered his breath, gasping in pain, and tried to move, but his leg . . . *Damnation,* that hurt.

Maya brushed his mind.

"I'm trying to get up," he said through gritted teeth. "Give me a sec. Storming sword." He had another coughing fit, then finally rolled off the rubble. He crawled out onto the street, half expecting Skar and Drehy to be there to pull him to his feet. Storms, he missed those bridgemen.

The street was empty around him, though maybe twenty feet away people crowded, trying to get up the thoroughfare to safety. They called and shouted in fear and urgency. If Adolin ran that way, the thunderclast would follow. It had proven *determined* to bring him down.

He sneered at the looming monster and—leaning against the wall of the small home he'd fallen into—pulled himself to his feet. Maya dropped into his hand. Though he was covered in dust, she still shone bright.

He steadied himself, then held Maya in two hands—his grip wetted by blood—and fell into Stonestance. The immovable stance.

"Come and get me, you bastard," he whispered.

"Adolin?" a familiar voice called from behind. "Storms, Adolin! What are you doing!"

Adolin started, then glanced over his shoulder. A glowing figure pushed through the crowd onto his street. Renarin carried a Shardblade, and his blue Bridge Four uniform was unstained.

Took you long enough.

As Renarin approached, the thunderclast actually took a step back, as if *afraid.* Well, that might help. Adolin clenched his teeth, trying to hold in his agony. He wobbled, then steadied himself. "All right, let's—"

"Adolin, don't be foolhardy!" Renarin grabbed his arm. A burst of healing moved through Adolin like cold water in his veins, causing his pains to retreat.

"But—"

"Get *away,*" Renarin said. "You're unarmored. You'll get yourself killed fighting this thing!"

"But—"

"I can handle it, Adolin. Just go! Please."

Adolin stumbled back. He'd never heard such forceful talk from Renarin—that was almost more amazing than the monster. Renarin, shockingly, *charged* at the thing.

A clatter announced Hrdalm climbing down from above, his Plate's helm cracked, but otherwise in good shape. He had lost his hammer, but carried one of the lances from the Fused, and his Plate fist was covered in blood.

Renarin! He didn't have Plate. How—

The thunderclast's palm crashed down on Renarin, smashing him. Adolin screamed, but his brother's Shardblade cut up through the palm, then separated the hand from the wrist.

The thunderclast trumpeted in anger as Renarin climbed from the rubble of the hand. He seemed to heal more quickly than Kaladin or Shallan did, as if being crushed wasn't even a bother.

"Excellent!" Hrdalm said, laughing inside his helm. "You, rest. Okay?"

Adolin nodded, stifling a groan of pain. Renarin's healing had stopped his insides from aching, and it was no longer painful to put weight on his leg, but his arms still ached, and some of his cuts hadn't closed.

As Hrdalm stepped toward the fight, Adolin took the man by the arm, then lifted Maya.

Go with him for now, Maya, Adolin thought.

He almost wished she'd object, but the vague sensation he received was a resigned agreement.

Hrdalm dropped his lance and took the Blade reverently. "Great Honor in you, Prince Adolin," he said. "Great Passion in me at this aid."

"Go," Adolin said. "I'll go see if I can help hold the streets."

Hrdalm charged off. Adolin chose an infantry spear from the rubble, then made toward the roadway behind.

⁂

Szeth of the Skybreakers had, fortunately, trained with all ten Surges.

The Fused transferred the enormous ruby to one of their number who could manipulate Abrasion—a woman who slid across the ground like Lift did. She infused the ruby, making it glow with her version of a Lashing. That would make the thing impossibly slick and difficult to carry for anyone but the Fused woman herself.

She seemed to think her enemies would have no experience with such a thing. Unfortunately for them, Szeth had not only carried an Honorblade that granted this power, he had practiced with skates on ice, a training exercise that somewhat mimicked an Edgedancer's movements.

And so, as he chased down the gemstone, he gave the Fused woman plenty of opportunities to underestimate him. He let her dodge, and was slow to reorient, acting surprised when she slipped this way, then that.

Once the Fused was confident she controlled this race, Szeth struck. When she leaped off a ledge of stone—soaring a short time in the air— Szeth swooped in with a sudden set of Lashings. He collided with her right as she landed. As his face touched her carapace, he Lashed her upward.

That sent her flying into the air with a scream. Szeth landed and prepared to follow, then cursed as the Fused *fumbled* with the gemstone. He whipped his jacket off as she dropped it. Though one of the flying Fused swept in to grab it, the ruby slipped out of his fingers.

Szeth caught it in the jacket, held like a pouch. A lucky turn; he had assumed he would need to attack her again to get it out of her hands.

Now, the real test. He Lashed himself eastward, toward the city. Here, a chaotic mix of soldiers fought on a painted battlefield. The Lightweaver was good; even the corpses looked authentic.

A Fused had begun gathering glowing-eyed soldiers who were real, then putting them with their backs to the city wall. They'd made ranks with spears bristling outward and yelled for soldiers to join them, but touched each one who approached. Illusions that tried to get in were disrupted. Soon the enemy would be able to ignore this distraction, regroup, and focus on getting through that wall.

Do what Dalinar told you. Get him this gemstone.

The ruby had finally stopped glowing, making it no longer slick. Above, many Fused swooped to intercept Szeth; they seemed happy to play this game, for as long as the gemstone was changing hands, it was not being delivered to Dalinar.

As the first Fused came for him, Szeth ducked into a roll and canceled his Lashing upward. He collided with a rock, acting dazed. He then shook his head, took up his pouch with the ruby, and launched into the air again.

Eight Fused gave chase, and though Szeth dodged between them, one eventually got close enough to seize his pouch and rip it out of his fingers. They swept away as a flock, and Szeth slowly floated down and landed beside Lift, who stepped out of the illusory rock. She held a bundle wrapped in clothing: the real gemstone, which she'd taken from his pouch during his feigned collision. The Fused now had a false ruby—a rock cut into roughly the same shape with a Shardblade, then covered in an illusion.

"Come," Szeth said, grabbing the girl and Lashing her upward, then towing her after him as he swept toward the northern edge of the plain. This place nearest the red mist had fallen into darkness—the Windrunner had consumed all of the Stormlight in gemstones on the ground. He fought against several enemies nearby.

Shadowed darkness. Whispered words. Szeth slowed to a halt.

"What?" Lift asked. "Crazyface?"

"I . . ." Szeth trembled, fearspren bubbling from the ground below. "I cannot go into that mist. I must be away from this place."

The *whispers*.

"I got it," she said. "Go back and help the redhead."

He dropped Lift to the ground and backed away. That churning red mist, those faces breaking and re-forming and screaming. Dalinar was still in there, somewhere?

The little girl with the long hair stopped at the border of the mist, then stepped inside.

⁂

Amaram was screaming in pain.

Kaladin sparred with the Fused who had the strange overgrown carapace, and couldn't spare a glance. He used the screaming to judge that he was staying far enough from Amaram to not be immediately attacked.

But storms, it was distracting.

Kaladin swept with the Sylblade, cutting through the Fused's forearms. That sheared the spurs completely free and disabled the hands. The creature backed up, growling a soft but angry rhythm.

Amaram's screaming voice approached. Syl became a shield—anticipating Kaladin's need—as he raised her toward his side, blocking a set of sweeping blows from the screaming highlord.

Stormfather. Amaram's helm was cracked from the wicked, sharp amethysts growing out of the sides of his face. The eyes still glowed deeply within, and the stone ground somehow *burned* beneath his crystal-covered feet, leaving flaming tracks behind.

The highprince battered against the Sylshield with two Shardblades. She, in turn, grew a latticework on the outside—with parts sticking out like the tines of a trident.

"What are you doing?" Kaladin asked.

Improvising.

Amaram struck again, and Helaran's sword got tangled in the tines. Kaladin spun the shield, wrenching the sword out of Amaram's grip. It vanished to smoke.

Now, press the advantage.

Kaladin!

The hulking Fused charged him. The creature's cut arms had regrown, and—even as it swung its hands—a large club formed there from carapace. Kaladin barely got Syl in place to block.

It didn't do much good.

The force of the club's sideways blow flung Kaladin against the remnants of a wall. He growled, then Lashed himself upward into the sky, Stormlight reknitting him. Damnation. The area around where they were fighting had grown dark and shadowed, the gemstones drained. Had he really used so much?

Uh-oh, Syl said, flying around him as a ribbon of light. *Dalinar!*

The red mist billowed, ominous in the gloom. Red on black. Within it Dalinar was a shadow, with two flying Fused besetting him.

Kaladin growled again. Amaram had gone hiking for his bow, which had fallen from the horse's saddle some ways off. Damnation. He couldn't defeat them all.

He shot down toward the ground. The hulking Fused came for him, and instead of dodging, Kaladin let the creature ram a knifelike spur into his stomach.

He grunted, tasting blood, but didn't flinch. He grabbed the creature's hand and Lashed him upward and toward the mist. The Fused flipped past his companions in the air, shouting something that sounded like a plea for help. They zipped after him.

Kaladin stumbled after Amaram, but his footsteps steadied as he healed. He got a little more Stormlight from some gemstones he'd missed earlier, then took to the sky. Syl became a lance, and Kaladin swooped down, causing Amaram to turn away from the bow—still a short distance from him—and track Kaladin. Crystals had broken through his armor all along his arms and back.

Kaladin made a charging pass. He wasn't accustomed to flying with a lance though, and Amaram batted the Syllance aside with a Shardblade. Kaladin rose up on the other side, considering his next move.

Amaram launched himself into the air.

He soared in an incredible leap, far higher and farther than even Shardplate would have allowed. And he *hung* for a time, sweeping close to Kaladin, who dodged backward.

"Syl," he hissed as Amaram landed. "Syl, that was a *Lashing.* What is he?"

I don't know. But we don't have much time before those Fused return.

Kaladin swept down and landed, shortening Syl to a halberd. Amaram spun on him, eyes within the helm trailing red light. "Can you feel it?" he demanded of Kaladin. "The beauty of the fight?"

Kaladin ducked in and rammed Syl at Amaram's cracked breastplate.

"It could have been so glorious," Amaram said, swatting aside the attack. "You, me, Dalinar. Together on the same side."

"The wrong side."

"Is it wrong to want to help the ones who truly own this land? Is it not *honorable?*"

"It's not Amaram I speak to anymore, is it? Who, or what, are you?"

"Oh, it's me," Amaram said. He dismissed one of his Blades, grabbed his helm. With a tug of the hand, it finally shattered, exploding away and revealing the face of Meridas Amaram—surrounded by amethyst crystals, glowing with a soft and somehow dark light.

He grinned. "Odium promised me something grand, and that promise has been kept. With honor."

"You still pretend to speak of honor?"

"Everything I do is for honor." Amaram swept with a single Blade, making Kaladin dodge. "It was honor that drove me to seek the return of the Heralds, of powers, and of our god."

"So you could join the *other side?*"

Lightning flashed behind Amaram, casting red light and long shadows as he resummoned his second Blade. "Odium showed me what the Heralds have become. We spent years trying to get them to return. But they were *here all along.* They *abandoned* us, spearman."

Amaram carefully circled Kaladin with his two Shardblades.

He's waiting for the Fused to come help, Kaladin thought. *That's why he's being cautious now.*

"I hurt, once," Amaram said. "Did you know that? After I was forced to kill your squad, I . . . hurt. Until I realized. It wasn't my fault." The color of his glowing eyes intensified to a simmering crimson. "None of this is my fault."

Kaladin attacked—unfortunately, he barely knew what he was facing. The ground rippled and became liquid, almost catching him again. Fire trailed behind Amaram's arms as he swung with both Shardblades. Somehow, he briefly ignited the very *air.*

Kaladin blocked one Blade, then the other, but couldn't get in an attack. Amaram was fast and brutal, and Kaladin didn't dare touch the ground, lest his feet freeze to the liquefied stone. After a few more exchanges, Kaladin was forced to retreat.

"You're outclassed, spearman," Amaram said. "Give in, and convince the city to surrender. That is for the best. No more need die today. Let me be merciful."

"Like you were merciful to my friends? Like you were merciful to me, when you gave me these brands?"

"I left you alive. I *spared* you."

"An attempt to assuage your conscience." Kaladin clashed with the highprince. "A failed attempt."

"*I* made you, Kaladin!" Amaram's red eyes lit the crystals that rimmed his face. "*I* gave you that granite will, that warrior's poise. This, the person you've become, was *my gift!*"

"A gift at the expense of everyone I loved?"

"What do you care? It made you strong! Your men died in the name of battle, so that the strongest man would have the weapon. Anyone would have done what I did, even Dalinar himself."

"Didn't you tell me you'd given up that grief?"

"Yes! I'm beyond guilt!"

"Then why do you still hurt?"

Amaram *flinched*.

"Murderer," Kaladin said. "You've switched sides to find peace, Amaram. But you won't ever have it. He'll *never* give it to you."

Amaram roared, sweeping in with his Shardblades. Kaladin Lashed himself upward, then—as Amaram passed underneath—twisted and came back down, swinging in a powerful, two-handed grip. In response to an unspoken command, Syl became a hammer, which crashed against the back of Amaram's Plate.

The cuirass-style breastplate—which was all one piece—exploded with an unexpected force, pushing Kaladin backward across the stone. Overhead, the lightning rumbled. They were fully in the Everstorm's shadow, which made it even more ghastly as he saw what had happened to Amaram.

The highprince's entire chest had collapsed inward. There was no sign of ribs or internal organs. Instead, a large violet crystal pulsed inside his chest cavity, overgrown with dark veins. If he'd been wearing a uniform or padding beneath the armor, it had been consumed.

He turned toward Kaladin, heart and lungs replaced by a gemstone that glowed with Odium's dark light.

"Everything I've done," Amaram said, blinking red eyes, "I've done for Alethkar. I'm a patriot!"

"If that is true," Kaladin whispered, "*why do you still hurt?*"

Amaram screamed, charging him.

Kaladin raised Syl, who became a Shardblade. "Today, what I do, I do for the men you killed. I am the man I've become because of *them*."

"*I* made you! I *forged* you!" He leaped at Kaladin, propelling himself off the ground, hanging in the air.

And in so doing, he entered Kaladin's domain.

Kaladin launched at Amaram. The highprince swung, but the winds themselves curled around Kaladin, and he anticipated the attack. He Lashed himself to the side, narrowly avoiding one Blade. Windspren streaked past him as he dodged the other by a hair's width.

Syl became a spear in his grip, matching his motions perfectly. He spun and slammed her against the gemstone at Amaram's heart. The amethyst cracked, and Amaram faltered in the air—then dropped.

Two Shardblades vanished to mist as the highprince fell some twenty feet to crash into the ground.

Kaladin floated downward toward him. "Ten spears go to battle," he whispered, "and nine shatter. Did that war *forge* the one that remained? No, Amaram. All the war did was *identify the spear that would not break.*"

Amaram climbed to his knees, howling with a bestial sound and clutching the flickering gemstone at his chest, which went out, plunging the area into darkness.

Kaladin! Syl shouted in Kaladin's mind.

He barely dodged as two Fused swooped past, their lances narrowly missing his chest. Two more came in from the left, one from the right. A sixth carried the hulking Fused back, rescued from Kaladin's Lashing.

They'd gone to fetch friends. It seemed the Fused had realized that their best path to stopping Dalinar was to first remove Kaladin from the battlefield.

⁂

Renarin puffed in and out as the thunderclast collapsed—crushing houses in its fall, but also breaking off its arm. It reached upward with its remaining arm, bleating a plaintive cry. Renarin and his companion—the Thaylen Shardbearer—had cut off both legs at the knees.

The Thaylen tromped up and slapped him—carefully—on the back with a Plated hand. "Very good fighting."

"I just distracted it while you cut chunks of its legs off."

"You did good," the Thaylen said. He nodded toward the thunderclast, which got to its knees, then slipped. "How to end?"

It will fear you! Glys said from within Renarin. *It will go. Make it so that it will go.*

"I'll see what I can do," Renarin said to the Thaylen, then carefully picked his way over to the street and up a level to get a better view of the thunderclast's head.

"So . . . Glys?" he asked. "What do I do?"

Light. You will make it go with light.

The thing pulled itself up across the rubble of a destroyed building. Stone rubbed stone as its enormous, wedge-shaped head turned to Renarin. Recessed molten eyes fluttered, like a sputtering fire.

It was in pain. It could hurt.

It will go! Glys promised, excitable as ever.

Renarin raised his fist and summoned Stormlight. It glowed as a powerful beacon. And . . .

The red molten eyes faded before that light, and the thing settled down with a last extinguishing sigh.

His Thaylen companion approached with a soft clinking of Plate. "Good. Excellent!"

"Go help with the fighting," Renarin said. "I need to open the Oathgate in person." The man obeyed without question, running for the main thoroughfare leading down to the Ancient Ward.

Renarin lingered with that stone corpse, troubled. *I was supposed to have died. I saw myself die. . . .*

He shook his head, then hiked toward the upper reaches of the city.

⁘

Shallan, Veil, and Radiant held hands in a ring. The three flowed, faces changing, identities melding. Together, they had raised an army.

It was dying now.

A hulking variety of Fused had organized the enemy. These refused to be distracted. Though Veil, Shallan, and Radiant had made copies of themselves—to keep the real ones from being attacked—those died as well.

Wavering. Stormlight running out.

We've strained ourselves too far, they thought.

Three Fused approached, cutting through the dying illusions, marching through evaporating Stormlight. People fell to their knees and puffed away.

"Mmmm . . ." Pattern said.

"Tired," Shallan said, her eyes drowsy.

"Satisfied," Radiant said, proud.

"Worried," Veil said, eyeing the Fused.

They wanted to move. Needed to move. But it hurt to watch their army die and puff into nothing.

One figure didn't melt like the others. A woman with jet-black hair that had escaped its usual braids. It blew free as she stepped between the enemy and Shallan, Radiant, and Veil. The ground turned glossy, the surface of the stone Soulcast into oil. Veil, Shallan, and Radiant were able to glimpse it in the Cognitive Realm. It changed so easily. How did Jasnah manage that?

Jasnah Soulcast a spark from the air, igniting the oil and casting up a field of flames. The Fused raised hands before their faces, stumbling back.

"That should buy us a few moments." Jasnah turned toward Radiant, Veil, and Shallan. She took Shallan by the arm—but Shallan wavered, then puffed away. Jasnah froze, then turned to Veil.

"Here," Radiant said, tired, stumbling to her feet. She was the one Jasnah could feel. She blinked away tears. "Are you . . . real?"

"Yes, Shallan. You did well out here." She touched Radiant's arm, then glanced toward the Fused, who were venturing into the fires despite the heat. "Damnation. Perhaps I should have opened a pit beneath them instead."

Shallan winced as the last of her army—like the shredded light of a setting sun—vanished. Jasnah proffered a gemstone, which Radiant drank eagerly.

Amaram's troops had begun to form ranks again.

"Come," Jasnah said, pulling Veil back to the wall, where steps grew from the stone itself.

"Soulcast?" Shallan asked.

"Yes." Jasnah stepped onto the first, but Shallan didn't follow.

"We shouldn't have ignored this," Radiant said. "We should have practiced this." She slipped—for a moment—into viewing Shadesmar. Beads rolled and surged beneath her.

"Not too far," Jasnah warned. "You can't bring your physical self into the realm, as I once assumed you could, but there are things here that can feast upon your mind."

"If I want to Soulcast the air. How?"

"Avoid air until you practice further," Jasnah said. "It is convenient, but difficult to control. Why don't you try to turn some stone into oil, as I did? We can fire it as we climb the steps, and further impede the enemy."

"I . . ." So many beads, so many *spren*, churning in the lake that marked Thaylen City. So overwhelming.

"That rubble near the wall will be easier than the ground itself," Jasnah said, "as you'll be able to treat those stones as distinct units, while the ground views itself all as one."

"It's too much," Shallan said, exhaustionspren spinning around her. "I can't, Jasnah. I'm sorry."

"It is well, Shallan," Jasnah said. "I merely wanted to see, as it seemed you were Soulcasting to give your illusions weight. But then, concentrated Stormlight has a faint mass to it. Either way, up the steps, child."

Radiant started up the stone steps. Behind, Jasnah waved her hand toward the approaching Fused—and stone formed from air, completely encasing them.

It was brilliant. Any who saw it in only the Physical Realm would be impressed, but Radiant saw so much more. Jasnah's absolute command and confidence. The Stormlight rushing to do her will. The air itself responding as if to the voice of God himself.

Shallan gasped in wonder. "It obeyed. The air obeyed your call to transform. When I tried to make a *single little stick* change, it refused."

"Soulcasting is a practiced art," Jasnah said. "Up, up. Keep walking."

She sliced the steps off as they walked. "Remember, you mustn't order stones, as they are more stubborn than men. Use coercion. Speak of freedom and of movement. But for a gas becoming a solid, you must impose discipline and will. Each Essence is different, and each offers advantages and disadvantages when used as a substrate for Soulcasting."

Jasnah glanced over her shoulder at the gathering army. "And perhaps . . . this is one time when a lecture isn't advisable. With all my complaints about not wanting wards, you'd think I would be able to resist instructing people at inopportune times. Keep moving."

Feeling exhausted, Veil, Shallan, and Radiant trudged up and finally reached the top of the wall.

❖

After how hard it had been for Renarin to get up to fight the thunderclast—he'd spent what seemed like an eternity caught in the press of people—he'd expected to have to work to cover the last distance to the Oathgate. However, people were moving more quickly now. The ones up above must have cleared off the streets, hiding in the many temples and buildings in the Royal Ward.

He was able to move with the flow of people. Near the top tier, he ducked into a building and walked to the back, past some huddled merchants. Most of the buildings here were a single story, so he used Glys to cut a hole in the roof. He then hollowed out some handholds in the rock wall and climbed up on top.

Beyond, he was able to get onto the street leading to the Oathgate platform. He was . . . unaccustomed to being able to do things like this. Not only using the Shardblade, but being physical. He'd always been afraid of his fits, always worried that a moment of strength would instantly become a moment of invalidity.

Living like that, you learned to stay back. Just in case. He hadn't suffered a fit in a while. He didn't know if that was just a coincidence—they could be irregular—or if they had been healed, like his bad eyesight. Indeed, he still saw the world differently from everyone else. He was still nervous talking to people, and didn't like being touched. Everyone else saw in each other things he never could understand. So much noise and destruction and people talking and cries for help and sniffles and muttering and whispering all like buzzing, buzzings.

At least here, on this street near the Oathgate, the crowds had diminished. Why was that? Wouldn't they have pressed up here, hoping for escape? Why . . .

Oh.

A dozen Fused hovered in the sky above the Oathgate, lances held formally before themselves, clothing draping beneath them and fluttering.

Twelve. *Twelve.*

This, Glys said, *would be bad.*

Motion caught his attention: a young girl standing in a doorway and waving at him. He walked over, worried the Fused would attack him. Hopefully his Stormlight—which he'd mostly used up fighting the thunderclast—wasn't bright enough to draw their ire.

He entered the building, another single-story structure with a large open room at the front. It was occupied by dozens of scribes and ardents, many of whom huddled around a spanreed. Children that he couldn't see crowded the back rooms, but he could hear their whimpers. And he heard the scratching, scratching, scratching of reeds on paper.

"Oh, bless the Almighty," Brightness Teshav said, appearing from the mass of people. She pulled Renarin deeper into the room. "Have you any news?"

"My father sent me up here to help," Renarin said. "Brightness, where are General Khal and your son?"

"In Urithiru," she said. "They transferred back to gather forces, but then . . . Brightlord, there's been an attack at Urithiru. We've been trying to get information via spanreed. It appears that a strike force of some kind arrived at the advent of the Everstorm."

"Brightness!" Kadash called. "Spanreed to Sebarial's scribes is responding again. They apologize for the long delay. Sebarial pulled back, following Aladar's command, to the upper levels. He confirms that the attackers are parshmen."

"The Oathgates?" Renarin asked, hopeful. "Can they reach those, and open the way here?"

"Not likely. The enemy is holding the plateau."

"Our armies have the advantage at Urithiru, Prince Renarin," Teshav said. "Reports agree that the enemy strike force isn't nearly large enough to defeat us there. This is obviously a delaying tactic to keep us from activating the Oathgate and bringing help to Thaylen City."

Kadash nodded. "Those Fused above the Oathgate held even when the stone monster outside was falling. They know their orders—keep that device from being activated."

"Radiant Malata is the only way for our armies to reach us through the Oathgate," Teshav said. "But we can't contact her, or any of the Kharbranth contingent. The enemy struck them first. They knew exactly what they had to do to cripple us."

Renarin took a deep breath, drawing in Stormlight that Teshav was carrying. His glow lit the room, and eyes all through the chamber looked up from spanreeds, turning toward him.

"The portal has to be opened," Renarin said.

"Your Highness . . ." Teshav said. "You can't fight them all."

"There's nobody else." He turned to go.

Shockingly, nobody called for him to stop.

All his life they'd done that. No, Renarin. That's not for you. You can't do that. You're not *well*, Renarin. Be *reasonable*, Renarin.

He'd always been reasonable. He'd always listened. It felt wonderful and terrifying at once to know that nobody did that today. The spanreeds continued their scratching, moving on their own, oblivious to the moment.

Renarin stepped outside.

Terrified, he strode down the street, summoning Glys as a Shardblade. As he approached the ramp up to the Oathgate, the Fused descended. Four landed on the ramp before him, then gave him a gesture not unlike a salute, humming to a frantic tune he did not know.

Renarin was so frightened, he worried he'd wet himself. Not very noble or brave, now was he?

Ah . . . what will come now? Glys said, voice thrumming through Renarin. *What emerges?*

One of his fits struck him.

Not the old fits, where he grew weak. He had new ones now, that neither he nor Glys could control. To his eyes, glass grew across the ground. It spread out like crystals, forming lattices, images, meanings and pathways. Stained-glass pictures, panel after panel.

These had always been right. Until today—until they had proclaimed that Jasnah Kholin's love would fail.

He read this latest set of stained-glass images, then felt his fear drain away. He smiled. This seemed to confuse the Fused as they lowered their salutes.

"You're wondering why I'm smiling," Renarin said.

They didn't respond.

"Don't worry," Renarin said. "You didn't miss something funny. I . . . well, I doubt you'll find it amusing."

Light exploded from the Oathgate platform in a wave. The Fused cried out in a strange tongue, zipping into the air. A luminous wall expanded from the Oathgate platform in a ring, trailing a glowing afterimage.

It faded to reveal an entire division of Alethi troops in Kholin blue standing upon the Oathgate platform.

Then, like a Herald from lore, a man rose into the air above them. Glowing white with Stormlight, the bearded man carried a long silver Shardspear with a strange crossguard shape behind the tip.

Teft.

Knight Radiant.

⁂

Shallan sat with her back against the battlement, listening to soldiers shout orders. Navani had given her Stormlight and water, but was currently distracted by reports from Urithiru.

Pattern hummed from the side of Veil's jacket. "Shallan? You did well, Shallan. Very well."

"An honorable stand," Radiant agreed. "One against many, and we held our ground."

"Longer than we should have," Veil said. "We were *already* exhausted."

"We're still ignoring too much," Shallan said. "We're getting too good at pretending." She had decided to stay with Jasnah in the first place to *learn*. But when the woman returned from the dead, Shallan had—instead of accepting training—immediately fled. What had she been thinking?

Nothing. She'd been trying to hide away things she didn't want to face. Like always.

"Mmm . . ." Pattern said, a concerned hum.

"I'm tired," Shallan whispered. "You don't have to worry. After I rest, I'll recover and settle down to being just one. I actually . . . actually don't think I'm quite as lost as I was before."

Jasnah, Navani, and Queen Fen whispered together farther along the wall. Thaylen generals joined them, and fearspren gathered around. The defense, in their opinion, was going poorly. Reluctantly, Veil pushed herself to her feet and surveyed the battlefield. Amaram's forces were gathering beyond bow range.

"We delayed the enemy," Radiant said, "but didn't defeat them. We still have an overwhelming army to face. . . ."

"Mmmm . . ." Pattern said, high pitched, worried. "Shallan, look. Beyond."

Out nearer the bay, thousands upon thousands of fresh parshman troops had begun to carry ladders off their ships to use in a full-on assault.

⁂

"Tell the men not to give chase to those Fused," Renarin said to Lopen. "We need to hold the Oathgate, first and foremost."

"Good enough, sure," Lopen said, launching into the sky and going to relay the order to Teft.

The Fused clashed with Bridge Four in the air over the city. This group of enemies seemed more skilled than the ones Renarin had seen below, but they didn't *fight* so much as *defend themselves*. They were progressively moving the clash farther out over the city, and Renarin worried they were deliberately drawing Bridge Four away from the Oathgate.

The Alethi division marched into the city with shouts of praise and joy from the surrounding people. Two thousand men wasn't going to do much if those parshmen outside joined the battle, but it was a start—plus, General Khal had brought not one, but *three* Shardbearers. Renarin did his best to explain the city situation, but was embarrassed to tell the Khals that he didn't know his father's status.

As they reunited with Teshav—turning her scribe station into a command post—Rock and Lyn landed next to Renarin.

"Ha!" Rock said. "What happened to uniform? Is needing my needle."

Renarin looked down at his tattered clothing. "I got hit by a large block of stone. Twenty times . . . You're not one to complain, anyway. Is that *your* blood on your uniform?"

"Is nothing!"

"We had to carry him all the way down to the Oathgate," Lyn said. "We were trying to get him to you, but he started drawing in Stormlight as soon as he got here."

"Kaladin is close," Rock agreed. "Ha! I feed him. But here, today, he fed me. With light!"

Lyn eyed Rock. "Storming Horneater weighs as much as a chull. . . ." She shook her head. "Kara will fight with the others—don't tell anyone, but she's been practicing with a spear since childhood, the little cheater. But Rock won't fight, and I've only been handling a spear for a few weeks now. Any idea where you want us?"

"I'm . . . um . . . not really in command or anything. . . ."

"Really?" Lyn said. "That's your best Knight Radiant voice?"

"Ha!" Rock said.

"I think I used up all my Radianting for the day," Renarin said. "Um, I'll work the Oathgate and get more troops here. Maybe you two could go down and help on the city wall, pull wounded out of the front lines?"

"Is good idea," Rock said. Lyn nodded and flew off, but Rock lingered, then grabbed Renarin in a very warm, suffocating, and *unexpected* embrace.

Renarin did his best not to squirm. It wasn't the first hug he'd endured from Rock. But . . . storms. You weren't supposed to just grab someone like that.

"Why?" Renarin said after the embrace.

"You looked like person who needed hug."

"I assure you, I *never* look like that. But, um, I am glad you guys came. Really, *really* glad."

"Bridge Four," Rock said, then launched into the air.

Renarin settled down nearby on some steps, trembling from it all, but grinning anyway.

◆◆◆

Dalinar drifted in the Thrill's embrace.

He'd once believed he had been four men in his life, but he now saw he'd grossly underestimated. He hadn't lived as two, or four, or six men—he had lived as thousands, for each day he became someone slightly different.

He hadn't changed in one giant leap, but across a million little steps.

The most important always being the next, he thought as he drifted in the red mist. The Thrill threatened to take him, control him, rip him apart and shred his soul in its eagerness to please him—to give him something it could never understand was dangerous.

A small hand gripped Dalinar's.

He started, looking down. "L-Lift? You shouldn't have come in here."

"But I'm the *best* at going places I'm not supposed to." She pressed something into his hand.

The large ruby.

Bless you.

"What is it?" she said. "Why do you need that rock?"

Dalinar squinted into the mists. *Do you know how we capture spren, Dalinar?* Taravangian had said. *You lure the spren with something it loves. You give it something familiar to draw it in . . .*

Something it knows deeply.

"Shallan saw one of the Unmade in the tower," he whispered. "When she got close, it was afraid, but I don't think the Thrill comprehends like it did. You see, it can only be bested by someone who deeply, sincerely, *understands it.*"

He lifted the gemstone above his head, and—one last time—embraced the Thrill.

War.

Victory.

The contest.

Dalinar's entire life had been a competition: a struggle from one conquest to the next. He accepted what he had done. It would always be part of him. And though he was determined to resist, he would not cast aside what he had learned. That very thirst for the struggle—the fight, the *victory*—had also prepared him to refuse Odium.

"Thank you," he whispered again to the Thrill, "for giving me strength when I needed it."

The Thrill churned close around him, cooing and exulting in his praise.

"Now, old friend, it is time to rest."

⁙

Keep moving.

Kaladin dodged and wove, avoiding some strikes, healing from others.

Keep them distracted.

He tried to take to the skies, but the eight Fused swarmed about him, knocking him back down. He hit the stone ground, then Lashed himself laterally, away from the stabbing lances or crushing clubs.

Can't actually escape.

He had to keep their attention. If he managed to slip away, all of these would turn against Dalinar.

You don't have to beat them. You simply have to last long enough.

He dodged to the right, skimming a few inches above the ground. But one of the hulking Fused—there were four fighting him now—grabbed him by the foot. She slammed him down, then carapace grew down along her arms, threatening to bind Kaladin to the ground.

He kicked her off, but another grabbed him by the arm and flung him to the side. Flying ones descended, and while he warded away their lances with the Sylshield, his side throbbed with pain. The healing was coming more slowly now.

Two other Fused swept along, scooping up nearby gemstones, leaving Kaladin in an ever-expanding ring of darkness.

Just buy time. Dalinar needs time.

Syl sang in his mind as he spun, forming a spear and ramming it through the chest of one of the hulking ones. Those could heal unless you stabbed them in exactly the right spot in the sternum, and he'd missed. So, he made Syl into a sword and—the weapon still embedded in the Fused woman's chest—swept upward through the head, burning her eyes. Another hulking Fused swung, but as it hit—the club being part of the thing's actual body—Kaladin used much of his remaining Stormlight to Lash this man upward, crashing him into a Fused above.

Another clobbered him from the side, sending him rolling. Red lightning pulsed overhead as he came to a rest on his back. He immediately summoned Syl as a spear, pointing straight up. That impaled the Fused dropping down to attack him, cracking its sternum within, causing its eyes to burn.

Another grabbed him by the foot and lifted him, then slammed him face-first into the ground. That knocked Kaladin's breath out. The monstrous Fused stomped a carapace-encrusted foot onto his back, shattering ribs. Kaladin screamed, and though the Stormlight healed what it could, the last of it fluttered inside.

Then went out.

A sudden sound rose behind Kaladin, like that of rushing air—accompanied by wails of pain. The Fused stumbled backward, muttering to a quick, worried rhythm. Then, remarkably, it *turned and ran*.

Kaladin twisted, looking behind himself. He couldn't make out Dalinar anymore, but the mist itself had begun to thrash. Surging and pulsing, it whipped about like it was caught in a powerful wind.

More Fused fled. That wailing grew louder, and the mist seemed to roar—a thousand faces stretching from it, mouths opened in agony. They were sucked back together, like rats pulled by their tails.

The red mist imploded, vanishing. All went dark, with the storm overhead growing still.

Kaladin found himself lying broken on the ground. Stormlight had healed his vital functions; his organs would probably be intact, though his cracked bones left him gasping with pain when he tried to sit up. The spheres around the area were dun, and the darkness prevented him from spotting whether Dalinar lived.

The mist was entirely gone. That seemed a good sign. And in the darkness, Kaladin could see something streaking from the city. Brilliant white lights flying in the air.

A scraping sound came from nearby, and then a violet light flickered in the darkness. A shadow stumbled to its feet, dark purple light pulsing alive in its chest cavity, which was empty save for that gemstone.

Amaram's glowing red eyes illuminated a distorted face: his jaw had broken as he'd fallen, and gemstones had pushed out the sides of his face at awkward angles, making the jaw hang limp from his mouth, drool leaking out the side. He stumbled toward Kaladin, gemstone heart pulsing with light. A Shardblade formed in his hand. The one that had killed Kaladin's friends so long ago.

"Amaram," Kaladin whispered. "I can see what you are. What you've always been."

Amaram tried to speak, but his drooping jaw only let out spittle and grunts. Kaladin was struck by a memory of the first time he'd seen the highlord at Hearthstone. So tall and brave. Seemingly perfect.

"I saw it in your eyes, Amaram," Kaladin whispered as the husk of a man stumbled up to him. "When you killed Coreb and Hab and my other friends. I *saw* the guilt you felt." He licked his lips. "You tried to break me as a slave. But you failed. They rescued me."

Maybe it's time for someone to save you, Syl had said in Shadesmar. But someone already had.

Amaram raised the Shardblade high.

"Bridge Four," Kaladin whispered.

An arrow slammed into Amaram's head from behind, going right through the skull, coming out his inhuman mouth. Amaram stumbled forward, dropping his Shardblade, the arrow stuck in his head. He made a choking sound, then turned about just in time to catch another arrow straight in the chest—right through the flickering gemstone heart.

The amethyst exploded, and Amaram dropped in a crumbled wreck beside Kaladin.

A glowing figure stood on some rubble beyond, holding Amaram's enormous Shardbow. The weapon seemed to match Rock, tall and brilliant, a beacon in the darkness.

Amaram's red eyes faded as he died, and Kaladin had the distinct impression of a dark smoke escaping his corpse. Two Shardblades formed beside him and clanged to the stone.

⁙

The soldiers made a space for Radiant on the wall as they prepared for the enemy assault. Amaram's army formed assault ranks while parshmen carried ladders, ready to charge.

It was hard to step atop the wall without squishing a fearspren. Thaylens whispered of Alethi prowess in battle, recalling stories like when Hamadin and his fifty had withstood ten thousand Vedens. This was the first battle the Thaylens had seen in a generation, but Amaram's troops had been hardened by constant war on the Shattered Plains.

They looked to Shallan as if she could save them. The Knights Radiant were the only edge this city had. Their best hope of survival.

That terrified her.

The armies started charging the wall. No pause, no breather. Odium would keep pushing forces at this wall as long as it took to crack Thaylen City. Bloodlusty men, controlled by . . .

The lights in their eyes started to go out.

That clouded sky made it unmistakable. All across the field, red faded from the eyes of Amaram's soldiers. Many immediately fell to their knees, retching on the ground. Others stumbled, holding themselves upright by sagging against spears. It was like the very life had been sucked out of them—and it was so abrupt and unexpected that Shallan had to blink several times before her mind admitted that—yes—this was happening.

Cheers erupted along the wall as the Fused inexplicably retreated back toward the ships. The parshmen rushed to follow, as did many of Amaram's troops—though some just lay on the broken stones.

Lethargically, the black storm faded until it was a mere overcast stain, rippling with drowsy red lightning. It finally rolled across the island—impotent, bereft of wind—and vanished to the east.

⁂

Kaladin drank Stormlight from Lopen's gemstones.

"Be lucky the Horneater was looking for you, gon," Lopen said. "The rest of us thought we'd just fight, you know?"

Kaladin glanced toward Rock, who stood over Amaram's body, looking down, the enormous bow held limply in one hand. How had he drawn it? Stormlight granted great endurance, but it didn't vastly improve strength.

"Whoa," Lopen said. "Gancho! Look!"

The clouds had thinned, and sunlight peeked through, illuminating the field of stone. Dalinar Kholin knelt not far away, clutching a large ruby that glowed with the same strange phantom light as the Fused. The Reshi girl stood with her diminutive hand resting on his shoulder.

The Blackthorn was crying as he cradled the gemstone.

"Dalinar?" Kaladin asked, worried, jogging over. "What happened?"

"It is over, Captain," Dalinar said. Then he smiled. So were they tears of joy? Why had he seemed so grieved? "It's over."

121

IDEALS

*It becomes the responsibility of every man, upon realizing he lacks
the truth, to seek it out.*

—From *The Way of Kings*, postscript

Moash found it easy to transition from killing men to breaking
apart rubble.

He used a pick to hack at pieces of fallen stone in the former east wing of the Kholinar palace, smashing fallen columns so they could
be carried off by other workers. Nearby, the floor was still red with dried
blood. That was where he'd killed Elhokar, and his new masters had ordered the blood to not be cleaned. They claimed that the death of a king
was a thing to regard with reverence.

Shouldn't Moash have felt pleasure? Or at least satisfaction? Instead,
killing Elhokar had only made him feel . . . cold. Like a man who had hiked
across half of Roshar with a caravan of stubborn chulls. At the top of the
last hill, you didn't feel satisfaction. You just felt tired. Maybe a sliver of
relief at being done.

He slammed his pick into a fallen pillar. Near the end of the battle
for Kholinar, the thunderclast had knocked down a large portion of
the palace's eastern gallery. Now, human slaves worked to clear out the
rubble. The others would often break down crying, or work with hunched
shoulders.

Moash shook his head, enjoying the peaceful rhythm of pick on stone.

A Fused strode past, covered in carapace armor as brilliant and wicked
as Shardplate. There were nine orders of them. Why not ten?

"Over there," the Fused said through an interpreter. He pointed at a section of wall. "Break this down."

Moash wiped his brow, frowning as other slaves began work there. Why break down that wall? Wouldn't it be needed to rebuild this portion of the palace?

"Curious, human?"

Moash jumped, startled to find a figure hovering down through the broken ceiling, swathed in black. Lady Leshwi still visited Moash, the man who had killed her. She was important among the singers, but not in a highprince sort of way. More like a field captain.

"I guess I am curious, Ancient Singer," Moash said. "Is there a reason you're ripping apart this section of the palace? More than just to clear away the rubble?"

"Yes. But you do not yet need to know why."

He nodded, then returned to his work.

She hummed to a rhythm he associated with being pleased. "Your passion does you credit."

"I have no passion. Just numbness."

"You have given him your pain. He will return it, human, when you need it."

That would be fine, so long as he could forget the look of betrayal he'd seen in Kaladin's eyes.

"Hnanan wishes to speak with you," the ancient one said. The name wasn't fully a word. It was more a hummed sound, with specific beats. "Join us above."

She flew off. Moash set aside his pick and followed in a more mundane manner, rounding to the front of the palace. Once away from the picks and the clatter of rocks, he could hear sobs and whimpers. Only the most destitute humans sheltered here, in the broken buildings near the palace.

Eventually, these would be rounded up and sent to work farms. For now, however, the grand city was a place of wails and heartache. The people thought the world had ended, but they were only half right. *Their* world had.

He entered the palace uncontested, and started up the stairwell. Fused didn't need guards. Killing them was difficult, and even if you succeeded, they would simply be reborn at the next Everstorm, assuming a willing parshman could be found to take the burden.

Near the king's chambers, Moash passed two Fused reading books in a library. They'd removed their lengthy coats, floating with bare feet peeking from loose, rippling trousers, toes pointed downward. He eventually found Hnanan out beyond the king's balcony, hovering in the air, her train blowing and rippling in the wind beneath.

"Ancient Singer," he said from the balcony. Though Hnanan was the equivalent of a highprince, they did not demand that Moash bow even to her. Apparently, by having killed one of their better fighters, he had obtained a level of respect.

"You did well," she said, speaking Alethi, her voice thickly accented. "You felled a king in this palace."

"King or slave, he was an enemy to me and mine."

"I have called myself wise," she said, "and felt pride for Leshwi at picking you out. For years, my brother, sister, and I will boast of having chosen you." She looked to him. "Odium has a command for you. This is rare for a human."

"Speak it."

"You have killed a king," she said, removing something from a sheath within her robes. A strange knife, with a sapphire set into the pommel. The weapon was of a bright golden metal, so light it was almost white. "Would you do the same to a god?"

⁙

Navani left through the sally port in the Thaylen City wall, and ran across the broken field, heedless of the calls of soldiers who scrambled after her. She'd waited as long as was reasonable to let the enemy army withdraw.

Dalinar walked with help from Lopen and Captain Kaladin, one under each arm. He towed jets of exhaustionspren like a swarm. Navani took him in a powerful embrace anyway. He was the Blackthorn. He'd survive a forceful hug.

Kaladin and Lopen hovered nearby. "He's mine," she said to them.

They nodded, and didn't move.

"People need your help inside," she said. "I can handle him, boys."

Finally they flew off, and Navani tried to get under Dalinar's arm. He shook his head, still holding her in the embrace, a large stone—wrapped in his coat—held in one hand and pressing against her back. What was that?

"I think I know why the memories came back," he whispered. "Odium was going to make me remember once I faced him. I needed to learn to stand up again. All my pain these last two months was a blessing."

She held to him on that open field of rock, broken by the thunderclasts, littered with men who wailed toward the empty sky, screaming for what they'd done, demanding to know why they'd been abandoned.

Dalinar resisted Navani's attempts to tug him toward the wall. Instead, teary eyed, he kissed her. "Thank you for inspiring me."

"Inspiring you?"

He released her and held up his arm, which was strapped with the clock and painrial she'd given him. It had cracked open, exposing the gemstones. "It reminded me," he said. "Of how we make fabrials."

He lethargically unwrapped his uniform jacket from around a large ruby. It glowed with a bizarre light, deep and dark. Somehow, it seemed to be trying to pull the light around it *in*.

"I want you to keep this safe for me," Dalinar said. "Study it. Find out why this gemstone specifically was capable of holding one of the Unmade. Don't break it though. We dare not let it out again."

She bit her lip. "Dalinar, I've seen something like this before. Much smaller, like a sphere." She looked up at him. "Gavilar made it."

Dalinar touched the stone with his bare finger. Deep within it, something seemed to stir. Had he really trapped an entire *Unmade* inside this thing?

"Study it," he repeated. "And in the meantime, there's something else I want you to do, dearest. Something unconventional, perhaps uncomfortable."

"Anything," she said. "What is it?"

Dalinar met her eyes. "I want you to teach me how to read."

⁙

Everyone started celebrating. Shallan, Radiant, and Veil just settled down on the wall walk, back to the stone.

Radiant worried they'd leave the city undefended in their reverie. And what had become of the enemy that had been fighting in the streets? The defenders had to make certain this wasn't an elaborate feint.

Veil worried about looting. A city in chaos often proved how feral it could become. Veil wanted to be out on the streets, looking for people likely to be robbed, and making sure they were cared for.

Shallan wanted to sleep. She felt . . . weaker . . . more tired than the other two.

Jasnah approached along the wall walk, then leaned down beside her. "Shallan? Are you well?"

"Just tired," Veil lied. "You have no idea how draining that was, Brightness. I could use a stiff drink."

"I suspect that would help very little," Jasnah said, rising. "Rest here a while yet. I want to make absolutely certain the enemy is not returning."

"I swear to do better, Brightness," Radiant said, taking Jasnah's hand. "I wish to fulfill my wardship—to study and learn until *you* determine I am ready. I will not flee again. I've realized I have very far to go yet."

"That is well, Shallan." Jasnah moved off.

Shallan. *Which . . . which am I . . . ?* She'd insisted she would be better soon, but that didn't seem to be happening. She grasped for an answer, staring into the nothingness until Navani approached and knelt down beside her. Behind, Dalinar accepted a respectful bow from Queen Fen, then bowed back.

"Storms, Shallan," Navani said. "You look like you can barely keep your eyes open. I'll get you a palanquin to the upper reaches of the city."

"The Oathgate is likely clogged," Radiant said. "I would not take a place from others who might be in greater need."

"Don't be foolish, child," Navani said, then gave her an embrace. "You must have been through so much. Devmrh, would you get a palanquin for Brightness Davar?"

"My own feet are good enough," Veil said, glaring at the scribe who jumped to obey Navani. "I'm stronger than you think—no offense, Brightness."

Navani pursed her lips, but then was pulled away by Dalinar and Fen's conversation; they were planning to write the Azish and explain what had happened. Veil figured he was rightly worried that today's events would spread as rumors of Alethi betrayal. Storms, if she hadn't been here herself, she'd have been tempted to believe them. It wasn't every day that an entire army went rogue.

Radiant decided they could rest for ten minutes. Shallan accepted that, leaning her head back against the wall. Floating . . .

"Shallan?"

That voice. She opened her eyes to find Adolin scrambling across the wall to her. He skidded a little as he fell to his knees beside her, then raised his hands—only to hesitate, as if confronted by something very fragile.

"Don't look at me like that," Veil said. "I'm not some delicate piece of crystal."

Adolin narrowed his eyes.

"Truly," Radiant said. "I'm a soldier as much as the men atop this wall. Treat me—other than in obvious respects—as you would treat them."

"Shallan . . ." Adolin said, taking her hand.

"What?" Veil asked.

"Something's wrong."

"Of course it is," Radiant said. "This fighting has left us all thoroughly worn out."

Adolin searched her eyes. She bled from one, to the other, and back. A moment of Veil. A moment of Radiant. Shallan peeking through—

Adolin's hand tightened around her own.

Shallan's breath caught. *There,* she thought. *That's the one. That's the one I am. He knows.*

Adolin relaxed, and for the first time she noticed how ragged his clothing was. She raised her safehand to her lips. "Adolin, are you all right?"

"Oh!" He looked down at his ripped uniform and scraped hands. "It's not as bad as it looks, Shallan. Most of the blood isn't mine. Well, I mean, I guess it is. But I'm feeling better."

She cupped his face with her freehand. "You'd better not have gotten too many scars. I'm expecting you to remain pretty, I'll have you know."

"I'm barely hurt, Shallan. Renarin got to me."

"Then it's all right if I do this?" Shallan asked, hugging him. He responded, pulling her tight. He smelled of sweat and blood—not the gentlest of scents, but this was *him* and she was *Shallan*.

"How are you?" he asked. "*Really?*"

"Tired," she whispered.

"You want a palanquin . . ."

"Everyone keeps asking that."

"I could carry you up," he said, then pulled back and grinned. "Course, you're a Radiant. So maybe you could carry me instead? I've already been all the way up to the top of the city and back down once. . . ."

Shallan smiled, until farther down the wall a glowing figure in blue landed on the battlements. Kaladin settled down, blue eyes shining, flanked by Rock and Lopen. Soldiers all along the walk turned toward him. Even in a battle with multiple Knights Radiant, there was something about the way Kaladin flew, the way he moved.

Veil immediately took over. She pulled herself to her feet as Kaladin strode along the wall to meet with Dalinar. *What happened to his boots?*

"Shallan?" Adolin asked.

"A palanquin sounds *great*," Veil said. "Thanks."

Adolin blushed, then nodded and strode toward one of the stairwells down into the city.

"Mmm . . ." Pattern said. "I'm confused."

"We need to approach this from a logical position," Radiant said. "We've been dancing around a decision for months, ever since those days we spent in the chasms with Stormblessed. I've begun to consider that a relationship between two Knights Radiant is likely to accomplish a more equitable union."

"Also," Veil added, "look at those *eyes*. Simmering with barely bridled emotion." She walked toward him, grinning.

Then slowed.

Adolin knows me.

What was she doing?

She shoved Radiant and Veil aside, and when they resisted, she stuffed them into the back part of her brain. They were not her. She was occasionally them. But they were *not her*.

Kaladin hesitated on the wall walk, but Shallan just gave him a wave, then went the other way, tired—but determined.

⁂

Venli stood by the railing of a fleeing ship.

The Fused boasted from within the captain's cabin. They talked about next time, promising what they'd do and how they'd win. They spoke of past victories, and subtly hinted at why they'd failed. Too few of them had awakened so far, and those who had awakened were unaccustomed to having physical bodies.

What a strange way to treat a failure. She attuned Appreciation anyway. An old rhythm. She loved being able to hear those again at will—she could attune either old or new, and could make her eyes red, except when she drew in Stormlight. Timbre had granted this by capturing the Voidspren within her.

This meant she could hide it from the Fused. From Odium. She stepped away from the cabin door and walked along the side of the ship, which surged through the water, heading back toward Marat.

"This bond was supposed to be impossible," she whispered to Timbre.

Timbre pulsed to Peace.

"I'm happy too," Venli whispered. "But why me? Why not one of the humans?"

Timbre pulsed to Irritation, then the Lost.

"That many? I had no idea the human betrayal had cost so many of your people's lives. And your own grandfather?"

Irritation again.

"I'm not sure how much I trust the humans either. Eshonai did though."

Nearby, sailors worked on the rigging, speaking softly in Thaylen. Parshmen, yes, but also Thaylens. "I don't know, Vldgen," one said. "Yeah, some of them weren't so bad. But what they did to us . . ."

"Does that mean we have to kill them?" his companion asked. She caught a tossed rope. "It doesn't seem right."

"They took our culture, Vldgen," the malen said. "They blustering took our *entire identity*. And they'll never let a bunch of parshmen remain free. Watch. They'll come for us."

"I'll fight if they do," Vldgen said. "But . . . I don't know. Can't we simply enjoy being able to *think*? Being able to *exist*?" She shook her head, lashing a rope tight. "I just wish I knew who we were."

Timbre pulsed to Praise.

"The listeners?" Venli whispered to the spren. "We didn't do that good a job of resisting Odium. As soon as we got a *hint* of power, we came running back to him." That had been her fault. She had driven them toward new information, new powers. She'd always hungered for it. Something new.

Timbre pulsed to Consolation, but then it blended, changing once again to Resolve.

Venli hummed the same transformation.

Something new.

But also something old.

She walked to the two sailors. They immediately stood at attention, saluting her as the only Regal on the ship, holding a form of power. "I know who you were," she said to the two of them.

"You . . . you do?" the femalen asked.

"Yes." Venli pointed. "Keep working, and let me tell you of the listeners."

* * *

I think you did a great job, Szeth, the sword said from Szeth's hand as they rose above Thaylen City. *You didn't destroy many of them, yes, but you just need some more practice!*

"Thank you, sword-nimi," he said, reaching Nin. The Herald floated with toes pointed downward, hands clasped behind his back, watching the disappearing ships of the parshmen in the distance.

"I am sorry, master," Szeth finally said. "I have angered you."

"I am not your master," Nin said. "And you have not angered me. Why would I be displeased?"

"You have determined that the parshmen are the true owners of this land, and that the Skybreakers should follow their laws."

"The very reason that we swear to something external is because we acknowledge that our own judgment is flawed. *My* judgment is flawed." He narrowed his eyes. "I used to be able to feel, Szeth-son-Neturo. I used to have compassion. I can remember those days, before . . ."

"The torture?" Szeth asked.

He nodded. "Centuries spent on Braize—the place you call Damnation—stole my ability to feel. We each cope somehow, but only Ishar survived with his mind intact. Regardless, you are certain you wish to follow a man with your oath?"

"It is not as perfect as the law, I know," Szeth said. "But it feels right."

"The law is made by men, so it is not perfect either. It is not perfection we seek, for perfection is impossible. It is instead consistency. You have said the Words?"

"Not yet. I swear to follow the will of Dalinar Kholin. This is my oath." At the Words, snow crystallized around him in the air, then fluttered down. He felt a surge of something. Approval? From the hidden spren who only rarely showed itself to him, even still.

"I believe that your Words have been accepted. Have you chosen your quest for the next Ideal?"

"I will cleanse the Shin of their false leaders, so long as Dalinar Kholin agrees."

"We shall see. You may find him a harsh master."

"He is a good man, Nin-son-God."

"That is precisely why." Nin saluted him quietly, then began to move away through the air. He shook his head when Szeth followed, and then he pointed. "You must protect the man you once tried to kill, Szeth-son-Neturo."

"What if we meet on the battlefield?"

"Then we will both fight with confidence, knowing that we obey the precepts of our oaths. Farewell, Szeth-son-Neturo. I will visit you again to oversee your training in our second art, the Surge of Division. You may access that now, but take care. It is dangerous."

He left Szeth alone in the sky, holding a sword that hummed happily to itself, then confided that it had never really liked Nin in the first place.

⁖

Shallan had found that no matter how bad things got, *someone* would be making tea.

Today it was Teshav, and Shallan gratefully took a cup, then peeked through the command post at the top of the city, still looking for Adolin. Now that she was moving, she found she could ignore her fatigue. Momentum could be a powerful thing.

Adolin wasn't here, though one of the runner girls had seen him a short time ago, so Shallan was on the right track. She walked back to the main thoroughfare, passing men carrying stretchers full of the wounded. Otherwise, the streets were mostly empty. People had been sent to stormshelters or homes as Queen Fen's soldiers gathered gemstones from the reserve, rounded up Amaram's troops, and made certain there was no looting.

Shallan idled in the mouth of an alleyway. The tea was bitter, but good. Knowing Teshav, it probably had something in it to keep her on her feet and alert—scribes always knew the best teas for that.

She watched the people for a time, then glanced upward as Kaladin landed on a rooftop nearby. He was next up for working the Oathgate, taking over from Renarin.

The Windrunner stood like a sentinel, surveying the city. Was that going to become a *thing* for him? Always standing around up high somewhere? She'd seen how envious he'd been as he'd watched those Fused, with their flowing robes, moving like the winds.

Shallan glanced toward the thoroughfare as she heard a familiar voice. Adolin hiked down the street, led by the messenger girl, who pointed him toward Shallan. Finally. The messenger girl bowed, then scampered off back toward the command post.

Adolin stepped over and ran his hand through his mop of hair, blond and black. It looked fantastic, despite his ripped uniform and scraped face. Perhaps that was the advantage to persistently messy hair—he managed to make it go with anything. Though she had no idea how he'd gotten so much dust on his uniform. Had he fought a bag of sand?

She pulled him against her in the mouth of the alleyway, then twisted and put his arm around her shoulders. "Where did you get off to?"

"Father asked me to check on each of the Thaylen Shardbearers and report. I left you a palanquin."

"Thank you," she said. "I've been surveying the aftermath of the fight. I think we did a good job. Only half the city destroyed—which is quite the step up from our work in Kholinar. If we keep this up, some people might actually live through the end of the world."

He grunted. "You seem in higher spirits than earlier."

"Teshav fed me tea," she said. "I'll probably be bouncing off the clouds soon. Don't get me laughing. I sound like an axehound puppy when I'm hyper."

"Shallan . . ." he said.

She twisted up to look at his eyes, then followed his gaze. Above, Kaladin rose into the air to inspect something that they couldn't see.

"I didn't mean to abandon you earlier," Shallan said. "I'm sorry. I should never have let you run off."

He took a deep breath, then removed his arm from her shoulders.

I've screwed it up! Shallan thought immediately. *Stormfather. I've gone and ruined it.*

"I've decided," Adolin said, "to step back."

"Adolin, I didn't mean to—"

"I have to say this, Shallan. Please." He stood up tall, stiff. "I'm going to let him have you."

She blinked. "*Let* him *have* me."

"I'm holding you back," Adolin said. "I see the way you two look at each other. I don't want you to keep forcing yourself to spend time with me because you feel sorry for me."

Storms. Now he's *trying to ruin it!* "No," Shallan said. "First off, you don't get to treat me like some kind of prize. You don't decide who *gets* me."

"I'm not trying to . . ." He took another deep breath. "Look, this is hard for me, Shallan. I'm trying to do the right thing. Don't make it harder."

"I don't get a choice?"

"You've made your choice. I see how you look at him."

"I'm an *artist*, Adolin. I appreciate a nice picture when I see one. Doesn't mean I want to pull it off the hook and go get intimate."

Kaladin landed on a roof in the distance, still looking the other way. Adolin waved toward him. "Shallan. He can *literally* fly."

"Oh? And is that what women are supposed to seek in a mate? Is it in the *Polite Lady's Handbook to Courtship and Family*? The Bekenah edition, maybe? 'Ladies, you can't *possibly* marry a man if he can't fly.' Never mind if the other option is as handsome as sin, kind to everyone he meets regardless of their station, passionate about his art, and genuinely humble in the weirdest, most confident way. Never mind if he actually seems to get you, and remarkably listens to your problems, encouraging you to be you—not to hide yourself away. Never mind if being *near* him makes you want to rip his shirt off and push him into the nearest alleyway, then kiss him until he can't breathe anymore. If he can't *fly*, then well, you just have to call it off!"

She paused for breath, gasping.

"And . . ." Adolin said. "That guy is . . . me?"

"You are such a fool." She grabbed his ripped coat and pulled him into a kiss, passionspren crystallizing in the air around them. The warmth of the kiss did more for her than the tea ever could. It made her bubble and boil inside. Stormlight was nice, but this . . . *this* was an energy that made it dun by comparison.

Storms, she loved this man.

When she let him out of the kiss, he grabbed her and pulled her close, breathing heavily.

"Are you . . . are you sure?" he asked. "I just . . . Don't glare at me, Shallan. I have to say this. The world is full of gods and Heralds now, and you're one of them. I'm practically a nobody. I'm not used to that feeling."

"Then it's probably the best thing that's ever happened to you, Adolin Kholin. Well. Except for *me*." She snuggled against him. "I will admit to you, in the interest of full honesty, that Veil *did* have a tendency to fawn over Kaladin Stormblessed. She has terrible taste in men, and I've convinced her to fall in line."

"That's worrisome, Shallan."

"I won't let her act on it. I promise."

"I didn't mean that," Adolin said. "I meant . . . you, Shallan. Becoming

other people."

"We're all different people at different times. Remember?"

"Not the same way as you."

"I know," she said. "But I . . . I think I've stopped leaking into new personas. Three for now." She turned around, smiling at him, his hands still around her waist. "How do you like that, though? Three betrotheds instead of one. Some men drool over the idea of such debauchery. If you wanted, I could be practically anyone."

"But that's the thing, Shallan. I don't want anyone. I want *you.*"

"That might be the hardest one. But I think I can do it, Adolin. With some help, maybe?"

He grinned that goofy grin of his. Storms, how could his hair look so good with *gravel* in it? "So . . ." he said. "You mentioned something about kissing me until I can't breathe. But here I am, not even winded—"

He cut off as she kissed him again.

⁘

Kaladin settled down on the edge of a roof, high at the top of Thaylen City.

This poor city. First the Everstorm, and its subsequent returns. The Thaylens had only just started figuring out how to rebuild, and now had to deal with more smashed buildings leading up to the corpse of the thunderclast, which lay like a toppled statue.

We can win, he thought. *But each victory scars us a little more.*

In his hand he rubbed a small stone with his thumb. Down below, in an alleyway off the main thoroughfare, a woman with flowing red hair kissed a man in a ragged and ripped uniform. Some people could celebrate despite the scars. Kaladin accepted that. He merely wished he knew how they did it.

"Kaladin?" Syl said. She wove around him as a ribbon of light. "Don't feel bad. The Words have to come in their own time. You'll be all right."

"I always am."

He squinted down at Shallan and Adolin, and found that he couldn't be bitter. He didn't feel resignation either. Instead he felt . . . agreement?

"Oh, them," Syl said. "Well, *I* know that you don't back down from fights. You've lost the round, but—"

"No," he said. "Her choice is made. You can see it."

"I can?"

"You should be able to." He rubbed his finger on the rock. "I don't think I loved her, Syl. I felt . . . something. A lightening of my burdens when I was near her. She reminds me of someone."

"Who?"

He opened his palm, and she landed on it, forming into the shape of a young woman with flowing hair and dress. She bent down, inspecting the rock in his palm, cooing over it. Syl could still be shockingly innocent—wide-eyed and excited about the world.

"That's a nice rock," she said, completely serious.

"Thank you."

"Where did you get it?"

"I found it on the battlefield below. If you get it wet it changes colors. It looks brown, but with a little water, you can see the white, black, and grey."

"Oooooh."

He let her inspect it for a moment more. "It's true, then?" he finally said. "About the parshmen. That this was their land, their *world*, before we arrived? That . . . that *we* were the Voidbringers?"

She nodded. "Odium is the void, Kaladin. He draws in emotion, and doesn't let it go. You . . . you brought him with you. I wasn't alive then, but I know this truth. He was your first god, before you turned to Honor."

Kaladin exhaled slowly, closing his eyes.

The men of Bridge Four were having trouble with this idea. As well they should. Others in the military didn't care, but his men . . . they knew.

You could protect your home. You could kill to defend the people inside. But what if you'd stolen that house in the first place? What if the people you killed were only trying to get back what was rightfully theirs?

Reports from Alethkar said that the parshman armies were pushing north, that Alethi armies in the area had moved into Herdaz. What would happen to Hearthstone? His family? Surely in the face of the invasion, he could convince his father to move to Urithiru. But what then?

It got so complicated. Humans had lived upon this land for thousands of years. Could anyone really be expected to let go because of what ancient people had done, no matter how dishonorable their actions?

Who did he fight? Who did he protect?

Defender? Invader?

Honorable knight? Hired thug?

"The Recreance," he said to Syl. "I always imagined it as a single event. A day the knights all gave up their Shards, like in Dalinar's vision. But I don't think it actually happened like that."

"Then . . . how?" Syl asked.

"Like this," Kaladin said. He squinted, watching the light of a setting sun play on the ocean. "They found out something they couldn't ignore. Eventually they had to face it."

"They made the wrong choice."

Kaladin pocketed the stone. "The oaths are about perception, Syl. You confirmed that. The only thing that matters is whether or not we are confident that we're obeying our principles. If we lose that confidence, then dropping the armor and weapons is only a formality."

"Kal—"

"I'm not going to do the same," he said. "I'd like to think that the past of Bridge Four will make us a little more pragmatic than those ancient Radiants. We won't abandon you. But finding out what we *will* do might end up being messy."

Kaladin stepped off the building, then Lashed himself so he soared in a wide arc over the city. He landed on a rooftop where most of Bridge Four was sharing a meal of flatbread with kuma—crushed lavis and spices. They could have demanded something far better than travel rations, but they didn't seem to realize it.

Teft stood apart, glowing softly. Kaladin waved to the other men, then walked up to join Teft at the edge of the rooftop, staring out over the ocean beyond.

"Almost time to get the men back to work," Teft noted. "King Taravangian wants us to fly wounded up from the triage stations to the Oathgate. The men wanted a break for food, not that they storming did much. You'd already won this battle when we got here, Kal."

"I'd be dead if you hadn't activated the Oathgate," Kaladin said softly. "Somehow I knew that you would, Teft. I knew you'd come for me."

"Knew better than I did, then." Teft heaved a breath.

Kaladin rested his hand on Teft's shoulder. "I know how it feels."

"Aye," Teft said. "I suppose you do. But isn't it supposed to feel better? The longing for my moss is still storming there."

"It doesn't change us, Teft. We're still who we are."

"Damnation."

Kaladin looked back at the others. Lopen was currently trying to impress Lyn and Laran with a story about how he lost his arm. It was the seventh rendition Kaladin had heard, each a little different.

Beard . . . Kaladin thought, feeling the loss like a stab to his side. *He and Lopen would have gotten along well.*

"It doesn't get easier, Teft," he said. "It gets harder, I think, the more you learn about the Words. Fortunately, you *do* get help. You were mine when I needed it. I'll be yours."

Teft nodded, but then pointed. "What about him?"

For the first time, Kaladin realized that Rock wasn't with the rest of the team. The large Horneater was sitting—Stormlight extinguished—on the steps of one of the temples down below. Shardbow across his lap. Head bowed. He obviously considered what he'd done to be an oath broken, despite it having saved Kaladin's life.

"We lift the bridge together, Teft," Kaladin said. "And we carry it."

⁕

Dalinar refused to leave Thaylen City immediately—but in compromise with Navani, he agreed to return to his villa in the Royal Ward and rest. On his way, he stopped in the temple of Talenelat—which had been cleared of people to make space for the generals to meet.

Those hadn't arrived yet, so he had a short time to himself, looking at the reliefs dedicated to the Herald. He knew that he should go up and sleep, at least until the Azish ambassador arrived. But something about those images of Talenelat'Elin, standing tall against overwhelming forces . . .

Did he ever have to fight humans in one of these last stands? Dalinar thought. *Worse, did he ever wonder about what he had done? What we all had done, in taking this world?*

Dalinar was still standing there when a frail figure darkened the doorway to the temple. "I brought my surgeons," Taravangian said, voice echoing in the large stone chamber. "They have already begun helping with the city's wounded."

"Thank you," Dalinar said.

Taravangian didn't enter. He stood, waiting, until Dalinar sighed softly. "You abandoned me," he said. "You abandoned this city."

"I assumed that you were going to fall," Taravangian said, "and so positioned myself in a way that I could seize control of the coalition."

Dalinar started. He turned toward the old man, who stood silhouetted in the doorway. "You *what*?"

"I assumed that the only way for the coalition to recover from your mistakes was for me to take command. I could not stand with you, my friend. For the good of Roshar, I stepped away."

Even after their discussions together—even *knowing* how Taravangian viewed his obligations—Dalinar was shocked. This was brutal, utilitarian politics.

Taravangian finally stepped into the chamber, trailing a wizened hand along one of the wall reliefs. He joined Dalinar, and together they studied a carving of a powerful man, standing tall between two pillars of stone— barring the way between monsters and men.

"You . . . didn't become king of Jah Keved by accident, did you?" Dalinar asked.

Taravangian shook his head. It seemed obvious to Dalinar now. Taravangian was easy to dismiss when you assumed he was slow of thought. But once you knew the truth, other mysteries began to fit into place.

"How?" Dalinar asked.

"There's a woman at Kharbranth," he said. "She goes by the name Dova, but we think she is Battah'Elin. A Herald. She told us the Desolation was approaching." He looked to Dalinar. "I had nothing to do with the death of your brother. But once I heard of what incredible things the assassin did, I sought him out. Years later, I located him, and gave him specific instructions. . . ."

⁘

Moash stepped down out of the Kholinar palace into the shadows of a night that had seemed far too long in coming.

People clogged the palace gardens—humans who had been cast out of homes to make way for parshmen. Some of these refugees had strung tarps between benches of shalebark, creating very low tents only a couple of feet tall. Lifespren bobbed among them and the garden plants.

Moash's target was a particular man who sat giggling in the darkness near the back of the gardens. A madman with eye color lost to the night.

"Have you seen me?" the man asked as Moash knelt.

"No," Moash said, then rammed the strange golden knife into the man's stomach. The man took it with a quiet grunt, smiled a silly smile, then closed his eyes.

"Were you really one of them?" Moash asked. "Herald of the Almighty?"

"Was, was, was . . ." The man started to tremble violently, his eyes opening wide. "Was . . . no. No, what is this death? *What is this death!*"

Huddled forms stirred, and some of the wiser ones scuttled away.

"It's taking me!" the man screamed, then looked down at the knife in Moash's hand. "What *is* that?"

The man trembled for a moment more, then jerked once, going motionless. When Moash pulled the yellow-white knife free, it trailed dark smoke and left a blackened wound. The large sapphire at the pommel took on a subdued glow.

Moash glanced over his shoulder toward the Fused hanging in the night sky behind the palace. This murder seemed a thing that they dared not do themselves. Why? What did they fear?

Moash held the knife aloft toward them, but there were no cheers. Nothing accompanied the act but a few muttered words from people trying to sleep. These broken slaves were the only other witnesses to this moment.

The final death of Jezrien. Yaezir. Jezerezeh'Elin, king of Heralds. A figure known in myth and lore as the greatest human who had ever lived.

◆◆◆

Lopen leaped behind a rock, then grinned, spotting the little spren in the shape of a leaf tucked there. "Found you, naco."

Rua transformed into the shape of a petulant young boy, maybe nine or ten years old. Rua was his name, but "naco" was—of course—what Lopen called him.

Rua zipped into the air as a ribbon of light. Bridge Four stood near some tents at the bottom of Thaylen City, in the Low Ward, right in the shadow of the walls. Here, a massive surgeons' station was caring for the wounded.

"Lopen!" Teft called. "Stop being crazy and get over here to help."

"I'm not crazy," Lopen yelled back. "Sure, I'm the *least* crazy of this whole lot! And you all know it!"

Teft sighed, then waved to Peet and Leyten. Together, they carefully Lashed a large platform—easily twenty feet square—into the air. It was filled with recuperating wounded. The three bridgemen flew with it toward the upper part of the city.

Rua zipped onto Lopen's shoulder and formed into the shape of a young man, then thrust a hand toward the bridgemen and tried the gesture that Lopen had taught him.

"Nice," Lopen said. "But wrong finger. Nope! Not that one either. Naco, that's your foot."

The spren turned the gesture toward Lopen.

"That's it," Lopen said. "You can thank me, naco, for inspiring this great advance in your learning. People—and little things made out of nothing too, sure—are often inspired near the Lopen."

He turned and strolled into a tent of wounded, the far wall of which was tied right onto a nice, shiny bronze portion of wall. Lopen hoped the Thaylens would appreciate how nice it was. Who had a metal wall? Lopen would put one on his palace when he built it. Thaylens were strange though. What else could you say about a people who liked it so far south, in the cold? The local language was practically chattering teeth.

This tent of wounded was filled with the people who had been deemed too healthy to deserve Renarin's or Lift's healing, but still needed a surgeon's care. They weren't dying, sure, *right now*. Maybe later. But everyone was dying maybe later, so it was probably all right to ignore them for someone whose guts got misplaced.

The moans and whimpers indicated that they found not dying immediately to be a small comfort. The ardents did what they could, but most of the real surgeons were set up higher in the city. Taravangian's forces had finally decided to join the battle, now that all the easy stuff—like dying, which really didn't take much skill—was through.

Lopen fetched his pack, then passed Dru—who was folding freshly boiled bandages. Even after all these centuries, sure, they did what the Heralds had told them. Boiling stuff killed rotspren.

Lopen patted Dru on the shoulder. The slender Alethi man looked up and nodded toward Lopen, showing reddened eyes. Loving a soldier was not easy, and now that Kaladin had returned from Alethkar alone . . .

Lopen moved on, and eventually settled down beside a wounded man in a cot. Thaylen, with drooping eyebrows and a bandage around his head. He stared straight ahead, not blinking.

"Want to see a trick?" Lopen asked the soldier.

The man shrugged.

Lopen lifted his foot up and put the boot on the man's cot. The laces had come undone, and Lopen—one hand behind his back—deftly grabbed the strings and looped them around his hand, twisted them, then pulled them tight, using his other foot to hold one end. He wound up with an excellent knot with a nice bow. It was even symmetrical. Maybe he could get an ardent to write a poem about it.

The soldier gave no reaction. Lopen settled back, pulling over his pack, which clinked softly. "Don't look like that. It's not the end of the world."

The soldier cocked his head.

"Well, sure. *Technically* it might be. But for the end of the world, it's not so bad, right? I figured that when everything ended, we'd sink into a noxious bath of pus and doom, breathing in agony as the air around us—sure—became molten, and we screamed a final burning scream, relishing the memories of the last time a woman loved us." Lopen tapped the man's cot. "Don't know about you, moolie, but my lungs aren't burning. The air doesn't seem very molten. Considering how bad this could have gone, you've got a lot to be thankful for. Remember that."

"I . . ." The man blinked.

"I meant, remember those exact words. That's the phrase to tell the woman you're seeing. Helps a ton." He fished in his pack and pulled out a bottle of Thaylen lavis beer he'd salvaged. Rua stopped zipping around the top of the tent long enough to float down and inspect it.

"Want to see a trick?" Lopen asked.

"A . . . another?" the man asked.

"Normally, I'd pop the cap off with one of my fingernails. I have great Herdazian ones, extra hard. You have weaker ones like most people. So here's the trick."

Lopen rolled up his trouser leg with one hand. He pressed the bottle—top first—to his leg and then, with a quick flick, twisted off the cap. He raised the bottle toward the man.

The man reached for it with the bandaged stump of his right arm, which ended above the elbow. He looked at it, grimaced, then reached with the left hand instead.

"If you need any jokes," Lopen said, "I've got a few I can't use anymore."

The soldier drank quietly, eyes flicking to the front of the tent, where Kaladin had entered, glowing softly, speaking with some of the surgeons. Knowing Kaladin, he was probably telling them how to do their jobs.

"You're one of them," the soldier said. "Radiant."

"Sure," Lopen said. "But not *really* one of them. I'm trying to figure out the next step."

"Next step?"

"I've got the flying," Lopen said, "and the spren. But I don't know if I'm good at saving people yet."

The man looked at his drink. "I . . . think you might be doing just fine."

"That's a beer, not a person. Don't get those mixed up. Very embarrassing, but I won't tell."

"How . . ." the man said. "How does one join up? They say . . . they say it heals you. . . ."

"Sure, it heals everything except what's in the rockbud on the end of your neck. Which is great for me. I'm the only sane one in this group. That might be a problem."

"Why?"

"They say you have to be broken," Lopen said, glancing toward his spren, who made a few loops of excitement, then shot off to hide again. Lopen would need to go looking for the little guy—he did enjoy the game. "You know that tall woman, the king's sister? The chortana with the glare that could break a Shardblade? She says that the power has to get into your soul somehow. So I've been trying to cry a lot, and moan about my life being so terrible, but I think the Stormfather knows I'm lying. Hard to act sad when you're the Lopen."

"I might be broken," the man said softly.

"Good, good! We don't have a Thaylen yet, and lately it looks like we're trying to collect one of everything. We even have a parshman!"

"I just ask?" the man said, then took a drink.

"Sure. Ask. Follow us around. Worked for Lyn. But you have to say the Words."

"Words?"

"'Life before death, strength before weakness, journey before pancakes.'

That's the easy one. The hard one is, 'I will protect those who cannot protect themselves,' and—"

A sudden flash of coldness struck Lopen, and the gemstones in the room flickered, then went out. A symbol crystallized in frost on the stones around Lopen, vanishing under the cots. The ancient symbol of the Windrunners.

"What?" Lopen stood up. "*What? Now?*"

He heard a far-off rumbling, like thunder.

"NOW?" Lopen said, shaking a fist at the sky. "I was saving that for a dramatic moment, you penhito! Why didn't you listen earlier? We were, sure, all about to die and things!"

He got a distinct, very distant impression.

YOU WEREN'T QUITE READY.

"Storm you!" Lopen made a double obscene gesture toward the sky— something he'd been waiting a long time to use properly for the first time. Rua joined him, making the same gesture, then grew two *extra* arms to give it more weight.

"Nice," Lopen said. "Hey gancho! I'm a full Knight Radiant now, so you can start complimenting me." Kaladin didn't seem to have even noticed. "Just a moment," Lopen said to the one-armed soldier, then stalked over to where Kaladin was speaking with a runner.

"You're sure?" Kaladin said to the scribe. "Does Dalinar know about this?"

"He sent me, sir," the woman said. "Here's a map with the location the spanreed listed."

"Gancho," Lopen said. "Hey, did you—"

"Congratulations, Lopen, good job. You're second-in-command after Teft until I return."

Kaladin burst from the tent and Lashed himself to the sky, streaking away, the tent's front flaps rustling in the wind of his passing.

Lopen put his hands on his hips. Rua landed on his head, then made a little squeal of angry delight while proffering toward Kaladin a double rude gesture.

"Don't wear it out, naco," Lopen said.

. .
. .

"Come on," Ash said, holding Taln's hand, pulling him up the last few steps.

He stared at her dully.

"Taln," she whispered. "*Please.*"

The last glimmers of his lucidity had faded. Once, nothing would have kept him from the battlefield when other men died. Today, he had hidden and whimpered during the fighting. Now he followed her like a simpleton.

Talenel'Elin had broken like the rest of them.

Ishar, she thought. *Ishar will know what to do.* She fought down the tears—watching him fade had been like watching the sun go out. All these years, she'd hoped that maybe . . . maybe . . .

What? That he'd be able to redeem them?

Someone nearby cursed by her name, and she wanted to slap him. *Don't swear by us. Don't paint pictures of us. Don't worship at our statues.* She'd stamp it all out. She would ruin every depiction. She . . .

Ash breathed in and out, then pulled Taln by the hand again, getting him into line with the other refugees fleeing the city. Only foreigners were allowed out right now, to prevent the Oathgate from being overworked. She'd get back to Azir, where their skin tones wouldn't stand out.

What a gift you gave them! he'd said. *Time to recover, for once, between Desolations. Time to progress . . .*

Oh, Taln. Couldn't he have just hated her? Couldn't he have let her—

Ash stopped in place as something *ripped* inside of her.

Oh God. Oh, Adonalsium!

What was that? *What was that?*

Taln whimpered and collapsed, a puppet with cut strings. Ash stumbled, then sank to her knees. She wrapped her arms around herself, trembling. It wasn't pain. It was something far, far worse. A loss, a hole inside of her, a piece of her soul being excised.

"Miss?" a soldier asked, jogging up. "Miss, are you all right? Hey, someone get one of the healers! Miss, what's wrong?"

"They . . . they killed him somehow. . . ."

"Who?"

She looked up at the man, tears blurring her vision. This wasn't like their other deaths. This was something horrible. She couldn't feel him at all.

They'd done something to Jezrien's soul.

"My father," she said, "is dead."

They caused a stir in the refugees, and someone detached themselves from the group of scribes up ahead. A woman in deep violet. The Blackthorn's niece. She looked at Ash, then at Taln, then at a piece of paper she'd been carrying. It contained shockingly accurate sketches of the two of them. Not as they were presented in iconography, but real sketches. Who . . . why?

That's his drawing style, a part of Ash noted. *Why has Midius been giving away pictures of us?*

The ripping sensation finally ended. So abruptly that—for the first time in thousands of years—Ash fell unconscious.

122

A DEBT REPAID

Yes, I began my journey alone, and I ended it alone.
But that does not mean that I walked alone.

—From *The Way of Kings*, postscript

Kaladin flew across the churning ocean. Dalinar had been able to summon the strength to overcharge him with Stormlight, though it was obviously exhausting to do so.

Kaladin had used up that charge getting to Kharbranth, where he'd stopped for a night's sleep. Even Stormlight could only push the body so far. After a long flight the next day, he'd reached the Tarat Sea.

He flew now using gemstones requisitioned from the royal treasury in Kharbranth. Smoke rose from several places along the coast of Alethkar, where cities still resisted the parshman invasion. Kaladin's map fluttered in his fingers, and he watched the coast for the rock formation the scribe had sketched for him.

By the time he spotted it, he worried he wouldn't have enough Stormlight left to make it back to safety. He dropped there and continued on foot, per the instructions, crossing a cold and rocky land that reminded him of the Shattered Plains.

Along a dried-out river, he found a little group of refugees huddled by a cavern in the stone. A very small fire laced the air with smoke, and lit ten people in brown cloaks. Nondescript, like many others he'd passed during his search. The only distinctive feature was a small symbol they'd painted on an old tarp pinned up between two poles at the front of the camp.

The symbol of Bridge Four.

Two of the figures rose from the fire, pulling back hoods. Two men: one tall and lanky, the other short and scrappy, silver-haired at the temples.

Drehy and Skar.

They gave Kaladin a pair of sharp salutes. Drehy had old cuts on his face and Skar looked like he hadn't slept in weeks. They'd had to cover their foreheads in ash to hide their tattoos, an act that wouldn't have worked in simpler times. It basically marked them as runaway slaves.

Syl let out a laugh of pure delight, zipping over to them—and from the way they reacted, it seemed she'd let them see her. Behind them, Shallan's three servants emerged from their cloaks. Kaladin didn't know the other people, but one of them would be the merchant they'd found—a man who still possessed a spanreed.

"Kal," Skar said as Kaladin slapped him on the back. "There's something we didn't mention by spanreed."

Kaladin frowned as Drehy returned to the fire and picked up one of the figures there. A child? In rags. Yes, a frightened little boy, maybe three or four years old, lips chapped, eyes haunted.

Elhokar's son.

"We protect those," Drehy said, "who cannot protect themselves."

⁜

Taravangian was unable to solve the first page of the day's puzzles.

Dukar, the stormwarden, took the paper and looked it over. He shook his head. Stupid today.

Taravangian rested back against his seat in Urithiru. He seemed to be stupid more and more often. Perhaps it was his perception.

Eight days had passed since the Battle of Thaylen Field. He wasn't certain Dalinar would ever trust him again, but giving him some truth had been a calculated risk. For now, Taravangian was still part of the coalition. It was good, even if . . . It . . .

Storms. Trying to think through the fuzz in his brain was . . . bothersome.

"He is weak of mind today," Dukar announced to Mrall, Taravangian's thick-armed bodyguard. "He can interact, but should not make important policy decisions. We cannot trust his interpretation of the Diagram."

"Vargo?" Adrotagia asked. "How would you like to spend the day? In the Veden gardens, perhaps?"

Taravangian opened his eyes and looked to his faithful friends. Dukar and Mrall. Adrotagia, who looked so old now. Did she feel as he did, shocked every time she looked in the mirror, wondering where the days had gone? When they'd been young, they'd wanted to conquer the world.

Or save it.

"Your Majesty?" Adrotagia asked.

Oh. Right. His mind did wander sometimes. "We cannot do anything until the Everstorm passes. Correct?"

Adrotagia nodded, proffering her calculations. "It is nearly here." People had spent the eight days since the battle vainly hoping that the Everstorm had blown itself out for good. "It's not as strong as it was during its previous cycle, but it *is* coming. It has already reached Azir, and should hit Urithiru within the hour."

"Then let us wait."

Adrotagia gave him a few letters that had come from his grandchildren in Kharbranth. He could read, even when he was stupid, though it took him longer to make out some of the words. Gvori had been accepted to study at the School of Storms, which had legacy access to the Palanaeum for all scholars. Karavaniga, the middle granddaughter, had been accepted for wardship, and had sketched him a picture of the three of them. Little Ruli grinned a gap-toothed smile in the center. She had drawn him a picture of flowers.

Taravangian touched the tears on his cheek as he finished reading. None of the three knew anything of the Diagram, and he was determined to keep it that way.

Adrotagia and Dukar conversed quietly in the corner of the room, confused by portions of the Diagram. They ignored Maben, the room servant, who felt Taravangian's forehead, as he'd been coughing lately.

What fools we can be, Taravangian said, resting fingers on the picture of flowers. *We never know as much as we think. Perhaps in that, the smart me has always been the more stupid one.*

He knew the Everstorm's arrival only by a *ding* from Adrotagia's clock—a magnificently small piece, gifted by Navani Kholin.

"The Diagram has been wrong too often," Mrall said to Adrotagia and Dukar. "It predicted Dalinar Kholin would fall, if pressured, and become the enemy's champion."

"Perhaps Graves was right," Dukar said, rubbing his hands together nervously. He glanced toward the window, shuttered despite the fact that the Everstorm didn't reach this high. "The Blackthorn could have been made an ally. This is what the Diagram meant."

"No," Taravangian said. "That is not what it meant."

They looked to him. "Vargo?" Adrotagia asked.

He tried to find the argument to explain himself, but it was like trying to hold a cupful of oil in his fist.

"We're in a dangerous position," Dukar said. "His Majesty revealed too much to Dalinar. We will be watched now."

. . . the . . . window . . .

"Dalinar doesn't know of the Diagram," Adrotagia countered. "Or that we brought the singers to Urithiru. He only knows that Kharbranth controlled the assassin—and thinks that the Herald's insanity prompted us. We're still well positioned."

Open . . . the . . . window. . . . None of the others heard the voice.

"The Diagram is growing too flawed," Mrall insisted. Though he was no scholar, he was a full participant in their scheme. "We've deviated too much from its promises. Our plans need to change."

"It's too late," Adrotagia said. "The confrontation will happen soon."

OPEN IT.

Taravangian rose from his seat, trembling. Adrotagia was right. The confrontation predicted by the Diagram would happen soon.

Sooner, even, than she thought.

"We must trust in the Diagram," Taravangian whispered, as he passed by them. "We must trust the version of myself that knew what to do. We must have faith."

Adrotagia shook her head. She didn't like it when any of them used words like "faith." He tried to remember that, and did remember it when he was smart.

Storms take you, Nightwatcher, he thought. *Odium's victory will kill you too. Couldn't you have just gifted me, and not cursed me?*

He'd asked for the capacity to save his people. He'd begged for compassion and acumen—and he'd gotten them. Just never at the same time.

He touched the window shutters.

"Vargo?" Adrotagia asked. "Letting in fresh air?"

"No, unfortunately. Something else."

He opened the shutters.

And was suddenly in a place of infinite light.

The ground beneath him glowed, and nearby, rivers flowed past, made of something molten colored gold and orange. Odium appeared to Taravangian as a twenty-foot-tall human with Shin eyes and a scepter. His beard was not wispy, like Taravangian's had been, but neither was it bushy. It almost looked like an ardent's beard.

"Now," Odium said. "Taravangian, is it?" He squinted, as if seeing Taravangian for the first time. "Little man. Why did you write to us? Why did you have your Surgebinder unlock the Oathgate, and allow our armies to attack Urithiru?"

"I wish only to serve you, Great God," Taravangian said, getting down onto his knees.

"Do not prostrate yourself," the god said, laughing. "I can see that you are no sycophant, and I will not be fooled by your attempts to seem one."

Taravangian drew in a deep breath, but remained on his knees. Today of all days, Odium finally contacted him in person? "I am not well today, Great God. I . . . um . . . am frail and of ill health. Might I meet with you again, when I am well?"

"Poor man!" Odium said.

A chair sprouted from the golden ground behind Taravangian, and Odium stepped over to him, suddenly smaller, more human sized. He gently pushed Taravangian up and into the chair. "There. Isn't that better?"

"Yes . . . thank you." Taravangian scrunched up his brow. This was not how he'd imagined this conversation.

"Now," Odium said, lightly resting his scepter on Taravangian's shoulder. "Do you think I will ever meet with you when you are feeling well?"

"I . . ."

"Do you not realize that I chose this day *specifically* because of your ailment, Taravangian? Do you really think you will *ever* be able to negotiate with me from a position of *power*?"

Taravangian licked his lips. "No."

"Good, good. We understand one another. Now, what is it you have been doing. . . ." He stepped to the side, and a golden pedestal appeared with a book on top of it. The Diagram. Odium began leafing through it, and the golden landscape changed, shifting to a bedroom with fine wooden furniture. Taravangian recognized it from the scribbled writing on every surface—from floor to ceiling, to the headboard of the bed.

"Taravangian!" Odium said. "This is *remarkable*." The walls and furniture faded, leaving behind the words, which hung in the air and started glowing with a golden light. "You did this *without* access to Fortune, or the Spiritual Realm? Truly incredible."

"Th-thank you?"

"Allow me to show you how far I see."

Golden words exploded outward from the ones Taravangian had written in the Diagram. Millions upon millions of golden letters burned into the air, extending into infinity. Each took one small element that Taravangian had written, and expanded upon it in volumes and volumes' worth of information.

Taravangian gasped as, for a moment, he saw into eternity.

Odium inspected words that Taravangian had once written on the side of a dresser. "I see. Take over Alethkar? Bold plan, bold plan. But why invite me to attack Urithiru?"

"We—"

"No need! I see. Give up Thaylen City to ensure that the Blackthorn fell, removing your opposition. An overture toward me, which worked, obviously." Odium turned to him and smiled. A knowing, confident smile.

Do you really think you will ever be able to negotiate with me from a position of power?

All that writing loomed over Taravangian, blocking off the landscape with millions of words. A smarter him would have tried to read it, but this dumber version was simply intimidated. And . . . could that be for his . . . his good? Reading that would consume him. Lose him.

My grandchildren, he thought. *The people of Kharbranth. The good people of the world.* He trembled to think of what might happen to them all.

Somebody had to make the difficult decisions. He slipped off his golden seat as Odium studied another portion of the Diagram. There. Behind where the bed had stood. A section of words that had faded from golden to black. What was that? As he drew near, Taravangian saw that the words were blacked out into eternity starting from this point on his wall. As if something had happened here. A ripple in what Odium could see . . .

At its root, a name. Renarin Kholin.

"Dalinar was not supposed to Ascend," Odium said, stepping up behind Taravangian.

"You need me," Taravangian whispered.

"I need nobody."

Taravangian looked up and there, glowing in front of him, was a set of words. A message from himself, in the past. Incredible! Had he somehow seen even this?

Thank you.

He read them out loud. "You have agreed to a battle of champions. You must withdraw to prevent this contest from occurring, and so must not meet with Dalinar Kholin again. Otherwise, he can force you to fight. This means you must let your agents do your work. You need me."

Odium stepped up, noting the words that Taravangian had read. Then he frowned at the tears on Taravangian's cheeks.

"Your Passion," Odium said, "does you credit. What is it you ask in barter?"

"Protect the people I rule."

"Dear Taravangian, do you not think I can see what you are planning?" Odium gestured toward writing where the ceiling had once stood. "You would seek to become king of all humans—and then I would need to preserve them all. No. If you help me, I will save your family. Anyone within two generations of you."

"Not enough."

"Then we have no deal."

The words started to fade all around them. Leaving him alone. Alone and stupid. He blinked tears from the corners of his eyes. "Kharbranth," he said. "Preserve only Kharbranth. You may destroy all other nations. Just leave my city. It is what I beg of you."

The world was lost, humankind doomed.

They had planned to protect so much more. But . . . he saw now how little they knew. One city before the storms. One land protected, even if the rest had to be sacrificed.

"Kharbranth," Odium said. "The city itself, and any humans who have been born into it, along with their spouses. This is whom I will spare. Do you agree to this?"

"Should we write . . . a contract?"

"Our word is the contract. I am not some spren of Honor, who seeks to obey only the strictest letter of a promise. If you have an agreement from me, I will keep it in spirit, not merely in word."

What else could he do? "I will take this deal," Taravangian whispered. "The Diagram will serve you, in exchange for the preservation of my people. But I warn you, the assassin has joined Dalinar Kholin. I was forced to reveal my association with him."

"I know," Odium said. "You are still of use. First, I will require that Honorblade which you have so cleverly stolen. And then you will find out for me what the Alethi have discovered about this tower. . . ."

* *

Shallan breathed out Stormlight, shaping an illusion possible only when she and Dalinar met. Spinning curls of mist swept out to form oceans and peaks—the entire continent of Roshar, a mass of vibrant colors.

Highprinces Aladar and Hatham waved for their generals and scribes to walk around the map, which filled the large room, hovering at about waist height. Dalinar stood in the very center of the thing, among the mountains near Urithiru, the illusion rippling and dissolving where it touched his uniform.

Adolin wrapped his arms around Shallan from behind. "It looks beautiful."

"*You* look beautiful," she replied.

"You *are* beautiful."

"Only because you're here. Without you, I fade."

Brightness Teshav stood near them, and though the woman normally maintained a stoic professionalism, Shallan thought she caught a hint of an eye roll. Well, Teshav was so old she probably forgot what it was like to *breathe* most days, let alone what it was like to love.

Adolin made Shallan giddy. With his warmth so close, she had trouble maintaining the illusion of the map. She felt silly—they'd been betrothed for months now, and she'd grown so comfortable with him. Yet something had still changed. Something incredible.

It was *finally* time. The wedding date had been set for only one week away—once the Alethi put their minds to something, they made it happen. Well, that was good. Shallan wouldn't want to go too far in a relationship without oaths, and storms, even one week was starting to sound like an eternity.

She still needed to explain some things to Adolin. Most notably, the entire mess with the Ghostbloods. She'd done too good a job of ignoring that one lately, but it would be a relief to finally have someone she could talk to about it. Veil could explain—Adolin was growing accustomed to her, though he wouldn't be intimate with her. He treated her like a drinking buddy, which was actually kind of working for both of them.

Dalinar walked through the illusion, holding his hand over Iri, Rira, and Babatharnam. "Change this part of the land to a burning gold."

It took her a moment to realize he was talking to her. Stupid Adolin and his stupid arms. Stupid strong yet gentle arms pressing against her, right beneath her breasts . . .

Right. Right. Illusion.

She did as Dalinar commanded, amused by how the scribes and generals pointedly did not look at her and Adolin. Some whispered about Adolin's Westerner heritage, which made him too public with his affection. His mixed parentage didn't seem to concern the Alethi in most cases—they were a pragmatic people, and saw his hair as a sign of other peoples conquered and brought into their superior culture. But they *would* look for excuses for why he didn't always act like they thought he should.

By reports via spanreed, most of the lesser kingdoms surrounding the Purelake had been captured by Iri—which had moved, accompanied by Fused, to secure land they'd eyed for generations. This secured for them three total Oathgates. Shallan painted those kingdoms on the map a vivid gold at Dalinar's request.

Azir and its protectorates she painted a pattern of blue and maroon, the symbol the Azish scribes had chosen for the coalition between their kingdoms. The emperor of Azir had agreed to continue negotiations; they weren't fully in the coalition. They wanted assurances that Dalinar could control his troops.

She continued shading the landscape colors at Dalinar's request. Marat and those around it went gold, as did—unfortunately—Alethkar. Lands that hadn't yet committed, like Shinovar and Tukar, she turned green. The result was a depressing view of a continent, with far too little of it colored the shades of their coalition.

The generals began discussing tactics. They wanted to invade Tu Bayla—

the large land that stretched between Jah Keved and the Purelake. The argument was that if the enemy took that, they'd divide the coalition in two. The Oathgates allowed quick access to the capitals, but many cities were far from the centers of power.

Dalinar crossed the room, forming a ripple that followed in his wake. He stopped near where Adolin and Shallan stood by Herdaz. And Alethkar.

"Show me Kholinar," he said softly.

"That's not how it works, Brightlord," she said. "I have to sketch something first, and . . ."

He touched her on the shoulder, and a thought entered her mind. Another pattern.

"This is what the Stormfather sees," Dalinar said. "It is not specific, so we won't be able to rely on the details, but it should give us an impression. If you please."

Shallan turned and waved her hand toward the wall, painting it with Stormlight. When the illusion took, the side of the room seemed to vanish— letting them look out, as if from a balcony in the sky, toward Kholinar.

The gate nearest them still hung broken, exposing ruined buildings inside—but some progress had been made toward cleaning those up. Parshmen walked the streets and patrolled the unbroken sections of wall. Fused coursed overhead, trailing long clothing. A flag flew from the tops of buildings, red lines on black. A foreign symbol.

"Kaladin said they weren't here to destroy," Adolin said, "but to occupy."

"They want their world back," Shallan said, pushing against him, wanting to feel his body against hers. "Could we . . . just let them have what they've taken?"

"No," Dalinar said. "So long as Odium leads the enemy, they will try to sweep us off this land, and make the world so it has no need of another Desolation. Because we'll be gone."

The three of them stood as if on a precipice, overlooking the city. The humans toiling outside, preparing for a planting. The lines of smoke curling from inside, where lighteyed keeps had tried to hold out against the invasion. The sights haunted Shallan, and she could only imagine how Adolin and Dalinar felt. They had protected Thaylenah, but had lost their homeland.

"There's a traitor among us," Dalinar said softly. "Someone attacked Bridge Four specifically to get the Honorblade—because they needed it to unlock the Oathgates and let the enemy in."

"That," Shallan said softly, "or it was unlocked by a Radiant who has changed sides."

Inexplicably, the Assassin in White had joined them. He sat outside the room, guarding the door as Dalinar's new bodyguard. He'd explained, frankly and without concern, that the majority of the Order of the Sky-breakers had chosen to serve Odium. Shallan wouldn't have thought that possible, but that—and Renarin's bonding of a corrupted spren—indicated that they couldn't trust someone simply because they'd spoken Ideals.

"You think," Adolin said, "Taravangian might have done it?"

"No," Dalinar said. "Why would he work with the enemy? Everything he's done so far has been to secure a safe Roshar—if through brutal means. Still, I have to wonder. I can't afford to be too trusting. Hopefully that's one thing Sadeas cured in me."

The Blackthorn shook his head, then looked to Shallan and Adolin. "Either way, Alethkar needs a *king*. More so now than ever."

"The heir—" Adolin began.

"Too young. This isn't the time for a regency. Gavinor can be named your heir, Adolin, but we must see you two married and the monarchy secured. For the good of Alethkar, but also the world." He narrowed his eyes. "The coalition needs more than I can provide. I will continue to lead it, but I have never been good at diplomacy. I need someone on the throne who can inspire Alethkar *and* command the respect of the monarchs."

Adolin grew tense, and Shallan took his hand, holding tight. *You can be this man, if you want,* she thought to him. *But you don't have to be what he makes of you.*

"I'll prepare the coalition for your coronation," Dalinar said. "Perhaps the day before the wedding." He turned to walk away. Dalinar Kholin was a force like a storm. He simply blew you over, and assumed you'd always *wanted* to lie down in the first place.

Adolin looked to Shallan, then set his jaw and seized his father by the arm. "I killed Sadeas, Father," Adolin whispered.

Dalinar froze.

"It was me," Adolin continued. "I broke the Codes of War and killed him in the corridor. For speaking against our family. For betraying us time and time again. I stopped him because it needed to be done, and because I knew you would never be able to do it."

Dalinar turned, speaking in a harsh whisper. "What? Son, *why* did you hide this from me?"

"Because you're you."

Dalinar took a deep breath. "We can fix this," he said. "We can see that atonement is made. It will hurt our reputation. Storms, this is *not* what I needed now. Nonetheless, we will fix it."

"It's already fixed. I'm not sorry for what I did—and I'd do it again, right now."

"We'll talk about this further once the coronation—"

"I'm *not* going to be king, Father," Adolin said. He glanced at Shallan, and she nodded to him, then squeezed his hand again. "Didn't you listen to what I just said? I broke the Codes."

"Everyone in this storming country breaks the Codes," Dalinar said, loudly, then looked over his shoulder. He continued, more softly. "*I* broke the Codes hundreds of times. You don't have to be perfect, you only have to do your duty."

"*No.* I'll be highprince, but not king. I just . . . no. I don't want that burden. And before you complain that none of us want it, I'd also be terrible at the job. You think the monarchs would listen to *me?*"

"I can't be king of Alethkar," Dalinar said softly. "I have to lead the Radiants—and need to divest myself of that power in Alethkar, to move away from that highking nonsense. We need a ruler in Alethkar who won't be pushed over, but who can also deal with diplomats in diplomatic ways."

"Well, that's not me," Adolin repeated.

"Who, then?" Dalinar demanded.

Shallan cocked her head. "Hey. Have you boys ever considered . . ."

⁂

Palona skimmed through the latest gossip reports out of Tashikk, looking for the juicy stuff.

Around her in the grand conference room of Urithiru, kings and princes squabbled with one another. Some complained that they weren't allowed to join whatever meeting Dalinar was having on the floor above, with his generals. The Natans still complained that they should be given control of the Oathgate at the Shattered Plains, while the Azish were talking—again—about how God himself had apparently prophesied that Surgebinders would destroy the world.

Everyone was quite persistent, and quite loud—even those who didn't speak Alethi. You had to be very dedicated to your grousing to wait for interpretation.

Sebarial—Turi—snored softly beside Palona. That was an act. He did the same fake snore when she tried to tell him about the latest novel she'd read. Then when she quit, he got annoyed. He seemed to like hearing the stories, but only as long as he could comment on how trite and feminine they were.

She nudged him, and he cracked an eye as she turned one of her gossip reports toward him, pointing at a drawing it included. "Yezier and Emul," she whispered. "The prince and princess were seen together in Thaylen City, speaking intimately while their guards worked on the rubble."

Turi grunted.

"Everyone thinks their romance is back on, though they can't talk about it, as head monarchs in Azir are forbidden marriage without the emperor's consent. But the rumors are wrong. *I* think she's been courting Halam Khal, the Shardbearer."

"You could just go *talk to* her," Turi said, pointing a lazy finger toward the princess of Yezier, whose translators were complaining forcefully about the dangers of Surgebinding.

"Oh, Turi," Palona said. "You can't just *ask* people about gossip. This is why you're hopeless."

"And here I thought I was hopeless because of my terrible taste in women."

The doors to the room slammed open, the noise of it sending a shock through the room, complaints falling silent. Even Turi sat up to note Jasnah Kholin standing in the doorway.

She wore a small but unmistakable crown on her head. The Kholin family, it seemed, had chosen their new monarch.

Turi grinned at the looks of worry on the faces of many of the others in the room. "Oh my," he whispered to Palona. "Now *this* should be interesting."

⁘

Moash pounded the pickaxe down again.

Two weeks of work, and he was still here clearing out rubble. Kill a god. Get back to work.

Well, he didn't mind. It would take months, maybe years, to clear all the rubble from this city. All of it out of Alethkar.

Most days this week, he was the only one here working at the palace. The city was slowly being reversed, humans shipped out, singers moved in— but they left him alone to break stones, with no overseer or guard in sight.

So he was surprised when he heard another pick fall beside him. He spun, shocked. "Khen?"

The beefy parshwoman started breaking rocks.

"Khen, you were freed from your slavery," Moash said. "Your assault on the palace earned you the Passion of Mercy."

Khen kept working. Nam and Pal stepped in, wearing warform—two others who had survived with him during the assault. Only a handful had.

They lifted picks and started breaking stones too.

"Pal," Moash said. "You—"

"They want us to farm," she said. "I'm tired of farming."

"And I'm no house servant," Khen said. "Running drinks." They were starting to speak to rhythms, like proper singers.

"So you'll break rocks?" Moash asked.

"We heard something. Made us want to be near you."

Moash hesitated, but then the numbness drove him to keep working, to hear that steady beat of metal on stone that let him pass between times.

It was maybe an hour later when they came for him. Nine flying Fused, rippling clothing pooling beneath them as they descended around Moash.

"Leshwi?" he asked. "Ancient One?"

She held something before herself in two hands. A long, slender weapon. A Shardblade with a gentle curve, its metal largely unornamented. Elegant, yet somehow humble, as Shardblades went. Moash had known it as the sword of the Assassin in White. Now he recognized it as something else. The Blade of Jezerezeh. Honorblade.

Moash reached for it, hesitant, and Leshwi hummed a warning rhythm. "If you take it, you die. Moash will be no more."

"Moash's world is no more," he said, taking the Blade by the hilt. "He might as well join it in the tomb."

"Vyre," she said. "Join us in the sky. You have a work." She and the others Lashed themselves upward.

Join us in the sky. The Honorblades, Graves had told him, gave their powers to any who held them.

Hesitant, Moash took the sphere that Khen offered. "What was that she said? Vyre?" She had said it in a way that rhymed with "fire."

"It's one of their names," Khen said. "I've been told it means He Who Quiets."

Vyre, He Who Quiets, sucked in the light of the sphere.

It was sweet and beautiful, and—as he'd been promised—brought Passion with it. He held to it, then Lashed himself upward into the sky.

⁂

Though Shallan had been given months to grow accustomed to the idea of getting married, on the actual day, she didn't feel ready.

It was such an ordeal and a hassle.

Everyone was determined that, after Dalinar and Navani's rushed wedding, they'd do this one *right*. So Shallan had to sit here and be fussed over, primped, her hair braided and her face painted by the royal Alethi makeup artists. Who'd known there even was such a thing?

She suffered it, then was deposited on a throne while scribes lined up and gave her piles of keteks and glyphwards. Noura delivered a box of incense from the Azish emperor, along with a dried fish from Lift. A Marati rug came from Queen Fen. Dried fruit. Perfumes.

A pair of boots. Ka seemed embarrassed as she opened the box and revealed them as a gift from Kaladin and Bridge Four, but Shallan just laughed. It was a much-needed moment of relief in the stress of the day.

She got gifts from professional organizations, family members, and one from each highprince except for Ialai—who had left Urithiru in disgrace. Though Shallan was grateful, she found herself trying to vanish into her dress. So many things that she didn't want—most of all, this attention.

Well, you're marrying an Alethi highprince, she thought as she squirmed on her wedding throne. *What did you expect?* At least she wasn't going to end up as queen.

Finally—after ardents arrived and pronounced blessings, anointings, and prayers—she was shuffled off into a little room by herself with a brazier, a window, and a mirror. The table held implements for her to paint a last prayer, so that she could meditate. Somewhere, Adolin was suffering gifts from the men. Probably swords. Lots and lots of swords.

The door closed, and Shallan stood facing herself in the mirror. Her sapphire gown was of an ancient style, with twin drooping sleeves that went far beyond her hands. Small rubies woven into the embroidery glowed with a complementary light. A golden vest draped over the shoulders, matched by the ornate headdress woven into her braids.

She wanted to shrink from it.

"Mmm . . ." Pattern said. "This is a good you, Shallan."

A good me. She breathed out. Veil formed on one side of the room, lounging against the wall. Radiant appeared near the table, tapping it with one finger, reminding her that she really should write a prayer—for tradition's sake, if nothing else.

"We're decided upon this," Shallan said.

"A worthy union," Radiant said.

"He's good for you, I suppose," Veil said. "Plus he knows his wine. We could do far worse."

"But not much better," Radiant said, giving Veil a pointed look. "This is good, Shallan."

"A celebration," Veil said. "A celebration of *you.*"

"It's okay for me to enjoy this," Shallan said, as if discovering something precious. "It's all right to celebrate. Even if things are terrible in the world, it's all right." She smiled. "I . . . I deserve this."

Veil and Radiant faded. When Shallan looked back into the mirror, she didn't feel embarrassed by the attention any longer. It was all right.

It was *all right* to be happy.

She painted her glyphward, but a knock at the door interrupted burning it. What? The time wasn't up.

She turned with a grin. "Come in." Adolin had probably found an excuse to come steal a kiss. . . .

The door opened.

Revealing three young men in worn clothing. Balat, tallest and round faced. Wikim, still gaunt, with skin as pale as Shallan's. Jushu, thinner than she recalled, but still plump. All three were somehow younger than she pictured them in her head, even though it had been over a year since she'd seen them.

Her brothers.

Shallan cried out in delight, throwing herself toward them, passing through a burst of joyspren like blue petals. She tried to embrace all three at once, heedless of what it might do to her carefully arranged dress. "How? When? What happened?"

"It was a long trek across Jah Keved," Nan Balat said. "Shallan . . . we didn't hear anything until we were transported here through that device. You're getting *married*? The son of the *Blackthorn*?"

So much to tell them. Storms, these tears were going to *ruin* her makeup. She'd have to go through it all again.

She found herself too overwhelmed to talk, to explain. She pulled them tight again, and Wikim even complained about the affection, as he always had. She hadn't seen them in how long, and he still complained? That made her even more giddy, for some reason.

Navani appeared behind them, looking over Balat's shoulder. "I will call for a delay of the festivities."

"No!" Shallan said.

No. She was going to *enjoy* this. She pulled her brothers tight, one after another. "I'll explain after the wedding. So *much* to explain . . ."

Balat, as she hugged him, handed her a slip of paper. "He said to give you this."

"Who?"

"He said you'd know." Balat still had the haunted look that had always shadowed him. "What is going on? How do you know people like *that*?"

She unfolded the letter.

It was from Mraize.

"Brightness," Shallan said to Navani, "will you provide my brothers with seats of honor?"

"Of course."

Navani drew the three boys away, joining Eylita, who had been waiting. Storms. Her brothers were back. *They were alive.*

A wedding gift, Mraize's note read.

In payment for work done. You will find that I do keep my promises. I apologize for the delay.

I congratulate you on your upcoming nuptials, little knife. You have done well. You have frightened away the Unmade who was in this tower, and in payment, we forgive a part of your debt owed from the destruction of our Soulcaster.

Your next mission is equally important. One of the Unmade seems willing to break from Odium. Our good and that of your Radiant friends align. You will find this Unmade, and you will persuade it to serve the Ghostbloods. Barring that, you will capture it and deliver it to us.

Details will be forthcoming.

She lowered the note, then burned it in the brazier meant for her prayer. So Mraize knew about Sja-anat, did he? Did he know about Renarin accidentally bonding one of her spren? Or was that a secret Shallan actually had over the Ghostbloods?

Well, she could worry about him later. Today, she had a wedding to attend. She pulled open the door and strode out. Toward a celebration.

Of being herself.

⁘

Dalinar entered his rooms, full of food from the wedding feast, glad to finally get some peace after the celebrations. The assassin settled down outside his door to wait, as was becoming his custom. Szeth was the only guard Dalinar had for the moment, as Rial and his other bodyguards were all in Bridge Thirteen—and that whole crew had gone up as squires to Teft.

Dalinar smiled to himself, then walked to his desk and settled down. A Shardblade hung on the wall before him. A temporary place; he'd find it a home. For now, he wanted it near. It was time.

He picked up the pen and started writing.

Three weeks had seen him progress far, though he still felt uncertain as he scratched out each letter. He worked at it a good hour before Navani returned, slipping into their rooms. She bustled over, opening the balcony doors, letting in the light of a setting sun.

A son married. Adolin was not the man Dalinar had thought he was— but then, couldn't he forgive someone for that? He dipped his pen and continued writing. Navani walked up and placed hands on his shoulders, looking at his paper.

"Here," Dalinar said, handing it to her. "Tell me what you think. I've run into a problem."

As she read, he resisted the urge to shift nervously. This was as bad as his first day with the swordmasters. Navani nodded to herself, then smiled at him, dipping her pen and making a few notes on his page to explain mistakes. "What's the problem?"

"I don't know how to write 'I.'"

"I showed you. Here, did you forget?" She wrote out a few letters. "No, wait. You used this several times in this piece, so you obviously know how to write it."

"You said pronouns have a gender in the women's formal script, and I realized that the one you taught me says 'I, being female.'"

Navani hesitated, pen in her fingers. "Oh. Right. I guess . . . I mean . . . Huh. I don't think there is a masculine 'I.' You can use the neuter, like an ardent. Or . . . no, here. I'm an idiot." She wrote some letters. "This is what you use when writing a quote by a man in the first person."

Dalinar rubbed his chin. Most words in the script were the same as the ones from spoken conversation, but small additions—that you wouldn't read out loud—changed the context. And that didn't even count the undertext— the writer's hidden commentary. Navani had explained, with some embarrassment, that that was never read to a man requesting a reading.

We took Shardblades from the women, he thought, glancing at the one hung on the wall above his desk. *And they seized literacy from us. Who got the better deal, I wonder?*

"Have you thought," Navani said, "about how Kadash and the ardents will respond to you learning to read?"

"I've been excommunicated already. There's not much more they could do."

"They could leave."

"No," Dalinar said. "I don't think they will. I actually think . . . I think I might be getting through to Kadash. Did you see him at the wedding? He's been reading what the ancient theologians wrote, trying to find justification for modern Vorinism. He doesn't want to believe me, but soon he won't be able to help it."

Navani seemed skeptical.

"Here," Dalinar said. "How do I emphasize a word?"

"These marks here, above and below a word you want to stress."

He nodded in thanks, dipped his pen, then rewrote what he'd given to Navani, substituting the proper changes.

The most important words a man can say are, "I will do better." These are not the most important words *any* man can say. I am a man, and they are what I needed to say.

The ancient code of the Knights Radiant says "journey before destination." Some may call it a simple platitude, but it is far more. A journey will have pain and failure. It is not only the steps forward that we must accept. It is the stumbles. The trials. The knowledge that we will fail. That we will hurt those around us.

But if we stop, if we accept the person we are when we fall, the journey ends. That failure *becomes* our destination.

To love the journey is to accept no such end. I have found, through painful experience, that the most important step a person can take is always the *next* one.

I'm certain some will feel threatened by this record. Some few may feel liberated. Most will simply feel that it should not exist.

I needed to write it anyway.

He sat back, pleased. It seemed that in opening this doorway, he had entered a new world. He could read *The Way of Kings*. He could read his niece's biography of Gavilar. He could write down his own orders for men to follow.

Most importantly, he could write this. His thoughts. His pains. His *life*. He looked to the side, where Navani had placed the handful of blank pages he'd asked her to bring. Too few. Far, far too few.

He dipped his pen again. "Would you close the balcony doors again, gemheart?" he asked her. "The sunlight is distracting me from the other light."

"Other light?"

He nodded absently. What next? He looked up again at the familiar Shardblade. Wide like him—and thick, also like him, at times—with a hook shape at the end. This was the best mark of both his honor and his disgrace. It should have belonged to Rock, the Horneater bridgeman. He'd killed Amaram and won it, along with two other Shards.

Rock had insisted that Dalinar take Oathbringer back. A debt repaid, the Windrunner had explained. Reluctantly, Dalinar had accepted, handling the Shardblade only through cloth.

As Navani shut the balcony doors, he closed his eyes and felt the warmth of a distant, unseen light. Then he smiled, and—with a hand still unsteady, like the legs of a child taking his first steps—he took another page and wrote a title for the book.

Oathbringer, My Glory and My Shame.
Written by the hand of Dalinar Kholin.

EPILOGUE

GREAT ART

"All great art is hated," Wit said.

He shuffled in line—along with a couple hundred other people—one dreary step.

"It is obscenely difficult—if not impossible—to make something that nobody hates," Wit continued. "Conversely, it is incredibly easy—if not expected—to make something that nobody loves."

Weeks after the fall of Kholinar, the place still smelled like smoke. Though the city's new masters had moved tens of thousands of humans out to work farms, complete resettlement would take months, if not years.

Wit poked the man in front of him in the shoulder. "This makes sense, if you think about it. Art is about *emotion, examination,* and *going places people have never gone before to discover and investigate new things.* The only way to create something that nobody hates is to ensure that it can't be loved either. Remove enough spice from soup, and you'll just end up with water."

The brutish man in front eyed him, then turned back to the line.

"Human taste is as varied as human fingerprints," Wit said. "Nobody will like everything, everybody dislikes something, someone loves that thing you hate—but at least being hated is better than nothing. To risk metaphor, a grand painting is often about contrast: brightest brights, darkest darks. Not grey mush. That a thing is hated is not proof that it's great art, but the lack of hatred is certainly proof that it is not."

They shuffled forward another step.

He poked the man in the shoulder again. "And so, dear sir, when I say that you are the very embodiment of repulsiveness, I am merely looking to improve my art. You look so ugly, it seems that someone tried—and failed—to get the warts off your face through aggressive application of sandpaper. You are less a human being, and more a lump of dung with aspirations.

If someone took a stick and beat you repeatedly, it could only serve to improve your features.

"Your face defies description, but only because it nauseated all the poets. You are what parents use to frighten children into obedience. I'd tell you to put a sack over your head, but think of the poor sack! Theologians use you as proof that God exists, because such hideousness can *only* be intentional."

The man didn't respond. Wit poked him again, and he muttered something in Thaylen.

"You . . . don't speak Alethi, do you?" Wit asked. "Of course you don't." Figured.

Well, repeating all that in Thaylen would be monotonous. So Wit cut in front of the man in line. This finally provoked a response. The beefy man grabbed Wit and spun him around, then punched him right in the face.

Wit fell backward onto the stone ground. The line continued its shuffling motion, the occupants refusing to look at him. Cautiously, he prodded at his mouth. Yes . . . it seemed . . .

One of his teeth popped out. "Success!" he said in Thaylen, speaking with a faint lisp. "Thank you, dear man. I'm glad you appreciate my performance art, accomplished by cutting in front of you."

Wit flicked the tooth aside and stood up, starting to dust off his clothing. He then stopped himself. After all, he'd worked hard to place that dust. He shoved hands in the pockets of his ragged brown coat, then slouched his way through an alley. He passed groaning humans crying for deliverance, for mercy. He absorbed that, letting it reflect in him.

Not a mask he put on. Real sorrow. Real pain. Weeping echoed around him as he moved into the section of town nearest the palace. Only the most desperate or the most broken dared remain here, nearest the invaders and their growing seat of power.

He rounded to the courtyard out in front of the steps leading up. Was it time for his big performance? Strangely, he found himself reluctant. Once he walked up those steps, he was committing to leave the city.

He'd found a much better audience among these poor people than he had among the lighteyes of Alethkar. He'd enjoyed his time here. On the other hand, if Rayse learned that Wit was in the city, he'd order his forces to level it—and would consider that a cheap price for even the slimmest chance of ending him.

Wit lingered, then moved through the courtyard, speaking softly with several of the people he'd come to know over the weeks. He eventually squatted next to Kheni, who still rocked her empty cradle, staring with haunted eyes across the square.

"The question becomes," he whispered to her, "how many people need to love a piece of art to make it worthwhile? If you're inevitably going to inspire hate, then how much enjoyment is needed to balance out the risk?"

She didn't respond. Her husband, as usual, hovered nearby.

"How's my hair?" Wit asked Kheni. "Or lack thereof?"

Again, no response.

"The missing tooth is a new addition," Wit said, poking at the hole. "I think it will add that special touch."

He had a few days, with his healing repressed, until the tooth grew back. The right concoction had made him lose his hair in patches.

"Should I put an eye out?"

Kheni looked at him, incredulous.

So you are *listening.* He patted her on the shoulder. *One more. One more, then I go.*

"Wait here," he told her, then went walking along an alley to the north. He scooped up some rags—the remnants of a spren costume. He didn't see many of those around anymore. He took a cord from his pocket and twisted it around the rags.

Nearby, several buildings had fallen to the thunderclast's attacks. He felt life from one, and when he drew close, a dirty little face poked out from some rubble.

He smiled at the little girl.

"Your teeth look funny today," she said to him.

"I take exception to that, as the funny part is not the teeth, but the lack of tooth." He held out his hand to her, but she ducked back in.

"I can't leave Mama," she whispered.

"I understand," Wit said. He took the rags and cord he'd worked with earlier, forming them into the shape of a little doll. "The answer to the question has been bothering me for some time."

The little face poked out again, looking at the doll. "The question?"

"I asked it earlier," Wit said. "You couldn't hear. Do you know the answer?"

"You're weird."

"Right answer, but wrong question." He walked the little doll along the broken street.

"For me?" the girl whispered.

"I need to leave the city," he said. "And I can't take her with me. Someone needs to care for her."

A grimy hand reached toward the doll, but Wit pulled it back. "She's afraid of the darkness. You've got to keep her in the light."

The hand vanished into the shadows. "I can't leave Mama."

"That's too bad," Wit said. He raised the doll to his lips, then whispered a choice set of words.

When he set it down, it started to walk on its own. A soft gasp sounded inside the shadows. The little doll toddled toward the street. Step by step by step . . .

The girl, maybe four years old, finally emerged from the shadows and ran to get the doll. Wit stood and dusted off his coat, which was now grey. The girl hugged the patchwork creation, and he picked her up, turning away from the broken building—and the bones of a leg sticking from the rubble just inside.

He carried the girl back to the square, then quietly pushed the empty cradle away from Kheni and knelt before her. "I think, in answer to my question . . . I think it only takes one."

She blinked, then focused on the child in his arms.

"I have to leave the city," Wit said. "And someone needs to take care of her."

He waited until, at long last, Kheni held out her arms. Wit put the child into them, then rose. Kheni's husband took him by the arm, smiling. "Can you not stay a little longer?"

"I should think you are the first to ever ask me that, Cob," Wit said. "And in truth, the sentiment frightens me." He hesitated, then leaned down and touched the doll in the child's hands. "Forget what I told you before," he whispered. "Instead, take care of *her*."

He turned and started up the steps toward the palace.

He adopted the act as he walked. The twitch of madness, the shuffle to his step. He squinted one eye and hunched over, changed his breathing to come raggedly, with occasional sharp intakes. He muttered to himself, and exposed his teeth—but not the one that was missing, for that was impossible.

He passed into the shadow of the palace, and the sentry hovering in the air nearby, wind rippling her long clothing. Vatwha was her name. Thousands of years ago, he'd shared a dance with her. Like all the others, she'd later been trained to watch for him.

But not well enough. As he passed underneath, she gave him the barest of glances. He decided not to take that as an insult, as it was what he wanted. He needed to be soup so bland, it was water. What a conundrum. In this case, his art was best when ignored.

Perhaps he would need to revise his philosophy.

He passed the sentry post, and wondered if anyone else thought it irregular that the Fused spent so much time here near this fallen section of the palace. Did anyone wonder why they worked so hard, clearing blocks, breaking down walls?

It was good to know that his heart could still flutter at a performance. He ducked in close to the work project, and a pair of more mundane singer guards cursed at him to move on toward the gardens, with the other beggars. He bowed several times, then tried to sell them some trinkets from his pocket.

One shoved him away, and so he acted panicked, scrambling past them and up a ramp into the work project itself. Nearby, some workers broke rocks, and a patch of blood stained the ground. The two singer guards shouted at him to get out. Wit adopted a frightened look, and hurried to obey, but tripped himself so he fell against the wall of the palace—a portion that was still standing.

"Look," he whispered to the wall, "you don't have many choices right now."

Above, the Fused turned to look at him.

"I know you'd rather have someone else," Wit said, "but it isn't the time to be picky. I'm certain now that the reason I'm in the city is to find you."

The two singer guards approached, one bowing apologetically to the Fused in the air. They still didn't realize that sort of behavior would not impress the ancient singers.

"It's either go with me now," Wit said to the wall, "or wait it out and get captured. I honestly don't even know if you've the mind to listen. But if you do, know this: I will give you truths. And I know some *juicy* ones."

The guards reached him. Wit pushed against them, slamming himself against the wall again.

Something slipped from one of the cracks in the wall. A moving Pattern that dimpled the stone. It crossed to his hand, which he tucked into his rags as the guards seized him under the arms and hauled him out into the gardens, then tossed him among the beggars there.

Once they were gone, Wit rolled over and looked at the Pattern that now covered his palm. It seemed to be trembling.

"Life before death, little one," Wit whispered.

THE END OF

Book Three of

THE STORMLIGHT ARCHIVE

ENDNOTE

United, new beginnings sing: "Defying truth, love.
Truth defy!" Sing beginnings, new unity.

Ketek written by Jasnah Kholin on the occasion of her
ward Shallan Davar's wedding celebration.

ARS ARCANUM

THE TEN ESSENCES AND THEIR HISTORICAL ASSOCIATIONS

NUMBER	GEMSTONE	ESSENCE	BODY FOCUS	SOULCASTING PROPERTIES	PRIMARY / SECONDARY DIVINE ATTRIBUTES
1 Jes	Sapphire	Zephyr	Inhalation	Translucent gas, air	Protecting / Leading
2 Nan	Smokestone	Vapor	Exhalation	Opaque gas smoke, fog	Just / Confident
3 Chach	Ruby	Spark	The Soul	Fire	Brave / Obedient
4 Vev	Diamond	Lucentia	The Eyes	Quartz, glass, crystal	Loving / Healing
5 Palah	Emerald	Pulp	The Hair	Wood, plants, moss	Learned / Giving
6 Shash	Garnet	Blood	The Blood	Blood, all non-oil liquid	Creative / Honest
7 Betab	Zircon	Tallow	Oil	All kinds of oil	Wise / Careful
8 Kak	Amethyst	Foil	The Nails	Metal	Resolute / Builder
9 Tanat	Topaz	Talus	The Bone	Rock and stone	Dependable / Resourceful
10 Ishi	Heliodor	Sinew	Flesh	Meats, flesh	Pious / Guiding

The preceding list is an imperfect gathering of traditional Vorin symbolism associated with the Ten Essences. Bound together, these form the Double Eye of the Almighty, an eye with two pupils representing the creation of plants and creatures. This is also the basis for the hourglass shape that was often associated with the Knights Radiant.

Ancient scholars also placed the ten orders of Knights Radiant on this list, alongside the Heralds themselves, who each had a classical association with one of the numbers and Essences.

I'm not certain yet how the ten levels of Voidbinding or its cousin the Old Magic fit into this paradigm, if indeed they can. My research suggests that, indeed, there should be another series of abilities that is even more esoteric than the Voidbindings. Perhaps the Old Magic fits into those, though I am beginning to suspect that it is something entirely different.

Note that I currently believe the concept of the "Body Focus" to be more a matter of philosophical interpretation than an actual attribute of this Investiture and its manifestations.

THE TEN SURGES

As a complement to the Essences, the classical elements celebrated on Roshar, are found the Ten Surges. These, thought to be the fundamental forces by which the world operates, are more accurately a representation of the ten basic abilities offered to the Heralds, and then the Knights Radiant, by their bonds.

Adhesion: The Surge of Pressure and Vacuum
Gravitation: The Surge of Gravity
Division: The Surge of Destruction and Decay
Abrasion: The Surge of Friction
Progression: The Surge of Growth and Healing, or Regrowth
Illumination: The Surge of Light, Sound, and Various Waveforms
Transformation: The Surge of Soulcasting
Transportation: The Surge of Motion and Realmatic Transition
Cohesion: The Surge of Strong Axial Interconnection
Tension: The Surge of Soft Axial Interconnection

ON THE CREATION OF FABRIALS

Five groupings of fabrial have been discovered so far. The methods of their creation are carefully guarded by the artifabrian community, but they appear to be the work of dedicated scientists, as opposed to the more mystical Surgebindings once performed by the Knights Radiant. I am more and more convinced that the creation of these devices requires forced enslavement of transformative cognitive entities, known as "spren" to the local communities.

ALTERING FABRIALS

Augmenters: These fabrials are crafted to enhance something. They can create heat, pain, or even a calm wind, for instance. They are powered—like all fabrials—by Stormlight. They seem to work best with forces, emotions, or sensations.

The so-called half-shards of Jah Keved are created with this type of fabrial attached to a sheet of metal, enhancing its durability. I have seen fabrials of this type crafted using many different kinds of gemstone; I am guessing that any one of the ten Polestones will work.

Diminishers: These fabrials do the opposite of what augmenters do, and generally seem to fall under the same restrictions as their cousins. Those artifabrians who have taken me into confidence seem to believe that even greater fabrials are possible than what have been created so far, particularly in regard to augmenters and diminishers.

PAIRING FABRIALS

Conjoiners: By infusing a ruby and using methodology that has not been revealed to me (though I have my suspicions), you can create a conjoined pair of gemstones. The process requires splitting the original ruby. The two halves will then create parallel reactions across a distance. Spanreeds are one of the most common forms of this type of fabrial.

Conservation of force is maintained; for instance, if one is attached to a heavy stone, you will need the same strength to lift the conjoined fabrial that you would need to lift the stone itself. There appears to be some sort of process used during the creation of the fabrial that influences how far apart the two halves can go and still produce an effect.

Reversers: Using an amethyst instead of a ruby also creates conjoined halves of a gemstone, but these two work in creating *opposite* reactions. Raise one, and the other will be pressed downward, for instance.

These fabrials have only just been discovered, and already the possibilities for exploitation are being conjectured. There appear to be some unexpected limitations to this form of fabrial, though I have not been able to discover what they are.

WARNING FABRIALS

There is only one type of fabrial in this set, informally known as the Alerter. An Alerter can warn one of a nearby object, feeling, sensation, or phenomenon. These fabrials use a heliodor stone as their focus. I do not know whether this is the only type of gemstone that will work, or if there is another reason heliodor is used.

In the case of this kind of fabrial, the amount of Stormlight you can infuse into it affects its range. Hence the size of gemstone used is very important.

WINDRUNNING AND LASHINGS

Reports of the Assassin in White's odd abilities have led me to some sources of information that, I believe, are generally unknown. The Windrunners were an order of the Knights Radiant, and they made use of two primary types of Surgebinding. The effects of these Surgebindings were known—colloquially among the members of the order—as the Three Lashings.

BASIC LASHING: GRAVITATIONAL CHANGE

This type of Lashing was one of the most commonly used Lashings among the order, though it was not the easiest to use. (That distinction belongs to the Full Lashing below.) A Basic Lashing involved revoking a being's or object's spiritual gravitational bond to the planet below, instead temporarily linking that being or object to a different object or direction.

Effectively, this creates a change in gravitational pull, twisting the energies of the planet itself. A Basic Lashing allowed a Windrunner to run up walls, to send objects or people flying off into the air, or to create similar effects. Advanced uses of this type of Lashing would allow a Windrunner to make himself or herself lighter by binding part of his or her mass upward. (Mathematically, binding a quarter of one's mass upward would halve a person's effective weight. Binding half of one's mass upward would create weightlessness.)

Multiple Basic Lashings could also pull an object or a person's body downward at double, triple, or other multiples of its weight.

FULL LASHING: BINDING OBJECTS TOGETHER

A Full Lashing might seem very similar to a Basic Lashing, but they worked on very different principles. While one had to do with gravitation, the other had to do with the force (or Surge, as the Radiants called them) of Adhesion—binding objects together as if they were one. I believe this Surge may have had something to do with atmospheric pressure.

To create a Full Lashing, a Windrunner would infuse an object with Stormlight, then press another object to it. The two objects would become bound together with an extremely powerful bond, nearly impossible to break. In fact, most materials would themselves break before the bond holding them together would.

I believe this may actually be a specialized version of the Basic Lashing. This type of Lashing required the least amount of Stormlight of any of the three Lashings. The Windrunner would infuse something, give a mental command, and create a *pull* to the object that yanked other objects toward it.

At its heart, this Lashing created a bubble around the object that imitated its spiritual link to the ground beneath it. As such, it was much harder for the Lashing to affect objects touching the ground, where their link to the planet was strongest. Objects falling or in flight were the easiest to influence. Other objects could be affected, but the Stormlight and skill required were much more substantial.

LIGHTWEAVING

A second form of Surgebinding involves the manipulation of light and sound in illusory tactics common throughout the cosmere. Unlike the variations present on Sel, however, this method has a powerful Spiritual element, requiring not just a full mental picture of the intended creation, but some level of Connection to it as well. The illusion is based not simply upon what the Lightweaver imagines, but upon what they *desire* to create.

In many ways, this is the most similar ability to the original Yolish variant, which excites me. I wish to delve more into this ability, with the hope to gain a full understanding of how it relates to cognitive and spiritual attributes.

SOULCASTING

Essential to the economy of Roshar is the art of Soulcasting, in which one form of matter is directly transformed into another by changing its spiritual nature. This is performed on Roshar via the use of devices known as Soulcasters, and these devices (the majority of which appear to be focused on turning stone into grain or flesh) are used to provide mobile supply for armies or to augment local urban food stores. This has allowed kingdoms on Roshar—where fresh water is rarely an issue, because of highstorm rains— to field armies in ways that would be unthinkable elsewhere.

What intrigues me most about Soulcasting, however, are the things we can infer about the world and Investiture from it. For example, certain gemstones are requisite in producing certain results—if you wish to produce grain, however, your Soulcaster must both be attuned to that transformation *and* have an emerald (not a different gemstone) attached. This creates an economy based on the relative values of what the gemstones can create, not upon their rarity. Indeed, as the chemical structures are identical for several of these gemstone varieties, aside from trace impurities, the *color* is the most important part—not their actual axial makeup. I'm certain you will find this relevance of hue quite intriguing, particularly in its relationship to other forms of Investiture.

This relationship must have been essential in the local creation of the table I've included above, which lacks some scientific merit, but is intrinsically tied to the folklore surrounding Soulcasting. An emerald can be used to create food—and thus is traditionally associated with a similar Essence. Indeed, on Roshar there are considered to be ten elements; not the traditional four or sixteen, depending upon local tradition.

Curiously, these gemstones seem tied to the original abilities of the Soulcasters who were an order of Knights Radiant—but they don't seem *essential* to the actual operation of the Investiture when performed by a living Radiant. I do not know the connection here, though it implies something valuable.

Soulcasters, the devices, were created to *imitate* the abilities of the Surge of Soulcasting (or Transformation). This is yet *another* mechanical imitation of something once only available only to a select few within the bounds of an Invested Art. The Honorblades on Roshar, indeed, may be the very first example of this—from thousands of years ago. I believe this has relevance to the discoveries being made on Scadrial, and the commoditization of Allomancy and Feruchemy.

ABOUT THE AUTHOR

Brandon Sanderson grew up in Lincoln, Nebraska. He lives in Utah with his wife and children and teaches creative writing at Brigham Young University. He is the author of such bestsellers as the Mistborn® trilogy and its sequels, *The Alloy of Law, Shadows of Self* and *The Bands of Mourning*; the Stormlight Archive novels, *The Way of Kings, Words of Radiance*, and *Oathbringer*, and other novels, including *The Rithmatist* and *Steelheart* for young adults, and the Alcatraz vs. the Evil Librarians series middle-grade readers. In 2013 he won a Hugo Award for Best Novella for *The Emperor's Soul*, set in the world of his acclaimed first novel, *Elantris*. Additionally, he was chosen to complete Robert Jordan's Wheel of Time® sequence. For behind-the-scenes information on all of Brandon Sanderson's books, visit brandonsanderson.com.